# THE WORKS
## OF
# EMILE ZOLA

One Volume Edition

WALTER J. BLACK, INC.
2 Park Avenue
NEW YORK, N. Y.

# Contents

# THE INUNDATION

## NANTAS

## COQUEVILLE

## NAIS MICOULIN

## ANGELINE

## MADAME NEIGEON

# A LOVE EPISODE

# L'ASSOMMOIR

# THE MYSTERIES OF MARSEILLES

# NANA

# Nana

## CHAPTER I

AT NINE o'clock in the evening the body of the house at the Théâtres des Variétés was still all but empty. A few individuals, it is true, were sitting quietly waiting in the balcony and stalls, but these were lost, as it were, among the ranges of seats whose coverings of cardinal velvet loomed in the subdued light of the dimly-burning lustre. A shadow enveloped the great red splash of the curtain, and not a sound came from the stage, the unlit footlights, the scattered desks of the orchestra. It was only high overhead, in the third gallery, round the domed ceiling, where nude females and children flew in heavens which had turned green in the gas-light, that calls and laughter were audible above a continuous hub-bub of voices, and heads in women's and workmen's caps were ranged, row above row, under the wide-vaulted bays with their gilt-surrounding adornments. Every few seconds an attendant would make her appearance, bustling along with tickets in her hand, and piloting in front of her a gentleman and a lady, who took their seats, he in his evening dress, she sitting slim and undulant beside him whilst her eyes wandered slowly round the house.

Two young men appeared in the stalls; they kept standing, and looked about them.

"Didn't I say so, Hector?" cried the elder of the two, a tall fellow with little black moustaches, "we're too early! You might quite well have allowed me to finish my cigar."

An attendant was passing.

"Oh, Monsieur Fauchery," she said, familiarly, "it won't begin for half an hour yet!"

"Then why do they advertise for nine o'clock?" muttered Hector, whose long thin face assumed an expression of vexation. "Only this morning, Clarisse, who's in the piece, swore that they'd begin at nine o'clock punctually."

For a moment they remained silent, and looking upwards scanned the shadowy boxes. But the green paper with which these were hung, rendered them more shadowy still. Down below, under the dress circle, the lower boxes were buried in utter night. In those on the second tier there was only one stout lady, who was stranded, as it were, on the velvet-covered balustrade in front of her. On the right hand and on the left, between lofty pilasters, the stage-boxes, bedraped with long-fringed scalloped hangings, remained untenanted. The house with its white and gold, relieved by soft green tones, lay only half disclosed to view, as though full of a fine dust shed from the little jets of flame in the great glass lustre.

"Did you get your stage-box for Lucy?" asked Hector.

"Yes," replied his companion; "but I had some trouble to get it. Oh, there's no danger of Lucy coming too early!"

He stifled a slight yawn; then, after a pause,—

"You're in luck's way, you are, since you haven't been at a first night before. The *Blonde Venus* will be the event of the year. People have been talking about it for six months. Oh, such music, my dear boy! Such a sly dog, Bordenave! He knows his business, and has kept this for the Exhibition season."

Hector was religiously attentive. He asked a question.

"And Nana, the new star, who's going to play Venus, d'you know her?"

"There you are, you're beginning again!" cried Fauchery, casting up his arms. "Ever since this morning people have been dreeing me with Nana. I've met more than twenty people, and it's Nana here and Nana there! What do *I* know? Am I acquainted with all the light ladies in Paris? Nana is an invention of Bordenave's! It must be a fine one!"

He calmed himself, but the emptiness of the house, the dim light of the lustre, the church-like sense of self-absorption, which the place inspired, full as it was of whispering voices and the sound of doors banging—all these got on his nerves.

"No, by Jove," said he, all of a sudden, "one's hair turns grey here. I— I'm going out. Perhaps we shall find Bordenave downstairs. He'll give us information about things."

Downstairs, in the great marble-paved entrance-hall, where the box office was, the public were beginning to shew themselves. Through the three open gates might have been observed, passing in, the ardent life of the boulevards, which were all astir and aflare under the fine April night. The sound of carriage wheels kept stopping suddenly, carriage doors were noisily shut again, and people began entering in small groups, taking their stand before the ticket bureau, and climbing the double flight of stairs at the end of the hall, up which the women loitered with swaying hips. Under the crude gas-light, round the pale, naked walls of the entrance-hall, which with its scanty First Empire decorations suggested the peristyle of a toy temple, there was a flaring display of lofty yellow posters, bearing the name of "Nana" in great black letters. Gentlemen, who seemed to be glued to the entry, were reading them; others, standing about, were engaged in talk, barring the doors of the house in so doing, while, hard by the box office, a thick-set man with an extensive, close-shaven visage was giving rough answers to such as pressed to engage seats.

"There's Bordenave," said Fauchery, as he came down the stairs. But the manager had already seen him.

"Ah, ah! you're a nice fellow!" he shouted at him from a distance. "That's the way you give me a notice, is it? Why, I opened my *Figaro* this morning —never a word!"

"Wait a bit," replied Fauchery. "I certainly must make the acquaintance of your Nana before talking about her. Besides, I've made no promises."

Then, to put an end to the discussion, he introduced his cousin, M. Hector de la Faloise, a young man who had come to finish his education in Paris. The manager took the young man's measure at a glance. But Hector returned his scrutiny with deep interest. This, then, was that Bordenave, that showman of the sex, who treated women like a convict-overseer, that clever fellow who was always at full steam over some advertising dodge, that shouting, spitting, thigh-slapping fellow, that cynic with the soul of a policeman! Hector was under the impression that he ought to discover some amiable observation for the occasion.

"Your theatre——" he began, in dulcet tones.

Bordenave interrupted him with a savage phrase, as becomes a man who dotes on frank situations.

"Call it my brothel!"

At this Fauchery laughed approvingly, while la Faloise stopped with his pretty speech strangled in his throat, feeling very much shocked, and striving to appear as though he enjoyed the phrase. The manager had dashed off to shake hands with a dramatic critic, whose column had considerable influence. When he returned, la Faloise was recovering. He was afraid of being treated as a provincial if he shewed himself too much nonplussed.

"I have been told," he began again, longing, positively, to find something to say, "that Nana has a delicious voice."

"Nana!" cried the manager, shrugging his shoulders, "the voice of a squirt!"

The young man made haste to add,—

"Besides being a first-rate comedian!"

"She! Why she's a lump! She has

no notion what to do with her hands and feet."

La Faloise blushed a little. He had lost his bearings. He stammered,—

"I wouldn't have missed this first representation to-night for the world. I was aware that your theatre——"

"Call it my brothel," Bordenave again interpolated, with the frigid obstinacy of a man convinced.

Meanwhile, Fauchery, with extreme calmness, was looking at the women as they came in. He went to his cousin's rescue when he saw him all at sea, and doubtful whether to laugh or to be angry.

"Do be pleasant to Bordenave—call his theatre what he wishes you to, since it amuses him. And you, my dear fellow, don't keep us waiting about for nothing. If your Nana neither sings nor acts, you'll find you've made a blunder, that's all. It's what I'm afraid of, and the truth be told."

"A blunder! A blunder!" shouted the manager, and his face grew purple. "Must a woman know how to act and sing? Oh, my chicken, you're too *stoopid:* Nana has other good points, by Heaven!—something which is as good as all the other things put together. I've smelt it out; it's deuced pronounced with her, or I've got the scent of an idiot. You'll see, you'll see! She's only got to come on, and all the house will be gaping at her."

He had held up his big hands which were trembling under the influence of his eager enthusiasm, and now, having relieved his feelings, he lowered his voice and grumbled to himself,—

"Yes, she'll go far! Oh yes, s'elp me,

she'll go far! A skin, oh what a skin she's got!"

Then, as Fauchery began questioning him, he consented to enter into a detailed explanation, couched in phraseology so crude that Hector de la Faloise felt slightly disgusted. He had been thick with Nana, and he was anxious to start her on the stage. Well, just about that time, he was in search of a Venus. He—he never let a woman encumber him for any length of time; he preferred to let the public enjoy the benefit of her forthwith. But there was a deuce of a row going on in his shop, which had been turned topsy-turvy by that big damsel's advent. Rose Mignon, his star, a comic actress of much subtlety and an adorable singer, was daily threatening to leave him in the lurch, for she was furious, and guessed the presence of a rival. And as for the bill, good God! what a noise there had been about it all! It had ended by his deciding to print the names of the two actresses in the same sized type. But it wouldn't do to bother him. Whenever any of his little women, as he called them—Simonne or Clarisse, for instance—wouldn't go the way he wanted her to, he just up with his foot and caught her one in the rear. Otherwise, life was impossible. Oh yes, he sold 'em; _he_ knew what they fetched, the wenches!

"Tut!" he cried, breaking off short; "Mignon and Steiner. Always together. You known Steiner's getting sick of Rose; that's why the husband dogs his steps now for fear of his slipping away."

On the pavement outside, the row of gas-jets, flaring on the cornice of the theatre, cast a patch of brilliant light. Two small trees, violently green, stood sharply out against it, and a column gleamed in such vivid illumination that one could read the notices thereon at a distance, as though in broad daylight, while the dense night of the boulevard beyond was dotted with lights above the vague outline of an ever-moving crowd. Many men did not enter the theatre at once, but stayed outside to talk while finishing their cigars under the rays of the line of gas-jets, which shed a sallow pallor on their faces and silhouetted their short black shadows on the asphalte. Mignon, a very tall, very broad fellow, with the square-shaped head of a strong man at a fair, was forcing a passage through the midst of the groups, and dragging on his arm the banker Steiner, an exceedingly small man with a corporation already in evidence, and a round face framed in a setting of beard which was already growing grey.

"Well," said Bordenave to the banker, "you met her yesterday in my office."

"Ah! it was she, was it?" ejaculated Steiner. "I suspected as much. Only I was coming out as she was going in, and I scarcely caught a glimpse of her."

Mignon was listening with half-closed eyelids, and nervously twisting a great diamond ring round his finger. He had quite understood that Nana was in question. Then as Bordenave was drawing a portrait of his new star which lit a flame in the eyes of the banker, he ended by joining in the conversation.

"Oh let her alone, my dear fellow: she's a low lot! The public will shew her the door in quick time. Steiner, my laddie, you know that my wife is waiting for you in her box."

He wanted to take possession of him

again. But Steiner would not quit Bordenave. In front of them, a stream of people was crowding and crushing against the ticket office, and there was a din of voices, in the midst of which the name of Nana sounded with all the melodious vivacity of its two syllables. The men who stood planted in front of the notices kept spelling it out loudly; others, in an interrogative tone, uttered it as they passed; while the women, at once restless and smiling, repeated it softly with an air of surprise. Nobody knew Nana. Whence had Nana fallen? And stories and jokes, whispered from ear to ear, went the round of the crowd. The name was a caress in itself; it was a pet name, the very familiarity of which suited every lip. Merely through enunciating it thus, the throng worked itself into a state of gaiety and became highly good-natured. A fever of curiosity urged it forward, that kind of Parisian curiosity which is as violent as an access of positive unreason. Everybody wanted to see Nana. A lady had the flounce of her dress torn off; a man lost his hat.

"Oh, you're asking me too many questions about it!" cried Bordenave, whom a score of men were besieging with their queries. "You're going to see her, and I'm off; they want me."

He disappeared, enchanted at having fired his public. Mignon shrugged his shoulders, reminding Steiner that Rose was awaiting him, in order to shew him the costume she was about to wear in the first act.

"By Jove! there's Lucy out there, getting down from her carriage," said la Faloise to Fauchery.

It was in fact Lucy Stewart, a plain little woman, some forty years old, with a disproportionately long neck, a thin, drawn face, a heavy mouth, but withal of such brightness, such graciousness of manner, that she was really very charming. She was bringing with her Caroline Héquet and her mother—Caroline a woman of a cold type of beauty, the mother a person of a most worthy demeanour, who looked as if she were stuffed with straw.

"You're coming with us? I've kept a place for you," said she to Fauchery.

"Oh, decidedly not! to see nothing!" he made answer. "I've a stall; I prefer being in the stalls."

Lucy grew nettled. Did he not dare shew himself in her company? Then suddenly restraining herself, and skipping to another topic,—

"Why haven't you told me that you knew Nana?"

"Nana! I've never set eyes on her."

"Honour bright? I've been told that you've been to bed with her."

But Mignon, coming in front of them, his finger to his lips, made them a sign to be silent. And, when Lucy questioned him, he pointed out a young man who was passing, and murmured,—

"Nana's fancy man."

Everybody looked at him. He was a pretty fellow. Fauchery recognised him; it was Daguenet, a young man who had run through three hundred thousand francs in the pursuit of women, and who now was dabbling in stocks, in order from time to time to treat them to bouquets and dinners. Lucy made the discovery that he had fine eyes.

"Ah, there's Blanche!" she cried. "It's she who told me that you had been to bed with Nana."

Blanche de Sivry, a great fair girl, whose good-looking face shewed signs of growing fat, made her appearance in the company of a spare, sedulously well-groomed, and extremely distinguished man. "The Count Xavier de Vandeuvres," Fauchery whispered in his companion's ear.

The Count and the journalist shook hands, while Blanche and Lucy entered into a brisk mutual explanation. One of them in blue, the other in rose-pink, they stood blocking the way with their deeply-flounced skirts, and Nana's name kept repeating itself so shrilly in their conversation that people began to listen to them. The Count de Vandeuvres carried Blanche off. But by this time Nana's name was echoing more loudly than ever round the four walls of the entrance-hall amid yearnings sharpened by delay. Why didn't the play begin? The men pulled out their watches, late-comers sprang from their conveyances before these had fairly drawn up, the groups left the sidewalk, where the passers-by were crossing the now vacant space of gas-lit pavement, craning their necks, as they did so, in order to get a peep into the theatre. A street-boy came up whistling and planted himself before a notice at the door, then cried out, "Woa, Nana!" in the voice of a tipsy man and hied on his way with a rolling gait and a shuffling of his old boots. A laugh had arisen at this. Gentlemen of unimpeachable appearance repeated "Nana, woa Nana!" People were crushing, a dispute arose at the ticket office, and there was a growing clamour caused by the hum of voices calling on Nana, demanding Nana in

one of those accesses of silly facetious-ness and sheer animalism which pass over mobs.

But, above all the din, the bell that precedes the rise of the curtain became audible. "They've rung, they've rung!" The rumour reached the boulevard; and thereupon followed a stampede, everyone wanting to pass in, while the servants of the theatre increased their forces. Mignon, with an anxious air, at last got hold of Steiner again, the latter not having been to see Rose's costume. At the very first tinkle of the bell, la Faloise had cloven a way through the crowd, pulling Fauchery with him, so as not to miss the opening scene. But all this eagerness on the part of the public irri-tated Lucy Stewart. What brutes were these people to be pushing women like that! She stayed in the rear of them all, with Caroline Héquet and her mother. The entrance-hall was now empty, while beyond it was still heard the long-drawn rumble of the boulevard.

"As though they were always funny, those pieces of theirs!" Lucy kept re-peating as she climbed the stair.

In the house, Fauchery and la Faloise, in front of their stalls, were gazing about them anew. By this time the house was resplendent. High jets of gas illumined the great glass chandelier with a rustling of yellow and rosy flames, which rained down a stream of brilliant light from dome to floor. The cardinal velvets of the seats were shot with hues of lake, while all the gilding shone again, the soft green decorations chastening its effect beneath the too-decided paintings of the ceiling. The footlights were turned up, and with a vivid flood of brilliance lit up the curtain, the heavy purple drapery of which had all the richness befitting a palace in a fairy tale, and contrasted with the meanness of the proscenium, where cracks shewed the plaster under the gilding. The place was already warm. At their music-stands the orchestra were tuning their instruments amid a delicate trilling of flutes, a stifled tooting of horns, a singing of violin notes, which floated forth amid the increasing uproar of voices. All the spectators were talking, jostling, settling themselves in a general assault upon seats; and the hustling rush in the side-passages was now so violent that every door into the house was laboriously admitting an inexhaustible flood of people. There were signals, rustlings of fabrics, a continual march-past of skirts and head-dresses, accentuated by the black hue of a dress-coat or a surtout. Notwithstanding this, the rows of seats were little by little getting filled up, while here and here a light toilette stood out from its surroundings, a head with a delicate profile bent forward under its chignon, where flashed the lightning of a jewel. In one of the boxes the tip of a bare shoulder glimmered like snowy silk. Other ladies, sitting at ease, languidly fanned themselves, following with their gaze the pushing movements of the crowd, while young gentlemen, standing up in the stalls, their waistcoats cut very low, gardenias in their button-holes, pointed their opera-glasses with gloved finger-tips.

It was now that the two cousins began searching for the faces of those they knew. Mignon and Steiner were together in a lower box, sitting side by side with their arms leaning for support on the velvet balustrade. Blanche de Sivry seemed to be in sole possession of a stage-box on the level of the stalls. But la Faloise examined Daguenet before anyone else, he being in occupation of a stall two rows in front of his own. Close to him, a very young man, seventeen years old at the outside, some truant from college, it may be, was straining wide a pair of fine eyes such as a cherub might have owned. Fauchery smiled when he looked at him.

"Who is that lady in the balcony?" la Faloise asked suddenly; "the lady with a young girl in blue beside her."

He pointed out a large woman, who was excessively tight-laced, a woman who had been a blonde and had now become white and yellow of tint, her broad face, reddened with paint, looking puffy under a rain of little childish curls.

"It's Gaga" was Fauchery's simple reply, and as this name seemed to astound his cousin, he added,—

"You don't know Gaga? She was the delight of the early years of Louis-Philippe. Nowadays, she drags her daughter about with her wherever she goes."

La Faloise never once glanced at the young girl. The sight of Gaga moved him; his eyes did not leave her again. He still found her very good-looking, but he dared not say so.

Meanwhile the conductor lifted his violin bow and the orchestra attacked the overture. People still kept coming in; the stir and noise were on the increase. Among that public, peculiar to first nights and never subject to change, there were little subsections composed of intimate friends, who smilingly foregathered again. Old first-nighters, hat on head, seemed familiar and quite at ease, and kept exchanging salutations. All Paris was there, the Paris of literature, of finance, and of pleasure. There were many journalists, several authors, a number of stock exchange people, and more courtesans than honest women. It was a singularly mixed world, composed, as it was, of all the talents, and tarnished by all the vices, a world where the same fatigue and the same fever played over every face. Fauchery, whom his cousin was questioning, shewed him the boxes devoted to the newspapers and to the clubs, and then named the dramatic critics—a lean, dried-up individual, with thin spiteful lips, and, chief of all, a big fellow, with a good-natured expression, lolling on the shoulder of his neighbour, a young miss over whom he brooded with tender and paternal eye.

But he interrupted himself on seeing la Faloise in the act of bowing to some persons who occupied the box opposite. He appeared surprised.

"What!" he queried, "you know the Count Muffat de Beuville?"

"Oh, for a long time back," replied Hector. "The Muffats had a property near us. I often go to their house. The Count's with his wife and his father-in-law, the Marquis de Chouard."

And, with some vanity—for he was happy in his cousin's astonishment—he entered into particulars. The Marquis was a Councillor of State, the Count had recently been appointed Chamberlain to the Empress. Fauchery, who had caught up his opera-glass, looked at the Countess, a plump brunette with a white skin and fine dark eyes.

"You shall present me to them between the acts," he ended by saying. "I have already met the Count, but I should like to go to them on their Tuesdays."

Energetic cries of "Hush" came from the upper galleries. The overture had begun, but people were still coming in. Late arrivals were obliging whole rows of spectators to rise, the doors of boxes were banging, loud voices were heard disputing in the passages. And there was no cessation of the sound of many conversations, a sound similar to the loud twittering of talkative sparrows at close of day. All was in confusion; the house was a medley of heads and arms which moved to and fro, their owners seating themselves or trying to make themselves comfortable, or, on the other hand, excitedly endeavouring to remain standing so as to take a final look-round. The cry of "Sit down, sit down!" came fiercely from the obscure depths of the pit. A shiver of expectation traversed the house: at last people were going to make the acquaintance of this famous Nana, with whom Paris had been occupying itself for a whole week!

Little by little, however, the buzz of talk dwindled softly down among occasional fresh outbursts of rough speech. And, amid this swooning murmur, these perishing sighs of sound, the orchestra struck up the small lively notes of a waltz with a vagabond rhythm bubbling with roguish laughter. The public were titillated; they were already on the grin. But the gang of clappers, in the foremost rows of the pit, applauded furiously. The curtain rose.

"By George!" exclaimed la Faloise,

still talking away, "there's a man with Lucy."

He was looking at the stage-box, on the second tier to his right, the front of which Caroline and Lucy were occupying. At the back of this box were observable the worthy countenance of Caroline's mother, and the side face of a tall young man, with a noble head of light hair and an irreproachable get-up.

"Do look!" la Faloise again insisted, "there's a man there."

Fauchery decided to level his opera-glass at the stage-box. But he turned round again directly.

"Oh! it's Labordette," he muttered, in a careless voice, as though that gentleman's presence ought to strike all the world as though both natural and immaterial.

Behind the cousins people shouted "Silence!" They had to cease talking. A motionless fit now seized the house, and great stretches of heads, all erect and attentive, sloped away from stalls to topmost gallery. The first act of the *Blonde Venus* took place in Olympus, a paste-board Olympus, with clouds in the wings and the throne of Jupiter on the right of the stage. First of all Iris and Ganymede, aided by a troupe of celestial attendants, sang a chorus while they arranged the seats of the gods for the council. Once again the prearranged applause of the clappers alone burst forth; the public, a little out of their depth, sat waiting. Nevertheless, la Faloise had clapped Clarisse Besnus, one of Bordenave's little women, who played Iris in a soft blue dress with a great scarf of the seven colours of the rainbow looped round her waist.

"You know she draws up her chemise to put that on," said he to Fauchery, loud enough to be heard by those around him. "We tried the trick this morning. It was all up under her arms and round the small of her back."

But a slight rustling movement ran through the house, Rose Mignon had just come on the stage as Diana. Now, though she had neither the face nor the figure for the part, being thin and dark, and of the adorable type of ugliness peculiar to a Parisian street child, she none the less appeared charming, and as though she were a satire on the personage she represented. Her song, at her entrance on the stage, was full of lines quaint enough to make you cry with laughter, and of complaints about Mars, who was getting ready to desert her for the companionship of Venus. She sang it with a chaste reserve so full of sprightly suggestiveness that the public warmed amain. The husband and Steiner, sitting side by side, were laughing complaisantly, and the whole house broke out in a roar when Prullière, that great favourite, appeared as a general, a masquerade Mars, decked with an enormous plume, and dragging along a sword the hilt of which reached to his shoulder. As for him, he had had enough of Diana; she had been a great deal too coy with him, he averred. Thereupon Diana promised to keep a sharp eye on him and to be revenged. The duet ended with a comic yodel which Prullière delivered very amusingly with the yell of an angry tomcat. He had about him all the entertaining fatuity of a young leading gentleman whose love affairs prosper, and he rolled around the most swaggering glances, which excited shrill feminine laughter in the boxes.

Then the public cooled again, for the ensuing scenes were found tiresome. Old Bosc, an imbecile Jupiter, with head crushed beneath the weight of an immense crown, only just succeeded in raising a smile among his audience, when he had a domestic altercation with Juno on the subject of the cook's accounts. The march-past of the gods, Neptune, Pluto, Minerva and the rest, was well-nigh spoiling everything. People grew impatient, there was a restless, slowly-growing murmur, the audience ceased to take an interest in the performance, and looked round at the house. Lucy began laughing with Labordette; the Count de Vandeuvres was craning his neck in conversation behind Blanche's sturdy shoulders, while Fauchery, out of the corners of his eyes, took stock of the Muffats, of whom the Count appeared very serious, as though he had not understood the allusions, and the Countess smiled vaguely, her eyes lost in reverie. But, on a sudden, in this uncomfortable state of things, the applause of the clapping contingent rattled out with the regularity of platoon-firing. People turned towards the stage. Was it Nana at last? This Nana made one wait with a vengeance.

It was a deputation of mortals whom Ganymede and Iris had introduced, respectable middle-class persons, deceived husbands all of them, and they came before the master of the gods to proffer a complaint against Venus, who was assuredly inflaming their good ladies with an excess of ardour. The chorus, in quaint dolorous tones, broken by silences full of pantomimic admissions, caused great amusement. A neat phrase went the round of the house: "The Cuckold's Chorus, the Cuckold's Chorus," and it "caught on," for there was an encore. The singers' heads were droll; their faces were discovered to be in keeping with the phrase, especially that of a fat man which was as round as the moon. Meanwhile, Vulcan arrived in a towering rage, demanding back his wife, who had slipped away three days ago. The chorus resumed their plaint, calling on Vulcan, the God of the Cuckolds. Vulcan's part was played by Fontan, a comic actor of talent, at once vulgar and original, and he had a *rôle* of the wildest whimsicality, and was got up as a village blacksmith, fiery red wig, bare arms tattooed with arrow-pierced hearts, and all the rest of it. A woman's voice cried in a very high key, "Oh, isn't he ugly?" and all the ladies laughed and applauded.

Then followed a scene which seemed interminable. Jupiter in the course of it seemed never to be going to finish assembling the Council of Gods, in order to submit thereto the deceived husband's requests. And still no Nana! Was the management keeping Nana for the fall of the curtain then? So long a period of expectancy had ended by annoying the public. Their murmurings began again.

"It's going badly," said Mignon radiantly to Steiner. "She'll get a pretty reception, you'll see!"

At that very moment the clouds at the back of the stage were cloven apart, and Venus appeared. Exceedingly tall, exceedingly strong for her eighteen years, Nana, in her goddess's white tunic, and with her light hair simply flowing unfastened over her shoulders, came down to the footlights, with a quiet certainty of movement, and a laugh of greeting for the public, and struck up her grand ditty,—

*"When Venus roams at eventide."*

From the second verse onward, people looked at each other all over the house. Was this some jest, some wager on Bordenave's part? Never had a more tuneless voice been heard, or one managed with less art. Her manager judged of her excellently; she certainly sang like a squirt. Nay, more, she didn't even know how to deport herself on the stage: she thrust her arms in front of her, while she swayed her whole body to and fro in a manner which struck the audience as unbecoming and disagreeable. Cries of "Oh, oh!" were already rising in the pit and the cheap places. There was a sound of whistling too, when a voice in the stalls, suggestive of a moulting cockerel cried out with great conviction,—

"That's very smart!"

All the house looked round. It was the cherub, the truant from the boarding-school, who sat with his fine eyes very wide open, and his fair face glowing very hotly at sight of Nana. When he saw everybody turning towards him, he grew extremely red at the thought of having thus unconsciously spoken aloud. Daguenet, his neighbour, smilingly examined him; the public laughed, as though disarmed, and no longer anxious to hiss; while the young gentlemen in white gloves, fascinated in their turn by Nana's gracious contours, lolled back in their seats and applauded.

"That's it! well done! Bravo!"

Nana, in the mean time, seeing the house laughing, began to laugh herself.

The gaiety of all redoubled itself. She was an amusing creature, all the same, was that fine girl! Her laughter made a love of a little dimple appear in her chin. She stood there waiting, not bored in the least, familiar with her audience, falling into step with them at once, as though she herself were admitting, with a wink, that she had not two farthings' worth of talent, but that it did not matter at all, that in fact she had other good points. And then, after having made a sign to the conductor which plainly signified, "Go ahead, old boy!" she began her second verse:—

*" 'Tis Venus who at midnight passes——"*

Still the same acidulated voice, only that now it tickled the public in the right quarter so deftly that momentarily it caused them to give a little shiver of pleasure. Nana still smiled her smile: it lit up her little red mouth, and shone in her great eyes, which were of the clearest blue. When she came to certain rather lively verses, a delicate sense of enjoyment made her tilt her nose, the rosy nostrils of which lifted and fell, while a bright flush suffused her cheeks. She still swung herself up and down, for she only knew how to do that. And the trick was no longer voted ugly; on the contrary, the men raised their opera-glasses. When she came to the end of a verse, her voice completely failed her, and she was well aware that she never would get through with it. Thereupon, rather than fret herself, she kicked up her leg, which forthwith was roundly outlined under her diaphanous tunic, bent sharply backwards, so that her bosom was thrown upward and forward, and stretched her arms out. Applause burst forth on all sides. In the twinkling of an eye she had turned on her heel, and was going up the stage, presenting the nape of her neck to the spectators' gaze, a neck where the red gold hair shewed like some animal's fell. Then the plaudits became frantic.

The close of the act was not so exciting. Vulcan wanted to slap Venus. The gods held a consultation, and decided to go and hold an enquiry on earth before granting the deceived husband satisfaction. It was then that Diana surprised a tender conversation between Venus and Mars, and vowed that she would not take her eyes off them during the whole of the voyage. There was also a scene where Love, played by a little twelve-year-old chit, answered every question put to her with—"Yes, mamma! No, mamma!" in a winey-piney tone, her fingers in her nose. At last Jupiter, with the severity of a master who is growing cross, shut Love up in a dark closet, bidding her conjugate the verb "I love" twenty times. The finale was more appreciated: it was a chorus which both troupe and orchestra performed with great brilliancy. But, the curtain once down, the clappers tried in vain to obtain a call, while the whole house was already up and making for the doors.

The crowd trampled and jostled, jammed, as it was, between the rows of seats, and in so doing exchanged expressions. One phrase only went round— "It's idiotic." A critic was saying that it would be one's duty to do a pretty bit of slashing. The piece, however, mattered very little; for people were talking about Nana before everything else. Fauchery and la Faloise, being among the earliest to emerge, met Steiner and Mignon in the passage outside the stalls. In this gas-lit gut of a place, which was as narrow and circumscribed as a gallery in a mine, one was well-nigh suffocated. They stopped a moment at the foot of the stairs on the right of the house, protected by the final curve of the balusters. The audience from the cheap places were coming down the steps with a continuous tramp of heavy boots, a stream of black dress-coats was passing, whilst an attendant was making every possible effort to protect a chair, on which she had piled up coats and cloaks, from the onward pushing of the crowd.

"Surely I know her," cried Steiner, the moment he perceived Fauchery. I'm certain I've seen her somewhere—at the Casino, I imagine, and she got herself taken up there—she was so drunk."

"As for me," said the journalist, "I don't quite know where it was; I am like you, I certainly have come across her."

He lowered his voice, and asked laughing,—

"At the Tricon's, perhaps."

"Egad, it was in a dirty place," Mignon declared. He seemed exasperated. "It's disgusting that the public give such a reception to the first trollop that comes by. There'll soon be no more decent women on the stage. Yes, I shall end by forbidding Rose to play."

Fauchery could not restrain a smile. Meanwhile the downward shuffle of the heavy shoes on the steps did not cease, and a little man in a workman's cap was heard crying, in a drawling voice,—

"Oh my, she ain't no wopper! There's some pickings there!"

In the passage, two young men, delicately curled and formally resplendent in turn-down collars and the rest, were disputing together. One of them was repeating the words, "Beastly, beastly!" without stating any reasons; the other was replying with the words, "Stunning, stunning!" as though he too disdained all argument.

La Faloise declared her to be quite the thing; only he ventured to opine that she would be better still if she were to cultivate her voice. Steiner, who was no longer listening, seemed to awake with a start. Whatever happens, one must wait, he thought. Perhaps everything will be spoilt in the following acts. The public had shewn complaisance, but it was certainly not yet taken by storm. Mignon swore that the piece would never finish, and when Fauchery and la Faloise left them in order to go up to the foyer, he took Steiner's arm, and leaning hard against his shoulder, whispered in his ear,—

"You're going to see my wife's costume for the second act, old fellow. It *is* just blackguardly."

Upstairs, in the foyer, three glass chandeliers burnt with a brilliant light. The two cousins hesitated an instant before entering, for the widely opened glazed doors afforded a view right through the gallery—a view of a surging sea of heads, which two currents, as it were, kept in a continuous eddying movement. But they entered after all. Five or six groups of men, talking very loud and gesticulating, were obstinately discussing the play amid these violent interruptions; others were filing round, their heels, as they turned, sounding sharply on the waxed floor. To right and left, between columns of variegated imitation marble, women were sitting on benches covered with red velvet, and viewing the passing movement of the crowd with an air of fatigue as though the heat had rendered them languid. In the lofty mirrors behind them one saw the reflection of their chignons. At the end of the room, in front of the bar, a man with a huge corporation was drinking a glass of fruit-syrup.

But Fauchery, in order to breathe more freely, had gone to the balcony. La Faloise, who was studying the photographs of actresses hung in frames alternating with the mirrors between the columns, ended by following him. They had extinguished the line of gas-jets on the façade of the theatre, and it was dark and very cool on the balcony, which seemed to them unoccupied. Solitary and enveloped in shadow, a young man was standing, leaning his arms on the stone balustrade, in the recess to the right. He was smoking a cigarette, of which the burning end shone redly. Fauchery recognised Daguenet. They shook hands warmly.

"What are you after there, my dear fellow?" asked the journalist. "You're hiding yourself in holes and crannies—you, a man who never leaves the stalls on a first night!"

"But I'm smoking, you see," replied Daguenet.

Then Fauchery, to put him out of countenance,—

"Well, well! what's your opinion of the new actress? She's being roughly handled enough in the passages."

"Bah!" muttered Daguenet, "they're people whom she'll have had nothing to do with!"

That was the sum of his criticism of Nana's talent. La Faloise leant forward, and looked down at the boulevard. Over against them the windows of a hotel and of a club were brightly lit up, whilst, on the pavement below, a dark mass of customers occupied the tables of the "Café de Madrid." Despite the lateness of the hour, the crowd were still crushing and being crushed; people were advancing with shortened step; a throng was constantly emerging from the Passage Jouffroy; individuals stood waiting five or six minutes before they could cross the roadway, to such a distance did the string of carriages extend.

"What a moving mass! And what a noise!" la Faloise kept reiterating, for Paris still astonished him.

The bell rang for some time, the foyer emptied. There was a hurrying of people in the passages. The curtain was already up when whole bands of spectators re-entered the house amid the irritated expressions of those who were once more in their places. Everyone took his seat again with an animated look and renewed attention. La Faloise directed his first glance in Gaga's direction, but he was dumbfounded at seeing by her side the tall fair man, who but recently had been in Lucy's stage-box.

"What *is* that man's name?" he asked.

Fauchery failed to observe him.

"Ah yes, it's Labordette," he said at last; with the same careless movement.

The scenery of the second act came as a surprise. It represented a suburban Shrove Tuesday dance at the "Boule Noire." Masqueraders were trolling a catch, the chorus of which was accompanied with a tapping of their heels. This 'Arryish departure, which nobody had in the least expected, caused so much amusement that the house encored

the catch. And it was to this entertainment that the divine band, led astray by Iris, who falsely bragged that he knew the Earth well, were now come in order to proceed with their enquiry. They had put on disguises so as to preserve their *incognito*. Jupiter came on the stage as King Dagobert, with his breeches inside out, and a huge tin crown on his head. Phœbus appeared as the Postillion of Lonjumeau, and Minerva as a Norman nurse-maid. Loud bursts of merriment greeted Mars, who wore an outrageous uniform suggestive of an Alpine Admiral. But the shouts of laughter became uproarious when Neptune came in view, clad in a blouse, a high, bulging workman's cap on his head, love-locks glued to his temples. Shuffling along in slippers, he cried in a thick brogue,—

"Well I'm blessed! when ye're a masher, it'll never do not to let 'em love yer!"

There were some shouts of "Oh! Oh!" while the ladies held their fans one degree higher. Lucy in her stage-box laughed so obstreperously that Caroline Héquet silenced her with a tap of her fan.

From that moment forth the piece was saved—nay more, promised a great success. This carnival of the gods, this dragging in the mud of their Olympus, this mock at a whole religion, a whole world of poetry, appeared in the light of a royal entertainment. The fever of irreverence gained the literary first-night world: legend was trampled under foot, ancient images were shattered. Jupiter's make-up was capital. Mars was a success. Royalty became a farce, and the Army a thing of folly. When Jupiter, grown suddenly amorous of a little laundress, began to knock off a mad cancan, Simonne, who was playing the part of the laundress launched a kick at the master of the immortals' nose, and addressed him so drolly as, "My big daddy!" that an immoderate fit of laughter shook the whole house. While they were dancing, Phœbus treated Minerva to salad-bowls of negus, and Neptune sat in state among seven or eight women, who regaled him with cakes. Allusions were eagerly caught, indecent meanings were attached to them, harmless phrases were diverted from their proper significations in the light of exclamations issuing from the stalls. For a long time past the theatrical public had not wallowed in folly more irreverent. It rested them.

Nevertheless the action of the piece advanced amid these fooleries. Vulcan, as an elegant young man, clad, down to his gloves, entirely in yellow, and with an eye-glass stuck in his eye, was for ever running after Venus, who at last made her appearance as a fish-wife, a kerchief on her head, and her bosom, covered with big gold trinkets, in great evidence. Nana was so white and plump, and looked so natural in a part demanding wide hips and a voluptuous mouth, that she straightway won the whole house. On her account Rose Mignon was forgotten, though she was made up as a delicious baby, with a wickerwork burlet on her head and a short muslin frock, and had just sighed forth Diana's plaints in a sweetly pretty voice. The other one, the big wench who slapped her thighs and clucked like a hen, shed round her an odour of life, a sovran feminine charm, with which the public grew intoxicated. From the second act onwards everything was permitted her. She might hold herself awkwardly, she might fail to sing some note in tune, she might forget her words—it mattered not: she had only to turn and laugh to raise shouts of applause. When she gave her famous kick from the hip, the stalls were fired, and a glow of passion rose upward, upward, from gallery to gallery, till its reached the gods. It was a triumph too when she led the dance. She was at home in that: hand on hip, she enthroned Venus in the gutter by the pavement-side. And the music, seemed made for her plebeian voice—shrill, piping music, with reminiscences of Saint-Cloud Fair, wheezings of clarinets, and playful trills on the part of the little flutes.

Two numbers were again encored. The opening waltz, that waltz with the naughty rhythmic beat, had returned, and swept the gods with it. Juno, as a peasant woman, caught Jupiter and his little laundress cleverly, and boxed his ears. Diana, surprising Venus in the act of making an assignation with Mars, made haste to indicate hour and place to Vulcan, who cried, "I've hit on a plan!" The rest of the act did not seem very clear. The enquiry ended in a final galop after which Jupiter, breathless, streaming with perspiration, and minus his crown, declared that the little women of Earth were delicious, and that the men were all to blame.

The curtain was falling, when certain voices, rising above the storm of bravos, cried uproariously,—

"All! All!"

Thereupon the curtain rose again, the artistes reappeared hand in hand. In the middle of the line Nana and Rose Mignon stood side by side, bowing and curtseying. The audience applauded, the clappers shouted acclamations. Then, little by little, the house emptied.

"I must go and pay my respects to the Countess Muffat," said la Faloise.

"Exactly so; you'll present me," replied Fauchery; "we'll go down afterwards."

But it was not easy to get to the first-tier boxes.· In the passage, at the top of the stairs, there was a crush. In order to get forward at all, among the various groups, you had to make yourself small and to slide along, using your elbows in so doing. Leaning under a copper lamp, where a jet of gas was burning, the bulky critic was sitting in judgment on the piece, in presence of an attentive circle. People in passing mentioned his name to each other in muttered tones. He had laughed the whole act through—that was the humour going the round of the passages: nevertheless he was now very severe, and spoke of taste and morals. Further off, the thin-lipped critic was brimming over with a benevolence which had an unpleasant after-taste, as of milk turned sour.

Fauchery glanced along, scrutinising the boxes through the round openings in each door. But the Count de Vandeuvres stopped him with a question, and when he was informed that the two cousins were going to pay their respects to the Muffats, he pointed out to them Box Seven, from which he had just emerged. Then, bending down and whispering in the journalist's ear,—

"Tell me, my dear fellow," said he, "this Nana—surely she's the girl we saw one evening at the corner of the Rue de Provençe?"

"By Jove, you're right!" cried Fauchery. "I was saying that I had come across her!"

La Faloise presented his cousin to Count Muffat de Beuville, who appeared very frigid. But, on hearing the name "Fauchery," the Countess raised her head, and with a certain reserve complimented the paragraphist on his articles in the *Figaro*. Leaning on the velvet-covered support in front of her, she turned half round with a pretty movement of the shoulders. They talked for a short time, and the Universal Exhibition was mentioned.

"It will be very fine," said the Count, whose square-cut, regular-featured face retained a certain gravity.

"I visited the Champ-de-Mars to-day, and returned thence truly astonished."

"They say that things won't be ready in time," la Faloise ventured to remark. "There's infinite confusion there——"

But the Count interrupted him in his severe voice,—

"Things will be ready. The Emperor desires it."

Fauchery gaily recounted how, one day, when he had gone down thither in search of a subject for an article, he had come near spending all his time in the aquarium, which was then in course of construction. The Countess smiled. Now and again she glanced down at the body of the house, raising an arm which a white glove covered to the elbow, and fanning herself with languid hand. The house dozed, almost deserted. Some gentlemen in the stalls had opened out newspapers, and ladies received visits quite comfortably, as though they were at their own homes. Only a well-bred whispering was audible under the great chandelier, the light of which was softened in

the fine cloud of dust raised by the confused movements of the interval. At
the different entrances men were crowding in order to talk to ladies who remained seated. They stood there motionless for a few seconds, craning forward somewhat and displaying the great
white bosoms of their shirt-fronts.

"We count on you next Tuesday," said
the Countess to la Faloise, and she invited Fauchery, who bowed.

Not a word was said of the play;
Nana's name was not once mentioned.
The Count was so glacially dignified that
he might have been supposed to be
taking part at a sitting of the Legislature.
In order to explain their presence that
evening, he remarked simply that his
father-in-law was fond of the theatre.
The door of the box must have remained
open, for the Marquis de Chouard, who
had gone out in order to leave his seat to
the visitors, was back again. He was
straightening up his tall, old figure. His
face looked soft and white under a broad-
brimmed hat, and with his restless eyes
he followed the movements of the women
who passed.

The moment the Countess had given
her invitation, Fauchery took his leave,
feeling that to talk about the play would
not be quite the thing. La Faloise was
the last to quit the box. He had just
noticed the fair-haired Labordette, comfortably installed in the Count de Vandeuvres's stage-box and, chatting at very
close quarters with Blanche de Sivry.

"Gad," said he, after rejoining his
cousin, "that Labordette knows all the
girls, then! He's with Blanche now."

"Doubtless, he knows them all," replied Fauchery, quietly. "What d'you
want to be taken for, my friend?"

The passage was somewhat cleared of
people, and Fauchery was just about to
go downstairs when Lucy Stewart called
him. She was quite at the other end of
the corridor, at the door of her stage-box.
They were getting cooked in there, she
said, and she took up the whole corridor
in company with Caroline Héquet and her
mother, all three nibbling burnt almonds
A box-opener was chatting maternally
with them. Lucy fell out with the journalist. He was a pretty fellow, to be
sure! He went up to see other women,
and didn't even come and ask if they
were thirsty! Then, changing the subject,—

"You know, dear boy, I think Nana
very nice."

She wanted him to stay in the stage-
box for the last act, but he made his
escape, promising to catch them at the
door afterwards. Downstairs, in front
of the theatre, Fauchery and la Faloise
lit cigarettes. A great gathering blocked
the sidewalk, a stream of men who had
come down from the theatre steps, and
were inhaling the fresh night air in the
boulevards, where the roar and battle
had diminished.

Meanwhile, Mignon had drawn Steiner
away to the "Café des Variétés." Seeing
Nana's success, he had set to work to
talk enthusiastically about her, all the
while observing the banker out of the
corners of his eyes. He knew him well;
twice he had helped him to deceive
Rose, and then, the caprice being over,
had brought him back to her, faithful and
repentant. In the café the too-numerous
crowd of customers were squeezing themselves round the marble-topped tables.
Several were standing up, drinking in a
great hurry. The tall mirrors reflected

this thronging world of heads to infinity, and magnified the narrow room beyond measure, with its three chandeliers, its moleskin-covered seats, and its winding staircase draped with red. Steiner went and seated himself at a table in the first saloon, which opened full on the boulevard, its doors having been removed rather early for the time of year. As Fauchery and la Faloise were passing, the banker stopped them. "Come and take a *bock* with us, eh?" they said.

But he was too preoccupied by an idea, he wanted to have a bouquet thrown to Nana. At last he called a waiter belonging to the café, whom he familiarly addressed as Auguste. Mignon, who was listening, looked at him so sharply that he lost countenance, and stammered out:

"Two bouquets, Auguste, and deliver them to the attendant. A bouquet for each of these ladies! Happy thought, eh?"

At the other end of the saloon, her shoulders resting against the frame of a mirror, a girl some eighteen years of age at the outside, was leaning motionless in front of her empty glass, as though she had been benumbed by long and fruitless waiting. Under the natural curls of her beautiful grey-gold hair, a virginal face looked out at you with velvety eyes, which were at once soft and candid.

She wore a dress of faded green silk, and a round hat which blows had dinted. The cool air of the night made her look very pale.

"Egad, there's Satin," murmured Fauchery when his eye lit upon her.

La Faloise questioned him. Oh dear yes, she was a street-walker—she didn't count. But she was such a scandalous sort, that people amused themselves by making her talk. And the journalist, raising his voice,—

"What are you doing there, Satin?"

"I'm bogging," replied Satin quietly, without changing position.

The four men were charmed, and fell a-laughing. Mignon assured them that there was no need to hurry; it would take twenty minutes to set up the scenery for the third act. But the two cousins, having drunk their beer, wanted to go up into the theatre again; the cold was making itself felt. Then Mignon remained alone with Steiner, put his elbows on the table, and spoke to him at close quarters.

"It's an understood thing, eh? We are to go to her house, and I'm to introduce you. You know the thing's quite between ourselves—my wife needn't know."

Once more in their places, Fauchery and la Faloise noticed a pretty, quietly-dressed woman in the second tier of boxes. She was with a serious-looking gentleman, a chief clerk at the Office of the Ministry of the Interior, whom la Faloise knew, having met him at the Muffats. As to Fauchery, he was under the impression that her name was Madame Robert, a lady of honourable repute, who had a lover, only one, and that always a person of respectability.

But they had to turn round for Daguenet was smiling at them. Now that Nana had had a success, he no longer hid himself: indeed, he had just been scoring triumphs in the passages. By his side was the young truant schoolboy, who had not quitted his seat, so stupefying was the state of admiration into which

Nana had plunged him. That was it, he thought; that was the woman! And he blushed as he thought so, and dragged his gloves on and off mechanically. Then, since his neighbour had spoken of Nana, he ventured to question him.

"Will you pardon me for asking you, sir, but that lady who is acting—do you know her?"

"Yes, I do a little," murmured Daguenet with some surprise and hesitation.

"Then you know her address?"

The question, addressed as it was to him, came so abruptly that he felt inclined to respond with a box on the ear.

"No," said he, in a dry tone of voice.

And with that he turned his back. The fair lad knew that he had just been guilty of some breach of good manners. He blushed more hotly than ever and looked scared.

The traditional three knocks were given, and among the returning throng, attendants, laden with pelisses and overcoats, bustled about at a great rate in order to put away people's things. The clappers applauded the scenery, which represented a grotto on Mount Etna, hollowed out in a silver mine and with sides glittering like new money. In the background Vulcan's forge glowed like a setting star. Diana, since the second act, had come to a good understanding with the god, who was to pretend that he was on a journey, so as to leave the way clear for Venus and Mars. Then, scarcely was Diana alone, than Venus made her appearance. A shiver of delight ran round the house. Nana was nude. With quiet audacity, she appeared in her nakedness, certain of the sovran power of her flesh. Some gauze enveloped her, but her rounded shoulders, her Amazonian bosom, her wide hips, which swayed to an fro voluptuously, her whole body, in fact, could be devined, nay discerned, in all its foamlike whiteness of tint, beneath the slight fabric she wore. It was Venus rising from the waves, with no veil save her tresses. And when Nana lifted her arms, the golden hairs in her arm-pits were observable in the glare of the footlights. There was no applause. Nobody laughed any more. The men strained forward with serious faces, sharp features, mouths irritated and parched. A wind seemed to have passed, a soft, soft wind, laden with a secret menace. Suddenly in the bouncing child the woman stood discovered, a woman full of restless suggestion, who brought with her the delirium of sex, and opened the gates of the unknown world of desire. Nana was smiling still, but her smile was now bitter, as of a devourer of men.

"By God," said Fauchery, quite simply, to la Faloise.

Mars in the meantime, with his plume of feathers, came hurrying to the trysting-place, and found himself between the two goddesses. Then ensued a passage which Prullière played with great delicacy. Petted by Diana, who wanted to make a final attack upon his feelings before delivering him up to Vulcan, wheedled by Venus, whom the presence of her rival excited, he gave himself up to these tender delights with the beatified expression of a man in clover. Finally, a grand trio brought the scene to a close, and it was then that an attendant appeared in Lucy Stewart's box and threw on the stage two immense bouquets of white lilac. There was applause, Nana and Rose Mignon bowed, while Prullière picked up the bouquets. Many of the occupants of the stalls turned smilingly towards the ground-floor occupied by Steiner and Mignon. The banker, his face blood-red, was suffering from little convulsive twitchings of the chin, as though he had a stoppage in his throat. What followed took the house by storm completely. Diana had gone off in a rage, and directly afterwards, Venus, sitting on a moss-clad seat, called Mars to her. Never yet had a more glowing scene of seduction been ventured on. Nana, her arms round Prullière's neck, was drawing him towards her, when Fontan, with comically-furious mimicry and an exaggerated imitation of the face of an outraged husband, who surprises his wife in *flagrante delicto,* appeared at the back of the grotto. He was holding the famous net with iron meshes. For an instant he poised and swung it, as a fisherman does when he is going to make a cast, and, by an ingenious twist, Venus and Mars were caught in the snare, the net wrapped itself round them, and held them motionless in the attitude of happy lovers.

A murmur of applause swelled and swelled, like a growing sigh. There was some hand-clapping, and every opera-glass was fixed on Venus. Little by little Nana had taken possession of the public, and now every man was her slave. A wave of lust had flowed from her as from an excited animal, and its influence had spread, and spread, and spread till the whole house was possessed by it. At that moment her slightest movements blew the flame of desire: with her little finger she ruled men's flesh. Backs were arched and quivered as though unseen violin-bows had been drawn across their muscles; upon men's shoulders appeared fugitive hairs, which flew in

air, blown by warm and wandering breaths, breathed one knew not from what feminine mouth. In front of him Fauchery saw the truant schoolboy half lifted from his seat by passion. Curiosity led him to look at the Count de Vandeuvres—he was extremely pale, and his lips looked pinched—at fat Steiner, whose face was purple to the verge of apoplexy—at Labordette, ogling away with the highly-astonished air of a horse-dealer admiring a perfectly-shaped mare—at Daguenet, whose ears were blood-red and twitching with enjoyment. Then, a sudden idea made him glance behind, and he marvelled at what he saw in the Muffats' box. Behind the Countess, who was white and serious as usual, the Count was sitting straight upright, with mouth agape and face mottled with red, while close by him, in the shadow, the restless eyes of the Marquis de Chouard had become cat-like phosphorescent, full of golden sparkles. The house was suffocating, people's very hair grew heavy on their perspiring heads. For three hours back, the breath of the multitude had filled and heated the atmosphere with a scent of crowded humanity. Under the swaying glare of the gas, the dust-clouds, in mid-air, had grown constantly denser as they hung motionless beneath the chandelier. The whole house seemed to be oscillating, to be lapsing towards dizziness, in its fatigue and excitement, full, as it was, of those drowsy midnight desires which flutter in the recesses of the bed of passion. And Nana, in front of this languorous public, these fifteen hundred human beings thronged and smothered in the exhaustion and nervous exasperation which belong to the close of a spectacle, Nana still triumphed by right of her marble flesh, and that sexual nature of hers, which was strong enough to destroy the whole crowd of her adorers and yet sustain no injury.

The piece drew to a close. In answer to Vulcan's triumphant summons, all the Olympians defiled before the lovers, with oh! and ahs! of stupefaction and gaiety. Jupiter said, "I think it is light conduct on your part, my son, to summon us to see such a sight as this." Then a reaction took place in favour of Venus. The Chorus of Cuckolds was again ushered in by Iris, and besought the master of the gods not to give effect to its petition, for since women had lived at home, domestic life had been becoming impossible for the men: the latter preferred being deceived and happy. That was the moral of the play. Then Venus was set at liberty, and Vulcan obtained a partial divorce from her. Mars was reconciled with Diana, and Jove, for the sake of domestic peace, packed his little laundress off into a constellation. And finally they extricated Love from his black hole, where, instead of conjugating the verb *amo,* he had been busy in the manufacture of "dollies." The curtain fell on an apotheosis, wherein the Cuckold's Chorus knelt and sang a hymn of gratitude to Venus, who stood there with smiling lips, her stature enhanced by her sovran nudity.

The audience, already on the feet, were making for the exits. The authors were mentioned, and, amid a thunder of applause there were two calls before the curtain. The shout of "Nana! Nana!" rang wildly forth. Then, no sooner was the house empty, than it grew dark: the footlights went out, the chandelier

was turned down, long strips of grey canvas slipped from the stage-boxes and swathed the gilt ornamentation of the galleries, and the house, lately so full of heat and noise, lapsed suddenly into a heavy sleep, while a musty, dusty odour began to pervade it. In the front of her box stood the Countess Muffat. Very erect and closely wrapped up in her furs, she stared at the gathering shadows and waited for the crowd to pass away.

In the passages the people were jostling the attendants, who hardly knew what to do among the tumbled heaps of out-door raiment. Fauchery and la Faloise had hurried in order to see the crowd pass out. All along the entrance-hall men formed a living hedge, while down the double staircase came slowly, and in regular complete formation, two interminable throngs of human beings. Steiner, in tow of Mignon, had left the house among the foremost. The Count de Vandeuvres took his departure with Blanche de Sivry on his arm. For a moment or two Gaga and her daughter seemed doubtful how to proceed, but Labordette made haste to go and fetch them a conveyance, the door whereof he gallantly shut after them. Nobody saw Daguenet go by. As the truant schoolboy, registering a mental vow to wait at the stage-door, was running with burning cheeks towards the Passage des Panoramas, of which he found the gate closed, Satin, standing on the edge of the pavement, moved forward and brushed him with her skirts, but he in his despair gave her a savage refusal, and vanished amid the crowd, tears of impotent desire in his eyes. Members of the audience were lighting their cigars, and walking off, humming—

*"When Venus roams at eventide."*

Satin had gone back in front of the "Café des Variétés," where Auguste let her eat the sugar that remained over from the customers' orders. A stout man, who came out in a very heated condition, finally carried her off in the shadow of the boulevard, which was now gradually going to sleep.

Still people kept coming downstairs. La Faloise was waiting for Clarisse; Fauchery had promised to catch up Lucy Stewart with Caroline Héquet and her mother. They came; they took up a whole corner of the entrance-hall, and were laughing very loud when the Muffats passed by them with an icy expression. Bordenave had just then opened a little door, and, peeping out, had obtained from Fauchery the formal promise of an article. He was dripping with perspiration, his face blazed, as though he were drunk with success.

"You're good for two hundred nights," said La Faloise to him with civility. "The whole of Paris will visit your theatre."

But Bordenave grew annoyed, and indicating with a jerk of his chin the public who filled the entrance-hall—a herd of men with parched lips and ardent eyes, still burning with the enjoyment of Nana, he cried out violently,—

"Say, 'my brothel,' you obstinate devil!"

## CHAPTER II

At ten o'clock the next morning, Nana was still asleep. She occupied the second floor of a large new house in the Boulevard Haussmann, the landlord of which let flats to single ladies in order by their means to dry the paint. A rich merchant from Moscow, who had come to pass a winter in Paris, had installed her there, after paying six months' rent in advance. The rooms were too big for her and had never been completely furnished. The vulgar sumptuosity of gilded consoles and gilded chairs formed a crude contrast therein to the *bric-à-bric* of a second-hand furniture shop—to mahogany round tables, that is to say, and zinc candelabras, which sought to imitate Florentine bronze. All of which smacked of the courtesan, too early deserted by her first serious protector, and fallen back on shabby lovers, of a precarious first appearance of a bad start, handicapped by refusals of credit and threats of eviction.

Nana was sleeping on her face, hugging in her bare arms a pillow, in which she was burying cheeks grown pale in sleep. The bedroom and the dressing-room were the only two apartments which had been properly furnished by a neighbouring upholsterer. A ray of light, gliding in under a curtain, rendered visible rose-wood furniture, and hangings and chairbacks of figured damask with a pattern of big blue flowers on a grey ground. But in the soft atmosphere of that slumbering chamber, Nana suddenly awoke with a start, as though surprised to find an empty place at her side. She looked at the other pillow, lying next to hers; there was the dint of a human head among its flounces: it was still warm. And groping with one hand, she pressed the knob of an electric bell by her bed's-head.

"He's gone, then?" she asked the maid who presented herself.

"Yes, *Madame*, Monsieur Paul went away, not ten minutes back. As *Madame* was tired, he did not wish to wake her. But he ordered me to tell *Madame* that he would come to-morrow."

As she spoke, Zoé, the lady's maid, opened the outer shutter. A flood of daylight entered. Zoé, a dark brunette, with hair in little plaits, had a long canine face, at once livid and full of seams, a snub nose, thick lips, and two black eyes in continual movement.

"To-morrow, to-morrow," repeated Nana, who was not yet wide awake, "is to-morrow the day?"

"Yes, *Madame*, Monsieur Paul has always come on the Wednesday."

"No, now I remember," said the young woman, sitting up. "It's all changed. I wanted to tell him so this morning. He would run against the nigger! We should have a nice to-do!"

"*Madame* did not warn me; I couldn't be aware of it," murmured Zoé. "When *Madame* changes her days, she will do well to tell me, so that I may know. Then the old miser is no longer due on the Tuesday?"

Between themselves they were wont thus gravely to nickname as "old miser" and "nigger" their two paying visitors, one of whom was a tradesman of economical tendencies from the Faubourg Saint-Denis, whilst the other was a Wallachian, a mock count, whose money, paid always at the most irregular intervals, never looked as though it had been honestly come by. Daguenet had made Nana give him the days subsequent to the old miser's visits, and as the trader had to be at home by eight o'clock in the morning, the young man would watch for his departure from Zoé's

kitchen, and would take his place, which was still quite warm, till ten o'clock. Then he too would go about his business. Nana and he were wont to think it a very comfortable arrangement.

"So much the worse," said Nana; "I'll write to him this afternoon. And, if he doesn't receive my letter, then to-morrow you will stop him coming in."

In the meantime Zoé was walking softly about the room. She spoke of yesterday's great hit. *Madame* had shewn such talent, she sang so well! Ah! *Madame* need not fret at all now!

Nana, her elbow dug into her pillow, only tossed her head in reply. Her nightdress had slipped down on her shoulders, and her hair, unfastened and entangled, flowed over them in masses.

"Without doubt," she murmured, becoming thoughtful; "but what's to be done to gain time? I'm going to have all sorts of bothers to-day. Now let's see, has the porter come upstairs yet this morning?"

Then both the women talked together seriously. Nana owed three quarters' rent; the landlord was talking of seizing the furniture. Then, too, there was a perfect downpour of creditors; there was a livery-stableman, a needlewoman, a ladies' tailor, a charcoal-dealer, and others besides, who came every day and settled themselves on a bench in the little hall. The charcoal-dealer especially was a dreadful fellow—he shouted on the staircase. But Nana's greatest cause of distress was her little Louis, a child she had given birth to when she was sixteen, and now left in charge of a nurse in a village in the neighbourhood of Rambouillet. This woman was clamouring for the sum of three hundred francs before she would consent to give the little Louis back to her. Nana, since her last visit to the child, had been seized with a fit of maternal love, and was desperate at the thought that she could not realise a project, which had now become a hobby with her. This was to pay off the nurse and to place the little man with his aunt, Madame Lerat, at the Batignolles, whither she could go and see him as often as she liked.

Meanwhile, the lady's maid kept hinting that her mistress ought to have confided her necessities to the "old miser."

"To be sure, I told him everything," cried Nana, "and he told me in answer that he had too many big liabilities. He won't go beyond his thousand francs a month. The nigger's beggared just at present; I expect he's lost at play. As to that poor Mimi, he stands in great need of a loan himself; a fall in stocks has cleaned him out—he can't even bring me flowers now."

She was speaking of Daguenet. In the self-abandonment of her awakening she had no secrets from Zoé, and the latter, inured to such confidences, received them with respectful sympathy. Since *Madame* condescended to speak to her of her affairs, she would permit herself to say what she thought. Besides, she was very fond of *Madame;* she had left Madame Blanche for the express purpose of taking service with her, and, Heaven knew, Madame Blanche was straining every nerve to have her again! Situations weren't lacking—she was pretty well known, but she would have stayed with *Madame,* even in narrow circumstances, because she believed in *Madame's* future. And she concluded by stating her advice with precision. When one was

young, one often did silly things. But this time it was one's duty to look alive, for the men only thought of having their fun. Oh dear, yes! things would right themselves. *Madame* had only to say one word in order to quiet her creditors and find the money she stood in need of.

"All that doesn't help me to three hundred francs," Nana kept repeating, as she plunged her fingers into the vagrant convolutions of her back hair. "I must have three hundred francs to-day, at once! It's stupid not to know anyone who'll give you three hundred francs."

She racked her brains. She would have sent Madame Lerat, whom she was expecting that very morning, to Rambouillet. The counteraction of her sudden fancy spoiled for her the triumph of last night. Among all those men who had cheered her, to think that there wasn't one to bring her fifteen louis! And then one couldn't accept money in that way! Dear Heaven! how unfortunate she was! And she kept harking back again to the subject of her baby—he had blue eyes like a cherub's; he could lisp "Mamma" in such a funny voice that you were ready to die of laughing!

But, at this moment, the electric bell at the outer door was heard to ring with its quick and tremulous vibration. Zoé returned, murmuring with a confidential air,—

"It's a woman."

She had seen this woman a score of times, only she made believe never to recognise her, and to be quite ignorant of the nature of her relations with ladies in difficulties.

"She has told me her name—Madame Tricon."

"The Tricon," cried Nana. "Dear me!

that's true. I'd forgotten her. Shew her in."

Zoé ushered in a tall old lady, who wore ringlets, and looked like a countess who haunts lawyers' offices. Then she effaced herself, disappearing noiselessly with the lithe serpentine movement, wherewith she was wont to withdraw from a room on the arrival of a gentleman. However, she might have stayed. The Tricon did not even sit down. Only a brief exchange of words took place.

"I have someone for you to-day. Do you care about it?"

"Yes. How much?"

"Twenty louis."

"At what o'clock?"

"At three. It's settled, then?"

'It's settled."

Straightway the Tricon talked of the state of the weather. It was dry weather, pleasant for walking. She had still four or five persons to see. And she took her departure, after consulting a small memorandum book. When she was once more alone, Nana appeared comforted. A slight shiver agitated her shoulders, and she wrapped herself softly up again in her warm bed-clothes, with the lazy movements of a cat who is susceptible to cold. Little by little her eyes closed, and she lay smiling at the thought of dressing Louiset prettily on the following day, while, in the slumber into which she once more sank, last night's long feverish dream of endlessly rolling applause returned like a sustained accompaniment to music, and gently soothed her lassitude.

At eleven o'clock, when Zoé shewed Madame Lerat into the room, Nana was still asleep. But she woke at the noise, and cried out at once,—

"It's you. You'll go to Rambouillet to-day."

"That's what I've come for," said the aunt. "There's a train at twenty past twelve. I've got time to catch it."

"No, I shall only have the money by-and-by," replied the young woman, stretching herself and throwing out her bosom. "You'll have lunch, and then we'll see."

Zoé brought a dressing-jacket.

"The hairdresser's here, *Madame*," she murmured.

But Nana did not wish to go into the dressing-room. And she herself cried out,—

"Come in, Francis."

A well-dressed man pushed open the door and bowed. Just at that moment Nana was getting out of bed, her bare legs in full view. But she did not hurry, and stretched her hands out so as to let Zoé draw on the sleeves of the dressing-jacket. Francis, on his part, was quite at his ease, and without turning away waited with a sober expression on his face.

"Perhaps *Madame* has not seen the papers. There's a very nice article in the *Figaro*."

He had brought the journal. Madame Lerat put on her spectacles, and read the article aloud, standing in front of the window as she did so. She had the build of a policeman, and she drew herself up to her full height, while her nostrils seemed to compress themselves whenever she uttered a gallant epithet. It was a notice by Fauchery, written just after the performance, and it consisted of a couple of very glowing columns, full of witty sarcasm about the artist and of broad admiration for the woman.

"Excellent!" Francis kept repeating.

Nana laughed good-humouredly at his chaffing her about her voice! He was a nice fellow was that Fauchery, and she would repay him for his charming style of writing. Madame Lerat, after having re-read the notice, roundly declared that the men all had the devil in their shanks; and she refused to explain herself further, being fully satisfied with a brisk allusion which she alone knew the meaning of. Francis finished turning up and fastening Nana's hair. He bowed, and said,—

"I'll keep my eye on the evening papers. At half-past five as usual, eh?"

"Bring me a pot of pomade, and a pound of burnt almonds from Boissier's," Nana cried to him across the drawing-room just as he was shutting the door after him.

Then the two women, once more alone, recollected that they had not embraced, and they planted big kisses on each other's cheeks. The notice warmed their hearts. Nana, who up till now had been half asleep, was again seized with the fever of her triumph. Dear, dear, 'twas Rose Mignon that would be spending a pleasant morning! Her aunt having been unwilling to go to the theatre, because, as she averred, sudden emotions ruined her stomach, Nana set herself to describe the events of the evening, and grew intoxicated at her own recital, as though all Paris had been shaken to the ground by the applause. Then, suddenly interrupting herself, she asked with a laugh if one would ever have imagined it all when she used to go trapesing about the Rue de la Goutte-d'Or. Madame Lerat shook her head. No, no, one never could have foreseen it! And she began talking in her turn, assuming a

serious air as she did so, and calling Nana "daughter." Wasn't she a second mother to her, since the first had gone to rejoin papa and grandmamma? Nana was greatly softened, and on the verge of tears. But Madame Lerat declared that the past was the past—oh yes, to be sure, a dirty past with things in it which it was as well not to stir up every day. She had left off seeing her niece for a long time, because, among the family, she was accused of ruining herself along with the little thing. Good God, as though that were possible! She didn't ask for confidences, she believed that Nana had always lived decently, and now it was enough for her to have found her again in a fine position, and to observe her kind feelings towards her son. Virtue and hard work were still the only things worth anything in this world.

"Who is the baby's father?" she said, interrupting herself, her eyes lit up with an expression of acute curiosity.

Nana was taken by surprise, and hesitated a moment.

"A gentleman," she replied.

"There now!" rejoined the aunt. "They declared that you had him by a stonemason who was in the habit of beating you. Indeed, you shall tell me all about it some day; you know I'm discreet! Tut, tut, I'll look after him as though he were a prince's son."

She had retired from business as a florist, and was living on her savings, which she had got together sou by sou, till now they brought her in an income of six hundred francs a year. Nana promised to rent some pretty little lodgings for her, and to give her a hundred francs a month besides. At the mention of this sum, the aunt forgot herself, and shrieked to her niece, bidding her squeeze their throats, since she had them in her grasp. She was meaning the men, of course. Then they both embraced again, but, in the midst of her rejoicing, Nana's face, as she led the talk back to the subject of Louiset, seemed to be overshadowed by a sudden recollection. "Isn't it a bore I've got to go out at three o'clock?" she muttered. "It *is* a nuisance!"

Just then Zoé came in to say that lunch was on the table. They went into the dining-room, where an old lady was already seated at table. She had not taken her hat off, and she wore a dark dress of an indecisive colour midway between puce and goose dripping. Nana did not seem surprised at sight of her. She simply asked her why she hadn't come into the bedroom.

"I heard voices," replied the old lady. "I thought you had company."

Madame Maloir, a respectable-looking and mannerly woman, was Nana's old friend, chaperon, and companion. Madame Lerat's presence seemed to fidget her at first. Afterwards, when she became aware that it was Nana's aunt, she looked at her with a sweet expression and a die-away smile. In the meantime, Nana, who averred that she was as hungry as a wolf, threw herself on the radishes, and gobbled them up without bread. Madame Lerat had become ceremonious; she refused the radishes as provocative of phlegm. By-and-by when Zoé had brought in the cutlets, Nana just chipped the meat, and contented herself with sucking the bones. Now and again she scrutinised her old friend's hat out of the corners of her eyes.

"It's the new hat I gave you?" she ended by saying.

"Yes, I made it up," murmured Madame Maloir, her mouth full of meat.

The hat was smart to distraction. In front it was greatly exaggerated, and it was adorned with a lofty feather. Madame Maloir had a mania for doing up all her hats afresh; she alone knew what really became her, and with a few stitches she could manufacture a toque out of the most elegant head-gear. Nana, who had brought her this very hat in order not to be ashamed of her when in her company out of doors, was very near being vexed.

"Push it up, at any rate," she cried.

"No, thank you," replied the old lady with dignity. "It doesn't get in my way: I can eat very comfortably as it is."

After the cutlets came cauliflowers and the remains of a cold chicken. But at the arrival of each successive dish Nana made a little face, hesitated, sniffed, and left her plateful untouched. She finished her lunch with the help of preserve.

Dessert took a long time. Zoé did not remove the cloth before serving the coffee. Indeed the ladies simply pushed back their plates before taking it. They talked continually of yesterday's charming evening. Nana kept rolling cigarettes, which she smoked, swinging up and down on her backward-tilted chair. And as Zoé had remained behind and was lounging idly against the sideboard, it came about that the company were favoured with her history. She said she was the daughter of a midwife at Bercy who had failed in business. First of all she had taken service with a dentist, and after that with an insurance agent, but neither place suited her; and she thereupon enumerated, not without a certain amount of pride, the names of the ladies with whom she had served as lady's maid. Zoé spoke of these ladies as one who had had the making of their fortunes. It was very certain that, without her, more than one would have had some queer tales to tell. Thus, one day, when Madame Blanche is with Monsieur Octave, in comes the old gentleman. What does Zoé do? She makes believe to tumble as she crosses the drawing-room; the old boy rushes up to her assistance, flies to the kitchen to fetch her a glass of water, and Monsieur Octave slips away.

"Oh, she's a good girl, you bet!" said Nana, who was listening to her with tender interest, and a sort of submissive admiration.

"Now, I've had my troubles," began Madame Lerat. And edging up to Madame Maloir, she imparted to her certain confidential confessions. Both ladies took lumps of sugar dipped in cognac, and sucked them. But Madame Maloir was wont to listen to other people's secrets without even confessing anything concerning herself. People said that she lived on a mysterious allowance in a room whither no one ever penetrated.

All of a sudden, Nana grew excited. "Don't play with the knives, aunt. You know it gives me a turn!"

Without thinking about it, Madame Lerat had crossed two knives on the table in front of her. Notwithstanding this, the young woman defended herself from the charge of superstition. Thus, if the salt were upset, it meant nothing, even on a Friday; but when it came to knives, that was too much of a good thing: that

had never proved fallacious. There could be no doubt that something unpleasant was going to happen to her. She yawned, and then with an air of profound boredom,—

"Two o'clock already. I must go out. What a nuisance!"

The two old ladies looked at one another. The three women shook their heads without speaking. To be sure, life was not always amusing. Nana had tilted her chair back anew and lit a cigarette, while the others sat pursing up their lips discreetly, thinking deeply philosophic thoughts.

"While waiting for you to return, we'll play a game of bézique," said Madame Maloir, after a short silence. "Does *Madame* play bézique?"

Certainly, Madame Lerat played it, and that to perfection. It was no good troubling Zoé, who had vanished—a corner of the table would do quite well. And they pushed back the tablecloth over the dirty plates. But as Madame Maloir was herself going to take the cards out of a drawer in the sideboard, Nana remarked that, before she sat down to her game, it would be very nice of her if she would write her a letter. It bored Nana to write letters; besides she was not sure of her spelling, whilst her old friend could turn out the most feeling epistles. She ran to fetch some good note paper in her bedroom. An inkstand consisting of a bottle of ink worth about three sous stood untidily on one of the pieces of furniture, with a pen deep in rust beside it. The letter was for Daguenet. Madame Maloir herself wrote in her bold English hand, "My darling little man," and then she told him not to come to-morrow, because "that could not be," but hastened to add that "she was with him in thought at every moment of the day, whether she were near or far away."

"And I end with 'a thousand kisses,'" she murmured.

Madame Lerat had shewn her approval of each phrase with an emphatic nod. Her eyes were sparkling; she loved to find herself in the midst of love affairs. Nay, she was seized with a desire to add some words of her own, and assuming a tender look, and cooing like a dove, she suggested,—

"A thousand kisses on thy beautiful eyes."

"That's the thing: 'a thousand kisses on thy beautiful eyes!'" Nana repeated, while the two old ladies assumed a beatified expression.

Zoé was rung for, and told to take the letter down to a commissionaire. She had just been talking with the theatre messenger, who had brought her mistress the day's playbill and rehearsal arrangements, which he had forgotten in the morning. Nana had this individual ushered in, and got him to take the latter to Daguenet on his return. Then she put questions to him. Oh, yes! Monsieur Bordenave was very pleased; people had already taken seats for a week to come; *Madame* had no idea of the number of people who had been asking her address since morning. When the man had taken his departure, Nana announced that at most she would only be out half an hour. If there were any visitors, Zoé would make them wait. As she spoke, the electric bell sounded. It was a creditor in the shape of the man of whom she jobbed her carriages. He had settled himself on the bench in the ante-room, and the

fellow was free to twiddle his thumbs till night—there wasn't the least hurry now.

"Come, buck up!" said Nana, still torpid with laziness, and yawning and stretching afresh. "I ought to be there now!"

Yet she did not budge, but kept watching the play of her aunt, who had just announced "four aces." Chin on hand, she grew quite engrossed in it, but gave a violent start on hearing three o'clock strike.

"Good God!" she cried roughly.

Then Madame Maloir, who was counting the tricks she had won with her tens and aces, said cheeringly to her in her soft voice,—

"It would be better, dearie, to give up your expedition at once."

"No, be quick about it," said Madame Lerat, shuffling the cards. "I shall take the half-past four o'clock train, if you're back here with the money before four o'clock."

"Oh! there'll be no time lost," she murmured.

Ten minutes after, Zoé helped her on with a dress and a hat. It didn't matter much if she were badly turned out. Just as she was about to go downstairs there was a new ring at the bell. This time it was the charcoal dealer. Very well, he might keep the livery-stable keeper company—it would amuse the fellows. Only, as she dreaded a scene, she crossed the kitchen, and made her escape by the back stairs. She often went that way, and in return had only to lift up her flounces.

"When one is a good mother, anything's excusable," said Madame Maloir sententiously, when left alone with Madame Lerat.

"Four kings," replied this lady, whom the play greatly excited.

And they both plunged into an interminable game.

The table had not been cleared. The smell of lunch and the cigarette smoke filled the room with an ambient steamy vapour. The two ladies had again set to work dipping lumps of sugar in brandy and sucking the same. For twenty minutes at least they played and sucked simultaneously when, the electric bell having rung a third time, Zoé bustled into the room, and roughly disturbed them, just as if they had been her own friends.

"Look here, that's another ring. You can't stay where you are. If many folks call I must have the whole flat. Now, off you go, off you go!"

Madame Maloir was for finishing the game; but Zoé looked as if she was going to pounce down on the cards, and so she decided to carry them off without in any way altering their positions, whilst Madame Lerat undertook the removal of the brandy bottle, the glasses, and the sugar. Then they both scudded to the kitchen, where they installed themselves at the table in an empty space between the dish-cloths, which were spread out to dry, and the bowl still full of dishwater.

"We said it was three hundred and forty. It's your turn."

"I play hearts."

When Zoé returned she found them once again absorbed. After a silence, as Madame Lerat was shuffling, Madame Maloir asked who it was.

"Oh! nobody to speak of," replied the servant carelessly; "a slip of a lad! I wanted to send him away again, but he's such a pretty boy with never a hair on his chin, and blue eyes, and a girl's face! So I told him to wait after all. He's got an enormous bouquet in his hand, which he never once consented to put down. One would like to catch him one—a brat like that who ought to be at school still!"

Madame Lerat went to fetch a water bottle to mix herself some brandy and water, the lumps of sugar having rendered her thirsty. Zoé muttered something to the effect that she really didn't mind if she drank something too. Her mouth, she averred, was as bitter as gall.

"So you put him?——" continued Madame Maloir.

"Oh, yes, I put him in the closet at the end of the room, the little unfurnished one. There's only one of my lady's trunks there and a table. It's there I stow the lubbers."

And she was putting plenty of sugar in her grog, when the electric bell made her jump. Oh drat it all! wouldn't they let her have a drink in peace? If they were to have a peal of bells things promised well. Nevertheless, she ran off to open the door. Returning presently she saw Madame Maloir questioning her with a glance.

"It's nothing," she said, "only a bouquet."

All three refreshed themselves, nodding to each other in token of salutation. Then, whilst Zoé was at length busy clearing the table, bringing the plates out one by one and putting them in the sink, two other rings followed close upon one another. But they weren't serious, for, whilst keeping the kitchen informed of what was going on, she twice repeated her disdainful expression.

"Nothing; only a bouquet."

Notwithstanding which, the old ladies laughed between two of their tricks, when they heard her describe the looks of the creditors in the ante-room after the flowers had arrived. *Madame* would find her bouquets on her toilet-table. What a pity it was they cost such a lot, and that you could only get ten sous for them! Oh dear yes, plenty of money was wasted!

"For my part," said Madame Maloir, "I should be quite content if every day of my life I got what the men in Paris had spent on flowers for the women."

"Now, you know, you're not hard to please," murmured Madame Lerat. "Why, one would have only just enough to buy thread with. Four queens, my dear."

It was ten minutes to four. Zoé was astonished—could not understand why her mistress was out so long. Ordinarily, when *Madame* found herself obliged to go out in the afternoons, she got it over in double-quick time. But Madame Maloir declared that one didn't always manage things as one wished. Truly, life was beset with obstacles, averred Madame Lerat. The best course was to wait. If her niece was long in coming, it was because her occupations detained her, wasn't it so? Besides, they weren't overworked—it was comfortable in the kitchen. And, as hearts were out, Madame Lerat threw down diamonds.

The bell began again, and when Zoé reappeared she was burning with excitement.

"My children, it's fat Steiner!" said she, in the doorway, lowering her voice as she spoke. "I've put *him* in the little sitting-room."

Thereupon Madame Maloir spoke about the banker to Madame Lerat, who knew no such gentleman. Was he getting ready to give Rose Mignon the go-by? Zoé shook her head; she knew a thing or two. But, once more, she had to go and open the door.

"Here's bothers!" she murmured, when she came back. "It's the nigger! 'Twasn't any good telling him that my lady's gone out, and so he's settled himself in the bedroom. We only expected him this evening."

At a quarter past four Nana was not in yet. What could she be after? It was silly of her! Two other bouquets were brought round, and Zoé, growing bored, looked to see if there were any coffee left. Yes, the ladies would willingly finish off the coffee; it would waken them up. Sitting hunched up on their chairs, they were beginning to fall asleep through dint of constantly taking their cards between their fingers with the accustomed movement. The half-hour sounded. Something must decidedly have happened to *Madame*. And they began whispering to each other.

Suddenly Madame Maloir forgot herself, and in a ringing voice announced,— "I've the five hundred! Trumps, Major Quint!"

"Oh, do be quiet!" said Zoé, angrily. "What will all those gentlemen think?"

And in the silence which ensued, and amid the whispered muttering of the two old women at strife over their game, the sound of rapid footsteps ascended from the back stairs. It was Nana at last. Before she had opened the door, her breathlessness became audible. She bounced abruptly in, looking very red in the face. Her skirt, the string of which must have been broken, was trailing over the stairs, and her flounces had just been dipped in a puddle of something unpleasant, which had oozed out on the landing of the first floor, where the servant girl was a regular slut.

"Here you are! It's lucky!" said Madame Lerat, pursing up her lips, for she was still vexed at Madame Maloir's "five hundred." "You may flatter yourself at the way you keep folks waiting."

"*Madame* isn't reasonable, indeed she isn't!" added Zoé.

Nana was already harassed, and these reproaches exasperated her. Was that the way people received her after the worry she had gone through?

"Will you blooming well leave me alone, eh?" she cried.

"Hush, ma'am, there are people in there," said the maid.

Then, in lower tones, the young woman stuttered breathlessly,—

"D'you suppose I've been having a good time? Why, there was no end to it. I should have liked to see you there! I was boiling with rage! I felt inclined to smack somebody. And never a cab to come home in! Luckily it's only a step from here, but never mind that, I did just run home."

"You have the money?" asked the aunt.

"Dear, dear! that question!" rejoined Nana.

She had sat herself down on a chair close up against the stove, for her legs had failed her after so much running; and without stopping to take breath, she drew from behind her stays an envelope in which there were four hundred-franc notes. They were visible through a large rent she had torn with savage fingers in order to be sure of the contents. The three women round about her stared

fixedly at the envelope, a big, crumpled, dirty receptacle, as it lay clasped in her small gloved hands.

It was too late now—Madame Lerat would not go to Rambouillet till tomorrow, and Nana entered into long explanations.

"There's company waiting for you," the lady's maid repeated.

But Nana grew excited again. The company might wait: she'd go to them all in good time when she'd finished. And, as her aunt began putting her hand out for the money,—

"Ah no! not all of it," said she. "Three hundred francs for the nurse, fifty for your journey and expenses, that's three hundred and fifty. Fifty francs I keep."

The big difficulty was how to find change. There were not ten francs in the house. But they did not even address themselves to Madame Maloir who, never having more than a six-sou omnibus fare upon her, was listening in quite a disinterested manner. At length Zoé went out of the room, remarking that she would go and look in her box, and she brought back a hundred francs in hundred-sou pieces. They were counted out on a corner of the table, and Madame Lerat took her departure at once, after having promised to bring Louiset back with her the following day.

"You say there's company there?" continued Nana, still sitting on the chair and resting herself.

"Yes, *Madame,* three people."

And Zoé mentioned the banker first. Nana made a face. Did that man Steiner think she was going to let herself be bored because he had thrown her a bouquet yesterday evening?"

"Besides, I've had enough of it," she

declared. "I shan't receive to-day. Go and say you don't expect me now."

"*Madame* will think the matter over; *Madame* will receive Monsieur Steiner," murmured Zoé, gravely, without budging from her place. She was annoyed to see her mistress on the verge of committing another foolish mistake.

Then she mentioned the Wallachian, who ought by now to find time hanging heavy on his hands in the bedroom. Whereupon Nana grew furious, and more obstinate than ever. No, she would see nobody, nobody! Who'd sent her such a blooming leech of a man?

"Chuck 'em all out! I—I'm going to play a game of bézique with Madame Maloir. I prefer doing that."

The bell interrupted her remarks. That was the last straw. Another of the beggars yet! She forbade Zoé to go and open the door, but the latter had left the kitchen without listening to her, and when she reappeared she brought back a couple of cards, and said authoritatively,—

"I told them that *Madame* was receiving visitors. The gentlemen are in the drawing-room."

Nana had sprung up raging, but the names of the Marquis de Chouard and of Count Muffat de Beuville, which were inscribed on the cards, calmed her down. For a moment or two she remained silent.

"Who are they?" she asked at last. "You know them?"

"I know the old fellow," replied Zoé, discreetly pursing up her lips.

And, her mistress continuing to question her with her eyes, she added simply,—

"I've seen him somewhere."

This remark seemed to decide the young woman. Regretfully she left the kitchen, that asylum of steaming warmth, where you could talk and take your ease amid the pleasant fumes of the coffee-pot, which was being kept warm over a handful of glowing embers. She left Madame Maloir behind her. That lady was now busy reading her fortune by the cards: she had never yet taken her hat off, but now in order to be more at her ease she undid the strings and threw them back over her shoulders.

In the dressing-room, where Zoé rapidly helped her on with a tea-gown, Nana revenged herself for the way in which they were all boring her, by muttering quiet curses upon the male sex. These big words caused the lady's maid not a little distress, for she saw with pain that her mistress was not rising superior to her origin as quickly as she could have desired. She even made bold to beg *Madame* to calm herself.

"You bet," was Nana's crude answer; "they're swine, they glory in that sort of thing."

Nevertheless, she assumed her princess-like manner, as she was wont to call it. But just when she was turning to go into the drawing-room, Zoé held her back, and herself introduced the Marquis de Chouard and the Count Muffat into the dressing-room. It was much better so.

"I regret having kept you waiting, gentlemen," said the young woman, with studied politeness.

The two men bowed and seated themselves. A blind of embroidered tulle kept the little room in twilight. It was the most elegant chamber in the flat, for it was hung with some light-coloured fabric and contained a cheval-glass framed in inlaid wood, a lounge chair, and some others with arms and blue satin upholsteries. On the toilet-table, the bouquets—roses, lilacs, and hyacinths—appeared like a very ruin of flowers. Their perfume was strong and penetrating, while through the dampish air of the place, which was full of the spoilt exhalations of the washstand, came occasional whiffs of a more pungent scent, the scent of some grains of dry patchouli ground to fine powder at the bottom of a cup. And as she gathered herself together, and drew up her dressing-jacket, which had been ill-fastened, Nana had all the appearance of having been surprised at her toilet: her skin was still damp, she smiled, and looked quite startled amid her frills and laces.

"Madam, you will pardon our insistence," said the Count Muffat, gravely. "We come on a quest. Monsieur and I are members of the Benevolent Organisation of the district."

The Marquis de Chouard hastened, gallantly, to add,—

"When we learnt that a great artiste lived in this house, we promised ourselves that we would put the claims of our poor people before her in a very special manner. Talent is never without a heart."

Nana pretended to be modest. She answered them with little assenting movements of her head, making rapid reflections at the same time. It must be the old man that had brought the other one: he had such wicked eyes. And yet the other was not to be trusted either: the veins near his temples were so queerly puffed up. He might quite well have come by himself. Ah, now that she thought of it, it was this way: the porter

had given them her name, and they had egged one another on, each with his own ends in view.

"Most certainly, gentlemen, you were quite right to come up," said she, with a very good grace.

But the electric bell made her tremble again. Another call, and that Zoé always opening the door! She went on,—

"One is only too happy to be able to give."

At bottom she was flattered.

"Ah, *Madame*," rejoined the Marquis, "if only you knew about it! There's such misery! Our district has more than three thousand poor people in it, and yet it's one of the richest. You cannot picture to yourself anything like the present distress—children with no bread, women ill, utterly without assistance, perishing of the cold——!"

"The poor souls!" cried Nana, very much moved.

Such was her feeling of compassion that tears flooded her fine eyes. No longer studying deportment, she leant forward with a quick movement, and under her open dressing-jacket her neck became visible, while the bent position of her knees served to outline the rounded contour of the thigh under the thin fabric of her skirt. A little flush of blood appeared in the Marquis's cadaverous cheeks. Count Muffat, who was on the point of speaking, lowered his eyes. The air of that little room was too hot: it had the close heavy warmth of a greenhouse. The roses were withering, and intoxicating odours floated up from the patchouli in the cup.

"One would like to be very rich on occasions like this," added Nana. "Well,

well, we each do what we can. Believe
me, gentlemen, if I had known——"

She was on the point of being guilty
of a silly speech, so melted was she at
heart. But she did not end her sentence,
and for a moment was worried at not being able to remember where she had put
her fifty francs on changing her dress.
But she recollected at last: they must be
on the corner of her toilet table under
an inverted pomatum-pot. As she was in
the act of rising, the bell sounded for
quite a long time. Capital! Another
of them still! It would never end. The
Count and the Marquis had both risen
too, and the ears of the latter seemed to
be pricked up, and, as it were, pointing
towards the door: doubtless he knew that
kind of ring. Muffat looked at him;
then they averted their gaze mutually.
They felt awkward, and once more assumed their frigid bearing, the one looking square-set and solid with his thick
head of hair, the other drawing back his
lean shoulders, over which fell his fringe
of thin white locks.

"My faith," said Nana, bringing the
ten big silver pieces, and quite determined to laugh about it, "I am going to
entrust you with this, gentlemen. It is
for the poor."

And the adorable little dimple in her
chin became apparent. She assumed her
favourite pose, her amiable baby expression, as she held the pile of five-franc
pieces on her open palm and offered it
to the men, as though she were saying
to them,—"Now then, who wants some?"
The Count was the sharper of the two.
He took the fifty francs, but left one
piece behind, and, in order to gain possession of it, had to pick it off the young
woman's very skin, a moist supple skin,

the touch of which sent a thrill through
him. She was thoroughly merry, and
did not cease laughing.

"Come, gentlemen," she continued.
"Another time I hope to give more."

The gentlemen no longer had any pretext for staying, and they bowed, and
went towards the door. But just as they
were about to go out, the bell rang anew.
The Marquis could not conceal a faint
smile, while a frown made the Count
look more grave than before. Nana detained them some seconds so as to give
Zoé time to find yet another corner for
the newcomers. She did not relish meetings at her house. Only, this time, the
whole place must be packed! She was
therefore much relieved when she saw
the drawing-room empty, and asked herself whether Zoé had really stuffed them
into the cupboards.

"*Au revoir,* gentlemen," said she, pausing on the threshold of the drawing-
room.

It was as though she lapped them in
her laughing smile and clear unclouded
glance. The Count Muffat bowed slightly. Despite his great social experience,
he felt that he had lost his equilibrium.
He needed air, he was overcome with the
dizzy feeling engendered in that dressing-
room, with a scent of flowers, with a
feminine essence which choked him.
And, behind his back, the Marquis de
Chouard, who was sure that he could
not be seen, made so bold as to wink at
Nana, his whole face suddenly altering
its expression, as he did so, and his
tongue nigh lolling from his mouth.

When the young woman re-entered
the little room, where Zoé was awaiting
her with letters and visiting cards, she

cried out, laughing more heartily than ever,—

"There are a pair of beggars for you! Why they've got away with my fifty francs!"

She wasn't vexed. It struck her as a joke that *men* should have got money out of her. All the same they were swine, for she hadn't a sou left. But at sight of the cards and the letters her bad temper returned. As to the letters, why, she said "pass" to them. They were from fellows who, after applauding her last night, were now making their declarations. And as to the callers, they might go about their business!

Zoé had stowed them all over the place, and she called attention to the great capabilities of the flat, every room in which opened on the corridor. That wasn't the case at Madame Blanche's, where people had all to go through the drawing-room. Oh yes, Madame Blanche had had plenty of bothers over it!

"You will send them all away," continued Nana, in pursuance of her idea. "Begin with the 'nigger.' "

"Oh, as to him, *Madame,* I gave him his marching orders a while ago," said Zoé, with a grin. "He only wanted to tell *Madame* that he couldn't come to-night."

There was vast joy at this announcement, and Nana clapped her hands. He wasn't coming, what good luck! She would be free then! And she emitted sighs of relief, as though she had been let off the most abominable of tortures. Her first thought was for Daguenet. Poor duck, why she had just written to tell him to wait till Thursday! Quick, quick, Madame Maloir should write a second letter! But Zoé announced that

Madame Maloir had slipped away unnoticed, according to her wont. Whereupon Nana, after talking of sending someone to him, began to hesitate. She was very tired. A long night's sleep— oh it would be so jolly! The thought of such a treat overcame her at last. For once in a way, she could allow herself that!

"I shall go to bed when I come back from the theatre," she murmured greedily, "and you won't wake me before noon."

Then raising her voice,—

"Now then, gee up! Shove the others downstairs!"

Zoé did not move. She would never have dreamt of giving her mistress overt advice, only now she made shift to give *Madame* the benefit of her experience, when *Madame* seemed to be running her hot head against a wall.

"Monsieur Steiner as well?" she queried curtly.

"Why, certainly!" replied Nana. "Before all the rest."

The maid still waited, in order to give her mistress time for reflection. *Would* not *Madame* be proud to get such a rich gentleman away from her rival, Rose Mignon—a man, moreover, who was known in all the theatres?

"Now, to make haste, my dear," rejoined Nana, who perfectly understood the situation, "and tell him he pesters me."

But suddenly there was a reversion of feeling. To-morrow she might want him. Whereupon she laughed, winked once or twice, and with a naughty little gesture cried out,—

"After all's said and done, if I want

him, the best way even now is to kick him out of doors."

Zoé seemed much impressed. Struck with a sudden admiration, she gazed at her mistress, and then went and chucked Steiner out of doors without further deliberation.

Meanwhile, Nana waited patiently for a second or two, in order to give her time to sweep the place out, as she phrased it. No one would ever have expected such a siege! She craned her head into the drawing-room, and found it empty. The dining-room was empty too. But as she continued her visitation in a calmer frame of mind, feeling certain that nobody remained behind, she opened the door of a closet and came suddenly upon a very young man. He was sitting on the top of a trunk, holding a huge bouquet on his knees, and looking exceeding quiet and extremely well-behaved.

"Goodness gracious me!" she cried. "There's one of 'em in there even now!"

The very young man had jumped down at sight of her, and was blushing as red as a poppy. He did not know what to do with his bouquet, which he kept shifting from one hand to the other, whilst his looks betrayed the extreme of emotion. His youth, his embarrassment, and the funny figure he cut in his struggles with his flowers, melted Nana's heart, and she burst into a pretty peal of laughter. Well now, the very children were coming, were they? Men were arriving in long clothes. So she gave up all airs and graces, became familiar and maternal, tapped her leg, and asked for fun,—

"You want me to wipe your nose, do you, baby?"

"Yes," replied the lad in a low supplicating tone.

This answer made her merrier than ever. He was seventeen years old, he said. His name was Georges Hugon. He was at the Variétés last night and now he had come to see her.

"These flowers are for me?"

"Yes."

"Then give 'em to me, booby!"

But, as she took the bouquet from him, he sprang upon her hands and kissed them with all the gluttonous eagerness peculiar to his charming time of life. She had to beat him to make him leave go. There was a dreadful little dribbling customer for you! But as she scolded him, she flushed rosy-red and began smiling. And with that she sent him about his business, telling him that he might call again. He staggered away; he could not find the doors.

Nana went back into her dressing-room, where Francis made his appearance almost simultaneously in order to dress her hair for the evening. Seated in front of her mirror, and bending her head beneath the hairdresser's nimble hands, she stayed silently meditative. Presently, however, Zoé entered, remarking,—

"There's one of them, *Madame,* who refuses to go."

"Very well, he must be left alone," answered she quietly.

"If that comes to that, they still keep arriving."

"Bah! tell 'em to wait. When they begin to feel too hungry they'll be off."

Her humour had changed, and she was now delighted to make people wait about for nothing. A happy thought struck her as very amusing: she escaped from

beneath Francis' hands, and ran and
bolted the doors. They might now crowd
in there, as much as they liked: they
would probably refrain from making a
hole through the wall. Zoé could come
in and out through the little doorway
leading to the kitchen. However, the
electric bell rang more lustily than ever.
Every five minutes a clear lively little
ting-ting recurred as regularly as if it
had been produced by some well-adjusted
piece of mechanism. And Nana counted
these rings to while the time away withal.
But suddenly she remembered something.
"I say, where are my burnt almonds?"
Francis, too, was forgetting about the
burnt almonds. But now he drew a
paper bag from one of the pockets of his
frock-coat, and presented it to her with
the discreet gesture of a man who is
offering a lady a present. Nevertheless,
whenever his accounts came to be settled, he always put the burnt almonds
down on his bill. Nana put the bag between her knees, and set to work munching her sweetmeats, turning her head
from time to time under the hairdresser's
gently-compelling touch.
"The deuce," she murmured, after a
silence, "there's a troop for you!"
Thrice, in quick succession, the bell
had sounded. Its summonses became
fast and furious. There were modest
tintinabulations, which seemed to stutter
and tremble like a first avowal: there
were bold rings which vibrated under
some rough touch, and hasty rings which
sounded through the house with shivering rapidity. It was a regular peal, as
Zoé said, a peal loud enough to upset
the neighbourhood, seeing that a whole
mob of men were jabbing at the ivory
button, one after the other. That old

joker, Bordenave, had really been far
too lavish with her address. Why, the
whole of yesterday's house was coming!
"By-the-by, Francis, have you five
louis?" said Nana.
He drew back, looked carefully at her
head-dress, and then quietly remarked,—
"Five louis, that's according!"
"Ah, you know if you want securi-
ties . . ." she continued.
And without finishing her sentence,
she indicated the adjoining rooms with
a sweeping gesture. Francis lent the
five louis. Zoé, during each momentary
respite, kept coming in to get *Madame's*
things ready. Soon she came to dressing
her, whilst the hairdresser lingered with
the intention of giving some finishing
touches to the head-dress. But the bell
kept continually disturbing the lady's
maid, who left *Madame* with her stays
half-laced and only one shoe on. Despite
her long experience, the maid was losing
her head. After bringing every nook and
corner into requisition, and putting men
pretty well everywhere, she had been
driven to stow them away in threes and
fours, which was a course of procedure
entirely opposed to her principles. So
much the worse for them if they ate each
other up! It would afford more room!
And Nana, sheltering behind her carefully bolted door, began laughing at them,
declaring that she could hear them pant.
They ought to be looking lovely in there,
with their tongues hanging out like a lot
of bow-wows sitting round on their be-
hinds. Yesterday's success was not yet
over, and this pack of men had followed
up her scent.
"Provided they don't break anything,"
she murmured.
She began to feel some anxiety, for

she fancied she felt their hot breath coming through chinks in the door. But Zoé ushered Labordette in, and the young woman gave a little shout of relief. He was anxious to tell her about an account he had settled for her at the Justice of Peace's Court. But she did not attend, and said,—

"I'll take you along with me. We'll have dinner together, and afterwards you shall escort me to the Variétés. I don't go on before half-past nine."

Good old Labordette, how lucky it was he had come! He was a fellow who never asked for any favours. He was only the friend of the women, whose little bits of business he arranged for them. Thus, on his way in, he had dismissed the creditors in the ante-room. Indeed, those good folks really didn't want to be paid. On the contrary, if they *had* been pressing for payment, it was only for the sake of complimenting *Madame,* and of personally renewing their offers of service, after her grand success of yesterday.

"Let's be off, let's be off," said Nana, who was dressed by now.

But, at that moment, Zoé came in again, shouting:

"I refuse to open the door any more. They're waiting in a crowd all down the stairs."

A crowd all down the stairs! Francis himself, despite the English stolidity of manner which he was wont to affect, began laughing as he put up his combs. Nana, who had already taken Labordette's arm, pushed him into the kitchen, and effected her escape. At last she was delivered from the men, and felt happily conscious that she might now enjoy his society anywhere, without fear of stupid interruptions.

"You shall see me back to my door," said she, as they went down the kitchen stairs. "I shall feel safe, in that case. Just fancy, I want to sleep a whole night quite by myself—yes, a whole night! It's a sort of infatuation, dear boy!"

## CHAPTER III

THE Countess Sabine, as it had become customary to call Madame Muffat de Beuville, in order to distinguish her from the Count's mother, who had died the year before, was wont to receive every Tuesday in her house, in the Rue Miromesnil, at the corner of the Rue de Pentièvre. It was a great square building, and the Muffats had lived in it for a hundred years and more. On the side of the street, its frontage seemed to slumber, so lofty was it and dark, so sad and convent-like, with its great outer shutters, which were nearly always closed. And at the back, in a little dark garden, some trees had grown up, and were straining towards the sunlight with such long slender branches that their tips were visible above the roof.

This particular Tuesday, towards ten o'clock in the evening, there were scarcely a dozen people in the drawing-room. When she was only expecting intimate friends, the Countess opened neither the little drawing-room nor the dining-room. One felt more at home on such occasions, and chatted round the fire. The drawing-room was very large and very lofty; its four windows looked out upon the garden, from which, on this rainy evening of the close of April, issued a sensation of damp, despite the great logs burning on the hearth. The sun never shone down into the room; in the daytime it was dimly lit up by a faint greenish light, but at night, when the lamps and the chandelier were burning, it looked merely a serious old chamber with its massive mahogany First Empire furniture, its hangings and chair coverings of yellow velvet, stamped with a large design. Entering it, one was in an atmosphere of cold dignity, of ancient manners, of a vanished age, the air of which seemed devotional.

Opposite the arm-chair, however, in which the Count's mother had died—a square arm-chair of formal design and inhospitable padding, which stood by the hearth-side—the Countess Sabine was seated in a deep and cozy lounge, the red silk upholsteries of which were soft as eider-down. It was the only piece of modern furniture there, a fanciful item introduced amid the prevailing severity, and clashing with it.

"So we shall have the Shah of Persia," the young woman was saying.

They were talking of the crowned heads who were coming to Paris for the Exhibition. Several ladies had formed a circle round the hearth, and Madame du Joncquoy, whose brother, a diplomat, had just fulfilled a mission in the East, was giving some details about the Court of Nazr-ed-Din.

"Are you out of sorts, my dear?" asked Madame Chantereau, the wife of an iron-master, seeing the Countess shivering slightly and growing pale as she did so.

"Oh no, not at all," replied the latter, smiling. "I felt a little cold. This drawing-room takes so long to warm."

And with that she raised her melancholy eyes, and scanned the walls from floor to ceiling. Her daughter Estelle, a slight, insignificant-looking girl of sixteen, the thankless period of life, quitted the large footstool on which she was sitting, and silently came and propped up one of the logs which had rolled from its place. But Madame de Chezelles, a convent friend of Sabine's, and her junior by five years, exclaimed,—

"Dear me, I would gladly be possessed of a drawing-room such as yours! At any rate, you are able to receive visitors. They only build boxes nowadays. Oh, if I were in your place!"

She ran giddily on, and with lively gestures explained how she would alter the hangings, the seats—everything, in fact. Then, she would give balls to which all Paris should run. Behind her seat, her husband, a magistrate, stood listening with serious air. It was rumoured that she deceived him quite openly, but people pardoned her offence, and received her just the same, because, said they, "she's not answerable for her actions."

"Oh that Léonide!" the Countess Sabine contented herself by murmuring, smiling her faint smile the while.

With a languid movement she eked out the thought that was in her. After having lived there seventeen years, she certainly would not alter her drawing-room now. It would henceforth remain just such as her mother-in-law had wished to preserve it during her lifetime. Then, returning to the subject of conversation,—

"I have been assured," said she, "that we shall also have the King of Prussia and the Emperor of Russia."

"Yes, some very fine fêtes are promised," said Madame du Joncquoy.

The banker Steiner, not long since introduced into this circle by Léonide de

Chezelles, who was acquainted with the whole of Parisian society, was sitting chatting on a sofa between two of the windows. He was questioning a Deputy, from whom he was endeavouring with much adroitness to elicit news about a movement on the Stock Exchange of which he had his suspicions, while the Count Muffat, standing in front of them, was silently listening to their talk, looking, as he did so, even greyer than was his wont.

Four or five young men formed another group, near the door, round the Count Xavier de Vandeuvres, who in a low tone was telling them an anecdote. It was doubtless a very risky one, for they were choking with laughter. Companionless in the centre of the room, a stout man, a chief clerk at the Ministry of the Interior, sat heavily in an armchair, dozing with his eyes open. But when one of the young man appeared to doubt the truth of the anecdote, Vandeuvres raised his voice.

"You are too much of a sceptic, Foucarmont; you'll spoil all your pleasures that way."

And he returned to the ladies with a laugh. Last scion of a great family, of feminine manners and witty tongue, he was at that time running through a fortune with a rage of life and appetite which nothing could appease. His racing stable, which was one of the best known in Paris, cost him a fabulous amount of money; his betting losses at the Imperial Club amounted monthly to an alarming number of pounds, whilst, taking one year with another, his mistresses would be always devouring now a farm, now some acres of arable land or forest, which amounted in fact to quite a respectable slice of his vast estates in Picardy.

"I advise you to call other people sceptics! Why you don't believe a thing yourself," said Léonide, making shift to find him a little space in which to sit down at her side. "It's you who spoil your own pleasures."

"Exactly," replied he. "I wish to make others benefit by my experience."

But the company imposed silence on him: he was scandalising Monsieur Venot. And, the ladies having changed their positions, a little old man of sixty, with bad teeth and a subtle smile, became visible in the depths of an easy-chair. There he sat as comfortably as in his own house, listening to everybody's remarks, and making none himself. With a slight gesture he announced himself by no means scandalised. Vandeuvres had once more assumed his dignified bearing, and added gravely,—

"Monsieur Venot is fully aware that I believe what it is one's duty to believe."

It was an act of faith, and even Léonide appeared satisfied. The young men at the end of the room no longer laughed: the company were old fogeys, and amusement was not to be found there. A cold breath of wind had passed over them, and amid the ensuing silence Steiner's nasal voice became audible. The Deputy's discreet answers were at last driving him to desperation. For a second or two, the Countess Sabine looked at the fire; then she resumed the conversation.

"I saw the King of Prussia at Baden-Baden last year. He's still full of vigour for his age."

"Count Bismarck is to accompany

him," said Madame du Joncquoy. "Do you know the Count? I lunched with him at my brother's ages ago, when he was representative of Prussia in Paris. There's a man now whose latest successes I cannot in the least understand."

"But why?" asked Madame Chantereau.

"Good gracious, how am I to explain! He doesn't please me. His appearance is boorish and underbred. Besides, so far as I am concerned, I find him stupid."

With that the whole room spoke of Count Bismarck, and opinions differed considerably. Vandeuvres knew him, and assured the company that he was great in his cups and at play. But when the discussion was at its height, the door was opened, and Hector de la Faloise made his appearance. Fauchery, who followed in his wake, approached the Countess, and bowing,—

"Madam," said he, "I have not forgotten your extremely kind invitation."

She smiled, and made a pretty little speech. The journalist, after bowing to the Count, stood for some moments in the middle of the drawing-room. He only recognised Steiner, and accordingly looked rather out of his element. But Vandeuvres turned, and came and shook hands with him. And, forthwith, in his delight at the meeting and with a sudden desire to be confidential, Fauchery buttonholed him, and said in a low voice,—

"It's to-morrow. Are you going?"

"Egad, yes."

"At midnight, at her house."

"I know, I know. I'm going with Blanche."

He wanted to escape and return to the ladies in order to urge yet another reason in Monsieur de Bismarck's favour. But Fauchery detained him.

"You never will guess whom she has charged me to invite."

And, with a slight nod, he indicated Count Muffat, who was just then discussing a knotty point in the Budget with Steiner and the Deputy.

"It's impossible," said Vandeuvres, stupefaction and merriment in his tones.

"My word on it! I had to swear that I would bring him to her. Indeed, that's one of my reasons for coming here."

Both laughed silently, and Vandeuvres, hurriedly rejoining the circle of ladies, cried out,—

"I declare that on the contrary Monsieur de Bismarck is exceedingly witty. For instance, one evening he said a charmingly epigrammatic thing in my presence——"

La Faloise meanwhile had heard the few rapid sentences thus whisperingly interchanged, and he gazed at Fauchery, in hopes of an explanation which was not vouchsafed him. Of whom were they talking, and what were they going to do at midnight to-morrow? He did not leave his cousin's side again. The latter had gone and seated himself. He was especially interested by the Countess Sabine. Her name had often been mentioned in his presence, and he knew that, having been married at the age of seventeen, she must now be thirty-four, and that since her marriage she had passed a cloistered existence with her husband and her mother-in-law. In society, some spoke of her as a woman of religious chastity, whilst others pitied her, and recalled to memory her charming bursts of laughter and the burning glances of her great eyes in the days prior to her imprisonment in this old town house. Fauchery scrutinised her, and yet hesitated. One of his friends, a captain who had recently died in Mexico, had, on the very eve of his departure, made him one of those gross post-prandial confessions, of which even the most prudent among men are occasionally guilty. But of this he only retained a vague recollection; they had dined not wisely but too well that evening; and when he saw the Countess, in her black dress and with her quiet smile, seated in that old-world drawing-room, he certainly had his doubts. A lamp, which had been placed behind her, threw into clear relief her dark, delicate, plump, side face, wherein a certain heaviness in the contours of the mouth alone indicated a species of imperious sensuality.

"What do they want with their Bismarck?" muttered la Faloise, whose constant pretence it was to be bored in good society. "One's ready to kick the bucket here. A pretty idea of yours it was to want to come!"

Fauchery questioned him abruptly.

"Now tell me, does the Countess admit someone to her embraces?"

"Oh dear, no, no! my dear fellow," he stammered, manifestly taken aback, and quite forgetting his pose. "Where d'you think we are?"

After which he was conscious of a want of up-to-dateness in this outburst of indignation, and throwing himself back on a great sofa, he added,—

"Gad! I say no! but I don't know much about it. There's a little chap out there, Foucarmont they call him, who's to be met with everywhere and at every turn. One's seen faster men than that, though, you bet. However, it doesn't concern me, and indeed all I know is that if the Countess indulges in high jinks, she's still pretty sly about it; for the thing never gets about—nobody talks."

Then, although Fauchery did not take the trouble to question him, he told him all he knew about the Muffats. Amid the conversation of the ladies, which still continued in front of the hearth, they both spoke in subdued tones, and, seeing them there with their white cravats and gloves, one might have supposed them to be discussing, in chosen phraseology, some really serious topic. Old Madame Muffat then, whom la Faloise had been well acquainted with, was an insufferable old lady always hand in glove with the priests. She had the grand manner besides, and an authoritative way of comporting herself which bent everybody to her will. As to Muffat, he was an old man's child; his father, a general, had been created count by Napoleon I., and naturally he had found himself in favour after the 2nd of December. He hadn't much gaiety of manner either, but he passed for a very honest man of straightforward intentions and understanding. Add to these a code of old aristocratic ideas, and such a lofty conception of his duties at Court, of his dignities and of his virtues, that he behaved like a God on wheels. It was the Mamma Muffat who had given him this precious education, with its daily visits to the confessional, its complete absence of escapades, and of all that is meant by youth. He was a practising Christian, and had attacks of faith of such fiery violence that they might be likened to accesses of burning fever. Finally, in order to add a last touch to the picture, la Faloise whispered something in his cousin's ear. "You don't say so!" said the latter. "On my word of honour, they swore it was true! He was still like that when he married." Fauchery chuckled as he looked at the Count, whose face, with its fringe of whiskers and absence of moustaches, seemed to have grown squarer and harder now that he was busy quoting figures to the writhing, struggling Steiner. "My word, he's got a phiz for it!" murmured Fauchery. "A pretty present he made his wife! Poor little thing, how he must have bored her! She knows nothing about anything, I'll wager!"

Just then the Countess Sabine was saying something to him. But he did not hear her, so amusing and extraordinary did he esteem the Muffats' case. She repeated the question.

"Monsieur Fauchery, have you not published a sketch of Monsieur de Bismarck? You spoke with him once?"

He got up briskly, and approached the circle of ladies, endeavouring to collect himself, and soon with perfect ease of manner finding an answer,—

"Dear me, madam, I assure you I wrote that 'Portrait' with the help of biographies which had been published in Germany. I have never seen Monsieur de Bismarck."

He remained beside the Countess, and, whilst talking with her, continued his meditations. She did not look her age; one would have set her down as being twenty-eight at most, for her eyes above all, which were filled with the dark blue shadow of her long eyelashes, retained the glowing light of youth. Bred in a divided family, so that she used to spend one month with the Marquis de Chouard,

another with the Marquise, she had been married very young, urged on doubtless by her father whom she embarrassed after her mother's death. A terrible man was the Marquis, a man about whom strange tales were beginning to be told, and that despite his lofty piety! Fauchery asked if he should have the honour of meeting him. Certainly her father was coming, but only very late; he had so much work on hand! The journalist thought he knew where the old gentleman passed his evenings, and looked grave. But a mole, which he noticed close to her mouth, on the Countess's left cheek, surprised him. Nana had precisely the same mole. It was curious. Tiny hairs curled up on it, only they were golden in Nana's case, black as jet in this. Ah, well, never mind! This woman enjoyed nobody's embraces.

"I have always felt a wish to know Queen Augusta," said she. "They say she is so good, so devout. Do you think she will accompany the King?"

"It is not thought that she will, madam," replied he.

She had no lovers: the thing was only too apparent. One had only to look at her there, by the side of that daughter of hers, sitting so insignificant and constrained on her foot-stool. That sepulchral drawing-room of hers, which exhaled odours suggestive of being in a church, spoke as plainly as words could of the iron hand, the austere mode of existence, that weighed her down. There was nothing suggestive of her own personality in that ancient abode, black with the damps of years. It was Muffat who made himself felt there, who dominated his surroundings with his devotional training, his penances, and his fasts. But the sight of the little old gentleman with the black teeth and subtle smile, whom he suddenly discovered in his arm-chair behind the group of ladies, afforded him a yet more decisive argument. He knew the personage. It was Théophile Venot, a retired lawyer who had made a specialty of church cases. He had left off practice with a handsome fortune, and was now leading a sufficiently mysterious existence, for he was received everywhere, treated with great deference, and even somewhat feared, as though he had been the representative of a mighty force, an occult power, which was felt to be at his back. Nevertheless, his behaviour was very humble. He was churchwarden at the Madeleine Church, and had simply accepted the post of deputy-mayor at the town house of the Ninth Arrondissement in order, as he said, to have something to do in his leisure time. Deuce take it! the Countess was well guarded; there was nothing to be done in that quarter.

"You're right, it's enough to make one kick the bucket here," said Fauchery to his cousin, when he had made good his escape from the circle of ladies. "We'll hook it!"

But Steiner, deserted at last by the Count Muffat and the Deputy, came up in a fury. Drops of perspiration stood on his forehead, and he grumbled huskily,—

"Gad! let 'em tell me nothing, if nothing they want to tell me. I shall find people who will talk."

Then he pushed the journalist into a corner, and altering his tone, said in accents of victory,—

"It's to-morrow, eh? I'm of the party, my bully!"

"Indeed!" muttered Fauchery, with some astonishment.

"You didn't know about it. Oh! I had lots of bother to find her at home. Besides, Mignon never would leave me alone."

"But they're to be there, are the Mignons."

"Yes, she told me so. In fact, she did receive my visit, and she invited me. Midnight punctually, after the play."

The banker was beaming. He winked, and added with a peculiar emphasis on the words,—

"You've worked it, eh?"

"Eh, what?" said Fauchery, pretending not to understand him. "She wanted to thank me for my article, so she came and called on me."

"Yes, yes. You fellows are fortunate. You get rewarded. By-the-by, who pays the piper to-morrow?"

The journalist made a slight outward movement with his arms, as though he would intimate that no one had ever been able to find out. But Vandeuvres called to Steiner, who knew Monsieur de Bismarck. Madame du Joncquoy had almost convinced herself of the truth of her suppositions: she concluded with these words:

"He gave me an unpleasant impression: I think his face is evil. But I am quite willing to believe that he has a deal of wit. It would account for his successes."

"Without doubt," said the banker with a faint smile. He was a Jew from Frankfort.

Meanwhile la Faloise at last made bold to question his cousin. He followed him up and got inside his guard:

"There's supper at a woman's to-mor-

row evening? With which of them, eh?
—with which of them?"
Fauchery motioned to him that they
were overheard, and must respect the
conventions here. The door had just
been opened anew, and an old lady had
come in, followed by a young man, in
whom the journalist recognised the truant schoolboy, perpetrator of the famous
and as yet unforgotten "*très chic*" of
the *Blonde Venus* first night. This lady's
arrival caused a stir among the company.
The Countess Sabine had risen briskly
from her seat in order to go and greet
her, and she had taken both her hands
in hers, and addressed her as her "dear
Madame Hugon." Seeing that his cousin
viewed this little episode with some curiosity, la Faloise sought to arouse his interest, and in a few brief phrases explained the position. Madame Hugon,
widow of a notary, lived in retirement
at Les Fondettes, an old estate of her
family's, in the neighbourhood of Orleans, but she also kept up a small establishment in Paris, in a house belonging
to her in the Rue de Richelieu, and was
now passing some weeks there in order
to settle her youngest son, who was reading the law and in his "first year." In
old times she had been a dear friend of
the Marquise de Chouard, and had assisted at the birth of the Countess, who,
prior to her marriage, used to stay at her
house for months at a time, and even
now was quite familiarly treated by her.

"I have brought Georges to see you,"
said Madame Hugon to Sabine. "He's
grown, I trust."

The young man, with his clear eyes,
and the fair curls which suggested a girl
dressed up as a boy, bowed easily to the
Countess and reminded her of a bout of
battledore and shuttlecock they had had
together, two years ago, at The Fondettes.

"Philippe is not in Paris?" asked Count
Muffat.

"Dear me, no!" replied the old lady.
"He is always in garrison at Bourges."

She had seated herself, and began talking with considerable pride of her eldest
son, a great big fellow, who, after enlisting in a fit of waywardness, had of late
very rapidly attained the rank of lieutenant. All the ladies behaved to her
with respectful sympathy, and conversation was resumed in a tone at once more
amiable and more refined. Fauchery,
at sight of that respectable Madame
Hugon, that motherly face lit up with
such a kindly smile beneath its broad
tresses of white hair, thought how foolish
he had been to suspect the Countess Sabine even for an instant.

Nevertheless, the big chair with the
red silk upholsteries, in which the Countess sat, had attracted his attention. Its
style struck him as crude, not to say fan-
tastically suggestive, in that dim old
drawing-room. Certainly, it was not the
Count who had inveigled thither that
nest of voluptuous idleness. One might
have described it as an experiment, marking the birth of an appetite and of an
enjoyment. Then he forgot where he
was, fell into a brown study, and in
thought even harked back to that vague,
confidential announcement, imparted to
him one evening in the dining-room of a
restaurant. Impelled by a sort of sensu-
ous curiosity, he had always wanted an
introduction into the Muffats' circle, and,
now that his friend was in Mexico
through all eternity, who could tell what
might happen? "We shall see," he

thought. It was a folly doubtless, but the idea kept tormenting him, he felt himself drawn on, and his animal nature aroused. The big chair had a rumpled look—its nether cushions had been tumbled, a fact which now amused him.

"Well, shall we be off?" asked la Faloise, mentally vowing that, once outside, he would find out the name of the woman with whom people were going to sup.

"All in good time," replied Fauchery. But he was no longer in any hurry, and excused himself on the score of the invitation he had been commissioned to give, and had as yet not found a convenient opportunity to mention. The ladies were chatting about an assumption of the veil, a very touching ceremony, by which the whole of Parisian society had for the last three days been greatly moved. It was the eldest daughter of the Baronne de Fougeray, who, under stress of an irresistible vocation, had just entered the Carmelite Convent. Madame Chantereau, a distant cousin of the Fougerays, told how the baroness had been obliged to take to her bed the day after the ceremony, so overdone was she with weeping.

"I had a very good place," declared Léonide. "I found it interesting."

Nevertheless, Madame Hugon pitied the poor mother. How sad to lose a daughter in such a way!

"I am accused of being over-religious," said she, in her quiet frank manner, "but that does not prevent me thinking the children very cruel who obstinately commit such suicide."

"Yes, it's a terrible thing," murmured the Countess, shivering a little, as became a chilly person, and huddling herself anew in the depths of her big chair in front of the fire.

Then the ladies fell into a discussion. But their voices were discreetly attuned, whilst light trills of laughter now and again interrupted the gravity of their talk. The two lamps on the chimney-piece, which had shades of rose-coloured lace, cast a feeble light over them, while, on scattered pieces of furniture, there burnt but three other lamps, so that the great drawing-room remained in soft shadow.

Steiner was getting bored. He was describing to Fauchery an escapade of that little Madame de Chezelles, whom he simply referred to as Léonide. "A blackguard woman," said he, lowering his voice behind the ladies' arm-chairs. Fauchery looked at her as she sat quaintly perched, in her voluminous ball-dress of pale blue satin, on the corner of her arm-chair. She looked as slight and impudent as a boy, and he ended by feeling astonished at seeing her there. People comported themselves better at Caroline Héquet's, whose mother had arranged her house on serious principles. Here was a perfect subject for an article. What a strange world was this world of Paris! The most rigid circles found themselves invaded. Evidently that silent Théophile Venot, who contented himself by smiling and shewing his ugly teeth, must have been a legacy from the late Countess. So, too, must have been such ladies of mature age as Madame Chantereau and Madame du Joncquoy, besides four or five old gentlemen, who sat motionless in corners. The Count Muffat attracted to the house a series of functionaries, distinguished by the immaculate personal appearance which was at that time required of the men at the Tuileries. Among others there was the chief clerk, who still sat solitary in the middle of the room, with his closely-shorn cheeks, his vacant glance, and his coat so tight of fit that he could scarce venture to move. Almost all the young men and certain individuals with distinguished aristocratic manners were the Marquis de Chouard's contribution to the circle, he having kept touch with the Legitimist party after making his peace with the Empire on his entrance into the Council of State. There remained Léonide de Chezelles and Steiner, an ugly little knot against which Madame Hugon's elderly and amiable serenity stood out in strange contrast. And Fauchery, having sketched out his article, named this last group "Countess Sabine's little clique."

"On another occasion," continued Steiner in still lower tones, "Léonide got her tenor down to Montauban. She was living in the Château de Beaurecueil, two leagues further off, and she used to come in daily in a carriage and pair in order to visit him at the 'Lion d'Or,' where he had put up. The carriage used to wait at the door, and Léonide would stay hours in the house, while a crowd gathered round and looked at the horses."

There was a pause in the talk, and some solemn moments passed silently by in the lofty room. Two young men were whispering, but they ceased in their turn, and the hushed step of Count Muffat was alone audible as he crossed the floor. The lamps seemed to have paled; the fire was going out; a stern shadow fell athwart the old friends of the house where they sat in the chairs they had occupied there for forty years back. It was as though, in a momentary pause of conversation, the invited guests had become suddenly aware that the Count's mother, in all her glacial stateliness, had returned among them.

But the Countess Sabine had once more resumed,—

"Well, at last the news of it got about. The young man was likely to die, and that would explain the poor child's adoption of the religious life. Besides, they say that Monsieur de Fougeray would never have given his consent to the marriage."

"They say heaps of other things, too," cried Léonide giddily.

She fell a-laughing: she refused to talk. Sabine was won over by this gaiety, and put her handkerchief up to her lips. And in the vast and solemn room their laughter sounded a note which struck Fauchery strangely, the note of delicate glass breaking. Assuredly here was the first beginning of the "little rift." Everyone began talking again. Madame du Joncquoy demurred; Madame Chantereau knew for certain that a marriage had been projected, but that matters had gone no further; the men even ventured to give their opinions. For some minutes the conversation was a Babel of opinions, in which the divers elements of the circle, whether Bonapartist, or Legitimist, or merely worldly and sceptical, appeared to jostle one another simultaneously. Estelle had rung to order wood to be put on the fire; the footman turned up the lamps; the room seemed to wake from sleep. Fauchery began smiling, as though once more at his ease.

"Egad, they become the brides of God when they couldn't be their cousin's," said Vandeuvres between his teeth.

The subject bored him, and he had rejoined Fauchery.

"My dear fellow, have you ever seen a woman who was really loved become a nun?"

He did not wait for an answer, for he had had enough of the topic, and in a hushed voice,—

"Tell me," said he, "how many of us will there be tomorrow? There'll be the Mignons, Steiner, yourself, Blanche and I: who else?"

"Caroline, I believe, and Simonne, and Gaga without doubt. One never knows exactly, does one? On such occasions, one expects the party will number twenty, and you're really thirty."

Vandeuvres, who was looking at the ladies, passed abruptly to another subject:

"She must have been very nice-looking, that du Joncquoy woman, some fifteen years ago. Poor Estelle has grown lankier than ever. What a nice lath to put into a bed!"

But, interrupting himself, he returned to the subject of to-morrow's supper.

"What's so tiresome of those shows is that it's always the same set of women. One wants a novelty. Do try and invent a new girl. By Jove, happy thought! I'll go and beseech that stout man to bring the woman he was trotting about the other evening at the Variétés."

He referred to the chief clerk, sound asleep in the middle of the drawing-room. Fauchery, afar off, amused himself by following this delicate negotiation. Vandeuvres had sat himself down by the stout man, who still looked very sedate. For some moments they both appeared to be discussing with much propriety the question before the house, which was,

"How can one discover the exact state of feeling that urges a young girl to enter into the religious life?" Then the Count returned with the remark,—

"It's impossible. He swears she's straight. She'd refuse; and yet I would have wagered that I once saw her at Laure's."

"Eh, what? You go to Laure's!" murmured Fauchery, with a chuckle. "You venture your reputation in places like that! I was under the impression that it was only we poor devils of outsiders who——"

"Ah, dear boy, one ought to see every side of life."

Then they sneered, and with sparkling eyes they compared notes about the *table d'hôte* in the Rue des Martyrs, where big Laure Piédefer ran a dinner at three francs a head for little women in difficulties. A nice hole, where all the little women used to kiss Laure on the lips! And as the Countess Sabine, who had overheard a stray word or two, turned towards them, they started back, rubbing shoulders in excited merriment. They had not noticed that Georges Hugon was close by, and that he was listening to them, blushing so hotly the while that a rosy flush had spread from his ears to his girlish throat. The infant was full of shame and of ecstasy. From the moment his mother had turned him loose in the room, he had been hovering in the wake of Madame de Chezelles, the only woman present who struck him as being the thing. But after all is said and done, Nana licked her to fits!

"Yesterday evening," Madame Hugon was saying, "Georges took me to the play. Yes, we went to the Variétés, where I certainly had not set foot for the last ten years. That child adores music. As to me, I wasn't in the least amused; but he was so happy! They put extraordinary pieces on the stage nowadays. Besides, music delights me very little, I confess."

"What! you don't love music, madam?" cried Madame du Joncquoy, lifting her eyes to heaven. "Is it possible there should be people who don't love music?"

The exclamation of surprise was general. No one had dropped a single word concerning the performance at the Variétés, at which the good Madame Hugon had not understood any of the allusions. The ladies knew the piece, but said nothing about it, and with that they plunged into the realm of sentiment, and began discussing the masters in a tone of refined and ecstatical admiration. Madame du Joncquoy was not fond of any of them save Weber, while Madame Chantereau stood up for the Italians. The ladies' voices had turned soft and languishing, and in front of the hearth one might have fancied one's self listening, in meditative religious retirement, to the faint, discreet music of a little chapel.

"Now, let's see," murmurea Vandeuvres, bringing Fauchery back into the middle of the drawing-room; "notwithstanding it all, we must invent a woman for to-morrow. Shall we ask Steiner about it?"

"Oh, when Steiner's got hold of a woman," said the journalist, "it's because Paris has done with her."

Vandeuvres, however, was searching about on every side.

"Wait a bit," continued he, "the other day I met Foucarmont with a charming

blonde. I'll go and tell him to bring her."

And he called to Foucarmont. They exchanged a few words rapidly. There must have been some sort of complication, for both of them, moving carefully forward and stepping over the dresses of the ladies, went off in quest of another young man, with whom they continued the discussion in the embrasure of a window. Fauchery was left to himself, and had just decided to proceed to the hearth, where Madame du Joncquoy was announcing that she never heard Weber played without at the same time seeing lakes, forests, and sunrises over landscapes steeped in dew, when a hand touched his shoulder and a voice behind him remarked,—

"It's not civil of you."

"What d'you mean?" he asked, turning round and recognising la Faloise.

"Why, about that supper to-morrow. You might easily have got me invited."

Fauchery was at length about to state his reasons, when Vandeuvres came back to tell him,—

"It appears it isn't a girl of Foucarmont's. It's that man's flame out there. She won't be able to come. What a piece of bad luck! But all the same I've pressed Foucarmont into the service, and he's going to try to get Louise from the Palais-Royal."

"Is it not true, Monsier de Vandeuvres," asked Madame Chantereau, raising her voice, "that Wagner's music was hissed last Sunday?"

"Oh, frightfully, madam," he made answer, coming forward with his usual exquisite politeness.

Then, as they did not detain him, he

moved off, and continued whispering in the journalist's ear,—

"I'm going to press some more of them. These young fellows must know some little ladies."

With that he was observed to accost men and to engage them in conversation, in his usual amiable and smiling way, in every corner of the drawing-room. He mixed with the various groups, said something confidential to everyone, and walked away again with a sly wink and a secret signal or two. It looked as though he were giving out a watchword in that easy way of his. The news went round, the place of meeting was announced, while the ladies' sentimental dissertations on music served to conceal the small feverish rumour of these recruiting operations.

"No, do not speak of your Germans," Madame Chantereau was saying. "Song is gaiety, song is light. Have you heard Patti in the *Barber of Seville?*"

"She was delicious!" murmured Léonide, who strummed none but operatic airs on her piano.

Meanwhile the Countess Sabine had rung. When, on Tuesdays, the number of visitors was small, tea was handed round the drawing-room itself. While directing a footman to clear a round table, the Countess followed the Count de Vandœuvres with her eyes. She still smiled that vague smile which slightly disclosed her white teeth, and, as the Count passed, she questioned him.

"What *are* you plotting, Monsieur de Vandeuvres?"

"What am I plotting, madam?" he answered, quietly, "nothing at all."

"Really! I saw you so busy. Pray, wait, you shall make yourself useful!"

She placed an album in his hands, and asked him to put it on the piano. But he found means to inform Fauchery, in a low whisper, that they would have Tatan Néné, the most finely-developed girl that winter, and Maria Blond, the same who had just made her first appearance at the Folies-Dramatiques. Meanwhile la Faloise stopped him at every step in hopes of receiving an invitation. He ended by offering himself, and Vandeuvres engaged him in the plot at once; only he made him promise to bring Clarisse with him, and when la Faloise pretended to scruple about certain points, he quieted him by the remark,—

"Since I invite you, that's enough!"

Nevertheless, la Faloise would have much liked to know the name of the hostess. But the Countess had recalled Vandeuvres, and was questioning him as to the manner in which the English made tea. He often betook himself to England, where his horses ran. Then, as though he had been inwardly following up quite a laborious train of thought during his remarks, he broke in with the question:

"And the Marquis, by-the-by? Are we not to see him?"

"Oh, certainly you will! My father made me a formal promise that he would come," replied the Countess. "But I'm beginning to be anxious. His duties will have kept him."

Vandeuvres smiled a discreet smile. He too seemed to have his doubts as to the exact nature of the Marquis de Chouard's duties. Indeed, he had been thinking of a pretty woman whom the Marquis occasionally took into the country with him. Perhaps they could get her too.

In the meantime Fauchery decided that the moment had come in which to risk giving Count Muffat his invitation. The evening, in fact, was drawing to a close.

"Are you serious?" asked Vandeuvres, who thought a joke was intended.

"Extremely serious. If I don't execute my commission, she'll tear my eyes out. It's a case of landing her fish, you know."

"Well then, I'll help you, dear boy."

Eleven o'clock struck. Assisted by her daughter, the Countess was pouring out the tea, and as hardly any guests save intimate friends had come, the cups and the platefuls of little cakes were being circulated without ceremony. Even the ladies did not leave their arm-chairs in front of the fire, and sat sipping their tea and nibbling cakes which they held between their finger-tips. From music the talk had declined to purveyors. Boissier was the only person for sweetmeats, and Catherine for ices. Madame Chantereau, however, was all for Latinville. Speech grew more and more indolent, and a sense of lassitude was lulling the room to sleep. Steiner had once more set himself secretly to undermine the Deputy, whom he held in a state of blockade in the corner of a settee. Monsieur Venot, whose teeth must have been ruined by sweet things, was eating little dry cakes, one after the other, with a small nibbling sound suggestive of a mouse, while the chief clerk, his nose in a teacup, seemed never to be going to finish its contents. As to the Countess, she went in a leisurely way from one guest to another, never pressing them,

indeed, only pausing a second or two before the gentlemen whom she viewed with an air of dumb interrogation before she smiled and passed on. The great fire had flushed all her face, and she looked as if she were the sister of her daughter, who appeared so withered and ungainly at her side. When she drew near Fauchery, who was chatting with her husband and Vandeuvres, she noticed that they grew suddenly silent: accordingly she did not stop, but handed the cup of tea she was offering to Georges Hugon beyond them.

"It's a lady who desires your company at supper," the journalist gaily continued, addressing Count Muffat.

The last-named, whose face had worn its grey look all the evening, seemed very much surprised. What lady was it?

"Oh, Nana!" said Vandeuvres, by way of forcing the invitation.

The Count became more grave than before. His eyelids trembled just perceptibly, while a look of discomfort, such as headache produces, hovered for a moment athwart his forehead.

"But I'm not acquainted with that lady," he murmured.

"Come, come, you went to her house," remarked Vandeuvres.

"What d'you say? I went to her house? Oh yes, the other day, in behalf of the Benevolent Association. I had forgotten about it. But, no matter, I am not acquainted with her, and I cannot accept."

He had adopted an icy expression in order to make them understand that this jest did not appear to him to be in good taste. A man of his position did not sit down at the tables of such women as that. Vandeuvres protested: it was to be a supper-party of dramatic and artistic people, and talent excused everything. But without listening further to the arguments urged by Fauchery, who spoke of a dinner where the Prince of Scots, the son of a queen, had sat down beside an ex-music-hall singer, the Count only emphasized his refusal. In so doing, he allowed himself, despite his great politeness, to be guilty of an irritated gesture.

Georges and la Faloise, standing in front of each other drinking their tea, had overheard the two or three phrases exchanged in their immediate neighbourhood.

"Jove, it's at Nana's then," murmured la Faloise. "I might have expected as much!"

Georges said nothing, but he was all aflame. His fair hair was in disorder, his blue eyes shone like tapers, so fiercely had the vice, which for some days past had surrounded him, inflamed and stirred his blood. At last he was going to plunge into all that he had dreamt of!

"I don't know the address," la Faloise resumed.

"She lives on a third floor in the Boulevard Haussmann, between the Rue de l'Arcade and the Rue Pasquier," said Georges, all in a breath.

And when the other looked at him in much astonishment, he added, turning very red, and fit to sink into the ground with embarrassment and conceit,—

"I'm of the party. She invited me this morning."

But there was a great stir in the drawing-room, and Vandeuvres and Fauchery could not continue pressing the Count. The Marquis de Chouard had just come in, and everyone was anxious to greet him. He had moved painfully forward, his legs failing under him, and he now stood in the middle of the room with pallid face and eyes blinking, as though he had just come out of some dark alley, and were blinded by the brightness of the lamps.

"I scarcely hoped to see you to-night, father," said the Countess. "I should have been anxious till the morning."

He looked at her without answering, as a man might who fails to understand. His nose, which loomed immense on his shorn face, looked like a swollen pimple, while his lower lip hung down. Seeing him such a wreck, Madame Hugon, full of kind compassion, said pitying things to him.

"You work too hard. You ought to rest yourself. At our age we ought to leave work to the young people."

"Work! Ah yes, to be sure, work!" he stammered at last. "Always plenty of work."

He began to pull himself together, straightening up his bent figure, and, passing his hand, as was his wont, over his scant grey hair, of which a few locks strayed behind his ears.

"At what are you working as late as this?" asked Madame du Joncquoy. "I thought you were at the Financial Minister's reception."

But the Countess intervened with,—

"My father had to study the question of a projected law."

"Yes, a projected law," said he; "exactly so, a projected law. I shut myself up for that reason. It refers to work in factories, and I was anxious for a proper observance of the Lord's Day of Rest. It is really shameful that the Government is unwilling to act with vigour in the matter. Churches are growing empty; we are running headlong to ruin."

Vandeuvres had exchanged glances with Fauchery. They both happened to be behind the Marquis, and they were scanning him suspiciously. When Vandeuvres found an opportunity to take him aside, and to speak to him about that good-looking creature he was in the habit of taking down into the country, the old man affected extreme surprise. Perhaps someone had seen him with the Baroness Decker, at whose house, at Viroflay, he sometimes spent a day or so. Vandeuvres's sole vengeance was an abrupt question:

"Tell me, where have you been straying to? Your elbow is covered with cobwebs and plaster."

"My elbow," muttered he, slightly disturbed. "Yes, indeed, it's true. A speck or two. I must have come in for them on my way downstairs from my office."

Several people were taking their departure. It was close on midnight. Two footmen were noiselessly removing the empty cups and the plates with cakes. In front of the hearth, the ladies had reformed and, at the same time, narrowed their circle, and were chatting more carelessly than before in the languid atmosphere peculiar to the close of a party. The very room was going to sleep, and slowly creeping shadows were cast by its walls. It was then Fauchery spoke of departure. Yet he once more forgot his intention at sight of the Countess Sabine. She was resting from her cares as hostess, and as she sat in her wonted seat, silent, her eyes fixed on a log which was turning into embers, her face appeared so white and so impassable that doubt again possessed him. In the glow of the fire, the small black hairs on the mole at the corner of her lip became white. It was Nana's very mole, down to the colour of the hair. He could not refrain from whispering something about it in Vandeuvres's ear. Gad, it was true, the other had never noticed it before. And both men continued this comparison of Nana and the Countess. They discovered a vague resemblance about the chin and the mouth, but the eyes were not at all like. Then, too, Nana had a good-natured expression, while, with the Countess, it was hard to decide—she might have been a cat, sleeping with claws withdrawn and paws stirred by a scarce perceptible nervous quiver.

"All the same, one could have her," declared Fauchery.

Vandeuvres stripped her at a glance. "Yes, one could, all the same," said he. "But I think nothing of the thighs, you know. Will you bet she has no thighs?"

He stopped, for Fauchery touched him briskly on the arm, and shewed him Estelle, sitting close to them on her footstool. They had raised their voices without noticing her, and she must have overheard them. Nevertheless, she continued sitting there stiff and motionless, not a hair having lifted on her thin neck, which was that of a girl who has shot up all too quickly. Thereupon they retired three or four paces, and Vandeuvres vowed that the Countess was a very honest woman. Just then voices were raised in front of the hearth. Madame du Joncquoy was saying,—

"I was willing to grant you that Monsieur de Bismarck was perhaps a witty man. Only, if you go as far as to talk of genius——"

The ladies had come round again to their earliest topic of conversation. "What the deuce! still Monsieur de Bismarck!" muttered Fauchery. "This time I make my escape for good and all." "Wait a bit," said Vandeuvres, "we must have a definite 'no' from the Count."

The Count Muffat was talking to his father-in-law and a certain serious-looking gentleman. Vandeuvres drew him away and renewed the invitation, backing it up with the information that he was to be at the supper himself. A man might go anywhere; no one could think of suspecting evil where at most there could only be curiosity. The Count listened to these arguments with downcast eyes and expressionless face. Vandeuvres felt him to be hesitating when the Marquis de Chouard approached with a look of interrogation. And when the latter was informed of the question in hand, and Fauchery had invited him in his turn, he looked at his son-in-law furtively. There ensued an embarrassed silence, but both men encouraged one another, and would doubtless have ended by accepting, had not Count Muffat perceived Monsieur Venot's gaze fixed upon him. The little old man was no longer smiling; his face was cadaverous, his eyes bright and keen as steel.

"No," replied the Count directly in so decisive a tone that further insistence became impossible.

Then the Marquis refused with even greater severity of expression. He talked morality. The aristocratic classes ought to set a good example. Fauchery smiled and shook hands with Vandeuvres. He did not wait for him, and took his de-

parture immediately, for he was due at his newspaper office.

"At Nana's at midnight, eh?"

La Faloise retired too. Steiner had made his bow to the Countess. Other men followed them, and the same phrase went round—"At midnight, at Nana's" —as they went to get their overcoats in the ante-room. Georges, who could not leave without his mother, had stationed himself at the door, where he gave the exact address. "Third floor, door on your left." Yet, before going out, Fauchery gave a final glance. Vandeuvres had again resumed his position among the ladies, and was laughing with Léonide de Chezelles. Count Muffat and the Marquis de Chouard were joining in the conversation, whilst the good Madame Hugon was falling asleep open-eyed. Lost among the petticoats, Monsieur Venot was his own small self again, and smiled as of old. Twelve struck slowly in the great solemn room.

"What—what do you mean?" Madame du Joncquoy resumed. "You imagine that Monsieur de Bismarck will make war on us and beat us! Oh, that's unbearable!"

Indeed, they were laughing round Madame Chantereau, who had just repeated an assertion she had heard made in Alsace, where her husband owned a foundry.

"We have the Emperor, fortunately," said Count Muffat, in his grave official way.

It was the last phrase Fauchery was able to catch. He closed the door, after casting one more glance in the direction of the Countess Sabine. She was talking sedately with the chief clerk, and seemed to be interested in that stout individual's conversation. Assuredly, he must have been deceiving himself. There was no "little rift" there at all. It was a pity.

"You're not coming down then?" la Faloise shouted up to him from the entrance-hall.

And out on the pavement, as they separated, they once more repeated,— "To-morrow, at Nana's."

## CHAPTER IV

SINCE morning Zoé had delivered up the flat to a managing man, who had come from Brebant's with a staff of helpers and waiters. Brebant was to supply everything, from the supper, the plates and dishes, the glass, the linen, the flowers, down to the seats and footstools. Nana could not have mustered a dozen napkins out of all her cupboards, and not having had time to get a proper outfit after her new start in life, and scorning to go to the restaurant, she had decided to make the restaurant come to her. It struck her as being more the thing. She wanted to celebrate her great success as an actress with a supper which should set people talking. As her dining-room was too small, the manager had arranged the table in the drawing-room, a table with twenty-five covers, placed somewhat close together.

"Is everything ready?" asked Nana, when she returned at midnight.

"Oh! I don't know," replied Zoé roughly, looking beside herself with worry. "The Lord be thanked, I don't bother about anything. They're making a fearful mess in the kitchen and all over the flat! I've had to fight my battles too. The other two came again. My eye! I did just chuck 'em out!"

She referred of course to her employer's old admirers, the tradesman and the Wallachian, to whom Nana, sure of her future and longing to shed her skin, as she phrased it, had decided to give the go-by.

"There are a couple of leeches for you!" she muttered.

"If they come back, threaten to go to the police."

Then she called Daguenet and Georges, who had remained behind in the anteroom, where they were hanging up their overcoats. They had both met at the stage-door, in the Passage des Panoramas, and she had brought them home with her in a cab. As there was nobody there yet, she shouted to them to come into the dressing-room whilst Zoé was touching up her toilet. Hurriedly and without changing her dress, she had her hair done up, and stuck white roses in her chignon and at her bosom. The little room was littered with the drawing-room furniture, which the workmen had been compelled to roll in there, and it was full of a motley assemblage of round tables, sofas, and arm-chairs, with their legs in air for the most part. Nana was quite ready when her dress caught on a castor and tore upwards. At this she swore furiously; such things only happened to her! Ragingly she took off her dress, a very simple affair of white foulard, of so thin and supple a texture that it clung about her like a long shift. But she put it on again directly, for she could not find another to her taste, and with tears in her eyes declared that she was dressed like a rag-picker. Daguenet and Georges had to patch up the rent with pins, while Zoé once more arranged her hair. All three hurried round her, especially the boy, who knelt on the floor with his hands among her skirts. And at last she calmed down again, when Daguenet assured her it could not be later than a quarter past twelve, seeing that by dint of scamping her words and skipping her lines she had effectually shortened the third act of the *Blonde Venus*.

"The play's still far too good for that crowd of idiots," said she. "Did you see? There were thousands there to-night. Zoé, my girl, you will wait in here. Don't go to bed, I shall want you. By gum, it is time they came. Here's company!"

She ran off, whilst Georges stayed where he was with the skirts of his coat brushing the floor. He blushed, seeing Daguenet looking at him. Notwithstanding which, they had conceived a tender regard the one for the other. They rearranged the bows of their cravats in front of the big dressing-glass, and gave each other a mutual dose of the clothes-brush, for they were all white from their close contact with Nana.

"One would think it was sugar," murmured Georges, giggling like a greedy little child.

A footman, hired for the evening, was ushering the guests into the small drawing-room, a narrow slip of a place, in which only four arm-chairs had been left in order the better to pack in the company. From the large drawing-room beyond came a sound as of the moving of plates and silver, while a clear and brilliant ray of light shone from under the door. At her entrance, Nana found Clarisse Besnus, whom la Faloise had brought, already installed in one of the arm-chairs.

"Dear me, you're the first of 'em!" said Nana, who, now that she was successful, treated her familiarly.

"Oh, it's his doing," replied Clarisse. "He's always afraid of not getting anywhere in time. If I'd taken him at his word, I shouldn't have waited to take off my paint and my wig."

The young man, who now saw Nana for the first time, bowed, paid her a compliment, and spoke of his cousin, hiding his agitation behind an exaggeration of politeness. But Nana, neither listening to him, nor recognising his face, shook hands with him, and then went briskly towards Rose Mignon, with whom she at once assumed a most distinguished manner.

"Ah! how nice of you, my dear madam! I was so anxious to have you here!"

"It's I who am charmed, I assure you," said Rose, with equal amiability.

"Pray sit down. Do you require anything?"

"Thank you, no! Ah, yes, I've left my fan in my pelisse, Steiner, just look in the right-hand pocket."

Steiner and Mignon had come in behind Rose. The banker turned back and reappeared with the fan, while Mignon embraced Nana fraternally, and forced Rose to do so also. Did they not all belong to the same family in the theatrical world? Then he winked as though to encourage Steiner, but the latter was disconcerted by Rose's clear gaze, and contented himself by kissing Nana's hand.

Just then the Count de Vandeuvres made his appearance with Blanche de Sivry. There was an interchange of profound bows, and Nana with the utmost ceremony conducted Blanche to an arm-chair. Meanwhile, Vandeuvres told them laughingly that Fauchery was engaged in a dispute at the foot of the stairs, because the porter had refused to allow Lucy Stewart's carriage to come in at the gate. They could hear Lucy telling the porter he was a dirty blackguard in the ante-room. But when the footman had opened the door, she came forward with her laughing grace of manner, announced her name herself, took both Nana's hands in hers, and told her that she had liked her from the very first, and considered her talent splendid. Nana, puffed up by her novel *rôle* of hostess, thanked her, and was veritably confused. Nevertheless, from the moment of Fauchery's arrival, she appeared preoccupied, and directly she could get near him, she asked him in a low voice,—

"Will he come?"

"No, he did not want to," was the journalist's abrupt reply, for he was taken by surprise, though he had got ready some sort of tale to explain Count Muffat's refusal.

Seeing the young woman's sudden pallor, he became conscious of his folly, and tried to retract his words.

"He was unable to; he is taking the Countess to the ball at the Ministry of the Interior to-night."

"All right," murmured Nana, who suspected him of ill-will, "you'll pay me out for that, my pippin."

She turned on her heel, and so did he; they were angry. Just then, Mignon was pushing Steiner up against Nana, and when Fauchery had left her, he said to her in a low voice, and with the good-natured cynicism of a comrade in arms, who wishes his friends to be happy,—

"He's dying of it, you know, only he's afraid of my wife. Won't you protect him?"

Nana did not appear to understand. She smiled, and looked at Rose, the husband, and the banker, and finally said to the latter,—

"Monsieur Steiner, you will sit next me."

With that there came from the ante-room a sound of laughter and whispering, and a burst of merry chattering voices, which sounded as if a runaway convent were on the premises. And Labordette appeared, towing five women in his rear, his boarding school, as Lucy Stewart cruelly phrased it. There was Gaga, majestic in a blue velvet dress which was too tight for her, and Caroline Héquet, clad as usual in ribbed black silk, trimmed with Chantilly lace. Léa de Horn came next, terribly dressed up, as her wont was, and after her the big Tatan Néné, a good-humoured fair girl with the bosom of a wet nurse, at which people laughed, and, finally, little Maria Blond, a young damsel of fifteen, as thin and vicious as a street child, yet on the high road to success owing to her recent first appearance at the Folies. Labordette had brought the whole collection in a single fly, and they were still laughing at the way they had been squeezed with Maria Blond on her knees. But, on entering the room, they pursed up their lips, and all grew very conventional as they shook hands and exchanged salutations. Gaga even affected the infantile, and lisped through excess of genteel deportment. Tatan Néné alone transgressed. They had been telling her as they came along that six absolutely naked Negroes would serve up Nana's supper, and she now grew anxious about them, and asked to see them. Labordette called her a goose, and besought her to be silent.

"And Bordenave?" asked Fauchery.

"Oh! you may imagine how miserable I am," cried Nana; "he won't be able to join us."

"Yes," said Rose Mignon, "his foot caught in a trap-door, and he's got a fearful sprain. If only you could hear him swearing, with his leg tied up and laid out on a chair!"

Thereupon everybody mourned over Bordenave's absence. No one ever gave a good supper without Bordenave. Ah well, they would try and do without him, and they were already talking about other matters, when a burly voice was heard,—

"What, eh what? Is that the way they're going to write my obituary notice?"

There was a shout, and all heads were turned round, for it was indeed Bordenave. Huge and fiery-faced, he was standing with his stiff leg in the doorway, leaning for support on Simonne Cabiroche's shoulder. Simonne was for the time being his mistress. This little creature had had a certain amount of education, and could play the piano and talk English. She was a blonde on a tiny, pretty scale, and so delicately formed that she seemed to bend under Bordenave's rude weight. Yet she was smilingly submissive withal. He postured there for some moments, for he felt that together they formed a tableau.

"One can't help liking ye, eh?" continued he. "Zounds, I was afraid I should get bored, and I said to myself, —'Here goes.'"

But he interrupted himself with an oath.

"Oh, damn!"

Simonne had taken a step too quickly forward, and his foot had just felt his full weight. He gave her a rough push, but she, still smiling away, and ducking her pretty head as some animal might that is afraid of a beating, held him up with all the strength a little plump blonde can command. Amid all these exclamations, there was a rush to his assistance. Nana and Rose Mignon rolled up an arm-chair, into which Bordenave let himself sink, whilst the other women slid a second one under his leg. And with that all the actresses present kissed him —as a matter of course. He kept grumbling and gasping.

"Oh, damn! Oh, damn! Ah well, the stomach's unhurt, you'll see."

Other guests had arrived by this time, and motion became impossible in the room. The noise of clinking plates and silver had ceased, and now a dispute was heard going on in the big drawing-room, where the voice of the manager grumbled angrily. Nana was growing impatient, for she expected no more invited guests, and wondered why they did not bring in supper. She had just sent Georges to find out what was going on, when, to her great surprise, she noticed the arrival of more guests, both male and female. She did not know them in the least. Whereupon, with some embarrassment, she questioned Bordenave, Mignon, and Labordette about them. They did not know them any more than she did; but when she turned to the Count de Vandeuvres he seemed suddenly to recollect himself. They were the young men he had pressed into her service at Count Muffat's. Nana thanked him. That was capital, capital! Only they would all be terribly crowded, and she begged

Labordette to go and have seven more covers set. Scarcely had he left the room than the footman ushered in three new-comers. Nay, this time the thing was becoming ridiculous; one certainly could never take them all in. Nana was beginning to grow angry, and, in her haughtiest manner announced that such conduct was scarcely in good taste. But, seeing two more arrive, she began laughing; it was really too funny. So much the worse. People would have to fit in anyhow! The company were all on their feet save Gaga, and Rose, and Bordenave, who alone took up two arm-chairs. There was a buzz of voices, people talking in low tones, and stifling slight yawns the while.

"Now what d'you say, my lass," asked Bordenave, "to our sitting down at table as if nothing had happened? We are all here, don't you think?"

"Oh yes, we're all here, I promise you!" she answered laughingly.

She looked round her, but grew suddenly serious, as though she were surprised at not finding someone. Doubtless there was a guest missing whom she did not mention. It was a case of waiting. But a minute or two later the company noticed in their midst a tall gentleman with a fine face and a beautiful white beard. The most astonishing thing about it was that nobody had seen him come in; indeed, he must have slipped into the little drawing-room through the bedroom door, which had remained ajar. Silence reigned, broken only by a sound of whispering. The Count de Vanduevres certainly knew who the gentleman was, for they both exchanged a discreet hand-grip; but to the questions which the women asked him he replied

by a smile only. Thereupon Caroline Héquet wagered in a low voice that it was an English lord, who was on the eve of returning to London to be married. She knew him quite well—she had had him. And this account of the matter went the round of the ladies present, Maria Blond alone asserting that, for her part, she recognised a German ambassador. She could prove it, because he often passed the night with one of her friends. Among the men his measure was taken in a few rapid phrases. A real swell, to judge by his looks! Perhaps he would pay for the supper! Most likely. It looked like it. Bah! provided only the supper was a good one! In the end the company remained undecided. Nay, they were already beginning to forget the old white-bearded gentleman, when the manager opened the door of the large drawing-room.

"Supper is on the table, madam."

Nana had already accepted Steiner's proffered arm without noticing a movement on the part of the old gentleman, who started to walk behind her in solitary state. Thus, the march-past could not be organised; and men and women entered anyhow, joking with homely good humour over this absence of ceremony. A long table stretched from one end to the other of the great room, which had been entirely cleared of furniture, and this same table was not long enough, for the plates thereon were touching one another. Four candelabra, with ten candles apiece, lit up the supper, and of these one was gorgeous in silver plate with sheaves of flowers to right and left of it. Everything was luxurious after the restaurant fashion; the china was ornamented with a gold line and lacked the customary monogram, the silver had become worn and tarnished through dint of continual washings, the glass was of the kind that you can complete an odd set of in any cheap emporium.

The scene suggested a premature house-warning in an establishment newly smiled on by Fortune, and as yet lacking the necessary conveniences. There was no central lustre, and the candelabra, whose tall tapers had scarcely burnt up properly, cast a pale yellow light among the dishes and stands, on which fruit, cakes, and preserves alternated symmetrically.

"You sit where you like, you know," said Nana. "It's more amusing that way."

She remained standing midway down the side of the table. The old gentleman, whom nobody knew, had placed himself on her right, while she kept Steiner on her left hand. Some guests were already sitting down, when the sound of oaths came from the little drawing-room. It was Bordenave. The company had forgotten him, and he was having all the trouble in the world to raise himself out of his two arm-chairs, for he was howling amain and calling for that cat of a Simonne, who had slipped off with the rest. The women ran in to him, full of pity for his woes, and Bordenave appeared, supported, nay, almost carried, by Caroline, Clarisse, Tatan Néné, and Maria Blond And there was much to-do over his installation at the table.

"In the middle, facing Nana!" was the cry. "Bordenave in the middle! He'll be our president!"

Thereupon the ladies seated him in the middle. But he needed a second chair

for his leg, and two girls lifted it up and stretched it carefully out. It wouldn't matter; he would eat sideways.

"God blast it all!" he grumbled. "We're squashed all the same! Ah, my kittens, papa recommends himself to your tender care!"

He had Rose Mignon on his right and Lucy Stewart on his left hand, and they promised to take good care of him. Everybody was now getting settled. Count de Vandeuvres placed himself between Lucy and Clarisse; Fauchery between Rose Mignon and Caroline Héquet. On the other side of the table, Hector de la Faloise had rushed to get next Gaga, and that despite the calls of Clarisse opposite; while Mignon, who never deserted Steiner, was only separated from him by Blanche, and had Tatan Néné on his left. Then came Labordette, and, finally, at the two ends of the table were irregular crowding groups of young men and of women, such as Simonne, Léa de Horn and Maria Blond. It was in this region that Daguenet and Georges foregathered more warmly than ever, whilst smilingly gazing at Nana.

Nevertheless, two people remained standing, and there was much joking about it. The men offered seats on their knees. Clarisse, who could not move her elbows, told Vandeuvres that she counted on him to feed her. And then that Bordenave did just take up space with his chairs! There was a final effort, and at last everybody was seated, but, as Mignon loudly remarked, they were confoundedly like herrings in a barrel.

"Thick asparagus soup *à la Comtesse,* clear soup *à la Deslignac,*" murmured the waiters, carrying about platesful in rear of the guests.

Bordenave was loudly recommending the thick soup, when a shout arose, followed by protests and indignant exclamations. The door had just opened, and three late arrivals, a woman and two men, had just come in. Oh, dear no! there was no space for them! Nana, however, without leaving her chair, began screwing up her eyes in the effort to find out whether she knew them. The woman was Louise Violaine, but she had never seen the men before.

"This gentleman, my dear," said Vandeuvres, "is a friend of mine, a naval officer, Monsieur de Foucarmont by name. I invited him."

Foucarmont bowed, and seemed very much at ease, for he added,—

"And I took leave to bring one of my friends with me."

"Oh, it's quite right, quite right!" said Nana. "Sit down, pray. Let's see, you —Clarisse—push up a little. You're a good deal spread out down there. That's it—where there's a will——"

They crowded more tightly than ever, and Foucarmont and Louise were given a little stretch of table, but the friend had to sit at some distance from his plate, and ate his supper through dint of making a long arm between his neighbours' shoulders. The waiters took away the soup plates, and circulated rissoles of young rabbit with truffles, and "niokys" and powdered cheese. Bordenave agitated the whole table with the announcement that at one moment he had had the idea of bringing with him Prullière, Fontan, and old Bosc. At this Nana looked sedate, and remarked dryly that she would have given them a pretty reception. Had

she wanted colleagues, she would certainly have undertaken to ask them herself. No, no, she wouldn't have third-rate play-actors. Old Bosc was always drunk; Prullière was fond of spitting too much, and as to Fontan, he made himself unbearable in society with his loud voice and his stupid doings. Then, you know, third-rate play-actors were always out of place when they found themselves in the society of gentlemen such as those around her.

"Yes, yes, it's true," Mignon declared.

All round the table the gentlemen in question looked unimpeachable in the extreme, what with their evening dress, and their pale features, the natural distinction of which was still further refined by fatigue. The old gentleman was as deliberate in his movements, and wore as subtle a smile, as though he were presiding over a diplomatic congress, and Vandeuvres, with his exquisite politeness towards the ladies next to him, seemed to be at one of the Countess Muffat's receptions. That very morning Nana had been remarking to her aunt that, in the matter of men, one could not have done better— they were all either well-born or wealthy, in fact quite the thing. And as to the ladies, they were behaving admirably. Some of them, such as Blanche, Léa, and Louise, had come in low dresses, but Gaga's only was perhaps a little too low, the more so because at her age she would have done well not to shew her neck at all. Now that the company were finally settled, the laughter and the light jests began to fail. Georges was under the impression that he had assisted at merrier dinner-parties among the good folks of Orleans. There was scarcely any conversation. The men, not being mutually acquainted, stared at one another, while the women sat quite quiet, and it was this which especially surprised Georges. He thought them all smugs—he had been under the impression that everybody would begin kissing at once.

The third course, consisting of a Rhine carp à la Chambord and a saddle of venison à l'Anglaise, was being served, when Blanche remarked aloud,—

"Lucy, my dear, I met your Ollivier on Sunday. How he's grown!"

"Dear me, yes! he's eighteen," replied Lucy. "It doesn't make me feel any younger. He went back to his school yesterday."

Her son Ollivier, whom she was wont to speak of with pride, was a pupil at the Ecole de Marine. Then ensued a conversation about the young people, during which all the ladies waxed very tender. Nana described her own great happiness. Her baby, the little Louis, she said, was now at the house of her aunt, who brought him round to her every morning at eleven o'clock, when she would take him into her bed, where he played with her griffon dog, Lulu. It was enough to make one die of laughing to see them both burying themselves under the clothes at the bottom of the bed. The company had no idea how cunning Louiset had already become.

"Oh! yesterday I did just pass a day!" said Rose Mignon, in her turn. "Just imagine, I went to fetch Charles and Henry at their boarding school; and I had positively to take them to the theatre at night. They jumped, they clapped their little hands: 'We shall see mamma act! We shall see mamma act!' Oh! it was a to-do!"

Mignon smiled complaisantly, his eyes moist with paternal tenderness.

"And at the play itself," he continued, "they were so funny! They behaved as seriously as grown men, devoured Rose with their eyes, and asked me why mamma had her legs bare like that."

The whole table began laughing, and Mignon looked radiant, for his pride as a father was flattered. He adored his children, and had but one object in life, which was to increase their fortunes by administering the money, gained by Rose at the theatre and elsewhere, with the business-like severity of a faithful steward. When, as first fiddle in the music hall where she used to sing, he had married her, they had been passionately fond of one another. Now, they were good friends. There was an understanding between them: she laboured hard to the full extent of her talent and of her beauty; he had given up his violin in order the better to watch over her successes as an actress and as a woman. One could not have found a more homely and united household anywhere!

"What age is your eldest?" asked Vandeuvres.

"Henry's nine," replied Mignon, "but such a big chap for his years!"

Then he chaffed Steiner, who was not fond of children, and with quiet audacity informed him that, were he a father, he would make a less stupid hash of his fortune. Whilst talking, he watched the banker over Blanche's shoulders to see if it was coming off with Nana. But for some minutes, Rose and Fauchery, who were talking very near him, had been getting on his nerves. Was Rose going to waste time over such a folly as that? In that sort of cases, by Jove, he blocked the way. And diamond on finger, and with his fine hands in great evidence, he finished discussing a filet of venison.

Elsewhere, the conversation about children continued. La Faloise, rendered very restless by the immediate proximity of Gaga, asked news of her daughter, whom he had had the pleasure of noticing in her company at the Variétés. Lili was quite well, but she was still such a tomboy! He was astonished to learn that Lili was entering on her nineteenth year. Gaga became even more imposing in his eyes, and when he endeavoured to find out why she had not brought Lili with her,—

"Oh! no, no, never!" said she stiffly. "Not three months ago she positively insisted on leaving her boarding school. I was thinking of marrying her off at once, but she loves me, so that I had to take her home—oh! so much against my will!"

Her blue eyelids, with their blackened lashes, blinked and wavered, while she spoke of the business of settling her young lady. If, at her time of life, she hadn't laid by a sou, but was still always working to minister to men's pleasures, especially those of very young men, whose grandmother she might well be, it was truly because she considered a good match of far greater importance than mere savings. And with that she leant over la Faloise, who reddened under the huge naked plastered shoulder with which she well nigh crushed him.

"You know," she murmured, "if she fails, it won't be my fault. But they're so strange when they're young!"

There was a considerable bustle round the table, and the waiters became very active. After the third course the *entrées*

had made their appearance; they consisted of pullets *à la maréchale*, fillets of sole with shallot sauce, and *escalopes* of Strasbourg *pâté*. The manager, who till then had been having Meursault served, now offered Chambertin and Léoville. Amid the slight hubbub which the change of plates involved, Georges, who was growing momentarily more astonished, asked Daguenet if all the ladies present were similarly provided with children, and the other, who was amused by this question, gave him some further details. Lucy Stewart was the daughter of a man of English origin, who greased the wheels of the trains at the Gare du Nord; she was thirty-nine years old and had the face of a horse, but was adorable withal, and, though consumptive, never died. In fact, she was the smartest woman there, and represented three princes and a duke. Caroline Héquet, born at Bordeaux, daughter of a little clerk long since dead of shame, was lucky enough to be possessed of a mother with a head on her shoulders, who, after having cursed her, had made it up again at the end of a year of reflection, being minded at any rate to save a fortune for her daughter. The latter was twenty-five years old, and very passionless, and was held to be one of the finest women it was possible to enjoy. Her price never varied. The mother, a model of orderliness, kept the accounts, and noted down receipts and expenditures with severe precision. She managed the whole household from some small lodging two stories above her daughter's, where, moreover, she had established a workroom for dressmaking and plain sewing. As to Blanche de Sivry, whose real name was Jacqueline Bandu, she hailed from a village near

Amiens. Magnificent in person, stupid and untruthful in character, she gave herself out as the grand-daughter of a general, and never owned to her thirty-two summers. The Russians had a great taste for her owing to her *embonpoint*. Then Daguenet added a rapid word or two about the rest. There was Clarisse Besnus, whom a lady had brought up from Saint-Aubin-sur-Mer in the capacity of maid, whilst the lady's husband had started her in quite another line. There was Simonne Cabiroche, the daughter of a furniture dealer in the Faubourg Saint-Antoine, who had been educated in a large boarding school with a view to becoming a governess. Finally, there were Maria Blond, and Louise Violaine, and Léa de Horn, who had all shot up to woman's estate on the pavements of Paris, not to mention Tatan Néné, who had herded cows in Champagne till she was twenty.

Georges listened and looked at these ladies, feeling dizzy and excited by the coarse recital thus crudely whispered in his ear, whilst, behind his chair, the waiters kept repeating in respectful tones,—

"Pullets *à la maréchale*: fillets of sole with *ravigote* sauce."

"My dear fellow," said Daguenet, giving him the benefit of his experience, "don't take any fish: it'll do you no good at this time of night. And be content with Léoville: it's less treacherous."

A heavy warmth floated upward from the candelabras, from the dishes which were being handed round, from the whole table where thirty-eight human beings were suffocating. And the waiters forgot themselves and ran when crossing the carpet, so that it was spotted with grease.

Nevertheless, the supper grew scarce any merrier. The ladies trifled with their meat, left half of it uneaten. Tatan Néné alone partook gluttonously of every dish. At that advance hour of the night, hunger was of the nervous order only, a mere whimsical craving born of an exasperated stomach.

At Nana's side, the old gentleman refused every dish offered him; he had only taken a spoonful of soup, and he now sat in front of his empty plate gazing silently about. There was some subdued yawning, and occasionally eyelids closed, and faces became haggard and white. It was unutterably slow, as it always was, according to Vandeuvres's dictum. This sort of supper should be served anyhow if it was to be funny, he opined. Otherwise, when elegantly and conventionally done, you might as well feed in good society, where you were not more bored than here. Had it not been for Bordenave, who was still bawling away, everybody would have fallen asleep. That rum old buffer, Bordenave, with his leg duly stretched on its chair, was letting his neighbours, Lucy and Rose, wait on him as though he were a sultan. They were entirely taken up with him, and they helped him and pampered him, and watched over his glass and his plate, and yet that did not prevent his complaining.

"Who's going to cut up my meat for me? I can't, the table's a league away."

Every few seconds Simonne rose, and took up a position behind his back in order to cut his meat and his bread. All the women took a great interest in the things he ate. The waiters were recalled, and he was stuffed to suffocation. Simonne having wiped his mouth for him, whilst Rose and Lucy were changing his plate, her act struck him as very pretty, and, deigning at length to shew contentment,—

"There, there, my daughter," said he, "that's as it should be. Women are made for that!"

There was a slight re-awakening, and conversation became general as they finished discussing some orange sherbet. The hot roast was a fillet with truffles, and the cold roast a galantine of guinea-fowls in jelly. Nana, annoyed by the want of go displayed by her guests, had begun talking with the greatest distinctness.

"You know the Prince of Scots has already had a stage-box reserved so as to see the *Blonde Venus* when he comes to visit the Exhibition."

"I very much hope that all the princes will come and see it," declared Bordenave with his mouth full.

"They are expecting the Shah of Persia next Sunday," said Lucy Stewart.

Whereupon Rose Mignon spoke of the Shah's diamonds. He wore a tunic entirely covered with gems: it was a marvel, a flaming star, it represented millions. And the ladies, with pale faces and eyes glittering with covetousness, craned forward, and ran over the names of the other kings, the other emperors, who were shortly expected. All of them were dreaming of some royal caprice, some night to be paid for by a fortune.

"Now tell me, dear boy," Caroline Héquet asked Vandeuvres, leaning forward as she did so, "how old's the Emperor of Russia?"

"Oh, he's 'present time,'" replied the Count, laughing. "Nothing to be done in that quarter, I warn you."

Nana made pretence of being hurt.

The witticism appeared somewhat too stinging, and there was a murmur of protest. But Blanche gave a description of the King of Italy, whom she had once seen at Milan. He was scarcely good-looking, and yet that did not prevent him enjoying all the women. She was put out somewhat when Fauchery assured her that Victor Emmanuel could not come to the Exhibition. Louise Violaine and Léa favoured the Emperor of Austria, and all of a sudden little Maria Blond was heard saying,—

"What an old stick the King of Prussia is! I was at Baden last year, and one was always meeting him about with Count Bismarck."

"Dear me, Bismarck!" Simonne interrupted. "I knew him once, I did. A charming man."

"That's what I was saying yesterday," cried Vandeuvres, "but nobody would believe me."

And, just as at Countess Sabine's, there ensued a long discussion about Bismarck. Vandeuvres repeated the same phrases, and for a moment or two one was again in the Muffats' drawing-room, the only difference being that the ladies were changed. Then, just as last night, they passed on to a discussion on music, after which, Foucarmont having let slip some mention of the assumption of the veil of which Paris was still talking, Nana grew quite interested, and insisted on details about Mademoiselle de Fougeray. Oh, the poor child, fancy her burying herself alive like that! Ah, well, when it was a question of vocation! All round the table the women expressed themselves much touched, and Georges, wearied at hearing these things a second time discussed, was beginning to ask

Daguenet about Nana's ways in private life, when the conversation veered fatefully back to Count Bismarck. Tatan Néné bent towards Labordette to ask him privily who this Bismarck might be, for she did not know him. Whereupon Labordette, in cold blood, told her some portentous anecdotes. This Bismarck, said he, was in the habit of eating raw meat, and when he met a woman near his den would carry her off thither on his back; at forty years of age he had already had as many as thirty-two children that way.

"Thirty-two children at forty!" cried Tatan Néné, stupefied and yet convinced. "He must be jolly well worn out for his age."

There was a burst of merriment, and it dawned on her that she was being made game of.

"You sillies! How am I to know if you're joking?"

Gaga, meanwhile, had stopped at the Exhibition. Like all these ladies, she was delightedly preparing for the fray. A good season, provincials and foreigners rushing into Paris! In the long run, perhaps, after the close of the Exhibition, she would, if her business had flourished, be able to retire to a little house at Jouvisy, which she had long had her eye on.

"What's to be done?" said she to la Faloise. "One never gets what one wants! Oh! if only one were still really loved!"

Gaga behaved meltingly because she had felt the young man's knee gently placed against her own. He was blushing hotly, and lisping as elegantly as ever. She weighed him at a glance. Not a very heavy little gentleman, to be sure;

but then she wasn't hard to please. La Faloise obtained her address.

"Just look there," murmured Vandeuvres to Clarisse. "I think Gaga's doing you out of your Hector."

"A good riddance, so far as I'm concerned," replied the actress. "That fellow's an idiot. I've already chucked him downstairs three times. You know, I'm disgusted when dirty little boys run after old women."

She broke off, and with a little gesture indicated Blanche, who from the commencement of dinner had remained in a most uncomfortable attitude, sitting up very markedly, with the intention of displaying her shoulders to the old distinguished-looking gentleman three seats beyond her.

"You're being left too," she resumed. Vandeuvres smiled his thin smile, and made a little movement to signify he did not care. Assuredly, 'twas not he who would ever have prevented poor dear Blanche scoring a success. He was more interested by the spectacle which Steiner was presenting to the table at large. The banker was noted for his sudden flames. That terrible German Jew, who brewed money, whose hands forged millions, was wont to turn imbecile whenever he became enamoured of a woman. He wanted them all too! Not one could make her appearance on the stage but he bought her, however expensive she might be. Vast sums were quoted. Twice had his furious appetite for courtesans ruined him. The courtesans, as Vandeuvres used to say, avenged public morality by emptying his money bags. A big operation in the salt works of the Landes had rendered him powerful on 'Change, and so for six weeks past the Mignons had been getting a pretty slice out of those same salt works. But people were beginning to lay wagers that the Mignons would not finish their slice, for Nana was shewing her white teeth. Once again Steiner was in the toils, and so deeply this time that, as he sat by Nana's side, he seemed stunned—he ate without appetite, his lip hung down, his face was mottled. She had only to name a figure. Nevertheless, she did not hurry, but continued playing with him, breathing her merry laughter into his hairy ear, and enjoying the little convulsive movements which kept traversing his heavy face. There would always be time enough to patch all that up if that ninny of a Count Muffat were really to treat her as Joseph did Potiphar's wife.

"Léoville or Chambertin?" murmured a waiter, who came craning forward between Nana and Steiner, just as the latter was addressing her in a low voice.

"Eh? what?" he stammered, losing his head. "Whatever you like—I don't care."

Vandeuvres gently nudged Lucy Stewart, who had a very spiteful tongue and a very fierce invention when once she was set going. That evening Mignon was driving her to exasperation.

"He would gladly be bottle-holder, you know," she remarked to the Count. "He's in hopes of repeating what he did with little Jonquier. You remember: Jonquier was Rose's man, but he was sweet on big Laure. Now Mignon procured Laure for Jonquier, and then came back arm in arm with him to Rose, as if he were a husband who had been allowed a little peccadillo. But this time the thing's going to fail. Nana doesn't give up the men who are lent her."

"What ails Mignon that he should be looking at his wife in that severe way?" asked Vandeuvres.

He leant forward, and saw Rose growing exceedingly amorous towards Fauchery. This was the explanation of his neighbour's wrath. He resumed laughingly,—

"The devil, are you jealous?"

"Jealous!" said Lucy in a fury. "Good gracious, if Rose is wanting Léon, I give him up willingly—for what he's worth! That's to say, for a bouquet a week, and the rest to match! Look here, my dear boy, these theatrical trollops are all made the same way. Why, Rose cried with rage when she read Léon's article on Nana; I know she did. So now, you understand, she must have an article too, and she's gaining it. As for me, I'm going to chuck Léon downstairs, you'll see!"

She paused to say "Léoville" to the waiter standing behind her with his two bottles, and then resumed in lowered tones,—

"I don't want to shout; it isn't my style. But she's a cocky slut all the same. If I were in her husband's place I should lead her a lovely dance. Oh! she won't be very happy over it. She doesn't know my Fauchery: a dirty gent he is, too, palling up with women like that so as to get on in the world. Oh, a nice lot they are!"

Vandeuvres did his best to calm her down, but Bordenave, deserted by Rose and by Lucy, grew angry, and cried out that they were letting papa perish of hunger and thirst. This produced a fortunate diversion. Yet the supper was flagging; no one was eating now, though platefuls of *cèpes à l'Italienne* and pineapple fritters à la *Pompadour* were being mangled. The champagne, however, which had been drunk ever since the soup course, was beginning little by little to warm the guests into a state of nervous exaltation. They ended by paying less attention to decorum than before. The women began leaning on their elbows amid the disordered table arrangements, whilst the men, in order to breathe more easily, pushed their chairs back; and soon the black coats appeared buried between the light-coloured bodices, and bare shoulders, half turned towards the table, began to gleam as soft as silk. It was too hot, and the glare of the candles above the table grew ever yellower and duller. Now and again, when a woman bent forward, the back of her neck glowed golden under a rain of curls, and the glitter of a diamond clasp lit up a lofty chignon. There was a touch of fire in the passing jests, in the laughing eyes, in the sudden gleam of white teeth, in the reflection of the candelabra, on the surface of a glass of champagne. The company joked at the tops of their voices, gesticulated, asked questions which no one answered, and called to one another across the whole length of the room. But the loudest din was made by the waiters; they fancied themselves at home in the corridors of their parent restaurant; they jostled one another, and served the ices and the dessert to an accompaniment of guttural exclamations.

"My children," shouted Bordenave, "you know we're playing to-morrow. Be careful! not too much champagne!"

"As far as I'm concerned," said Foucarmont, "I've drunk every imaginable kind of wine in all the four quarters of the globe. Extraordinary liquors some of 'em, containing alcohol enough to kill a corpse! Well, and what d'you think? why it never hurt me a bit. I can't make myself drunk. I've tried and I can't."

He was very pale, very calm and collected, and he lolled back in his chair, drinking without cessation.

"Never mind that," murmured Louise Violaine. "Leave off: you've had enough. It would be a funny business if I had to look after you the rest of the night."

Such was her state of exaltation that Lucy Stewart's cheeks were assuming a red consumptive flush, whilst Rose Mignon with moist eyelids was growing excessively melting. Tatan Néné, greatly astonished at the thought that she had overeaten herself, was laughing vaguely over her own stupidity. The others, such as Blanche, Caroline, Simonne, and Maria, were all talking at once, and telling each other about their private affairs —about a dispute with a coachman, a projected picnic, and innumerable complex stories of lovers stolen or restored. Meanwhile, a young man near Georges, having evinced a desire to kiss Léa de Horn, received a sharp rap, accompanied by a "Look here, you, let me go!" which was spoken in a tone of fine indignation; and Georges, who was now very tipsy and greatly excited by the sight of Nana, hesitated about carrying out a project which he had been gravely maturing. He had been planning, indeed, to get under the table on all-fours and to go and crouch at Nana's feet like a little dog. Nobody would have seen him, and he would have stayed there in the quietest way. But when, at Léa's urgent request, Daguenet had told the young man to sit still, Georges all at once felt grievously chagrined, as though the reproof had just been levelled at him. Oh, it was all silly, and slow, and there was nothing worth living for! Daguenet, nevertheless, began chaffing, and obliged him to swallow a big glassful of water, asking him, at the same time, what he would do if he were to find himself alone with a woman, seeing that three glasses of champagne were able to bowl him over. "Why, in Havana," resumed Foucarmont, "they make a spirit with a certain wild berry; you think you're swallowing fire! Well now, one evening I drank more than a litre of it, and it didn't hurt me one bit. Better than that, another time when we were on the coast of Coromandel, some savages gave us I don't know what sort of a mixture of pepper and vitriol; and that didn't hurt me one bit. I can't make myself drunk."

For some moments past la Faloise's face opposite had excited his displeasure. He began sneering, and giving vent to disagreeable witticisms. La Faloise, whose brain was in a whirl, was behaving very restlessly, and squeezing up against Gaga. But at length he became the victim of anxiety; somebody had just taken his handkerchief, and with drunken obstinacy he demanded it back again, asked his neighbours about it, stooped down in order to look under the chairs and the guests' feet. And when Gaga did her best to quiet him,—

"It's a nuisance," murmured he, "my initials and my coronet are worked in the corner. They may compromise me."

"I say, Monsieur Falamoise, Lamafoise, Mafaloise!" shouted Foucarmont, who thought it exceedingly witty thus to disfigure the young man's name *ad infinitum.*

But la Faloise grew wroth, and talked with a stutter about his ancestry. He threatened to send a water bottle at Foucarmont's head, and Count de Vandeuvres had to interfere in order to assure him that Foucarmont was a great joker. Indeed, everybody was laughing. This did for the already flurried young man, who was very glad to resume his seat, and to begin eating with childlike submissiveness, when, in a loud voice, his cousin ordered him to feed. Gaga had taken him back to her ample side; only from time to time he cast sly and anxious glances at the guests, for he ceased not to search for his handkerchief.

Then Foucarmont, being now in his witty vein, attacked Labordette right at the other end of the table. Louise Violaine strove to make him hold his tongue, for, said she, "when he goes nagging at other people like that, it always ends in mischief for me." He had discovered a witticism which consisted in addressing Labordette as *"Madame,"* and it must have amused him greatly, for he kept on repeating it, while Labordette tranquilly shrugged his shoulders, and as constantly replied,—

"Pray hold your tongue, my dear fellow, it's stupid."

But as Foucarmont failed to desist, and even became insulting, without his neighbours knowing why, he left off answering him, and appealed to Count Vandeuvres.

"Make your friend hold his tongue, *Monsieur.* I don't wish to become angry."

Foucarmont had twice fought duels, and he was in consequence most politely treated, and admitted into every circle. But there was now a general uprising against him. The table grew merry at his sallies, for they thought him very witty; but that was no reason why the evening should be spoilt. Vandeuvres, whose subtle countenance was darkening visibly, insisted on his restoring Labordette his sex. The other men—Mignon, Steiner, and Bordenave—who were by this time much exalted, also intervened with shouts which drowned his voice. Only the old gentleman, sitting forgotten next to Nana, retained his stately demeanour, and, still smiling in his tired silent way, watched with lack-lustre eyes the untoward finish of the dessert.

"What do you say to our taking coffee in here, duckie?" said Bordenave. "We're very comfortable."

Nana did not give an immediate reply. Since the beginning of supper, she had seemed no longer in her own house. All this company had overwhelmed and bewildered her with their shouts to the waiters, the loudness of their voices, and the way in which they put themselves at their ease, just as though they were in a restaurant. Forgetting her *rôle* of hostess, she busied herself exclusively with bulky Steiner, who was verging on apoplexy beside her. She was listening to his proposals, and continually refusing them with shakes of the head, and that temptress's laughter which is peculiar to a voluptuous blonde. The champagne she had been drinking had flushed her a rosy-red; her lips were moist, her eyes sparkled, and the banker's offers rose with every kittenish movement of her shoulders, with every little voluptuous lift and fall of her throat, which occurred when she turned her head. Close by her ear, he kept espying a sweet little satiny corner which drove him crazy. Occasionally Nana was interrupted, and then,

remembering her guests, she would try and be as pleased as possible in order to shew that she knew how to receive. Towards the end of supper she was very tipsy. It made her miserable to think of it, but champagne had a way of intoxicating her almost directly! Then an exasperating notion struck her. In behaving thus improperly at her table, these ladies were shewing themselves anxious to do her an ugly turn. Oh yes! she could see it all distinctly. Lucy had given Foucarmont a wink in order to egg him on against Labordette, whilst Rose, Caroline, and the others, were doing all they could to stir up the men. Now there was such a din you couldn't hear your neighbour speak, and so the story would get about that you might allow yourself every kind of liberty when you supped at Nana's. Very well then! they should see! She might be tipsy, if you like, but she was still the smartest and most lady-like woman there.

"Do tell them to serve the coffee here, duckie," resumed Bordenave. "I prefer it here because of my leg."

But Nana had sprung savagely to her feet, after whispering into the astonished ears of Steiner and the old gentleman,—

"It's quite right: it'll teach me to go and invite a dirty lot like that."

Then she pointed to the door of the dining-room, and added at the top of her voice,—

"If you want coffee, it's there, you know."

The company left the table, and crowded towards the dining-room without noticing Nana's indignant outburst. And soon no one was left in the drawing-room save Bordenave, who advanced cautiously, supporting himself against the wall, and cursing away at the confounded women, who chucked papa the moment they were chock-full. The waiters behind him were already busy removing the plates and dishes, in obedience to the loudly-voiced orders of the manager. They rushed to and fro, jostled one another, caused the whole table to vanish, as a pantomime property might at sound of the chief scene-shifter's whistle. The ladies and gentlemen were to return to the drawing-room after drinking their coffee.

"By gum, it's less hot here," said Gaga with a slight shiver as she entered the dining-room.

The window here had remained open. Two lamps illuminated the table, where coffee and liqueurs were set out. There were no chairs, and the guests drank their coffee standing, while the hubbub the waiters were making in the next room grew louder and louder. Nana had disappeared, but nobody fretted about her absence. They did without her excellently well, and everybody helped himself, and rummaged in the drawers of the side-board in search of teaspoons, which were lacking. Several groups were formed; people separated during supper rejoined each other; and there was an interchange of glances, of meaning laughter, and of phrases which summed up recent situations.

"Ought not Monsieur Fauchery to come and lunch with us one of these days, Auguste?" said Rose Mignon.

Mignon, who was toying with his watch-chain, eyed the journalist for a second or two with his severe glance. Rose was out of her senses. As became a good manager, he would put a stop to such spendthrift courses. In return for

a notice well and good, but afterwards decidedly not. Nevertheless, as he was fully aware of his wife's wrong-headedness, and as he made it a rule to wink paternally at a folly now and again, when such was necessary, he answered amiably enough,—

"Certainly, I shall be most happy. Pray come to-morrow, Monsieur Fauchery."

Lucy Stewart heard this invitation given while she was talking with Steiner and Blanche, and, raising her voice, she remarked to the banker,—

"It's a mania they've all of them got. One of them even went so far as to steal my dog. Now, dear boy, am I to blame if you chuck her?"

Rose turned round. She was very pale, and gazed fixedly at Steiner as she sipped her coffee. And then all the concentrated anger she felt at his abandonment of her flamed out in her eyes. She saw more clearly than Mignon; it was stupid in him to have wished to begin the Jonquier ruse a second time—those dodgers never succeeded twice running. Well, so much the worse for him! She would have Fauchery! She had been getting enamoured of him since the beginning of supper, and if Mignon was not pleased, it would teach him greater wisdom!

"You are not going to fight?" said Vandeuvres, coming over to Lucy Stewart.

"No, don't you be afraid of that! Only, she must mind and keep quiet, or I let the cat out of the bag!"

Then signing imperiously to Fauchery,—

"I've got your slippers at home, my

little man. I'll get them taken to your porter's lodge for you to-morrow."

He wanted to joke about it, but she swept off, looking like a queen. Clarisse, who had propped herself against a wall in order to drink a quiet glass of kirsch, was seen to shrug her shoulders. A pleasant business for a man! Wasn't it true that the moment two women were together in the presence of their lovers their first idea was to do one another out of them? It was a law of nature! As to herself, why, in Heaven's name, if she had wanted to, she would have torn out Gaga's eyes on Hector's account! But la! she despised him. Then, as la Faloise passed by, she contented herself by remarking to him,—

"Listen, my friend, you like 'em well advanced, you do! You don't want 'em ripe, you want 'em mildewed!"

La Faloise seemed much annoyed, and not a little anxious. Seeing Clarisse making game of him, he grew suspicious of her.

"No humbug, I say," he muttered. "You've taken my handkerchief. Well then, give it back!"

"He's dreeing us with that handkerchief of his!" she cried. "Why, you ass, why should I have taken it from you?"

"Why should you?" said he suspiciously, "why that you may send it to my people and compromise me."

In the mean time, Foucarmont was diligently attacking the liqueurs. He continued to gaze sneeringly at Labordette, who was drinking his coffee in the midst of the ladies. And occasionally he gave vent to fragmentary assertions, as thus: "He's the son of a horse-dealer; some say the illegitimate child of a countess. Never a penny of income, yet always got twenty-five louis in his pocket! Footboy to the ladies of the town! A big lubber, who never goes with any of 'em! Never, never, never!" he repeated, growing furious. "No, by Jove! I must box his ears."

He drained a glass of Chartreuse. The Chartreuse had not the slightest effect upon him; it didn't affect him "even to that extent," and he clicked his thumbnail against the edge of his teeth. But suddenly, just as he was advancing upon Labordette, he grew ashy white and fell down in a heap in front of the side-board. He was dead drunk. Louise Violaine was beside herself. She had been quite right to prophesy that matters would end badly; and now she would have her work cut out for the remainder of the night. Gaga reassured her. She examined the officer with the eye of a woman of experience, and declared that there was nothing much the matter, and that the gentleman would sleep like that for at least a dozen or fifteen hours without any serious consequences. Foucarmont was carried off.

"Well, where's Nana gone to?" asked Vandeuvres.

Yes, she had certainly flown away somewhere on leaving the table. The company suddenly recollected her, and everybody asked for her. Steiner, who for some seconds had been uneasy on her account, asked Vandeuvres about the old gentleman, for he too had disappeared. But the Count reassured him—he had just brought the old gentleman back. He was a stranger, whose name it was useless to mention. Suffice it to say that he was a very rich man, who was quite pleased to pay for suppers! Then, as Nana was once more being forgotten, Vandeuvres saw Daguenet looking out of an open door and beckoning to him. And in the bedroom he found the mistress of the house sitting up, white-lipped and rigid, while Daguenet and Georges stood gazing at her with an alarmed expression. "What *is* the matter with you?" he asked in some surprise.

She neither answered nor turned her head, and he repeated his question.

"Why, this is what's the matter with me," she cried out at length; "I won't let them make bloody sport of me!"

Thereupon she gave vent to any expression that occurred to her. Yes, oh yes, *she* wasn't a ninny—*she* could see clearly enough. They had been making devilish light of her during supper, and saying all sorts of frightful things, to shew that they thought nothing of her! A pack of sluts, who weren't fit to black her boots! Catch her bothering herself again, just to be badgered for it after! She really didn't know what kept her from chucking all that dirty lot out of the house! And, with this, rage choked her, and her voice broke down in sobs.

"Come, come, my lass, you're drunk," said Vandeuvres, growing familiar. "You must be reasonable."

No, she would give her refusal now; she would stay where she was.

"I am drunk—it's quite likely! But I want people to respect me!"

For a quarter of an hour past, Daguenet and Georges had been vainly beseeching her to return to the drawing-room. She was obstinate, however; her guests might do what they liked; she despised them too much to come back amongst them.

No, she never would, never. They might tear her in pieces before she would leave her room!

"I ought to have had my suspicions," she resumed.

"It's that cat of a Rose who's got the plot up! I'm certain Rose'll have stopped that respectable woman coming, whom I was expecting to-night."

She referred to Madame Robert. Vandeuvres gave her his word of honour that Madame Robert had given a spontaneous refusal. He listened, and he argued with much gravity, for he was well accustomed to similar scenes, and knew how women in such a state ought to be treated. But the moment he tried to take hold of her hands in order to lift her up from her chair and draw her away with him, she struggled free of his clasp, and her wrath redoubled. Now, just look at that! They would never get her to believe that Fauchery had not put the Count Muffat off coming! A regular snake was that Fauchery; an envious sort, a fellow capable of growing mad against a woman and of destroying her whole happiness. For she knew this— the Count had become madly devoted to her! She could have had him!

"Him, my dear, never!" cried Vandeuvres, forgetting himself and laughing aloud.

"Why not!" she asked, looking serious and slightly sobered.

"Because he's thoroughly in the hands of the priests, and if he were only to touch you with the tips of his fingers, he would go and confess it the day after. Now listen to a bit of good advice. Don't let the other man escape you!"

She was silent and thoughtful for a moment or two. Then she got up, and went and bathed her eyes. Yet, when they wanted to take her into the dining-room, she still shouted "No!" furiously.

Vandeuvres left the bedroom, smiling and without further pressing her, and, the moment he was gone, she had an access of melting tenderness, threw herself into Daguenet's arms, and cried out,—

"Ah, my sweetie, there's only you in the world. I love you! *Yes,* I love you from the bottom of my heart! Oh, it would be too nice if we could always live together. My God! how unfortunate women are!"

Then her eye fell upon Georges, who, seeing them kiss, was growing very red, and she kissed him too. Sweetie could not be jealous of a baby! She wanted Paul and Georges always to agree, because it would be so nice for them all three to stay like that, knowing all the time that they loved one another very much. But an extraordinary noise disturbed them: someone was snoring in the room. Whereupon, after some searching, they perceived Bordenave, who, since taking his coffee, must have comfortably installed himself there. He was sleeping on two chairs, his head propped on the edge of the bed, and his leg stretched out in front. Nana thought him so funny with his open mouth and his nose moving with each successive snore, that she was shaken with a mad fit of laughter. She left the room, followed by Daguenet and Georges, crossed the dining-room, entered the drawing-room, her merriment increasing at every step.

"Oh, my dear, you've no idea!" she cried, almost throwing herself into Rose's arms. "Come and see it."

All the women had to follow her. She took their hands coaxingly, and drew them along with her, willy-nilly, accompanying her action with so frank and outburst of mirth that they all of them began laughing on trust. The band vanished, and returned, after standing breathlessly for a second or two round Bordenave's lordly, outstretched form. And then there was a burst of laughter, and when one of them told the rest to be quiet, Bordenave's distant snorings became audible.

It was close on four o'clock. In the dining-room, a card-table had just been set out, at which Vandeuvres, Steiner, Mignon, and Labordette had taken their seats. Behind them Lucy and Caroline stood making bets, whilst Blanche, nodding with sleep and dissatisfied about her night, kept asking Vandeuvres at intervals of five minutes if they weren't going soon. It the drawing-room there was an attempt at dancing. Daguenet was at the piano, or "chest of drawers," as Nana called it. She did not want a "thumper," for Mimi would play as many waltzes and polkas as the company desired. But the dance was languishing, and the ladies were chatting drowsily together in the corners of sofas. Suddenly, however, there was an outburst of noise. A band of eleven young men had arrived and were laughing loudly in the ante-room and crowding to the drawing-room. They had just come from the ball at the Ministry of the Interior, and were in evening dress and wore various unknown orders. Nana was annoyed at this riotous entry, called to the waiters who still remained in the kitchen, and ordered them to throw these individuals out of doors. She vowed that she had never seen any of them before. Fauchery, Labordette, Daguenet, and the rest of the men had all come forward in order to enforce respectful behaviour towards their hostess. Big words flew about, arms were outstretched, and for some seconds a general exchange of fisticuffs was imminent. Notwithstanding this, however, a little sickly-looking light-haired man kept insistently repeating,—

"Come, come, Nana, you saw us the other evening at Peters's in the great red saloon! Pray remember you invited us."

The other evening at Peters's? She did not remember it all. To begin with, what evening?

And when the little light-haired man had mentioned the day, which was Wednesday, she distinctly remembered having supped at Peters's on the Wednesday, but she had given no invitation to anyone, she was almost sure of that.

"However, suppose you *have* invited them, my good girl," murmured Labordette, who was beginning to have his doubts. "Perhaps you were a little elevated."

Then Nana fell a-laughing. It was quite possible, she really didn't know. So then, since these gentlemen were on the spot, they had her leave to come in. Everything was quietly arranged, several of the newcomers found friends in the drawing-room, and the scene ended in hand-shakings. The little sickly-looking, light-haired man bore one of the greatest names in France. Furthermore, the eleven announced that others were to follow them, and, in fact, the door opened every few moments, and men in white gloves and official garb presented themselves. They were still coming from the ball at the Ministry. Fauchery jestingly enquired whether the Minister was not coming too, but Nana answered in a huff that the Minister went to the houses of people she didn't care a pin for. What she did not say was, that she was possessed with a hope of seeing Count Muffat enter her room among all that stream of people. He might quite have reconsidered his decision; and so, whilst talking to Rose, she kept a sharp eye on the door.

Five o'clock struck. The dancing had ceased, and the card-players alone persisted in their game. Labordette had vacated his seat, and the women had returned into the drawing-room. The air there was heavy with the somnolence which accompanies a long vigil, and the lamps cast a wavering light, whilst their burnt-out wicks glowed red within their globes. The ladies had reached that vaguely melancholy hour when they felt it necessary to tell each other their histories. Blanche de Sivry spoke of her grandfather, the general, whilst Clarisse invented a romantic story about a Duke seducing her at her uncle's house, whither he used to come for the boar-hunting. Both women, looking different ways, kept shrugging their shoulders, and asking themselves how the deuce the other could tell such woppers! As to Lucy Stewart, she quietly confessed to her origin, and of her own accord spoke of her childhood, and of the days when her father, the wheel-greaser at the Northern Railway Terminus, used to treat her to an apple puff on Sundays.

"Oh! I must tell you about it!" cried the little Maria Blond, abruptly. "Opposite to me there lives a gentleman, a Russian, an awfully rich man! Well, just fancy, yesterday I received a basket of fruit—oh! it just was a basket! Enormous peaches, grapes as big as that, simply wonderful for the time of year! And

in the middle of them six thousand-franc
notes! It was the Russian's doing. Of
course, I sent the whole thing back again,
but I must say my heart ached a little
—when I thought of the fruit!"

The ladies looked at one another and
pursed up their lips. At her age little
Maria Blond had a pretty cheek! Besides,
to think that such things should happen
to trollops like her! Infinite was their
contempt for her among themselves. It
was Lucy of whom they were particularly
jealous, for they were besides themselves
at the thought of her three princes. Since
Lucy had begun taking a daily morning
ride in the Bois, they all had become
Amazons, as though a mania possessed
them.

Day was about to dawn, and Nana
turned her eyes away from the door, for
she was relinquishing all hope. The
company were bored to distraction. Rose
Mignon had refused to sing the "Slipper,"
and sat huddled up on a sofa, chatting
in a low voice with Fauchery and waiting for Mignon, who had by now won
some fifty louis from Vandeuvres. A
fat gentleman, with a decoration and a
serious cast of countenance, had certainly given a recitation, in Alsatian accents, of "Abraham's Sacrifice," a piece
in which the Almighty says, "By My
blasted Name" when He swears, and
Isaac always answers with a "Yes, papa!"
Nobody, however, understood what it
was all about, and the piece had been
voted stupid. People were at their wits'
end how to make merry and to finish the
night with fitting hilarity. For a moment
or two Labordette conceived the idea
of denouncing different women in a whisper to la Faloise, who still went prowling
round each individual lady, looking to
see if she were hiding his handkerchief
in her bosom. Soon, as there were still
some bottles of champagne on the sideboard, the young men again fell to drinking. They shouted to one another; they
stirred each other up; but a dreary species of intoxication, which was stupid
enough to drive one to despair, began to
overcome the company beyond hope of
recovery. Then the little fair-haired fellow, the man who bore one of the greatest names in France, and had reached
his wits' end and was desperate at the
thought that he could not hit upon something really funny, conceived a brilliant
notion: he snatched up his bottle of
champagne and poured its contents into
the piano. His allies were convulsed
with laughter.

"La now! why's he putting champagne
into the piano?" asked Tatan Néné, in
great astonishment as she caught sight
of him.

"What, my lass, you don't know why
he's doing that?" replied Labordette solemnly. "There's nothing so good as
champagne for pianos. It gives 'em
tone."

"Ah," murmured Tatan Néné with
conviction.

And when the rest began laughing at
her, she grew angry. How should she
know? They were always confusing her.

Decidedly, the evening was becoming
a big failure. The night threatened to
end in the unloveliest way. In a corner
by themselves, Maria Blond and Léa de
Horn had begun squabbling at close
quarters, the former accusing the latter
of consorting with people of insufficient
wealth. They were getting vastly abusive over it, their chief stumbling-block
being the good looks of the men in ques-

tion. Lucy, who was plain, got them to hold their tongues. Good looks were nothing, according to her: good figures were what was wanted. Further off, on a sofa, an attaché had slipped his arm round Simonne's waist, and was trying to kiss her neck; but Simonne, sullen and thoroughly out of sorts, pushed him away at every fresh attempt with cries of "You're pestering me!" and sound slaps of the fan across his face. For the matter of that, not one of the ladies allowed herself to be touched. Did people take them for light women? Gaga, in the mean time, had once more caught la Faloise, and had almost hoisted him upon her knees, whilst Clarisse was disappearing from view between two gentlemen, shaking with nervous laughter as women will when they are tickled. Round about the piano they were still busy with their little game, for they were suffering from a fit of stupid imbecility, which caused each man to jostle his fellow in his frantic desire to empty his bottle into the instrument. It was a simple process and a charming.

"Now then, old boy, drink a glass! Devil take it, he's a thirsty piano! Hi! 'tenshun! here's another bottle! You mustn't lose a drop!"

Nana's back was turned, and she did not see them. Emphatically, she was now falling back on the bulky Steiner, who was seated next to her. So much the worse! It was all on account of that Muffat, who had refused what was offered him. Sitting there in her white foulard dress, which was as light and full of folds as a shift, sitting there with drooped eyelids and cheeks pale with the touch of intoxication from which she was suffering, she offered herself to him with that quiet expression which is peculiar to a good-natured courtesan. The roses in her hair and at her throat had lost their leaves, and their stalks alone remained. Presently, Steiner withdrew his hand quickly from the folds of her skirt, where he had come in contact with the pins that Georges had stuck there. Some drops of blood appeared on his fingers, and one fell on Nana's dress, and stained it.

"Now, the bargain's struck," said Nana, gravely.

The day was breaking apace. An uncertain glimmer of light, fraught with a poignant melancholy, came stealing through the windows. And with that the guests began to take their departure. It was a most sour and uncomfortable retreat. Caroline Héquet, annoyed at the loss of her night, announced that it was high time to be off unless you were anxious to assist at some pretty scenes. Rose pouted as if her womanly character had been compromised. It was always so with these girls; they didn't know how to behave, and were guilty of disgusting conduct when they made their first appearance in society! And Mignon having cleaned Vandeuvres out completely, the family took their departure. They did not trouble about Steiner, but renewed their invitation for to-morrow to Fauchery. Lucy thereupon refused the journalist's escort home, and sent him back shrilly to his "strolling actress." At this Rose turned round immediately, and hissed out a "Dirty sow" by way of answer. But Mignon, who in feminine quarrels was always paternal, for his experience was a long one, and rendered him superior to them, had already pushed her out of the house, telling her, at the same time, to have done. Lucy came downstairs in solitary state behind them. After which, Gaga had to carry off la Faloise, ill, sobbing like a child, calling after Clarisse, who had long since gone off with her two gentlemen. Simonne, too, had vanished. Indeed, none remained save Tatan, Léa, and Maria, whom Labordette complaisantly took under his charge.

"Oh, but I don't the least bit want to go to bed!" said Nana. "One ought to find something to do."

She looked at the sky through the window-panes. It was a livid sky, and sooty clouds were scudding across it. It was six o'clock in the morning. Over the way, on the opposite side of the Boulevard Haussmann, the glistening roofs of the still slumbering houses were sharply outlined against the twilight sky, whilst, along the deserted roadway, a gang of street-sweepers passed with a clatter of wooden shoes. As she viewed Paris thus grimly awakening, she was overcome by tender girlish feelings, by a yearning for the country, for idyllic scenes, for things soft and white.

"Now, guess what you're to do," said she, coming back to Steiner. "You're going to take me to the Bois de Boulogne, and we'll drink milk there."

She clapped her hands in childish glee. Without waiting for the banker's reply—he naturally consented, though he was really rather bored and inclined to think of other things—she ran off to throw a pelisse over her shoulders. In the drawing-room there was now no one with Steiner save the band of young men. These had by this time dropped the very dregs of their glasses into the piano, and were talking of going, when one of their number ran in triumphantly. He held

in his hands a last remaining bottle, which he had brought back with him from the pantry.

"Wait a minute, wait a minute!" he shouted. "Here's a bottle of Chartreuse; that'll pick him up! And now my young friends, let's hook it. We're blooming idiots."

In the dressing-room Nana was compelled to wake up Zoé, who had dozed off on a chair. The gas was still alight, and Zoé shivered as she helped her mistress on with her hat and pelisse.

"Well, it's over; I've done what you wanted me to," said Nana, speaking familiarly to the maid in a sudden burst of expansive confidence, and much relieved at the thought that she had at last made her election. "You were quite right; the banker's as good as another."

The maid was cross, for she was still heavy with sleep. She grumbled something to the effect that Madame ought to have come to a decision the first evening. Then, following her into the bedroom, she asked what she was going to do with "those two," meaning Bordenave, who was snoring away as usual, and Georges, who had slipped in slyly, buried his head in a pillow, and finally falling asleep there, was now breathing as lightly and regularly as a cherub. Nana in reply told her that she was to let them sleep on. But seeing Daguenet come into the room, she again grew tender. He had been watching her from the kitchen, and was looking very wretched.

"Come, my sweetie, be reasonable," said she, taking him in her arms, and kissing him with all sorts of little wheedling caresses. "Nothing's changed; you know that it's sweetie whom I always adore! Eh, dear? I had to do it. Why

I swear to you we shall have even nicer times now. Come to-morrow, and we'll arrange about hours. Now, be quick, kiss and hug me as you love me. Oh! tighter, tighter than that!"

And she escaped, and rejoined Steiner, feeling happy and once more possessed with the idea of drinking milk. In the empty room the Count de Vandeuvres was left alone with the "decorated" man who had recited "Abraham's Sacrifice." Both seemed glued to the card-table; they had lost count of their whereabouts, and never once noticed the broad light of day without, whilst Blanche had made bold to put her feet up on a sofa in order to try and get a little sleep.

"Oh! Blanche is with them!" cried Nana. "We are going to drink milk, dear. Do come; you'll find Vandeuvres here when we return."

Blanche got up lazily. This time the banker's fiery face grew white with annoyance at the idea of having to take that big wench with him too. She was certain to bore him. But the two women had already got him by the arms, and were reiterating,—

"We want them to milk the cow before our eyes, you know."

## CHAPTER V

At the Variétés they were giving the thirty-fourth performance of the *Blonde Venus*. The first act had just finished, and in the green-room, Simonne, dressed as the Little Laundress, was standing in front of a console-table, surmounted by a looking-glass, and situated between the two corner doors which opened obliquely on the end of the dressing-room passage. No one was with her, and she was scrutinising her face, and rubbing her finger up and down below her eyes, with a view to putting the finishing touches to her make-up. The gas-jets on either side of the mirror flooded her with warm crude light.

"Has he arrived?" asked Prullière, entering the room in his Alpine Admiral's costume, which was set off by a big sword, enormous top-boots, and a vast tuft of plumes.

"Who d'you mean?" said Simonne, taking no notice of him, and laughing into the mirror in order to see how her lips looked.

"The Prince."

"I don't know; I've just come down. Oh, he's certainly due here to-night; he comes every time!"

Prullière had drawn near the hearth opposite the console-table, where a coke fire was blazing, and two more gas-jets were flaring brightly. He lifted his eyes, and looked at the clock and the barometer on his right hand and on his left. They had gilded sphinxes by the way of adornment in the style of the First Empire. Then he stretched himself out in a huge arm-chair with ears, the green velvet of which had been so worn by four generations of comedians that it looked yellow in places, and there he stayed, with moveless limbs and vacant eyes, in that weary and resigned attitude peculiar to actors who are used to long waits before their turn for going on the stage.

Old Bosc, too, had just made his appearance. He came in dragging one foot behind the other, and coughing. He was wrapped in an old box-coat, part of which had slipped from his shoulder in such a way as to uncover the gold-laced cloak of King Dagobert. He put his crown on the piano, and for a moment or two stood moodily stamping his feet. His hands were trembling slightly with the first beginnings of alcoholism, but he looked a sterling old fellow for all that, and a long white beard lent that fiery tippler's face of his a truly venerable appearance. Then, in the silence of the room, while the shower of hail was whipping the panes of the great window that looked out on the court-yard, he shook himself disgustedly.

"What filthy weather!" he growled.

Simonne and Prullière did not move. Four or five pictures—a landscape, a portrait of the actor Vernet—hung yellowing in the hot glare of the gas, and a bust of Potier, one of the bygone glories of the Variétés, stood gazing vacant-eyed from its pedestal. But just then there was a burst of voices outside. It was Fontan, dressed for the second act. He was a young dandy, and his habiliments, even to his gloves, were entirely yellow.

"Now say you don't know!" he shouted, gesticulating. "To-day's my patron saint's day!"

"What?" asked Simonne, coming up smilingly, as though attracted by the huge nose and the vast, comic mouth of the man. "D'you answer to the name of Achille?"

"Exactly so! and I'm going to get 'em to tell Madame Bron to send up champagne after the second act."

For some seconds a bell had been ringing in the distance. The long-drawn sound grew fainter, then louder, and when the bell ceased a shout ran up the stair and down it till it was lost along the passages. "All on the stage for the second act! All on the stage for the second act!" The sound drew near, and a little pale-faced man passed by the green-room doors, outside each of which he yelled at the top of his shrill voice, "On the stage for the second act!"

"The deuce, it's champagne!" said Prullière, without appearing to hear the din. "You're prospering!"

"If I were you I should have it in from the café," old Bosc slowly announced. He was sitting on a bench covered with green velvet, with his head against the wall.

But Simonne said that it was one's duty to consider Madame Bron's small perquisites. She clapped her hands excitedly, and devoured Fontan with her gaze, whilst his long goat-like visage kept up a continuous twitching of eyes and nose and mouth.

"Oh, that Fontan!" she murmured. "There's no one like him, no one like him!"

The two green-room doors stood wide open to the corridor leading to the wings. And along the yellow wall, which was brightly lit up by a gas-lamp out of view, passed a string of rapidly-moving shadows—men in costume, women with shawls over their scant attire, in a word the whole of the characters in the second act, who would shortly make their appearance as masqueraders in the ball at the "Boule Noire." And at the end of the corridor became audible a shuffling of feet as these people clattered down the five wooden steps which led to the stage. As the big Clarisse went running by, Simonne called to her, but she said she would be back directly. And indeed she reappeared almost at once, shivering in the thin tunic and scarf which she wore as Iris.

"God bless me!" she said. "It isn't warm, and I've left my furs in my dressing-room!"

Then as she stood toasting her legs, in their warm rose-coloured tights, in front of the fire-place, she resumed,— "The Prince has arrived."

"Oh!" cried the rest, with the utmost curiosity.

"Yes, that's why I ran down: I wanted to see. He's in the first stage-box to the right, the same he was in on Thursday. It's the third time he's been this week, eh? That's Nana; well, she's in luck's way! I was willing to wager he wouldn't come again."

Simonne opened her lips to speak, but her remarks were drowned by a fresh shout, which arose close to the greenroom. In the passage the call-boy was yelling at the top of his shrill voice,— "They've knocked!"

"Three times!" said Simonne, when she was again able to speak. "It's getting exciting. You know he won't go to her place; he takes her to his. And it seems that he has to pay for it too!"

"Egad! it's a case of when one 'has to go out,'" muttered Prullière wickedly, and he got up to have a last look at the mirror as became a handsome fellow whom the boxes adored.

"They've k n o c k e d ! They've knocked!" the call-boy kept repeating, in tones that died gradually away in the distance, as he passed through the various stories and corridors.

Fontan thereupon, knowing how it had all gone off on the first occasion the Prince and Nana met, told the two women the whole story whilst they in their turn crowded against him and laughed at the tops of their voices whenever he stooped to whisper certain details in their ears. Old Bosc had never budged an inch—he was totally indifferent. That sort of thing no longer interested him now. He was stroking a great tortoiseshell cat, which was lying curled up on the bench. He did so quite beatifically, and ended by taking her in his arms with the tender good-nature becoming a worn-out monarch. The cat arched its back, and then, after a prolonged sniff at the big white beard, the gluey odour of which doubtless disgusted her, she turned, and curling herself up, went to sleep again on the bench beside him. Bosc remained grave and absorbed.

"That's all right, but if I were you I should drink the champagne at the restaurant—it's better there," said he, suddenly addressing Fontan when he had finished his recital.

"The curtain's up!" cried the callboy, in cracked and long-drawn accents. "The curtain's up! The curtain's up!"

The shout sounded for some moments, during which there had been a noise of rapid footsteps. Through the suddenly-opened door of the passage came a burst of music and a far-off murmur of voices, and then the door shut to again, and you could hear its dull thud as it wedged itself into position once more.

A heavy peaceful atmosphere again pervaded the green-room, as though the place were situated a hundred leagues from the house where crowds were applauding. Simonne and Clarisse were still on the topic of Nana. There was a girl who never hurried herself! Why, yesterday she had again come on too late! But there was a silence; for a tall damsel had just craned her head in at the door, and seeing that she had made a mistake, had departed to the other end of the passage. It was Satin. Wearing a hat and a small veil, for the nonce, she was affecting the manner of a lady about to pay a call.

"A pretty trollop!" muttered Prullière, who had been coming across her for a year past at the "Café des Variétés." And at this Simonne told them how Nana had recognised in Satin an old school-mate, had taken a vast fancy to her, and was now plaguing Bordenave to let her make a first appearance on the stage.

"How d'ye do!" said Fontan, shaking hands with Mignon and Fauchery, who now came into the room.

Old Bosc himself gave them the tips of his fingers, whilst the two women kissed Mignon.

"A good house this evening?" queried Fauchery.

"Oh, a splendid one!" replied Prullière. "You should see 'em gaping."

"I say, my little dears," remarked Mignon, "it must be your turn!"

Oh, all in good time! They were only at the fourth scene as yet, but Bosc got up in obedience to instinct as became a rattling old actor who felt that his cue was coming. At that very moment the call-boy was opening the door.

"Monsieur Bosc!" he called, "Mademoiselle Simonne!"

Simonne flung a fur-lined pelisse briskly over her shoulders, and went out. Bosc, without hurrying at all, went and got his crown, which he settled on his brow with a rap. Then, dragging himself unsteadily along in his great coat, he took his departure, grumbling and looking as annoyed as a man who has been rudely disturbed.

"You were very amiable in your last notice," continued Fontan, addressing Fauchery. "Only why do you say that comedians are vain?"

"Yes, my little man, why d'you say that?" shouted Mignon, bringing down his huge hands on the journalist's slender shoulders with such force as almost to double him up.

Prullière and Clarisse refrained from laughing aloud. For some time past, the whole company had been deriving amusement from a comedy which was going on in the wings. Mignon, rendered frantic by his wife's caprice, and annoyed at the thought that this man Fauchery brought nothing but a certain doubtful notoriety to his household, had conceived the idea of revenging himself on the journalist by overwhelming him with tokens of friendship. Every evening, therefore, when he met him behind scenes, he would shower friendly slaps on his back and shoulders, as though fairly carried away by an outburst of tenderness; and Fauchery, who was a frail, small man in comparison to such a giant, was fain to take the raps with a strained smile in order not to quarrel with Rose's husband.

"Ah, ha! my buck, you've insulted Fontan," resumed Mignon, who was doing his best to force the joke. "Stand on guard! One—two—got him right in the middle of his chest!"

He lunged and struck the young man with such force that the latter grew very pale, and could not speak for some seconds. With a wink Clarisse showed the others where Rose Mignon was standing on the threshold of the green-room. Rose had witnessed the scene, and she marched straight up to the journalist, as though she had failed to notice her husband, and standing on tiptoe, bare-armed and in baby costume, she held her face up to him with a caressing infantine pout.

"Good evening, Baby," said Fauchery, kissing her familiarly.

Thus he indemnified himself. Mignon, however, did not seem to have observed this kiss, for everybody kissed his wife at the theatre. But he laughed, and gave the journalist a keen little look. The latter would assuredly have to pay for Rose's bravado.

In the passage the tightly-shutting door opened and closed again, and a tempest of applause was blown as far as the green-room. Simonne came in after her scene.

"Oh! Father Bosc *has* just scored!" she cried. "The Prince was writhing with laughter, and applauded with the rest as though he had been paid to. I say, do you know the big man sitting beside the Prince in the stage-box? A handsome man, with a very sedate expression and splendid whiskers!"

"It's Count Muffat," replied Fauchery. "I know that the Prince, when he was at the Empress's the day before yesterday, invited him to dinner for to-night. He'll have corrupted him afterwards!"

"So that's Count Muffat! We know his father-in-law, eh, Auguste?" said Rose, addressing her remark to Mignon. "You know the Marquis de Chouard, at whose place I went to sing? Well, he's in the house, too. I noticed him at the back of a box. There's an old boy for you——!"

Prullière, who had just put on his huge plume of feathers, turned round and called her.

"Hi, Rose! let's go now!"

She ran after him, leaving her sentence unfinished. At that moment, Madame Bron, the portress of the theatre, passed by the door with an immense bouquet in her arms. Simonne asked cheerfully if it was for her, but the porter-woman did not vouchsafe an answer, and only pointed her chin towards Nana's dressing-room at the end of the passage. Oh, that Nana! they were loading her with flowers! Then, when Madame Bron returned, she handed a letter to Clarisse, who allowed a smothered oath to escape her. That beggar la Faloise again! There was a fellow who wouldn't let her alone! And when she learnt the gentleman in question was waiting for her at the porter's lodge, she shrieked,——

"Tell him I'm coming down after this act. I'm going to catch him one on the face."

Fontan had rushed forward, shouting,——

"Madame Bron, just listen. Please listen, Madame Bron. I want you to send up six bottles of champagne between the acts."

But the call-boy had again made his appearance. He was out of breath, and in a sing-song voice he called out,——

"All to go on the stage! It's your turn, Monsieur Fontan. Make haste, make haste!"

"Yes, yes, I'm going, Father Barillot," replied Fontan in a flurry.

And he ran after Madame Bron, and continued,——

"You understand, eh? Six bottles of champagne, in the green-room, between the acts. It's my patron saint's day, and I'm standing the racket."

Simonne and Clarisse had gone off

with a great rustling of skirts. Everybody was swallowed up in the distance, and when the passage-door had banged with its usual hollow sound, a fresh hail shower was heard beating against the windows in the now silent green-room. Barillot, a small, pale-faced ancient, who for thirty years had been a servant in the theatre, had advanced familiarly towards Mignon, and had presented his open snuff-box to him. This proffer of a pinch and its acceptance allowed him a minute's rest in his interminable career up and down stairs, and along the dressing-room passage. He certainly had still to look up Madame Nana, as he called her; but she was one of those who followed her own sweet will, and didn't care a pin for penalties. Why, if she chose to be too late, she was too late! But he stopped short, and murmured in great surprise,—

"Well I never, she's ready; here she is! She must know that the Prince is here."

Indeed Nana appeared in the corridor. She was dressed as a fish-hag: her arms and face were plastered with white paint, and she had a couple of red dabs under her eyes. Without entering the green-room, she contented herself by nodding to Mignon and Fauchery.

"How do? You're all right?"

Only Mignon shook her outstretched hand, and she hied royally on her way, followed by her dresser, who almost trod on her heels whilst stooping to adjust the folds of her skirt. In the rear of the dresser came Satin, closing the procession, and trying to look quite the lady, though she was already bored to death.

"And Steiner?" asked Mignon sharply.

"Monsieur Steiner has gone away to the Loiret," said Barillot, preparing to return to the neighbourhood of the stage. "I expect he's gone to buy a country place in those parts."

"Ah yes, I know, Nana's country place."

Mignon had grown suddenly serious. Oh, that Steiner! He had promised Rose a fine house in the old days! Well, well, it wouldn't do to grow angry with anybody. Here was a position that would have to be won again. From fire-place to console-table Mignon paced, sunk in thought yet still unconquered by circumstances. There was no one in the green-room now save Fauchery and himself. The journalist was tired, and had flung himself back into the recesses of the big arm-chair. There he stayed with half-closed eyes, and as quiet as quiet could be, whilst the other glanced down at him as he passed. When they were alone Mignon scorned to slap him at every turn. What good would it have done, since nobody would have enjoyed the spectacle? He was far too disinterested to be personally entertained by the farcical scenes in which he figured as a bantering husband. Glad of this short-lived respite, Fauchery stretched his feet out languidly towards the fire, and let his upturned eyes wander from the barometer to the clock. In the course of his march Mignon planted himself in front of Potier's bust, looked at it without seeming to see it, and then turned back to the window, outside which yawned the darkling gulf of the court-yard. The rain had ceased, and there was now a deep silence in the room, which the fierce heat of the coke fire and the flare of the gas-jets rendered still more oppressive. Not a sound came from the wings: the staircase and the passages were deadly still.

That choking sensation of quiet, which behind the scenes immediately precedes the end of an act, had begun to pervade the empty green-room. Indeed, the place seemed to be drowsing off through very breathlessness, amid that faint murmur which the stage gives forth when the whole troupe are raising the deafening uproar of some grand finale.

"Oh, the cows!" Bordenave suddenly shouted in his hoarse voice.

He had only just come up, and he was already howling complaints about two chorus-girls who had nearly fallen flat on the stage because they were playing the fool together. When his eye lit on Mignon and Fauchery, he called them—he wanted to shew them something. The Prince had just notified a desire to compliment Nana in her dressing-room, during the next interval. But, as he was leading them into the wings, the stage-manager passed.

"Just you fine those hags Fernande and Maria!" cried Bordenave savagely.

Then calming down, and endeavouring to assume the dignified expression worn by "heavy fathers," he wiped his face with his pocket-handkerchief, and added,—

"I am now going to receive his highness."

The curtain fell amid a long-drawn salvo of applause. Then across the twilight stage, which was no longer lit up by the footlights, there followed a disorderly retreat. Actors, and supers, and chorus, made haste to get back to their dressing-rooms, whilst the scene-shifters rapidly changed the scenery. Simonne and Clarisse, however, had remained "at the top," talking together in whispers. On the stage, in an interval between their lines, they had just settled a little matter. Clarisse, after viewing the thing in every light, found she preferred not to see la Faloise, who could never decide to leave her for Gaga, and so Simonne was simply to go and explain that a woman ought not to be palled up to in that fashion! At last she agreed to undertake the mission.

Then Simonne, in her theatrical laundress's attire, but with furs over her shoulders, ran down the greasy steps of the narrow winding stair which led between damp walls to the porter's lodge. This lodge, situated between the actors' staircase and that of the management, was shut in to right and left by large glass partitions, and resembled a huge transparent lantern, in which two gasjets were flaring.

There was a set of pigeon-holes in the place in which were piled letters and newspapers, whilst on the table various bouquets lay awaiting their recipients in close proximity to neglected heaps of dirty plates and to an old pair of stays, the eyelets of which the portress was busy mending. And in the middle of this untidy, ill-kept store-room sat four fashionable, white-gloved society men. They occupied as many ancient straw-bottomed chairs, and, with an expression at once patient and submissive, kept sharply turning their heads in Madame Bron's direction every time she came down from the theatre overhead, for on such occasions she was the bearer of replies. Indeed she had but now handed a note to a young man who had hurried out to open it beneath the gas-light in the vestibule, where he had grown slightly pale on reading the classic phrase—how often had others read it in that very place!—"Impossible to-night, my dearie! I'm booked!" La Faloise sat on one of these chairs, at the back of the room, between the table and the stove. He seemed bent on passing the evening there, and yet he was not quite happy. Indeed he kept tucking up his long legs in his endeavours to escape from a whole litter of black kittens who were gambolling wildly round them, whilst the mother cat sat bolt upright staring at him with yellow eyes.

"Ah, it's you, Mademoiselle Simonne! What can I do for you?" asked the portress.

Simonne begged her to send la Faloise out to her. But Madame Bron was unable to comply with her wishes all at once. Under the stairs in a sort of deep cupboard she kept a little bar, whither the supers were wont to descend for drinks between the acts, and seeing that just at that moment there were five or six tall lubbers there who, still dressed as "Boule Noire" masqueraders, were dying of thirst and in a great hurry, she lost her head a bit. A gas-jet was flaring in the cupboard, within which it was possible to descry a tin-covered table, and some shelves garnished with half-emptied bottles. Whenever the door of this coal-hole was opened, a violent whiff of alcohol mingled with the scent of stale cooking in the lodge, as well as with the penetrating scent of the flowers upon the table.

"Well, now," continued the portress when she had served the supers, "is it the little dark chap out there you want?"

"No, no; don't be silly!" said Simonne. "It's the lanky one by the side of the stove. Your cat's sniffing at his trouser-legs!"

And with that she carried la Faloise off into the lobby, whilst the other gentlemen once more resigned themselves to their fate and to semi-suffocation, and the masqueraders drank on the stairs, and indulged in rough horse-play and guttural drunken jests.

On the stage above Bordenave was wild with the scene-shifters, who seemed never to have done changing scenes. They appeared to be acting of set purpose—the Prince would certainly have some set-piece or other tumbling on his head.

"Up with it! Up with it!" shouted the foreman.

At length the canvas at the back of the stage was raised into position, and the stage was clear. Mignon, who had kept his eye on Fauchery, seized this opportunity in order to start his pummelling matches again. He hugged him in his long arms, and cried,—

"Oh, take care! that mast just missed crushing you!"

And he carried him off, and shook him before setting him down again. In view of the scene-shifters' exaggerated mirth, Fauchery grew white. His lips trembled, and he was ready to flare up in anger, whilst Mignon, shamming good nature, was clapping him on the shoulder with such affectionate violence as nearly to pulverise him.

"I value your health, I do!" he kept repeating. "Egad! I should be in a pretty pickle if anything serious happened to you!"

But just then a whisper ran through their midst: "The Prince! The Prince!" and everybody turned and looked at the little door which opened out of the main body of the house. At first nothing was visible save Bordenave's round back and beefy neck, which bobbed down and arched up in a series of obsequious obeisances. Then the Prince made his appearance. Largely and strongly built, light of beard and rosy of hue, he was not lacking in the kind of distinction peculiar to a sturdy man of pleasure, the square contours of whose limbs are clearly defined by the irreproachable cut of a frock-coat. Behind him walked Count Muffat and the Marquis de Chouard, but this particular corner of the theatre being dark, the group were lost to view amid huge moving shadows.

In order fittingly to address the son of a queen, who would some day occupy a throne, Bordenave had assumed the tone of a man exhibiting a bear in the street. In a voice tremulous with false emotion he kept repeating,—

"If his highness will have the goodness to follow me—would his highness deign to come this way?—His highness will take care!"

The Prince did not hurry in the least. On the contrary, he was greatly interested, and kept pausing in order to look at the scene-shifters' manœuvres. A batten had just been lowered, and the group of gas-lights high up among its iron cross-bars illuminated the stage with a wide beam of light. Muffat, who had never yet been behind scenes at a theatre, was even more astonished than the rest. An uneasy feeling of mingled fear and vague repugnance took possession of him. He looked up into the heights above him, where more battens, the gas-jets on which were burning low, gleamed like galaxies of little bluish stars amid a chaos of iron rods, connecting-lines of all sizes, hanging stages, and canvases spread out in space, like huge cloths hung out to dry.

"Lower away!" shouted the foreman, unexpectedly.

And the Prince himself had to warn the Count, for a canvas was descending. They were setting the scenery for the third act, which was the grotto on Mount Etna. Men were busy planting masts in the sockets, whilst others went and took frames, which were leaning against the walls of the stage, and proceeded to lash them with strong cords to the poles already in position. At the back of the stage, with a view to producing the bright rays thrown by Vulcan's glowing forge, a stand had been fixed by a lime-light man, who was now lighting various burners under red glasses. The scene was one of confusion, verging to all appearances on absolute chaos, but every little move had been prearranged. Nay, amid all the scurry, the whistle-blower even took a few turns, stepping short as he did so, in order to rest his legs.

"His highness overwhelms me," said Bordenave, still bowing low. "The theatre is not large, but we do what we can. Now, if his highness deigns to follow me——"

Count Muffat was already making for the dressing-room passage. The really sharp downward slope of the stage had surprised him disagreeably, and he owed no small part of his present anxiety to a feeling that its boards were moving under his feet. Through the open sockets gas was descried burning in the "dock." Human voices and blasts of air, as from a vault, came up thence, and, looking down into the depths of gloom, one became aware of a whole subterranean existence. But just as the Count was going up the stage, a small incident occurred to stop him. Two little women, dressed for the third act, were chatting by the peep-hole in the curtain. One of them, straining forward, and widening the hole with her fingers in order the better to observe things, was scanning the house beyond.

"I see him," said she sharply. "Oh, what a mug!"

Horrified, Bordenave had much ado not to give her a kick. But the Prince smiled, and looked pleased and excited by the remark. He gazed warmly at the little woman who did not care a button for his highness, and she, on her part, laughed unblushingly. Bordenave, however, persuaded the Prince to follow him. Muffat was beginning to perspire: he had taken his hat off. What inconvenienced him most was the stuffy dense, overheated air of the place, with its strong haunting smell, a smell peculiar to this part of a theatre, and, as such, compact of the reek of gas, of the glue used in the manufacture of the scenery, of dirty dark nooks and corners, and of questionably cleanly chorus-girls. In the passage the air was still more suffocating, and one seemed to breathe a poisoned atmosphere, which was occasionally relieved by the acid scents of toilet-waters and the perfumes of various soaps emanating from the dressing-rooms. The Count lifted his eyes as he passed and glanced up the stair-case, for he was well-nigh startled by the keen flood of light and warmth which flowed down upon his back and shoulders. High up above him there was a clicking of ewers and basins, a sound of laughter and of people calling to one another, a banging of doors, which in their continual opening and shutting allowed an odour of womankind to escape—a musky scent of oils and essences mingling with the natural pungency exhaled from human tresses. He did not stop. Nay, he hastened his walk: he almost ran, his skin tingling with the breath of that fiery approach to a world he knew nothing of.

"A theatre's a curious sight, eh?" said the Marquis de Chouard, with the enchanted expression of a man who once more finds himself amid familiar surroundings.

But Bordenave had at length reached Nana's dressing-room at the end of the passage. He quietly turned the doorhandle; then, cringing again:

"If his highness will have the goodness to enter——"

They heard the cry of a startled woman, and caught sight of Nana as, stripped to the waist, she slipped behind a curtain, whilst her dresser, who had been in the act of drying her, stood towel in air before them.

"Oh, it *is* silly to come in that way!" cried Nana from her hiding-place. "Don't come in: you see you mustn't come in!"

Bordenave did not seem to relish this sudden flight.

"Do stay where you were, my dear. Why it doesn't matter," said he. "It's his highness. Come, come, don't be childish."

And, when she still refused to make her appearance—for she was startled as yet, though she had begun to laugh—he added in peevish paternal tones,—

"Good Heavens, these gentlemen

know perfectly well what a woman looks like. They won't eat you."

"I'm not so sure of that," said the Prince, wittily.

With that the whole company began laughing in an exaggerated manner in order to pay him proper court.

"An exquisitely witty speech—an altogether Parisian speech," as Bordenave remarked.

Nana vouchsafed no further reply, but the curtain began moving. Doubtless she was making up her mind. Then Count Muffat, with glowing cheeks, began to take stock of the dressing-room. It was a square room with a very low ceiling, and it was entirely hung with a light-coloured Havana stuff. A curtain of the same material depended from a copper rod, and formed a sort of recess at the end of the room, whilst two large windows opened on the courtyard of the theatre, and were faced, at a distance of three yards at most, by a leprous-looking wall, against which the panes cast squares of yellow light amid the surrounding darkness. A large dressing-glass faced a white marble toilet-table, which was garnished with a disorderly array of flasks and glass boxes, containing oils, essences, and powders. The Count went up to the dressing-glass and discovered that he was looking very flushed, and had small drops of perspiration on his forehead. He dropped his eyes, and came and took up a position in front of the toilet-table, where the basin, full of soapy water, the small scattered ivory toilet utensils, and the damp sponges, appeared for some moments to absorb his attention. The feeling of dizziness, which he had experienced when he first visited Nana in the Boulevard Haussmann, once more overcame him. He felt the thick carpet soften under foot, and the gas-jets burning by the dressing-table and by the glass seemed to shoot whistling flames about his temples. For one moment, being afraid of fainting away under the influence of those feminine odours which he now re-encountered intensified by the heat under the low-pitched ceiling, he sat down on the edge of a softly-padded divan between the two windows. But he got up again almost directly, and, returning to the dressing-table, seemed to gaze with vacant eyes into space, for he was thinking of a bouquet of tuberoses which had once faded in his bedroom, and had nearly killed him in their death. When tuberoses are turning brown, they have a human smell.

"Make haste!" Bordenave whispered, putting his head in behind the curtain.

The Prince, however, was listening complaisantly to the Marquis de Chouard, who had taken up a hare's-foot on the dressing-table and had begun explaining the way grease paint is put on. In a corner of the room, Satin, with her pure virginal face, was scanning the gentlemen keenly, whilst the dresser, Madame Jules by name, was getting ready Venus's tights and tunic. Madame Jules was a woman of no age. She had the parchment skin and changeless features peculiar to old maids whom no one ever knew in their younger years. She had indeed shrivelled up in the burning atmosphere of the dressing-rooms and amid the most famous thighs and bosoms in all Paris. She wore everlastingly a faded black dress, and on her flat and sexless chest a perfect forest of pins clustered above the spot where her heart should have been.

"I beg your pardon, gentlemen," said Nana, drawing aside the curtain, "but you took me by surprise."

They all turned round. She had not clothed herself at all, had in fact only buttoned on a little pair of linen stays which half revealed her bosom. When the gentlemen had put her to flight, she had scarcely begun undressing, and was rapidly taking off her fish-wife's costume. Through the opening in her drawers behind, a corner of her shift was even now visible. There she stood, bare-armed, bare-shouldered, bare-breasted, in all the adorable glory of her youth and plump fair beauty, but she still held the curtain with one hand, as though ready to draw it to again upon the slightest provocation.

"Yes, you took me by surprise! I never shall dare—"she stammered in pretty mock confusion, while rosy blushes crossed her neck and shoulders, and smiles of embarrassment played about her lips.

"Oh, don't apologise," cried Bordenave, "since these gentlemen approve of your good looks!"

But she still tried the hesitating, innocent, girlish game, and, shivering as though someone were tickling her, she continued:

"His highness does me too great an honour. I beg his highness will excuse my receiving him thus——"

"It is I who am importunate," said the Prince, "but madam, I could not resist the desire of complimenting you."

Thereupon, in order to reach her dressing-table, she walked very quietly, and just as she was, through the midst of the gentlemen, who made way for her to pass.

She had strongly-marked hips, which filled her drawers out roundly, whilst, with swelling bosom, she still continued bowing, and smiling her delicate little smile. Suddenly she seemed to recognise Count Muffat, and she extended her hand to him as an old friend. Then she scolded him for not having come to her supper-party. His highness deigned to chaff Muffat about this, and the latter stammered and thrilled again at the thought that, for one second, he had held in his own feverish clasp a little fresh and perfumed hand. The Count had dined excellently at the Prince's, who indeed was a heroic eater and drinker. Both of them were even a little intoxicated, but they behaved very creditably. To hide the commotion within him, Muffat could only remark about the heat.

"Good Heavens, how hot it is here!" said he. "How do you manage to live in such a temperature, madam?"

And conversation was about to ensue on this topic, when noisy voices were heard at the dressing-room door. Bordenave drew back the slide over a grated peep-hole of the kind used in convents. Fontan was outside with Prullière and Bosc, and all three had bottles under their arms and their hands full of glasses. He began knocking, and shouting out that it was his patron saint's day, and that he was standing champagne round. Nana consulted the Prince with a glance. Eh! oh, dear yes! His highness did not want to be in anyone's way; he would be only too happy! But without waiting for permission, Fontan came in, repeating in baby accents,—

"Me not a cad, me pay for champagne!"

Then, all of a sudden, he became aware of the Prince's presence, of which he had been totally ignorant. He stopped short, and assuming an air of farcical solemnity, announced,—

"King Dagobert is in the corridor, and is desirous of drinking the health of his royal highness."

The Prince having made answer with a smile, Fontan's sally was voted charming. But the dressing-room was too small to accommodate everybody, and it became necessary to crowd up anyhow, Satin and Madame Jules standing back against the curtain at the end, and the men clustering closely round the half-naked Nana. The three actors still had on the costumes they had been wearing in the second act, and whilst Prullière took off his Alpine Admiral's cocked hat, the huge plume of which would have knocked the ceiling, Bosc, in his purple cloak and tinware crown, steadied himself on his tipsy old legs and greeted the Prince as became a monarch receiving the son of a powerful neighbour. The glasses were filled, and the company began clinking them together.

"I drink to Your Highness!" said ancient Bosc, royally.

"To the Army!" added Prullière.

"To Venus!" cried Fontan.

The Prince complaisantly poised his glass, waited quietly, bowed thrice, and murmured,—

"Madam! Admiral! your Majesty!"

Then he drank it off. Count Muffat and the Marquis de Chouard had followed his example. There was no more jesting now—the company were at Court. Actual life was prolonged in the life of the theatre, and a sort of solemn farce was enacted under the hot flare of the gas. Nana, quite forgetting that she was in her drawers, and that a corner of her shift stuck out behind, became the great lady, the Queen of Love, in act to open her most private palace chambers to State dignitaries. In every sentence she used the words "royal highness," and bowing with the utmost conviction, treated the masqueraders, Bosc and Prullière, as if the one were a sovereign and the other his attendant minister. And no one dreamt of smiling at this strange contrast, this real prince, this heir to a throne, drinking a petty actor's champagne, and taking his ease amid a carnival of gods, a masquerade of royalty, in the society of dressers and courtesans, shabby players and showmen of venal beauty. Bordenave was simply ravished by the dramatic aspects of the scene, and began dreaming of the receipts which would have accrued had his highness only consented thus to appear in the second act of the *Blonde Venus*.

"I say, shall we have our little women down?" cried he, becoming familiar.

Nana would not hear of it. But, notwithstanding this, she was giving way herself. Fontan attracted her with his comic make-up. She brushed against him, and eyeing him as a woman in the family-way might do when she fancies some unpleasant kind of food, she suddenly became extremely familiar:

"Now then, fill up again, ye great brute!"

Fontan charged the glasses afresh, and the company drank, repeating the same toasts.

"To His Highness!"

"To the Army!"

"To Venus!"

But with that Nana made a sign and obtained silence. She raised her glass, and cried,—

"No, no! to Fontan! It's Fontan's day; to Fontan! to Fontan!"

Then they clinked glasses a third time, and drank Fontan with all the honours. The Prince, who had noticed the young woman devouring the actor with her eyes, saluted him with a "Monsieur Fontan, I drink to your success!" This he said with his customary lofty courtesy.

But meanwhile the tail of his highness's frock-coat was sweeping the marble of the dressing-table. The place, indeed, was like an alcove, or narrow bathroom, full as it was of the steam of hot water and sponges, and of the strong scent of essences which mingled with the tartish intoxicating fumes of the champagne. The Prince and Count Muffat, between whom Nana was wedged, had to lift up their hands so as not to brush against her hips or her breast with every little movement. And there stood Madame Jules, waiting, cool and rigid as ever, whilst Satin, marvelling in the depths of her vicious soul to see a prince and two gentlemen in black coats going after a naked woman in the society of dressed-up actors, secretly concluded that fashionable people were not so very particular after all.

But Father Barillot's tinkling bell approached along the passage. At the door of the dressing-room he stood amazed when he caught sight of the three actors still clad in the costumes which they had worn in the second act.

"Gentlemen, gentlemen," he stammered, "do please make haste. They've just rung the bell in the public foyer."

"Bah! the public will have to wait," said Bordenave placidly.

However, as the bottles were now empty the comedians went upstairs to dress after yet another interchange of civilities. Bosc having dipped his beard in the champagne had taken it off, and under his venerable disguise the drunkard had suddenly reappeared. His was the haggard empurpled face of the old actor who has taken to drink. At the foot of the stairs he was heard remarking to Fontan in his boozy voice,—

"I pulverised him, eh?"

He was alluding to the Prince.

In Nana's dressing-room none now remained save his highness, the count, and the marquis. Bordenave had withdrawn with Barillot, whom he advised not to knock without first letting madam know.

"You will excuse me, gentlemen?" asked Nana, again setting to work to make up her arms and face, of which she was now particularly careful owing to her nude appearance in the third act.

The Prince seated himself by the Marquis de Chouard on the divan, and Count Muffat alone remained standing. In that suffocating heat, the two glasses of champagne they had drunk had increased their intoxication. Satin, when she saw the gentlemen thus closeting themselves with her friend, had deemed it discreet to vanish behind the curtain, where she sat waiting on a trunk, much annoyed at being compelled to remain motionless, whilst Madame Jules came and went quietly without word or look.

"You sang your numbers marvellously," said the Prince.

And with that they began a conversation, but their sentences were short and their pauses frequent. Nana indeed was not always able to reply. After rubbing cold cream over her arms and face with the palm of her hand, she laid on the grease paint with the corner of a towel. For one second only she ceased looking in the glass, and smilingly stole a glance at the Prince.

"His highness is spoiling me," she murmured, without putting down the grease paint.

Her task was a complicated one, and the Marquis de Chouard followed it with an expression of devout enjoyment. He spoke in his turn.

"Could not the band accompany you more softly?" said he. "It drowns your voice, and that's an unpardonable crime."

This time Nana did not turn round. She had taken up the hare's-foot, and was lightly manipulating it. All her attention was concentrated on this action, and she bent forward over her toilet-table so very far that the white round contour of her drawers and the little patch of chemise stood out with the unwonted tension. But she was anxious to prove that she appreciated the old man's compliment, and therefore made a little swinging movement with her hips.

Silence reigned. Madame Jules had noticed a tear in the right leg of her drawers. She took a pin from over her heart, and for a second or so knelt on the ground, busily at work about Nana's leg, whilst the young woman, without seeming to notice her presence, applied the rice-powder, taking extreme pains, as she did so, to avoid putting any on the upper part of her cheeks. But when the Prince remarked that if she were to come and sing in London all England

would want to applaud her, she laughed amiably, and turned round for a moment, with her left cheek looking very white, amid a perfect cloud of powder. Then she became suddenly serious; for she had come to the operation of rouging. And, with her face once more close to the mirror, she dipped her finger in a jar, and began applying the rouge below her eyes, and gently spreading it back towards her temples. The gentlemen maintained a respectful silence.

Count Muffat, indeed, had not yet opened his lips. He was thinking perforce of his own youth. The bedroom of his childish days had been quite cold, and later, when he had reached the age of sixteen, and would give his mother a good-night kiss every evening, he used to carry the icy feeling of the embrace into the world of dreams. One day, in passing a half-open door, he had caught sight of a maid-servant washing herself; and that was the solitary recollection which had in any way troubled his peace of mind from the days of puberty till the time of marriage. Afterwards, he had found his wife strictly obedient to her conjugal duties, but had himself felt a species of religious dislike to them. He had grown to man's estate, and was now ageing, in ignorance of the flesh, in the humble observance of rigid devotional practices, and in obedience to a rule of life full of precepts and moral laws. And now, suddenly, he was dropped down in this actress's dressing-room, in the presence of this undraped courtesan. He, who had never seen the Countess Muffat putting on her garters, was witnessing, amid that wild disarray of jars and basins, and that strong sweet perfume, the intimate details of a woman's toilet. His whole being was in turmoil; he was terrified by the stealthy, all-pervading influence which for some time past Nana's presence had been exercising over him, and he recalled to mind the pious accounts of diabolic possession which had amused his early years. He was a believer in the devil, and, in a confused kind of way, Nana was he; with her laughter, and her bosom, and her hips, which seemed swollen with many vices. But he promised himself that he would be strong—nay, he would know how to defend himself.

"Well, then, it's agreed," said the Prince, lounging quite comfortably on the divan. "You will come to London next year, and we shall receive you so cordially that you will never return to France again. Ah, my dear Count, you don't value your pretty women enough. We shall take them all from you!"

"That won't make much odds to him," murmured the Marquis de Chouard wickedly, for he occasionally said a risky thing among friends. "The Count is virtue itself."

Hearing his virtue mentioned, Nana looked at him so comically that Muffat felt a keen twinge of annoyance. But directly afterwards he was surprised and angry with himself. Why, in the presence of this courtesan, should the idea of being virtuous embarrass him? He could have struck her. But in attempting to take up a brush, Nana had just let it drop on the ground, and as she stooped to pick it up he rushed forward. Their breath mingled for one moment, and the loosened tresses of Venus flowed over his hands. But remorse mingled with his enjoyment, a kind of enjoyment, moreover, peculiar to good Catholics, whom the fear of hell torments in the midst of their sin.

At this moment Father Barillot's voice was heard outside the door.

"May I give the knocks, madam? The house is growing impatient."

"All in good time," answered Nana, quietly.

She had dipped her paint-brush in a pot of kohl, and, with the point of her nose close to the glass, and her left eye closed, she passed it delicately along between her eyelashes. Muffat stood behind her, looking on. He saw her reflection in the mirror, with her rounded shoulders and her bosom half hidden by a rosy shadow. And despite all his endeavours he could not turn away his gaze from that face so merry with dimples and so worn with desire, which the closed eye rendered more seductive. When she shut her right eye and passed the brush along it, he understood that he belonged to her.

"They are stamping their feet, madam," the call-boy once more cried. "They'll end by smashing the seats. May I give the knocks?"

"Oh, bother!" said Nana, impatiently. "Knock away: I don't care! If I'm not ready, well! they'll have to wait for me!"

She grew calm again, and turning to the gentlemen, added with a smile,—

"It's true: we've only got a minute left for our talk."

Her face and arms were now finished, and with her fingers she put two large dabs of carmine on her lips. Count Muffat felt more excited than ever. He was ravished by the perverse transformation wrought by powders and paints, and filled by a lawless yearning for those young painted charms, for the too red mouth and the too white face, and the exaggerated eyes, ringed round with black, and burning and dying for very love. Meanwhile, Nana went behind the curtain for a second or two in order to take off her drawers and slip on Venus's tights. After which, with tranquil immodesty, she came out and undid her little linen stays, and held out her arms to Madame Jules, who drew the short-sleeved tunic over them.

"Make haste; they're growing angry!" she muttered.

The Prince with half-closed eyes marked the swelling lines of her bosom with an air of connoisseurship, whilst the Marquis de Chouard wagged his head involuntarily. Muffat gazed at the carpet in order not to see any more. At length, Venus, with only her gauze veil over her shoulders, was ready to go on the stage. Madame Jules, with vacant, unconcerned eyes and an expression suggestive of a little elderly wooden doll, still kept circling round her. With brisk movements she took pins out of the inexhaustible pin-cushion over her heart, and pinned up Venus's tunic, but as she ran over all those plump nude charms with her shrivelled hands, nothing was suggested to her. She was as one whom her sex does not concern.

"There!" said the young woman, taking a final look at herself in the mirror.

Bordenave was back again. He was anxious, and said the third act had begun.

"Very well! I'm coming," replied Nana. "Here's a pretty fuss! Why, it's usually I that waits for the others."

The gentlemen left the dressing-room,

but they did not say good-bye, for the Prince had expressed a desire to assist behind the scenes at the performance of the third act. Left alone, Nana seemed greatly surprised, and looked round her in all directions.

"Where can she be?" she queried.

She was searching for Satin. When she had found her again, waiting on her trunk behind the curtain, Satin quietly replied,—

"Certainly, I didn't want to be in your way with all those men there!"

And she added further that she was going now. But Nana held her back. What a silly girl she was! Now that Bordenave had agreed to take her on! Why, the bargain was to be struck after the play was over! Satin hesitated. There were too many bothers; she was out of her element! Nevertheless, she stayed.

As the Prince was coming down the little wooden stair-case, a strange sound of smothered oaths and stamping scuffling feet became audible on the other side of the theatre. The actors waiting for their cues were being scared by quite a serious episode. For some seconds past, Mignon had been renewing his jokes and smothering Fauchery with caresses. He had at last invented a little game of a novel kind, and had begun flicking the other's nose, in order, as he phrased it, to keep the flies off him. This kind of game naturally diverted the actors to any extent.

But success had suddenly thrown Mignon off his balance. He had launched forth into extravagant courses, and had given the journalist a box on the ear, an actual, a vigorous box on the ear. This time he had gone too far: in the presence of so many spectators, it was impossible for Fauchery to pocket such a blow with laughing equanimity. Whereupon the two men had desisted from their farce, had sprung at one another's throats, their faces livid with hate, and were now rolling over and over behind a set of sidelights, pounding away at each other as though they weren't breakable.

"Monsieur Bordenave, Monsieur Bordenave!" said the stage-manager, coming up in a terrible flutter.

Bordenave made his excuses to the Prince, and followed him. When he recognised Fauchery and Mignon in the men on the floor, he gave vent to an expression of annoyance. They had chosen a nice time, certainly, with his highness on the other side of the scenery, and all that houseful of people who might have overheard the row! To make matters worse, Rose Mignon arrived out of breath at the very moment she was due on the stage. Vulcan, indeed, was giving her the cue, but Rose stood rooted to the ground, marvelling at sight of her husband and her lover as they lay wallowing at her feet, strangling one another, kicking, tearing their hair out, and whitening their coats with dust. They barred the way. A scene-shifter had even stopped Fauchery's hat just when the devilish thing was going to bound onto the stage in the middle of the struggle. Meanwhile Vulcan, who had been gagging away to amuse the audience, gave Rose her cue a second time. But she stood motionless, still gazing at the two men.

"Oh, don't look at *them!*" Bordenave furiously whispered to her. "Go on the stage, go on, do! It's no business of yours! Why, your missing your cue!"

And with a push from the manager,

Rose stepped over the prostrate bodies, and found herself in the flare of the footlights and in the presence of the audience. She had quite failed to understand why they were fighting on the floor behind her. Trembling from head to foot and with a humming in her ears, she came down to the footlights, Diana's sweet amorous smile on her lips, and attacked the opening lines of her duet with so feeling a voice that the public gave her a veritable ovation.

Behind the scenery she could hear the dull thuds caused by the two men. They had rolled down to the wings, but fortunately the music covered the noise made by their feet as they kicked against them.

"By God!" yelled Bordenave in exasperation, when at last he had succeeded in separating them, "why couldn't you fight at home? You know as well as I do that I don't like this sort of thing. You, Mignon, you'll do me the pleasure of staying over here on the prompt side, and you, Fauchery, if you leave the O.P. side, I'll chuck you out of the theatre. You understand, eh?—prompt side and O.P. side, or I forbid Rose to bring you here at all."

When he returned to the Prince's presence, the latter asked what was the matter.

"Oh, nothing at all," murmured he quietly.

Nana was standing wrapped in furs, talking to these gentlemen, whilst awaiting her cue. As Count Muffat was coming up in order to peep between two of the wings at the stage, he understood from a sign made him by the stage-manager that he was to step softly. Drowsy warmth was streaming down from the flies, and in the wings, which were lit by vivid patches of light, only a few people remained talking in low voices, or making off on tip-toe. The gasman was at his post amid an intricate arrangement of cocks; a fireman, leaning against the side-lights, was craning forward, trying to catch a glimpse of things; whilst, on his seat, high up, the curtain-man was watching with resigned expression, careless of the play, constantly on the alert for the bell to ring him to his duty among the ropes. And amid the close air, and the shuffling of feet, and the sound of whispering, the voices of the actors on the stage sounded strange, deadened, surprisingly discordant. Further off, again, above the confused noises of the band, a vast breathing sound was audible. It was the breath of the house, which sometimes swelled up till it burst in vague rumors, in laughter, in applause. Though invisible, the presence of the public could be felt, even in the silences.

"There's something open," said Nana, sharply, and with that she tightened the folds of her fur cloak. "Do look, Barillot. I bet they've just opened a window. Why, one might catch one's death of cold here!"

Barillot swore that he had closed every window himself, but suggested that possibly there were broken panes about. The actors were always complaining of draughts. Through the heavy warmth of that gas-lit region blasts of cold air were constantly passing—it was a regular influenza-trap, as Fontan phrased it.

"I should like to see *you* in a low-cut dress," continued Nana, growing annoyed.

"Hush!" murmured Bordenave.

On the stage Rose rendered a phrase in her duet so cleverly that the stalls burst into universal applause. Nana was silent at this, and her face grew grave. Meanwhile the Count was venturing down a passage when Barillot stopped him and said he would make a discovery there. Indeed he obtained an oblique back-view of the scenery, and of the wings which had been strengthened, as it were, by a thick layer of old posters. Then he caught sight of a corner of the stage, of the Etna cave hollowed out in a silver mine, and of Vulcan's forge in the background. Battens, lowered from above, lit up a sparkling substance which had been laid on with large dabs of the brush. Side-lights, with red glasses and blue, were so placed as to produce the appearance of a fiery brazier, whilst, on the floor of the stage, in the far background, long lines of gas-light had been laid down in order to throw a wall of dark rocks into sharp relief. Hard by, on a gentle "practicable" incline, amid little points of light resembling the illumination-lamps scattered about in the grass on the night of a public holiday, old Madame Drouard, who played Juno, was sitting dazed and sleepy, waiting for her cue.

Presently there was a commotion, for Simonne, whilst listening to a story Clarisse was telling her, cried out,—

"My! It's the Tricon!"

It was indeed the Tricon, wearing the same old curls and looking as like a litigious great lady as ever.

When she saw Nana, she went straight up to her.

"No," said the latter after some rapid phrases had been exchanged, "not now."

The old lady looked grave. Just then Prullière passed by and shook hands with her, whilst two little chorus-girls stood gazing at her with looks of deep emotion. For a moment she seemed to hesitate. Then she beckoned to Simonne, and the rapid exchange of sentences began again.

"Yes," said Simonne at last. "In half an hour."

But as she was going upstairs again to her dressing-room, Madame Bron, who was once more going the rounds with letters, presented one to her. Bordenave lowered his voice, and furiously reproached the portress for having allowed the Tricon to come in. That woman! And on such an evening of all others! It made him so angry because his highness was there! Madame Bron, who had been thirty years in the theatre, replied quite sourly. How was she to know? she asked. The Tricon did business with all the ladies—Monsieur de Directeur had met her a score of times without making remarks. And whilst Bordenave was muttering oaths, the Tricon stood quietly by, scrutinising the Prince as became a woman who weighs a man at a glance. A smile lit up her yellow face. Presently she paced slowly off through the crowd of deeply-deferential little women.

"Immediately, eh?" she queried, turning round again to Simonne.

Simonne seemed much worried. The letter was from a young man to whom she had engaged herself for that evening. She gave Madame Bron a scribbled note, in which were the words, "Impossible to-night, darling—I'm booked." But she was still apprehensive—the young man might possibly wait for her in spite of everything. As she was not playing in the third act, she had a mind to be off at once, and accordingly begged Clarisse to go and see if the man were there. Clarisse was only due on the stage towards the end of the act, and so she went downstairs, whilst Simonne ran up for a minute to their common dressing-room.

In Madame Bron's drinking-bar downstairs a super, who was charged with the part of Pluto, was drinking in solitude, amid the folds of a great red robe diapered with golden flames. The little business plied by the good portress must have been progressing finely, for the cellar-like hole under the stairs was wet with emptied heel-taps and water. Clarisse picked up the tunic of Iris, which was dragging over the greasy steps behind her, but she halted prudently at the turn in the stairs, and was content simply to crane forward and peer into the lodge. She certainly had been quick to scent things out! Just fancy! That idiot la Faloise was still there, sitting on the same old chair between the table and the stove! He had made pretence of sneaking off in front of Simonne, and had returned after her departure. For the matter of that, the lodge was still full of gentlemen, who sat there gloved, elegant, submissive, and patient as ever. They were all waiting, and viewing each other gravely, as they waited. On the table there were now only some dirty plates, Madame Bron having recently distributed the last of the bouquets. A single fallen rose was withering on the floor in the neighbourhood of the black cat, who had lain down and curled herself up, whilst the kittens ran wild races and danced fierce gallops among the gentlemen's legs. Clarisse was momentarily inclined to turn la Faloise out. The idiot wasn't fond of animals, and that put the finishing touch to him! He was busy drawing in his legs because the cat was there, and he didn't want to touch her. "He'll nip you: take care!" said Pluto, who was a joker, as he went upstairs, wiping his mouth with the back of his hand.

After that, Clarisse gave up the idea of hauling la Faloise over the coals. She had seen Madame Bron giving the letter to Simonne's young man, and he had gone out to read it under the gas-light in the lobby. "Impossible to-night, darling—I'm booked." And with that he had peaceably departed, as one who was doubtless used to the formula. He at any rate knew how to conduct himself! Not so the others, the fellows who sat there doggedly, on Madame Bron's battered straw-bottomed chairs, in the great glazed lantern, where the heat was enough to roast you, and there was an unpleasant odour. What a lot of men it must have held! Clarisse went upstairs again in disgust, crossed over behind scenes, and nimbly mounted three flights of steps which led to the dressing-rooms, in order to bring Simonne her reply.

Downstairs, the Prince had withdrawn from the rest and stood talking to Nana. He never left her; he stood brooding over her through half-shut eyelids. Nana did not look at him, but smiling nodded "yes." Suddenly, however, Count Muffat obeyed an overmastering impulse, and leaving Bordenave, who was explaining to him the working of the rollers and windlasses, he came up in order to interrupt their confabulations. Nana lifted her eyes, and smiled at him as she smiled at his highness. But she kept

her ears open notwithstanding, for she was waiting for her cue.

"The third act is the shortest, I believe," the Prince began saying, for the Count's presence embarrassed him.

She did not answer: her whole expression altered: she was suddenly intent on her business. With a rapid movement of the shoulders, she had let her furs slip from her, and Madame Jules, standing behind, had caught them in her arms. And then, after passing her two hands to her hair as though to make it fast, she went on the stage in all her nudity.

"Hush, hush!" whispered Bordenave.

The Count and the Prince had been taken by surprise. There was profound silence, and then a deep sigh and the far-off murmur of a multitude became audible. Every evening when Venus entered in her god-like nakedness the same effect was produced. Then Muffat was seized with a desire to see; he put his eye to a peep-hole. Above and beyond the glowing arc formed by the footlights the dark body of the house seemed full of ruddy vapour, and against this neutral-tinted background, where row upon row of faces struck a pale, uncertain note, Nana stood forth white and vast, so that the boxes from the balcony to the flies were blotted from view. He saw her from behind—noted her swelling hips, her outstretched arms, whilst down on the floor, on the same level as her feet, the prompter's head—an old man's head with a humble, honest face—stood on the edge of the stage looking as though it had been severed from the body. At certain points in her opening number an undulating movement seemed to run from her neck to her waist, and to die out in the trailing border of her tunic. When amid a tempest of applause she had sung her last note, she bowed, and the gauze floated forth round about her limbs, and her hair swept over her waist as she bent sharply backwards. And seeing her thus as, with bending form and with exaggerated hips, she came backing towards the Count's peep-hole, he stood upright again, and his face was very white. The stage had disappeared, and he now saw only the reverse side of the scenery with its display of old posters pasted up in every direction. On the practicable slope, among the lines of gas-jets, the whole of Olympus had rejoined the dozing Madame Drouard. They were waiting for the close of the act. Bosc and Fontan sat on the floor with their knees drawn up to their chins, and Prullière stretched himself and yawned before going on. Everybody was worn out; their eyes were red, and they were longing to go home to sleep.

Just then Fauchery, who had been prowling about on the O.P. side ever since Bordenave had forbidden him the other, came and buttonholed the Count in order to keep himself in countenance, and offered, at the same time, to shew him the dressing-rooms. An increasing sense of languor had left Muffat without any power of resistance, and after looking round for the Marquis de Chouard, who had disappeared, he ended by following the journalist. He experienced a mingled feeling of relief and anxiety as he left the wings whence he had been listening to Nana's songs.

Fauchery had already preceded him up the staircase, which was closed on the first and second floors by low panelled doors. It was one of those stairways which you find in miserable tene-

ments. Count Muffat had seen many such during his rounds as member of the Benevolent Organisation. It was bare and dilapidated: there was a wash of yellow paint on its walls, its steps had been worn by the incessant passage of feet, and its iron balustrade had grown smooth under the friction of many hands. On a level with the floor, on every stair-head, there was a low window which resembled a deep square vent-hole, whilst in lanterns fastened to the walls flaring gas-jets crudely illuminated the surrounding squalor, and gave out a glowing heat, which, as it mounted up the narrow stair-well, grew ever more intense.

When he reached the foot of the stairs, the Count once more felt that hot breath upon his neck and shoulders. As of old it was laden with the odour of women, wafted amid floods of light and sound, from the dressing-rooms above; and now, with every upward step he took, the musky scent of powders and the tart perfume of toilet vinegars heated and bewildered him more and more. On the first floor two corridors ran backward, branching sharply off and presenting a set of doors to view which were painted yellow and numbered with great white numerals in such a way as to suggest a hotel with a bad reputation. The tiles on the floor had been many of them unbedded, and the old house, being in a state of subsidence, they stuck up like hummocks. The Count dashed recklessly forward, glanced through a half-open door, and saw a very dirty room, which resembled a barber's shop in a poor part of the town. It was furnished with two chairs, a mirror, and a small table containing a drawer which had been black-

ened by the grease from brushes and
combs. A great perspiring fellow, with
smoking shoulders, was changing his linen
there, whilst in a similar room, next door,
a woman was drawing on her gloves
preparatory to departure. Her hair was
damp and out of curl, as though she had
just had a bath. But Fauchery began
calling the Count, and the latter was
rushing up without delay, when a furious
"damn!" burst from the corridor on the
right. Mathilde, a little drab of a miss,
had just broken her wash-hand basin,
the soapy water from which was flowing
out to the stair-head. A dressing-room
door banged noisily. Two women in
their stays skipped across the passage,
and another, with the hem of her shift
in her mouth, appeared and immediately
vanished from view. Then followed a
sound of laughter; a dispute, the snatch
of a song, which was suddenly broken
off short. All along the passage, naked
gleams, sudden visions of white skin and
wan underlinen, were observable through
chinks in doorways. Two girls were
making very merry, shewing each other
their birth-marks. One of them, a very
young girl, almost a child, had drawn her
skirts up over her knees in order to sew
up a rent in her drawers, and the dressers,
catching sight of the two men, drew
some curtains half to, for decency's sake.
The wild stampede which follows the
end of a play had already begun, the
grand removal of white paint and rouge,
the reassumption amid clouds of rice-
powder of ordinary attire. The strange
animal scent came in whiffs of redoubled
intensity through the lines of banging
doors. On the third story, Muffat abandoned himself to the feeling of intoxication which was overpowering him. For

the chorus-girls' dressing-room was there,
and you saw a crowd of twenty women,
and a wild display of soaps and flasks of
lavender water. The place resembled
the common room in a slum lodging-
house. As he passed by he heard fierce
sounds of washing behind a closed door,
and a perfect storm raging in a wash-
hand basin. And, as he was mounting
up to the topmost story of all, curiosity
led him to risk one more little peep
through an open loop-hole. The room
was empty, and, under the flare of the
gas, a solitary chamber pot stood forgotten among a heap of petticoats trailing
on the floor. This room afforded him
his ultimate impression. Upstairs, on the
fourth floor, he was well-nigh suffocated.
All the scents, all the blasts of heat, had
found their goal there. The yellow
ceiling looked as if it had been baked,
and a lamp burned amid fumes of russet-
coloured fog. For some seconds he leant
upon the iron balustrade, which felt
warm and damp, and well-nigh human
to the touch. And he shut his eyes, and
drew a long breath, and drank in the
sexual atmosphere of the place. Hitherto he had been utterly ignorant of it, but
now it beat full in his face.

"Do come here," shouted Fauchery,
who had vanished some moments ago.
"You're being asked for."

At the end of the corridor was the
dressing-room belonging to Clarisse and
Simonne. It was a long, ill-built room
under the roof, with a garret ceiling and
sloping walls. The light penetrated to
it from two deep-set openings high up in
the wall, but at that hour of the night
the dressing-room was lit by flaring gas.
It was papered with a paper at seven sous
a roll, with a pattern of roses twining

over green trellis-work. Two boards, placed near one another and covered with oilcloth, did duty for dressing-tables. They were black with spilt water, and underneath them was a fine medley of dinted zinc jugs, slop-pails, and coarse yellow earthenware crocks. There was an array of fancy articles in the room— a battered, soiled, and well-worn array of chipped basins, of toothless combs, of all those manifold untidy trifles, which, in their hurry and carelessness, two women will leave scattered about when they undress and wash together amid purely temporary surroundings, the dirty aspect of which has ceased to concern them.

"Do come here," Fauchery repeated, with the good-humoured familiarity which men adopt among their fallen sisters, "Clarisse is wanting to kiss you."

Muffat entered the room at last. But what was his surprise when he found the Marquis de Chouard snugly esconced on a chair between the two dressing-tables. The Marquis had withdrawn thither some time ago. He was spreading his feet apart because a pail was leaking and letting a whitish flood spread over the floor. He was visibly much at his ease, as became a man who knew all the snug corners, and had grown quite merry in the close dressing-room, where people might have been bathing, and amid those quietly immodest feminine surroundings which the uncleanness of the little place rendered at once natural and poignant.

"D'you go with the old boy?" Simonne asked Clarisse, in a whisper.

"Rather!" replied the latter, aloud.

The dresser, a very ugly and extremely familiar young girl, who was helping Simonne into her coat, positively writhed with laughter. The three pushed each other, and babbled little phrases which redoubled their merriment.

"Come, Clarisse, kiss the gentleman," said Fauchery. "You know, he's got the rhino."

And turning to the Count,—

"You'll see, she's very nice! She's going to kiss you!"

But Clarisse was disgusted by the men. She spoke in violent terms of the dirty lot waiting at the porter's lodge down below. Besides, she was in a hurry to go downstairs again—they were making her miss her last scene. Then, as Fauchery blocked up the doorway, she gave Muffat a couple of kisses on the whiskers, remarking as she did so,—

"It's not for you at any rate! It's for that nuisance Fauchery!"

And with that she darted off, and the Count remained much embarrassed in his father-in-law's presence. The blood had rushed to his face. In Nana's dressing-room, amid all the luxury of hangings and mirrors, he had not experienced the sharp physical sensation which the shameful wretchedness of that sorry garret excited within him, redolent as it was of these two girls' self-abandonment. Meanwhile the Marquis had hurried in the rear of Simonne, who was making off at the top of her pace; and he kept whispering in her ear, whilst she shook her head in token of refusal. Fauchery followed them laughing. And with that the Count found himself alone with the dresser, who was washing out the basins. Accordingly, he took his departure too, his legs almost failing under him. Once more he put up flights of half-dressed women, and caused doors to bang, as he advanced. But amid the disorderly disbanded troops of girls to be found on each of the four stories, he was only distinctly aware of a cat, a great tortoiseshell cat, which went gliding upstairs through the oven-like place, where the air was poisoned with musk, rubbing its back against the banisters, and keeping its tail exceedingly erect.

"Yes, to be sure!" said a woman, hoarsely. "I thought they'd keep us back to-night! What a nuisance they are with their calls!"

The end had come, the curtain had just fallen. There was a veritable stampede on the staircase—its walls rang with exclamations, and everyone was in a savage hurry to dress and be off. As Count Muffat came down the last step or two, he saw Nana and the Prince passing slowly along the passage. The young woman halted, and lowered her voice as she said with a smile,—

"All right then—by-and-by!"

The Prince returned to the stage, where Bordenave was awaiting him. And, left alone with Nana, Muffat gave way to an impulse of anger and desire. He ran up behind her, and as she was on the point of entering her dressing-room, imprinted a rough kiss on her neck, among little golden hairs curling low down between her shoulders. It was as though he had returned the kiss that had been given him upstairs. Nana was in a fury—she lifted her hand, but when she recognised the Count, she smiled.

"Oh, you frightened me" said she simply.

And her smile was adorable in its embarrassment and submissiveness, as though she had despaired of this kiss and were happy to have received it. But she could do nothing for him either that evening or the day after. It was a case of waiting. Nay, even if it had been in her power she would still have let herself be desired. Her glance said as much. At length she continued,—

"I'm a landowner, you know. Yes, I'm buying a country house near Orleans, in a part of the world to which you sometimes betake yourself. Baby told me you did—little Georges Hugon, I mean. You know him? So come and see me down there."

The Count was a shy man, and the thought of his roughness had frightened him—he was ashamed of what he had done, and he bowed ceremoniously, promising, at the same time, to take advantage of her invitation. Then he walked off as one who dreams.

He was rejoining the Prince when, passing in front of the foyer, he heard Satin screaming out,—

"Oh, the dirty old thing! Just you bloody well leave me alone!"

It was the Marquis de Chouard, who was tumbling down over Satin. The girl had decidedly had enough of the fashionable world! Nana had certainly introduced her to Bordenave, but the necessity of standing with sealed lips, for fear of allowing some awkward phrase to escape her, had been too much for her feelings, and now she was anxious to regain her freedom, the more so as she had run against an old flame of hers in the wings. This was the super, to whom the task of impersonating Pluto had been entrusted, a pastry-cook, who had already treated her to a whole week of love and flagellation. She was waiting for him, much irritated at the things the Marquis was saying to her as though she were one of those theatrical ladies! And so at last she assumed a highly respectable expression, and jerked out this phrase: "My husband's coming! You'll see."

Meanwhile, the worn-looking artistes, were dropping off one after the other, in their outdoor coats. Groups of men and women were coming down the little winding staircase, and the outlines of battered hats and worn-out shawls were visible in the shadows. They looked colourless and unlovely as became poor play-actors who have got rid of their paint. On the stage, where the side-lights and battens were being extinguished, the Prince was listening to an anecdote Bordenave was telling him. He was waiting for Nana, and when at length she made her appearance, the stage was dark, and the fireman on duty was finishing his round, lantern in hand. Bordenave, in order to save his highness going about by the Passage des Panoramas, had made them open the corridor which led from the porter's lodge to the entrance-hall of the theatre. Along this narrow alley little women were racing pell-mell, for they were delighted to escape from the men who were waiting for them in the other passage. They went jostling and elbowing along, casting apprehensive glances behind them, and only breathing freely when they got outside. Fontan, Bosc and Prullière, on the other hand, retired at a leisurely pace, joking at the figure cut by the serious, paying admirers who were striding up and down the Galerie des Variétés at a time when the little dears were escaping along the boulevard with the men of their hearts. But Clarisse was especially sly. She had her suspicions about la Faloise, and, as a matter of fact, he was still in his place, in the lodge, among the gentlemen obstinately waiting on Madame Bron's chairs. They all stretched forward, and, with that, she passed brazenly by, in the wake of a friend. The gentlemen were blinking in bewilderment over the wild whirl of petticoats eddying at the foot of the narrow stairs. It made them desperate to think they had waited so long only to see them all flying away like this without being able to recognise a single one. The litter of little black cats were sleeping on the oil-cloth nestled against their mother's belly, and the latter was stretching her paws out in a state of beatitude, whilst the big tortoise-shell cat sat at the other end of the table, her tail stretched out behind her, and her yellow eyes solemnly following the flight of the women.

"If his highness will be good enough to come this way," said Bordenave, at the bottom of the stairs, and he pointed to the passage.

Some chorus-girls were still crowding along it. The Prince began following Nana, whilst Muffat and the Marquis walked behind.

It was a long narrow passage lying between the theatre and the house next door, a kind of contracted by-lane, which had been covered with a sloping glass roof. Damp oozed from the walls, and the footfall sounded as hollow on the tiled floor as in an underground vault. It was crowded with the kind of rubbish usually found in a garret. There was a work-bench on which the porter was wont to plane such parts of the scenery as required it, besides a pile of wooden barriers which at night were placed at the doors of the theatre for the purpose of regulating the incoming stream of people. Nana had to pick up her dress as she passed a hydrant, which, through having been carelessly turned off, was flooding the tiles underfoot. In the entrance-hall the company bowed and said good-bye. And when Bordenave was alone, he summed up his opinion of the Prince in a shrug of eminently philosophic disdain.

"He's a bit of a duffer all the same," said he to Fauchery, without entering on further explanations; and with that Rose Mignon carried the journalist off with her husband in order to effect a reconciliation between them at home.

Muffat was left alone on the sidewalk. His highness had handed Nana quietly into his carriage, and the Marquis had slipped off after Satin and her super. In his excitement he was content to follow this vicious pair in vague hopes of some stray favour being granted him. Then, with brain on fire, Muffat decided to walk home. The struggle within him had wholly ceased. The ideas and beliefs of the last forty years were being drowned in a flood of new life. Whilst he was passing along the boulevards, the roll of the last carriages deafened him with the name of Nana: the gas-lights set nude limbs dancing before his eyes— the nude limbs, the lithe arms, the white shoulders of Nana. And he felt that he was hers utterly: he would have abjured everything, sold everything, to possess her for a single hour that very night. Youth, a lustful puberty of early manhood, was stirring within him at last, flaming up suddenly in the chaste heart of the Catholic and amid the dignified traditions of middle age.

# CHAPTER VI

COUNT MUFFAT, accompanied by his wife and daughter, had arrived overnight at The Fondettes, where Madame Hugon, who was staying there with only her son Georges, had invited them to come and spend a week. The house, which had been built at the end of the eighteenth century, stood in the middle of a huge square enclosure. It was perfectly unadorned, but the garden possessed magnificent shady trees, and a chain of tanks fed by running spring water. It stood at the side of the road which leads from Orleans to Paris, and with its rich verdure and high-embowered trees broke the monotony of that flat countryside, where fields stretched to the horizon's verge.

At eleven o'clock, when the second lunch-bell had called the whole household together, Madame Hugon, smiling in her kindly maternal way, gave Sabine two great kisses, one on each cheek, and said as she did so,—

"You know it's my custom in the country. Oh, seeing you here makes me feel twenty years younger. Did you sleep well in your old room?"

Then, without waiting for her reply, she turned to Estelle:

"And this little one, has she had a nap too? Give me a kiss, my child."

They had taken their seats in the vast dining-room, the windows of which looked out on the park. But they only occupied one end of the long table, where they sat somewhat crowded together for company's sake. Sabine, in high good spirits, dwelt on various childish memories which had been stirred up within her—memories of months passed at The Fondettes, of long walks, of a tumble into one of the tanks on a summer evening, of an old romance of chivalry discovered by her on the top of a cupboard and read, during the winter, before fires made of vine-branches. And Georges, who had not seen the Countess for some months, thought there was something curious about her. Her face seemed changed somehow, whilst, on the other hand, that stick of an Estelle seemed more insignificant, and dumb, and awkward than ever.

Whilst such simple fare as cutlets and boiled eggs was being discussed by the company, Madame Hugon, as became a good housekeeper, launched out into complaints. The butchers, she said, were becoming impossible. She bought everything at Orleans, and yet they never brought her the pieces she asked for. Yet, alas! if her guests had nothing worth eating, it was their own fault: they had come too late in the season.

"There's no sense in it," said she. "I've been expecting you since June, and now we're half through September. You see, it doesn't look pretty."

And with a movement, she pointed to the trees on the grass outside, the leaves of which were beginning to turn yellow. The day was covered, and the distance was hidden by a bluish haze, which was fraught with a sweet and melancholy peacefulness.

"Oh, I'm expecting company," she continued. "We shall be gayer then! The first to come will be two gentlemen whom Georges has invited—Monsieur Fauchery and Monsieur Daguenet: you know them, do you not? Then we shall have Monsieur de Vandeuvres, who has promised me a visit these five years past.

This time, perhaps, he'll make up his mind!"

"Oh, well and good!" said the Countess, laughing; "if we only can get Monsieur de Vandeuvres! But he's too much engaged."

"And Philippe?" queried Muffat.

"Philippe has asked for a furlough," replied the old lady; "but without doubt you won't be at The Fondettes any longer when he arrives."

The coffee was served. Paris was now the subject of conversation, and Steiner's name was mentioned, at which Madame Hugon gave a little cry.

"Let me see," said she, "Monsieur Steiner is that stout man I met at your house one evening. He's a banker, is he not? Now there's a detestable man for you! Why, he's gone and bought an actress an estate, about a league from here, over Gumières way, beyond the Choue. The whole countryside's scandalised. Did you know about that, my friend?"

"I knew nothing about it," replied Muffat. "Ah, then, Steiner's bought a country place in the neighbourhood!"

Hearing his mother broach the subject, Georges looked into his coffee-cup, but, in his astonishment at the Count's answer, he glanced up at him and stared. Why was he lying so glibly? The Count, on his side, noticed the young fellow's movement, and gave him a suspicious glance. Madame Hugon continued to go into details: the country place was called La Mignotte. In order to get there one had to go up the bank of the Choue as far as Gumières in order to cross the bridge; otherwise one got one's feet wet and ran the risk of a ducking.

"And what is the actress's name?" asked the Countess.

"Oh, I wasn't told," murmured the old lady. "Georges, you were there the morning the gardener spoke to us about it."

Georges appeared to rack his brains. Muffat waited, twirling a teaspoon between his fingers. Then the Countess addressed her husband:

"Isn't Monsieur Steiner with that singer at the Variétés, that Nana?"

"Nana, that's the name! A horrible woman!" cried Madame Hugon, with growing annoyance. 'And they are expecting her at The Mignotte. I've heard all about it from the gardener. Didn't the gardener say they were expecting her this evening, Georges?"

The Count gave a little start of astonishment, but Georges replied with much vivacity,—

"Oh, mother, the gardener spoke without knowing anything about it. Directly afterwards, the coachman said just the opposite. Nobody's expected at The Mignotte before the day after to-morrow."

He tried hard to assume a natural expression, whilst he slyly watched the effect of his remarks on the Count. The latter was twirling his spoon again as though reassured. The Countess, her eyes fixed dreamily on the blue distances of the park, seemed to have lost all interest in the conversation. The shadow of a smile on her lips, she seemed to be following up a secret thought which had been suddenly awakened within her. Estelle, on the other hand, sitting stiffly on her chair, had heard all that had been said about Nana, but her white virginal face had not betrayed a trace of emotion.

"Dear me, dear me! I've got no right to grow angry," murmured Madame Hugon, after a pause, and with a return to her old good humour, she added,— "Everybody's got a right to live. If we meet this said lady on the road, we shall not bow to her—that's all!"

And as they got up from table she once more gently upbraided the Countess Sabine for having been so long in coming to her that year. But the Countess defended herself, and threw the blame of the delays upon her husband's shoulders. Twice on the eve of departure, when all the trunks were locked, he counter-ordered their journey on the plea of urgent business. Then he had suddenly decided to start just when the trip seemed shelved. Thereupon the old lady told them how Georges in the same way had twice announced his arrival without arriving, and had finally cropped up at The Fondettes the day before yesterday, when she was no longer expecting him. They had come down into the garden, and the two men, walking beside the ladies, were listening to them in consequential silence.

"Never mind," said Madame Hugon, kissing her son's sunny locks, "Zizi is a very good boy to come and bury himself in the country with his mother. He's a dear Zizi not to forget me!"

In the afternoon she expressed some anxiety for Georges, directly after leaving the table had complained of a heavy feeling in his head, and now seemed in for an atrocious sick headache. Towards four o'clock he said he would go upstairs to bed: it was the only remedy. After sleeping till to-morrow morning he would be perfectly himself again. His mother was bent on putting him to bed herself, but, as she left the room, he ran and locked the door, explaining that he was shutting himself in so that no one should come and disturb him. Then caressingly he shouted "Good night till to-morrow, little mother!" and promised to take a nap. But he did not go to bed again, and with flushed cheeks and bright eyes noiselessly put on his clothes. Then he sat on a chair and waited. When the dinner-bell rang, he listened for Count Muffat, who was on his way to the dining-room, and ten minutes later, when he was certain that no one would see him, he slipped from the window to the ground with the assistance of a rain-pipe. His bedroom was situated on the first floor, and looked out upon the rear of the house. He threw himself among some bushes, and got out of the park, and then galloped across the fields with empty stomach and heart beating with excitement. Night was closing in, and a small fine rain was beginning to fall.

It was the very evening that Nana was due at The Mignotte. Ever since, in the preceding May, Steiner had bought her this country place, she had from time to time been so filled with the desire of taking possession, that she had wept hot tears about; but on each of these occasions Bordenave had refused to give her even the shortest leave, and had deferred her holiday till September on the plea that he did not intend putting an understudy in her place, even for one evening, now that the Exhibiton was on. Towards the close of August he spoke of October. Nana was furious, and declared that she would be at The Mignotte in the middle of September. Nay, in order to dare Bordenave, she even invited a crowd of guests in his very presence. One after-

noon, in her rooms, as Muffat, whose advances she still adroitly resisted, was beseeching her with tremulous emotion to yield to his entreaties, she at length promised to be kind, but not in Paris; and to him, too, she named the middle of September. Then, on the twelfth, she was seized by a desire to be off forthwith, with Zoé as her sole companion. It might be that Bordenave had got wind of her intentions, and was about to discover some means of detaining her. She was delighted at the notion of putting him in a fix, and she sent him a doctor's certificate. When once the idea had entered her head of being the first to get to The Mignotte, and of living there two days without anybody knowing anything about it, she rushed Zoé through the operation of packing, and finally pushed her into a cab, where, in a sudden burst of extreme contrition, she kissed her and begged her pardon. It was only when they got to the station refreshment-room that she thought of writing Steiner of her movements. She begged him to wait till the day after to-morrow before rejoining her, if he wanted to find her quite bright and fresh. And then, suddenly conceiving another project, she wrote a second letter, in which she besought her aunt to bring little Louis to her at once. It would do baby so much good! And how happy they would be together in the shade of the trees! In the railway carriage between Paris and Orleans she spoke of nothing else; her eyes were full of tears, she had an unexpected attack of maternal tenderness, and mingled together, flowers, birds, and child in her every sentence.

La Mignotte was more than three

leagues away from the station, and Nana lost a good hour over the hire of a carriage, a huge dilapidated calash, which rumbled slowly along to an accompaniment of rattling old iron. She had at once taken possession of the coachman, a little taciturn old man, whom she overwhelmed with questions. Had he often passed by La Mignotte? It was behind this hill, then? There ought to be lots of trees there, eh? And the house, could one see it at a distance? The little old man answered with a succession of grunts. Down in the calash Nana was almost dancing with impatience, whilst Zoé, in her annoyance at having left Paris in such a hurry, sat stiffly sulking beside her. The horse suddenly stopped short, and the young woman thought they had reached their destination. She put her head out of the carriage-door, and asked,—

"Are we there, eh?"

By way of answer the driver whipped up his horse, which was in the act of painfully climbing a hill. Nana gazed ecstatically at the vast plain beneath the grey sky where great clouds were banked up.

"Oh, do look, Zoé! There's greenery! Now, is that all wheat? Good Lord, how pretty it is!"

"One can quite see that *Madame* doesn't come from the country," was the servant's prim and tardy rejoinder. "As for me, I knew the country only too well, when I was with my dentist. He had a house at Bougival. No, it's cold, too, this evening. It's damp in these parts."

They were driving under the shadow of a wood, and Nana sniffed up the scent of the leaves as a young dog might. All of a sudden, at a turn of the road, she caught sight of the corner of a house among the trees. Perhaps it was there! And with that she began a conversation with the driver, who continued shaking his head by way of saying no. Then, as they drove down the other side of the hill, he contented himself by holding out his whip and muttering,—" 'Tis down there."

She got up, and stretched herself almost bodily out of the carriage-door.

"Where is it? Where is it?" she cried, with pale cheeks, but as yet she saw nothing.

At last she caught sight of a bit of wall. And then followed a succession of little cries and jumps, the ecstatic behaviour of a woman overcome by a new and vivid sensation.

"I see it! I see it, Zoé! Look out at the other side. Oh, there's a terrace, with brick ornaments on the roof! And there's a hothouse down there! But the place is immense: oh, how happy I am! Do look, Zoé! Now, do look!"

The carriage had by this time pulled up before the park gates. A side-door was opened, and the gardener, a tall dry fellow, made his appearance, cap in hand. Nana made an effort to regain her dignity, for the driver seemed now to be suppressing a laugh behind his dry, speechless lips. She refrained from setting off at a run, and listened to the gardener, who was a very talkative fellow. He begged *Madame* to excuse the disorder in which she found everything, seeing that he had only received *Madame's* letter that very morning. But, despite all his efforts, she flew off at a tangent, and walked so quickly that Zoé could scarcely follow her. At the end of the avenue she paused for a moment, in order to take the house in at a glance. It was a great pavilion-like building in the Italian manner, and it was flanked by a smaller construction, which a rich Englishman, after two years' residence in Naples had caused to be erected and had forthwith become disgusted with.

"I'll take *Madame* over the house," said the gardener.

But she had outrun him entirely, and she shouted back that he was not to put himself out, and that she would go over the house by herself. She preferred doing that, she said. And, without removing her hat, she dashed into the different rooms, calling to Zoé as she did so, shouting her impressions from one end of each corridor to the other, and filling the empty house, which for long months had been uninhabited, with exclamations and bursts of laughter. In the first place, there was the hall. It was a little damp, but that didn't matter; one wasn't going to sleep in it. Then came the drawing-room, quite the thing the drawing-room, with its windows opening on the lawn. Only the red upholsteries there were hideous: she would alter all that. As to the dining-room— well, it was a lovely dining-room, eh? What big blow-outs you might give in Paris if you had a dining-room as large as that! As she was going upstairs to the first floor it occurred to her that she had not seen the kitchen, and she went down again and indulged in ecstatic exclamations. Zoé ought to admire the beautiful dimensions of the sink and the width of the hearth, where you might have roasted a sheep! When she had gone upstairs again, her bedroom especially enchanted her. It had been hung with delicate rose-coloured Louis XVI. cretonne by an Orleans upholsterer. Dear me, yes! One ought to sleep jolly sound in such a room as that: why, it was a real best bedroom! Then came four or five guest chambers, and then some splendid garrets, which would be extremely convenient for trunks and boxes. Zoé looked very gruff, and cast a frigid glance into each of the rooms as she lingered in *Madame's* wake. She saw Nana disappearing up the steep garret ladder, and said, "Thanks, I haven't the least wish to break my legs." But the sound of a voice reached her from far away; indeed, it seemed to come whistling down a chimney.

"Zoé, Zoé, where are you? Come up, do! You've no idea! It's like fairyland!"

Zoé went up grumbling. On the roof she found her mistress leaning against the brick-work balustrade, and gazing at the valley which spread out into the silence. The horizon was immeasurably wide, but it was now covered by masses of gray vapour, and a fierce wind was driving fine rain before it. Nana had to hold her hat on with both hands to keep it from being blown away, whilst her petticoats streamed out bchind her, flapping like a flag.

"Not if I know it!" said Zoé, drawing her head in at once. "*Madame* will be blown away. What beastly weather!"

*Madame* did not hear what she said. With her head over the balustrade she was gazing at the grounds beneath. They consisted of seven or eight acres of land, enclosed within a wall. Then the view of the kitchen garden entirely engrossed her attention. She darted back, jostling the lady's maid at the top of the stairs, and bursting out,—

"It's full of cabbages! Oh, such woppers! And lettuces, and sorrel, and onions, and everything! Come along, make haste!"

The rain was falling more heavily now, and she opened her white silk sunshade, and ran down the garden walks.

"*Madame* will catch cold," cried Zoé, who had stayed quietly behind under the awning over the garden-door.

But *Madame* wanted to see things, and at each new discovery there was a burst of wonderment.

"Zoé, here's spinach! Do come. Oh! look at the artichokes! They are funny. So they grow in the ground, do they? Now, what can that be? I don't know it. Do come, Zoé, perhaps you know."

The lady's maid never budged an inch. *Madame* must really be raving mad. For now the rain was coming down in torrents, and the little white silk sunshade was already dark with it. Nor did it shelter *Madame*, whose skirts were wringing wet. But that didn't put her out in the smallest degree, and in the pouring rain she visited the kitchen garden and the orchard, stopping in front of every fruit tree, and bending over every bed of vegetables. Then she ran and looked down the well, and lifted up a frame to see what was underneath it, and was lost in the contemplation of a huge pumpkin. She wanted to go along every single garden walk, and to take immediate possession of all the things she had been wont to dream of in the old days, when she was a slipshod workgirl on the Paris pavements. The rain redoubled, but she never heeded it, and was only miserable at the thought that the daylight was fading. She could not see clearly now, and touched things with her fingers to find out what they were. Suddenly, in the twilight, she caught sight of a bed of strawberries, and all that was childish in her awoke.

"Strawberries! Strawberries! There are some here: I can feel them. A plate, Zoé! Come and pick strawberries."

And, dropping her sunshade, Nana crouched down in the mire under the full force of the downpour. With drenched hands she began gathering the fruit among the leaves. But Zoé in the meantime brought no plate, and when the young woman rose to her feet again she was frightened. She thought she had seen a shadow close to her.

"It's some beast!" she screamed.

But she stood rooted to the path in utter amazement. It was a man, and she recognized him.

"Gracious me, it's Baby! What *are* you doing there, Baby?"

" 'Gad, I've come—that's all!" replied Georges.

Her head swam.

"You knew I'd come through the gardener telling you? Oh, that poor child! Why, he's soaking!"

"Oh, I'll explain that to you! The rain caught me on my way here, and then, as I didn't wish to go up stream as far as Gumières, I crossed the Choue, and fell into a blessed hole."

Nana forgot the strawberries forthwith. She was trembling and full of pity. That poor dear Zizi in a hole full of water! And she drew him with her in the direction of the house, and spoke of making up a roaring fire.

"You know," he murmured, stopping her among the shadows, "I was in hiding, because I was afraid of being scolded, like in Paris, when I come and see you and you're not expecting me."

She made no reply, but burst out laughing, and gave him a kiss on the forehead. Up till to-day she had always treated him like a naughty urchin, never taking his declarations seriously, and amusing herself at his expense as though he were a little man of no consequence whatever. There was much ado to instal him in the house. She absolutely insisted on the fire being lit in her bedroom, as being the most comfortable place for his reception. Georges had not surprised Zoé, who was used to all kinds of encounters; but the gardener, who brought the wood upstairs, was greatly nonplussed at sight of this dripping gentleman to whom he was certain he had not opened the front door. He was, however, dismissed, as he was no longer wanted.

A lamp lit up the room, and the fire burnt with a great bright flame.

"He'll never get dry, and he'll catch cold," said Nana, seeing Georges beginning to shiver.

And there were no men's trousers in her house! She was on the point of calling the gardener back, when an idea struck her. Zoé, who was unpacking the trunks in the dressing-room, brought her mistress a change of underwear, consisting of a shift and some petticoats, with a dressing-jacket.

"Oh, that's first rate!" cried the young woman. "Zizi can put 'em all on. You're not angry with me, eh? When your clothes are dry, you can put them on again, and then off with you, as fast as fast can be, so as not to have a scolding from your mamma. Make haste! I'm

going to change my things too, in the dressing-room."

Ten minutes afterwards, when she reappeared in a tea-gown, she clasped her hands in a perfect ecstasy.

"Oh, the darling! How sweet he looks dressed like a little woman!"

He had simply slipped on a long night-gown with an insertion front, a pair of worked drawers, and the dressing-jacket, which was a long cambric garment trimmed with lace. Thus attired, and with his delicate young arms shewing, and his bright damp hair falling almost to his shoulders, he looked just like a girl.

"Why, he's as slim as I am!" said Nana, putting her arm round his waist. "Zoé, just come here and see how it suits him. It's made for him, eh?—all except the bodice part, which is too large. He hasn't got as much as I have, poor dear Zizi!"

"Oh, to be sure, I'm a bit wanting there," murmured Georges, with a smile.

All three grew very merry about it. Nana had set to work buttoning the dressing-jacket from top to bottom, so as to make him quite decent. Then she turned him round as though he were a doll, gave him little thumps, made the skirt stand well out behind. After which she asked him questions. Was he comfortable? Did he feel warm? Zounds, yes, he was comfortable! Nothing fitted more closely and warmly than a woman's shift: had he been able, he would always have worn one. He moved round and about therein, delighted with the fine linen and the soft touch of that unmanly garment, in the folds of which he thought he discovered some of Nana's own warm life.

Meanwhile, Zoé had taken the soaked clothes down to the kitchen in order to dry them as quickly as possible in front of a vine-branch fire. Then Georges, as he lounged in an easy chair, ventured to make a confession.

"I say, are you going to feed this evening? I'm dying of hunger. I haven't dined."

Nana was vexed. The great silly thing to go sloping off from mamma's with an empty stomach, just to chuck himself into a hole full of water! But she was as hungry as a hunter, too. They certainly must feed! Only they would have to eat what they could get. Whereupon a round table was rolled up in front of the fire, and the queerest of dinners was improvised thereon. Zoé ran down to the gardener's, he having cooked a mess of cabbage soup in case *Madame* should not dine at Orleans before her arrival. *Madame*, indeed, had forgotten to tell him what he was to get ready in the letter she had sent him. Fortunately the cellar was well furnished. Accordingly they had cabbage soup, followed by a piece of bacon. Then Nana rummaged in her hand-bag, and found quite a heap of provisions which she had taken the precaution of stuffing into it. There was a Strasbourg *pâté*, for instance, and a bag of sweetmeats, and some oranges. So they both ate away like ogres, and, whilst they satisfied their healthy young appetites, treated one another with easy good fellowship. Nana kept calling Georges "dear old girl," a form of address which struck her as at once tender and familiar. At dessert, in order not to give Zoé any more

trouble, they used the same spoon turn and turn about, whilst demolishing a pot of preserve they had discovered at the top of a cupboard.

"Oh, you dear old girl!" said Nana, pushing back the round table, "I haven't made such a good dinner these ten years past!"

Yet it was growing late, and she wanted to send her boy off for fear he should be suspected of all sorts of things. But he kept declaring that he had plenty of time to spare. For the matter of that his clothes were not drying well, and Zoé averred that it would take an hour longer at least; and, as she was dropping with sleep after the fatigues of the journey, they sent her off to bed. After which they were alone in the silent house.

It was a very charming evening. The fire was dying out amid glowing embers, and in the great blue room, where Zoé had made up the bed before going upstairs, the air felt a little oppressive. Nana, overcome by the heavy warmth, got up to open the window for a few minutes, and, as she did so, she uttered a little cry.

"Great heavens, how beautiful it is! Look, dear old girl!"

Georges had come up, and as though the window-bar had not been sufficiently wide, he put his arm round Nana's waist, and rested his head against her shoulder. The weather had undergone a brisk change: the skies were clearing, and a full moon lit up the country with its golden disc of light. A sovran quiet reigned over the valley. It seemed wider and larger as it opened on the immense distances of the plain, where the trees loomed like little shadowy islands amid a shining and waveless lake. And Nana grew tender-hearted, felt herself a child again. Most surely she had dreamed of nights like this at an epoch which she could not recall. Since leaving the train, every object of sensation —the wide countryside, the green things with their pungent scents, the house, the vegetables—had stirred her to such a degree that now it seemed to her as if she had left Paris twenty years ago. Yesterday's existence was far, far away, and she was full of sensations of which she had no previous experience. Georges, meanwhile, was giving her neck little coaxing kisses, and this again added to her sweet unrest. With hesitating hand she pushed him from her, as though he were a child whose affectionate advances are fatiguing, and once more she told him that he ought to take his departure. He did not gainsay her. All in good time —he would go all in good time!

But a bird raised its song, and again was silent. It was a robin, in an elder tree, below the window.

"Wait one moment," whispered Georges; "the lamp's frightening him; I'll put it out."

And when he came back and took her waist again, he added—

"We'll relight it in a minute."

Then as she listened to the robin, and the boy pressed against her side, Nana remembered. Ah, yes, it was in novels that she had got to know all this! In other days she would have given her heart to have a full moon, and robins, and a lad dying of love for her. Great God! she could have cried, so good and charming did it all seem to her! Beyond a doubt she had been born to live

honestly! So she pushed Georges away again, and he grew yet bolder.

"No, let me be: I don't care about it. It would be very wicked at your age. Now listen—I'll always be your mamma."

A sudden feeling of shame overcame her. She was blushing exceedingly, and yet not a soul could see her. The room behind them was full of black night, whilst the country stretched before them in silence and lifeless solitude. Never had she known such a sense of shame before. Little by little, she felt her power of resistance ebbing away, and that despite her embarrassed efforts to the contrary. That disguise of his, that woman's shift and that dressing-jacket, set her laughing again. It was as though a girl-friend were teasing her.

"Oh, it's not right, it's not right!" she stammered, after a last effort.

And with that, in face of the lovely night, she sank like a young virgin into the arms of this mere child. The house slept.

Next morning, at The Fondettes, when the bell rang for lunch, the dining-room table was no longer too big for the company. Fauchery and Daguenet had been driven up together in one carriage, and after them another had arrived with the Count de Vandeuvres, who had followed by the next train. Georges was the last to come downstairs. He was looking a little pale, and his eyes were sunken, but, in answer to questions, he said that he was much better, though he was still somewhat shaken by the violence of the attack. Madame Hugon looked into his eyes with an anxious smile, and adjusted his hair, which had been carelessly combed that morning, but he drew back as though embarrassed by this tender little action. During the meal she chaffed Vandeuvres very pleasantly, and declared that she had expected him for five years past.

"Well, here you are at last! How have you managed it?"

Vandeuvres took her remarks with equal pleasantry. He told her that he had lost a fabulous sum of money at the club yesterday, and thereupon had come away with the intention of ending up in the country.

"'Pon my word, yes, if only you can find me an heiress in these rustic parts! There must be delightful women hereabouts."

The old lady rendered equal thanks to Daguenet and Fauchery for having been so good as to accept her son's invitation, and then, to her great and joyful surprise, she saw the Marquis de Chouard enter the room. A third carriage had brought him.

"Dear me, you've made this your trysting-place to-day!" cried she. "You've passed word round! But what's happening? For years I've never succeeded in bringing you all together, and now you all drop in at once. Oh, I certainly don't complain."

Another place was laid. Fauchery found himself next the Countess Sabine, whose liveliness and gaiety surprised him when he remembered her drooping languid state in the austere Rue Miromesnil drawing-room. Daguenet, on the other hand, who was seated on Estelle's left, seemed slightly put out by his propinquity to that tall silent girl. The angularity of her elbows was disagreeable to him. Muffat and Chouard had exchanged a sly glance, whilst Vandeuvres continued joking about his coming marriage.

"Talking of ladies," Madame Hugon ended by saying, "I have a new neighbour whom you probably know."

And she mentioned Nana. Vaudeuvres affected the liveliest astonishment.

"Well, that is strange! Nana's property near here!"

Fauchery and Daguenet indulged in a similar demonstration, whilst the Marquis de Chouard discussed the breast of a chicken without appearing to comprehend their meaning. Not one of the men had smiled.

"Certainly," continued the old lady, "and the person in question arrived at The Mignotte yesterday evening, as I was saying she would. I got my information from the gardener this morning."

At these words the gentlemen could not conceal their very real surprise. They all looked up. Eh? what? Nana had come down! But they were only expecting her next day: they were privately under the impression that they would arrive before her! Georges alone sat looking at his glass with drooped eyelids and a tired expression. Ever since the beginning of lunch, he had seemed to be sleeping with open eyes and a vague smile on his lips.

"Are you still in pain, my Zizi?" asked his mother, who had been gazing at him throughout the meal.

He started, and blushed as he said that he was very well now, but the worn-out insatiate expression of a girl who has danced too much did not fade from his face.

"What's the matter with your neck?"

resumed Madame Hugon, in an alarmed tone. "It's all red."

He was embarrassed, and stammered. He did not know—he had nothing the matter with his neck. Then, drawing his shirt-collar up,—

"Ah, yes, some insect stung me there!"

The Marquis de Chouard had cast a sidelong glance at the little red place. Muffat, too, looked at Georges. The company was finishing lunch, and planning various excursions. Fauchery was growing increasingly excited with the Countess Sabine's laughter. As he was passing her a dish of fruit, their hands touched, and for one second she looked at him with eyes so full of dark meaning that he once more thought of the secret, which had been communicated to him one evening after an uproarious dinner. Then, too, she was no longer the same woman. Something was more pronounced than of old, and her grey foulard gown, which fitted loosely over her shoulders, added a touch of license to her delicate, high-strung elegance.

When they rose from the table, Daguenet remained behind with Fauchery in order to impart to him the following crude witticism about Estelle: "A nice broomstick that to shove into a man's hands!" Nevertheless, he grew serious when the journalist told him the amount she was worth in the way of dowry.

"Four hundred thousand francs."

"And the mother?" queried Fauchery. "She's all right, eh?"

"Oh! she'll work the oracle! But it's no go, my dear man!"

"Bah! How are we to know? We must wait and see."

It was impossible to go out that day, for the rain was still falling in heavy showers. Georges had made haste to disappear from the scene, and had double-locked his door. These gentlemen avoided mutual explanations, though they were none of them deceived as to the reasons which had brought them together. Vandeuvres, who had had a very bad time at play, had really conceived the notion of lying fallow for a season, and he was counting on Nana's presence in the neighborhood as a safeguard against excessive boredom. Fauchery had taken advantage of the holidays granted him by Rose, who just then was extremely busy. He was thinking of discussing a second notice with Nana, in case country air should render them reciprocally affectionate. Daguenet, who had been just a little sulky with her since Steiner had come upon the scene, was dreaming of resuming the old connection, or at least of snatching some delightful opportunities, if occasion offered. As to the Marquis de Chouard, he was watching for times and seasons. But, among all those men who were busy following in the tracks of Venus—a Venus with the rouge scarce washed from her cheeks—Muffat was at once the most ardent and the most tortured by the novel sensations of desire and fear and anger warring in his anguished members. A formal promise had been made him; Nana was awaiting him. Why, then, had she taken her departure two days sooner than was expected?

He resolved to betake himself to The Mignotte after dinner that same evening.

At night, as the Count was leaving the park, Georges fled forth after him. He left him to follow the road to Gumières, crossed the Choue, rushed into Nana's presence, breathless, furious, and with tears in his eyes. Ah yes, he understood everything! That old fellow, now on his way to her, was coming to keep an appointment! Nana was dumbfounded by this ebullition of jealousy; and, greatly moved by the way things were turning out, she took him in her arms, and comforted him to the best of her ability. Oh, no, he was quite beside the mark; she was expecting no one. If the gentleman came it would not be her fault. What a great ninny that Zizi was to be taking on so about nothing at all! By her child's soul she swore she loved nobody except her own Georges. And with that she kissed him, and wiped away his tears.

"Now just listen! You'll see that it's all for your sake," she went on, when he had grown somewhat calmer. "Steiner has arrived—he's up above there now. You know, duckie, I can't turn *him* out of doors."

"Yes, I know, I'm not talking of *him*," whispered the boy.

"Very well then, I've stuck him into the room at the end. I said I was out of sorts. He's unpacking his trunk. Since nobody's seen you, be quick and run up, and hide in my room, and wait for me."

Georges sprang at her and threw his arms round her neck. It was true after all! She loved him a little! So they would put the lamp out as they did yesterday, and be in the dark till daytime! Then, as the front-door bell sounded, he quietly slipped away. Upstairs, in the bedroom, he at once took off his shoes so as not to make any noise, and straightway crouched down behind a curtain and waited soberly.

Nana welcomed Count Muffat, who, though still shaken with passion, was now somewhat embarrassed. She had pledged her word to him, and would even have liked to keep it since he struck her as a serious, practicable lover. But truly, who could have foreseen all that happened yesterday? There was the voyage, and the house she had never set eyes on before, and the arrival of the drenched little lover! How sweet it had all seemed to her, and how delightful it would be to continue in it! So much the worse for the gentleman! For three months past she had been keeping him dangling after her whilst she affected conventionality in order the further to inflame him. Well, well! He would have to continue dangling, and if he didn't like that he could go! She would sooner have thrown up everything than have played false to Georges.

The Count had seated himself with all the ceremonious politeness becoming a country caller. Only his hands were trembling slightly. Lust, which Nana's skilful tactics daily exasperated, had at last wrought terrible havoc in that sanguine, uncontaminated nature. The grave man, the chamberlain who was wont to tread the state apartments at the Tuileries with slow and dignified step, was now nightly driven to plunge his teeth into his bolster, whilst, with sobs of exasperation, he pictured to himself a sensual shape which never changed. But this time he was determined to make an end of the torture. Coming along the highroad, in the deep quiet of the gloaming, he had meditated a fierce course of action. And the moment he had finished his opening remarks he tried to take hold of Nana with both hands.

"No, no! take care!" she said, simply. She was not vexed; nay, she even smiled.

He caught her again, clenching his teeth as he did so. Then, as she struggled to get free, he coarsely and crudely reminded her that he had come to stay the night. Though much embarrassed at this, Nana did not cease to smile. She took his hands, and spoke very familiarly in order to soften her refusal.

"Come now, darling, do be quiet! Honour bright, I can't: Steiner's upstairs."

But he was beside himself. Never yet had she seen a man in such a state. She grew frightened, and put her hand over his mouth in order to stifle his cries. Then, in lowered tones, she besought him to be quiet and to let her alone. Steiner was coming downstairs. Things were getting stupid, to be sure! When Steiner entered the room, he heard Nana remarking,—

"I adore the country."

She was lounging comfortably back in her deep easy chair, and she turned round and interrupted herself.

"It's Monsieur le Comte Muffat, darling. He saw a light here while he was strolling past, and he came in to bid us welcome."

The two men clasped hands. Muffat, with his face in shadow, stood silent for a moment or two. Steiner seemed sulky. Then they chatted about Paris: business there was at a standstill; abominable things had been happening on 'Change. When a quarter of an hour had elapsed, Muffat took his departure, and, as the young woman was seeing him to the door, he tried, without success to make an assignation for the following night. Steiner went up to bed almost directly afterwards, grumbling, as he did so, at the everlasting little ailments that seemed to afflict the genus courtesan. The two old boys had been packed off at last! When she was able to rejoin him, Nana found Georges still hiding exemplarily behind the curtain. The room was dark. He pulled her down on to the floor, as she sat near him, and together they began playfully rolling on the ground, stopping now and again, and smothering their laughter with kisses whenever they struck their bare feet against some piece of furniture. Far away, on the road to Gumières, Count Muffat walked slowly home, and, hat in hand, bathed his burning forehead in the freshness and silence of the night.

During the days that followed, Nana found life adorable. In the lad's arms she was once more a girl of fifteen, and under the caressing influence of this renewed childhood, love's white flower once more blossomed forth in a nature which had grown hackneyed and disgusted in the service of the other sex. She would experience sudden fits of shame, sudden vivid emotions which left her trembling. She wanted to laugh and to cry, and she was beset by nervous maidenly feelings, mingled with warm desires that made her blush again. Never yet had she felt anything comparable to this. The country filled her with tender thoughts. As a little girl she had long wished to dwell in a meadow, tending a goat, because one day, on the talus of the fortifications, she had seen a goat bleating at the end of its tether. Now, this estate, this stretch of land belonging to her, simply swelled her heart to bursting, so utterly had her old ambition been surpassed. Once again she tasted the novel sensations experienced by chits of girls, and at night, when she went upstairs, dizzy with her day in the open air, and intoxicated by the scent of green leaves, and rejoined her Zizi behind the curtain, she fancied herself a school-girl enjoying a holiday escapade. It was an amour, she thought, with a young cousin, to whom she was going to be married. And so she trembled at the slightest noise, and dread lest parents should hear her, whilst making the delicious experiments and suffering the voluptuous terrors attendant on a girl's first slip from the path of virtue.

Nana in those days was subject to the fancies a sentimental girl will indulge in. She would gaze at the moon for hours. One night she had a mind to go down into the garden with Georges, when all the household was asleep. When there, they strolled under the trees, their arms round each other's waists, and finally went and laid down in the grass, where the dew soaked them through and through. On another occasion, after a long silence up in the bedroom, she fell sobbing on the lad's neck, declaring in broken accents that she was afraid of dying. She would often croon a favourite ballad of Madame Lerat's, which was full of flowers and birds. The song would melt her to tears, and she would break off in order to clasp Georges in a passionate embrace, and to extract from him vows of undying affection. In short she was extremely silly, as she herself would admit when they both became jolly good fellows again, and sat up smoking cigarettes on the edge of the bed, dangling their bare legs over it the while, and tapping their heels against its wooden side.

But what utterly melted the young woman's heart was Louiset's arrival. She had an access of maternal affection which was as violent as a mad fit. She would carry off her boy into the sunshine outside to watch him kicking about; she would dress him like a little prince and roll with him in the grass. The moment he arrived she decided that he was to sleep near her, in the room next hers, where Madame Lerat, whom the country greatly affected, used to begin snoring the moment her head touched the pillow. Louiset did not hurt Zizi's position in the least. On the contrary, Nana said that she had now two children, and she treated them with the same wayward tenderness. At night, more than ten times running, she would leave Zizi to go and see if Louiset were breathing properly, but on her return she would re-embrace her Zizi, and lavish on him the caresses that had been destined for the child. She played at being mamma, whilst he wickedly enjoyed being dandled in the arms of the great wench and allowed himself to be rocked to and fro like a baby that is being sent to sleep. It was all so delightful, and Nana was so charmed with her present existence, that she seriously proposed to him never to leave the country. They would send all the other people away, and he, she, and the child would live alone. And with that they would make a thousand plans till day-break, and never once hear Madame Lerat as she snored vigorously after the fatigues of a day spent in picking country flowers.

This charming existence lasted nearly

a week. Count Muffat used to come every evening, and go away again with disordered face and burning hands. One evening he was not even received, as Steiner had been obliged to run up to Paris. He was told that *Madame* was not well. Nana grew daily more disgusted at the notion of deceiving Georges. He was such an innocent lad, and he had such faith in her! She would have looked on herself as the lowest of the low had she played him false. Besides, it would have sickened her to do so! Zoé, who took her part in this affair in mute disdain, believed that *Madame* was growing senseless.

On the sixth day a band of visitors suddenly blundered into Nana's idyl. She had, indeed, invited a whole swarm of people under the belief that none of them would come. And so, one fine afternoon, she was vastly astonished and annoyed to see an omnibus full of people pulling up outside the gate of La Mignotte.

"It's us!" cried Mignon, getting down first from the conveyance, and extracting then his sons, Henri and Charles.

Labordette thereupon appeared, and began handing out an interminable file of ladies—Lucy Stewart, Caroline Héquet, Tatan Néné, Maria Blond. Nana was in hopes that they would end there, when la Faloise sprang from the step in order to receive Gaga and her daughter Amélie in his trembling arms. That brought the number up to eleven people. Their installation proved a laborious undertaking. There were five spare rooms at The Mignotte, one of which was already occupied by Madame Lerat and Louiset. The largest was devoted to the Gaga and la Faloise establishment, and it was

decided that Amélie should sleep on a truckle bed in the dressing-room at the side. Mignon and his two sons had the third room, Labordette the fourth. There thus remained one room, which was transformed into a dormitory with four beds in it, for Lucy, Caroline, Tatan and Maria. As to Steiner, he would sleep on the divan in the drawing-room. At the end of an hour, when everyone was duly settled, Nana, who had begun by being furious, grew enchanted at the thought of playing hostess on a grand scale. The ladies complimented her on The Mignotte. "It's a stunning property, my dear!" And then too they brought her quite a whiff of Parisian air, and talking all together with bursts of laughter, and exclamation, and emphatic little gestures, they gave her all the petty gossip of the week just past. By-the-by, and how about Bordenave? What had he said about her prank? Oh, nothing much! After bawling about having her brought back by the police, he had simply put somebody else in her place at night. Little Violaine was the understudy, and she had even obtained a very pretty success as the Blonde Venus. Which piece of news made Nana rather serious.

It was only four o'clock in the afternoon, and there was some talk of taking a stroll around.

"Oh, I haven't told you," said Nana, "I was just off to get up potatoes when you arrived."

Thereupon they all wanted to go and dig potatoes without even changing their dresses first. It was quite a party. The gardener and two helpers were already in the potato field at the end of the grounds. The ladies knelt down, and began fumbling in the mould with their be-ringed fingers, shouting gaily whenever they discovered a potato of exceptional size. It struck them as so amusing! But Tatan Néné was in a state of triumph! So many were the potatoes she had gathered in her youth, that she forgot herself entirely, and gave the others much good advice, treating them like geese the while. The gentlemen toiled less strenuously. Mignon looked every inch the good citizen and father, and made his stay in the country an occasion for completing his boys' education. Indeed, he spoke to them of Parmentier!

Dinner that evening was wildly hilarious. The company ate ravenously. Nana, in a state of great elevation, had a warm disagreement with her butler, an individual who had been in service at the bishop's palace in Orleans. The ladies smoked over their coffee. An ear-splitting noise of merry-making issued from the open windows, and died out far away under the serene evening sky, whilst peasants, belated in the lanes, turned and looked at the flaring rooms.

"It's most tiresome that you're going back the day after to-morrow," said Nana. "But never mind, we'll get up an excursion all the same!"

They decided to go on the morrow, Sunday, and visit the ruins of the old Abbey of Chamont, which were some seven kilomètres distant. Five carriages would come out from Orleans, take up the company after lunch, and bring them back to dinner at The Mignotte at about seven. It would be delightful.

That evening, as his wont was, Count Muffat mounted the hill to ring at the outer gate. But the brightly-lit windows and the shouts of laughter astonished him. When, however, he recognised Mignon's voice, he understood it all, and went off, raging at this new obstacle, driven to extremities, bent on some violent act. Georges passed through a little door, of which he had the key, slipped along the staircase walls, and went quietly up into Nana's room. Only he had to wait for her till past midnight. She appeared at last in a high state of intoxication, and more maternal even than on the previous nights. Whenever she had drunk anything she became so amorous as to be absurd. Accordingly, she now insisted on his accompanying her to the Abbaye de Chamont. But he stood out against this; he was afraid of being seen: if he were to be seen driving with her, there would be an atrocious scandal. But she burst into tears, and evinced the noisy despair of a slighted woman. And he thereupon consoled her, and formally promised to be one of the party.

"So you do love me very much," she blurted out. "Say you love me very much. Oh, my darling old bear, if I were to die, would you feel it very much? Confess!"

At The Fondettes, the near neighbourhood of Nana had utterly disorganised the party. Every morning, during lunch, good Madame Hugon returned to the subject despite herself, told her guests the news the gardener had brought her, and gave evidence of the absorbing curiosity with which notorious courtesans are able to inspire even the worthiest old ladies. Tolerant though she was, she was revolted and maddened by a vague presentiment of coming ill, which frightened her in the evenings as thoroughly as if a wild beast had escaped from a menagerie and were known to be lurking in the countryside.

She began trying to pick a little quarrel with her guests, whom she each and all accused of prowling round The Mignotte. Count Vandeuvres had been seen laughing on the high road with a golden-haired lady; but he defended himself against the accusation, he denied that it was Nana, the fact being that Lucy had been with him and had told him how she had just turned her third prince out of doors. The Marquis de Chouard used also to go out every day, but his excuse was doctor's orders. Towards Daguenet and Fauchery Madame Hugon behaved unjustly too. The former especially never left The Fondettes, for he had given up the idea of renewing the old connection, and was busy paying the most respectful attentions to Estelle. Fauchery also stayed with the Muffat ladies. On one occasion only he had met Mignon with an armful of flowers, putting his sons through a course of botanical instruction in a by-path. The two men had shaken hands, and given each other the news about Rose. She was perfectly well and happy: they had both received a letter from her that morning, in which she besought them to profit by the fresh country air for some days longer. Among all her guests the old lady spared only Count Muffat and Georges. The Count, who said he had serious business in Orleans, could certainly not be running after the bad woman, and as to Georges, the poor child was at last causing her grave anxiety, seeing that every evening he was seized with atrocious sick

headaches which kept him to his bed in broad daylight.

Meanwhile, Fauchery had become the Countess Sabine's faithful attendant in the absence, during each afternoon, of Count Muffat. Whenever they went to the end of the park, he carried her camp-stool and her sunshade. Besides, he amused her with the original witticisms peculiar to a second-rate journalist, and in so doing he prompted her to one of those sudden intimacies which are allowable in the country. She had apparently consented to it from the first, for she had grown quite a girl again in the society of a young man whose noisy humour seemed unlikely to compromise her. But now and again, when for a second or two they found themselves alone behind the shrubs, their eyes would meet, they would pause amid their laughter, grow suddenly serious, and view one another darkly, as though they had fathomed and divined their inmost hearts.

On Friday a fresh place had to be laid at lunch-time. Monsieur Théophile Venot, whom Madame Hugon remembered to have invited at the Muffats' last winter, had just arrived. He sat stooping humbly forward, and behaved with much good nature, as became a man of no account, nor did he seem to notice the anxious deference with which he was treated. When he had succeeded in getting the company to forget his presence, he sat nibbling small lumps of sugar during dessert, looking sharply up at Daguenet as the latter handed Estelle strawberries, and listening to Fauchery, who was making the Countess very merry over one of his anecdotes. Whenever anyone looked at *him*, he smiled in his quiet way. When the guests rose from table, he took the Count's arm, and drew him into the park. He was known to have exercised great influence over the latter ever since the death of his mother. Indeed, singular stories were told about the kind of dominion which the ex-lawyer enjoyed in that household. Fauchery, whom his arrival doubtless embarassed, began explaining to Georges and Daguenet the origin of the man's wealth. It was a big lawsuit, with the management of which the Jesuits had entrusted him in days gone by. In his opinion, the worthy man was a terrible fellow, despite his gentle plump face, and at this time of day had his finger in all the intrigues of the priesthood. The two young men had begun joking at this, for they thought the little old gentleman had an idiotic expression. The idea of an unknown Venot, a gigantic Venot, acting for the whole body of the clergy, struck them in the light of a comical invention. But they were silenced when, still leaning on the old man's arm, Count Muffat reappeared with blanched cheeks and eyes reddened as if by recent weeping.

"I bet they've been chatting about hell," muttered Fauchery, in a bantering tone.

The Countess Sabine overheard the remark. She turned her head slowly, and their eyes met in that long gaze with which they were accustomed to sound one another prudently before venturing once for all.

After the breakfast it was the guests' custom to betake themselves to a little flower-garden on a terrace overlooking the plain. This Sunday afternoon was exquisitely mild. There had been signs

of rain towards ten in the morning, but the sky, without ceasing to be covered, had, as it were, melted into milky fog, which now hung like a cloud of luminous dust in the golden sunlight. Soon Madame Hugon proposed that they should step down through a little doorway below the terrace, and take a walk on foot in the direction of Gumières and as far as the Choue. She was fond of walking, and, considering her threescore years, was very active. Besides, all her guests declared that there was no need to drive. So, in a somewhat straggling order, they reached the wooden bridge over the river. Fauchery and Daguenet headed the column with the Muffat ladies, and were followed by the Count and the Marquis, walking on either side of Madame Hugon, whilst Vandeuvres, looking fashionable and out of his element on the high road, marched in the rear, smoking a cigar. Monsieur Venot, now slackening, now hastening his pace, passed smilingly from group to group, as though bent on losing no scrap of conversation.

"To think of poor dear Georges at Orleans!" said Madame Hugon. "He was anxious to consult old Doctor Tavernier, who never goes out now, on the subject of his sick headaches. Yes, you were not up, as he went off before seven o'clock. But it'll be a change for him all the same."

She broke off, exclaiming,—

"Why, what's making them stop on the bridge?"

The fact was the ladies, and Fauchery and Daguenet, were standing stock-still on the crown of the bridge. They seemed to be hesitating as though some obstacle or other rendered them uneasy, and yet the way lay clear before them. "Go on!" cried the Count.

They never moved, and seemed to be watching the approach of something, which the rest had not yet observed. Indeed the road wound considerably, and was bordered by a thick screen of poplar trees. Nevertheless, a dull sound began to grow momentarily louder, and soon there was a noise of wheels, mingled with shouts of laughter and the cracking of whips. Then, suddenly, five carriages came into view, driving one behind the other. They were crowded to bursting, and bright with a galaxy of white, blue, and pink costumes.

"What is it?" said Madame Hugon, in some surprise.

Then her instinct told her, and she felt indignant at such an untoward invasion of her road.

"Oh, that woman!" she murmured. "Walk on, pray walk on. Don't appear to notice——"

But it was too late. The five carriages, which were taking Nana and her circle to the ruins of Chamont, rolled on to the narrow wooden bridge. Fauchery, Daguenet, and the Muffat ladies were forced to step backward, whilst Madame Hugon and the others had also to stop in Indian file, along the roadside. It was a superb ride-past! The laughter in the carriages had ceased, and faces were turned with an expression of curiosity. The rival parties took stock of each other amid a silence broken only by the measured trot of the horses. In the first carriage, Maria Blond and Tatan Néné were lolling backwards like a pair of duchesses, their skirts swelling forth over the wheels, and as they passed they cast disdainful glances at the honest women who were walking afoot. Then came Gaga, filling up a whole seat, and half smothering la Faloise beside her, so that little but his small anxious face was visible. Next followed Caroline Héquet with Labordette, Lucy Stewart with Mignon and his boys, and at the close of all Nana in a victoria with Steiner, and on a bracket-seat in front of her, that poor darling Zizi, with his knees jammed against her own.

"It's the last of them, isn't it?" the Countess placidly asked Fauchery, pretending, at the same time, not to recognise Nana.

The wheel of the victoria came near grazing her, but she did not step back. The two women had exchanged a deeply significant glance. It was, in fact, one of those momentary scrutinies which are at once complete and definite. As to the men, they behaved unexceptionably. Fauchery and Daguenet looked icy, and recognised no one. The Marquis, more nervous than they, and afraid of some farcical ebullition on the part of the ladies, had plucked a blade of grass and was rolling it between his fingers. Only Vandeuvres, who had stayed somewhat apart from the rest of the company, winked imperceptibly at Lucy, who smiled at him as she passed.

"Be careful!" Monsieur Venot had whispered, as he stood behind Count Muffat.

The latter in extreme agitation gazed after this illusive vision of Nana, whilst his wife turned slowly round and scrutinised him. Then he cast his eyes on the ground as though to escape the sound of galloping hoofs which were sweeping away both his senses and his heart. He could have cried aloud in his agony, for, seeing Georges among Nana's skirts, he understood it all now. A mere child! He was broken-hearted at the thought that she should have preferred a mere child to him! Steiner was his equal, but that child——!

Madame Hugon, in the mean time, had not at once recognised Georges. Crossing the bridge, he was fain to jump into the river, but Nana's knees restrained him. Then white as a sheet, and icy cold, he sat rigidly up in his place, and looked at no one. It was just possible no one would notice him.

"Oh, my God!" said the old lady, suddenly, "Georges is with her!"

The carriages had passed quite through the uncomfortable crowd of people who recognised and yet gave no sign of recognition. The short critical encounter seemed to have been going on for ages. And now the wheels whirled away the carriage-loads of girls more gaily than ever. Towards the fair open country they went, amid the buffetings of the fresh air of heaven. Bright-coloured fabrics fluttered in the wind, and the merry laughter burst forth anew, as the voyagers began jesting and glancing back at the respectable folk halting with looks of annoyance at the roadside. Turning round, Nana could see the walking party hesitating, and then returning the way they had come, without crossing the bridge. Madame Hugon was leaning silently on Count Muffat's arm, and so sad was her look that no one dared comfort her.

"I say, did you see Fauchery, dear?" Nana shouted to Lucy, who was leaning out of the carriage in front. "What a brute he was! He shall pay out for that. And Paul, too, a fellow I've been

so kind to! Not a sign! They're polite, *I'm* sure!"

And with that she gave Steiner a terrible dressing, he having ventured to suggest that the gentlemen's attitude had been quite as it should be. So then, they weren't even worth a bow? The first blackguard that came by might insult them? Thanks! He was the right sort, too, he was! It couldn't be better! One ought always to bow to a woman.

"Who's the tall one?" asked Lucy at random, shouting through the noise of the wheels.

"It's the Countess Muffat," answered Steiner.

"There now! I suspected as much," said Nana. "Now, my dear fellow, it's all very well her being a Countess, for she's no better than she should be. Yes, yes, she's no better than she should be. You know I've got an eye for such things, I have! And now I know your Countess as well as if I had been at the making of her! I'll bet you that she's the mistress of that viper Fauchery! I tell you she's his mistress! Between women, you guess that sort of thing at once!"

Steiner shrugged his shoulders. Since the previous day his irritation had been hourly increasing. He had received letters which necessitated his leaving the following morning, added to which he did not much appreciate coming down to the country in order to sleep on the drawing-room divan.

"And this poor baby boy!" Nana continued, melting suddenly at sight of Georges's pale face, as he still sat rigid and breathless in front of her.

"D'you think Mamma recognised me?" he stammered at last.

"Oh, most surely she did! Why, she cried out! But it's my fault. He didn't want to come with us: I forced him to. Now listen, Zizi, would you like me to write to your mamma? She looks such a kind, decent sort of lady! I'll tell her that I never saw you before, and that it was Steiner who brought you with him for the first time to-day."

"No, no, don't write," said Georges, in great anxiety. "I'll explain it all myself. Besides, if they bother me about it, I shan't go home again."

But he continued plunged in thought, racking his brains for excuses against his return home in the evening. The five carriages were rolling through a flat country, along an interminable straight road bordered by fine trees. The country was bathed in a silvery grey atmosphere. The ladies still continued shouting remarks from carriage to carriage behind the backs of the drivers, who chuckled over their extraordinary fares. Occasionally one of them would rise to her feet to look at the landscape, and, supporting herself on neighbour's shoulder, would grow extremely excited till a sudden jolt brought her down to the seat again. Caroline Héquet, in the mean time, was having a warm discussion with Labordette. Both of them were agreed that Nana would be selling her country house before three months were out, and Caroline was urging Labordette to buy it back for her for as little as it was likely to fetch. In front of them, la Faloise, who was very amorous, and could not get at Gaga's apopletic neck, was imprinting kisses on her spine, through her dress, the strained fabric of which was nigh splitting, whilst Amélie, perching stiffly on the bracket-

seat, was bidding them be quiet, for she was horrified to be sitting idly by watching her mother being kissed. In the next carriage, Mignon, in order to astonish Lucy, was making his sons recite a fable by La Fontaine. Henri was prodigious at this exercise: he could spout you one without pause or hesitation. But Maria Blond, at the head of the procession, was beginning to feel extremely bored. She was tired of hoaxing that blockhead of a Tatan Néné with a story to the effect that the Parisian dairy-women were wont to fabricate eggs with a mixture of paste and saffron. The distance was too great: were they never going to get to their destination? And the question was transmitted from carriage to carriage, and finally reached Nana, who, after questioning her driver, got up and shouted,—

"We've not got a quarter of an hour more to go. You see that church behind the trees down there."

Then she continued,—

"Do you know, it appears the owner of the Château de Chamont is an old lady of Napoleon's time? Oh, *she* was a merry one! At least, so Joseph told me, and he heard it from the servants at the bishop's palace. There's no one like it nowadays, and for the matter of that, she's become goody-goody."

"What's her name?" asked Lucy.

"Madame d'Anglars."

"Irma d'Anglars, I knew her!" cried Gaga.

Admiring exclamations burst from the line of carriages, and were borne down the wind, as the horses quickened their trot. Heads were stretched out in Gaga's direction; Maria Blond and Tatan Néné turned round an knelt on the seat, while they leant over the carriage-hood; and the air was full of questions and cutting remarks, tempered by a certain obscure admiration. Gaga had known her! The idea filled them all with respect for that far-off past. "Dear me, I was young then," continued Gaga. "But never mind, I remember it all: I saw her pass. They said she was disgusting in her own house, but, driving in her carriage, she *was* just smart! And the stunning tales about her! Dirty doings and money flung about like one o'clock! I don't wonder at all that she's got a fine place. Why she used to clean out a man's pockets as soon as look at him. Irma d'Anglars still in the land of the living! Why, my little pets, she must be near ninety."

At this the ladies became suddenly serious. Ninety years old! The deuce, there wasn't one of them, as Lucy loudly declared, who would live to that age. They were all done for. Besides, Nana said she didn't want to make old bones; it wouldn't be amusing. They were drawing near their destination, and the conversation was interrupted by the cracking of whips as the drivers put their horses to their best paces. Yet, amid all the noise, Lucy continued talking, and, suddenly changing the subject, urged Nana to come to town with them all tomorrow. The Exhibition was soon to close, and the ladies must really return to Paris, where the season was surpassing their expectations. But Nana was obstinate. She loathed Paris; she wouldn't set foot there yet!

"Eh, darling, we'll stay?" said she, giving Georges's knees a squeeze, as though Steiner were of no account.

The carriages had pulled up abruptly, and, in some surprise, the company got out on some waste ground at the bottom of a small hill. With his whip one of the drivers had to point them out the ruins of the old Abbey of Chamont, where they lay hidden among trees. It was a great sell! The ladies voted them silly. Why, they were only a heap of old stones, with briers growing over them, and part of a tumble-down tower. It really wasn't worth coming a couple of leagues to see that! Then the driver pointed out to them the country-seat, the park of which stretched away from the Abbey, and he advised them to take a little path and follow the walls surrounding it. They would thus make the tour of the place, whilst the carriages would go and await them in the village square. It was a delightful walk, and the company agreed to the proposition.

"Lord love me, Irma knows how to take care of herself!" said Gaga, halting before a gate at the corner of the park wall abutting on the high road.

All of them stood silently gazing at the enormous bush which stopped up the gateway. Then, following the little path, they skirted the park wall, looking up from time to time to admire the trees, whose lofty branches stretched out over them and formed a dense vault of greenery. After three minutes or so they found themselves in front of a second gate. Through this a wide lawn was visible, over which two venerable oaks cast dark masses of shadow. Three minutes further on yet another gate afforded them an extensive view of a great avenue, a perfect corridor of shadow, at the end of which a bright spot of sunlight gleamed like a star. They stood in silent, wondering admiration, and then, little by little, exclamations burst from their lips. They had been trying hard to joke about it all, with a touch of envy at heart, but this decidedly and immeasurably impressed them. What a genius that Irma was! A sight like this gave you a rattling notion of the woman! The trees stretched away and away, and there were endlessly recurrent patches of ivy along the will, with glimpses of lofty roofs, and screens of poplars interspersed with dense masses of elms and aspens. Was there no end to it, then? The ladies would have liked to catch sight of the mansion-house, for they were weary of circling on and on, weary of seeing nothing but leafy recesses through every opening they came to. They took the rails of the gate in their hands, and pressed their faces against the iron-work. And thus excluded and isolated, a feeling of respect began to overcome them, as they thought of the castle lost to view in surrounding immensity. Soon, being quite unused to walking, they grew tired. And the wall did not leave off; at every turn of the small deserted path the same range of grey stones stretched ahead of them. Some of them began to despair of ever getting to the end of it, and began talking of returning. But the more their long walk fatigued them, the more respectful they became, for at each successive step they were increasingly impressed by the tranquil, lordly dignity of the domain.

"It's getting silly, this is!" said Caroline Héquet, grinding her teeth.

Nana silenced her with a shrug. For some moments past she had been rather pale and extremely serious, and had not spoken a single word. Suddenly the path

gave a final turn, the wall ended, and as they came out on the village square, the mansion-house stood before them, on the further side of its grand outer court. All stopped to admire the proud sweep of the wide steps, the twenty frontage windows, the arrangement of the three wings, which were built of brick framed by courses of stone. Henri IV. had erewhile inhabited this historic mansion, and his room, with its great bed hung with Genoa velvet, was still preserved there. Breathless with admiration, Nana gave a little childish sigh.

"Great God!" she whispered very quietly to herself.

But the party were deeply moved when Gaga suddenly announced that Irma herself was standing yonder, in front of the church. She recognised her perfectly. She was as upright as of old, the hoary campaigner, and that despite her age, and she still had those eyes which flashed when she moved in that proud way of hers! Vespers were just over, and, for a second or two, *Madame* stood in the church porch. She was dressed in a dark brown silk, and looked very simple and very tall, her venerable face reminding one of some old marquise who had survived the horrors of the Great Revolution. In her right hand a huge Book of Hours shone in the sunlight, and very slowly, she crossed the square, followed some fifteen paces off by a footman in livery. The church was emptying, and all the inhabitants of Chamont bowed before her with extreme respect. An old man even kissed her hand, and a woman wanted to fall on her knees. Truly this was a potent queen, full of years and honours. She mounted her flight of steps, and vanished from view. "That's what one attains to when one has methodical habits!" said Mignon, with an air of conviction, looking at his sons and improving the occasion. Then everybody said his say. Labordette thought her extraordinarily well preserved. Maria Blond let slip a foul expression, and vexed Lucy, who declared that one ought to honour grey hairs. All the women, to sum up, agreed that she was a perfect marvel. Then the company got into their conveyances again. From Chamont all the way to La Mignotte Nana remained silent. She had twice turned round to look back at the house, and now, lulled by the sound of the wheels, she forgot that Steiner was at her side and that Georges was in front of her. A vision had come up out of the twilight, and the great lady seemed still to be sweeping by with all the majesty of a potent queen, full of years and of honours.

That evening Georges re-entered The Fondettes in time for dinner. Nana, who had grown increasingly absent-minded and singular in point of manner, had sent him to ask his mamma's forgiveness. It was his plain duty, she remarked severely, growing suddenly solicitious for the decencies of family life. She even made him swear not to return for the night; she was tired, and, in shewing proper obedience, he was doing no more than his duty. Much bored by this moral discourse, Georges appeared in his mother's presence with heavy heart and downcast head.

Fortunately for him, his brother Philippe, a great merry devil of a military man, had arrived during the day, a

fact which greatly curtailed the scene he was dreading. Madame Hugon was content to look at him with eyes full of tears, whilst Philippe, who had been put in possession of the facts, threatened to go and drag him home by the scruff of the neck if ever he went back into that woman's society. Somewhat comforted, Georges began slyly planning how to make his escape towards two o'clock next day in order to arrange about future meetings with Nana.

Nevertheless, at dinner-time, the house party at The Fondettes seemed not a little embarrassed. Vandeuvres had given notice of departure, for he was anxious to take Lucy back to Paris with him. He was amused at the idea of carrying off this girl whom he had known for ten years, yet never desired. The Marquis de Chouard bent over his plate, and meditated on Gaga's young lady. He could well remember dandling Lili on his knee. What a way children had of shooting up! This little thing was becoming extremely plump! But Count Muffat especially was silent and absorbed. His cheeks glowed, and he had given Georges one long look. Dinner over, he went upstairs, intending to shut himself in his bedroom, his pretext being a slight feverish attack. Monsieur Venot had rushed after him, and upstairs, in the bedroom, a scene ensued. The Count threw himself upon the bed, and strove to stifle a fit of nervous sobbing in the folds of the pillow, whilst Monsieur Venot, in a soft voice, called him brother, and advised him to implore Heaven for mercy. But he heard nothing: there was a rattle in his throat. Suddenly he sprang off the bed, and stammered:

"I am going there. I can't resist any longer."

"Very well," said the old man, "I go with you."

As they left the house, two shadows were vanishing into the dark depths of a garden walk, for every evening now Fauchery and the Countess Sabine left Daguenet to help Estelle make tea. Once on the high road the Count walked so rapidly that his companion had to run in order to follow him. Though utterly out of breath, the latter never ceased showering on him the most conclusive arguments against the temptations of the flesh. But the other never opened his mouth as he hurried away into the night. Arrived in front of The Mignotte, he said simply,—

"I can't resist any longer. Go!"

"God's will be done, then!" muttered Monsieur Venot. "He uses every method to assure His final triumph. Your sin will become His weapon."

At The Mignotte there was much wrangling during the evening meal. Nana had found a letter from Bordenave awaiting her, in which he advised rest, just as though he were anxious to be rid of her. Little Violaine, he said, was being encored twice nightly. But when Mignon continued urging her to come away with them on the morrow, Nana grew exasperated, and declared that she did not intend taking advice from anybody. In other ways, too, her behaviour at table was ridiculously stuck-up. Madame Lerat having made some sharp little speech or other, she loudly announced that, God willing, she wasn't going to let anyone—no, not even her own aunt—make improper remarks in her presence. After which, she dreed her guests with honourable sentiments. She seemed to be suffering from a fit of stupid right-mindedness, and she treated them all to projects of religious education for Louiset and to a complete scheme of regeneration for herself. When the company began laughing, she gave vent to profound opinions, nodding her head like a grocer's wife who knows what she is saying. Nothing but Order could lead to Fortune! And, so far as she was concerned, she had no wish to die like a beggar! She set the ladies' teeth on edge. They burst out in protest. Could anyone have been converting Nana? No, it was impossible! But she sat quite still, and with absent looks once more plunged into dreamland, where the vision of an extremely-wealthy and greatly-courted Nana rose up before her.

The household were going upstairs to bed when Muffat put in an appearance. It was Labordette who caught sight of him in the garden. He understood it all at once, and did him a service, for he got Steiner out of the way, and, taking his hand, led him along the dark corridor as far as Nana's bedroom. In affairs of this kind, Labordette was wont to display the most perfect tact and cleverness. Indeed he seemed delighted to be making other people happy. Nana shewed no surprise: she was only somewhat annoyed by the excessive heat of Muffat's pursuit. Life was a serious affair, was it not? Love was too silly: it led to nothing. Besides, she had her scruples in view of Zizi's tender age. Indeed, she had scarcely behaved quite fairly towards him. Dear me yes, she was choosing the proper course again in taking up with an old fellow.

"Zoé," said she to the lady's maid, who was enchanted at the thought of leaving the country, "pack the trunks when you get up to-morrow. We are going back to Paris."

And she went to bed with Muffat, but experienced no pleasure.

## CHAPTER VII

ONE December evening, three months afterwards, Count Muffat was strolling in the Passage des Panoramas. The evening was very mild, and owing to a passing shower the passage had just become crowded with people. There was a perfect mob of them, and they thronged slowly and laboriously along between the shops on either side. Under the windows, white with reflected light, the pavement was violently illuminated. A perfect stream of brilliancy emanated from white globes, red lanterns, blue transparencies, lines of gas-jets, gigantic watches and fans, outlined in flame and burning in the open. And the motley displays in the shops, the gold ornaments of the jewellers, the glass ornaments of the confectioners, the light-coloured silks of the modistes, seemed to shine again in the crude light of the reflectors behind the clear plate glass windows; whilst, among the bright-coloured disorderly array of shop-signs, a huge purple glove loomed in the distance, like a bleeding hand which had been severed from an arm and fastened to a yellow cuff.

Count Muffat had slowly returned as far as the boulevard. He glanced out at the roadway, and then came sauntering back along the shop-windows. The damp and heated atmosphere filled the narrow passage with a slight luminous mist. Along the flagstones, which had been wetted by the drip-drop of umbrellas, the footsteps of the crowd rang continually, but there was no sound of voices. Passers-by elbowed him at every turn, and cast enquiring looks at his silent face, which the gaslight rendered pale. And to escape these curious manifestations the Count posted himself in front of a stationer's, where with profound attention he contemplated an array of paper-weights in the form of glass bowls containing floating landscapes and flowers.

He was conscious of nothing: he was thinking of Nana. Why had she lied to him again? That morning she had written and told him not to trouble about her in the evening, her excuse being that Louiset was ill, and that she was going to pass the night at her aunt's in order to nurse him. But he had felt suspicious, and had called at her house, where he learnt from the porter that *Madame* had just gone off to her theatre. He was astonished at this, for she was not playing in the new piece. Why then should she have told him this falsehood, and what could she be doing at the Variétés that evening? Hustled by a passer-by, the Count unconsciously left the paper-weights, and found himself in front of a glass case full of toys, where he grew absorbed over an array of pocket-books and cigar-cases, all of which had the same blue swallow stamped on one corner. Nana was most certainly not the same woman! In the early days after his return from the country, she used to drive him wild with delight, as with pussy-cat caresses she kissed him all round his face and whiskers, and vowed that he was her own dear pet and the only little man she adored. He was no longer afraid of Georges, whom his mother kept down at The Fondettes. There was only fat Steiner to reckon with, and he believed he was really ousting him, but he did not dare provoke an explanation on his score. He knew he was once more in an extraordinary financial scrape, and on the verge of being declared bankrupt on 'Change, so much so that he was clinging fiercely to the shareholders in the Landes Salt Pits, and striving to sweat a final subscription out of them. Whenever he met him at Nana's, she would explain, reasonably enough, that she did not wish to turn him out of doors like a dog, after all he had spent on her. Besides, for the last three months, he had been living in such a whirl of sensual excitement, that, beyond the need of possessing her, he had felt no very distinct impressions. His was a tardy awakening of the fleshly instinct, a childish greed of enjoyment, which left no room for either vanity or jealousy. Only one definite feeling could affect him now, and that was Nana's decreasing kindness. She no longer kissed him on the beard! It made him anxious; and as became a man quite ignorant of womankind, he began asking himself what possible cause of offence he could have given her. Besides, he was under the impression that he was satisfying all her desires. And so he harked back again and again to the letter he had received that morning with its tissue of falsehoods, invented for the extremely simple purpose of passing an evening at her own theatre. The crowd had pushed him forward again, and he had crossed the passage and was puzzling his brain in front of the entrance to a restaurant, his eyes fixed on some plucked larks and on a huge salmon laid out inside the window.

At length he seemed to tear himself away from this spectacle. He shook himself, looked up, and noticed that it was close on nine o'clock. Nana would soon be coming out, and he would make her tell the truth. And with that he walked on, and recalled to memory the evenings he once passed in that region in the days when he used to meet her at the door of the theatre.

He knew all the shops, and in the gas-laden air he recognized their different scents, such, for instance, as the strong savour of Russia leather, the perfume of vanilla emanating from a chocolate-dealer's basement, the savour of musk blown in whiffs from the open doors of the perfumers. But he did not dare linger under the gaze of the pale shop-women, who looked placidly at him as though they knew him by sight. For one instant he seemed to be studying the line of little round windows above the shops, as though he had never noticed them before among the medley of signs. Then, once again, he went up to the boulevard, and stood still a minute or two. A fine rain was now falling, and the cold feel of it on his hands calmed him. He thought of his wife who was staying in a country house near Mâcon, where her friend Madame de Chezelles had been ailing a good deal since the autumn. The carriages in the roadway were rolling through a stream of mud. The country, he thought, must be detestable in such vile weather. But suddenly he became anxious and re-entered the hot, close passage, down which he strode among the strolling people. A thought had struck him: if Nana were suspicious of his presence there, she would be off along the Galerie Montmartre.

After that, the Count kept a sharp look-out at the very door of the theatre, though he did not like this passage-end, where he was afraid of being recognised. It was at the corner between the Galerie des Variétés and the Galerie Saint-Marc, an equivocal corner full of obscure little shops. Of these last one was a shoemaker's, where customers never seemed to enter. Then there were two or three upholsterers', deep in dust, and a smoky, sleepy reading-room and library, the shaded lamps in which cast a green and slumbrous light all the evening through. There was never anyone in this corner save well-dressed, patient gentlemen, who prowled about the wreckage peculiar to a stage-door, where drunken scene-shifters and ragged chorus-girls congregate. In front of the theatre, a single gas-jet, in a ground-glass globe, lit up the doorway. For a moment or two Muffat thought of questioning Madame Bron; then he grew afraid lest Nana should get wind of his presence and escape by way of the boulevard. So he went on the march again, and determined to wait till he was turned out at the closing of the gates, an event which had happened on two previous occasions. The thought of returning home to his solitary bed simply wrung his heart with anguish. Every time that golden-haired girls and men in dirty linen came out and stared at him, he returned to his post in front of the reading-room, where, looking in between two advertisements posted on a window-pane, he was always greeted by the same sight. It was a little old man, sitting stiff and solitary at the vast table, and holding a green newspaper in his green hands under the green light of one of the lamps. But shortly before ten o'clock, another gentleman, a tall, good-looking, fair man, with well-fitting gloves, was also walking up and down in front of the stage-door. Thereupon, at each successive turn, the pair treated each other to a suspicious sidelong glance. The Count walked to the corner of the two galleries, which was adorned with a high mirror, and when he saw himself therein, looking grave and elegant, he was both ashamed and nervous.

Ten o'clock struck, and suddenly it occurred to Muffat that it would be very easy to find out whether Nana were in her dressing-room or not. He went up the three steps, crossed the little yellow-painted lobby, and slipped into the court by a door which simply shut with a latch. At that hour of the night, the narrow damp well of a court, with its pestiferous water-closets, its fountain, its back view of the kitchen stove, and the collection of plants with which the portress used to litter the place, was drenched in dark mist; but the two walls, rising pierced with windows on either hand, were flaming with light, since the property room and the firemen's office were situated on the ground floor, with the managerial bureau on the left, and on the right and upstairs the dressing-rooms of the company. The mouths of furnaces seemed to be opening on the outer darkness from top to bottom of this well. The Count had at once marked the light in the windows of the dressing-room on the first floor; and, as a man who is comforted and happy, he forgot where he was, and stood gazing upward amid the foul mud and faint decaying smell peculiar to the premises of this antiquated Parisian building. Big drops were dripping from a broken water-spout, and a ray of gas-light slipped from Madame Bron's window, and cast a yellow glare over a patch of moss-clad pavement, over the base of a wall which had been rotted by water from a sink, over a whole corner-ful of nameless filth amid which old pails and broken crocks lay in fine confusion round a spindling tree, growing mildewed in its pot. A window-fastening creaked, and the Count fled.

Nana was certainly going to come down. He returned to his post in front of the reading-room; among its slumbering shadows, which seemed only broken by the glimmer of a night-light, the little old man still sat motionless, his side-face sharply outlined against his newspaper. Then Muffat walked again, and this time took a more prolonged turn, and, crossing the large gallery, followed the Galerie des Variétés as far as that of Feydeau. The last-mentioned was cold and deserted, and buried in melancholy shadow. He returned from it, passed by the theatre, turned the corner of the Galerie Saint-Marc, and ventured as far as the Galerie Montmartre, where a sugar-chopping machine in front of a grocer's interested him a while. But when he was taking his third turn, he was seized with such dread lest Nana should escape behind his back that he lost all self-respect. Thereupon he stationed himself beside the fair gentleman, in front of the very theatre. Both

exchanged a glance of fraternal humility, with which was mingled a touch of distrust, for it was possible they might yet turn out to be rivals. Some scene-shifters, who came out smoking their pipes between the acts, brushed rudely against them, but neither one nor the other ventured to complain. Three big wenches with untidy hair and dirty gowns appeared on the doorstep. They were munching apples and spitting out the cores, but the two men bowed their heads, and patiently braved their impudent looks and rough speeches, though they were hustled, and as it were soiled, by these trollops, who amused themselves by pushing each other down upon them.

At that very moment Nana descended the three steps. She grew very pale when she noticed Muffat.

"Oh, it's you!" she stammered.

The sniggering extra ladies were quite frightened when they recognised her, and they formed in line, and stood up looking as stiff and serious as servants whom their mistress has caught behaving badly. The tall fair gentleman had moved away; he was at once reassured and sad at heart.

"Well, give me your arm," Nana continued impatiently.

They walked quietly off. The Count had been getting ready to question her, and now found nothing to say.

It was she who in rapid tones told a story to the effect that she had been at her aunt's as late as eight o'clock, when, seeing Louiset very much better, she had conceived the idea of going down to the theatre for a few minutes.

"On some important business?" he queried.

"Yes, a new piece," she replied, after

some slight hesitation. "They wanted my advice."

He knew that she was not speaking the truth, but the warm touch of her arm, as it leant firmly on his own, left him powerless. He felt neither anger nor rancour after his long, long wait: his one thought was to keep her where she was now that he had got hold of her. To-morrow, and not before, he would try and find out what she had come to her dressing-room after. But Nana still appeared to hesitate: she was manifestly a prey to the sort of secret anguish that besets people when they are trying to regain lost ground and to initiate a plan of action. Accordingly, as they turned the corner of the Galerie des Variétés, she stopped in front of the show in a fan-seller's window.

"I say, that's pretty," she whispered; "I mean that mother-of-pearl mount with the feathers."

Then, indifferently,—

"So you're seeing me home?"

"Of course," said he, with some surprise, "since your child's better."

She was sorry she had told him that story. Perhaps Louiset was passing through another crisis! She talked of returning to the Batignolles. But when he offered to accompany her she did not insist on going. For a second or two she was possessed with the kind of white-hot fury which a woman experiences when she feels herself entrapped and must nevertheless behave prettily. But in the end she grew resigned, and determined to gain time. If only she could get rid of the Count towards midnight, everything would happen as she wished.

"Yes, it's true, you're a bachelor to-night," she murmured. "Your wife doesn't return till to-morrow, eh?"

"Yes," replied Muffat. It embarrassed him somewhat to hear her talking familiarly about the Countess.

But she pressed him further, asking at what time the train was due, and wanting to know whether he were going to the station to meet her. She had begun to walk more slowly than ever, as though the shops interested her very much.

"Now do look!" said she, pausing anew before a jeweller's window, "what a funny bracelet!"

She adored the Passage des Panoramas. The tinsel of the *article de Paris*, the false jewellery, the gilded zinc, the cardboard made to look like leather, had been the passion of her early youth. It remained, and when she passed the shop-windows she could not tear herself away from them. It was the same with her to-day as when she was a ragged, slouching child, who fell into reveries in front of the chocolate-maker's sweet-stuff shows, or stood listening to a musical box in a neighbouring shop, or fell into supreme ecstasies over cheap, vulgarly-designed knick-knacks, such as nutshell work-boxes, rag-pickers' baskets for holding toothpicks, Vendôme Columns and Luxor Obelisks on which thermometers were mounted. But that evening she was too much agitated, and looked at things without seeing them. When all was said and done, it bored her to think she was not free. An obscure revolt raged within her, and amid it all she felt a wild desire to do something foolish. It was a great thing gained, forsooth, to be mistress of men of position! She had been devouring the Prince's substance, and Steiner's too, with her childish caprices, and yet she had no notion where her money went. Even, at this time of day, her flat in the Boulevard Haussmann was not entirely furnished. The drawing-room alone was finished, and with its red satin upholsteries and excess of ornamentation and furniture it struck a decidedly false note. Her creditors, moreover, would now take to tormenting her more than ever before whenever she had no money in hand, a fact which caused her constant surprise, seeing that she was wont to quote herself as a model of economy. For a month past that thief Steiner had been scarcely able to pay up his thousand francs on the occasions when she threatened to kick him out of doors in case he failed to bring them. As to Muffat, he was an idiot: he had no notion as to what it was usual to give, and she could not therefore grow angry with him on the score of miserliness. Oh, how gladly she would have turned all these folks off, had she not repeated to herself, a score of times daily, a whole string of economical maxims!

One ought to be sensible, Zoé kept saying every morning, and Nana herself was constantly haunted by the queenly vision seen at Chamont. It had now become an almost religious memory with her, and through dint of being ceaselessly recalled it grew even more grandiose. And for these reasons, though trembling with repressed indigation, she now hung submissively on the Count's arm as they went from window to window among the fast-diminishing crowd. The pavement was drying outside, and a cool wind blew along the gallery, swept the close hot air up beneath the glass that

imprisoned it, and shook the coloured lanterns, and the lines of gas-jets, and the giant fan which was flaring away like a set piece in an illumination. At the door of the restaurant a waiter was putting out the gas, while the motionless attendants in the empty glaring shops looked as though they had dropped off to sleep with their eyes open.

"Oh, what a duck!" continued Nana, retracing her steps as far as the last of the shops in order to go into ecstasies over a porcelain greyhound, standing with raised fore paw in front of a nest hidden among roses.

At length they quitted the passage, but she refused the offer of a cab. It was very pleasant out she said; besides, they were in no hurry, and it would be charming to return home on foot. When they were in front of the Café Anglais she had a sudden longing to eat oysters. Indeed, she said that owing to Louiset's illness she had tasted nothing since morning. Muffat dared not oppose her. Yet, as he did not in those days wish to be seen about with her, he asked for a private supper-room, and hurried to it along the corridors. She followed him with the air of a woman familiar with the house, and they were on the point of entering a private room, the door of which a waiter held open, when from a neighbouring saloon, whence issued a perfect tempest of shouts and laughter, a man rapidly emerged. It was Daguenet.

"By Jove, it's Nana!" cried he.

The Count had briskly disappeared into the private room, leaving the door ajar behind him. But Daguenet winked behind his round shoulders, and added in chaffing tones,—

"The deuce, but you're doing nicely! You catch 'em in the Tuileries nowadays!"

Nana smiled and laid a finger on her lips to beg him to be silent. She could see he was very much exalted, and yet she was glad to have met him, for she still felt tenderly towards him, and that despite the nasty way he had cut her when in the company of fashionable ladies.

"What are you doing now?" she asked amicably.

"Becoming respectable. Yes, indeed, I'm thinking of getting married."

She shrugged her shoulders with a pitying air. But he jokingly continued to the effect that to be only just gaining enough on 'Change to buy ladies bouquets could scarcely be called an income, provided you wanted to look respectable too! His three hundred thousand francs had only lasted him eighteen months! He wanted to be practical, and he was going to marry a girl with a huge dowry, and end off as a *préfèt*, like his father before him! Nana still smiled incredulously. She nodded in the direction of the saloon: "Who are you with in there?"

"Oh! a whole gang," said he, forgetting all about his projects under the influence of returning intoxication. "Just think! Léa is telling us about her trip in Egypt. Oh, it's screaming! There's a bathing story——"

And he told the story, while Nana lingered complaisantly. They had ended by leaning up against the wall in the corridor, facing one another. Gas-jets were flaring under the low ceiling, and a vague smell of cookery hung about the folds of the hangings. Now and again, in order to hear each other's voices,

when the din in the saloon became louder than ever, they had to lean well forward. Every few seconds, however, a waiter with an armful of dishes found his passage barred, and disturbed them. But they did not cease their talk for that; on the contrary, they stood close up to the walls, and, amid the uproar of the supper-party and the jostlings of the waiters, chatted as quietly as if they were by their own firesides.

"Just look at that," whispered the young man, pointing to the door of the private room, through which Muffat had vanished.

Both looked. The door was quivering slightly; a breath of air seemed to be disturbing it, and at last, very, very slowly, and without the least sound, it was shut-to. They exchanged a silent chuckle. The Count must be looking charmingly happy, all alone in there!

"By-the-by," she asked, "have you read Fauchery's article about me?"

"Yes, 'The Golden Fly,'" replied Daguenet; "I didn't mention it to you, as I was afraid of paining you."

"Paining me—why? His article's a very long one."

She was flattered to think that the *Figaro* should concern itself about her person. But failing the explanations of her hairdresser Francis, who had brought her the paper, she would not have understood that it was she who was in question. Daguenet scrutinised her slyly, sneering in his chaffing way. Well, well, since she was pleased, everybody else ought to be.

"By your leave!" shouted a waiter, holding a dish of iced cheese in both hands, as he separated them.

Nana had stepped towards the little saloon, where Muffat was waiting.

"Well, good-bye!" continued Daguenet. "Go and find your cuckold again." But she halted afresh.

"Why d'you call him cuckold?"

"Because he is a cuckold, by Jove!"

She came and leant against the wall again; she was profoundly interested.

"Ah!" said she, simply.

"What, d'you mean to say you didn't know that? Why, my dear girl, his wife's Fauchery's mistress. It probably began in the country. Some time ago, when I was coming here, Fauchery left me, and I suspect he's got an assignation with her at his place to-night. They've made up a story about a journey, I fancy."

Overcome with surprise, Nana remained voiceless.

"I suspected it," said she at last, slapping her leg. "I guessed it by merely looking at her on the high road that day. To think of its being possible for an honest woman to deceive her husband, and with that blackguard Fauchery too! He'll teach her some pretty things!"

"Oh, it isn't her trial trip," muttered Daguenet, wickedly. "Perhaps she knows as much about it as he does."

At this Nana gave vent to an indignant exclamation.

"Indeed she does! What a nice world! It's too foul!"

"By your leave!" shouted a waiter, laden with bottles, as he separated them.

Daguenet drew her forward again, and held her hand for a second or two. He adopted his crystalline tone of voice, the voice with notes as sweet as those of a harmonica, which had gained him his success among the ladies of Nana's type.

"Good-bye, darling! You know I love you always."

She disengaged her hand from his, and while a thunder of shouts and bravos, which made the door in the saloon tremble again, almost drowned her words, she smilingly remarked,—

"It's over between us, stupid! But that doesn't matter. Do come up one of these days, and we'll have a chat."

Then she became serious again, and in the outraged tones of a respectable woman,—

"So he's a cuckold, is he?" she cried. "Well, that *is* a nuisance, dear boy. They've always sickened me, cuckolds have."

When at length she went into the private room she noticed that Muffat was sitting resignedly on a narrow divan with pale face and twitching hands. He did not reproach her at all, and she, greatly moved, was divided between feelings of pity and of contempt. The poor man! To think of his being so unworthily cheated by a vile wife! She had a good mind to throw her arms round his neck and comfort him. But it was only fair all the same! He was a fool with women, and this would teach him a lesson! Nevertheless, pity overcame her. She did not get rid of him as she had determined to do after the oysters had been discussed. They scarcely stayed a quarter of an hour in the Café Anglais, and together they went into the house in the Boulevard Haussmann. It was then eleven. Before midnight she would easily have discovered some means of getting rid of him kindly.

In the ante-room, however, she took the precaution of giving Zoé an order.

"You'll look out for him, and you'll

tell him not to make a noise if the other man's still with me."

"But where shall I put him, *Madame?*"

"Keep him in the kitchen. It's more safe."

In the room inside, Muffat was already taking off his overcoat. A big fire was burning on the hearth. It was the same room as of old, with its rose-wood furniture and its hangings and chair coverings of figured damask with the large blue flowers on a grey background. On two occasions Nana had thought of having it re-done, the first in black velvet, the second in white satin, with bows; but directly Steiner consented, she demanded the money that these changes would cost simply with a view to pillaging him. She had, indeed, only indulged in a tiger-skin rug for the hearth and a cut-glass hanging-lamp.

"I'm not sleepy: I'm not going to bed," said she, the moment they were shut in together.

The Count obeyed her submissively as became a man no longer afraid of being seen. His one care now was to avoid vexing her.

"As you will," he murmured.

Nevertheless, he took his boots off, too, before seating himself in front of the fire. One of Nana's pleasures consisted in undressing herself in front of the mirror on her wardrobe door, which reflected her whole height. She would let everything slip off her in turn, and then would stand perfectly naked, and gaze and gaze in complete oblivion of all around her. Passion for her own body, ecstasy over her satin skin and the supple contours of her shape, would keep her serious, attentive, and absorbed in the love of herself. The hair-dresser

frequently found her standing thus, and would enter without her once turning to look at him. Muffat used to grow angry then, but he only succeeded in astonishing her. What was coming over the man? She was doing it to please herself, not other people.

That particular evening, she wanted to have a better view of herself, and she lit the six candles attached to the frame of the mirror. But while letting her shift slip down, she paused. She had been preoccupied for some moments past, and a question was on her lips.

"You haven't read the *Figaro* article, have you? The paper's on the table."

Daguenet's laugh had recurred to her recollections, and she was harassed by a doubt. If that Fauchery had slandered her, she would be revenged.

"They say that it's about me," she continued, affecting indifference. "What's your notion, eh, darling?"

And letting go her shift, and waiting till Muffat should have done reading, she stood naked. Muffat was reading slowly Fauchery's article, entitled "The Golden Fly," describing the life of a harlot, descended from four or five generations of drunkards, and tainted in her blood by a cumulative inheritance of misery and drink, which in her case has taken the form of a nervous exaggeration of the sexual instinct. She has shot up to womanhood in the slums and on the pavements of Paris and tall, handsome, and as superbly grown as a dung-hill plant, she avenges the beggars and outcasts of whom she is the ultimate product. With her the rottenness that is allowed to ferment among the populace is carried upwards and rots the aristocracy. She becomes a blind power of nature, a leaven of destruction, and unwittingly she corrupts and disorganises all Paris, churning it between her snow-white thighs as milk is monthly churned by housewives. And it was at the end of this article that the comparison with a fly occurred, a fly of sunny hue, which has flown up out of the dung, a fly which sucks in death on the carrion tolerated by the roadside, and then buzzing, dancing, and glittering like a precious stone, enters the windows of palaces and poisons the men within by merely settling on them in her flight.

Muffat lifted his head; his eyes stared fixedly; he gazed at the fire.

"Well?" asked Nana.

But he did not answer. It seemed as though he wanted to read the article again. A cold shivering feeling was creeping from his scalp to his shoulders. This article had been written anyhow. The phrases were wildly extravagant, the unexpected epigrams and quaint collocations of words went beyond all bounds. Yet, notwithstanding this, he was struck by what he had read, for it had rudely awakened within him much that for months past he had not cared to think about.

He looked up. Nana had grown absorbed in her ecstatic self-contemplation. She was bending her neck and was looking attentively in the mirror at a little brown mark above her right haunch. She was touching it with the tip of her finger, and by dint of bending backward was making it stand out more clearly than ever. Situated where it was, it doubtless struck her as both quaint and pretty. After that she studied other parts of her body with an amused expression, and much of the vicious curiosity of a child. The sight of herself always astonished her, and she would look as surprised and ecstatic as a young girl who has discovered her puberty. Slowly, slowly she spread out her arms in order to give full value to her figure, which suggested the torso of a plump Venus. She bent herself this way and that, and examined herself before and behind, stooping to look at the side-view of her bosom and at the sweeping contours of her thighs. And she ended with a strange amusement, which consisted of swinging to right and left, her knees apart, and her body swaying from the waist with the perpetual jogging, twitching movements peculiar to an Oriental dancer in the *danse du ventre*.

Muffat sat looking at her. She frightened him. The newspaper had dropped from his hand. For a moment he saw her as she was, and he despised himself. Yes, it was just that; she had corrupted his life, he already felt himself tainted to his very marrow by impurities hitherto undreamt of. Everything was now destined to rot within him, and in the twinkling of an eye he understood what this evil entailed. He saw the ruin brought about by this kind of "leaven" —himself poisoned, his family destroyed, a bit of the social fabric cracking and crumbling. And, unable to take his eyes from the sight, he sat looking fixedly at her, striving to inspire himself with loathing for her nakedness.

Nana no longer moved. With an arm behind her neck, one hand clasped in the other, and her elbows far apart, she was throwing back her head, so that he could see a fore-shortened reflection of her half-closed eyes, her parted lips, her face clothed with amorous laughter.

Her masses of yellow hair were unknotted behind, and they covered her back with the fell of a lioness.

Bending back thus, she displayed her solid Amazonian waist and firm bosom, where strong muscles moved under the satin texture of the skin. A delicate line, to which the shoulder and the thigh added their slight undulations, ran from one of her elbows to her foot, and Muffat's eyes followed this tender profile, and marked how the outlines of the fair flesh vanished in golden gleams, and how its rounded contours shone like silk in the candle-light. He thought of his old dread of Woman, of the Beast of the Scriptures, at once lewd and wild. Nana was all covered with fine hair, a russet down made her body velvety; whilst the Beast was apparent in the almost equine development of her flanks, in the fleshy exuberances and deep hollows of her body, which lent her sex the mystery and suggestiveness lurking in their shadows. She was, indeed, that Golden Creature, blind as brute force, whose very odour ruined the world. Muffat gazed and gazed as a man possessed, till, at last, when he had shut his eyes in order to escape it, the Brute reappeared in the darkness of the brain, larger, more terrible, more suggestive in its attitude. Now, he understood, it would remain before his eyes, in his very flesh, forever.

But Nana was gathering herself together. A little thrill of tenderness seemed to have traversed her members. Her eyes were moist; she tried, as it were, to make herself small, as though she could feel herself better thus. Then she threw her head and bosom back, and melting, as it were, in one great bodily caress, she rubbed her cheeks coaxingly first against one shoulder then against the other. Her lustful mouth breathed desire over her limbs. She put out her lips, kissed herself long and long in the neighbourhood of her armpit, and laughed at the other Nana who, also, was kissing herself in the mirror.

Then Muffat gave a long sigh. This solitary pleasure exasperated him. Suddenly all his resolutions were swept away as though by a mighty wind. In a fit of brutal passion he caught Nana to his breast and threw her down on the carpet.

"Leave me alone!" she cried. "You're hurting me!"

He was conscious of his undoing; he recognised in her stupidity, vileness, and falsehood, and he longed to possess her, poisoned though she was.

"Oh, you're a fool!" said she savagely, when he let her get up.

Nevertheless, she grew calm. He would go now. She slipped on a nightgown, trimmed with lace, and came and sat down on the floor in front of the fire. It was her favourite position. When she again questioned him about Fauchery's article, Muffat replied vaguely, for he wanted to avoid a scene. Besides, she declared that she had found a weak spot in Fauchery. And with that she relapsed into a long silence, and reflected on how to dismiss the Count. She would have liked to do it in an agreeable way, for she was still a good-natured wench, and it bored her to cause others pain, especially in the present instance where the man was a cuckold. The mere thought of his being that had ended by rousing her sympathies!

"So you expect your wife to-morrow morning?" said she at last.

Muffat had stretched himself in an arm-chair. He looked drowsy, and his limbs were tired. He gave a sign of assent. Nana sat gazing seriously at him, with a dull tumult in her brain. Propped on one leg, among her slightly-rumpled laces, she was holding one of her bare feet between her hands, and was turning it mechanically about and about.

"Have you been married long?" she asked.

"Nineteen years," replied the Count.

"Ah! And is your wife amiable? Do you get on comfortably together?"

He was silent. Then, with some embarrassment,—

"You know I've begged you never to talk of those matters."

"Dear me, why's that?" she cried, beginning to grow vexed directly. "I'm sure I won't eat your wife if I *do* talk about her. Dear boy, why every woman's worth——"

But she stopped for fear of saying too much. She contented herself by assuming a superior expression, since she considered herself extremely kind. The poor fellow, he needed delicate handling! Besides, she had been struck by a laughable notion, and she smiled as she looked him carefully over.

"I say," she continued, "I haven't told you the story about you that Fauchery's circulating. There's a viper, if you like! I don't bear him any ill-will, because his article may be all right, but he's a regular viper all the same."

And laughing more gaily than ever, she let go her foot, and, crawling along the floor, came and propped herself against the Count's knees.

"Now just fancy, he swears you were still like a babe when you married your wife. You were still like that, eh? Is it true, eh?"

Her eyes pressed for an answer, and she raised her hands to his shoulders, and began shaking him in order to extract the desired confession.

"Without doubt," he at last made answer gravely.

Thereupon she again sank down at his feet. She was shaking with uproarious laughter, and she stuttered, and dealt him little slaps.

"No, it's too funny! There's no one like you; you're a marvel. But, my poor pet, you must just have been stupid! When a man doesn't know, oh, it is so comical! Good heavens, I should have liked to have seen you! And it came off well, did it? Now tell me something about it! Oh, do, do tell me!"

She overwhelmed him with questions, forgetting nothing, and requiring the veriest details. And she laughed such sudden merry peals, which doubled her up with mirth, and her chemise slipped and got turned down to such an extent, and her skin looked so golden in the light of the big fire that, little by little, the Count described to her his bridal night. He no longer felt at all awkward. He himself began to be amused at last as he spoke. Only he kept choosing his phrases, for he still had a certain sense of modesty. The young woman, now thoroughly interested, asked him about the Countess. According to his account she had a marvellous figure, but was a regular iceberg for all that.

"Oh! get along with you!" he muttered, indolently. "You have no cause to be jealous."

Nana had ceased laughing, and she now resumed her former position, and, with her back to the fire, brought her knees up under her chin with her clasped hands. Then, in a serious tone, she declared,—

"It doesn't pay, dear boy, to look like a ninny with one's wife the first night."

"Why?" queried the astonished Count.

"Because," she replied, slowly, assuming a doctorial expression.

And with that she looked as if she were delivering a lecture, and shook her head at him. In the end, however, she condescended to explain herself more lucidly.

"Well, look here! I know how it all happens. Yes, dearie, women don't like a man to be foolish. They don't say anything, because there's such a thing as modesty, you know, but you may be sure they think about it for a jolly long time to come. And sooner or later, when a man's been an ignoramus, they go and make other arrangements. That's it, my pet."

He did not seem to understand. Whereupon she grew more definite still. She became maternal, and taught him his lesson out of sheer goodness of heart, as a friend might do. Since she had discovered him to be a cuckold, the information had weighed on her spirits; she was madly anxious to discuss his position with him.

"Good heavens! I'm talking of things that don't concern me. I've said what I have because everybody ought to be happy. We're having a chat, eh? Well,

then, you're to answer me as straight as you can."

But she stopped to change her position, for she was burning herself.

"It's jolly hot, eh? My back's roasted. Wait a second. I'll cook my tummy a bit. That's what's good for the aches!"

And when she had turned round with her breast to the fire, and her feet tucked under her,—

"Let me see," she said, "you don't sleep with your wife any longer?"

"No, I swear to you I don't," said Muffat, dreading a scene.

"And you believe she's really a stick?"

He bowed his head in the affirmative.

"And that's why you love me? Answer me! I shan't be angry."

He repeated the same movement.

"Very well then," she concluded. "I suspected as much! Oh! the poor pet. Do you know my aunt Lerat? When she comes, get her to tell you the story about the fruiterer who lives opposite her. Just fancy that man—— Damn it, how hot this fire is! I must turn round. I'm going to roast my left side now."

And as she presented her side to the blaze, a droll idea struck her, and like a good-tempered thing, she made fun of herself, for she was delighted to see that she was looking so plump and pink in the light of the coal fire.

"I look like a goose, eh? Yes, that's it! I'm a goose on the spit, and I'm turning, turning, and cooking in my own juice, eh?"

And she was once more indulging in a merry fit of laughter, when a sound of voices and slamming doors became audible. Muffat was surprised, and he questioned her with a look. She grew serious, and an anxious expression came over her face. It must be Zoé's cat, a cursed beast that broke everything. It was half-past twelve o'clock. How long was she going to bother herself in her cuckold's behalf? Now that the other man had come, she ought to get him out of the way, and that quickly.

"What were you saying?" asked the Count complaisantly, for he was charmed to see her so kind to him.

But in her desire to be rid of him, she suddenly changed her mood, became brutal, and did not take care what she was saying.

"Oh yes! the fruiterer and his wife. Well, my dear fellow, they never once touched one another! Not the least bit! She was very keen on it, you understand, but he, the ninny, didn't know it. He was so green that he thought her a stick, and so he went elsewhere, and took up with streetwalkers, who treated him to all sorts of nastiness, whilst she, on her part, made up for it beautifully with fellows who were a lot slyer than her green-horn of a husband. And things always turn out that way through people not understanding one another. I know it, I do!"

Muffat was growing pale. At last he was beginning to understand her allusions, and he wanted to make her keep silence. But she was in full swing.

"No, hold your tongue, will you? If you weren't brutes you would be as nice with your wives as you are with us, and if your wives weren't geese they would take as much pains to keep you as we do to get you. That's the way to behave. Yes, my duck, you can put that in your pipe and smoke it."

"Do not talk of honest women," said he, in a hard voice. "You do not know them."

At that Nana rose to her knees.

"I don't know them! Why, they aren't even clean, your honest women aren't! They aren't even clean! I defy you to find me one who would dare show herself as I am doing. Oh, you make me laugh with your honest women! Don't drive me to it; don't oblige me to tell you things I may regret afterwards."

The Count, by way of answer, mumbled something insulting. Nana became quite pale in her turn. For some seconds she looked at him without speaking. Then, in her decisive way,—

"What would you do if your wife were deceiving you?"

He made a threatening gesture.

"Well, and if I were to?"

"Oh! you," he muttered, with a shrug of his shoulders.

Nana was certainly not spiteful. Since the beginning of the conversation, she had been strongly tempted to throw his cuckold's reputation in his teeth, but she had resisted. She would have liked to confess him quietly on the subject, but he had begun to exasperate her at last. The matter ought to stop now.

"Well then, my dearie," continued she, "I don't know what you're getting at with me. For two hours past you've been worrying my life out. Now do just go and find your wife, for she's at it with Fauchery. Yes, it's quite correct; they're in the Rue Taitbout, at the corner of the Rue de Provençe. You see, I'm giving you the address."

Then, triumphantly, as she saw Muffat stagger to his feet like an ox under the hammer,—

"If honest women must meddle in our affairs and take our sweethearts from us——! Oh, you bet they're a nice lot, those honest women!"

But she was unable to proceed. With a terrible push he had cast her full length on the floor, and lifting his heel he seemed on the point of crushing in her head in order to silence her. For the twinkling of an eye she felt sickening dread. Blinded with rage he had begun beating about the room like a maniac. Then his choking silence and the struggle with which he was shaken melted her to tears. She felt a mortal regret, and rolling herself up in front of the fire so as to roast her right side, she undertook the task of comforting him.

"I take my oath, darling, I thought you knew it all. Otherwise I shouldn't have spoken, you may be sure. But perhaps it isn't true. I don't say anything for certain. I've been told it, and people are talking about it; but what does that prove? Oh, get along! You're very silly to grow riled about it. If I were a man I shouldn't care a rush for the women! All the women are alike, you see, high or low; they're all rowdy and the rest of it."

In a fit of self-abnegation she was severe on womankind, for she wished thus to lessen the cruelty of her blow. But he did not listen to her or hear what she said. With fumbling movements he had put on his boots and his overcoat. For a moment longer he raved round, and then, in a final outburst, finding himself near the door, he rushed from the room. Nana was very much annoyed.

"Well, well! A prosperous trip to you!" she continued aloud, though she was now alone. "He's polite, too, that fellow is, when he's spoken to! And I had to defend myself at that! Well, I was the first to get back my temper, and I made plenty of excuses, I'm thinking! Besides, he had been getting on my nerves!"

Nevertheless, she was not happy, and sat scratching her legs with both hands. Then she took high ground:

"Tut, tut, it isn't my fault if he is a cuckold!"

And toasted on every side, and as hot as a roast bird, she went and buried herself under the bedclothes, after ringing for Zoé to usher in the other man, who was waiting in the kitchen.

Once outside, Muffat began walking at a furious pace. A fresh shower had just fallen, and he kept slipping on the greasy pavement. When he looked mechanically up into the sky, he saw ragged, soot-coloured clouds scudding in front of the moon. At this hour of the night passers-by were becoming few and far between in the Boulevard Haussmann. He skirted the enclosures round the opera-house in his search for darkness, and, as he went along, he kept mumbling inconsequent phrases. That girl had been lying. She had invented her story out of sheer stupidity and cruelty. He ought to have crushed her head when he had it under his heel. After all was said and done, the business was too shameful. Never would he see her, never would he touch her again, or, if he did, he would be miserably weak. And with that he breathed hard, as though he were free once more. Oh, that naked, cruel monster, roasting away like any goose, and slavering over everything that he had respected for forty years back. The moon had come out, and the empty street was bathed in white light. He felt afraid, and he burst into a great fit of sobbing, for he had grown suddenly hopeless and maddened as though he had sunk into a fathomless void.

"My God!" he stuttered out. "It's finished! There's nothing left now!"

Along the boulevards belated people were hurrying. He tried hard to be calm, and as the story told him by that courtesan kept recurring to his burning consciousness, he wanted to reason the matter out. The Countess was coming up from Madame de Chezelle's country house to-morrow morning. Yet nothing, in fact, could have prevented her from returning to Paris the night before, and passing it with that man. He now began recalling to mind certain details of their stay at The Fondettes. One evening, for instance, he had surprised Sabine in the shade of some trees, when she was so much agitated as to be unable to answer his questions. The man had been present; why should she not be with him now? The more he thought about it the more possible the whole story became, and he ended by thinking it natural and even inevitable. Whilst he was in his shirt-sleeves in the house of a harlot, his wife was undressing in her lover's room. Nothing could be simpler or more logical! Reasoning in this way he forced himself to keep cool. He felt as if there were a great downward movement in the direction of fleshly madness, a movement which, as it grew, was overcoming the whole world round about him. Warm images pursued him in imagination. A

naked Nana suddenly evoked a naked Sabine. At this vision, which seemed to bring them together in shameless relationship, and under the influence of the same lusts, he literally stumbled, and in the road a cab nearly ran over him. Some women who had come out of a café jostled him amid loud laughter. Then a fit of weeping once more overcame him, despite all his efforts to the contrary, and, not wishing to shed tears in the presence of others, he plunged into a dark and empty street. It was the Rue Rossini, and along its silent length he wept like a child.

"It's over with us," said he in hollow tones. "There's nothing left us now, nothing left us now!"

He wept so violently that he had to lean up against a door as he buried his face in his wet hands. A noise of footsteps drove him away. He felt a shame and a fear which made him fly before people's faces with the restless step of a bird of darkness. When passers-by met him on the pavement he did his best to look and walk in a leisurely way, for he fancied they were reading his secret in the very swing of his shoulders. He had followed the Rue de la Grange Batelière as far as the Rue du Faubourg Montmartre, where the brilliant lamplight surprised him, and he retraced his steps. For nearly an hour he traversed the district thus, choosing always the darkest corners. Doubtless there was some goal whither his steps were patiently, instinctively, leading him through a labyrinth of endless turnings. At length he lifted his eyes up at a street-corner. He had reached his destination, the point where the Rue Taitbout and the Rue de la Provençe met. He had taken an hour, amid his painful mental sufferings to arrive at a place he could have reached in five minutes. One morning, a month ago, he remembered going up to Fauchery's rooms to thank him for a notice of a ball at the Tuileries, in which the journalist had mentioned him. The flat was between the ground floor and the first story, and had a row of small square windows which were half-hidden by the colossal signboard belonging to a shop. The last window on the left was bisected by a brilliant band of lamplight coming from between the half-closed curtains. And he remained, absorbed and expectant, with his gaze fixed on this shining streak.

The moon had disappeared in an inky sky, whence an icy drizzle was falling. Two o'clock struck at the Trinité. The Rue de Provençe and the Rue Taitbout lay in shadow, bestarred at intervals by bright splashes of light from the gaslamps, which in the distance were merged in yellow mist. Muffat did not move from where he was standing. That was the room. He remembered it now: it had hangings of red "andrinople," and a Louis XIII. bed stood at one end of it. The lamp must be standing on the chimney-piece to the right. Without doubt they had gone to bed, for no shadows passed across the window, and the bright streak gleamed as motionless as the light of a night-lamp. With his eyes still uplifted, he began forming a plan; he would ring the bell, go upstairs despite the porter's remonstrances, break the doors in with a push of his shoulder, and fall upon them in the very bed without giving them time to unlace their arms. For one moment the thought that he had no weapon upon him gave

him pause, but directly afterwards he decided to throttle them. He returned to the consideration of his project, and he perfected it, whilst waiting for some sign, some indication, which should bring certainty with it.

Had a woman's shadow only shewn itself at that moment, he would have rung. But the thought that perhaps he was deceiving himself froze him. How could he be certain? Doubts began to return. His wife could not be with that man. It was monstrous and impossible. Nevertheless he stayed where he was, and was gradually overcome by a species of torpor which merged into sheer feebleness, whilst he waited long and long, and the fixity of his gaze induced hallucinations.

A shower was falling. Two policemen were approaching, and he was forced to leave the doorway where he had taken shelter. When these were lost to view in the Rue de Provençe, he returned to his post, wet and shivering. The luminous streak still traversed the window, and this time he was going away for good when a shadow crossed it. It moved so quickly, that he thought he had deceived himself. But first one and then another black thing followed quickly after it, and there was a regular commotion in the room. Riveted anew to the pavement, he experienced an intolerable burning sensation in his inside as he waited to find out the meaning of it all. Outlines of arms and legs flitted after one another; and an enormous hand travelled about with the silhouette of a water-jug. He distinguished nothing clearly, but he thought he recognised a woman's head-dress. And he disputed the point with himself; it might well have been Sabine's hair, only the neck did not seem sufficiently slim. At that hour of the night he had lost the power of recognition and of action. In this terrible agony of uncertainty, his inside caused him such acute suffering that he pressed against the door in order to calm himself, shivering like a man in rags, as he did so. Then seeing that, despite everything, he could not turn his eyes away from the window, his anger changed into a fit of moralising. He fancied himself a Deputy; he was haranguing an assembly, loudly denouncing debauchery, prophesying national ruin. And he reconstructed Fauchery's article on the poisoned fly, and he came before the house and declared that morals such as these, which could only be paralleled in the days of the later Roman Empire, rendered society an impossibility: that did him good. But the shadows had meanwhile disappeared. Doubtless they had gone to bed again, and, still, watching, he continued waiting where he was.

Three o'clock struck, then four, but he could not take his departure. When showers fell, he buried himself in a corner of the doorway, his legs splashed with wet. Nobody passed by now, and occasionally his eyes would close, as though scorched by the streak of light, which he kept watching obstinately, fixedly, with idiotic persistence. On two subsequent occasions the shadows flitted about, repeating the same gestures and agitating the silhouette of the same gigantic jug; and twice quiet was re-established, and the nightlamp again glowed discreetly out. These shadows only increased his uncertainty. Then, too, a sudden idea soothed his brain,

whilst it postponed the decisive moment. After all, he had only to wait for the woman when she left the house. He could quite easily recognise Sabine. Nothing could be simpler, and there would be no scandal, and he would be sure of things one way or the other. It was only necessary to stay where he was. Among all the confused feelings which had been agitating him, he now merely felt a dull need of certain knowledge. But sheer weariness and vacancy began lulling him to sleep under his doorway, and by way of distraction he tried to reckon up how long he would have to wait. Sabine was to be at the station towards nine o'clock; that meant about four hours and a half more. He was very patient; he would even have been content not to move again; and he found a certain charm in fancying that his night-vigil would last through eternity.

Suddenly the streak of light was gone. This extremely simple event was to him an unforeseen catastrophe, at once troublesome and disagreeable. Evidently they had just put the lamp out, and were going to sleep. It was reasonable enough at that hour, but he was irritated thereat, for now the darkened window ceased to interest him. He watched it for a quarter of an hour longer, and then grew tired, and leaving the doorway took a turn upon the pavement. Until five o'clock he walked to and fro looking upwards from time to time. The window seemed a dead thing, and now and then he asked himself if he had not dreamed that shadows had been dancing up there behind the panes. An intolerable sense of fatigue weighed him down, a dull heavy feeling, under the influence of which he forgot what he was waiting for at that particular street-corner. He kept stumbling on the pavement, and starting into wakefulness with the icy shudder of a man who does not know where he is. Nothing seemed to justify the painful anxiety he was inflicting on himself. Since those people were asleep—well then, let them sleep! What good could it do mixing in their affairs? It was very dark; no one would ever know anything about this night's doings. And with that every sentiment within him, down to curiosity itself, took flight before the longing to have done with it all and to find relief somewhere. The cold was increasing, and the street was becoming insufferable. Twice he walked away and slowly returned, dragging one foot behind the other, only to walk further away next time. It was all over; nothing was left him now, and so he went down the whole length of the boulevard and did not return.

His was a melancholy progress through the streets. He walked slowly, never changing his pace, and simply keeping along the walls of the houses.

His boot-heels re-echoed, and he saw nothing but his shadow moving at his side. As he neared each successive gaslight it grew taller, and immediately afterwards diminished. But this lulled him and occupied him mechanically. He never knew afterwards where he had been; it seemed as if he had dragged himself round and round in a circle for hours. One reminiscence only was very distinctly retained by him. Without his being able to explain how it came about he found himself with his face pressed close against the gate at the end of the

Passage des Panoramas and his two hands grasping the bars. He did not shake them, but his whole heart swelling with emotion, he simply tried to look into the passage. But he could make nothing out clearly, for shadows flooded the whole length of the deserted gallery, and the wind, blowing hard down the Rue Saint-Marc, puffed in his face with the damp breath of a cellar. For a time he tried doggedly to see into the place, and then, awakening from his dream, he was filled with astonishment, and asked himself what he could possibly be seeking for at that hour and in that position, for he had pressed against the railings so fiercely that they had left their mark on his face. Then he went on tramp once more. He was hopeless, and his heart was full of infinite sorrow, for he felt, amid all those shadows, that he was evermore betrayed and alone.

Day broke at last. It was the murky dawn that follows winter nights, and looks so melancholy from muddy Paris pavements. Muffat had returned into the wide streets, which were then in course of construction on either side of the New Opera House. Soaked by the rain and cut up by cart-wheels, the chalky soil had become a lake of liquid mire. But he never looked to see where he was stepping, and walked on and on, slipping and regaining his footing as he went. The awakening of Paris, with its gangs of sweepers and early workmen trooping to their destinations, added to his troubles as day brightened. People stared at him in surprise, as he went by with scared look, and soaked hat, and muddy clothes. For a long while he sought refuge against palings and among scaffoldings, his desolate brain haunted by the single remaining thought that he was very miserable. Then he thought of God. The sudden idea of Divine help, of superhuman consolation, surprised him, as though it were something unforeseen and extraordinary. The image of Monsieur Venot was evoked thereby, and he saw his little plump face and ruined teeth. Assuredly Monsieur Venot, whom for months he had been avoiding and thereby rendering miserable, would be delighted were he to go and knock at his door and fall weeping into his arms. In the old days God had been always so merciful towards him. At the least sorrow, the slightest obstacle on the path of life, he had been wont to enter a church, where, kneeling down, he would humble his littleness in the presence of Omnipotence. And he had been used to go forth thence, fortified by prayer, fully prepared to give up the good things of this world, possessed by the single yearning for eternal salvation. But at present he only practised by fits and starts, when the terror of hell came upon him. All kinds of weak inclinations had overcome him, and the thought of Nana disturbed his devotions. And now the thought of God astonished him. Why had he not thought of God before, in the hour of that terrible agony when his feeble humanity was breaking up in ruin?

Meanwhile, with slow and painful steps, he sought for a church. But he had lost his bearings; the early hour had changed the face of the streets. Soon, however, as he turned the corner of the Rue de la Chaussée-d'Antin, he noticed a tower looming vaguely in the fog at the end of the Trinité Church. The white statues, overlooking the bare garden, seemed like so many chilly Venuses among the yellow foliage of a park. Under the porch he stood and panted a little, for the ascent of the wide steps had tired him. Then he went in. The church was very cold, for its heating-apparatus had been fireless since the previous evening, and its lofty vaulted aisles were full of a fine damp vapour which had come filtering through the windows. The aisles were deep in shadow; not a soul was in the church, and the only sound audible, amid the unlovely darkness, was that made by the old shoes of some verger or other, who was dragging himself about in sulky semi-wakefulness. Muffat, however, after knocking forlornly against an untidy collection of chairs, sank on his knees with bursting heart, and propped himself against the rails in front of a little chapel, close by a font. He clasped his hands, and began searching within himself for suitable prayers, whilst his whole being yearned towards a transport. But only his lips kept stammering empty words; his heart and brain were far away, and with them he returned to the outer world, and began his long unresting march through the streets, as though lashed forward by implacable necessity. And he kept repeating, "O my God, come to my assistance! O my God, abandon not Thy creature, who delivers himself up to Thy justice! O my God, I adore Thee: Thou wilt not leave me to perish under the buffetings of mine enemies!" Nothing answered: the shadows and the cold weighed upon him, and the noise of the old shoes continued in the distance, and prevented him praying. Nothing indeed save that tiresome noise was audible in the deserted church, where the matutinal sweeping was unknown before the early masses had somewhat warmed the air of the place. After that he rose to his feet with the help of a chair, his knees cracking under him as he did so. God was not yet there. And why should he weep in Monsieur Venot's arms? The man could do nothing.

And then, mechanically, he returned to Nana's house. Outside he slipped, and he felt the tears welling to his eyes again, but he was not angry with his lot—he was only feeble and ill. Yes, he was too tired, the rain had wetted him too much, he was nipped with cold, but the idea of going back to his great dark house in the Rue Miromesnil froze his heart. The house-door at Nana's was not open as yet, and he had to wait till the porter made his appearance. He smiled as he went upstairs, for he already felt penetrated by the soft warmth of that cosy retreat, where he would be able to stretch his limbs and go to sleep.

When Zoé opened the door to him, she gave a start of most uneasy astonishment. *Madame* had been taken ill with an atrocious sick headache, and she hadn't closed her eyes all night. Still, she could quite go and see whether *Madame* had gone to sleep for good. And with that she slipped into the bedroom, whilst he sank back into one of the arm-chairs in the drawing-room. But almost at that very moment Nana appeared. She had just jumped out of bed, and had scarce had time to slip on a petticoat. Her feet were bare, her hair in wild disorder, her night-gown all crumpled.

"What! you here again!" she cried, with a red flush on her cheeks.

Up she rushed, stung by sudden indignation, in order herself to thrust him out of doors. But when she saw him in such sorry plight—nay, so utterly done for, she felt infinite pity.

"Well, you are a pretty sight, my dear fellow!" she continued more gently. "But what's the matter? You've spotted them, eh? And it's given you the hump?"

He did not answer: he looked like a broken-down animal. Nevertheless, she came to the conclusion that he still lacked proofs, and, to hearten him up, she said,—

"You see now I was on the wrong tack. Your wife's an honest woman, on my word of honour! And now, my little friend, you must go home to bed. You want it badly."

He did not stir.

"Now then, be off! I can't keep you here. But perhaps you won't presume to stay at such a time as this?"

"Yes, let's go to bed," he stammered. She repressed a violent gesture, for her patience was deserting her. Was the man going crazy?

"Come, be off!" she repeated.

"No."

But she flared up in exasperation, in utter rebellion.

"It's sickening! Don't you understand I'm jolly tired of your company? Go and find your wife, who's making a cuckold of you. Yes, she's making a cuckold of you. I say so—yes, I do now. There, you've got the sack! Will you leave me, or will you not?"

Muffat's eyes filled with tears. He clasped his hands together.

"Oh, let's go to bed!"

At this Nana suddenly lost all control over herself, and was choked by nervous sobs. She was being taken advantage of, when all was said and done! What had these stories to do with her? She certainly had used all manner of delicate methods in order to teach him his lesson gently. And now he was for making her pay the damages! No, thank you! She was kind-hearted, but not to that extent.

"The devil, but I've had enough of this!" she swore, bringing her fist down on the furniture. "Yes, yes, I wanted to be faithful—it was all I could do to be that! Yet, if I spoke the word, I could be rich to-morrow, my dear fellow!"

He looked up in surprise. Never once had he thought of the monetary question. If she only expressed a desire, he would realise it at once; his whole fortune was at her service.

"No, it's too late now," she replied, furiously. "I like men who give without being asked. No, if you were to offer me a million for a single interview, I should say no! It's over between us: I've got other fish to fry there! So be off, or I shan't answer for the consequences. I shall do something dreadful."

She advanced threateningly towards him, and whilst she was raving as became a good courtesan, who, though driven to desperation, was yet firmly convinced of her rights and her superiority over tiresome, honest folk, the door opened suddenly, and Steiner presented himself. That proved the finishing touch. She shrieked aloud:

"Well, I never. Here's the other one!"

Bewildered by her piercing outcry,

Steiner stopped short. Muffat's unexpected presence annoyed him, for he feared an explanation and had been doing his best to avoid it these three months past. With blinking eyes, he stood first on one leg, then on the other, looking embarrassed the while, and avoiding the Count's gaze. He was out of breath, and as became a man who had rushed across Paris with good news only to find himself involved in unforeseen trouble, his face was flushed and distorted.

"Que veux-tu, toi?" asked Nana, roughly, using the second person singular in open mockery of the Count.

"What—what do I—?" he stammered. "I've got it for you—you know what."

"Eh?"

He hesitated. The day before yesterday she had given him to understand that, if he could not find her a thousand francs to pay a bill with, she would not receive him any more. For two days he had been loafing about the town in quest of the money, and had at last made the sum up that very morning.

"The thousand francs!" he ended by declaring, as he drew an envelope from his pocket.

Nana had not remembered.

"The thousand francs!" she cried. "D'you think I'm begging alms? Now, look here, that's what I value your thousand francs at!"

And, snatching the envelope, she threw it full in his face. As became a prudent Hebrew, he picked it up slowly and painfully, and then looked at the young woman with a dull expression of face. Muffat and he exchanged a despairing glance, whilst she put her arms akimbo in order to shout more loudly than before.

"Come now, will you soon have done insulting me? I'm glad you've come too, dear boy, because now you see the clearance'll be quite complete. Now then, gee up! Out you go!"

Then, as they did not hurry in the least, for they were paralysed,—

"D'you mean to say I'm acting like a fool, eh? It's likely enough! But you've bored me too much! And, hang it all! I've had enough of swelldom! If I die of what I'm doing—well, it's my fancy!"

They sought to calm her; they begged her to listen to reason.

"Now then, once, twice, thrice!—— Won't you go? Very well! Look there! I've got company."

And with a brisk movement she flung wide the bedroom door. Whereupon, in the middle of the tumbled bed, the two men caught sight of Fontan. He had not expected to be shewn off in this situation; nevertheless, he took things very easily, for he was used to sudden surprises on the stage. Indeed, after the first shock, he even hit upon a grimace calculated to tide him honourably over his difficulty: he "turned rabbit," as he phrased it, and stuck out his lips, and wrinkled up his nose, so as completely to transform the lower half of his face. His base, satyr-like head seemed to exude incontinence. It was this man Fontan, then, whom Nana had been to fetch at the Variétiés every day for a week past, for she was smitten with that fierce sort of passion which the grimacing ugliness of a low comedian is wont to inspire in the genus courtesan.

"There!" said she, pointing him out with tragic gesture.

Muffat, who hitherto had pocketed everything, rebelled at this affront.

"Bitch!" he stammered.

But Nana, who was once more in the bedroom, came back in order to have the last word.

"How am I a bitch? What about your wife?"

And she was off, and slamming the door with a bang she noisily pushed to the bolt. Left alone, the two men gazed at one another in silence. Zoé had just come into the room, but she did not drive them out. Nay, she spoke to them in the most sensible manner. As became a woman with a head on her shoulders, she decided that *Madame's* conduct was rather too much of a good thing. But she defended her none the less: this union with the play actor couldn't last: the madness must be allowed to pass off! The two men retired without uttering a sound. On the pavement outside they shook hands silently, as though swayed by a mutual sense of fraternity. Then they turned their backs on one another, and went crawling off in opposite directions.

When at last Muffat entered his town house in the Rue Miromesnil, his wife was just arriving. The two met on the great staircase, whose walls exhaled an icy chill. They lifted up their eyes and beheld one another. The Count still wore his muddy clothes, and his pale, bewildered face betrayed the prodigal returning from his debauch. The Countess looked as though she were utterly fagged out by a night in the train. She was dropping with sleep, but her hair had been brushed anyhow, and her eyes were deeply sunken.

## CHAPTER VIII

WE are in a little set of lodgings on the fourth floor in the Rue Véron at Montmartre. Nana and Fontan have invited a few friends to cut their Twelfth-Night cake with them. They are giving their house-warming, though they have been only three days settled.

They had no fixed intention of keeping house together, but the whole thing had come about suddenly in the first glow of the honeymoon. After her grand blow-up, when she had turned the Count and the banker so vigorously out of doors, Nana felt the world crumbling about her feet. She estimated the situation at a glance; the creditors would swoop down on her ante-room, would mix themselves up with her love affairs, and threaten to sell her little all unless she continued to act sensibly. Then, too, there would be no end of disputes and carking anxieties if she attempted to save her furniture from their clutches. And so she preferred giving up everything. Besides the flat in the Boulevard Haussmann was plaguing her to death. It was so stupid with its great gilded rooms! In her access of tenderness for Fontan, she began dreaming of a pretty little bright chamber. Indeed, she returned to the old ideals of the florist days, when her highest ambition was to have a rosewood cupboard with a plate-glass door, and a bed hung with blue "reps." In the course of two days she sold what she could smuggle out of the house in the way of knick-knacks and jewellery, and then disappeared, taking with her ten

thousand francs, and never even warning the porter's wife. It was a plunge into the dark, a merry spree; never a trace was left behind. In this way she would prevent the men from coming dangling after her. Fontan was very nice. He did not say No to anything, but just let her do as she liked. Nay, he even displayed an admirable spirit of comradeship. He had, on his part, nearly seven thousand francs, and, despite the fact that people accused him of stinginess, he consented to add them to the young woman's ten thousand. The sum struck them as a solid foundation on which to begin housekeeping. And so they started away, drawing from their common hoard, in order to hire and furnish the two rooms in the Rue Véron, and sharing everything together like old friends. In the early days it was really delicious.

On Twelfth Night Madame Lerat and Louiset were the first to arrive. As Fontan had not yet come home, the old lady ventured to give expression to her fears, for she trembled to see her niece renouncing the chance of wealth.

"Oh, aunt, I love him so dearly!" cried Nana, pressing her hands to her heart with the prettiest of gestures.

This phrase produced an extraordinary effect on Madame Lerat, and tears came into her eyes.

"That's true," said she with an air of conviction. "Love before all things!"

And with that she went into raptures over the prettiness of the rooms. Nana took her to see the bedroom, the parlour, and the very kitchen. Gracious goodness, it wasn't a vast place, but then they had painted it afresh, and put up new wall-papers. Besides, the sun shone merrily into it during the daytime.

Thereupon Madame Lerat detained the young woman in the bedroom, whilst Louiset installed himself behind the charwoman in the kitchen in order to watch a chicken being roasted. If, said Madame Lerat, she permitted herself to say what was in her mind, it was because Zoé had just been at her house. Zoé had stayed courageously in the breach, because she was devoted to her mistress. *Madame* would pay her later on: she was in no anxiety about that! And amid the break-up of the Boulevard Haussmann establishment, it was she who shewed the creditors a bold front; it was she who conducted a dignified retreat, saving what she could from the wreck, and telling everyone that her mistress was travelling. She never once gave them her address. Nay, through fear of being followed, she even deprived herself of the pleasure of calling on *Madame*. Nevertheless, that same morning she had run round to Madame Lerat's because matters were taking a new turn. The evening before, creditors in the persons of the upholsterer, the charcoal merchant, and the laundress, had put in an appearance, and had offered to give *Madame* an extension of time. Nay, they had even proposed to advance *Madame* a very considerable amount, if only *Madame* would return to her flat and conduct herself like a sensible person. The aunt repeated Zoé's words. Without doubt there was a gentleman behind it all.

"I'll never consent!" declared Nana, in great disgust. "Ah, they're a pretty lot those trademen! Do they think I'm to be sold so that they can get their bills

paid? Why look here, I'd rather die of hunger than deceive Fontan."

"That's what I said," averred Madame Lerat. "My niece," said I, "is too noble-hearted!"

Nana, however, was much vexed to learn that La Mignotte was being sold, and that Labordette was buying it for Caroline Héquet at an absurdly low price. It made her angry with that clique. Oh, they were a regular cheap lot, in spite of their airs and graces! Yes, by Jove, she was worth more than the whole lot of them!

"They can have their little joke out," she concluded, "but money will never give them true happiness! Besides, you know, aunt, I don't even know now whether all that set are alive or not: I'm much too happy."

At that very moment Madame Maloir entered, wearing one of those hats of which she alone understood the shape. It was delightful meeting again. Madame Maloir explained that magnificence frightened her, and that *now*, from time to time, she would come back for her game of bézique. A second visit was paid to the different rooms in the lodgings, and in the kitchen Nana talked of economy in the presence of the charwoman, who was basting the fowl, and said that a servant would have cost too much, and that she was herself desirous of looking after things. Louiset was gazing beatifically at the roasting process.

But presently there was a loud outburst of voices. Fontan had come in with Bosc and Prullière, and the company could now sit down to table. The soup had been already served when Nana for the third time shewed off the lodgings.

"Ah, dear children, how comfortable

you are here!" Bosc kept repeating, simply for the sake of pleasing the chums who were standing the dinner. At bottom, the subject of the "nook," as he called it, nowise touched him. In the bedroom he harped still more vigorously on the amiable note. Ordinarily he was wont to treat women like cattle, and the idea of a man bothering himself about one of the dirty brutes excited within him the only angry feelings of which, in his comprehensive, drunken disdain of the universe, he was still capable.

"Ah, ah! the villains," continued he, with a wink, "they've done this on the sly. Well, you were certainly right. It will be charming, and, by Heaven, we'll come and see you!"

But when Louiset arrived on the scene, astride upon a broomstick, Prullière chuckled spitefully, and remarked,—

"Well I never! You've got a baby already?"

This struck everybody as very droll, and Madame Lerat and Madame Maloir shook with laughter. Nana, far from being vexed, laughed tenderly, and said that unfortunately this was not the case. She would very much have liked it, both for the little one's sake and for her own, but perhaps one would arrive all the same. Fontan, in his *rôle* of honest citizen, took Louiset in his arms, and began playing with him and lisping.

"Never mind! It loves its daddy! Call me 'papa,' you little blackguard!"

"Papa, papa!" stammered the child.

The company overwhelmed him with caresses, but Bosc was bored, and talked of sitting down to table. That was the only serious business in life. Nana asked her guests' permission to put Louiset's

chair next her own. The dinner was very merry, but Bosc suffered from the near neighbourhood of the child, from whom he had to defend his plate. Madame Lerat bored him too. She was in a melting mood, and kept whispering to him all sorts of mysterious things about gentlemen of the first fashion who were still running after Nana. Twice he had to push away her knee, for she was positively invading him in her gushing, tearful mood. Prullière behaved with great incivility towards Madame Maloir, and did not once help her to anything. He was entirely taken up with Nana, and looked annoyed at seeing her with Fontan. Besides, the turtle-doves were kissing so excessively as to be becoming positive bores. Contrary to all known rules they had elected to sit side by side.

"Devil take it! Why don't you eat? You've got plenty of time ahead of you!" Bosc kept repeating with his mouth full. "Wait till we are gone!"

But Nana could not restrain herself. She was in a perfect ecstasy of love. Her face was as full of blushes as an innocent young girl's, and her looks and her laughter seemed to overflow with tenderness. Gazing on Fontan, she overwhelmed him with pet names—"my doggie! my old bear! my kitten!"—and, whenever he passed her the water or the salt she bent forward and kissed him at random on lips, eyes, nose, or ear. Then, if she met with reproof, she would return to the attack with the cleverest manœuvres, and with infinite submissiveness, and the supple cunning of a beaten cat, would catch hold of his hand, when no one was looking, in order to kiss it again. It seemed she must be touching something belonging to him. As to Fontan, he gave himself airs, and let himself be adored with the utmost condescension. His great nose sniffed with entirely sensual content: his goat face, with its quaint monstrous ugliness, positively glowed in the sunlight of devoted adoration lavished upon him by that superb woman, who was so fair and so plump of limb. Occasionally he gave a kiss in return, as became a man who is having all the enjoyment, and is yet willing to behave prettily.

"Well, you're growing maddening!" cried Prullière. "Get away from her, you fellow there!"

And he dismissed Fontan, and changed covers, in order to take his place at Nana's side. The company shouted and applauded at this, and gave vent to some stiffish epigrammatic witticisms. Fontan counterfeited despair, and assumed the quaint expression of Vulcan crying for Venus. Straightway Prullière became very gallant, but Nana, whose foot he was groping for under the table, caught him a slap to make him keep quiet. No, no, she was certainly not going to become his mistress. A month ago she had begun to take a fancy to him because of his good looks, but now she detested him. If he pinched her again under pretense of picking up her napkin, she would throw her glass in his face!

Nevertheless the evening passed off well. The company had naturally begun talking about the Variétés. Wasn't that cad of a Bordenave going to go off the hooks after all? His nasty diseases kept reappearing, and causing him such suffering that you couldn't come within six yards of him nowadays. The day before, during rehearsal, he had been incessantly yelling at Simonne. There was a fellow whom the theatrical people wouldn't shed many tears over. Nana announced that if he were to ask her to take another part she would jolly well send him to the right-about. Moreover, she began talking of leaving the stage; the theatre was not to compare with her home. Fontan, who was not in the present piece nor in that which was then being rehearsed, also talked big about the joy of being entirely at liberty and of passing his evenings, with his feet on the fender, in the society of his little pet. And at this the rest exclaimed delightedly, treating their entertainers as lucky people and pretending to envy their felicity.

The Twelfth-Night cake had been cut and handed round. The bean had fallen to the lot of Madame Lerat, who popped it into Bosc's glass. Whereupon there were shouts of "The King drinks! The King drinks!" Nana took advantage of this outburst of merriment, and went and put her arms round Fontan's neck again, kissing him and whispering in his ear. But Prullière, laughing angrily as became a pretty man, declared that they were not playing the game. Louiset, meanwhile, slept soundly on two chairs. It was nearing one o'clock when the company separated, shouting *Au revoir* as they went downstairs.

For three weeks the existence of the pair of lovers was really charming. Nana fancied she was returning to those early days when her first silk dress had caused her infinite delight. She went out little, and affected a life of solitude and simplicity. One morning early, when she had gone down to buy fish *in propria persona* in the La Rochefoucauld Market, she was vastly surprised to meet

NANA 159

her old hairdresser Francis, face to face. His get-up was as scrupulously careful as ever: he wore the finest linen and his frock-coat was beyond reproach; in fact, Nana felt ashamed that he should see her in the street with a dressing-jacket, and disordered hair, and down-at-heel shoes. But he had the tact, if possible, to intensify his politeness towards her. He did not permit himself a single enquiry, and affected to believe that *Madame* was at present on her travels. Ah, but *Madame* had rendered many persons unhappy when she decided to travel! All the world had suffered loss. The young woman, however, ended by asking him questions, for a sudden fit of curiosity had made her forget her previous embarrassment. Seeing that the crowd was jostling them, she pushed him into a doorway, and, still holding her little basket in one hand, stood chatting in front of him. What were people saying about her high jinks? Good heavens! The ladies to whom he went said this, and that, and all sorts of things. In fact, she had made a great noise, and was enjoying a real boom. And Steiner? Monsieur Steiner was in a very bad way—would make an ugly finish, if he couldn't hit on some new commercial operation. And Daguenet? Oh, *he* was getting on swimmingly. Monsieur Daguenet was settling down. Nana, under the exciting influence of various recollections, was just opening her mouth with a view to a further examination, when she felt it would be awkward to utter Muffat's name. Thereupon Francis smiled, and spoke instead of her. As to Monsieur le Comte, it was all a great pity, so sad had been his sufferings since *Madame's* departure.

He had been like a soul in pain—you might have met him wherever *Madame* was likely to be found. At last Monsieur Mignon had come across him, and had taken him home to his own place. This piece of news caused Nana to laugh a good deal. But her laughter was not of the easiest kind.

"Ah, he's with Rose now," said she. "Well then, you must know, Francis, I've done with him! Oh, the canting thing! Its learnt some pretty habits—can't even go fasting for a week now! And to think that he used to swear he wouldn't have any woman after me!"

She was raging inwardly.

"My leavings, if you please!" she continued. "A pretty Johnnie for Rose to go and treat herself to! Oh, I understand it all now: she wanted to have her revenge because I got that brute of a Steiner away from her. Ain't it sly to get a man to come to her when I've chucked him out of doors?"

"Monsieur Mignon doesn't tell that tale," said the hairdresser. "According to his account, it was Monsieur le Comte who chucked you out. Yes, and in a pretty disgusting way too—with a kick on the bottom!"

Nana became suddenly very pale.

"Eh, what?" she cried, "with a kick on my bottom? He's going too far, he is! Look here, my little friend, it was I who threw him downstairs, the cuckold, for he is a cuckold, I must inform you. His countess is making him one with every man she meets—yes, even with that good-for-nothing of a Fauchery. And that Mignon, who goes loafing about the pavement in behalf of his harridan of a wife, whom nobody wants because she's so lean! What a foul lot! What a foul lot!"

She was choking, and she paused for breath.

"Oh, that's what they say, is it? Very well, my little Francis, I'll go and look 'em up, I will. Shall you and I go to them at once? Yes, I'll go, and we'll see whether they will have the cheek to go telling about kicks on the bottom. Kicks! I never took one from anybody! And nobody's ever going to strike me—d'ye see?—for I'd smash the man who laid a finger on me!"

Nevertheless, the storm subsided at last. After all, they might jolly well say what they liked! She looked upon them as so much filth underfoot! It would have soiled her to bother about people like that. She had a conscience of her own, she had! And Francis, seeing her thus giving herself away, what with her housewife's costume and all, became familiar, and, at parting, made so bold as to give her some good advice. It was wrong of her to be sacrificing everything for the sake of an infatuation: such infatuations ruined existence. She listened to him with bowed head, whilst he spoke to her with a pained expression, as became a connoisseur who could not bear to see so fine a girl making such a hash of things.

"Well, that's my affair," she said at last. "Thanks all the same, dear boy."

She shook his hand, which despite his perfect dress, was always a little greasy, and then went off to buy her fish. During the day, that story about the kick on the bottom occupied her thoughts. She even spoke about it to Fontan, and again posed as a sturdy woman who was not going to stand the slightest flick

from anybody. Fontan, as became a philosophic spirit, declared that all men of fashion were beasts whom it was one's duty to despise. And from that moment forth Nana was full of very real disdain.

That same evening they went to the Bouffes-Parisiens Theatre to see a little woman of Fontan's acquaintance make her *début* in a part of some ten lines. It was close on one o'clock when they once more trudged up the heights of Montmartre. They had purchased a cake, a "Moka," in the Rue de la Chaussée-d'-Antin; and they ate it in bed, seeing that the night was not warm and it was not worth while lighting a fire. Sitting up, side by side, with the bed-clothes pulled up in front, and the pillows piled up behind, they supped and talked about the little woman. Nana thought her plain and lacking in style. Fontan, lying on his stomach, passed up the pieces of cake, which had been put between the candle and the matches on the edge of the night-table. But they ended by quarrelling.

"Oh, just to think of it!" cried Nana. "She's got eyes like gimlet holes, and her hair's the colour of tow."

"Hold your tongue, do!" said Fontan. "She has a superb head of hair and such fire in her looks! It's lovely the way you women always tear each other to pieces!"

He looked annoyed.

"Come now, we've had enough of it!" he said at last, in savage tones. "You know I don't like being bored. Let's go to sleep, or things'll take a nasty turn."

And he blew out the candle, but Nana was furious, and went on talking. She was not going to be spoken to in that voice—she was accustomed to being treated with respect! As he did not vouchsafe any further answer, she was silenced, but she could not go to sleep, and lay tossing to and fro.

"Great God! have you done moving about?" cried he suddenly, giving a brisk jump upwards.

"It isn't my fault if there are crumbs in the bed," said she curtly.

In fact, there were crumbs in the bed. She felt them down to her middle, she was everywhere devoured by them. One single crumb was scorching her, and making her scratch herself till she bled. Besides, when one eats a cake, isn't it usual to shake out the bed-clothes afterwards? Fontan, white with rage, had re-lit the candle, and they both got up, and bare-footed and in their night-dresses, they turned down the clothes and swept up the crumbs on the sheet with their hands. Fontan went to bed again shivering, and told her to go to the devil when she advised him to wipe the soles of his feet carefully. And in the end she came back to her old position, but scarce had she stretched herself out than she danced again. There were fresh crumbs in the bed!

"By Jove, it was sure to happen!" she cried. "You've brought them back again under your feet. I can't go on like this! No, I tell you, I can't go on like this!"

And with that she was on the point of stepping over him in order to jump out of bed again, when Fontan in his longing for sleep grew desperate, and dealt her a ringing box on the ear. The blow was so smart that Nana suddenly found herself lying down again with her head on the pillow.

She lay half stunned.

"Oh!" she ejaculated simply, sighing a child's big sigh.

For a second or two he threatened her with a second slap, asking her at the same time if she meant to move again. Then he put out the light, settled himself squarely on his back, and in a trice was snoring. But she buried her face in the pillow and began sobbing quietly to herself. It was cowardly of him to take advantage of his superior strength! She had experienced very real terror all the same, so terrible had that quaint mask of Fontan's become. And her anger began dwindling down as though the blow had calmed her. She began to feel respect towards him, and accordingly squeezed herself against the wall in order to leave him as much room as possible. She even ended by going to sleep, her cheek tingling, her eyes full of tears, and feeling so deliciously depressed, and wearied, and submissive, that she no longer noticed the crumbs. When she woke up in the morning she was holding Fontain in her naked arms and pressing him tightly against her breast. He would never begin it again, eh? Never again? She loved him too dearly. Why, it was even nice to be beaten if he struck the blow!

After that night a new life began. For a mere trifle—a yes, a no—Fontan would deal her a blow. She grew accustomed to it, and pocketed everything. Sometimes she shed tears and threatened him, but he would pin her up against the wall and talk of strangling her, which had the effect of rendering her extremely obedient. As often as not, she sank down on a chair, and sobbed for five minutes on end. But afterwards, she would forget all about it, grow very merry, fill the little lodgings with the sound of song, and laughter, and the rapid rustle of skirts. The worst of it was that Fontan was now in the habit of disappearing for the whole day and never returning home before midnight, for he was going to cafés and meeting his old friends again. Nana bore with everything. She was tremulous and caressing, her only fear being that she might never see him again if she reproached him. But on certain days, when she had neither Madame Maloir, nor her aunt and Louiset with her, she grew mortally dull. Thus, one Sunday, when she was bargaining for some pigeons at the La Rochefoucauld Market, she was delighted to meet Satin, who, in her turn, was busy purchasing a bunch of radishes. Since the evening when the Prince had drunk Fontan's champagne, they had lost sight of one another. "What? It's you! D'you live in our parts?" said Satin, astounded at seeing her in the street at that hour of the morning, and in slippers too. "Oh, my poor dear girl, you're really ruined then!"

Nana knitted her brows as a sign that she was to hold her tongue, for they were surrounded by other women who wore dressing-gowns, and were without linen, whilst their dishevelled tresses were white with fluff. In the morning, when the man picked up overnight had been newly dismissed, all the courtesans of the quarter were wont to come marketing here, their eyes heavy with sleep, their feet in old down-at-heel shoes, and themselves full of the weariness and ill-humour entailed by a night of boredom. From the four converging streets they came down into the market, looking still rather young in some cases, and very pale and charming in their utter unconstraint, in others, hideous and old, with bloated faces and peeling skin. The latter did not the least mind being seen thus outside working hours, and not one of them deigned to smile when the passers-by on the side-walk turned round to look at them. Indeed they were all very full of business, and wore a disdainful expression as became good housewives for whom men had ceased to exist. Just as Satin, for instance, was paying for her bunch of radishes, a young man, who might have been a shop-boy going late to his work, threw her a passing greeting:

"Good morning, duckie."

She straightened herself up at once, and with the dignified manner becoming an offended queen, remarked,—

"What's up with that swine there?"

Then she fancied she recognized him. Three days ago, towards midnight, as she was coming back alone from the boulevards, she had talked to him at the corner of the Rue Labruyère for nearly half an hour, with a view to persuading him to come home with her. But this recollection only angered her the more.

"Fancy they're brutes enough to shout things to you in broad daylight!" she continued. "When one's out on business, one ought to be respectfully treated, eh?"

Nana had ended by buying her pigeons, although she certainly had her doubts of their freshness. After which Satin wanted to shew her where she lived in the Rue Rochefoucauld close by. And the moment they were alone, Nana told her of her passion for Fontan. Arrived in front of the house, the girl stopped, with her bundle of radishes under her arm, and listened eagerly to a final detail which the other imparted to her. Nana fibbed away, and vowed that it was she who had turned Count Muffat out of doors with a perfect hail of kicks on the posterior.

"Oh, how smart!" Satin repeated; "how very smart! Kicks, eh? And he never said a word, did he? What a blooming coward! I wish I'd been there to see his ugly mug! My dear girl, you were quite right. A pin for the coin! When *I'm* on with a mash, I starve for it! You'll come and see me, eh? You promise? It's the left-hand door. Knock three knocks, for there's a whole heap of damned squints about."

After that, whenever Nana grew too weary of life, she went down and saw Satin. She was always sure of finding her, for the girl never went out before six in the evening. Satin occupied a couple of rooms, which a chemist had furnished for her in order to save her from the clutches of the police; but in little more than a twelvemonth she had broken the furniture, knocked in the chairs, dirtied the curtains, and that in a manner so furiously filthy and untidy, that the lodgings seemed as though inhabited by a pack of mad cats. On the mornings when she grew disgusted with herself, and thought about cleaning up a bit, chair-rails and strips of curtain would come off in her hands during her struggle with superincumbent dirt. On such days the place was fouler than ever, and it was impossible to enter it owing to the things which had fallen down across the doorway. At length she ended by leaving her house severely alone. When the lamp was lit, the cupboard with plate-glass doors, the

clock, and what remained of the curtains, still served to impose on the men. Besides, for six months past, her landlord had been threatening to evict her. Well then, for whom should she be keeping the furniture nice? For him more than anyone else, perhaps! And so, whenever she got up in a merry mood, she would shout "Gee up!" and give the sides of the cupboard and the chest of drawers such a tremendous kick that they cracked again.

Nana nearly always found her in bed. Even on the days when Satin went out to do her marketing, she felt so tired on her return upstairs that she flung herself down on the bed and went to sleep again. During the day she dragged herself about, and dozed off on chairs. Indeed, she did not emerge from this languid condition till the evening drew on, and the gas was lit outside. Nana felt very comfortable at Satin's, sitting doing nothing on the untidy bed, whilst basins stood about on the floor at her feet, and petticoats which had been bemired last night hung over the backs of arm-chairs and stained them with mud. They had long gossips together, and were endlessly confidential, whilst Satin lay on her stomach in her night-gown, waving her legs above her head, and smoking cigarettes as she listened. Sometimes, on such afternoons as they had troubles to retail, they treated themselves to absinthe in order, as they termed it, "to forget." Satin did not go downstairs or put on a petticoat, but simply went and leant over the banisters, and shouted her order to the portress's little girl, a chit of ten, who when she brought up the absinthe in a glass would look furtively at the lady's bare legs. Every conversation led up to one subject—the beastliness of the men. Nana was overpowering on the subject of Fontan. She could not say a dozen words without lapsing into endless repetitions of his sayings and his doings. But Satin, like a good-natured girl, would listen unwearyingly to everlasting accounts of how Nana had watched for him at the window, how they had fallen out over a burnt dish of hash, and how they had made it up in bed after hours of silent sulking. In her desire to be always talking about these things, Nana had got to tell of every slap that he dealt her. Last week he had given her a swollen eye; nay, the night before he had given her such a box on the ear as to throw her across the night-table, and all because he could not find his slippers. And the other woman did not evince any astonishment, but blew out cigarette smoke, and only paused a moment to remark that, for her part, she always ducked under, which sent the gentleman pretty nearly sprawling. Both of them settled down with a will to these anecdotes about blows: they grew supremely happy and excited over these same idiotic doings, about which they told one another a hundred times or more, whilst they gave themselves up to the soft and pleasing sense of weariness which was sure to follow the drubbings they talked of. It was the delight of rediscussing Fontan's blows, and of explaining his works and his ways, down to the very manner in which he took off his boots, which brought Nana back daily to Satin's place. The latter, moreover, used to end by growing sympathetic in her turn, and would cite even more violent cases, as for instance, that of a pastrycook, who had left her for dead on the floor.

Yet she loved him, spite of it all! Then came the days on which Nana cried, and declared that things could not go on as they were doing. Satin would escort her back to her own door, and would linger an hour out in the street to see that he did not murder her. And the next day the two women would rejoice over the reconciliation the whole afternoon through. Yet, though they did not say so, they preferred the days when thrashings were, so to speak, in the air, for then their comfortable indignation was all the stronger.

They became inseparable. Yet, Satin never went to Nana's, Fontan having announced that he would have no trollops in his house. They used to go out together, and thus it was that Satin one day took her friend to see another woman. This woman turned out to be that very Madame Robert who had interested Nana, and inspired her with a certain respect, ever since she had refused to come to her supper. Madame Robert lived in the Rue Mosnier, a silent new street in the Quartier de l'Europe, where there were no shops, and the handsome houses, with their small limited flats, were peopled by ladies. It was five o'clock, and along the silent pavements, in the quiet aristocratic shelter of the tall white houses, were drawn up the broughams of Stock Exchange people and merchants, whilst men walked hastily about, looking up at the windows, where women in dressing-jackets seemed to be awaiting them. At first Nana refused to go up, remarking with some constraint that she had not the pleasure of the lady's acquaintance. But Satin would take no refusal. She was only desirous of paying a civil call, for Madame Robert, whom she had met in a restaurant the day before, had made herself extremely agreeable, and had got her to promise to come and see her. And at last Nana consented. At the top of the stairs a little drowsy maid informed them that *Madame* had not come home yet, but she ushered them into the drawing-room notwithstanding, and left them there.

"The deuce, it's a smart show!" whispered Satin. It was a stiff, middle-class room, hung with dark-coloured fabrics, and suggested the conventional taste of a Parisian shopkeeper who has retired on his fortune. Nana was struck, and did her best to make merry about it. But Satin shewed annoyance, and spoke up for Madame Robert's strict adherence to the proprieties. She was always to be met with in the society of elderly, grave-looking men, on whose arms she leaned. At present, she had a retired chocolate-seller in tow, a serious soul. Whenever he came to see her he was so charmed by the solid, handsome way in which the house was arranged, that he had himself announced and addressed its mistress as "dear child."

"Look! here she is!" continued Satin, pointing to a photograph which stood in front of the clock. Nana scrutinised the portrait for a second or so. It represented a very dark brunette, with a longish face and lips pursed up in a discreet smile. "A thoroughly fashionable lady," one might have said of the likeness, "but one who is rather more reserved than the rest."

"It's strange," murmured Nana at length, "but I've certainly seen that face somewhere. Where I don't remember. But it can't have been in a pretty place

—oh no, I'm sure it wasn't in a pretty place."

And turning towards her friend, she added, "So she's made you promise to come and see her? What does she want with you?"

"What does she want with me? 'Gad! to talk, I expect—to be with me a bit. It's her politeness."

Nana looked steadily at Satin: "Tut, tut," she said softly. After all, it didn't matter to her! Yet, seeing that the lady was keeping them waiting, she declared that she would not stay longer, and accordingly they both took their departure.

The next day Fontan informed Nana that he was not coming home to dinner, and she went down early to find Satin, with a view to treating her at a restaurant. The choice of the restaurant involved infinite debate. Satin proposed various brewery bars, which Nana thought detestable, and at last persuaded her to dine at Laure's. This was a *table d'hôte* in the Rue des Martyrs, where the dinner cost three francs.

Tired of waiting for the dinner-hour and not knowing what to do out in the street, the pair went up to Laure's twenty minutes too early. The three dining-rooms there were still empty, and they sat down at a table, in the very saloon where Laure Piédefer was enthroned on a high bench behind a bar. This Laure was a lady of some fifty summers, whose swelling contours were tightly laced by belts and corsets. Women kept entering in quick procession, and each, in passing, craned upward so as to overtop the saucers raised on the counter, and kissed Laure on the mouth with tender familiarity, whilst the monstrous creature tried, with tears in her eyes, to divide her attentions among them in such a way as to make no one jealous. On the other hand, the servant, who waited on the ladies, was a tall, lean woman. She seemed wasted with disease, and her eyes were ringed with dark lines and glowed with sombre fire. Very rapidly the three saloons filled up. There were some hundred customers, and they had seated themselves wherever they could find vacant places. The majority were nearing the age of forty: their flesh was puffy, and so bloated by vice as almost to hide the outlines of their flaccid mouths. But amid all these gross bosoms and figures, some slim, pretty girls were observable. These still wore a modest expression, despite their impudent gestures, for they were only beginners in their art, who had started life in the ball-rooms of the slums, and had been brought to Laure's by some customer or other. Here the tribe of bloated women, excited by the sweet scent of their youth, jostled one another, and, whilst treating them to dainties, formed a perfect court round them, much as old amorous bachelors might have done. As to the men, they were not numerous. There were ten or fifteen of them at the outside, and, if we except four tall fellows who had come to see the sight, and were cracking jokes and taking things easy, they behaved humbly enough amid this, whelming flood of petticoats.

"I say, their stew's very good, ain't it?" said Satin.

Nana nodded with much satisfaction. It was the old substantial dinner you get in a country hotel, and consisted of *vol-au-vent à la financière,* fowls boiled in rice, beans with a sauce, and vanilla creams, iced and flavoured with burnt

sugar. The ladies made an especial onslaught on the boiled fowl and rice: their stays seemed about to burst, they wiped their lips with slow luxurious movements. At first Nana had been afraid of meeting old friends, who might have asked her silly questions; but she grew calm at last, for she recognised no one she knew among that extremely motley throng, where faded dresses and lamentable hats contrasted strangely with handsome costumes, the wearers of which fraternised in vice with their shabbier neighbours. She was momentarily interested, however, at the sight of a young man, with short curly hair and insolent face, who kept a whole tableful of vastly fat women breathlessly attentive to his slightest caprice. But when the young man began to laugh, his bosom swelled.

"Good lack, it's a woman!"

She let a little cry escape as she spoke, and Satin, who was stuffing herself with boiled fowl, lifted up her head and whispered,—

"Oh, yes! I know her. A smart lot, eh? They do just fight for her."

Nana pouted disgustingly. She could not understand the thing as yet. Nevertheless, she remarked, in her sensible tone, that there was no disputing about tastes or colours, for you never could tell what you yourself might one day have a liking for. So she ate her cream with an air of philosophy, though she was perfectly well aware that Satin with her great blue virginal eyes was throwing the neighbouring tables into a state of great excitement. There was one woman in particular, a powerful fair-haired person who sat close to her and made herself extremely agreeable. She seemed all aglow with affection, and pushed towards the girl so eagerly that Nana was on the point of interfering.

But at that very moment a woman who was entering the room gave her a shock of surprise. Indeed, she had recognised Madame Robert. The latter, looking as was her wont like a pretty brown mouse, nodded familiarly to the tall, lean serving-maid, and came and leant upon Laure's counter. Then both women exchanged a long kiss. Nana thought such an attention on the part of a woman so distinguished-looking very amusing, the more so because Madame Robert had quite altered her usual modest expression. On the contrary, her eye roved about the saloon as she kept up a whispered conversation. Laure had resumed her seat, and once more settled herself down with all the majesty of an old image of Vice, whose face has been worn and polished by the kisses of the faithful. Above the range of loaded plates she sat enthroned in all the opulence which an hotel-keeper enjoys after forty years of activity, and as she sat there she swayed her bloated following of large women, in comparison with the biggest of whom she seemed monstrous.

But Madame Robert had caught sight of Satin, and leaving Laure she ran up and behaved charmingly, telling her how much she regretted not having been at home the day before. When Satin, however, who was ravished at this treatment, insisted on finding room for her at the table, she vowed she had already dined. She had simply come up to look about her. As she stood talking behind her new friend's chair, she leant lightly on her shoulders, and in a smiling, coaxing manner remarked,—

"Now, when shall I see you? If you were free——"

Nana unluckily failed to hear more. The conversation vexed her, and she was dying to tell this honest lady a few home truths. But the sight of a troop of new arrivals paralysed her. It was composed of smart, fashionably-dressed women, who were wearing their diamonds. Under the influence of perverse impulse, they had made up a party to come to Laure's—whom, by-the-by, they all treated with great familiarity—to eat the three-franc dinner, whilst flashing their jewels of great price in the jealous and astonished eyes of poor bedraggled prostitutes. The moment they entered, talking and laughing in their shrill clear tones, and seeming to bring sunshine with them from the outside world, Nana turned her head rapidly away. Much to her annoyance, she had recognised Lucy Stewart and Maria Blond amongst them, and for nearly five minutes, during which the ladies chatted with Laure before passing into the saloon beyond, she kept her head down, and seemed deeply occupied in rolling bread pills on the cloth in front of her. But, when at length she was able to look round, what was her astonishment to observe the chair next to hers vacant! Satin had vanished.

"Gracious, where can she be?" she loudly ejaculated.

The sturdy fair woman, who had been overwhelming Satin with civil attentions, laughed ill-temperedly, and when Nana, whom the laugh irritated, looked threatening, she remarked in a soft drawling way,—

"It's certainly not me that's done you this turn; it's the other one!"

Thereupon, Nana understood that they would most likely make game of her, and so said nothing more. She even kept her seat for some moments, as she did not wish to shew how angry she felt. She could hear Lucy Stewart laughing at the end of the next saloon, where she was treating a whole table of little women, who had come from the public balls at Montmartre and la Chapelle. It was very hot; the servant was carrying away piles of dirty plates with a strong scent of boiled fowl and rice, whilst the four gentlemen had ended by regaling quite half a dozen couples with capital wine in the hope of making them tipsy and hearing some pretty stiffish things. What at present most exasperated Nana was the thought of paying for Satin's dinner. There was a wench for you, who allowed herself to be amused, and then made off with never a thank-you in company with the first petticoat that came by! Without doubt it was only a matter of three francs, but she felt it was hard lines all the same—her way of doing it was too disgusting. Nevertheless she paid up, throwing the six francs at Laure, whom at the moment she despised more than the mud in the street. In the Rue des Martyrs Nana felt her bitterness increasing. She was certainly not going to run after Satin! It was a nice filthy business for one to be poking one's nose into! But her evening was spoilt, and she walked slowly up again towards Montmartre, raging against Madame Robert in particular. Gracious goodness, that woman had a fine cheek to go playing the lady—yes, the lady in the dust-bin! She now felt sure she had met her at the "Papillon," a wretched public-house ball in the Rue des Poisson-

niers, where men conquered her scruples for thirty sous. And to think a thing like that got hold of important functionaries with her modest looks! And to think she refused suppers to which one did her the honour of inviting her, because forsooth she was playing the virtuous game! Oh, yes, she'd get virtued! It was always those conceited prudes who went the most fearful lengths in low corners nobody knew anything about.

Revolving these matters, Nana at length reached her home in the Rue Véron, and was taken aback on observing a light in the window. Fontan had come home in a sulk, for he too had been deserted by the friend who had been dining with him. He listened coldly to her explanations, whilst she trembled lest he should strike her. It scared her to find him at home, seeing that she had not expected him before one in the morning, and she told him a fib, and confessed that she had certainly spent six francs, but in Madame Maloir's society. He was not ruffled, however, and he handed her a letter, which, though addressed to her, he had quietly opened. It was a letter from Georges, who was still a prisoner at The Fondettes, and comforted himself weekly with the composition of glowing pages. Nana loved to be written to, especially when the letters were full of grand, lover-like expressions, with a sprinkling of vows. She used to read them to everybody. Fontan was familiar with the style employed by Georges, and appreciated it. But that evening she was so afraid of a scene that she affected complete indifference, skimming through the letter with a sulky expression and flinging it aside as soon as read. Fontan had begun beating a tattoo on a window-pane: the thought of going to bed so early bored him, and yet he did not know how to employ his evening. He turned briskly round:

"Suppose we answer that young vagabond at once," said he.

It was the custom for him to write the letters in reply. He was wont to vie with the other in point of style. Then, too, he used to be delighted when Nana, grown enthusiastic after the letter had been read over aloud, would kiss him with the announcement that nobody but he could "say things like that." Thus their latent affections would be stirred, and they would end with mutual adoration.

"As you will," she replied. "I'll make tea, and we'll go to bed after."

Thereupon Fontan installed himself at the table, on which pen, ink, and paper were at the same time grandly displayed. He curved his arm: he drew a long face.

"My Heart's Own," he began aloud.

And, for more than an hour he applied himself to his task, polishing here, weighing a phrase there, whilst he sat with his head between his hands, and laughed inwardly whenever he hit upon a peculiarly tender expression. Nana had already consumed two cups of tea in silence, when at last he read out the letter in the level voice, and with the two or three emphatic gestures peculiar to such performances on the stage. It was five pages long, and he spoke therein of "the delicious hours passed at The Mignotte, those hours of which the memory lingered like subtle perfume." He vowed "eternal fidelity to that springtide of Love," and ended by declaring that his sole wish was to "recommence that

happy time, if indeed, happiness can recommence."

"I say that out of politeness, y'know," he explained. "The moment it becomes laughable—eh, what! I think she's felt it, she has!"

He glowed with triumph. But Nana was unskilful: she still suspected an outbreak, and now was mistaken enough not to fling her arms round his neck in a burst of admiration. She thought the letter a respectable performance, nothing more. Thereupon he was much annoyed. If his letter did not please her, she might write another! And so, instead of bursting out in lover-like speeches and exchanging kisses, as their wont was, they sat coldly facing one another at the table. Nevertheless, she poured him out a cup of tea.

"Here's a filthy mess," he cried, after dipping his lips in the mixture. "You've put salt in it, you have!"

Nana was unlucky enough to shrug her shoulders, and at that he grew furious.

"Ah, ha! things are taking a wrong turn to-night!"

And with that the quarrel began. It was only ten by the clock, and this was a way of killing time. So he lashed himself into a rage, and threw in Nana's teeth a whole string of insults and all kinds of accusations, which followed one another so closely that she had no time to defend herself. She was dirty, she was stupid, she had knocked about in all sorts of low places! After that, he waxed frantic over the money question. Did he spend six francs when he dined out? No, somebody was treating him to a dinner; otherwise he would have eaten his ordinary meal at home. And to think of spending them on that old procuress of a Maloir, a jade he would chuck out of the house to-morrow! Yes, by Jingo! they would get into a nice mess if he and she were to go throwing six francs out of window every day!

"Now, to begin with, I want your accounts," he shouted. "Let's see; hand over the money! Now, where do we stand?"

All his sordid avaricious instincts came to the surface. Nana was cowed and scared, and she made haste to fetch their remaining cash out of the desk, and to bring it him. Up to that time the key had lain on this common treasury, from which they had drawn as freely as they wished.

"How's this?" said he, when he had counted up the money, "there are scarcely seven thousand francs remaining out of seventeen thousand, and we've only been together three months. The thing's impossible."

He rushed forward, gave the desk a savage shake, and brought the drawer forward in order to ransack it in the light of the lamp. But it actually contained only six thousand eight hundred and odd francs. Thereupon the tempest burst forth.

"Ten thousand francs in three months!" he yelled. "By God! what have you done with it all? Eh? Answer! It all goes to your jade of an aunt, eh? Or you're keeping men, that's plain! Will you answer?"

"Oh, well! if you must get in a rage!" said Nana. "Why, the calculation's easily made! You haven't allowed for the furniture; besides, I've had to buy linen. Money goes quickly when one's settling in a new place."

But while requiring explanations he refused to listen to them.

"Yes, it goes a deal too quickly!" he rejoined more calmly. "And look here, little girl, I've had enough of this mutual housekeeping. You know those seven thousand francs are mine. Yes, and as I've got 'em, I shall keep 'em! Hang it, the moment you become wasteful I get anxious not to be ruined. To each man his own."

And he pocketed the money in a lordly way, whilst Nana gazed at him dumbfounded. He continued speaking complaisantly,—

"You must understand I'm not such a fool as to keep aunts and likewise children who don't belong to me. You were pleased to spend your own money —well, that's your affair! But my money—no, that's sacred! When in future you cook a leg of mutton, I'll pay for half of it. We'll settle up to-night—there!"

Straightway Nana rebelled. She could not help shouting,—

"Come, I say, it's you who've run through my ten thousand francs. It's a dirty trick, I tell you!"

But he did not stop to discuss matters further, for he dealt her a random box on the ear across the table, remarking as he did so,—

"Let's have that again!"

She let him have it again, despite his blow. Whereupon he fell upon her, and kicked and cuffed her heartily. Soon he had reduced her to such a state that she ended, as her wont was, by undressing and going to bed in a flood of tears.

He was out of breath, and was going to bed in his turn, when he noticed the letter he had written to Georges lying on the table. Whereupon he folded it up carefully, and, turning towards the bed, remarked in threatening accents,—

"It's very well written, and I'm going to post it myself, because I don't like women's fancies. Now don't go moaning any more; it puts my teeth on edge."

Nana, who was crying and gasping, thereupon held her breath. When he was in bed she choked with emotion, and threw herself upon his breast with a wild burst of sobs. Their scuffles always ended thus, for she trembled at the thought of losing him, and, like a coward, wanted always to feel that he belonged entirely to her, despite everything. Twice he pushed her magnificently away, but the warm embrace of this woman, who was begging for mercy with great tearful eyes as some faithful brute might do, finally aroused desire. And he became royally condescending, without, however, lowering his dignity before any of her advances. In fact, he let himself be carressed and taken by force, as became a man whose forgiveness is worth the trouble of winning. Then he was seized with anxiety, fearing that Nana was playing a part with a view to regaining possession of the treasury key. The light had been extinguished when he felt it necessary to reaffirm his will and pleasure.

"You must know, my girl, that this is really very serious and that I keep the money."

Nana, who was falling asleep with her arms round his neck, uttered a sublime sentiment.

"Yes, you need fear nothing! I'll work for both of us!"

But from that evening onwards, their life in common became more and more difficult. From one week's end to the other the noise of slaps filled the air, and resembled the ticking of a clock by which they regulated their existence. Through dint of being much beaten, Nana became as pliable as fine linen; her skin grew delicate, and pink and white, and so soft to the touch and clear to the view that she may be said to have grown more good-looking than ever. Prullière, moreover, began running after her like a madman, coming in when Fontan was away, and pushing her into corners in order to snatch an embrace. But she used to struggle out of his grasp, full of indignation, and blushing with shame. It disgusted her to think of him wanting to deceive a friend. Prullière would thereupon begin sneering with a wrathful expression. Why, she was growing jolly stupid nowadays! How could she take up with such an ape? For indeed Fontan was a regular ape, with that great swingeing nose of his. Oh, he had an ugly mug! Besides, the man knocked her about too!

"It's possible: I like him as he is," she one day made answer, in the quiet voice peculiar to a woman who confesses to an abominable taste.

Bosc contented himself by dining with them as often as possible. He shrugged his shoulders behind Prullière's back— a pretty fellow to be sure, but a frivolous! Bosc had on more than one occasion assisted at domestic scenes, and at dessert, when Fontan slapped Nana, he went on chewing solemnly, for the thing struck him as being quite in the course of nature. In order to give some return for his dinner, he used always to go into ecstasies over their happiness. He declared himself a philosopher, who had given up everything, glory included. At times Prullière and Fontan lolled back in their chairs, losing count of time in front of the empty table, whilst with theatrical gestures and intonation they discussed their former successes till two in the morning. But he would sit by, lost in thought, finishing the brandy bottle in silence, and only occasionally emitting a little contemptuous sniff. Where was Talma's tradition? Nowhere. Very well, let them leave him jolly well alone! It was too stupid to go on as they were doing!

One evening he found Nana in tears. She took off her dressing-jacket in order to shew him her back and her arms, which were black and blue. He looked at her skin without being tempted to abuse the opportunity, as that ass of a Prullière would have been. Then, sententiously,—

"My dear girl, where there are women there are sure to be ructions. It was Napoleon who said that, I think. Wash yourself with salt water. Salt water's the very thing for those little knocks. Tut, tut, you'll get others as bad, but don't complain so long as no bones are broken. I'm inviting myself to dinner, you know; I've spotted a leg of mutton."

But Madame Lerat had less philosophy. Every time Nana shewed her a fresh bruise on the white skin she screamed aloud. They were killing her niece: things couldn't go on as they were doing. As a matter of fact, Fontan had turned Madame Lerat out of doors, and had declared that he would not have her at his house in the future, and ever since that day, when he returned home and she happened to be there, she had to make off through the kitchen, which was a horrible humilia-

tion to her. Accordingly, she never ceased inveighing against that brutal individual. She especially blamed his ill-breeding, pursing up her lips, as she did so, like a highly respectable lady, whom nobody could possibly remonstrate with on the subject of good manners.

"Oh, you notice it at once," she used to tell Nana; "he hasn't the barest notion of the very smallest proprieties. His mother must have been common! Don't deny it—the thing's obvious! I don't speak on my own account, though a person of my years has a right to respectful treatment: but *you*—how do *you* manage to put up with his bad manners? For, though I don't want to flatter myself, I've always taught you how to behave, and, among our own people you always enjoyed the best possible advice. We were all very well-bred in our family, weren't we now?"

Nana used never to protest, but would listen with bowed head.

"Then, too," continued the aunt, "you've only known perfect gentlemen hitherto. We were talking of that very topic with Zoé, at my place, yesterday evening. She can't understand it any more than I can. 'How is it,' said she, 'that *Madame*, who used to have that perfect gentleman, Monsieur le Comte, at her beck and call'—for between you and me it seems you drove him silly—'how is it that *Madame* lets herself be made into mince-meat by that clown of a fellow?' I remarked at the time that you might put up with the beatings, but that I would never have allowed him to be lacking in proper respect. In fact, there isn't a word to be said for him. I wouldn't have his portrait in my room even! And you ruin yourself for such a bird as that; yes, you ruin yourself, my darling; you toil and you moil, when there are so many others, and such rich men too, some of them even connected with the Government! Ah, well, it's not I who ought to be telling you this, of course! But, all the same, when next he tries any of his dirty tricks on, I should cut him short with a 'Monsieur, what d'you take me for?' You know how to say it in that grand way of yours! It would downright cripple him."

Thereupon Nana burst into sobs, and stammered out,—

"Oh, aunt, I love him!"

The fact of the matter was that Madame Lerat was beginning to feel anxious at the painful way her niece doled out the sparse occasional francs, destined to pay for little Louis's board and lodging. Doubtless she was willing to make sacrifices, and to keep the child by her whatever might happen, whilst waiting for more prosperous times, but the thought that Fontan was preventing her, and the brat, and its mother, from swimming in a sea of gold, made her so savage that she was ready to deny the very existence of true love. Accordingly she ended up with the following severe remarks:

"Now listen, some fine day when he's taken the skin off your back, you'll come and knock at my door, and I'll open it to you."

Soon, money began to engross Nana's whole attention. Fontan had caused the seven thousand francs to vanish away. Without doubt they were quite safe: indeed, she would never have dared ask him questions about them, for she was wont to be blushingly diffident with that bird, as Madame Lerat called him. She trembled lest he should think her capable of quarrelling with him about halfpence. He had certainly promised to subscribe towards their common household expenses, and in the early days he had given out three francs every morning. But he was as exacting as a boarder: he wanted everything for his three francs—butter, meat, early fruit and early vegetables—and if she ventured to make an observation, if she hinted that you could not have everything in the market for three francs, he flew into a temper and treated her as a useless wasteful woman, a confounded donkey, whom the tradespeople were robbing. Moreover, he was always ready to threaten that he would take lodgings somewhere else. At the end of a month, on certain mornings, he had forgotten to deposit the three francs on the chest of drawers, and she had ventured to ask for them in a timid roundabout way. Whereupon there had been such bitter disputes, and he had seized every pretext to render her life so miserable, that she had found it best no longer to count upon him. Whenever, however, he had omitted to leave behind the three one-franc pieces, and found a dinner awaiting him all the same, he grew as merry as a sand-boy, kissed Nana gallantly, and waltzed with the chairs. And she was so charmed by this conduct that she at length got to hope that nothing would be found on the chest of drawers, despite the difficulty she experienced in making both ends meet. One day she even returned him his three francs, telling him a tale to the effect that she still had yesterday's money. As he had given her nothing then, he hesitated for some moments, as though he dreaded a lecture. But she gazed at him with her loving eyes, and hugged him in such utter self-surrender, that he pocketed the money again with that little convulsive twitch of the fingers peculiar to a miser when he regains possession of that which has been well-nigh lost. From that day forth he never troubled himself about money again, nor enquired whence it came. But when there were potatoes on the table he looked intoxicated with delight, and would laugh and smack his lips before her turkeys and legs of mutton, though of course this did not prevent his dealing Nana sundry sharp smacks, as though to keep his hand in, amid all his happiness.

Nana had indeed found means to provide for all needs, and the place on certain days overflowed with good things. Twice a week regularly, Bosc had indigestion. One evening as Madame Lerat was withdrawing from the scene in high dudgeon because she had noticed a copious dinner she was not destined to eat in process of preparation, she could not prevent herself asking brutally who paid for it all. Nana was taken by surprise: she grew foolish, and began crying.

"Ah! that's a pretty business," said the aunt, who had divined her meaning.

Nana had resigned herself to it for the sake of enjoying peace in her own home. Then, too, the Tricon was to blame. She had come across her in the Rue de Laval, one fine day when Fontan had gone out raging about a dish of cod. She had accordingly consented to the proposals made her by the Tricon, who happened just then to be in a difficulty. As Fontan never came in before six o'clock, she made arrangements for her afternoons, and used to bring back forty francs, sixty francs, sometimes more.

She might have made it a matter of ten and fifteen louis had she been able to maintain her former position, but, as matters stood she was very glad thus to earn enough to keep the pot boiling. At night she used to forget all her sorrows, when Bosc sat there bursting with dinner, and Fontan leant on his elbows, and with an expression of lofty superiority becoming a man who is loved for his own sake, allowed her to kiss him on the eyelids.

In due course Nana's very adoration of her darling, her dear old duck, which was all the more passionately blind seeing that now she paid for everything, plunged her back into the muddiest depths of her calling. She roamed the streets, and loitered on the pavement in quest of a five-franc piece, just as when she was a slipshod baggage years ago. One Sunday, at the La Rochefoucauld Market, she had made her peace with Satin, after having flown at her with furious reproaches about Madame Robert. But Satin had been content to answer that, when one didn't like a thing, there was no reason why one should want to disgust others with it. And Nana, who was by way of being wide-minded, had accepted the philosophic view that you never can tell where your tastes will lead you, and had forgiven her. Her curiosity was even excited, and she began questioning her about obscure vices, and was astounded to be adding to her information at her time of life and with her knowledge. She burst out laughing and gave vent to various expressions of surprise. It struck her as so queer, and yet she was a little shocked by it, for she was really quite the Philistine outside the pale of her own habits. So she went back to Laure's and fed there when Fontan was dining out. She derived much amusement from the stories, and the amours, and the jealousies, which inflamed the female customers without hindering their appetites in the slightest degree. Nevertheless, she still was not quite in it, as she herself phrased it. The vast Laure, meltingly maternal as ever, used often to invite her to pass a day or two at her Asnières Villa, a country house containing seven spare bedrooms. But she used to refuse: she was afraid. Satin, however, swore she was mistaken about it, that gentlemen from Paris swung you in swings, and played *tonneau* with you, and so she promised to come at some future time, when it would be possible for her to leave town.

At that time Nana was much tormented by circumstances, and not at all festively inclined. She needed money, and when the Tricon did not want her, which too often happened, she had no notion where to bestow her charms. Then began a series of wild descents upon the Parisian pavement, plunges into the baser sort of vice, whose votaries prowl in muddy by-streets under the restless flicker of gas-lamps. Nana went back to the public-house balls in the suburbs, where she had kicked up her heels in the early ill-shod days. She revisited the dark corners on the outer boulevards, where, when she was fifteen years old, men used to hug her, whilst her father was looking for her in order to give her a hiding. Both the women would speed along, visiting all the ballrooms and restaurants in a quarter, and climbing innumerable staircases, which were wet with spittle and spilt beer, or they would

stroll quietly about, going up streets and planting themselves in front of carriage-gates. Satin, who had served her apprenticeship in the Quartier Latin, used to take Nana to Bullier's and the public-houses in the Boulevard Saint-Michel. But the vacations were drawing on, and the "Quarter" looked too starved. Eventually they always returned to the principal boulevards, for it was there they ran the best chance of getting what they wanted. From the heights of Montmartre to the Observatory plateau, they scoured the whole town in the way we have been describing. They were out on rainy evenings, when their boots got worn down, and on hot evenings when their linen clung to their skins. There were long periods of waiting and endless periods of walking; there were jostlings and disputes, and the nameless brutal caresses of the stray passer-by who was taken by them to some miserable furnished room, and came swearing down the greasy stairs afterwards.

The summer was drawing to a close, a stormy summer of burning nights. The pair used to start out together after dinner towards nine o'clock. On the pavements of the Rue Notre Dame de la Lorette two long files of women scudded along with tucked-up skirts and bent heads, keeping close to the shops, but never once glancing at the displays in the shop-windows, as they hurried busily down towards the boulevards. This was the hungry exodus from the Quartier Breda which took place nightly when the street lamps had just been lit. Nana and Satin used to skirt the church and then march off along the Rue le Peletier. When they were some hundred yards from the Café Riche, and had fairly reached their scene of operations, they would shake out the skirts of their dresses which up till that moment they had been holding carefully up, and begin sweeping the pavements, regardless of dust. With much swaying of the hips they strolled delicately along, slackening their pace when they crossed the bright light thrown from one of the great cafés. With shoulders thrown back, shrill and noisy laughter, and many backward glances at the men who turned to look at them, they marched about and were completely in their element. In the shadow of night, their artificially whitened faces, their rouged lips, and their darkened eyelids became as charming and suggestive as if the inmates of a make-believe trumpery Oriental bazaar had been sent forth into the open street. Till eleven at night they sauntered gaily along among the rudely-jostling crowds, contenting themselves with an occasional "dirty ass!" hurled after the clumsy people whose boot-heels had torn a flounce or two from their dresses. Little familiar salutations would pass between them and the café waiters, and at times they would stop and chat in front of a small table and accept of drinks, which they consumed with much deliberation, as became people not sorry to sit down for a bit whilst waiting for the theatres to empty. But, as night advanced, if they had not made one or two trips in the direction of the Rue la Rochefoucauld, they became abject strumpets, and their hunt for men grew more ferocious than ever. Beneath the trees, in the darkening and fast-emptying boulevards, fierce bargainings took place, accompanied by oaths and blows. Respectable family parties—fathers, mothers, and daughters —who were used to such scenes, would pass quietly by the while, without quickening their pace. Afterwards, when they had walked from the Opera to the Gymnase some half score times, and, in the deepening night, men were rapidly dropping off homewards for good and all, Nana and Satin kept to the side-walk in the Rue du Faubourg Montmartre. There, up till two o'clock in the morning, restaurants, bars, and ham-and-beef shops were brightly lit up, whilst a noisy mob of women hung obstinately round the doors of the cafés. This suburb was the only corner of night Paris which was still alight and still alive, the only market still open to nocturnal bargains. These last were openly struck between group and group, and from one end of the street to the other, just as in the wide and open corridor of a disorderly house. On such evenings as the pair came home, without having had any success, they used to wrangle together. The Rue Notre Dame de la Lorette stretched dark and deserted in front of them. Here and there the crawling shadow of a woman was discernible; for the quarter was going home, and going home late, and poor creatures, exasperated at a night of fruitless loitering, were unwilling to give up the chase, and would still stand disputing in hoarse voices with any strayed reveller they could catch at the corner of the Rue Breda or the Rue Fontaine.

Nevertheless, some windfalls came in their way now and then, in the shape of louis picked up in the society of elegant gentlemen, who slipped their decorations into their pockets as they went upstairs with them. Satin had an especially keen scent for these. On rainy evenings, when the dripping city exhaled an unpleasant odour suggestive of a great untidy bed, she knew that the soft weather and the fetid reek of the town's holes and corners were sure to send the men mad. And so she watched the best dressed among them, for she knew by their pale eyes what their state was. On such nights it was as though a fit of fleshly madness were passing over Paris. The girl was rather nervous certainly, for the most modish gentlemen were always the most obscene. All the varnish would crack off a man, and the brute beast would shew itself, exacting, monstrous in lust, a past master in corruption. But besides being nervous, that trollop of a Satin was lacking in respect. She would blurt out awful things in front of dignified gentlemen in carriages, and assure them that their coachmen were better bred than they, because they behave respectfully towards the women and did not half kill them with their diabolical tricks and suggestions. The way in which smart people sprawled head over heels into all the cesspools of vice still caused Nana some surprise, for she had a few prejudices remaining, though Satin was rapidly destroying them.

"Well, then," she used to say, when talking seriously about the matter, "there's no such thing as virtue left, is there?"

From one end of the social ladder to the other everybody was on the loose! Good gracious! Some nice things ought to be going on in Paris between nine o'clock in the evening and three in the morning! And with that she began making very merry and declaring that, if one could only have looked into every room, one would have seen some funny sights—the little people going it head over ears, and a good lot of swells, too, playing the swine rather harder than the rest. Oh, she was finishing her education!

One evening when she came to call for Satin she recognised the Marquis de Chauard. He was coming downstairs with quaking legs—his face was ashen white and he leant heavily on the banisters. She pretended to be blowing her nose. Upstairs she found Satin amid indescrible filth. No household work had been done for a week, her bed was disgusting, and ewers and basins were standing about in all directions. Nana expressed surprise at her knowing the Marquis. Oh, yes, she knew him! He had jolly well bored her confectioner and her when they were together. At present, he used to come back now and then, but he nearly bothered her life out, going sniffing into all the dirty corners—yes, even into her slippers!

"Yes, dear girl, my slippers! Oh! he's the dirtiest old beast, always wanting one to do things!"

The sincerity of these low debauches rendered Nana especially uneasy. Seeing the courtesans around her slowly dying of it every day, she recalled to mind the comedy of pleasure she had taken part in when she was in the heyday of success. Moreover, Satin inspired her with an awful fear of the police. She was full of anecdotes about them. Formerly she had been the mistress of a plain-clothes man—had consented to this in order to be left in peace, and on two occasions he had prevented her from being put "on the lists." But, at present, she was in a great fright, for, if she were to be nabbed again, there was a clear case against her. You had only to listen to her! For the sake of perquisites, the police used to take up as many women as possible. They laid hold of everybody, and quieted you with a slap if you shouted, for they were sure of being defended in their actions and rewarded, even when they had taken a virtuous girl amongst the rest. In the summer they would swoop upon the boulevard in parties of twelve or fifteen, surround a whole long reach of side-walk and fishing up as many as thirty women in an evening. Satin, however, knew the likely places, and the moment she saw a plain-clothes man heaving in sight she took to her heels, while the long lines of women on the pavements scattered in consternation and fled through the surrounding crowd. The dread of the law and of the magistracy was such that certain women would stand as though paralysed in the doorways of the cafés, whilst the raid was sweeping the avenue without. But Satin was even more afraid of being denounced; for her pastrycook had proved blackguard enough to threaten to sell her when she had left him. Yes, that was a fake by which men lived on their mistresses! Then, too, there were the dirty women who delivered you up out of sheer treachery, if you were prettier than they! Nana listened to these recitals, and felt her terrors growing upon her. She had always trembled before the Law, that unknown power, that form of revenge practised by men able and willing to crush her in the certain absence of all defenders. Saint-Lazare she pictured as a grave, a dark hole, in which they buried live women after they had cut off their hair. She admitted that it was only necessary to leave Fontan and seek powerful protectors. But as matters stood, it was in vain that Satin talked to her of certain lists of women's names, which it was the duty of the plain-clothes men to consult, and of certain photographs accompanying the lists, the originals of which were on no account to be touched. The reassurance did not make her tremble the less, and she still saw herself hustled and dragged along, and finally subjected to the official medical inspection. The thought of the official armchair filled her with shame and anguish, for had she not bade it defiance a score of times?

Now it so happened that, one evening towards the close of September, as she was walking with Satin in the Boulevard Poissonnière, the latter suddenly began tearing along at a terrible pace. And when Nana asked her what she meant thereby,—

"It's the plain-clothes men!" whispered Satin. "Off with you! Off with you!"

A wild stampede took place amid the surging crowd. Skirts streamed out behind, and were torn. There were blows and shrieks. A woman fell down. The crowd of bystanders stood hilariously watching this rough police raid, whilst the plain-clothes men rapidly narrowed their circle. Meanwhile, Nana had lost Satin. Her legs were failing her, and she would have been taken up for a certainty, had not a man caught her by the arm and led her away in front of the angry police. It was Prullière, and he had just recognised her. Without saying a word, he turned down the Rue Rougemont with her. It was just then quite deserted, and she was able to regain breath there, but at first her faintness and exhaustion were such that he had to support her. She did not even thank him.

"Look here," said he, "you must recover a bit. Come up to my rooms." He lodged in the Rue Bergère close by. But she straightened herself up at once.

"No, I don't want to."

Thereupon he waxed coarse, and rejoined,—

"Why don't you want to, eh? Why, everybody visits my rooms."

"Because I don't."

In her opinion that explained everything. She was too fond of Fontan to betray him with one of his friends. The other people ceased to count the moment there was no pleasure in the business, and necessity compelled her to it. In view of her idiotic obstinacy, Prullière, as became a pretty fellow whose vanity had been wounded, did a cowardly thing.

"Very well, do as you like!" he cried "Only I don't side with you, my dear. You must get out of the scrape by yourself."

And with that he left her. Terrors got hold of her again, and scurrying past shops and turning white whenever a man drew nigh, she fetched an immense compass before reaching Montmartre.

On the morrow, whilst still suffering from the shock of last night's terrors, Nana went to her aunt's, and, at the foot of a small empty street in the Batignolles, found herself face to face with Labordette. At first they both appeared embarrassed, for with his usual complaisance he was busy on a secret errand. Nevertheless, he was the first to regain his self-possession and to announce him-

self fortunate in meeting her. Yes, certainly, everybody was still wondering at Nana's total eclipse. People were asking for her, and old friends were pining. And with that he grew quite paternal, and ended by sermonising.

"Frankly speaking, between you and me, my dear, the thing's getting stupid. One can understand a mash, but to go to that extent, to be trampled on like that, and to get nothing but knocks! Are you playing up for the 'Virtue Prizes' then?"

She listened to him with an embarrassed expression. But when he told her about Rose, who was triumphantly enjoying her conquest of Count Muffat, a flame came into her eyes.

"Oh! if I wanted to——" she muttered.

As became an obliging friend, he at once offered to act as intercessor. But she refused his help, and he thereupon attacked her in an opposite quarter.

He informed her that Bordenave was busy mounting a play of Fauchery's, containing a splendid part for her.

"What! a play with a part!" she cried in amazement. "But he's in it, and he's told me nothing about it!"

She did not mention Fontan by name. However, she grew calm again directly, and declared that she would never go on the stage again. Labordette doubtless remained unconvinced, for he continued with smiling insistence.

"You know you need fear nothing with me. I get your Muffat ready for you, and you go on the stage again, and I bring him to you like a little dog!"

"No!" cried she, decisively.

And she left him. Her heroic conduct made her tenderly pitiful towards herself. No blackguard of a man would ever have sacrificed himself like that without trumpeting the fact abroad. Nevertheless, she was struck by one thing: Labordette had given her exactly the same advice as Francis had given her. That evening, when Fontan came home, she questioned him about Fauchery's piece. The former had been back at the Variétés for two months past. Why, then, had he not told her about the part?

"What part?" said he, in his ill-humoured tone. "The grand lady's part, maybe? The deuce, you believe you've got talent then! Why, such a part would utterly do for you, my girl! You're meant for comic business—there's no denying it!"

She was dreadfully wounded. All that evening he kept chaffing her, calling her Mademoiselle Mars. But the harder he hit, the more bravely she suffered, for she derived a certain bitter satisfaction from this heroic devotion of hers, which rendered her very great and very loving in her own eyes. Ever since she had gone with other men in order to supply his wants, her love for him had increased, and the fatigues and disgusts encountered outside only added to the flame. He was fast becoming a sort of pet vice for which she paid, a necessity of existence it was impossible to do without, seeing that blows only stimulated her desires. He, on his part, seeing what a good tame thing she had become, ended by abusing his privileges. She was getting on his nerves, and he began to conceive so fierce a loathing for her that he forgot to keep count of his real interests. When Bosc made his customary remarks to him, he cried

out in exasperation, for which there was no apparent cause, that he had had enough of her and of her good dinners, and that he would shortly chuck her out of doors if only for the sake of making another woman a present of his seven thousand francs. Indeed, that was how their liaison ended.

One evening Nana came in towards eleven o'clock, and found the door bolted. She tapped once—there was no answer; twice—still no answer. Meanwhile, she saw light under the door, and Fontan inside did not trouble to move. She rapped again unwearyingly; she called him, and began to get annoyed. At length Fontan's voice became audible; he spoke slowly and rather unctuously, and uttered but this one word:

"*Merde!*"

She beat on the door with her fists.

"*Merde!*"

She banged hard enough to smash in the woodwork.

"*Merde!*"

And for upwards of a quarter of an hour the same foul expression buffeted her, answering like a jeering echo to every blow wherewith she shook the door. At length, seeing that she was not growing tired, he opened sharply, planted himself on the threshold, folded his arms, and said in the same cold, brutal voice,—

"By God! have you done yet? What d'you want? Are you going to let us sleep in peace, eh? You can quite see I've got company to-night."

He was certainly not alone, for Nana perceived the little woman from the Bouffes, with the untidy tow hair and the gimlet-hole eyes, standing enjoying herself in her shift among the furni-

ture she had paid for. But Fontan
stepped out on the landing. He looked
terrible, and he spread out and crooked
his great fingers as if they were pincers.

"Hook it, or I'll strangle you!"

Thereupon Nana burst into a nervous
fit of sobbing. She was frightened, and
she made off. This time it was she that
was being kicked out of doors. And in
her fury the thought of Muffat suddenly
occurred to her. Ah, to be sure, Fontan
of all men ought never to have done her
such a turn!

When she was out in the street, her
first thought was to go and sleep with
Satin, provided the girl had no one with
her. She met her in front of her house,
for she, too, had been turned out of
doors by her landlord. He had just had
a padlock affixed to her door—quite il-
legally, of course, seeing that she had
her own furniture. She swore, and talked
of having him up before the commissary of police. In the mean time, as
midnight was striking, they had to begin
thinking of finding a bed. And Satin,
deeming it unwise to let the plain-clothes
men into her secrets, ended by taking
Nana to a woman who kept a little hotel
in the Rue Laval. Here they were assigned a narrow room on the first floor,
the window of which opened on the court-
yard. Satin remarked,—

"I should gladly have gone to Madame
Robert's. There's always a corner there
for me. But with you it's out of the
question. She's getting absurdly jealous; she beat me the other night."

When they had shut themselves in,
Nana, who had not yet relieved her feelings, burst into tears and again and again
recounted Fontan's dirty behaviour. Satin

listened complaisantly, comforted her,
grew even more angry than she in denunciation of the male sex.

"Oh, the pigs, the pigs! Look here,
we'll have nothing more to do with
them!"

Then she helped Nana to undress with
all the small busy attentions becoming a
humble little friend. She kept saying
coaxingly,—

"Let's go to bed as fast as we can,
pet. We shall be better off there! Oh,
how silly you are to get crusty about
things! I tell you they're dirty brutes.
Don't think any more about 'em. I—I
love you very much. Don't cry, and
oblige your own little darling girl."

And, once in bed, she forthwith took
Nana in her arms, and soothed and comforted her. She refused to hear Fontan's name mentioned again, and each
time it recurred to her friend's lips, she
stopped it with a kiss. Her lips pouted
in pretty indignation, her hair lay loose
about her, and her face glowed with tenderness and childlike beauty. Little by
little her soft embrace compelled Nana
to dry her tears. She was touched, and
replied to Satin's caresses. When two
o'clock struck the candle was still burning, and a sound of soft smothered laughter and lovers' talk was audible in the
room.

But suddenly a loud noise came up
from the lower floors of the hotel, and
Satin, with next to nothing on, got up
and listened intently.

"The police!" said she, growing very
pale.

"Oh, blast our bad luck! We're bloody
well done for!"

Often and often had she told stories
about the raids on hotels made by the

plain-clothes men. But that particular night neither of them had suspected anything when they took shelter in the Rue Laval. At the sound of the word "police," Nana lost her head. She jumped out of bed, and ran across the room with the scared look of a mad woman about to jump out of the window. Luckily, however, the little courtyard was roofed with glass, which was covered with an iron-wire grating at the level of the girls' bedroom. At sight of this, she ceased to hesitate; she stepped over the window prop, and with her chemise flying and her legs bared to the night air, she vanished in the gloom.

"Stop! stop!" said Satin in a great fright. "You'll kill yourself."

Then, as they began hammering at the door, she shut the window like a good-natured girl, and threw her friend's clothes down into a cupboard. She was already resigned to her fate, and comforted herself with the thought that after all if she were to be put on the official list, she would no longer be so "beastly frightened" as of yore. So she pretended to be heavy with sleep. She yawned, she palavered, and ended by opening the door to a tall burly fellow with an unkempt beard, who said to her,—

"Shew your hands! You've got no needle-pricks on them: you don't work. Now then, dress!"

"But I'm not a dressmaker, I'm a burnisher," Satin brazenly declared.

Nevertheless, she dressed with much docility, knowing that argument was out of the question. Cries were ringing through the hotel, a girl was clinging to doorposts, and refusing to budge an inch. Another girl, in bed with a lover, who was answering for her legality, was acting the honest woman who had been grossly insulted, and spoke of bringing an action against the Prefect of Police. For close on an hour there was a noise of heavy shoes on the stairs, of fists hammering on doors, of shrill disputes terminating in sobs, of petticoats rustling along the walls, of all the sounds, in fact, attendant on the sudden awakening and scared departure of a flock of women, as they were roughly packed off by three plain-clothes men, headed by a little oily-mannered, fair-haired commissary of police. After they had gone, the hotel relapsed into deep silence.

Nobody had betrayed her; Nana was saved. Shivering and half dead with fear, she came groping back into the room. Her bare feet were cut and bleeding, for they had been torn by the grating. For a long while she remained sitting on the edge of the bed, listening and listening. Towards morning, however, she went to sleep again, and at eight o'clock, when she woke up, she escaped from the hotel and ran to her aunt's. When Madame Lerat, who happened just then to be drinking her morning coffee with Zoé, beheld her bedraggled plight and haggard face, she took note of the hour, and at once understood the state of the case.

"It's come to it, eh?" she cried. "I certainly told you that he would take the skin off your back one of these days. Well, well, come in; you'll always find a kind welcome here."

Zoé had risen from her chair, and was muttering with respectful familiarity,—

"Madame is restored to us at last. I was waiting for Madame."

But Madame Lerat insisted on Nana's

going and kissing Louiset at once, because, said she, the child took delight in his mother's nice ways. Louiset, a sickly child with poor blood, was still asleep, and when Nana bent over his white scrofulous face, the memory of all she had undergone during the last few months brought a choking lump into her throat. "Oh! my poor little one, my poor little one!" she gasped, bursting into a final fit of sobbing.

## CHAPTER IX

THE *Petite Duchesse* was being rehearsed at the Variétés. The first act had just been carefully gone through, and the second was about to begin. Seated in old arm-chairs in the front of the stage, Fauchery and Bordenave were discussing various points, whilst the prompter, Father Cossard, a little hump-backed man, perched on a straw-bottomed chair, was turning over the pages of the manuscript, a pencil between his lips.

"Well, what are they waiting for?" cried Bordenave on a sudden, tapping the floor savagely with his heavy cane. "Barillot, why don't they begin?"

"It's Monsieur Bosc that has disappeared," replied Barillot, who was acting as second stage manager.

Then there arose a tempest, and everybody shouted for Bosc, while Bordenave swore.

"Always the same thing, by God! It's all very well ringing for 'em: they're always where they've no business to be. And then they grumble when they're kept till after four o'clock."

But Bosc just then came in with supreme tranquillity.

"Eh? What? What do they want

me for? Oh, it's my turn! You ought to have said so. All right! Simonne gives the cue: 'Here are the guests,' and I come in—which way must I come in?"

"Through the door, of course," cried Fauchery in great exasperation.

"Yes, but where is the door?"

At this, Bordenave fell upon Barillot, and once more set to work swearing and hammering the boards with his cane.

"By God! I said a chair was to be put there to stand for the door, and every day we have to get it done again. Barillot? Where's Barillot? Another of 'em! Why, they're all going!"

Nevertheless, Barillot came and planted the chair down in person, mutely weathering the storm as he did so. And the rehearsal began again. Simonne, in her hat and furs, began moving about like a maid-servant busy arranging furniture. She paused to say,—

"I'm not warm, you know, so I keep my hands in my muff."

Then, changing her voice, she greeted Bosc with a little cry:

"La, it's *Monsieur le Comte*. You're the first to come, *Monsieur le Comte*, and *Madame* will be delighted."

Bosc had muddy trousers and a huge yellow overcoat, round the collar of which a tremendous comforter was wound. On his head he wore an old hat, and he kept his hands in his pockets. He did not act, but dragged himself along, remarking in a hollow voice,—

"Don't disturb your mistress, Isabelle; I want to take her by surprise."

The rehearsal took its course. Bordenave knitted his brows. He had slipped down low in his arm-chair, and was listening with an air of fatigue.

Fauchery was nervous, and kept shifting about in his seat. Every few minutes he itched with the desire to interrupt, but he restrained himself. He heard a whispering in the dark and empty house behind him.

"Is she there?" he asked, leaning over towards Bordenave.

The latter nodded affirmatively. Before accepting the part of Géraldine which he was offering her, Nana had been anxious to see the piece, for she hesitated to play a courtesan's part a second time. She, in fact, aspired to an honest woman's part. Accordingly she was hiding in the shadows of a corner box in company with Labordette, who was managing matters for her with Bordenave. Fauchery glanced in her direction, and then once more set himself to follow the rehearsal.

Only the front of the stage was lit up. A flaring gas-burner on a support, which was fed by a pipe from the footlights, burnt in front of a reflector, and cast its full brightness over the immediate foreground. It looked like a big yellow eye glaring through the surrounding semi-obscurity, where it flamed in a doubtful, melancholy way. Cossard was holding up his manuscript against the slender stem of this arrangement. He wanted to see more clearly, and in the flood of light his hump was sharply outlined. As to Bordenave and Fauchery, they were already drowned in shadow. It was only in the heart of this enormous structure, on a few square yards of stage, that a faint glow suggested the light cast by some lantern nailed up in a railway station. It made the actors look like eccentric phantoms, and set their shadows dancing after them. The remainder of the stage was full of mist, and suggested a house in process of being pulled down, a church nave in utter ruin. It was littered with ladders, with set-pieces, and with scenery, of which the faded painting suggested heaped-up rubbish. Hanging high in air, the scenes had the appearance of great ragged clouts suspended from the rafters of some vast old-clothes shop, whilst above these again a ray of bright sunlight fell from a window and clove the shadow round the flies with a bar of gold.

Meanwhile actors were chatting at the back of the stage, whilst awaiting their cues. Little by little they had raised their voices.

"Confound it, will you be silent?" howled Bordenave, raging up and down in his chair. "I can't hear a word. Go outside, if you want to talk: we are at work. Barillot, if there's any more talking, I clap on fines all round!"

They were silent for a second or two. They were sitting in a little group on a bench and some rustic chairs in the corner of a scenic garden, which was standing ready to be put in position as it would be used in the opening act the same evening. In the middle of this group Fontan and Prullière were listening to Rose Mignon, to whom the manager of the Folies-Dramatique Theatre had been making magnificent offers. But a voice was heard shouting,—

"The Duchess! Saint-Firmin! The Duchess and Saint-Firmin are wanted!"

Only when the call was repeated did Prullière remember that he was Saint-Firmin! Rose, who was playing the Duchess Hélène, was already waiting to go on with him, whilst old Bosc slowly returned to his seat, dragging one foot after the other over the sonorous and deserted boards. Clarisse offered him a place on the bench beside her. "What's he bawling like that for?" said she, in allusion to Bordenave. "Things will be getting rosy soon! A piece can't be put on nowadays without its getting on his nerves."

Bosc shrugged his shoulders; he was above such storms. Fontan whispered,— "He's afraid of a fiasco. The piece strikes me as idiotic."

Then he turned to Clarisse, and again referred to what Rose had been telling them:

"D'you believe in the offers of the Folies people, eh? Three hundred francs an evening for a hundred nights! Why not a country-house into the bargain? If his wife were to be given three hundred francs, Mignon would chuck my friend Bordenave, and do it jolly sharp too!"

Clarisse was a believer in the three hundred francs. That man Fontan was always picking holes in his friend's successes! Just then Simonne interrupted her. She was shivering with cold. Indeed, they were all buttoned up to the ears and had comforters on, and they looked up at the ray of sunlight, which shone brightly above them, but did not penetrate the cold gloom of the theatre. In the streets outside there was a frost under a November sky.

"And there's no fire in the greenroom!" said Simonne. "It's disgusting; he *is* just becoming a skinflint! I want to be off; I don't want to get seedy."

"Silence, I say!" Bordenave once more thundered.

Then, for a minute or so, a confused murmur alone was audible as the actors went on repeating their parts. There was scarcely any appropriate action, and they spoke in even tones so as not to tire themselves. Nevertheless, when they did emphasise a particular shade of meaning, they cast a glance at the house, which lay before them like a yawning gulf. It was suffused with vague ambient shadow, which resembled the fine dust floating pent in some high windowless loft. The deserted house, whose sole illumination was the twilight radiance of the stage, seemed to slumber in melancholy and mysterious effacement. Near the ceiling dense night smothered the frescoes, whilst from the several tiers of stage-boxes on either hand huge widths of grey canvas stretched down to protect the neighbouring hangings. In fact there was no end to these coverings; bands of canvas had been thrown over the velvet-covered ledges in front of the various galleries which they shrouded thickly. Their pale hue stained the surrounding shadows, and of the general decorations of the house only the dark recesses of the boxes were distinguishable. These served to outline the framework of the several stories, where the seats were so many stains of red velvet turned black. The chandelier had been let down as far as it would go, and it so filled the region of the stalls with its pendants as to suggest a flitting, and to set one thinking that the public had started on a journey from which they would never return.

Just about then, Rose, as the little Duchess who has been misled into the society of a courtesan, came to the footlights, lifted up her hands and pouted adorably at the dark and empty theatre, which was as sad as a house of mourning.

"Good Heavens, what queer people!" said she, emphasizing the phrase, and confident that it would have its effect.

Far back in the corner box, in which she was hiding, Nana sat enveloped in a great shawl. She was listening to the play, and devouring Rose with her eyes. Turning towards Labordette, she asked him in a low tone,—

"You are sure he'll come?"

"Quite sure. Without doubt, he'll come with Mignon, so as to have an excuse for coming. As soon as he makes his appearance, you'll go up into Mathilde's dressing-room, and I'll bring him to you there."

They were talking of Count Muffat. Labordette had arranged this interview with him on neutral ground. He had had a serious talk with Bordenave, whose affairs had been gravely damaged by two successive failures. Accordingly Bordenave had hastened to lend him his theatre and to offer Nana a part, for he was anxious to win the Count's favour, and hoped to be able to borrow from him.

"And this part of Géraldine, what d'you think of it?" continued Labordette.

But Nana sat motionless, and vouchsafed no reply. After the first act, in which the author shewed how the Duc de Beaurivage played his wife false with the blonde Géraldine, a comic-opera celebrity, the second act witnessed the Duchess Hélène's arrival at the house of the actress on the occasion of a masked ball being given by the latter. The Duchess has come to find out by what magical process ladies of that sort

conquer and retain their husbands' affections. A cousin, the handsome Oscar de Saint-Firmin, introduces her, and hopes to be able to debauch her. And her first lesson causes her great surprise, for she hears Géraldine swearing like a hodman at the Duke, who suffers with most ecstatic submissiveness. The episode causes her to cry out, "Dear me, if that's the way one ought to talk to the men!" Géraldine had scarce any other scene in the act save this one. As to the Duchess, she was very soon punished for her curiosity, for an old buck, the Baron de Tardiveau, took her for a courtesan and became very gallant, whilst, on her other side, Beaurivage sat on a lounging chair and made his peace with Géraldine by dint of kisses and caresses. As this last lady's part had not yet been assigned to anyone. Father Cossard had got up to read it, and he was now figuring away in Bosc's arms and emphasising it despite himself. At this point, whilst the rehearsal was dragging monotonously on, Fauchery suddenly jumped from his chair. He had restrained himself up to that moment, but now his nerves got the better of him.

"That's not it!" he cried.

The actors paused awkwardly enough, whilst Fontan sneered, and asked in his most contemptuous voice,—

"Eh? What's not it? Who's not doing it right?"

"Nobody is! You're quite wrong, quite wrong!" continued Fauchery, and, gesticulating wildly, he came striding over the stage, and began himself to act the scene.

"Now look here, you Fontan, do please comprehend the way Tardiveau gets packed off. You must lean forward like this in order to catch hold of the Duchess. And then you, Rose, must change your position like that, but not too soon—only when you hear the kiss."

He broke off, and in the heat of explanation shouted to Cossard,—

"Géraldine, give the kiss! Loudly, so that it may be heard!"

Father Cossard turned towards Bosc, and smacked his lips vigorously.

"Good! That's the kiss," said Fauchery triumphantly. "Once more, let's have it once more. Now you see, Rose, I've had time to move, and then I give a little cry—so: 'Oh, she's given him a kiss.' But, before I do that, Tardiveau must go up the stage. D'you hear, Fontan, you go up. Come, let's try it again, all together."

The actors continued the scene again, but Fontan played his part with such an ill grace that they made no sort of progress. Twice Fauchery had to repeat his explanation, each time acting it out with more warmth than before. The actors listened to him with melancholy faces, gazed momentarily at one another as though he had asked them to walk on their heads, and then awkwardly essayed the passage only to pull up short directly afterwards, looking as stiff as puppets whose strings have just been snapped.

"No, it beats me; I can't understand it," said Fontan at length, speaking in the insolent manner peculiar to him.

Bordenave had never once opened his lips. He had slipped quite down in his arm-chair, so that only the top of his hat was now visible in the doubtful flicker of the gas-light on the stand. His cane had fallen from his grasp, and lay slantwise across his waistcoat. Indeed

he seemed to be asleep. But suddenly he sat bolt upright.

"It's idiotic, my boy," he announced quietly to Fauchery.

"What d'you mean? Idiotic!" cried the author, growing very pale. "It's you that are the idiot, my dear boy!"

Bordenave began to get angry at once. He repeated the word "idiotic," and, seeking a more forcible expression, hit upon "imbecile" and "damned foolish." The public would hiss, and the act would never be finished! And when Fauchery, without indeed being very deeply wounded by these big phrases, which always recurred when a new piece was being put on, grew savage and called the other a brute, Bordenave went beyond all bounds, brandished his cane in the air, snorted like a bull, and shouted,—

"Good God! why the hell can't you shut up? We've lost a quarter of an hour over this folly. Yes, folly! There's no sense in it. And it's so simple, after all's said and done! You, Fontan, mustn't move. You, Rose, must make your little movement; just that, no more, d'ye see? And then you come down. Now, then let's get it done this journey. Give the kiss, Cossard."

Then ensued confusion. The scene went no better than before. Bordenave, in his turn, shewed them how to act it about as gracefully as an elephant might have done, whilst Fauchery sneered and shrugged pityingly. After that Fontan put his word in, and even Bosc made so bold as to give advice. Rose, thoroughly tired out, had ended by sitting down on the chair which indicated the door. No one knew where they had got to, and by way of finish to it all Simonne made a premature entry, under the impression that her cue had been given her, and arrived amid the confusion. This so enraged Bordenave that he whirled his stick round in a terrific manner, and caught her a sounding thwack to the rearward. At rehearsal he used frequently to drub his former mistress. Simonne ran away, and this furious outcry followed her:

"Take that, and, by God! if I'm annoyed again I shut the whole shop up at once!"

Fauchery pushed his hat down over his forehead, and pretended to be going to leave the theatre. But he stopped at the top of the stage, and came down again when he saw Bordenave perspiringly resuming his seat. Then he too took up his old position in the other arm-chair. For some seconds they sat motionlessly side by side, while oppressive silence reigned in the shadowy house. The actors waited for nearly two minutes. They were all heavy with exhaustion, and felt as though they had performed an overwhelming task.

"Well, let's go on," said Bordenave at last. He spoke in his usual voice, and was perfectly calm.

"Yes, let's go on," Fauchery repeated. "We'll arrange the scene to-morrow."

And with that they dragged on again, and rehearsed their parts with as much listlessness and as fine an indifference as ever. During the dispute between manager and author, Fontan and the rest had been taking things very comfortably on the rustic bench and seats at the back of the stage, where they had been chuckling, grumbling, and saying fiercely cutting things. But when Simonne came back, still smarting from her blow and choking with sobs, they grew melodramatic and declared that had they been in her place they would have strangled the swine. She began wiping her eyes and nodding approval. It was all over between them, she said. She was leaving him, especially as Steiner had offered to give her a grand start in life only the day before. Clarisse was much astonished at this, for the banker was quite ruined; but Prullière began laughing and reminded them of the neat manner in which that confounded Israelite had puffed himself alongside of Rose, in order to get his Landes Saltworks afloat on 'Change. Just at that time he was airing a new project, namely, a tunnel under the Bosphorus. Simonne listened with the greatest interest to this fresh piece of information.

As to Clarisse, she had been raging for a week past. Just fancy, that beast la Faloise, whom she had succeeded in chucking into Gaga's venerable embrace, was coming into the fortune of a very rich uncle! It was just her luck; she had always been destined to make things cosy for other people. Then, too, that pig Bordenave had once more given her a mere scrap of a part, a paltry fifty lines, just as if she could not have played Géraldine! She was yearning for the *rôle*, and hoping that Nana would refuse it.

"Well, and what about me?" said Prullière, with much bitterness. "I haven't got more than two hundred lines. I wanted to give the part up. It's too bad to make me play that fellow Saint-Firmin: why it's a regular failure! And then what a style it's written in, my dears! It'll fall dead flat, you may be sure."

But just then Simonne, who had been

chatting with Father Barillot, came back breathless, and announced,—

"By-the-by, talking of Nana, she's in the house."

"Where, where?" asked Clarisse briskly, getting up to look for her.

The news spread at once, and everyone craned forward. The rehearsal was, as it were, momentarily interrupted. But Bordenave emerged from his quiescent condition, shouting,—

"What's up, eh? Finish the act, I say. And be quiet out there: it's unbearable!"

Nana was still following the piece from the corner box. Twice Labordette shewed an inclination to chat, but she grew impatient and nudged him to make him keep silent. The second act was drawing to a close, when two shadows loomed at the back of the theatre. They were creeping softly down, avoiding all noise, and Nana recognised Mignon and Count Muffat. They came forward and silently shook hands with Bordenave.

"Ah, there they are," she murmured with a sigh of relief.

Rose Mignon delivered the last sentences of the act. Thereupon Bordenave said that it was necessary to go through the second again before beginning the third. With that he left off attending to the rehearsal, and greeted the Count with looks of exaggerated politeness, whilst Fauchery pretended to be entirely engrossed with his actors, who now grouped themselves round him. Mignon stood whistling carelessly, with his hands behind his back and his eyes fixed complacently on his wife, who seemed rather nervous.

"Well, shall we go upstairs?" Labordette asked Nana. "I'll install you in the dressing-room, and come down again and fetch him."

Nana forthwith left the corner box. She had to grope her way along the passage outside the stalls, but Bordenave guessed where she was as she passed along in the dark, and caught her up at the end of the corridor passing behind the scenes, a narrow tunnel where the gas burnt day and night. Here, in order to bluff her into a bargain, he plunged into a discussion of the courtesan's part.

"What a part it is, eh? What a wicked little part! It's made for you. Come and rehearse to-morrow."

Nana was frigid. She wanted to know what the third act was like.

"Oh! it's superb the third act is! The Duchess plays the courtesan in her own house, and this disgusts Beaurivage, and makes him amend his way. Then there's an awfully funny *quid pro quo*, when Tardiveau arrives and is under the impression that he's at an opera dancer's house."

"And what does Géraldine do in it all?" interrupted Nana.

"Géraldine?" repeated Bordenave, in some embarrassment. "She has a scene, not a very long one, but a great success. It's made for you, I assure you! Will you sign?"

She looked steadily at him, and at length made answer,—

"We'll see about that, all in good time."

And she rejoined Labordette, who was waiting for her on the stairs. Everybody in the theatre had recognised her, and there was now much whispering, especially between Prulliére, who was scandalised at her return, and Clarisse, who was very desirous of the part. As to Fontan, he looked coldly on, pretending unconcern, for he did not think it becoming to round on a woman he had loved. Deep down in his heart, though, his old love had turned to hate, and he nursed the fiercest rancour against her in return for the constant devotion, the personal beauty, the life in common, of which his perverse and monstrous tastes had made him tire.

In the mean time, when Labordette reappeared and went up to the Count, Rose Mignon, whose suspicions Nana's presence had excited, understood it all forthwith. Muffat was bothering her to death, but she was beside herself at the thought of being left like this. She broke the silence which she usually maintained on such subjects in her husband's society, and said bluntly,—

"You see what's going on? My word, if she tries the Steiner trick on again, I'll tear her eyes out!"

Tranquilly and haughtily, Mignon shrugged his shoulders, as became a man from whom nothing could be hidden.

"Do be quiet," he muttered. "Do me the favour of being quiet, won't you?"

He knew what to rely on now. He had drained his Muffat dry, and he knew that at a sign from Nana he was ready to lie down and be a carpet under her feet. There is no fighting against passions such as that. Accordingly, as he knew what men were, he thought of nothing but how to turn the situation to the best possible account.

It would be necessary to wait on the course of events. And he waited on them.

"Rose, it's your turn!" shouted Bordenave. "The second act's being begun again."

"Off with you, then," continued Mignon, "and let me arrange matters."

Then he began bantering, despite all his troubles, and was pleased to congratulate Fauchery on his piece. A very strong piece! Only why was his great lady so chaste? It wasn't natural! With that he sneered, and asked who had sat for the portrait of the Duke of Beaurivage, Géraldine's worn-out *roué*. Fauchery smiled—he was far from annoyed. But Bordenave glanced in Muffat's direction, and looked vexed, and Mignon was struck at this and became serious again.

"Let's begin, for God's sake!" yelled the manager. "Now then, Barillot? Eh? What? Isn't Bosc there? Is he bloody well making game of me now?"

Bosc, however, made his appearance quietly enough, and the rehearsal began again just as Labordette was taking the Count away with him. The latter was tremulous at the thought of seeing Nana once more. After the rupture had taken place between them, there had been a great void in his life. He was idle, and fancied himself about to suffer through the sudden change his habits had undergone, and accordingly he had let them take him to see Rose. Besides, his brain had been in such a whirl that he had striven to forget everything, and had strenuously kept from seeking out Nana whilst avoiding an explanation with the Countess. He thought, indeed, that he owed his dignity such a measure of forgetfulness. But mysterious forces were at work within, and Nana began slowly to reconquer him. First came thoughts of her, then fleshly cravings, and finally a new set of exclusive, tender, well-nigh paternal feelings.

The abominable events attendant on their last interview were gradually effacing themselves. He no longer saw Fontan, he no longer heard the stinging taunt about his wife's adultery with which Nana cast him out of doors. These things were as words whose memory vanishes. Yet, deep down in his heart, there was a poignant smart which wrung him with such increasing pain that it nigh choked him. Childish ideas would occur to him; he imagined that she would never have betrayed him if he had really loved her, and he blamed himself for this. His anguish was becoming unbearable; he was really very wretched. His was the pain of an old wound, rather than the blind present desire which puts up with everything for the sake of immediate possession. He felt a jealous passion for the woman, and was haunted by longings for her and her alone, her hair, her mouth, her body. When he remembered the sound of her voice, a shiver ran through him; he longed for her as a miser might have done, with refinements of desire beggaring description. He was in fact so dolorously possessed by his passion, that when Labordette had begun to broach the subject of an assignation, he had thrown himself into his arms in obedience to irresistible impulse. Directly afterwards he had, of course, been ashamed of an act of self-abandonment which could not but seem very ridiculous in a man of his position; but Labordette was one who knew when to see and when not to see things, and he gave a further proof of his tact when he left the Count at the foot of the stairs, and without effort let slip only these simple words:

"The right-hand passage on the second floor. The door's not shut."

Muffat was alone in that silent corner of the house. As he passed before the players' waiting-room, he had peeped through the open doors and noticed the utter dilapidation of the vast chamber, which looked shamefully stained and worn in broad daylight. But what surprised him most, as he emerged from the darkness and confusion of the stage, was the pure clear light and deep quiet at present pervading the lofty staircase, which one evening, when he had seen it before, had been bathed in gas-fumes and loud with the footsteps of women scampering over the different floors. He felt that the dressing-rooms were empty, the corridors deserted; not a soul was there; not a sound broke the stillness; whilst, through the square windows on the level of the stairs, the pale November sunlight filtered and cast yellow patches of light, full of dancing dust, amid the dead, peaceful air which seemed to descend from the regions above.

He was glad of this calm and the silence, and he went slowly up, trying to regain breath as he went, for his heart was thumping, and he was afraid lest he might behave childishly and give way to sighs and tears. Accordingly, on the first-floor landing, he leant up against a wall—for he was sure of not being observed—and pressed his handkerchief to his mouth, and gazed at the warped steps, the iron balustrade bright with the friction of many hands, the scraped paint on the walls—all the squalor, in fact, which that house of tolerance so crudely displayed at the pale afternoon hour when courtesans are asleep. When he reached the second floor he had to step over a big yellow cat, which was lying curled up on a step. With half-closed eyes this cat was keeping solitary watch over the house, where the close and now frozen odours which the women nightly left behind them had rendered him somnolent.

In the right-hand corridor, the door of the dressing-room had indeed not been closed entirely. Nana was waiting. That little Mathilde, a drab of a young girl, kept her dressing-room in a filthy state. Chipped jugs stood about anyhow; the dressing-table was greasy, and there was a chair covered with red stains, which looked as if someone had bled over the straw. The paper pasted on walls and ceiling was splashed from top to bottom with spots of soapy water, and this smelt so disagreeably of lavender scent turned sour that Nana opened the window, and for some moments stayed leaning on the sill, breathing the fresh air, and craning forward to catch sight of Madame Bron underneath. She could hear her broom wildly at work on the mildewed pantiles of the narrow court, which was buried in shadow. A canary, whose cage hung on a shutter, was trilling away piercingly. The sound of carriages in the boulevard and neighbouring streets was no longer audible, and the quiet and the wide expanse of sleeping sunlight suggested the country. Looking further afield, her eye fell on the small buildings and glass roofs of the galleries in the Passage, and beyond these, on the tall houses in the Rue Vivienne, the backs of which rose silent and apparently deserted over against her. There was a succession of terrace-roofs close by, and on one of these a photographer had perched a big cage-like construction of blue glass. It was all very gay, and Nana was becoming absorbed in contemplation, when it struck her someone had knocked at the door.

She turned round and shouted,—
"Come in!"

At sight of the Count she shut the window, for it was not warm, and there was no need for the eavesdropping Madame Bron to listen. The pair gazed at one another gravely. Then, as the Count still kept standing stiffly in front of her, looking ready to choke with emotion, she burst out laughing, and said,—

"Well! So you're here again, you silly big beast!"

The tumult going on within him was so great that he seemed a man frozen to ice. He addressed Nana as "madam," and esteemed himself happy to see her again. Thereupon, she became more familiar than ever, in order to bounce matters through.

"Don't do it in the dignified way! You wanted to see me, didn't you? But you didn't intend us to stand looking at one another like a couple of chinaware dogs. We've both been in the wrong—— Oh, I certainly forgive you!"

And herewith they agreed not to talk of that affair again, Muffat nodding his assent as Nana spoke. He was calmer now, but as yet could find nothing to say, though a thousand things rose tumultuously to his lips. Surprised at his apparent coldness, she began acting a part with much vigour.

"Come," she continued with a faint smile; "you're a sensible man! Now that we've made our peace, let's shake hands and be good friends in future." "What? Good friends?" he murmured in sudden anxiety. "Yes; it's idiotic, perhaps, but I should like you to think well of me. We've had our little explanation out, and if we meet again we shan't at any rate look like a pair of boobies." He tried to interrupt her with a movement of the hand. "Let me finish! There's not a man, you understand, able to accuse me of doing him a blackguardly turn: well, and it struck me as horrid to begin in your case. We all have our sense of honour, dear boy."

"But that's not my meaning!" he shouted violently. "Sit down—listen to me!"

And as though he were afraid of seeing her take her departure, he pushed her down on the solitary chair in the room. Then he paced about in growing agitation. The little dressing-room was airless and full of sunlight, and no sound from the outside world disturbed its pleasant, peaceful, dampish atmosphere. In the pauses of conversation the shrillings of the canary were alone audible, and suggested the distant piping of a flute.

"Listen," said he, planting himself in front of her, "I've come to possess myself of you again. Yes, I want to begin again. You know that well, then why do you talk to me as you do? Answer me; tell me you consent."

Her head was bent, and she was scratching the blood-red straw of the seat underneath her. Seeing him so anxious, she did not hurry to answer. But at last she lifted up her face. It had assumed a grave expression, and into the beautiful eyes she had succeeded in infusing a look of sadness.

"Oh, it's impossible, little man. Never, never, will I live with you again."

"Why?" he stuttered, and his face seemed contracted in unspeakable suffering.

"Why? Hang it all, because——! It's impossible, that's about it. I don't want to."

He looked ardently at her for some seconds longer. Then his legs curved under him, and he fell on the floor. In a bored voice she added this simple advice:

"Ah, don't be a baby!"

But he was one already. Dropping at her feet, he had put his arms round her waist, and was hugging her closely, pressing his face hard against her knees. When he felt her thus—when he once more divined the presence of her velvety limbs beneath the thin fabric of her dress, he was suddenly convulsed, and trembled, as it were, with fever, whilst madly, savagely, he pressed his face against her knees as though he had been anxious to force through her flesh. The old chair creaked, and beneath the low ceiling, where the air was pungent with stale perfumes, smothered sobs of desire were audible.

"Well, and after?" Nana began saying, letting him do as he would. "All this doesn't help you a bit, seeing that the thing's impossible. Good God, what a child you are!"

His energy subsided, but he still stayed on the floor, nor did he relax his hold of her, as he said in a broken voice,—

"Do at least listen to what I came to

offer you. I've already seen a town house close to the Parc Monceau—I would gladly realise your smallest wish——in order to have you all to myself, I would give my whole fortune. Yes, that would be my only condition, that I should have you all to myself! Do you understand? And if you were to consent to be mine only, oh then I should want you to be the loveliest, the richest woman on earth. I should give you carriages, and diamonds, and dresses!"

At each successive offer Nana shook her head proudly. Then seeing that he still continued them, that he even spoke of settling money on her—for he was at loss what to lay at her feet—she apparently lost patience.

"Come, come, have you done bargaining with me? I'm a good sort, and I don't mind giving in to you for a minute or two, as your feelings are making you so ill; but I've had enough of it now, haven't I? So let me get up. You're tiring me."

She extricated herself from his clasp, and once on her feet,—

"No, no, no!" said she. "I don't want to!"

With that he gathered himself up painfully, and feebly dropped into a chair, in which he leant back with his face in his hands. Nana began pacing up and down in her turn. For a second or two she looked at the stained wall-paper, the greasy toilet-table, the whole dirty little room as it basked in the pale sunlight. Then she paused in front of the Count, and spoke with quiet directness.

"It's strange, how rich men fancy they can have everything for their money. Well, and if I don't want to consent—what then? I don't care a pin for your presents! You might give me Paris, and yet I should say no! Always no! Look here, it's scarcely clean in this room, yet I should think it very nice if I wanted to live in it with you. But one's fit to kick the bucket in your palaces, if one isn't in love. Ah, as to money, my poor pet, I can lay my hands on that if I want to, but I tell you, I trample on it, I spit on it!"

And with that she assumed a disgusted expression. Then she became sentimental, and added in a melancholy tone,—

"I know of something worth more than money. Oh, if only someone were to give me what I long for!"

He slowly lifted his head, and there was a gleam of hope in his eyes.

"Oh, you can't give it me," she continued; "it doesn't depend on you, and that's the reason I'm talking to you about it. Yes, we're having a chat, so I may as well mention to you that I should like to play the part of the respectable woman in that show of theirs."

"What respectable woman?" he muttered in astonishment.

"Why, their Duchess Hélène! If they think I'm going to play Géraldine, a part with nothing in it, a scene, and nothing besides—if they think that! Besides, that isn't the reason. The fact is I've had enough of courtesans. Why there's no end to 'em! They'll be fancying I've got 'em on the brain, to be sure they will! Besides, when all's said and done, it's annoying, for I can quite see they seem to think me uneducated. Well, my boy, they're jolly well in the dark about it, I can tell you! When I want to be a perfect lady, why then I am a swell, and no mistake! Just look at this."

And she withdrew as far as the window, and then came swelling back, with the mincing gait and circumspect air of a portly hen that fears to dirty her claws. As to Muffat, he followed her movements with eyes still wet with tears. He was stupefied by this sudden transition from anguish to comedy. She walked about for a moment or two in order the more thoroughly to shew off her paces, and as she walked she smiled subtly, closed her eyes demurely, and managed her skirts with great dexterity. Then she posted herself in front of him again.

"I guess I've hit it, eh?"

"Oh, thoroughly," he stammered with a broken voice and a troubled expression.

"I tell you I've got hold of the honest woman! I've tried at my own place. Nobody's got my little knack of looking like a duchess who don't care a damn for the men. Did you notice it when I passed in front of you? Why, the thing's in my blood! Besides, I want to play the part of an honest woman. I dream about it day and night—I'm miserable about it. I must have the part, d'you hear!"

And with that she grew serious, speaking in a hard voice and looking deeply moved, for she was really tortured by her stupid, tiresome wish. Muffat, still smarting from her late refusals, sat on without appearing to grasp her meaning. There was a silence, during which the very flies abstained from buzzing through the quiet, empty place.

"Now look here," she resumed bluntly, "you're to get them to give me the part."

He was dumfounded, and with a despairing gesture,—

"Oh, it's impossible! You yourself were saying just now that it didn't depend on me."

She interrupted him with a shrug of the shoulders.

"You'll just go down, and you'll tell Bordenave you want the part. Now don't be such a silly! Bordenave wants money—well, you'll lend him some, since you can afford to make ducks and drakes of it."

And as he still struggled to refuse her, she grew angry.

"Very well, I understand; you're afraid of making Rose angry. I didn't mention the woman when you were crying down on the floor—I should have had too much to say about it all. Yes, to be sure, when one has sworn to love a woman for ever, one doesn't usually take up with the first creature that comes by directly after. Oh, that's where the shoe pinches, I remember! Well, dear boy, there's nothing very savoury in the Mignons' leavings! Oughtn't you to have broken it off with that dirty lot, before coming and squirming on my knees?"

He protested vaguely, and at last was able to get out a phrase.

"Oh, I don't care a jot for Rose; I'll give her up at once."

Nana seemed satisfied on this point. She continued,—

"Well, then, what's bothering you? Bordenave's master here. You'll tell me there's Fauchery after Bordenave——"

She had sunk her voice, for she was coming to the delicate part of the matter. Muffat sat silent, his eyes fixed on the ground. He had remained voluntarily ignorant of Fauchery's assiduous attentions to the Countess, and time had lulled his suspicions, and set him hoping that he had been deceiving himself during that fearful night passed in a doorway of the Rue Taitbout. But he still felt a dull angry repugnance to the man.

"Well, what then? Fauchery isn't the devil!" Nana repeated, feeling her way cautiously and trying to find out how matters stood between husband and lover. "One can get over his soft side. I promise you he's a good sort at bottom! So it's a bargain, eh? You'll tell him that it's for my sake?"

The idea of taking such a step disgusted the Count.

"No, no! Never!" he cried.

She paused, and this sentence was on the verge of utterance:

"Fauchery can refuse you nothing."

But she felt that by way of argument it was rather too much of a good thing. So she only smiled a queer smile which spoke as plainly as words. Muffat had raised his eyes to her, and now once more lowered them, looking pale and full of embarrassment.

"Ah, you're not good-natured," she muttered at last.

"I cannot," said he, with a voice and a look of the utmost anguish. "I'll do whatever you like, but not that, dear love! Oh, I beg you not to insist on that!"

Thereupon she wasted no more time in discussion, but took his head between her small hands, pushed it back a little, bent down, and glued her mouth to his in a long long kiss. He shivered violently; he trembled beneath her touch; his eyes were closed, and he was beside himself. She lifted him to his feet.

"Go," said she simply.

He walked off, making towards the door. But as he passed out she took him in her arms again, became meek and coaxing, lifted her face to his, and rubbed her cheek against his waistcoat, much as a cat might have done.

"Where's the fine house?" she whispered in laughing embarrassment, like a little girl who returns to the pleasant things she has previously refused.

"In the Avenue de Villiers."

"And there are carriages there?"

"Yes."

"Lace? Diamonds?"

"Yes."

"Oh, how good you are, my old pet! You know it was all jealousy just now! And this time I solemnly promise you it won't be like the first, for now you understand what's due to a woman. You give all, don't you? Well, then, I don't want anybody but you! Why, look here, there's some more for you! There, and there, and there!"

When she had pushed him from the room, after firing his blood with a rain of kisses on hands and on face, she panted awhile. Good heavens! what an unpleasant smell there was in that slut Mathilde's dressing-room! It was warm, if you will, with the tranquil warmth peculiar to rooms in the South when the winter sun shines into them, but really it smelt far too strong of stale lavender water, not to mention other less cleanly things! She opened the window, and again leaning on the window-sill began watching the glass roof of the passage below in order to kill time.

Muffat went staggering downstairs. His head was swimming. What should he say? How should he broach the matter, which, moreover, did not concern him? He heard sounds of quarrelling as he reached the stage. The second act was being finished, and Prullière was beside himself with wrath, owing to an attempt on Fauchery's part to cut short one of his speeches. "Cut it all out then," he was shouting. "I should prefer that! Just fancy I haven't two hundred lines, and they're still cutting me down. No, by Jove, I've had enough of it: I give the part up."

He took a little crumpled manuscript book out of his pocket, and fingered its leaves feverishly as though he were just about to throw it on Cossard's lap. His pale face was convulsed by outraged vanity; his lips were drawn and thin, his eyes flamed; he was quite unable to conceal the struggle that was going on inside him. To think that he, Prullière, the idol of the public, should play a part of only two hundred lines!

"Why not make me bring in letters on a tray?" he continued bitterly.

"Come, come, Prullière, behave decently," said Bordenave, who was anxious to treat him tenderly because of his influence over the boxes. "Don't begin making a fuss. We'll find some points. Eh, Fauchery, you'll add some points? In the third act it would even be possible to lengthen a scene out."

"Well, then, I want the last speech of all," the comedian declared. "I certainly deserve to have it."

Fauchery's silence seemed to give consent, and Prullière, still greatly agitated, and discontented despite everything, put his part back into his pocket. Bosc and Fontan had appeared profoundly indifferent during the course of this explanation. Let each man fight for his own hand, they reflected; the present dispute had nothing to do with them; they had no interest therein! All the actors clustered round Fauchery, and began questioning him and fishing for praise, whilst Mignon listened to the last of Prullières' complaints without, however, losing sight of Count Muffat, whose return he had been on the watch for.

Entering in the half light, the Count had paused at the back of the stage, for he hesitated to interrupt the quarrel. But Bordenave caught sight of him, and ran forward.

"Aren't they a pretty lot?" he muttered. "You can have no idea what I've got to undergo with that lot, Monsieur le Comte. Each man's vanier than his neighbour, and they're wretched players all the same, a scabby lot, always mixed up in some dirty business or other! Oh, they'd be delighted if I were to come to smash. But I beg pardon—I'm getting beside myself."

He ceased speaking, and silence reigned, whilst Muffat sought how to broach his announcement gently. But he failed, and, in order to get out of his difficulty the more quickly, ended by an abrupt announcement:

"Nana wants the Duchess's part."

Bordenave gave a start, and shouted,—

"Come now, it's sheer madness!"

Then looking at the Count, and finding him so pale and so shaken, he was calm at once.

"Devil take it!" he said simply.

And with that there ensued a fresh silence. At bottom he didn't care a pin about it. That great thing Nana playing the Duchess might possibly prove amusing! Besides, now that this had happened, he had Muffat well in his grasp. Accordingly, he was not long in coming to a decision, and so he turned round and called out,—

"Fauchery!"

The Count had been on the point of stopping him. But Fauchery did not hear him, for he had been pinned against the curtain by Fontan, and was being compelled to listen patiently to the comedian's reading of the part of Tardiveau. Fontan imagined Tardiveau to be a native of Marseilles with a dialect; and he imitated the dialect. He was repeating whole speeches. Was that right? Was this the thing? Apparently he was only submitting ideas to Fauchery of which he was himself uncertain, but as the author seemed cold and raised various objections, he grew angry at once.

Oh, very well, the moment the spirit of the part escaped him, it would be better for all concerned that he shouldn't act it at all!

"Fauchery!" shouted Bordenave once more.

Thereupon the young man ran off, delighted to escape from the actor, who was wounded not a little by his prompt retreat.

"Don't let's stay here," continued Bordenave. "Come this way, gentlemen."

In order to escape from curious listeners, he led them into the property-room, behind the scenes, whilst Mignon watched their disappearance in some surprise. They went down a few steps, and entered a square room, whose two windows opened upon the court-yard. A faint light stole through the dirty panes, and hung wanly under the low ceiling. In pigeon-holes and shelves which filled the whole place up lay a collection of the most varied kind of *bric-à-brac*. Indeed it suggested an old clothes' shop in the Rue de Lappe in process of selling off, so indescribable was the hotch-potch of plates, gilt paste-board cups, old red umbrellas, Italian jars, clocks in all styles, platters and ink-pots, fire-arms and squirts, which lay chipped and broken, and in unrecognisable heaps, under a layer of dust an inch deep. An unendurable odour of old iron, rags, and damp cardboard, emanated from the various piles, where the *débris* of forgotten dramas had been collecting for half a century.

"Come in," Bordenave repeated. "We shall be alone at any rate."

The Count was extremely embarrassed, and he contrived to let the manager risk his proposal for him. Fauchery was astonished.

"Eh? What?" he asked.

"Just this," said Bordenave finally. "An idea has occurred to us. Now whatever you do, don't jump! It's most serious. What do you think of Nana for the Duchess's part?"

The author was bewildered; then he burst out with,—

"Ah, no, no! You're joking, aren't you? People would laugh far too much."

"Well, and it's a point gained already if they do laugh! Just reflect, my dear boy. The idea pleases Monsieur le Comte very much."

In order to keep himself in countenance Muffat had just picked out of the dust on a neighbouring shelf an object which he did not seem to recognise. It was an egg-cup, and its stem had been mended with plaster. He kept hold of it unconsciously, and came forward muttering,—

"Yes, yes, it would be capital."

Fauchery turned towards him with a brisk, impatient gesture. The Count had nothing to do with his piece, and he said decisively,—

"Never! Let Nana play the courtesan as much as she likes, but a lady—— No, by Jove!"

"You are mistaken, I assure you," rejoined the Count, growing bolder. "This very minute she has been playing the part of a pure woman for my benefit."

"Where?" queried Fauchery, with growing surprise.

"Upstairs in a dressing-room. Yes, she has indeed, and with such distinction! She's got a way of glancing at you as she goes by you—something like this, you know!"

And, egg-cup in hand, he endeavoured to imitate Nana, quite forgetting his dignity in his frantic desire to convince the others. Fauchery gazed at him in a state of stupefaction. He understood it all now, and his anger had ceased. The Count felt that he was looking at him, mockingly and pityingly, and he paused with a slight blush on his face.

" 'Egad, it's quite possible!" muttered the author complaisantly. "Perhaps she would do very well, only the part's been assigned. We can't take it away from Rose."

"Oh, if that's all the trouble," said Bordenave, "I'll undertake to arrange matters."

But presently, seeing them both against him, and guessing that Bordenave had some secret interest at stake, the young man thought to avoid acquiescence by redoubling the violence of his refusal. The consultation was on the verge of being broken up.

"Oh, dear! No, no! Even if the part were unassigned, I should never give it her! There, is that plain? Do let me alone: I have no wish to ruin my play!"

He lapsed into silent embarrassment. Bordenave deeming himself *de trop*, went away, but the Count remained with bowed head. He raised it with an effort, and said in a breaking voice,—

"Supposing, my dear fellow, I were to ask this of you as a favour?"

"I cannot, I cannot," Fauchery kept repeating as he writhed to get free.

Muffat's voice became harder.

"I pray and beseech you for it! I want it!"

And with that he fixed his eyes on him. The young man read menaces in that darkling gaze, and suddenly gave way with a splutter of confused phrases:

"Do what you like—I don't care a pin about it. Yes, yes, you're abusing your power, but you'll see, you'll see!"

At this the embarrassment of both increased. Fauchery was leaning up against a set of shelves, and was tapping nervously on the ground with his foot. Muffat seemed busy examining the egg-cup, which he was still turning round and about.

"It's an egg-cup," Bordenave obligingly came and remarked.

"Yes, to be sure! it's an egg-cup," the Count repeated.

"Excuse me, you're covered with dust," continued the manager, putting the thing back on a shelf. "If one had to dust every day, there'd be no end to it, you understand. But it's hardly clean here —a filthy mess, eh? Yet, you may believe me or not, when I tell you there's money in it. Now look, just look at all that!"

He walked Muffat round in front of the pigeon-holes and shelves, and in the greenish light which filtered through the court-yard, told him the names of different properties, for he was anxious to interest him in his marine-stores inventory, as he jocosely termed it.

Presently, when they had returned into Fauchery's neighbourhood, he said carelessly enough,—

"Listen, since we're all of one mind, we'll finish the matter at once. Here's Mignon, just when he's wanted."

For some little time past Mignon had been prowling in the adjoining passage, and the very moment Bordenave began talking of a modification of their agreement he burst into wrathful protest. It was infamous—they wanted to spoil his wife's career—he'd go to law about it! Bordenave meanwhile was extremely calm and full of reasons. He did not think the part worthy of Rose, and he preferred to reserve her for an operetta, which was to be put on after the *Little Duchess*. But when her husband still continued shouting, he suddenly offered to cancel their arrangement in view of the offers which the Folies-Dramatiques had been making the singer. At this Mignon was momentarily put out, so without denying the truth of these offers he loudly professed a vast disdain for money. His wife, he said, had been engaged to play the Duchesse Hélène, and she would play the part even if he, Mignon, were to be ruined over it. His dignity, his honour, were at stake! Starting from this basis, the discussion grew interminable. The manager, however, always returned to the following argu-

ment: since the Folies had offered Rose three hundred francs a night during a hundred performances, and since she only made a hundred and fifty with him, she would be the gainer by fifteen thousand francs the moment he let her depart. The husband, on his part, did not desert the artist's position. What would people say if they saw his wife deprived of her part? Why, that she was not equal to it; that it had been deemed necessary to find a substitute for her! And this would do great harm to Rose's reputation as an artist; nay, it would diminish it. Oh, no, no! Glory before gain! Then without a word of warning he pointed out a possible arrangement: Rose, according to the terms of her agreement, was pledged to pay a forfeit of ten thousand francs in case she gave up the part. Very well, then, let them give her ten thousand francs, and she would go to the Folies-Dramatiques. Bordenave was utterly dumfounded, whilst Mignon, who had never once taken his eyes off the Count, tranquilly awaited results.

"Then everything can be settled," murmured Muffat in tones of relief; "we can come to an understanding."

"The deuce, no! that would be too stupid!" cried Bordenave, mastered by his commercial instincts. "Ten thousand francs to let Rose go! Why, people would make game of me!"

But the Count, with a multiplicity of nods, bade him accept. He hesitated, and at last with much grumbling and infinite regret over the ten thousand francs, which, by-the-by, were not destined to come out of his own pocket, he bluntly continued,—

"After all, I consent. At any rate I shall have you off my hands."

For a quarter of an hour past Fontan had been listening in the court-yard. Such had been his curiosity that he had come down and posted himself there; but, the moment he understood the state of the case, he went upstairs again and enjoyed the treat of telling Rose. Dear me! They were just haggling in her behalf! He dinned his words into her ears; she ran off to the property-room. They were silent as she entered. She looked at the four men. Muffat hung his head; Fauchery answered her questioning glance with a despairing shrug of the shoulders; as to Mignon, he was busy discussing the terms of the agreement with Bordenave.

"What's up?" she demanded curtly.

"Nothing," said her husband. "Bordenave here is giving ten thousand francs in order to get you to give up your part."

She grew tremulous with anger, and very pale, and she clenched her little fists. For some moments she stared at him; her whole nature in revolt. Ordinarily, in matters of business, she was wont to trust everything obediently to her husband, leaving him to sign agreements with managers and lovers. Now she could but cry,—

"Oh, come, you're too base for anything!"

The words fell like a lash. Then she sped away, and Mignon, in utter astonishment, ran after her. What next? Was she going mad? He began explaining to her in low tones that ten thousand francs from one party, and fifteen thousand from the other, came to twenty-five thousand. A splendid deal! Muffat was getting rid of her in every sense

of the word; it was a pretty trick to have plucked him of this last feather! But Rose in her anger vouchsafed no answer. Whereupon Mignon in disdain left her to her feminine spite, and turning to Bordenave, who was once more on the stage with Fauchery and Muffat, said,—

"We'll sign to-morrow morning. Have the money in readiness."

At this moment Nana, to whom Labordette had brought the news, came down to the stage in triumph. She was quite the honest woman now, and wore a most distinguished expression, in order to overwhelm her friends and prove to the idiots that when she chose she could give them all points in the matter of smartness. But she nearly got into trouble, for at the sight of her Rose darted forward, choking with rage and stuttering,—

"Yes, you, I'll pay you out! Things can't go on like this, d'you understand!"

Nana forgot herself in face of this brisk attack, and was going to put her arms akimbo and give her what for. But she controlled herself, and looking like a marquise who is afraid of treading on an orange peel, fluted in still more silvery tones.

"Eh, what?" said she. "You're mad, my dear!"

And with that she continued in her graceful affectation, whilst Rose took her departure, followed by Mignon, who now refused to recognise her. Clarisse was enraptured, having just obtained the part of Géraldine from Bordenave. Fauchery, on the other hand, was gloomy: he shifted from one foot to the other: he could not decide whether to leave the theatre or no. His piece was bedevilled, and he was seeking how best to save it. But Nana came up, took him by both hands, and drawing him towards her, asked whether he thought her so very atrocious after all. She wasn't going to eat his play—not she! Then she made him laugh, and gave him to understand that he would be foolish to be angry with her in view of his relationship to the Muffats. If, said she, her memory failed her she would take her lines from the prompter. The house, too, would be packed in such a way as to ensure applause. Besides, he was mistaken about her, and he would soon see how she would rattle through her part. By-and-by it was arranged that the author should make a few changes in the *rôle* of the Duchess so as to extend that of Prullière. The last-named personage was enraptured. Indeed, amid all the joy which Nana now quite naturally diffused, Fontan alone remained unmoved. In the middle of the yellow lamp-light, against which the sharp outline of his goat-like profile shone out with great distinctness, he stood shewing off his figure and affecting the pose of one who has been cruelly abandoned. Nana went quietly up and shook hands with him.

"How are you getting on?"

"Oh! pretty fairly. And how are you?"

"Very well, thank you."

That was all. They seemed to have only parted at the doors of the theatre the day before. Meanwhile, the players were waiting about, but Bordenave said that the third act would not be rehearsed. And so it chanced that old Bosc went grumbling away at the proper time, whereas usually the company were needlessly detained and lost whole afternoons

in consequence. Everyone went off. Down on the pavement they were blinded by the broad daylight, and stood blinking their eyes in a dazed sort of way, as became people who had passed three hours squabbling with tight-strung nerves in the depths of a cellar. The Count, with racked limbs and vacant brain, got into a conveyance with Nana, whilst Labordette took Fauchery off and comforted him.

A month later the first night of the *Petite Duchesse* proved supremely disastrous to Nana. She was atrociously bad, and displayed such pretentions towards high comedy that the public grew mirthful. They did not hiss— they were too amused. From a stagebox Rose Mignon kept greeting her rival's successive entrances with a shrill laugh, which set the whole house off. It was the beginning of her revenge. Accordingly, when at night Nana, greatly chagrined, found herself alone with Muffat, she said furiously,—

"What a conspiracy, eh? It's all owing to jealousy. Oh! if they only knew how I despise 'em! What do I want them for nowadays? Look here! I'll bet a hundred louis that I'll bring all those who made fun to-day and make 'em lick the ground at my feet! Yes, I'll fine-lady your Paris for you, I will!"

## CHAPTER X

THEREUPON Nana became a smart woman, mistress of all that is foolish and filthy in man, marquise in the ranks of her calling. It was a sudden but decisive start, a plunge into the garish day of gallant notoriety and mad expenditure, and that dare-devil wastefulness peculiar to beauty. She at once became queen among the most expensive of her kind. Her photographs were displayed in shop-windows, and she was mentioned in the papers. When she drove in her carriage along the boulevards, the people would turn and tell one another who that was, with all the unction of a nation saluting its sovereign, whilst the object of their adoration lolled easily back in her diaphanous dresses, and smiled gaily under the rain of little golden curls which ran riot above the blue of her made-up eyes and the red of her painted lips. And the wonder of wonders was that the great creature, who was so awkward on the stage, so very absurd the moment she sought to act the chaste woman, was able without effort to assume the *rôle* of an enchantress in the outer world. Her movements were lithe as a serpent's, and the studied and yet seemingly involuntary carelessness with which she dressed was really exquisite in its elegance. There was a nervous distinction in all she did which suggested a well-born Persian cat; she was an aristocrat in vice, and proudly and rebelliously trampled upon a prostrate Paris like a sovereign whom none dare disobey. She set the fashion, and great ladies imitated her.

Nana's fine house was situated at the corner of the Rue Cardinet, in the Avenue de Villiers. The avenue was part of the luxurious quarter at that time springing up in the vague district which had once been the Plaine Monceau. The house had been built by a young painter, who was intoxicated by a first success, and had been perforce resold almost as soon as it was habitable. It was in the palatial Renaissance manner, and had

fantastic interior arrangements which consisted of modern conveniences framed in a setting of somewhat artificial originality. Count Moffat had bought the house ready furnished, and full of hosts of beautiful objects—lovely Eastern hangings, old credences, huge chairs of the Louis XIII. epoch. And thus Nana had come into artistic surroundings of the choicest kind and of the most extravagantly various dates. But since the studio, which occupied the central portion of the house, could not be of any use to her, she had upset existing arrangements, establishing a small drawing-room on the first floor, next to her bedroom and dressing-room, and leaving a conservatory, a large drawing-room, and a dining-room, to look after themselves underneath. She astonished the architect with her ideas, for, as became a Parisian work-girl who understands the elegancies of life by instinct, she had suddenly developed a very pretty taste for every species of luxurious refinement. Indeed she did not spoil her house overmuch; nay, she even added to the richness of the furniture, save here and there, where certain traces of tender foolishness and vulgar magnificence betrayed the ex-flower-seller who had been wont to dream in front of shop-windows in the arcades.

A carpet was spread on the steps beneath the great awning over the front door in the court, and the moment you entered the hall you were greeted by a perfume as of violets and a soft warm atmosphere which thick hangings helped to produce. A window, whose yellow and rose-coloured panes suggested the warm pallor of human flesh, gave light to the wide staircase, at the foot of which a Negro in carved wood held out a silver tray full of visiting cards, and four white marble women, with bosoms displayed, raised lamps in their uplifted hands. Bronzes and Chinese vases full of flowers, divans covered with old Persian rugs, arm-chairs upholstered in old tapestry, furnished the entrance-hall, adorned the stair-heads, and gave the first-floor landing the appearance of an ante-room. Here men's overcoats and hats were always in evidence, and there were thick hangings which deadened every sound. It seemed a place apart: on entering it you might have fancied yourself in a chapel, whose very air was thrilling with devotion, whose very silence and seclusion were fraught with mystery.

Nana only opened the large and somewhat too-sumptuous Louis XVI. drawing-room on those gala nights when she received society from the Tuileries or strangers of distinction. Ordinarily, she only came downstairs at meal-times, and she would feel rather lost on such days as she lunched by herself in the lofty dining-room, with its Gobelins tapestry, and its monumental sideboard, adorned with old porcelain and marvellous pieces of ancient plate. She used to go upstairs again as quickly as possible, for her home was on the first floor, in the three rooms, the bed, dressing, and small drawing-room above described. Twice already she had done the bed-chamber up anew; on the first occasion in mauve satin, on the second in blue silk under lace. But she had not been satisfied with this; it had struck her as "nohowish," and she was still unsuccessfully seeking for new colours and designs. On the elaborately-upholstered bed, which was as low as a sofa, there were

twenty thousand francs'-worth of *point de Venise* lace. The furniture was lacquered blue and white under designs in silver filigree; and everywhere lay such numbers of white bearskins that they hid the carpet. This was a luxurious caprice on Nana's part, she having never been able to break herself of the habit of sitting on the floor to take her stockings off. Next door to the bedroom the little saloon was full of an amusing medley of exquisitely artistic objects. Against the hangings of pale rose-coloured silk—a faded Turkish rose-colour, embroidered with gold thread—a whole world of them stood sharply outlined. They were from every land and in every possible style. There were Italian cabinets, Spanish and Portuguese coffers, models of Chinese pagodas, a Japanese screen of precious workmanship, besides china, bronzes, embroidered silks, hangings of the finest needlework. Arm-chairs wide as beds, and sofas deep as alcoves, suggested voluptuous idleness and the somnolent life of the seraglio. The prevailing tone of the room was old gold, blended with green and red, and nothing it contained too forcibly indicated the presence of the courtesan save the luxuriousness of the seats. Only two "biscuit" statuettes, a woman in her shift hunting for fleas, and another with nothing at all on walking on her hands and waving her feet in the air, sufficed to sully the room with a note of stupid originality.

Through a door, which was nearly alway ajar, the dressing-room was visible. It was all in marble and glass, with a white bath, silver jugs and basins, and crystal and ivory appointments. A drawn curtain filled the place with a clear twilight, which seemed to slumber in the warm scent of violets, that suggestive perfume peculiar to Nana wherewith the whole house from the roof to the very court-yard was penetrated.

The furnishing of the house was a most important undertaking. Nana certainly had Zoé with her, that girl so devoted to her fortunes. For months she had been tranquilly awaiting this abrupt new departure as became a woman who was certain of her powers of prescience, and now she was triumphant; she was mistress of the house, and was putting by a round sum whilst serving *Madame* as honestly as possible. But a solitary lady's maid was no longer sufficient. A butler, a coachman, a porter, and a cook were wanted. Besides, it was necessary to fill the stables. It was then that Labordette made himself most useful. He undertook to perform all sorts of errands which bored the Count; he made a comfortable job of the purchase of horses, he visited the coach-builders, he guided the young woman in her choice of things. She was to be met with at the shops, leaning on his arm. Labordette even got in the servants—Charles, a great tall coachman, who had been in service with the Duc de Corbreuse; Julien, a little, smiling, much-becurled butler; and a married couple, of whom the wife, Victorine, became cook, whilst the husband, François, was taken on as porter and footman. The last mentioned in powder and breeches wore Nana's livery, which was a sky-blue one adorned with silver lace, and he received visitors in the hall. The whole thing was princely in the correctness of its style.

At the end of two months the house was set going. The cost had been more than three hundred thousand francs. There were eight horses in the stables, and five carriages in the coach-houses, and of these five one was a landau with silver embellishments, which for the moment occupied the attention of all Paris. And, amid this great wealth, Nana began settling down, and making her nest. After the third representation of the *Petite Duchesse* she had quitted the theatre, leaving Bordenave to struggle on against a bankruptcy which, despite the Count's money, was imminent. Nevertheless, she was still bitter about her failure. It added to that other bitterness, the lesson Fontan had given her, a shameful lesson for which she held all men responsible. Accordingly, she now declared herself very firm, and quite proof against sudden infatuations, but thoughts of vengeance took no hold of her volatile brain. What did maintain a hold on it, in the hours when she was not indignant, was an ever-wakeful lust of expenditure, added to a natural contempt for the man who paid, and to a perpetual passion for consumption and waste, which took pride in the ruin of her lovers.

At starting, Nana put the Count on a proper footing, and clearly mapped out the conditions of their relationship. The Count gave twelve thousand francs monthly, presents excepted, and demanded nothing in return save absolute fidelity. She swore fidelity, but insisted also on being treated with the utmost consideration, on enjoying complete liberty as mistress of the house, and on having her every wish respected. For instance, she was to receive her friends every day, and he was to come only at stated times. In a word, he was to repose a blind confidence in her in everything. And when he was seized with jealous anxiety, and hesitated to grant what she wanted, she stood on her dignity, and threatened to give him back all he had given, or even swore by little Louiset to perform what she promised. This was to suffice him. There was no love where mutual esteem was wanting. At the end of the first month Muffat respected her.

But she desired and obtained still more. Soon she began to influence him as became a good-natured courtesan. When he came to her in a moody condition she cheered him up, confessed him, and then gave him good advice. Little by little she interested herself in the annoyances of his home life, in his wife, in his daughter, in his love affairs and financial difficulties; she was very sensible, very fair, and right-minded. On one occasion only did she let anger get the better of her, and that was when he confided to her that doubtless Daguenet was going to ask for his daughter Estelle in marriage. When the Count began making himself notorious, Daguenet had thought it a wise move to break off with Nana. He had treated her like a base hussy, and had sworn to snatch his future father-in-law out of the creature's clutches. In return, Nana abused her old Mimi in a charming fashion. He was a renegade who had devoured his fortune in the company of vile women; he had no moral sense. True, he did not let them pay him money, but he profited by that of others, and only repaid them at rare intervals with a bouquet or a dinner. And when the Count seemed inclined to find excuses for these failings she bluntly informed him that Daguenet

had enjoyed her favours, and she added disgusting particulars. Muffat had grown ashen-pale. There was no question of the young man now. This would teach him to be lacking in gratitude!

Meanwhile, the house had not been entirely furnished, when, one evening after she had lavished the most energetic promises of fidelity on Muffat, Nana kept the Count Xavier de Vandeuvres for the night. For the last fortnight he had been paying her assiduous court, visiting her and sending presents of flowers, and now she gave way not so much out of sudden infatuation as to prove that she was a free woman. The idea of gain followed later, when, the day after, Vandeuvres helped her to pay a bill which she did not wish to mention to the other man. From Vandeuvres she would certainly derive from eight to ten thousand francs a month, and this would prove very useful as pocket-money. In those days he was finishing the last of his fortune in an access of burning, feverish folly. His horses and Lucy had devoured three of his farms, and at one gulp Nana was going to swallow his last château, near Amiens. He seemed in a hurry to sweep everything away, down to the ruins of the old tower, built by a Vandeuvres under Philip Augustus. He was mad for ruin, and thought it a great thing to leave the last golden bezants of his coat-of-arms in the grasp of this courtesan, whom the world of Paris desired. He, too, accepted Nana's conditions, leaving her entire freedom of action and claiming her caresses only on certain days. He was not even naïvely impassioned enough to require her to make vows. Muffat suspected nothing. As to Vandeuvres, he knew things would take place for a certainty, but he never made the least allusion to them, and pretended total ignorance, whilst his lips wore the subtle smile of the sceptical man of pleasure, who does not seek the impossible provided he can have his day and that Paris is aware of it.

From that time forth Nana's house was really properly appointed. The staff of servants was complete in the stable, in the kitchen, and in my lady's chamber. Zoé organised everything, and passed successfully through the most unforeseen difficulties. The household moved as easily as the scenery in a theatre, and was regulated like a grand administrative concern. Indeed, it worked with such precision that during the early months there were no jars and no derangements. *Madame,* however, pained Zoé extremely with her imprudent acts, her sudden fits of unwisdom, her mad bravado. Still the lady's maid grew gradually lenient, for she had noticed that she made increased profits in seasons of wanton waste when *Madame* had committed a folly which must be made up for. It was then that the presents began raining on her, and she fished up many a louis out of the troubled waters.

One morning when Muffat had not yet left the bedroom, Zoé ushered a gentleman into the dressing-room, where Nana was changing her underwear. He was trembling violently.

"Good gracious! It's Zizi!" said the young woman, in great astonishment.

It was indeed Georges. But when he saw her in her shift, with her golden hair over her bare shoulders, he threw his arms round her neck and round her waist, and kissed her in all directions.

She began struggling to get free, for she was frightened, and in smothered tones she stammered,—

"Do leave off! He's there! Oh, it's silly of you! And you, Zoé, are you out of your senses? Take him away, and keep him downstairs: I'll try and come down."

Zoé had to push him in front of her. When Nana was able to rejoin them in the drawing-room downstairs, she scolded them both, and Zoé pursed up her lips, and took her departure with a vexed expression, remarking that she had only been anxious to give *Madame* a pleasure. Georges was so glad to see Nana again, and gazed at her with such delight, that his fine eyes began filling with tears. The miserable days were over now; his mother believed him to have grown reasonable, and had allowed him to leave The Fondettes. Accordingly, the moment he had reached the terminus, he had got a conveyance in order the more quickly to come and kiss his sweet darling. He spoke of living at her side in future, as he used to do down in the country, when he waited for her barefooted in the bedroom at The Mignotte. And as he told her about himself, he let his fingers creep forward, for he longed to touch her after that cruel year of separation. Then he got possession of her hands, felt about in the wide sleeves of her dressing-jacket, travelled up as far as her shoulders.

"You still love your baby?" he asked, in his child-voice.

"Oh, I certainly love him!" answered Nana, briskly getting out of his clutches; "but you come popping in without warning. You know, my little man, I'm not my own mistress; you must be good!"

Georges, when he got out of his cab, had been so dizzy with the feeling that his long desire was as last about to be satisfied, that he had not even noticed what sort of house he was entering. But now he became conscious of a change in the things around him. He examined the sumptuous dining-room, with its lofty decorated ceiling, its Gobelins hangings, its buffet blazing with plate.

"Yes, yes!" he remarked sadly.

And with that she made him understand that he was never to come in the mornings, but between four and six in the afternoon, if he cared to. That was her reception-time. Then, as he looked at her with suppliant questioning eyes and craved no boon at all, she, in her turn, kissed him on the forehead in the most amiable way.

"Be very good," she whispered. "I'll do all I can."

But the truth was that this remark now meant nothing. She thought Georges very nice, and would have liked him as a companion, but as nothing else. Nevertheless, when he arrived daily at four o'clock, he seemed so wretched, that she was often fain to be as compliant as of old, and would hide him in cupboards, and constantly allow him to pick up the crumbs from Beauty's table. He hardly ever left the house now, and became as much one of its inmates as the little dog Bijou. Together they nestled among mistress's skirts and enjoyed a little of her at a time, even when she was with another man, whilst doles of sugar and stray caresses not seldom fell to their share in her hours of loneliness and boredom.

Doubtless Madame Hugon found out that the lad had again returned to that wicked woman's arms, for she hurried up to Paris, and came and sought aid from her other son, the Lieutenant Philippe, who was then in garrison at Vincennes. Georges, who was hiding from his elder brother, was seized with despairing apprehension, for he feared the latter might adopt violent tactics, and as his tenderness for Nana was so nervously expansive that he could not keep anything from her, he soon began talking of nothing but his big brother, a great strong fellow who was capable of all kinds of things.

"You know," he explained, "mamma won't come to you whilst she can send my brother. Oh, she'll certainly send Philippe to fetch me."

The first time he said this Nana was deeply wounded. She said frigidly,—

"Gracious me, I should like to see him come! For all that he's a lieutenant in the army, François will chuck him out in double-quick time!"

Soon, as the lad kept returning to the subject of his brother, she ended by taking a certain interest in Philippe, and in a week's time she knew him from head to foot—knew him as very tall and very strong, and merry and somewhat rough. She learnt intimate details, too, and found out that he had hair on his arms and a birthmark on his shoulder. So thoroughly did she learn her lesson that one day, when she was full of the image of the man who was to be turned out of doors by her orders, she cried out,—

"I say, Zizi, your brother's not coming. He's a base deserter!"

The next day, when Georges and Nana were alone together, François came upstairs to ask whether *Madame* would receive Lieutenant Philippe Hugon. Georges grew extremely white, and murmured,—

"I suspected it; mamma was talking about it this morning."

And he besought the young woman to send down word that she could not see visitors. But she was already on her feet, and seemed all aflame as she said,—

"Why should I not see him? He would think me afraid. Dear me, we'll have a good laugh! Just leave the gentleman in the drawing-room for a quarter of an hour, François; afterwards bring him up to me."

She did not sit down again, but began pacing feverishly to and fro between the fire-place and a Venetian mirror hanging above an Italian chest. And each time she reached the latter she glanced at the glass and tried the effect of a smile, whilst Georges sat nervously on a sofa, trembling at the thought of the coming scene. As she walked up and down she kept jerking out such little phrases as,—

"It will calm the fellow down if he has to wait a quarter of an hour. Besides, if he thinks he's calling on a Tottie, the drawing-room will stun him! Yes, yes, have a good look at everything, my fine fellow! It isn't imitation, and it'll teach you to respect the lady who owns it. Respect's what men need to feel! The quarter of an hour's gone by, eh? No? Only ten minutes? Oh! we've got plenty of time."

She did not stay where she was, however. At the end of the quarter of an hour she sent Georges away, after making him solemnly promise not to listen at the door, as such conduct would

scarcely look proper in case the servants saw him. As he went into her bedroom, Zizi ventured, in a choking sort of way to remark,—

"It's my brother, you know——"

"Don't you fear," she said, with much dignity; "if he's polite, I'll be polite."

François ushered in Philippe Hugon, who wore morning dress. Georges began crossing on tiptoe on the other side of the room, for he was anxious to obey the young woman. But the sound of voices retained him, and he hesitated in such anguish of mind that his knees gave way under him. He began imagining that a dread catastrophe would befall, that blows would be struck, that something abominable would happen, which would make Nana everlastingly odious to him. And so he could not withstand the temptation to come back and put his ear against the door. He heard very ill, for the thick *portières* deadened every sound; but he managed to catch certain words spoken by Philippe, stern phrases in which such terms as "mere child," "family," "honour," were distinctly audible. He was so anxious about his darling's possible answers that his heart beat violently and filled his head with a confused buzzing noise. She was sure to give vent to a "Dirty blackguard!" or to a "Leave me bloody well alone! I'm in my own house!" But nothing happened—not a breath came from her direction. Nana seemed dead in there! Soon even his brother's voice grew gentler, and he could not make it out at all, when a strange murmuring sound finally stupefied him. Nana was sobbing! For a moment or two he was the prey of contending feelings, and knew not whether to run away or to fall upon Philippe. But just then Zoé came into the room, and he withdrew from the door, ashamed at being thus surprised.

She began quietly to put some linen away in a cupboard, whilst he stood mute and motionless, pressing his forehead against a window-pane. He was tortured by uncertainty. After a short silence the woman asked,—

"It's your brother that's with *Madame?*"

"Yes," replied the lad, in a choking voice.

There was a fresh silence.

"And it makes you anxious, doesn't it, Monsieur Georges?"

"Yes," he rejoined in the same painful, suffering tone.

Zoé was in no hurry. She folded up some lace, and said slowly,—

"You're wrong: *Madame* will manage it all."

And then the conversation ended: they said not another word. Still she did not leave the room. A long quarter of an hour passed, and she turned round again without seeming to notice the look of exasperation overspreading the lad's face, which was already white with the effects of uncertainty and constraint. He was casting sidelong glances in the direction of the drawing-room.

Maybe Nana was still crying. The other must have grown savage and have dealt her blows. Thus, when Zoé finally took her departure, he ran to the door, and once more pressed his ear against it. He was thunderstruck; his head swam, for he heard a brisk outburst of gaiety, tender whispering voices, and the smothered giggles of a woman who is being tickled. Besides, almost directly afterwards, Nana conducted Philippe to the head of the stairs, and there was an exchange of cordial and familiar phrases.

When Georges again ventured into the drawing-room the young woman was standing before the mirror, looking at herself.

"Well?" he asked in utter bewilderment.

"Well, what?" said she, without turning round. Then negligently,—

"What did you mean? He's very nice, is your brother!"

"So it's all right, is it?"

"Oh, certainly it's all right! Goodness me, what's over you? One would have thought we were going to fight!"

Georges still failed to understand.

"I thought I heard—that is, you didn't cry?" he stammered out.

"Me cry!" she exclaimed, looking fixedly at him. "Why, you're dreaming! What makes you think I cried?"

Thereupon the lad was treated to a distressing scene for having disobeyed and played Paul Pry behind the door. She sulked, and he returned with coaxing submissiveness to the old subject, for he wished to know all about it.

"And my brother, then?"

"Your brother saw where he was at once. You know I might have been a Tottie, in which case his interference would have been accounted for by your age and the family honour! Oh yes, I understand those kinds of feelings! But a single glance was enough for him, and he behaved like a well-bred man at once. So don't be anxious any longer, it's all over—he's gone to quiet your mamma!"

And she went on laughingly,—

"For that matter, you'll see your

brother here. I've invited him, and he's going to return."

"Oh, he's going to return," said the lad, growing white. He added nothing, and they ceased talking of Philippe. She began dressing to go out, and he watched her with his great sad eyes. Doubtless he was very glad that matters had got settled, for he would have preferred death to a rupture of their connection, but deep down in his heart there was a silent anguish, a profound sense of pain, which he had no experience of and dared not talk about. How Philippe quieted their mother's fears he never knew, but three days later she returned to The Fondettes, apparently satisfied. On the evening of her return, at Nana's house, he trembled when François announced the lieutenant, but the latter jested gaily, and treated him like a young rascal, whose escapade he had favoured as something not likely to have any consequences. The lad's heart was sore within him, he scarcely dared move, and blushed girlishly at the least word that was spoken to him. He had not lived much in Philippe's society, he was ten years his junior, and he feared him as he would a father, from whom stories about women are concealed. Accordingly, he experienced an uneasy sense of shame when he saw him so free in Nana's company, and heard him laugh uproariously as became a man who was plunging into a life of pleasure with the gusto born of magnificent health. Nevertheless, when his brother shortly began to present himself every day, Georges ended by getting somewhat used to it all. Nana was radiant.

This her latest installation had been involving all the riotous waste attend-ant on the life of gallantry; and now her housewarming was being defiantly celebrated in a grand mansion positively overflowing with males and with furni-ture.

One afternoon when the Hugons were there, Count Muffat arrived out of hours. But when Zoé told him that *Madame* was with friends, he refused to come in and took his departure discreetly, as became a gallant gentleman. When he made his appearance again in the eve-ning, Nana received him with the frigid indignation of a grossly-affronted woman.

"Sir," said she, "I have given you no cause why you should insult me. You must understand this: when I am at home to visitors, I beg you to make your appearance just like other people."

The Count simply gaped in astonish-ment. "But my dear——?" he endeav-oured to explain.

"Perhaps it was because I had visi-tors! Yes, there were men here, but what d'you suppose I was doing with those men? You only advertise a wo-man's affairs when you act the discreet lover, and I don't want to be advertised, I don't!"

He obtained his pardon with difficulty, but at bottom he was enchanted. It was with scenes such as these that she kept him in unquestioning and docile submission. She had long since suc-ceeded in imposing Georges on him as a young vagabond who, she declared, amused her. She made him dine with Philippe, and the Count behaved with great amiability. When they rose from table, he took the young man on one side, and asked news of his mother. From that time forth the young Hugons, Van-deuvres, and Muffat were openly about the house, and shook hands as guests and intimates might have done. It was a more convenient arrangement than the previous one. Muffat alone still abstained discreetly from too frequent visits, thus adhering to the ceremonious policy of an ordinary strange caller. At night when Nana was sitting on her bearskins drawing off her stockings, he would talk amicably about the other three gentlemen, and lay especial stress on Philippe, who was loyalty itself.

"It's very true; they're nice," Nana would say, as she lingered on the floor to change her shift. "Only, you know, they see what I am. One word about it, and I should chuck 'em all out of doors for you!"

Nevertheless, despite her luxurious life and her group of courtiers, Nana was nearly bored to death. She had men for every minute of the night, and money overflowed even among the brushes and combs in the drawers of her dressing-table. But all this had ceased to satisfy her; she felt that there was a void somewhere or other, an empty place provocative of yawns. Her life dragged on devoid of occupation, and successive days only brought back the same monotonous hours. To-morrow had ceased to be; she lived like a bird: sure of her food, and ready to perch and roost on any branch which she came to. This certainty of food and drink left her lolling effortless for whole days, lulled her to sleep in conventual idleness and submission as though she were the prisoner of her trade. Never going out except to drive, she was losing her walking powers. She reverted to low childish tastes, would kiss Bijou from morning to night and kill time with stupid pleasures, whilst

waiting for the man whose caresses she tolerated with an appearance of complaisant lassitude. Amid this species of self-abandonment she now took no thought about anything save her personal beauty; her sole care was to look after herself, to wash and to perfume her limbs, as became one who was proud of being able to undress at any moment and in face of anybody without having to blush for her imperfections.

At ten in the morning Nana would get up. Bijou, the Scotch griffon dog, used to lick her face and wake her, and then would ensue a game of play lasting some five minutes, during which the dog would race about over her arms and legs, and cause Count Muffat much distress. Bijou was the first little male he had ever been jealous of. It was not at all proper, he thought, that an animal should go poking its nose under the bed-clothes like that! After this Nana would proceed to her dressing-room, where she took a bath. Towards eleven o'clock, François would come and do up her hair before beginning the elaborate manipulations of the afternoon.

At breakfast, as she hated feeding alone, she nearly always had Madame Maloir at table with her. This lady would arrive from unknown regions in the morning, wearing her extravagantly quaint hats, and would return at night to that mysterious existence of hers, about which no one ever troubled. But the hardest to bear were the two or three hours between lunch and the toilet. On ordinary occasions she proposed a game of bézique to her old friend, on others she would read the *Figaro*, in which the theatrical echoes and the fashionable news interested her. Sometimes she even opened a book, for she fancied herself in literary matters. Her toilet kept her till close on five o'clock, and then only she would wake from her day-long drowse, and drive out or receive a whole mob of men at her own house. She would often dine abroad, and always go to bed very late, only to rise again on the morrow with the same languor as before, and to begin another day differing in nothing from its predecessor.

The great distraction was to go to the Batignolles and see her little Louis at her aunt's. For a fortnight at a time she forgot all about him, and then would follow an access of maternal love, and she would hurry off on foot with all the modesty and tenderness becoming a good mother. On such occasions she would be the bearer of snuff for her aunt and of oranges and biscuits for the child, the kind of presents one takes to a hospital. Or again she would drive up in her landau on her return from the Bois, decked in costumes, the resplendence of which greatly excited the dwellers in the solitary street. Since her niece's magnificent elevation, Madame Lerat had been puffed up with vanity. She rarely presented herself in the Avenue Villiers, for she was pleased to remark that it wasn't her place to do so, but she enjoyed triumphs in her own street. She was delighted when the young woman arrived in dresses that had cost four or five thousand francs, and would be occupied during the whole of the next day in shewing off her presents and in citing prices which quite stupefied the neighbours. As often as not, Nana kept Sunday free for the sake of "her family"; and on such occasions, if Muffat invited her, she would refuse with the smile of a good little shopwoman. It was impossible, she would answer; she was dining at her aunt's, she was going to see baby. Moreover, that poor little man Louiset was always ill. He was almost three years old, growing quite a great boy! But he had had an eczema on the back of his neck, and now concretions were forming in his ears, which pointed, it was feared, to decay of the bones of the skull. When she saw how pale he looked, with his spoilt blood and his flabby flesh all out in yellow patches, she would become serious, but her principal feeling would be one of astonishment. What could be the matter with the little love that he should grow so weakly? She, his mother, was so strong and well!

On the days when her child did not engross attention, Nana would again sink back into the noisy monotony of her existence, with its drives in the Bois, first nights at the theatre, dinners and suppers at the Maison-d'Or, or the Café Anglais, not to mention all the places of public resort, all the spectacles to which crowds rushed—Mabille, the reviews, the races. But whatever happened she still felt that stupid, idle void, which caused her, as it were, to suffer internal cramps. Despite the incessant infatuations that possessed her heart, she would stretch out her arms with a gesture of immense weariness the moment she was left alone. Solitude rendered her low spirited at once, for it brought her face to face with the emptiness and boredom within her. Extremely gay by nature and profession, she became dismal in solitude, and would sum up her life in the following ejaculation, which recurred incessantly between her yawns:

"Oh, how the men bother me!"

One afternoon, as she was returning home from a concert, Nana, on the sidewalk in the Rue Montmartre, noticed a woman trotting along in down-at-heel boots, dirty petticoats, and a hat utterly ruined by the rain. She recognised her suddenly.

"Stop, Charles!" she shouted to the coachman, and began calling: "Satin, Satin!"

Passers-by turned their heads, the whole street stared. Satin had drawn near, and was still further soiling herself against the carriage wheels.

"Do get in, my dear girl," said Nana tranquilly, disdaining the onlookers.

And with that she picked her up and carried her off, though she was in disgusting contrast to her light blue landau and her dress of pearl-grey silk, trimmed with Chantilly, whilst the street smiled at the coachman's loftily dignified demeanour.

From that day forth Nana had a passion to occupy her thoughts. Satin became her vicious foible. Washed and dressed, and duly installed in the house in the Avenue de Villiers, during three days the girl talked of Saint-Lazare, and the annoyances the sisters had caused her, and how those dirty police people had put her down on the official list. Nana grew indignant, and comforted her, and vowed she would get her name taken off, even though she herself should have to go and find out the Minister of the Interior. Meanwhile, there was no sort of hurry: nobody would come and search for her at Nana's—that was certain. And thereupon the two women began to pass tender afternoons together, making numberless endearing little speeches, and mingling their kisses with laughter. The same little sport, which the arrival of the plain-clothes men had interrupted in the Rue de Laval, was beginning again in a jocular sort of spirit. One fine evening, however, it became serious, and Nana, who had been so disgusted at Laure's, now understood what it meant. She was upset and enraged by it, the more so because Satin disappeared on the morning of the fourth day. No one had seen her go out. She had, indeed, slipped away in her new dress, seized by a longing for air, full of sentimental regret for her old street existence.

That day there was such a terrible storm in the house that all the servants hung their heads in sheepish silence. Nana had come near beating François for not throwing himself across the door through which Satin escaped. She did her best, however, to control herself, and talked of Satin as a dirty swine. Oh, it would teach her to pick filthy things like that out of the gutter!

When *Madame* shut herself up in her room in the afternoon, Zoé heard her sobbing. In the evening she suddenly asked for her carriage and had herself driven to Laure's. It had occurred to her that she would find Satin at the *table d'hôte* in the Rue des Martyrs. She was not going there for the sake of seeing her again, but in order to catch her one in the face! As a matter of fact, Satin was dining at a little table with Madame Robert. Seeing Nana, she began to laugh; but the former, though wounded to the quick, did not make a scene. On the contrary, she was very sweet and very compliant. She paid for champagne, made five or six tablefuls tipsy, and then carried off Satin when Madame

Robert was in the closets. Not till they were in the carriage did she make a mordant attack on her, threatening to kill her if she did it again. After that day, the same little business began again continually. On twenty different occasions, Nana, tragically furious as only a jilted woman can be, ran off in pursuit of this sluttish creature, whose flights were prompted by the boredom she suffered amid the comforts of her new home. Nana began to talk of boxing Madame Robert's ears; one day she even meditated a duel: there was one woman too many, she said.

In these latter times, whenever she dined at Laure's, she donned her diamonds, and occasionally brought with her Louise Violaine, Maria Blond, and Tatan Néné, all of them ablaze with finery; and whilst the sordid feast was progressing in the three saloons, and the yellow gaslight flared overhead, these four resplendent ladies would demean themselves with a vengeance, for it was their delight to dazzle the little local courtesans and to carry them off when dinner was over. On days such as these, Laure, sleek and tight-laced as ever, would kiss everyone with an air of expanded maternity. Yet notwithstanding all these circumstances, Satin's blue eyes and pure virginal face remained as calm as heretofore; torn, beaten, and pestered by the two women, she would simply remark that it was a funny business, and they would have done far better to make it up at once. It did no good to slap her; she couldn't cut herself in two, however much she wanted to be nice to everybody. It was Nana who finally carried her off in triumph, so assiduously had she loaded Satin with kind-nesses and presents. In order to be revenged, however, Madame Robert wrote abominable, anonymous letters to her rival's lovers.

For some time past Count Muffat had appeared suspicious, and one morning, with considerable show of feeling, he laid before Nana an anonymous letter, where, in the very first sentences, she read that she was accused of deceiving the Count with Vandeuvres and the young Hugons. "It's false! It's false!" she loudly exclaimed in accents of extraordinary candour.

"You swear?" asked Muffat, already willing to be comforted.

"I'll swear by whatever you like—yes! by the head of my child!"

But the letter was long. Soon her connection with Satin was described in the broadest and most ignoble terms. When she had done reading, she smiled.

"Now I know who it comes from," she remarked simply.

And, as Muffat wanted her denial to the charges therein contained, she resumed quietly enough,—

"That's a matter which doesn't concern you, dear old pet. How can it hurt you?"

She did not deny anything. He used some horrified expressions. Thereupon she shrugged her shoulders. Where had he been all this time? Why it was done everywhere! And she mentioned her friends, and swore that fashionable ladies went in for it. In fact, to hear her speak, nothing could be commoner or more natural. But a lie was a lie, and so, a moment ago, he had seen how angry she grew in the matter of Vandeuvres and the young Hugons! Oh, if that had been true, he would have been justified in throttling her! But what was the good of lying to him about a matter of no consequence? And with that she repeated her previous expression:

"Come now, how can it hurt you?"

Then, as the scene still continued, she closed it with a rough speech:

"Besides, dear boy, if the thing doesn't suit you, it's very simple: the house-door's open! There now you must take me as you find me!"

He hung his head, for the young woman's vows of fidelity made him happy at bottom. She, however, now knew her power over him, and ceased to consider his feelings. And from that time forth Satin was openly installed in the house, on the same footing as the gentlemen. Vandeuvres had not needed anonymous letters in order to understand how matters stood, and accordingly he joked and tried to pick jealous quarrels with Satin. Philippe and Georges, on their parts, treated her like a jolly good fellow, shaking hands with her, and cracking the riskiest jokes imaginable.

Nana had an adventure one evening when this slut of a girl had given her the go-by, and she had gone to dine in the Rue des Martyrs without being able to catch her. Whilst she was dining by herself, Daguenet had appeared on the scene, for, although he had reformed, he still occasionally dropped in, under the influnce of his old vicious inclinations. He hoped of course that no one would meet him in these black recesses, dedicated to the town's lowest depravity. Accordingly even Nana's presence seemed to embarrass him at the outset. But he was not the man to run away, and coming forward with a smile, he asked if *Madame* would be so kind as to allow him to dine at her table. Noticing his jocular tone, Nana assumed her magnificently frigid demeanour, and icily replied:

"Sit down where you please, sir. We are in a public place."

Thus begun, the conversation proved amusing. But, at dessert, Nana, bored and burning for a triumph, put her elbows on the table, and began in the old familiar way:

"Well, what about your marriage, my lad? Is it getting on all right?"

"Not much," Daguenet averred.

As a matter of fact, just when he was about to venture on his request at the Muffats', he had met with such a cold reception from the Count that he had prudently refrained. The business struck him as a failure. Nana fixed her clear eyes on him: she was sitting leaning her chin on her hand, and there was an ironical curve about her lips.

"Oh yes! I'm a baggage," she resumed slowly. "Oh yes, the future father-in-law will have to be dragged from between my claws! Dear me, dear me, for a fellow with *nous,* you're jolly stupid! What! d'you mean to say you're going to tell your tales to a man who adores me and tells me everything! Now just listen: you shall marry if I wish it, my little man!"

For a minute or two, he had felt the truth of this, and now he began scheming out a method of submission. Nevertheless, he still talked jokingly, not wishing the matter to grow serious, and after he had put on his gloves, he demanded the hand of Mlle. Estelle de Beuville in the strict regulation manner. Nana ended by laughing, as though she had been tickled. Oh, that Mimi! it was impossible to bear him a grudge! Daguenet's great successes with ladies of her class were due to the sweetness of his voice, a voice of such musical purity and pliancy as to have won him among courtesans the sobriquet of "Velvet-Mouth." Every woman would give way to him when he lulled her with his sonorous caresses. He knew this power, and rocked Nana to sleep with endless words, telling her all kinds of idiotic anecdotes. When they left the *table d'hôte,* she was blushing rosy-red; she trembled as she hung on his arm; he had reconquered her. As it was very fine, she sent her carriage away, and walked with him as far as his own place, where she went upstairs with him naturally enough. Two hours later, as she was dressing again, she said,—

"So, you hold to this marriage of yours, Mimi?"

"Egad," he muttered; "it's the best thing I could possibly do after all! You know I'm stony broke."

She summoned him to button her boots, and after a pause,—

"Good heavens! I've no objection. I'll shove you on! She's as dry as a lath is that little thing, but since it suits your game—oh! I'm agreeable: I'll run the thing through for you."

Then, with bosom still uncovered, she began laughing:

"Only, what will you give me?"

He had caught her in his arms and was kissing her on the shoulders in a perfect access of gratitude, whilst she quivered with excitement and struggled merrily, and threw herself backwards in her efforts to be free.

"Oh! I know," she cried, excited by the contest. "Listen to what I want in the way of commission. On your wedding day, you shall make me a present of your innocence. Before your wife, d'you understand?"

"That's it! That's it!" said he, laughing even louder than Nana.

The bargain amused them — they thought the whole business very good indeed.

Now, as it happened, there was a dinner at Nana's next day. For the matter of that, it was the customary Thursday dinner, and Muffat, Vandeuvres, the young Hugons, and Satin were present. The Count arrived early. He stood in need of eighty thousand francs wherewith to free the young woman from two or three debts and to give her a set of sapphires she was dying to possess. As he had already seriously lessened his capital, he was in search of a lender, for he did not dare to sell another property. With the advice of Nana herself, he had addressed himself to Labordette, but the latter, deeming it too heavy an undertaking, had mentioned it to the hairdresser Francis, who willingly busied himself in such affairs in order to oblige his lady clients. The Count put himself into the hands of these gentlemen, but expressed a formal desire not to appear in the matter; and they both undertook to keep in hand the bill for a hundred thousand francs which he was to sign, excusing themselves at the same time for charging a matter of twenty thousand francs interest, and loudly denouncing the blackguard usurers, to whom, they declared, it had been necessary to have recourse. When Muffat had himself announced, Francis was putting the last touches to Nana's coiffure.

Labordette also was sitting familiarly in the dressing-room as became a friend of no consequence. Seeing the Count, he discreetly placed a thick bundle of bank-notes among the powders and pomades, and the bill was signed on the marble-topped dressing-table. Nana was anxious to keep Labordette to dinner, but he declined—he was taking a rich foreigner about Paris. Muffat, however, led him aside, and begged him to go to Becker, the jeweller, and bring him back thence the set of sapphires, which he wanted to present the young woman by way of surprise that very evening. Labordette willingly undertook the commission, and half an hour later Julien handed the jewel-case mysteriously to the Count.

During dinner-time Nana was nervous. The sight of the eighty thousand francs had excited her. To think all that money was to go to tradespeople! It was a disgusting thought. After soup had been served she grew sentimental, and in the splendid dining-room, glittering with plate and glass, she talked of the bliss of poverty. The men were in evening dress, Nana in a gown of white embroidered satin, whilst Satin made a more modest appearance in black silk, with a simple gold heart at her throat, which was a present from her kind friend. Julien and François waited behind the guests, and were assisted in this by Zoé. All three looked most dignified.

"It's certain I had far greater fun when I hadn't a cent!" Nana repeated.

She had placed Muffat on her right hand and Vandeuvres on her left, but she scarcely looked at them so taken up was she with Satin, who sat in state between Philippe and Georges on the opposite side of the table.

"Eh, duckie?" she kept saying at every turn. "How we did use to laugh, in those days, when we went to Mother Josse's school in the Rue Polonceau!"

When the roast was being served the two women plunged into a world of reminiscences. They used to have regular chattering fits of this kind when a sudden desire to stir the muddy depths of their childhood would possess them. These fits always occurred when men were present: it was as though they had given way to a burning desire to treat them to the dunghill on which they had grown to woman's estate. The gentlemen paled visibly and looked embarrassed. The young Hugons did their best to laugh, whilst Vandeuvres nervously toyed with his beard, and Muffat redoubled his gravity.

"You remember Victor?" said Nana. "There was a wicked little fellow for you! Why, he used to take the little girls into cellars!"

"I remember him perfectly," replied Satin. "I recollect the big court-yard at your place very well. There was a portress there with a broom!"

"Mother Boche: she's dead."

"And I can still picture your shop. Your mother was a great fatty. One evening when we were playing your father came in drunk. Oh, so drunk!"

At this point Vandeuvres tried to intercept the ladies' reminiscences and to effect a diversion.

"I say, my dear, I should be very glad to have some more truffles. They're simply perfect. Yesterday I had some at the house of the Duc de Corbreuse, which did not come up to them at all."

"The truffles, Julien!" said Nana roughly.

Then returning to the subject:

"By Jove, yes, dad hadn't any sense! And then what a smash there was! You should have seen it—down, down, down we went, starving away all the time. I can tell you I've had to bear pretty well everything, and it's a miracle I didn't kick the bucket over it, like daddy and mammy."

This time Muffat, who was playing with his knife in a state of infinite exasperation, made so bold as to intervene.

"What you're telling us isn't very cheerful."

"Eh, what? Not cheerful!" cried she, with a withering glance. "I believe you, it isn't cheerful! Somebody had to earn a living for us, dear boy. Oh yes, you know, I'm the right sort; I don't mince matters. Mammy was a laundress; daddy used to get drunk, and he died of it! There! if it doesn't suit you—if you're ashamed of my family——"

They all protested. What was she after now? They had every sort of respect for her family! But she went on:

"If you're ashamed of my family, you'll please leave me, because I'm not one of those women who deny their father and mother. You must take me and them together, d'you understand?"

They took her as required; they accepted the dad, the mammy, the past; in fact, whatever she chose. With their eyes fixed on the table-cloth, the four now sat shrinking and insignificant, whilst Nana, in a transport of omnipotence, trampled on them in the old muddy boots worn long since in the Rue Goutte-d'Or. She was determined not to lay down the cudgels just yet. It was all very fine to bring her fortunes, to build her palaces, she would never leave off regretting the time when she munched apples! Oh, what bosh that stupid thing money was! It was made for the tradespeople! Finally her outburst ended in a sentimentally-expressed desire for a simple, open-hearted existence, to be passed in an atmosphere of universal benevolence.

When she got to this point she noticed Julien waiting idly by.

"Well, what's the matter? Hand the champagne, then!" said she. "Why d'you stand staring at me like a goose?"

During this scene the servants had never once smiled. They apparently heard nothing, and the more their mistress let herself down, the more majestic they became. Julien set to work to pour out the champagne, and did so without mishap, but François, who was handing round the fruit, was so unfortunate as to tilt the fruit-dish too low, and the apples, the pears, and the grapes rolled on the table.

"You bloody clumsy lot!" cried Nana.

The footman was mistaken enough to try and explain that the fruit had not been firmly piled up. Zoé had disarranged it by taking out some oranges.

"Then it's Zoé that's the goose!" said Nana.

"*Madame*——," murmured the lady's maid in an injured tone.

Straightway *Madame* rose to her feet, and in a sharp voice, and with royally-authoritative gesture,—

"We've had enough of this, haven't we? Leave the room all of you! We don't want you any longer!"

This summary procedure calmed her

down, and she was forthwith all sweetness and amiability. The dessert proved charming, and the gentlemen grew quite merry waiting on themselves. But Satin, having peeled a pear, came and ate it behind her darling, leaning on her shoulder the while, and whispering sundry little remarks in her ear, at which they both laughed very loudly. By-and-by she wanted to share her last piece of pear with Nana, and presented it to her between her teeth. Whereupon there was a great nibbling of lips, and the pear was finished amid kisses. At this there was a burst of comic protest from the gentlemen, Philippe shouting to them to take it easy, and Vandeuvres asking if one ought to leave the room. Georges, meanwhile, had come and put his arm round Satin's waist, and had brought her back to her seat.

"How silly of you!" said Nana; "you're making her blush, the poor darling duck. Never mind, dear girl, let them chaff. It's our own little private affair."

And turning to Muffat, who was watching them with his serious expression,—

"Isn't it, my friend?"

"Yes, certainly," he murmured with a slow nod of approval.

He no longer protested now. And so, amid that company of gentlemen with the great names and the old upright traditions, the two women sat face to face, exchanging tender glances, conquering, reigning, in tranquil defiance of the laws of sex, in open contempt for the male portion of the community. The gentlemen burst into applause.

The company went upstairs to take coffee in the little drawing-room, where a couple of lamps cast a soft glow over the rosy hangings and the lacquer and old gold of the knick-knacks. At that hour of the evening the light played discreetly over coffers, bronzes, and china, lighting up silver or ivory inlaid work, bringing into view the polished contours of a carved stick, and gleaming over a panel with glossy silky reflections. The fire, which had been burning since the afternoon, was dying out in glowing embers. It was very warm—the air behind the curtains and hangings was languid with warmth. The room was full of Nana's intimate existence: a pair of gloves, a fallen handkerchief, an open book, lay scattered about, and their owner seemed present in careless attire with that well-known odour of violets, and that species of untidiness which became her in her character of good-natured courtesan, and had such a charming effect among all those rich surroundings. The very arm-chairs, which were as wide as beds, and the sofas, which were as deep as alcoves, invited to slumber oblivious of the flight of time, and to tender whispers in shadowy corners.

Satin went and lolled back in the depths of a sofa near the fire-place. She had lit a cigarette; but Vandeuvres began amusing himself by pretending to be ferociously jealous. Nay, he even threatened to send her his seconds if she still persisted in keeping Nana from her duty. Philippe and Georges joined him, and teased her and badgered her so mercilessly that at last she shouted out,—

"Darling! Darling! Do make 'em keep quiet! They're still after me!"

"Now then, let her be," said Nana seriously. "I won't have her tormented, you know that quite well. And you, my pet, why d'you always go mixing yourself up with them when they've got so little sense?"

Satin, blushing all over and putting out her tongue, went into the dressing-room, through the widely-open door of which you caught a glimpse of pale marbles gleaming in the milky light of a gas-flame in a globe of rough glass. After that Nana talked to the four men as charmingly as hostess could. During the day she had read a novel, which was at that time making a good deal of noise. It was the history of a courtesan; and Nana was very indignant, declaring the whole thing to be untrue, and expressing angry dislike to that kind of monstrous literature which pretends to paint from nature. "Just as though one could describe everything," she said. Just as though a novel ought not to be written so that the reader may while away an hour pleasantly! In the matter of books and of plays Nana had very decided opinions: she wanted tender and noble productions, things that would set her dreaming and would elevate her soul. Then allusion being made in the course of conversation to the troubles agitating Paris, the incendiary articles in the papers, the incipient popular disturbances which followed the calls to arms nightly raised at public meetings, she waxed wroth with the Republicans. What on earth did those dirty people who never washed really want? Were folks not happy? Had not the Emperor done everything for the People? A nice filthy lot of People! She knew 'em, she could talk about 'em, and, quite forgetting the respect which at dinner she had just been insisting should be paid to her humble circle in the Rue de la Goutte-d'Or, she began blackguarding her own class with all the terror and disgust peculiar to a woman who had risen successfully above it. That very afternoon she had read in the *Figaro* an account of the proceedings at a public meeting which had verged on the comic. Owing to the slang words that had been used, and to the piggish behaviour of a drunken man who had got himself chucked, she was laughing at those proceedings still.

"Oh, those drunkards!" said she with a disgusted air. "No, look you here, their Republic would be a great misfortune for everybody! Oh, may God preserve us the Emperor as long as possible!"

"God will hear your prayer, my dear," Muffat replied gravely. "To be sure, the Emperor stands firm."

He liked her to express such excellent views. Both, indeed, understood one another in political matters. Vandeuvres and Captain Hugon likewise indulged in endless jokes against the "cads," the quarrelsome set who scuttled off the moment they clapped eyes on a bayonet. But Georges that evening remained pale and sombre.

"What can be the matter with that baby?" asked Nana, noticing his troubled appearance.

"With me? Nothing—I am listening," he muttered.

But he was really suffering. On rising from table, he had heard Philippe joking with the young woman, and now it was Philippe, and not himself, who sat beside her. His heart, he knew not why, swelled to bursting. He could not bear to see them so close together; such vile thoughts oppressed him that shame mingled with his anguish. He who laughed at Satin, who had accepted Steiner, and

Muffat, and all the rest, felt outraged and murderous at the thought that Philippe might some day touch that woman.

"Here, take Bijou," said she, to comfort him, and she passed him the little dog which had gone to sleep on her dress. And with that Georges grew happy again, for with the beast still warm from her lap in his arms, he held, as it were, part of her.

Allusion had been made to a considerable loss which Vandeuvres had last night sustained at the Imperial Club. Muffat, who did not play, expressed great astonishment, but Vandeuvres smilingly alluded to his imminent ruin, about which Paris was already talking. The kind of death you chose did not much matter, he averred; the great thing was to die handsomely. For some time past, Nana had noticed that he was nervous, and had a sharp downward droop of the mouth, and a fitful gleam in the depths of his clear eyes. But he retained his haughty aristocratic manner, and the delicate elegance of his impoverished race; and as yet these strange manifestations were only, so to speak, momentary fits of vertigo overcoming a brain already sapped by play and by debauchery. One night, as he lay beside her, he had frightened her with a dreadful story. He had told her he contemplated shutting himself up in his stable and setting fire to himself and his horses at such time as he should have devoured all his substance. His only hope at that period was a horse, Lusignan by name, which he was training for the Prix de Paris. He was living on this horse, which was the sole stay of his shaken credit, and, whenever Nana grew exacting, he would put her off till June and

to the probability of Lusignan's winning.

"Bah! he may very likely lose," said she merrily, "since he's going to clear them all out at the races."

By way of reply he contented himself by smiling a thin mysterious smile. Then, carelessly,—

"By-the-by, I've taken the liberty of giving your name to my outsider, the filly. Nana, Nana—that sounds well. You're not vexed?"

"Vexed, why?" said she, in a state of inward ecstasy.

The conversation continued, and some mention was made of an execution shortly to take place. The young woman said she was burning to go to it, when Satin appeared at the dressing-room door, and called her in tones of entreaty. She got up at once, and left the gentlemen lolling lazily about, whilst they finished their cigars and discussed the grave question as to how far a murderer subject to chronic alcoholism is responsible for his act. In the dressing-room Zoé sat helpless on a chair, crying her heart out, whilst Satin vainly endeavoured to console her.

"What's the matter?" said Nana, in surprise.

"Oh, darling, do speak to her!" said Satin. "I've been trying to make her listen to reason for the last twenty minutes. She's crying because you called her a goose."

"Yes, *Madame*, it's very hard—very hard," stuttered Zoé, choked by a fresh fit of sobbing.

This sad sight melted the young woman's heart at once. She spoke kindly, and when the other woman still refused to grow calm, she sank down in front of her, and took her round the waist with truly cordial familiarity:

"But, you silly, I said 'goose' just as I might have said anything else. How shall I explain? I was in a passion—it was wrong of me: now calm down."

"I who love *Madame* so," stuttered Zoé; "after all I've done for *Madame*."

Thereupon Nana kissed the lady's maid, and, wishing to shew her she wasn't vexed, gave her a dress she had worn three times. Their quarrels always ended up in the giving of presents! Zoé plugged her handkerchief into her eyes. She carried the dress off over her arm, and added, before leaving, that they were very sadly in the kitchen, and that Julien and François had been unable to eat, so entirely had *Madame's* anger taken away their appetites. Thereupon *Madame* sent them a louis as a pledge of reconciliation. She suffered too much if people around her were sorrowful.

Nana was returning to the drawing-room, happy in the thought that she had patched up a disagreement, which was rendering her quietly apprehensive of the morrow, when Satin came and whispered vehemently in her ear. She was full of complaint, threatened to be off if those men still went on teasing her, and kept insisting that her darling should turn them all out of doors for that night, at any rate. It would be a lesson to them. And then it would be so nice to be alone, both of them! Nana, with a return of anxiety, declared it to be impossible. Thereupon, the other shouted at her like a violent child, and tried hard to overrule her.

"I wish it, d'you see? Send 'em away, or I'm off!"

And she went back into the drawing-room, stretched herself out in the recesses of a divan, which stood in the background near the window, and lay waiting, silent and death-like, with her great eyes fixed upon Nana.

The gentlemen were deciding against the new criminological theories. Granted that lovely invention of irresponsibility in certain pathological cases and criminals ceased to exist, and sick people alone remained. The young woman, expressing approval with an occasional nod, was busy considering how best to dismiss the Count. The others would soon be going, but he would assuredly prove obstinate. In fact, when Philippe got up to withdraw, Georges followed him at once—he seemed only anxious not to leave his brother behind. Vandeuvres lingered some minutes longer, feeling his way, as it were, and waiting to find out if, by any chance, some important business would oblige Muffat to cede him his place. Soon, however, when he saw the Count deliberately taking up his quarters for the night, he desisted from his purpose, and said good-bye as became a man of tact. But, on his way to the door, he noticed Satin staring fixedly at Nana, as usual. Doubtless he understood what this meant, for he seemed amused, and came and shook hands with her.

"We're not angry, eh?" he whispered. "Pray pardon me. You're the nicer attraction of the two, on my honour!"

Satin deigned no reply. Nor did she take her eyes off Nana and the Count, who were now alone. Muffat, ceasing to be ceremonious, had come to sit beside the young woman. He took her fingers, and began kissing them. Whereupon, Nana, seeking to change the current of his thoughts, asked him if his daughter Estelle were better. The previous night he had been complaining of the child's melancholy behaviour—he could not even spend a day happily at his own house, with his wife always out and his daughter icily silent.

In family matters of this kind Nana was always full of good advice, and when Muffat abandoned all his usual self-control under the influence of mental and physical relaxation, and once more launched out into his former plaints, she remembered the promise she had made. "Suppose you were to marry her?" said she. And with that she ventured to talk of Daguenet. At the mere mention of the name the Count was filled with disgust. "Never," said he, after what she had told him!

She pretended great surprise and then burst out laughing and put her arm round his neck.

"Oh, the jealous man! To think of it! Just argue it out a little. Why, they slandered me to you—I was furious. At present I should be ever so sorry if——"

But over Muffat's shoulder she met Satin's gaze. And she left him anxiously and in a grave voice continued,—

"This marriage must come off, my friend; I don't want to prevent your daughter's happiness. The young man's most charming; you could not possibly find a better sort."

And she launched into extraordinary praise of Daguenet. The Count had again taken her hands; he no longer refused now; he would see about it, he said; they would talk the matter over. By-and-by, when he spoke of going to bed, she sank her voice and excused her-

self. It was impossible; she was not well. If he loved her at all he would not insist! Nevertheless, he was obstinate; he refused to go away, and she was beginning to give in when she met Satin's eyes once more. Then she grew inflexible. No, the thing was out of the question! The Count, deeply moved and with a look of suffering, had risen and was going in quest of his hat. But in the doorway he remembered the set of sapphires; he could feel the case in his pocket. He had been wanting to hide it at the bottom of the bed, so that, when she entered it before him, she should feel it against her legs. Since dinner-time he had been meditating this little surprise like a school-boy, and now, in trouble and anguish of heart at being thus dismissed, he gave her the case without further ceremony.

"What is it?" she queried. "Sapphires? dear me! Oh yes, it's that set. How sweet you are! But I say, my darling, d'you believe it's the same one? In the shop-window it made a much greater show."

That was all the thanks he got, and she let him go away. He noticed Satin stretched out silent and expectant, and with that he gazed at both women, and without further insistence submitted to his fate and went downstairs. The hall door had not yet closed when Satin caught Nana round the waist, and danced and sang. Then she ran to the window.

"Oh, just look at the figure he cuts down in the street!" The two women leant upon the wrought-iron window-rail in the shadow of the curtains. One o'clock struck. The Avenue de Villiers was deserted, and its double file of gas-lamps stretched away into the darkness of the damp March night, through which great gusts of wind kept sweeping, laden with rain. There were vague stretches of land on either side of the road, which looked like gulfs of shadow, whilst scaffoldings round mansions in process of construction loomed upward under the dark sky. They laughed uncontrollably as they watched Muffat's rounded back and glistening shadow disappearing along the wet sidewalk into the glacial desolate plains of new Paris. But Nana silenced Satin.

"Take care: there are the police!"

Thereupon they smothered their laughter, and gazed in secret fear at two dark figures walking with measured tread on the opposite side of the Avenue. Amid all her luxurious surroundings, amid all the royal splendours of the woman whom all must obey, Nana still stood in horror of the police, and did not like to hear them mentioned any oftener than death. She felt distinctly unwell when a policeman looked up at her house. One never knew what such people might do! They might easily take them for loose women if they heard them laughing at that hour of the night. Satin, with a little shudder, had squeezed herself up against Nana. Nevertheless, the pair stayed where they were, and were soon interested in the approach of a lantern, the light of which danced over the puddles in the road. It was an old rag-picker woman who was busy raking in the gutters. Satin recognized her.

"Dear me," she exclaimed, "it's Queen Pomaré with her wickerwork shawl!"

And while a gust of wind lashed the fine rain in their faces, she told her beloved the story of Queen Pomaré. Oh! she had been a splendid girl once upon a time: all Paris had talked of her beauty. And such devilish go, and such cheek! Why, she led the men about like dogs, and great people stood blubbering on her stairs! Now, she was in the habit of getting tipsy, and the women round about would make her drink absinthe for the sake of a laugh, after which the street-boys would throw stones at her and chase her. In fact, it was a regular smash-up: the queen had tumbled into the mud! Nana listened, feeling cold all over.

"You shall see," added Satin.

She whistled a man's whistle, and the rag-picker, who was then below the window, lifted her head and shewed herself by the yellow flare of her lantern. Framed among rags, a perfect bundle of them, a face looked out from under a tattered kerchief—a blue seamed face with a toothless cavernous mouth, and fiery bruises where the eyes should be. And Nana, seeing the frightful old woman, the wanton drowned in drink, had a sudden fit of recollection, and saw far back amid the shadows of consciousness the vision of Chamont,—Irma d'Anglars, the old harlot crowned with years and honours, ascending the steps in front of her château amid abjectly reverential villagers. Then, as Satin whistled again, making game of the old hag, who could not see her—

"Do leave off, there are the police!" she murmured in changed tones. "In with us, quick, my pet!"

The measured steps were returning, and they shut the window. Turning round again, shivering, and with the damp of night on her hair, Nana was momentarily astounded at sight of her drawing-room. It seemed as though she had forgotten it, and were entering an unknown chamber. So warm, so full of perfume was the air she encountered, that she experienced a sense of delighted surprise. The heaped-up wealth of the place, the old-world furniture, the fabrics of silk and gold, the ivory, the bronzes, were slumbering in the rosy light of the lamps, whilst from the whole of the silent house a rich feeling of great luxury ascended, the luxury of the solemn reception-rooms, of the comfortable ample dining-room, of the vast retired staircase, with their soft carpets and seats. Her individuality, with its longing for domination and enjoyment, and its desire to possess everything that she might destroy everything, was suddenly increased. Never before had she felt so profoundly the puissance of her sex. She gazed slowly round, and remarked with an expression of grave philosophy,—

"Ah well, all the same, one's jolly well right to profit by things when one's young!"

But now Satin was rolling on the bearskins in the bedroom, and calling her.

"Oh, do come! do come!"

Nana undressed in the dressing-room, and, in order to be quicker about it, she took her thick fell of blonde hair in both hands, and began shaking it above the silver wash-hand basin, whilst a downward hail of long hair-pins rang a little chime on the shining metal.

## CHAPTER XI

One Sunday, the race for the Grand Prix de Paris was being run in the Bois de Boulogne beneath skies rendered sultry by the first heats of June. The sun, that morning, had risen amid a mist of dun-coloured dust, but towards eleven o'clock, just when the carriages were reaching the Longchamps course, a southerly wind had swept away the clouds, long streamers of grey vapour were disappearing across the sky, and gaps shewing an intense blue beyond were spreading from one end of the horizon to the other. In the bright bursts of sunlight which alternated with the clouds, the whole scene shone again, from the field which was gradually filling with a crowd of carriages, horsemen and pedestrians, to the still vacant course, where the judge's box stood, together with the "posts," and the masts for signalling numbers, and thence on to the five symmetrical stands of brickwork and timber, rising gallery upon gallery in the middle of the weighing-enclosure opposite. Beyond these, bathed in the light of noon, lay the vast level plain, bordered with little trees, and shut in to the westward by the wooded heights of Saint-Cloud and the Suresnes, which, in their turn, were dominated by the severe outlines of Mont-Valérien.

Nana, as excited as if the Grand Prix were going to make her fortune, wanted to take up a position by the railing next the winning post. She had arrived very early—she was in fact one of the first to come—in a landau adorned with silver, and drawn, à la Daumont, by four splendid white horses. This landau was a present from Count Muffat. When she had made her appearance at the entrance to the field, with two postillions jogging blithely on the near horses, and two footmen perching motionless behind the carriage, the people had rushed to look as though a queen were passing.

She sported the blue and white colours of the Vandeuvres stable, and her dress was remarkable. It consisted of a little blue silk bodice and tunic, which fitted closely to the body and bulged out enormously behind her waist, thereby bringing her lower limbs into bold relief in such a manner as to be extremely noticeable in that epoch of voluminous skirts. Then there was a white satin dress with white satin sleeves, and a sash worn crosswise over the shoulders, the whole ornamented with silver guipure which shone in the sun. In addition to this, in order to be still more like a jockey, she had stuck a blue toque with a white feather jauntily upon her chignon, the fair tresses from which flowed down beyond her shoulders and resembled an enormous russet pigtail.

Twelve struck. The public would have to wait more than three hours for the Grand Prix to be run. When the landau had drawn up beside the barriers, Nana settled herself comfortably down as though she were in her own house. A whim had prompted her to bring Bijou and Louiset with her, and the dog crouched among her skirts, shivering with cold despite the heat of the day, whilst, amid a bedizenment of ribbons and laces, the child's poor little face looked waxen and dumb and white in the open air. Meanwhile the young woman, without troubling about the people near her, talked at the top of her voice with Georges and Philippe Hugon, who were seated opposite on the front seat among such a mountain of bouquets of white roses and blue myosotis that they were buried up to their shoulders.

"Well, then," she was saying, "as he bored me to death, I shewed him the door. And now it's two days that he's been sulking."

She was talking of Muffat, but she took care not to confess to the young men the real reason for this first quarrel, which was that one evening he had found a man's hat in her bedroom. She had indeed brought home a passer-by out of sheer ennui—a silly infatuation.

"You have no idea how funny he is," she continued, growing merry over the particulars she was giving. "He's a regular bigot at bottom, so he says his prayers every evening. Yes, he does. He's under the impression I notice nothing because I go to bed first so as not to be in his way; but I watch him out of the corner of my eye. Oh! he jaws away, and then he crosses himself, when he turns round to step over me and get to the inside of the bed."

"Jove; it's sly," muttered Philippe. "That's what happens before, but afterwards, what then?"

She laughed merrily.

"Yes, just so, before and after! When I'm going to sleep I hear him jawing away again. But the biggest bore of all is that we can't argue about anything now without his growing 'pi.' I've always been religious. Yes, chaff as much as you like, that won't prevent me believing what I do believe! Only he's too much of a nuisance: he blubbers, he talks about remorse. The day before yesterday, for instance, he had a regular fit of it after our usual row, and I wasn't the least bit reassured when all was over."

But she broke off, crying out,—

"Just look at the Mignons arriving. Dear me, they've brought the children!

Oh, how those little chaps are dressed up!"

The Mignons were in a landau of severe hue; there was something substantially luxurious about their turn-out, suggesting rich retired tradespeople. Rose was in a grey silk gown, trimmed with red knots and with puffs; she was smiling happily at the joyous behaviour of Henri and Charles, who sat on the front seat, looking awkward in their ill-fitting collegians' tunics. But, when the landau had drawn up by the rails, and she perceived Nana sitting in triumph among her bouquets, with her four horses, and her liveries, she pursed up her lips, sat bolt upright, and turned her head away. Mignon, on the other hand, looking the picture of freshness and gaiety, waved her a salutation. He made it a matter of principle to keep out of feminine disagreements.

"By-the-by," Nana resumed, "d'you know a little old man who's very clean and neat and has bad teeth—a Monsieur Venot? He came to see me this morning."

"Monsieur Venot," said Georges, in great astonishment, "it's impossible! Why, the man's a Jesuit!"

"Precisely; I spotted that. Oh, you have no idea what our conversation was like! It was just funny! He spoke to me about the Count, about his divided house, and begged me to restore a family its happiness. He was very polite, and very smiling for the matter of that. Then I answered to the effect that I wanted nothing better, and I undertook to reconcile the Count and his wife. You know it's not humbug. I should be delighted to see them all happy again, the poor things! Besides it would be a re-lief to me, for there are days—yes, there are days when he bores me to death."

The weariness of the last months escaped her in this heartfelt outburst. Moreover, the Count appeared to be in big money difficulties; he was anxious, and it seemed likely that the bill which Labordette had put his name to would not be met.

"Dear me, the Countess is down yonder," said Georges, letting his gaze wander over the stands.

"Where, where?" cried Nana. "What eyes that baby's got! Hold my sunshade, Philippe."

But with a quick forward dart Georges had outstripped his brother. It enchanted him to be holding the blue silk sunshade with its silver fringe. Nana was scanning the scene through a huge pair of field-glasses.

"Ah, yes! I see her," said she at length. "In the right-hand stand, near a pillar, eh? She's in mauve, and her daughter in white by her side. Dear me, there's Daguenet going to bow to them."

Thereupon, Philippe talked of Daguenet's approaching marriage with that lath of an Estelle. It was a settled matter—the banns were being published. At first the Countess had opposed it, but the Count, they said, had insisted. Nana smiled.

"I know, I know," she murmured. "So much the better for Paul. He's a nice boy—he deserves it."

And leaning towards Louiset,—

"You're enjoying yourself, eh? What a grave face!"

The child never smiled. With a very old expression he was gazing at all those crowds, as though the sight of them filled him with melancholy reflections.

Bijou, chased from the skirts of the young woman, who was moving about a great deal, had come to nestle shivering against the little fellow.

Meanwhile, the field was filling up. Carriages, a compact, interminable file of them, were continually arriving through the Porte de la Cascade. There were big omnibuses such as the *Pauline,* which had started from the Boulevard des Italiens, freighted with its fifty passengers, and was now going to draw up to the right of the stands. Then, there were dogcarts, victorias, landaus, all superbly well turned out, mingled with lamentable cabs, which jolted along behind sorry old hacks, and four-in-hands, sending along their four horses, and mail-coaches, where the masters sat on the seats above and left the servants to take care of the hampers of champagne inside, and "spiders," the immense wheels of which were a flash of glittering steel, and light tandems, which looked as delicately formed as the works of a clock and slipped along amid a peel of little bells. Every few seconds an equestrian rode by, and a swarm of people on foot rushed in a scared way among the carriages. On the green, the far-off rolling sound which issued from the avenues in the Bois died out suddenly in dull rustlings, and now nothing was audible save the hubbub of the ever-increasing crowds, and cries, and calls, and the crackings of whips in the open. When the sun, amidst bursts of wind, reappeared at the edge of a cloud, a long ray of golden light ran across the field, lit up the harness and the varnished coach-panels, and touched the ladies' dresses with fire, whilst, amid the dusty radiance, the coachmen, high up on their boxes, flamed beside their great whips.

Labordette was getting out of an open carriage where Gaga, Clarisse, and Blanche de Sivry had kept a place for him. As he was hurrying to cross the course and enter the weighing-enclosure, Nana got Georges to call him. Then when he came up,—

"What's the betting on me?" she asked, laughingly.

She referred to the filly, Nana, the Nana who had let herself be shamefully beaten in the race for the Prix de Diane, and had not even been placed in April and May last when she ran for the Prix des Cars and the Grand Poule des Produits, both of which had been gained by Lusignan, the other horse in the Vandeuvres stable. Lusignan had all at once become prime favourite, and since yesterday he had been currently taken at two to one.

"Always fifty to one against," replied Labordette.

"The deuce! I'm not worth much," rejoined Nana, amused by the jest. "I don't back myself, then; no, by Jingo! I don't put a single louis on myself."

Labordette went off again in a great hurry, but she recalled him. She wanted some advice. Since he kept in touch with the world of trainers and jockeys, he had special information about various stables. His prognostications had come true a score of times already, and people called him the "King of Tipsters."

"Let's see, what horses ought I to choose?" said the young woman. "What's the betting on the Englishman?"

"Spirit? three to one against. Valerio II. the same. As to the others, they're laying twenty-five to one against Cosinus, forty to one against Hazard, thirty to one against Boum, thirty-five to one against Pichenette, ten to one against Frangipane."

"No, I don't bet on the Englishman, I don't. I'm a patriot. Perhaps Valerio II. would do, eh? The Duc de Corbreuse was beaming a little while ago. Well, no, after all! Fifty louis on Lusignan, what do you say to that?"

Labordette looked at her with a singular expression. She leant forward and asked him questions in a low voice, for she was aware that Vandeuvres commissioned him to arrange matters with the bookmakers so as to be able to bet the more easily. Supposing him to have got to know something, he might quite well tell it her. But without entering into explanations Labordette persuaded her to trust to his sagacity. He would put on her fifty louis for her as he might think best, and she would not repent of his arrangement.

"All the horses you like!" she cried gaily, letting him take his departure; "but no 'Nana'; she's a jade!"

There was a burst of uproarious laughter in the carriage. The young men thought her sally very amusing, whilst Louiset in his ignorance lifted his pale eyes to his mother's face, for her loud exclamations surprised him. However, there was no escape for Labordette as yet. Rose Mignon had made a sign to him, and was now giving him her commands, whilst he wrote figures in a notebook. Then Clarisse and Gaga called him back, in order to change their bets; for they had heard things said in the crowd, and now they didn't want to have anything more to do with Valerio II. and were choosing Lusignan. He wrote

down their wishes with an impassible expression, and at length managed to escape. He might be seen disappearing between two of the stands on the other side of the course.

Carriages were still arriving. They were by this time drawn up five rows deep, and a dense mass of them spread along the barriers, chequered by the light coats of white horses. Beyond them, other carriages stood about in comparative isolation, looking as though they had stuck fast in the grass. Wheels and harness were here, there, and everywhere, according as the conveyances to which they belonged were side by side, at an angle, across and across, or head to head. Over such spaces of turf as still remained unoccupied cavaliers kept trotting, and black groups of pedestrians moved continually. The scene resembled the field where a fair is being held, and above it all, amid the confused motley of the crowd, the drinking-booths raised their grey canvas roofs, which gleamed white in the sunshine. But a veritable tumult, a mob, an eddy of hats surged round the several bookmakers, who stood in open carriages, gesticulating like itinerant dentists, while their odds were pasted up on tall boards beside them.

"All the same, it's stupid not to know on what horse one's betting," Nana was remarking. "I really must risk some louis in person."

She had stood up to select a bookmaker with a decent expression of face, but forgot what she wanted on perceiving a perfect crowd of her acquaintance. Besides the Mignons, besides Gaga, Clarisse, and Blanche, there were present, to the right and left, behind and in the middle of the mass of carriages now hemming in her landau, the following ladies: Tatan Néné and Maria Blond in a victoria, Caroline Héquet with her mother and two gentlemen in an open carriage, Louise Violaine quite alone, driving a little basket-chaise, decked with orange and green ribbons, the colours of the Méchain stables, and finally, Léa de Horn on the lofty seat of a mail-coach, where a band of young men were making a great din. Further off, in a *huit ressorts* of aristocratic appearance, Lucy Stewart, in a very simple black silk dress, sat, looking distinguished beside a tall young man in the uniform of a naval cadet. But what most astounded Nana was the arrival of Simonne in a tandem, which Steiner was driving, whilst a footman sat motionless, with folded arms, behind them. She looked dazzling in white satin, striped with yellow, and was covered with diamonds from waist to hat. The banker, on his part, was handling a tremendous whip, and sending along his two horses, which were harnessed tandemwise, the leader being a little warm-coloured chestnut, with a mouse-like trot, the shaft horse a big brown bay, a stepper, with a fine action.

"Deuce take it!" said Nana. "So that thief Steiner has cleared the Bourse again, has he? I say, isn't Simonne a swell! It's too much of a good thing, he'll get into the clutches of the law!"

Nevertheless, she exchanged greetings at a distance. Indeed, she kept waving her hand, and smiling, turning round and forgetting no one in her desire to be seen by everybody. At the same time she continued chatting.

"It's her son Lucy's got in tow! He's charming in his uniform. That's why she's looking so grand, of course! You know she's afraid of him, and that she passes herself off as an actress. Poor young man, I pity him all the same! He seems quite unsuspicious."

"Bah," muttered Philippe, laughing, "she'll be able to find him an heiress in the country when she likes."

Nana was silent, for she had just noticed the Tricon amid the thick of the carriages. Having arrived in a cab, whence she could not see anything, the Tricon had quietly mounted the coach-box. And there, straightening up her tall figure, with her noble face enshrined in its long curls, she dominated the crowd, as though enthroned amid her feminine subjects. All the latter smiled discreetly at her, whilst she, in her superiority, pretended not to know them. She wasn't there for business purposes: she was watching the races for the love of the thing, as became a frantic gambler with a passion for horseflesh.

"Dear me, there's that idiot la Faloise!" said Georges, suddenly.

It was a surprise to them all. Nana did not recognise her la Faloise, for since he had come into his inheritance he had grown extraordinarily up to date. He wore a low collar, and was clad in a cloth of delicate hue, which fitted close to his meagre shoulders. His hair was in little *bandeaux,* and he affected a weary kind of swagger, a soft tone of voice, and slang words and phrases which he did not take the trouble to finish.

"But he's quite the thing!" declared Nana, in perfect enchantment.

Gaga and Clarisse had called la Faloise, and were throwing themselves at him in their efforts to regain his allegiance, but he left them immediately, rolling off in a chaffing, disdainful manner. Nana dazzled him. He rushed up to her and stood on the carriage-step, and when she twitted him about Gaga he murmured,—

"Oh, dear no! We've seen the last of the old lot! Mustn't play her off on me any more. And then, you know, it's you now, Juliet mine!"

He had put his hand to his heart. Nana laughed a good deal at this exceedingly sudden out-of-doors declaration. She continued,—

"I say, that's not what I'm after. You're making me forget that I want to lay wagers. Georges, you see that bookmaker down there, a great red-faced man with curly hair. He's got a dirty blackguard expression which I like. You're to go and choose—— Oh! I say, what can one choose?"

"I'm not a patriotic soul—oh, dear no!" la Faloise blurted out. "I'm all for the Englishman. It will be ripping if the Englishman gains! The French may go to Jericho!"

Nana was scandalised. Presently the merits of the several horses began to be discussed, and la Faloise, wishing to be thought very much in the swim, spoke of them all as sorry jades. Frangipane, Baron Verdier's horse, was by The Truth out of Lenore. A big bay horse he was, who would certainly have stood a chance if they hadn't let him get foundered during training. As to Valerio II., from the Corbreuse stable, he wasn't ready yet; he'd had the colic in April. Oh, yes! they were keeping that dark, but he was sure of it, on his honour! In the end he advised Nana to choose Hazard, the most defective of the

lot, a horse nobody would have anything to do with. Hazard, by jingo—such superb lines, and such an action! That horse was going to astonish the people.

"No," said Nana, "I'm going to put ten louis on Lusignan and five on Boum."

La Faloise burst forth at once:

"But, my dear girl, Boum's all rot! Don't choose him! Gasc himself is chucking up backing his own horse. And your Lusignan—never! Why, it's all humbug! By Lamb and Princess—just think! By Lamb and Princess—no, by Jove! All too short in the legs!"

He was choking. Philippe pointed out that, notwithstanding this, Lusignan had won the Prix des Cars and the Grande Poule des Produits. But the other ran on again. What did that prove? Nothing at all. On the contrary, one ought to distrust him. And besides, Gresham rode Lusignan; well then, let them jolly well dry up! Gresham had bad luck: he would never get to the post.

And, from one end of the field to the other, the discussion raging in Nana's landau seemed to spread and increase. Voices were raised in a scream; the passion for gambling filled the air, set faces glowing, and arms waving excitedly, whilst the bookmakers, perched on their conveyances, shouted odds and jotted down amounts right furiously. Yet these were only the small fry of the betting world; the big bets were made in the weighing-enclosure. Here, then, raged the keen contest of people with light purses, who risked their five-franc pieces and displayed infinite covetousness for the sake of a possible gain of a few louis. In a word, the battle would be between Spirit and Lusignan. Englishmen, plainly recognisable as such, were strolling about among the various groups. They were quite at home, their faces were fiery with excitement, they were already triumphant. Bramah, a horse belonging to Lord Reading, had gained the Grand Prix the previous year, and this had been a defeat over which hearts were still bleeding. This year it would be terrible if France were beaten anew. Accordingly, all the ladies were wild with national pride. The Vandeuvres stable became the rampart of our honour, and Lusignan was pushed, and defended, and applauded exceedingly. Gaga, Blanche, Caroline, and the rest betted on Lusignan. Lucy Stewart abstained from this on account of her son, but it was bruited abroad that Rose Mignon had commissioned Labordette to risk two hundred louis for her. The Tricon, as she sat alone next her driver, waited till the last moment. Very cool indeed amid all these disputes, very far above the ever-increasing uproar in which horses' names kept recurring, and lively Parisian phrases mingled with guttural English exclamations, she sat listening, and taking notes majestically.

"And Nana?" said Georges. "Does no one want her?"

Indeed, nobody was asking for the filly; she was not even being mentioned. The outsider of the Vandeuvres's stud was swamped by Lusignan's popularity. But la Faloise flung his arms up, crying,—

"I've an inspiration. I'll bet a louis on Nana."

"Bravo! I bet a couple," said Georges.

"And I three," added Philippe.

And they mounted up and up, bidding against one another good-humouredly, and naming prices as though they had been haggling over Nana at an auction. La Faloise said he would cover her with gold. Besides, everybody was to be made to back her; they would go and pick up backers. But as the three young men were darting off to propagandise, Nana shouted after them,—

"You know I don't want to have anything to do with her; I don't for the world! Georges, ten louis on Lusignan and five on Valerio II."

Meanwhile they had started fairly off, and she watched them gaily as they slipped between wheels, ducked under horses' heads, and scoured the whole field. The moment they recognised anyone in a carriage they rushed up and urged Nana's claims. And there were great bursts of laughter among the crowd when sometimes they turned back triumphantly signalling amounts with their fingers, whilst the young woman stood and waved her sunshade. Nevertheless, they made poor enough work of it. Some men let themselves be persuaded; Steiner, for instance, ventured three louis, for the sight of Nana stirred him. But the women refused point blank. "Thanks," said they, "to lose for a certainty!" Besides, they were in no hurry to work for the benefit of a dirty wench who was overwhelming them all with her four white horses, her postillions, and her outrageous assumption of side. Gaga and Clarisse looked exceedingly prim, and asked la Faloise whether he was jolly well making fun of them. When Georges boldly presented himself before the Mignons' carriage, Rose turned her head away in the most marked manner and did not answer him. One must be a pretty foul sort to let one's name be given to a horse! Mignon, on the contrary, followed the young man's movements with a look of amusement, and declared that the women always brought luck.

"Well?" queried Nana, when the young men returned after a prolonged visit to the bookmakers.

"The odds are forty to one against you," said la Faloise.

"What's that? Forty to one!" she cried astounded. "They were fifty to one against me. What's happened?"

Labordette had just then reappeared. The course was being cleared, and the pealing of a bell announced the first race. Amid the expectant murmur of the bystanders, she questioned him about this sudden rise in her value. But he replied evasively; doubtless a demand for her had arisen. She had to content herself with this explanation. Moreover, Labordette announced with a preoccupied expression that Vandeuvres was coming, if he could get away.

The race was ending unnoticed, people were all waiting for the Grand Prix to be run—when a storm burst over the Hippodrome. For some minutes past the sun had disappeared, and a wan twilight had darkened over the multitude. Then the wind rose, and there ensued a sudden deluge. Huge drops, perfect sheets of water, fell. There was a momentary confusion, and people shouted, and joked, and swore, whilst those on foot scampered madly off to find refuge under the canvas of the drinking-booths. In the carriages the women did their best to shelter themselves, grasping their sunshades with both hands, whilst the bewildered footmen ran to the hoods. But the shower was already nearly over, and the sun began shining brilliantly through escaping clouds of fine rain. A blue cleft opened in the stormy mass, which was blown off over the Bois, and the skies seemed to smile again and to set the women laughing in a reassured manner, whilst, amid the snorting of horses and the disarray and agitation of the drenched multitude that was shaking itself dry, a broad flush of golden light lit up the field, still dripping and glittering with crystal drops.

"Oh, that poor dear Louiset!" said Nana. "Are you very drenched, my darling?"

The little thing silently allowed his hands to be wiped. The young woman had taken out her handkerchief. Then she dabbed it over Bijou, who was trembling more violently than ever. It would not matter in the least; there were a few drops on the white satin of her dress, but she didn't care a pin for them. The bouquets, refreshed by the rain, glowed like snow, and she smelt one ecstatically, drenching her lips in it as though it were wet with dew.

Meanwhile, the burst of rain had suddenly filled the stands. Nana looked at them through her field-glasses. At that distance you could only distinguish a compact, confused mass of people, heaped up, as it were, on the ascending ranges of steps, a dark background relieved by light dots which were human faces. The sunlight filtered in through openings near the roof at each end of the stand, and detached and illumined portions of the seated multitude, where the ladies' dresses seemed to lose their distinguishing colours. But Nana was especially amused by the ladies whom the shower had driven from the rows of chairs, ranged on the sand at the base of the stands. As courtesans were absolutely forbidden to enter the enclosure, she began making exceedingly bitter remarks about all the fashionable women therein assembled. She thought them fearfully dressed up, and such guys!

There was a rumour that the Empress was entering the little central stand, a pavilion built like a châlet, with a wide balcony furnished with red arm-chairs. "Why, there he is!" said Georges. "I didn't think he was on duty this week."

The stiff and solemn form of the Count Muffat had appeared behind the Empress. Thereupon the young men jested, and were sorry that Satin wasn't there to go and dig him in the ribs. But Nana's field-glass focussed the head of the Prince of Scots in the imperial stand.

"Gracious, it's Charles!" she cried.

She thought him stouter than formerly. In eighteen months he had broadened, and with that she entered into particulars. Oh, yes, he was a big, solidly-built fellow!

All round her, in the ladies' carriages, they were whispering that the Count had given her up. It was quite a long story. Since he had been making himself noticeable, the Tuileries had grown scandalised at the Chamberlain's conduct. Whereupon, in order to retain his position, he had recently broken it off with Nana. La Faloise bluntly reported this account of matters to the young woman, and addressing her as his Juliet, again offered himself. But she laughed merrily, and remarked,—

"It's idiotic! you don't know him; I've only to say 'Come here,' for him to chuck up everything."

For some seconds past she had been examining the Countess Sabine and Estelle. Daguenet was still at their side. Fauchery had just arrived, and was disturbing the people round in his desire to make his bow to them. He, too, stayed smilingly beside them. After that Nana pointed with disdainful action at the stands, and continued,—

"Then, you know, those people don't fetch me any longer now! I know 'em too well. You should see 'em behind scenes. No more honour! It's all up with honour! Filth below stairs, filth above stairs, filth everywhere. That's why I won't be bothered about 'em!"

And with a comprehensive gesture she took in everybody, from the grooms leading the horses on to the course, to the sovereign lady busy chatting with Charles, a prince and a dirty fellow to boot.

"Bravo, Nana! Awfully smart, Nana!" cried la Faloise, enthusiastically.

The tolling of a bell was lost in the wind; the races continued. The Prix d'Ispahan had just been run for and Berlingot, a horse belonging to the Méchain stable, had won. Nana recalled Labordette in order to obtain news of the hundred louis, but he burst out laughing, and refused to let her know the horses he had chosen for her, so as not to disturb the luck, as he phrased it. Her money was well placed; she would see that all in good time. And when she confessed her bets to him, and told him how she had put ten louis on Lusignan, and five of Valerio II., he shrugged his shoulders, as who should say that women did stupid things whatever happened. His action surprised her; she was quite at sea.

Just then the field grew more animated than before. Open-air lunches were arranged in the interval before the Grand Prix. There was much eating and more drinking in all directions, on the grass, on the high seats of the four-in-hands and mail-coaches, in the victorias, the broughams, the landaus. There was a universal spread of cold viands, and a fine disorderly display of champagne baskets which footmen kept handing down out of the coach-boots. Corks came out with feeble pops, which the wind drowned. There was an interchange of jests, and the sound of breaking glasses imparted a note of discord to the high-strung gaiety of the scene. Gaga and Clarisse, together with Blanche, were making a serious repast, for they were eating sandwiches on the carriage-rug with which they had been covering their knees. Louise Violaine had got down from her basket-carriage, and had joined Caroline Héquet. On the turf, at their feet, some gentlemen had instituted a drinking-bar, whither Tatan, Maria, Simonne, and the rest came to refresh themselves, whilst high in air and close at hand bottles were being emptied on Léa de Horn's mail-coach, and, with infinite bravado and gesticulation, a whole band were making themselves tipsy in the sunshine, above the heads of the crowd. Soon, however, there was an especially large crowd by Nana's landau. She had risen to her feet, and had set herself to pour out glasses of champagne for the men who came to pay her their respects. François, one of the footmen, was passing up the bottles, whilst la Faloise, trying hard to imitate a coster's accents, kept pattering away:

" 'Ere y're, given away, given away! There's some for everybody!"

"Do be still, dear boy," Nana ended by saying. "We look like a set of tumblers."

She thought him very droll, and was greatly entertained. At one moment she conceived the idea of sending Georges with a glass of champagne to Rose Mignon, who was affecting temperance. Henri and Charles were bored to distraction; they would have been glad of some champagne, the poor little fellows. But Georges drank the glassful, for he feared an argument. Then Nana remembered Louiset, who was setting forgotten behind her. Maybe he was thirsty, and she forced him to take a drop or two of wine, which made him cough dreadfully.

" 'Ere y'are, 'ere y'are, gemmen!" la Faloise reiterated. "It don't cost two sous: it don't cost one. We give it away."

But Nana broke in with an exclamation,—

"Gracious, there's Bordenave down there! Call him. Oh, run, please, please do!"

It was indeed Bordenave. He was strolling about with his hands behind his back, wearing a hat that looked rusty in the sunlight, and a greasy frock-coat that was glossy at the seams. It was Bordenave shattered by bankruptcy, yet furious despite all reverses, a Bordenave who flaunted his misery among all the fine folks with the hardihood becoming a man every ready to take Dame Fortune by storm.

"The deuce, how smart we are!" said he, when Nana extended her hand to him like the good-natured wench she was.

Presently, after emptying a glass of

champagne, he gave vent to the following profoundly regretful phrase:

"Ah! if only I were a woman! But, by God, that's nothing! Would you like to go on the stage again? I've a notion: I'll hire the Gaîté, and we'll gobble up Paris between us. You certainly owe it me, eh?"

And he lingered grumbling beside her, though glad to see her again; for, said he, that confounded Nana was balm to his feelings. Yes, it was balm to them merely to exist in her presence! She was his daughter: she was blood of his blood!

The circle increased, for now la Faloise was filling glasses, and Georges and Philippe were picking up friends. A stealthy impulse was gradually bringing in the whole field. Nana would fling everyone a laughing smile or an amusing phrase. The groups of tipplers were drawing near, and all the champagne scattered over the place was moving in her direction. Soon there was only one noisy crowd, and that was round her landau, where she queened it among outstretched glasses, her yellow hair floating on the breeze, and her snowy face bathed in the sunshine. Then, by way of finishing touch, and to make the other women, who were mad at her triumph, simply perish of envy, she lifted a brimming glass on high, and assumed her old pose as Venus Victrix.

But somebody touched her shoulder, and she was surprised, on turning round, to see Mignon on the seat. She vanished from view an instant, and sat herself down beside him, for he had come to communicate a matter of importance. Mignon had everywhere declared that it was ridiculous of his wife to bear Nana

a grudge: he thought her attitude stupid and useless.

"Look here, my dear," he whispered. "Be careful: don't madden Rose too much. You understand, I think it best to warn you. Yes, she's got a weapon in store, and, as she's never forgiven you the *Petite Duchesse* business——"

"A weapon," said Nana; "what's that blooming well got to do with me?"

"Just listen: it's a letter she must have found in Fauchery's pocket, a letter written to that screw Fauchery by the Countess Muffat. And by Jove! it's clear the whole story's in it. Well then, Rose wants to send the letter to the Count so as to be revenged on him and on you."

"What the deuce has that got to do with me?" Nana repeated. "It's a funny business. So the whole story about Fauchery's in it! Very well, so much the better: the woman has been exasperating me! We shall have a good laugh!"

"No, I don't wish it," Mignon briskly rejoined. "There'll be a pretty scandal! Besides, we've got nothing to gain."

He paused fearing lest he should say too much, whilst she loudly averred that she was most certainly not going to get a chaste woman into trouble.

But when he still insisted on his refusal, she looked steadily at him. Doubtless he was afraid of seeing Fauchery again introduced into his family in case he broke with the Countess. Whilst avenging her own wrongs, Rose was anxious for that to happen, since she still felt a kindness towards the journalist. And Nana waxed meditative, and thought of Monsieur Venot's call, and a plan began to take shape in her brain, whilst

Mignon was doing his best to talk her over.

"Let's suppose that Rose sends the letter, eh? There's food for scandal: you're mixed up in the business, and people say you're the cause of it all. Then, to begin with, the Count separates from his wife."

"Why should he?" said she. "On the contrary——"

She broke off, in her turn. There was no need for her to think aloud. So, in order to be rid of Mignon, she looked as though she entered into his view of the case, and when he advised her to give Rose some proof of her submission —to pay her a short visit on the racecourse, for instance, where everybody would see her—she replied that she would see about it, that she would think the matter over.

A commotion caused her to stand up again. On the course the horses were coming in amid a sudden blast of wind. The prize given by the City of Paris had just been run for, and Cornemuse had gained it. Now the Grand Prix was about to be run, and the fever of the crowd increased and they were tortured by anxiety, and stamped and swayed as though they wanted to make the minutes fly faster. At this ultimate moment the betting world was surprised and startled by the continued shortening of the odds against Nana, the outsider of the Vandeuvres stables. Gentlemen kept returning every few moments with a new quotation: the betting was thirty to one against Nana; it was twenty-five to one against Nana, then twenty to one, then fifteen to one. No one could understand it. A filly beaten on all the race-courses! a filly which that same

morning no single sportsman would take at fifty to one against! What did this sudden madness betoken? Some laughed at it, and spoke of the pretty doing awaiting the duffers who were being taken in by the joke. Others looked serious and uneasy, and sniffed out something ugly under it all. Perhaps there was a "deal" in the offing. Allusion was made to well-known stories about the robberies which are winked at on racecourses, but on this occasion the great name of Vandeuvres put a stop to all such accusations, and the sceptics in the end prevailed when they prophesied that Nana would come in last of all.

"Who's riding Nana?" queried la Faloise.

Just then the real Nana reappeared, whereat the gentleman lent his question an indecent meaning, and burst into an uproarious fit of laughter. Nana bowed.

"Price is up," she replied.

And with that the discussion began again. Price was an English celebrity. Why had Vandeuvres got this jockey to come over, seeing that Gresham ordinarily rode Nana? Besides, they were astonished to see him confiding Lusignan to this man Gresham, who according to la Faloise never got a place. But all these remarks were swallowed up in jokes, contradictions, and an extraordinarily noisy confusion of opinions. In order to kill time the company once more set themselves to drain bottles of champagne. Presently a whisper ran round, and the different groups opened outwards. It was Vandeuvres. Nana affected vexation.

"Dear me, you're a nice fellow to come at this time of day! Why, I'm burning to see the enclosure."

"Well, come along then," said he; "there's still time. You'll take a stroll round with me. I just happen to have a permit for a lady about me."

And he led her off on his arm, whilst she enjoyed the jealous glances with which Lucy, Caroline, and the others followed her. The young Hugons and la Faloise remained in the landau behind her retreating figure, and continued to do the honours of her champagne. She shouted to them that she would return immediately.

But Vandeuvres caught sight of Labordette and called him, and there was an interchange of brief sentences.

"You've scraped everything up?"

"Yes."

"To what amount?"

"Fifteen hundred louis—pretty well all over the place."

As Nana was visibly listening, and that with much curiosity, they held their tongues. Vandeuvres was very nervous, and he had those same clear eyes, shot with little flames, which so frightened her the night he spoke of burning himself and his horses together. As they crossed over the course, she spoke low and familiarly.

"I say, do explain this to me. Why are the odds on your filly changing?"

He trembled, and this sentence escaped him:

"Ah, they're talking, are they? What a set those betting men are! When I've got the favourite, they all throw themselves upon him, and there's no chance for me. After that, when an outsider's asked for, they give tongue, and yell as though they were being skinned."

"You ought to tell me what's going to happen—I've made my bets," she rejoined. "Has Nana a chance?"

A sudden, unreasonable burst of anger overpowered him.

"Won't you deuced well let me be, eh? Every horse has a chance. The odds are shortening, because, by Jove! people have taken the horse. Who, I don't know. I should prefer leaving you if you must needs badger me with your idiotic questions."

Such a tone was not germane either to his temperament or to his habits, and Nana was rather surprised than wounded. Besides, he was ashamed of himself directly afterwards, and when she begged him in a dry voice to behave politely, he apologised. For some time past he had suffered from such sudden changes of temper. No one in the Paris of pleasure or of society was ignorant of the fact that he was playing his last trump-card to-day. If his horses did not win, if, moreover, they lost him the considerable sums wagered upon them, it would mean utter disaster and collapse for him, and the bulwark of his credit and the lofty appearance which, though undermined, he still kept up, would come ruining noisily down. Moreover, no one was ignorant of the fact that Nana was the devouring siren who had finished him off, who had been the last to attack his crumbling fortunes and to sweep up what remained of them. Stories were told of wild whims and fancies, of gold scattered to the four winds, of a visit to Baden-Baden, where she had not left him enough to pay the hotel bill, of a handful of diamonds cast on the fire during an evening of drunkenness in order to see whether they would burn like coal. Little by little her great limbs and her coarse, plebeian way of laughing had gained complete mastery over this elegant degenerate son of an ancient race. At that time he was risking his all, for he had been so utterly overpowered by his taste for ordure and stupidity as to have even lost the vigour of his scepticism. A week before Nana had made him promise her a château on the Norman coast between Havre and Trouville, and now he was staking the very foundations of his honour on the fulfilment of his word. Only she was getting on his nerves, and he could have beaten her, so stupid did he feel her to be.

The man at the gate, not daring to stop the woman hanging on the Count's arm, had allowed them to enter the enclosure. Nana, greatly puffed up at the thought that at last she was setting foot on the forbidden ground, put on her best behaviour, and walked slowly by the ladies seated at the foot of the stands. On ten rows of chairs the toilets were densely massed, and in the blithe open air their bright colours mingled harmoniously. Chairs were scattered about, and, as people met one another, friendly circles were formed, just as though the company had been sitting under the trees in a public garden. Children had been allowed to go free, and were running from group to group, whilst, overhead, the stands rose tier above crowded tier, and the light-coloured dresses therein fading into the delicate shadows of the timber-work. Nana stared at all these ladies. She stared steadily and markedly at the Countess Sabine. After which, as she was passing in front of the imperial stand, the sight of Muffat, looming in all his official stiffness by the side of the Empress, made her very merry.

"Oh, how silly he looks!" said she at the top of her voice to Vandeuvres.

She was anxious to pay everything a visit. This small park-like region, with its green lawns and groups of trees, rather charmed her than otherwise. A vendor of ices had set up a large buffet near the entrance-gates, and beneath a rustic thatched roof a dense throng of people were shouting and gesticulating. This was the Ring. Close by were some empty stalls, and Nana was disappointed at discovering only a gendarme's horse there. Then there was the paddock, a small course some hundred mètres in circumference, where a stable-help was walking about Valerio II. in his horse-cloths. And oh, what a lot of men on the gravelled side-walks, all of them with their tickets forming an orange-coloured patch in their button-holes! And what a continual parade of people in the open galleries of the grand stands! The scene interested her for a moment or two, but truly, it was not worth while getting the spleen because they didn't admit you inside here.

Daguenet and Fauchery passed by and bowed to her. She made them a sign, and they had to come up. Thereupon she made hay of the weighing-in enclosure. But she broke off abruptly:

"Dear me, there's the Marquis de Chouard! How old he's growing! That old man's killing himself! Is he still as mad about it as ever?"

Thereupon Daguenet described the old man's last brilliant stroke. The story dated from the day before yesterday, and no one knew it as yet. After dangling about for months, he had bought her daughter Amélie from Gaga for thirty thousand francs, they said. "Good gracious! that's a nice business!" cried Nana in disgust. "Go in for the regular thing, please! But now that I come to think of it, that must be Lili down there on the grass, with a lady in a brougham. I recognised the face. The old boy will have brought her out."

Vandeuvres was not listening—he was impatient and longed to get rid of her. But Fauchery having remarked at parting that if she had not seen the bookmakers she had seen nothing, the Count was obliged to take her to them in spite of his obvious repugnance. And she was perfectly happy at once; that truly was a curious sight, she said!

Amid lawns bordered by young horse-chestnut trees, there was a round open enclosure, where, forming a vast circle under the shadow of the tender green leaves, a dense line of bookmakers was waiting for betting men, as though they had been hucksters at a fair. In order to overtop and command the surrounding crowd, they had taken up positions on wooden benches, and they were advertising their prices on the trees beside them. They had an ever-vigilant glance, and they booked wagers in answer to a single sign, a mere wink, so rapidly that certain curious onlookers watched them open-mouthed, without being able to understand it all. Confusion reigned; prices were shouted, and any unexpected change in a quotation was received with something like tumult. Occasionally scouts entered the place at a run, and redoubled the uproar as they stopped at the entrance to the rotunda and, at the tops of their voices, announced depart-

ures and arrivals. In this place, where the gambling fever was pulsing in the sunshine, such announcements were sure to raise a prolonged muttering sound.

"They *are* funny!" murmured Nana, greatly entertained.

"Their features look as if they had been put on the wrong way. Just you see that big fellow there; I shouldn't care to meet him all alone in the middle of a wood."

But Vandeuvres pointed her out a bookmaker, once a shopman in a fancy repository, who had made three million francs in two years. He was slight of build, delicate, and fair, and people all round him treated him with great respect. They smiled when they addressed him, whilst others took up positions close by in order to catch a glimpse of him.

They were at length leaving the ring, when Vandeuvres nodded slightly to another bookmaker, who thereupon ventured to call him. It was one of his former coachmen, an enormous fellow with the shoulders of an ox, and a high colour. Now that he was trying his fortunes at race-meetings, on the strength of some mysteriously-obtained capital, the Count was doing his utmost to push him, confiding to him his secret bets, and treating him on all occasions as a servant to whom one shews one's true character. Yet, despite this protection, the man had in rapid succession lost very heavy sums, and to-day he too was playing his last card. There was blood in his eyes; he looked fit to drop with apoplexy.

"Well, Maréchal," queried the Count in the lowest of voices, "to what amount have you laid odds?"

"To five thousand louis, Monsieur

le Comte," replied the bookmaker, like-wise lowering his voice. "A pretty job, eh? I'll confess to you that I've in-creased the odds; I've made it three to one."

Vandeuvres looked very much put out. "No, no, I don't want you to do that: put it at two to one again directly. I shan't tell you any more, Maréchal."

"Oh, how can it hurt, Monsieur le Comte, at this time o' day?" rejoined the other, with the humble smile be-fitting an accomplice. "I had to attract the people so as to lay your two thousand louis."

At this Vandeuvres silenced him. But as he was going off, Maréchal remem-bered something, and was sorry he had not questioned him about the shorten-ing of the odds on the filly. It would be a nice business for him if the filly stood a chance, seeing that he had just laid fifty to one about her in two hun-dreds.

Nana, though she did not understand a word of what the Count was whispering, dared not, however, ask for new explana-tions. He seemed more nervous than before, and abruptly handed her over to Labordette, whom they came upon in front of the weighing-in room.

"You'll take her back," said he. "I've got something on hand. Au revoir!"

And he entered the room, which was narrow and low-pitched, and half filled with a great pair of scales. It was like a waiting-room in a suburban station, and Nana was again hugely disillusioned, for she had been picturing to herself something on a very vast scale, a monu-mental machine, in fact, for weighing horses. Dear me, they only weighed the jockeys! Then it wasn't worth while

making such a fuss with their weighing! In the scale, a jockey with an idiotic expression was waiting, harness on knee, till a stout man in a frock-coat should have done verifying his weight. At the door, a stable-help was holding a horse, Cosinus, round which a silent and deeply-interested throng was clustering.

The course was about to be cleared. Labordette hurried Nana, but retraced his steps in order to shew her a little man talking with Vandeuvres at some distance from the rest.

"Dear me, there's Price!" said he.

"Ah, yes! the man who's mounting me," she murmured laughingly.

And she declared him to be exquisitely ugly. All jockeys struck her as look-ing idiotic, doubtless, said she, because they were prevented from growing bigger. This particular jockey was a man of forty, and with his long, thin, deeply furrowed, hard, dead countenance, he looked like an old shrivelled-up child. His body was knotty, and so reduced in size that his blue jacket with its white sleeves looked as if it had been thrown over a lay figure.

"No," she resumed as she walked away, "he would never make me very happy, you know."

A mob of people were still crowd-ing the course, the turf of which had been wetted and trampled on, till it had grown black. In front of the two telegraphs, which hung very high up on their cast-iron pillars, the crowd were jostling together, with upturned faces, uproariously greeting the numbers of the different horses as an electric wire in connection with the weighing-room made them appear. Gentlemen were pointing at programmes: Pichenette had been scratched by his owner, and this caused some noise. However, Nana did not do more than cross over the course on Labordette's arm. The bell hanging on the flat-staff was ringing persistently to warn people to leave the course.

"Ah! my little dears," said she, as she got up into her landau again, "their enclosure's all humbug!"

She was welcomed with acclamation; people around her clapped their hands.

"Bravo Nana! Nana's ours again!"

What idiots they were, to be sure! Did they think she was the sort to cut old friends? She had come back just at the auspicious moment. Now then, 'tenshun! The race was beginning! And the champagne was accordingly forgotten, and everyone left off drinking.

But Nana was astonished to find Gaga in her carriage, sitting with Bijou and Louiset on her knees. Gaga had indeed decided on this course of action in order to be near la Faloise, but she told Nana that she had been anxious to kiss baby. She adored children.

"By-the-by, what about Lili?" asked Nana. "That's certainly she over there, in that old fellow's brougham. They've just told me something very nice!"

Gaga had adopted a lachrymose expression.

"My dear, it's made me ill," said she dolorously. "Yesterday I had to keep my bed, I cried so, and to-day I didn't think I should be able to come. You know what my opinions were, don't you? I didn't desire that kind of thing at all. I had her educated in a convent with a view to a good marriage. And, then, to think of the strict advice she had, and the constant watching! Well, my dear, it was she who wished it.

We had such a scene—tears—disagreeable speeches! It even got to such a point that I caught her a box on the ear. She was too much bored by existence, she said; she wanted to get out of it. By-and-by, when she began to say, ' 'Tisn't you, after all, who've got the right to prevent me,' I said to her: 'You're a miserable wretch: you're bringing dishonour upon us: begone!' and it was done. I consented to arrange about it. But my last hope's blooming well blasted, and oh, I used to dream about such nice things!"

The noise of a quarrel caused them to rise. It was Georges, in the act of defending Vandeuvres against certain vague rumours which were circulating among the various groups.

"Why should you say that he's laying off his own horse?" the young man was exclaiming. "Yesterday, in the Salon des Courses, he took the odds on Lusignan for a thousand louis."

"Yes, I was there," said Philippe in affirmation of this. "And he didn't put a single louis on Nana. If the bettings ten to one against Nana, he's got nothing to win there. It's absurd to imagine people are so calculating. Where would his interest come in?"

Labordette was listening with a quiet expression. Shrugging his shoulders, he said,—

"Oh, leave them alone; they must have their say. The Count has again laid at least as much as five hundred louis on Lusignan, and if he's wanted, Nana to run to a hundred louis, it's because an owner ought always to look as if he believes in his horses."

"Oh, bosh! What the deuce does that matter to us?" shouted la Faloise, with a wave of his arms. "Spirit's going to win! Down with France—bravo England!"

A long shiver ran through the crowd, whilst a fresh peal from the bell announced the arrival of the horses upon the race-course. At this, Nana got up and stood on one of the seats of her carriage so as to obtain a better view, and in so doing she trampled the bouquets of roses and myosotis under-foot. With a sweeping glance she took in the wide, vast horizon. At this last feverish moment the course was empty, and closed by grey barriers, between the posts of which stood a line of policemen. The strip of grass, which lay muddy in front of her, grew brighter as it stretched away, and turned into a tender green carpet in the distance. In the middle landscape, as she lowered her eyes, she saw the field swarming with vast numbers of people, some on tip-toe, others perched on carriages, and all heaving and jostling in sudden passionate excitement.

Horses were neighing, tent-canvases flapped, whilst equestrians urged their hacks forward amid a crowd of pedestrians rushing to get places along the barriers. When Nana turned in the direction of the stands on the other side, the faces seemed diminished, and the dense masses of heads were only a confused and motley array, filling gangways, steps, and terraces, and looming in deep, dark, serried lines against the sky. And beyond these again, she overlooked the plain surrounding the course. Behind the ivy-clad mill to the right, meadows, dotted over with great patches of umbrageous wood, stretched away into the distance; whilst opposite to her, as far as

the Seine flowing at the foot of a hill, the avenues of the Park intersected one another, filled at that moment with long motionless files of waiting carriages; and, in the direction of Boulogne, on the left, the landscape widened anew, and opened out towards the blue distances of Meudon through an avenue of pawlonias, whose rosy, leafless tops were one stain of brilliant lake colour. People were still arriving, and a long procession of human ants kept coming along the narrow ribbon of road which crossed the distance, whilst, very far away, on the Paris side, the non-paying public, herding like sheep among the woods, loomed in a moving line of little dark spots under the trees on the skirts of the Bois.

Suddenly a cheering influence warmed the hundred thousand souls who covered this part of the plain like insects swarming madly under the vast expanse of heaven. The sun, which had been hidden for about a quarter of an hour, made his appearance again, and shone out amid a perfect sea of light. And everything flamed afresh: the women's sunshades turned into countless golden targets above the heads of the crowd. The sun was applauded, saluted with bursts of laughter. And people stretched their arms out as though to brush apart the clouds.

Meanwhile, a solitary police officer advanced down the middle of the deserted race-course, whilst higher up, on the left, a man appeared with a red flag in his hand.

"It's the starter, the Baron de Mauriac," said Labordette in reply to a question from Nana. All round the young woman exclamations were bursting from the men who were pressing to her very carriage-step. They kept up a disconnected conversation, jerking out phrases under the immediate influence of passing impressions. Indeed, Philippe and Georges, Bordenave and la Faloise, could not be quiet.

"Don't shove! Let me see! Ah, the judge is getting into his box. D'you say it's Monsieur de Souvigny? You must have good eyesight—eh? to be able to tell what half a head is out of a fakement like that! Do hold your tongue—the banner's going up. Here they are—'tenshun! Cosinus is the first!"

A red and yellow banner was flapping in mid-air, at the top of a mast. The horses came on the course one by one, they were led by stable-boys, and the jockeys were sitting idle-handed in the saddles, the sunlight making them look like bright dabs of colour. After Cosinus appeared Hazard and Boum. Presently a murmur of approval greeted Spirit, a magnificent big brown bay, the harsh citron-colour and black of whose jockey were cheerlessly Britannic. Valerio II. scored a success as he came in; he was small and very lively, and his colours were soft green bordered with pink. The two Vandeuvres' horses were slow to make their appearance, but at last, in Frangipane's rear, the blue and white shewed themselves. But Lusignan, a very dark bay, of irreproachable shape, was almost forgotten amid the astonishment caused by Nana. People had not seen her looking like this before, for now the sudden sunlight was dyeing the chestnut filly the brilliant colour of a girl's red-gold hair. She was shining in the light like a new gold coin; her chest was deep, her head and neck tapered lightly from the delicate, high-strung line of her long back.

"Gracious, she's got my hair!" cried Nana in an ecstasy. "You bet you know I'm proud of it!"

The men clambered up on the landau, and Bordenave narrowly escaped putting his foot on Louiset, whom his mother had forgotten. He took him up with an outburst of paternal grumbling and, hoisted him on his shoulder, muttering at the same time:

"The poor little brat, he must be in it too! Wait a bit, I'll shew you mamma. Eh? Look at mummy out there."

And, as Bijou was scratching his legs, he took charge of him too, whilst Nana, rejoicing in the brute that bore her name, glanced round at the other women to see how they took it. They were all raging madly. Just then, on the summit of her cab, the Tricon, who had not moved till that moment, began waving her hand and giving her bookmaker her orders above the heads of the crowd. Her instinct had at last prompted her; she was backing Nana.

La Faloise meanwhile was making an insufferable noise. He was getting wild over Frangipane.

"I've an inspiration," he kept shouting. "Just look at Frangipane. What an action, eh? I back Frangipane at eight to one. Who'll take me?"

"Do keep quiet now," said Labordette at last. "You'll be sorry for it, if you do."

"Frangipane's a screw," Philippe declared. "He's been utterly blown upon already. You'll see the canter."

The horses had gone up to the right, and they now started for the preliminary canter, passing in loose order before the stands. Thereupon there was a passionate fresh burst of talk, and people all spoke at once.

"Lusignan's too long in the back, but he's very fit. Not a cent, I tell you, on Valerio II.; he's nervous—gallops with his head up—it's a bad sign. Jove! Burne's riding Spirit. I tell you he's got no shoulders. A well-made shoulder —that's the whole secret. No, decidedly, Spirit's too quiet. Now listen, Nana, I saw her after the Grande Poule des Produits, and she was dripping, and draggled, and her sides were trembling like one o'clock. I lay twenty louis she isn't placed! Oh, shut up! He's boring us with his Frangipane. There's no time to make a bet now; there, they're off!"

Almost in tears, la Faloise was struggling to find a bookmaker. He had to be reasoned with. Everyone craned forward, but the first go-off was bad; the starter, who looked in the distance like a slim dash of blackness, not having lowered his flag. The horses came back to their places after galloping a moment or two. There were two more false starts. At length the starter got the horses together and sent them away with such address as to elicit shouts of applause.

"Splendid! No, it was mere chance! Never mind—it's done it!"

The outcries were smothered by the anxiety which tortured every breast. The betting stopped now, and the game was being played on the vast course itself. Silence reigned at the outset as though everyone were holding his breath. White faces and trembling forms were stretched forward in all directions. At first Hazard and Cosinus made the running at the head of the rest; Valerio II. followed close by, and the field came on in a confused mass behind. When they passed in front of the stands, thundering over the ground in their course like a sudden storm-wind, the mass was already some fourteen lengths in extent. Frangipane was last, and Nana was slightly behind Lusignan and Spirit.

"Egad!" muttered Labordette, "how the Englishman is pulling it off out there!"

The whole carriage-load again burst out with phrases and exclamations. Everyone rose on tiptoe and followed the bright splashes of colour, which were the jockeys as they rushed through the sunlight.

At the rise Valerio II. took the lead, whilst Cosinus and Hazard lost ground, and Lusignan and Spirit were running neck and neck with Nana still behind them.

"By jingo, the Englishman's gained! it's palpable!" said Bordenave. "Lusignan's in difficulties, and Valerio II. can't stay."

"Well, it will be a pretty biz if the Englishman wins!" cried Philippe, in an access of patriotic grief.

A feeling of anguish was beginning to choke all that crowded multitude. Another defeat! And with that a strange ardent prayer, which was almost religious, went up for Lusignan, whilst people heaped abuse on Spirit and his dismal mute of a jockey. Among the crowd scattered over the grass the wind of excitement put up whole groups of people and set their boot-soles flashing in air as they ran. Horsemen crossed the green at a furious gallop. And Nana, who was slowly revolving on her own axis, saw beneath her a surging waste of beasts and men, a sea of heads swayed and stirred, all round the course, by the whirlwind of the race, which clove the horizon with the bright lightning flash of the jockeys. She had been following their movement from behind, whilst the cruppers sped away and the legs seemed to grow longer as they raced, and then diminished till they looked slender as strands of hair. Now the horses were running at the end of the course, and she caught a side view of them looking minute and delicate of outline against the green distances of the Bois. Then, suddenly, they vanished behind a great clump of trees growing in the middle of the Hippodrome.

"Don't talk about it!" cried Georges, who was still full of hope. "It isn't over yet. The Englishman's touched."

But la Faloise was again seized with contempt for his country, and grew positively outrageous in his applause of Spirit. Bravo! That was right! France needed it! Spirit first and Frangipane second—that would be a nasty one for his native land! He exasperated Labordette, who threatened seriously to throw him off the carriage.

"Let's see how many minutes they'll be about it," said Bordenave peaceably, for, though holding up Louiset, he had taken out his watch.

One after the other the horses reappeared from behind the clump of trees. There was stupefaction: a long murmur arose among the crowd. Valerio II. was still leading, but Spirit was gaining on him, and behind him Lusignan had slackened, whilst another horse was taking his place. People could not make this out all at once: they were confused about the colours. Then there was a burst of exclamations.

"But it's Nana! Nana? Get along! I tell you Lusignan hasn't budged. Dear me, yes, it's Nana. You can certainly recognise her by her golden colour. D'you see her now? She's blazing away. Bravo Nana! What a ripper she is! Bah, it doesn't matter a bit: she's making the running for Lusignan!"

For some seconds this was everybody's opinion. But little by little, the filly kept gaining and gaining, spurting hard all the while. Thereupon a vast wave of feeling passed over the crowd, and the tail of horses in the rear ceased to interest. A supreme struggle was beginning between Spirit, Nana, Lusignan, and Valerio II. They were pointed out: people estimated what ground they had gained or lost in disconnected, gasping phrases. And Nana, who had mounted up on the coach-box, as though some power had lifted her thither, stood white and trembling, and so deeply moved as not to be able to speak. At her side Labordette smiled as of old.

"The Englishman's in trouble, eh?" said Philippe joyously. "He's going badly."

"In any case, it's all up with Lusignan," shouted la Faloise. "Valerio II. is coming forward. Look, there they are all four together."

The same phrase was in every mouth. "What a rush, my dears! By God, what a rush!"

The squad of horses was now passing in front of them like a flash of lightning. Their approach was perceptible—the breath of it was as a distant muttering which increased at every second. The whole crowd had thrown themselves impetuously against the barriers, and a deep clamour issued from innumerable chests before the advance of the horses, and drew nearer and nearer like the sound of a foaming tide. It was the last fierce outburst of colossal partisanship— a hundred thousand spectators were possessed by a single passion, burning with the same gambler's lust, as they gazed after the beasts, whose galloping feet were sweeping millions with them. The crowd pushed and crushed—fists were clenched, people gaped, open-mouthed; every man was fighting for himself, every man with voice and gesture was madly speeding the horse of his choice. And the cry of all this multitude, a wild beast's cry despite the garb of civilisation, grew ever more distinct,—

"Here they come! Here they come! Here they come!"

But Nana was still gaining ground, and now Valerio II. was distanced, and she was heading the race, with Spirit two or three necks behind. The rolling thunder of voices had increased. They were coming in; a storm of oaths greeted them from the landau.

"Gee up, Lusignan, you great coward! The Englishman's stunning! Do it again, old boy, do it again! Oh, that Valerio! it's sickening! Oh, the carcass! My ten louis damned well lost! Nana's the only one! Bravo, Nana! Bravo!"

And without being aware of it Nana, upon her seat, had begun jerking her hips and waist as though she were racing herself. She kept striking her side—she fancied it was a help to the filly. With each stroke she sighed with fatigue, and said in low anguished tones,—

"Go it, go it!"

Then a splendid sight was witnessed.

Price, rising in his stirrups and brandishing his whip, flogged Nana with an arm of iron. The old shrivelled-up child, with his long, hard, dead face, seemed to breath flame. And in a fit of furious audacity and triumphant will, he put his heart into the filly, held her up, lifted her forward drenched in foam, with eyes of blood. The whole rush of horses passed with a roar of thunder: it took away people's breaths; it swept the air with it, whilst the judge sat frigidly waiting, his eye adjusted to its task. Then there was an immense re-echoing burst of acclamation. With a supreme effort, Price had just flung Nana past the post, thus beating Spirit by a head.

There was an uproar as of a rising tide. "Nana! Nana! Nana!" The cry rolled up and swelled with the violence of a tempest, till, little by little, it filled the distance, the depths of the Bois as far as Mont Valérien, the meadows of Longchamps and the Plaine de Boulogne. In all parts of the field the wildest enthusiasm declared itself. "Vive Nana! Vive la France! Down with England!" The women waved their sunshades; men leapt and spun round, vociferating as they did so, whilst others with shouts of nervous laughter threw their hats in the air. And from the other side of the course, the enclosure made answer, the people on the stands were stirred, though nothing was distinctly visible save a tremulous motion of the air, as though an invisible flame were burning in a brazier above the living mass of gesticulating arms, and little, wildly-moving faces, where the eyes and gaping mouths looked like black dots. The noise did not cease, but swelled up and recommenced in the recesses of far-

away avenues and among the people encamped under the trees, till it spread on
and on and attained its climax in the
imperial stand, where the Empress herself had applauded. "Nana! Nana!
Nana!" The cry rose heavenward in the
glorious sunlight, whose golden rain beat
fiercely on the dizzy heads of the multitude.

Then Nana, looming large on the seat
of her landau, fancied that it was she
whom they were applauding. For a
moment or two she had stood devoid
of motion, stupefied by her triumph,
gazing at the course as it was invaded
by so dense a flood of people that the
turf became invisible beneath the sea of
black hats. By-and-by, when this crowd
had become somewhat less disorderly,
and a lane had been formed as far as
the exit, and Nana was again applauded
as she went off with Price hanging life-
lessly and vacantly over her neck, she
smacked her thigh energetically, lost
all self-possession, triumphed in crude
phrases:

"Oh, by God, it's me, it's me. Oh, by
God, what luck!"

And, scarce knowing how to give expression to her overwhelming joy, she
hugged and kissed Louiset, whom she
now discovered high in air on Bordenave's shoulder.

"Three minutes and fourteen seconds,"
said the latter as he put his watch back
in his pocket.

Nana kept hearing her name; the whole
plain was echoing it back to her. Her
people were applauding her whilst she
towered above them in the sunlight, in
the splendour of her starry hair, and
white and sky-blue dress. Labordette,
as he made off, had just announced to

her a gain of two thousand louis, for
he had put her fifty on Nana, at forty to
one. But the money stirred her less than
this unforeseen victory, the fame of
which made her Queen of Paris. All the
other ladies were losers. With a raging
movement Rose Mignon had snapped her
sunshade; and Caroline Héquet, and
Clarisse, and Simonne—nay, Lucy Stewart herself, despite the presence of her
son, were swearing low in their exasperation at that great wench's luck, whilst the
Tricon, who had made the sign of the
cross at both start and finish, straightened up her tall form above them, went
into an ecstasy over her intuition, and
damned Nana admiringly as became an
experienced matron.

Meanwhile, round the landau the crush
of men increased. The band of Nana's
immediate followers had made a fierce
uproar, and now Georges, choking with
emotion, continued shouting all by himself in breaking tones. As the champagne had given out, Philippe, taking
the footmen with him, had run to the
wine-bars. Nana's court was growing
and growing, and her present triumph
caused many loiterers to join her. Indeed, that movement which had made
her carriage a centre of attraction to
the whole field was now ending in an
apotheosis, and Queen Venus was enthroned amid suddenly-maddened subjects. Bordenave, behind her, was muttering oaths, for he yearned to her as a
father. Steiner himself had been reconquered—he had deserted Simonne and
had hoisted himself up on one of Nana's
carriage-steps. When the champagne had
arrived, when she lifted her brimming
glass, such applause burst forth, and
"Nana! Nana! Nana!" was so loudly

repeated, that the crowd looked round in astonishment for the filly, nor could any tell whether it was the horse or the woman that filled all hearts.

Whilst this was going on, Mignon came hastening up in defiance of Rose's terrible frown. That confounded girl simply maddened him, and he wanted to kiss her. Then after imprinting a paternal salute on both her cheeks,—

"What bothers me," said he, "is that now Rose is certainly going to send the letter. She's raging, too, fearfully."

"So much the better! It'll do my business for me!" Nana let slip.

But noting his utter astonishment, she hastily continued,—

"No, no, what am I saying? Indeed, I don't rightly know what I'm saying now! I'm drunk."

And drunk indeed, drunk with joy, drunk with sunshine, she still raised her glass on high and applauded herself.

"To Nana! To Nana!" she cried, amid a redoubled uproar of laughter and bravos, which little by little overspread the whole Hippodrome.

The races were ending, and the Prix Vaublanc was run for. Carriages began driving off one by one. Meanwhile, amid much disputing, the name of Vandeuvres was again mentioned. It was quite evident now: for two years past Vandeuvres had been preparing his final stroke, and had accordingly told Gresham to hold Nana in, whilst he had only brought Lusignan forward in order to make play for the filly. The losers were vexed, the winners shrugged their shoulders. After all, wasn't the thing permissable? An owner was free to run his stud in his own way. Many others had done as he had! In fact the majority thought Van-

deuvres had displayed great skill in raking in all he could get about Nana through the agency of friends, a course of action which explained the sudden shortening of the odds. People spoke of his having laid two thousand louis on the horse, which, supposing the odds to be thirty to one against, gave him twelve hundred thousand francs, an amount so vast as to inspire respect and to excuse everything.

But other rumours of a very serious nature were being whispered about: they issued in the first instance from the enclosure, and the men who returned thence were full of exact particulars. Voices were raised, an atrocious scandal began to be openly canvassed. That poor fellow Vandeuvres was done for; he had spoilt his splendid hit with a piece of flat stupidity, an idiotic robbery, for he had commissioned Maréchal, a shady bookmaker, to lay two thousand louis on his account against Lusignan, in order thereby to get back his thousand and odd openly wagered louis. It was a miserable business, and it proved to be the last rift necessary to the utter break-up of his fortune. The bookmaker being thus warned that the favourite would not win, had realized some sixty thousand francs over the horse. Only Labordette, for lack of exact and detailed instructions, had just then gone to him to put two hundred louis on Nana, which the bookmaker, in his ignorance of the stroke actually intended, was still quoting at fifty to one against. Cleared of one hundred thousand francs over the filly, and a loser to the tune of forty thousand, Maréchal, who felt the world crumbling under his feet, had suddenly divined the situation when he saw the Count and

Labordette talking together in front of the enclosure, just after the race was over. Furious, as became an ex-coachman of the Count's, and brutally frank as only a cheated man can be, he had just made a frightful scene in public, had told the whole story in atrocious terms, and had thrown everyone into angry excitement. It was further stated that the stewards were about to meet.

Nana, whom Philippe and Georges were whisperingly putting in possession of the facts, gave vent to a series of reflections, and yet ceased not to laugh and drink. After all it was quite likely; she remembered such things, and then that Maréchal had a dirty, hangdog look. Nevertheless, she was still rather doubtful when Labordette appeared. He was very white.

"Well?" she asked in a low voice.

"Bloody well smashed up!" he replied simply.

And he shrugged his shoulders. That Vandeuvres was a mere child! She made a bored little gesture.

That evening at the Bal Mabille Nana obtained a colossal success. When, towards ten o'clock, she made her appearance, the uproar was already formidable. That classic night of madness had brought together all that was young and pleasure-loving, and now this smart world was wallowing in the coarseness and imbecility of the servants' hall. There was a fierce crush under the festoons of gas-lamps, and men in evening coats and women in outrageous low-necked old toilets, which they did not mind soiling, were howling and surging to and fro under the maddening influence of a vast drunken fit. At a distance of thirty paces the brass instruments of the orchestra were inaudible. Nobody was dancing. Stupid witticisms, repeated no one knew why, were going the round of the various groups. People were straining after wit without succeeding in being funny. Seven women, imprisoned in the cloak-room, were crying to be set free. A shallot had been found, put up to auction, and knocked down at two louis. Just then Nana arrived, still wearing her blue-and-white race-course costume, and amid a thunder of applause the shallot was presented to her. People caught hold of her in her own despite, and three gentlemen bore her triumphantly into the garden, across ruined grass-plats and ravaged masses of greenery. As the band-stand presented an obstacle to her advance, it was taken by storm, and chairs and music-stands were smashed. A paternal police organised the disorder.

It was only on Tuesday that Nana recovered from the excitements of victory. That morning, she was chatting with Madame Lerat, the old lady having come in to bring her news of Louiset, whom the open air had upset. A long story, which was occupying the attention of all Paris, interested her beyond measure. Vandeuvres, after being warned off all race-courses and posted at the Cercle Imperial on the very evening after the disaster had set fire to his stable on the morrow, and had burnt himself and his horses to death.

"He certainly told me he was going to," the young woman kept saying. "That man was a regular maniac! Oh, how they did frighten me when they told me about it yesterday evening! You see he might easily have murdered me some fine night. And besides, oughtn't he to have given me a hint about his horse? I should at any rate have made my fortune! He said to Labordette that if I knew about the matter I would immediately inform my hairdresser and a whole lot of other men. How polite, eh? Oh dear no, I certainly can't grieve much for him."

After some reflection, she had grown very angry. Just then Labordette came in; he had seen about her bets, and was now the bearer of some forty thousand francs. This only added to her bad temper, for she ought to have gained a million. Labordette, who during the whole of this episode had been pretending entire innocence, abandoned Vandeuvres in decisive terms. Those old families, he opined, were worn out, and apt to make a stupid ending.

"Oh, dear no!" said Nana; "it isn't stupid to burn one's self in one's stable as he did. For my part, I think he made a dashing finish; but oh, you know, I'm not defending that story about him and Maréchal. It's too silly. Just to think that Blanche has had the cheek to want to lay the blame of it on me! I said to her: 'Did I tell him to steal?' Don't you think one can ask a man for money without urging him to commit crime? If he had said to me, 'I've got nothing left,' I should have said to him, 'All right, let's part.' And the matter wouldn't have gone further."

"Just so," said the aunt gravely. "When men are obstinate about a thing, so much the worse for them!"

"But as to the merry little finish up, oh, that was awfully smart!" continued Nana. "It appears to have been terrible enough to give you the shudders! He sent everybody away, and boxed himself up in the place with a lot of petroleum. And it blazed! you should have seen it! Just think a great big affair, almost all made of wood, and stuffed with hay and straw! The flames simply towered up, and the finest part of the business was that the horses didn't want to be roasted. They could be heard plunging, throwing themselves against the doors, crying aloud just like human beings. Yes, people haven't got rid of the horror of it yet."

Labordette let a low, incredulous whistle escape him. For his part he did not believe in the death of Vandeuvres. Somebody had sworn he had seen him escaping through a window. He had set fire to his stable in a fit of aberration, but when it had begun to grow too warm it must have sobered him. A man so besotted about the women and so utterly worn out could not possibly die so pluckily.

Nana listened in her disillusionment, and could only remark:

"Oh! the poor wretch, it was so beautiful!"

## CHAPTER XII

Towards one in the morning, in the great bed of the Venice point draperies. Nana and the Count lay still awake. He had returned to her that evening after a three days' sulking fit. The room, which was dimly illumined by a lamp, seemed to slumber amid a warm, damp odour of love, whilst the furniture, with its white lacquer and silver incrustations, loomed vague and wan through the gloom. A curtain had been drawn to, so that the bed lay flooded with shadow. A sigh became audible; then a kiss broke the silence, and Nana, slipping off the coverlet, sat for a moment or two, barelegged, on the edge of the bed. The Count let his head fall back on the pillow, and remained in darkness.

"Dearest, you believe in the good God, don't you?" she queried after some moments' reflection. Her face was serious; she had been overcome by pious terrors on quitting her lover's arms.

Since morning, indeed, she had been complaining of feeling uncomfortable, and all her stupid notions, as she phrased it, notions about death and hell, were secretly torturing her. From time to time she had nights such as these, during which childish fears and atrocious fancies would thrill her with waking nightmares. She continued,—

"I say, d'you think I shall go to heaven?"

And with that she shivered, whilst the Count, in his surprise at her putting such singular questions at such a moment, felt his old religious remorse returning upon him. Then, with her chemise slipping from her shoulders and her hair unpinned, she again threw herself upon his breast, sobbing and clinging to him as she did so.

"I'm afraid of dying! I'm afraid of dying!" He had all the trouble in the world to disengage himself. Indeed, he was himself afraid of giving in to the sudden madness of this woman clinging to his body in her dread of the Invisible. Such dread is contagious, and he reasoned with her. Her conduct was perfect—she had only to conduct herself well in order one day to merit pardon. But she shook her head. Doubtless she was doing no one any harm; nay, she was even in the constant habit of wearing a medal of the Virgin, which she shewed to him as it hung by a red thread between her breasts. Only it had been foreordained that all unmarried women who held conversation with men would go to hell. Scraps of her catechism recurred to her remembrance. Ah! if one only knew for certain; but, alas! one was sure of nothing; nobody ever brought back any information; and then, truly, it would be stupid to bother one's self about things if the priests were talking foolishness all the time. Nevertheless, she religiously kissed her medal, which was still warm from contact with her skin, as though by way of charm against death, the idea of which filled her with icy horror. Muffat was obliged to accompany her into the dressing-room, for she shook at the idea of being alone there one moment, even though she had left the door open. When he had lain down again she still roamed about the room, visiting its several corners, and starting and shivering at the slightest noise. A mirror stopped her, and as of old she lapsed into obvious contemplation of her nakedness. But the sight of her breast, her waist, and her thighs only doubled her terror, and she ended by feeling with both hands very slowly over the bones of her face.

"You're ugly when you're dead," said she in deliberate tones.

And she pressed her cheeks, enlarging her eyes and pushing down her jaw, in order to see how she would look. Thus disfigured she turned towards the Count:

"Do look! my head'll be quite small, it will!"

At this he grew vexed.

"You're mad; come to bed!"

He fancied he saw her in a grave, emaciated by a century of sleep, and he joined his hands and stammered a prayer. It was some time ago that the religious sense had reconquered him, and now his daily access of faith had again assumed the apopletic intensity which was wont to leave him well-nigh stunned. The joints of his fingers used to crack, and he would repeat without cease these words only: "My God, my God, my God!" It was the cry of his impotence, the cry of that sin against which, though his damnation was certain, he felt powerless to strive. When Nana returned, she found him hidden beneath the bedclothes; he was haggard, he had dug his nails into his bosom, and his eyes stared upward as though in search of heaven. And with that she started to weep again. Then they both embraced, and their teeth chattered they knew not why, as the same imbecile obsession overmastered them. They had already passed a similar night, but on this occasion, the thing was utterly idiotic, as Nana declared when she ceased to be frightened. She suspected something, and this caused her to question the Count in a prudent sort of way. It might be that Rose Mignon had sent the famous letter! But that was not the case; it was sheer fright, nothing more, for he was still ignorant whether he was a cuckold or no.

Two days later, after a fresh disappearance, Muffat presented himself in the morning, a time of day at which he never came. He was livid; his eyes were red, and his whole man still shaken by a great internal struggle. But Zoé being scared herself, did not notice his troubled state. She had run to meet him, and now began crying,—

"Oh, *Monsieur,* do come in! *Madame* nearly died yesterday evening!"

And, when he asked for particulars,—

"Something it's impossible to believe has happened—a miscarriage, *Monsieur.*"

Nana had been in the family way for the past three months. For long she had simply thought herself out of sorts, and Doctor Boutarel had himself been in doubt. But when afterwards he made her a decisive announcement, she felt so bored thereby that she did all she possibly could to disguise her condition. Her nervous terrors, her dark humours, sprang to some extent from this unfortunate state of things, the secret of which she kept very shamefacedly, as became a courtesan-mother who is obliged to conceal her plight. The thing struck her as a ridiculous accident, which made her appear small in her own eyes, and would, had it been known, have led people to chaff her.

"A poor joke, eh?" said she. "Bad luck, too, certainly."

She was necessarily very sharp-set when she thought her last hour had come. There was no end to her surprise, too; her sexual economy seemed to her to have got out of order, it produced children, then, even when one did not want them, and when one employed it for quite other purposes! Nature drove her to exasperation; this appearance of serious motherhood in a career of pleasure, this gift of life amid all the deaths she was spreading around, exasperated her. Why could one not dispose of one's self as fancy dictated, without all this fuss? And whence had this brat come? She could not even suggest a father. Ah, dear heaven! the man who made him would have a splendid notion had he kept him in his own hands, for nobody asked for him, he was in everybody's way, and he would certainly not have much happiness in life!

Meanwhile Zoé described the catastrophe.

"*Madame* was seized with colic towards four o'clock. When she didn't come back out of the dressing-room, I went in, and found her lying stretched on the floor in a faint. Yes, *Monsieur*, on the floor, in a pool of blood, as though she had been murdered. Then I understood, you see. I was furious; *Madame* might quite well have confided her trouble to me. As it happened, Monsieur Georges was there, and he helped me to lift her up, and directly a miscarriage was mentioned he felt ill in his turn! Oh, it's true I've had the hump since yesterday!"

In fact the house seemed utterly upset. All the servants were galloping upstairs, downstairs, and through the rooms. Georges had passed the night on an arm-chair in the drawing-room. It was he who had announced the news to *Madame's* friends at that hour of the evening when *Madame* was in the habit of receiving. He had still been very pale, and he had told his story very feelingly and as though stupefied. Steiner, la Faloise, Philippe, and others besides, had presented themselves, and, at the end of the lad's first phrase, they burst into exclamations. The thing was impossible! It must be a farce! After which they grew serious, and gazed with an embarrassed expression at her bedroom-door. They shook their heads: it was no laughing matter.

Till midnight a dozen gentlemen had stood talking in low voices in front of the fire-place. All were friends, all were deeply exercised by the same idea of paternity. They seemed to be mutually excusing themselves, and they looked as confused as if they had done something clumsy. Eventually, however, they put a bold face on the matter. It had nothing to do with them: the fault was hers! What a stunner that Nana was, eh? One would never have believed her capable of such a fake! And with that they departed one by one, walking on tip-toe as though in a chamber of death where you cannot laugh.

"Come up all the same, *Monsieur*," said Zoé to Muffat. "*Madame* is much better, and will see you. We are expecting the doctor, who promised to come back this morning."

The lady's maid had persuaded Georges to go back home to sleep, and upstairs in the drawing-room only Satin remained. She lay stretched on a divan, smoking a cigarette, and scanning the ceiling. Amid the household scare which had followed the accident, she had been white with rage, had shrugged her shoulders violently, and had made ferocious remarks. Accordingly, when Zoé was passing in front of her and telling Monsieur that poor dear *Madame* had suffered a great deal,—

"That's right; it'll teach him!" said Satin curtly.

They turned round in surprise, but she had not moved a muscle; her eyes were still turned towards the ceiling, and her cigarette was still wedged tightly between her lips.

"Dear me, you're charming, you are!" said Zoé.

But Satin sat up, looked savagely at the Count, and once more hurled her remark at him.

"That's right; it'll teach him!"

And she lay down again, and blew forth a thin jet of smoke, as though she had no interest in present events and were resolved not to meddle in any of them. No, it was all too silly!

Zoé, however, introduced Muffat into the bedroom, where a scent of ether lingered amid warm heavy silence, scarce broken by the dull roll of occasional carriages in the Avenue de Villiers. Nana, looking very white on her pillow, was lying awake with wide-open, meditative eyes. She smiled when she saw the Count, but did not move.

"Ah, dear pet!" she slowly murmured; "I really thought I should never see you again."

Then, as he leant forward to kiss her on the hair, she grew tender towards him, and spoke frankly about the child, as though he were its father.

"I never dared tell you, I felt so happy about it! Oh, I used to dream about it; I should have liked to be worthy of you! And now there's nothing left. Ah well, perhaps that's best. I don't want to bring a stumbling-block into your life."

Astounded by this story of paternity, he began stammering vague phrases. He had taken a chair, and had sat down by the bed, leaning one arm on the coverlet. Then the young woman noticed his wild expression, the blood reddening his eyes, the fever that set his lips aquiver.

"What's the matter, then?" she asked. "You're ill, too."

"No," he answered with extreme difficulty.

She gazed at him with a profound expression. Then she signed to Zoé to retire, for the latter was lingering round arranging the medicine bottles. And when they were alone she drew him down to her and again asked,—

"What's the matter with you, darling? The tears are ready to burst from your eyes—I can see that quite well. Well, now, speak out; you've come to tell me something."

"No, no, I swear I haven't," he blurted out. But he was choking with suffering, and this sick-room, into which he had suddenly entered unawares, so worked on his feelings that he burst out sobbing, and buried his face in the bedclothes to smother the violence of his grief. Nana understood. Rose Mignon had most assuredly decided to send the letter. She let him weep for some moments, and he was shaken by convulsions so fierce that the bed trembled under her. At length, in accents of motherly compassion, she queried,—

"You've had bothers at your home?"

He nodded affirmatively. She paused anew, and then very low,—

"Then you know all?"

He nodded assent. And a heavy silence fell over the chamber of suffering. The night before, on his return from a party given by the Empress, he had received the letter Sabine had written her lover. After an atrocious night passed in the meditation of vengeance, he had gone out in the morning in order to resist a longing which prompted him to kill his wife. Outside, under a sudden sweet influence of a fine June morning, he had lost the thread of his thoughts, and had come to Nana's as he always came at terrible moments in his life.

There only he gave way to his misery, for he felt a cowardly joy at the thought that she would console him.

"Now look here, be calm!" the young woman continued, becoming at the same time extremely kind. "I've known it a long time, but it was certainly not I that would have opened your eyes. You remember you had your doubts last year, but then things arranged themselves owing to my prudence. In fact, you wanted proofs. The deuce you've got one to-day, and I know it's hard lines. Nevertheless, you must look at the matter quietly: you're not dishonoured because it's happened."

He had left off weeping. A sense of shame restrained him from saying what he wanted to, although he had long ago slipped into the most intimate confessions about his household. She had to encourage him. Dear me, she was a woman; she could understand everything. When in a dull voice he exclaimed,—

"You're ill. What's the good of tiring you? It was stupid of me to have come. I'm going——"

"No," she answered briskly enough. "Stay! Perhaps I shall be able to give you some good advice. Only don't make me talk too much: the medical man's forbidden it."

He had ended by rising, and he was now walking up and down the room. Then she questioned him.

"Now what are you going to do?"

"I'm going to box the man's ears— by heavens, yes!"

She pursed up her lips disapprovingly. "That's not very wise. And about your wife?"

"I shall go to law: I've proofs."

"Not at all wise, my dear boy. It's stupid even. You know I shall never let you do that!"

And in her feeble voice she shewed him decisively how useless and scandalous a duel and a trial would be. He would be a nine days' newspaper sensation—his whole existence would be at stake, his peace of mind, his high situation at Court, the honour of his name, and all for what? That he might have the laughers against him.

"What will it matter?" cried he. "I shall have had my revenge."

"My pet," said she, "in a business of that kind one never has one's revenge if one doesn't take it directly."

He paused and stammered. He was certainly no poltroon, but he felt that she was right. An uneasy feeling was growing momentarily stronger within him, a poor shameful feeling which softened his anger now that it was at its hottest. Moreover, in her frank desire to tell him everything, she dealt him a fresh blow.

"And d'you want to know what's annoying you, dearest? Why, that you are deceiving your wife yourself. You don't sleep away from home for nothing, eh? Your wife must have her suspicions. Well, then, how can you blame her? She'll tell you that you've set her the example, and that'll shut you up. There, now, that's why you're stamping about here instead of being at home murdering both of 'em."

Muffat had again sunk down on the chair; he was overwhelmed by these home thrusts. She broke off and took breath, and then in a low voice,—

"Oh, I'm a wreck! Do help me sit

up a bit. I keep slipping down, and my head's too low."

When he had helped her she sighed and felt more comfortable. And with that she harked back to the subject. What a pretty sight a divorce suit would be! Couldn't he imagine the advocate of the Countess amusing Paris with his remarks about Nana? Everything would have come out—her fiasco at the Variétés, her house, her manner of life. Oh, dear no! she had no wish for all that amount of advertising. Some dirty women might, perhaps, have driven him to it for the sake of getting a thundering big advertisement, but she—she desired his happiness before all else. She had drawn him down towards her, and, after passing her arm round his neck, was nursing his head close to hers, on the edge of the pillow. And with that she whispered softly:

"Listen, my pet, you shall make it up with your wife."

But he rebelled at this. It could never be! His heart was nigh breaking at the thought: it was too shameful. Nevertheless, she kept tenderly insisting.

"You shall make it up with your wife. Come, come, you don't want to hear all the world saying that I've tempted you away from you home? I should have too vile a reputation! What would people think of me? Only swear that you'll always love me, because the moment you go with another woman——"

Tears choked her utterance, and he intervened with kisses, and said,—

"You're beside yourself: it's impossible!"

"Yes, yes," she rejoined, "you must. But I'll be reasonable. After all, she's your wife, and it isn't as if you were to play me false with the first comer."

And she continued in this strain, giving him the most excellent advice. She even spoke of God, and the Count thought he was listening to Monsieur Venot, when that old gentleman endeavoured to sermonise him out of the grasp of sin. Nana, however, did not speak of breaking it off entirely: she preached indulgent good nature, and suggested that, as became a dear nice old fellow, he should divide his attentions between his wife and his mistress, so that they would all enjoy a quiet life, devoid of any kind of annoyance, something, in fact, in the nature of a happy slumber amid the inevitable miseries of existence. Their life would be nowise changed: he would still be the little man of her heart. Only he would come to her a bit less often and would give the Countess the nights not passed with her. She had got to the end of her strength, and left off speaking under her breath.

"After that, I shall feel I've done a good action, and you'll love me all the more."

Silence reigned. She had closed her eyes, and lay wan upon her pillow. The Count was patiently listening to her, not wishing her to tire herself. A whole minute went by before she reopened her eyes, and murmured,—

"Besides, how about the money? Where would you get the money from, if you must grow angry and go to law? Labordette came for the bill yesterday. As for me, I'm out of everything; I have nothing to put on now."

Then she shut her eyes again, and looked like one dead. A shadow of deep anguish had passed over Muffat's brow.

Under the present stroke, he had since yesterday forgotten the money troubles, from which he knew no how to escape. Despite formal promises to the contrary, the bill for a hundred thousand francs had been put in circulation after being once renewed, and Labordette, pretending to be very miserable about it, threw all the blame on Francis, declaring that he would never again mix himself up in such a matter with an uneducated man. It was necessary to pay, for the Count would never have allowed his signature to be protested. Then, in addition to Nana's novel demands, his home expenses were extraordinarily confused. On their return from The Fondettes, the Countess had suddenly manifested a taste for luxury, a longing for worldly pleasures, which was devouring their fortune. Her ruinous caprices began to be talked about. Their whole household management was altered, and five hundred thousand francs were squandered in utterly transforming the old house in the Rue Miromesnil. Then there were extravagantly magnificent gowns, and large sums disappeared, squandered, or perhaps given away, without her ever dreaming of accounting for them. Twice Muffat ventured to mention this, for he was anxious to know how the money went: but on these occasions she had smiled and gazed at him with so singular an expression that he dared not interrogate her further for fear of a too unmistakable answer. If he were taking Daguenet as son-in-law as a gift from Nana it was chiefly with the hope of being able to reduce Estelle's dower to two hundred thousand francs and of then being free to make any arrangements he chose about the remainder with a young man who was still rejoicing in this unexpected match.

Nevertheless for the last week, under the immediate necessity of finding Labordette's hundred thousand francs, Muffat had been able to hit on but one expedient, from which he recoiled. This was that he should sell the Bordes, a magnificent property, valued at half a million, which an uncle had recently left the Countess. However, her signature was necessary, and she herself, according to the terms of the deed, could not alienate the property without the Count's authorisation. The day before he had indeed resolved to talk to his wife about this signature. And now everything was ruined; at such a moment he would never accept of such a compromise. This reflection added bitterness to the frightful disgrace of the adultery. He fully understood what Nana was asking for, since in that ever-growing self-abandonment which prompted him to put her in possession of all his secrets, he had complained to her of his position, and had confided to her the tiresome difficulty he was in with regard to the signature of the Countess.

Nana, however, did not seem to insist. She did not open her eyes again; and seeing her so pale, he grew frightened and made her inhale a little ether. She gave a sigh, and, without mentioning Daguenet, asked him some questions.

"When is the marriage?"

"We sign the contract on Tuesday in five days' time," he replied.

Then, still keeping her eyelids closed as though she were speaking from the darkness and silence of her brain,—

"Well, then, pet, see to what you've got to do. As far as I'm concerned,

I want everybody to be happy and comfortable."

He took her hand and soothed her. Yes, he would see about it; the important thing now was for her to rest. And the revolt within him ceased, for this warm and slumbrous sick-room, with its all-pervading scent of ether, had ended by lulling him into a mere longing for happiness and peace. All his manhood, erewhile maddened by wrong, had departed out of him in the neighbourhood of that warm bed and that suffering woman, whom he was nursing under the influence of her feverish heat and of remembered delights. He leant over her and pressed her in a close embrace, whilst, despite her unmoved features, her lips wore a delicate victorious smile. But the Docteur Boutarel made his appearance.

"Well, and how's this dear child?" said he familiarly to Muffat, whom he treated as her husband. "The deuce but we've made her talk!"

The Doctor was a good-looking man, and still young. He had a superb practice among the gay world, and being very merry by nature, and ready to laugh and joke in the friendliest way with the *demi-monde* ladies, with whom however, he never went further, he charged very high fees and got them paid with the greatest punctuality. Moreover, he would put himself out to visit them on the most trivial occasions, and Nana, who was always trembling at the fear of death, would send and fetch him two or three times a week, and would anxiously confide to him little infantile ills which he would cure to an accompaniment of amusing gossip and harebrained anecdotes. The ladies all adored

him. But this time the little ill was serious.

Muffat withdrew deeply moved. Seeing his poor Nana so very weak, his sole feeling was now one of tenderness. As he was leaving the room she motioned him back, and gave him her forehead to kiss. In a low voice, and with a playfully-threatening look, she said,—

"You know what I've allowed you to do. Go back to your wife, or it's all over and I shall grow angry!"

The Countess Sabine had been anxious that her daughter's wedding contract should be signed on a Tuesday in order that the renovated house, where the paint was still scarcely dry, might be reopened with a grand entertainment. Five hundred invitations had been issued to people in all kinds of sets. On the morning of the great day the upholsterers were still nailing up hangings, and towards nine at night, just when the lustres were going to be lit, the architect, accompanied by the eager and interested Countess, was given his final orders.

It was one of those spring festivities which have a delicate charm of their own. Owing to the warmth of the June nights it had become possible to open the two doors of the great drawing-room and to extend the dancing floor to the sanded paths of the garden. When the first guests arrived and were welcomed at the door by the Count and the Countess, they were positively dazzled. One had only to recall to mind the drawing-room of the past, through which flitted the icy, ghostly presence of the Countess Muffat, that antique room full of an atmosphere of religious austerity with its massive First Empire mahogany furniture, its yellow velvet hangings, its mouldy ceiling through which the damp had soaked. Now from the very threshold of the entrance-hall, mosaics set off with gold were glittering under the lights of lofty candelabras, whilst the marble staircase unfurled, as it were, a delicately chiselled balustrade. Then, too, the drawing-room looked splendid; it was hung with Genoa velvet, and a huge decorative design by Boucher covered the ceiling, a design for which the architect had paid a hundred thousand francs at the sale of the Château de Dampierre. The lustres and the crystal ornaments lit up a luxurious display of mirrors and precious furniture. It seemed as though Sabine's long chair, that solitary red silk chair, whose soft contours were so marked in the old days, had grown and spread till it filled the whole great house with voluptuous idleness and a sense of tense enjoyment not less fierce and hot than a fire which has been long in burning up.

People were already dancing. The band, which had been located in the garden, in front of one of the open windows, was playing a waltz, the supple rhythm of which came softly into the house through the intervening night air. And the garden seemed to spread away and away, bathed in transparent shadow and lit by Venetian lamps, whilst in a purple tent, pitched on the edge of a lawn, a table for refreshments had been established. The waltz, which was none other than the quaint vulgar one in the *Blonde Venus*, with its laughing, blackguard lilt, penetrated the old hotel with sonorous waves of sound, and sent a feverish thrill along its walls. It was as though some fleshly wind had come up out of the common street and were sweeping the relics of a vanished epoch out of the proud old dwelling, bearing away the Muffats' past, the age of honour and religious faith which had long slumbered beneath the lofty ceilings.

Meanwhile, near the hearth, in their accustomed places, the old friends of the Count's mother were taking refuge. They felt out of their element—they were dazzled and they formed a little group amid the slowly-invading mob. Madame du Joncquoy, unable to recognise the various rooms, had come in through the dining-saloon. Madame Chantereau was gazing with a stupefied expression at the garden, which struck her as immense. Presently there was a sound of low voices, and the corner gave vent to all sorts of bitter reflections."

"I declare," murmured Madame Chantereau, "just fancy if the Countess were to return to life. Why, can you not imagine her coming in among all these crowds of people! And then there's all this gilding, and this uproar! It's scandalous!"

"Sabine's out of her senses," replied Madame du Joncquoy. "Did you see her at the door? Look, you can catch sight of her here; she's wearing all her diamonds."

For a moment or two they stood up in order to take a distant view of the Count and Countess. Sabine was in a white dress, trimmed with marvellous English point lace. She was triumphant in beauty; she looked young and gay, and there was a touch of intoxication in her continual smile. Beside her stood Muffat, looking aged and a little pale, but he too was smiling in his calm and worthy fashion.

"And just to think that he was once master," continued Madame Chantereau, "and that not a single rout seat would have come in without his permission! Ah well, she's changed all that; it's her house now. D'you remember when she did not want to do her drawing-room up again? She's done up the entire house."

But the ladies grew silent, for Madame de Chezelles was entering the room, followed by a band of young men. She was going into ecstasies, and marking her approval with a succession of little exclamations.

"Oh, it's delicious, exquisite! What taste!" And she shouted back to her followers:

"Didn't I say so? There's nothing equal to these old places when one takes them in hand. They become dazzling! It's quite in the grand seventeen century style. Well, *now* she can receive."

The two old ladies had again sat down, and with lowered tones began talking about the marriage, which was causing astonishment to a good many people. Estelle had just passed by them. She was in a pink silk gown, and was as pale, flat, silent, and virginal as ever. She had accepted Daguenet very quietly; and now evinced neither joy nor sadness, for she was still as cold and white as on those winter evenings when she used to put logs on the fire. This whole fête given in her honour, these lights and flowers and tunes, left her quite unmoved.

"An adventurer," Madame du Joncquoy was saying. "For my part I've never seen him."

"Take care, here he is," whispered Madame Chantereau.

Daguenet, who had caught sight of Madame Hugon and her sons, had eagerly offered her his arm. He laughed and was effusively affectionate towards her, as though she had had a hand in his sudden good fortune.

"Thank you," said she, sitting down near the fire-place. "You see it's my old corner."

"You know him?" queried Madame du Joncquoy, when Daguenet had gone.

"Certainly I do—a charming young man. Georges is very fond of him. Oh, they're a most respected family."

And the good lady defended him against the mute hostility which was apparent to her. His father, held in high esteem by Louis-Philippe, had been a *préfêt* up to the time of his death. The son had been a little dissipated, perhaps; they said he was ruined; but, in any case, one of his uncles, who was a great landowner, was bound to leave him his fortune. The ladies, however, shook their heads, whilst Madame Hugon, herself somewhat embarrassed, kept harking back to the extreme respectability of his family. She was very much fatigued, and complained of her feet. For some months she had been occupying her house in the Rue Richelieu, having, as she said, a whole lot of things on hand. A look of sorrow overshadowed her smiling, motherly face.

"Never mind," Madame Chantereau concluded, "Estelle could have aimed at something much better."

There was a flourish. A quadrille was about to begin, and the crowd flowed back to the sides of the drawing-room in order to leave the floor clear. Bright dresses flitted by and mingled together amid the dark evening coats, whilst the intense light set jewels flashing, and white plumes quivering, and lilacs and roses gleaming and flowering amid the sea of many heads. It was already very warm, and a penetrating perfume was exhaled from light tulles and crumpled silks and satins, from which bare shoulders glimmered white, whilst the orchestra played its lively airs. Through open doors ranges of seated ladies were visible in the background of adjoining rooms: they flashed a discreet smile, their eyes glowed, and they made pretty mouths as the breath of their fans caressed their faces. And guests still kept arriving, and a footman announced their names, whilst gentlemen advanced slowly amid the surrounding groups, striving to find places for ladies, who hung with difficulty on their arms, and stretching forward in quest of some far-off vacant arm-chair. The house kept filling, and crinolined skirts got jammed together with a little rustling sound. There were corners where an amalgam of laces, bunches, and puffs would completely bar the way, whilst all the other ladies stood waiting, politely resigned and imperturbably graceful, as became people who were made to take part in these dazzling crushes. Meanwhile, across the garden, couples, who had been glad to escape from the close air of the great drawing-room, were wandering away under the roseate gleam of the Venetian lamps, and shadowy dresses kept flitting along the edge of the lawn, as though in rhythmic time to the music of the quadrille, which sounded sweet and distant behind the trees.

Steiner had just met with Foucarmont and la Faloise, who were drinking a glass of champagne in front of the buffet.

"It's beastly smart," said la Faloise as he took a survey of the purple tent, which was supported by gilded lances. "You might fancy yourself at the Ginger-bread Fair. That's it?—the Ginger-bread Fair!"

In these days he continually affected a bantering tone, posing as the young man who has abused every mortal thing and now finds nothing worth taking seriously.

"How surprised poor Vandeuvres would be if he were to come back," murmured Foucarmont. "You remember how he simply nearly died of boredom in front of the fire in there. Egad, it was no laughing matter."

"Vandeuvres—oh, let him be. He's a gone coon!" la Faloise disdainfully rejoined. "He jolly well choused himself, he did, if he thought he could make us sit up with his roast meat story! Not a soul mentions it now. Blotted out, done for, buried—that's what's the matter with Vandeuvres! Here's to the next man!"

Then, as Steiner shook hands with him,—

"You know Nana's just arrived. Oh, my boys, it was a state entry. It was too brilliant for anything! First of all she kissed the Countess. Then, when the children came up, she gave them her blessing, and said to Daguenet,—'Listen, Paul, if you go running after the girls, you'll have to answer for it to me.' What, d'you mean to say you didn't see that? Oh, it *was* smart. A success, if you like!"

The other two listened to him open-mouthed, and at last burst out laughing. He was enchanted, and thought himself in his best vein.

"You thought it had really happened, eh? Confound it, since Nana's made the match! Any way, she's one of the family."

The young Hugons were passing, and Philippe silenced him. And with that they chatted about the marriage from the male point of view. Georges was vexed with la Faloise for telling an anecdote. Certainly, Nana had fubbed off on Muffat one of her old flames as son-in-law; only it was not true that she had been to bed with Daguenet as lately as yesterday. Foucarmont made bold to shrug his shoulders. Could anyone ever tell when Nana was in bed with anyone? But Georges grew excited, and answered with an "I can tell, sir!" which set them all laughing. In a word, as Steiner put it, it was all a very funny kettle of fish!

The buffet was gradually invaded by the crowd, and still keeping together they vacated their positions there. La Faloise stared brazenly at the women as though he, believed himself to be Mabille. At the end of a garden walk the little band was surprised to find Monsieur Venot busily conferring with Daguenet, and with that they indulged in some facile pleasantries which made them very merry. He was confessing him, giving him advice about the bridal night! Presently they returned in front of one of the drawing-room doors, within which a polka was sending the couples whirling to and fro till they seemed to leave a wake behind them among the crowd of men who remained standing about. In the slight puffs of air which came from outside, the tapers flared up brilliantly, and when a dress floated by in time to the rat-tat of the measure, a little gust of wind cooled the sparkling heat which streamed down from the lustres.

"Egad, they're not cold in there!" muttered la Faloise.

They blinked after emerging from the mysterious shadows of the garden. Then they pointed out to one another the Marquis de Chouard where he stood apart, his tall figure towering over the bare shoulders which surrounded him. His face was pale and very stern, and beneath its crown of scant white hair it wore an expression of lofty dignity. Scandalised by Count Muffat's conduct, he had publicly broken off all intercourse with him, and was by way of never again setting foot in the house. If he had consented to put in an appearance that evening it was because his granddaughter had begged him to. But he disapproved of her marriage, and had inveighed indignantly against the way in which the governing classes were being disorganised by the shameful compromises engendered by modern debauchery.

"Ah! it's the end of all things," Madame du Joncquoy whispered in Madame Chantereau's ear as she sat near the fireplace. "That bad woman has bewitched the unfortunate man. And to think we once knew him such a true believer, such a noble-hearted gentleman!"

"It appears he is ruining himself," continued Madame Chantereau. "My husband has had a bill of his in his hands. At present he's living in that house in the Avenue de Villiers; all Paris is talking about it. Good heavens! I don't make excuses for Sabine, but you must admit that he gives her infinite cause of complaint, and, dear me, if she throws money out of the window, too——"

"She does not only throw money," interrupted the other. "In fact, between them, there's no knowing where they'll stop; they'll end in the mire, my dear."

But just then a soft voice interrupted them. It was Monsieur Venot and he had come and seated himself behind them, as though anxious to disappear from view. Bending forward he murmured,—

"Why despair. God manifests Himself when all seems lost."

He was assisting peacefully at the downfall of the house which he erewhile governed. Since his stay at The Fondettes, he had been allowing the madness to increase, for he was very clearly aware of his own powerlessness. He had, indeed, accepted the whole position—the Count's wild passion for Nana, Fauchery's presence, even Estelle's marriage with Daguenet. What did these things matter? He even became more supple and mysterious, for he nursed a hope of being able to gain the same mastery over the young as over the disunited couple, and he knew that great disorders lead to great conversions. Providence would have its opportunity.

"Our friend," he continued in a low voice, "is always animated by the best religious sentiments. He has given me the sweetest proofs of this."

"Well," said Madame du Joncquoy, "he ought first to have made it up with his wife."

"Doubtless. At this moment I have hopes that the reconciliation will be shortly effected."

Whereupon the two old ladies questioned him.

But he grew very humble again. "Heaven," he said, "must be left to act." His whole desire in bringing the Count and the Countess together again was to avoid a public scandal, for religion tolerated many faults when the proprieties were respected.

"In fact," resumed Madame du Joncquoy, "you ought to have prevented this union with an adventurer."

The little old gentleman assumed an expression of profound astonishment.

"You deceive yourself. Monsieur Daguenet is a young man of the greatest merit. I am acquainted with his thoughts; he is anxious to live down the errors of his youth. Estelle will bring him back to the path of virtue, be sure of that."

"Oh, Estelle!" Madame Chantereau murmured disdainfully. "I believe the dear young thing to be incapable of willing anything; she is so insignificant!"

This opinion caused Monsieur Venot to smile. However, he went into no explanations about the young bride, and shutting his eyes, as though to avoid seeming to take any further interest in the matter, he once more lost himself in his corner behind the petticoats. Madame Hugon, though weary and absentminded, had caught some phrases of the conversation, and she now intervened, and summed up in her tolerant way by remarking to the Marquis de Chouard, who just then bowed to her,—

"These ladies are too severe. Existence is so bitter for every one of us! Ought we not to forgive others much, my friend, if we wish to merit forgiveness ourselves?"

For some seconds the Marquis appeared embarrassed, for he was afraid of allusions. But the good lady wore so sad a smile that he recovered almost at once, and remarked,—

"No; there is no forgiveness for certain faults. It is by reason of this kind of accommodating spirit that a society sinks into the abyss of ruin."

The ball had grown still more animated. A fresh quadrille was imparting a slight swaying motion to the drawing-room floor, as though the old dwelling had been shaken by the impulse of the dance. Now and again, amid the wan confusion of heads, a woman's face with shining eyes and parted lips stood sharply out, as it was whirled away by the dance, the light of the lustres gleaming on the white skin. Madame du Joncquoy declared that the present proceedings were senseless. It was madness to crowd five hundred people into a room which would scarcely contain two hundred. In fact, why not sign the wedding contract on the Place du Carrousel? This was the outcome of the new code of manners, said Madame Chantereau. In old times these solemnities took place in the bosom of the family; but to-day one must have a mob of people, the whole street must be allowed to enter quite freely, and there must be a great crush, or else the evening seems a chilly affair. People now advertised their luxury and introduced the mere foam on the wave of Parisian society into their houses, and accordingly it was only too natural if illicit proceedings such as they had been discussing afterwards polluted the hearth. The ladies complained that they could not recognise more than fifty people. Where

did all this crowd spring from? Young girls with low necks were making a great display of their shoulders. A woman had a golden dagger stuck in her chignon, whilst a bodice thickly embroidered with jet beads clothed her in what looked like a coat of mail. People's eyes kept following another lady smilingly, so singularly marked were her clinging skirts. All the luxuriant splendour of the departing winter was there—the over-tolerant world of pleasure, the scratch gathering a hostess can get together after a first introduction, the sort of society in fact, in which great names and great shames jostle together in the same fierce quest of enjoyment. The heat was increasing, and amid the over-crowded rooms the quadrille unrolled the cadenced symmetry of its figures.

"Very smart—the Countess!" la Faloise continued at the garden door. "She's ten years younger than her daughter. By-the-by, Foucarmont, you must decide on a point. Vandeuvres once betted that she had no thighs."

This affectation of cynicism bored the other gentlemen, and Foucarmont contented himself by saying,—

"Ask your cousin, dear boy. Here he is."

"Jove, it's a happy thought!" cried la Faloise. "I bet ten louis she has thighs."

Fauchery did indeed come up. As became a constant inmate of the house, he had gone round by the dining-room in order to avoid the crowded doors. Rose had taken him up again at the beginning of the winter, and he was now dividing himself between the singer and the Countess, but he was extremely fatigued, and did not know how to get rid of one of them. Sabine flattered his vanity, but Rose amused him more than she. Besides, the passion Rose felt was a real one: her tenderness for him was marked by a conjugal fidelity which drove Mignon to despair.

"Listen, we want some information," said la Faloise, as he squeezed his cousin's arm. "You see that lady in white silk."

Ever since his inheritance had given him a kind of insolent dash of manner, he had affected to chaff Fauchery, for he had an old grudge to satisfy, and wanted to be revenged for much bygone raillery, dating from the days when he was just fresh from his native province.

"Yes, that lady with the lace."

The journalist stood on tiptoe, for as yet he did not understand.

"The Countess?" he said at last.

"Exactly, my good friend. I've bet ten louis—now, has she thighs?"

And he fell a-laughing, for he was delighted to have succeeded in snubbing a fellow who had once come heavily down on him for asking whether the Countess slept with anyone. But Fauchery, without shewing the very slightest astonishment, looked fixedly at him.

"Get along, you idiot!" he said finally, as he shrugged his shoulders.

Then he shook hands with the other gentlemen, whilst la Faloise, in his discomfiture, felt rather uncertain whether he had said something funny. The men chatted. Since the races the banker and Foucarmont had formed part of the set in the Avenue de Villiers. Nana was going on much better, and every evening the Count came and asked how she did. Meanwhile, Fauchery, though he

listened, seemed preoccupied; for, during a quarrel that morning, Rose had roundly confessed to the sending of the letter. Oh, yes, he might present himself at his great lady's house: he would be well received! After long hesitation, he had come despite of everything—out of sheer courage. But la Faloise's imbecile pleasantry had upset him in spite of his apparent tranquillity.

"What's the matter?" asked Philippe. "You seem in trouble."

"I do? Not at all. I've been working: that's why I came so late."

Then coldly, in one of those heroic moods which, although unnoticed, are wont to solve the vulgar tragedies of existence,—

"All the same, I haven't made my bow to our hosts. One must be civil."

He even ventured on a joke, for he turned to la Faloise, and said,—

"Eh, you idiot?"

And with that he pushed his way through the crowd. The valet's full voice was no longer shouting out names, but, close to the door, the Count and Countess were still talking, for they were detained by ladies coming in. At length he joined them, whilst the gentlemen who were still on the garden steps stood on tiptoe so as to watch the scene. Nana, they thought, must have been chattering.

"The Count hasn't noticed him," muttered Georges. "Look out! He's turning round: there, it's done!"

The band had again taken up the waltz in the *Blonde Venus*. Fauchery had begun by bowing to the Countess, who was still smiling in ecstatic serenity. After which he had stood motionless a moment, waiting very calmly behind the

Count's back. That evening the Count's deportment was one of lofty gravity: he held his head high, as became the official and the great dignitary. And when at last he lowered his gaze in the direction of the journalist, he seemed still further to emphasize the majesty of his attitude. For some seconds the two men looked at one another. It was Fauchery who first stretched out his hand. Muffat gave him his. Their hands remained clasped, and the Countess Sabine with downcast eyes stood smiling before them, whilst the waltz continually beat out its mocking vagabond rhythm.

"But the thing's going on wheels!" said Steiner.

"Are their hands glued together?" asked Foucarmont, surprised at this prolonged clasp. A memory he could not forget brought a faint glow to Fauchery's pale cheeks, and in his mind's eye he saw the property-room bathed in greenish twilight and filled with dusty bric-à-brac. And Muffat was there, eggcup in hand, making a clever use of his suspicions. At this moment Muffat was no longer suspicious, and the last vestige of his dignity was crumbling in ruin. Fauchery's fears were assuaged, and when he saw the frank gaiety of the Countess he was seized with a desire to laugh. The thing struck him as comic.

"Ah ha, here she is at last!" cried la Faloise, who did not abandon a jest when he thought it a good one. "D'you see Nana coming in over there?"

"Hold your tongue, do, you idiot!" muttered Philippe.

"But I tell you it is Nana! They're playing her waltz for her, by Jove! She's making her entry. And she takes part

in the reconciliation, the devil she does! What? You don't see her! She's squeezing all three of 'em to her heart—my cousin Fauchery, my lady cousin, and her husband, and she's calling 'em her dear kitties. Oh, those family scenes give me a turn!"

Estelle had come up, and Fauchery complimented her whilst she stood stiffly up in her rose-coloured dress, gazing at him with the astonished look of a silent child, and constantly glancing aside at her father and mother. Daguenet, too, exchanged a hearty shake of the hand with the journalist. Together they made up a smiling group, whilst Monsieur Venot came gliding in behind them. He gloated over them with a beatified expression, and seemed to envelop them in his pious sweetness, for he rejoiced in these last instances of self-abandonment which were preparing the means of grace.

But the waltz still beat out its swinging, laughing, voluptuous measure; it was like a shrill continuation of the life of pleasure which was beating against the old house like a rising tide. The band blew louder trills from their little flutes; their violins sent forth more swooning notes. Beneath the Genoa velvet hangings, the gilding and the paintings, the lustres exhaled a living heat and a great glow of sunlight, whilst the crowd of guests, multiplied in the surrounding mirrors, seemed to grow and increase as the murmur of many voices rose ever louder. The couples who whirled round the drawing-room, arm about waist, amid the smiles of the seated ladies, still further accentuated the quaking of the floors. In the garden a dull fiery glow fell from the Venetian lanterns, and threw a distant reflection of flame over the dark shadows moving in search of a breath of air about the walks at its further end. And this trembling of walls, and this red glow of light, seemed to betoken a great ultimate conflagration in which the fabric of an ancient honour was cracking and burning on every side. The shy early beginnings of gaiety, of which Fauchery one April evening had heard the vocal expression in the sound of breaking glass, had little by little grown bolder, wilder, till they had burst forth in this festival. Now the rift was growing; it was crannying the house, and announcing approaching downfall. Among drunkards in the slums it is black misery, an empty cupboard, which put an end to ruined families; it is the madness of drink which empties the wretched beds. Here the waltz-tune was sounding the knell of an old race amid the suddenly-ignited ruins of accumulated wealth, whilst Nana, although unseen, stretched her lithe limbs above the dancers' heads, and sent corruption through their caste, drenching the hot air with the ferment of her exhalations and the vagabond lilt of the music.

On the evening after the celebration of the church marriage Count Muffat made his appearance in his wife's bedroom, where he had not entered for the last two years. At first, in her great surprise, the Countess drew back from him. But she was still smiling the intoxicated smile, which she now always wore. He began stammering in extreme embarrassment; whereupon she gave him a short moral lecture. However, neither of them risked a decisive explanation. It was religion, they pre-

tended, which required this process of mutual forgiveness, and they agreed by a tacit understanding to retain their freedom. Before going to bed, seeing that the Countess still appeared to hesitate, they had a business conversation, and the Count was the first to speak of selling the Bordes. She consented at once. They both stood in great want of money, and they would share and share alike. This completed the reconciliation, and Muffat, remorseful though he was, felt veritably relieved.

That very day, as Nana was dozing towards two in the afternoon, Zoé made so bold as to knock at her bedroom door. The curtains were drawn to, and a hot breath of wind kept blowing through a window into the fresh twilight stillness within. During these last days the young woman had been getting up and about again, but she was still somewhat weak. She opened her eyes, and asked,—

"Who is it?"

Zoé was about to reply, but Daguenet pushed by her, and announced himself in person. Nana forthwith propped herself up on her pillow, and, dismissing the lady's maid,—

"What! is that you?" she cried. "On the day of your marriage? What can be the matter?"

Taken aback by the darkness, he stood still in the middle of the room. However, he grew used to it, and came forward at last. He was in evening dress, and wore a white cravat and gloves.

"Yes, to be sure, it's me!" he said. "You don't remember?"

No, she remembered nothing, and in his chaffing way he had to offer himself frankly to her.

"Come now, here's your commission.

I've brought you the handsel of my innocence!"

And with that, as he was now by the bedside, she caught him in her bare arms, and shook with merry laughter, and almost cried, she thought it so pretty of him.

"Oh, that Mimi, how funny he is! He's thought of it after all! And to think I didn't remember it any longer! So you've slipped off: you're just out of church. Yes, certainly, you've got a scent of incense about you. But kiss me, kiss me! Oh, harder than that, Mimi dear! Bah! perhaps it's for the last time."

In the dim room, where a vague odour of ether still lingered, their tender laughter died away suddenly. The heavy, warm breeze swelled the window-curtains, and children's voices were audible in the Avenue without. Then the lateness of the hour tore them asunder and set them joking again. Daguenet took his departure with his wife directly after the breakfast.

## CHAPTER XIII

Towards the end of September Count Muffat, who was to dine at Nana's that evening, came at nightfall to inform her of a summons to the Tuileries. The lamps in the house had not been lit yet, and the servants were laughing uproariously in the kitchen regions, as he softly mounted the stairs where the tall windows gleamed in warm shadow. The door of the drawing-room upstairs opened noiselessly. A faint pink glow was dying out on the ceiling of the room, and the red hangings, the deep divans, the lacquered furniture, with their medley of embroidered fabrics, and bronzes and china, were already sleeping under a slowly-creeping flood of shadows, which drowned nooks and corners, and blotted out the gleam of ivory and the glint of gold. And there in the darkness, on the white surface of a wide outspread petticoat, which alone remained clearly visible, he saw Nana lying stretched in the arms of Georges. Denial in any shape or form was impossible. He gave a choking cry and stood gaping at them.

Nana had bounded up, and now she pushed him into the bedroom in order to give the lad time to escape.

"Come in," she murmured, with reeling senses, "I'll explain."

She was exasperated at being thus surprised. Never before had she given way like this in her own house, in her own drawing-room, when the doors were open. It was a long story: Georges and she had had a disagreement: he had been mad with jealousy of Philippe, and he had sobbed so bitterly on her bosom that she had yielded to him, not knowing how else to calm him, and really very full of pity for him at heart. And, on this solitary occasion, when she had been stupid enough to forget herself thus with a little rascal, who could not even now bring her bouquets of violets, so short did his mother keep him—on this solitary occasion, the Count turned up and came straight down on them. 'Gad, she had very bad luck! That was what one got if one was a good-natured wench!

Meanwhile in the bedroom, into which she had pushed Muffat, the darkness was complete. Whereupon, after some groping, she rang furiously and asked for a lamp. It was Julien's fault, too!

If there had been a lamp in the drawing-room, the whole affair would not have happened. It was the stupid nightfall which had got the better of her heart.

"I beseech you to be reasonable, my pet," said she, when Zoé had brought in the lights.

The Count, with his hands on his knees, was sitting gazing at the floor. He was stupefied by what he had just seen. He did not cry out in anger. He only trembled, as though overtaken by some horror which was freezing him. This dumb misery touched the young woman, and she tried to comfort him.

"Well, yes, I've done wrong. It's very bad what I did. You see I'm sorry for my fault. It makes me grieve very much because it annoys you. Come now, be nice, too, and forgive me."

She had crouched down at his feet, and was striving to catch his eye with a look of tender submission. She was fain to know whether he was very vexed with her. Presently, as he gave a long sigh and seemed to recover himself, she grew more coaxing, and with grave kindness of manner added a final reason:

"You see, dearie, you must try and understand how it is: I can't refuse it to my poor friends."

The Count consented to give way, and only insisted that Georges should be dismissed once for all. But all his illusions had vanished, and he no longer believed in her sworn fidelity. Next day Nana would deceive him anew, and he only remained her miserable possessor in obedience to a cowardly necessity and to terror at the thought of living without her.

This was the epoch in her existence when Nana flared upon Paris with redoubled splendour. She loomed larger than heretofore on the horizon of vice, and swayed the town with her impudently flaunted splendour, and that contempt of money, which made her openly squander fortunes. Her house had become a sort of glowing smithy, where her continual desires were the flames, and the slightest breath from her lips changed gold into fine ashes, which the wind hourly swept away. Never had eye beheld such a rage of expenditure. The great house seemed to have been built over a gulf, in which men—their worldly possessions, their fortunes, their very names—were swallowed up without leaving even a handful of dust behind them. This courtesan, who had the tastes of a parrot, and gobbled up radishes and burnt almonds, and pecked at the meat upon her plate, had monthly table-bills amounting to five thousand francs. The wildest waste went on in the kitchen: the place, metaphorically speaking, was one great river, which stove in cask upon cask of wine and swept great bills with it, swollen by three or four successive manipulators. Victorine and François reigned supreme in the kitchen, whither they invited friends. In addition to these, there was quite a little tribe of cousins, who were cockered up in their homes with cold meats and strong soup. Julien made the tradespeople give him commissions, and the glaziers never put up a pane of glass at a cost of a franc and a half but he had a franc put down to himself. Charles devoured the horses' oats, and doubled the amount of their provender, re-selling at the back door what came in at the carriage-gate; whilst, amid the general pillage, the sack of the town after the storm, Zoé, by dint of cleverness, succeeded in saving appearances, and covering the thefts of all in order the better to slur over and make good her own. But the household waste was worse than the household dishonesty. Yesterday's food was thrown into the gutter, and the collection of provisions in the house was such that the servants grew disgusted with it. The glass was all sticky with sugar, and the gas-burners flared and flared till the rooms seemed ready to explode. Then, too, there were instances of negligence and mischief and sheer accident—of everything, in fact, which can hasten the ruin of a house devoured by so many mouths. Upstairs, in *Madame's* quarters, destruction raged more fiercely still. Dresses, which cost ten thousand francs and had been twice worn, were sold by Zoé: jewels vanished as though they had crumbled deep down in their drawers; stupid purchases were made; every novelty of the day was brought, and left to lie forgotten in some corner the morning after, or swept up by rag-pickers in the street. She could not see any very expensive object without wanting to possess it, and so she constantly surrounded herself with the wrecks of bouquets, and costly knick-knacks, and was the happier the more her passing fancy cost. Nothing remained intact in her hands, she broke everything; and this object withered, and that grew dirty, in the clasp of her lithe white fingers. A perfect heap of nameless *débris,* of twisted shreds and muddy rags, followed her and marked her passage. Then, amid this utter squandering of pocket-money, cropped up a question about the big bills and

their settlement. Twenty thousand francs were due to the *modiste,* thirty thousand to the linen-draper, twelve thousand to the boot-maker. Her stable devoured fifty thousand for her, and in six months she ran up a bill of a hundred and twenty thousand francs at her ladies' tailor. Though she had not enlarged her scheme of expenditure, which Labordette reckoned at four hundred thousand francs on an average, she ran up that same year to a million. She was herself stupefied by the amount, and was unable to tell whither such a sum could have gone. Heaps upon heaps of men, barrowsful of gold, failed to stop up the hole, which, amid this ruinous luxury, continually gaped under the floor of her house.

Meanwhile Nana had cherished her latest caprice. Once more exercised by the notion that her room needed redoing, she fancied she had hit on something at last. The room should be done in velvet of the colour of tea-roses, with silver buttons, and golden cords, tassels and fringes, and the hangings should be caught up to the ceiling after the manner of a tent. This arrangement ought to be both rich and tender, she thought, and would form a splendid background to her blonde *vermeil*-tinted skin. However, the bedroom was only designed to serve as a setting to the bed, which was to be a dazzling affair, a prodigy. Nana meditated a bed such as had never before existed; it was to be a throne, an altar, whither Paris was to come in order to adore her sovran nudity. It was to be all in gold and silver beaten-work —it should suggest a great piece of jewellery with its golden roses climbing on a trellis-work of silver. On the headboard a band of Loves should peep forth laughing from amid the flowers as though they were watching the voluptuous dalliance within the shadow of the bed-curtains. Nana had applied to Labordette who had brought two goldsmiths to see her. They were already busy with the designs. The bed would cost fifty thousand francs, and Muffat was to give it her as a New Year's present.

What most astonished the young woman was that she was endlessly short of money amid a river of gold, the tide of which almost enveloped her. On certain days she was at her wit's end for want of ridiculously small sums—sums of only a few louis. She was driven to borrow from Zoé, or she scraped up cash as well as she could on her own account. But before resignedly adopting extreme measures, she tried her friends, and in a joking sort of way got the men to give her all they had about them, even down to their coppers. For the last three months she had been emptying Philippe's pockets especially, and now, on days of passionate enjoyment, he never came away but he left his purse behind him. Soon she grew bolder, and asked him for loans of two hundred francs, three hundreds francs—never more than that—wherewith to pay the interest of bills or to stave off outrageous debts. And Philippe, who in July had been appointed paymaster to his regiment, would bring the money the day after, apologising at the same time for not being rich, seeing that good mamma Hugon now treated her sons with singular financial severity. At the close of three months these little oft-renewed loans mounted up to a sum of ten thousand francs. The captain still laughed his hearty sounding laugh, but he was growing visibly thinner, and sometimes he seemed absent-minded, and a shade of suffering would pass over his face. But one look from Nana's eyes would transfigure him in a sort of sensual ecstasy. She had a very coaxing way with him and would intoxicate him with furtive kisses, and yield herself to him in sudden fits of self-abandonment, which tied him to her apron-strings the moment he was able to escape from his military duties.

One evening, Nana having announced that her name too was Thérèse, and that her fête-day was the fifteenth of October, the gentlemen all sent her presents. Captain Philippe brought his himself; it was an old comfit-dish in Dresden china, and it had a gold mount. He found her alone in her dressing-room. She had just emerged from the bath, had nothing on save a great red and white flannel bathing-wrap, and was very busy examining her presents, which were ranged on a table. She had already broken a rock-crystal flask in her attempts to un-stopper it.

"Oh, you're too nice!" said she. "What is it? Let's have a peep! What a baby you are to spend your pennies in little fakements like that!"

She scolded him, seeing that he was not rich, but at heart she was delighted to see him spending his whole substance for her. Indeed, this was the only proof of love which had power to touch her. Meanwhile, she was fiddling away at the comfit-dish, opening it and shutting it, in her desire to see how it was made.

"Take care," he murmured, "it's brittle."

But she shrugged her shoulders. Did he think her as clumsy as a street-porter? And all of a sudden the hinge came off between her fingers and the lid fell and was broken. She was stupefied, and remained gazing at the fragments, as she cried,—

"Oh, it's smashed!"

Then she burst out laughing. The fragments lying on the floor tickled her fancy. Her merriment was of the nervous kind, the stupid spiteful laughter of a child who delights in destruction. Philippe had a little fit of disgust, for the wretched girl did not know what anguish this curio had cost him. Seeing him thoroughly upset, she tried to contain herself.

"Gracious me, it isn't my fault! It was cracked; those old things barely hold together. Besides, it was the cover! Didn't you see the bound it gave?"

And she once more burst into uproarious mirth.

But, though he made an effort to the contrary, tears appeared in the young man's eyes and with that she flung her arms tenderly round his neck.

"How silly you are! You know I love you all the same. If one never broke anything the tradesmen would never sell anything. All that sort of thing's made to be broken. Now look at this fan; it's only held together with glue!"

She had snatched up a fan and was dragging at the blades so that the silk was torn in two. This seemed to excite her, and in order to shew that she scorned the other presents, the moment she had ruined his, she treated herself to a general massacre, rapping each successive object and proving clearly that not one was solid in that she had broken them all. There was a lurid glow in her

vacant eyes, and her lips, slightly drawn back, displayed her white teeth. Soon, when everything was in fragments, she laughed cheerily again, and with flushed cheeks beat on the table with the flat of her hands, lisping like a naughty little girl:

"All over! Got no more! Got no more!"

Then Philippe was overcome by the same mad excitement, and pushing her down he merrily kissed her bosom. She abandoned herself to him, and clung to his shoulders with such gleeful energy that she could not remember having enjoyed herself so much for an age past. Without letting go of him she said caressingly,—

"I say, dearie, you ought certainly to bring me ten louis to-morrow. It's a bore, but there's the baker's bill worrying me awfully."

He had grown pale. Then, imprinting a final kiss on her forehead, he said simply,—

"I'll try."

Silence reigned. She was dressing, and he stood pressing his forehead against the window-panes. A minute passed, and he returned to her and deliberately continued,—

"Nana, you ought to marry me."

This notion straightway so tickled the young woman that she was unable to finish tying on her petticoats.

"My poor pet, you're ill! D'you offer me your hand because I ask you for ten louis? No, never! I'm too fond of you. Good gracious, what a silly question!"

And, as Zoé entered in order to put her boots on, they ceased talking of the matter. The lady's maid at once espied the presents lying broken in pieces on the table. She asked if she should put those things away, and *Madame* having bidden her get rid of them, she carried the whole collection off in the folds of her dress. In the kitchen, a sorting-out process began, and *Madame's débris* were shared among the servants.

That day Georges had slipped into the house despite Nana's orders to the contrary. François had certainly seen him pass, but the servants had now got to laugh among themselves at their good lady's embarrassing situations. He had just slipped as far as the little drawing-room, when his brother's voice stopped him, and, as one powerless to tear himself from the door, he overheard everything that went on within, the kisses, the offer of marriage. A feeling of horror froze him, and he went away in a state bordering on imbecility, feeling as though there were a great void in his brain. It was only in his own room, above his mother's flat, in the Rue Richelieu, that his heart broke in a storm of furious sobs. This time there could be no doubt about the state of things; a horrible picture of Nana in Philippe's arms kept rising before his mind's eye. It struck him in the light of an incest. When he fancied himself calm again, the remembrance of it all would return, and in fresh access of raging jealousy he would throw himself on the bed, biting the coverlet, shouting infamous accusations which maddened him the more. Thus the day passed. In order to stay shut up in his room, he spoke of having a sick headache. But the night proved more terrible still; a murder-fever shook him amid continual nightmares. Had his brother lived in the house, he would have gone and killed him with the stab of a knife. When day returned he tried to reason things out. It was he who ought to die, and he determined to throw himself out of the window when an omnibus was passing. Nevertheless, he went out towards ten o'clock, and traversed Paris, wandered up and down on the bridges, and at the last moment felt an unconquerable desire to see Nana once more. With one word, perhaps, she would save him. And three o'clock was striking when he entered the house in the Avenue de Villiers.

Towards noon a frightful piece of news had simply crushed Madame Hugon. Philippe had been in prison since the evening of the previous day, accused of having stolen twelve thousand francs from the chest of his regiment. For the last three months he had been withdrawing small sums therefrom in the hope of being able to repay them, whilst he had covered the deficit with false money. Thanks to the negligence of the administrative committee, this fraud had been constantly successful. The old lady, humbled utterly by her child's crime, had at once cried out in anger against Nana. She knew Philippe's connection with her, and her melancholy had been the result of this miserable state of things, which kept her in Paris in constant dread of some final catastrophe. But she had never looked forward to such shame as this, and now she blamed herself for refusing him money, as though such refusal had made her accessory to his act. She sank down on an arm-chair; her legs were seized with paralysis, and she felt herself to be useless, incapable of action, and destined to stay where she was till she died. But the sudden thought of Georges comforted her. Georges was still left her; he would be able to act, perhaps to save them. Thereupon, without seeking aid of anyone else—for she wished to keep these matters shrouded in the bosom of her family—she dragged herself up to the next story, her mind possessed by the idea that she still had someone to love about her. But upstairs she found an empty room. The porter told her that Monsieur Georges had gone out at an early hour. The room was haunted by the ghost of yet another calamity; the bed with its gnawed bed-clothes bore witness to someone's anguish, and a chair, which lay amid a heap of clothes on the ground, looked like something dead. Georges must be at that woman's house; and so, with dry eyes and feet that had regained their strength, Madame Hugon went downstairs. She wanted her sons; she was starting to reclaim them.

Since morning Nana had been much worried. First of all it was the baker, who at nine o'clock had turned up bill in hand. It was a wretched story. He had supplied her with bread to the amount of a hundred and thirty-three francs, and, despite her royal housekeeping, she could not pay it. In his irritation at being put off, he had presented himself a score of times since the day he had refused further credit, and the servants were now espousing his cause. François kept saying that *Madame* would never pay him unless he made a fine scene; Charles talked of going upstairs, too, in order to get an old unpaid straw bill settled, whilst Victorine advised them to wait till some gentleman was with her, when they would get the money out of her by suddenly asking for it in the middle of conversation. The kitchen was in a savage mood—the tradesmen were all kept posted in the course events were taking, and there were gossiping consultations, lasting three or four hours on a stretch, during which *Madame* was stripped, plucked, and talked over with the wrathful eagerness peculiar to an idle, over-prosperous servants' hall. Julien, the house-steward, alone pretended to defend his mistress. She was quite the thing, whatever they might say! And when the others accused him of sleeping with her, he laughed fatuously, thereby driving the cook to distraction, for she would have liked to be a man in order to "spit on such women's backsides," so utterly would they have disgusted her. François, without informing *Madame* of it, had wickedly posted the baker in the hall, and when she came downstairs at lunch-time, she found herself face to face with him. Taking the bill, she told him to return towards three o'clock, whereupon, with many foul expressions, he departed, vowing that he would have things properly settled and get his money by hook or by crook.

Nana made a very bad lunch, for the scene had annoyed her. Next time the man would have to be definitely got rid of. A dozen times she had put his money aside for him, but it had as constantly melted away, sometimes in the purchase of flowers, at others in the shape of a subscription got up for the benefit of an old *gendarme*. Besides, she was counting on Philippe, and was astonished not to see him make his appearance with his two hundred francs. It was regular bad luck, seeing that the day before yesterday she had again given Satin an outfit, a perfect trousseau this time, some twelve hundred francs' worth of dresses and linen, and now she had not a louis remaining.

Towards two o'clock, when Nana was beginning to be anxious, Labordette presented himself. He brought with him the designs for the bed, and this caused a diversion, a joyful interlude which made the young woman forget all her troubles. She clapped her hands and danced about. After which, her heart bursting with curiosity, she leant over a table in the drawing-room, and examined the designs, which Labordette proceeded to explain to her.

"You see," said he, "this is the body of the bed. In the middle here, there's a bunch of roses in full bloom, and then comes a garland of buds and flowers. The leaves are to be in yellow and the roses in red gold. And here's the grand design for the bed's-head; Cupids dancing in a ring on a silver trellis-work."

But Nana interrupted him, for she was beside herself with ecstasy.

"Oh, how funny that little one is, that one in the corner, with his behind in the air! Isn't he now? And what a sly laugh! They've all got such dirty wicked eyes! You know, dear boy, I shall never dare play any silly tricks before *them!*"

Her pride was flattered beyond measure. The goldsmiths had declared that no queen anywhere slept in such a bed. However, a difficulty presented itself. Labordette showed her two designs for the foot-board, one of which reproduced the pattern on the sides, whilst the other, a subject by itself, represented Night wrapt in her veil, and discovered by a faun in all her splendid nudity. He added that, if she chose this last subject, the goldsmiths intended making Night in her own likeness. This idea, the taste of which was rather risky, made her grow white with pleasure, and she pictured herself as a silver statuette symbolic of the warm voluptuous delights of darkness.

"Of course you will only sit for the head and shoulders," said Labordette.

She looked quietly at him.

"Why? The moment a work of art's in question, I don't mind the sculptor that takes my likeness a blooming bit!"

Of course it must be understood that she was choosing the subject. But at this he interposed.

"Wait a moment; it's six thousand francs extra."

"It's all the same to me, by Jove!" cried she, bursting into a laugh. "Hasn't my little rough got the rhino?"

Nowadays among her intimates, she always spoke thus of Count Muffat, and the gentlemen had ceased to enquire after him otherwise.

"Did you see your little rough last night?" they used to say.

"Dear me, I expected to find the little rough here!"

It was a simple familiarity enough, which nevertheless she did not as yet venture on in his presence.

Labordette began rolling up the designs as he gave the final explanations. The goldsmiths, he said, were undertaking to deliver the bed in two months' time, towards the 25th of December, and next week a sculptor would come to make a model for the Night. As she accompanied him to the door, Nana remembered the baker, and briskly enquired:

"By-the-by, you wouldn't be having ten louis about you?"

Labordette made it a solemn rule, which stood him in good stead, never to lend women money. He used always to make the same reply.

"No, my girl, I'm short. But would you like me to go to your little rough?"

She refused; it was useless. Two days before she had succeeded in getting five thousand francs out of the Count. However, she soon regretted her discreet conduct, for the moment Labordette had gone the baker reappeared, though it was barely half-past two and with many loud oaths roughly settled himself on a bench in the hall. The young woman listened to him from the first floor. She was pale, and it caused her especial pain to hear the servants' secret rejoicings swelling up louder and louder till they even reached her ears. Down in the kitchen they were dying of laughter. The coachman was staring across from the other side of the court, François was crossing the hall without any apparent reason. Then he hurried off to report progress, after sneering knowingly at the baker. They didn't care a damn for *Madame:* the walls were echoing to their laughter, and she felt that she was deserted on all hands and despised by the servants' hall, the inmates of which were watching her every movement and liberally bespattering her with the filthiest of chaff. Thereupon she abandoned the intention of borrowing the hundred and thirty-three francs from Zoé; she already owed the maid money, and she was too proud to risk a refusal now. Such a burst of feeling stirred her that she

went back into her room, loudly remarking,—

"Come, come, my girl, don't count on anyone but yourself. Your body's your own property, and it's better to make use of it than to let yourself be insulted."

And without even summoning Zoé she dressed herself with feverish haste in order to run round to the Tricon's. In hours of great embarrassment this was her last resource. Much sought after and constantly solicited by the old lady, she would refuse or resign herself according to her needs; and on these increasingly frequent occasions when both ends would not meet in her royally-conducted establishment, she was sure to find twenty-five louis awaiting her at the other's house. She used to betake herself to the Tricon's with the ease born of use, just as the poor go to the pawnshop.

But as she left her own chamber Nana came suddenly upon Georges, standing in the middle of the drawing-room. Not noticing his waxen pallor and the sombre fire in his wide eyes, she gave a sigh of relief.

"Ah! you've come from your brother."

"No," said the lad, growing yet paler.

At this she gave a despairing shrug. What did he want? Why was he barring her way? She was in a hurry—yes, she was. Then, returning to where he stood,—

"You've no money, have you?"

"No."

"That's true. How silly of me! Never a stiver; not even their omnibus fares. Mamma doesn't wish it! Oh, what a set of men!"

And she escaped. But he held her back; he wanted to speak to her. She was fairly under way, and again declared she had no time, but he stopped her with a word.

"Listen; I know you're going to marry my brother."

Gracious! the thing was too funny! And she let herself down into a chair in order to laugh at her ease.

"Yes," continued the lad, "and I don't wish it. It's I you're going to marry. That's why I've come."

"Eh, what? You too?" she cried. "Why, it's a family disease, is it? No, never! What a fancy, to be sure! Have I ever asked you to do anything so nasty? Neither one nor t'other of you! No, never!"

The lad's face brightened. Perhaps he had been deceiving himself! He continued:

"Then swear to me that you don't go to bed with my brother."

"Oh, you're beginning to bore me now!" said Nana, who had risen with renewed impatience. "It's amusing for a little while, but when I tell you I'm in a hurry——! I go to bed with your brother if it pleases me. Are you keeping me—are you paymaster here, that you insist on my making a report? Yes, I go to bed with your brother."

He had caught hold of her arm, and squeezed it hard enough to break it, as he stuttered:

"Don't say that! Don't say that!"

With a slight blow she disengaged herself from his grasp.

"He's maltreating me now! Here's a young ruffian for you! My chicken, you'll leave this jolly sharp. I used to keep you about out of niceness. Yes, I did! You may stare! Did you think I was going to be your mammy till I

died? I've got better things to do than to bring up brats."

He listened to her stark with anguish, yet in utter submission. Her every word cut him to the heart so sharply that he felt he should die. She did not so much as notice his suffering, and continued delightedly to revenge herself on him for the annoyances of the morning.

"It's like your brother; he's another pretty Johnny, he is! He promised me two hundred francs. Oh, dear me; yes, I can wait for 'em. It isn't his money I care for! I've not got enough to pay for hair oil. Yes, he's leaving me in a jolly fix! Look here, d'you want to know how matters stand? Here goes, then: it's all owing to your brother that I'm going out to earn twenty-five louis with another man."

At these words his head spun, and he barred her egress. He cried, he besought her not to go, clasping his hands together, and blurting out:

"Oh no! oh no!"

"I want to, I do," said she. "Have you the money?"

No, he had not got the money. He would have given his life to have the money! Never before had he felt so miserable, so useless, so very childish. All his wretched being was shaken with weeping, and gave proof of such heavy suffering that at last she noticed it and grew kind. She pushed him away softly.

"Come, my pet, let me pass: I must. Be reasonable. You're a baby boy, and it was very nice for a week, but nowadays I must look after my own affairs. Just think it over a bit. Now, your brother's a man: what I'm saying doesn't apply to him. Oh, please do me a favour; it's no good telling him all this.

He needn't know where I'm going. I always let out too much when I'm in a rage."

She began laughing. Then taking him in her arms, and kissing him on the forehead,—

"Good-bye baby," she said; "it's over, quite over between us, d'you understand. And now I'm off!"

And she left him, and he stood in the middle of the drawing-room. Her last words rang like the knell of a tocsin in his ears: "It's over, quite over!" and he thought the ground was opening beneath his feet. There was a void in his brain, from which the man awaiting Nana had disappeared. Philippe alone remained there in the young woman's bare embrace, for ever and ever. She did not deny it: she loved him, since she wanted to spare him the pain of her infidelity. It was over, quite over. He breathed heavily, and gazed round the room, suffocating beneath a crushing weight. Memories kept recurring to him one after the other—memories of merry nights at The Mignotte, of amorous hours during which he had fancied himself her child, of pleasures stolen in this very room. And now these things would never, never recur! He was too small, he had not grown up quickly enough; Philippe was supplanting him because he was a bearded man. So then, this was the end; he could not go on living. His vicious passion had become transformed into an infinite tenderness, a sensual adoration, in which his whole being was merged. Then, too, how was he to forget it all if his brother remained —his brother, blood of his blood, a second self, whose enjoyment drove him

mad with jealousy? It was the end of all things; he wanted to die.

All the doors remained open, as the servants noisily scattered over the house, after seeing *Madame* make her exit on foot. Downstairs, on the bench in the hall, the baker was laughing with Charles and François. Zoé come running across the drawing-room and seemed surprised at sight of Georges. She asked him if he were waiting for *Madame*. Yes, he was waiting for her; he had forgotten to give her an answer to a question. And when he was alone, he set to work and searched. Finding nothing else to suit his purpose, he took up in the dressing-room a pair of very sharply-pointed scissors, with which Nana had a mania for ceaselessly trimming herself either by polishing her skin or cutting off little hairs. Then for a whole hour he waited patiently, his hand in his pocket, and his fingers tightly clasped round the scissors.

"Here's *Madame*," said Zoé returning. She must have espied her through the bedroom window.

There was a sound of people racing through the house, and laughter died away, and doors were shut. Georges heard Nana paying the baker, and speaking in the curtest way. Then she came upstairs.

"What, you're here still!" said she as she noticed him. "Ah ha! we're going to grow angry, my good man!"

He followed her as she walked towards her bedroom.

"Nana, will you marry me?"

She shrugged her shoulders. It was too stupid: she refused to answer any more, and conceived the idea of slamming the door in his face.

"Nana, will you marry me?"

She slammed the door. He opened it with one hand, whilst he brought the other and the scissors out of his pocket. And, with one great stab, he simply buried them in his breast.

Nana, meanwhile, had felt conscious that something dreadful would happen, and she had turned round. When she saw him stab himself she was seized with indignation.

"Oh, what a fool he is! what a fool! And with my scissors! Will you leave off, you naughty little rogue? Oh, my God! Oh, my God!"

She was scared. Sinking on his knees, the boy had just given himself a second stab, which sent him down at full length on the carpet. He blocked the threshold of the bedroom. With that Nana lost her head utterly, and screamed with all her might, for she dared not step over his body, which shut her in and prevented her from running to seek assistance.

"Zoé! Zoé! Come at once. Make him leave off. It's getting stupid—a child like that! He's killing himself now! And in my place too! Did you ever see the like of it!"

He was frightening her. He was all white, and his eyes were shut. There was scarcely any bleeding—only a little blood, a tiny stain which was oozing down into his waistcoat. She was making up her mind to step over the body, when an apparition sent her starting back. An old lady was advancing through the drawing-room door, which remained wide open opposite. And in her terror she recognized Madame Hugon, but could not explain her presence. Still wearing her gloves and hat, Nana

kept edging backwards, and her terror grew so great that she sought to defend herself, and in a shaky voice,—

"Madame," cried she, "it isn't I, I swear to you it isn't. He wanted to marry me, and I said no, and he's killed himself!"

Slowly Madame Hugon drew near—she was in black, and her face shewed pale under her white hair. In the carriage, as she drove thither, the thought of Georges had vanished, and that of Philippe's misdoing had again taken complete possession of her. It might be that this woman could afford explanations to the judges which would touch them, and so she conceived the project of begging her to bear witness in her son's favour. Downstairs, the doors of the house stood open, but as she mounted to the first floor her sick feet failed her, and she was hesitating as to which way to go when suddenly horror-stricken cries directed her. Then, upstairs, she found a man lying on the floor with blood-stained shirt. It was Georges—it was her other child.

Nana, in idiotic tones, kept saying,—

"He wanted to marry me, and I said no, and he's killed himself."

Uttering no cry, Madame Hugon stooped down. Yes, it was the other one, it was Georges. The one was brought to dishonour, the other murdered! It caused her no surprise, for her whole life was ruined. Kneeling on the carpet, utterly forgetting where she was, noticing no one else, she gazed fixedly at her boy's face, and listened with her hand on his heart. Then she gave a feeble sigh—she had felt the heart beating. And with that she lifted her head and scrutinised the room and the woman, and seemed to remember. A fire glowed forth in her vacant eyes, and she looked so great and terrible in her silence that Nana trembled as she continued to defend herself above the body that divided them.

"I swear it, *Madame!* If his brother were here, he could explain it to you."

"His brother has robbed—he is in prison," said the mother, in a hard voice.

Nana felt a choking sensation. Why, what was the reason of it all? The other had turned thief now! They were mad in that family! She ceased struggling in self-defence: she seemed no longer mistress in her own house, and allowed Madame Hugon to give what orders she liked. The servants had at last hurried up, and the old lady insisted on their carrying the fainting Georges down to her carriage. She preferred killing him rather than letting him remain in that house. With an air of stupefaction Nana watched the retreating servants as they supported poor dear Zizi by his legs and shoulders. The mother walked behind them in a state of collapse; she supported herself against the furniture; she felt as if all she held dear had vanished in the void. On the landing a sob escaped her: she turned, and twice ejaculated,—

"Oh, but you've done us infinite harm! You've done us infinite harm!"

That was all. In her stupefaction Nana had sat down: she still wore her gloves and her hat. The house once more lapsed into heavy silence; the carriage had driven away; and she sat motionless, not knowing what to do next, her head swimming after all she had gone through. A quarter of an hour later, Count Muffat found her thus, but at sight of him she relieved her feelings in an overflowing current of talk. She told him all about the sad incident, repeated the same details twenty times over, picked up the blood-stained scissors in order to imitate Zizi's gesture when he stabbed himself. And above all she nursed the idea of proving her own innocence.

"Look you here, dearie, is it my fault? If you were the judge, would you condemn me? I certainly didn't tell Philippe to meddle with the till any more than I urged that wretched boy to kill himself. I've been most unfortunate throughout it all. They come and do stupid things in my place, they make me miserable, they treat me like a hussy."

And she burst into tears. A fit of nervous expansiveness rendered her soft and doleful, and her immense distress melted her utterly.

"And you, too, look as if you weren't satisfied. Now do just ask Zoé if I'm at all mixed up in it. Zoé, do speak: explain to *Monsieur*——"

The lady's maid, having brought a towel and a basin of water out of the dressing-room, had for some moments past been rubbing the carpet in order to remove the blood-stains before they dried.

"Oh, *Monsieur*," she declared, "*Madame* is utterly miserable!"

Muffat was still stupefied; the tragedy had frozen him, and his imagination was full of the mother weeping for her sons. He knew her greatness of heart, and pictured her in her widow's weeds, withering solitarily away at The Fondettes. But Nana grew ever more despondent, for now the memory of Zizi, lying stretched on the floor, with a red hole in his shirt, almost drove her senseless.

"He used to be such a darling, so sweet and caressing. Oh, you know, my pet —I'm sorry if it vexes you—I loved that baby! I can't help saying so: the words must out. Besides, now it ought not to hurt you at all. He's gone. You've got what you wanted: you're quite certain never to surprise us again."

And this last reflection tortured her with such regret that he ended by turning comforter. Well, well, said he, she ought to be brave; she was quite right, it wasn't her fault! But she checked her lamentations of her own accord in order to say,—

"Listen, you must run round and bring me news of him. At once! I wish it!"

He took his hat and went to get news of Georges. When he returned, after some three quarters of an hour, he saw Nana leaning anxiously out of a window; and he shouted up to her from the pavement that the lad was not dead, and that they even hoped to bring him through. At this she immediately exchanged grief for excess of joy, and began to sing, and dance, and vote existence delightful. Zoé, meanwhile, was still dissatisfied with her washing. She kept looking at the stain, and every time she passed it she repeated,—

"You know it's not gone yet, Madame."

As a matter of fact, the pale red stain kept reappearing on one of the white roses in the carpet pattern. It was as though, on the very threshold of the room, a splash of blood were barring the doorway.

"Bah!" said the joyous Nana, "that'll be rubbed out under people's feet."

After the following day, Count Muffat had likewise forgotten the incident. For a moment or two, when in the cab which drove him to the Rue Richelieu, he had busily sworn never to return to that woman's house. Heaven was warning him; the misfortunes of Philippe and Georges were, he opined, prophetic of his proper ruin. But neither the sight of Madame Hugon in tears, nor that of the boy burning with fever, had been strong enough to make him keep his vow, and the short-lived horror of the situation had only left behind it a sense of secret delight at the thought that he was now well quit of a rival, the charm of whose youth had always exasperated him. His passion had by this time grown exclusive; it was, indeed, the passion of a man who has had no youth. He loved Nana as one who yearned to be her sole possessor, to listen to her, to touch her, to be breathed on by her. His was now a super-sensual tenderness, verging on pure sentiment; it was an anxious affection, and as such was jealous of the past, and apt at times to dream of a day of redemption and pardon received, when both should kneel before God the Father. Every day, religion kept regaining its influence over him. He again became a practising Christian; he confessed himself and communicated, whilst a ceaseless struggle raged within him, and remorse redoubled the joys of sin and of repentance. Afterwards, when his director gave him leave to spend his passion, he had made a habit of this daily perdition, and would redeem the same by ecstasies of faith, which were full of pious humility. Very naïvely he offered Heaven, by way of expiatory anguish, the abominable torment from which he was suffering. This torment grew and increased, and he would climb his Calvary with the deep and solemn feelings of a believer, though steeped in a harlot's fierce sensuality. That which made his agony most poignant was this woman's continued faithlessness. He could not share her with others, nor did he understand her imbecile caprices. Undying, unchanging love was what he wished for. However, she had sworn, and he paid her as having done so. But he felt that she was untruthful, incapable of common fidelity, apt to yield to friends, to stray passersby, like a good-natured animal, born to live minus a shift.

One morning when he saw Foucarmont emerging from her bedroom at an unusual hour, he made a scene about it. But, in her weariness of his jealousy, she grew angry directly. On several occasions ere that she had behaved rather prettily. Thus the evening when he surprised her with Georges she was the first to regain her temper and to confess herself in the wrong. She had loaded him with caresses and dosed him with soft speeches in order to make him swallow the business. But he had ended by boring her to death with his obstinate refusals to understand the feminine nature, and now she was brutal.

"Very well, yes! I've slept with Foucarmont. What then? That's flattened you out a bit, my little rough, hasn't it?"

It was the first time she had thrown "my little rough" in his teeth. The frank directness of her avowal took his breath away; and when he began clench-ing his fists, she marched up to him, and looked him full in the face.

"We've had enough of this, eh? If it doesn't suit you, you'll do me the pleasure of leaving the house. I don't want you to go yelling in my place. Just you get it into your noodle that I mean to be quite free. When a man pleases me I go to bed with him. Yes, I do—that's my way! And you must make up your mind directly. Yes or no! If it's no, out you may walk!"

She had gone and opened the door, but he did not leave. That was her way now of binding him more closely to her. For no reason whatever, at the slightest approach to a quarrel, she would tell him he might stop or go, as he liked; and she would accompany her permission with a flood of odious reflections. She said she could always find better than he; she had only too many from whom to choose; men in any quantity could be picked up in the street, and men a good deal smarter too, whose blood boiled in their veins. At this he would hang his head, and wait for those gentler moods when she wanted money. She would then become affectionate, and he would forget it all, one night of tender dalliance making up for the tortures of a whole week. His reconciliation with his wife had rendered his home unbearable. Fauchery, having again fallen under Rose's dominion, the Countess was running madly after other loves. She was entering on the forties, that restless, feverish time in the life of women, and ever hysterically nervous, she now filled her mansion with the maddening whirl of her fashionable life. Estelle, since her marriage, had seen nothing of her father: the undeveloped, insignificant girl had suddenly become a woman of iron will, so imperious withal that Daguenet trembled in her presence. In these days he accompanied her to mass: he was converted, and he raged against his father-in-law for ruining them with a courtesan. Monsieur Venot alone still remained kindly inclined towards the Count, for he was biding his time. He had even succeeded in getting into Nana's immediate circle. In fact he frequented both houses, where you encountered his continual smile behind doors. So Muffat, wretched at home, driven out by ennui and shame, still preferred to live in the Avenue de Villiers, even though he was abused there.

Soon there was but one question between Nana and the Count, and that was "money." One day, after having formally promised her ten thousand francs, he had dared keep his appointment empty-handed. For two days past she had been surfeiting him with love, and such a breach of faith, such a waste of caresses, made her ragingly abusive. She was white with fury.

"So you've not got the money, eh? Then go back where you came from, my little rough, and look sharp about it! There's a bloody fool for you! He wanted to kiss me again! Mark my words—no money, no nothing!"

He explained matters; he would be sure to have the money the day after to-morrow. But she interrupted him violently:

"And my bills! They'll sell me up while Monsieur's playing the fool. Now then, look at yourself. D'ye think I love you for your figure? A man with a mug like yours has to pay the women who are kind enough to put up with him.

By God, if you don't bring me that ten thousand francs to-night, you shan't even have the tip of my little finger to suck. I mean it! I shall send you back to your wife!"

At night he brought the ten thousand francs. Nana put up her lips, and he took a long kiss which consoled him for the whole day of anguish. What annoyed the young woman was to have him continually tied to her apron strings. She complained to Monsieur Venot, begging him to take her little rough off to the Countess. Was their reconciliation good for nothing, then? She was sorry she had mixed herself up in it, since, despite everything, he was always at her heels. On the days when, out of anger, she forgot her own interest, she swore to play him such a dirty trick that he would never again be able to set foot in her place. But when she slapped her leg and yelled at him, she might quite as well have spat in his face too: he would still have stayed and even thanked her. Then the rows about money matters kept continually recurring. She demanded money savagely; she rowed him over wretched little amounts; she was odiously stingy with every minute of her time; she kept fiercely informing him that she slept with him for his money, not for any other reasons, and that she did not enjoy it a bit; that, in fact, she loved another and was awfully unfortunate in needing an idiot of his sort! They did not even want him at Court now, and there was some talk of requiring him to send in his resignation. The Empress had said,— "He is too disgusting." It was true enough. So Nana repeated the phrase by way of closure to all their quarrels.

"Look here! You disgust me!"

Nowadays she no longer minded her p's and q's; she had regained the most perfect freedom.

Every day she did her round of the lake, beginning acquaintanceships which ended elsewhere. Here was the happy hunting ground *par excellence,* where courtesans of the first water spread their nets in open daylight, and flaunted themselves amid the tolerating smiles and brilliant luxury of Paris. Duchesses pointed her out to one another with a passing look—rich shopkeepers' wives copied the fashion of her hats. Sometimes her landau, in its haste to get by, stopped a file of puissant turn-outs, wherein sat plutocrats able to buy up all Europe, or cabinet ministers with plump fingers tight-pressed to the throat of France. She belonged to this Bois society, occupied a prominent place in it, was known in every capital, and asked about by every foreigner. The splendours of this crowd were enhanced by the madness of her profligacy as though it were the very crown, the darling passion, of the nation. Then there were unions of a night, continual passages of desire, which she lost count of the morning after, and these sent her touring through the grand restaurants, and on fine days, as often as not, to "Madrid." The staffs of all the embassies visited her, and she, Lucy Stewart, Caroline Héquet, and Maria Blond would dine in the society of gentlemen who murdered the French language and paid to be amused, engaging them by the evening with orders to be funny, and yet proving so *blasés* and so worn-out that they never

even touched them. This the ladies called "going on a spree," and they would return home happy at having been despised, and would finish the night in the arms of the lovers of their choice.

When she did not actually throw the men at his head, Count Muffat pretended not to know about all this. However, he suffered not a little from the lesser indignities of their daily life. The mansion in the Avenue de Villiers was becoming a hell, a house full of mad people, in which every hour of the day wild disorders led to hateful complications. Nana even fought with her servants. One moment she would be very nice with Charles, the coachman. When she stopped at a restaurant she would send him out beer by the waiter, and would talk with him from the inside of her carriage when he slanged the cabbies at a block in the traffic, for then he struck her as funny, and cheered her up. Then, the next moment, she called him a fool for no earthly reason. She was always squabbling over the straw, the bran, or the oats; in spite of her love for animals she thought her horses ate too much. Accordingly, one day, when she was settling up, she accused the man of robbing her. At this Charles got in a rage and called her a whore right out; his horses, he said, were distinctly better than she was, for they did not sleep with everybody. She answered him in the same strain, and the Count had to separate them and give the coachman the sack. This was the beginning of a rebellion among the servants. When her diamonds had been stolen, Victorine and François left. Julien himself disappeared; and the tale ran that the master had given him a big bribe, and had begged him to go, because he slept with the mistress. Every week there were new faces in the servants' hall. Never was there such a mess; the house was like a passage down which the scum of the registry offices galloped, destroying everything in their path. Zoé alone kept her place; she always looked clean, and her only anxiety was how to organise this riot until she had got enough together to set up on her own account in fulfilment of a plan she had been hatching for some time past.

These, again, were only the anxieties he could own to. The Count put up with the stupidity of Madame Maloir, playing bézique with her in spite of her musty smell. He put up with Madame Lerat and her encumbrances, with Louiset and the mournful complaints peculiar to a child who is being eaten up with the rottenness inherited from some unknown father. But he spent hours worse than these. One evening he had heard Nana angrily telling her maid that a man pretending to be rich had just swindled her—a handsome man calling himself an American, and owning gold mines in his own country, a beast who had gone off while she was asleep without giving her a copper, and had even taken a packet of cigarette papers with him. The Count had turned very pale, and had gone downstairs again on tiptoe so as not to hear more. But later he had to hear all. Nana having been smitten with a baritone in a music-hall and having been thrown over by him, wanted to commit suicide during a fit of sentimental melancholia. She swallowed a glass of water, in which she had soaked a box of matches. This made her terribly sick, but did not kill her. The Count had to nurse her, and to listen to the whole story of her passion, her tearful protests, and her oaths never to take to any man again. In her contempt for those swine, as she called them, she could not, however, keep her heart free, for she always had some sweetheart round her, and her exhausted body inclined to incomprehensible fancies and perverse tastes. As Zoé designedly relaxed her efforts, the service of the house had got to such a pitch that Muffat did not dare to push open a door, to pull a curtain, or to unclose a cupboard. The bells did not ring; men lounged about everywhere, and at every moment knocked up against one another. He had now to cough before entering a room, having almost caught the girl hanging round Francis' neck one evening that he had just gone out of the dressing-room for two minutes to tell the coachman to put the horses to, whilst her hairdresser was finishing her hair. She gave herself up suddenly behind his back; she took her pleasure in every corner, quickly, with the first man she met. Whether she was in her chemise or in full dress did not matter. She would come back to the Count red all over, happy at having cheated him. As for him, he was plagued to death; it was an abominable infliction!

In his jealous anguish the unhappy man was comparatively at peace when he left Nana and Satin alone together. He would have willingly urged her on to this vice, to keep the men off her. But all was spoilt in this direction, too. Nana deceived Satin as she deceived the Count, going mad over some monstrous fancy or other, and picking up girls at the street corners. Coming back in her carriage, she would suddenly be taken with a little slut that she saw on the pavement; her senses would be captivated; her imagination excited. She would take the little slut in with her, pay her, and send her away again. Then, disguised as a man, she would go to infamous houses, and look on at scenes of debauch to while away hours of boredom. And Satin, angry at being thrown over every moment, would turn the house topsy-turvy with the most awful scenes. She had at last acquired a complete ascendancy over Nana, who now respected her. Muffat even thought of an alliance between them. When he dared not say anything, he let Satin loose. Twice she had compelled her darling to take up with him again; whilst he shewed himself obliging, and effaced himself in her favour at the least sign. But this good understanding lasted no time, for Satin, too, was a little cracked. On certain days she would very nearly go mad, and would smash everything, wearing herself out in tempest of love and anger, but pretty all the time. Zoé must have excited her, for the maid took her into corners as if she wanted to tell her about her great design of which she as yet spoke to no one.

At times, however, Count Muffat was still singularly revolted. He who had tolerated Satin for months, who had at last shut his eyes to the unknown herd of men that scampered so quickly through Nana's bedroom, became terribly enraged at being deceived by one of his own set, or even by an acquaintance. When she confessed her relations with Foucarmont, he suffered so acutely, he thought the treachery of the young man so base, that he wished to insult

him and fight a duel. As he did not know where to find seconds for such an affair, he went to Labordette. The latter, astonished, could not help laughing.

"A duel about Nana? But, my dear sir, all Paris would be laughing at you. Men do not fight for Nana; it would be ridiculous."

The Count grew very pale, and made a violent gesture.

"Then I shall slap his face in the open street."

For an hour Labordette had to argue with him. A blow would make the affair odious; that evening everyone would know the real reason of the meeting; it would be in all the papers. And Labordette always finished with the same expression:

"It is impossible; it would be ridiculous."

Each time Muffat heard these words they seemed sharp and keen as a stab. He could not even fight for the woman he loved; people would have burst out laughing. Never before had he felt more bitterly the misery of his love, the contrast between his heavy heart and the absurdity of this life of pleasure in which it was now lost. This was his last rebellion; he allowed Labordette to convince him, and he was present afterwards at the procession of his friends, who lived there as if at home.

Nana in a few months finished them up greedily, one after the other. The growing needs, entailed by her luxurious way of life, only added fuel to her desires, and she finished a man up at one mouthful. First she had Foucarmont, who did not last a fortnight. He was thinking of leaving the Navy, having saved about thirty thousand francs, in his ten years of service, which he wished to invest in the United States. His instincts, which were prudential, even miserly, were conquered; he gave her everything, even his signature to notes of hand, which pledged his future. When Nana had done with him he was penniless. But then she proved very kind, she advised him to return to his ship. What was the good of getting angry? Since he had no money, their relations were no longer possible. He ought to understand that, and to be reasonable. A ruined man fell from her hands like a ripe fruit, to rot on the ground by himself.

Then Nana took up with Steiner, without disgust but without love. She called him a dirty Jew; she seemed to be paying back an old grudge, of which she had no distinct recollection. He was fat; he was stupid, and she got him down and took two bites at a time in order the quicker to do for this Prussian. As for him, he had thrown Simonne over. His Bosphorous scheme was getting shaky, and Nana hastened the downfall by wild expenses. For a month he struggled on, doing miracles of finance. He filled Europe with posters, advertisements, and prospectuses of a colossal scheme, and obtained money from the most distant climes. All these savings, the pounds of speculators, and the pence of the poor, were swallowed up in the Avenue de Villiers. Again he was partner in an iron works in Alsace; where, in a small provincial town, workmen, blackened with coal dust and soaked with sweat, day and night strained their sinews and heard their bones crack to satisfy Nana's pleasures. Like a huge fire, she devoured all the fruits of stock-exchange swindling and the profits of labour. This time she did for Steiner; she brought him to the ground, sucked him dry to the core, left him so cleaned out that he was unable to invent a new roguery. When his bank failed, he stammered and trembled at the idea of prosecution. His bankruptcy had just been published, and the simple mention of money flurried him, and threw him into a childish embarrassment. And this was he who had played with millions. One evening, at Nana's, he began to cry and asked her for a loan of a hundred francs wherewith to pay his maid-servant. And Nana, much affected and amused at the end of this terrible old man, who had squeezed Paris for twenty years, brought it to him and said,—

"I say, I'm giving it you because it seems so funny! But, listen to me, my boy, you are too old for me to keep. You must find something else to do."

Then Nana started on la Faloise at once. He had for some time been longing for the honour of being ruined by her in order to put the finishing stroke on his smartness. He needed a woman to launch him properly; it was the one thing still lacking. In two months all Paris would be talking of him, and he would see his name in the papers. Six weeks were enough. His inheritance was in landed estate, houses, fields, woods and farms. He had to sell all, one after the other, as quickly as he could. At every mouthful Nana swallowed an acre. The foliage trembling in the sunshine, the wide fields of ripe grain, the vineyards so golden in September, the tall grass in which the cows stood knee-deep, all passed through her hands as if engulfed by an abyss. Even fishing rights, a stone quarry, and three mills disappeared. Nana passed over them like an invading army, or one of those swarms of locusts whose flight scours a whole province. The ground was burnt up where her little foot had rested. Farm by farm, field by field, she ate up the man's patrimony very prettily and quite inattentively, just as she would have eaten a box of sweetmeats flung into her lap between mealtimes. There was no harm in it all; they were only sweets! But at last, one evening, there only remained a single little wood. She swallowed it up disdainfully, as it was hardly worth the trouble opening one's mouth for. La Faloise laughed idiotically and sucked the top of his stick. His debts were crushing him, he was not worth a hundred francs a year, and he saw that he would be compelled to go back into the country and live with his maniacal uncle. But that did not matter; he had achieved smartness; the *Figaro* had printed his name twice. And with his meagre neck sticking up between the turn-down points of his collar, and his figure squeezed into all too short a coat, he would swagger about, uttering his parrot-like exclamations and affecting a solemn listlessness suggestive of an emotionless marionette. He so annoyed Nana that she ended by beating him.

Meanwhile Fauchery had returned; his cousin having brought him. Poor Fauchery had now set up housekeeping. After having thrown over the Countess, he had fallen into Rose's hands, and she treated him as a lawful wife would have done. Mignon was simply *Madame's* major-domo. Installed as master of the house, the journalist lied to Rose, and took all sorts of precautions when he deceived her. He was as scrupulous as a good husband, for he really wanted to settle down at last. Nana's triumph consisted in possessing and in ruining a newspaper that he had started with a friend's capital. She did not proclaim her triumph; on the contrary, she delighted in treating him as a man who had to be circumspect; and when she spoke of Rose it was as "poor Rose." The newspaper kept her in flowers for two months. She took all the provincial subscriptions; in fact she took everything, from the column of news and gossip down to the dramatic notes. Then, the editorial staff having been turned topsy-turvy and the management completely disorganised, she satisfied a fanciful caprice and had a winter garden constructed in a corner of her house: that carried off all the type. But then it was no joke after all! When, in his delight at the whole business, Mignon came to see if he could not saddle Fauchery on her altogether, she asked him if he took her for a fool. A penniless fellow living by his articles and his plays—not if she knew it! That sort of foolishness might be all very well for a clever woman like her poor dear Rose! She grew distrustful: she feared some treachery on Mignon's part, for he was quite capable of preaching to his wife, and so she gave Fauchery his *congé* as he now only paid her in fame.

But she always recollected him kindly. They had both enjoyed themselves so much at the expense of that fool of a la Faloise! They would never have thought of seeing each other again if the delight of fooling such a perfect idiot had not egged them on! It seemed an

awfully good joke to kiss each other under his very nose. They cut a regular
dash with his coin; they would send him
off full speed to the other end of Paris
in order to be alone, and then, when he
came back, they would crack jokes and
make allusions he could not understand.
One day, urged by the journalist, she bet
that she would smack his face, and that
she did the very same evening, and went
on to harder blows, for she thought it a
good joke, and was glad of the opportunity of shewing how cowardly men
were. She called him her "slapjack,"
and would tell him to come and have his
smack! The smacks made her hands
red, for as yet she was not up to the
trick. La Faloise laughed in his idiotic,
languid way, though his eyes were full
of tears. He was delighted at such
familiarity; he thought it simply stunning.

One night when he had received sundry cuffs, and was greatly excited,—

"Now, d'you know," said he, "you
ought to marry me. We should be as
jolly as grigs together, eh?"

This was no empty suggestion. Seized
with a desire to astonish Paris, he had
been slyly projecting this marriage.
"Nana's husband! Wouldn't that sound
smart, eh?" Rather a stunning apotheosis that! But Nana gave him a fine
snubbing.

"Me marry you! Lovely! If such an
idea had been tormenting me, I should
have found a husband a long time ago!
And he'd have been a man worth twenty
of you, my pippin! I've had a heap
of proposals. Why look here, just
reckon 'em up with me: Philippe,
Georges, Foucarmont, Steiner — that
makes four, without counting the others

you don't know. It's a chorus they all
sing. I can't be nice but they forthwith begin yelling, 'Will you marry me?
Will you marry me?' "

She lashed herself up, and then burst
out in fine indignation.

"Oh, dear no! I don't want to!
D'you think I'm built that way? Just
look at me a bit! Why I shouldn't be
Nana any longer if I fastened a man on
behind! And, besides, it's too foul!"

And she spat and hiccoughed with
disgust, as though she had seen all the
dirt in the world spread out beneath
her.

One evening la Faloise vanished, and
a week later it became known that he
was in the country with an uncle whose
mania was botany. He was pasting his
specimens for him, and stood a chance
of marrying a very plain pious cousin.
Nana shed no tears for him. She simply
said to the Count,—

"Eh, little rough, another rival less!
You're chortling to-day. But he was
becoming serious! He wanted to marry
me."

He waxed pale, and she flung her arms
round his neck and hung there laughing,
whilst she emphasised every little cruel
speech with a caress.

"You can't marry Nana! Isn't that
what's fetching you, eh? When they're
all bothering me with their marriages,
you're raging in your corner. It isn't
possible; you must wait till your wife
kicks the bucket. Oh! if she were only
to do that, how you'd come rushing
round! How you'd fling yourself on the
ground and make your offer with all the
grand accompaniments—sighs, and tears,
and vows! Wouldn't it be nice, darling,
eh?"

Her voice had become soft, and she was chaffing him in a ferociously wheedling manner. He was deeply moved, and began blushing as he paid her back her kisses. Then she cried,—

"By God! to think I should have guessed! He's thought about it; he's waiting for his wife to go off the hooks! Well, well, that's the finishing touch! Why, he's even a bigger rascal than the others!"

Muffat had resigned himself to "the others." Nowadays he was trusting to the last relics of his personal dignity in order to remain *"Monsieur"* among the servants and intimates of the house, the man, in fact, who because he gave most was the official lover. And his passion grew fiercer. He kept his position because he paid for it, buying even smiles at a high price. He was even robbed, and he never got his money's worth; but a disease seemed to be gnawing his vitals from which he could not prevent himself suffering. Whenever he entered Nana's bedroom he was simply content to open the windows for a second or two, in order to get rid of the odours the others left behind them, the essential smells of fair-haired men and dark, the smoke of cigars, of which the pungency choked him. This bedroom was becoming a veritable thoroughfare, so continually were boots wiped on its threshold. Yet never a man among them was stopped by the blood-stain barring the door. Zoé was still preoccupied by this stain; it was a simple mania with her, for she was a clean girl, and it horrified her to see it always there. Despite of everything, her eyes would wander in its direction, and she now never entered *Madame's* room without remarking,—

"It's strange that don't go. All the same, plenty of folk come in this way."

Nana kept receiving the best news from Georges, who was by that time already convalescent in his mother's keeping at The Fondettes, and she used always to make the same reply.

"Oh, hang it, time's all that's wanted. It's apt to grow paler as feet cross it."

As a matter of fact, each of the gentlemen, whether Foucarmont, Steiner, la Faloise, or Fauchery, had borne away some of it on their boot-soles. And Muffat, whom the blood-stain preoccupied as much as it did Zoé, kept studying it in his own despite, as though in its gradual rosy disappearance he would read the number of men that passed. He secretly dreaded it, and always stepped over it out of a vivid fear of crushing some live thing, some naked limb lying on the floor.

But in the bedroom within he would grow dizzy and intoxicated, and would forget everything—the mob of men which constantly crossed it, the sign of mourning which barred its door. Outside, in the open air of the street, he would weep occasionally out of sheer shame and disgust, and would vow never to enter the room again. And, the moment the portière had closed behind him, he was under the old influence once more, and felt his whole being melting in the damp warm air of the place, felt his flesh penetrated by a perfume, felt himself overborne by a voluptuous yearning for self-annihilation. Pious, and habituated to ecstatic experiences in sumptuous chapels, he there re-encountered precisely the same mystical sensations as when he knelt under some painted window, and gave way to the intoxication of organ music and incense. Woman swayed him as jealously and despotically as the God of wrath, terrifying him, granting him moments of delight, which were like spasms in their keenness, in return for hours filled with frightful, tormenting visions of hell and eternal tortures. In Nana's presence, as in church, the same stammering accents were his, the same prayers and the same fits of despair—nay, the same paroxysms of humility peculiar to an accursed creature, who is crushed down in the mire from whence he has sprung. His fleshly desires, his spiritual needs, were confounded together, and seemed to spring from the obscure depths of his being, and to bear but one blossom on the tree of his existence. He abandoned himself to the power of love and of faith, those twin levers which move the world. And despite all the struggles of his reason, this bedroom of Nana's always filled him with madness, and he would sink shuddering under the almighty dominion of sex, just as he would swoon before the vast unknown of Heaven.

Then, when she felt how humble he was, Nana grew tyrannously triumphant. The rage for debasing things was inborn in her. It did not suffice her to destroy them, she must soil them too. Her delicate hands left abominable traces, and themselves decomposed whatever they had broken. And he in his imbecile condition lent himself to this sort of sport, for he was possessed by vaguely-remembered stories of saints who were devoured by vermin, and in turn devoured their own excrements. When once she had him fast in her room, and the doors were shut, she treated herself to a man's infamy. At first they joked together, and she would deal him light blows, and impose quaint tasks on him, making him lisp like a child, and repeat tags of sentences.

"Say as I do:——'tonfound it! Ickle man dam vell don't tare about it!"

He would prove so docile as to reproduce her very accent.

"——'tonfound it! Ickle man dam vell don't tare about it!"

Or again she would play bear, walking on all fours on her rugs, when she had only her chemise on, and turning round with a growl as though she wanted to eat him. She would even nibble his calves for the fun of the thing. Then, getting up again,—

"It's your turn now, try it a bit. I bet you don't play bear like me."

It was still charming enough. As bear she amused him with her white skin and her fell of ruddy hair. He used to laugh, and go down on all fours too, and growl, and bite her calves, whilst she ran from him with an affectation of terror.

"Are we beasts, eh?" she would end by saying. "You've no notion how ugly you are, my pet! Just think, if they were to see you like that at the Tuileries!"

But ere long these little games were spoilt. It was not cruelty in her case, for she was still a good-natured girl; it was as though a passing wind of madness were blowing ever more strongly in the shut-up bedroom. A storm of lust disordered their brains, plunged them into the delirious imaginations of the flesh. The old pious terrors of their sleepless nights were now transforming themselves into a thirst for bestiality, a furious longing to walk on all fours, to growl and to bite. One day, when he was playing bear, she pushed him so roughly that he fell against a piece of furniture, and when she saw the lump on his forehead, she burst into involuntary laughter. After that, her experiments on la Faloise having whetted her appetite, she treated him like an animal, thrashing him and chasing him to an accompaniment of kicks.

"Gee up! Gee up! You're a horse. Hoi! gee up! Won't you hurry up, you dirty screw!"

At other times he was a dog. She would throw her scented handkerchief to the far end of the room, and he had to run and pick it up with his teeth, dragging himself along on hands and knees.

"Fetch it, Cæsar! Look here, I'll give you what for if you don't look sharp! Well done, Cæsar! Good dog! Nice old fellow! Now behave pretty!"

And he loved his abasement, and delighted in being a brute beast. He longed to sink still further, and would cry,—

"Hit harder. On, on! I'm wild! Hit away!"

She was seized with a whim, and insisted on his coming to her one night clad in his magnificent Chamberlain's costume. Then how she did laugh and make fun of him when she had him there in all his glory, with the sword, and the cocked hat, and the white breeches, and the full-bottomed coat of red cloth laced with gold, and the symbolic key hanging on its left-hand skirt. This key made her especially merry, and urged her to a wildly fanciful and extremely filthy discussion of it. Laughing without cease, and carried away by her irreverence for pomp and by the joy

of debasing him in the official dignity of his costume, she shook him, pinched him, shouted, "Oh, get along with ye, Chamberlain!" and ended by an accompaniment of swinging kicks behind. Oh, those kicks! How heartily she rained them on the Tuileries, and the majesty of the Imperial Court, throning on high above an abject and trembling people. That's what she thought of society! That was her revenge! It was an affair of unconscious hereditary spite; it had come to her in her blood. Then, when once the Chamberlain was undressed and his coat lay spread on the ground, she shrieked, "Jump!" and he jumped; she shrieked, "Spit!" and he spat. With a shriek she bade him walk on the gold, on the eagles, on the decorations, and he walked on them. Hi tiddly hi ti! Nothing was left; everything was going to pieces. She smashed a Chamberlain just as she smashed a flask or a comfit-box, and she made filth of him, reduced him to a heap of mud at a street-corner.

Meanwhile, the goldsmiths had failed to keep their promise, and the bed was not delivered till one day about the middle of January. Muffat was just then in Normandy, whither he had gone to sell a last stray shred of property, but Nana demanded four thousand francs forthwith. He was not due in Paris till the day after to-morrow, but when his business was once finished, he hastened his return, and without even paying a flying visit in the Rue Miromesnil, came direct to the Avenue de Villiers. Ten o'clock was striking. As he had a key of a little door opening on the Rue Cardinet, he went up unhindered. In the drawing-room upstairs, Zoé, who was polishing the bronzes, stood dumfounded at sight of him, and not knowing how to stop him she began with much circumlocution informing him that Monsieur Venot, looking utterly beside himself, had been searching for him since yesterday, and that he had already come twice to beg her to send *Monsieur* to his house, if *Monsieur* arrived at *Madame's* before going home. Muffat listened to her without in the least understanding the meaning of her recital; then he noticed her agitation, and was seized by a sudden fit of jealousy of which he no longer believed himself capable. He threw himself against the bedroom door, for he heard the sound of laughter within. The door gave, its two flaps flew asunder, whilst Zoé withdrew, shrugging her shoulders. So much the worse for *Madame!* As *Madame* was bidding goodbye to her wits, she might arrange matters for herself.

And, on the threshold, Muffat uttered a cry at the sight that was presented to his view.

"My God! My God!"

The renovated bedroom was resplendent in all its royal luxury. Silver buttons gleamed like bright stars on the tearose velvet of the hangings. These last were of that pink flesh tint which the skies assume on fine evenings, when Venus lights her fires on the horizon against the clear background of fading daylight. The golden cords and tassels hanging in corners, and the gold lacework surrounding the panels, were like little flames or ruddy strands of loosened hair, and they half covered the wide nakedness of the room whilst they emphasised its pale voluptuous tone. Then, over against him, there was the gold and silver bed, which shone in all the fresh splendour of its chiselled workmanship, a throne this of sufficient extent for Nana to display the outstretched glory of her naked limbs, an altar of Byzantine sumptuousness, worthy of the almighty puissance of Nana's sex, which at this very hour lay nudely displayed there in the religious immodesty befitting an idol of all men's worship. And close by, beneath the snowy reflections of her bosom, and amid the triumph of the goddess, lay wallowing a shameful decrepit thing, a comic and lamentable ruin, the Marquis de Chouard in his night-shirt.

The Count had clasped his hands together and, shaken by a paroxysmal shuddering, he kept crying,—

"My God! My God!"

It was for the Marquis de Chouard, then, that the golden roses flourished on the side-panels, those bunches of golden roses blooming among the golden leaves; it was for him that the Cupids leaned forth with amorous roguish laughter from their tumbling ring on the silver trellis-work. And it was for him that the faun at his feet discovered the nymph sleeping, tired with dalliance, the figure of Night copied down to the exaggerated thighs—which caused her to be recognisable of all—from Nana's renowned nudity. Cast there like the rag of something human, which has been spoilt and dissolved by sixty years of debauchery, he suggested the charnel-house amid the glory of the woman's dazzling contours. Seeing the door open, he had risen up, smitten with sudden terror as became an infirm old man. This last night of passion had rendered him imbecile; he was entering on his second childhood; and, his speech failing him, he remained in an attitude of flight, half-paralysed, stammering, shivering, his night-shirt half up his skeleton shape, and one leg outside the clothes, a livid leg, covered with grey hair. Despite her vexation, Nana could not keep from laughing.

"Do lie down! Stuff yourself into the bed," said she, pulling him back and burying him under the coverlet, as though he were some filthy thing she could not shew anyone.

Then she sprang up to shut the door again. She was decidedly never lucky with her little rough. He was always coming when least wanted. And why had he gone to fetch money in Normandy? The old man had brought her the four thousand francs, and she had let him have his will of her. She pushed back the two flaps of the door and shouted,—

"So much the worse for you! It's your fault. Is that the way to come into a room? I've had enough of this sort of thing. Ta ta!"

Muffat remained standing before the closed door, thunderstruck by what he had just seen. His shuddering fit increased. It mounted from his feet to his heart and brain. Then, like a tree shaken by a mighty wind, he swayed to and fro, and dropped on his knees, all his muscles giving way under him. And with hands despairingly outstretched he stammered,—

"This is more than I can bear, my God! more than I can bear!"

He had accepted every situation but he could do so no longer. He had come to the end of his strength, and was plunged in the dark void where man and

his reason are together overthrown. In an extravagant access of faith he raised his hands ever higher and higher, searching for heaven—calling on God.

"Oh, no, I do not desire it! Oh, come to me, my God! Succour me; nay, let me die sooner! Oh, no, not that man, my God! It is over: take me, carry me away, that I may not see, that I may not feel any longer! Oh, I belong to you, my God! Our Father which art in heaven——"

And, burning with faith, he continued his supplication, and an ardent prayer escaped from his lips. But someone touched him on the shoulder. He lifted his eyes; it was Monsieur Venot. He was surprised to find him praying before that closed door. Then, as though God Himself had responded to his appeal, the Count flung his arms round the little old gentleman's neck. At last he could weep, and he burst out sobbing, and repeated,—

"My brother, my brother."

All his suffering humanity found comfort in that cry. He drenched Monsieur Venot's face with tears; he kissed him, uttering fragmentary ejaculations.

"Oh, my brother, how I am suffering! You only are left me, my brother. Take me away for ever—oh, for mercy's sake, take me away!"

Then Monsieur Venot pressed him to his bosom, and called him "brother" also. But he had a fresh blow in store for him. Since yesterday he had been searching for him in order to inform him that the Countess Sabine, in a supreme fit of moral aberration, had but now taken flight with the manager of one of the departments in a large fancy emporium. It was a fearful scandal, and all Paris was already talking about it. Seeing him under the influence of such religious exaltation, Venot felt the opportunity to be favourable, and at once told him of the meanly tragic shipwreck of his house. The Count was not touched thereby. His wife had gone? That meant nothing to him; they would see what would happen later on. And again he was seized with anguish, and gazing with a look of terror at the door, the walls, the ceiling, he continued pouring forth his single supplication:

"Take me away! I cannot bear it any longer! take me away!"

Monsieur Venot took him away as though he had been a child. From that day forth Muffat belonged to him entirely; he again became strictly attentive to the duties of religion; his life was utterly blasted. He had resigned his position as Chamberlain out of respect for the outraged modesty of the Tuileries, and soon Estelle, his daughter, brought an action against him for the recovery of a sum of sixty thousand francs, a legacy left her by an aunt to which she ought to have succeeded at the time of her marriage. Ruined, and living narrowly on the remains of his great fortune, he let himself be gradually devoured by the Countess, who ate up the husks Nana had rejected. Sabine was indeed ruined by the example of promiscuity set her by her husband's intercourse with the wanton. She was prone to every excess, and proved the ultimate ruin and destruction of his very hearth. After sundry adventures she had returned home, and he had taken her back in a spirit of Christian resignation and forgiveness. She haunted him as his living disgrace, but he grew more

and more indifferent, and at last ceased suffering from these distresses. Heaven took him out of his wife's hands in order to restore him to the arms of God, and so the voluptuous pleasures he had enjoyed with Nana were prolonged in religious ecstasies, accompanied by the old stammering utterances, the old prayers and despairs, the old fits of humility which befit an accursed creature who is crushed beneath the mire whence he sprang. In the recesses of churches, his knees chilled by the pavement, he would once more experience the delights of the past, and his muscles would twitch, and his brain would whirl deliciously, and the satisfaction of the obscure necessities of his existence would be the same as of old.

On the evening of the final rupture Mignon presented himself at the house in the Avenue de Villiers. He was growing accustomed to Fauchery, and was beginning at last to find the presence of his wife's husband infinitely advantageous to him. He would leave all the little household cares to the journalist, and would trust him in the active superintendence of all their affairs. Nay, he devoted the money gained by his dramatic successes to the daily expenditure of the family, and as, on his part, Fauchery behaved sensibly, avoiding ridiculous jealousy, and proving not less pliant than Mignon himself whenever Rose found her opportunity, the mutual understanding between the two men constantly improved. In fact they were happy in a partnership which was so fertile in all kinds of amenities, and they settled down side by side, and adopted a family arrangement which no longer proved a stumbling-block. The whole thing was conducted according to rule; it suited admirably; and each man vied with the other in his efforts for the common happiness. That very evening, Mignon had come by Fauchery's advice to see if he could not steal Nana's lady's maid from her, the journalist having formed a high opinion of the woman's extraordinary intelligence. Rose was in despair; for a month past she had been falling into the hands of inexperienced girls who were causing her continual embarrassment. When Zoé received him at the door he forthwith pushed her into the dining-room. But at his opening sentence she smiled. The thing was impossible, she said, for she was leaving *Madame* and establishing herself on her own account. And she added with an expression of discreet vanity that she was daily receiving offers, that the ladies were fighting for her, and that Madame Blanche would give a pile of gold to have her back.

Zoé was taking the Tricon's establishment. It was an old project and had been long brooded over. It was her ambition to make her fortune thereby, and she was investing all her savings in it. She was full of great ideas, and meditated increasing the business, and hiring a house, and combining all the delights within its walls. It was with this in view that she had tried to entice Satin, a little pig at that moment dying in hospital, so terribly had she done for herself.

Mignon still insisted with his offer, and spoke of the risks run in the commercial life, but Zoé, without entering into explanations about the exact nature of her establishment, smiled a pinched smile, as though she had just put a sweetmeat in her mouth, and was content to remark,—

"Oh, luxuries always pay. You see I've been with others quite long enough, and now I want others to be with me."

And a fierce look set her lip curling. At last she would be *"Madame,"* and, for the sake of earning a few louis, all those women, whose slops she had emptied during the last fifteen years, would prostrate themselves before her.

Mignon wished to be announced, and Zoé left him for a moment, after remarking that *Madame* had passed a miserable day. He had only been at the house once before, and he did not know it at all. The dining-room with its Gobelins tapestry, its sideboard, and its plate, filled him with astonishment. He opened the doors familiarly, and visited the drawing-room, and the winter garden, returning thence into the hall. This overwhelming luxury, this gilded furniture, these silks and velvets, gradually filled him with such a feeling of admiration that it set his heart beating. When Zoé came down to fetch him, she offered to show him the other rooms, the dressing-room, that is to say, and the bedroom. In the latter, Mignon's feelings overcame him, he was carried away by them; they filled him with tender enthusiasm.

That damned Nana was simply stupefying him, and yet he thought he knew a thing or two. Amid the downfall of the house, and the servants' wild wasteful race to destruction, massed-up riches still filled every gaping hole and overtopped every ruined wall. And Mignon, as he viewed this lordly monument of wealth, began recalling to mind the various great works he had seen. Near

Marseilles they had shown him an aqueduct, the stone arches of which bestrode an abyss, a Cyclopean work which cost millions of money and ten years of intense labour. At Cherbourg he had seen the new harbour, with its enormous works, where hundreds of men sweated in the sun, whilst cranes filled the sea with huge squares of rock, and built up a wall where a workman now and again remained crushed into bloody pulp. But all that now struck him as insignificant. Nana excited him far more. Viewing the fruit of her labours, he once more experienced the feelings of respect that had overcome him one festal evening in a sugar refiner's château. This château had been erected for the refiner, and its palatial proportions and royal splendour had been paid for by a single material—sugar. It was with something quite different, with a little laughable folly, a little delicate nudity—it was with this shameful trifle, which is so powerful as to move the universe, that she alone, without workmen, without the inventions of engineers, had shaken Paris to its foundations, and had built up a fortune on the bodies of dead men.

"Oh, by God, what an implement!"

Mignon let the words escape him in his ecstasy, for he felt a return of personal gratitude.

Nana had gradually lapsed into a most mournful condition. To begin with, the meeting of the Marquis and the Count had given her a severe fit of feverish nervousness, which verged at times on laughter. Then the thought of this old man going away half dead in a cab, and of her poor rough, whom she would never set eyes on again, now that she had driven him so wild, brought on what looked like the beginnings of melancholia. After that, she grew vexed to hear about Satin's illness. The girl had disappeared about a fortnight ago, and was now ready to die at Lariboisière, to such a damnable state had Madame Robert reduced her. When she ordered the horses to be put to in order that she might have a last sight of this vile little wretch, Zoé had just quietly given her a week's notice. The announcement drove her to desperation at once! it seemed to her she was losing a member of her own family. Great heavens! what was to become of her when left alone? And she besought Zoé to stay, and the latter, much flattered by *Madame's* despair, ended by kissing her to shew that she was not going away in anger. No, she had positively to go: the heart could have no voice in matters of business.

But that day was one of annoyances. Nana was thoroughly disgusted, and gave up the idea of going out. She was dragging herself wearily about the little drawing-room, when Labordette came up to tell her of a splendid chance of buying magnificent lace, and in the course of his remarks casually let slip the information that Georges was dead. The announcement froze her.

"Zizi dead!" cried she.

And, involuntarily, her eyes sought the pink stain on the carpet, but it had vanished at last; passing footsteps had worn it away. Meanwhile, Labordette entered into particulars. It was not exactly known how he died. Some spoke of a wound reopening, others of suicide. The lad had plunged, said they, into a tank at The Fondettes. Nana kept repeating:

"Dead! dead!"

She had been choking with grief since

morning, and now she burst out sobbing, and thus sought relief. Hers was an infinite sorrow: it overwhelmed her with its depth and immensity. Labordette wanted to comfort her as touching Georges, but she silenced him with a gesture, and blurted out,—

"It isn't only he; it's everything, everything. I'm very wretched. Oh, yes, I know! They'll again be saying I'm a hussy. To think of the mother mourning down there, and of the poor man who was groaning in front of my door this morning, and of all the other people that are now ruined after running through all they had with me! That's it; punish Nana; punish the beastly thing! Oh, I've got a broad back! I can hear them as if I were actually there! 'That dirty wench who lies with everybody, and cleans out some, and drives others to death, and causes a whole heap of people pain!'"

She was obliged to pause, for tears choked her utterance, and in her anguish she flung herself athwart a divan, and buried her face in a cushion. The miseries she felt to be around her, miseries of which she was the cause, overwhelmed her with a warm continuous stream of self-pitying tears; and her voice failed as she uttered a little girl's broken plaint:

"Oh, I'm wretched! Oh, I'm wretched! I can't go on like this: it's choking me. It's too hard to be misunderstood, and to see them all siding against you because they're the stronger. However, when you've got nothing to reproach yourself with, and your conscience is clear, why then I say, 'I won't have it! I won't have it!'"

In her anger she began rebelling against circumstances, and getting up,

she dried her eyes, and walked about in much agitation.

"I won't have it! They can say what they like, but it's not my fault! Am I a bad lot, eh? I give away all I've got; I wouldn't crush a fly! It's they who are bad! Yes, it's they! *I* never wanted to be horrid to them. And they came dangling after me, and to-day they're kicking the bucket, and begging, and going to ruin on purpose."

Then she paused in front of Labordette, and tapped his shoulders.

"Look here," said she, "you were there all along, now speak the truth: did I urge them on? Weren't there always a dozen of 'em squabbling who could invent the dirtiest trick? They used to disgust me, they did! I did all I knew not to copy them: I was afraid to. Look here, I'll give you a single instance: they all wanted to marry me! A pretty notion, eh? Yes, dear boy, I could have been countess or baroness a dozen times over, and more, if I'd consented. Well now, I refused, because I was reasonable. Oh, yes, I saved 'em some crimes and other foul acts! They'd have stolen, murdered, killed father and mother. I had only to say one word, and I didn't say it. You see what I've got for it to-day. There's Daguenet, for instance, I married that chap off! I made a position for the beggarly fellow, after keeping him gratis for weeks! And I met him yesterday, and he looks the other way! Oh, get along, you swine! I'm less dirty than you!"

She had begun pacing about again, and now she brought her fist violently down on a round table.

"By God, it isn't fair! Society's all wrong. They come down on the women when it's the men who want you to do things. Yes, I can tell you this now: when I used to go with them—see? I didn't enjoy it, no, I didn't enjoy it one bit. It bored me, on my honour. Well then, I ask you whether I've got anything to do with it! Yes, they bored me to death! If it hadn't been for them and what they made of me, dear boy, I should be in a convent saying my prayers to the good God, for I've always had my share of religion. Dash it, after all if they have dropped their money and their lives over it, what do I care? It's their fault. I've had nothing to do with it!"

"Certainly not," said Labordette with conviction.

Zoé ushered in Mignon, and Nana received him smilingly. She had cried a good deal, but it was all over now. Still glowing with enthusiasm, he complimented her on her installation; but she let him see that she had had enough of her mansion, and that now she had other projects, and would sell everything up one of these days. Then, as he excused himself for calling on the ground that he had come about a benefit performance in aid of old Bosc, who was tied to his arm-chair by paralysis, she expressed extreme pity, and took two boxes. Meanwhile Zoé announced that the carriage was waiting for *Madame,* and she asked for her hat, and as she tied the strings told them about poor dear Satin's mishap, adding,—

"I'm going to the hospital. Nobody ever loved me as she did. Oh, they're quite right when they accuse the men of heartlessness! Who knows; perhaps I shan't see her alive. Never mind, I shall ask to see her: I want to give her a kiss."

Labordette and Mignon smiled, and, as Nana was no longer melancholy, she smiled too. Those two fellows didn't count; they could enter into her feelings. And they both stood and admired her in silent abstraction, whilst she finished buttoning her gloves. She alone kept her feet amid the heaped-up riches of her mansion, while a whole generation of men lay stricken down before her. Like those antique monsters whose redoubtable domains were covered with skeletons, she rested her feet on human skulls. She was ringed round with catastrophes. There was the furious immolation of Vandeuvres; the melancholy state of Foucarmont, who was lost in the China seas; the smash-up of Steiner, who now had to live like an honest man; the satisfied idiocy of la Faloise; and the tragic shipwreck of the Muffats. Finally, there was the white corpse of Georges, over which Philippe was not watching, for he had come out of prison but yesterday. She had finished her labour of ruin and death. The fly that had flown up from the ordure of the slums, bringing with it the leaven of social rottenness, had poisoned all these men by merely alighting on them. It was well done—it was just. She had avenged the beggars and the wastrels from whose caste she issued. And whilst, metaphorically speaking, her sex rose in a halo of glory and beamed over prostrate victims like a mounting sun shining brightly over a field of carnage, the actual woman remained as unconscious as a splendid animal, and in her ignorance of her mission was the good-natured courtesan to the last. She was still big, she was still plump, her health was excellent, her spirits capital. But this went for nothing now, for her house struck her as ridiculous. It was too small; it was full of furniture which got in her way. It was a wretched business, and the long and the short of the matter was she would have to make a fresh start. In fact she was meditating something much better, and so she went off to kiss Satin for the last time. She was in all her finery, and looked clean, and solid, and as brand-new as if she had never seen service before.

## CHAPTER XIV

NANA suddenly disappeared. It was a fresh plunge, an escapade, a flight into barbarous regions. Before her departure she had treated herself to a new sensation: she had held a sale, and had made a clean sweep of everything—house, furniture, jewellery, nay, even dresses and linen. Prices were cited—the five days' sale produced more than six hundred thousand francs. For the last time Paris had seen her in a fairy piece. It was called *Mélusine,* and it played at the Théâtre de la Gaîté, which the penniless Bordenave had taken out of sheer audacity. Here she again found herself in company with Prullière and Fontan. Her part was simply spectacular, but it was the great attraction of the piece, consisting, as it did, of three *poses plastiques,* each of which represented the same dumb and puissant fairy. Then one fine morning, amid his grand success, when Bordenave, who was mad after advertisement, kept firing the Parisian imagination with colossal posters, it became known that she must have started for Cairo the previous day.

She had simply had a few words with her manager. Something had been said which did not please her; the whole thing was the caprice of a woman who is too rich to let herself be annoyed. Besides, she had indulged an old infatuation, for she had long meditated visiting the Turks.

Months passed—she began to be forgotten. When her name was mentioned, among the ladies and gentlemen we wot of, the strangest stories were told, and everybody gave the most contradictory and at the same time prodigious information. She had made a conquest of the Viceroy, she was reigning, in the recesses of a palace, over two hundred slaves whose heads she now and then cut off for the sake of a little amusement. No, not at all! She had ruined herself with a great big nigger! A filthy passion this, which had left her wallowing without a chemise to her back in the crapulous debauchery of Cairo. A fortnight later, much astonishment was produced when someone swore to having met her in Russia. A legend began to be formed, she was the mistress of a prince, and her diamonds were mentioned. All the women were soon acquainted with them from the current descriptions, but nobody could cite the precise source of all this information. There were finger-rings, earrings, bracelets, a rivière of phenomenal width, a queenly diadem, surmounted by a central brilliant the size of one's thumb. In the retirement of those far-away countries she began to gleam forth as mysteriously as a gem-laden idol. People now mentioned her without laughing, for they were full of meditative respect for this fortune acquired among the barbarians.

One evening in July, towards eight o'clock, Lucy, whilst getting out of her carriage in the Rue du Faubourg-Saint-Honoré, noticed Caroline Héquet, who had come out on foot to order something at a neighbouring tradesman's. Lucy called her, and at once burst out with,—

"Have you dined? Are you disengaged? Oh! then come with me, my dear. Nana's back."

The other got in at once, and Lucy continued,—

"And you know, my dear, she may be dead while we're gossiping."

"Dead! What an idea!" cried Caroline, in stupefaction. "And where is she? And what's it of?"

"At the Grand Hôtel, of small-pox. Oh! it's a long story!"

Lucy had bidden her coachman drive fast, and, whilst the horses trotted rapidly along the Rue Royale and the Boulevards, she told what had happened to Nana in jerky breathless sentences.

"You can't imagine it. Nana plumps down out of Russia. I don't know why —some dispute with her prince. She leaves her traps at the station; she lands at her aunt's—you remember the old thing. Well, and then she finds her baby dying of small-pox. The baby dies next day, and she has a row with the aunt about some money she ought to have sent, of which the other one has never seen a sou. Seems the child died of that: in fact, it was neglected and badly cared for. Very well; Nana slopes; goes to a hotel, then meets Mignon just as she was thinking of her traps. She has all sorts of queer feelings, shivers, wants to be sick, and Mignon takes her back to her place, and promises to look after her affairs. Isn't it odd, eh? Doesn't it all happen pat? But this is the best part of the story: Rose finds out about Nana's illness, and gets indignant at the idea of her being alone in furnished apartments. So she rushes off, crying, to look after her. You remember how they used to detest one another —like regular furies! Well then, my dear, Rose has had Nana transported to the Grand Hôtel, so that she should at any rate die in a smart place, and now she's already passed three nights there and is free to die of it after. It's Labordette who told me all about it. Accordingly, I wanted to see for myself——"

"Yes, yes," interrupted Caroline, in great excitement. "We'll go up to her."

They had arrived at their destination. On the boulevard the coachman had had to rein in his horses amid a block of carriages and people on foot. During the day the Corps Législatif had voted for war; and now a crowd was streaming down all the streets, flowing along all the pavements, invading the middle of the roadway. Beyond the Madeleine the sun had set behind a blood-red cloud, which cast a reflection as of a great fire and set the lofty windows flaming. Twilight was falling, and the hour was oppressively melancholy, for now the avenues were darkening away into the distance, but were not as yet dotted over by the bright sparks of the gas-lamps. And, among the marching crowds, distant voices swelled and grew ever louder, and eyes gleamed from pale faces, whilst a great spreading wind of anguish and stupor set every head whirling.

"Here's Mignon," said Lucy. "He'll give us news."

Mignon was standing under the vast porch of the Grand Hôtel. He looked nervous, and was gazing at the crowd. After Lucy's first few questions, he grew impatient and cried out,—

"How should I know! These last two days I haven't been able to tear Rose away from up there. It's getting stupid, when all's said, for her to be risking her life like that! She'll be charming, if she gets over it, with holes in her face! It'll suit us to a tee!"

The idea that Rose might lose her beauty was exasperating him. He was giving up Nana in the most downright fashion, and he could not in the least understand these stupid feminine devotions. But Fauchery was crossing the boulevard, and he too came up anxiously and asked for news. The two men egged each other on. They addressed one another familiarly in these days.

"Always the same business, my sonny," declared Mignon. "You ought to go upstairs; you would force her to follow you."

"Come now, you're kind, you are!" said the journalist. "Why don't you go upstairs yourself?"

Then, as Lucy began asking for Nana's number, they besought her to make Rose come down; otherwise, they would end by getting angry.

Nevertheless, Lucy and Caroline did not go up at once. They had caught sight of Fontan, strolling about with his hands in his pockets, and greatly amused by the quaint expressions of the mob. When he became aware that Nana was lying ill upstairs, he affected sentiment and remarked,—

"The poor girl! I'll go and shake her

by the hand. What's the matter with her, eh?"

"Small-pox," replied Mignon.

The actor had already taken a step or two in the direction of the court but he came back, and simply murmured with a shiver,—

"Oh, damn it!"

The small-pox was no joke. Fontan had been near having it when he was five years old, whilst Mignon gave them an account of one of his nieces who had died of it. As to Fauchery, he could speak of it from personal experience, for he still bore marks of it in the shape of three little lumps at the base of his nose, which he shewed them. And when Mignon again egged him on to the ascent, on the pretext that you never had it twice, he violently combated this theory, and with infinite abuse of the doctors instanced various cases. But Lucy and Caroline interrupted them, for the growing multitude filled them with astonishment.

"Just look! Just look what a lot of people!" The night was deepening, and in the distance, the gas-lamps were being lit one by one. Meanwhile, interested spectators became visible at windows, whilst, under the trees, the human flood grew every minute more dense, till it ran in one enormous stream from the Madeleine to the Bastille. Carriages rolled slowly along. A roaring sound went up from this compact and as yet inarticulate mass. Each member of it had come out impelled by the desire to form a crowd, and was now trampling along, steeping himself in the pervading fever. But a great movement caused the mob to flow asunder. Among the jostling, scattering groups, a band of

men in workmen's caps and white blouses
had come in sight, uttering a rhythmical
cry which suggested the beat of hammers upon an anvil.

"To Ber—lin! To Ber—lin! To
Ber—lin!" And the crowd stared in
gloomy distrust, yet felt themselves already possessed and inspired by heroic
imaginings, as though a military band
were passing.

"Oh, yes, go and get your throats cut!"
muttered Mignon, overcome by an access of philosophy.

But Fontan thought it very fine indeed, and spoke of enlisting. When the
enemy was on the frontier, all citizens
ought to rise up in defence of the father-
land! And with that he assumed an attitude suggestive of Bonaparte at
Austerlitz.

"Look here, are you coming up with
us?" Lucy asked him.

"Oh, dear no! to catch something
horrid?" said he.

On a bench, in front of the Grand
Hôtel, a man sat hiding his face in a
handkerchief. On arriving Fauchery had
indicated him to Mignon with a wink of
the eye. Well, he was still there; yes,
he was always there. And the journalist
detained the two women also in order
to point him out to them. When the
man lifted his head they recognised him,
an exclamation escaped them. It was
the Count Muffat, and he was giving
an upward glance at one of the windows.

"You know he's been waiting there
since this morning," Mignon informed
them. "I saw him at six o'clock, and
he hasn't moved since. Directly Labordette spoke about it he came there
with his handkerchief up to his face.
Every half hour he comes dragging him-

self to where we're standing to ask if the
person upstairs is doing better, and then
he goes back and sits down. Hang it,
that room isn't healthy! It's all very
well being fond of people, but one doesn't
want to kick the bucket."

The Count sat with uplifted eyes, and
did not seem conscious of what was going on around him. Doubtless he was
ignorant of the declaration of war, and
he neither felt nor saw the crowd.

"Look, here he comes!" said Fauchery.
"Now you'll see."

The Count had, in fact, quitted his
bench and was entering the lofty porch.
But the porter, who was getting to know
his face at last did not give him time to
put his question. He said sharply,—

"She's dead, *Monsieur*, this very
minute."

Nana dead! It was a blow to them
all. Without a word Muffat had gone
back to the bench, his face still buried
in his handkerchief. The others burst
into exclamations, but they were cut
short, for a fresh band passed by howling,
"*A Berlin! à Berlin! à Berlin!*" Nana
dead! Hang it, and such a fine girl too!
Mignon sighed and looked relieved, for
at last Rose would come down. A chill
fell on the company. Fontan, meditating
a tragic *rôle*, had assumed a look of woe,
and was drawing down the corners of
his mouth, and rolling his eyes askance,
whilst Fauchery chewed his cigar nervously, for despite his cheap journalistic
chaff he was really touched. Nevertheless, the two women continued to give
vent to their feelings of surprise. The
last time Lucy had seen her was at the
Gaîté; Blanche, too, had seen her in
*Mélusine*. Oh, how stunning it was, my
dear, when she appeared in the depths

of the crystal grot! The gentlemen remembered the occasion perfectly. Fontan had played the Prince Cocorico. And, their memories once stirred up, they launched into interminable particulars. How ripping she looked with that rich colouring of hers in the crystal grot? Didn't she, now? She didn't say a word: the authors had even deprived her of a line or two, because it was superfluous. No, never a word! It was grander that way, and she drove her public wild by simply shewing herself. You wouldn't find another body like hers! Such shoulders as she had, and such legs, and such a figure! Strange that she should be dead! You know, above her tights, she had nothing on but a golden girdle which hardly concealed her behind and in front. All round her, the grotto, which was entirely of glass, shone like day. Cascades of diamonds were flowing down, strings of brilliant pearls glistened among the stalactites in the vault overhead, and amid the transparent atmosphere and flowing fountain water, which was crossed by a wide ray of electric light, she gleamed like the sun with that flame-like skin and hair of hers. Paris would always picture her thus—would see her shining high up among crystal glass like the good God Himself. No, it was too stupid to let herself die under such conditions! She must be looking pretty by this time, in that room up there!

"And what a lot of pleasures bloody well wasted!" said Mignon in melancholy tones, as became a man who did not like to see good and useful things lost.

He sounded Lucy and Caroline in order to find out if they were going up after all. Of course they were going up; their curiosity had increased. Just then Blanche arrived, out of breath and much exasperated at the way the crowds were blocking the pavement, and when she heard the news there was a fresh outburst of exclamations, and with a great rustling of skirts the ladies moved towards the stair-case. Mignon followed them, crying out,—

"Tell Rose that I'm waiting for her. She'll come at once, eh?"

"They do not exactly know whether the contagion is to be feared at the beginning or near the end," Fontan was explaining to Fauchery. "A medical I know was assuring me that the hours immediately following death are particularly dangerous. There are miasmatic exhalations then. Ah! but I do regret this sudden ending; I should have been so glad to shake hands with her for the last time."

"What good would it do you now?" said the journalist.

"Yes, what good?" the two others repeated.

The crowd was still on the increase. In the bright light thrown from shop-windows and beneath the wavering glare of the gas, two living streams were distinguishable as they flowed along the pavement, innumerable hats apparently drifting on their surface. At that hour the popular fever was gaining ground rapidly, and people were flinging themselves in the wake of the bands of men in blouses. A constant forward movement seemed to sweep the roadway, and the cry kept recurring; obstinately, abruptly, there rang from thousands of throats,—

"*A Berlin! A Berlin! A Berlin!*"

The room on the fourth floor upstairs cost twelve francs a day, since Rose had wanted something decent and yet not luxurious, for sumptuousness is not necessary when one is suffering. Hung with Louis XIII. cretonne, which was adorned with a pattern of large flowers, the room was furnished with the mahogany commonly found in hotels. On the floor there was a red carpet variegated with black foilage. Heavy silence reigned save for an occasional whispering sound caused by voices in the corridor.

"I assure you we're lost. The waiter told us to turn to the right. What a barrack of a house!"

"Wait a bit: we must have a look. Room No. 401, Room No. 401!"

"Oh, it's this way: 405, 403. We ought to be there. Ah, at last, 401! This way! Hush now, hush!"

The voices were silent. Then there was a slight coughing, and a moment or so of mental preparation. Then the door opened slowly, and Lucy entered, followed by Caroline and Blanche. But they stopped directly; there were already five women in the room; Gaga was lying back in the solitary arm-chair, which was a red velvet Voltaire. In front of the fire-place, Simonne and Clarisse were standing talking to Léa de Horn, who was seated, whilst, by the bed, to the left of the door, Rose Mignon, perched on the edge of a chest, sat gazing fixedly at the body where it lay hidden in the shadow of the curtains. All the others had their hats and gloves on, and looked as if they were paying a call: she alone sat there with bare hands and untidy hair, and cheeks rendered pale by three nights of watching. She

felt stupid in the face of this sudden death, and her eyes were swollen with weeping. A shaded lamp, standing on the corner of the chest of drawers, threw a bright flood of light over Gaga.

"What a sad misfortune, is it not?" whispered Lucy, as she shook hands with Rose. "We wanted to bid her good-bye."

And she turned round, and tried to catch sight of her, but the lamp was too far off, and she did not dare bring it nearer. On the bed lay stretched a grey mass, but only the ruddy chignon was distinguishable and a pale blotch which might be the face. Lucy added:

"I never saw her since that time at the Gaîté, when she was at the end of the grotto."

At this Rose awoke from her stupor, and smiled as she said:

"Ah, she's changed, she's changed."

Then she once more lapsed into contemplation, and neither moved nor spoke. Perhaps they would be able to look at her presently! And with that the three women joined the others in front of the fire-place. Simonne and Clarisse were discussing the dead woman's diamonds in low tones. Well, did they really exist— those diamonds? Nobody had seen them; it must be a bit of humbug. But Léa de Horn knew someone who knew all about them. Oh, they were monster stones! Besides, they weren't all; she had brought back lots of other precious property from Russia—embroidered stuffs, for instance, valuable knick-knacks, a gold dinner service, nay, even furniture. "Yes, my dear, fifty-two boxes, enormous cases some of them, three truck-loads of them!" They were all lying at the station. "Wasn't it hard lines, eh?—to die without even having time to unpack one's traps." Then, she had a lot of tin besides—something like a million! Lucy asked who was going to inherit it all. Oh, distant relations— the aunt, without doubt! It would be a pretty surprise for that old body. She knew nothing about it yet, for the sick woman had obstinately refused to let them warn her, for she still owed her a grudge over her little boy's death. Thereupon, they were all moved to pity about the little boy, and they remembered seeing him at the races. Oh, it was a wretchedly sickly baby; it looked so old and so sad. In fact, it was one of those poor brats who never asked to be born!

"He's happier under the ground," said Blanche.

"Bah, and so's she!" added Caroline. "Life isn't so funny!"

In that gloomy room melancholy ideas began to take possession of their imaginations. They felt frightened. It was silly to stand talking so long, but a longing to see her kept them rooted to the spot. It was very hot—the lampglass threw a round moon-like patch of light upon the ceiling, but the rest of the room was drowned in steamy darkness. Under the bed, a deep plate, full of phenol, exhaled an insipid smell. And, every few moments, tiny gusts of wind swelled the window-curtains. The window opened on the boulevard, whence rose a dull roaring sound.

"Did she suffer much?" asked Lucy, who was absorbed in contemplation of the clock, the design of which represented the Three Graces as nude young women, smiling like opera-dancers.

Gaga seemed to wake up,—

"My word, yes! I was present when she died. I promise you it was not at all pleasant to see. Why, she was taken with a shuddering fit——"

But she was unable to proceed with her explanation for a cry arose outside,——

"A Berlin! A Berlin! A Berlin!"

And Lucy, who felt suffocated, flung wide the window, and leant upon the sill. It was pleasant there; the air came fresh from the starry sky. Opposite her the windows were all aglow with light and the gas sent dancing reflections over the gilt lettering of the shop-signs.

Beneath these, again, a most amusing scene presented itself. The streams of people were discernible rolling torrent-wise along the sidewalks, and in the roadway, where there was a confused procession of carriages. Everywhere there were vast moving shadows in which lanterns and lamp-posts gleamed like sparks. But the band which now came roaring by carried torches, and a red glow streamed down from the direction of the Madeleine, crossed the mob like a trail of fire, and spread out over the heads in the distance like the vivid reflection of a burning house. Lucy called Blanche and Caroline, forgetting where she was, and shouting,—

"Do come! You get a capital view from this window!"

They all three leant out, greatly interested. The trees got in their way, and occasionally the torches disappeared under the foliage. They tried to catch a glimpse of the men of their own party below, but a protruding balcony hid the door, and they could only make out Count Muffat, who looked like a dark parcel thrown down on the bench where he sat. He was still burying his face in his handkerchief. A carriage had stopped in front, and yet another woman hurried up, in whom Lucy recognised Maria Blond. She was not alone: a stout man got down after her. "It's that thief of a Steiner," said Caroline. "How is it they haven't sent him back to Cologne yet? I want to see how he looks when he comes in." They turned round, but when, after the lapse of ten minutes, Maria Blond appeared, she was alone. She had twice mistaken the staircase. And when Lucy, in some astonishment, questioned her,—

"What he!" said she. "My dear, don't you go fancying that he'll come upstairs! It's a great wonder he's escorted me as far as the door. There are nearly a dozen of them smoking cigars."

As a matter of fact, all the gentlemen were meeting downstairs. They had come strolling thither in order to have a look at the boulevards, and they hailed one another and commented loudly on that poor girl's death. Then they began discussing politics and strategy. Bordenave, Daguenet, Labordette, Prulliére and others besides, had swollen the group, and now they were all listening to Fontan, who was explaining his plan for taking Berlin within a week.

Meanwhile, Maria Blond was touched as she stood by the bedside, and murmured, as the others had done before her,—

"Poor pet! the last time I saw her was in the grotto at the Gaîté."

"Ah, she's changed, she's changed!" Rose Mignon repeated with a smile of gloomiest dejection.

Two more women arrived. These were Tatan Néné and Louise Violaine. They had been wandering about the Grand Hôtel for twenty minutes past, bandied from waiter to waiter, and had ascended and descended more than thirty flights of stairs, amid a perfect stampede of travellers who were hurrying to leave Paris amid the panic caused by the war and the excitement on the boulevards. Accordingly they just dropped down on chairs when they came in, for they were too tired to think about the dead. At that moment a loud noise came from the room next door where people were pushing trunks about and striking against furniture to an accompaniment of strident outlandish syllables. It was a young Austrian couple, and Gaga told how during her agony the neighbours had played a game of catch as catch can, and how, as only an unused door divided the two rooms, they had heard them laughing and kissing when one or the other was caught.

"Come, it's time we were off," said Clarisse. "We shan't bring her to life again. Are you coming, Simonne?"

They all looked at the bed out of the corners of their eyes, but they did not budge an inch. Nevertheless, they began getting ready, and gave their skirts various little pats. Lucy was again leaning out of window. She was alone now, and a sorrowful feeling began little by little to overpower her, as though an intense wave of melancholy had mounted up from the howling mob. Torches still kept passing, shaking out clouds of sparks, and far away in the distance the various bands stretched into the shadows, surging unquietly to and fro like flocks being driven to the slaughter-house at night. A dizzy feeling emanated from these confused masses as the human flood rolled them along,—a dizzy feeling, a sense of terror, and all the pity of the massacres to come. The people were going wild; their voices broke; they were drunk with a fever of excitement which sent them rushing towards the unknown "out there" beyond the dark wall of the horizon.

"*A Berlin! A Berlin! A Berlin!*"

Lucy turned round. She leant her back against the window, and her face was very pale.

"Good God! what's to become of us?"

The ladies shook their heads. They were serious, and very anxious about the turn events were taking.

"For my part," said Caroline Héquet in her decisive way, "I start for London the day after to-morrow. Mamma's already over there getting a house ready for me. I'm certainly not going to let myself be massacred in Paris."

Her mother, as became a prudent woman, had invested all her daughters' money in foreign lands. One never knows how a war may end! But Maria Blond grew vexed at this. She was a patriot, and spoke of following the army.

"There's a coward for you! Yes, if they wanted me, I should put on man's clothes just to have a good shot at those pigs of Prussians! And if we all die after? What of that? Our wretched skins aren't so valuable!"

Blanche de Sivry was exasperated.

"Please don't speak ill of the Prussians! They are just like other men, and they're not always running after the women, like your Frenchmen. They've just expelled the little Prussian who was with me. He was an awfully rich fellow and so gentle: he couldn't have hurt a soul. It's disgraceful: I'm ruined by it. And, you know you mustn't say a word, or I go and find him out in Germany!"

After that, whilst the two were at loggerheads, Gaga began murmuring in dolorous tones,—

"It's all over with me; my luck's always bad. It's only a week ago that I finished paying for my little house at Juvisy. Ah, God knows what trouble it cost me! I had to go to Lili for help! And now here's the war declared, and the Prussians'll come, and they'll burn everything. How am I to begin again at my time of life, I should like to know?"

"Bah!" said Clarisse, "I don't care a damn about it. I shall always find what I want."

"Certainly you will," added Simonne. "It'll be a joke. Perhaps, after all, it'll be good biz."

And her smile hinted what she thought. Tatan Néné and Louise Violaine were of her opinion. The former told them that she had enjoyed the most roaring jolly good times with soldiers. Oh! they were good fellows, and would have done any mortal thing for the girls. But as the ladies had raised their voices unduly, Rose Mignon, still sitting on the chest by the bed, silenced them with a softly-whispered "Hush!" They stood quite still at this, and glanced obliquely towards the dead woman, as though this request for silence had emanated from the very shadows of the curtains. In the heavy peaceful stillness which ensued, a void, deathly stillness which made them conscious of the stiff dead body lying stretched close by them, the cries of the mob burst forth,—

"*A Berlin! A Berlin! A Berlin!*"

But soon they forgot. Léa de Horn, who had a political *salon* where former ministers of Louis-Philippe were wont to indulge in delicate epigrams, shrugged her shoulders and continued the conversation in a low tone:

"What a mistake this war is! What a bloodthirsty piece of stupidity!"

At this Lucy forthwith took up the cudgels for the Empire. She had been the mistress of a Prince of the Imperial House, and its defence became a point of family honour with her.

"Do leave them alone, my dear. We couldn't let ourselves be further insulted! Why, this war concerns the honour of France. Oh, you know, I don't say that because of the Prince. He *was* just mean! Just imagine, at night, when he was going to bed, he hid his gold in his boots, and when we played at bézique he used beans, because one day I pounced down on the stakes for fun. But that doesn't prevent my being fair. The Emperor was right."

Léa shook her head with an air of superiority, as became a woman who was repeating the opinions of important personages. Then, raising her voice,—

"This is the end of all things. They're out of their minds at the Tuileries. France ought to have driven them out yesterday. Don't you see?"

They all violently interrupted her. What was up with her? Was she mad about the Emperor? Were people not happy? Was business doing badly? Paris would never enjoy itself so thoroughly again.

Gaga was beside herself: she woke up and was very indignant.

"Be quiet! It's idiotic! You don't know what you're saying. I—I've seen Louis-Philippe's reign: it was full of beggars and misers, my dear. And then came 'Forty-eight!' Oh, it was a pretty disgusting business was their Republic! After 'February,' I was simply dying of starvation—yes, I, Gaga. Oh, if only you'd been through it all, you would go down on your knees before the Emperor, for he's been a father to us; yes, a father to us."

She had to be soothed, but continued with pious fervour:

"O my God, do Thy best to give the Emperor the victory. Preserve the Empire to us!"

They all repeated this aspiration, and Blanche confessed that she burnt candles for the Emperor. Caroline had been smitten by him, and for two whole months had walked where he was likely to pass, but had failed to attract his attention. And with that the others burst forth into furious denunciations of the Republicans, and talked of exterminating them on the frontiers, so that Napoleon III., after having beaten the enemy, might reign peacefully amid universal enjoyment.

"That dirty Bismarck—there's another cad for you!" Maria Blond remarked.

"To think that I should have known him!" cried Simonne. "If only I could have foreseen, I'm the one that would have put some poison in his glass."

But Blanche, on whose heart the expulsion of her Prussian still weighed, ventured to defend Bismarck. Perhaps he wasn't such a bad sort. To every man his trade!

"You know," she added, "he adores women."

"What the hell has that got to do with us?" said Clarisse. "We don't want to cuddle him, eh?"

"There's always too many men of that

sort!" declared Louise Violaine, gravely. "It's better to do without 'em than to mix one's self up with such monsters!"

And the discussion continued, and they stripped Bismarck, and, in her Bonapartist zeal, each of them gave him a sounding kick, whilst Tatan Néné kept saying,—

"Bismarck! Why they've simply driven me crazy with the chap! Oh, I hate him! *I* didn't know that there Bismarck! One can't know everybody."

"Never mind," said Léa de Horn, by way of conclusion, "that Bismarck will give us a jolly good thrashing."

But she could not continue. The ladies were all down on her at once. Eh, what? A thrashing? It was Bismarck they were going to escort home, with blows from the butt-ends of their muskets. What was this bad Frenchwoman going to say next!

"Hush," whispered Rose, for so much noise hurt her.

The cold influence of the corpse once more overcame them, and they all paused together. They were embarrassed; the dead woman was before them again, a dull thread of coming ill possessed them. On the boulevard the cry was passing, hoarse and wild,—

"*A Berlin! A Berlin! A Berlin!*"

Presently, when they were making up their minds to go, a voice was heard calling from the passage,—

"Rose! Rose!"

Gaga opened the door in astonishment, and disappeared for a moment. When she returned,—

"My dear," said she, "it's Fauchery. He's out there at the end of the corridor. He won't come any further, and

he's beside himself because you still stay near that body."

Mignon had at last succeeded in urging the journalist upstairs. Lucy, who was still at the window, leant out, and caught sight of the gentlemen out on the pavement. They were looking up, making energetic signals to her. Mignon was shaking his fists in exasperation, and Steiner, Fontan, Bordenave, and the rest were stretching out their arms with looks of anxious reproach, whilst Daguenet simply stood smoking a cigar, with his hands behind his back, so as not to compromise himself.

"It's true, dear," said Lucy, leaving the window open, "I promised to make you come down. They're all calling us now."

Rose slowly and painfully left the chest.

"I'm coming down, I'm coming down," she whispered. "It's very certain she no longer needs me. They're going to send in a Sister of Mercy."

And she turned round searching for her hat and shawl. Mechanically she filled a basin of water on the toilet-table, and whilst washing her hands and face, continued,—

"I don't know! It's been a great blow to me. We used scarcely to be nice to one another. Ah, well! you see I'm quite silly over it now. Oh! I've got all sorts of strange ideas—I want to die myself—I feel the end of the world's coming. Yes, I need air."

The corpse was beginning to poison the atmosphere of the room. And after long heedlessness there ensued a panic.

"Let's be off, let's be off, my little

pets!" Gaga kept saying. "It isn't wholesome here."

They went briskly out, casting a last glance at the bed as they passed it. But whilst Lucy, Blanche, and Caroline still remained behind, Rose gave a final look round, for she wanted to leave the room in order. She drew a curtain across the window, and then it occurred to her that the lamp was not the proper thing, and that a taper should take its place. So she lit one of the copper candelabra on the chimney-piece and placed it on the night-table beside the corpse. A brilliant light suddenly illumined the dead woman's face. The women were horror-struck. They shuddered and escaped.

"Ah, she's changed, she's changed!" murmured Rose Mignon, who was the last to remain.

She went away; she shut the door. Nana was left alone, with upturned face in the light cast by the candle. She was fruit of the charnel-house, a heap of matter and blood, a shovelful of corrupted flesh thrown down on the pillow. The pustules had invaded the whole of the face, so that each touched its neigh-bour. Fading and sunken, they had assumed the greyish hue of mud, and on that formless pulp, where the features had ceased to be traceable, they already resembled some decaying damp from the grave. One eye, the left eye, had completely foundered among bubbling purulence, and the other, which remained half open, looked like a deep black ruinous hole. The nose was still suppurating. Quite a reddish crush was peeling from one of the cheeks, and invading the mouth, which it distorted into a horrible grin. And over this loathsome and grotesque mask of death, the hair, the beautiful hair, still blazed like sunlight and flowed downwards in rippling gold. Venus was rotting. It seemed as though the poison she had assimilated in the gutters, and on the carrion tolerated by the roadside, the leaven with which she had poisoned a whole people, had but now remounted to her face and turned it to corruption.

The room was empty. A great despairing breath came up from the boulevard, and swelled the curtain.

"*A Berlin! A Berlin! A Berlin!*"

THE END

# A LOVE EPISODE
## AND
# OTHER STORIES

# The Miller's Daughter

## CHAPTER I

### THE BETROTHAL

Père Merlier's mill, one beautiful summer evening, was arranged for a grand fête. In the courtyard were three tables, placed end to end, which awaited the guests. Every one knew that Françoise, Merlier's daughter, was that night to be betrothed to Dominique, a young man who was accused of idleness, but whom the fair sex for three leagues around gazed at with sparkling eyes, such a fine appearance had he.

Père Merlier's mill was pleasing to look upon. It stood exactly in the centre of Rocreuse, where the highway made an elbow. The village had but one street, with two rows of huts, a row on each side of the road; but, at the elbow, meadows spread out and huge trees, which lined the banks of the Morelle, covered the extremity of the valley with lordly shade. There was not, in all Lorraine, a corner of nature more adorable. To the right and to the left, thick woods, centenarian forests, towered up from gentle slopes, filling the horizon with a sea of verdure, while, towards the south, the plain stretched away, of marvellous fertility, displaying as far as the eye could reach patches of ground divided by green hedges. But what constituted the special charm of Rocreuse was the coolness of that cut of verdure in the most sultry days of July and August. The Morelle descended from the forests of Gagny, and seemed to have gathered the cold from the foliage beneath which it flowed for leagues; it brought with it the murmuring sounds, the icy and concentrated shade of the woods. And it was not the sole source of coolness: all sorts of flowing streams gurgled through the forest; at each step, springs bubbled up; one felt, on following the narrow pathways, that there must exist subterranean lakes which pierced through beneath the moss and availed themselves of the smallest crevices, at the feet of trees or between the rocks, to burst forth in crystalline fountains. The whispering voices of these brooks were so numerous and so loud that they drowned the song of the bullfinches. It was like some enchanted park, with cascades falling from every portion.

Below, the meadows were damp. Gigantic chestnut trees cast dark shadows. On the borders of the meadows, long hedges of poplars exhibited in lines their rustling branches. Two avenues of enormous plane trees

1

stretched across the fields towards the ancient Château de Gagny, then a mass of ruins. In this constantly watered district, the grass grew to an extraordinary height. It resembled a garden between two wooded hills, a natural garden, of which the meadows were the lawns, the giant trees marking the colossal flower-beds. When the sun's rays, at noon, poured straight downward, the shadows assumed a bluish tint, scorched grass slept in the heat, while an icy shiver passed beneath the foliage.

And there it was that Père Merlier's mill enlivened with its tic-tac a corner of wild verdure. The structure, built of plaster and planks, seemed as old as the world. It dipped partially in the Morelle, which rounded at that point into a transparent basin. A sluice had been made, and the water fell from a height of several mètres upon the mill wheel, which cracked as it turned, with the asthmatic cough of a faithful servant grown old in the house. When Père Merlier was advised to change it, he shook his head, saying that a new wheel would be lazier and would not so well understand the work; and he mended the old one with whatever he could put his hands on: cask staves, rusty iron, zinc and lead. The wheel appeared gayer than ever for it, with its profile grown odd, all plumed with grass and moss. When the water beat upon it with its silvery flood, it was covered with pearls, its strange carcass wore a sparkling attire of necklaces of mother-of-pearl.

The part of the mill which dipped in the Morelle had the air of a barbaric arch, stranded there. A full half of

the structure was built on piles. The water flowed beneath the floor, and deep places were there, renowned throughout the district for the enormous eels and cray-fish caught in them. Below the fall, the basin was as clear as a mirror, and, when the wheel did not cover it with foam, schools of huge fish could be seen, swimming with the slowness of a squadron. Broken steps led down to the river, near a stake to which a boat was moored. A wooden gallery passed above the wheel. Windows opened, pierced irregularly. It was a pellmell of corners, of little walls, of constructions added too late, of beams and of roofs, which gave the mill the aspect of an old, dismantled citadel. But ivy had grown; all sorts of clinging plants stopped the too wide chinks and threw a green cloak over the ancient building. The young ladies who passed by sketched Père Merlier's mill in their albums.

On the side facing the highway, the structure was more solid. A stone gateway opened upon the wide courtyard, which was bordered to the right and to the left by sheds and stables. Beside a well, an immense elm covered half the courtyard with its shadow. In the backround, the building displayed the four windows of its second-story, surmounted by a pigeon house. Père Merlier's sole vanity was to have this front plastered every ten years. It had just received a new coating, and dazzled the village when the sun shone on it at noon.

For twenty years, Père Merlier had been mayor of Rocreuse. He was esteemed for the fortune he had acquired. His wealth was estimated at something like eighty thousand francs, amassed sou by sou. When he married Madeleine Guillard, who brought him the mill as her dowry, he possessed only his two arms. But Madeleine never repented of her choice, so briskly did he manage the business. Now, his wife was dead, and he remained a widower with his daughter Françoise. Certainly, he might have rested, allowed the mill wheel to slumber in the moss; but that would have been too dull for him, and in his eyes the building would have seemed dead. He toiled on for pleasure.

Père Merlier was a tall old man, with a long, still face, who never laughed, but who possessed, notwithstanding, a very gay heart. He had been chosen mayor because of his money, and also on account of the imposing air he could assume during a marriage ceremony.

Françoise Merlier was just eighteen. She did not pass for one of the handsome girls of the district, as she was not robust. Up to her fifteenth year, she had been even ugly.

The Rocreuse people had not been able to understand why the daughter of Père and Mère Merlier, both of whom had always enjoyed excellent health, grew ill and with an air of regret. But, at fifteen, though yet delicate, her little face became one of the prettiest in the world. She had black hair, black eyes, and was as rosy as a peach; her lips constantly wore a smile, there were dimples in her cheeks, and her fair forehead seemed crowned with sunlight. Although not considered robust in the district, she was far from thin; the idea was simply that she could not lift a sack of grain; but she would become

plump as she grew older—she would eventually be as round and dainty as a quail. Her father's long periods of silence had made her thoughtful very young. If she smiled constantly, it was to please others. By nature she was serious.

Of course, all the young men of the district paid court to her, more on account of her ècus than her pretty ways. At last, she made a choice which scandalized the community.

On the opposite bank of the Morelle lived a tall youth named Dominique Penquer. He did not belong to Rocreuse. Ten years before, he had arrived from Belgium as the heir of his uncle, who had left him a small property upon the very border of the forest of Gagny, just opposite the mill, a few gunshots distant. He had come to sell this property, he said, and return home. But the district charmed him, it appeared, for he did not quit it. He was seen cultivating his little field, gathering a few vegetables upon which he subsisted. He fished and hunted; many times, the forest guards nearly caught him and were on the point of drawing up procès-verbaux against him. This free existence, the resources of which the peasants could not clearly discover, at length gave him a bad reputation. He was vaguely styled a poacher. At any rate, he was lazy, for he was often found asleep on the grass when he should have been at work. The hut he inhabited, beneath the last trees on the edge of the forest, did not seem at all like the dwelling of an honest young fellow. If he had had dealings with the wolves of the ruins of Gagny, the old women would not have been the least bit surprised. Nevertheless, the young girls sometimes risked defending him, for this doubtful man was superb; supple and tall as a poplar, he had a very white skin, with flaxen hair and beard which gleamed like gold in the sun.

One fine morning, Françoise declared to Père Merlier that she loved Dominique and would never wed any other man.

It may well be imagined what a blow this was to Père Merlier. He said nothing, according to his custom, but his face grew thoughtful and his internal gayety no longer sparkled in his eyes. He looked gruff for a week. Françoise also was exceedingly grave. What tormented Père Merlier was to find out how this rogue of a poacher had managed to fascinate his daughter. Dominique had never visited the mill. The miller watched and saw the gallant, on the other side of the Morelle, stretched out upon the grass and feigning to be asleep. Françoise could see him from her chamber window. Everything was plain: they had fallen in love by casting sheep's eyes at each other over the mill wheel.

Another week went by. Françoise became more and more grave. Père Merlier still said nothing. Then, one evening, he himself silently brought in Dominique. Françoise, at that moment, was setting the table. She did not seem astonished; she contented herself with putting on an additional plate, knife and fork; but the little dimples were again seen in her cheeks and her smile reappeared. That morning, Père Merlier, had sought out Dominique in his hut on the border of the wood.

There, the two men had talked for three hours, with doors and windows closed. What was the purport of their conversation no one ever knew. Certain it was, however, that Père Merlier, on taking his departure, already called Dominique his son-in-law. Without doubt, the old man had found the youth he had gone to seek—a worthy youth—in the lazy fellow who stretched himself out upon the grass to make the girls fall in love with him.

All Rocreuse clamored. The women at the doors had plenty to say on the subject of the folly of Père Merlier, who had thus introduced a reprobate into his house. The miller let people talk on. Perhaps, he remembered his own marriage. He was without a sou when he wedded Madeleine and her mill; this, however, had not prevented him from making a good husband. Besides, Dominique cut short the gossip by going so vigorously to work that all the district was amazed. The miller's assistant had just been drawn to serve as a soldier, and Dominique would not suffer another to be engaged. He carried the sacks, drove the cart, fought with the old mill wheel when it refused to turn, and all this with such good will that people came to see him out of curiosity. Père Merlier had his silent laugh. He was excessively proud of having formed a correct estimate of this youth. There is nothing like love to give courage to young folks. Amid all these heavy labors, Françoise and Dominique adored each other. They did not indulge in lovers' talks, but there was a smiling gentleness in their glances.

Up to that time, Père Merlier had not spoken a single word on the subject of marriage, and they respected this silence, awaiting the old man's will. Finally, one day towards the middle of July, he caused three tables to be placed in the courtyard, beneath the great elm, and invited his friends of Rocreuse to come in the evening and drink a glass of wine with him.

When the courtyard was full and all had their glasses in their hands, Père Merlier raised his very high and said:

"I have the pleasure to announce to you that Françoise will wed this young fellow here in a month, on Saint-Louis' Day."

Then, they drank noisily. Everybody smiled. But Père Merlier, again lifting his voice, exclaimed:

"Dominique, embrace your fiancée. It is your right."

They embraced, blushing to the tips of their ears, while all the guests laughed joyously. It was a genuine fête. They emptied a small cask of wine. Then, when all were gone but intimate friends, the conversation was carried on without noise. The night had fallen, a starry and cloudless night. Dominique and Françoise, seated side by side on a bench, said nothing.

An old peasant spoke of the war the Emperor had declared against Prussia. All the village lads had already departed. On the preceding day troops had again passed through the place. There was going to be hard fighting. "Bah!" said Père Merlier, with the selfishness of a happy man, "Dominique is a foreigner; he will not go to the war. And, if the Prussians come here, he will be on hand to defend his wife!"

The idea that the Prussians might come there seemed a good joke. They were going to receive a sound whipping, and the affair would soon be over.

"I have already seen them, I have already seen them," repeated the old peasant, in a hollow voice.

There was silence. Then, they drank again. Françoise and Dominique had heard nothing; they had gently taken each other by the hand, behind the bench, so that nobody could see them, and it seemed so delightful that they remained where they were, their eyes plunged into the depths of the shadows.

What a warm and superb night it was! The village slumbered on both edges of the white highway in infantile quietude. From time to time was heard the crowing of some chanticleer aroused too soon. From the huge woods near by came long breaths, which passed over the roofs like caresses. The meadows, with their dark shadows, assumed a mysterious and dreamy majesty, while all the springs, all the flowing waters which gurgled in the darkness seemed to be the cool and rhythmical respiration of the sleeping country. Occasionally, the ancient mill wheel, lost in a doze, appeared to dream like those old watchdogs that bark while snoring; it cracked, it talked to itself, rocked by the fall of the Morelle, the surface of which gave forth the musical and continuous sound of an organ pipe. Never had more profound peace descended upon a happier corner of nature.

## CHAPTER II

### THE ATTACK ON THE MILL

A MONTH later, on the day preceding that of Saint-Louis, Rocreuse was in a state of terror. The Prussians had beaten the Emperor and were advancing by forced marches towards the village. For a week past, people who hurried along the highway had been announcing them thus: "They are at Lormière—they are at Novelles!" and, on hearing that they were drawing near so rapidly, Rocreuse, every morning, expected to see them descend from the woods of Gagny. They did not come, however, and that increased the fright. They would surely fall upon the village during the night and slaughter everybody.

That morning, a little before sunrise, there was an alarm. The inhabitants were awakened by the loud tramp of men on the highway. The women were already on their knees, making the sign of the cross, when some of the people, peering cautiously through the partially opened windows, recognized the red pantaloons. It was a French detachment. The captain immediately asked for the mayor of the district, and remained at the mill, after having talked with Père Merlier.

The sun rose gayly, that morning. It would be hot at noon. Over the woods floated a golden brightness, while, in the distance, white vapors arose from the meadows. The neat and pretty village awoke amid the fresh air, and the country, with its river and its springs, had the moist sweetness of a bouquet. But that beautiful day caused nobody to smile. The captain was seen to take a turn around the mill, examine the neighboring houses, pass to the other side of the Morelle, and from there study the district with a fieldglass; Père Merlier, who accompanied him, seemed to be giving him explanations. Then, the captain posted soldiers behind the walls, behind the trees and in the ditches. The main body of the detachment encamped in the courtyard of the mill. Was there going to be a battle? When Père Merlier returned, he was questioned. He nodded his head, without speaking. Yes, there was going to be a battle!

Françoise and Dominique were in the courtyard; they looked at him. At last, he took his pipe from his mouth, and said:

"Ah! my poor young ones, you cannot get married to-morrow!"

Dominique, his lips pressed together, with an angry frown on his forehead, at times raised himself on tip-toe and fixed his eyes upon the woods of Gagny, as if he wished to see the Prussians arrive. Françoise, very pale and serious came and went, furnishing the soldiers with what they needed. The troops were making soup in a corner of the courtyard; they joked while waiting for it to get ready.

The captain was delighted. He had visited the chambers and the huge hall of the mill which looked out upon the river. Now, seated beside the well, he was conversing with Père Merlier.

"Your mill is a real fortress," said he. "We can hold it without difficulty until evening. The bandits are late. They ought to be here."

The miller was grave. He saw his mill burning like a torch; but he uttered no complaint, thinking such a course useless. He merely said:

"You had better hide the boat behind the wheel; there is a place there just fit for that purpose. Perhaps, it will be useful to have the boat."

The captain gave the requisite order.

This officer was a handsome man of forty; he was tall and had an amiable countenance. The sight of Françoise and Dominique seemed to please him. He contemplated them as if he had forgotten the coming struggle. He followed Françoise with his eyes and his look told plainly that he thought her charming. Then, turning towards Dominique, he asked, suddenly:

"Why are you not in the army, my good fellow?"

"I am a foreigner," answered the young man.

The captain evidently did not attach much weight to this reason. He winked his eye and smiled. Françoise was more agreeable company than a cannon. On seeing him smile, Dominique added:

"I am a foreigner, but I can put a ball in an apple at five hundred mètres. There is my hunting gun behind you."

"You may have use for it," responded the captain dryly.

Françoise had approached, somewhat agitated. Without heeding the strangers present, Dominique took and grasped in his the two hands she extended to him as if to put herself under his protection. The captain smiled again, but said not a word. He remained seated, his sword across his knees and his eyes plunged into space, lost in a reverie.

It was already ten o'clock. The heat had become very great. A heavy silence prevailed. In the courtyard, in the shadows of the sheds, the soldiers had begun to eat their soup. Not a sound came from the village; all its inhabitants had barricaded the doors and windows of their houses. A dog, alone upon the highway, howled. From the neighboring forests and meadows, swooning in the heat, came a prolonged and distant voice, made up of all the scattered breaths. A cuckoo sang. Then, the silence grew more intense.

Suddenly, in that slumbering air, a shot was heard. The captain leaped briskly to his feet, the soldiers left their plates of soup, yet half full. In a few seconds everybody was at the post of duty; from bottom to top the mill was occupied. Meanwhile, the captain, who had gone out upon the road, had discovered nothing; to the right and to the left, the highway stretched out, empty and white. A second shot was heard, and still nothing visible, not even a shadow. But, as he was returning, the captain perceived in the direction of Gagny, between two trees, a light puff of smoke whirling away like thistledown. The wood was calm and peaceful.

"The bandits have thrown themsleves into the forest," muttered he. "They know we are here."

Then the firing continued, growing more and more vigorous, between the French soldiers, posted around the mill, and the Prussians, hidden behind the trees. The balls whistled above the Morelle, without damaging either side. The fusillade was irregular, the shots coming from every bush; and still only the little puffs of smoke, tossed gently by the breeze, were seen. This lasted nearly two hours. The officer hummed a tune with an air of indifference. Françoise and Dominique, who had remained in the court yard, raised themselves on tiptoe and looked over a low wall. They were particularly interested in a little soldier, posted on the shore of the Morelle, behind the remains of an old batteau; he stretched himself out flat on the ground, watched, fired, and then glided into a ditch a trifle further back to reload his gun; and his movements were so droll, so tricky and so supple, that they smiled as they looked at him. He must have perceived the head of a Prussian, for he arose quickly and brought his weapon to his shoulder; but, before he could fire, he uttered a cry, fell and rolled into the ditch, where, for an instant, his legs twitched convulsively like the claws of a chicken just killed. The little soldier had received a ball full in the breast. He was the first man slain. Instinctively, Françoise seized Dominique's hand and clasped it with a nervous contraction.

"Move away," said the captain. "You are within range of the balls."

At that moment, a sharp little thud was heard in the old elm, and a fragment of a branch came whirling down. But the two young folks did not stir; they were nailed to the spot by anxiety to see what was going on. On the edge of the wood, a Prussian had suddenly come out from behind a tree as from a theatre stage entrance, beating the air with his hands and falling backwards. Nothing further moved; the two corpses seemed asleep in the broad sunlight; not a living soul was seen in the scorching country. Even the crack of the fusillade had ceased. The Morelle alone whispered in its clear tones.

Père Merlier looked at the captain with an air of surprise, as if to ask him if the struggle was over.

"They are getting ready for something worse," muttered the officer. "Don't trust appearances. Move away from there."

He had not finished speaking when there was a terrible discharge of musketry. The great elm was riddled and a host of leaves shot into the air. The Prussians had happily fired too high. Dominique dragged, almost carried Françoise away, while Père Merlier followed them, shouting:

"Go down into the cellar; the walls are solid!"

But they did not heed him; they entered the huge hall, where ten soldiers were waiting in silence, watching through the chinks in the closed window-shutters. The captain was alone in the courtyard, crouching behind the little wall, while the furious discharges continued. Without, the soldiers he had posted gave ground only foot by foot. However, they re-entered one by one, crawling, when the enemy had dislodged them from their hiding-places. Their orders were to gain time, and not show themselves that the Prussians might remain in ignorance as to what force was before them. Another hour went by. As a sergeant arrived, saying that but two or three more men remained without, the captain glanced at his watch, muttering:

"Half-past two o'clock. We must hold the position four hours longer."

He caused the great gate of the courtyard to be closed, and every preparation was made for an energetic resistance. As the Prussians were on the opposite side of the Morelle, an immediate assault was not to be feared. There was a bridge two kilomètres away, but they evidently were not aware of its existence, and it was hardly likely that they would attempt to ford the river. The officer, therefore, simply ordered the highway to be watched. Every effort would be made in the direction of the country.

Again the fusillade had ceased. The mill seemed dead beneath the glowing sun. Not a shutter was open; no sound came from the interior. At length, little by little, the Prussians showed themselves at the edge of the forest of Gagny. They stretched their necks, and grew bold. In the mill, several soldiers had already raised their guns to their shoulders; but the captain cried: "No, no; wait. Let them come nearer."

They were exceedingly prudent, gazing at the mill with a suspicious air. The silent and sombre old structure, with its curtains of ivy, filled them with uneasiness. Nevertheless, they advanced. When fifty of them were in the opposite meadow, the officer uttered the single word:

"Fire!"

A crash was heard, isolated shots followed. Françoise, all of a tremble, had mechanically put her hands to her ears. Dominique, behind the soldiers, looked on; when the smoke had somewhat lifted, he saw three Prussians stretched upon their backs in the centre of the meadow. The others had thrown themselves behind the willows and poplars. Then, the siege began.

For more than an hour, the mill was riddled with balls. They dashed against the old walls like hail. When they struck the stones they were heard to flatten and fall into the water. They buried themselves in the wood with a hollow sound. Occasionally, a sharp crack announced that the mill wheel had been hit. The soldiers in the interior were careful of their shots; they fired only when they could take aim. From time to time, the captain consulted his watch. As a ball broke a shutter and ploughed into the ceiling, he said to himself:

"Four o'clock. We shall never be able to hold out!"

Little by little, the terrible fusillade weakened the old mill. A shutter fell into the water, pierced like a bit of lace, and it was necessary to replace it with a mattress. Père Merlier constantly exposed himself to ascertain the extent of the damage done to his poor wheel, the cracking of which made his heart ache. All would be over with it this time; never could he repair it. Dominique had implored Françoise to withdraw, but she had refused to leave him; she was seated behind a huge oaken clothes-press, which protected her. A ball, however, struck the clothes-press, the sides of which gave forth a hollow sound. Then, Dominique placed himself in front of Françoise. He had not yet fired a shot; he held his gun in his hand, but was unable to approach the windows, which were altogether occupied by the soldiers. At each discharge, the floor shook.

"Attention! attention!" suddenly cried the captain.

He had just seen a great dark mass emerge from the wood. Immediately a formidable platoon fire opened. It was like a water-spout passing over the mill. Another shutter was shattered, and, through the gaping opening of the window, the balls entered. Two soldiers rolled upon the floor. One of them lay like a stone; they pushed the body against the wall because it was in the way. The other twisted in agony, begging his comrades to finish him; but they paid no attention to him. The balls entered in a constant stream; each man took care of himself and strove to find a loop-hole through which to return the fire. A third soldier was hit; he uttered not a word; he fell on the edge of a table, with eyes fixed and haggard. Opposite these dead men, Françoise, stricken with horror, had mechanically pushed away her chair to sit on the floor against the wall; she thought she would take up less room there and not be in so much danger. Meanwhile, the soldiers had collected all the mattresses of the household and partially stopped up the window with them. The hall was filled with wrecks, with broken weapons and demolished furniture.

"Five o'clock," said the captain, "Keep up your courage! They are about to try to cross the river!"

At that moment, Françoise uttered a cry. A ball which had ricochetted had grazed her forehead. Several drops of blood appeared. Dominique stared at her; then, approaching the window, he fired his first shot. Once started, he did not stop. He loaded and fired without heeding what was pasisng around him, but from time to time he glanced at Françoise. He was very deliberate and aimed with care. The Prussians, keeping beside the poplars, attempted the passage of the Morelle, as the captain had predicted; but, as soon as a man strove to cross, he fell, shot in the head by Dominique. The captain, who had his eyes on the young man, was amazed. He complimented him, saying that he should be glad to have many

such skilful marksmen. Dominique did not hear him. A ball cut his shoulder, another wounded his arm, but he continued to fire.

There were two more dead men. The mangled mattresses no longer stopped the windows. The last discharge seemed as if it would have carried away the mill. The position had ceased to be tenable. Nevertheless, the captain said, firmly:

"Hold your ground for half an hour more!"

Now, he counted the minutes. He had promised his chiefs to hold the enemy in check there until evening, and he would not give an inch before the hour he had fixed on for the retreat. He preserved his amiable air and smiled upon Françoise to reassure her. He had picked up the gun of a dead soldier and himself was firing.

Only four soldiers remained in the hall. The Prussians appeared in a body on the other side of the Morelle, and it was clear that they intended speedily to cross the river. A few minutes more elapsed. The stubborn captain would not order the retreat. Just then, a sergeant hastened to him and said:

"They are upon the highway; they will take us in the rear!"

The Prussians must have found the bridge. The captain pulled out his watch and looked at it.

"Five minutes longer," said he. "They cannot get here before that time!"

Then, at six o'clock exactly, he at last consented to lead his men out through a little door which opened into a lane. From there they threw themselves into a ditch; they gained the forest of Sauval. Before taking his departure, the captain bowed very politely to Père Merlier and made his excuses, adding:

"Amuse them! We will return!"

Dominique was now alone in the hall. He was still firing, hearing nothing, understanding nothing. He felt only the need of defending Françoise. He had not the least suspicion in the world that the soldiers had retreated. He aimed and killed his man at every shot. Suddenly, there was a loud noise. The Prussians had entered the courtyard from behind. Dominique fired a last shot, and they fell upon him while his gun was yet smoking.

Four men held him. Others vociferated around him in a frightful language. They were ready to slaughter him on the spot. Françoise, with a supplicating look, had cast herself before him. But an officer entered and ordered the prisoner to be delivered up to him. After exchanging a few words in German with the soldiers, he turned towards Dominique and said to him, roughly, in very good French:

"You will be shot in two hours!"

## CHAPTER III

### THE FLIGHT

IT was a settled rule of the German staff that every Frenchman, not belonging to the regular army, taken with arms in his hands should be shot. The militia companies themselves were not recognized as belligerents. By thus making terrible examples of the peasants who defended their homes, the Germans hoped to prevent the levy en masse, which they feared.

The officer, a tall, lean man of fifty, briefly questioned Dominique. Although he spoke remarkably pure French, he had a stiffness altogether Prussian.

"Do you belong to this district?" asked he.

"No; I am a Belgian," answered the young man.

"Why then did you take up arms? The fighting did not concern you!"

Dominique made no reply. At that moment, the officer saw Françoise who was standing by, very pale, listening; upon her white forehead her slight would had put a red bar. He looked at the young folks, one after the other, seemed to understand matters and contented himself with adding:

"You do not deny having fired, do you?"

"I fired as often as I could!" responded Dominique, tranquilly.

This confession was useless, for he was black with powder, covered with sweat and stained with a few drops of blood which had flowed from the scratch on his shoulder.

"Very well," said the officer. "You will be shot in two hours!"

Françoise did not cry out. She clasped her hands and raised them with a gesture of mute despair. The officer noticed this gesture. Two soldiers had taken Dominique to a neighboring apartment, where they were to keep watch over him. The young girl had fallen upon a chair, totally overcome; she could not weep, she was suffocating. The officer had continued to examine her. At last he spoke to her

"Is that young man your brother?" he demanded.

She shook her head negatively. The

German stood stiffly on his feet, without a smile. Then, after a short silence, he again asked:

"Has he lived long in the district?"

She nodded affirmatively.

"In that case, he ought to be thoroughly acquainted with the neighboring forests."

This time, she spoke.

"He is thoroughly acquainted with them, Monsieur," said she, looking at him with considerable surprise.

He said nothing further to her, but turned upon his heel, demanding that the mayor of the village should be brought to him. But Françoise had arisen, with a slight blush on her countenance; thinking that she had seized the aim of the officer's questions, she had recovered hope. She herself ran to find her father.

Perè Merlier, as soon as the firing had ceased, had quickly descended to the wooden gallery to examine his wheel. He adored his daughter; he had a solid friendship for Dominique, his future son-in-law; but his wheel also held a large place in his heart. Since the two young ones, as he called them, had come safe and sound out of the fight, he thought of his other tenderness, which had suffered greatly. Bent over the huge wooden carcass, he was studying its wounds with a sad air. Five buckets were shattered to pieces; the central framework was riddled. He thrust his fingers in the bullet holes to measure their depth; he thought how he could repair all these injuries. Françoise found him already stopping up the clefts with rubbish and moss.

"Father," said she, "you are wanted."

And she wept, at last, as she told him what she had just heard. Père Merlier tossed his head. People were not shot in such a summary fashion. The matter must be looked after. He re-entered the mill, with his silent and tranquil air. When the officer demanded of him provisions for his men, he replied that the inhabitants of Rocreuse were not accustomed to be treated roughly, and that nothing would be obtained from them if violence were employed. He would see to everything but on condition that he was not interfered with. The officer at first seemed irritated by his calm tone; then, he gave way before the old man's short and clear words. He even called him back and asked him:

"What is the name of that wood opposite?"

"The forest of Sauval."

"What is its extent?"

The miller looked at him fixedly.

"I do not know," he answered.

And he went away. An hour later, the contribution of war in provisions and money, demanded by the officer, was in the courtyard of the mill. Night came on. Françoise watched with anxiety the movements of the soldiers. She hung about the room in which Dominique was imprisoned. Towards seven o'clock, she experienced a poignant emotion. She saw the officer enter the prisoner's apartment, and, for a quarter of an hour, heard their voices in loud conversation. For an instant, the officer reappeared upon the threshold to give an order in German, which she did not understand; but, when twelve men ranged themselves in the courtyard, their guns on their shoulders, she trembled and felt as if about to faint. All then was over: the execution was going to take place. The twelve men stood there ten minutes, Dominique's voice continuing to be raised in a tone of violent refusal. Finally, the officer came out, saying, as he roughly shut the door: "Very well; reflect. I give you until to-morrow morning."

And, with a gesture, he ordered the twelve men to break ranks. Françoise was stupefied. Père Merlier, who had been smoking his pipe and looking at the platoon simply with an air of curiosity, took her by the arm with paternal gentleness. He led her to her chamber.

"Be calm," said he, "and try to sleep. To-morrow, when it is light, we will see what can be done."

As he withdrew, he prudently locked her in. It was his opinion that women are good for nothing, and that they spoil everything when they take a hand in a serious affair. But Françoise did not retire. She sat for a long while upon the side of her bed, listening to the noises of the house. The German soldiers, encamped in the courtyard, sang and laughed; they must have been eating and drinking until eleven o'clock, for the racket did not cease an instant. In the mill itself, heavy footsteps resounded from time to time, without doubt those of the sentinels who were being relieved. But she was interested most by the sounds she could distinguish in the apartment beneath her chamber. Many times she stretched herself out at full length and put her ear to the floor. That apartment was the one in which Dominique was confined. He must have been walking back and forth from

the window to the wall, for she long heard the regular cadence of his steps. Then, deep silence ensued; he had, doubtless, seated himself. Finally, every noise ceased and all was as if asleep. When slumber appeared to her to have settled on the house, she opened her window as gently as possible and leaned her elbows on the sill.

Without, the night had a warm serenity. The slender crescent of the moon, which was sinking behind the forest of Sauval, lighted up the country with the glimmer of a night-lamp. The lengthened shadows of the tall trees barred the meadows with black, while the grass in uncovered spots assumed the softness of greenish velvet. But Françoise did not pause to admire the mysterious charms of the night. She examined the country, searching for the sentinels whom the Germans had posted obliquely. She clearly saw their shadows extending like the rounds of a ladder along the Morelle. Only one was before the mill, on the other shore of the river, beside a willow the branches of which dipped in the water. Françoise saw him plainly. He was a tall man and was standing motionless, his face turned towards the sky, with the dreamy air of a shepherd.

When she had carefully inspected the locality, she again seated herself on her bed. She remained there an hour, deeply absorbed. Then, she listened once more: there was not a sound in the mill. She returned to the window and glanced out; but, doubtless, one of the horns of the moon, which was still visible behind the trees, made her uneasy, for she resumed her waiting attitude. At last, she thought the proper time had come. The night was as black as jet; she could no longer see the sentinel opposite; the country spread out like a pool of ink. She strained her ear for an instant and made her decision. Passing near the window, was an iron ladder, the bars fastened to the wall, which mounted from the wheel to the garret, and formerly enabled the millers to reach certain machinery; afterwards, the mechanism had been altered, and for a long while, the ladder had been hidden under the thick ivy which covered that side of the mill.

Françoise bravely climbed out of her window and grasped one of the bars of the ladder. She began to descend. Her skirts embarrassed her greatly. Suddenly a stone was detached from the wall and fell into the Morelle with a loud splash. She stopped, with an icy shiver of fear. Then, she realized that the waterfall, with its continuous roar, would drown every noise she might make, and she descended more courageously, feeling the ivy with her foot, assuring herself that the rounds were firm. When she was at the height of the chamber which served as Dominique's prison, she paused. An unforeseen difficulty nearly caused her to lose all her courage: the window of the chamber was not directly below that of her apartment. She hung off from the ladder, but, when she stretched out her arm, her hand encountered only the wall. Must she, then, ascend without pushing her plan to completion? Her arms were fatigued; the murmur of the Morelle beneath her commenced to make her dizzy. Then, she tore from the wall little fragments of plaster and threw them against Dominique's window. He did not hear; he was, doubtless, asleep. She crumbled more plaster from the wall, scraping the skin off her fingers. She was utterly exhausted; she felt herself falling backwards, when Dominique, at last, softly opened the window.

"It is I!" murmured she. "Catch me quickly; I am falling!"

It was the first time that she had addressed him familiarly. Leaning out, he seized her and drew her into the chamber. There, she gave vent to a flood of tears, stifling her sobs that she might not be heard. Then, by a supreme effort, she calmed herself.

"Are you guarded?" asked she, in a low voice.

Dominique, still stupefied at seeing her thus, nodded his head affirmatively, pointing to the door. On the other side they heard some one snoring; the sentinel, yielding to sleep, had thrown himself on the floor, against the door, arguing that, by disposing himself thus, the prisoner could not escape.

"You must fly," resumed Françoise, excitedly. "I have come to beg you to do so and to bid you farewell."

But he did not seem to hear her. He repeated:

"What! is it you, is it you? Oh! what fear you caused me! You might have killed yourself!"

He seized her hands; he kissed them.

"How I love you, Françoise!" murmured he. "You are as courageous as good. I had only one dread: that I should die without seeing you again. But you are here, and now they can shoot me. When I have passed a quarter of an hour with you, I shall be ready."

Little by little, he had drawn her to him, and she leaned her head upon his shoulder. The danger made them dearer to each other. They forgot everything in that warm clasp.

"Ah! Françoise," resumed Dominique, in a caressing voice, "this is Saint-Louis' Day, the day so long awaited of our marriage. Nothing has been able to separate us, since we are both here alone, faithful to the appointment. Is not this our wedding morning?"

"Yes, yes," repeated she, " it is our wedding morning."

They tremblingly exchanged a kiss. But, all at once, she disengaged herself from Dominique's arms; she remembered the terrible reality.

"You must fly, you must fly," whispered she. "There is not a minute to be lost!"

And, as he stretched out his arms in the darkness to clasp her again, she said, tenderly:

"Oh! I implore you to listen to me! If you die, I shall die also! In an hour it will be light. I want you to go at once."

Then, rapidly, she explained her plan. The iron ladder descended to the mill wheel; there he could climb down the buckets and get into the boat which was hidden away in a nook. Afterwards, it would be easy for him to reach the other bank of the river and escape.

"But what of the sentinels?" asked he.

"There is only one, opposite, at the foot of the first willow."

"What if he should see me and attempt to give an alarm?"

Françoise shivered. She placed in his hand a knife she had brought with her. There was a brief silence.

"What is to become of your father and yourself?" resumed Dominique. "No, I cannot fly! When I am gone, those soldiers will, perhaps, massacre you both! You do not know them. They offered me my life if I would consent to guide them through the forest of Sauval. When they discover my escape, they will be capable of anything!"

The young girl did not stop to argue. She said, simply, in reply to all the reasons he advanced:

"Out of love for me, fly! If you love me, Dominique, do not remain here another moment!"

Then, she promised to climb back to her chamber. No one would know that she had helped him. She finally threw her arms around him, to convince him with an embrace, with a burst of extraordinary love. He was vanquished. He asked but one more question:

"Can you swear to me that your father knows what you have done and that he advises me to fly?"

"My father sent me!" answered Françoise, boldly.

She told a falsehood. At that moment, she had only one immense need: to know that he was safe, to escape from the abominable thought that the sun would be the signal for his death. When he was far away every misfortune might fall upon her; that would seem delightful to her, from the moment he was secure. The selfishness of her tenderness desired that he should live, before everything.

"Very well," said Dominique; "I will do what you wish."

They said nothing more. Dominique

re-opened the window. But, suddenly, a sound froze them. The door was shaken, and they thought that it was about to be opened. Evidently, a patrol had heard their voices. Standing, locked in each other's arms, they waited in unspeakable anguish. The door was shaken a second time, but it did not open. They uttered low sighs of relief; they comprehended that the soldier who was asleep against the door must have turned over. In fact, silence succeeded; the snoring was resumed.

Dominique exacted that Françoise should ascend to her chamber before he departed. He clasped her in his arms and bade her a mute adieu. Then, he aided her to seize the ladder and clung to it in his turn. But he refused to descend a single round until convinced that she was in her apartment. When Françoise had entered her window, she let fall, in a voice as light as a breath: "Au revoir, my love!"

She leaned her elbows on the sill and strove to follow Dominique with her eyes. The night was yet very dark. She searched for the sentinel, but could not see him; the willow alone made a pale stain in the midst of the gloom. For an instant, she heard the sound produced by Dominique's body in passing along the ivy. Then, the wheel cracked, and there was a slight agitation in the water which told her that the young man had found the boat. A moment afterwards, she distinguished the sombre silhouette of the bateau on the gray surface of the Morelle. Terrible anguish seized upon her. Each instant, she thought she heard the sentinel's cry of alarm; the smallest sounds scattered through the gloom seemed to

her the hurried tread of soldiers, the clatter of weapons, the charging of guns. Nevertheless, the seconds elapsed and the country maintained its profound peace. Dominique must have reached the other side of the river. Françoise saw nothing more. The silence was majestic. She heard a shuffling of feet, a hoarse cry and the hollow fall of a body. Afterwards, the silence grew deeper. Then, as if she had felt Death pass by, she stood, chilled through and through, staring into the thick night.

## CHAPTER IV

### A TERRIBLE EXPERIENCE

At dawn, a clamor of voices shook the mill. Père Merlier opened the door of Françoise's chamber. She went down into the courtyard, pale and very calm. But, there, she could not repress a shiver, as she saw the corpse of a Prussian soldier, stretched out on a cloak beside the well.

Around the body, troops gesticulated, uttering cries of fury. Many of them shook their fists at the village. Meanwhile, the officer had summoned Père Merlier as the mayor of the commune.

"Look!" said he to him, in a voice almost choking with anger. "There lies one of our men who was found assassinated upon the bank of the river. We must make a terrible example, and I count on you to aid us in discovering the murderer."

"As you choose," answered the miller, with his usual stoicism; "but you will find it no easy task."

The officer stooped and drew aside

a part of the cloak which hid the face of the dead man. Then, appeared a horrible wound. The sentinel had been struck in the throat, and the weapon had remained in the cut. It was a kitchen knife with a black handle.

"Examine that knife," said the officer to Père Merlier; "perhaps, it will help us in our search."

The old man gave a start, but recovered control of himself immediately. He replied, without moving a muscle of his face:

"Everybody in the district has similar knives. Doubtless, your man was weary of fighting and put an end to his own life. It looks like it!"

"Mind what you say!" cried the officer, furiously. "I do not know what prevents me from setting fire to the four corners of the village!"

Happily, in his rage, he did not notice the deep trouble pictured on Françoise's countenance. She had been forced to sit down on a stone bench near the well. Despite herself, her eyes were fixed upon the corpse, stretched out on the ground almost at her feet. It was that of a tall and handsome man, who resembled Dominique, with flaxen hair and blue eyes. This resemblance made her heart ache. She thought that, perhaps, the dead soldier had left behind him, in Germany, a sweetheart who would weep her eyes out for him. She recognized her knife in the throat of the murdered man. She had killed him.

The officer was talking of striking Rocreuse with terrible measures, when soldiers, came running to him. Dominique's escape had just been discovered. It caused an extreme agitation. The officer went to the apartment in which

the prisoner had been confined, looked out of the window which had remained open, understood everything and returned exasperated.

Père Merlier seemed greatly vexed by Dominique's flight.

"The imbecile!" he muttered. "He has ruined all!"

Françoise heard him and was overcome with anguish. But the miller did not suspect her of complicity in the affair. He tossed his head, saying to her in an undertone:

"We are in a nice scrape!"

"It was that wretch who assassinated the soldier! I am sure of it!" cried the officer. "He has undoubtedly reached the forest. But he must be found for us, or the village shall pay for him!"

Turning to the miller, he said:

"See here; you ought to know where he is hidden!"

Père Merlier laughed silently, pointing to the wide stretch of wooden hills.

"Do you expect to find a man in there?" said he.

"Oh! there must be nooks there with which you are acquainted. I will give you ten men. You must guide them."

"As you please. But it will take a week to search all the woods in the vicinity."

The old man's tranquillity enraged the officer. In fact, the latter comprehended the absurdity of this search. At that moment, he saw Françoise, pale and trembling, on the bench. The anxious attitude of the young girl struck him. He was silent for an instant, during which he in turn examined the miller and his daughter.

At length, he demanded roughly of the old man:

"Is not that fellow your child's lover?"

Père Merlier grew livid, and seemed about to hurl himself upon the officer to strangle him. He stiffened himself, but made no answer. Françoise buried her face in her hands.

"Yes, that's it!" continued the Prussian, "and you or your daughter helped him to escape! One of you is his accomplice! For the last time, will you give him up to us?"

The miller uttered not a word. He turned away and looked into space with an air of indifference, as if the officer had not addressed him. This brought the latter's rage to a head.

"Very well!" shouted he. "You shall be shot in his place!"

And he again ordered out the platoon of execution. Père Merlier remained as stoical as ever. He hardly even shrugged his shoulders; all this drama appeared to him in bad taste. Without doubt, he did not believe that they would shoot a man so lightly. But, when the platoon drew up before him, he said, gravely:

"So, it is serious, is it? Go on with you bloody work, then! If you must have a victim, I will do as well as another!"

But Françoise started up, terrified, stammering:

"In pity, Monsieur, do no harm to my father! Kill me in his stead! I aided Dominique to fly! I alone am guilty!"

"Hush, my child!" cried Père Merlier. "Why do you tell an untruth? She passed the night locked in her chamber, Monsieur. She tells a falsehood, I assure you!"

"No, I do not tell a falsehood!" resumed the young girl, ardently. "I climbed out of my window and went down the iron ladder; I urged Dominique to fly. This is the truth, the whole truth!"

The old man became very pale. He saw clearly in her eyes that she did not lie, and her story terrified him. Ah! these children, with their hearts, how they spoil everything! Then, he grew angry and exclaimed:

"She is mad; do not heed her. She tells you stupid tales. Come, finish your work!"

She still protested. She knelt, clasping her hands. The officer tranquilly watched this dolorous struggle.

"Mon Dieu!" said he, at last, "I take your father because I have not the other. Find the fugitive and the old man shall be set at liberty!"

She gazed at him with staring eyes, astonished at the atrocity of the proposition.

"How horrible!" murmured she. "Where do you think I can find Dominique at this hour? He has departed; I know no more about him."

"Come, make your choice—him or your father."

"Oh! mon Dieu! how can I choose! If I knew where Dominique was, I could not choose! You are cutting my heart. I would rather die at once. Yes, it would be the sooner over. Kill me, I implore you, kill me!"

This scene of despair and tears finally made the officer impatient. He cried out:

"Enough! I will be merciful: I consent to give you two hours. If, in that time, your lover is not here, your father will be shot in his place!"

He caused Père Merlier to be taken to the chamber which had served as Dominique's prison. The old man demanded tobacco and began to smoke. Upon his impassible face not the slightest emotion was visible. But, when alone, as he smoked, he shed two big tears which ran slowly down his cheeks. His poor, dear child, how she was suffering!

Françoise remained in the middle of the courtyard. Prussian soldiers passed, laughing. Some of them spoke to her, uttered jokes she could not understand. She stared at the door through which her father had disappeared. With a slow movement she put her hand to her forehead, as if to prevent it from bursting.

The officer turned upon his heel, saying:

"You have two hours. Try to utilize them."

She had two hours. This phrase buzzed in her ears. Then, mechanically, she quitted the courtyard; she walked straight ahead. Where should she go? —what should she do? She did not even try to make a decision, because she well understood the inutility of her efforts. However, she wished to see Dominique. They could have an understanding together; they might, perhaps, find an expedient. And, amid the confusion of her thoughts, she went down to the shore of the Morelle, which she crossed below the sluice, at a spot where there were huge stones. Her feet led her beneath the first willow, in the corner of the meadow. As she stooped, she saw a pool of blood which made

her turn pale. It was there the murder had been committed. She followed the track of Dominique in the trodden grass; he must have run, for she perceived a line of long footprints stretching across the meadow. Then, further on, she lost these traces. But, in a neighboring field, she thought she found them again. The new trail conducted her to the edge of the forest, where every indication was effaced.

Françoise, nevertheless, plunged beneath the trees. It solaced her to be alone. She sat down for an instant; but, at the thought that time was passing, she leaped to her feet. How long had it been since she left the mill? Five minutes?—half an hour? She had lost all conception of time. Perhaps, Dominique had concealed himself in a copse she knew of, where they had, one afternoon, eaten filberts together. She hastened to the copse, searched it. Only a blackbird flew away, uttering its soft, sad note. Then, she thought he might have taken refuge in a hollow of the rocks, where it had sometimes been his custom to lie in wait for game; but the hollow of the rocks was empty. What good was it to hunt for him?—she would never find him; but, little by little, the desire to discover him took entire possession of her, and she hastened her steps. The idea that he might have climbed a tree suddenly occurred to her. She advanced with uplifted eyes, and, that he might be made aware of her presence, she called him every fifteen or twenty steps. Cuckoos answered; a breath of wind which passed through the branches made her believe that he was there and was descending. Once, she even imagined she saw him; she stopped, almost choked, and wished to fly. What was she to say to him? Had she come to take him back to be shot? Oh! no, she would not tell him what had happened. She would cry out to him to escape, not to remain in the neighborhood. Then, the thought that her father was waiting for her gave her a sharp pain. She fell upon the turf, weeping, crying aloud:

"Mon Dieu! mon Dieu! Why am I here!"

She was mad to have come. And, as if seized with fear, she ran, she sought to leave the forest. Three times, she deceived herself; she thought she never again would find the mill, when she entered a meadow just opposite Rocreuse. As soon as she saw the village, she paused. Was she going to return alone?

She was still hesitating, when a voice softly called:

"Françoise! Françoise!"

And she saw Dominique, who had raised his head above the edge of a ditch. Just God! she had found him! Did Heaven wish his death? She restrained a cry; she let herself glide into the ditch.

"Are you searching for me?" asked the young man.

"Yes," answered she, her brain in a whirl, not knowing what she said.

"What has happened?"

She lowered her eyes stammered:

"Nothing. I was uneasy; I wanted to see you."

Then, reassured, he explained to her that he had resolved not to go away. He was doubtful about the safety of herself and her father. Those Prussian

wretches were fully capable of taking vengeance upon women and old men. But everything was getting on well. He added, with a laugh:

"Our wedding will take place in a week—I am sure of it."

Then, as she remained overwhelmed, he grew grave again and said:

"But what ails you? You are concealing something from me!"

"No; I swear it to you. I am out of breath from running."

He embraced her, saying that it was imprudent for them to be talking, and he wished to climb out of the ditch to return to the forest. She restrained him. She trembled.

"Listen," said she: "it would, perhaps, be wise for you to remain where you are. No one is searching for you; you have nothing to fear."

"Françoise, you are concealing something from me," repeated he.

Again she swore that she was hiding nothing. She had simply wished to know that he was near her. And she stammered forth still further reasons. She seemed so strange to him that he now could not be induced to flee. Besides, he had faith in the return of the French. Troops had been seen in the direction of Sauval.

"Ah! let them hurry, let them get here as soon as possible;" murmured she, fervently.

At that moment, eleven o'clock sounded from the belfry of Rocreuse. The strokes were clear and distinct. She arose, with a terrified look; two hours had passed since she quitted the mill.

"Hear me," said she, rapidly: "if we have need of you, I will wave my handkechief from my chamber window."

And she departed on a run, while Dominique, very uneasy, stretched himself out upon the edge of the ditch to watch the mill. As she was about to enter Rocreuse, Françoise met an old beggar, Père Bontemps, who knew everybody in the district. He bowed to her; he had just seen the miller in the midst of the Prussians; then, making the sign of the cross, and muttering broken words, he went on his way.

"The two hours have passed," said the officer when Françoise appeared.

Père Merlier was there, seated upon the bench, beside the well. He was smoking. The young girl again begged, wept, sank on her knees. She wished to gain time. The hope of seeing the French return had increased in her, and, while lamenting, she thought she heard in the distance the measured tramp of an army. Oh! if they would come, if they would deliver them all!

"Listen, Monsieur," said she: "an hour, another hour; you can grant us another hour!"

But the officer remained inflexible. He even ordered two men to seize her and take her away, that they might quietly proceed with the execution of the old man. Then, a frightful struggle took place in Françoise's heart. She could not allow her father to be thus assassinated. No, no; she would die rather with Dominique. She was running towards her chamber, when Dominique himself entered the courtyard.

The officer and the soldiers uttered a shout of triumph. But the young man, calmly, with a somewhat severe look, went up to Françoise, as if she had been the only person present.

"You did wrong," said he. "Why did you not bring me back? It remained for Père Bontemps to tell me everything. But I am here!"

## CHAPTER V

### THE RETURN OF THE FRENCH

IT was three o'clock in the afternoon. Great black clouds, the trail of some neighboring storm, had slowly filled the sky. The yellow heavens, the brass covered uniforms, had changed the valley of Rocreuse, so gay in the sunlight, into a den of cut-throats full of sinister gloom. The Prussian officer had contented himself with causing Dominique to be imprisoned, without announcing what fate he reserved for him. Since noon, Françoise had been torn by terrible anguish. Despite her father's entreaties, she would not quit the courtyard. She was awaiting the French. But the hours sped on, night was approaching, and she suffered the more as all the time gained did not seem to be likely to change the frightful dénouement.

About three o'clock, the Prussians made their preparations for departure. For an instant past, the officer had, as on the previous day, shut himself up with Dominique. Françoise realized that the young man's life was in the balance. She clasped her hands, she prayed. Père Merlier, beside her, maintained silence and the rigid attitude of an old peasant, who does not struggle against fate.

"Oh! mon Dieu! oh! mon Dieu!" murmured Françoise, "they are going to kill him!"

The miller drew her to him, and

took her on his knees as if she had been a child.

At that moment, the officer came out, while, behind him, two men brought Dominique.

"Never! never!" cried the latter. "I am ready to die!"

"Think well," resumed the officer. "The service you refuse me another will render us. I am generous: I offer you your life. I want you simply to guide us through the forest to Montredon. There must be pathways leading there."

Dominique was silent.

"So, you persist in your infatuation, do you?"

"Kill me and end all this!" replied the young man.

Françoise, her hands clasped, supplicated him from afar. She had forgotten everything; she would have advised him to commit an act of cowardice. But Père Merlier seized her hands that the Prussians might not see her wild gestures.

"He is right," whispered he: "it is better to die!"

The platoon of execution was there. The officer awaited a sign of weakness on Dominique's part. He still expected to conquer him. No one spoke. In the distance violent crashes of thunder were heard. Oppressive heat weighed upon the country. But, suddenly, amid the silence, a cry broke forth:

"The French! the French!"

Yes, the French were at hand. Upon the Sauval highway, at the edge of the wood, the line of red pantaloons could be distinguished. In the mill there was an extraordinary agitation. The Prussian soldiers ran hither and thither, with guttural exclamations. Not a shot had yet been fired.

"The French! the French!" cried Françoise, clapping her hands.

She was wild with joy. She escaped from her father's grasp; she laughed and tossed her arms in the air. At last, they had come and come in time, since Dominique was still alive!

A terrible platoon fire, which burst upon her ears like a clap of thunder, caused her to turn. The officer muttered between his teeth:

"Before everything, let us settle this affair!"

And, with his own hand pushing Dominique against the wall of a shed, he ordered his men to fire. When Françoise looked, Dominique lay upon the ground, with blood streaming from his neck and shoulders.

She did not weep; she stood stupefied. Her eyes grew fixed and she sat down under the shed, a few paces from the body. She stared at it, wringing her hands. The Prussians had seized Père Merlier as a hostage.

It was a stirring combat. The officer had rapidly posted his men, comprehending that he could not beat a retreat without being cut to pieces. Hence, he would fight to the last. Now, the Prussians defended the mill and the French attacked it. The fusillade began with unusual violence. For half an hour, it did not cease. Then, a hollow sound was heard, and a ball broke a main branch of the old elm. The French had cannon. A battery, stationed just above the ditch in which Dominique had hidden himself, swept the wide street of Rocreuse. The struggle could not last long.

Ah! the poor mill! Balls pierced it in every part. Half of the roof was carried away. Two walls were battered down. But it was on the side of the Morelle that the destruction was most lamentable. The ivy, torn from the tottering edifice, hung like rags; the river was encumbered with wrecks of all kinds, and, through a breach, was visible Françoise's chamber with its bed, the white curtains of which were carefully closed. Shot followed shot; the old wheel received two balls and gave vent to an agonizing groan: the buckets were borne off by the current, the framework was crushed. The soul of the gay mill had left it!

Then, the French began the assault. There was a furious fight with swords and bayonets. Beneath the rust-colored sky, the valley was choked with the dead. The broad meadows had a wild look, with their tall, isolated trees and their hedges of poplars which stained them with shade. To the right and to the left, the forests were like the walls of an ancient amphitheatre which enclosed the fighting gladiators, while the springs, the fountains and the flowing brooks seemed to sob amid the panic of the country.

Beneath the shed, Françoise still sat near Dominique's body; she had not moved. Père Merlier had received a slight wound. The Prussians were exterminated, but the ruined mill was on fire in a dozen places. The French rushed into the courtyard, headed by their captain. It was his first success of the war. His face beamed with triumph. He waved his sword, shouting:

"Victory! victory!"

On seeing the wounded miller, who was endeavoring to comfort Françoise, and noticing the body of Dominique, his joyous look changed to one of sadness. Then, he knelt beside the young man, and, tearing open his blouse, put his hand to his heart.

"Thank God!" he cried, "it is yet beating! Send for the surgeon!"

At the captain's words, Françoise leaped to her feet.

"There is hope!" she cried. "Oh! tell me there is hope!"

At that moment, the surgeon appeared. He made a hasty examination, and said:

"The young man is severely hurt, but life is not extinct, he can be saved!"

By the surgeon's orders, Dominique was transported to a neighboring cottage, where he was placed in bed. His wounds were dressed, restoratives were administered and he soon recovered consciousness. When he opened his eyes, he saw Françoise sitting beside him and, through the open window, caught sight of Père Merlier talking with the French captain. He passed his hand over his forehead with a bewildered air, and said:

"They did not kill me, after all!"

"No," replied Françoise. "The French came and their surgeon saved you."

Père Merlier turned and said through the window:

"No talking yet, my young ones!"

In due time Dominique was entirely restored, and, when peace again blessed the land he wedded his beloved Françoise.

The mill was rebuilt, and Père Merlier had a new wheel upon which to bestow whatever tenderness was not engrossed by his daughter and her husband.

————

# Captain Burle

## CHAPTER I

### THE SWINDLE

It was nine o'clock. The little town of Vauchamp, dark and silent, had just retired to bed amid a chilly November rain. In the Rue des Recollets, one of the narrowest and most deserted streets of the district of Saint-Jean, a single window was still alight on the third floor of an old house, from whose damaged gutters torrents of water were falling into the street. Madame Burle was sitting up before a meagre fire of vine-stocks, while her little grandson Charles pored over his lessons by the pale light of a lamp.

The apartment, rented at one hundred and sixty francs per annum, consisted of four large rooms which it was absolutely impossible to keep warm during the wi ter. Madame Burle slept in the largest chamber, her son, Captain and Quarter-Master Burle, occupying a somewhat smaller one overlooking the street, while little Charles had his iron cot at the further end of a spacious drawing-room with mildewed hangings, which was never used. The few pieces of furniture belonging to the captain and his mother, furniture of the massive style of the First Empire, dented and worn by continuous transit from one garrison town to another, almost disappeared from view beneath the lofty ceilings whence darkness fell. The flooring of red-coloured tiles was cold and hard to the feet; before the chairs there were merely a few threadbare little rugs of poverty-stricken aspect; and athwart this desert all the winds of heaven blew through the disjointed doors and windows.

Near the fire-place sat Madame Burle, leaning back in her old yellow velvet arm-chair, and watching the last vine-branch smoke, with that stolid, blank stare of the aged who live within themselves. She would sit thus for whole days together, with her tall figure, her long stern face, and her thin lips that never smiled. The widow of a colonel who had died just as he was on the point of becoming a general, the mother of a captain whom she had followed even in his campaigns, she had acquired a military stiffness of bearing, and formed for herself a code of honor, duty, and patriotism which kept her rigid, desiccated as it were by the stern application of discipline. She seldom, if ever, complained. When her son had become a widower after five years of married life, she had undertaken the education of little Charles as a matter of course, performing her duties with the severity of a sergeant drilling recruits. She watched over the child, never tolerated the slightest waywardness or irregularity, but compelling him to sit up till midnight when his exercises were not finished, and sitting up herself until he had completed them. Under such implacable despotism Charles, whose constitution was delicate, grew up pale and thin, with beautiful eyes, inordinately large and clear, shining in his white pinched face.

During the long hours of silence, Madame Burle dwelt continuously upon one and the same idea. she had been disappointed in her son. This thought sufficed to occupy her mind; and under its influence she would live her whole life over again, from the birth of her son whom she had pictured rising amid glory to the highest rank, till she came down to mean and narrow garrison life, the dull monotonous existence of nowadays, that stranding in the post of a quarter-master, from which Burle would never rise, and in which he seemed to sink more and more heavily. And yet his first efforts had filled her with pride, and she had hoped to see her dreams realised. Burle had only just left St. Cyr when he distinguished himself at the battle of Solferino, where he had captured a whole battery of the enemy's artillery with merely a handful of men. For this feat he had won the cross, the papers had recorded his

heroism, and he had become known as one of the bravest soldiers in the army. But gradually the hero had grown stout, embedded in flesh, timorous, lazy and satisfied. In 1870, still a captain, he had been made a prisoner in the first encounter; and he returned from Germany quite furious, swearing that he would never be caught fighting again, for it was too absurd. Being prevented from leaving the army as he was incapable of embracing any other profession, he applied for and obtained the position of captain quarter-master, "a kennel," as he called it "in which he would be left to kick the bucket in peace." That day Madame Burle experienced a great internal disruption. She felt that it was all over, and she ever afterwards preserved a rigid attitude with tightened lips.

A blast of wind shook the Rue des Recollets, and drove the rain angrily against the window-panes. The old lady lifted her eyes from the smoking vine-roots now dying out, to make sure that Charles was not falling asleep over his Latin exercise. This lad, twelve years of age, had become the old lady's supreme hope, the one human being in whom she centred her obstinate yearning for glory. At first she had hated him with all the loathing she had felt for his mother, a weak and pretty young lace-maker whom the captain had been foolish enough to marry when he found out that she would not listen to his passionate addresses on any other condition. Later on, when the mother had died, and the father had begun to wallow in vice, Madame Burle dreamt again in presence of that little ailing child whom she found it so hard to rear. She wanted to see him robust, so that he might grow into the hero that Burle had declined to be, and for all her cold ruggedness she watched him anxiously, feeling his limbs and instilling courage into his soul. By degrees, blinded by her passionate desires, she imagined that she had at last found the man of the family. The boy, whose temperament was of a gentle, dreamy character, had a physical horror of soldiering, but as he lived in mortal dread of his grandmother, and was extremely shy and submissive, he would echo all she said, and resignedly express his intention of entering the army when he grew up.

Madame Burle observed that the exercise was not progressing. In fact little Charles, overcome by the deafening noise of the storm, was dozing, albeit his pen was between his fingers and his eyes were staring at the paper. The old lady at once struck the edge of the table with her bony hand; whereupon the lad started, opened his dictionary and hurriedly began to turn over the leaves. Then, still preserving silence, his grandmother drew the vine-roots together on the hearth and unsuccessfully attempted to rekindle the fire.

At the time when she had still believed in her son she had sacrificed her small income, which he had squandered in pursuits she dared not investigate. Even now he drained the household, all its resources went to the streets, and it was through him that she lived in penury, with empty rooms and cold kitchen. She never spoke to him of all those things, for with her sense of discipline he remained the master. Only, at times, she shuddered at the sudden fear that Burle might some day commit some foolish misdeed which would prevent Charles from entering the army.

She was rising up to fetch a fresh piece of wood in the kitchen when a fearful hurricane fell upon the house, making the doors rattle, tearing off a shutter and whirling the water in the broken gutters like a spout against the window. In the midst of the uproar a ring at the bell startled the old lady. Who could it be at such an hour and in such weather? Burle never returned till after midnight, if he came home at all. However, she went to the door. An officer stood before her, dripping with rain and swearing savagely.

"Hell and thunder!" he growled, "what cursed weather!"

It was Major Laguitte, a brave old soldier who had served under Colonel Burle during Madame Burle's palmy days. He had started in life as a drummer-boy, and, thanks to his courage rather than his intellect, had attained to the command of a battalion, when a painful infirmity—the contraction of the muscles of one of his thighs due to a wound—obliged him to accept the post of major. He was slightly lame, but it would have been imprudent to tell him so, as he refused to own it.

"What, you, major?" said Madame Burle with growing astonishment.

"Yes, thunder," grumbled Laguitte, "and I must be confoundedly fond of you to roam the streets on such a night as this. One would think twice before sending even a parson out."

He shook himself, and little rivulets fell from his huge boots on to the floor. Then he looked round him.

"I particularly want to see Burle. Is the lazy beggar already in bed?"

"No, he is not in yet," said the old woman in her harsh voice.

The major looked furious; and, raising his voice, he shouted: "What, not at home! But in that case they hoaxed me at the café, Mélanie's establishment, you know. I went there, and a maid grinned at me, saying that the captain had gone home to bed. Curse the girl! I suspected as much, and felt like pulling her ears!"

After this outburst he became somewhat calmer, stamping about the room in an undecided way; withal seeming greatly disturbed. Madame Burle looked at him attentively.

"Is it the captain personally whom you want to see?" she said at last.

"Yes," he answered.

"Can I not tell him what you have to say?"

"No."

She did not insist, but remained standing without taking her eyes off the major, who did not seem able to make up his mind to leave. Finally, in a fresh burst of rage, he exclaimed with an oath: "It can't be helped. As I am here you may as well know—after all it is, perhaps, best."

He sat down before the chimneypiece, stretching out his muddy boots as if a bright fire had been burning. Madame Burle was about to resume her own seat when she remarked that Charles, overcome by fatigue, had dropped his head between the open pages of his dictionary. The arrival of the major had at first interested him, but seeing that he remained unnoticed he had been unable to struggle against his sleepiness. His grandmother turned towards the table to slap his frail little hands, whitening in the lamplight, when Laguitte stopped her.

"No—no!" said he. "Let the poor little man sleep. I haven't got anything funny to say. There's no need for him to hear me."

The old lady sat down in her armchair; deep silence reigned, and they looked at one another.

"Well, yes," said the major at last, punctuating his words with an angry motion of his chin, "he has been and done it; that hound Burle has been and done it!"

Not a muscle of Madame Burle's face moved, but she became livid, and her figure stiffened. Then the major continued: "I had my doubts. I had intended mentioning the subject to you. Burle was spending too much money, and he had an idiotic look which I did not fancy. Thunder and lightning! what a fool a man must be to behave so filthily!"

Then he thumped his knee furiously with his clenched fist, and seemed to choke with indignation. The old woman put the straightforward question:

"He has stolen?"

"You can't have an idea of it. You see, I never examined his accounts; I approved and signed them. You know how those things are managed. However, just before the inspection—as the colonel is a crotchety old maniac—I said to Burle: 'I say, old man, look to your accounts; I am answerable, you know,' and then I felt perfectly secure. Well, about a month ago, as he seemed queer, and some nasty stories were circulating, I peered a little closer into the books and pottered over the entries. I thought everything looked straight and very well kept——"

At this point he stopped, convulsed by such a fit of rage that he had to relieve himself by a volley of appalling oaths. Finally he resumed: "It isn't the swindle that angers me, it is his disgusting behaviour to me. He has gammoned me, Madame Burle. By God! does he take me for an old fool?"

"So he stole?" the mother again questioned.

"This evening," continued the major, more quietly, "I had just finished my dinner when Gagneux came in—you know Gagneux, the butcher at the corner of the Place aux Herbes? Another dirty beast who got the meat contract, and makes our men eat all the diseased cowflesh in the neighbourhood! Well, I received him like a dog, and then he let it all out—blurted out the whole thing, and a pretty mess it is! It appears that Burle only paid him in driblets and had got himself into a muddle—a confusion of figures which the devil himself couldn't disentangle. In short, Burle owes the butcher two thousand francs, and Gagneux threatens that he'll inform the colonel if he is not paid. To make matters worse, Burle, just to blind me, handed me every week a forged receipt which he had squarely signed with Gagneux' name. To think he did that to me, his old friend! Ah, curse him!"

With increasing profanity the major rose to his feet, shook his fist at the ceiling, and then fell back in his chair. Madame Burle again repeated: "He has stolen. It was inevitable."

Then, without a word of judgment or condemnation, she added simply: "Two thousand francs—we have not got them. There are barely thirty francs in the house."

"I expected as much," said Laguitte. "And do you know where all the money goes? Why, Mélanie gets it—yes, Mélanie; a creature who has turned Burle into a perfect fool. Ah, those women! those fiendish women! I always said they would do for him! I cannot conceive what he is made of! He is only five years younger than I am, and yet he is as mad as ever. What a womanhunter he is!"

Another long silence followed. Outside the rain was increasing in violence, and throughout the sleepy little town one could hear the crashing of slates and chimneypots as they were dashed by the blast on to the pavements of the streets.

"Come," suddenly said the major, rising up, "my stopping here won't mend matters. I have warned you—and now I'm off."

"What is to be done? To whom can we apply?" muttered the old woman drearily.

"Don't give way—we must consider. If I only had the two thousand francs—but you know that I am not rich."

The major stopped short in confusion. This old bachelor, wifeless and childless spent his pay in drink and gambled away at écarté whatever money his cognac and absinthe left in his pocket. Despite that, however, he was scrupulously honest. from a sense of discipline.

"Never mind," he added, as he reached the threshold, "I'll begin by

stirring him up. I shall move heaven
and earth! What! Burle, Colonel
Burle's son, condemned for theft! That
cannot be! I would sooner burn down
the town! Now, thunder and lightning!
don't worry; it is far more annoying
for me than for you."

He shook the old lady's hand roughly
and vanished into the shadows of the
staircase, while she held the lamp aloft
to light the way. When she returned
and replaced the lamp on the table she
stood for a moment motionless in front
of Charles, who was still asleep with his
face lying on the dictionary. His pale
cheeks and long fair hair made him look
like a girl, and she gazed at him
dreamily, a shade of tenderness passing
over her harsh countenance. But it was
only a passing emotion; her features
regained their look of cold obstinate
determination, and, giving the youngster
a sharp rap on his little hand, she said:

"Charles—your lessons."

The boy awoke, dazed and shivering,
and again rapidly turned over the
leaves. At the same moment Major
Laguitte, slamming the house door behind him, received on his head a quantity of water falling from the gutters
above, whereupon he began to swear in
so loud a voice that he could be heard
above the storm. And after that no
sound broke upon the pelting downpour
save the slight rustle of the boy's pen
travelling over the paper. Madame
Burle had resumed her seat near the
chimneypiece, still rigid, with her eyes
fixd on the dead embers, preserving, indeed, her habitual attitude, and absorbed in her one idea.

# CHAPTER II

### THE CAFÉ

THE Café de Paris, kept by Mélanie
Cartier, a widow, was situated on the
Place du Palais, a large irregular square
planted with meagre, dusty elm trees.
The place was so well known in Vauchamp that it was customary to say,
"Are you coming to Mélanie's?" At the
further end of the first room, which was
a spacious one, there was another called
"the divan," a narrow apartment having
sham leather benches placed against the
walls, while at each corner there stood
a marble-topped table. The widow, deserting her seat in the front room,
where she left her little servant
Phrosine, spent her evenings in the
inner apartment, ministering to a few
customers, the usual frequenters of the
place, those who were currently styled
"the gentlemen of the divan." When
a man belonged to that set it was as if
he had a label on his back; he was
spoken of with smiles of mingled contempt and envy.

Madame Cartier had become a widow
when she was five-and-twenty. Her husband, a wheelwright, who, on the death
of an uncle, had amazed Vauchamp by
taking the Café de Paris, had one fine
day brought her back with him from
Montpellier, where he was wont to repair twice a year to purchase liqueurs.
As he was stocking his establishment
he selected, together with divers bever-
ages, a woman of the sort he wanted—
of an engaging aspect, and apt to
stimulate the trade of the house. It
was never known where he had picked
her up, but he married her after trying

her in the café during six months or so. Opinions were divided in Vauchamp as to her merits, some folks declaring that she was superb, while others asserted that she looked like a drum-major. She was a tall woman, with large features and coarse hair falling low over her forehead. However, everyone agreed that she knew very well how to fool the sterner sex. She had fine eyes, and was wont to fix them with a bold stare on the gentlemen of the divan, who coloured and became like wax in her hands. She also had the reputation of possessing a wonderfully fine figure, and Southerners appreciate a statuesque style of beauty.

Cartier had died in a singular way. Rumour hinted at a conjugal quarrel; a kick, producing some internal tumour. Whatever may have been the truth, Mélanie found herself encumbered with the café, which was far from doing a prosperous business. Her husband had wasted his uncle's inheritance in drinking his own absinthe, and wearing out the cloth of his own billiard-table. For a while it was believed that the widow would have to sell out, but she liked the life and the establishment just as it was. If she could secure a few customers the bigger room might remain deserted. So she limited herself to re-papering the divan in white and gold and re-covering the benches. She began by entertaining a chemist. Then a vermicelli maker, a lawyer, and a retired magistrate put in an appearance; and thus it was that the café remained open, although the waiter did not receive twenty orders a day. No objections were raised by the authorities, as appearances were kept up; and, indeed it was not deemed advisable to interfere, for some respectable folks might have been worried.

Of an evening, five or six well-to-do citizens would enter the front room and play at dominoes there. Although Cartier was dead, and the Café de Paris had got a queer name, they saw nothing, and kept up their old habits. In course of time, the waiter having nothing to do, Mélanie dismissed him, and made Phrosine light the solitary gas burner in the corner where the domino-players congregated. Occasionally a party of young men, attracted by the gossip that circulated through the town, would come in, wildly excited, and laughing loudly and awkwardly. But they were received there with icy dignity. As a rule they did not even see the widow, and even if she happened to be present, she treated them with withering disdain, so that they withdrew stammering and confused. Mélanie was too astute to indulge in any compromising whims. While the front room remained obscure, save in the corner where the few townsfolk rattled their dominoes, she personally waited on the gentlemen of the divan, showing herself amiable without being free, merely venturing in moments of familiarity to lean on the shoulder of one or another of them, the better to watch a skilfully played game of écarté.

One evening the gentlemen of the divan, who had ended by tolerating each other's presence, experienced a disagreeable surprise on finding Captain Burle at home there. He had casually entered the café that same morning to get a glass of vermouth, so it seemed, and he had found Mélanie there. They had conversed, and in the evening, when he returned, Phrosine immediately showed him to the inner room.

Two days later Burle reigned there supreme; still he had not frightened the chemist, the vermicelli-maker, the lawyer, or the retired magistrate away. The captain, who was short and dumpy, worshipped tall plump women. In his regiment he had been nicknamed "Petticoat Burle," on account of his constant philandering. Whenever the officers, and even the privates, met some monstrous-looking creature, some giantess puffed out with fat, whether she were in velvet or in rags, they would invariably exclaim, "There goes one to Petticoat Burle's taste!" Thus Mélanie, with her opulent presence, quite conquered him. He was lost—quite wrecked. In less than a fortnight he had fallen to vacuous imbecility. With much the expression of a whipped hound in the tiny sunken eyes which lighted up his bloated face, he was incessantly watching the widow in mute adoration before her masculine features and stubby hair. For fear that he might be dismissed, he put up with the presence of the other gentlemen of the divan, and spent his pay in the place down to the last copper. A sergeant reviewed the situation in one sentence —"Petticoat Burle is done for; he's a buried man!"

It was nearly ten o'clock when Major Laguitte furiously flung the door of the café open. For a moment those inside could see the deluged square transformed into a dark sea of liquid mud, bubbling under the terrible downpour. The major, now soaked to the skin and leaving a stream behind him,

strode up to the small counter where Phrosine was reading a novel.

"You little wretch," he yelled, "you have dared to gammon an officer; you deserve——"

And then he lifted his hand as if to deal a blow such as would have felled an ox. The little maid shrank back terrified, while the amazed dominoplayers looked open-mouthed. However, the major did not linger there— he pushed the divan door open, and appeared before Mélanie and Burle just as the widow was playfully making the captain sip his grog in small spoonfuls, as if she were feeding a pet canary. Only the ex-magistrate and the chemist had come that evening, and they had retired early in a melancholy frame of mind. Then Mélanie, being in want of three hundred francs for the morrow, had taken advantage of the opportunity to cajole the captain.

"Come," said she, "open your mouth; ain't it nice you greedy piggy-wiggy?"

Burle, flushing scarlet, with glazed eyes and sunken figure, was sucking the spoon with an air of intense enjoyment.

"Good heavens!" roared the major from the threshold, "you now play tricks on me, do you? I'm sent to the round-about and told that you never came here, and yet all the while here you are, addling your silly brains?"

Burle shuddered, pushing the grog away, while Mélanie stepped angrily in front of him as if to shield him with her portly figure; but Laguitte looked at her with that quiet, resolute expression well known to women who are familiar with bodily chastisement.

"Leave us," he said curtly.

She hesitated for the space of a

second. She almost felt the gust of the expected blow; and then, white with rage, she joined Phrosine in the outer room.

When the two men were alone, Major Laguitte walked up to Burle, looked at him, and slightly stooping, yelled into his face these two words—"You pig!"

The captain, quite dazed, endeavoured to retort; but he had not time to do so.

"Silence!" resumed the major. "You have bamboozled a friend. You palmed off on me a lot of forged receipts which might have sent both of us to the gallows. Do you call that proper behaviour? Is that the sort of trick to play a friend of thirty years' standing?"

Burle, who had fallen back in his chair, was livid; his limbs shook as if with ague. Meanwhile the major, striding up and down, and striking the tables wildly with his fists, continued: "So you have become a thief like the veriest scribbling cur of a clerk, and all for the sake of that creature here! If at least you had stolen for your mother's sake it would have been honourable! But, curse it, to play tricks and bring the money into this shanty, is what I cannot understand! Tell me —what are you made of at your age to go to the dogs as you are going all for the sake of a creature like a grenadier!"

"*You* gamble——" stammered the captain.

"Yes—I do—curse it!" thundered the major, lashed into still greater fury by this remark, "and I am a pitiful rogue to do so, because it swallows up all my pay and doesn't redound to the honour of the French army. However, I don't steal. Kill yourself, if it pleases you, starve your mother and the boy, but respect the regimental cash-box, and don't drag your friends down with you."

He stopped. Burle was sitting there with fixed eyes and a stupid air. Nothing was heard for a moment save the clatter of the major's heels.

"And not a single copper," he continued aggressively. "Can you picture yourself between two gendarmes, eh?"

He then grew a little calmer, caught hold of Burle's wrists and forced him to rise up.

"Come!" he said gruffly. "Something must be done at once, for I cannot go to bed with this affair on my mind— I have an idea."

In the front room Mélanie and Phrosine were talking eagerly in low voices. When the widow saw the two men leaving the divan, she moved towards Burle, and said coaxingly: "What, are you going already, captain?"

"Yes, he's going," brutally answered Laguitte, "and I don't intend to let him set foot here again."

The little maid felt frightened and pulled her mistress back by the skirt of her dress; in doing so she imprudently murmured the word "drunkard," and thereby brought down the slap which the major's hand had been itching to deal for some time past. Both women having stooped, however, the blow only fell on Phrosine's back hair, flattening her cap and breaking her comb. The domino-players were indignant.

"Let's cut it," shouted Laguitte, and

he pushed Burle on the pavement. "If I remained I should smash every one in the place."

To cross the square they had to wade up to their ankles in mud. The rain, driven by the wind, poured off their faces. The captain walked on in silence, while the major kept on reproaching him with his cowardice and its disastrous consequences. Wasn't it sweet weather for tramping the streets? If he hadn't been such an idiot they would both be warmly tucked in bed instead of paddling about in the mud. Then he spoke of Gagneux—a scoundrel whose diseased meat had on three separate occasions made the whole regiment ill. In a week, however, the contract would come to an end, and the fiend himself would not get it renewed.

"It rests with me," the major grumbled. "I can select whomsoever I choose, and I'd rather cut off my right arm than put that poisoner in the way of earning another copper."

Just then he slipped into a gutter, and, half-choked by a string of oaths, he gasped:

"You understand—I am going to rout up Gagneux. You must stop outside while I go in. I must know what the rascal is up to, and if he'll dare to carry out his threat of informing the colonel to-morrow. A butcher—curse him! The idea of compromising oneself with a butcher! Ah, you aren't over proud, and I shall never forgive you for all this."

They had now reached the Place aux Herbes. Gagneux' house was quite dark, but Laguitte knocked so loudly that he was eventually admitted. Burle remained alone in the dense obscurity,

and did not even attempt to seek any shelter. He stood at a corner of the market, under the pelting rain, his head filled with a loud buzzing noise which prevented him from thinking. He did not feel impatient, for he was unconscious of the flight of time. He stood there looking at the house, which, with its closed door and windows, seemed quite lifeless. When at the end of an hour the major came out again it appeared to the captain as if he had only just gone in.

Laguitte was so grimly mute that Burle did not venture to question him. For a moment they sought each other, groping about in the dark; then they resumed their walk through the sombre streets, where the water rolled as in the bed of a torrent. They moved on in silence side by side, the major being so abstracted that he even forgot to swear. However as they again crossed the Place du Palais, at the sight of the Café de Paris, which was still lighted up, he dropped his hand on Burle's shoulder and said, "If you ever re-enter that hole, I——"

"No fear!" answered the captain, without letting his friend finish his sentence.

Then he stretched out his hand.

"No, no," said Laguitte, "I'll see you home; I'll at least make sure that you'll sleep in your bed to-night."

They went on, and as they ascended the Rue des Recollets they slackened their pace. When the captain's door was reached and Burle had taken out his latch key, he ventured to ask:—

"Well?"

"Well," answered the major, gruffly, "I am as dirty a rogue as you are,

Yes! I have done a scurrilous thing. The fiend take you! Our soldiers will eat carrion for three months longer."

Then he explained that Gagneux, the disgusting Gagneux, had a horribly level head, and that he had persuaded him—the major—to strike a bargain. He would refrain from informing the colonel, and he would even make a present of the two thousand francs and replace the forged receipts by genuine ones, on condition that the major bound himself to renew the meat contract. It was a settled thing.

"Ah!" continued Laguitte, "calculate what profits the brute must make out of the meat, to part with such a sum as two thousand francs."

Burle, choking with emotion, grasped his old friend's hands, stammering confused words of thanks. The vileness of the action committed for his sake brought tears into his eyes.

"I never did such a thing before," growled Laguitte, "but I was driven to it—curse it, to think that I haven't those two thousand francs in my drawer! It is enough to make one hate cards. It is my own fault. I am not worth much; only, mark my words— don't begin again, for, curse it — *I* sha'n't."

The captain embraced him, and when he had entered the house, the major stood a moment before the closed door, to make certain that he had gone upstairs to bed. Then as midnight was striking, and the rain was still belabouring the dark town, he slowly turned homewards. The thought of his men almost broke his heart, and stopping short he said aloud in a voice full of compassion:

"Poor devils! what a lot of cow beef they'll have to swallow for those two thousand francs!"

## CHAPTER III

### AGAIN?

THE regiment was altogether nonplussed: Petticoat Burle had quarrelled with Mélanie. When a week had elapsed it became a proved and undeniable fact; the captain no longer set foot inside the Café de Paris, where the chemist, it was averred, once more reigned in his stead, to the profound sorrow of the retired magistrate. An even more incredible statement was that Captain Burle led the life of a recluse in the Rue des Recollects. He was becoming a reformed character; he spent his evenings at his own fireside, hearing little Charles repeat his lessons. His mother, who had never breathed a word to him of his manipulations with Gagneux, maintained her old severity of demeanour as she sat opposite to him in her arm-chair, but her looks seemed to imply that she believed him reclaimed.

A fortnight later Major Laguitte came one evening to invite himself to dinner. He felt some awkwardness at the prospect of meeting Burle again, not on his own account, but because he dreaded awakening painful memories. However, as the captain was mending his ways he wished to shake hands and break a crust with him. He thought this would please his old friend.

When Laguitte arrived, Burle was in his room, so it was the old lady who received the major. The latter, after announcing that he had come to have a plate of soup with them, added, lowering his voice:

"Well, how goes it?"

"It is all right," answered the old lady.

"Nothing queer?"

"Absolutely nothing. Never away—in bed at nine — and looking quite happy."

"Ah! confound it," replied the major, "I knew very well he only wanted a shaking. He has some heart left, the dog!"

When Burle appeared he almost crushed the major's hands in his grasp; and standing before the fire, waiting for the dinner, they conversed peacefully, honestly together, extolling the charms of home life. The captain vowed he wouldn't exchange his home for a kingdom, and declared that when he had removed his braces, put on his slippers, and settled himself in his arm-chair, no king was fit to hold a candle to him. The major assented and examined him. At all events his virtuous conduct had not made him any thinner; he still looked bloated, his eyes were bleared, and his mouth was heavy. He seemed to be half asleep as he repeated mechanically: "Home life! there's nothing like home life, nothing in the world!"

"No doubt," said the major; "still, one mustn't exaggerate—take a little exercise and come to the café now and then."

"To the café, why?" asked Burle. "Do I lack anything here? No, no, I remain at home."

When Charles had laid his books aside, Laguitte was surprised to see a maid come in to lay the cloth.

"So you keep a servant now," he remarked to Madame Burle.

"I had to get one," she answered with a sigh. "My legs are not what they used to be, and the household was going to rack and ruin. Fortunately Cabrol let me have his daughter. You know old Cabrol, who sweeps the market? He did not know what to do with Rose—I am teaching her how to work."

Just then the girl left the room.

"How old is she?" asked the major.

"Barely seventeen. She is stupid and dirty, but I only give her ten francs a month, and she eats nothing but soup."

When Rose returned with an armful of plates, Laguitte, though he did not care about women, began to scrutinise her and was amazed at seeing so ugly a creature. She was very short, very dark, and slightly deformed, with a face like an ape's: a flat nose, a huge mouth, and narrow greenish eyes. Her broad back and long arms gave her an appearance of great strength.

"What a snout!" said Laguitte laughing, when the maid had again left the room to fetch the cruets.

"Never mind," said Burle carelessly, "she is very obliging and does all one asks her. She suits us well enough as a scullion."

The dinner was very pleasant. It consisted of boiled beef and mutton hash. Charles was encouraged to relate some stories of his school, and Madame Burle repeatedly asked him the same question: "Don't you want to be a soldier?" A faint smile hovered over the child's wan lips as he answered with the frightened obedience of a trained dog, "O yes, grandmother." Captain Burle, with his elbows on the table, was masticating slowly with an absent-minded expression. The big room was getting warmer, the single lamp placed on the table left the corners in vague gloom. There was a certain amount of heavy comfort, the familiar intimacy of penurious people who do not change their plates at every course, but become joyously excited at the unexpected appearance of a bowl of whipped egg cream, at the close of the meal.

Rose, whose heavy tread shook the floor as she paced round the table, had not yet opened her mouth. At last she stopped behind the captain's chair, and asked in a gruff voice: "Cheese, sir?"

Burle started. "What, eh? Oh yes —cheese. Hold the plate tight."

He cut a piece of Gruyère, the girl watching him the while with her narrow eyes. Laguitte laughed; Rose's unparalleled ugliness amused him immensely. He whispered in the captain's ear, "She is ripping! there never was such a nose and such a mouth! You ought to send her to the colonel's some day as a curiosity. It would amuse him to see her."

More and more struck by this phenomenal ugliness, the major felt a paternal desire to examine the girl more closely.

"Come here," said he, "I want some cheese too."

She brought the plate, and Laguitte, sticking the knife in the Gruyère, stared at her, grinning the while because he discovered that she had one

nostril broader than the other. Rose gravely allowed herself to be looked at, waiting till the gentleman had done laughing.

She removed the cloth and disappeared. Burle immediately went to sleep in the chimney-corner, while the major and Madame Burle began to chat. Charles had returned to his exercises. Quietude fell from the lofty ceiling, the quietude of a middle-class household gathered in concord around their fireside. At nine o'clock Burle woke up, yawned, and announced that he was going off to bed; he apologized, but declared that he could not keep his eyes open. Half an hour later, when the major took his leave, Madame Burle vainly called for Rose to light him downstairs; the girl must have gone up to her room; she was, indeed, a regular hen, snoring the round of the clock without waking.

"No need to disturb anybody," said Laguitte on the landing; "my legs are not much better than yours, but if I get hold of the banisters I sha'n't break any bones. Now, my dear lady, I leave you happy; your troubles are ended at last. I watched Burle closely, and I'll take my oath that he's guileless as a child. Dash it—after all it was high time for Petticoat Burle to reform; he was going downhill fast."

The major went away fully satisfied with the house and its inmates; the walls were of glass, and could harbour no equivocal conduct. What particularly delighted him in his friend's return to virtue was that it absolved him from the obligation of verifying the accounts. Nothing was more distasteful to him than the inspection of a number of ledgers, and as long as Burle kept steady, he—Laguitte—could smoke his pipe in peace and sign the books in all confidence. However, he continued to keep one eye open for a little while longer, and found the receipts genuine, the entries correct, the columns admirably balanced. A month later he contented himself with glancing at the receipts and running his eye over the totals. Then one morning, without the slightest suspicion of there being anything wrong, simply because he had lit a second pipe and had nothing to do, he carelessly added up a row of figures and fancied that he detected an error of thirteen francs. The balance seemed perfectly correct, and yet he was not mistaken; the total outlay was thirteen francs more than the various sums for which receipts were furnished. It looked queer, but he said nothing to Burle, just making up his mind to examine the next accounts closely. On the following week he detected a fresh error of nineteen francs, and then, suddenly becoming alarmed, he shut himself up with the books and spent a wretched morning poring over them, perspiring, swearing, and feeling as if his very skull were bursting with the figures. At every page he discovered thefts of a few francs—the most miserable petty thefts —ten, eight, eleven francs, latterly, three and four; and, indeed, there was one column showing that Burle had pilfered just one franc and a half. For two months, however, he had been steadily robbing the cash-box; and, by comparing dates, the Major found to his disgust that the famous lesson respecting Gagneux had only kept him

straight for one week! This last discovery infuriated Laguitte, who struck the books with his clenched fists, yelling through a shower of oaths:

"This is more abominable still! At least there was some pluck about those forged receipts of Gagneux. But this time he is as contemptible as a cook charging two-pence extra for her cabbages. Powers of hell! to pilfer a franc and a half and clap it in his pocket! Hasn't the brute got any pride, then? Couldn't he run away with the safe, or play the fool with actresses?"

The pitiful meanness of these pilferings revolted the major, and, moreover, he was enraged at having been duped a second time, deceived by the simple stupid dodge of falsified additions. He rose up at last and paced his office for a whole hour growling aloud.

"This gives me his measure. Even if I were to thrash him to a jelly every morning, he would still drop a couple of coins into his pocket every afternoon. But where can he spend it all? He is never seen abroad, he goes to bed at nine, and everything looks so clean and proper over there. Can the brute have vices that nobody knows of?"

He returned to the desk, added up the subtracted money and found a total of five hundred and forty-five francs. Where was this deficiency to come from? The inspection was close at hand, and if the crotchety colonel should take it into his head to examine a single page, the murder would be out, and Burle would be done for.

This idea froze the major, who left off cursing, picturing Madame Burle erect and despairing, and at the same time he felt his heart swell with personal grief and shame.

"Well," he muttered, "I must first of all look into the rogue's business; I will act afterwards."

As he walked over to Burle's office he caught sight of a skirt vanishing through the doorway. Fancying that he had a clue to the mystery, he slipped up quietly and listened, and speedily recognized Mélanie's shrill voice. She was complaining of the gentlemen of the divan. She had signed a promissory-note which she was unable to meet; the bailiffs were in the house, and all her goods would be sold. The captain, however, barely replied to her. He alleged that he had no money, whereupon she burst into tears and began to coax him. But her blandishments were apparently ineffectual, for Burle's husky voice could be heard repeating "Impossible! impossible!" and finally the widow withdrew in a towering passion. The major, amazed at the turn affairs were taking, waited a few moments longer before entering the office, where Burle had remained alone. He found him very calm, and despite his furious inclination to call him names he also remained calm, determined to begin by finding out the exact truth.

The office certainly did not look like a swindler's den. A cane-seated chair, covered with an honest leather cushion, stood before the captain's desk, and in a corner there was the locked safe. Summer was coming on, and the song of a canary sounded through the open window. The apartment was very neat and tidy, redolent of old papers, and altogether its appearance inspired one with confidence.

"Wasn't it Mélanie who was leaving here as I came along?" asked Laguitte.

Burle shrugged his shoulders.

"Yes," he mumbled. "She has been dunning me for two hundred francs, but she can't screw ten out of me— not even ten pence."

"Indeed!" said the major, just to try him. "I heard that you had made up with her."

"I? Certainly not. I have done with the likes of her for good."

Laguitte went away, feeling greatly perplexed. Where had the five hundred and forty-five francs gone? Had the idiot taken to drinking or gambling? He decided to pay Burle a surprise visit that very evening at his own house, and, may be, by questioning his mother, he might learn something. However, during the afternoon his leg became very painful; latterly he had been feeling in ill-health, and he had to use a stick so as not to limp too outrageously. This stick grieved him sorely, and he declared with angry despair that he was now no better than a pensioner. However, towards the evening, making a strong effort, he pulled himself out of his arm-chair and, leaning heavily on his stick, dragged himself through the darkness to the Rue des Recollets, which he reached about nine o'clock. The street door was still unlocked, and on going up he stood panting on the third landing, when he heard voices on the upper floor. One of these voices was Burle's. so he fancied: and out of curiosity he ascended another flight of stairs. Then, at the end of a passage on the left, he saw a ray of light coming from a door, which stood ajar. As the creaking of his boots resounded, this door was sharply closed, and he found himself in the dark.

"Some cook going to bed!" he muttered angrily. "I'm a fool."

All the same, he groped his way as gently as possible to the door and listened. Two people were talking in the room, and he stood aghast; for it was Burle and that fright Rose! Then he listened, and the conversation he heard left him no doubt of the awful truth. For a moment he lifted his stick as if to beat down the door. Then he shuddered, and, staggering back, leant against the wall. His legs were trembling under him, while in the darkness of the staircase he brandished his stick as if it had been a sabre.

What was to be done? After his first moment of passion there had come thoughts of the poor old lady below. And these made him hesitate. It was all over with the captain now; when a man sank as low as that he was hardly worth the few shovelfuls of earth that are thrown over carrion to prevent them from polluting the atmosphere. Whatever might be said of Burle, however much one might try to shame him, he would assuredly begin the next day. Ah, heavens, to think of it! the money! the honour of the army! the name of Burle, that respected name, dragged through the mire! By all that was holy, this could and should not be!

Presently the major softened. If he had only possessed five hundred and forty-five francs! But he had not got such an amount. On the previous day he had drunk too much cognac, just

like a mere sub., and had lost shockingly at cards. It served him right— he ought to have known better! And if he was so lame, he richly deserved it too; by rights, in fact, his leg ought to be much worse.

At last he crept downstairs and rang at the bell of Madame Burle's flat. Five minutes elapsed and then the old lady appeared.

"I beg your pardon for keeping you waiting," she said; "I thought that dormouse Rose was still about. I must go and shake her."

But the major detained her.

"Where is Burle?" he asked.

"Oh, he has been snoring since nine o'clock. Would you like to knock at his door?"

"No, no, I only wanted to have a chat with you."

In the parlour Charles sat at his usual place, having just finished his exercises. He looked terrified, and his poor little white hands were tremulous. In point of fact, his grandmother, before sending him to bed, was wont to read some martial stories aloud so as to develop the latent family heroism in his bosom. That night she had selected the episode of the *Vengeur*, the man-of-war freighted with dying heroes and sinking into the sea. The child, while listening, had become almost hysterical, and his head was racked as with some ghastly nightmare.

Madame Burle asked the major to let her finish the perusal, "Long live the Republic!" she solemnly closed the volume. Charles was as white as a sheet.

"You see," said the old lady, "the

duty of every French soldier is to die for his country."

"Yes, grandmother."

Then the lad kissed her on the forehead, and, shivering with fear, went to bed in his big room, where the faintest creak of the panelling threw him into a cold sweat.

The major had listened with a grave face. Yes, by heavens! honour was honour, and he would never permit that wretched Burle to disgrace the old woman and the boy! As the lad was so devoted to the military profession, it was necessary that he should be able to enter St. Cyr with his head erect.

When Madame Burle took up the lamp to show the major out, she passed the door of the captain's room, and stopped short, surprised to see the key outside, which was a most unusual occurrence.

"Do go in," she said to Laguitte, "it is bad for him to sleep so much."

And before he could interpose, she had opened the door, and stood transfixed on finding the room empty. Laguitte turned crimson and looked so foolish that she suddenly understood everything, enlightened by the sudden recollection of several little incidents to which she had previously attached no importance.

"You knew it—you knew it!" she stammered. "Why was I not told? Oh, my God, to think of it! Ah! he has been stealing again—I feel it!"

She remained erect, white and rigid. Then she added in a harsh voice:

"Look you—I wish he were dead!"

Laguitte caught hold of both her hands, which for a moment he kept tightly clasped in his own. Then he left her hurriedly, for he felt a lump rising in his throat, and tears coming to his eyes. Ah, by all the powers! this time his mind was quite made up.

## CHAPTER IV

### INSPECTION

THE regimental inspection was to take place at the end of the month. The major had ten days before him. On the very next morning, however, he crawled, limping, as far as the Café de Paris, where he ordered some beer. Mélanie grew pale when she saw him enter, and it was with a lively recollection of a certain slap that Phrosine hastened to serve him. The major seemed very calm, however; he called for a second chair to rest his bad leg upon, and drank his beer quietly like any other thirsty man. He had sat there for about an hour when he saw two officers crossing the Place du Palais —Morandot, who commanded one of the battalions of the regiment, and Captain Doucet. Thereupon he excitedly waved his cane and shouted: "Come in and have a glass of beer with me!"

The officers dared not refuse, but when the maid had brought the beer Morandot said to the major: "So you patronise this place now?"

"Yes—the beer is good."

Captain Doucet winked, and asked archly: "Do you belong to the divan, major?"

Laguitte chuckled, but did not answer. Then the others began to chaff him about Mélanie, and he took their remarks good-naturedly, simply shrugging his shoulders. The widow was undoubtedly a fine woman, however much people might talk. Some of those who disparaged her would, in reality, be only too pleased to win her good graces. Then turning to the little counter and assuming an engaging air, he shouted:

"Three more glasses, madame."

Mélanie was so taken aback that she rose and brought the beer herself. The major detained her at the table, and forgot himself so far as to softly pat the hand which she had carelessly placed on the back of a chair. Used as she was to alternate brutality and flattery, she immediately became confident, believing in a sudden whim of gallantry on the part of the "old wreck" as she was wont to style the major when talking with Phrosine. Doucet and Morandot looked at each other in surprise. Was the major actually stepping into Petticoat Burle's shoes? The regiment would be convulsed if that were the case.

Suddenly, however, Laguitte, who kept his eye on the square, gave a start. "Hallo, there's Burle!" he exclaimed.

"Yes, it is his time," explained Phrosine. "The captain passes every afternoon on his way from the office."

In spite of his lameness the major had risen to his feet, pushing aside the chairs as he called out: "Burle! I say —come along—and have a glass."

The captain, quite aghast, and unable to understand why Laguitte was at the widow's, advanced mechanically. He was so perplexed that he again hesitated at the door.

"Another glass of beer," ordered the major; and then turning to Burle, he

added, "What's the matter with you? Come in. Are you afraid of being eaten alive?"

The captain took a seat, and an awkward pause followed. Mélanie, who brought the beer with trembling hands, dreaded some scene which might result in the closing of her establishment. The major's gallantry made her uneasy, and she endeavoured to slip away, but he invited her to drink with them, and before she could refuse he had ordered Phrosine to bring a liqueur glass of anisette, doing so with as much coolness as if he had been master of the house. Mélanie was thus compelled to sit down between the captain and Laguitte, who exclaimed aggressively: "I *will* have ladies respected. We are French officers! Let us drink madame's health!"

Burle, with his eyes fixed on his glass, smiled in an embarrassed way. The two officers, shocked at the proceedings, had already tried to get off. Fortunately the café was deserted, save that the domino-players were having their afternoon game. At every fresh oath which came from the major they glanced around, scandalised by such an unusual accession of customers, and ready to threaten Mélanie that they would leave her for the Café de la Gare if the soldiery was going to invade her place, like the flies that buzzed about, attracted by the stickiness of the tables which Phrosine only scoured on Saturdays. She was now reclining behind the counter already reading a novel again.

"How's this—you are not drinking with madame?" roughly said the major to Burle. "Be civil at least!"

Then, as Doucet and Morandot were again preparing to leave, he stopped them.

"Why can't you wait? We'll go together. It is only this brute who never knows how to behave himself."

The two officers looked surprised at the major's sudden bad temper. Mélanie attempted to restore peace, and with a light laugh placed her hands on the arms of both men. However, Laguitte disengaged himself.

"No," he roared, "leave me alone. Why does he refuse to chink glasses with you? I shall not allow you to be insulted—do you hear? I am quite sick of him."

Burle, paling under the insult, turned slightly and said to Morandot, "What does this mean? He calls me in here to insult me. Is he drunk?"

With a wild oath the major rose on his trembling legs and struck the captain's cheek with his open hand. Mélanie dived and thus escaped one half of the smack. An appalling uproar ensued. Phrosine screamed behind the counter as if she herself had received the blow; the domino-players also entrenched themselves behind their table in fear lest the soldiers should draw their swords and massacre them. However, Doucet and Morandot pinioned the captain to prevent him from springing at the major's throat, and forcibly led him to the door. When they got him outside they succeeded in quieting him a little by repeating that Laguitte was quite in the wrong. They would lay the affair before the colonel, having witnessed it, and the colonel would give his decision. As soon as they had got Burle away they returned to the café where they found Laguitte in reality greatly disturbed, with tears in his eyes, but affecting stolid indifference and slowly finishing his beer.

"Listen, major," began Morandot; "that was very wrong on your part. The captain is your inferior in rank, and you know that he won't be allowed to fight you."

"That remains to be seen," answered the major.

"But how has he offended you? He never uttered a word. Two old comrades too; it is absurd."

The major made a vague gesture. "No matter. He annoyed me."

He could never be made to say anything else. Nothing more as to his motive was ever known. All the same, the scandal was a terrible one. The regiment was inclined to believe that Mélanie, incensed by the captain's defection, had contrived to entrap the major, telling him some abominable stories, and prevailing upon him to insult and strike Burle publicly. Who would have thought it of that old fogey Laguitte, who professed to be a woman-hater? they said. So he too had been caught at last. Despite the general indignation against Mélanie, this adventure made her very conspicuous; and her establishment soon drove a flourishing business.

On the following day the colonel summoned the major and the captain into his presence. He censured them sternly, accusing them of disgracing their uniform by frequenting unseemly haunts. What resolution had they come to, he asked, as he could not authorise them to fight? This same question had occupied the whole regiment for the last twenty-four hours. Apologies were unacceptable on account of the blow, but as Laguitte was almost unable to stand, it was hoped that, should the colonel insist upon it, some reconciliation might be patched up.

"Come," said the colonel, "will you accept me as arbitrator?"

"I beg your pardon, colonel," interrupted the major, "I have brought you my resignation. Here it is. That settles everything. Please name the day for the duel."

Burle looked at Laguitte in amazement, and the colonel thought it his duty to protest.

"This is a most serious step, major," he began. "Two years more and you would be entitled to your full pension."

But again did Laguitte cut him short, saying gruffly, "That is my own affair."

"Oh, certainly! Well, I will send in your resignation, and as soon as it is accepted I will fix a day for the duel."

The unexpected turn that events had taken startled the regiment. What possessed that lunatic major to persist in cutting the throat of his old comrade Burle? The officers again discussed Mélanie: they even began to dream of her. There must surely be something wonderful about her since she had completely fascinated two such tough old veterans, and brought them to a deadly feud. Morandot having met Laguitte, did not disguise his concern. If he—the major—was not killed, what would he live upon? He had no fortune, and the pension to which his cross of the Legion of Honour entitled him, with the half of a full regimental pension which he would obtain on resigning, would

barely find him in bread. While Morandot was thus speaking, Laguitte simply stared before him with his round eyes, persevering in the dumb obstinacy born of his narrow mind; and when his companion tried to question him respecting his hatred for Burle, he simply made the same vague gesture as before, and once again repeated:

"He annoyed me; so much the worse."

Every morning at mess, and at the canteen, the first words were: "Has the acceptance of the major's resignation arrived?" The duel was impatiently expected, and ardently discussed. The majority believed that Laguitte would be run through the body in three seconds, for it was madness for a man to fight with a paralysed leg which did not even allow him to stand upright. A few, however, shook their heads. Laguitte had never been a marvel of intellect, that was true; for the last twenty years, indeed, he had been held up as an example of stupidity, but there had been a time when he was known as the best fencer of the regiment; and although he had begun as a drummer, he had won his epaulets as the commander of a battalion by the sanguine bravery of a man who is quite unconscious of danger. On the other hand, Burle fenced indifferently, and passed for a poltroon. However, they would soon know what to think.

Meanwhile the excitement became more and more intense as the acceptance of Laguitte's resignation was so long in coming. The major was unmistakably the most anxious and upset of everybody. A week had passed by, and the general inspection would commence two days later. Nothing, however, had come as yet. He shuddered at the thought that he had, perhaps, struck his old friend and sent in his resignation all in vain, without delaying the exposure for a single minute. He had in reality reasoned thus: If he himself were killed, he would not have the worry of witnessing the scandal; and if he killed Burle, as he expected to do, the affair would undoubtedly be hushed up. Thus he would save the Honour of the Army, and the little chap would be able to get in at St. Cyr. Ah! why wouldn't those wretched scribblers at the War Office hurry up a bit? The major could not keep still but was for ever wandering about before the post office stopping the estafettes and questioning the colonel's orderly to find out if the acceptance had arrived. He lost his sleep, and, careless as to people's remarks, he leant more and more heavily on his stick, hobbling about with no attempt to steady his gait.

On the day before that fixed for the inspection he was as usual on his way to the colonel's quarters, when he paused startled, to see Madame Burle (who was taking Charles to school) a few paces ahead of him. He had not met her since the scene at the Café de Paris, for she had remained in seclusion at home. Unmanned at thus meeting her, he stepped down to leave the whole side-walk free. Neither he nor the old lady bowed, and the little boy lifted his large inquisitive eyes in mute surprise. Madame Burle, cold and erect, brushed past the major without the least sign of emotion or recognition. When she had passed he looked

after her with an expression of stupefied compassion.

"Confound it, I am no longer a man," he growled, dashing away a tear.

When he arrived at the colonel's quarters, a captain in attendance greeted him with the words: "It's all right at last. The papers have come."

"Ah!" murmured Laguitte, growing very pale.

And again he beheld the old lady walking on, relentlessly rigid, and holding the little boy's hand. What! he had longed so eagerly for those papers for eight days past, and now, when the scraps had come, he felt his brain on fire and his heart lacerated.

The duel took place on the morrow, in the barrack-yard behind a low wall. The air was keen, the sun shining brightly. Laguitte had almost to be carried to the ground; one of his seconds supported him on one side, while on the other he leant heavily on his stick. Burle looked half asleep, his face was puffy with unhealthy fat, as if he had spent a night of debauchery. Not a word was spoken. They were all anxious to have it over.

Captain Doucet crossed the swords of the two adversaries and then drew back, saying: "Set-to, gentlemen."

Burle was the first to attack; he wanted to test Laguitte's strength and ascertain what he had to expect. For the last ten days, the encounter had seemed to him a ghastly nightmare which he could not fathom. At times a hideous suspicion assailed him, but he put it aside with terror, for it meant death, and he refused to believe that a friend could play him such a trick, even to set things right. Besides, Laguitte's leg reassured him; he would prick the major on the shoulder, and then all would be over.

During well-nigh a couple of minutes the swords clashed, and then the captain lunged, but the major, recovering his old suppleness of wrist, parried in a masterly style, and if he had returned the attack Burle would have been pierced through. The captain now fell back; he was livid, for he felt that he was at the mercy of the man who had just spared him. At last he understood that this was an execution.

Laguitte, squarely poised on his infirm legs and seemingly turned to stone, stood waiting. The two men looked at each other fixedly. In Burle's blurred eyes there arose a supplication—a prayer for pardon. He knew why he was going to die, and like a child he promised not to transgress again. But the major's eyes remained implacable; honour had spoken, and he silenced his emotion and his pity.

"Let it end," he muttered between his teeth.

Then it was he who attacked. Like a flash of lightning his sword flamed, flying from right to left, and then with a resistless thrust it pierced the breast of the captain, who fell like a log without even a groan.

Laguitte had released his hold upon his sword and stood gazing at that poor old rascal Burle, who was stretched upon his back with his fat stomach bulging out.

"Oh, my God! my God!" repeated the major furiously and desparingly, and then he began to swear.

They led him away, and, both his legs failing him, he had to be supported on either side, for he could not even use his stick.

Two months later the ex-major was crawling slowly along in the sunlight down a lonely street of Vauchamp, when he again found himself face to face with Madame Burle and little Charles. They were both in deep mourning. He tried to avoid them; but he now only walked with difficulty, and they advanced straight upon him without hurrying or slackening their steps. Charles still had the same gentle, girlish, frightened face, and Madame Burle retained her stern, rigid demeanour, looking even harsher than ever.

As Laguitte shrank into the corner of a doorway, to leave the whole street to them, she abruptly stopped in front of him and stretched out her hand. He hesitated and then took it and pressed it, but he trembled so violently that he made the old lady's arm shake. They exchanged glances in silence.

"Charles," said the boy's grandmother at last, "shake hands with the major."

The boy obeyed without understanding. The major, who was very pale, barely ventured to touch the child's frail fingers; then, feeling that he ought to speak, he stammered out: "You still intend to send him to St. Cyr?"

"Of course, when he is old enough," answered Madame Burle.

But during the following week Charles was carried off by typhoid fever. One evening his grandmother had again read him the story of the *Vengeur,* to make him bold, and in the night he had become delirious. The poor little fellow died of fright.

# The Death of Olivier Becaille

## CHAPTER I

### MY PASSING

It was on a Saturday, at six in the morning, that I died, after a three days' illness. My wife was searching a trunk for some linen, and when she rose and turned she saw me rigid, with open eyes and silent pulses. She ran to me, fancying that I had fainted, touched my hands, and bent over me. Then she suddenly grew alarmed, burst into tears, and stammered:

"My God my God! he is dead!"

I heard everything, but the sounds seem to come from a great distance. My left eye still detected a faint glimmer, a whitish light in which all objects melted, but my right eye was quite bereft of sight. It was the coma of my whole being, as if a thunderbolt had struck me. My will was annihilated, not a fibre of flesh obeyed my bidding. And yet amid the impotency of my inert limbs my thoughts subsisted, sluggish and lazy, still perfectly clear.

My poor Marguerite was crying; she had dropped on her knees beside the bed, repeating in heartrending tones:

"He is dead! my God! he is dead!"

Was this strange state of torpor, this immobility of the flesh, really death, although the functions of the intellect were not arrested? Was my soul only lingering for a brief space before it soared away for ever. From my childhood upwards I had been subject to hysterical attacks, and twice, in early youth, I had nearly succumbed to nervous fevers. By degrees all those who surrounded me had got accustomed to consider me an invalid, and to see me sickly. So much so, that I myself had forbidden my wife to call in a doctor when I had taken to my bed on the day of our arrival at the cheap lodging house of the Rue Dauphine in Paris. A little rest would soon set me right again; it was only the fatigue of the journey which had caused my intolerable weariness. And yet I was conscious of having felt singularly uneasy. We had left our province somewhat abruptly; we were very poor, and had barely enough money to support ourselves till I drew my first month's salary in the office where I had obtained a situation. And now a sudden seizure was carrying me off!

Was it really death? I had pictured to myself a darker night, a deeper silence. As a little child I had already felt afraid to die. Being weak and compassionately petted by everyone, I had concluded that I had not long to live, that I should soon be buried; and the thought of the cold earth filled me with a dread I could not master

46

—a dread which haunted me day and night. As I grew older the same terror pursued me. Sometimes, after long hours spent in reasoning with myself, I thought that I had conquered my fear. I reflected, "After all, what does it matter? one dies and all is over. It is the common fate; nothing could be better or easier."

I then prided myself on being able to look death boldly in the face; but suddenly a shiver froze my blood, and my dizzy anguish returned as if a giant hand had swung me over a dark abyss. It was some vision of the earth returning and setting reason at naught. How often at night did I start up in bed, not knowing what cold breath had swept over my slumbers, but clasping my despairing hands and moaning, "Must I die?" In those moments an icy horror would stop my pulses, while an appalling vision of dissolution rose before me. It was with difficulty that I could get to sleep again. Indeed, sleep alarmed me, it so closely resembled death. If I closed my eyes they might never open again—I might slumber on for ever.

I cannot tell if others have endured the same torture; I only know that my own life was made a torment by it. Death ever rose between me and all I loved; I can remember how the thought of it poisoned the happiest moments I spent with Marguerite. During the first months of our marrried life, when she lay sleeping by my side and I dreamed of a fair future for her and with her, the foreboding of some fatal separation dashed my hopes aside and embittered my delights. Perhaps we should be parted on the morrow—

nay, perhaps in an hour's time. Then utter discouragement assailed me; I wondered what the bliss of being united availed me if it were to end in so cruel a disruption.

My morbid imagination revelled in scenes of mourning. I speculated as to who would be the first to depart, Marguerite or I. Either alternative caused me harrowing grief, and tears rose to my eyes at the thought of our shattered lives. At the happiest periods of my existence I often became a prey to grim dejection such as nobody could understand, but which was caused by the thought of impending nihility. When I was most successful I was to general wonder most depressed. The fatal question, "What avails it?" rang like a knell in my ears. But the sharpest sting of this torment was that it came with a secret sense of shame, which rendered me unable to confide my thoughts to another. Husband and wife lying side by side in the darkened room may quiver with the same shudder and yet remain mute; for people do not mention death any more than they pronounce certain obscene words. Fear makes it nameless.

I was musing thus while my dear Marguerite knelt sobbing at my feet. It grieved me sorely to be unable to comfort her by telling her that I suffered no pain. If death were merely the annihilation of the flesh it had been foolish of me to harbour so much dread. I experienced a selfish kind of restfulness in which all my cares were forgotten. My memory had become extraordinarily vivid. My whole life passed before me rapidly like a play in which I no longer acted a part; it was a curious and enjoyable sensation —I seemed to hear a far-off voice relating my own history.

I saw in particular a certain spot in the country near Guérande, on the way to Piriac. The road turns sharply, and some scattered pine-trees carelessly dot a rocky slope. When I was seven years old I used to pass through those pines with my father as far as a crumbling old house, where Marguerite's parents gave me pancakes. They were salt-gatherers, and earned a scanty livelihood by working the adjacent salt marshes. Then I remembered the school at Nantes, where I had grown up, leading a monotonous life within its ancient walls and yearning for the broad horizon of Guérande, and the salt marshes stretching to the limitless sea widening under the sky.

Next came a blank—my father was dead. I entered the hospital as clerk to the managing board and led a dreary life with one solitary diversion: my Sunday visits to the old house on Piriac road. The salt works were doing badly; poverty reigned in the land, and Marguerite's parents were nearly penniless. Marguerite, when merely a child, had been fond of me because I trundled her about in a wheelbarrow, but on the morning when I asked her in marriage she shrank from me with a frightened gesture, and I realised that she thought me hideous. Her parents, however, consented at once; they looked upon my offer as a godsend, and the daughter submissively acquiesced. When she became accustomed to the idea of marrying me she did not seem to dislike it so much. On our wedding day at Guérande the rain fell in torrents, and when we got home my bride had to take off her dress, which was soaked through, and sit in her petticoats.

That was all the youth I ever had. We did not remain long in our province. One day I found my wife in tears. She was miserable, life was so dull, she wanted to get away. Six months later I had saved a little money by taking in extra work after office hours, and through the influence of a friend of my father's I obtained a petty appointment in Paris. I started off to settle there with the dear little woman so that she might cry no more. During the night, which we spent in the third-class railway carriage, the seats being very hard, I took her in my arms in order that she might sleep.

That was the past, and now I had just died on the narrow couch of a Paris lodging-house, and my wife was crouching on the floor, crying bitterly. The white light before my left eye was growing dim, but I remembered the room perfectly. On the left there was a chest of drawers, on the right a mantelpiece surmounted by a damaged clock without a pendulum, the hands of which marked ten minutes past ten. The window overlooked the Rue Dauphine, a long dark street. All Paris seemed to pass below, and the noise was so great that the window shook.

We knew nobody in the city; we had hurried our departure, but I was not expected at the office till the following Monday. Since I had taken to my bed I had wondered at my imprisonment in this narrow room into which we had tumbled after a railway journey of fifteen hours, followed by a hurried, confusing transit through the noisy streets. My wife had nursed me with smiling tenderness, but I knew that she was anxious. She would walk to the window, glance out and return to the bedside, looking very pale and startled by the sight of the busy thoroughfare, the aspect of the vast city of which she did not know a single stone, and which deafened her with its continuous roar. What would happen to her if I never woke up again—alone, friendless, and unknowing as she was?

Marguerite had caught hold of one of my hands which lay passive on the coverlet, and covering it with kisses she repeated wildly: "Olivier, answer me. Oh, my God, he is dead, dead!"

So death was not complete annihilation. I could hear and think. I had been uselessly alarmed all those years. I had not dropped into utter vacancy as I had anticipated. I could not picture the dissapearance of my being, the suppression of all that I had been, without the possibility of renewed existence. I had been wont to shudder whenever in any book or newspaper I came across a date of a hundred years hence. A date at which I should no longer be alive, a future which I should never see, filled me with unspeakable uneasiness. Was I not the whole world, and would not the universe crumble away when I was no more?

To dream of life had been a cherished vision, but this could not possibly be death. I should assuredly awake presently. Yes, in a few moments I would lean over, take Marguerite in my arms, and dry her tears. I would rest a little while longer before going to my office; and then a new life would

begin, brighter than the last. However, I did not feel impatient; the commotion had been too strong. It was wrong of Marguerite to give way like that when I had not even the strength to turn my head on the pillow and smile at her. The next time that she moaned out "He is dead! dead!" I would embrace her, and murmur softly so as not to startle her: "No, my darling, I was only asleep. You see I am alive, and I love you."

## CHAPTER II

### FUNERAL PREPARATIONS

MARGUERITE'S cries had attracted attention, for all at once the door was opened, and a voice exclaimed: "What is the matter, neighbour? Is he worse?"

I recognized the voice; it was that of an elderly woman, Madame Gabin, who occupied a room on the same floor. She had been most obliging since our arrival, and had evidently become interested in our concerns. On her own side she had lost no time in telling us her history. A stern landlord had sold her furniture during the previous winter to pay himself his rent, and since then she had resided at the lodging-house in the Rue Dauphine with her daughter Dédé, a child of ten. They both cut and pinked lamp-shades; and between them they earned at the utmost only two francs a day.

"Heavens! is it all over?" cried Madame Gabin, looking at me.

I realized that she was drawing nearer. She examined me, touched me, and turning to Marguerite, murmured compassionately: "Poor girl! poor girl!"

My wife, wearied out, was sobbing like a child. Madame Gabine lifted her, placed her in a dilapidated arm-chair near the fireplace, and proceeded to comfort her.

"Indeed, you'll do yourself harm if you go on like this, my dear. It's no reason because your husband is gone that you should kill yourself with weeping. Sure enough, when I lost Gabin I was just like you. I remained three days without swallowing a morsel of food. But that didn't help me—on the contrary, it pulled me down. Come, for the Lord's sake, be sensible!"

By degrees Marguerite grew calmer; she was exhausted, and it was only at intervals that she gave way to a fresh flow of tears. Meanwhile the old woman had taken possession of the room with a sort of rough authority.

"Don't worry yourself," she said, as she bustled about. "Neighbours must help each other. Luckily Dédé has just gone to take the work home. Ah, I see, your trunks are not yet all un-packed, but I suppose there is some linen in the chest of drawers—isn't there?"

I heard her pull a drawer open; she must have taken out a napkin which she spread on the little table at the bedside. She then struck a match, which made me think that she was lighting one of the candles on the man-telpiece, and placing it near me as a religious rite. I could follow her move-ments in the room and divine all her ac-tions.

"Poor gentleman," she muttered. "Luckily I heard you sobbing, poor dear!"

Suddenly the vague light which my left eye had detected vanished. Madame Gabin had just closed my eyelids, but I had not felt her finger on my face. When I understood this I felt chilled.

The door had opened again, and Dédé, the child of ten, now rushed in, calling out in her shrill voice: "Mother, mother! Ah, I knew you would be here! Look here, there's the money—three francs and four sous. I took back three dozen lamp-shades."

"Hush, hush! Hold your tongue," vainly repeated the mother, who, as the little girl chattered on, must have pointed to the bed, for I guessed that the child felt perplexed, and was back-ing towards the door.

"Is the gentleman asleep?" she whis-pered.

"Yes, yes—go and play," Madame Gabin.

But the child did not go. She was, no doubt, staring at me with widely opened eyes, startled and vaguely com-prehending. Suddenly she seemed con-vulsed with terror, and ran out, upset-ting a chair.

"He is dead, mother, he is dead!" she gasped.

Profound silence followed. Mar-guerite, lying back in the arm-chair, had left off crying. Madame Gabin was still rummaging about the room, and talking under her breath.

"Children know everything now-adays. Look at that girl. Heaven knows how carefully she's brought up! When I send her on an errand, or take the shades back, I calculate the time to a minute so that she can't loiter about, but for all that she learns everything. She saw at a glance what had happened here—and yet I never showed her but one corpse, that of her uncle Francois, and she was then only four years old

Ah, well! there are no children left—it can't be helped."

She paused, and without any transition passed to another subject.

"I say, dearie, we must think of the formalities—there's the declaration at the municipal offices to be made, and the seeing about the funeral. You are not in a fit state to attend to business. What do you say if I look in at Monsieur Simoneau's to find out if he's at home?"

Marguerite did not reply. It seemed to me that I watched her from afar, and at times changed into a subtle flame hovering above the room, while a stranger lay heavy and unconscious on my bed. I wished that Marguerite had declined the assistance of Simoneau. I had seen him three or four times during my brief illness, for he occupied a room close to ours, and had been civil and neighbourly. Madame Gabin had told us that he was merely making a short stay in Paris, having come to collect some old debts due to his father, who had settled in the country and recently died. He was a tall, strong, handsome young man, and I hated him, perhaps on account of his healthy appearance. On the previous evening he had come in to make inquiries, and I had much disliked seeing him at Marguerite's side; she had looked so fair and pretty, and he had gazed so intently into her face when she smilingly thanked him for his kindness.

"Ah! here is Monsieur Simoneau," said Madame Gabin, introducing him.

He gently pushed the door ajar, and as soon as Marguerite saw him enter she burst into a flood of tears. The presence of a friend, of the only person she knew in Paris besides the old woman, recalled her bereavement. I could not see the young man, but in the darkness that encompassed me I conjured up his appearance. I pictured him distinctly, grave and sad at finding poor Marguerite in such distress. How lovely she must have looked with her golden hair unbound, her pale face and her dear little baby hands burning with fever!

"I am at your disposal, madame," he said softly. "Pray allow me to manage everything."

She only answered him with broken words, but as the young man was leaving, accompanied by Madame Gabin, I heard the latter mention money. These things were always expensive, she said, and she feared that the poor little body hadn't a farthing—anyhow, he might ask her. But Simoneau silenced the old woman; he did not want to have the widow worried; he was going to the municipal office and to the undertakers.

When silence reigned once more I wondered if my nightmare would last much longer. I was certainly alive, for I was conscious of passing incidents, and I began to realise my condition. I must have fallen into one of those cataleptic states that I had read of. As a child I had suffered from syncopes which had lasted several hours, but surely my heart would beat anew, my blood circulate and my muscles relax. Yes, I should wake up and comfort Marguerite; and, reasoning thus, I tried to be patient.

Time passed. Madame Gabin had brought in some breakfast, but Marguerite refused to taste any food. Later on the afternoon waned. Through the open window I heard the rising clamour of the Rue Dauphine. Byand-by a slight ringing of the brass candlestick on the marble-topped table made me think that a fresh candle had been lighted. At last Simoneau returned.

"Well?" whispered the old woman.

"It is all settled," he answered; "the funeral is ordered for to-morrow at eleven. There is nothing for you to do, and you needn't talk of these things before the poor lady."

Nevertheless Madame Gabin remarked: "The doctor of the dead hasn't come yet."

Simoneau took a seat beside Marguerite, and after a few words of encouragement remained silent. The funeral was to take place at eleven! Those words rang in my brain like a passing bell. And the doctor coming— the doctor of the dead, as Madame Gabin had called him. *He* could not possibly fail to find out that I was only in a state of lethargy; he would do whatever might be necessary to rouse me, so I longed for his arrival with feverish anxiety.

The day was drawing to a close. Madame Gabin, anxious to waste no time had brought in her lamp-shades and summoned Dédé without asking Marguerite's permission. "To tell the truth," she observed, "I do not like to leave children too long alone."

"Come in, I say," she whispered to the little girl, "come in, and don't be frightened. Only don't look towards the bed, or you'll catch it."

She thought it decorous to forbid Dédé to look at me, but I was convinced that the child was furtively glancing at the corner where I lay, for every now and then I heard her mother rap her knuckles and repeat angrily: "Get on with your work, or you shall leave the room, and the gentleman will come during the night and pull you by the feet."

The mother and daughter had sat down at our table. I could plainly hear the click of their scissors as they clipped the lamp-shades, which no doubt required very delicate manipulation, for they did not work rapidly. I counted the shades one by one as they were laid aside, while my anxiety grew more and more intense.

The clicking of the scissors was the only noise in the room so I concluded that Marguerite had been overcome by fatigue and was dozing. Twice Simoneau rose up, and the torturing thought flashed through me that he might be taking advantage of her slumbers to touch her hair with his lips. I hardly knew the man, and yet felt sure that he loved my wife. At last little Dédé began to giggle, and her laugh exasperated me.

"Why are you sniggering, you idiot?" asked her mother. "Do you want to be turned out on the landing? Come, out with it; what makes you laugh so?"

The child stammered: she had not laughed, she had only coughed; but I felt certain she had seen Simoneau bending over Marguerite, and had felt amused.

The lamp had been lit, when a knock was heard at the door.

"It must be the doctor at last," said the old woman.

It was the doctor; he did not apologise for coming so late, for he had no doubt ascended many flights of stairs during the day. The room being but imperfectly lighted by the lamp, he inquired: "Is the body here?"

"Yes, it is," answered Simoneau.

Marguerite had risen, trembling violently. Madame Gabin dismissed Dédé, saying it was useless that a child should be present, and then she tried to lead my wife to the window, to spare her the sight of what was about to take place.

The doctor quickly approached the bed. I guessed that he was bored, tired, and impatient. Had he touched my wrist? had he placed his hand on my heart? I could not tell; but I fancied that he had only carelessly bent over me.

"Shall I bring the lamp, so that you may see better?" asked Simoneau obligingly.

"No, it is not necessary," quietly answered the doctor.

Not necessary! That man held my life in his hands, and he did not think it worth while to proceed to a careful examination! I was not dead! I wanted to cry out that I was not dead!

"At what o'clock did he die?" asked the doctor.

"At six this morning," volunteered Simoneau.

A feeling of frenzy and rebellion rose within me, bound as I was in seemingly iron chains. Oh, for the power of uttering one word, of moving a single limb!

"This close weather is unhealthy," resumed the doctor; "nothing is more trying than these early spring days."

And then he moved away. It was like my life departing. Screams, sobs, and insults were choking me, struggling in my convulsed throat, in which even my breath was arrested. The wretch! Turned into a mere machine by professional habits, he only came to a deathbed to accomplish a perfunctory formality; he knew nothing, his science was a lie, since he could not at a glance distinguish life from death— and now he was going—going!

"Good-night, sir," said Simoneau.

There came a moment's silence, the doctor was probably bowing to Marguerite, who had turned while Madame Gabin was fastening the window. He left the room, and I heard his footsteps descending the stairs.

It was all over; I was condemned. My last hope had vanished with that man. If I did not wake before eleven on the morrow I should be buried alive. The horror of that thought was so great that I lost all consciousness of my surroundings—'twas something like a fainting fit in death. The last sound I heard was the clicking of the scissors handled by Madame Gabin and Dédé. The funeral vigil had begun; nobody spoke.

Marguerite had refused to retire to rest in the neighbour's room. She remained reclining in her arm-chair, with her beautiful face pale, her eyes closed, and her long lashes wet with tears, while before her in the gloom Simoneau sat silently watching her.

## CHAPTER III

### THE PROCESSION

I CANNOT describe my agony during the morning of the following day.

I remember it as a hideous dream, in which my impressions were so ghastly and so confused that I could not formulate them. The persistent yearning for a sudden awakening increased my torture; and as the hour for the funeral drew nearer, my anguish became more poignant still.

It was only at daybreak that I had recovered a fuller consciousness of what was going on around me. The creaking of hinges startled me out of my stupor. Madame Gabin had just opened the window. It must have been about seven o'clock, for I heard the cries of hawkers in the street, the shrill voice of a girl offering groundsel, and the hoarse voice of a man shouting "Carrots!" The clamorous awakening of Paris pacified me at first. I could not believe that I should be laid under the sod in the midst of so much life; and, besides, a sudden thought helped to calm me. It had just occurred to me that I had witnessed a case similar to my own when I was employed at the hospital of Guérande. A man had been sleeping twenty-eight hours, the doctors hesitating in presence of his apparent lifelessness, when suddenly he had sat up in bed, and was almost at once able to rise. I myself had already been asleep for some twenty-five hours; if I awoke at ten I should still be in time.

I endeavoured to ascertain who was in the room and what was going on there. Dédé must have been playing on the landing, for once when the door opened I heard her shrill childish laughter outside. Simoneau must have retired, for nothing indicated his presence. Madame Gabin's slipshod tread was still audible over the floor. At last she spoke.

"Come, my dear," she said. "It is wrong of you not to take it while it is hot. It would cheer you up."

She was addressing Marguerite, and a slow trickling sound as of something filtering indicated that she had been making some coffee.

"I don't mind owning," she continued, "that I needed it. At my age sitting up *is* trying. The night seems so dreary when there is a misfortune in the house. *Do* have a cup of coffee, my dear—just a drop."

She persuaded Marguerite to taste it.

"Isn't it nice and hot?" she continued; "and doesn't it set one up? Ah! you'll be wanting all your strength presently for what you've got to go through to-day. Now, if you were sensible you'd step into my room and just wait there."

"No; I want to stay here," said Marguerite resolutely.

Her voice, which I had not heard since the previous evening, touched me strangely. It was changed, broken as by tears. To feel my dear wife near me was a last consolation. I knew that her eyes were fastened on me, and that she was weeping with all the anguish of her heart.

The minutes flew by. An inexplicable noise sounded from beyond the door. It seemed as if some people were bringing a bulky piece of furniture upstairs, and knocking against the walls as they did so. Suddenly I understood, as I heard Marguerite begin to sob: it was the coffin.

"You are too early," said Madame

Gabin crossly. "Put it behind the bed."

What o'clock was it? Nine perhaps. So the coffin had come. Amid the opaque night around me I could see it plainly, quite new, with roughly planed boards. Heavens! was this the end, then? Was I to be borne off in that box which I realised was lying at my feet?

However I had one supreme joy. Marguerite, in spite of her weakness, insisted upon discharging all the last offices. Assisted by the old woman, she dressed me with all the tenderness of a wife and a sister. Once more I felt myself in her arms as she clothed me in various garments. She paused at times, overcome by grief; she clasped me convulsively, and her tears rained on my face. Oh! how I longed to return her embrace, and cry, "I live!" And yet I was lying there powerless, motionless, inert!

"You are foolish," suddenly said Madame Gabin; "it is all wasted."

"Never mind," answered Marguerite, sobbing. "I want him to wear his very best things."

I understood that she was dressing me in the clothes I had worn on my wedding-day. I had kept them carefully for great occasions. When she had finished she fell back exhausted in the arm-chair.

Simoneau now spoke; he had probably just entered the room.

"They are below," he whispered.

"Well, it ain't any too soon," answered Madame Gabin, also lowering her voice. "Tell them to come up and get it over."

"But I dread the despair of the poor little wife."

The old woman seemed to reflect and presently resumed: "Listen to me, Monsieur Simoneau. You must take her off to my room. I wouldn't have her stop here. It is for her own good. When she is out of the way we'll get it done in a jiffy."

These words pierced my heart, and my anguish was intense when I realised that a struggle was actually taking place. Simoneau had walked up to Marguerite imploring her to leave the room.

"Do, for pity's sake, come with me!" he pleaded. "Spare yourself useless pain."

"No, no!" she cried, "I will remain till the last minute. Remember that I have only him in the world, and when he is gone I shall be all alone!"

From the bedside Madame Gabin was prompting the young man.

"Don't parley—take hold of her — carry her off in your arms."

Was Simoneau about to lay his hands on Marguerite and bear her away? She screamed. I wildly endeavoured to rise, but the springs of my limbs were broken. I remained rigid, unable to lift my eyelids to see what was going on. The struggle continued, and my wife clung to the furniture, repeating—"Oh don't, don't! Have mercy! Let me go! I will not——"

He must have lifted her in his stalwart arms, for I heard her moaning like a child. He bore her away, her sobs were lost in the distance, and I fancied I saw them both—he, tall and strong, pressing her to his breast; she fainting, powerless and conquered, following him wherever he listed.

"Drat it all! what a to-do!" muttered Madame Gabin. "Now for the tug of war, as the coast is clear at last."

In my jealous madness I looked upon this incident as a monstrous outrage. I had not been able to see Marguerite for twenty-four hours, but at least I had still heard her voice. Now even this was denied me; she had been torn away, a man had eloped with her even before I was laid under the sod. He was alone with her, on the other side of the wall, comforting her—embracing her perhaps!

But the door opened once more, and heavy footsteps shook the floor.

"Quick, make haste," repeated Madame Gabin. "Get it done before the lady comes back."

She was speaking to some strangers, who merely answered her with uncouth grunts.

"You understand," she went on, "I am not a relation, I'm only a neighbour. I have no interest in the matter. It is out of pure good-nature that I have mixed myself up in their affairs. And I ain't over cheerful, I can tell you. Yes, yes, I sat up the whole blessed night—it was pretty cold, too, about four o'clock. That's a fact. Well, I have always been a fool—I'm too soft-hearted."

The coffin had been dragged into the centre of the room. As I had not awakened I was condemned. All clearness departed from my ideas; everything seemed to revolve in a black haze; and I experienced such utter lassitude that it seemed almost a relief to leave off hoping.

"They haven't spared the material," said one of the undertaker's men in a gruff voice. "The box is too long."

"He'll have all the more room," said the other laughing.

I was not heavy, and they chuckled over it since they had three flights of stairs to descend. As they were seizing me by the shoulders and feet, I heard Madame Gabin fly into a violent passion.

"You cursed little brat," she screamed, " what do you mean by poking your nose where you're not wanted? Look here, I'll teach you to spy and pry."

Dédé had slipped her tousled head through the doorway to see how the gentleman was being put into the box. Two ringing slaps resounded, however, by an explosion of sobs. And as soon as the mother returned she began to gossip about her daughter for the benefit of the two men who were settling me in the coffin.

"She is only ten, you know. She is not a bad girl, but she is frightfully inquisitive. I do not beat her often, only I *will* be obeyed."

"Oh," said one of the men, "all kids are alike. Whenever there is a corpse lying about they always want to see it."

I was commodiously stretched out, and I might have thought myself still in bed, had it not been that my left arm felt a trifle cramped from being squeezed against a board. The men had been right. I was pretty comfortable inside on account of my diminutive stature.

"Stop!" suddenly exclaimed Madame Gabin. "I promised his wife to put a pillow under his head."

The men, who were in hurry, stuffed in the pillow roughly. One of them, who had mislaid his hammer, began to swear. He had left the tool below, and went to fetch it, dropping the lid; and when two sharp blows of the hammer drove in the first nail, a shock ran through my being—I had ceased to live. The nails then entered in rapid succession with a rhythmical cadence. It was as if some packers had been closing a case of dried fruit with easy dexterity. After that such sounds as reached me were deadened and strangely prolonged, as if the deal coffin had been changed into a huge musical-box. The last words spoken in the room of the Rue Dauphine—at least the last ones that I heard distinctly—were uttered by Madame Gabin.

"Mind the staircase," she said; "the banister of the second flight isn't safe, so be careful."

While I was being carried down, I experienced a sensation similar to that of pitching, as when one is on board a ship in a rough sea. However, from that moment my impressions became more and more vague. I remember that the only distinct thought that still possessed me was an imbecile impulsive curiosity as to the road by which I should be taken to the cemetery. I was not acquainted with a single street of Paris, and I was ignorant of the position of the large burial grounds (though, of course, I had occasionally heard their names), and yet every effort of my mind was directed towards ascertaining whether we were turning to the right or to the left. Meanwhile, the jolting of the hearse, over the paving stones, the rumbling of passing vehicles, the steps of the foot-passengers, all created a confused clamour, intensified by the acoustical properties of the coffin.

At first I followed our course pretty closely; then came a halt. I was again lifted and carried about, and I concluded that we were in church; but when the funeral procession once more moved onwards, I lost all consciousness of the road we took. A ringing of bells informed me that we were passing another church, and then the softer and easier progress of the wheels indicated that we were skirting a garden or park. I was like a victim being taken to the gallows, awaiting in stupor a death-blow that never came.

At last they stopped and pulled me out of the hearse. The business proceeded rapidly. The noises had ceased; I knew that I was in a deserted space amid avenues of trees, and with the broad sky over my head. No doubt a few persons followed the bier, some of the inhabitants of the lodging house perhaps—Simoneau and others, for instance—for faint whisperings reached my ear. Then I heard a psalm chanted, and some Latin words mumbled by a priest, and afterwards I suddenly felt myself sinking, while the ropes rubbing against the edges of the coffin elicited lugubrious sounds as if a bow were being drawn across the strings of a cracked violoncello. It was the end. On the left side of my head I felt a violent shock like that produced by the

bursting of a bomb; with another under
my feet, and a third more violent still
on my chest. So forcible indeed was
this last one that I thought the lid
was cleft atwain. I fainted from it.

## CHAPTER IV

### THE NAIL

IT IS impossible for me to say how
long my swoon lasted. Eternity is not
of longer duration than one second
spent in nihility. I was no more. It
was slowly and confusedly that I regained some degree of consciousness.
I was still asleep, but I began to dream;
a nightmare started into shape amidst
the blackness of my horizon; a nightmare compounded of a strange fancy
which in other days had haunted my
morbid imagination, whenever with my
propensity for dwelling upon hideous
thoughts I had conjured up catastrophes.

Thus I dreamed that my wife was
expecting me somewhere—at Guérande,
I believe—and that I was going to join
her by rail. As we passed through a
tunnel a deafening roll thundered over
our head, and a sudden subsidence
blocked up both issues of the tunnel,
leaving our train intact in the centre.
We were walled up by blocks of rock
in the heart of a mountain. Then a
long and fearful agony commenced. No
assistance could possibly reach us; even
with powerful engines and incessant labour it would take a month to clear
the tunnel. We were prisoners there
with no outlet, and so our death was
only a question of time.

My fancy had often dwelt on that
hideous drama and had constantly varied
the details and touches. My actors
were men, women and children; their
number increased to hundreds, and they
were ever furnishing me with new incidents. There were some provisions in
the train, but these were soon exhausted, and the hungry passengers, if
they did not actually devour human
flesh, at least fought furiously over the
last piece of bread. Sometimes an
aged man was driven back with blows
and slowly perished; a mother struggled
like a she-wolf to keep three or four
mouthfuls for her child. In my own
compartment a bride and bridegroom
were dying, clasped in each other's arms
in mute despair.

The line was free along the whole
length of the train, and people came
and went, prowling round the carriages
like beasts of prey in search of carrion.
All classes were mingled together. A
millionaire, a high functionary, it was
said, wept on a workman's shoulder.
The lamps had been extinguished from
the first, and the engine fire was nearly
out. To pass from one carriage to another it was necessary to grope about,
and thus, too, one slowly reached the
engine, recognizable by its enormous
barrel, its cold motionless flanks, its
useless strength, its grim silence in the
overwhelming night. Nothing could
be more appalling than this train entombed alive with its passengers perishing one by one.

I gloated over the ghastliness of each
detail; howls resounded through the
vault; somebody, whom one could not
see, whose vicinity was not even sus-

jected, would suddenly drop upon another's shoulder. But what affected me most of all was the cold and the want of air. I have never felt so chilled; a mantel of snow seemed to enwrap me, heavy moisture rained upon my skull, I was gasping; the rocky vault seemed to crush my chest, the whole mountain was seemingly weighing upon me.

Suddenly a cry of deliverance sounded. For some time past we fancied that we could hear a dull sound, and we tried to hope that men were at work and that help was coming; but it came not thus. One of the passengers, however, had discovered an air shaft in the tunnel, and crowding round we all saw this shaft, above which we could discern a blue patch about the size of a wafer. That blue patch filled us with rapture, for it was the sky. We stretched ourselves and stood on tiptoes to breathe more freely. Then we distinguished some black specks moving about, specks that must surely be workmen about to deliver us. A furious clamour arose. The cry, "Saved! Saved!" burst from every mouth, while trembling arms were uplifted towards the tiny azure patch above.

That roar of voices aroused me. Where was I? In the tunnel, of course. I was lying at full length, hard walls were pressing against my ribs. Then I attempted to rise and struck my head roughly. Was it the rock closing in on all sides? The blue speck had vanished—ay, the sky had disappeared—and I was still suffocating, shivering, with chattering teeth.

All at once I remembered. Intense horror raised my hair on end. I felt the hideous truth freeze me from head to foot like ice. I had shaken off the long coma which for many hours had stricken me with corpselike rigidity. Yes, I could move; my hands could feel the boards of my coffin, my lips parted, words came to me, and instinctively I called out Marguerite's name. It was a scream I raised. In that deal box my voice took so hoarse and weird a sound that it terrified me. Oh, my God! was this thing true? I was able to walk, speak, cry out that I was living, and yet my voice could not be heard; I was entombed under the earth.

I made a desperate effort to remain calm and reflect. Was there no means of getting out? Then my dream began afresh in my troubled brain. The fanciful air-shaft with the blue bit of sky overhead, was mingled with the real grave in which I was lying. I stared at the darkness with widely opened eyes; perhaps I might discover a hole, a slit, a glimmer of light; but only sparks of fire flitted through that night, with rays that broadened and then faded away. I was in a sombre abyss again. With returning lucidity I struggled against these fatal visions. Indeed, I should need all my reason if I meant to try to save myself.

The most immediate peril lay in an increasing sense of suffocation. If I had been able to live so long without air, it was owing to suspended animation, which had changed all the normal conditions of my existence; but now that my heart beat and my lungs breathed, I should die asphyxiated if

I did not promptly liberate myself. I also suffered from cold, and dreaded lest I should succumb to the mortal numbness of those who fall asleep in the snow never to wake again. Still, while unceasingly realizing the necessity of remaining calm, I felt maddening blasts sweep through my brain; and to quiet my senses I exhorted myself to patience, trying to remember the circumstances of my burial. Probably the ground had been bought for five years, and this would be against my chances of self-deliverance, for I remembered having noticed at Nantes that in the trenches of the common graves one end of the last lowered coffins protruded into the next open cavity, in which case I should only have had to break through one plank. But if I were in a separate hole, filled up above me with earth, the obstacles would prove too great. Had I not been told that the dead were buried six feet deep in Paris? How was I to get through the enormous mass of soil above me? Even if I succeeded in slitting the lid of my bier open, the mould would drift in like fine sand and fill my mouth and eyes. That would be death again, a ghastly death, like drowning in mud.

However, I began to feel the planks carefully. The coffin was roomy, and I found that I was able to move my arms with tolerable ease. On both sides the roughly planed boards were stout and resistive. I slipped my arm on to my chest to raise it over my head. There I discovered in the top plank a knot in the wood which yielded slightly at my pressure. Working laboriously I finally succeeded in driving out this knot, and on passing my finger through the hole I found that the earth was wet and clayey. But that availed me little. I even regretted having removed the knot, vaguely dreading the irruption of the mould. A second experiment occupied me for a while. I tapped all over the coffin to ascertain if perhaps there were any vacuum outside. But the sound was everywhere the same. At last, as I was slightly kicking the foot of the coffin, I fancied that it gave out a clearer echoing noise; but that might merely be produced by the sonority of the wood.

At any rate I began to press against the boards with my arms and my closed fists. In the same way too I used my knees, my back, and my feet without eliciting even a creak from the wood. I strained with all my strength; indeed with so desperate an effort of my whole frame, that my bruised bones seemed breaking. But nothing moved and I became insane.

Until that moment I had held delirium at bay. I had mastered the intoxicating rage which was mounting to my head like the fumes of alcohol; I had silenced my screams, for I feared that if I again cried out aloud I should be undone. But now I yelled, I shouted; unearthly howls which I could not repress came from my relaxed throat. I called for help in a voice that I did not recognize, growing wilder with each fresh appeal, and crying out that I would not die. I also tore at the wood with my nails; I writhed with the contortions of a caged wolf. I do not know how long this fit of madness lasted, but I can still feel the relentless hardness of the box that imprisoned me; I can still hear the storm of shrieks and sobs with which I filled it; a remaining glimmer of reason made me try to stop, but I could not do so.

Great exhaustion followed. I lay waiting for death in a state of somnolent pain. The coffin was like stone, which no effort could break, and the conviction that I was powerless left me unnerved, without courage to make any fresh attempts. Another suffering—hunger—was presently added to cold and want of air. The torture soon became intolerable. With my finger I tried to pull small pinches of earth through the hole of the dislodged knot, and I swallowed them eagerly, only increasing my torment. Tempted by my flesh, I bit my arms and sucked my skin with a fiendish desire to drive my teeth in; but I was afraid of drawing blood.

Then I ardently longed for death. All my life long I had trembled at the thought of dissolution, but I had come to yearn for it, to crave for an everlasting night that could never be dark enough. How childish it had been of me to dread the long dreamless sleep, the eternity of silence and gloom! Death was kind, for in suppressing life it put an end to suffering. Oh! to sleep like the stones, to be no more!

With groping hands I still continued feeling the wood, and suddenly I pricked my left thumb. That slight pain roused me from my growing numbness. I felt again, and found a nail—a nail which the undertaker's men had driven in crookedly and which had not caught in the lower wood. It was long and very sharp; the head was secured to the lid, but it moved. Henceforth I

had but one idea—to possess myself of that nail; and I slipped my right hand across my body and began to shake it. I made but little progress, however, it was a difficult job; for my hands soon tired, and I had to use them alternately. The left one, too was of little use, on account of the nail's awkward position.

While I was obstinately persevering, a plan dawned on my mind. That nail meant salvation, and I must have it. But should I get it in time? Hunger was torturing me, my brain was swimming, my limbs were losing their strength, my mind was becoming confused. I had sucked the drops that trickled from my punctured finger, and suddenly I bit my arm and drank my own blood! Thereupon, spurred on by pain, revived by the tepid acrid liquor that moistened my lips, I tore desperately at the nail and at last I wrenched it off!

I then believed in success. My plan was a simple one; I pushed the point of the nail into the lid, dragging it along as far as I could in a straight line, and working it so as to make a slit in the wood. My fingers stiffened, but I doggedly persevered, and when I fancied that I had sufficiently cut into the board I turned on my stomach, and lifting myself on my knees and elbows thrust the whole strength of my back against the lid. But although it creaked, it did not yield; the notched line was not deep enough. I had to resume my old position—which I only managed to do with infinite trouble—and work afresh. At last, after another supreme effort, the lid was cleft from end to end.

I was not saved as yet, but my heart beat with renewed hope. I had ceased pushing and remained motionless, lest a sudden fall of earth should bury me. I intended to use the lid as a screen, and thus protected to open a sort of shaft in the clayey soil. Unfortunately I was assailed by unexpected difficulties. Some heavy clods of earth weighed upon the boards and made them unmanageable: I foresaw that I should never reach the surface in that way, for the mass of soil was already bending my spine and crushing my face.

Once more I stopped affrighted; then suddenly, while I was stretching my legs trying to find something firm against which I might rest my feet, I felt the end board of the coffin yielding. I at once gave a desperate kick with my heels, in the faint hope that there might be a freshly dug grave in that direction.

It was so. My feet abruptly forced their way into space. An open grave was there; I had only a slight partition of earth to displace, and soon I rolled into the cavity. I was saved!

I remained for a time lying on my back in the open grave, with my eyes raised to heaven. It was dark, the stars were shining in a sky of velvety blueness. Now and then the rising breeze wafted a spring-like freshness, a perfume of foliage upon me. I was saved! I could breathe, I felt warm; and I wept, and I stammered, with my arms prayerfully extended towards the starry sky. O God! how sweet seemed life!

# CHAPTER V

## MY RESURRECTION

MY FIRST impulse was to find the custodian of the cemetery and ask him to have me conducted home, but various thoughts that came to me restrained me from following that course. My return would create general alarm; why should I hurry now that I was master of the situation? I felt my limbs; I had only an insignificant wound on my left arm, where I had bitten myself; and a slight feverishness lent me unhoped-for strength. I should no doubt be able to walk unaided.

Still I lingered; all sorts of dim visions confused my mind. I had felt beside me in the open grave some sextons' tools which had been left there, and I conceived a sudden desire to repair the damage I had done, to close up the hole through which I had crept, so as to conceal all traces of my resurrection. I do not believe that I had any positive motive in doing so. I only deemed it useless to proclaim my adventure aloud, feeling ashamed to find myself alive when the whole world thought me dead. In half an hour every trace of my escape was obliterated, and then I climbed out of the hole.

The night was splendid, and deep silence reigned in the cemetery; the black trees threw motionless shadows over the white tombs. When I endeavoured to ascertain my bearings, I noticed that one half of the sky was ruddy as if lit by a huge conflagration; Paris lay in that direction, and I moved towards it, following a long avenue, amid the darkness of the branches.

However, after I had gone some fifty yards I was compelled to stop, feeling faint and weary. I then sat down on a stone bench, and for the first time looked at myself. I was fully attired with the exception that I had no hat. I blessed my beloved Marguerite for the pious thought which had prompted her to dress me in my best clothes—those which I had worn at our wedding. That remembrance of my wife brought me to my feet again. I longed to see her without delay.

At the further end of the avenue I had taken, a wall arrested my progress. However I climbed to the top of a monument, reached the summit of the wall, and then dropped over the other side. Although roughly shaken by the fall, I managed to walk for a few minutes along a broad deserted street skirting the cemetery. I had no notion as to where I might be, but with the reiteration of monomania I kept saying to myself that I was going towards Paris, and that I should find the Rue Dauphine somehow or other. Several people passed me but, seized with sudden distrust, I would not stop them and ask my way. I have since realized that I was then in a burning fever, and already nearly delirious. Finally, just as I reached a large thoroughfare, I became giddy and fell heavily upon the pavement.

Here there is a blank in my life. For three whole weeks I remained unconscious. When I awoke at last I found myself in a strange room. A man who was nursing me told me quietly that he had picked me up one morning on the Boulevard Montparnasse, and had brought me to his house. He was an old doctor who had given up practising.

When I attempted to thank him, he sharply answered that my case had seemed a curious one, and that he had wished to study it. Moreover, during the first days of my convalescence he would not allow me to ask a single question; and later on, he never put one to me. For eight days longer I remained in bed, feeling very weak, and not even trying to remember, for memory was a weariness and a pain. I felt half ashamed and half afraid. As soon as I could leave the house I would go and find out whatever I wanted to know. Possibly in the delirium of fever a name had escaped me; however, the doctor never alluded to anything I may have said. His charity was not only generous, it was discreet.

The summer had come at last, and one warm June morning I was at last permitted to take a short walk. The sun was shining with that joyous brightness which imparts renewed youth to the streets of old Paris. I went along slowly, questioning the passers-by at every crossing I came to, and asking the way to Rue Dauphine. When I reached the street I had some difficulty in recognising the lodging-house where we had alighted on our arrival in the capital. A childish terror made me hesitate. If I appeared suddenly before Marguerite, the shock might kill her. It might be wiser to begin by revealing myself to our neighbour, Madame Gabin; still I shrank from taking a third party into confidence. I seemed unable to arrive at a resolution, and yet in my innermost heart I felt a great void, like that left by some sacrifice long since consummated.

The building looked quite yellow in the sunshine. I had just recognised it by a shabby eating-house on the ground floor, where we had ordered our meals, having them sent up to us. Then I raised my eyes to the last window of the third floor on the left-hand side, and as I looked at it a young woman with tumbled hair, wearing a loose dressing gown, appeared and leant her elbows on the sill. A young man followed and printed a kiss upon her neck. It was not Marguerite. Still I felt no suprise. It seemed to me that I had dreamt all this, with other things too, which I was to learn presently.

For a moment I remained in the street, uncertain whether I had better go upstairs and question the lovers, who were still laughing in the sunshine. However, I decided to enter the little restaurant below. When I started on my walk, the old doctor had placed a five-franc piece in my hand. No doubt I was changed beyond recognition, for my beard had grown during the brain fever, and my face was wrinkled and haggard. As I took a seat at a small table, I saw Madame Gabin come in carrying a cup; she wished to buy a penny-worth of coffee. Standing in front of the counter, she began to gossip with the land-lady of the establishment.

"Well," asked the latter, "so the poor little woman of the third floor has made up her mind at last, eh?"

"How could she help herself?" answered Madame Gabin "it was the very best thing for her to do. Monsieur Simoneau showed her so much kindness. You see, he had finished his business in Paris to his satisfaction, for he has inherited a pot of money. Well, he offered to take her away with him to his own part of the country, and place her with an aunt of his, who wants a housekeeper and companion."

The landlady laughed archly. I buried my face in a newspaper which I picked off the table. My lips were white and my hands shook.

"It will end in a marriage of course," resumed Madame Gabin. "The little widow mourned for her husband very properly, and the young man was extremely well-behaved. Well, they left last night—and after all they were free to please themselves."

Just then the side door of the restaurant communicating with the passage of the house opened, and Dédé appeared.

"Mother, ain't you coming?" she cried. "I'm waiting, you know; do be quick."

"Presently," said the mother testily. "Don't bother."

The girl stood listening to the two women with the precocious shrewdness of a child born and reared amid the streets of Paris.

"When all is said and done," explained Madame Gabin, "the dear departed did not come up to Monsieur Simoneau. I didn't fancy him over much; he was a puny sort of a man, a poor fretful fellow—and he hadn't a penny to bless himself with. No, candidly, he wasn't the kind of husband for a young and healthy wife, whereas Monsieur Simoneau is rich, you know, and as strong as a Turk."

"Oh, yes!" interrupted Dédé, "I saw him once when he was washing—his door was open. His arms are so hairy!"

"Get along with you," screamed the old woman, shoving the girl out of the restaurant. "You are always poking your nose where it has no business to be."

Then she concluded with these words: "Look here, to my mind the other one did quite right to take himself off. It was fine luck for the little woman!"

When I found myself in the street again, I walked along slowly with trembling limbs. And yet I was not suffering much; I think I smiled once at my shadow in the sun. It was quite true. I *was* very puny. It had been a queer notion of mine to marry Marguerite. I recalled her weariness at Guérande, her impatience, her dull, monotonous life. The dear creature had been very good to me, but I had never been a real lover; she had mourned for me as a sister for her brother, not otherwise. Why should I again disturb her life? A dead man is not jealous.

When I lifted my eyelids I saw the garden of the Luxembourg before me. I entered it, and took a seat in the sun, dreaming with a sense of infinite restfulness. The thought of Marguerite stirred me softly. I pictured her in the provinces beloved, petted, and very happy. She had grown handsomer, and she was the mother of three boys and two girls. It was all right. I had behaved like an honest man in dying, and I would not commit the cruel folly of coming to life again.

Since then I have travelled a good deal. I have been a little everywhere. I am an ordinary man who has toiled and eaten like anybody else. Death no longer frightens me, but it does not seem to care for me now that I have no motive in living; and I sometimes fear that I have been forgotten upon earth.

# Jacques Damour

## CHAPTER I

### FÉLICIE

OVER yonder at Nouméa, when Jacques Damour gazed at the blank horizon of the sea, he sometimes fancied he saw passing over it all his past history—the miseries of the German seige, the wrath of the Commune, the disruption which had cast him so far, bruised and stunned. It was not a clear vision of memories over which he lingered tenderly; his was the dull brooding of a darkened intellect returning mechanically to certain facts which alone started out sharp and precise from amidst general ruin.

At twenty-seven years of age Jacques had married Félicie, a tall, handsome girl of eighteen, the niece of a fruiterer at La Villette, of whom he had hired a room. Jacques was an engraver on metals, and at times earned as much as twelve francs a day. His wife had tried dress-making, but a baby having come, it was as much as she could do to nurse her boy and look after her household. Eugène was a strong, healthy little fellow, but nine years later a girl was born, who for a long time remained so puny and sickly that she cost a great deal in doctors and physic. Still they were not unhappy. Damour, it is true, would now and then loaf about on a Monday, but when he had been drinking he had the good sense to go to bed, and on the following morning he would return to his work, blaming himself severely as a ne'er-do-well. When Eugène was twelve years old he had learned enough of his father's calling to earn his living, although he could barely read or write. Félicie kept her rooms scrupulously clean; she became a thrifty and clever housewife, somewhat of a screw, the father would say, giving them more vegetables than meat, so as to put by something for a rainy day. They lived at Menilmontant, in the Rue des Envierges, occupying a set of three rooms, one for the father and mother, one for Eugène, and a sitting-room, where the vice, benches, and tools were kept; they also had a kitchen, and a small closet for Louise. The flat was reached by a yard, and was situated in a rear building, but they had plenty of air, as the windows overlooked an open stretch of waste ground, where from morning till night carts came and emptied bricks, stones, and old boards, the refuse of demolished houses.

When war broke out with Germany the Damours had been living for ten years in the Rue des Envierges. Félicie was now nearly forty, but she was still young-looking and plump; indeed, the roundness of her hips and shoulders made her the handsomest woman in the neighbourhood. Jacques, on the contrary, was, as it were, desiccated, and the eight years' difference in age between them made him already look like an old man beside his wife. Louise, although no longer in danger, was still thin and delicate, resembling her father, while Eugène, then nineteen years old, had his mother's tall figure and broad back. They lived in perfect union, save for those unfortunate Mondays, when father and son lingered in the wine shops, and Félicie sulked, furious at the misspent money. Two or three times they even came to blows, but it did not amount to much, and on the whole there was not a more respectable or more united family in the house. They were quoted as a bright example. When the Germans marched upon Paris, and the terrible stoppage of work began, they had over a thousand francs in the savings bank. This was a large sum for a working couple who had reared two children.

Thus the first months of the seige were not very hard to bear. In the parlour, where the tools lay idle, bread and meat still appeared upon the table. Touched also by the penury of a neighbour, a stalwart house-painter called Berru, who was starving, Damour asked him to share their dinner several times, and soon, indeed, the neighbour dropped in regularly at all the meals. He was a larky fellow, full of chaff and fun, and contrived to get round Félicie, who at first had looked angrily and distrustfully at his big hungry mouth, in which the largest and best morsels vanished. At night they played cards and abused the Prussians. Berru, who was a patriot, talked of digging tunnels, subterranean passages through the country abutting under the enemy's batteries at Châtillon and Montretout, and then blowing them all up. He denounced the Government as a pack of cowards, who would throw open the gates of Paris to Bismark in view of placing Henri V.—the Count de Chambord—on the throne. The Republic as managed by those traitors made him shrug his shoulders. Ah, the Republic! Then, with both elbows on the table and his short pipe in his mouth, he explained to Damour his own ideas of what a Government ought to be—all brothers—all free—all rich—justice and equality reigning everywhere amid high and low. "Like '93!" he added squarely, not knowing, however, what he meant.

Damour remained grave. He, too, was a Republican, for from his cradle he had heard it asserted that the Republic would one day bring about the triumph of the working classes and universal bliss; however, he had no real notion of the manner in which it was all to happen. He listened attentively to Berru, finding his reasoning exceedingly good, and admitting that such a Republic as he expected would no doubt come some day. He became interested, and even excited in the controversy, firmly believing that if all the Parisians,

men, women, and children, had marched to Versailles singing the *Marseillaise,* the Prussians would have been routed. Yes, the Parisians would have shaken hands with the provinces, and the Government of the people, which was bound to give every citizen an income, would have been established.

"Beware!" said Félicie, with secret misgivings; "your Berru will lead you into mischief. Feed him, if you want to do so, but let him go and get his skull cracked without your help."

She, too, wanted the Republic. In '48 her father had been killed on a barricade, but the memory of that death, instead of maddening her, made her reasonable. If *she* had been the mob, she knew how she would have compelled the Government to be just—she would have behaved irreproachably. Berru's speeches caused her as much indignation as alarm; she found them deficient in honesty. She also noticed uneasily that Damour was changed; that he assumed a manner and used words she did not like; and she became still more anxious when she remarked the sombre ardent looks with which her son Eugène listened to Berru. At night time, when Louise had fallen asleep with her head on the table, the young man, after slowly sipping a little glass of brandy, would fold his arms and mutely fix his eyes on the painter, who daily returned from his rambles through Paris with some extraordinary tale of treachery—Bonapartists had signalled to the Germans from Montmartre, or sacks of flour and barrels of powder had been cast into the Seine, so that the city might be forced to surrender.

"What nonsense!" said Félicie to her

son as soon as Berru had made up his mind to leave them; "don't put such stuff into your head, my boy; you know he lies."

"I know what I know," answered Eugène, with a furious gesture.

Towards the middle of December the Damours had got to the end of their savings, but as it was hourly proclaimed that the Germans had been defeated in the provinces, or that a victorious sortie had at last liberated Paris, the little household was at first not much alarmed, being upheld by the daily hope that work would soon begin again. Félicie accomplished miracles of thrift, and they lived as best they could on the black seige bread, which little Louise alone could not digest. It was about this time that Damour and Eugène became distracted, or, as the mother said, completely lost their heads. Having nothing to do from morning to night, with all their habits altered, they spent their days in a wearied, troubled idleness, haunted by dreams full of grotesque and sanguinary visions. They had both enlisted in a marching battalion, which, like many others, never left the fortifications, remaining quartered at a spot, where the men spent their time playing cards. It was there that Damour, suffering from hunger, his heart rent by the thought of his family's misery, listened to the reports bandied about on all sides, and acquired the conviction that the Government was determined to exterminate the people and do away with the Republic. Berru was right; everyone knew that Henri V. was at St. Germain, in a house over which the white flag was flying. But all this could not last much

longer. Some fine morning they would go and shoot the vermin that starved the working classes and allow them to be bombarded—just to make room for priests and nobles. When Damour and Eugène came home, fevered by the insane delirium of the streets, they talked of nothing but wholesale butchery; while Félicie, pale and dumb, tended little Louise, who had fallen ill again, affected by the bad diet.

At last the seige ended, the armistice was signed, and one day the Germans trouped along the Champs-Elysées. In the Rue des En, vierges they again ate white bread which Félicie had gone to buy at St. Denis; still, the dinner proved dreary. Eugène, who had been to look at the Germans, was giving some particulars, when Damour, waving his fork, shouted out furiously that all the generals ought to be guillotined. Félicie thereupon got angry and took his fork away. The following days, as the workshops did not open, Damour decided to begin work on his own account; he had a few articles on hand, among others, a pair of candlesticks, which he meant to finish carefully and try to sell. At the end of an hour, however, Eugène, who felt unable to remain quiet, threw down his tools. As for Berru, he had disappeared since the armistice, having no doubt found liberal board elsewhere. One morning, however, he returned in a state of great excitement, and related the story of the cannon of Montmartre. Barricades were being erected on all sides, said he, the triumph of the people was at hand, and he had come to fetch Damour, as all good citizens were wanted. Damour at once rose from his bench, utterly disregarding the anxious, troubled looks of Félicie.

The days of March, April, and May followed. When Damour was worn out with fatigue, and his wife implored him to stop at home, he answered: "And my thirty sous? Who would give us bread?"

Félicie silently bowed her head. The thirty sous of the father and the thirty sous of the son, occasionally supplemented by distributions of bread and salted meat, were all they had to live upon. Damour was convinced of the righteousness of his cause, and he fired on the Versailles troops as he would have fired on the Prussians, persuaded that he was saving the Republic and assuring the welfare of the people. After the misery and the fatigues of the German siege, the commotion of civil war gave him a sensation of nightmare amid which he struggled, like an obscure hero who was resolved to die for the defense of Liberty. He did not enter into any of the complex theories about the Commune; in his eyes the Commune was simply the prophesied golden era, the dawn of the universal felicity; and he believed with even greater obstinacy that somewhere, at St. Germain or Versailles, there was a king ready to revive the Inquisition and feudal privileges, provided he were permitted to enter Paris. He, who would not willingly have crushed an insect at home, picked off the gendarmes at the outposts without the slightest hesitation. When he returned to Menilmontant exhausted, grimy with sweat and powder, he sat for hours by the side of little Louise's cot, listening to her laboured breathing. Félicie no longer attempted

to oppose him, but waited for the end of the cataclysm with the calm shrewdness of her practical mind.

One day, however, she ventured to remark that that big, hulking Berru who bragged so loudly had not been such a simpleton as to put himself within gun-shot. He had been shrewd enough to get a post in the commissariat, which did not prevent him, whenever he came in his belaced uniform, from exciting Damour with fanatical speeches, talking freely of shooting Ministers, the members of the Legislature, in fact, all the Reactionaries, as soon as they should be captured at Versailles.

"Why doesn't he go himself, instead of sending others?" argued Félicie, after some such speech.

"Hold your tongue," answered Damour. "I am doing my duty; so much the worse for those who don't do theirs."

One morning, towards the close of April, Eugène was brought back to the Rue des Envierges on a stretcher. A bullet had struck him in the chest, and he expired as they were carrying him up the stairs. When Damour came home at night he found Félicie standing in silence by the corpse of their son. It was a terrible blow for him; he sank to the floor, and remained there sobbing, huddled against the wall. His wife did not attempt to comfort him, she never spoke, for she had nothing to say; still, if she had opened her lips involuntarily, she would have cried, "It is your doing!" She had closed the door of Louise's closet, so that the noise would not frighten the child. Even now she went to see if the father's sobs had not wakened Louise. When Damour rose up he walked to the mantel-piece, and gazed at a photograph of Eugène, representing the young man in his uniform of the National Guard. Then he took a pen and wrote at the back of the portrait, "I will avenge you!" adding the date and his signature. After that he felt relieved. The next day a hearse draped with large red flags conveyed the body to the Père Lachaise Cemetery, followed by an enormous crowd. The father walked bare-headed behind the coffin, and the sight of the flags, of their bloody purple adorning the black bier, swelled his heart with wild, sinister thoughts. Félicie had remained at home with Louise. That same evening Damour returned to the outposts to pick off some more gendarmes.

At last the days of May began. The army of Versailles entered Paris. Damour did not come home for two days, but fell back with his battalion, defending the barricades amid the conflagration. He knew nothing of what went on, but fired through the smoke because it was his duty to do so. On the morning of the third day he reappeared in the Rue des Envierges; his clothes were in rags, and he staggered and seemed stupefied like a drunken man. Félice was helping him to undress, and washing his hands with a wet towel, when a neighbour rushed in saying that the Communists still held Père Lachaise Cemetery, and that the Versaillais were unable to dislodge them.

"I'll go there, then," said Damour simply.

He again dressed and caught up his gun. But the last defenders of the Commune were not on the plateau, near the spot where Eugène slept. Damour had vaguely hoped to get killed on his son's grave, but he did not get so far. Bombs were falling, splintering the big tombs. Between the beeches, hidden by the marble whitening in the sun, a few National Guardsmen were still firing in a desultory fashion on the soldiers, whose red trousers were seen advancing. Damour joined his confederates just in time to be captured. Thirty-seven of his companions were shot at once; he himself escaping this summary justice almost by a miracle. As his wife had washed his hands and his gun was not loaded, his life was spared; but in the stupor of his exhaustion and horror he never quite remembered the events that followed, they hovered about in his memory like the perplexing dreams of delirium; long hours passed in dark cells, dreary marches under the sun, yells, blows, staring crowds opening to see him pass. . . . When he at last shook off his crazy imbecility he was a prisoner at Versailles.

Félicie, always pale and calm, came to see him; but when she had told him that Louise was better, they remained speechless, having nothing more to say. As she was going away she informed him, by way of encouragement, that his case was being investigated, and that he would surely come out safe.

"And Berrru?" he asked.

"'Oh! Berru is all right," she answered. "He got away on the day before the troops entered Paris; they won't even trouble him."

A month later Damour started for

New Caledonia; he had been condemned to transportation. As he held no rank, the court-martial before which he appeared would probably have acquitted him, had he not quietly admitted that he had fought and fired from the beginning of the insurrection. During their last interview he said to Félicie; "I shall come back. Wait for me with the little ones."

And these were the words that Damour heard most clearly amid the confusion of his memory, as he sat with drooping head, before the blank horizon of the sea. At times night fell and found him still in the same spot. Afar a brighter line lingered like the furrow of a ship cutting athwart the increasing darkness, and it seemed to him as if he must rise and walk on that white road, since he had promised to return.

## CHAPTER II

### CONVALESCENT

At Nouméa Damour behaved fairly well. He found work, and was told that he might expect a pardon. He was gentle and fond of playing with children; he no longer meddled with politics; he kept aloof from his companions, living quite alone. His only failing was that he drank occasionally; still, even in his cups he remained quiet and good-natured, shedding copious tears and retiring to bed of his own accord. His pardon appeared certain, when suddenly he disappeared. The surprise was great when it was found that he had run away with four of his comrades. During his two years of exile he had received several letters from Félicie, regularly at first, but less frequently later on. He himself wrote often. At last, three months having elapsed without bringing him any news, he grew desperate at the thought of waiting for a pardon that might be delayed for two years longer, and in one of those moments of frenzy which are so bitterly rued afterwards he risked everything. A week later, some leagues off, a shattered boat was found on the shore, and near it were the bodies of three of the fugitives— quite naked and in an advanced state of decomposition. Some witnesses declared that one of the corpses was Damour's; it was of the same stature, and the beard looked like his. After a hasty inquiry the necessary formalities were carried out: a cerificate of death was drawn up, and at the request of the widow who had been duly informed by the authorities, a duplicate was sent to her. The whole press teemed with this adventure, and a dramatic account of the escape and its tragic ending circulated through the newspapers of the whole world.

Nevertheless Damour was alive. One of his fellow-prisoners had been mistaken for him—a circumstance which was all the more singular as the two men were not in the least like one another; only each wore a long beard. Damour and the fourth man, who also had miraculously survived, parted company as soon as they reached Australia. They never met again, and probably the other poor devil died of yellow fever, which very nearly carried off Damour himself. His first intention had been to inform Félicie of his whereabouts by letter, but, having come across a newspaper narrating his escape and death, he thought to himself that it would be imprudent to write; a letter might be intercepted—read, and then the truth revealed. Would it not be better to remain dead to the world? Nobody would then suspect him, and he might quietly return to France and wait for an amnesty before confessing his identity. It was just then that a severe attack of yellow fever prostrated him for many weeks on a hospital bed.

When Damour became convalescent he experienced unconquerable lassitude; for many months he remained very weak and absolutely purposeless. The fever had seemingly swept all his old desires away; he cared for nothing, he wanted nothing; the images of Félicie and Louise were blurred; he still saw them, but at a great distance, in a fog, as it were, and at times he hardly recognised them. Certainly, as soon as his strength returned he meant to start and seek them, but suddenly, when he found himself once more on his legs, another idea possessed him. Before joining his wife and daughter he would make a fortune. What could he do in Paris? Starve over his engraving work, and he might not even find any to do; besides, he felt dreadfully aged. On the other hand, if he went to America, he might, in a few months, gain a hundred thousand francs; a modest sum with which he would rest content, notwithstanding the prodigious tales of millions which were constantly buzzing in his ears. He had been told of a gold mine where every man, even the humblest navvy, had been able to drive a coach and pair before six months had passed. He arranged his future life:

he would go back to France with his little pile, buy a small house near Vincennes, and, forgotten, happy, and well rid of politics, settle down there on an income of four or five thousand francs with Félicie and Louise. Four weeks later Damour was in America.

Then began an up-and-down existence, in which chance whirled him at haphazard into a turmoil of adventures at once vulgar and strange; he knew every kind of misery, touched every kind of fortune; three times he thought he had grasped his hundred thousand francs, three times they melted in his fingers; he was robbed, or he ruined himself in the last supreme effort. He suffered, toiled, and at last remained without a shirt on his back. After wandering to the four corners of the world, fate finally threw him on English soil; thence he drifted to Belgium, to the very frontier of France, but he no longer wished to cross it. From America he had written to Félice, but, as three letters had elicited no answer, he felt justified in thinking that she was either dead or had left Paris. A year later he made another fruitless attempt to get some news of her. In order not to betray himself, if his correspondence were opened, he had written under an assumed name about some fictitious business, calculating that Félicie would recognise his handwriting, and understand. Her continued silence paralysed his memory, as it were; he felt dead, as if he belonged to nobody, as if nothing mattered any more. During the year that he spent in Belgium he worked in a coal mine, underground, without seeing the sun, just sleeping and eating, and wishing for naught else. At last, one evening in a pothouse he heard some one say that an amnesty had just been voted, and that all the exiled Communists were returning home. This roused him; he felt a sudden thrill, a desire to look once more upon the street where he had lived so long.

At first it was merely an instinctive impulse; but while he was in the train carrying him to Paris his brain worked, and he realised that he might once again resume his place in the broad daylight, if he could only succeed in finding Félicie and Louise. New hopes dawned in his heart; he was free, he could boldly search for them, and he began to think that he would find them seated quitely in the parlour in the Rue des Envierges, with the cloth laid and waiting for him. Their silence would be explained by some simple mishap. Then he would report himself at the municipal offices, and the happy home life would recommence as of yore.

When he alighted at the Northern Terminus in Paris the station was filled with a boisterous crowd. As soon as the travellers appeared, loud acclamations arose, wild enthusiasm prevailed, hats were waved, and names shouted. Damour felt frightened; he could not understand—he fancied that all these people had assembled to hoot him. But presently he caught the name so noisily cheered; it belonged to a member of the Commune who had been with him in the train; an illustrious exile, who was greeted by the crowd with riotous ovations. Damour saw him pass, looking very much stouter, with moist eyes, smiling, and feeling flattered by his reception. When the hero had got into

a cab there was a rush to take out the horses; then the mob swayed, and finally the human billows dashed into the Rue Lafayette, the cab slowly rolling along like a triumphal car above a sea of heads. Damour, hurried, hustled, and crushed, experienced great difficulty in reaching the outer boulevards. Nobody noticed *him*. All his sufferings, Versailles, the voyage, Nouméa, rose up in his throat with a bitter nauseous taste.

When he found himself on the outer boulevards he was strangely affected. He forgot his trials, for it seemed to him that he had just taken back some finished work and was quietly returning to his home in the Rue des Envierges. Ten years of his life, so full of trouble and perplexity, were now closing behind him. And yet he felt a certain wondering strangeness in thus reverting to former habits. Surely the boulevards were wider; and he stopped to read some new inscriptions, surprised at finding them there. Truth to tell, he did not experience any frank delight in setting foot on that much-regretted ground; the sensation that came to him was half of tenderness musical with old refrains and half of covert apprehension: the uneasiness that one feels in presence of the unknown, and this although the scene before him was a familiar one. His disquietude increased as he neared the Rue des Envierges; his courage wavered, and he felt half-inclined to go no further, as if he dreaded some impending catastrophe. Why had he returned? What was he to do?

When he at last found himself in the Rue des Envierges, he halted before the house three times without entering it. The pork-butcher's shop, formerly just opposite, had disappeared, being replaced by a greengrocer's; the woman standing at the door seemed so buxom, and so thoroughly at home, that he did not venture to address her as had been his first intention. He preferred to get it all over, and walk boldly to the house-porter's den. How often he had turned to the left at the end of the passage and knocked at the little window-pane!

"Madame Damour, if you please," he stammered.

"Don't know her. There's no one of that name in the house."

He stood transfixed. Instead of the door-keeper of his time, who had been extremely stout, he had before him a cross, dried-up little woman who surveyed him distrustfully.

"Madame Damour," he resumed; "lived at the back—ten years ago."

"Ten years!" screamed the woman. "Well, plenty of water has passed under the bridges since then. We only came here last January."

"Maybe Madame Damour has left her address?"

"No; don't know her." And then, as he insisted, she got angry and threatened to call her husband. "Haven't you soon done prying and spying?" she said. "There are lots of people who sneak in here, anyhow—"

Damour colored and went away stammering apologies. He was ashamed of his frayed trousers and his soiled old blouse. He went off along the foot pavement with hanging head, but he soon retraced his steps as if he could not make up his mind to depart; it was like taking an eternal farewell that tore his heart. He lifted his eyes, looked at the windows and examined the shops, trying to reconnoitre the surroundings. In those houses, divided into petty lodgings amongst which evictions rain like hail, ten years had sufficed to change nearly all the tenants; and besides, from a vague sense of prudence not unmixed with shame and terror, he did not wish to be recognised. As he went down the street again, he at last came across some people he had known; the tobacconist, a grocer, a laundress, the baker's wife, with whom he had once dealt. For another fifteen minutes he wavered, passing before the shops, uncertain which to enter, while perspiration came to his forehead from the pain of his inward struggles. With failing heart he finally decided in favour of the baker's wife, a sleepy kind of woman, who looked as white as if she slept in her own flour-bags. She gazed at him without leaving her counter, and she evidently did not know him, with his tanned skin, his bald head scorched by the burning suns, and his long rough beard covering half his face. Emboldened by her manner, he asked for a halfpenny roll, paid for it, and then ventured to ask:

"Haven't you among your customers, madame, a woman and a little girl—Madame Damour?"

The baker's wife pondered a while, and then in her slumberous way answered, "Well, yes; once upon a time, possibly. But that's very long ago. I don't remember; so many people come and go."

He had to rest satisfied with that answer and go off. During the following days he came to the neighbourhood again and questioned other tradespeople with less timidity; but he always found the same careless indifference, the same oblivion, together with contradictory statements that confused him. All things considered, it seemed positive that Félicie had left the neighbourhood some two years after his own departure for Nouméa, and just about the time of his escape. Nobody knew her address; some asserted that she had gone to the Gros Caillou, others that she was at Bercy, while, as for little Louise, she was not even remembered. It was a hopeless case. Damour sat down one evening on a bench on the outer boulevard, and wept as he decided to give up his search. What was he to do? Paris seemed empty now, and the little money that he had brought with him was nearly all spent. Once he thought of returning to Belgium and the coal mine, where it was so dark, and where, remembering nothing, he had lived the vacuous happy life of a dumb brute amidst the slumbering earth. However, he stayed on, miserable and starving, unable to procure work, for he was repulsed everywhere, being judged too old. He was only fifty-five, but the decrepitude brought about by ten long years of suffering made him look five-and-seventy. He prowled about like a wolf, roaming over the building-yards of the monuments fired by the Commune, and now in course of re-erection, begging for such jobs as are usually given to children and cripples. A stone-mason employed at the Hôtel de Ville works at last promised to procure him the keeping of the tools there, but the promise was slow of fulfilment, and Damour was hungry.

One day he stood on the bridge of Notre Dame looking at the water with the dizziness of those unfortunates who are fascinated by the idea of suicide. But by a mechanical instinct of self-preservation he suddenly loosened his hold of the railings, and threw himself back so violently that he nearly knocked down a passer-by, a tall man in a white blouse, who began to abuse him.

"You brute!"

But Damour had paused aghast, his eyes riveted on the tall fellow.

"Berru!" he stammered at last.

It was indeed Berru—Berru, altered no doubt but to his advantage, for he had a blooming face and looked younger than ever. Damour had frequently thought of him since his return, but then where was he to find the old comrade who had been wont to flit every fortnight? The painter opened his eyes wide, and even remained incredulous, when Damour in faltering accents revealed his name.

"Impossible! What a cracker!"

However, he recognized him at last, and his noisy ejaculations began to attract a crowd around them.

"But you were dead! The deuce, if I expected this!" said he. "It ain't fair to play such tricks. Come, come, is it quite true that you are alive?"

Thereupon Damour, lowering his own voice, begged Berru to be silent. The painter, who thought the whole thing a capital joke, took his arm and led him off to a wineshop in the Rue St. Martin, plying him with questions and wishing to know all the particulars.

"Presently," said Damour, as soon as they were seated at a small table in a private room. "But, first of all, where is my wife?"

Berru looked at him in amazement.

"What do you mean—your wife?"

"Yes. Where is she? Do you know her address?"

The painter's stupefaction increased, and he answered slowly, "Certainly—I know her address. But you—don't you know the story?"

"No—what story?"

"Ah, there's a go!" burst out Berru. "A rum go it is, sure enough! So you know nothing, eh? Why, your wife is married again, old man."

Damour, who had just lifted his glass to drink, replaced it on the table; he trembled so violently that the wine trickled between his fingers, which he wiped upon his blouse while he repeated in a dull, toneless voice, "What do you say? married again? married? Are you sure?"

"Positive. You were dead, and she married again; there's nothing strange in that! Only it's deucedly queer, now that you have come to life again!"

Then while the poor fellow sat there, pale and with tremulous lips, the painter spared him no details. Félicie was perfectly happy. She had married a butcher in the Rue des Moines at Batignolles, a widower whose business she managed with a high hand and level head. Sagnard — the husband's name was Sagnard—was a stout, florid man of sixty, extremely well preserved for his age. The shop—a corner one at the angle of the Rue Nollet—was one of the best patronized in the district; it had tall iron railings painted red, and on either side of the signboard there were two large gilded ox-heads.

"And now what do you intend doing?" asked Berru after each explanation.

The poor wretch, dazzled by the description of the fine shop, answered by vaguely wagging his head—he could not tell.

"And Louise?" he asked abruptly.

"The little one? Ah! I don't know! They have probably sent her somewhere to get rid of her, for I have never seen her with them. That's it. Well, they might anyhow return you the child, as they don't want her. Only, what will you do with a big girl of twenty—for you don't look as if you were in clover, eh? No offense, old man, but anyone passing you in the street would chuck you a copper."

Damour's head drooped, his throat tightened, and he felt unable to speak a word. Berru ordered a second bottle of wine and began to comfort him.

"The deuce!" he cried. "As you are alive let us be jolly. It ain't a desperate case—things will mend. What do you propose doing?"

Then the two men plunged into an interminable discussion, in which the same arguments were incessantly repeated. The painter had omitted to mention that immediately after the convict's departure he had attempted o make love to Félicie, and that he harboured a secret grudge against the butcher Sagnard, whom she had preferred to himself, probably because he was well off. After Berru had ordered a third bottle he became excited.

"If I were you," he said aggressively, "I'd look them up: square myself in the place and keep Sagnard out if he annoyed me. You are the master; after all the law's on your side."

By degrees Damour, flushed with wine, felt a glow rise to his white cheeks; he loudly declared that he certainly would do something. Berru kept on urging him to action, slapping his shoulders, and asking him if he were a man! Of course he was a man!—and he had loved that woman so fondly! He loved her still, enough to set Paris on fire in order to get her back. Well, then, in that case, why delay? As she was his, he had only to step out and take her. The two men were nearly drunk by this time, and shouted incoherently in each other's face.

"I'm off," suddenly said Damour, rising with difficulty to his feet.

"Well done!" cried Berru. "Don't be a coward! I'll go with you!"

And thereupon they started for Batignolles.

## CHAPTER III

### THE CHANGE

THE shop at the corner of the Rue des Moines and the Rue Nollet had a very prosperous appearance, with its red railings and gilded ox-heads. Quartered animals hung there against white sheets, while legs of mutton, partly wrapped in lace-edged paper like nosegays, formed circular garlands round about. Piles of ruddy flesh, joints already cut and trimmed, roseate veal, purple mutton, and scarlet beef streaked with fat covered the marble slabs. The brass pans, the large scales, the steel hooks, shone brightly. The plentifulness of everything, the healthy atmosphere of the premises, paved with white marble and open to the light, the invigorating smell of the fresh meat—all seemed to send a warmer blood to the cheeks of those employed in the shop.

In the centre, and in full view of the street, Félicie sat enthroned behind a tall counter, partitioned off so as to shield her from the draughts. Behind the glass panes and amid the cheerful reflections of all the pink colouring she herself looked young and fresh, with the full mature freshness of a woman who is past forty. And apart from her clear complexion, her smooth skin, her dark hair, and her white neck, she displayed the amiable busy gravity of a clever business woman, who, with a pen in one hand while with the other she fingers the money in the till, represents a shop's integrity and prosperity. Under her eyes the men cut and weighed the meat, and called out the amounts; then the customers passed before the counter; she received payment, and in a deferential voice talked over the news of the neighbourhood. A short, sickly-looking woman was at that moment paying for two cutlets, at which she gazed languidly.

"Fifteen sous, isn't it?" said Félicie. "So you are not any better, Madame Vernier?"

"No, not any better. It is always my digestion—my food never agrees with me. The doctor has at last ordered me to eat meat, but it is dreadfully expensive. Ah! you know that the coal dealer is dead?"

"You don't say so!"

"It wasn't the stomach with him—it was internal disease, I hear. Two cutlets, fifteen sous! Why, poultry is cheaper!"

"Well, it is not our fault, Madame Vernier. We hardly know ourselves how to make both ends meet. What is the matter, Charles?" she added, turning to one of the men.

While Félicie had been chatting and giving change she had not relaxed in her watchfulness, and had just noticed one of the men talking with two fellows on the foot pavement. As he did not seem to have heard her, she raised her voice to call "Charles, what is wanted?"

But she did not wait for an answer, for as the two men entered she recognised the one who walked ahead.

"Ah! so it's you, Monsieur Berru?" She did not seem at all pleased, for her lips met with a slightly contemptuous expression. The two men, on their way from the Rue St. Martin to Batignolles, had halted at various wine-shops, for the distance was considerable, and having talked loudly, earnestly, and incessantly, they had frequently felt parched. It was easy to see that the wine had affected them. Moreover, Damour had received a sudden shock when, from across the street, Berru had suddenly stretched out his hand and pointed to Félicie, looking so comely and even young as she sat there at her little counter. "There she is!" said the painter.

It could not be. That must be Louise, who had always resembled her mother. Félicie was much older. And the sight of the flourishing shop, of the ruddy carcases, of the dazzling brasses, of that well-dressed woman with her air of middle-class prosperity whose hand was rattling piles of money, robbed Damour of both his anger and his courage, and indeed inspired him

with terror. That lady would never consent to take him back; he looked too wretched and abject, with his unkempt beard and filthy blouse. He had already turned on his heels, and was going off in the direction of the Rue des Moines so as to escape notice, when Berru forcibly detained him.

"Thunder!" he cried, "haven't you any blood in your veins? If I was in your skin I'd make that fine madame wince. I wouldn't go away unless I had share and share alike—yes, half of the joints, and half of everything else. Go ahead, I say, don't be so timid!"

He then compelled Damour to cross the street; and asked one of the men if Monsieur Sagnard was in. And having ascertained that the master had gone to the slaughter-house, he entered the shop, determined to have it over. Damour followed, feeling dazed.

"What is it you want, Monsieur Berru?" asked Félicie, coldly and unpleasantly.

"*I* don't want anything," answered the painter, "but my mate does. He has got some news for you."

Then Berru stepped aside, and Damour faced Félicie, who looked at him. Suffering tortures, cruelly embarrassed, he lowered his eyes. At first she viewed him with disgust, her calm, happy face expressed strong repugnance for that old drunkard who looked like a pauper; but as she continued gazing at him without a word being spoken on either side, she suddenly turned quite white, stifled a scream, and dropped the money she had been handling, which fell with a silvery ring into the drawer of the till.

"What is the matter? Are you ill?' asked Madame Vernier, who had purposely lingered out of curiosity.

Félicie motioned her away with her hand; she could not speak. With a painful effort she rose up, and walked slowly into the parlour at the back of the shop. Without being told to follow, the two men disappeared behind her, Berru chuckling, and Damour with his eyes still fixed on the sawdust strewing the floor, as if he were afraid of stumbling.

"Well, it's mighty queer," said Madame Vernier, half aloud, when she found herself alone with the assistants.

They had stopped carving and weighing, and looked at each other in astonishment. However, not caring to compromise themselves, they soon resumed their occupations, carelessly indifferent as to the hint of the customer, who went off with her two cutlets in her hand, examining them crossly.

Félicie did not seem to think herself sufficiently alone in the parlour, for she opened a second door and ushered the two men into her bedroom. It was a comfortable, warm, silent apartment, with white curtains to the window and bed; there was a gilt clock, and on the mahogany furniture, shining with polish, not a speck of dust was to be seen. Félicie dropped into a blue rep armchair, repeating mechanically: "You—it is you!"

Damour found nothing to say. He glanced round the room, not daring to sit down, because the chairs looked too fine. Once more Berru took the lead.

"Yes," he said, airily. "He has been hunting after you for a fortnight past.

He met me by chance, and I brought him here."

And as if he instinctively felt the necessity of apologizing to her, he added: "You must see that I couldn't help myself. He's an old chum, and it made my heart jump to see him with one foot in the gutter."

Félicie was slowly recovering herself. She was stronger-minded and more practical than Damour. When the choking sensation in her throat relaxed, she nerved herself for an explanation which might put an end to this intolerable situation.

"Come, Jacques," she asked firmly but not unkindly, "what do you want with me."

He did not answer.

"It is true," she continued, "I married again, but it was no fault of mine, and you know it. I thought you were dead—you did nothing to undeceive me."

At last Damour spoke.

"I did—I wrote to you."

"I swear that I did not receive your letter. You know me—you know that I never lie, and I have the certificate of your death—here—in a drawer."

She went to a desk, opened it feverishly, and pulled out a paper which she handed to Damour, who began to read it with dazed eyes. It was the proof of his death.

Then Félicie resumed: "I found myself quite alone. I yielded to the solicitations of a man who offered to raise me out of my misery and loneliness. That is my only crime—I allowed myself to be tempted by the prospect of happiness. It was not a sin, was it?"

He listened with bowed head, more humble and more ill at ease than she was. At length, however, he lifted his eyes.

"And my daughter?" he asked.

Félicie started and trembled.

"Your daughter?" she stammered. "I don't know—I haven't got her."

"What?"

"I sent her to my aunt, but she ran away, and—and—went to the bad!"

For an instant Damour remained mute; he looked very calm, as if he had not understood. Then suddenly losing his embarrassment, he let his closed fist fall on the chest of drawers with such force that a shell box clattered on the marble top. But before he had time to speak, two children, a boy of six and a girl of four, flung the door open and rushed into Félicie's arms with shouts of delight.

"Good evening, little mother; we have been in the gardens, over there, at the end of the street. Françoise said it was time to come home. Oh, if you only knew—there is some sand there—and ducks on the water!"

"Hush! hush! run away now," said the mother sharply; and calling the servant she added: "Take them out again, Françoise—it is stupid of you to come in so early."

The children turned away regretfully, and the girl, displeased by her mistress's manner, pushed them angrily before her. Félicie had been seized with the insane fear that Jacques might kidnap the little ones, fling them across his back and hurry away. Berru, who had not been asked to take a seat, but who had unceremoniously stretched himself in the second arm-chair, now whispered to his friend:

"The little Sagnards. Nothing grows so fast as children, eh?"

When the door had closed again behind the little ones, Damour once more struck the marble with his fist and shouted: "It's neither here nor there— I want my daughter; and I have come to fetch you."

Félicie shivered from head to foot.

"Sit down," she said faintly, "and let us talk. It won't help you to make a fuss. So you have come for me?"

"Yes—you must come with me and at once. I am your husband, the only real one. Oh! I know my rights. I say, Berru, is it not my right? Come, put on your bonnet, and don't kick up a row if you don't want everybody to know what's up."

She looked at him, and unconsciously her anguish-stricken face plainly expressed that she loved him no longer, that he frightened and horrified her with his hideous, loathsome, old age. Was it possible that she, so fair and clean, accustomed to the comforts of middle-class prosperity, would have to return to the rough, miserable existence of the past with that man who had appeared before her like a ghost?

"You refuse," said Damour, who read her thoughts in her face. "Oh! I understand; you have got used to playing the lady behind your counter, and I haven't a fine shop, and a drawer full of money to finger and rattle at will. Besides, there are the children that were here just now; they seem better looked after than Louise was. When a woman has lost her daughter, she scorns her husband. But I don't care.

I want you to come, and you shall come; or else I'll go to the police and have you brought away between two gendarmes. It is my right, Berru—is it not?"

The painter nodded approvingly. He enjoyed the scene exceedingly. However, when he saw Damour beside himself, intoxicated with excitement, and Félicie exhausted, half fainting and sobbing, he thought it advisable to assume a conciliatory attitude.

"Yes, yes," he said, in a sententious tone, "it is your right, but you must pause awhile and consider. I have always conducted myself with propriety, and I say that before coming to a decision it would only be proper to consult Monsieur Sagnard. As he is not here——"

He stopped, and resumed in a different voice, tremulous with affected emotion: "Of course it is hard on my mate to have to wait. Naturally he's in a hurry. Ah, madame! if you knew what he has gone through! And now he hasn't a farthing—not a crust—he's starving—repulsed on all sides. When I met him just now he had not eaten since yesterday."

Félicie, passing from terror to sudden pity, could not keep back her blinding tears; she was overcome by intense grief, the regret and weariness of life. Involuntarily she exclaimed: "Forgive me, Jacques!"

Then, when she could command her voice, she continued: "What is done is done, but I cannot bear to see you so poor. Let me help you."

Damour made a frantic gesture of refusal.

"Of course," quickly interposed Berru, "this house is so plentifully stocked that your wife need not dismiss you with an empty stomach. Admitting that you refuse cash, you can at least accept a present. Supposing you only gave him a bit of gravy beef, eh, Madame Sagnard?"

"Anything he fancies, Monsieur Berru."

But Damour, still furiously striking the chest of drawers, shouted out: "Thanks—that's not the sort of grub I live on."

And walking up close to his wife, he fixed his eyes on hers, saying: "It is you alone that I want—and I will have you. Keep your meat."

Félicie had recoiled with renewed fear and loathing. Damour, losing all restraint, became terrible, threatening to smash the whole concern, and vociferating shameful accusations. He would get at his daughter's address, he said; and he shook his wife in her chair, yelling out that she had sold Louise. Félicie, in the awed stupor caused by this outburst, did not attempt to exonerate herself; merely repeating in a broken voice that she did not know the address, but that no doubt it might be discovered. Damour at last took a seat, swearing that the devil himself should not make him leave it; but suddenly he rose, and after a last and still more violent blow on the drawers, he said, hoarsely:

"Well, thunder and hell! I am going. Yes—I go, because I choose to go. But you'll lose nothing for waiting. I shall come back when your butcher is at home and I will square you all—he, you, the brats, and the shanty! Just wait, and you'll see."

He went out, still threatening her with his clenched fist, but in his heart he was relieved to end the scene thus.

Berru, who was delighted at being mixed up in this family affair, lingered behind, to say soothingly: "Don't alarm yourself; I sha'n't leave him. I'll see that he does no mischief."

He even ventured to kiss Félicie's hand, but she did not seem to notice it. She was so dazed and exhausted that if at that moment Damour had taken her by the arm she would have followed him unresistingly. She listened to the footsteps of the two men crossing the shop; and heard one of her apprentices sharply chopping a joint of mutton while he hurriedly shouted out some amount. Her business instincts brought her back to her counter, and she sat down, very pale but very calm, as though nothing strange had occurred.

"How much is there to take?" she asked.

"Seven francs and a half, madame." Then she gave the change.

## CHAPTER IV

### GOOD-BYE!

THE next day Damour had a stroke of luck. His acquaintance the stonemason got him the place of custodian of the building-yard of the Hôtel de Ville, and he was set to watch over the edifice which he had helped to burn down ten years previously. His task was easy, his occupation stupid, benumbing, and yet soothing. At night-time he wandered about at the foot of the scaffoldings, listening for stray noises and sometimes falling asleep on the bags of plaster. He never spoke of returning to Batignolles till one day after Berru took him off to lunch, and then he declared after the third bottle that the great flare-up should take place on the morrow. However, when the morrow came he never stirred from the yard. And henceforth it was a regular thing: whenever he was in his cups he got excited and asserted his rights, when he was sober he remained thoughtful and half-ashamed. The painter often chaffed him, and sneeringly declared that he wasn't a man; but he remained gravely indifferent, merely muttering between his teeth: "That means that I ought to kill them. Well, I'll wait till the fancy takes me."

One evening he went as far as the Place Moncey, then after spending an hour seated on a bench there he quietly returned to his yard; that afternoon he had thought he had seen his daughter drive past the Hôtel de Ville, reclining on the cushions of an elegant landau. Berru had offered to make inquiries, declaring that he could procure Louise's address in twenty-four hours, but Damour had refused the proposal. Why should he know? And yet the supposition that the handsome woman he had seen, beautifully dressed and carried along by two big grey horses, might be his daughter, affected him strangely. His sadness increased, and at last he bought a knife and showed it to Berru, saying that he meant to bleed the butcher with it. This sentence pleased him; he repeated it frequently, adding with a grim enjoyment of his own facetiousness: "I'll bleed the butcher. His turn next, eh?"

Berru, feeling somewhat alarmed, kept him for some hours in a wine-shop of the Rue du Temple trying to convince him that it was needless to bleed anybody. It would, in fact, be idiotic to do so, for at that game a fellow might run his neck into a noose. Then he wrung his friend's hands, trying to obtain a solemn promise that he would not get himself into trouble; but Damour repeated with a dogged chuckle: "No, no; his turn next. I'll bleed the butcher!"

The days passed and the bleeding did not take place. But an incident occurred which seemed likely to hasten the end. Damour was dismissed from the yard for inefficiency; for one night during a thunder-storm he had fallen asleep and a shovel had been stolen. He now once more dragged himself about the streets, half-starved but still too proud to beg, though he looked with hungry eyes into the windows of the eating-houses. His poverty, instead of exciting him, made him apathetic with repect to his wife; his shoulders drooped, he walked along meditating. It seemed as if he dared not return to Batignolles now that he no longer had a clean blouse to wear.

At Batignolles Félicie was living in continual terror. She had not dared to mention Damour's visit to Sagnard when the latter came home; and on the next day, frightened by her previous silence, she had felt remorseful, but still had lacked the courage to speak. She every moment expected to see her first husband walk into the shop, and in her distress she conjured up appalling scenes. She fancied, too, that the suspicions of the establishment were aroused, for the men grinned together at times, and Madame Vernier, when she called for her two cutlets, assumed a most unpleasant look while waiting for her change.

At last, one evening Félicie flung her arms around Sagnard's neck, and sobbingly confessed everything. She repeated what she had already said to Damour: it was not her fault, for when people are dead they ought not to come to life again. Sagnard, who was an honest man, hale and hearty, in spite of his sixty years, comforted her. Gracious goodness! it was certainly no joke, but it would all come right. Most things came right in time. Being securely settled in life with plenty of money for his needs, his feelings were principally those of curiosity. He would interview the ghost, and reason with him. The affair interested him; so much so, that a week later, as Damour did not put in an appearance, the butcher said to his wife: "Well, what's up? Does he mean to cut us? If I knew where he lived I'd go and look him up myself."

Then, as she implored him to remain quiet, he added: "But, my dear it's only to ensure your peace and happiness. You are fretting and worrying. Let's have it over."

Félicie was indeed becoming thin, such disquietude did she feel at the thought of the impending tragedy, the postponement of which only made her the more anxious. However, one day, just as the butcher was blowing up one of his men, who had neglected to change the water of a calf's head, she came up to him, deadly pale, and stammered out: "There he is!"

"All right," answered Sagnard, suddenly calming down; "take him into the parlour."

And then, without hurrying himself, he quietly added, turning to his man: "Wash it thoroughly, mind—in plenty of water, too; it stinks."

He then went into the parlour, where he found Damour and Berru. They had met by chance in the Rue de Clichy. Berru had seen less of his old chum lately, having felt bored by his increasing wretchedness. When he discovered that Damour was actually on his way to the Rue des Moines, he became very abusive, declaring that this business was his also. He argued with him, swearing that he would stop his going over yonder to make a fool of himself, and he even stepped in front of him to compel him to give up his knife. However, Damour shrugged his shoulders, obstinately refusing to disclose his intentions, and merely answering again and again, "Come with me if you like, but don't bother."

Sagnard did not ask the two men to be seated. As for Félicie, she had fled to her room with her children, and double-locked the door; then she crouched against it, frightened, dazed, and clasping the little ones to her bosom as if to guard and defend them. She listened intently, but could hear nothing as yet. In the parlor the two husbands were looking at each other in awkward silence.

"So it is you?' began Sagnard at last, just to say something.

"Yes, it is," answered Damour.

He was thinking how good-looking the butcher was, and he felt very small before him. Sagnard did not appear to be more than fifty; he was handsome and fresh-complexioned; he wore his hair short, his cheeks and chin were clean shaven. Standing there in his shirt-sleeves with a large apron of snowy whiteness tied round him, he had a joyous air of prosperity.

"However," said Damour, hesitatingly, "it is not with you that I want to talk; it is with Félicie."

At these words Sagnard recovered his composure.

"Come, my friend," he said quietly, "let us understand each other. Dash it all, we have nothing to reproach ourselves with—you or I. Why should we quarrel when no one is in fault?"

Damour, with his head bent, fixed his eyes doggedly on the legs of the table. At last he muttered drearily: "I am not angry with you. Leave me alone; go away. I want to see Félicie."

"No, you shall not see her," calmly answered the butcher. "I don't choose to have her made ill again, as you made her last time. We can settle this without her. Besides, if you are sensible, everything will be all right. You say you love her still; well, consider her position—think it over, and act for her happiness."

"Hold your tongue," interrupted Damour, with a sudden burst of rage. "Don't interfere, or there will be mischief done."

Berru, feeling convinced that his friend was about to draw his knife, threw himself in front of him with a great show of zeal. However, Damour pushed him aside.

"Hold your tongue, I say! What are you afraid of, you fool?"

"Be calm," repeated Sagnard. "When

a man is angry he doesn't know what he's about. Listen to me. If I call in Félicie, will you promise to keep quiet? She is very sensitive, you know that as well as I do. We don't want to kill her between us, do we—neither you nor I? Will you promise to behave decently?"

"Eh! if I had come to misbehave myself, I should have strangled you ere this, and stopped all your fine talk."

He spoke these words in so deep and pained a tone, that the butcher felt sincerely touched.

"Well, then," he said, "I'll call Félicie. By nature I'm very impartial, and I quite understand that you wish to discuss the matter with her. It is your right."

He then stepped up to the bedroom door and knocked.

"Félicie, Félicie!" he called.

Nothing stirred. Félicie, chilled and affrighted by the prospect of the coming interview, was silently pressing her children still closer to her breast. The butcher, however, repeated impatiently: "Félicie, do come! You are very silly. He has promised to behave sensibly."

At last the key turned in the lock, and she appeared, carefully closing the door behind her to ensure the safety of her children. Fresh silence and another awkward pause followed. It was the beginning of the end, as Berru styled it.

Damour began to speak in slow entangled sentences, while Sagnard, who had walked to the window and lifted one of the short blinds, pretended to be looking out, as if to show that he was both discreet and magnanimous in this affair.

"Listen, Félicie," Damor was saying. "You know that I have never been a bad man; you must own that. Well, I don't mean to begin to-day. True, at first I wanted to smash and murder you all. Then I asked myself how that would better me. I would rather leave you free to choose. We'll do just what you say. Yes, as the tribunals can't help us with their justice, you shall decide what you like best. Answer, Félicie; with whom will you go—him or me?"

But she could not answer; she was speechless with emotion.

"Just so," resumed Damour, in the same husky, desolate voice. "I understand—you'll remain with him. When I came here I knew how it would be. Oh, I'm not angry with you—you are right after all. I am done for—I have nothing left, and you love me no longer; whereas *he* makes you happy; and besides there are the two little ones."

Félicie was weeping uncontrollably.

"Don't cry," he continued. "I am not reproaching you. It has happened so—well, that is all; and I had a sort of wish to see you once more, just to tell you that you might sleep in peace. Now that you have chosen, I won't torment you again. It's all over: you'll never hear of me any more."

He turned to the door, but Sagnard, who felt deeply moved, stopped him, exclaiming: "Dash it, you are a brick, and no mistake! It is out of the question that we should part like this. Stay and dine with us."

Berru, amazed at this unlooked-for conclusion, which he considered very droll, looked quite shocked when his friend refused the invitation.

"At least let us drink a glass together," insisted the butcher. "The deuce, you can't refuse a glass of wine under our roof!"

Damour did not accept at once. His eyes wandered round the parlour, a clear and cheerful room with its light oak furniture; and when at last they rested on Félicie's tear-stained face, and her imploring earnest glance, he said simply: "Well, I don't mind if I do."

Sagnard was delighted.

"Glasses, Félicie," he shouted. "We can do without the servant. Bring out four glasses, for you must drink with us. Ah! mate, you are a good fellow to have accepted. You don't know what pleasure it gives me! I love a true heart; and yours is a true heart. I'll take my oath on it."

Félicie was taking the glasses and a bottle of wine out of the sideboard with trembling hands. Her head was swimming; she could do nothing, and Sagnard had to go to her assistance. When the wine was poured out, and they were all seated round the table, they touched glasses.

"Your health."

Damour, who sat opposite Félicie, had to stretch out his arm to clink glasses with her. They both looked at each other mutely; all their past was in their eyes. She shook so nervously that, as the crystal rang, one could hear the chattering of her teeth as though she were in a high fever. They were now dead to each other, living only in their memories.

"Your health."

Then, as they drank, the voices of the children in the next room broke upon the silence. The little ones were playing, chasing each other about with shouts and laughter. Suddenly, too, they knocked at the door, calling: "Mamma! mamma!"

"Enough," said Damour, setting his glass on the table. "Good-bye, all of you."

He went away. Félicie, erect and pale, watched him leave the room, while Sagnard politely escorted both gentlemen through the shop to the street.

## CHAPTER V

### HIS ONLY JOY

As soon as Damour got into the street he began to walk so fast that Berru found it difficult to keep up with him. The painter was indignant. On the Boulevard des Batignolles, when his friend finally sank upon a bench, and remained there, with pallid cheeks, dilated eyes, and weary limbs, the painter at last exploded and relieved his feelings. Good heavens! for his part he would at least have boxed the butcher's ears, and the woman's too. It was revolting to see a man give up his wife to another fellow without any conditions. It was the act of an idiot, a simpleton, not to use any other word. He quoted various examples in support of his opinion. It was a case for an agreement; none in their senses would allow themselves to be duped and swindled in that manner.

"You can't understand," answered Damour drearily. "Go away, go, since you are no friend of mine."

"What! not your friend, after all I have done for you? Look at it squarely—what is to become of you? You haven't a soul to look after you; you are like a lost dog in the streets, and you'll starve if I don't come to the rescue. Not your friend? But if I were to forsake you now, all you could do would be to poke your head under your foot, like a fowl weary of living."

Damour made a gesture of despair. It was true; he had no alternative but to throw himself into the Seine or give himself up to the police as a destitute vagabond.

"Well," continued the painter, "I am so much your friend that I'm going to take you somewhere where you'll get a bed and a bite."

He rose as if impelled by a sudden resolve, and forced his companion to follow him. Damour, half-persuaded, repeated in a dazed way: "Where? where do you mean?"

"You'll see. As you refuse to dine with your wife, you shall dine elsewhere. Depend upon it, I won't allow you to play the fool twice in one day."

He walked rapidly down the Rue d'Amsterdam, and when he reached the Rue de Berlin he stopped before a small house, rang the bell, and asked the footman who came to the door if Madame de Sauvigny were at home. On seeing the servant hesitate, he added:

"Go and tell her that Berru is here."

Damour followed the painter mechanically. This unexpected visit to this sumptuous residence increased his confusion and perplexity. At last he ascended a flight of stairs and abruptly found himself in the arms of a very pretty, fair, diminutive, young woman, clad in a lace gown.

"Papa! it is papa!" she exclaimed joyfully. "Ah, how kind of you, Berru, to have persuaded him to come at last!"

She seemed an unsophisticated creature, and did not attach any importance to the old man's grimy blouse; indeed, she was delighted, and clapped her hands in a sudden fit of filial love. Her father, who was greatly startled, had not even recognised her.

"Yes, yes, it's Louise!" said Berru.

Then Damour stammered vaguely, "Ah, yes! you are too kind!"

He did not attempt to be familiar. Louise, however, made him sit down on a sofa, and rang the bell to give orders that she was at home to nobody. Then Damour glanced about the room, which was hung with Indian fabrics, and felt strangely moved. Berru, meanwhile, triumphantly slapped him on the shoulder, saying, "Will you dare to say again that I'm not your friend? I knew that you'd want your daughter some time or other; so I got hold of her address, and came to tell her all about you. She at once exclaimed, 'Bring him to me!' "

"Why, certainly I did, poor dear father!" added Louise. "Oh, you know, I abhor your Republic! The Communists are a dirty lot, who would ruin us all if they had the chance. But you are my papa. I remember how good you were to me when I was quite little, and so ill. You'll see how comfortably we'll get on together, provided we never talk politics. To begin with, we'll all three of us dine together. Won't it be jolly?"

Her clear eyes were full of laughter, and her pale hair flew round her ears. Damour remained nerveless; he wanted to refuse because he did not think it quite right to accept a meal there; but he had already lost the energy which had hurried him away from the butcher's without once turning his head. His daughter was too soft and gentle, and her little white hands placed on his own held him so fast.

"Now, do say yes," she pleaded.

"Yes," he said at last, while two big tears coursed down the furrows with which misery had marked his cheeks.

Berru thought this decision very practical. As the three of them were passing into the dining-room, a footman came to tell his mistress that "Monsieur" was there.

"I can't see him," she said quietly: "tell him that I am with my father."

The dinner was delightful. Berru enlivened it by relating all sorts of stories, and Louise laughed till the tears ran down her cheeks. She fancied herself back in the Rue des Envierges, and enjoyed herself exceedingly. Damour ate heartily and grew heavy with fatigue and food; but each time his eyes met his daughter's his smile became very soft. At dessert they drank some sweet foaming wine like champagne, which affected them all. As soon as the servants had retired they rested their elbows on the table and began to speak of the past with half-maudlin melancholy. Berru had rolled a cigarette for Louise, who smoked it slowly with partly closed eyes and humid lashes while judging her mother's conduct with great severity.

"You understand," she said to her father, "I do not see her any more—her conduct has been too outrageous. Still, if you like I will go and tell her what I think of the dirty trick she played upon you——"

However, Damour gravely declared that Félicie no longer existed for him.

Then Louise rose, exclaiming, "Wait a bit; I must show you something that will give you pleasure!"

She left the room, but presently returned with her cigarette still between her teeth, and handed her father an old yellow photograph broken at the edges. The workman started violently, and, fixing his dim eyes upon the portrait, stammered, "Eugène, my poor Eugène!"

He passed the photograph to Berru, who looked at it with emotion and murmured feelingly: "It is very like him."

Then it was Louise's turn. She kept the portrait for a moment in her hand, and then returned it to her father, saying in a tearful voice: "Oh, I remember him well—he was so kind!"

Overcome by their feelings, they all three began to cry. Twice the photograph went round the table, eliciting pathetic comments. It had become very pale from exposure; poor Eugène in his uniform of the National Guard looked like a phantom rebel. At last, having turned the card round, the father suddenly read what he had written long ago upon the back, "I will avenge you!" and thereupon, brandishing a dessert-knife over his head, he repeated his oath: "Yes—yes! I will avenge you!"

Then Damour propped the photograph against his glass, and again gazed

at it. By degrees, however, they all
became quieter and more practical.
Louise, who was easy-going and open-
handed, wanted to help her father, and
at last she had an inspiration; she
asked him if he would consent to look
after a small etsate which had been
bought for her near Mantes in Normandy. There was a small house on
the property where he could live very
comfortably on two hundred francs a
month.

"Come now, that will be a perfect
paradise!" shouted Berru, who accepted for his friend. "And if he feels
dull there, I'll go and cheer him up."

The following week Damour was
settled at Bel Air, his daughter's property; and it is there that he now lives
in blissful repose, such as Providence
owed him after all his vicissitudes. He
is growing stout and florid; he dresses
like a well-to-do citizen, and has the
honest good-natured face of an old
soldier. The peasants salute him respectfully. He shoots and angles; he
is often seen sunning himself in the
lanes, or watching the growth of the
corn with the tranquil conscience of
a man who has cheated nobody, but
lives on an income laboriously earned.
Whenever his daughter visits Bel Air
with her friends, he maintains a dignified reserve; his happiest moments
are when she runs down alone to see
him and they lunch together in the
little house. Then he talks to her with
the fond foolish prattle of a doting
nurse, he looks at her pretty dresses
with admiration, and prepares with his
own hands various wonderful and delicate dishes, while Louise brings sweets
and cakes for dessert in her pockets.

Damour has never tried to see his
wife again. His daughter is everything to him; she took pity on him,
and she is his only joy. He has obstinately refused to attempt to recover
his civil rights. What good would it
do to confuse the Government regis-
ters? His peace and security are all
the more assured since he is unknown.
He lives in his nook, lost and forgotten.
Being nobody, he accepts the bounty
on which he lives without a blush;
whereas if he were to resuscitate legally, ill-natured and envious people
might comment unfavourably on his
position, and he would possibly wince
under their blame.

There are times, however, when the
little house becomes boisterous. This
is when Berru spends four or five days
in the country with his old pal. He
has, at last, found under Damour's
roof a pleasant corner where he can
eat his fill and enjoy himself. He
shoots and fishes, or else during whole
afternoons he lies on his back near the
river. At night the two friends talk
politics. Berru brings Anarchist papers
from Paris, and after reading them
they both agree upon the radical measures which are imperatively required,
such as shooting the Government, burning Paris again, and rebuilding another
city, the real metropolis of the people.
They invariably select general exter-
mination as the basis of universal happiness. Finally, when it is time to go
to bed, Damour, who has had Eugène's
photograph framed, walks up to it,
gazes on the faded likeness, and, brandishing his pipe, exclaims: "Yes—yes,
I will avenge you"

And the next morning, with bent

shoulders and placid face, he returns to his fishing; while Berru, stretched out at full length, sleeps buried in the grass.

---

# The Inundation

## CHAPTER I

### GLORIOUS DAYS

MY name is Louis Roubieu. I am seventy years of age, and was born in the village of St. Jory, at a few leagues from Toulouse, on the banks of the Garonne. During fourteen years I battled with the soil in order to obtain from it enough bread to feed me. Affluence came at last, and, only a month ago, I was the richest farmer of the whole country-side.

Our home was blessed. Happiness had its abode under our roof. The sun was our ally, and I do not remember a bad harvest. We were nearly a dozen at the farm, all sharing the same happiness: myself still hale and hearty, teaching the young ones how to work; my younger brother, Pierre, a bachelor, and formerly a sergeant in the army; my sister, Agathe, a shrewd housewife, extremely stout and gay, who had come to live with us after her husband's death, and whose laughter rang out from one end of the village to the other. Next came the whole brood: my son Jacques, and Rose, his wife; with their three daughters, Aimée, Véronique, and Marie. The first was married to Cyprien Bouis-

son, a strapping young fellow, to whom she had given two babies, one two years old and the other ten months old; Véronique, on her side, had just become engaged to Gaspard Rabuteau: while Marie, white and very fair, looked more like a town-born lady than a farmer's daughter. This made up ten; I was both a grandfather and a great-grandfather.

When we assembled round the supper-table I used to place my sister Agathe on my right, my brother Pierre on my left, and the children completed the circle, seated by order of seniority, down to the mite but ten months old. The whole lot ate heartily, and how gay they all were between each mouthful! I felt both pride and pleasure glowing in my veins when the little ones, stretching out their hands to me, shouted:

"Grandfather, give us some more bread. A big piece, grandfather, please!"

Those were glorious days. The busy house sang through all its windows; in the evenings Pierre invented new games or told old stories of his regiment; on Sundays Aunt Agathe baked cakes for the girls, and Marie knew some beautiful hymns which she sang with the voice of a young chorister, looking like a saint too, with her fair hair falling low on her neck, and her hands folded in her lap. At the time of Aimée's marriage with Cyprien I had added a storey to the house, and I used to say jokingly that when Véronique married Gaspard I should have to add another, and that if I did so at each successive wedding the house would end by reaching the sky. None of us wanted to leave it; we would rather have erected a town in the enclosure behind the farm. When the members of a large family agree, it is good to live and die on the spot where one was born.

This last Spring, the month of May was superb; the crops had not looked so promising for years. That day I went the round of the land with my son Jacques. We started at about three o'clock. Our meadows, still of a tender green, stretched alongside the Garonne; the grass had nearly reached its full height, and in a willow copse planted only last year there were shoots a yard long. We passed on, examining our corn-fields and vineyards, the land bought bit by bit as our means increased. The wheat was growing apace, the vines were in full bloom, heralding a rich vintage. Jacques laughed his hearty laugh, and, slapping me on the shoulder, said: "Well, father, we sha'n't lack bread or wine. You must be in the good graces of God Almighty, as He lets money rain upon your land like this."

Jacques was right. I had no doubt gained the good graces of some saint in heaven, for all the good luck of the district appeared to fall on us. During a storm the hail would stop at the edge of our fields; if our neighbours' vines were ailing, a protecting wall seemed to rise around ours, and gradually I had come to deem this just. Harming no one, I believed happiness to be my due.

On our way home we crossed some land belonging to us on the opposite side of the village. A plantation of mulberry trees was coming on splendidly, and the almond trees in a grove were bearing all they could. We chatted gaily and made plans for the future. As soon as we had saved the necessary capital we would purchase certain patches of ground lying between our various lots, and thus become the owners of an entire corner of the parish. If the crops turned out as well as they promised, our dream could be realised in the autumn.

As we drew near the farm we saw Rose gesticulating and shouting: "Come on, hurry up!"

One of our cows had just calved, and the whole household was astir. Aunt Agathe went rolling about, while the girls watched the little calf, whose advent seemed like an additional benison. Quite recently we had been compelled to enlarge our sheds, which contained nearly a hundred head of cattle, without reckoning the horses.

"Another lucky day," I said. "We must have a bottle of good wine to-night."

Just then Rose took us aside to inform us that as Gaspard, Véronique's lover, had come to fix the wedding-day, she had kept him to dinner. Gaspard, the eldest son of a farmer of Moranges, was a young man of twenty, known all through our part for his prodigious strength. At a public *fête* at Toulouse he had wrestled with and defeated Martial, the Lion of the South. Withal he was extremely good-natured and tender-hearted, and so shy, indeed, that he blushed whenever Vèronique's calm eyes met his own.

I told Rose to call him. He had stayed in the yard helping the maids to hang out the linen of a three months' washing. When he entered the parlour where we were all assembled, Jacques turned to me saying, "It's for you to speak, father."

"Well, my boy, you have come to settle the day," I said.

"Yes, that's why I came," he answered with a deep colour on his cheeks.

"Don't blush, my lad," I resumed. "Shall we say the 10th of July, the day of Saint Félicité? To-day's the 28th of June, so you won't have long to wait. My poor dead wife's name was Félicité—it will be a good omen. Well, is it a settled thing?"

"Yes, all right; the day of Sainte Fèlicité will do," replied Gaspard.

Then as he came up to Jacques and me his hand fell on our outstretched palms with a might sufficient to fell an ox. Next he kissed Rose, calling her "mother." This stalwart young fellow with such redoubtable fists was losing sleep and flesh for love of Véronique; he told us that he should have fallen ill if we had not consented to let him have her.

"Now," I resumed, "let us go to our meal. All of you to your places. Thunder and lightning! I am as hungry as a wolf!"

That evening we sat down eleven. We had placed Gaspard and Véronique side by side, and he kept gazing at her, forgetting his supper, and so disturbed by the thought that she was his that big tears moistened his eyelashes. Cyprien and Aimée, who had been married three years, smiled as they watched them; Jacques and Rose, with their twenty-five years of wedlock, were graver; still they stealthily exchanged moist glances, born of long-abiding tenderness. As for myself, I felt as if I were growing young again, and living anew in those lovers, whose happiness seemed to bring a nook of paradise to our board. How excellent the soup tasted that evening! Aunt Agathe, who was always one for laughing, ventured to make a few jocose remarks, whereupon Pierre insisted upon relating his love passages with a lady of Lyons. Fortunately we had got to the dessert and were all talking at the same time. I had brought two bottles of sweet wine from the cellar and we drank to Gaspard and Véronique's good luck, as the fashion is with us. Luck is never to quarrel, to have heaps of children, and put by bags of money. Later on we had some singing; Gaspard knew some love ballads in our dialect, and by way of conclusion we asked Marie for a hymn. She stood up and began at once, her flutelike and delicate voice falling like a caress on the ear.

I had moved towards the window, and as Gaspard joined me I said, "There is nothing new over your way, is there?"

"No," he answered; "they talk a good deal about the heavy rains of the

# THE INUNDATION

93

last few days; some say they might turn out badly."

It had, indeed, recently been raining during sixty consecutive hours, and since the previous day the Garonne had been greatly swollen; still we trusted her, and as long as she did not overflow we could not think of her as a dangerous neighbour. She was so useful, her expanse of water was so broad and gentle; and, moreover, peasants do not readily quit their homes even if the roof be about to fall.

"Nonsense," I said; "nothing will happen; it's the same every year. The river puts up its back as if it were in a rage, then it quiets down in a single night, and subsides as gently as a lamb. Take my word, lad, it's only a joke. Just look out of the window, and see what splendid weather we are having!"

Then with my hand I pointed to the sky.

It was seven o'clock; the sun was setting. All was blue; the sky showed like an immense expanse of azure, through which the sunset swam like golden dust. From above there slowly descended a delight, reaching to the verge of the distant horizon. I had never seen the village in such tender restfulness. A pink glow was fading under the eaves. I could hear a neighbour laughing and children chattering at the bend of the road opposite our house; while from further off the lowing of herds returning to their sheds reached us, softened by the distance.

Meanwhile the deep roar of the Garonne sounded incessantly; but I was so used to the voice of the river that it seemed to be merely the voice of silence. By degrees the sky whitened and the village seemed falling into a serener sleep. It was the end of a beautiful day, and I fancied that all our happiness, our rich harvests, Véronique's engagement, came to us wafted from above, in the purity of the dying light. A benediction spread over us with the farewell of day.

I had returned to the centre of the room where the girls were chatting merrily, and we were listening to them with smiling lips, when suddenly, through the great peace of the twilight, an appalling shriek rang out—a shriek of terror and of death:

"The Garonne! the Garonne!"

## CHAPTER II

### THE GARONNE!

WE ran to the yard.

St. Jory lies at the very bottom of a dip in the land, lower than the river, and some five hundred yards away from it. A screen of poplars dividing some meadows shuts out all view of the water.

We could see nothing, but the shriek still resounded: "The Garonne! the Garonne!"

Then, coming from the road in front of us, two men and three women abruptly appeared, one of the latter holding a child in her arms. They were shouting, frenzied with terror, and running as fast as they could over the hard ground. Every now and then they looked back with scared faces, as if they were being pursued by a pack of wolves.

"What has happened?" cried Cyprien. "Can you make out anything, grandfather?"

"No," I answered; "the leaves are not even stirring."

The low line of the horizon lay still and peaceful, but before I had done speaking a sharp exclamation broke from the others. Behind the fugitives, between the trunks of the poplars, over the tall grass, we caught sight of something resembling a pack of grey, yellowish spotted animals racing onwards. They appeared on all sides—waves hurrying upon waves, an invasion of masses of water crested with foam, shaking white saliva, and making the ground quiver with the heavy gallop of their serried ranks.

Then we also echoed the despairing cry, "The Garonne! the Garonne!"

The two men and the three women were still flying along the road, and they could hear the hideous gallop gaining upon them. Presently the waves formed in a single line, rolling and crashing with the thunder of charging battalions. Under their first onset three poplars snapped; their tall foliage tottered and disappeared. Then a shed was swollen up; a wall burst; unharnessed carts were carried away like wisps of straw. But the water seemed specially to pursue the fugitives. At a bend of the road, which is very steep at that particular spot, the flood suddenly fell in immense volume, cutting off their retreat. We saw them still attempting to run, splashing in the water, but silent now and maddened with fear. The waves rose to their knees; at last a huge billow dashed upon the woman who was carrying the child. Then all were submerged.

"Quick, quick!" I cried. "Come in! the house is strong. We have nothing to fear."

However, out of prudence, we at once ascended to the first floor, making the girls pass before us; I was determined to be the last. Our house was built on a bank above the road, and the water was now slowly invading the yard with a soft little ripple. We were not much alarmed.

"Never mind," said Jacques reassuringly; "there is no danger. Do you remember, father, how, in '55, the water came into the yard just as it does now? It rose to a foot, and then receded."

"It's a pity for the crops, anyhow," muttered Cyprien, half aloud.

"No, no; it won't be much," I said, noting the dilated, questioning eyes of the women. Aimée had laid her children on her bed and sat close to them with Véronique and Marie. Aunt Agathe talked of warming some wine which she had brought with her, in order to cheer us. Jacques and Rose looked out of the window and I stood at the other with my brother Cyprien and Gaspard.

"Come up, can't you?" I called to the two maids who were paddling about in the yard. "Don't stop there and get your legs wet."

"But the poor beasts," they answered; "they are frightened and will get killed in the sheds."

"Never mind! Come up. We will look after the cattle presently."

If the water continued to rise it would be impossible to save the cattle, but I thought it best not to alarm the servants. I tried to appear quite at ease, and leaning over the window-sill I gave an account of the progress of the flood. After rushing to the assault of the village, the river had taken possession of even its narrowest lanes. The race of the charging waves had ceased; there was now a stealthy invincible invasion. The hollow in which St. Jory lies was being transformed into a lake. In our yard the water had risen to a height of three feet already: I watched its ascent, but I affirmed that it remained stationary, and once I even hinted that it was subsiding.

"You will have to sleep here tonight, my boy," I said, turning to Gaspard, "that is, unless the roads get clear in a few hours, which might easily be the case."

He looked at me; his face was very pale, and I saw his eyes turn to Véronique, gleaming the while with intolerable anguish.

It was half-past eight. Out of doors it was still light—a white glimmer, unspeakably mournful, dropping from the pale sky. Before the maids joined us they had thought of bringing two lamps. I had them lit, hoping that they would brighten the darkening room in which we had taken refuge. Aunt Agathe now pushed a table forward and suggested a game of cards. The excellent woman, whose eyes sought mine anxiously every now and then, was especially desirous of diverting the children: her cheerfulness was grandly brave, and she laughed to conjure away the terror which she felt was creeping over all the others. The game was arranged; Aunt Agathe forced Aimée, Véronique, and Marie

into their chairs, placed the cards in their resistless fingers, and began shuffling, dealing, and cutting with such a flow of words that she almost stifled the sound of the rising flood. But our daughters could not fix their minds on the game; they remained pale, with feverish hands, bending their heads to listen. Every now and then one or another of them would turn uneasily and whisper:

"Grandfather, is it still rising?"

It *was* rising with fearful rapidity, but I answered carelessly, "No, no; go on playing—there is no danger."

Never before had I felt my heart wrung by such cruel dread. All the men had grouped themselves in front of the windows to shut out the appalling scene; we tried to look unconcerned when our faces were turned to the room, facing the lamps whose circular light fell on the table as amidst the gentle peace of homely vigils. I remembered winter evenings when we had sat thus at the table. It was the same quiet picture, full of the soft warmth of affection. But while perfect peace dwelt within, I could hear behind my back the bellowing of the overflowing river, which was ever rising and rushing onward.

"Louis," whispered my brother Pierre, "the water is only three feet from the window; something must be done."

I pressed his arm to silence him, but it was too late to conceal our peril. The cattle had become frantic in the outhouses: we plainly heard the bleating and lowing of the maddened animals, and particularly the wild shrieks of the horses who felt themselves in danger.

"O my God! my God!" murmured Aimée, who stood up, convulsed by a long shudder, and with her closed fists pressed to her temples.

The women had all risen, and we were powerless to keep them from the windows; they stood there erect and mute their hair lifted by a wind of terror. The twilight had come; a treacherous gleam hovered above the watery sheet, the pale sky looked like a white pall thrown over the earth; afar off some smoke was trailing; then everything became blurred: it was the close of a day of horror, sinking into a night of death. And not a human sound—only the dull roar of the infinitely widening expanse of water, and the lowing and neighing of the frenzied animals!

"O God! O God!" repeated the women under their breath, as if afraid to speak aloud.

A loud crash silenced them. The infuriated cattle had broken through the stable doors: they passed by in the yellow flood, rolling as they were carried away by the current; the sheep were hurled along in droves like dead leaves whirling in pools; the cows and the horses struggled, trying to feel the ground but losing their footing; our big grey horse refused to die: he reared, stretched out his long neck and panted like the bellows of a forge, till the eager waters dashed on his hindquarters, and then we saw him yield himself up and disappear.

Then for the first time we screamed; our cries seemed to come unconsciously, propelled by some alien will. With hands outstretched towards all those dear animals hurried away for ever, we moaned and wept, sobbing aloud, giving vent to the tears and lamentations we had restrained. It was indeed our ruin! the crops lost, the cattle drowned, our fortune gone in a few brief hours! Oh, God was not just! We had not offended Him, and yet He had taken back all He had given! I shook my fist at Heaven! I recalled our afternoon walk, the meadows, the wheat-fields, the vineyards, all so promising! They had all lied! Happiness had lied! The very sun, when he had set so gently and calmly in the deep serenity of evening, had lied.

The flood was still rising, and all at once my brother Pierre, who had been watching it, exclaimed sharply: "Louis, look out! The water has reached the windows. We can't stay here."

These words broke upon our despair. I pulled myself together, and shrugging my shoulders said, "After all, money is nothing. As long as we are all together and safe, there is nothing to regret. We must begin work afresh, that is all."

"Yes, yes—you are right, father," returned Jacques feverishly, "and we *are* safe—the walls are solid. Let us get upon the roof."

It was our only refuge. The water, after mounting the staircase step by step with a persevering gurgle, was entering at the door. We repaired to the loft, keeping close together, with the vague instinct which makes people in peril anxious to remain side by side. Cyprien alone had vanished. I called to him and he came out of an adjoining room with a white scared face.

Then as I suddenly became aware of the absence of the two maids, and stopped to wait for them, he looked at me strangely and whispered:

"Dead—the outbuilding where their room was has just given way."

The poor creatures must have gone to get their savings out of their boxes. Cyprien, in the same tone, told me that they had managed to throw a ladder across to the building where they slept, and had used it as a bridge. I warned him to say nothing, but I felt a great chill at the back of my neck. It was the breath of death entering our house.

We did not even think of turning out the lamps, when we went up to the roof in our turn; the cards remained spread out on the table; there was a foot of water in the room.

## CHAPTER III

### A CRISIS

FORTUNATELY the roof was broad and the incline a gentle one. It was reached by a skylight opening on t a little platform, upon which our party took refuge. The women sat down, and presently the men stepped out on the tiles to reconnoitre, going as far as the two tall chimney-stacks at either end of the roof. I remained leaning against the aperture of the skylight, looking towards the four points of the horizon.

"Help cannot fail to come soon," I said, with forced hopefulness. "The folks of Saintin have some boats, and they will pass this way. See over there, isn't that a lantern on the water?"

I received no answer. Pierre had mechanically lighted his pipe, and was smoking so furiously that with every puff he spat out bits of the stem which he had broken between his teeth. Jacques and Cyprien stared into the distance with mournful faces, while Gaspard, with clenched fists, went on pacing the roof as if seeking for some outlet. The women, crouching and shuddering at our feet, covered their eyes to avoid the terible sight. Presently, however, Rose, raising her head, looked round her.

"Where are the servants?" she asked. "Why don't they come up?"

I pretended not to hear, but she turned to me and fixed her eyes on mine.

"Where are the girls?" she repeated.

I turned away. I could not lie to her, and I felt that the deadly chill which had already touched me was passing over our wives and daughters. They had understood. Marie rose to her full height; a deep sigh parted her lips; and then sinking down she burst into a passion of tears. Aimée kept the heads of her two children in her lap, covering them up with her skirts as if to shield them. Véronique, who had her face in her hands, remained motionless. Aunt Agathe, growing paler, was repeatedly making the sign of the Cross and muttering *Paters* and *Aves*.

All around us the scene was one of supreme grandeur. The night, which had now completely fallen, had the clear limpidity of summer darkness. There was no moon as yet, but the sky was studded with countless stars, and it was of so pure a blue that all the surrounding space was filled with an azure light. The horizon was so clearly defined that it seemed to harbour the twilight; and meanwhile the immense sheet of water, spreading out under the soft skies, became quite white, luminous as with a glow of its own, a phosphorescence which tipped the crest of every wave with tiny flamelets. Land was nowhere visible, the whole plain must have been submerged. One evening, on the coast near Marseilles, I had seen the sea looking like this, and had remained gazing at it transfixed with admiration.

"The water rises, the water rises," repeated my brother Pierre, still biting the stem of his pipe, which he had allowed to go out.

Indeed, the water was now only a yard from the edge of the roof. It was losing its tranquillity, its lake-like quietude, and currents were forming. When it reached a certain height we were no longer sheltered by the rising ground before the village; and as soon as this was covered, in less than an hour's time, the flood became threatening, lashing the houses with all the wreckage, staved-in barrels, timbers, and trusses of hay, which it carried on its bosom. In the distance we heard the deafening shocks of the onsets against the walls. Poplars snapped and fell with a sinister splash, and houses crashed down like cartfuls of stones turned over on the roadside.

Jacques, unnerved by the women's sobs, kept on repeating: "We cannot stop here. Something must be done. Father, I implore you, let us try something."

Hesitating and stammering, I repeat-

ed after him: "Yes, yes, let us try something."

And none of us knew what to try. Gaspard proposed that he should take Véronique on his back, and swim away with her. Pierre suggested a raft. They were both crazy. At last, however, Cyprien said: "If we could only reach the church."

And indeed high above the flood the church still rose up intact with its little square tower. We were separated from it by seven dwellings. Our house, the first of the village, adjoined a taller building, which in its turn leant against its neighbour. It might be feasible to reach the presbytery by the roofs, and thence it would be easy to get into the church. Many of the villagers had already sought that refuge probably, for the neighbouring roofs were deserted, and we heard a murmur of voices which certainly came from the belfry. But at best it was a perilous and uncertain undertaking.

"It is impossible," said Pierre. "Raimbeau's house is too lofty; we should need some ladders."

"At any rate, I'll go and see," said Cyprien. "If we cannot get across I'll return; if we can we must all go, the men carrying the women."

I let him start. He was right: situated as we were, everything must be attempted. With the help of an iron clamp fixed to a chimney-stack he had just succeeded in climbing on to the next house when his wife, Aimée, raised her eyes, and saw that he was gone.

"Where is he?" she said. "I will not let him leave me. We are one— we must die together."

Then as she caught sight of him on

the other roof she darted across the tiles, still carrying her children.

"Wait for me, Cyprien," she panted; "I am coming with you. I will die with you."

She would not be denied. Her husband, leaning over, implored her to remain with us, promising to return, and assuring her that he was only acting for our common rescue. But, shaking her head, and with a wild look in her eyes, she still repeated excitedly: "I am coming with you. I will die with you."

He yielded: first he took the children, and then he helped his wife to climb up to him. We could see them walking slowly on the apex of the roof. Aimée had again taken her weeping children in her arms, and at every step Cyprien turned and supported her.

"As soon as she is in safety," I shouted, "come back to us."

I saw him wave his hand, but the roar of the water did not allow me to hear his answer. They were soon out of sight; they had descended on to the house beyond, the roof of which was lower. Five minutes later they again appeared on the third roof, which must have been very steep, for we could see that they were crawling up it on their knees. A sudden dread possessed me, and raising my hands to my mouth I shouted out with all my strength: "Come back, come back!"

All of us, Pierre, Jacques, and Gaspard, called to them to return; our voices seemed to stay them for a moment, but they soon moved on. They had reached the corner where the street turned in front of Raimbeau's house, a tall building rising nearly nine feet

above all the neighbouring roofs. For a moment they wavered, and then Cyprien began to climb up a chimney with catlike agility. Aimée, who had evidently consented to wait for him, remained erect amid the tiles. We could plainly distinguish her clasping her babies to her bosom, standing out black against the clear sky, and looking much taller than she really was. It was then that the awful catastrophe began.

Rambeau's house, originally intended for some business purposes, was very flimsily built, and, moreover, its frontage received the full shock of the current in the street. I fancied I could see it tremble under the onset of flood, and with bated breath I watched Cyprien's progress along the roof. Suddenly we heard a deep growl. The round moon had risen, freely pacing the sky, her yellow disc lighting up the immense lake with the clear brightness of a lamp. Not a single detail was lost to us. That growl was the noise of Rambeau's house falling in. A scream of terror escaped us as we saw Cyprien sink down. In that tempestuous crash we could only see the splashing of the waves under the remnants of the roof. Then all was calm again, the lake became level once more, with the black carcass of the submerged house bristling above the water with its snapped floors—a confused mass of tangled timbers, looking like the framework of some half-destroyed cathedral. Between those timbers I thought I could see a body moving, a living form wrestling with superhuman efforts.

"He lives!" I cried. "Ah blessed be God, he lives! There, above that white sheet of water lit up by the moon!"

We shook with hysterical laughter and clapped our hands for joy, as if all danger had passed away.

"He will get up again," said Pierre. "Yes, yes," explained Gaspard. "See, he is trying to catch hold of the beam on his left."

But our laughter was suddenly hushed. We remained dumb, silenced by anxiety. We had just realised in what an awful position Cyprien had now found himself. In the fall of the house his feet had been caught between two beams, and he was hanging head downwards at a few inches above the water, and quite unable to free himself. His agony was horrible. On the roof of the other house stood Aimée with her two children, shaken by convulsive shudders. There she remained a witness of her husband's death-struggle, never once taking her eyes off him. From her rigid lips there came a continuous lugubrious sound, like the howl of a dog frenzied by terror.

"We cannot let him die like that," said Jacques in distraction. "We must go to him."

"One might crawl down the beams, perhaps," muttered Pierre, "and disengage him."

They were already moving towards the nearest roof when the house it covered suddenly shook and crumbled in its turn. The way was cut off. Our blood froze in our veins. We seized each other's hands and pressed them nervously, unable to turn our eyes away from the ghastly sight.

Cyprien had at first attempted to stiffen himself, and with extraordinary muscular strength he had finally succeeded in getting further away from the water and maintaining a sidelong position. But fatigue was mastering him; he tried to resist, to lay hold of the beams, beating the air with his arms in the hope of finding something to which he might cling; then accepting death, he fell back and again hung down quite motionless. Death was slow to come; his hair barely touched the water, which was patiently rising— he must have felt its coolness on his head. A first wave wetted his brow, another closed his eyes — slowly his head vanished from our view.

The women, huddled at our feet, hid their faces with their clasped hands. We fell on our knees with out-stretched arms, stammering supplications and crying bitterly. On the other roof Aimée, still erect, with her children close pressed to her bosom, shrieked still louder and louder amid the night.

## CHAPTER IV

### THE BATTLE

I CANNOT tell how long the stupor of that crisis lasted. When I recovered my senses the water was higher still; it now reached the tiles, and our roof was only a narrow island barely emerging from the immense watery expanse. On the right and left the houses had fallen. The sea was widening on all sides.

"We are moving," whispered Rose, as she clutched at the tiles.

And, indeed, we all felt a pitching motion, as if the roof had changed into a floating raft; the heavy swell seemed to carry us along. It was only by turning to the motionless church tower that we got rid of this delusion, and realised that we were on the same spot amid the angry surf.

It was then that the siege began in earnest. The current so far had followed the street, but the increasing wreckage that barred the way now caused it to flow back. A furious onset commenced. As soon as a plank or beam passed within the current's grasp it was seized, swung round, and hurled like a ram against our house; the water never loosened its grasp; the current sucked the wreckage back merely to launch it again at our walls, which it assailed with regular repeated blows. Sometimes ten or twelve large pieces of wood would attack us at once on all sides. The water hissed, foamy splashes wetted our feet. We heard the dull moan of the sonorous house filling with water, and the creaking of the broken partitions; and whenever a more savage assault made the whole building quiver, we fancied that it was all over—that the walls were opening and giving us up to the river through their yawning breaches.

Gaspard, who had ventured to the very edge of the roof, succeeded in catching a passing beam, which he dragged out of the water with his powerful athletic arms.

"We must defend ourselves," he shouted.

Then Jacques, with the assistance of Pierre, endeavoured to stop a long pole. I cursed my old age, which left me useless and as weak as a child. However, the defence was being organised; it was the fight of three men against the flood. Gaspard, armed with his beam, waited for the passing timbers which the current turned into battering rams, and kept them off at some little distance from the walls. The shock at times was so great that he fell down. Meantime Pierre and Jacques were manœuvring with their long pole, shoving away the nearer wreckage.

This fierce and senseless battle lasted during nearly an hour. As the time passed the combatants grew wildly excited; they beat the water, insulted it, and swore at it. Gaspard hacked at it as if in a bodily struggle, lunged out with his beam as if he were trying to pierce a human breast. And all this time the water remained quietly obstinate, without a wound — invincible. Jacques and Pierre at last sank down on the roof exhausted, and Gaspard, while making a final effort, saw the current wrest his beam from his grasp and hurl it against us. The struggle had become impossible.

Marie and Véronique, clasped in each other's arms, were repeating the same words in broken tones—words of terror,' the echo of which still sounds incessantly in my ears: "I will not die! I will not die!"

Rose embraced them both, trying to reassure and comfort them; but at last she herself, trembling and shivering, lifted her white face and unconsciously cried aloud, "I will not die!"

Aunt Agathe alone remained quite silent. She had ceased praying and crossing herself. In a sort of dumb stupor she now let her eyes wander over the scene — and whenever they chanced to meet mine, she still attempted a smile.

The water was lapping the tiles. No help could reach us now. We still heard the sound of voices issuing from the church—two lanterns had gleamed for an instant in the distance, then again the silence deepened amid the desolate immensity of the yellow expanse. In all probability the people of Saintin who owned some boats had been surprised by the flood before us.

Gaspard was still wandering about the roof; and suddenly he called to us, saying: "Look out! Help me—hold me tight!

He had again snatched hold of a passing timber, and was lying in wait for a huge black mass which was slowly swimming towards us. It was the broad, solid plank-roof of a shed, wrenched away entire, and floating like a raft. When it came within reach Gaspard arrested it, and feeling that he was being dragged off he called to us to help him. We seized him round the waist and clasped him tight. As soon as the wreck entered the current it advanced of its own accord against our roof, coming forward with so much violence that for a moment we feared we should see it fly asunder.

However, Gaspard boldly jumped upon this raft thus sent to us by Providence; he walked all over it to make sure of its strength, while Jacques and Pierre maintained it in position at the edge of our roof. Then he began to laugh, and said exultingly, "You see, grandfather, we are saved. Come, you women, leave off crying! It is as good as a real boat. Look here, my feet are dry. It can carry us all, too. It feels like home already."

However, he thought it better to strengthen it, and securing some more beams he bound them with some ropes which Pierre had happened to bring up with him on the chance of their being wanted. While thus engaged, Gaspard once fell overboard, but he soon came up again, and answered our cry of alarm with renewed hilarity.

"The Garonne knows me," he laughed; "I have often swum it for a league at a time." Then when he had got on the roof again he shook himself and exclaimed, "Come aboard—there's no time to lose!"

The women had fallen on their knees, and Gaspard had to carry Véronique and Marie to the middle of the raft, where he made them sit down. Rose and Agathe slipped off the tiles unaided and joined the girls. At that moment I again glanced towards the church. Aimée was still on the same roof, only she was now leaning against a chimney-stack, holding her children aloft with rigidly uplifted arms. The water had risen to her waist.

"Do not worry, grandfather," said Gaspard. "I promise you that we'll pick her up as we pass by."

Pierre and Jacques were already on the raft. I jumped after them. It tilted over a little on one side, but seemed strong enough to carry us all. Gaspard was the last to leave the roof, and gave each of us one of the poles which he had in readiness to be used as oars, he himself keeping a very long one, which he handled with great dexterity. He had taken command, and by his instructions we all pressed against the tiles with our poles, trying to shove off. But our efforts were fruitless; the raft seemed to adhere to the roof; at every fresh attempt we made the current hurled us back against the house. We were incurring great danger, for every fresh shock threatened to shatter the boards on which we stood.

Once more we became conscious of our impotency. We had thought ourselves saved, but we still belonged to the greedy river. I even began to regret that the women had left the roof, for I expected, every minute, to see them hurled into the furious water and carried away. But when I suggested that we should return to the house they one and all rebelled.

"No, no, let us try again," they pleaded, "or die here."

Gaspard was not laughing now. We multiplied our efforts, weighing on the poles with feverish strength, but all in vain. At last Pierre had an idea. He climbed on to the roof again, and with a long rope managed to pull the raft to the left and get it out of the current. Then after he had jumped on to the raft again a few strokes of our poles enabled us to get into the open.

But Gaspard remembered his promise to rescue my poor Aimée, whose plaintive wail had not once ceased. To effect the rescue it was necessary to cross the street where raged that terrible current against which we had fought so desperately. He cast a questioning look at me. I was overcome. Never had I been placed in so cruel an alternative. Eight lives must be endangered, and yet, if for their sakes I hesitated just one moment, I lacked the strength to resist the mother's lugubrious call.

"Yes, yes," I said to Gaspard. "We cannot go without her."

He bent his head in silence and began to ply his pole, taking advantage of such walls as were still standing. We slowly skirted the adjoining house, passing over our own cow-sheds, but as soon as we turned the bend of the street we shrieked aloud. The current had captured us again, and was carrying us off, forcing us back to our roof.

It lasted only a few seconds. We were indeed whirled away so suddenly that the screams we immediately raised expired amid the deafening crash of the raft against the tiles. It was rent asunder, the shivered boards were scattered, and we were hurled into the foaming whirlpool. I do not know what followed. I only remember that as I fell I saw Aunt Agathe lying at full length on the water buoyed up by her skirts. Then without a struggle she slowly sank, her head thrown backwards.

A sharp pain made me open my eyes. Pierre was dragging me by the hair along the tiles. I remained lying there stupefied, with open eyes. Pierre had left me to dive again, and in the confusion of my mind I thought it strange when I espied Gaspard on the spot just vacated by my brother. The young man had Vèronique in his arms. He laid her near me, plunged in again, and brought up Marie, who was so white, rigid, and motionless that I thought her dead. Then for the third time he threw himself into the water, but now he sought in vain and returned empty-handed. Pierre had joined him: they were talking low, and I could not hear what they said. As they were coming, seemingly quite exhausted, up the incline of the roof I moaned out—"And Aunt Agathe, and Jacques, and Rose?"

They shook their heads; big tears were welling in their eyes. From the brief, husky words they spoke, I gathered that Jacques' brains had been dashed out by a passing beam. Rose had clung to her husband's corpse and been dragged away with it. As for Aunt Agathe, she had not reappeared; we presumed that her body, driven forward by the current, had entered the house beneath us through one of the open windows.

Raising myself up, I turned towards the chimney-stack which Aimée had been clutching hold of a few moments previously. The flood had risen higher still; Aimée was no longer wailing; I only saw her two stiffened arms holding the children above the water. Then all collapsed: the sheet of water closed over her arms and her babes amid the sleepy glimmer of the full moon.

## CHAPTER V

### DARKNESS

THERE were now only five of us on the roof. The water had left us but a narrow dry strip on the crest of the tiles. One of the chimney-stacks had been swept away. We had to raise Véronique and Marie, who had fainted, and keep them erect, to prevent the surf from wetting their legs. At last they regained consciousness, and our anguish increased as we saw them shivering in their soaked garments, and

heard them wailing that they would not die. We comforted them as one quiets children, assuring them that they were not going to die; that we would prevent Death from taking them. But they no longer believed us; they realised that their life was nearly spent. Each time that the word "die" fell like a knell from their lips their teeth chattered, and mutual dread threw them into each other's arms.

It was the end. A few ruined walls marked here and there the spot where the submerged village had stood. The church, alone intact, raised its belfry on high, and a sound of voices still proceeded from it, telling of people who were safely sheltered. In the distance the vast overflow of the raging waters roared continuously. We no longer heard the crash of crumbling houses, resembling the rough unloading of gravel on a road. The wreck was forsaken as if it were in mid-ocean, a thousand miles from land.

Once we fancied that we detected a splash of oars on our left: it was like a rhythmical gentle beat growing clearer and nearer. Ah! what a hopeful music it seemed! We craned our necks forward to question space. We held our breath. But we saw nothing. The yellow expanse stretched out, spotted with black shadowy things, but none of those things, crests of trees, fragments of shattered walls, were stirring. Tufts of herbage, empty barrels, planks, brought us delusive joys. We waved our handkerchiefs, till, recognising our error, we again became the prey of anxiety, wondering whence came the sound that ever fell upon our ears.

"Ah, I see it!" suddenly cried Gaspard; "a large boat—look! over there."

And with his outstretched arm he pointed to a distant spot. Neither Pierre nor I could distinguish anything, but Gaspard obstinately insisted that it was a boat. The strokes of the oars became more distinct, and finally we all saw it. It was moving slowly, and it seemed to be circling round us without drawing any nearer. I remember that we then became almost mad, waving our arms, raving, shouting, insanely apostrophising the boat, insulting it, and calling it a coward. The craft, still silent and dark, appeared to turn more slowly. Was it really a boat? I cannot tell; I only know that when we realised that it was gone, we felt that it had carried our last hope away.

After that we expected every second to be engulfed in the fall of the house. But this time it must be undermined, and was probably only held up by some stouter wall, which would drag down the whole building when it gave way. What especially terrified me was to feel the roof sinking under our weight; the house might possibly have resisted all night, but the tiles were loosened and broken by the attacking beams. We took refuge on the left, where the rafters seemed to be less impaired, but even there they soon seemed to weaken, and would infallibly yield if the five of us remained together on so narrow a space.

For the last few moments my brother Pierre had mechanically placed his pipe between his lips again. He was twisting his thick, military-looking moustache, and muttering confusedly, with his dark brows knit. The increasing peril which surrounded us on all sides, and against which there was no possible fighting, made him more and more irritated. He had two or three times spat into the water with angry contempt; then, as we were sinking more and more, he made up his mind, and walked down the slope of the roof.

"Pierre! Pierre!" I cried, afraid to understand.

He turned and answered quietly, "Good-bye, Louis; this lasts too long to suit me, and my going will give you more room."

Then, having thrown his pipe into the water, he resolutely flung himself after it, adding: "Good-night; I've had enough of it!"

He did not rise again; he was but an indifferent swimmer, and no doubt he surrendered himself to the flood, broken-hearted by our ruin, the loss of those he loved, and feeling unwilling to survive them.

Two o'clock struck at the church tower. The night was almost over; that horrible night, so full of agony and tears. The dry strip under our feet was gradually becoming smaller. There was a soft gurgle of running water, with little caressing wavelets playing and tossing. Then again the current changed; the wreckage was carried to the right of the village, floating lazily along, as if the flood, now seemingly about to reach its greatest height, were resting, weary and satisfied.

All at once Gaspard removed his shoes and coat. During the last moment or two I had watched him wringing his hands and crushing his fingers. In answer to my question he said:

"Listen, grandfather. It kills me to wait here. I cannot stop any longer. Let me act—I can save her!"

He was alluding to Véronique. I attempted to reason with him, saying that he would never be strong enough to swim with the girl as far as the church. But he obstinately insisted, repeating: "I love her—I shall save her!"

I remained silent, simply drawing Marie to my breast. He thought no doubt that I was reproaching him with his lover-like selfishness.

"I will come back for Marie," he stammered; "I swear it. I will find a boat somehow, and manage to get help. Trust me, grandfather!"

He stripped, merely retaining his trousers, and then in a low and hurried voice he gave some urgent advice to Véronique, telling her not to struggle, but to yield herself to him, and, above all, not to get alarmed. The girl stared at him, and huskily answered "Yes" to each sentence he spoke.

At last, having made the sign of the Cross, although he was not habitually devout, he let himself slide down the roof, holding Véronique by a rope which he had passed under her arms. She gave a loud scream, beat the water with her limbs, and fainted away.

"It is best so!" shouted Gaspard. "Now I can answer for her."

With unspeakable anguish I watched their progress. On the white water I easily discerned Gaspard's slightest movements: he supported the girl by means of the rope which he had also twined around himself, and he had thrown her partially across his right shoulder. Her dead weight occasion-ally made him sink, but he rallied, swimming on with supernatural energy.

I was getting hopeful, for he had already covered one third of the distance, when he struck against some obstacle—some wall hidden below the water's surface. The shock was appalling; they both disappeared. Then I saw Gaspard rise alone; the rope had broken. He plunged twice, and finally he reappeared, again carrying Véronique. He slung her upon his back, but as the supporting rope was gone, she weighed him down more heavily than before. In spite of this he was still advancing. A moment later, as they neared the church, I began to tremble violently; then suddenly I attempted to call out, for I had caught sight of some floating timber coming upon them sideways. My mouth remained wide open—a second concussion parted them; then the waters met again, but they were gone.

From that moment I remained stupefied, retaining merely the animal instinct of self-preservation, and shrinking back whenever the water gained on me. Amidst this stupor I continued hearing a sound of laughter without understanding whence it came. The day was rising in a great white dawn; the air was pleasant, very fresh and very calm, as it is beside a mere before the sunrise. But laughter still rang out, and on turning round I saw Marie standing near me in her dripping garments. It was she who was laughing!

How sweet and gentle she looked, poor darling, amid the advent of the morning! I saw her stoop, take a little water in the hollow of her palm and bathe her face. Then she twisted her rich golden hair and bound it round her head. She was dressing: she fancied herself back in her little room preparing for church on a Sunday morning, while the bells were ringing merrily; and still she laughed her childish laughter, with a happy face and serene clear eyes.

Her madness was contagious, for I began to laugh with her; terror had demented her, and it was a mercy vouchsafed by Heaven, for she seemed conscious only of the enchanting beauty of the spring-tide dawn.

I watched her quietly, nodding gently, and without comprehending. She went on with her toilet till she considered herself ready to start, and then raising her pure crystalline voice she began to sing one of her favourite hymns. Presently, however, she stopped, and, as if answering a call which she alone could hear, she cried: "I am coming! I am coming!"

Then resuming her chant she descended the incline of the roof, and stepped into the water, which softly, tenderly closed over her without shock or struggle. For myself, I continued to smile, looking with a happy, contented face on the spot where she had disappeared.

After that I do not remember. I was quite alone on the roof, the water touching me. A single chimney-stack remained standing, and I think I must have clung to it with all my strength, like an animal who refuses to perish. Beyond that I know nothing—nothing —all is black and vacant in my mind.

# CHAPTER VI

### HEROIC LOVE

WHY am I here? I have been told that the people of Saintin arrived at about six o'clock with their boats, and found me in a dead faint hanging on to the chimney. The water had been so cruel as not to take me away with those I loved while I remained unconscious of my bereavement.

I — the old one — have obstinately lived on. All the others are gone, the children in swaddling-clothes, the girls and their lovers, the young and the old married couples. And yet I remain living like a coarse dry weed rooted to the stones. If I had the courage, I would do what Pierre did. Like him, I would say, "Good-night, I have had enough of this," and then I would fling myself into the Garonne, following the course that all the others have taken. I have not one child left me; my house is a ruin; my fields lie waste. Oh, for the nights when we all sat at the table, the elders in the centre, the young ones in a row, when their merriment warmed my blood! Oh, for the grand days of harvest and vintage, when we all toiled together and came home in the gloaming, exultant in the pride of our wealth! Oh, for the handsome children and the fair vines, the lovely girls and the golden corn, the joy of my old age, the living reward of my whole life! Now that all this is dead and gone, tell me, O God! why wilt Thou have me stay?

I cannot be comforted. I want no help. I shall give my land to those of the village folk who possess children—for they will have the heart to clear it and till it afresh. Those who have no children need but a corner wherein to die.

I have had one wish, a last desire—I wanted to find the corpses of my dear ones and to bury them in our churchyard under a stone which would some day cover me also. I heard that a great many bodies which had been washed away by the river had been recovered at Toulouse; so I started to go and see them.

Was there ever so ghastly a scene? Nearly two thousand houses destroyed, seven hundred victims, all the bridges swept away, a whole district of the city razed, drowned in the mud; poignant tragedies, twenty thousand wretches half naked and dying of starvation, the town poisoned by the stench of unburied corpses, and terrified by the fear of typhus. And mourning everywhere, funerals in all the streets, distress such as no alms could allay. But I walked on among the ruins of others, regardless of aught save my own—my own dear dead, the thought of whom weighed me down.

People told me that many bodies had been found and that they had already been buried in long rows in the cemetery. However, the precaution had been taken to photograph the unrecognised ones. It was among the piteous portraits shown me that I came across those of Gaspard and Véronique. The lovers were still clasped in a passionate embrace; they had given and received their nuptial kiss in death. They clung to each other so closely, mouth pressed to mouth, and arms entwined, that it would have been impossible to part them without breaking their limbs. So they had been photographed together, and they slept united beneath the sod.

And that is all I have left, that horrible picture of those two fair children, disfigured and swollen by the water, but still bearing on their livid faces the imprint of their heroic love. I gaze upon them and I weep.

# *Nantas*

## CHAPTER I

### HIS ROOM

THE room in which Nantas had resided since his arrival from Marseilles was on the top floor of a house in the Rue de Lille, next to the mansion of Baron Danvilliers, a member of the Council of State. This house belonged to the baron, who had built it on the site of some old out-buildings. By leaning out of his window, Nantas could see a corner of the baron's garden, across which some magnificent trees cast their shade. Beyond, by looking over their leafy crests, a glimpse of Paris was to be had: the open space left by the Seine, with the Tuileries, the Louvre, the quays, a whole sea of roofs, and the Père Lachaise Cemetery in the dim distance.

Nantas's room was a small attic, with a dormer-window amid the tiles. He had furnished it simply with a bed, a table, and a chair. He had taken up his abode there because he was attracted by the low rent, and had made up his mind to rough it until he found a situation of some kind. The dirty paper, the black ceiling, the general misery and barrenness of this garret did not deter him. Living in sight of the Louvre and the Tuileries, he compared himself to a general sleeping in some miserable inn at the roadside within

view of the weathy city which he means to carry by assault on the morrow.

Nantas's story was a short one. The son of a Marseilles mason, he had begun his studies at the Lycée in that city, stimulated by the ambitious affection of his mother, who had set her heart upon making a gentleman of him. His parents had stinted themselves to give him a good education; but, his mother having died, Nantas had been obliged to accept an unprofitable situation in the office of a merchant, where for twelve years he had led a life of exasperating monotony. He would have taken himself off a score of times, if his sense of filial duty had not tied him to Marseilles, for his father, who had fallen from a scaffolding, was quite unable to work. One night, however, when Nantas returned home, he found the old fellow dead, with his pipe lying still warm at his side. Three days later the young man had sold the few sticks about the place, and started for Paris, with just two hundred francs in his pocket.

Nantas had inherited boundless ambition from his mother. He was a young fellow of ready decision and firm will; and even when quite a boy he had been wont to say that he was a power. He was often laughed at when he so far forgot himself as to repeat his favourite expression confidingly, "I am a power," an expression which sounded comical indeed when one looked at him in his thin black coat, all out at the elbows, and with the cuffs half-way up his arms. However, he had gradually made power a religion, seeing nothing else in the world, and feeling convinced that the strong are necessarily the successful. According to his idea, to be willing and able ought to suffice one. All the rest was of no importance.

One Sunday, while he was walking about alone, in the scorching suburbs of Marseilles, he felt genius within him; in his innermost being there was, as it were, an instinctive impulse driving him onwards; and when he went home to eat a plateful of potatoes with his bedridden father, he determined in his own mind that some day or other he would carve his own way in that world in which, at the age of thirty, he was still a nonentity. This was no low greed, no appetite for vulgar pleasures on his part; it was the clearly-defined longing of a will and intellect which, not being in their proper sphere, strove to attain to that sphere by the natural force of logic.

As soon as Nantas felt the paving-stones of Paris under his feet, he thought that he had merely to put forth his hands to find a situation worthy of him. On the very first day he began his search. He had been given various letters of introduction, which he presented; and, moreover, he called upon several of his own countrymen, thinking that they would help him. But at the end of a month there was still no result. The times were bad, people said; besides which, they merely made promises to break them. His little store of money was swiftly diminishing—indeed, at the most, some twenty francs

were left him. It was upon those twenty francs, however, that he was forced to live for another month, eating nothing but bread, scouring Paris from morning till evening, and going home to bed without a light, feeling tired to death, and still as poor as ever. His courage did not fail him; but mute anger arose within him. Destiny appeared to be illogical and unjust.

One evening Nantas returned home supperless. He had finished his last morsel of bread on the day before. No money, and not a friend to lend him even a franc. Rain had been falling all day, one of those raw downfalls which are so cold in Paris. Rivers of mud were running in the streets, and Nantas, drenched to the skin, had gone to Bercy and afterwards to Montmartre, where he had been told of employment. But the situation at Bercy was filled up and at Montmartre they had decided that his handwriting was not good enough. Those were his two last hopes. He would have accepted anything, with the certainty that he would soon command success. He only asked for bread at first, something to live upon in Paris, a foundation-stone upon which he might build his fortune. He walked slowly from Montmartre to the Rue de Lille with his heart full of bitterness. The rain had ceased falling, and busy throngs crowded the streets. He stopped for a few minutes in front of a money-changer's office. Five francs would perhaps suffice him to become one day the master of them all. On five francs he could indeed live for a week, and in a week a man may achieve great things. While he was dreaming thus a cab ran against him and splashed him with mud.

He then walked on more quickly, setting his teeth and experiencing a savage
desire to rush with clenched fists upon
the crowd which barred his way. It
would have been taking a kind of vengeance for the cruelty of fate.

In the Rue Richelieu he was almost
run over by an omnibus, but he made
his way to the Place du Carrousel,
whence he threw a jealous glance at the
Tuileries. On the Saints-Pères Bridge
a little well-dressed girl obliged him to
deviate from the straight path which he
was following with the obstinacy of a
wild boar tracked by hounds, and this
deviation appeared to him a supreme
humiliation. The very children im-
peded his progress! Finally, when he
had taken refuge in his room, as a
wounded animal returns to its lair to
die, he threw himself heavily upon his
chair, dead-beat, gazing at his trousers
which the mud had stiffened, and at his
worn-out boots which had left wet
marks along the floor.

The end had come then. Nantas
debated how he should kill himself. His
pride held good, and he imagined that
his suicide would injure Paris. To be
a power, to feel one's own worth, and
not to find a soul to appreciate you,
not one to give you the first crown
which you have ever wanted! It seemed
monstrous to him, and his whole being
revolted at the thought. Then he felt
immense regret as his glance fell upon
his useless arms. No work had any
terror for him. With the tip of his
little finger he would have raised the
world; and yet there he was, cast into
a corner, reduced to impotence, and
fuming with impatience like a caged
lion! But presently he became calmer,

death seemed to him grander. When he
was a little boy he had been told the
story of an inventor who, having constructed a marvellous machine, had one
day smashed it to pieces with a hammer because of the indifference of the
world. Well, he was like that man, he
bore within him a new force, a rare
mechanism of intelligence and will, and
he was about to destroy his machine
by dashing out his brains in the street.

The sun was going down behind the
tall trees of the Danvilliers mansion; an
autumn sun it was, with golden rays
lighting up the yellow leaves. Nantas
rose as if attracted by the farewell
beams of the heavenly body. He was
about to die, he wanted light. For a
moment he leant out of the window. Between the masses of foliage he had often
seen a tall, fair young girl walking with
a queenly step in the garden. He was
not romantic, he had passed that age
when young men in garrets dream that
well-born ladies approach them with
their love and fortunes. Yet it chanced
that, at this supreme hour of suicide, he
suddenly recollected that fair and
haughty girl. What could be her name?
He knew not. But at the same time he
clenched his fists, for his only feeling
was one of hatred for the inhabitants
of that mansion, glimpses of whose
luxury were afforded him by the partially opened windows; and he muttered
in a burst of rage:

"I would sell myself, I would sell myself, if some one would only give me the
first coppers I need for my fortune to
come!"

This idea of selling himself occupied
his mind for a moment. If there
had been such a place as a pawn-shop

where people advanced money on energy and willingness, he would have gone and pledged himself. He set about imagining cases: a politician might buy him to make a tool of him, a banker to make use of every atom of his intelligence; and he accepted, scorning honour, and telling himself that it would suffice if he some day acquired strength and ended by winning the fight. Then he smiled. Did a man ever get a chance to sell himself? Rogues, who watch every opportunity, die of want, without finding a purchaser. Now that suicide seemed his only course, he was fearful lest he should be overcome by cowardice, and he tried in this way to divert his thoughts. He had sat down again, swearing that he would throw himself out of the window as soon as it was dark.

So great was his fatigue, however, that he fell asleep upon his chair. Suddenly he was awakened by the sound of a voice. It was the doorkeeper of the house, who was showing a lady into his room.

"Sir," the doorkeeper began, "I took the liberty to come up——"

Then, seeing no light in the room, she quickly went downstairs and fetched a candle. She seemed to know the person whom she had brought with her, and showed herself at once complaisant and respectful.

"There," said she, on leaving the room, after placing the candle on the table, "you can talk at your ease: nobody will disturb you."

Nantas, who had awoke with a start, looked with astonishment at the lady who had called upon him. She had now raised her veil, and appeared to be about five-and-forty, short, very stout, and with the face of a devotee. He had never seen her before. When he offered her the only chair, casting an inquiring glance at her, she gave her name: "Mademoiselle Chuin—I have come, sir, to talk to you about a very important matter."

Nantas had sat down on the edge of the bed. The name of Mademoiselle Chuin told him nothing, and his only course was to wait until she should think fit to explain herself. But she seemed in no hurry to do so; she had given a glance round the tiny room, and appeared to be hesitating as to the way in which she might start the conversation. Finally she spoke in a very gentle voice, emphasising her remarks with a smile.

"Well, sir, I come as a friend. I have been told your touching story. Do not think that I am a spy; my only wish is to be of use to you. I know how full of trials your life has been till now, with what courage you have struggled to find a situation, and the final result of all your painful efforts. Once more, sir, forgive me for intruding upon you. I assure you that sympathy alone——"

Nantas, however, did not interrupt her; his curiosity was aroused, and he surmised that the doorkeeper of the house had furnished the lady with all those particulars. Mademoiselle Chuin, being at liberty to continue, seemed solely desirous of paying compliments and putting things in the most attractive way.

"You have a great future before you, sir," she resumed. "I have taken the liberty to follow your endeavors, and I have been greatly struck by your praiseworthy courage in misfortune. In one word, in my opinion there is a great future before you, if some one gives you a helping hand."

She stopped again. She was waiting for a word. The young man, who believed that the lady had come to offer him a situation, replied that he would accept anything. But she, now that the ice was broken, asked him point-blank: "Would you have any objection to marry?"

"Marry!" cried Nantas. "Goodness, madame! who would have me? Some poor girl that I could not even feed!"

"No; a very pretty girl, very rich, splendidly connected, and who will at once put you in possession of the means to attain to the highest position."

Nantas laughed no longer.

"Then what are the terms?" he asked, instinctively lowering his voice.

"The girl has had a misfortune and you must assume responsibility," said Mademoiselle Chuin; and, putting aside her unctuous phraseology in her desire to come straight to the point, she gave some details.

Nantas's first impulse was to turn her out of doors.

"It's an infamous thing to propose," he muttered.

"Infamous!" exclaimed Mademoiselle Chuin, affecting her honied tones again, "I can't admit that ugly word. The truth is, sir, that you will save a family from despair. Her father knows nothing as yet; this misfortune has not long fallen upon her, and it was I myself who conceived the idea of thus marrying her as soon as possible. I know her father; it would kill him if nothing were done. My plan would soften the

blow; he would think the wrong half-redressed. The unfortunate part of it is that the real culprit is married. Ah! sir, there are men who really have no moral sense."

She might have gone on like this for a long while, for Nantas was not listening to her. He was thinking, why should he refuse? Had he not been proposing to sell himself a little while back? Very well, here was a buyer. Fair exchange is no robbery. He would give his name, and he would be given a situation. It was an ordinary contract. He looked at his muddy trousers, and felt that he had eaten nothing since the day before; all the disgust born of two months' struggling and humiliation rose up within him. At last he was about to set his foot on the world which had repulsed him, and driven him to the verge of suicide!

"I accept," he said curtly.

Then he asked for clear explanations from Mademoiselle Chuin. What did she want for her services? She protested at first that she wanted nothing. However, she ended by claiming twenty thousand francs out of the dowry which the young man would receive. And as he did not haggle over the terms, she became expansive.

"Listen," she said, "it was I who thought of you, and the young lady did not refuse when I mentioned your name. Oh! you will thank me later on. I might have got a title; I know a man who would have jumped at the chance. But I preferred to choose some one outside of the poor child's sphere. It will appear more romantic. And then I like you. You are good-looking, and have plenty of sense. You will make your way; and you mustn't forget me. Remember that I am devoted to you."

So far, no name had been mentioned, and upon Nantas making an inquiry in this respect the old maid stood up and said, introducing herself afresh:

"Mademoiselle Chuin; I have been living as governess in Baron Danvilliers' family since the baroness's death. I educated Mademoiselle Flavie — the baron's daughter. Mademoiselle Flavie is the young lady in question."

Then she withdrew, after formally placing on the table an envelope containing a five hundred franc note. It was an advance which she herself made to defray preliminary expenses.

When Nantas found himself alone he went to the window again. The night was very dark; nothing was to be seen but the dark masses of shadow cast by the trees; one window only in the gloomy frontage of the mansion showed a light. So it was that tall fair girl who walked with such a queenly step, and did not deign to notice him. She or some other, what mattered it? The girl was no part of the bargain. Then Nantas raised his eyes still higher, upon Paris roaring in the gloom, upon the quays, the streets, the squares, upon the whole left bank of the river, illuminated by the flickering gaslights: and like a superior being he addressed the city, saying:

"Now you are mine!"

## CHAPTER II

### THE BARON

BARON DANVILLIERS was sitting in the room which served him as a study,

a cold lofty apartment, furnished with old-fashioned leather-covered furniture. For the last two days he had been in a state of stupor, Mademoiselle Chuin having informed him of what had befallen Flavie. In vain had she softened and toned down the facts; the old man had been overcome by the blow, and it was only the thought that the culprit was in a position to offer the sole reparation possible that kept him from death. That morning he was waiting the visit of this man, who was utterly unknown to him, but who had robbed him of his daughter. He rang the bell.

"Joseph, a young man will call, whom you will show in here at once. I am not at home to anybody else," he said.

Sitting alone at his fireside he brooded bitterly. The son of a mason, a starveling without any position! Mademoiselle Chuin had certainly spoken of him as a promising youth, but what a disgrace to a family whose honour had hitherto been stainless! Flavie had accused herself with a kind of passionate eagerness, so as to acquit her governess of the slightest blame. Since the painful scene between them she had kept her room, and, indeed, the baron had refused to see her. Before forgiving her he was determined to look into the matter. All his plans were laid. But his hair had grown whiter, and his head shook with age.

"Monsieur N a n t a s," announced Joseph.

The baron did not rise. He simply turned his head and looked fixedly at Nantas, who walked forward. The latter had had the good sense not to yield to any desire to dress himself up; he had simply bought a black coat and a

pair of trousers, which were decent but
very worn, and gave him the appearance of a poor but careful student, with
nothing of the adventurer about him.
He stopped in the middle of the room
and waited, standing up, but without
humility.

"So it is you, sir," stammered the
old man.

But he could not continue, for his
emotion choked him, and he feared lest
he might commit some act of violence.
After a pause, he said, simply, "You
have committed a wicked deed, sir."

Then when Nantas was about to
make some excuse, he repeated more
emphatically—"A wicked deed. I wish
to know nothing, I request you to explain nothing to me. In fact no explanation can lessen your crime. Only
robbers break in upon families in this
way."

Nantas hung his head again.

"It is making money very easily, setting a trap in which one is certain of
catching both child and father."

"Allow me, sir," interrupted the
young man, stung by these words.

But the baron made a violent gesture.

"What? Why should I allow anything? It is not for you to speak here.
I am telling you what I am in duty
bound to tell you, and what you are
bound to hear, since you come before
me as a culprit. Look at this house.
Our family has lived here for more than
three centuries without reproach. Standing here, are you not conscious of our
ancient honour and dignity? Well, sir,
you have trifled with all that. It nearly
killed me; and to-day my hands tremble
as if I had suddenly grown ten years
older. Be silent and listen to me."

Nantas had turned very pale. He had
taken a difficult part upon himself. He
felt anxious to make the blindness of
passionate love serve as his pretext.

"I lost my head," he muttered, trying
to make up some tale. "I could not
look at Mademoiselle Flavie——"

At his daughter's name the baron rose
and cried in a voice like thunder:

"Silence! I have told you that I do
not wish to know anything. Whatever
happened matters little to me. I have
asked her nothing, and I ask you nothing. Keep you confessions to yourselves, I will have nothing to do with
them."

Then he sat down again, trembling
and exhausted. Nantas bent his head,
feeling deeply moved, in spite of the
command he had over himself. After
a pause the old man continued in the
dry tone of a person discussing business
matters:

"I beg pardon, sir. I had determined
to keep cool but failed. You are not at
my disposal; I am at yours, since I am
in your power. You are here to carry
out a transaction which has become
necessary. To business, sir."

And thenceforward he affected to
speak like a lawyer, settling as agreeably as possible some shameful case in
which he was loath to dabble. He began formally: "Mademoiselle Flavie
Danvilliers inherited at the death of her
mother a sum of two hundred thousand
francs, which she was not to receive
until her marriage. That sum has produced interest; but here are the accounts of my guardianship which I will
communicate to you."

He opened a book and began to read
some figures. Nantas in vain tried to

stop him. Emotion seized him in the presence of this old man, who appeared so upright and simple, and who seemed to him so great because he was so calm.

"Finally," the baron concluded, "I bestow on you, by an agreement which my notary drew up this morning, another sum of two hundred thousand francs. I know that you have nothing. You can draw those two hundred thousand francs at my banker's on the day after the marriage."

"But I don't ask for your money, sir," said Nantas, "I only want your daughter."

The baron cut him short.

"You have not the right to refuse," he said, "and my daughter could not marry a man with less money than herself. I give you the dowry which I intended for her, that is all. Possibly you reckoned on more, for I have the credit of being richer than I really am."

And as the young man remained mute at this last thrust, the baron put an end to the interview by ringing the bell.

"Joseph, tell Mademoiselle Flavie that I want her in my room at once."

He had risen from his chair, and now began to walk slowly about the room. Nantas remained motionless. He was deceiving this old man, and he felt small and powerless before him. At last Flavie appeared.

"My child," said the baron, "here is the man. The marriage will take place as soon as possible."

Then he went out of the room, leaving them alone, as if, so far as he was concerned, the marriage were over.

When the door was shut, silence reigned. Nantas and Flavie looked at one another. They had never met before. He thought her very handsome, with her pale and haughty face, and her large grey eyes which never drooped. Perhaps she had been crying during the three days that she had spent in her room; however, the coldness of her cheeks must have frozen her tears. She it was who spoke first.

"Then the matter is settled, sir," said she.

"Yes, madame," replied Nantas simply.

Her face contracted involuntarily as she cast a long look at him, a look which seemed to be fathoming his baseness.

"Well, so much the better," she continued. "I was afraid I should not find anyone to agree to such a bargain."

Nantas could distinguish in her voice all the scorn which she felt for him, but he raised his head. If he had trembled before the father, knowing that he was deceiving him, he determined to be firm with the daughter, who was his accomplice.

"Excuse me, madame," he said calmly, and with the greatest politeness. "I think you misconceive the position in which what you rightly call the bargain has placed us. I apprehend that, from to-day forth, we are on a footing of perfect equality."

"Indeed!" interrupted Flavie, with a scornful smile.

"Yes, perfect equality. You require a name, in order to conceal a fault which I do not presume to condemn, and I give you my name. On my side I require money, and a certain social position, in order to carry out some great enterprise, and you furnish me with that money and position. We thus become two partners whose capitals balance. It only remains for us to express our mutual thanks for the service which we are rendering to one another."

She smiled no longer; indeed, a look of irritated pride appeared upon her face. After a pause she asked him, "You know my conditions?"

"No, madame," said Nantas, preserving perfect calmness. "Be good enough to name them. I agree to them in advance."

Upon this she spoke as follows, without hesitating or blushing: "Our lives will remain completely distinct and separate. You will give up all rights over me, and I shall owe no duty towards you."

At each sentence Nantas made an affirmative sign. This was precisely what he desired.

"If I thought it part of my duty to be gallant," he said, "I should assert that such conditions would drive me to despair. But we are above empty compliments. I am pleased to see that you have such a correct appreciation of our respective positions. We are not entering upon life by the path of roses. I only ask one thing of you, madame, which is, that you will not make use of the liberty I shall accord you in such a way as to necessitate any interference on my part."

"What, sir!" exclaimed Flavie, violently, her pride revolting.

Nantas bowed respectfully, and entreated her not to be offended. Their position was a delicate one; they must both of them put up with certain allusions, without which a perfect under-standing would be impossible. He refrained from insisting further. Mademoiselle Chuin, in a second interview, had given him further particulars and had named to him a certain Monsieur des Fondettes as the person to whom all the trouble was due.

Suddenly Nantas felt a friendly impulse. Like all those who are conscious of their own power, he was fond of being good-natured.

"Listen, madame," he exclaimed. "We don't know one another, but it would be really wrong of us to hate one another at first sight. Perhaps we are made to understand each other. I can see that you despise me, but perhaps that is because you do not know my story."

Then he began to talk feverishly, throwing himself into a state of excitement as he spoke of his life, his ambition, and his desperate fruitless efforts in Paris. Then he displayed his scorn of what he called social conventionalism, in which ordinary men became entangled. What mattered the opinion of the world, he asked, when a man had his foot on it? He must show his superiority. Power was an excuse for all. And in glowing terms he painted the sovereign existence which he would make for himself. He feared no further obstacle; nothing prevailed against power. He would be powerful, and therefore he would be happy.

"Don't imagine that I am miserably sordid," he continued. "I am not selling myself for your fortune; I only take your money as a means to rise. Oh, if you only knew what is working within me! if you only knew the burning nights which I have spent, always meditating over the same idea, which was only swept away by the reality of the morrow, then you would understand me! You would then, perhaps, be proud to lean on my arm, saying to yourself that you at least had furnished me with the means to become some one!"

She listened to him in silence, without a single movement of her features. And he asked himself a question which he had been turning over in his mind for three days past, without being able to find answer to it: Had she noticed him at his window, that she had so readily accepted Mademoiselle Chuin's scheme when the latter had mentioned him? The singular idea occurred to him that perhaps she might have loved him with a romantic love if he had indignantly refused the bargain which the governess had proposed to him.

He stopped at last, and Flavie maintained an icy silence. Then, as if he had not made his confession, she repeated in a dry voice: "Then, it is understood, our lives completely distinct, absolute liberty."

Nantas at once resumed his ceremonious air, and in the curt voice of a man discussing an agreement, replied: "It is settled, madame."

Ill-pleased with himself, he then withdrew. How was it that he had yielded to the foolish desire to overcome that woman? She was very handsome; but it was better that there should be nothing in common between them, for she might hamper him in life.

# CHAPTER III

## THE QUESTION

TEN years had passed. One morning Nantas was sitting in the study in which Baron Danvilliers had given him such a formidable reception on the occasion of their first meeting. That study was now his own; the baron, after being reconciled to his daughter and his son-in-law, had given up the house to them, merely reserving for his own use a little building situated at the other end of the garden and overlooking the Rue de Beaune. In ten years' time Nantas had won for himself one of the highest positions attainable in the financial and mercantile worlds. Having a hand in all the great railway enterprises, engaged in all the land speculations which signalised the earlier period of the Second Empire, he had rapidly accumulated an immense fortune. But his ambition did not halt at that; he was determined to play a part in politics, and he had succeeded to get elected as a deputy in a department where he had several farms. Since taking his seat in the Corps Législatif, he had posed as a future Finance Minister. Thanks to his practical knowledge and his ready tongue, he was day by day acquiring a more important position. He was skilful enough to effect absolute devotion to the Empire, but at the same time he professed theories on financial subjects which made a great stir, and which he knew gave the Emperor a deal to think of.

On that particular morning Nantas was overladen with business. The greatest activity prevailed in the spacious offices which he had arranged on the ground-floor of the mansion. There was a crowd of clerks, some sitting motionless at wickets, and others constantly going backwards and forwards, to the sound of banging doors. Bags of gold lay open and overflowing on the tables. There was a constant ring of precious metal, a tinkling music of wealth such as might have flooded the streets. In the ante-rooms a crowd was surging; place-hunters, financial agents, politicians, all Paris on its knees before power. Great men frequently waited there patiently for an hour at a stretch. And he, sitting at his table, in correspondence with people far and near, able to grasp the world with his outstretched arms, was carrying his former dream of force into fulfilment, conscious that he was the intelligent motor of a colossal machine which moved kingdoms and empires.

Suddenly he rang for his usher. He seemed anxious.

"Germain," he said, "do you know whether your mistress has come in?"

And when the man replied that he did not know, he told him to summon his wife's maid. But Germain did not move.

"Excuse me, sir," he whispered; "the President of the Corps Législatif insists on seeing you."

Nantas made an impatient gesture and replied: "Well, show him in, and do as I told you."

On the previous day, a speech which Nantas had made on an important budgetary question had produced such an impression that the matter had been referred to a commission to be amended according to his views. After the sitting of the Chamber a rumour had spread that the Finance Minister intended to resign, and Nantas was at once spoken of as his probable successor. For his part he shrugged his shoulders: nothing had been done, he had only had an interview with the Emperor with regard to certain special points. However, the President's visit might have vast significance. At this thought Nantas tried to throw off the feeling of worry which was weighing on him, and rose to grasp his President's hand.

"Ah, Monsieur le Duc," he said, "I beg your pardon. I did not know you were here. Believe me, I am deeply sensible of the honour which you are paying me."

For a minute they talked cordially; then the President, without saying anything definite, gave him to understand that he had been sent by the Emperor to sound him. Would he accept the Finance portfolio, and what would be his programme? Upon this, Nantas, with superb calmness, named his conditions. But beneath the impassibility of his face mute triumph was swelling. At last he had mounted the final rung, he was at the top of the ladder. Another step, and he would have all heads save that of the sovereign beneath him. As the President concluded, saying that he was going at once to the Emperor to communicate Nantas's programme, a small door which communicated with the private part of the house opened, and the maid of the financier's wife appeared.

Nantas, suddenly turning pale, stopped short in the middle of a sentence and hurried to the girl, saying to the duke:

"Pray excuse me."

Then he questioned the servant in whispers. Madame had gone out early? Had she said where she was going? When was she expected home? The maid replied vaguely, like a clever girl who did not wish to compromise herself. Understanding the absurdity of the situation, Nantas concluded by remarking, "Tell your mistress as soon as she comes in that I wish to speak to her."

The President of the Chamber, somewhat surprised, had stepped up to a window and was looking into the courtyard. Nantas returned to him, again apologising. But he had lost his self-possession, he stammered, and astonished the duke by his clumsy remarks.

"There, I've spoilt the whole business," he exclaimed aloud, when the other had gone. "I've missed the portfolio."

He sat down, feeling disgusted and angry. Several more visitors were then shown in. An engineer had a report to present to him, showing that enormous profits would arise from the working of a certain mine. A diplomatist interviewed him on the subject of a loan which a foreign Power wanted to negotiate in Paris. His tools flocked in, rendering account of twenty different schemes. Finally he received a large number of his colleagues of the Chamber, all of whom went into raptures about his speech of the day before.

Leaning back in his chair, he accepted all this flattery without a smile. The clink of gold was still audible in the neighbouring rooms; the house seemed to tremble like a factory, as if all that money were manufactured there. He had only to take up a pen to despatch telegrams which would have spread joy or consternation through the markets of Europe; he could prevent or precipitate war, by supporting or opposing the loan of which he had been told; he even held the fate of the French Budget in his hands, and he would soon know whether it would be best for him to support or oppose the Empire. This was his triumph, his formidable personality had become the axis upon which a world was turning. And yet he did not enjoy his triumph, as he had thought he would. He experienced a feeling of listlessness, his mind was elsewhere, on the alert at the slightest audible sound. Scarcely had a flame, a flush of satisfied ambition, risen to his cheeks than he felt himself turn pale again as if a cold hand from behind had been laid upon his neck.

Two hours had passed and Flavie had not yet appeared. Nantas at last called Germain, and gave him orders to summon Baron Danvilliers if the old gentleman were at home. Then he began to pace his study, refusing to see anyone else that day. Little by little his agitation had increased. His wife had evidently been to keep some appointment. She must have renewed her acquaintance with Monsieur des Fondettes. The latter's wife had died six months previously. True, Nantas disclaimed any idea of being jealous; during ten years he had strictly observed the agreement to which he had been a party; but he drew the line, as he said, at being made a dupe of. Never would he allow his wife to compromise his position by making him a laughing-stock. His strength forsook him as he became a prey to the feelings of a husband who requires respect. He experienced agony such as he had never endured, not even in his most hazardous speculations, at the commencement of his career.

At last Flavie entered the room, still in her outdoor costume; she had merely taken off her gloves and hat. Nantas, whose voice trembled, told her that he would have gone to her if he had known that she had come in. But, without sitting down, she motioned to him to have done quickly.

"Madame," he began, "an explanation has become necessary between us. Where were you this morning?"

Her husband's quivering voice and the pointedness of his question, astonished her profoundly.

"Where it pleased me to go," she replied in a cold tone.

"That is exactly what, in future, I must object to," he resumed, turning very pale. "It is your duty to recollect what I said to you: I will not allow you to make use of the liberty I grant you, in a way which may bring disgrace upon my name."

Flavie smiled in sovereign disdain.

"Disgrace your name, sir? but that is a question which regards yourself. It is a thing which no longer remains to be done."

Upon this, Nantas, wild with passion, advanced, as if to strike her.

"You wretched creature!" he stammered, "you have just left Monsieur des Fondettes. You have a lover, I know it!"

"You are wrong," she replied, without recoiling; "I have never seen Monsieur des Fondettes again. But even if I had a lover, it would not be for you to reproach me. What difference would it make to you? You forget our compact."

He looked at her for a moment with wild eyes; then, choking with sobs, and throwing into one cry all the passion which he had so long stifled, he flung himself at her feet.

"Oh, Flavie, I love you!"

Unbending still, she drew back, for he had touched the hem of her dress. But the wretched man followed her, dragging himself upon his knees with his hands uplifted.

"I love you, Flavie, I love you to madness! How it happened I know not. It began years ago, and it grew and grew, till now it has absorbed my whole being. Oh! I have struggled. I thought this passion unworthy of me. I called our first interview to mind. But now I suffer too much. I must speak——"

For a long time he continued thus. It was the shattering of all his principles. This man, who had put his trust in force, who maintained that violation was the sole lever capable of moving the world, was crushed, feeble like a child, disarmed by a woman. And his dream of fortune realized, his present high position, he would have given all for that woman to have raised him by a kiss upon his brow! She marred his triumph. He no longer heard the gold which sounded in his office, he no longer thought of the end-

less procession of flatterers who came
to bow their knees to him; he forgot
that the Emperor, at that moment, perhaps, was summoning him to power.
All those things had no existence for
him. He possessed everything, save
the only thing he wished for—his wife's
love. And if she denied it, then he had
nothing left him!

"Listen," he continued; "whatever I
have done, I have done for you. At
first, it is true, you were for nothing in
it; I simply worked to gratify my own
pride. But soon you became the one
object of all my thoughts, of all my
efforts. I told myself that I must
mount as high as possible, in order to
become worthy of you. I hoped to
make you unbend on the day when I
should lay my power at your feet. See
what I now am. Have I not won your
forgiveness? Do not despise me any
longer, I entreat you."

As yet she had not spoken. Now,
however, she said calmly: "Get up, sir.
Somebody might come in."

He refused, and still went on entreating. Perhaps he would have bided his
time if he had not been jealous of
Monsieur des Fondettes. It was that
torture which maddened him. At last
he became very humble.

"I see that you still despise me. Very
well, wait, do not bestow your love on
anybody. I can promise you so much
that I shall know how to move you.
You must forgive me if I was harsh
just now. I am out of my senses. Oh,
let me hope that you will love me some
day!"

"Never!" she answered energetically.

Then, as he still remained upon the
floor seemingly crushed, she would have

left the room; but suddenly beside
himself with fury, he sprang up and
caught her by the wrists. A woman
braved him thus when the world was
at his feet! He was capable of anything, could overthrow States, rule
France as he pleased, and yet he could
not obtain his wife's love! He, so
strong, so powerful, he whose slightest
desires were orders, he had but one
longing now, and that longing would
never be gratified, because a creature,
who was as weak as a child, spurned
him! He grasped her arms, and repeated in a hoarse whisper: "You must,
you must—"

"And I will not," replied Flavie, pale
and obstinate.

The struggle was still going on when
Baron Danvilliers opened the door. On
seeing him, Nantas released Flavie,
and cried:

"Your daughter has just come from
her lover, sir! Tell her that a woman
should respect her husband's name,
even if she does not love him,
even if the thought of her own honour
does not stand in the way."

The baron, who was greatly aged,
remained standing on the theshold,
gazing at this violent scene. It was a
melancholy surprise for him. He had
believed them to be united, and he
looked with approval on their ceremonious intercourse in public, considering
that to be a mere matter of form. His
son-in-law and he belonged to different
generations; but although he disliked
the financier's somewhat unscrupulous
activity, although he condemned certain undertakings which he regarded as
undesirable, he was forced to recognise
Nantas's strength of will and his quick

intellect. And now he suddenly came upon this drama, which he had never even suspected.

When Nantas accused Flavie of having a lover, the baron, who still treated his married daughter with the same severity as he had shown her when a child, advanced with a stately step.

"I swear to you that she has just come from her lover's," repeated Nantas; "and, look at her, she defies me."

Flavie turned away her head disdainfully. She was arranging her cuffs, which her husband had crushed in his roughness. Not a blush was to be seen on her face. Her father spoke to her.

"My child," said he, "why do you not defend yourself? Can your husband be speaking the truth? Can you have reserved this last grief for my old age? The offence would fall on me as well; for the fault of one member of a family falls upon the others."

Flavie made a gesture of impatience. Her father had well chosen his time to accuse her! For a moment longer she bore his questions, wishing to spare him the shame of an explanation. But as he in his turn lost patience, seeing her mute and obstinate, she finally replied, "Father, let this man play his part. You do not know him. For your own sake do not force me to speak out."

"He is your husband," said the old man, "the father of your child."

Flavie started, stung to the quick. "No, no, he is not the father of my child. I will tell you everything now. This man was never my lover, for it would be at least some excuse for him if he had loved me. This man simply

sold himself and agreed to hide another's sin."

The baron turned towards Nantas, who had recoiled, deadly pale.

"Do you hear me, father?" continued Flavie, more violently. "He sold himself, sold himself for money! I have never loved him, and he has never been anything to me. I wished to spare you a great sorrow. I bought him so that he might lie to you. Look at him now. See whether I am not telling you the truth."

Nantas hid his face in his hands.

"And now," resumed the young woman, "he actually wants me to love him. He went down on his knees just now and wept. Some comedy, no doubt! Forgive me for having deceived you, father; but how can I love such a man? Now that you know all, take me away. Indeed, he treated me with violence just now, and I will not remain here a moment longer."

The baron straightened his bent figure. In silence he stepped forward and gave his arm to his daughter. The two crossed the room, without Nantas making a movement to detain them. Then, upon reaching the door, the old man spoke these two words: "Farewell, sir."

The door closed. Nantas remained alone, crushed, gazing wildly into the void around him. Germain came in and placed a letter on the table; Nantas opened it mechanically, and cast his eyes over it. This letter, written by the Emperor in person, gave him the appointment of Finance Minister, and was couched in the most flattering terms. He could hardly understand it;

the realisation of all his ambition did not affect him in the least.

Meanwhile, in the neighboring rooms the rattle of money had grown louder; it was the busiest hour of the day, the hour when Nantas's house seemed to shake the world. And he, amid that colossal machinery which was his work, he, at the apogee of his power, with his eyes stupidly fixed on the Emperor's letter, gave vent to a childish complaint, the negation of his whole life: "Ah! how unhappy I am! how unhappy I am!"

Then, resting his head upon the table, he wept, and the hot tears that gushed forth from his eyes blotted the letter which appointed him Minister of Finance.

## CHAPTER IV

### TOIL

DURING the whole of the eighteen months that Nantas had been a Minister, he had been trying to drown the past by superhuman toil. On the day after the scene in his study he had had an interview with Baron Danvilliers; and Flavie, acting on her father's advice, had consented to return to her husband's roof. But they spoke no word together, except when they were forced to play a comedy in the eyes of the world. Nantas had determined not to leave his home. In the evening his secretaries came to him from the Ministry, and he got through all his work in his own study.

It was at this period of his life that he performed his greatest deeds. A secret voice suggested lofty and fruit-ful aspirations to him. Whenever he passed by, a murmur of sympathy and admiration was heard. But he remained insensible to eulogy. It may be said that he worked without hope of reward, with the sole idea of performing prodigies, of which the only aim was to compass the impossible. At each step on his upward career he consulted Flavie's face. Was she touched at last? Did she pardon him his former baseness? Had she still any thought save of the development of his intellect? But never did he detect any emotion on that woman's mute countenance, and he said to himself, as he redoubled his efforts: "I am not high enough for her yet; I must climb, still climb."

He was determined to compel happiness, as he had compelled fortune. All his old belief in his power returned, he would not admit that there was any other lever in this world; it was will which produced humanity. When discouragement seized on him at times, he shut himself up, so that nobody should witness the weakness of his flesh. His struggles could only be read in his deep-set, dark-circled eyes, in which an ardent fire blazed.

He was devoured by jealousy now. To fail to win Flavie's love was a torture; but the thought that she might care for another drove him mad. By way of asserting her liberty, it was quite possible that she might intrigue with Monsieur des Fondettes. Her husband affected not to occupy himself with her, but all the time he endured agony whenever she absented herself, even if it were only for an hour. If he had not feared to make himself look ridiculous, he would have followed her in the streets. That course displeasing him, he determined to have some one beside her whose devotion he could purchase.

Mademoiselle Chuin had remained an inmate of the house. The baron was used to her, not to mention that she knew too many things to make it advisable to get rid of her. At one time the old maid had resolved to retire on the twenty thousand francs that Nantas had paid her on the day after his marriage. But she had no doubt calculated that there would be further pickings in such a household. So she awaited her opportunity, having found, moreover, that she needed yet another twenty thousand francs to buy the long-desired notary's house at Roinville, the little market town she came from.

There was no occasion for Nantas to mince matters with this old lady, whose pious mien no longer deceived him. However, on the morning when he called her into his study and openly proposed to her that she should keep him informed as to his wife's slightest actions, she professed to be insulted, and asked him what he took her for.

"Come," said he impatiently, "I'm very busy, some one is waiting for me; let us be brief, please."

But she would listen to nothing which was not couched in proper terms. One of her principles was, that things are not ugly in themselves, that they only become ugly or cease to be so according to the way in which they are presented.

"Very well," said Nantas, "a good action is involved in this. I am fearful that my wife is hiding some sorrow

from me. For the last few weeks I have observed that she has been very much depressed, and I thought that you could find out the cause of it."

"You can rely on me," said Mademoiselle Chuin, with a maternal outburst on hearing these words. "I am devoted to your wife, I will do anything for her sake or yours. From tomorrow we will keep a watch on her."

Nantas promised to reward the old maid for her services. She pretended to be angry at first, but she had the adroitness to make him fix a sum, and it was agreed that he should give her ten thousand francs upon her furnishing him with positive proof of his wife's conduct whatever it might be. Little by little they had come to call things by their proper names.

From that time forward Nantas was less uneasy. Three months passed and he was engaged upon a great task—the preparation of the Budget. With the Emperor's sanction he had introduced some important modifications into the financial system. He knew that he would be fiercely attacked in the Chamber, and he had to prepare a large quantity of documents. Frequently he sat up all night, and this hard work deadened him as it were to emotion, and made him patient. Whenever he saw Mademoiselle Chuin he questioned her briefly. Did she know anything? Had his wife paid many visits? Had she stopped long at certain houses? Mademoiselle Chuin kept a journal of the slightest incidents, but so far she had not succeeded in making any important discovery. Nantas felt reassured, whilst the old woman occasionally blinked her eyes, saying that she should perhaps have some news for him soon.

The truth was that Mademoiselle Chuin had indulged in further reflection. Ten thousand francs was not enough; she needed twenty thousand to purchase the notary's house. She at first thought of selling herself to the wife, after having sold herself to the husband. But she knew Flavie, and she was fearful of being dismissed at the first word. For a long time past, before she had even been charged with this matter, she had kept watch over Madame Nantas on her own account, remarking to herself that a servant's profits lie in the master's or mistress's vices. However, she had discovered that she had to deal with a virtue which was all the more rigid since it was based upon pride One effect of Flavie's stumble had been that it had inspired her with positive hatred for the other sex. So Mademoiselle Chuin was in despair, when one day she met Monsieur des Fondettes in the street, and after they had had some conversation together, realising that he desired to be reconciled to her mistress, she made up her mind: she would serve both him and Nantas—a combination worthy of genius.

Everything favoured her. Monsieur des Fondettes had met Flavie in society and had been scorned by her. He was in despair thereat. At the end of a week's time, after a great parade of feeling on his side and of scruples on that of Mademoiselle Chuin, the matter was settled; he was to give her ten thousand francs, and she was to smuggle him into the house one evening so that he might have a private interview with Flavie.

The arrangement having been effected, Mademoiselle Chuin sought Nantas.

"What have you learnt?" he asked, turning pale.

She would not say anything definite at first. But Nantas displayed such furious impatience that before long she told him that Monsieur des Fondettes had an appointment with Flavie that evening in her private apartments.

"Very good—thank you," stammered Nantas. And he sent her off with a wave of the hand; he was afraid of giving way before her.

This abrupt dismissal astonished and delighted the old woman, for she had prepared herself for a long cross-examination, and had even pre-arranged her answers, so that she might not contradict herself. She made a bow, and then retired, putting on a mournful face.

Nantas had risen. As soon as he was alone he said aloud:

"This evening, in her private apartments."

Then he carried his hands to his head, as if he feared it would burst. That appointment under his own roof seemed to him monstrous audacity. He clenched his fists, and his rage made him think of murder. And yet he had his task to finish—those budgetary documents to complete. Three times did he sit down at his table, and three times a heaving of his whole body raised him to his feet again; whilst, behind him, something seemed to be urging him to go at once to his wife, and denounce her. At last, however, he conquered himself, and resumed his work, swearing that he would strangle them both that very evening. It was the greatest victory that he had ever won over his feelings.

That same afternoon Nantas went to submit to the Emperor the definite plan of the Budget. The sovereign having raised certain objections, he discussed them with perfect clearness. But it became necessary that he should modify an important part of his programme—a difficult matter, as the debate was to take place on the next day.

"I will pass the night over it," he said.

And on his way home he thought, "I'll kill them at midnight, and I shall have the whole night afterwards to finish this task."

At dinner that evening Baron Danvilliers began talking about the Budget, which was making some little stir. He did not approve of all his son-in-law's views on financial matters, but he admitted that they were very broad and very remarkable. Whilst Nantas was replying to the Baron, he fancied, on several occasions, that he noticed his wife's eyes fixed upon him. She frequently looked at him in that way now. Her glance was not softened, however; she simply listened, and seemed to be trying to read his thoughts. Nantas fancied that she feared she was betrayed. Accordingly he made an effort to appear careless; he talked a good deal, affected great animation, and finally overcame the objections of his great intellect. Flavie was still looking at him, and suddenly a hardly perceptible glimpse of tenderness darted across her face.

Nantas worked in his study until midnight. Little by little he had become absorbed in his task, and soon he lost consciousness of everything save that creation of his brain, that great financial scheme which he had painfully built up piece by piece, in the midst of innumerable obstacles. When the clock struck twelve he instinctively raised his head. Deep silence reigned in the house. Suddenly he recollected everything. But it was a trial for him to leave his chair; he laid his pen down regretfully, and at last took a few steps as if in obedience to a will which had forsaken him. Then his face flushed, and a flame blazed forth in his eyes. He started for his wife's rooms.

That evening Flavie had dismissed her maid early, saying that she wished to be alone. She had a suite of rooms for her own use. Until midnight she remained in a little boudoir, where, stretched upon a sofa, she took up a book and began to read. But again and again the book fell from her hands, and, closing her eyes at last, she became absorbed in thought. Her face still wore a softened expression, and a faint smile played upon it at intervals. Suddenly she started up. There was a knock outside.

"Who is there?" she asked.

"Open the door," replied Nantas.

She was so surprised that she opened it mechanically. Never before had her husband presented himself in this way. He entered the room half-distracted; his rage had mastered him while he ascended the stairs. Mademoiselle Chuin, who was watching for him on the landing, had just told him that Monsieur des Fondettes had been there for some hours. Accordingly he was determined to show his wife no mercy.

"There is a man concealed in your rooms," said he.

Flavie did not reply at first, so greatly did these words surprise her. At last she grasped their meaning. "You are mad, sir!" she answered.

But, without stopping to argue, he was already looking about him. Then he made his way to the next room. With one bound, however, she threw herself before the door, crying: "You shall not go in. These are my rooms, and you have no right here."

Quivering with passion and looking taller in her pride, she guarded the door. For a moment they stood thus motionless, speechless, gazing into one another's eyes. Nantas with his head thrust forward, his arms opened, seemed about to throw himself upon her to force a passage.

"Come away," he said, in a hoarse whisper. "I'm stronger than you, and go in I will!"

"You shall not; I will not permit it."

And as Nantas kept on repeating accusations, she, without even deigning to deny them, shrugged her shoulders, and replied, "Even if it were true what difference can it make to you? Am I not free?"

He recoiled at these words, which struck him like a blow. It was quite true, she was free. A cold shudder ran through him, he plainly realised that she had the best of the argument, and that he was playing the part of a feeble and illogical child. He was not observing their compact; his foolish passion had made it hateful to him. Why had he not remained at work in his study? The blood fled from his cheeks, and an indefinable expression of suffering overspread his face. When Flavie saw his pitiable condition she left the door before which she had been standing, whilst a tender gleam came into her eyes. "Look," she said, simply.

And then she passed into the adjoining room herself carrying a lamp in her hand, whilst Nantas remained standing at the door. He had made her a sign as if to say that it was sufficient, that he did not wish to enter. But it was she who insisted now. When she had drawn aside the curtains, and perceived Monsieur des Fondettes who had been concealed behind them, so intense was her amazement and horror that she shrieked.

"It was true," she stammered, "it was true this man was here; but I did not know it. On my life I swear it!"

Then, with an effort, she calmed herself, and even seemed to regret the impulse which had prompted her to defend herself.

"You were right, sir, and I crave your pardon," she said to Nantas, endeavouring to speak in her usual tone of voice.

Monsieur des Fondettes, however, felt somewhat foolish, and would have given a good deal if the husband had only flown into a passion. But Nantas remained silent. He had simply turned very pale. When he had carried his eyes from Monsieur des Fondettes to Flavie, he bowed to the latter, merely saying:

"Excuse me, madame, you are free."

Then he turned and walked away. Something seemed to have broken within him; merely a machinery of muscle and bone still worked. When he reached his study again he walked straight to a drawer where he kept a revolver. Having examined the weapon, he said aloud, as if making a formal engagement with himself: "That suffices; I will kill myself presently."

He turned up his lamp, sat down at his table, and quietly resumed his work. Amid the deep silence he completed, without an instant's hesitation, a sentence that he had previously left unfinished. One by one were fresh sheets of paper covered with writing and set in a heap. Two hours later, when Flavie, who had driven Monsieur des Fondettes from the house, came down with bare feet to listen at the door, she only heard her husband's pen scratching as it travelled over the paper. She bent down and applied her eye to the keyhole. Nantas was still calmly writing, his face was expressive of peace and satisfaction at his work; but a ray of the lamp fell upon the barrel of the revolver at his side.

## CHAPTER V

### HER REASON

THE house adjoining the garden of the mansion was now the property of Nantas, who had bought it from his father-in-law. By a personal caprice he had refrained from letting the wretched garret where he had struggled against want for two months after his arrival in Paris. Since he had acquired an enormous fortune he had on more than one occasion felt impelled to go and shut himself up in that little room

for hours at a time. It was there that he had suffered, and it was there that he liked to enjoy his triumph. Again, whenever he met with any obstacle he was wont to go there to reflect and to form great resolutions. Once there he again became what he had formerly been. And now, when the hand of death hovered over him, it was in that attic that he determined to meet it.

He did not finish his work until eight o'clock in the morning. Fearing that fatigue might overcome him, he took a cold bath. Then he summoned several of his clerks for the purpose of giving them instructions. When his secretary arrived he had an interview with him, and the secretary received orders to take the plan of the Budget to the Tuileries, and to furnish certain explanations if the Emperor should raise any fresh objections. That settled, Nantas considered that he had done enough. He had left everything in order; he was not going off like a demented bankrupt. After all, he was his own property; he could dispose of himself without being accused of selfishness or cowardice.

Nine o'clock struck. The time had come. But, just as he was leaving his study, taking the revolver with him, he had to put up with the final humiliation. Mademoiselle Chuin presented herself, to claim the ten thousand francs which he had promised her. He paid her, and was forced to put up with her familiarity. She assumed a maternal air, and seemed to treat him as a successful pupil. Even if he had had any hesitation left, this shameful complicity would have confirmed him in his intentions. He sought the garret quickly, and in his haste he left the door unlocked.

Nothing was changed there. There were the same rents in the wall-paper; the bed, the table, and the chair were still there, with their same old look of poverty. For a moment he inhaled the atmosphere which reminded him of his former struggles. Then he approached the window and caught sight of the same stretch of Paris as formerly; the trees in the garden, the Seine the quays, and a part of the right bank of the river, where the houses rose up in confused masses until they were lost to sight at the point where the Père-Lachaise Cemetery appeared in the far distance.

The revolver was lying within his reach on the rickety table. There was no hurry now; he felt certain that nobody would disturb him, and that he might kill himself whenever he pleased. He became absorbed in thought, and he reflected that he was at precisely the same point as formerly—led back to the same spot, with the same intention of suicide. One evening before, in that very room, he had determined to dash his brains out. In those days he had been too poor to purchase a pistol; he had only had the stones in the streets at his disposal, but death was awaiting him now as then. Thus in this world death is the only thing which never fails, which is always sure and always ready. Nothing that he knew of was like death; he sought in vain, all else had given way beneath him: death alone remained a certainty. He regretted that he had lived ten years too long. The experience that he had acquired of life, in his ascent

to fortune and power, seemed to him puerile. Why had he put himself to that expenditure of will, what purpose had been served by that waste of force, since will and force were as nothing? One passion had sufficed to destroy him: he had foolishly allowed himself to love Flavie, and now the edifice which he had built up was cracking, collapsing like a mere house of cards swept away by the breath of a child. It was lamentable—it resembled the punishment that overtakes a marauding schoolboy, under whom a branch snaps, and who perishes on the spot where he has sinned. Life was a mistake; the best men ended it as tamely as the biggest fools.

Nantas had taken the revolver from the table, and slowly raised it. At that supreme moment one last regret made him hesitate for a second. What great things would he not have accomplished if Flavie had understood him! Had she but thrown herself on his neck one day, saying, "I love you!" he would have found a lever to move the world. And his last thought was one of distain for force and strength; since they which were to have given him everything had not been able to give him Flavie.

He raised the revolver. The morning was a glorious one. Through the open window the sun poured in, lending even a look of brightness to that wretched garret. In the distance, Paris was awakening to its giant life. Nantas pressed the weapon to his temple.

But the door was suddenly flung open, and Flavie entered. With one movement she dashed the revolver aside, and the bullet lodged itself in the ceiling. They looked at one another. She was so out of breath, so choked with emotion, that she could not articulate. At last, embracing Nantas for the first time, she spoke the words for which he longed, the only words which could have determined him to live.

"I love you!" she cried, sobbing on his breast, and tearing the avowal from her pride, her mastered being. "I love you, for you are truly strong."

---

# Coqueville

## CHAPTER I

### A LONELY SPOT

COQUEVILLE is a little villiage situated in a cleft of the rocks, a couple of leagues from Grandport, with a fine sandy beach, stretching out before the hovels which cling half-way up the side of the cliff, like shells left there by the tide. When one climbs the heights of Grandport on the left, one can see westward, plainly enough, the smooth yellow sands which suggest a stream of gold dust pouring from the cloven rocks; and anyone with good eyes can even distinguish the reddish-coloured houses whose smoke ascends in bluish coils to the summit of the huge cliff, barring the sky.

It is a lonely spot, and the inhabitants have never reached the number of two hundred. The ravine which opens on to the sands, and on the threshold of which the village is perched, winds through the country with such sudden bends and such steep slopes, that it is almost impossible to pass through it except on foot. This cuts off most communication and isolates the little village, which might be a hundred miles from the neighbouring hamlets. Thus the only intercourse of the inhabitants with Grandport is by water. Nearly all are fishermen, gaining their livelihood from the sea, and each day they convey their fish to Grandport in their boats. A big firm —that of Dufeu & Co.—buys of them by the catch. Old Dufeu has been dead some years, but his widow carries on the business with the help of an assistant, M. Mouchel, a tall fair fellow, whose duty it is to scour the coast and make arrangements with the fishermen. This M. Mouchel is the one link between Coqueville and the civilized world.

Coqueville deserves a historian. It seems certain that some time during the dark ages the village was founded by the Mahés, a family who established themselves and multiplied exceedingly at the foot of the cliff. They must originally have been prosperous and have married among themselves, as for centuries there is no mention of anyone besides the Mahés in the place. Then, during the reign of Louis XIII., a man named Floche appeared upon the scene. It is not exactly known whence he came, but he married a Mahé girl, and from that moment a phenomenon was witnessed—the Floches prospered in their turn, and multiplied to such an extent that they gradually absorbed the Mahés, whose number diminished, and whose fortune passed into the hands of the new-comers. No doubt the Floches had the advantage of possessing fresher blood, more vigorous physiques, and temperaments which were better adapted to the inclemency of wind and waves. At any rate, the Floches are nowadays the masters of Coqueville.

It can be understood that this displacement of position and wealth was not accomplished without many terrible struggles. The Mahés and the Floches detest one another. Theirs is a century old hatred. In spite of their fall, the Mahés are still proud of having been the first conquerors, rulers, and ancestors of the place, and they speak in terms of contempt of the first Floche as a beggar, a vagrant whom they had taken in and sheltered from pity, and to whom, to their eternal regret, they had given one of their daughters. According to them, the descendants of this Floche have never been anything but libertines and thieves; and with the bitter rage of ruined, fallen nobles who see the swarming progeny of *bourgeois* lording it over their *châteaux* and lands, there is no insult that the Mahés do not heap upon the powerful tribe of Floche.

Naturally, the Floches, on their side,

are insolently triumphant. They enjoy life, and this gives them a jeering disposition. They jeer at the ancient race of Mahé, and swear that they will drive the others from the village if they do not bow to their rule. In their eyes the older family are starvelings, who would do far better to mend their rags rather than proudly drape them round their shoulders; and thus Coqueville is divided into two ferocious factions—that is to say, about a hundred and thirty of the inhabitants are quite determined to demolish the other fifty, simply because they are stronger. A struggle between two empires is carried on upon exactly the same lines.

Amongst the most recent quarrels which have shaken Coqueville, people quote the famous enmity between the two brothers, Fouasse and Tupain, and the uproarious battles of the Rouget household. It must be stated that each inhabitant formerly received a nickname, which, with time, has become a real family surname, for it was difficult to find one's way amidst the labyrinth of marriages between the Mahés and the Floches. Rouget ("Carrots") certainly had an ancestor of ruddy hair and complexion, but one cannot account for such names as Fouasse and Tupain, many cognomens having lost all sense and significance as time passed on.

Now, old Francoise, a jolly old woman of eighty, still living, had had Fouasse by a Mahé, then, her husband dying, she had taken a Floche as her second partner, and had given birth to Tupain. Thence came the hatred between the two brothers, which was all the more lively on account of dispute about some inheritance. The Rougets, too, were always fighting, because Rouget accused Marie, his wife, of partiality for a Floche, big Brisemotte, a dark sturdy fellow upon whom he, Rouget (a little nervous and very quarrelsome man), had already twice dashed, knife in hand, swearing that he would cut his heart out.

However Coqueville's chief concern was neither Rouget's fits of passion nor the disputes between Tupain and Fouasse. There was a much more important rumour about, viz., that Delphin, a young fellow of twenty, and a Mahé, had dared to fall in love with the beautiful Margot, the daughter of La Queue, who was the richest of the Floches, and mayor of the village. He was called La Queue (Pig-tail), because his father had, in Louis Philippe's time, been the last to wear his hair plaited, with the obstinate determination of an old man who clung to the fashions of his youth.

Now, La Queue owned one of the two biggest fishing-boats in Coqueville, the *Zephyr*, which was by far the best of all the smacks, and still new and in perfect order. The other large boat, the *Whale*, a leaking pinnace, belonged to Rouget, and was manned by Delphin and Fouasse; while La Queue took with him Tupain and Brisemotte. The latter was never tired of laughing contemptuously at the *Whale*, an old tub, so they said, which would some day disappear beneath the waves like a handful of mud. So when La Queue learnt that that vagabond Delphin, belonging to the *Whale*, was daring to hang about his daughter Margot, he gave the girl two sounding smacks, simply to warn

her that she should never be the wife of a Mahé.

Margot, in a furious rage, vowed that she would pass the blows to Delphin if he ever came near her, for it was indeed aggravating to be clouted on account of a fellow she never even looked at. Margot, who at sixteen was as strong as a man and as handsome as a real lady, was said to be very hard on anyone who made love to her, and to hold sweethearts in contempt. So one can understand the amount of gossip that went on in Coqueville about Delphin's audacity, Margot's anger, and the two smacks that she had received.

Still, there were some who said that Margot in her heart, was not really so very angry at seeing Delphin come after her. He was a short, fair fellow, with a sea-tanned skin, and thick curly hair which strayed over his eyes and down his neck. And he was very strong, too, in spite of his slender figure—quite capable, indeed, of beating a man three times his size. It was said that sometimes he went off to have a spree at Grandport, and this gave him a somewhat alarming reputation among the girls, who accused him, between themselves, of leading a fast life—a vague expression which denoted any and every unknown pleasure.

Whenever Margot spoke of Delphin she waxed too wrathful; but he always smiled knowingly, and gazed at her calmly with his small, bright eyes, never troubling in the least either about her contempt or her anger. He walked up and down before her house, and stealthily followed her under cover of brambles and thickets, watching her for hours with the patience and the cunning of a cat after a tom-tit. Whenever she suddenly found him behind her, so close that the warmth of his breath suffered to betray him, he did not take to his heels, but put on a gentle, sorrowful air, which took Margot by surprise, and made her forget her anger until he was already a long way off. If her father had seen her he would certainly have hit her again. Such a state of affairs could not last, and yet Margot seemed to have sworn to no purpose that Delphin should one day have the smacks she had promised him, for she never seized the opportunity of bestowing them on him when he was there; in such wise that people said she should not talk so much about doing it, since she kept the clouts for herself.

No one, however, ever dreamt that she could possibly become Delphin's wife. Her behaviour was simply regarded as the weakness of a born coquette, for a marriage between the most beggarly of all the Mahés—a fellow who had not six shirts to his back —and the mayor's daughter, the heiress of the richest of all the Floches, seemed simply monstrous and absurd. Illdisposed people said that she might keep company with him, but would certainly never marry him. In short, all Coqueville was interested in the affair, and felt anxious to know how things would end. Would Delphin have his ears boxed? Or would Margot allow herself to be kissed in some quiet corner among the rocks? That was what time alone would prove, but pending the result Coqueville was in a state of revolution, some being for the clouts and others for the kisses.

Two people only, in the village, belonged neither to the Mahés nor the Floches, and those were the priest and the rural constable. The latter—a tall, thin man, whose real name nobody seemed to know, but who was called the Emperor, probably because he had served under Charles X.—did not in reality exercise the slightest surveillance over the parish, whose land consisted chiefly of bare rocks and barren heath. A sub-prefect, who befriended him, had created this sinecure for his benefit, in order that he might live in peace on a microscopical salary. As for Abbé Radiguet, he was one of those simple-minded priests whom bishops are only too glad to get rid of by burying them in some far-away village. He lived the life of an honest peasant, tilling the small garden he had managed to form on the rock, and smoking his pipe as he watched the growth of his vegetables. His only fault was his partiality for good cheer which he did not know how to satisfy, reduced as he was to worship mackerel and to drink cider in far larger quantities at times than was good for him. Still, he was a father to his parishioners, and every now and then they came to hear mass just by way of pleasing him.

However, the priest and the constable, after long succeeding in remaining neutral, were in the end forced to take sides in the village. And now the Emperor stood up for the Mahés, while Abbé Radiguet lent his support to the Floches, whence arose various complications. As the Emperor had nothing to do from morning to night, and grew tired of counting the boats coming out of Grandport harbour, he constituted himself the village detective. Since becoming a partisan of the Mahés he upheld Fouasse against Tupain, tried to catch Rouget's wife flirting with Brisemotte, and, above all else, closed his eyes whenever he saw Delphin slip into the courtyard of Margot's house.

The worst of all this was that it led to violent quarrels between the Emperor and his natural superior, Mayor La Queue. In his respect for discipline, the former duly listened to the latter's reprimands, but then went and did exactly as he pleased, thus disorganizing public authority in Coqueville. It was impossible to pass before the barn, which by courtesy was termed the municipal building, without being half-deafened by the noise of a dispute. Abbé Radiguet, on the other hand, now that he had reinforced the ranks of the triumphant Floches (who showered superb mackerel upon him), stealthily encouraged Rouget's wife in the resistance she offered to her husband, and threatened Margot with flames should she ever dare allow Delphin to touch her with the tip of his finger. It was simply utter anarchy—the army in revolt against civil authority, religion winking at the misdeeds of the *bourgeoise,* and a whole nation, numbering a hundred and eighty souls, ready to devour one another in a mouse-hole, situated between the immense sea and the infinite vastness of the sky.

Delphin was the only one who still smiled amiably in the midst of the general agitation of Coqueville, for he was in love and only cared about winning Margot. He laid snares for her much as if he had been trying to catch

a rabbit, and he aimed at getting the priest to marry them.

One evening Margot found him watching for her in a lane, and then at last she raised her hand to strike. But she suddenly turned very red, for, without waiting for the blow to fall, Delphin had caught hold of the hand which threatened him, and was passionately kissing it.

She began to tremble, while he whispered to her:

"I love you. Will you have me?"

"Never!" she cried, in revolt at the idea.

Delphin shrugged his shoulders, then went on in a quiet tender voice: "Don't say that. We suit each other very well, and you'd see how nice it would be."

## CHAPTER II

### A FATAL DAY

THAT Sunday was a terrible day. One of those sudden September storms, which set such awful tempests raging round the rocky coast of Grandport, had arisen; and, as the light began to fade, a ship in distress was espied from Coqueville. But the darkness increased and it was not possible to attempt to render any aid. The *Zephyr* and the *Whale* had been anchored since the previous evening in a little natural harbour lying between two granite walls to the left of the beach; neither La Queue nor Rouget daring to go out in such weather, which the more to be regretted, as M. Mouchel, Madame Dufeu's representative, had taken the trouble to come in person on the Saturday, to offer them particularly good terms if they would make every effort, for the catches had not been very good lately, and the markets were complaining.

So Coqueville muttered and grumbled as it went to bed that Sunday evening, amidst the torrents of rain pouring down around it. It was the old, old tale; whenever fish was not to be got from the sea, orders came in. And between its grumblings, the village talked of the ship which had been seen driving before the hurricane, and which, now, must certainly be lying at the bottom of the sea.

On the following day, Monday, the sky was still overcast, and the sea still ran high, without growing calm, although the wind had fallen. It ceased blowing entirely, yet the waves still dashed on. Then, towards the afternoon, the two boats put out, in spite of everything. At about four o'clock the *Zephyr* returned, having caught nothing; and while Tupain and Brisemotte anchored it in the little harbour, La Queue stood on the beach, shaking his fist at the ocean in his exasperation. Was not M. Mouchel waiting? he said. Margot was there—with half Coqueville, indeed—watching the last billows, and sharing her father's rancour against sea and sky.

"But where's the *Whale?*" asked somebody.

"Down there behind that point," replied La Queue. "And if that old tub returns to-day without being smashed, it will be by sheer good luck."

He spoke in tones of great contempt, and then he allowed it to be understood that it was all very well for the Mahés to risk their lives in that fash-

ion; it didn't so much matter when a man hadn't a copper to call his own; but, for his part, he would rather fail in his promise to M. Mouchel.

All this was said while Margot stood observing the rocks, behind which the *Whale* was supposed to be.

"Father," she said at last, "have they caught anything?"

"They!" he cried. "Not a thing!"

He restrained himself as he caught sight of the Emperor smiling in a jeering way, and then went on more softly: "I don't know whether they have caught anything or not; but as they never do catch anything—"

"Perhaps, though, they have caught something to-day," said the Emperor, maliciously. "Such things have happened before now."

La Queue was on the point of making an angry reply, but Abbé Radiguet came up at that moment, and succeeded in soothing him. He, the Abbé, had just seen the *Whale* from the kind of platform on which the church stood, and the boat seemed to be after some big fish. This news caused great excitement. The group on the beach included both Mahés and Floches; the former wishing that the boat might return with a marvellous catch, and the others praying that it might come in empty.

Margot was standing perfectly erect, attentively watching the sea.

"Here they are," she said quietly.

There was, indeed, a black speck coming round the point, towards which they all turned their eyes. It looked like a cork dancing on the water, and the Emperor, whose eyesight was failing, could not see even that much. It needed a native of Coqueville to recognise the *Whale* and its crew at such a distance.

"Why," cried Margot, who had the best eyes in the village, "Fouasse and Rouget are rowing, and the boy is standing in the bows."

She called Delphin "the boy," to avoid mentioning his name. After that, however, every one watched the boat and tried to account for its strange movements. As the priest had said, it appeared to be after some fish which had fled before it. That seemed extraordinary, but the Emperor declared that no doubt the fish had carried the net away with it. Thereupon La Queue exclaimed that they were idle rogues, and were only amusing themselves. They certainly were not fishing for seals! All the Floches laughed at this joke, while the Mahés, in their vexation, protested that Rouget was a plucky fellow, ever ready to risk his life, when others would rather make for land at the least capful of wind. Then Abbé Radiguet again had to interfere, for matters threatened to come to blows.

"What is the matter with them?" exclaimed Margot, suddenly. "They've gone off again."

Every one then ceased to menace his neighbour, and all eyes were turned to the horizon. The *Whale* was again hidden behind the point, and this time La Queue himself became uneasy. He could not account for such manœuvres, and the fear that Rouget was really catching some fish made him lose all control over himself.

No one left the beach, though there was nothing to be seen, and for two hours the group stood there waiting for the boat, which came just in sight from time to time, and then again disappeared. At last it did not reappear at all, and La Queue in his rage declared that it had gone to the bottom, really wishing that it might be so. As Rouget's wife happened to be there with Brisemotte, the mayor looked at them both with a chuckle, and patted Tupain on the shoulder to console him for the death of his brother Fouasse. But his laughter ceased when he saw his daughter Margot standing still and silent, gazing out to sea. Perhaps she was looking for Delphin.

"What are you doing here?" he scolded. "Get back to the house, Margot, and take care what you're up to."

She did not move, but suddenly exclaimed: "Ah! Here they are!"

There was a cry of surprise. Margot, who had such good eyes, vowed that she could not see a soul on board, neither Rouget, nor Fouasse, nor anybody! The *Whale* was running before the wind as if forsaken, tacking at every minute, and lazily rocking from side to side. Fortunately a westerly wind had arisen and was driving the boat towards land, though in a strange, capricious, zigzag fashion. Then all Coqueville came down on to the beach, some calling the others, until there was not a girl left in all the houses to look after the dinners. Some catastrophe had happened, something inexplicable, which turned everybody's head. Marie, Rouget's wife, thought she ought to burst into tears, and did so; Tupain only succeeded in putting on an air of sorrow. All the Mahés began lamenting, while the Floches tried to behave decorously. Margot had sat down as if her legs had given way under her.

"What are you up to now?" cried La Queue, when he found her under his feet.

"I am tired," she answered quietly.

And she turned her face towards the sea, her cheeks in her hands and her eyes peeping between the tips of her fingers towards the boat which was rocking still more lazily, like a good-tempered craft that has drunk too much.

Different suppositions were still forthcoming. Perhaps the three men had fallen into the water, only, in that case, it seemed odd that they should have all fallen in together. La Queue would have liked to make everyone believe that the *Whale* had gone to pieces like a rotten egg, but the boat was still floating, and people shrugged their shoulders at the mayor's words. Then suddenly the latter remembered that he was the mayor, and he spoke of the formalities that would have to be gone through, as if the men had really perished.

"Don't talk like that!" cried the Emperor. "Do people ever die in such a stupid, senseless fashion? Why, if they had fallen into the water, little Delphin would have been here by now."

All Coqueville was obliged to own that little Delphin swam like a fish. But then where could the three men be? There were cries of: "I tell you they are drowned!" "I tell you they're not!" "You are a big fool!" "Fool yourself!" and sundry blows were also exchanged.

Abbé Radiguet had to entreat his parishioners to refrain from quarreling, and the Emperor proceeded to restore order by pushing everybody about. All this while the boat was dancing on the waves in sight of them; the tide, which was bringing it in, making it salute the shore with a series of long, measured bows. The craft had certainly gone mad.

Margot was still sitting with her cheeks between her hands, watching it. A skiff had just put out from the harbour to go and meet the *Whale*. It was Brisemotte to whom this idea had occurred, for he was too impatient to wait any longer, and wanted to relieve the suspense of Rouget's wife. Then everyone's interest became centred in the smaller boat, and voices were raised once more. Well! could Brisemotte see anything? The *Whale* was still coming on, in its mysterious, facetious way, and at last, from the shore, they saw Brisemotte rise and look into the fishing-boat, one of the ropes of which he had caught hold of. All the people on the beach held their breath, but all at once Brisemotte burst out laughing. That was indeed a surprise; what could there be to amuse him?

"What is it? what is it?" shouted every one at the top of their voices.

He did not reply, but laughed still louder, and made signs to them that they would soon see for themselves what the matter was. Then, having fastened the *Whale* to his own boat, he towed it to land, and Coqueville was stupefied by a totally unexpected sight.

Rouget, Delphin, and Fouasse were lying on their backs at the bottom of the craft, snoring heavily, and dead drunk. Beside them there was a little barrel staved in, a barrel which they had found full, and the contents of which they had tasted. Whatever it had contained had no doubt been very good, for they had drunk every drop of it except about a pint which had run out, and which was now mixed with some sea-water in the boat.

"Oh, the pig!" cried Rouget's wife roughly, drying her eyes.

"Well, their catch is something to be proud of," said La Queue, affecting great disgust.

"Well!" replied the Emperor, "people catch what they can, and at any rate they have caught a barrel, while others have caught nothing at all."

The mayor was greatly put out, but he said no more. All Coqueville was talking; they understood it now. When boats are tipsy they reel about like men, and that one was indeed full of liquor. Half Coqueville thereupon laughed, and the other half gave way to ill-temper —the Mahés thinking the incident very droll, while the Floches deemed it disgusting. Both factions crowded round the *Whale,* their necks stretched out and their eyes wide open to look at those three jubilant-faced men, who slept calmly on, unconscious of the crowd leaning over them. The scolding and the laughter did not disturb them in the slightest degree; Rouget did not hear his wife accuse him of always drinking all that he could lay his hands on, and Fouasse did not feel the stealthy kicks which his brother Tupain was bestowing on his ribs. As for Delphin, he looked quite pretty when he was drunk, with his fair hair and pink face with its rapturous expression. Margot had risen to her feet, and silently contemplated the lad with an air of severity.

"They ought to be put to bed!" exclaimed somebody.

But at that very moment Delphin opened his eyes, and looked around. He was at once assailed with eager questions, which somewhat dazed him, for he was still very tipsy.

"Well, what's the matter?" he stammered. "It's a little cask—there's no fish, so we caught a little barrel."

That was all that could be got from him, and at the end of every sentence he added:

"It was very nice."

"But what was there in the barrel?"

"Oh, I don't know, but it was very nice."

Now, everyone was burning with curiosity as to what the liqueur might be, and every nose in Coqueville was sniffing at the boat. It was unanimously agreed that it smelt like some liqueur, only nobody could say what liqueur it was. The Emperor, who flattered himself that he had tasted everything possible for man to drink, said that he would soon see, and in the hollow of his hand he gravely scooped up a little of the liquid lying in the bottom of the boat. The crowd stood silently awaiting his verdict, but after the first mouthful he shook his head, as though he had not yet arrived at a conclusion. He tasted the stuff again twice, and became more and more embarrassed and surprised.

"It's funny, but I don't know what it is," he was forced to admit. "No doubt I should know if there weren't any sea-water mixed with it, but upon my word it's funny."

People looked at each other, for it must be something remarkable if the

Emperor himself could not say what it was. All Coqueville gazed at the little empty barrel with respect.

"It was very nice," said Delphin again, who seemed utterly regardless of the people around him.

Then, designating the sea with a broad wave of the hand, he added: "If you want any, there's some more left. I saw any number of little casks—little casks—little casks—"

And he rocked himself to and fro, humming this refrain, and gazing at Margot, whose presence he had only just noticed. She was furious, and raised her hand to give him a box on the ears, but he did not even close his eyes; he awaited the blow with a tender look on his face.

Puzzled as to what the unknown beverage might be, Abbé Radiguet also dipped his finger in the liquid, and then sucked it, but, like the Emperor, he shook his head; no, it was very astonishing, he could not tell what it might be. There was only one point on which every one was agreed, which was that the barrel must have been part of the cargo of the vessel in distress which had been seen on the Sunday evening. English ships often brought liqueurs and wines to Grandport.

The day gradually closed in, and, in the deepening shadows, the crowd withdrew. But La Queue, tormented by an idea he had not revealed, still stood thinking, and as they carried Delphin away he still seemed to hear the lad saying in his sing-song voice, "Little casks—little casks—little casks. If you want any there are plenty left."

## CHAPTER III

### THE WOLF

DURING the night there came a complete change in the weather, and Coqueville awoke the next morning to a bright sun, a sea as smooth as a huge piece of green satin, and a warm autumn day.

La Queue was the first to rise, his head still full of the dreams of the night. For a long time he gazed at the sea in all directions, and at last he said, with a grumble, that M. Mouchel's wants must after all be satisfied. Then he set off with Tupain and Brisemotte, threatening Margot before he went that he would give her a thrashing if she didn't keep straight. However, when the *Zephyr* had left the harbour, and he saw the *Whale* still swinging at anchor, he became a little better tempered, and cried:

"Ah, to-day we've got the start."

As soon as the *Zephyr* was well out at sea, La Queue dropped his nets overboard, and then went to visit his baskets, which he used more particularly to catch lobsters and red mullet. But, in spite of the calmness of the sea, he found every one empty except the last, at the bottom of which there was a tiny mackerel, which he threw back into the water in a passion. It was regular bad luck; there were weeks like that when every fish seemed to avoid Coqueville, and it was always during those very weeks that M. Mouchel wanted all that could be caught. La Queue swore roundly when, an hour later, he pulled up his nets and found they contained nothing but a bundle of sea-weed.

His anger was all the greater since the ocean was perfectly smooth and calm, and lay under the blue sky like a sheet of burnished silver. The *Zephyr* glided so smoothly over the water, that it hardly seemed to be moving at all, and La Queue decided to go back to shore after once more setting his baskets. He would visit them again in the afternoon, and, with awful oaths, he threatened to revenge himself on the Divinity and all the saints should he find them empty.

Meantime Rouget, Fouasse, and Delphin were still asleep, and no one was able to arouse them until just before the mid-day meal. They could remember nothing, being merely conscious that they had regaled themselves with something strange, with which they had previously been totally unacquainted. That afternoon, as they were all three standing near the water-side, having regained their senses, the Emperor tried to question them. Well, perhaps the stuff they had drunk had been like brandy with liquorice juice in it, or rather, it had resembled sugared rum with a burnt flavour about it. They said yes and no, and from their answers the Emperor suspected that the liqueur was ratafia, though he would not have sworn to it. Rouget and his men were all too tired and dazed that day to go fishing; besides, they knew that La Queue had caught nothing in the morning, and so they talked of waiting till the following day before visiting their own traps.

They were all three seated on the rocks half-asleep, and feeling queer from their debauch, when Delphin suddenly jumped to his feet, crying: "Look there, governor! Over there!"

"What?" asked Rouget, stretching his limbs.

"A barrel."

The words were hardly out of his mouth before Rouget and Fouasse were on their feet, scanning the horizon with eager glistening eyes.

"Where is it, lad? Where is the barrel?" asked Rouget, excitedly.

"Over yonder, to the left; that black spot."

At first the others could see nothing, then Rouget muttered an oath.

Amidst an oblique ray of the declining sun he had just seen the barrel, which looked about the size of a bean on the white water, and he at once hastened to the *Whale,* followed by Delphin and Fouasse, who rushed along as fast as their legs would carry them.

The *Whale* was just leaving the harbour when the news that there was a barrel in sight spread through Coqueville.

Men, women, and children ran down to the beach, crying:

"A barrel! a barrel!"

"Can you see it? Is the current carrying it to Grandport?"

"Oh, yes; there it is on the left. Come along, there's a barrel in sight."

And Coqueville hastened down from its rock; the children turning cartwheels on the way, while the women gathered up their petticoats with both hands to get along as quickly as possible. Soon, as on the previous evening, the whole village was on the beach.

Margot had come out for a moment, and had then hastened back to the house to communicate the news to her father, who was just then arguing with the Emperor about some municipal matters.

At last La Queue appeared upon the scene white with passion.

"Shut up, will you?" he exclaimed to the constable. "Rouget sent you to me to keep me out of the way, but you'll see that he won't get the cask this time."

When, however, he saw the *Whale* three hundred yards out at sea, rowing as hard as it could go towards the black speck in the distance, his rage increased, and, pushing Tupain and Brisemotte into the *Zephyr*, he in his turn put off, repeating: "No, they shan't have it. I'll go to the bottom first."

Then Coqueville had the pleasure of seeing an exciting race between the *Whale* and the *Zephyr*. When the former saw the other boat leave the harbour, she understood the danger and made off as quickly as she could go. She may have been about four hundred yards ahead, but the chances were equal, for the *Zephyr* was the lighter and the quicker craft, and thus the excitement on the beach reached a climax. The Mahés and the Floches instinctively formed into two groups, each member supporting his particular party's boat, while they all eagerly watched the struggle.

At first the *Whale* kept her advantage, but it was soon seen that the *Zephyr* was gradually gaining upon her. Thereupon she made a supreme effort and succeeded for some minutes in again maintaining her distance from her adversary; but again it was diminished, the *Zephyr* drawing near with marvellous rapidity. From that moment it became clear that the two boats would meet just as they both reached the barrel. The victory would depend on an accident, on the slightest mistake.

"The *Whale* wins! The *Whale* wins!" cried the Mahés.

But all at once their cries ceased. The *Whale* was almost touching the barrel, when the *Zephyr*, by a bold manœuvre, succeeded in passing before her and in throwing the barrel to the left, where La Queue harpooned it with a boat-hook.

"Hurrah for the *Zephyr!*" screamed the Floches.

The Emperor said something about cheating, while Margot clapped her hands, and harsh words were exchanged, but Abbé Radiguet, who had come down to the beach, breviary in hand, suddenly quieted his parishioners, throwing them all into a state of consternation by a remark of great profundity.

"Perhaps they'll drink it all up like the others did," he said with a melancholy look.

Meantime out at sea a violent quarrel was raging between the *Whale* and the *Zephyr*. Rouget stigmatised La Queue as a thief, and the latter retorted by calling the master of the *Whale* a scoundrel. The men even took up their oars to strike one another, and the adventure was within an ace of becoming a naval battle. However, they finally contented themselves with shaking their fists and oars, and threatening to knock all the breath out of one another's bodies the first time they met on land.

"The rogue!" muttered Rouget. "That cask's bigger than the one we caught yesterday, and it's painted yellow. There must be some capital stuff inside it."

Then he resumed despondently: "Let's go and look at the traps. Perhaps we shall find some lobsters in them."

The *Whale* then went off heavily towards the little promontory on the left.

On board the *Zephyr* La Queue had to exert all his authority to keep Tupain and Brisemotte from the barrel. The boat-hook had broken one of its hoops, and a red liquid was oozing out, which the two men licked off the tips of their fingers and thought delicious. One glass wouldn't make much difference, surely, said they; but La Queue wouldn't hear of it. He stood the cask on end, and declared that the first who touched it would have to deal with him. He would see about giving them some when they had landed.

"Well then," asked Tupain, sulkily, "are we going to take up the traps?"

"Yes, by-and-by. There's no hurry," answered La Queue.

He himself was looking longingly at the barrel, and he wanted to go back at once to taste its contents; fishing bothered him.

"Bah!" he said after a pause. "It's getting late, and we had better go back. We'll come again tomorrow."

They had turned round, giving up all idea of fishing, when suddenly he caught sight of another barrel on his right—a tiny one, which was floating on end, and turning round and round. That settled the question of looking after the nets and baskets. Not a word was said, but the *Zephyr* gave chase to the little cask, which it easily captured.

Meanwhile a similar thing had happened to the *Whale*. Rouget had already visited five traps, and found them empty, when Delphin, always on the alert, cried out that he could see something, but it looked too long to be a barrel.

"It's a beam of wood," said Fouasse.

Rouget let his sixth lobster-trap drop back before he had quite lifted it out of the water.

"Well, we'll go and see what it is, at any rate," he replied.

As they advanced, they thought it a plank, a chest, or the trunk of a tree. Then they uttered a cry of delight. It was a cask, but a cask such as they had never seen before. It looked like a pipe swollen in the middle and closed at both ends by a layer of plaster.

"Oh, isn't it funny?" cried Rouget in delight. "I want the Emperor to taste this one, so let's go in, boys."

They all agreed that they would not touch it, and the *Whale* returned to Coqueville at the very moment when the *Zephyr* was anchoring in the little harbour. Not one of the inquisitive crowd had left the beach, and this unexpected catch of three barrels was hailed with shouts of joy. Boys threw their caps into the air, and the women ran off to get glasses. It was at once decided to taste the liqueurs then and there; all wreckage belonged to the whole village, so that no question of proprietorship was raised, but two groups were formed, the Mahés surrounding Rouget, while the Floches never quitted La Queue.

"The first glass is for you, Emperor," cried Rouget. "Tell us what it is."

The fluid was of a bright golden colour, and the constable raised the glass, looked, smelt, and finally decided to drink.

"That comes from Holland," he said, after a long silence.

He added no other information, but all the Mahés drank reverentially. The liqueur was rather thick, and had a flowery taste which surprised them. The women thought it very nice, but the men would have liked it better if it had not been so sweet. However, the more they drank of it the more they appreciated it, and at the third or fourth glass the men began to get merry, and the women funny.

In spite of his recent quarrel with the mayor, the Emperor now went and hung round the Floches. The larger barrel gave forth a dark red liquid, while from the smaller one there came a stream as white as spring water, and so strong and peppery that it burnt the tongue. Not one of the Floches knew what either the red or the white liquid might be, and yet there were some knowing ones among them. It vexed them not to know the name of what they were enjoying.

"Here, Emperor, taste that," said La Queue at last, thus making the first advance.

The Emperor, who was waiting for the invitation, again posed as a connoisseur.

"There is orange in that," he said, when he had tasted the red drink. The white he declared to be tip-top stuff.

Every one had to be contented with these answers, for he put on the happy look of a man who has fully satisfied his audience. Abbé Radiguet was the only person who did not seem convinced; he wanted to know the names. According to his own account, he had those names on the tip of his tongue but could not recall them. To help his memory, he drank several glasses one after the other, saying as he did so: "Wait a minute, I know what it is. I shall be able to tell you presently."

Meantime the two groups were gradually getting very merry. The Floches, especially, were very gay, for they were mixing the liqueurs. Both Floches and Mahés kept entirely to themselves and their own barrels, merely casting longing glances at each other, from time to time, for they felt a desire which they would not confess, which was to taste their neighbours' drink, as no doubt it was better than their own. The two hostile brothers, Tupain and Fouasse, stood near each other the whole evening without even shaking their fists, and it was also remarked that Rouget and his wife were drinking out of the same cup. As for Margot, she served the drink to the Floches, and, as she filled the glasses too full and the liqueur ran over her hands, she was constantly sucking her fingers until at last, although obeying her father's injunctions not to drink, she became as intoxicated as a woman vintaging. It rather improved her than otherwise, for her face became a rosy pink, and her eyes shone like candles.

The sun set, but the evening proved mild and spring-like. Coqueville had emptied its casks, and yet it did not think of going in to dinner. It was so pleasant on the beach. When it grew dark, Margot, who sat apart from the others, felt someone breathing on her neck. It was Delphin, who, feeling very lively, was prowling about behind her, like a wolf. She stifled an exclamation so as not to rouse her father, who would have kicked him away if he had seen him.

"Be off, you idiot!" she whispered, half angry, half laughing. "You'll be caught if you don't!"

## CHAPTER IV

### THE SEVENTH DAY

COQUEVILLE did not awake on the following day until the sun was well above the horizon. It was warmer even than before, and the sea lay dozing under a cloudless sky; in fact, it was just the sort of day when most pleasure is to be found in remaining absolutely idle.

Until lunch-time Coqueville rested after the treat of the evening before; then everyone went down to the beach to keep a look-out, and that Wednesday, fishing, Madame Dufeu, and M. Mouchel were all forgotten. La Queue and Rouget did not even speak of going to pull up their baskets. About three o'clock some casks were sighted. Four were dancing on the waves opposite the village, whereupon both the *Zephyr* and the *Whale* gave chase; but there was no dispute, as there was enough liquor for all, and each boat had its share.

After scouring the little gulf, Rouget and La Queue came back at six o'clock with three barrels each, and once again the festival began. The women carried out some tables, to be more comfortable; then seats were brought and two open-air *cafés*, such as there are at Grand-port, were at once established. The Mahés remained on the left and the Floches on the right, and between them there was a heap of sand. That evening, however, the Emperor went from one group to the other with full glasses

in his hands, so that everybody might taste the contents of all six barrels. By nine o'clock the scene was even gayer than on the previous evening; and the next day, try as it would, Coqueville could not remember how it had managed to get to bed.

On the Thursday, the *Zephyr* and the *Whale* only took two barrels apiece, but those were huge ones. On Friday, the catch was superb and quite surpassed everybody's hopes; seven barrels were brought to land, three by Rouget and four by La Queue. Then came golden hours for Coqueville. Nobody did any work. The fishermen lay in bed till noon, sleeping off their potations, and then sauntered down to the shore and gazed at the sea. Their only anxiety was as to the kind of liqueur which the tide might bring them, and they stood on the sand for hours giving shouts of delight as soon as any wreckage appeared. The women and children, perched on the tops of the rocks, pointed out everything floating on the water, even to the smallest bundle of seaweed, and the *Zephyr* and the *Whale* were always kept in readiness to go out to sea. They set off, tacked about the gulf, fishing for casks as they might have fished for tunny, quite despising the mackerel, which leapt in the sunlight, and the soles, which floated lazily along on the surface of the water. Coqueville meantime watched the fishers from the shore, and burst its sides with laughing; then, in the evening, the catch was drunk.

What delighted Coqueville most was that the supply of casks did not cease. The wrecked vessel must have had a large cargo, and Coqueville, now selfish and gay, joked about the lost ship, which had been, folks said, a regular wine-cellar, containing enough liquor to intoxicate all the fish in the sea. They never caught two barrels alike; the casks were of all shapes, sizes, and colours, and each contained a different liquid. The Emperor fell into profound reveries—he, who had drunk everything, could no longer give an opinion; and La Queue himself declared he had never seen such a cargo. Abbé Radiguet believed it had been destined for some savage king, who had wished to stock his cellar; but the rest of Coqueville no longer troubled to find out what it was that they were drinking.

The elder ladies preferred the liqueurs flavoured with mocha, peppermint, and vanilla; and Marie Rouget drank so much aniseed one evening that she became quite ill. Margot and the other young ladies devoted themselves to curaçoa, Bénédictine, Trappistine, and Chartreuse, while the cassis was given to the children. The men were naturally most pleased when the catch included cognac, rum, or gin. A barrel of raki from Chio stupefied Coqueville, for it thought that it had got hold of a cask of turpentine. Of course it was drunk, because it is not right to waste anything; still it was talked about for a long time. Batavian "arrack," Swedish brandy flavoured with cumin, Roumanian "tuica calugaresca," Servian "sliwowitz," also upset Coquevillian ideas about what was fit to drink. At bottom was a general leaning towards kümmel and kirsch, liqueurs clear as water and strong enough to kill a man. How could so many good things have been invented? At Coqueville. brandy had been

the only spirit known, and all the inhabitants were not even acquainted with that. A veritable worship for the inexhaustible variety of intoxicants began to spring up. Oh, to get drunk every evening on something different, of which even the name was unknown! It all seemed like a fairy tale, in which there was a magic fountain spouting forth strange alcoholic fluids, perfumed and flavoured with all the flowers and fruits in creation.

As has been said already, there were seven barrels on the shore on Friday evening. Coqueville now simply lived there, and, thanks to the mildness of the weather, it could do so with comfort. Never had there been so fine a week in September. The feast had lasted since Monday, and there was no reason why it should not last for ever, if only Providence (for in this affair Abbé Radiquet discerned the hand of Providence) would continue to send them casks. All work was suspended, and everybody for the time being became a gentleman, a gentleman who drank expensive liqueurs without having to pay for them. Coqueville idly thrust its hands in its pockets and basked in the sun, while waiting for the evening carouse. Besides, it was never sober. One after another it tried the delights of kümmel, kirsch, and ratafia. In the course of a week it experienced the anger born of gin, the soft-heartedness coming from curaçoa, and the laughter formented by cognac. And withal Coqueville retained the innocent ways of a new-born child, knowing nothing about any thing, but thankfully drinking whatever heaven sent it.

It was on the Friday that the Mahés

and the Floches at last fraternised. Every one was very merry that evening, and even on the night before the distance between the two groups had been lessened, for the more intoxicated among them had trodden down the heap of sand, and there was now only about a foot of it left between the two parties. The Floches were emptying their four casks, while the Mahés were making an end of three little barrels of liqueurs, the colours of which happened to be the same as those of the French flag—red, white, and blue. The Floches were filled with envy and jealousy whenever they saw the blue liqueur, for the blueness seemed to them something wonderful; and at last La Queue, who had turned quite good-natured now that he was never sober, came forward, glass in hand, thinking that it was his place as mayor to make the first advances.

"I say, Rouget," he stuttered, "will you drink with me?"

"Certainly," replied Rouget, whose emotion made him reel.

They fell on each other's necks, and everybody wept, the scene was so touching! Then the Mahés and the Floches, who had been ready to devour each other for the last three hundred years, kissed and shook each other by the hand; and Abbé Radiguet, who was very much affected, again spoke of the hand of Providence. Finally, they all toasted one another in the red, white, and blue liqueurs, and the Emperor cried, "Here's to France!"

The blue was not up to much, and the white was hardly any better, but the red was really first-rate. The Floches' barrels were next attacked, and then a dance was got up. As there was no music, some of the young fellows whistled and clapped their hands to keep time, and the girls danced with spirit. The spree was really assuming magnificent proportions. The seven casks were placed side by side, and everyone took what he liked best. Those who had had enough lay down on the sand and slept for a time, and when they woke up feeling parched they began to drink again. Meantime the number of dancers increased, and the ball was continued until midnight. The waves broke on the beach with a faint murmur, the stars shone in the deep blue sky—it was like the peacefulness of a newly-created world around a tribe of savages intoxicated by their first draught of brandy.

However, when there was nothing left to drink, Coqueville at last went indoors, Floches and Mahés helping one another to the best of their ability, and ending by somehow finding their beds.

On the Saturady, the spree was kept till nearly two o'clock in the morning. Six casks, two of which were huge ones, had been caught that day, and during the evening Fouasse and Tupain almost came to blows. Tupain, who was very bad-tempered when he got drunk, talked of making an end of his brother, but this quarrel shocked everybody—Floches as well as Mahés. Was there any sense in still disagreeing when the whole village had embraced and forgotten old scores? The two brothers were forced to drink together, and, as they still looked sulky, the Emperor determined to keep his eye on them. However, the Rougets did not get on very well together either. When Marie had drunk some anisette liqueur, she behaved towards Brisemotte in a manner which Rouget was unable to witness unmoved; besides, drink made him affectionate, and he wanted to be loved himself. It was in vain that Abbé Radiguet exhorted them to forgive all injuries; an accident was feared.

"Bah!" said La Queue, "you'll see, they'll make it up if there's a good catch to-morrow. Your health!"

But La Queue himself was not perfect. He still kept a watch on Delphin, and whenever he saw him near Margot he gave him a kick. This made the Emperor very indignant, for it was not reasonable to prevent two young people from laughing together; but La Queue still swore that he would kill Margot rather than give her to the boy. Besides, Margot herself did not want him.

"You don't, do you? You are too proud to marry a beggar, aren't you?" he cried.

"Yes, papa," answered Margot.

On Saturday, Margot drank a great deal of some syrupy liqueur. Nothing so sweet could be imagined, and, as she had no idea of the strength of the beverage, she soon found herself seated on the ground beside the cask. She remained laughing to herself, for she felt as if she were in paradise; she could see stars around her, and it seemed as if dance-music were being played inside her head. While she was in this state Delphin slipped into the shadow cast by the barrels, and, taking her hand, asked: "Tell me, Margot, will you?"

She still smiled and finally answered: "It's papa who won't hear of it."

"Oh, that doesn't matter," said the lad. "Old people, you know, are always against it; but if you are willing——"

And, getting bolder, he dropped a kiss on her neck. She drew up her head, but a little shiver ran down her back.

"Have done! You tickle me," she exclaimed.

However, she no longer said anything about boxing his ears; in the first place, because she would not have been able to do so, her hands felt so lazy, and, secondly, because it seemed nice to her to have her neck kissed. It made her feel deliciously drowsy, like the liqueurs, and after a time she began moving her head, and holding out her chin, like a cat who wants to be caressed.

"There, just under the ear," she murmured. "Oh, it's lovely!"

They both forgot La Queue, but fortunately, the Emperor was on the watch. "Look there, your reverence," he said, pointing them out to Abbé Radiguet. "It would be better to marry them."

"It certainly would," answered the priest.

And he undertook to speak to La Queue on the subject the very next day. In the meantime, La Queue had drunk so much that the Emperor and the priest had to carry him home. On the way they tried to talk to him about his daughter, but they could get nothing from him but a grunt. Behind them walked Delphin, with Margot on his arm.

By four o'clock the next day the *Zephyr* and the *Whale* had hooked up seven barrels; by six o'clock the *Zephyr* had found two more, which made nine altogether, and so Coqueville had a merry Sunday. It was the seventh day running that it had got drunk. And the spree was perfect—such a spree as had never been seen before, and would never be seen again. Just mention it in Lower Normandy, and people will answer you with a laugh: "Ah, yes! We know all about the spree at Coqueville."

## CHAPTER V

### THE ENDING

WHEN Tuesday had gone by, M. Mouchel was very much astonished to see neither Rouget nor La Queue arrive at Grandport. What could the rascals be thinking of? The sea was calm, and the catch must have been enormous; perhaps, though, they wanted to bring a big cargo of lobsters and soles all at once, and so he patiently waited until Wednesday.

That day M. Mouchel began to get angry. It must be stated that Madame Dufeu was not a good-tempered woman; at the least thing she flew into a rage, and although Mouchel was a big, strong, handsome fellow, he trembled before her—all the more as he aimed at marrying her later on, and was always on the alert to anticipate and gratify her wishes, meaning to make up for his present life if he ever became the master. Now, on the Wednesday morning, Madame Dufeu stormed and complained that they were missing the market for want of fish, and she accused Mouchel of running after girls, instead of giving his attention to whiting and mackerel, which they ought to have had in abundance. Thereupon M. Mouchel, in his vexation, shielded himself behind the strange failure of the Coqueville fishers. For a moment, surprise struck Madame Dufeu dumb. What could Coqueville be dreaming about? It had

never done such a thing before. Then she declared that she didn't care about Coqueville; that it was M. Mouchel's business to look after the supply, and that she would do so herself if he allowed the fisherman to play the fool with him again. Mouchel heartily wished Rouget and La Queue at the devil; but perhaps, after all, they would come on the morrow.

But on the next day, which was Thursday, neither one nor the other appeared; and M. Mouchel, in despair, went up in the evening to the rocks on the left of Grandport, whence Coqueville and its stretch of yellow sand can be seen. For a long time he gazed. The village seemed perfectly quiet; smoke was ascending from the chimneys, and no doubt the women were getting their dinners ready as usual. When M. Mouchel had ascertained that Coqueville still existed, and that no rock from the cliff had fallen and crushed it, he felt more puzzled than ever. However, just as he was about to go down again, he thought he discerned two black specks in the bay—the *Whale* and the *Zephyr* —whereupon he returned to soothe Madame Dufeu. It was all right, Coqueville was fishing.

The night passed, however, and Friday dawned, but still no news came from Coqueville. M. Mouchel climbed up on the rock a dozen times. He was beginning to lose his head. Madame Dufeu treated him shamefully, and he could find nothing to say to her. Coqueville still lay basking in the sun, like a lazy lizard, only there was no longer any smoke. The village seemed dead; could all the inhabitants have perished without any one knowing of it? There was, indeed, a black mass moving on the shore; but that might be seaweed thrown up by the waves.

No news on Saturday. Madame Dufeu no longer stormed, but her eyes were fixed and her lips white. M. Mouchel stayed two hours on the rock, feeling an ever-increasing desire to find out for himself the why and wherefore of the village's strange stillness. Those houses, sleeping so quietly in the sunlight, irritated him, and he made up his mind to start off very early on Monday morning, so as to reach Coqueville by nine o'clock.

The village was not within walking distance, but M. Mouchel preferred to go by land so that he might catch it unawares. A vehicle took him to Robigneux, where he left it under a shed, for it would have been dangerous to take it through the ravines. Then he cheerfully set off to walk some seven miles along the most abominable roads imaginable, though they are surrounded by a landscape full of wild beauty. The path—so narrow, that in places three men could not walk abreast—goes winding down between enormous walls of rock; then a little further on it skirts precipices; then the ravine suddenly widens, and through the opening one catches glimpses of the sea. But M. Mouchel was in no mood to admire scenery, and he only swore when the pebbles rolled away from beneath his feet. It was all Coqueville's fault, and he promised himself to call those vagabonds to account! However, while he pondered, he had drawn near the end of his journey, and suddenly as he turned round the last rock he saw the twenty houses of the village perched on the side of the cliff.

Nine o'clock was striking. It might have been June, the sky was so blue and clear; it was a magnificent day indeed, and there was a soft breeze, which brought with it a pleasant smell of the sea. M. Mouchel turned down the one street which the village possessed, and along which he had so often previously walked, and as he passed Rouget's house he looked in. It was empty. Then he went to Fouasse's, Tupain's, and Brisemotte's. Not a soul was to be found; all the doors were open, but there was nobody in the rooms. What did it mean? A slight shiver ran through him. Then he thought of the authorities; the Emperor would surely be able to tell what had happened.

But the Emperor's house was empty, like the others! Even the constable was missing! The deserted village frightened M. Mouchel now. He ran to the mayor's, but there another surprise awaited him; everything was in a terrible litter, the beds had evidently not been made for three days past, dirty china was lying about and chairs were overturned, as though there had been a fight. M. Mouchel felt thoroughly upset, but he determined to go on to the end, and accordingly visited the church. But there was no priest to be found any more than any mayor. All the authorities, both civil and religious, had disappeared, and Coqueville was utterly forsaken; there was not even a dog, or a cat, or a fowl about the place. Only emptiness, silence, and slumber remained under the vast blue sky.

It was not astonishing, then, that Coqueville had not brought any fish!

Coqueville had removed, Coqueville was dead, and the police must be informed. M. Mouchel was working himself into a state of great excitement over this mysterious catastrophe, when he thought of going down to the shore, and at the sight he saw there he uttered a cry of amazement. The entire population of the village was lying on the sands. At first he thought there had been a general massacre, but the deep snores he heard soon undeceived him. Coqueville had kept up the spree so late on Sunday night that it had found it impossible to go to bed; so it had slept on the seashore, lying just where it had fallen round the nine barrels, which were quite empty!

Yes, all Coqueville was snoring there —men, women, old folks, and children. Some were on their backs, others on their stomachs, not one was on his feet. They lay about like leaves scattered by the wind.

The moon, it so happened, had been a new one, and Coqueville, thinking it had blown out its candle, had fallen asleep in the dark. Then day had dawned, and now the sun was shining full on the sleepers' faces, though their eyelids did not even quiver. They were sleeping soundly with a happy expression, in the utter innocence of fuddle. The fowls must have come down early in the morning and pecked at the barrels, for they, too, were lying in the sand, drunk; and there were even five cats and three dogs on their backs, with their paws in the air, tipsy, from having licked the syrup remaining in the glasses.

For a few minutes M. Mouchel walked amidst those sleepers, taking care to tread on nobody. He understood what had happened, for some casks from the wreck of an English vessel had also been washed up at Grandport. All his anger evaporated. What a touching and moral spectacle lay before him! Coqueville reconciled! The Mahés and the Floches lying side by side! For at the last glass the bitterest enemies had embraced one another. Tupain and Fouasse were snoring hand in hand, like brothers incapable of ever again disputing over an inheritance, and the Rouget household formed a most amiable picture, for Marie was sleeping between Rouget and Brisemotte, as if to indicate that henceforth they would all live happily together.

But one group in particular supplied a touching scene of family affection: Delphin and Margot were lying with their arms round one another's necks; at their feet the Emperor was stretched, as if watching over their security; then just above them La Queue snored away like a father well pleased at having settled his daughter's future; while Abbé Radiguet, who had dropped like the others, lay with outstretched arms as though to bless them all.

The spree ended by a wedding a little later on, and M. Mouchel himself married Madame Dufeu, whom he then beat unmercifully. Just mention the affair in Lower Normandy, and people will answer with a laugh: "Oh, yes! We know all about the spree at Coqueville."

# Naïs Micoulin

## CHAPTER I

### NAÏS

DURING the fruit season a brown-skinned little girl with bushy black hair used to come every month to the house of Monsieur Rostand, a lawyer of Aix, in Provence, bringing with her a huge basket of apricots or peaches, so heavy that she had hardly strength enough to carry it. She would wait in the large entrance-hall, whither all the family went to greet her.

"So it's you, Naïs," the lawyer would say. "You've brought us some fruit, eh? Come, you're a good girl. And how is your father?"

"Quite well, sir," replied the little girl, showing her white teeth.

Then Madame Rostand would take her into the kitchen and ask her about the olives, the almonds, and the vines. But the most important question was whether there had been any rain at L'Estaque, where the Rostands' estate was situated, a place called La Blancarde, which was cultivated by the Micoulins. There were but a few dozen almond and olive trees, but the question of rain was none the less an important one in this province, where everything perishes from drought.

"There have been a few drops," Naïs would say. "The vines want more."

Then, having imparted her news, she ate a piece of bread and some scraps of meat, and set out again for L'Estaque in a butcher's cart which came to Aix every fortnight. Frequently she brought some shell-fish, a lobster, a fine eel, for Micoulin fished more than he tilled the ground. When she came during the holidays, Frédéric, the lawyer's son, used to rush into the kitchen to tell her that the family would soon take up their quarters at La Blancarde, and that she must get some nets and lines ready. He was almost like a brother to her. for they had played together as children. Since the age of twelve, however, she had called him "Monsieur Frédéric," out of respect. Every time old Micoulin heard her speak familiarly to the young man he boxed her ears, but in spite of this the two children were sworn allies.

"Don't forget to mend the nets," repeated the schoolboy.

"No fear, Monsieur Frédéric," replied Naïs. "They'll be ready for you."

Monsieur Rostand was very wealthy. He had bought a splendid seignorial mansion in the Rue du Collège at a very low price. The Hôtel de Coiron, built during the latter part of the seventeenth century, had twelve windows in its frontage, and contained enough rooms to house a religious order. Amid those vast rooms the family, consisting of five persons, including the two old servants, seemed lost. The lawyer occupied merely the first floor. For ten years he had tried, without success, to let the ground and second floors, and finally he had decided to lock them up, thus abandoning two-thirds of the house to the spiders. Echoes like those of a cathedral resounded through the empty sonorous mansion at the least noise in the entrance-hall, an enormous hall with a staircase from which one could easily have obtained sufficient material to build a modern dwelling.

Immediately after his purchase, Monsieur Rostand had divided the grand drawing-room into two offices, by means of a partition. It was a room thirty-six feet long by twenty-four broad, lighted by six windows. Of one of the two parts he had formed his own private room, the other being allotted to his clerks. The first floor contained four other apartments, the smallest of which measured twenty feet by fifteen. Madame Rostand, Frédéric, and the two old servants had bedrooms as lofty as churches. The lawyer had been forced, for convenience's sake, to convert an old boudoir into a kitchen; for at an earlier stage, when they had made use of the kitchen on the ground floor, the food, after passing through the chilly atmosphere of the entrance-hall and staircase, had come to table quite cold. To make matters worse, the gigantic apartments were furnished in the most sparing manner. In the lawyer's private room an ancient suite of furniture, upholstered in green Utrecht velvet, and of the stiff and comfortless-looking Empire style, did its best to fill up the space, with its sofa and eight chairs; a little round table, belonging to the same period, looked like a toy in that immensity; on the chimney-piece there was nothing beyond a horrible modern marble clock between two vases, whilst the tiled floor, looking much the worse for age, showed a dirty red. The bedrooms were more empty still. The whole house brought home to one the tranquil disdain which Southern families—even the richest of them—display for comfort

and luxury, in that happy land of the sun, where life is mainly spent out of doors. The Rostands were certainly not conscious of the sad, mortal chilliness which brooded over those huge rooms, mainly though the scantiness and poverty-stricken aspect of the furniture.

Yet the lawyer was a shrewd man. His father had left him one of the best practices in Aix, and he had managed to improve it considerably by displaying an amount of activity rare in that land of indolence. Small, brisk, weasel-faced, his sole thought was of his work. No other matters troubled his brain; he never even looked at a paper during the rare hours of idleness he spent at his club. His wife, on the contrary, had the reputation of being one of the cleverest and most accomplished women in the town. She was a De Villebonne, a fact which invested her with a certain amount of dignity, in spite of her *mésalliance*. But she was strait-laced to such a point, she practised her religious duties with such bigoted fortitude, that she had, as it were, become shrivelled up by the methodical life she led.

As for Frédéric, he grew up between his busy father and rigid mother. During his schoolboy days he was a dunce of the first water, trembling before his mother, but having such a distaste for work that he would often sit in the drawing-room during the evening poring for hours over his books without reading a single line, his mind wandering, whilst his parents imagined from the look of him that he was preparing his lessons. Irritated by his laziness, they put him to board at the college; but he then worked less than ever, being less looked after than at home, and delighted to feel that he was no longer under his parents' stern eyes. Accordingly, alarmed by the airs of liberty which he put on, they took him away, in order to have him under their ferule again. So narrowly did they look after him that he was forced to work: his mother examined his exercises, made him repeat his lessons, and mounted guard over him unremittingly like a gendarme. Thanks to this supervision, Frédéric failed but twice in passing the examination for his degree.

Aix is celebrated for its law school, and young Rostand was naturally sent to it. In that ancient town the population is largely composed of barristers, notaries, and solicitors practicing at the Appeals Court. A youth takes a law degree as a matter of course, following it up or not as he pleases. So Frédéric remained at the college, working as little as possible, but trying to make his parents believe that he was working a great deal. Madame Rostand, to her great sorrow, had been forced to give him more liberty. He now went out when he chose in the daytime, and was only expected to be at home to meals. He had, however, to be in by nine o'clock in the evening, except on those days when he was allowed to go to the theatre. Thus began that country student's life, so full of vice when it is not entirely devoted to work.

A person must know Aix, be acquainted with the quiet grass-grown streets, the state of torpor which enwraps the whole town, in order to understand the purposeless life which the students lead there. Those who work can manage to kill time over their books; but those who refuse to exert themselves steadily have no other places where they can while away their leisure save the cafés and other resorts, where people gamble and drink, and call it "seeing life." Thus Frédéric soon became an inveterate gambler: he passed the greater part of his evenings at cards, and finished them elsewhere. When he found his evenings too short for him he managed, by stealing a key of the house door, to have all night as well. In this way his years of probation passed pleasantly enough.

Frédéric had sense enough to see that he must play the part of a tractable son. The hypocrisy of a child curbed by fear had little by little grown upon him. His mother now declared herself satisfied; he took her to church, behaved most properly with her, told her with the greatest calmness the most unheard-of lies, which she believed, thanks to his air of candour. And so clever did he become in this respect that he never allowed himself to be outwitted, being always ready with an excuse, always prepared in advance with the most extraordinary stories in support of his statements. He paid his gaming debts with money borrowed from his cousins, and his pecuniary transactions would have filled a book. Once, after an unhoped-for stroke of good luck, he was able to turn a dream he had of spending a week in Paris into reality, by getting himself invited thither by a friend who had a little estate near the Durance.

Frédéric was a fine young fellow, tall, with regular features, and a black beard. His vices made him good company, especially with ladies. He was quoted for his good manners. Those who knew his goings on smiled a little, but, as he had the sense to throw a veil over this side of his life, he came in for a certain amount of credit for not making an exhibition of his excesses, as did other students who were the scandal of the town.

Frédéric was nearly twenty-one, and was soon to pass his last examination. His father, who was still young and not inclined as yet to hand his pratice over to him, talked of making him enter the magistrature to begin with. He had friends in Paris to whom he could apply to get him an appointment as public prosecutor's assessor. The young man raised no objection; for he never openly opposed his parents; but a certain expressive smile on his face betokened his firm determination to prolong the pleasant existence which suited him so well. He knew that his father was rich, that he was his only son, so why should he trouble himself? In the meantime he smoked his cigar on the Promenade, gambled in the neighbouring cafés, and paid his attentions to a variety of damsels, though all this did not prevent him from holding himself at his mother's orders, and loading her with attentions. At times when he felt out of sorts he stayed at home in the huge gloomy mansion in the Rue du Collège, and enjoyed delicious repose. The emptiness of the rooms, the sense of constraint perceptible on every side, seemed to him to possess a soothing influence. There he collected himself afresh, making his mother believe that he was stopping at home for her sake, until the day when, health and appetite having returned, he devised some fresh escapade. In one word, he was the best fellow in the world, so long as his pleasures were not interfered with.

Every year, however, Naïs came to the Rostands with her fish and fruit, and every year she grew. She was of the same age as Frédéric, or, to be correct, she was just three months older. Madame Rostand would often say to her:

"What a big girl you are growing, Naïs!"

And Naïs would smile, showing her white teeth. As a rule, Frédéric was not there; but one day, during the last year of his probation, he was going out, when he found Naïs standing in the hall with her basket. He stopped short in astonishment. He did not recognise the girl, though he had seen her only the year before at La Blancarde. Naïs looking superb, with her dark face beneath a swarthy covering of thick black hair, her broad shoulders, her supple waist, and her magnificent arms, of which the bare wrists were exposed. In a single year she had grown like a young tree.

"You!" said he, in hesitating voice.

"Yes, Monsieur Frédéric," replied Naïs, looking him in the face with her big eyes, in which a sombre fire smouldered. "I've brought some sea-urchins. When are you coming? Shall I get the nets ready?"

He was still looking at her, and muttering, as if he had not heard her speak: "How handsome you are, Naïs! What is there in you?"

The compliment made her smile. Then, as he took her hands playfully, as he had done in the days gone by, she became serious, and said in a hoarse whisper: "No, no; not here. Take care! here comes your mother."

## CHAPTER II

### FRÈDÈRIC

A FORTNIGHT later the Rostand family started for La Blancarde. The lawyer had to rest during the vacation, and September was a charming month at the seaside. The great heat was past, and the nights were deliciously cool.

La Blancarde was not actually in L'Estaque, a village situated on the extreme outskirts of Marseilles, and nestling among the rocks which bound the bay. The house was built on a cliff overlooking the village, and its yellow walls, glistening amongst the pines, could be seen from any part of the bay. It was one of those heavy square buildings, pierced with irregular windows, and called "châteaux" in Provence. In front of the house a broad terrace extended, rising almost perpendicularly above the pebbly beach. Behind, there was a vast enclosure of poor land, upon which nothing but a few vines, almond or olive trees would grow. One of the inconveniences, indeed, one of the dangers, of La Blancarde was the fact that the sea was gradually eating away the cliff; infiltrations, proceeding from neighbouring springs, were constantly at work in that softening mountain of clay and rock; and every year enormous masses fell away, being precipitated with a deafening crash into the sea. The property was thus becoming smaller and smaller; the pines had already begun to fall.

The Micoulins had been settled at La Blancarde for forty years. According to the Provençal custom, they cultivated the land and shared the crops with the landlord. These crops were scanty, and they would have died of starvation if, during the summer, they had not turned their attention to the sea. Between tilling and sowing there came an interval of fishing. The family consisted of Micoulin, a stern old man, with a black and seamy face, before whom the others trembled; of his wife, a tall woman, whose intellect was dulled by hard toil in the blazing sun; of a son, who at that time was serving on board the *Arrogant*, man-of-war; and of Naïs, whom her father, in spite of her numerous tasks at home, sent to work at a tile manufactory. Rarely did the sound of a laugh or a song enliven the tenants' dwelling, a hovel built against one of the sides of La Blancarde. Micoulin, buried in his reflections, preserved gloomy silence. The two women exhibited towards him that cringing respect which Southern wives and daughters always display for the head of the family. It was not often that silence was broken, except it were by the mother's calls, as she stood with her hands on her hips, her throat ready to burst, shouting out the name of Naïs whenever her daughter disappeared. Naïs heard her a mile away, and returned home pale with stifled anger.

The handsome Naïs, as they call her at L'Estaque, was by no means happy. At the age of sixteen, Micoulin, on the slightest provocation, would strike her so roughly in the face as to make the blood fly from her nose; and even now, in spite of her twenty years, her bruised shoulders bore the marks of her father's brutality for weeks together. Not that he was cruel; he simply exercised a rigorous rule, insisting on implicit obedience, having in his blood the old Roman feeling of authority over his own family—the authority of life and death. One day Naïs, on being unmercifully thrashed, dared to raise her hand to defend herself, and her father came near killing her. After a correction of this kind, the girl would throw herself trembling into a dark corner, and, with dry eyes, brood over the insult. Black rage would hold her there mute for hours together, gloating over revenge, which lay beyond her power. It was her father's blood which rose within her —his blind passion, his furious determination to be the master. When she saw her trembling and submissive mother humble herself before Micoulin, she looked at her with scorn. She would often say, "If I'd a husband like that, I'd kill him."

And yet Naïs preferred those days when she was beaten, for his violence was a diversion. At other times she led such a dreary, monotonous life that it almost killed her. Her father forbade her to go down to L'Estaque, keeping her constantly at work at home; even when she had nothing to do, it was his will that she should stay there beneath his eyes. Accordingly, she looked forward impatiently to September; for as soon as the family took up their quarters at La Blancarde Micoulin's surveillance necessarily became less strict, and Naïs, who was wont to run errands for Madame Rostand, was only too glad to make up for all her imprisonment.

One day the idea struck old Micoulin that this big girl might bring him in a franc or two a day. So he emancipated her, and sent her to work at a tile manufactory. Although the labour was severe, Naïs felt delighted. She left home early, proceeded to the other side of L'Estaque, and remained until evening in the hot sun, turning over the tiles set out to dry. Sad work it made with her hands, but she was freed from her father, and she used to joke with the boys. Here it was, in the midst of this rough toil, that she filled out and became a handsome woman. The blazing sun tinted her face and decked her neck with a ring of amber; her black hair grew and enveloped her, as if to protect her with its flying tresses; her body, continually on the move during the progress of her work, acquired the supple vigour of a young warrior's frame. When she stood up on the beaten ground at her full height amid the ruddy tiles, she looked like some Amazon, like a statue suddenly imbued with life by the rain of fire falling from the sky. Micoulin glowered at her with his little eyes on seeing her so fair. She laughed too much; it did not seem to him natural that a girl should be so happy. And he swore to himself he would throttle all lovers, should any ever venture to dangle around her!

Lovers! Naïs might have had them by the dozen, but she gave them no encouragement. She tossed her head at all the youths. Her only friend was a hunchback who was employed at the same manufactory as herself—a little fellow called Toine, whom the Foundling Hospital of Aix had sent to L'Estaque, and who had remained there, adopted, so to say, by the district. This hunchback had a ringing laugh and a comical profile. Naïs found an attraction in his gentleness. She did what she liked with him, and often tormented him when she felt inclined to take vengeance on someone for her father's violence towards herself. All this, however, had no further consequences. People used to make sport of Toine, and Micoulin himself said: "She's welcome to Toine: I know her, she's too proud."

That year, when Madame Rostand came to La Blancarde, she asked Micoulin to lend her Naïs, one of her servants being ill. Work was slack just then at the manufactory, and moreover, Micoulin, although brutal towards his own family, was politeness with his master's; he would not have refused, even if the request had been against his wishes. But that very day Monsieur Rostand was forced to go to Paris on sudden and important business, and Frédéric was thus left alone with his mother.

As a rule, on his arrival the young man was mad after outdoor exercise, and, intoxicated by the seaside air, he would go with Micoulin to set or draw up the nets; or take long walks with Naïs in the gorges which abound in the neighbourhood of L'Estaque. Then his ardour cooled down, and he remained for whole days lying under the pines on the edge of the terrace, half asleep and gazing at the sea, of which the monotonous azure finally palled upon him. As a rule, he had had enough of La Blancarde at the end of a fortnight, and was wont to invent some excuse in order to slip off to Marseilles.

That year, on the day after their arrival, Micoulin called Frédéric at sunrise. He was going to take up the traps, the long baskets with a narrow opening,

in which deep-water fish are caught. But the young man turned a deaf ear to him. Fishing appeared to have lost its attraction, for when he got up he threw himself on his back under the pines, and fixed his eyes on the sky. His mother was astonished not to see him set off for one of the long walks from which he usually returned as hungry as a wolf.

"You are not going out?" she asked.

"No, mother," he replied. "I shall stop with you, as father is not here."

Micoulin, who heard this, muttered in his dialect: "It won't be long before Monsieur Frédéric's off to Marseilles."

But Frédéric did not go to Marseilles. The week passed by and found him still stretched on his back, simply changing his position, whenever the sun rays fell on him. For appearance sake he had taken a book, but it was little he read; the greater part of the time the book remained lying on the dry pine-spikes. The young man did not even look at the sea; with his face turned towards the house, he appeared to be interested in the domestic arrangements, in watching the servants go backwards and forwards, crossing the terrace at every moment; and whenever it was Naïs who happened to pass him, a flash shot from his eyes. But Naïs, although she would slacken her pace, and move off with the rhythmical sway of her body, never cast a look behind her.

For several days this comedy went on. In his mother's presence Frédéric treated Naïs almost roughly, as if she had been some awkward servant. Then the young girl would cast her eyes down in pleased bashfulness, as if enjoying the harsh words.

One morning at breakfast she broke a salad bowl, and Frédéric flew into a rage.

"How clumsy she is!" he cried. "Wherever is her head?"

And he jumped up furiously, saying that his trousers were spoiled. A drop of oil had stained his knee, and it sufficed to make him raise the house.

"What are you staring at? Give me a napkin and some water. Come and help me," he said to the girl.

Naïs dipped the corner of a napkin in some water, and went down on her knees in front of Frédéric to rub the spot.

"Don't bother," said Madame Rostand. "That will do no good."

But the girl did not let go of her young master's trousers, which she went on rubbing with all the strength of her shapely arms, whilst he continued scolding her.

"I never saw such clumsiness. She must have brought it close to me on purpose to smash it. If she waited on us at Aix our china would soon be all in pieces," he grumbled.

These reproaches were so out of proportion to the gravity of the offence that Madame Rostand thought proper to try and appease her son as soon as Naïs had gone.

"What have you against the poor girl? One would think that you could not endure her. Be more gentle with her. She is an old playmate of yours, and she is not in the position of an ordinary servant here."

"Oh, she's a nuisance!" replied Frédéric, affecting a rough manner.

That evening at dusk, however, Naïs and Frédéric met in a shady spot at the end of the terrace. They had not yet spoken to one another alone. No one could hear them from the house. The pines filled the still air with a warm resinous odour. Then Naïs asked in a whisper, in the familiar way of their childhood:

"Why did you scold me so, Frédéric? You were unkind."

Without replying he caught hold of her hands, drew her towards him, and kissed her. She made no resistance, but afterwards went off, whilst he sat down on the parapet, in order not to appear before his mother in his then excited state. Ten minutes afterwards the girl was waiting at table with perfect and somewhat proud calmness.

Frédéric and Naïs made no appointments. Late one evening they found themselves together under an olive-tree, near the edge of the cliff. During dinner their eyes had several times exchanged glances. Then Naïs had gone home, and Frédéric had begun to roam about, possessed by a strange feeling. And indeed, when after a while he came to the old olive-tree, he found her there as if waiting for him. He sat down by her side and put his arm round her waist whilst she let her head fall upon his shoulder. For a moment they remained silent. The old olive-tree, with its gnarled limbs, covered them with a roof of grey leaves. Before them stretched the sea, motionless beneath the twinkling stars. Marseilles, on the far side of the bay, was hidden by a cloud; on the left the revolving Planier light shone out every minute, piercing the gloom with a yellow ray which suddenly disappeared; and nothing could be softer or more tender than this light, constantly vanishing on the horizon, and constantly returning.

"Is your father away?" asked Frédéric.

"I got out of the window," she said in her quiet voice.

They spoke no word of their love. That love came from afar, from the days of their infancy. The dawn was almost rising when they sought their rooms again.

## CHAPTER III

### LAND OF FIRE

WHAT a glorious month it was! Not one day of rain. The sky, invariably blue, displayed a satiny sheen unflecked by any cloud. The sun rose a ruddy crystal and sank in a cloud of golden dust. Yet it was not hot, for the sea breeze came with the sun, and though it died away when he set, the nights were deliciously cool, and balmy with the scent of aromatic plants diffusing the sweetness gathered during the day. The country is splendid. From both sides of the bay rocky arms jut out, whilst in the distance the islands seem to bound the horizon. In fine weather the sea appears to be nothing but a vast basin, a lake of an intense blue. In the distance, at the foot of the mountains, the houses of Marseilles climb up the low hills. When the atmosphere is clear one can see from L'Estaque the grey Joliette pier and the slender masts of the vessels in the port; beyond, houses peep out from amongst clumps of trees and the chapel of Notre-Dame-de-la-Garde glitters white

against the sky. The coastline winds about and takes broad sweeps before reaching L'Estaque, where manufactories throw out intermittent clouds of smoke. When the sun sinks below the horizon, the sea, almost black, looks as if it were slumbering between the two rocky promontories, whose whiteness is relieved by tinges of yellow and brown; pines, too, showing the dark green foliage against the reddish soil beyond. It is a vast panorama, a glimpse of the East, which departs, however, with the dazzling heat of day.

But L'Estaque has other sights besides the sea. The village, clinging to the mountain-side, is traversed by roads which wind through a chaos of shattered rocks. The railway line between Marseilles and Lyons passes amid those masses, crosses bridges thrown over ravines, and plunges under the cliffs themselves, remaining there for a distance of some four miles in what is called the tunnel of La Nerthe, the longest tunnel in France. Nothing can equal the savage grandeur of those gorges hollowed out amongst the hills, those narrow paths winding along at the foot of precipices, those barren mountains, planted with pines, uprearing ramparts tinged as with rust and blood. Now and then a pass widens, a field of struggling olive-trees fills the hollow of a valley, a lonely house shows its white frontage and closed shutters. Then come other rugged paths, impenetrable thickets, overturned rocks, dried-up torrents—all the surprises of a desert march. Over all, above the black fringe of pines, the sky stretches its expanse of silky blue.

Then there is the narrow line of coast between the rocks and the sea, the red soil pitted with immense holes, from which is taken the clay for tile-making, the chief industry of the district. Everywhere the ground is cracked and sundered, supporting with difficulty a few sickly trees, and seemingly parched by a breath of burning passion. The roads are like beds of plaster, in which the traveller sinks to the ankles at every step; and flying clouds of dust powder the hedges at the least puff of wind. Little grey lizards sleep along side the hot walls, which reverberate like ovens, whilst from the scorched grass rise whirring clouds of locusts. In the still and heavy air of the sleepy South there is no other sign of life than the grasshopper's monotonous song.

It was in this land of fire that Nais and Frédéric loved one another for a month. It was as if all the heat of the sky had entered their veins. For the first week they were satisfied with their nightly meetings under the same olive-tree on the edge of the cliff. There they tasted untold bliss. The cool night soothed their fever; they offered their burning cheeks and hands to the passing breeze, refreshing as a mountain spring. The sea broke with its slow voluptuous dirge over the rocks at their feet; the penetrating odour of seaweed intoxicated them with passion.

Then, leaning on one another's arms, they would watch across the bay the lights of Marseilles, tingling the water at the mouth of the port with a reflection as of blood; the twinkling gas-lights, outlining the streets in many a graceful curve; while in the midst of all, above the town, it seemed as if there were a mass of sparkling flame. The garden on the Colline Bonaparte was plainly distinguishable by a double row of lights mounting heavenwards. Those innumerable lights above the slumbering bay appeared to be illuminating some fairy town which the dawn would presently sweep away. And the sky, stretching over the black chaos of the horizon, also had its charm for them, a charm which alarmed and made them cling closer to one another. A rain of stars fell. On those clear Provencal nights the constellations resemble living flames. Shuddering beneath the vast space, they bowed their heads, turning their gaze on the solitary flicker of the Planier lighthouse, whose dancing scintillations stirred them, whilst their lips met again in a kiss.

But one night their eyes fell on the gigantic disc of the moon, glaring upon them with her yellow face. Out at sea a train of fire glittered, as if some enormous fish, some serpent from the depths, were trailing endless folds of golden scales; and then the glitter of Marseilles and the outlines of the gulf were obscured. As the moon rose the light increased, the shadows became more sharply defined. That heavenly witness was unwelcome to them. They feared they might be surprised if they remained so near La Blancarde. So when they next met they left the spot and walked into the shadowy open country. They found a meeting-place in a deserted tile-field; a ruined shed there concealed a pit in which two kilns remained still open. But the hovel saddened them; they preferred to have the open sky above their heads. So they explored the clay-pits, they discovered delightful nooks, perfect little deserts, whence they could hear nothing but the barking of watch-dogs. They prolonged their walks, wandering along the rocky coast in the direction of Niolon, following the course of the narrow gorges in search of distant grottoes and crevasses. For a fortnight they thus spent their nights. The moon had now disappeared, the sky had become dark again; but it seemed to them as if La Blancarde were too small to hold their love, as if they needed all the limitless expanse beyond it.

One night, as they were following a path above L'Estaque in order to gain the gorges of La Nerthe, they fancied they could hear a muffled step keeping pace with their own behind a plantation of pines stretching beside the road. They stopped in alarm.

"Do you hear that?" asked Frédéric.

"Yes; some stray dog," whispered Nais.

And they continued on their way. But, at the first bend in the road, after leaving the pines, they distinctly saw a dark object glide behind the rocks. It was certainly a human being, curiously shaped, looking indeed as if it were humpbacked. Nais uttered an exclamation.

"Wait here," she said quickly.

And then she darted in pursuit of the shadow. Presently Frédéric heard the sound of rapid whispering. She returned composed, but rather pale.

"What is it?" he asked.

"Nothing," she replied.

Then after a moment's silence she continued: "If you hear any steps, don't be alarmed. It's Toine—you know the hunchback. He wants to keep watch over us."

And in fact Frédéric was occasionally conscious of someone following them in the darkness. It was as if a protecting arm were stretched over them. More than once Naïs tried to drive Toine away; but the poor fellow merely asked to be her dog: he would not be seen, he would not be heard, why should he not be allowed to do as he pleased? From that time forward, if the lovers had listened attentively as they kissed in the lonely gorges, they would have caught the sound of smothered sobs behind them. It was Toine, their watchdog, weeping in his horny hands.

But at last those walks no longer sufficed them. They grew emboldened and took advantage of other opportunities to meet. Madame Rostand, who saw nothing, still blamed her son for being over-rough towards his old playmate. Yet one day she almost surprised them kissing.

After dinner, when the evening was cool, Madame Rostand often liked to go for a walk. She then took her son's arm and went down to L'Estaque, telling Naïs to bring her shawl as a measure of precaution. They went all three of them to see the sardine-fishers come in. Out at sea the lanterns danced, and soon the dark silhouettes of the boats could be discerned, nearing the beach, amid a muffled sound of oars. On good days joyous voices would ring out, and the women would hurry down, laden with baskets; while the three men who manned each boat set to work to empty the net, which, as it lay under the thwarts, looked like a broad dark ribbon dotted with flashes of silver. The sardines, hanging by the gills to the meshes, still struggled and threw out a metallic lustre. Then they fell linto the baskets, like a shower of crown pieces, amid the pale light of the lanterns. Madame Rostand would often leave her son's arm to talk to the fishermen standing near a boat, interested by the sight, whilst Frédéric, standing at Naïs's side, outside the radius of light, clasped the girl's hands in a burst of passion. Meanwhile old Micoulin preserved stubborn silence. He went out fishing and came home to do a day's work, with ever the same deep look on his face. But at last his little grey eyes assumed an uneasy expression. He threw side glances at Naïs without saying a word. She seemed to him changed, there was something about her that he could not quite understand. One day she ventured to argue with him, and he thereupon gave her a blow which cut her lip.

That evening, when Frédéric saw her mouth swollen he questioned her anxiously.

"It's nothing; only a blow my father gave me," she said.

Her tone was gloomy. And as the young man became angry and declared that he would see into it, "No, never mind," she said, "it's my business. There'll soon be an end to it."

She never told him of the beatings which she received. Only on the days when her father had treated her cruelly she kissed her lover with more ardour, as if to avenge herself on the old man.

Naïs had at first taken the most minute precautions in going to meet Frédéric; but at last rashness seized hold of her. Then, imagining from her father's manner that he suspected something, her prudence returned. She mised two appointments, as her mother told her that Micoulin did not sleep at night, but got up and went about from one door to another. However, on the third day, seeing Frédéric's distress, the girl once more forgot all prudence. She went out at about eleven o'clock, resolving that she would not remain more than an hour absent; and she was in hopes that her father being in his first sleep, would not hear her.

Frédéric was waiting for her under the olive-trees. Without telling her fears, she refused to go farther. They sat down in their usual place looking at the sea and the glow of Marseilles. The Planier light was beaming. As Naïs watched it she fell asleep on Frédéric's shoulder. He did not move, and gradually yielding to fatigue himself, his own eyes closed.

No sound; only the chirrup of the grasshopper. The sea slept like the lovers. But suddenly a dark form came forth from the gloom and approached them. It was Micoulin, who awakened by the creaking of a window, had missed Naïs from her room. He had left the house, taking a small hatchet with him. When he saw a dark mass under the olive-tree he grasped the handle of the implement. But the children did not stir, he was able to walk up to them, bend down, and look in their faces. A slight exclamation escaped him as he recognized his young master. No, no,

he could not kill him thus: the blood
spilt on the ground would leave traces
behind it, and would cost him too dear.
A peasant does not openly murder his
master, for the master, even when he
lies under the ground, is always the
stronger. As Micoulin stood there, however, a look of savage determination
came over his tanned face. At last he
shook his head and went off steathily,
leaving the lovers asleep.

When Naïs returned to her room
shortly before day-break, much alarmed
at having stayed away so long, she
found her window just as she had left
it. At breakfast Micoulin calmly
watched her eat her bread. She felt
safe, her father certainly knew nothing.

## CHAPTER IV

### PICNICING

"AREN'T you coming out fishing any
more, Monsieur Frédéric?" asked Micoulin one evening.

Madame Rostand was sitting on the
terrace in the shade of the pines, em-
broidering a handkerchief, whilst her
son, lying at her feet, was amusing himself by throwing pebbles.

"Not I," replied the young man. "I'm
getting lazy."

"You are wrong," continued Micoulin.
"The traps were full of fish yesterday.
You can catch as many as you like just
now. You'd like it. Come with me to-
morrow morning."

He said this so good-humoredly that
Frédéric, who thought of Naïs, and did
not want to fall out with the father,
finally exclaimed: "Very well, then.
But you'll have to call me. I shall

still be sound asleep at five o'clock."

Madame Rostand, feeling rather uneasy, had ceased working.

"Mind you are careful," she said.
"I am always anxious when you are on
the water."

Next morning Micoulin shouted to
Frédéric in vain; the young man's window remained closed. Upon this he
said to his daughter, with a savage
irony which she did not detect: "You
go. He'll hear you, perhaps."

Thus it was Naïs who woke Frédéric that morning. Ten minutes later
the young man appeared, clad from head
to foot in grey canvas. Old Micoulin
was sitting on the parapet of the terrace,
patiently waiting for him.

"It's cool, you'd better take a wrap-
per," he said.

Naïs went to fetch one, and afterwards the two men descended the steep
steps, which led to the sea, whilst the
girl, standing above, followed them with
her eyes. At the bottom old Micoulin
raised his head and looked at Naïs;
there were deep creases at the corners
of his mouth.

For the last five days the north-east
wind, the mistral, had been blowing.
On the previous day it had fallen at
evening, but when the sun rose it returned, at first rather gently. At that
early hour the sea, lashed by the sudden gusts, was of a deep mottled blue;
and the white-crested waves, illumined
by the first slanting rays, chased one
another over the bosom of the deep.
The sky was almost white, and clear as
crystal. In the distance Marseilles
stood out with a distinctness which enabled one to count the windows in the
fronts of the houses, whilst the rocks ir

the gulf were bathed in a delicate rosy haze.

"We shall have our work cut out to get back again," said Frédéric.

"Very likely," replied Micoulin.

He plied his oars silently, without turning his head. The young man looked for a moment at his bent back, noting his sunburnt neck and red ears, from which little rings of gold were hanging. Then he leant over the side of the boat gazing into the depths. The sea became rougher, and big shadowy weeds floated by, looking like tufts of some drowned man's hair. This saddened and even alarmed Frédéric a little.

"I say, Micoulin," he remarked, after a long silence, "the wind's getting stronger. Be careful; you know that I swim like a lump of lead."

"Yes, yes; I know," replied the old man, in a dry voice.

Still he continued rowing, in mechanical fashion. Then the boat began to pitch, the white foam on the crests of the waves turned into clouds of spray, which flew before the wind. Frédéric did not want to exhibit his alarm, but he felt very uncomfortable, and would have given a great deal to have been on land again. At last he grew angry and exclaimed: "Where the devil have you stuck your traps? Are we bound for Algiers?"

But old Micoulin, without seeming to trouble himself, again replied: "We're all right; we're all right."

All at once he let go the oars, stood up in the boat, and looked toward the shore, as if for certain guiding marks; there was still some five minutes' rowing to be accomplished before getting among the cork buoys which showed where the traps were placed. Once there, while Micoulin was drawing up the baskets, he remained for a few seconds with his face turned towards La Blancarde. Frédéric, following the direction of his eyes, distinctly saw a white form under the pines. It was Naïs, still leaning on the parapet.

"How many traps have you?" asked Frédéric.

"Thirty-five; and we mustn't stop here any longer than we can help," said Micoulin.

He laid hold of the buoy nearest to him, and drew the first basket in. The depth was enormous, there was no end to the rope. At last the trap appeared, with the large stone which had kept it at the bottom, and as soon as it left the water three fish began to leap about like birds in a cage. It seemed as if one could hear the beating of wings. In a second basket there was nothing; but in the third was found a somewhat rare capture—a small lobster, which flourished its tail violently. Frédéric was all attention now, forgetting his fears, leaning over the side of the boat, and awaiting the baskets with beating heart. Whenever he heard a sound as of wings, he felt like a sportsman who had just brought down his game. One by one, however, the baskets were drawn into the boat, the water meantime streaming around; and soon the whole thirty-five were secured. There were at least fifteen pounds of fish—a splendid catch for the Gulf of Marseilles, which from several causes, especially the extremely fine mesh of the nets which are used, has been yielding less and less fish for many years past.

"That's the lot," said Micoulin. "Now we can make for home."

He had carefully arranged his baskets in the stern; but when Frédéric saw him prepare to set the sail, he remarked that, with such a wind blowing, it would be more prudent to row. The old man shrugged his shoulders. He knew what he was about. And, before hoisting the sail, he cast a last look in the direction of La Blancarde. Naïs's white dress was still there.

Then came the catastrophe, as sudden as a thunderbolt. Afterwards, when Frédéric tried to think over what had happened, he remembered that all at once a gust had caught the sail, and that all had then overturned. He could not call anything else to mind, save a feeling of intense cold and bitter agony. He owed his life to a miracle; he had fallen on the sail, which kept him afloat. Some fishermen, having seen the accident, hastened to his help, and picked him up, as well as old Micoulin, who was already swimming towards the shore.

Madame Rostand was still asleep, and they concealed from her the danger which her son had incurred. At the foot of the terrace, Frédéric and Micoulin, dripping with water, found Naïs, who had witnessed the scene.

"Devil take it!" cried the old man. "We'd taken up the traps and were coming home. Bad luck to it all!"

Naïs, who was deadly pale, looked fixedly at her father.

"Yes," she muttered, "it's bad luck. But when you sail in a wind like that, you know what to expect."

Micoulin flew into a rage.

"What's that to do with you, lazybones? Can't you see Monsieur Frédéric's shivering? Help me get him indoors."

The young man escaped with a day in bed, and told his mother that he had a headache. The next day he found Naïs very dispirited. She refused to meet him out of doors again, though one evening, in the passage, she kissed him passionately. She never told him of her suspicions, but from that day forward she watched over him. Then, at the end of a week, her fears began to diminish. Her father went about as usual; he even seemed kinder, and beat her less often.

Every year the Rostands used to go to eat a *bouillabaisse* in a hollow of the rocks on the shore, in the direction of Niolon. Afterwards, as partridges abounded amongst the hills, the gentlemen would organize a shooting party. That year Madame Rostand wanted to take Naïs to wait on them, and refused to listen to Micoulin's remarks when the old savage attempted to raise some objection.

They set out early. The morning was a charming one. Lying like a mirror beneath the gleaming sun was the blue expanse of the sea; ripples appeared amid the currents, where the blue was tinged with violet, whilst in apparently stagnant spots the azure faded away into a milky transparency. You might have imagined the sea to be an immense piece of shot satin, whose changing colours grew more and more indistinct as the limpid horizon was reached. And over that slumbering lake the boat glided very softly.

The narrow beach on which they landed was at the mouth of a gorge, and they settled down on a strip of scorched grass which was to serve as a table.

How enjoyable that picnic was! First of all Micoulin set off alone in the boat to take up the baskets which he had set the day before. By the time he came back Naïs had gathered some thyme and lavender and enough dry wood to make a large fire. That day the old man was to make the *bouillabaisse,* the classic fish soup, the secret of which the coast fisherman transmit from father to son. And a terrible *bouillabaisse* it was, with its strong doses of pepper, and odour of crushed garlic. The Rostands were greatly interested in the preparation of the savoury mess.

"Micoulin," said Madame Rostand, "do you think you will be as successful as last year?"

The old man seemed to be in excellent spirits. First of all he washed the fish in sea water, whilst Naïs took the large pan out of the boat. Soon all was in progress: the fish at the bottom of the vessel, just covered with some water, with some onion, oil, garlic, a handful of pepper, and a tomato; then the whole was placed on the fire, a formidable fire, large enough to roast a sheep. Fishermen say that the goodness of *bouillabaisse* lies in the cooking: the pan must disappear amid the flames. Micoulin gravely cut some slices of bread into a salad bowl, and at the end of half an hour he poured the liquor on the slices, serving up the fish separately.

"Come along," he said. "It's not good unless it's hot."

Then the *bouillabaisse* was devoured with the usual jokes.

"I say, Micoulin, did you put any gunpowder in it?"

"It's very good, but it wants a throat of brass to swallow it."

Micoulin devoured his share tranquilly, swallowing a slice of bread at each mouthful, and showing at the same time how flattered he felt at eating with his masters.

Having finished, they sat there waiting for the heat of the day to pass off. The glistening rocks covered with ruddy streaks threw grateful shadows around. Clumps of evergreen oaks showed sombre foliage, whilst on the slopes the rows of pines ascended in regular lines, looking like little soldiers on the march. An oppressive silence filled the quivering air.

Madame Rostand had brought the endless embroidery, which was never seen to leave her hands. Naïs, seated at her side, seemed to be interested in the movements, of her needle. But her eyes were really on her father. He was lying on his back a few paces away enjoying a siesta. Then, farther still, Frédéric also was sleeping beneath the protecting shade of his broad-brimmed straw hat.

At about four o'clock they awoke, and Micoulin declared that he knew of a covey of partridges at the bottom of a ravine. He had seen them three days previously, so Frédéric allowed himself to be tempted, and they both took their guns.

"Pray be careful," said Madame Rostand. "You might slip and hurt yourself."

"Yes, that does happen sometimes," said Micoulin quietly.

They then went off, and as they disappeared behind the rocks, Naïs jumped up and followed them at a distance, muttering: "I'm going to see."

Instead of keeping to the pathway at the bottom of the gorge, she turned to the left among the bushes, hurrying along and avoiding the loose stones for fear of setting them rolling. At length, at a bend of the road, she espied Frédéric walking quickly, slightly bent, and ready to lift his gun to his shoulder. As yet she saw nothing of her father, but presently she discovered him on the same slope as herself: he was crouching down, looking towards the gorge, and he seemed to be waiting for something. Twice he raised his gun. Supposing the partridges flew up between the two sportsmen, Micoulin and Frédéric might shoot one another. Naïs, gliding from bush to bush, anxiously took up a position behind the old man.

Some minutes passed. On the other side Frédéric had disappeared in a dip in the ground, but finally he reappeared, and remained for an instant motionless. Then Micoulin, still crouching down, took a long aim at the young man. But with a kick Naïs knocked the barrel of his gun upward, and the charge went off in the air with a fearful report which brought down all the echoes of the gorge.

The old man sprang to his feet. On seeing Naïs, he seized the gun by its smoking barrel, as if he meant to dash her to the earth with one blow. But the girl stood her ground, her cheeks as white as death, her eyes darting fire. He dared not strike her, and, trembling with rage, he could stammer out in dialect: "I'll kill him, never you fear!"

At the report of the gun the partridges had flown off, Frédéric winging two of them. And about six o'clock the Rostands returned to La Blancarde, old Micoulin rowing with his accustomed air of sullen, stubborn brutishness.

## CHAPTER V

### THE FINDING OF THE BODY

SEPTEMBER was drawing to an end. After a violent storm the air had become very cool. The days grew shorter, and Naïs refused to meet Frédéric out of doors at night-time. However, as she reached the house every morning at six o'clock, and Madame Rostand did not get up till nine, the lovers still had opportunities for converse.

It was now that Naïs showed the greatest affection for Frédéric. She would take hold of his neck, draw his face towards hers, and look into it with a passion which filled her eyes with tears. It was as if she feared that she might never see him more. And she showered kisses upon him as if to protest and swear that she would guard him.

"What is the matter with Naïs?" Madame Rostand would often remark. "She changes every day."

Indeed she was becoming thinner, and quite pale. The fire in her eyes was dying away. She often remained for a long while silent, and then would give a start, looking alarmed like a girl awakening from a bad dream.

"You are ill, my child; you must take care of yourself," repeated her mistress.

But Naïs would smile and answer:

"Oh, no, madame, I'm quite well and happy! I've never been so happy."

One morning, as she was helping to count the linen, she ventured to ask a question.

"Are you going to stop late at La Blancarde this year?"

"Till the end of October," replied Madame Rostand.

Naïs stood still for a moment with fixed eyes; then she unconsciously said aloud: "Twenty days more."

A continual struggle was going on within her. She wished to keep Frédéric near her, and yet at the same time she was constantly tempted to cry out, "Go!"

He was lost to her; never would that season of love return; she had felt it from their first meeting. One night of gloomy despair she had even gone so far as to wonder whether she ought not to allow her father to kill Frédéric, so that he might never love another; but the idea of seeing him dead—he so delicate, so fair, more like a girl than herself—was unbearable to her, and the evil thought filled her with horror. No, she would save him, and he should never know of it. He might love her no longer, but she would be happy in the thought that he still lived.

She would often say to him, "Don't go to sea to-day; the weather will be rough." At other times she pressed him to leave La Blancarde: "You must be sick of being here; you won't love me any longer. Go to town for a few days."

These changes of humour surprised him. He thought her less handsome, now that her face had become drawn; and besides his was a very fickle temperament. He began to pine for the eau de Cologne and the rice powder of the beauties of Aix and Marseilles.

Meantime the old man's words were constantly ringing in Naïs' ears: "I'll kill him, I'll kill him!" In the middle of the night she would wake up, thinking that she had heard shots fired. She became timid, and screamed whenever a stone rolled away from under her feet. When Frédéric was out of her sight, she was always worrying about him; and what terrified her most was that from morning to night she still seemed to hear Micoulin repeating, "I'll kill him!" The old man however, preserved stubborn silence, he never made any allusion to what had passed, either by word or gesture; but for her, his every look, his every movement implied that he would kill his young master at the first opportunity he might have of doing so without being disturbed. And afterwards he would deal with Naïs. In the meantime he kicked her about like some disobedient dog.

"Does your father still use you badly?" Frédéric asked the girl one morning.

"Yes," she replied; "he's going mad."

And after showing him her arms, which were black with bruises, she muttered these words, which she often whispered to herself: "It'll soon be over, it'll soon be over."

At the beginning of October she became more gloomy than ever. She was absent-minded, and one could often see her lips move as if she were talking to herself. On several occasions Frédéric perceived her standing on the cliff, seemingly examining the trees around her and measuring the depth of the abyss. A few days later he discovered her with Toine the hunchback, plucking figs on the farthest part of the estate. Toine used to come and help her whenever she had too much to do. He was under the fig-tree, and Naïs, who had mounted on a thick branch, was joking with him, calling to him to open his mouth, and then throwing down figs which burst upon his face. The poor fellow opened his mouth as he was bidden, and closed his eyes in ecstasy, whilst his huge face expressed complete beatitude. Frédéric was certainly not jealous, but he could not refrain from taking Naïs to task.

"Toine would cut off his hand for us," she said curtly. "We mustn't ill-treat him, he may be useful later on."

The hunchback continued coming to La Blancarde every day. He worked on the cliff, where he was cutting a narrow canal to bring some water to the end of an experimental kitchen garden. Naïs used to go and watch him, and lively talk would ensue between them. He was so long over the task that old Micoulin finally called him a lazybones and kicked his legs, as he would have done his daughter's.

Rain fell on two successive days. Frédéric, who had to return to Aix the following week, determined that before leaving he would once more go out fishing with Micoulin. And seeing Naïs turn pale he laughed and replied "that he should not choose a day when the mistral was blowing." Then, as he was to leave so soon, the young girl consented to meet him once more. They met late at night on the terrace. The rain had cleansed the earth, and a strong odour rose from all the freshened vegetation. When that usually parched country is thoroughly soaked, all its colours and odours become intensified: the red earth looks like blood, the pines are of an emerald green, the rocks of the whiteness of freshly-washed linen. However, that night, all that the lovers could detect was the enhanced perfume of the thyme and lavender bushes.

Old associations led them to the olive-trees. Frédéric was walking towards one which had sheltered their first love-meeting—it stood quite at the edge of the cliff—when Naïs, as if aroused from a reverie, caught hold of his arm, dragged him from the edge, and said, trembling, "No, no; not there!"

"Why, what is the matter?" he asked.

She hesitated, and finally remarked that after such a fall of rain the cliff was not safe. And she added: "Last winter there was a landslip here."

They sat down farther back, under another olive-tree. And at last Naïs convulsively burst into tears, and would not say why she was crying. Afterwards a frigid silence took possession of her, and when Frédéric joked her about her sadness and apathy in his company she murmured:

"No, don't say that. I love you too much. But I'm not in good health: and, besides, it's all over. You're going away."

He vainly tried to comfort her, telling her that he would come again from time to time, and that next autumn he would spend two months there. But she shook her head; she knew very well that all was over now.

Their meeting ended in embarrassing silence; they gazed at the sea; Marseilles was glittering with gas lamps, but the Planier lighthouse showed only a solitary mournful gleam; and gradually the horizon imparted to them some of its own melancholy. At three o'clock, when Frédéric quitted Naïs, kissing her, he felt her shudder.

He could not sleep when he got back into the house; he read till dawn, and then, feeling feverish, he took up a position at the window. Just at that moment Micoulin was starting off to take up his traps. As the old man passed along the terrace he raised his head and asked Frédéric if he were coming with him that morning.

"No," replied Frédéric; "I've slept too badly. To-morrow."

The old fellow went off with a slouching gait. He had to go down to his boat at the foot of the cliff, just under the olive-tree where he had surprised his daughter. When he had disappeared, Frédéric, on turning his head, was astonished to see Toine already at work; the hunchback was standing near the olive-tree with a pickaxe in his hand, repairing the narrow channel which the rain had damaged. The air was cool; it was pleasant at the window. Frédéric went to make a cigarette, and as he lounged back to the casement a terrible crash—a roll of thunder as it seemed—was suddenly heard. He rushed to the window. It was a landslip. He could only distinguish Toine, who was running for his life, flourishing his pickaxe, amid a cloud of red dust. At the edge of the abyss the old olive-tree, with its gnarled branches, had pitched forward, crashing into the sea. A cloud of spray flew up, while a terrible cry rent the air. Then Frédéric saw Naïs leaning over the parapet, her stiffened hands clutching at

the stonework, while her eyes peered into the depths below. There she stood, motionless and expectant, with her hands pressed to the low wall. Still, she no doubt divined that somebody was looking at her, for she turned her head, saw Frédéric, and cried: "My father! my father!"

An hour afterwards they found Micoulin's mutilated body under the stones. Toine, almost crazy, related how he had almost been carried away himself; and everybody declared that it was wrong to carry a stream along the top of the cliff, on account of the infiltrations.

The old wife wept a great deal. As for Naïs, she followed her father to the cemetery with tearless eyes.

On the day after the catastrophe, Madame Rostand had insisted upon returning to Aix. Frédéric was very pleased to leave, for the terrible drama had disturbed his peace of mind; and, moreover, in his opinion, peasant girls with all their good looks were not equal to their town-bred sisters. He resumed his old mode of life. His mother, touched by his attentiveness to her at La Blancarde, gave him more liberty, so that he passed a very pleasant winter, and fondly hoped that his life would always thus glide smoothly away.

Monsieur Rostand had to go to La Blancarde at Easter, and wished his son to accompany him; but the young man made various excuses. When the lawyer came back, he said the next morning at breakfast: "Oh! by the way, Naïs is going to be married."

"Never!" cried Frédéric in amazement.

"And you'd never guess to whom,"

continued Monsieur Rostand. "She gave me such good reasons, however."

The fact was Naïs was marrying Toine. In that way nothing would be changed at La Blancarde. Toine would still manage the property, as he had done since Micoulin's death.

The young man listened with an awkward smile. Presently he expressed the opinion that the arrangement was the best one possible for everybody concerned.

"Naïs has grown very old and plain," continued Monsieur Rostand. "I didn't know her again. It is astonishing how quickly girls age on the coast; and she used to be quite pretty, too."

"Yes, a feast of sunlight," said Frédéric composedly, and he quietly went on eating his cutlet.

# Angeline

## CHAPTER I

### ORGEVAL

NEARLY two years ago I was spinning on my bicycle over a deserted road towards Orgeval, above Poissy, when the sudden sight of a wayside house caused me such surprise that I sprang from my machine to take a better look at it. It was a brick-built house, with no marked characteristics, and it stood under the grey November sky, amid the cold wind which was sweeping away the dead leaves, in the centre of spacious grounds planted with old trees. That which rendered it remarkable, which lent it an aspect of fierce, wild, savage strangeness of a nature to oppress the heart, was the frightful abandonment into which it had fallen. And as part of the iron gate was torn away, and a huge notice-board, with lettering half-effaced by the rain, announced that the place was for sale, I entered the garden, yielding to curiosity mingled with uneasiness and anguish.

The house must have been unoccupied for thirty or, perhaps, forty years. The bricks of the cornices and facings had been disjointed by past winters, and were overgrown with moss and lichen. Cracks, suggestive of precocious wrinkles, scarred the frontage of the building, which still looked strong, though no care whatever was now taken of it. The steps below, split by frost, and shut off by nettles and brambles, formed, as it were, a threshold of desolation and death. But the frightful mournfulness of the place came more particularly from its bare, curtainless, glaucous windows, whose panes had been broken by stone-throwing urchins, and which, one and all, revealed the desolate emptiness of the rooms, like dim eyes that had remained wide open in some soulless corpse. Then, too, the spacious garden all around was a scene of devastation; the old flower-beds could scarce be discerned beneath the growth of rank weeds; the paths had disappeared, devoured by hungry plants; the shrubberies had grown to virgin forests; there was all the wild vegetation of some abandoned cemetery in the damp gloom beneath the huge and ancient trees, whose last leaves were that day being swept off by the autumn wind, which ever shrieked its doleful plaint.

Long did I linger there amidst that despairing wail of Nature, for though my heart was oppressed by covert fear, by growing anguish, I was detained by a feeling of ardent pity, a longing to know and to sympathise with all the woe and grief that I felt around me. And when at last I had left the spot and perceived across the road, at a point where the latter forked, a kind of tavern, a hovel where drink was sold, I entered it, fully resolved to question the folks of the neighbourhood.

But I only found there an old woman who sighed and whimpered as she served me a glass of beer. She complained of living on that out-of-the-way road, along which not even a couple of cyclists passed each day. And she talked on interminably, telling me her story, relating that she was called Mother Toussaint, that she and her man had come from Vernon to take that tavern, that things had turned out fairly well at first, but that all had been going from bad to worse since she had become a widow. When, after her rush of words, I began

to question her respecting the neighbouring house, she suddenly became circumspect, and glanced at me suspiciously as if she thought that I wished to tear some dread secret from her.

"Ah, yes," said she, "La Sauvagière, the haunted house, as people say hereabout. . . . For my part, I know nothing, monsieur, it doesn't date from my time. I shall have only been here thirty years come next Easter, and those things go back to well-nigh forty years now. When we came here the house was already much as you see it. The summers pass, the winters pass, and nothing stirs unless it be the stones that fall."

"But why," I asked—"why is the place not sold, since it is for sale?"

"Ah! why? Why? Can I tell? People say so many things."

I was doubtless beginning to inspire her with some confidence. Besides, at heart she must have been burning to tell me the many thing: that people said. She began by relating that not one of the girls of the neighbouring village ever dared to enter La Sauvagière after twilight, for rumour had it that some poor wandering soul returned thither every night. And, as I expressed astonishment that such a story could still find any credit so near to Paris, she shrugged her shoulders, tried to talk like a strong-minded woman, but finally betrayed by her manner the terror she did not confess.

"There are 'acts that can't be denied, monsieur. You ask why the place is not sold? I've seen many purchasers arrive, and all have gone off quicker than they came; not one of them has ever put in a second appearance. Well, one matter that's certain is that as soon as a visitor dares venture inside the house some extraordinary things happen. The doors swing to and fro and close by themselves with a bang, as if a hurricane were sweeping past. Cries, moans, and sobs ascend from the cellars, and if the visitor obstinately remains, a heart-rending voice raises a continuous cry of "Angeline! Angeline! Angeline!" in such distressful, appealing tones that one's very bones are frozen. I repeat to you that this has been proved, nobody will tell you otherwise."

I must own that I was now growing impassioned myself, and could feel a little chilly quiver coursing under my skin. "And this Angeline, who is she?" I asked.

"Ah! monsieur, it would be necessary to tell you all. And, once again, for my part I know nothing."

Nevertheless, the old woman ended by telling me all. Some forty years previously—in or about 1858—at the time when the triumphant Second Empire was ever *en fête*, Monsieur de G——, a Tuileries functionary, lost his wife, by whom he had a daughter some ten years old—Angeline, a marvel of beauty, the living portrait of her mother. Two years later, Monsieur de G—— married again, espousing another famous beauty, the widow of a general. And it was asserted, that from the very moment of those second nuptials, atrocious jealousy had sprung up between Angeline and her stepmother: the former stricken in the heart at finding her own mother already forgotten, replaced so soon by a stranger; and the other tortured, maddened, by always having before her that living portrait of a woman whose memory she feared, she would never be able

to efface. La Sauvagière was the property of the new Madame de G——, and there one evening, on seeing the father passionately embrace his daughter, she, in her jealous madness, it was said, had dealt the child so violent a blow, that the poor girl had fallen to the floor dead, her collar-bone broken. Then the rest was frightful: the distracted father consenting to bury his daughter with his own hands in a cellar of the house in order to save the murderess; the remains lying there for years, whilst the child was said to be living with an aunt; and at last the howls of a dog and its persistent scratching of the ground leading to the discovery of the crime, which was, however, at once hushed up by command of the Tuileries. And now Monsieur and Madame de G—— were both dead, while Angeline again returned each night at the call of the heartrending voice that ever cried for her from out of the mysterious spheres beyond the darkness.

"Nobody will contradict me," concluded Mother Toussaint. "It is all as true as that two and two make four."

I had listened to her in bewilderment, resenting certain improbabilities, but won over by the brutal and sombre strangeness of the tragedy. I had heard of this Monsieur de G——, and it seemed to me that he had indeed married a second time, and that some family grief had overclouded his life. Was the tale true, then? What a tragical and affecting story! Every human passion stirred up, heightened, exasperated to madness the most terrifying love tale there could be, a little girl as beautiful as daylight, adored, and yet killed by her stepmother, and buried by her father in the corner of a cellar! There was here more matter for horror and emotion than one might dare to hope for. I was again about to question and discuss things. Then I asked myself what would be the use of it? Why not carry that frightful story away with me in its flower—such indeed as it had sprouted from popular imagination?

As I again sprang upon my bicycle I gave La Sauvagière a last glance. The night was falling and the woeful house gazed at me with its dim and empty windows akin to the eyes of a corpse, whilst the wail of the autumn wind still swept through the ancient trees.

## CHAPTER II

### PALE, BLUE EYES

WHY did this story so fix itself in my brain as to lead to real obsession, perfect torment? This is one of those intellectual problems that are difficult to solve. In vain I told myself that similar legends overrun the rural districts, and that I had no direct concern in this one. In spite of all, I was haunted by that dead child, that lovely and tragic Angeline, to whom every night for forty years past a desolate voice had called through the empty rooms of the forsaken house.

Thus, during the first two months of the winter I made researches. It was evident that if anything, however little, had transpired of such a dramatic disappearance, the newspapers of the period must have referred to it. However, I ransacked the collections of the National Library without discovering a line about any such story. Then I questioned contemporaries, men who had formerly had intercourse with Tuileries society; but none could give me a positive reply, I only obtained contradictory information. So much so that, although still and ever tortured by the mystery, I had abandoned all hope of getting to the truth, when chance one morning set me on a fresh track.

Every two or three weeks I paid a visit of good-fellowship, affection, and admiration to the old poet V——, who died last April on the threshold of his seventieth year. Paralysis of the legs had, for many years previous, riveted him to an armchair in his study of the Rue d'Assas, whose window overlooked the garden of the Luxembourg. He there peacefully finished a dreamy life, for he had ever lived on imagination, building for himself a palace of ideality, in which he had loved and suffered far away from the real. Who of us does not remember his refined and amiable features, his white hair curly like a child's, his pale blue eyes, which had retained the innocence of youth? One could not say that he invariably told falsehoods. But the truth is that he was prone to invention, in suchwise that one never exactly knew at what point reality ceased to exist for him and at what point dreaming began. He was a very charming old man, long since detached from life, one whose words often filled me with emotion as if indeed they were a vague, discreet revelation of the unknown.

One day, then, I was chatting with him near the window of the little room which a blazing fire ever warmed. It was freezing terribly out of doors. The

Luxembourg gardens stretched away white with snow, displaying a broad horizon of immaculate purity. And I know not how, but at last I spoke to him of La Sauvagière, and of the story that still worried me—that father who had re-married, and that stepmother, jealous of the little girl; then the murder perpetrated in a fit of fury, and the burial in a cellar. V—— listened to me with the quiet smile which he retained even in moments of sadness. Then silence fell, his pale blue eyes wandered away over the white immensity of the Luxembourg, whilst a shade of dreaminess, emanating from him, seemed to set a faint quiver all around.

"I knew Monsieur de G—— very well," he said. "I knew his first wife, whose beauty was superhuman; I knew the second one, who was no less wondrously beautiful; and I myself passionately loved them both without ever telling it. I also knew Angeline, who was yet more beautiful than they, and whom all men a little later would have worshipped on the their knees. But things did not happen quite as you say."

My emotion was profound. Was the unexpected truth that I despaired of at hand, then? At first I felt no distrust, but said to him, "Ah! what a service you render me, my friend! I shall at last be able to quiet my poor mind. Make haste to tell me all."

But he was not listening, his glance still wandered far away. And he began to speak in a dreamy voice, as if creating things and beings in his mind as he proceeded with his narrative.

"At twelve years of age Angeline was one in whom all woman's love, with every impulse of joy and grief, had already flowered. She it was who felt desperately jealous of the new wife whom every day she saw in her father's arms. She suffered from it as from some frightful act of betrayal; it was not her mother only who was insulted by that new union, she herself was tortured, her own heart was pierced. Every night, too, she heard her mother calling her from her tomb, and one night, eager to rejoin her, overcome by excess of suffering and excess of love, this child, who was but twelve years old, thrust a knife into her heart."

A cry burst from me. "God of heaven! Is it possible?"

"How great was the fright and horror," he continued, without hearing me, "when on the morrow Monsieur and Madame de G—— found Angeline in her little bed with that knife plunged to its very handle in her breast! They were about to start for Italy; of all their servants, too, there only remained in the house an old nurse who had reared the child. In their terror, fearing that they might be accused of a crime, they induced the woman to help them, and they did indeed bury the body, but in a corner of the conservatory behind the house, at the foot of a huge orange-tree. And there it was found on the day when, the parents being dead, the old servant told the story."

Doubts had come to me while he spoke, and I scrutinised him anxiously, wondering if he had not invited this. "But," said I, "do you also think it possible that Angeline can come back each night in response to the heart-rending, mysterious voice that calls her?"

This time he looked at me and smiled indulgently once more.

"Come back, my friend? Why, everyone comes back! Why should not the soul of that dear dead child still dwell in the spot where she loved and suffered? If a voice is heard calling her 'tis because life has not yet begun afresh for her. Yet it will begin afresh, be sure of it; for all begins afresh. Nothing is lost, love no more than beauty. Angeline! Angeline! Angeline! She is called, and will be born anew to the sunlight and the flowers."

Decidedly, neither belief nor tranquillity came to my mind. Indeed, my old friend V——, the child-poet, had but increased my torment. He had assuredly been inventing things. And yet, like all visionaries, he could, perhaps, divine the truth.

"Is it all true, what you have been telling me?" I ventured to ask him with a laugh.

He in his turn broke into gentle mirth. "Why, certainly it is true. Is not the infinite all true?"

That was the last time I saw him, for soon afterwards I had to quit Paris. But I can still picture him, glancing thoughtfully over the white expanse of the Luxembourg, so tranquil in the convictions born of his endless dream, whereas I am consumed by my desire to arrest and for all time determine Truth, which ever and ever flees.

## CHAPTER III

### LIFE'S GUST

EIGHTEEN months went by. I had been obliged to travel; great trials and great joys had impassioned my life amidst the tempest-gust which carries us all towards the Unknown. But at certain moments still I heard the woeful cry, "Angeline! Angeline! Angeline!" approach from afar and penetrate me. And then I trembled, full of doubt once more, tortured by my desire to know. I could not forget; for me there is no worse hell than uncertainty.

I cannot say how it was that one splendid June evening I again found myself on my bicycle on the lonely road that passes La Sauvagière. Had I expressly wished to see the place again, or was it mere instinct that had impelled me to quit the highway and turn in that direction? It was nearly eight o'clock, but, those being the longest days of the year, the sky was still radiant with a triumphal sunset, cloudless, all gold and azure. And how light and delicious was the atmosphere, how pleasant was the scent of foliage and grass, how softly and sweetly joyous was the far-stretching peacefulness of the fields!

As on the first occasion, amazement made me spring from my machine in front of La Sauvagière. I hesitated for a moment. The place was no longer the same. A fine new iron gate glittered in the sunset, the walls had been repaired, and the house, which I could scarce distinguish among the trees, seemed to have regained the smiling gaiety of youth. Was this, then, the predicted resurrection? Had Angeline returned to life at the call of the distant voice?

I had remained on the road, thunderstruck, still gazing, when a halting footfall made me start. I turned and saw Mother Toussaint bringing her cow back from a neighbouring patch of lucerne. "So those folks were not frightened, eh?" said I, pointing to the house.

She recognised me and stopped her beast. "Ah, monsieur!" she answered, "there are people who would tread on God Himself! The place has been sold for more than a year now. But it was a painter who bought it, a painter named B——, and those artists, you know, are capable of anything!"

Then she drove on her cow, shaking her head and adding: "Well, well, we must see how it will all turn out."

B——, the painter, the delicate and skillful artist who had portrayed so many amiable Parisiennes! I knew him a little; we shook hands when we met at theatres and shows, wherever, indeed, people are apt to meet. Thus, all at once, an irresistible longing seized me to go in, make my confession to him, and beg him to tell me what he knew of this Sauvagière, whose mystery ever haunted me. And without reasoning, without thought even of my dusty cycling suit, which custom, by the way, is now rendering permissible, I opened the gate and rolled my bycicle as far as the mossy trunk of an old tree. At the clear call of the bell affixed to the gate a servant came; I handed him my card and he left me for a moment in the garden.

My surprise increased still more when I glanced around me. The housefront had been repaired, there were no more cracks, no more disjointed bricks; the steps, girt with roses, were once more like a threshold of joyous welcome; and now the living windows smiled and spoke of the happiness behind their snowy curtains. Then, too, there was the garden rid of its nettles and brambles, the flowerbed reviviscent, resembling a huge and fragrant nosegay, and the old trees, standing amid the quietude of centuries, rejuvenated by the golden rain of the summer sun.

When the servant returned he led me to a drawing-room, saying that his master had gone to the neighbouring village, but would soon be home. I would have waited for hours. At first I took patience in examining the room, which was elegantly furnished, with heavy carpets, and window and door curtains of cretonne similar to that which upholstered the large settee and the deep arm-chairs. The hangings were, indeed, so full that I felt astonished at the sudden fall of the daylight. Then came darkness almost perfect. I know not how long I stayed there; I had been forgotten, no lamp even was brought me. Seated in the gloom, I once again yielded to my dreams and lived through the whole tragic story. Had Angeline been murdered? Or had she herself thrust a knife into her heart? And I must confess it, in that haunted house, where all had become so black, fear seized upon me—fear which was at the outset but slight uneasiness, a little creeping of the flesh, and which afterwards grew, froze me from head to foot, till I was filled with insane fright.

It seemed to me at first that vague sounds were echoing somewhere. 'Twas doubtless in the depths of the cellars. There were low moans, stifled sobs, footsteps as of some phantom. Then it all ascended and drew nearer, the whole dark house seemed to me full of that frightful anguish. All at once the terrible call rose, "Angeline! Angeline! Angeline!" with such increasing force that I fancied I could feel a puff of icy breath sweep across my face. A door of the drawing-room was flung open violently, Angeline entered and crossed the room without seeing me. I recognised her in the flash of light which came in with her from the hall, where a lamp was burning. 'Twas really she, the poor dead child, twelve years of age, so marvellously beautiful. Her splendid fair hair fell over her shoulders, and she was clad in white; she had come all white from the grave, whence every night she rose. Mute, scared, she passed before me, and vanished through another door, whilst again the cry rang out farther away, "Angeline! Angeline! Angeline!" And I—I remained erect, my brow wet with perspiration, in a state of horror, which made my hair stand on end, beneath the terror-striking blast that had come from the Mysterious.

Almost immediately afterwards, I fancy, at the moment when a servant at last brought a lamp, I became conscious that B——, the painter was beside me, shaking my hand and apologising for having kept me waiting so long. I showed no false pride, but, still quivering with dread, I at once told him my story. And with what astonishment did he not at first listen to me, and then with what kindly laughter did he not seek to reassure me!

"You were doubtless unaware, my dear fellow, that I am a cousin of the second Madame de G——. Poor woman! To accuse her of having murdered that child, she who loved her and wept for her as much as the father himself did! For the only point that is true is that the poor little girl did die here, not, thank Heaven! by her own hand, but from a sudden fever which struck her down like a thunderbolt, in such wise that the parents forsook this house in horror and would never return to it. This explains why it so long remained empty even in their lifetime. After their death came endless lawsuits, which prevented it from being sold. I wished to secure it myself, I watched for it for years, and I assure you that since we have been here we have seen no ghost."

The little quiver came over me again, and I stammered, "But Angeline, I have just seen her, here, this moment! The terrible voice was calling her, and she passed by, she crossed this room!"

He looked at me in dismay, fancying that my mind was affected. Then, all at once, he again broke into a sonorous, happy laugh.

"It was my daughter whom you saw. It so happens that Monsieur de G—— was her godfather; and in memory of his own dear daughter he chose for her the name of Angeline. No doubt her mother was calling her just now, and she passed through this room."

Then he himself opened a door, and once more raised the cry: "Angeline! Angeline! Angeline!"

The child returned, not dead, but living, sparkling with juvenile gaiety. 'Twas she in her white gown, with her splendid hair falling over her shoulders, and so beautiful, so radiant with hope, that she looked like an incarnation of all the springtide of life, bearing in the bud the promise of love and the promise of long years of happiness.

Ah! the dear *revenante*, the new child that had sprung from the one that was no more! Death was vanquished. My old friend, the poet V——, had told no

falsehood. Nothing is lost, renascerce comes to all, to beauty as well as love. Mothers' voices call them, those lasses of to-day, those sweethearts of to-morrow, and they live afresh beneath the sun, amid the flowers. And 'twas that awakening of youth that now haunted the house—the house which had once more become young and happy, in the joy at last regained that springs from life the eternal.

# Madame Neigeon

## CHAPTER I

### LIFE IN PARIS

EIGHT days have gone by since my father, M. de Vaugelade, allowed me to leave Le Boquet, the mournful old château where I was born, in Lower Normandy. My father has strange ideas about the present times; he is a good half-century behindhand. However, I am at last living in Paris, which I scarcely knew at all, having simply passed through it on two previous occasions. Fortunately, I am not over awkward in my ways. Félix Budin, my old schoolfellow at the College of Caen, pretended, on seeing me here, that I was superb, and that the Parisiennes would surely dote on me. This made me laugh. But when Félix had left, I

caught myself standing before a looking-glass, contemplating my five feet six inches, and smiling at my white teeth and black eyes. Then, however, I shrugged my shoulders, for I'm not conceited.

Yesterday for the first time in my life I spent an evening in a Parisian drawing-room. Countess de P——, who is in some degree my aunt, had asked me to dinner. It was her last Saturday. She wanted to introduce me to Monsieur Neigeon, a deputy for our constituency of Gommerville, who had just been appointed Under-Secretary of State, and is on the high road, so people say, to become a Minister. My aunt, who is far more tolerant than my father, plainly declared to me that a young man of my age must not sulk with his country, even if its government were republican. She wishes to get me an official appointment.

"'I will undertake to talk to that obstinate old Vaugelade," she said; "leave everything to me, my dear George."

Precisely at seven o'clock I reached the Countess's house. But it seems that people dine very late in Paris. The guests arrived one by one, and some had not yet put in an appearance when half-past seven struck. The Countess informed me with an expression of distress that she had been unable to secure Monsieur Neigeon's company; he was retained at Versailles by some parliamentary imbroglio. Nevertheless, she still hoped that he might look in for a moment during the evening. As a stop-gap she had invited another deputy of our department, "fat Gaucheraud," as we call him down there. I knew him already, as we had once gone shooting together.

This Gaucheraud is a short jovial fellow, who has lately let his whiskers grow in the hope of thereby giving himself a serious appearance. He was born in Paris, where his father was a petty solicitor of small means; but, down our way, he has a rich and very influential uncle, whom he somehow prevailed upon to run him as candidate. I was not aware that he was married; but at table my aunt placed me beside a young fair-haired lady, who looked very pretty and shy, and whom fat Gaucheraud called "Berthe" at the top of his voice.

We were all assembled at last. It was still daylight in the drawing-room, which looks towards the west, when all at once we entered the dining-room, which had its curtains drawn and was lit up by a chandelier and several lamps. The change seemed very singular, and as we took our seats some remarks were made about the way in which the last dinners of the winter season are saddened by the lingering twilight. My aunt detested it. And the conversation on the subject was kept up: how mournful, said somebody, did Paris look when you drove across it in the waning light on your way to an invitation. I said nothing myself, but I had not experienced any such impression in my cab, though it had jolted roughly over the paving stones for a half-hour. As a matter of fact, Paris, seen amidst the first gleams of the gaslight, had filled me with a passionate desire to partake of all the enjoyment with which it would presently blaze.

By the time the *entrées* were served, people raised their voices and politics were discussed. I was surprised to hear my aunt expressing political opinions. However, the other ladies were all conversant with State affairs, called prominent men by their names without any such prefix as "monsieur," and debated and passed judgment on everything and everybody. In front of me Gaucheraud was taking up an enormous amount of room and talking at the top of his voice whilst steadily eating and drinking. But all those political matters did not interest me; I did not even understand the true sense of many remarks, and so I ended by devoting all my attention to Madame Gaucheraud, Berthe, as I already called her in my own mind for brevity's sake. She was really very pretty. As she sat beside me her ear struck me as being particularly charming: a pretty little wounded ear it was, with light yellowish hair curling around it. She had one of those fair necks, covered behind with little wavy locks which quite upset one. Every now and then, when her shoulders moved, her dress-body, which was cut very low, gaped a little, and I noticed a supple, feline undulation about her back. I did not admire her profile so much, as it was rather sharp. She talked politics with even greater eagerness than any of the others.

"Madame, may I pour you out some wine? Shall I pass you the salt, madame?" I asked, striving to be as polite as possible, forestalling her slightest desires and interpreting her every glance and gesture. She had given me a long look as we sat down to table, as if to judge me once and for all.

"Politics bore you, do they not?" she said to me at last. "They plague *me* to death. But then one has to talk about something, and nowadays in society politics are the only thing that people care for."

Then she darted off to another subject.

"Is Gommerville a pretty place?" she asked. "Last summer my husband wanted to take me to see his uncle there, but I felt frightened and pretended that I was ill."

"The country is very fertile," I replied; "there are some beautiful plains."

"Ah! good. Now I know the truth," she resumed with a laugh. "It is a frightful spot, eh? A perfectly flat country with fields following fields, and ever the same fringes of poplar trees rising up at intervals."

I wanted to protest, but she had started off again, discussing some proposed law on secondary education with the guest seated on her right hand, a solemn-looking man with a white beard. At last, however, the conversation turned to theatricals. Whenever she leant foward to answer a question asked from the other end of the table, the feline undulations of her neck filled me with emotion. At Le Boquet, amidst the covert impatience of solitude, I had dreamt of a fair-haired beauty, but she was slow of gesture and had a noble face; and Berthe's mouse-like mein and curly hair quite revolutionised my dream. Nevertheless, while the vegetables were being served, I glided into some wild fancies. We were alone, she and I, and I kissed her on the neck and she turned round and smiled at me; whereupon we started together for some very distant land. But the dessert was served, and at that moment she said to me in a whisper, "Pass me that dish of sweetmeats there, in front of you."

It seemed to me that there was a caressing softness in her eyes, and the light pressure of her arm on the sleeve of my dress coat gave me a delightful thrill.

"I'm awfully fond of sweetmeats: aren't you?" she resumed, as she nibbled at some candied fruit.

Those simple words stirred me to such a degree that I fancied myself in love with her. As I raised my eyes I noticed Gaucheraud, who had been looking at me while I whispered with his wife. He wore his usual gay expression and smiled in an encouraging manner. The idea of the husband smiling calmed me.

But the dinner was drawing to an end. It did not seem to me that a Paris dinner party sparkled with more wit than one at Caen. Berthe alone surprised me. My aunt having complained of the warmth, the company reverted to their first subject of conversation, discussing the spring receptions, and finally opining that it was only at winter-time that one really dined well. Then we went off to the little drawing-room to take coffee there.

By degrees a great many people arrived. The three drawing-rooms and the dining-room like-wise became crowded. I had sought refuge in a corner, and as my aunt passed near me she said to me hurriedly: "Don't go away yet, George. His wife has arrived. He has promised to fetch her, and I will introduce you."

She was still talking of Monsieur Neigeon, but I scarcely listened. I had heard two young men near me exchanging hasty remarks which filled me with emotion. They were standing on tip-toes at a door of the big drawing-room, and at the moment when Félix Budin, my old school-fellow at Caen, came in and bowed to Madame Gaucheraud, the shorter of the two asked the other: "Are they still on the same terms?"

"Yes," the taller one answered, "more so than ever. It will last till the winter now. I have never known her keep an admirer so long."

This did not cause me any particular pang, but I felt hurt in my self-esteem. Why had she told me in so soft a voice that she was fond of sweet-meats? I certainly had no intention of contending against Félix, yet I ended by persuading myself that those young men had slandered

Madame Gaucheraud. I knew my aunt; she was a person of very rigid principles, and would not suffer women of doubtful repute in her house. Gaucheraud, as it happened, had just sprung forward to greet Félix, whom he tapped in a friendly way on the shoulder whilst eyeing him affection-ately.

"Ah! here you are," said Félix as soon as he discovered me. "I came on your account. Well, will you let me pilot you?"

We remained together in a recess formed by a doorway. I should greatly have liked to question him about Madame Gaucheraud, but I did not know how to do so in an off hand, indifferent way. Whilst seeking a transition I questioned him about a number of other people for whom I cared nothing at all. He named them to me, and gave precise particulars about each of them. He was, I should say, a Parisian by birth, and had merely spent a couple of years at the college at Caen at the time when his father was Prefect of the Department of Calvados. I found him very free in his language, and a smile appeared on his lips when I asked him for information about some of the women present.

"Are you looking at Madame Neigeon?" he suddenly asked me.

To tell the truth I was looking at Madame Gaucheraud. And so, somewhat foolishly, I answered: "'Madame Neigeon, ah! where is she?"

"She's that dark woman yonder, near the chimney-piece. She's talking with a fair woman in a low dress."

Near Madame Gaucheraud, indeed, there stood a lady whom I had not previously noticed, and who was laughing gaily.

"Ah! so that's Madame Neigeon," I repeated.

Then I examined her. It was a great pity that she was dark, for she struck me as being charming, not quite so tall as Berthe, but with a magnificent crown of black hair. Her eyes were both bright and soft. Her little nose, her finely modelled mouth, and her dimpled cheeks indicated a lively and yet thoughtful disposition. Such at least was my first impression. But my views became confused as I looked at her, for I soon saw her laughing more loudly and freely than even her friend.

"Do you know Neigeon?" Félix asked me.

"I? Not at all. My aunt is to introduce me to him."

"Oh! he's a nullity, a downright fool," Félix contiued. "Political mediocrity in all its perfection—one of those stop-gaps that are so useful in parliamentary government. As he does not possess two ideas of his own, and every prime minister can therefore employ him, he figures in the most contradictory ministerial combinations."

"And his wife?" I asked.

"His wife? Well, you see her. She is charming. If you want to obtain anything from him, pay court to his wife."

Félix affected some unwillingness to say anything further. But at last he gave me to understand that Madame Neigeon had made her husband's fortune, and continued watching over the home with a view to its prosperity. All Paris attributed lovers to her.

"And the fair lady?" I suddenly inquired.

"The fair lady," Félix answered without the faintest show of feeling, "is Madame Gaucheraud."

"She is a respectable woman, isn't she?"

"Oh! no doubt she's respectable."

Félix assumed a serious demeanour, but was unable to preserve it. His smile appeared once more, and I even fancied that I could detect on his features an expression of conceit which annoyed me. The two women had doubtless noticed that we were occupying ourselves with them, for they forced their laughter. I remained alone, a lady having led Fèlix away, and I spent the evening in comparing Madame Neigeon with Madame Gaucheraud, feeling at once hurt and attracted, failing to understand things aright, and experiencing the anxiety of a man who fears lest he may be guilty of some act of foolishness in venturing into a sphere of which he has no knowledge.

"Neigeon hasn't come; what a nuisance he is!" exclaimed my aunt when she again found me in the same corner by the door. "But it's always like that. True, it is barely midnight as yet, and his wife is still waiting for him."

I went round through the dining-room and took up a position at the other door of the *salon*. In this wise I found myself behind the two ladies I have mentioned. Just as I reached the spot I heard Berthe calling her friend "Louise." That is a pretty name. Louise was not wearing a low dress. Under her heavy coils of hair I could only see a white strip of neck, but that glimpse

of whiteness seemed to me for a moment to be far more fascinating than
the exhibition which Berthe was making
of her back. Then, however, I no
longer knew what to think; they both
seemed adorable, and in the perturbed
state in which I found myself it appeared to me impossible to choose between them.

But my aunt was looking for me
everywhere. It was already one
o'clock.

"Have you changed doors?" said she.
"Well, he won't come. Every evening
that man Neigeon has to save France.
At all events, I will introduce you to
his wife before she leaves. And mind
that you are amiable, for that is important."

Without awaiting my answer the
Countess placed me in front of Madame
Neigeon, giving her my name and briefly acquainting her with my position. I
felt rather awkward, and could scarcely find a few words. Louise waited
with that smile of hers on her face, and
then, seeing that I remained embarrassed, she simply bowed. It seemed
to me that Madame Gaucheraud was
looking at me contemptuously. Both
rose, however, and withdrew. In the
antechamber, used as a cloak-room, a
fit of wild merriment came over them.
However, their free and easy, bold,
masculine ways astonished nobody but
me. As they passed, the other men
drew back and bowed to them with a
commingling of extreme politeness and
social goodfellowship which stupefied
me.

Félix offered me a seat in his cab.
But I escaped from him, for I wished
to be alone; and I did not hail any
driver, for it pleased me to go on foot
through the silence and solitude of the
streets. I felt feverish, just as one feels
at the approach of some severe illness.
Was a passion springing up within me?
Like the travelers who pay tribute to
new climes, I was about to be sorely
tried by the atmosphere of Paris.

## CHAPTER II

### LOUISE

IT WAS only this afternoon that I
met those ladies again, this time at the
Salon de Peinture, which, it so happened, opened to-day. I confess that
I knew I should meet them there, and
that it would be very difficult for me
to pronounce an opinion on the value
of the three or four thousand paintings
before which I promenaded for four
successive hours. Félix had promised
me yesterday that he would call for
me about noon; we were to lunch at
a restaurant in the Champs-Elysées
and then repair to the Salon.

I have reflected a great deal since
the Countess's *soirée* took place, but
I must own that reflection has not
brought me much enlightenment. How
strange a world is Parisian society, at
once so polished and so corrupt! I am
not a rigid moralist, but none the less
I feel embarrassed when I think of
the fearful things that I heard men
saying to one another in my aunt's
drawing-room. If one was to believe
their muttered comments, more than
half the women present were disreput-
able. How was one to tell the truth
amidst all those assertions? I had at
first thought that, in spite of all my

father had said on the subject, my aunt really received a very questionable set. But Félix asserted that things were just the same in most Parisian drawing-rooms. Ladies, even the most severely inclined among them, were compelled to show a great deal of tolerance lest they should find their houses forsaken. Then, my first feeling of revolt having calmed down, I simply felt an impulse to snatch at the facile pleasures placed within my reach.

For the last four days I had never awoke in my little flat in the Rue Laffitte without thinking of Louise and Berthe, as I familiarly called them. A singular phenomenon was at work within me; I ended by confounding them together. I was now certain that Félix was Berthe's lover, but this, instead of wounding my feelings, seemed a kind of encouragement, and though my thoughts and plans remained very vague, I was convinced that I had only to choose between Berthe and Louise to become the master of one or the other.

When we entered the first gallery of the Fine Art show I was amazed at the great crowd that was stifling there. "The Devil," muttered Félix; "we are rather late. We shall have to use our elbows."

It was a very mixed throng of artists, bourgeois and society people. In the midst of overcoats badly brushed, and frockcoats black and gloomy, there were many light gowns, those spring Paris gowns which look so gay with their soft silk and their bright trimmings. And I was particularly delighted by the quiet assurance of the women, who cut through the thickest of the throng without even a thought of their trains, whose waves of lace always ended by effecting a passage. In this wise they went from one picture to another as if they were simply crossing their drawing-rooms. Only Parisiennes can thus retain a goddess-like serenity in a public crush, as if the words they hear, and the contact they have to put up with, could not possibly reach and soil them. For a moment I watched one lady who Félix told me was the Duchesse d'A——. She was accompanied by two daughters of from sixteen to eighteen years of age; and the three of them examined a 'Leda' without so much as blinking, whilst a party of young painters behind them made merry over the picture with the greatest freedom of language.

But Félix turned into the left-hand galleries, a succession of large square rooms where the crowd was less compact. A white light fell from the glazed roof, a crude light softened by linen hangings. The dust raised by the tramping of the people set, as it were, some slight smoke above the sea of heads. The women needed to be very pretty to bear the effect of that light, that uniform tone, with which the paintings on the four surrounding walls contrasted violently. There one perceived an extraordinary medley of colours, reds, yellows and blues all clashing and running riot amidst the bright gold of the picture-frames. It was becoming very warm. Some bald-headed gentlemen with polished glistening craniums puffed as they walked about, hat in hand. Every nose was raised upward. There was quite a crush in front of certain canvases. And one incessantly heard the tramping of feet over the floor boards, accompanied by a vague, endless clamour like the roaring of waves.

"Ah!" Félix suddenly remarked to me, "there's the big affair that folks talk so much about."

People stood, five rows deep, in contemplation before "the big affair." There were ladies with glasses, artists talking spitefully, and a tall lean gentleman taking notes. But I scarcely gave a glance in that direction, for in a neighbouring room I had caught sight of two ladies leaning against the handrail and inquisitively examining a little picture on the line. At first there was but a flash of thick black tresses and a mass of fair fluffy hair, showing under stylish hats. Then this vision vanished; a wave of the crowd, a sea of heads hid both ladies from my view. But I could have sworn to them. After taking a few steps, I again caught sight now of the fair hair, now of the black tresses between the ever-moving heads in front of me. I said nothing to Félix; I contented myself with leading him into the next room, manœuvring in such wise that it might seem as if he were the first to recognise the ladies. Had he already noticed them, as I had done? I almost believed so, for he gave me a glance full of delicate irony.

"Ah! what a fortunate meeting!" he exclaimed as he bowed.

The ladies turned and smiled. I awaited the effect of this second interview; it was decisive. Madame Neigeon quite upset me with a mere glance of her black eyes, whereas I seemed to be simply meeting a friend again in the person of Madame Gaucheraud.

This time, then, it was the lightning flash. *She* — Madame Neigeon — was wearing a small yellow hat trimmed with a branch of glycine, and her gown was of mauve silk with trimmings of straw-coloured satin, the whole forming a very soft yet showy toilette. However, it was only later that I really scrutinised her. At the first moment she appeared to me in a blaze of light, as if she scattered sunbeams around her.

But Félix was talking. "Nothing remarkable, eh?" said he; "I have seen nothing yet."

"It is the same, *mon Dieu,* as it is every year," Berthe declared.

Then, turning towards the wall, she added: "Look at this little painting which Louise discovered. The gown is so beautifully done! Madame de Rochetaillé wore one exactly like it at the ball at the Elysée."

"Yes," murmured Louise, "only the *ruches* fell squarewise over the *tablior*."

They again studied the little picture, which represented a lady standing before a boudoir mantelpiece, reading a letter. The painting seemed to me very commonplace, but somehow I felt full of sympathy for the painter.

"Why, where is he?" suddenly asked Berthe, as she looked around her. "He loses us at every dozen yards!"

She was speaking of her husband.

"Oh! Gaucheraud is over yonder," quietly exclaimed Félix, who could see everybody. "He is looking at that big Christ in sugar-candy, hanging from a gingerbread cross."

In a peaceful, disinterested way the husband with his hands behind him was indeed making the round of the room on his own account. On catching sight of us he came up to shake hands, and said in his jovial fashion: "There's a Crucifixion yonder which shows remarkable religious sentiment. Have you noticed it?"

The ladies, however, were walking on. We followed them with Gaucheraud. His presence authorised us to accompany them. We spoke of Monsieur Neigeon, who would no doubt look in at the show if he could only escape early enough from a committee meeting, at which he was to give the Government's opinion on a very important question. Gaucheraud meantime took possession of me with many expressions of friendship. This embarrassed me, for it was necessary that I should answer him. Félix smiled, and gently nudged my elbow, but I failed to understand him. For his part, profiting by the fact that I was keeping the fat man occupied, he walked on in front with the ladies. I only caught snatches of their conversation.

"So you are going to the Variétés this evening?"

"Yes, I have taken a corner box; the piece is said to be amusing. . . . I shall take you, Louise—Oh! I insist on it."

And further on:

"So now the season is over. The opening of the Salon is the final Parisian solemnity."

"But you forget the races!"

"Ah! yes, I've an idea of going to the races at Maisons-Laffitte. It's a very pretty place, I'm told."

Meantime Gaucheraud was talking to me about Le Boquet, a superb estate, said he, the value of which had been more than doubled by my father. I could tell that he was bent on flattery. But I barely listened to him. I was stirred to the depths of my being each time that Louise's long train brushed against me, as she suddenly stopped before some picture. Under her black hair, her white neck looked as delicate as a child's. However, she retained her masculine ways, which somewhat annoyed me. A great many people bowed to her, and she laughed at them and attracted general attention by her outbursts of gaiety and the quick motions of her skirts. On two occasions she turned around and looked at me fixedly. I walked on as in a dream; I could not say how many hours I followed her in this fashion, dazed by Gaucheraud's chatter and the leagues of paintings which spread out on right and left. I only knew that towards the end we were all chewing dust, and that for my own part I felt horribly fatigued, whereas the women bore up and smiled with all bravery.

At six o'clock Félix carried me off to dinner. And at dessert he suddenly exclaimed: "I've got to thank you."

"What for?" I asked him in great surprise.

"Why, for the delicacy you have shown in not paying court to Madame Gaucheraud. So you prefer dark women?"

I could not help flushing, but he hastily added: "Oh! I don't desire your confidence. You must have noticed that I abstained from intervening. In my opinion, a man ought to make his apprenticeship in life alone."

He was no longer smiling, but wore a serious, friendly air.

"So you think——" I began.

"I think nothing," he answered. "Do as you fancy. You will soon see how things turn out."

ᐟ I regarded this remark as a piece of encouragement. Félix had reverted to his ironical tone, and lightly, as if jesting, he pretended that Gaucheraud would have liked to see me fall in love with his wife.

"Oh! you don't know the beggar! You didn't understand why he flung himself so eagerly on your neck. The fact is that his uncle's influence is declining in your district, and if he had to face another election he would be heartily glad of your father's support. Well, as you can understand, I felt frightened directly I saw that you might be useful to him, for he has used me up already."

"But that's abominable!" I exclaimed.

"Why abominable?" Félix resumed in so quiet a fashion that I could not tell whether he was in earnest or not. "When a woman is bound to have friends, it is just as well that they should prove useful to the home."

On rising from table Félix talked of going to the Variétés. I had seen the piece there two days previously; but I dissembled, and expressed a keen desire to become acquainted with it. And what a charming evening we spent; The ladies happened to be in a corner box quite close to our stalls. On turning my head I could read on Louise's features the pleasure she took in the actors' jests. A couple of evenings previously I had found those jests idiotic. But they no longer offended me; I enjoyed them, since they seemed to foster a kind of complicity between Louise and myself. It was a very broad piece, and it was at the most questionable passages that she laughed the loudest. Whenever our eyes met

amidst the laughter she refrained from lowering them. I could not help thinking that the piece helped on my interests. Truth to tell, the whole house enjoyed itself; many women in the balcony stalls laughed outright, without even indulging in any fan play by way of hiding their blushes.

We went to pay our respects to the ladies during one of the entr'actes. Gaucheraud had just gone out, so we were able to sit down. The box was very gloomy, and I could feel Louise near me. Her skirts were spread out, and at a sudden movement she made they quite covered my knees. It was entrancing to be thus near her. That contact seemed to me like a first, secret avowal, which bound us one to the other.

## CHAPTER III

### A BARGAIN

TEN days have now gone by. Félix has disappeared, and I can devise no pretext that might bring me and Madame Neigeon together again. My only resource is to buy five or six daily papers in which I read her husband's name. He intervened lately in a serious debate in the Chamber, and delivered a speech about which people are still talking. At any other time that speech would have bored me to death, but nowadays it interests me, because it seems as if I could distinguish Louise's white neck and black tresses behind all the verbose phraseology. I have even had a violent discussion about Monsieur Neigeon— whose incapacity I defended—with a gentleman whom I scarcely know. The malicious attacks of the newspapers quite upset me. That man is an imbecile, no doubt, but then this only proves the superior intelligence of his wife, if indeed it be true, as people say, that she has been the good fairy to whom he owes his fortune.

During these ten days of vain impatience and fruitless rambles I have called quite five times on my aunt, ever in the hope of some piece of good luck, some unforeseen meeting. On the occasion of my last call I managed to displease the countess so seriously that it will be a long time before I shall dare to return to her house. She had taken it into her head to procure me an appointment in the diplomatic service by Monsieur Neigeon's influence; and her stupefaction was intense when I refused the offer on account of my political opinions. The worst was that I accepted it originally, that is, before I had fallen in love with Louise, and had come to the conclusion that I could not decently accept any favours from her husband's hands.

My aunt, who had no notion of the motives of delicacy which actuated me, expressed profound astonishment at what she called my childish capriciousness. Did not many Legitimists, who were quite as scrupulous as myself, represent the Republic abroad? she asked. Indeed, diplomacy was the refuge of the Legitimists. They filled the embassies and rendered useful service to the good cause by keeping possession of high positions which the Republicans envied them.

I was, for good reasons, greatly embarrassed as to how I might answer my aunt, and at last I sought a refuge in ridiculous rigidity of principles, whereupon my aunt ended by calling me a fool, for she felt all the more furious since she had already mentioned the affair to Monsieur Neigeon. But no matter! At all events, Louise will never have cause to think that I court her simply in order to secure a berth from the Government.

People would laugh at me if I were to relate through what a strange succession of feelings I have passed during the last ten days. At first I felt convinced that Louise had noticed the emotion with which she inspired me, and that it was not displeasing to her. Thus conquest on my part seemed quite possible. But on reflection I began to doubt all this. Surely I must be a fool to think that a woman would throw herself at my head so openly and quickly. Madame Neigeon could have no thought of me. It was quite possible that she had already had lovers, but assuredly any intrigue in which she had engaged had been a far more intricate affair than this. There must be a great distance between such a woman as I had dreamt of, a creature of mere elementary passions and instincts, and an artful Parisienne, expert in concealment, such as Louise doubtless was.

Thus she seemed to escape me entirely. I no longer saw her, I no longer knew even if it were indeed true that I had spent five minutes with her in a gloomy box in a theatre, feeling her palpitate beside me. And I became very wretched—to such a point, in fact, that for a moment I thought of hurrying back to Le Boquet and shutting myself up there.

But on the day before yesterday there

came to me an idea which I was astonished at not having had before. It was to attend a sitting of the Chamber. Perhaps Monsieur Neigeon would speak, perhaps his wife would be there. But it was written that I was not yet to set eyes upon that singular man. Though it had been decided that he should speak, he did not even put in an appearance. It was related that he had been detained by some committee business at the Senate. On the other hand, as I was sitting down in the rear of one of the galleries I experienced keen emotion, for I perceived Madame Gaucheraud in the front row of the gallery facing me. She saw me and looked at me with a smile. Louise, alas! was not with her. My delight fell. On leaving, however, I contrived to meet Madame Gaucheraud in a passage. She displayed a familiar manner. Félix had certainly spoken to her about me.

"Have you been absent from Paris?" she inquired.

I remained speechless, indignant at such a question. Absent! when I had been scouring the city so furiously!

"Well, one meets you nowhere!" she resumed. "The last reception at the Ministry was superb, and the Horse Show was marvellous."

Then, noticing my expression of despair, she began to laugh.

"Well, till to-morrow," she said, as she walked away. "We shall see you over yonder, shan't we?"

I answered "Yes" in a stupid fashion, never daring to ask a question for fear that I might again hear her laugh. She had turned around, and looked at me with a malicious expression. "Come,"

she murmured, in the discreet tone of a friend who had some pleasant surprise in store for one.

A wild impulse came upon me to run off after her and question her. But she had already turned into another passage, and I bitterly reproached myself with my foolish pride, which had prevented me from acknowledging my ignorance. I was certainly quite ready to go "yonder;" but where might "yonder" be? The vagueness of the appointment tortured me, and at the same time I felt ashamed at not knowing what everybody else seemed to know. In the evening I hastened to Félix's rooms, with the view of skilfully extracting from him the information which I needed. But Félix was not at home. Then, in my grief, I plunged into the perusal of the newspapers, selecting those which gave the most society news, and striving to guess, amongst the announcements for the morrow, what spot *le bon ton* would select as a meeting-place. But my perplexity increased, for all sorts of functions were announced: an exhibition of paintings by some of the old masters, a charity bazaar at a big club, a musical mass at Sainte-Clotilde, a general rehearsal, two concerts, the veil-taking of an aristocratic novice, without mentioning horse races in all sorts of directions. How could a new arrival in Paris, a provincial conscious of his shortcomings, hope to arrive at the truth amidst such confusion! I understood perfectly well that the proper thing was to attend one of those functions, but which one was it, O heaven? Finally, at the risk of wandering about all day consumed with vain impatience if I were mistaken, I dared to make a choice. It occurred to me that I had heard the ladies speak of the races at Maisons-Laffitte, and, an inspiration coming to me, I resolved to repair thither. This decision taken, I began to feel calmer.

What a delightful stretch of country is that formed by the environs of Paris! I was not acquainted with Maisons-Laffitte, which charmed me with its houses so gay of aspect, built on a slope which borders the Seine. Now that we have reached the first days of May, the apple-trees, which are all white, look like big bouquets amidst the tender greenery of poplar and elm.

At first, however, I quite lost my bearings between the walls and the quick-set hedges, for I was unwilling to ask anybody the way. On seeing a great many people take the same train I had felt overjoyed, but the ladies were not there, and as I scanned the passers-by in Maisons-Laffitte itself my heart contracted. I was really losing myself alongside the Seine, beyond all the houses, when all at once keen emotion brought me to a standstill, near a big tuft of nettles. A group of people, still some fifty yards away, was slowly coming towards me, and I recognized Louise and Berthe. Gaucheraud and Félix, those inseparables, followed them at a distance of a few paces. So I had guessed rightly! This filled me with pride. But my emotion was so great that I behaved like a nincompoop. I hid myself behind the tall clump of nettles, full of a nameless shame, dreading lest I should appear ridiculous. When Louise passed, the hem of her skirt brushed against the bushes. How-

ever, I at once realised the folly of my first impulse. And so I made all haste to cut across the fields, and as the others reached a bend in the road I came up in the most natural manner possible—like a man, indeed, who thinking himself alone is yielding to the dreamy mood inspired by the open air.

"Oh! is it you?" cried Gaucheraud.

I bowed, affecting extreme surprise. We all raised exclamations and shook hands. But Félix laughed in his singular fashion, whilst Berthe positively winked at me, thereby establishing additional complicity between us. As we walked on, I remained for a few seconds with her, behind the others.

"So you have come?" she said to me gaily, in an undertone.

And without giving me time to answer, she began to jest, saying that I was very happy in still being so young. I felt that I had an ally in her; it seemed to me that she would have been well pleased to help me with her friend. Then as Félix turned round to inquire, "What are you laughing about?" she replied in all tranquillity: "Oh, Monsieur de Vaugelade has been telling me of his journey in the company of a whole family of English tourists."

Gaucheraud, however, had again taken Félix by the arm, and was leading him off as if to avoid troubling my tête-à-tête with his wife. I remained between her and Louise, and spent a most entrancing hour on the shady road which followed the banks of the Seine. Louise was wearing a light silk gown, and her sunshade with its pink lining steeped her face in a warm, shadowless glow. Here in the country there was more freedom than ever in her demeanour; she talked in a loud voice, and looked me full in the face whilst replying to Berthe, who turned the conversation to rather venturesome subjects with a pertinacity which greatly struck me later on.

"Give Madame Neigeon your arm," she ended by saying to me. "You are certainly not gallant; you can surely see that she is tired."

I offered Louise my arm and she leant on it at once. Then, Berthe having joined her husband and Félix, we two remained together more than forty paces behind. The road ascended the slope, and we walked very slowly. Down below flowed the Seine between meadows stretching out like carpets of green velvet. There was a long slender island, too, intersected by two bridges, over which the trains rushed with a noise like distant thunder. Then across the water there was a vast cultivated plain stretching to Mont Valérien, whose grey buildings could be seen amidst a dust of sunshine on the very fringe of the sky. But what affected me almost to tears was an odour of springtide, spreading all around us as it rose from the herbage on either side of the road.

"Shall you soon go back to Le Boquet?" Louise asked me.

I was foolish enough to answer "No," for I did not foresee that she would add: "Ah! that's annoying, for next week we are going to Les Mûreaux, my husband's property, which is only some two leagues from your place, and my husband meant to ask you to call and see us there."

At this I began to stammer that my father might possibly recall me sooner than I had expected. It had seemed to me that I could feel her arm pressing my own. Was she giving me an assignation, then? With the ideas that I had formed of this Parisienne, so free and coquettish in her ways, I at once built up a perfect romance: an intrigue in the country, a whole month of passion under the trees. Yes, it was doubtless thus; she found in me the qualities of a young squire, and would grant me her love amidst suitable surroundings.

"I have to scold you," she suddenly resumed, assuming an affectionate, almost maternal manner.

"How is that?" I murmured.

"Yes, your aunt has spoken to me about you. It seems that you will not accept anything from us. That is very discourteous. Why do you refuse—tell me?"

I blushed again; I was on the point of making a declaration, of exclaiming, "I refuse because I love you." But she made a gesture as if she understood my intention and wished me to remain silent. And then she added with a laugh: "If you are proud, if you wish to render service for service, we will willingly accept your protection over yonder. You know that a General Councillor has to be elected. My husband is a candidate, but he fears defeat, which in our position would be very unpleasant. Will you help us?"

It was impossible to be more charming. That election story seemed to me to be a mere pretext devised by a clever woman to enable us to meet again in the country.

"But certainly I'll help you," I answered.

"And if you succeed in getting my husband returned, it is understood that he in his turn will give you a helping hand."

"It is a bargain."

"Yes, a bargain."

She offered me her little hand, and I tapped it, as the custom goes, by way of sealing our agreement. We made merry together. It really seemed to me most delightful. We had passed the last of the trees, the sunlight streamed down on the crest of the hill, and we walked on, silent, amidst the great heat. But of course that imbecile Gaucheraud must come to disturb that quivering silence under the flaming sky. He had heard us mention the General Council, and he gave me no more peace, but began to tell me all about his uncle, and to manœuvre for an introduction to my father. At last we reached the race ground. They found the races superb. For my part, I stood all the time behind Louise, looking at her delicate neck. And how delightful was the return homeward after a sudden shower! Beneath the rain the greenery had become softer still, the leaves and the earth sent forth a delightful smell, the very scent of love. Louise half closed her eyes, as if tired and penetrated by all the voluptuousness of spring-time.

"Remember our bargain," she said to me at the railway station, as she entered her carriage which was waiting there. "At Les Mûreaux in a fortnight's time, eh?"

I pressed the hand she offered and I fear that I must have been a little rough, as for the first time I saw her become grave, with two little creases as of displeasure about her lips.

But Berthe still seemed bent on encouraging me to be bold, and Félix retained his enigmatical smile, whilst Gaucheraud slapped me on the shoulder, exclaiming, "At Les Mûreaux in a fortnight, Monsieur de Vaugelade. We shall all be there."

The devil take him!

## CHAPTER IV

### NEWS

I HAVE just come back from Les Mûreaux, and such contradictory ideas and impressions fill my mind that it is needful I should recapitulate the day I have spent with Louise in order to arrive at a clear opinion.

Although the estate of Les Mûreaux is only two leagues from Le Boquet, I knew little of that part of our district. Our own shooting is in the direction of Gommerville, and, as a rather long round has to be made to cross the little Béage river, I had not gone there a dozen times in my life. Yet the slope is delightful, with its climbing road edged by big walnut-trees. Then, after reaching the plateau you dip down again, and Les Mûreaux lies at the entry of a dale, whose slopes soon contract into a narrow gorge. The house, a square building of the seventeenth century, is of no great importance, but the grounds are magnificent, with their broad lawns and the snatch of forest land at the far end—such a tangle of trees that the very paths are barred by the branches.

When I arrived on horseback two big dogs greeted me with a prolonged barking and jumping. At the end of the avenue I caught sight of a white spot. It was Louise in a light gown and a straw hat. She did not come down to meet me, but remained motionless and smiling on the large flight of steps that leads to the hall. It was nine o'clock at the latest.

"Ah, how nice of you!" she called to me; "you, at all events are an early riser. I am the only one up at the château, as you see."

I complimented her, saying that for a Parisienne she was really courageous. But she added with a laugh: "It is true that I have only been here five days. I would get up with the chickens the first mornings. Only, as soon as the second week arrives, I gradually relapse into my sluggardly ways and end by coming down at ten o'clock, the same as in Paris. This morning, however, I am still a country woman."

I had never seen her looking so charming. In her haste to leave her room she had negligently knotted her hair, and slipped into the first morning wrap she found. And with her eyes still moist with sleep and her cheeks quite fresh she seemed a young girl again. Some little locks of hair were waving over her neck, and whenever her broad sleeves gaped I could see her bare arms as far as the elbows.

"Do you know where I was going?" she resumed. "Well, I was going to inspect a screen of convolvuli on that arbour yonder. It is marvellous, it seems, when the sun has not yet closed the flowers. The gardener told me of it, and as I missed the sight yesterday, I don't want to do so to-day. You will come with me, won't you?"

I felt a great inclination to offer her my arm, but I understood in time that it would be ridiculous. She ran on like a school-girl enjoying a holiday. On reaching the arbour she gave a cry of admiration. From aloft hung quite a drapery of convolvuli, a shower of little bells, pearly with dew, and of delicate hues ranging from vivid rose colour to violet and pale blue. The whole suggested one of those phantasies of exquisite grace and strangeness that one finds in Japanese albums.

"This is one's reward when one gets up early," said Louise merrily.

Then she sat down under the arbour, and on seeing that she drew back her skirts to make a little room, I ventured to place myself beside her. I was in a state of keen emotion, for the thought had come to me of bringing matters to a crisis by catching her round the waist and kissing her on the neck. I felt well enough that such roughness was better suited to a young lieutenant dealing with a housemaid, but I could think of nothing else. I don't know whether Louise understood what was passing in my mind; but though she did not get up, her face assumed a very grave expression.

"First of all, shall we talk of our business?" she said.

There was a buzzing in my ears, but I tried to listen to her. It was dim and rather cold in the arbour. Sparks of golden sunshine came in here and there between the foliage of the convolvuli, and on Louise's white wrap they looked like golden flies, golden insects, settling there.

"Well, what is the position?" she asked me with the air of an accomplice.

I thereupon told her of the singular

change which I had noticed at my father's. He, who for ten years had never ceased railing at the new state of things and had forbidden me to serve the Republic, had now given me to understand, on the very evening of my return, that a young man of my age owed duty to his country. I suspected my aunt of having effected this conversion. Some women must have been set on him. Louise smiled as she listened, and she ended by saying: "I met Monsieur de Vaugelade three days ago at a neighbouring château where I was making a call. We had a little conversation."

Then she quickly added: "You know that the election for the General Council will take place next Sunday. You must start on your campaign at once. With your father's help my husband's success will be certain."

"Is Monsieur Neigeon here?" I inquired after some slight hesitation.

"Yes; he arrived last night. But you won't see him this morning, for he has gone off in the direction of Gommerville to take *déjeuner* with a friend, a landowner who has a good deal of influence."

She rose up, but I remained seated for yet another moment, deeply regretting that I had not kissed her on the neck, for never should I again find such a dim little nook and such an early propitious hour. It was too late now, and I understood so thoroughly that I should simply make her laugh by falling at her feet on the damp ground, that I put off my declaration till a more favourable moment.

Besides, I had just perceived Gauch-

eraud's bulky silhouette at the end of the path. On seeing Louise and myself come out of the arbour he gave a little sneer. Then he expressed astonishment at our courage in rising so early. For his part, he had only just come down.

"And Berthe?" Louise asked him; "did she sleep well?"

"Well, I really don't know," he answered; "I haven't seen her yet."

Then, noticing my astonishment, he explained that his wife had a headache for the whole day whenever she was disturbed in the morning. And he added that they had long found it most convenient to have separate rooms, one for him and one for her. I must confess that this gave me food for thought. I recalled all manner of stories that I had heard and read of Parisiennes in country houses, and when I saw Berthe and my friend Félix come together out of the hall, I could not help thinking that my surmises might be true.

I shook hands with Félix; and, I can hardly account for it, but by the smile which Louise and Berthe exchanged whilst Gaucheraud stood by, quietly whistling, the idea occurred to me that Louise was not ignorant of the matter I have referred to. And more than ever now I regretted not having kissed her while we were in the dim little arbour.

We had *déjeuner* at eleven o'clock. After the meal Gaucheraud took himself off for his siesta. He had unbosomed himself to me, telling me that he feared he might not be successful at the next elections, and that he proposed remaining three weeks in the district in the hope of gaining support. Thus, after staying with his uncle, he had desired to spend a few days at Les Mûreaux in order to show everybody that he was on the best of terms with the Neigeons, for this, in his opinion, might win him a good many votes. I understood that he was also extremely desirous of being invited to my father's. Unfortunately, it seemed that I did not care for fair-haired women.

I spent a very gay afternoon with the ladies and Félix. Château life, with Parisian graces frolicking in the open air amidst the sunshine of early summer, is really charming. The drawing-room spreads out over the lawns. It is no longer the winter drawing-room, where you are virtually cooped up, where the women in low dresses ply their fans while the men in black swallow-tails stand up alongside the walls. It is a kind of holiday drawing-room, with women in light garb scampering freely hither and thither, while the men in their short jackets show themselves amiable and natural: a setting aside, as it were, of society etiquette, a familiarity which banishes the boredom of the stereotyped conversation that one hears at the winter gatherings. Nevertheless, I must confess that the behaviour of the ladies still surprised me, reared as I was in the provinces among pious folk. When we took coffee on the terrace after *déjeuner,* Louise allowed herself a cigarette, and Berthe talked slang in the most natural manner possible. Later on they took themselves off amidst a great rustling of skirts, and one heard them laughing

in the distance, and calling one another, full of a flightiness which greatly disturbed me. It is foolish to own it, but these manners, so novel to one like myself, made me hope that Louise would give me an early assignation. As for Félix, he quietly went on smoking cigarettes, but at times I caught him looking at me in his almost sarcastic way.

At half-past four I spoke of leaving. But Louise immediately protested: "No, no; you can't go yet. I shall keep you to dinner. My husband will certainly come back, and then you will see him. Really, now, I must introduce you to him."

I explained to her that my father was expecting me. I was compelled to be present at a dinner he was giving at Le Boquet, and with a laugh I continued: "It is an election dinner; I have got to work for you."

"Oh! in that case," said she, "make haste. And if you succeed, you know, come for your reward."

It seemed to me that she blushed as she spoke those words. Did she simply refer to the appointment in the diplomatic service which my father is urging me to accept? I thought I might attribute another meaning to her words, and no doubt I assumed a very conceited air, for all at once, for the second time, I saw her become very grave, with those little creases about the lips which gave her such an expression of proud displeasure.

But I had no time to reflect upon that sudden change of expression. As I was starting a little conveyance drew up before the house steps. I already imagined that the husband had returned. But there were only two children, a little girl about five, and a little boy of four, in the vehicle, accompanied by a maid. They stretched out their arms and laughed, and as soon as they could spring to the ground they threw themselves among Louise's skirts. She kissed them on the hair.

"Whose pretty children are these?" I asked.

"Why, mine," she replied with an air of surprise.

Hers! I cannot express in words what a blow that simple answer dealt me. It seemed to me as if she were all at once escaping from me, as if those little beings with puny hands were digging an impassable abyss between her and me. What! she was a mother, and I had known nothing of it! I could not restrain the cry: "So you have children?"

"No doubt," she quietly responded. "They went to see their godmother, two leagues from here, this morning. Allow me to introduce them, Monsieur Lucien, Mademoiselle Marguerite."

The little ones smiled at me. I must have looked very stupid. No, I could not accustom myself to the idea of it. It upset all my notions. I went off with my head in a whirl, and even at this moment I don't know what to think. I see Louise in the arbour draped with convolvuli, and I see her kissing the hair of Lucien and Marguerite. Decidedly, those Parisiennes are far too intricate for provincials like me. I must get to sleep. I will try to understand things to-morrow.

# CHAPTER V

## A LESSON

THIS is the finish of my adventure. Oh, what a lesson! But let me try to relate things calmly.

Last Sunday Monsieur Neigeon was elected as General Councillor. After the counting of the votes it became evident that without our support he would have failed. My father, who, for his part, has seen Monsieur Neigeon, gave me to understand that a man of such utter mediocrity was not to be feared. Besides, it was a question of beating a Radical candidate. However, after dinner in the evening the old Adam reappeared in my father and he contented himself with saying to me:

"All that is not very clean business. But everybody repeated to me that I was working for you. Well, do what you think fit. For me the only course left is to take myself off, for I no longer understand things."

On the Monday and Tuesday I hesitated about going to Les Mûreaux. It seemed to me that it would be bad taste to go in search of thanks so quickly. The thought of the children no longer inconvenienced me. I had persuaded myself that there was very little motherliness about Louise. Besides, did not people say in our part of the country that the Parisiennes never allowed children to interfere with their amusements, but handed them over to the care of servants, so as to enjoy perfect liberty themselves? So yesterday, Wednesday, all my scruples disappeared. I was consumed with impatience, and set off for the battle at eight o'clock in the morning.

My plan was to reach Les Mûreaux as on the first occasion, at an early hour, so as to find Louise alone. But when I dismounted from my horse, a servant told me that Madame had not yet left her room, and made no offer to go and warn her of my arrival. So I simply replied that I would wait.

And, indeed, I waited two long hours. I don't know how many times I made the round of the flower-beds. Every now and again I raised my eyes to the first-floor windows, but the shutters remained closed. Tired, enervated by this long promenade, I ended by sitting down in the bower of convolvuli. The sky was overcast that morning, and the sunshine did not glide in golden dust between the foliage. It was almost night, indeed, amidst the verdure. I reflected, resolving that I must risk everything. I was convinced that if I should again hesitate I should lose Louise for ever. As soon as I should be alone with her I would take hold of her hands and affect great emotion so as not to frighten her too much, but afterwards I would kiss her on the neck, as I had thought of doing on the former occasion. I was for the tenth time perfecting my plan when all at once Louise herself appeared before me.

"Where are you hiding?" she gaily called, looking for me in the dark arbour. "Oh! you are here, are you? I have been hunting for you for the last ten minutes. I must apoligise for having kept you waiting."

Somewhat huskily I answered that there was nothing unpleasant in having

to wait when one's thoughts were of her.

"I warned you," she replied, without paying attention to my silly compliment, "that I'm not a country woman for more than the first week. I've now become a Parisian again, and can no longer leave my bed."

She had remained at the entrance of the arbour, as if she did not wish to risk herself amidst the gloom falling from the foliage.

"Well, aren't you coming?" she ended by asking me. "We have to talk, you know."

"But one is very comfortable here," said I, in a quivering voice. "We can talk on this bench."

She again hesitated, just for a second, then bravely replied: "Oh! as you like. It is rather dark here, still we don't need to see our words."

Thereupon she sat down near me. I felt like fainting. So the fateful hour had come! Yet another minute and I should take hold of her hands. She, however, still perfectly at ease, continued chatting in her clear voice, in which there was not the faintest sign of emotion.

"I won't thank you in ready-made phrases," said she. "You have given us good help, without which we should have been beaten."

I was in no condition to interrupt her. I was trembling, and exhorting myself to be brave.

"Besides, there is no need of words between us," she resumed. "We concluded a bargain, you know."

She laughed as she said this, and her laugh suddenly emboldened me. I caught hold of her hands and she did not withdraw them. I could feel them so little and so warm in my own. She surrendered them to me in a friendly, familiar way, whilst repeating: "Yes, that is so, isn't it? And now it is my turn to carry out my part of the agreement."

Thereupon I suddenly became audacious and rough, drawing her hands towards my lips. The gloom had increased; a cloud must have been passing over us, and the strong scent of all the plant-life around us intoxicated me in that nest of foliage. But before my lips could reach her, she freed herself with a nervous strength which I should never have suspected, and in her turn caught me roughly by the wrists. And she held me like that without any show of anger, her voice remaining calm, though it assumed somewhat of a scolding tone.

"Come, no childishness," said she. "This is what I feared. Will you allow me to give you a lesson whilst I hold you here, in this little corner?"

She showed the smiling severity of a mother reprimanding a boy.

"I understood you from the very first day. You had been told horrors about me, had you not? And so you conceived fancies which I forgive you, for you know nothing of our sphere of society. You landed in Paris with the ideas of this wolfish region, and perhaps you may say that it is in some measure my fault if you made a mistake. I ought to have stopped you, for you would have withdrawn at a word from me. That's true, and I did not speak that word; I let you go on and you must regard me as an abominable coquette. Do you know, how-

ever, why I did not speak that word?"

I began to stammer. The strangeness of the scene paralysed me with astonishment. She held my wrists yet more tightly and shook me, whilst remaining so close to me that I could feel her breath on my face.

"I did not say it, because I felt interested in you and wished to give you this lesson. Young men fresh to the world form very erroneous and foolish ideas of women. You don't understand, as yet, but you will reflect and guess. We women are very much slandered. Perhaps we do all that is needed to bring that about. Only, you see, there are some who are perfectly virtuous even amongst those who seem to be the wildest and most compromised. All that is a very delicate matter; but, I repeat, you will reflect and end by understanding."

"Let me go," I murmured in confusion.

"No, I will not let you go. Beg my pardon, if you wish me to do so."

In spite of her jesting tone I could feel that she was growing irritated, that tears of anger were rising to her eyes beneath the affront she had received from me. Within me was springing up a feeling of esteem, of genuine respect for that woman who was at once so charming and so capable. Her amazonian grace in virtuously enduring her husband's imbecility, her blending of coquetry and rigour, her disdain for evil tittle-tattle, and her skill in playing a man's part in the household amidst seeming flightiness of conduct—all made her a very complex creature, and filled me with admiration.

*"Pardon!"* I humbly said.

She released me. I at once rose to my feet whilst she remained quietly seated on the bench, fearing nothing more from the dimness of the disturbing odour of the greenery. And it was in her usual gay voice that she said to me: "Now, let us come back to our bargain. As I am very honest, I pay my debts. Here is your appointment as a junior diplomatic secretary. I received it last night."

Then, seeing that I hesitated to take the envelope which she held out to me, she exclaimed with just a touch of irony: "Well, it seems to me that you may well be my husband's *obligé*, now."

Such was the finish of my first adventure. When we came out of the arbour Félix was on the terrace with Gaucheraud and Berthe. He pursed his lips as he saw me approach carrying my nomination. He was doubtless aware of everything, and thought me a fool. I took him aside and reproached him bitterly for having allowed me to perpetrate such a blunder, but he answered that experience alone can form young men. And when with a gesture I designated Berthe, who was walking in front of us, by way of questioning him also about her, he shrugged his shoulders with a significance which was extremely clear. Matters being like this, I must confess that in spite of everything I do not yet fully understand the strange morality of society in which the most respectable women show such singular complaisance towards others.

But the last blow was to learn from Gaucheraud himself that my father had invited him and his wife to spend three days at Le Boquet. Félix again began to smile as he announced that for his part he was returning to Paris on the morrow.

Thereupon I ran off, pretending that I had positively promised my father that I would be home for *déjeuner*. I was already at the end of the avenue when I perceived a gentleman in a gig. It must have been Monsieur Neigeon. No matter! I prefer having again missed him. It is on Sunday that Gaucheraud and his wife are to arrive at Le Boquet. What a horrid nuisance!

# A Love Episode

## CHAPTER I

### THE LAMP

THE night-lamp with a bluish shade was burning on the chimney-piece, behind a book, whose shadows plunged more than half the chamber in darkness. There was a quiet gleam of light cutting across the round table and the couch, streaming over the heavy folds of the velvet curtains, and imparting an azure hue to the mirror of the rosewood wardrobe placed between the two windows. The quiet simplicity of the room, the blue tints on the hangings, furniture, and carpet, served at this hour of night to invest everything with the delightful vagueness of cloudland. Facing the windows, and within sweep of the shadow, loomed the velvet-curtained bed, a black mass, relieved only by the white of the sheets. With hands crossed on her bosom, and breathing lightly, lay Héléne, asleep—mother and widow alike personified by the quiet unrestraint of her attitude.

In the midst of the silence one o'clock chimed from the timepiece. The noises of the neighborhood had died away; the dull, distant roar of the city was the only sign of life that disturbed those Trocadéro heights. Héléne's breathing, so light and gentle, did not ruffle the chaste repose of her bosom. She was in a beauteous sleep, peaceful yet sound, her profile perfect, her nut-brown hair twisted into a knot, and

her head leaning forward somewhat, as though she had fallen asleep while eagerly listening. At the farther end of the room the open door of an adjoining closet seemed but a black square in the wall.

Still there was not a sound. The half-hour struck. The pendulum gave but a feeble tick-tack amid the general drowsiness that brooded over the whole chamber. Everything was sleeping, night-lamp and furniture alike; on the table, near an extinguished lamp, some woman's handiwork was disposed also in slumber. Héléne in her sleep retained her air of gravity and kindliness.

Two o'clock struck, and the stillness was broken. A deep sigh issued from the darkness of the closet. There was a rustling of linen sheets, and then silence reigned again. Anon labored breathing broke through the gloom. Héléne had not moved. Suddenly, however, she started up, for the moanings and cries of a child in pain had roused her. Dazed with sleep, she pressed her hands against her temples, but hearing a stifled sob, she leaped from her couch on to the carpet.

"Jeanne! my Jeanne! what ails you? tell me, love," she asked; and as the child remained silent, she murmured, while running towards the night-light, "Gracious Heaven! why did I go to bed when she was so ill?"

Quickly she entered the closet, where deep silence had again fallen. The feeble gleam of the lamp threw but a circular patch of light on the ceiling. Bending over the iron cot, she could at first make out nothing, but amidst the bed-clothes, tossed about in disorder, the dim light soon revealed Jeanne, with limbs quite stiff, her head flung back, the muscles of her neck swollen and rigid. Her sweet face was distorted, her eyes were open and fixed on the curtain-rod above.

"My child!" cried Hélène. "My God! my God! she is dying."

Setting down the lamp, Hélène touched her daughter with trembling hands. The throbbing of the pulse and the heart's action seemed to have died away. The child's puny arms and legs were stretched out convulsively, and the mother grew frantic at the sight.

"My child is dying! Help, help!" she stammered. "My child! my child!"

She wandered back to her room, brushing against the furniture, and unconscious of her movements; then, distracted, she again returned to the little bed, throwing herself on her knees, and ever appealing for help. She took Jeanne in her arms, rained kisses on her hair, and stroked her little body, begging her to answer, and seeking one word—only one word— from her silent lips. Where was the pain? Would she have some of the cooling drink she had liked the other day? Perhaps the fresh air would revive her? She rattled on, bent on making the child speak.

"Speak to me, Jeanne! speak to me, I entreat you!"

Oh God! and not to know what to do in this sudden terror born of the night! There was no light even. Then her ideas grew confused, though her supplications to the child continued— at one moment she was beseeching, at another answering in her own person. Thus, the pain gripped her in the stomach; no, no, it must be in the breast. It was nothing at all; she need merely keep quiet. Then Hélène tried to collect her scattered senses; but as she felt her daughter stark and stiff in her embrace, her heart sickened unto death. She tried to reason with herself, and to resist the yearning to scream. But all at once, despite herself, her cry rang out:

"Rosalie, Rosalie! my child is dying. Quick, hurry for the doctor."

Screaming out these words, she ran through dining-room and kitchen to a room in the rear, where the maid started up from sleep, giving vent to her surprise. Hélène speeded back again. Clad only in her night-dress she moved about, seemingly not feeling the icy cold of the February night. Pah! this maid would loiter, and her child would die! Back again she hurried through the kitchen to the bedroom before a minute had elapsed. Violently, and in the dark, she slipped on a petticoat, and threw a shawl over her shoulders. The furniture in her way was overturned; the room so still and silent was filled with the echoes of her despair. Then leaving the doors open, she rushed down three flights of stairs in her slippers, consumed with the thought that she alone could bring back a doctor.

After the house-porter had opened the door Hélène found herself upon the pavement, with a ringing in her ears and her mind distracted. However, she quickly ran down the Rue Vineuse and pulled the door-bell of Doctor Bodin, who had already tended Jeanne; but a servant — after an interval which seemed an eternity—informed her that the doctor was attending a woman in childbed. Hélène remained stupefied on the footway; she knew no other doctor in Passy. For a few moments she rushed about the streets, gazing at the houses. A slight but keen wind was blowing, and she was walking in slippers through the light snow that had fallen during the evening. Ever before her was her daughter, with the agonizing thought that she was killing her by not finding a doctor at once. Then, as she retraced her steps along the Rue Vineuse, she rang the bell of another house. She would inquire, at all events; some one would perhaps direct her. She gave a second tug at the bell; but no one seemed to come. The wind meanwhile played with her petticoat, making it cling to her legs, and tossed her dishevelled hair.

At last a servant answered her summons. "Doctor Deberle was in bed asleep." It was a doctor's house at which she had rung, so Heaven had not abandoned her! Straightway, intent upon entering, she pushed the servant aside, still repeating her prayer: "My child, my child is dying! Oh, tell him he must come!"

The house was small and seemed full of hangings. She reached the first floor, despite the servant's opposition, always answering his protest with the words, "My child is dying!" In the apartment she entered she would have been content to wait; but the moment she heard the doctor stirring in the next room she drew near and appealed to him through the doorway: "Oh, sir, come at once, I beseech you. My child is dying!"

When the doctor at last appeared in a short coat and without a neckcloth, she dragged him away without allowing him to finish dressing. He at once recognized her as a resident in the next-door house, and one of his own tenants; so when he induced her to cross a garden—to shorten the way by using a side-door between the two houses—memory suddenly awoke within her.

"True, you are a doctor!" she murmured, "and I knew it. But I was distracted. Oh, let us hurry!"

On the staircase she wished him to go first. She could not have admitted the Divinity to her home in a more reverent manner. Upstairs Rosalie had remained near the child and had lit the large lamp on the table. After the doctor had entered the room he took up this lamp and cast its light upon the body of the child, which retained its painful rigidity; the head, however, had slipped forward, and nervous twitchings were ceaselessly drawing the face. For a minute he looked on in silence, his lips compressed. Hélène anxiously watched him, and on noticing the mother's imploring glance, he muttered: "It will be nothing. But she must not lie here. She must have air."

Hélène grasped her child in a strong embrace, and carried her away on her shoulder. She could have kissed the doctor's hand for his good tidings, and a wave of happiness rippled through her. Scarcely, however, had Jeanne been placed in the larger bed than the poor little frame was again seized with violent convulsions. The doctor had removed the shade from the lamp, and a white light was streaming through the room. Then, opening a window, he ordered Rosalie to drag the bed away from the curtains. Hélène's heart was again filled with anguish. "Oh, sir, she is dying," she stammered. "Look! Look! Ah! I scarcely recognize her."

The doctor did not reply, but watched the paroxysm attentively.

"Step into the alcove," he at last exclaimed. "Hold her hands to prevent her from tearing herself. There now, gently, quietly! Don't make yourself uneasy. The fit must be allowed to run its course."

They both bent over the bed, supporting and holding Jeanne, whose limbs shot out with sudden jerks. The doctor had buttoned up his coat to hide his bare neck, and Hélène's shoulders had till now been enveloped in her shawl, but Jeanne in her struggles dragged a corner of the shawl away, and unbuttoned the top of the coat. Still they did not notice it; they never even looked at one another.

At last the convulsion ceased, and the little one then appeared to sink into deep prostration. Doctor Deberle was evidently ill at ease, though he had assured the mother that there was no danger. He kept his gaze fixed on the sufferer, and put some brief questions to Hélène as she stood by the bedside.

"How old is the child?"

"Eleven years and six months, sir," was the reply.

Silence again fell between them. He shook his head, and stooped to raise one of Jeanne's lowered eyelids and examine the mucus. Then he resumed his questions, but without raising his eyes to Hélène.

"Did she have convulsions when she was a baby?"

"Yes, sir; but they left her after she reached her sixth birthday. Ah! she is very delicate. For some days past she had seemed ill at ease. She was at times taken with a cramp, and plunged in a stupor."

"Do you know of any members of your family that have suffered from nervous affections?"

"I don't know. My mother was carried off by consumption."

Here shame made her pause. She could not confess that she had a grandmother who was an inmate of a lunatic asylum. There was something tragic connected with all her ancestry.

"Take care! the convulsions are coming on again!" now hastily exclaimed the doctor.

Jeanne had just opened her eyes, and for a moment she gazed around her with a vacant look, never speaking a word. Her glance then grew fixed, her body was violently thrown backwards, and her limbs became distended and rigid. Her skin, fiery-red, all at once turned livid. Her pallor was the pallor of death; the convulsions began once more.

"Do not loose your hold of her," said the doctor. "Take her other hand!"

He ran to the table, where, on entering, he had placed a small medicine-case. He came back with a bottle, the contents of which he made Jeanne inhale; but the effect was like that of a terrible lash; the child gave such a violent jerk that she slipped from her mother's hands.

"No, no, don't give her ether," exclaimed Hélène, warned by the odor. "It drives her mad."

The two had now scarcely strength enough to keep the child under control. Her frame was racked and distorted, raised by the heels and the nape of the neck, as if bent in two. But she fell back again and began tossing from one side of the bed to the other. Her fists were clenched, her thumbs bent against the palms of her hands. At times she would open the latter, and with fingers wide apart, grasp at phantom bodies in the air, as though to twist them. She touched her mother's shawl and fiercely clung to it. But Hélène's greatest grief was that she no longer recognized her daughter. The suffering angel, whose face was usually so sweet, was transformed in every feature, while her eyes swam, showing balls of a nacreous blue.

"Oh, do something, I implore you!" she murmured. "My strength is exhausted, sir."

She had just remembered how a child of a neighbor at Marseilles had died of suffocation in a similar fit. Perhaps from feeling of pity the doctor was deceiving her. Every moment she believed she felt Jeanne's last breath against her face; for the child's halting respiration seemed suddenly to cease. Heartbroken and overwhelmed

with terror, Hélène then burst into tears, which fell on the body of her child, who had thrown off the bed-clothes.

The doctor meantime was gently kneading the base of the neck with his long supple fingers. Gradually the fit subsided, and Jeanne, after a few slight twitches, lay there motionless. She had fallen back in the middle of the bed, with limbs outstretched, while her head, supported by the pillow, inclined towards her bosom. One might have thought her an infant Jesus. Hélène stooped and pressed a long kiss on her brow.

"Is it over?" she asked in a whisper. "Do you think she'll have another fit?"

The doctor made an evasive gesture, and then replied:

"In any case the others will be less violent."

He had asked Rosalie for a glass and water-bottle. Half-filling the glass with water, he took up two fresh medicine phials, and counted out a number of drops. Hélène assisted in raising the child's head, and the doctor succeeded in pouring a spoonful of the liquid between the clenched teeth. The white flame of the lamp was leaping up high and clear, revealing the disorder of the chamber's furnishings. Hélène's garments, thrown on the back of an armchair before she slipped into bed, had now fallen and were littering the carpet. The doctor had trodden on her stays, and had picked them up lest he might again find them in his way. An odor of vervain stole through the room. The doctor himself went for the basin, and soaked a linen cloth in it, which he then pressed to Jeanne's temples.

"Oh, madame, you'll take cold!" expostulated Rosalie as she stood there shivering. "Perhaps the window might be shut? The air is too raw."

"No, no!" cried Hélène; "leave the window open. Should it not be so?" she appealed to the doctor.

The wind entered in slight puffs, rustling the curtains to and fro; but she was quite unconscious of it. Yet the shawl had slipped off her shoulders, and her hair had become unwound, some wanton tresses sweeping down to her hips. She had left her arms free and uncovered, that she might be the more ready; she had forgotten all, absorbed entirely in her love for her child. And on his side, the doctor, busy with his work, no longer thought of his unbuttoned coat, or of the shirt-collar that Jeanne's clutch had torn away.

"Raise her up a little," said he to Hélène. "No, no, not in that way! Give me your hand."

He took her hand and placed it under the child's head. He wished to give Jeanne another spoonful of the medicine. Then he called Hélène close to him, made use of her as his assistant; and she obeyed him reverently on seeing that her daughter was already more calm.

"Now, come," he said. "You must let her head lean against your shoulder, while I listen."

Hélène did as he bade her, and he bent over her to place his ear against Jeanne's bosom. He touched her bare shoulder with his cheek, and as the pulsation of the child's heart struck his ear he could also have heard the throbbing of the mother's breast. As he rose up his breath mingled with Hélène's.

"There is nothing wrong there," was the quiet remark that filled her with delight. "Let her down again. We must not worry her more."

However, another, though much less violent, paroxysm followed. From Jeanne's lips burst some broken words. At short intervals two fresh attacks seemed about to convulse her, and then a great prostration, which again appeared to alarm the doctor, fell on the child. He had placed her so that her head lay high, with the clothes carefully tucked under her chin; and for nearly an hour he remained there watching her, as though awaiting the return of a healthy respiration. On the other side of the bed Hélène also waited, never moving a limb.

Little by little a great calm settled on Jeanne's face. The lamp cast a sunny light upon it, and it regained its exquisite though somewhat lengthy oval. Jeanne's fine eyes, now closed, had large, bluish, transparent lids, which veiled—one could divine it—a sombre, flashing glance. A light breathing came from her slender nose, while round her somewhat large mouth played a vague smile. She slept thus, amidst her outspread tresses, which were inky black.

"It has all passed away now," said the doctor in a whisper; and he turned to arrange his medicine bottles prior to leaving.

"Oh, sir!" exclaimed Hélène, approaching him, "don't leave me yet; wait a few minutes. Another fit might come on, and you, you alone, have saved her!"

He signed to her that there was nothing to fear; yet he tarried, with the idea of tranquillizing her. She had already sent Rosalie to bed; and now the dawn soon broke, still and grey, over the snow which whitened the housetops. The doctor proceeded to close the window, and in the deep quiet the two exchanged a few whispers.

"There is nothing seriously wrong with her I assure you," said he; "only with one so young great care must be taken. You must see that her days are spent quietly and happily, and without shock of any kind."

"She is so delicate and nervous," replied Hélène after a moment's pause. "I cannot always control her. For the most trifling reasons she is so overcome by joy or sorrow that I grow alarmed. She loves me with a passion, a jealousy, which makes her burst with tears when I caress another child."

"So, so—delicate, nervous, and jealous," repeated the doctor as he shook his head. "Doctor Bodin has attended her, has he not? I'll have a talk with him about her. We shall have to adopt energetic treatment. She has reached an age that is critical in one of her sex."

Recognizing the interest he displayed, Hélène gave vent to her gratitude. "How I must thank you, sir, for the great trouble you have taken!"

The loudness of her tones frightened her, however; she might have woke Jeanne, and she bent down over the bed. But no; the child was sound asleep, with rosy cheeks, and a vague smile playing round her lips. The air of the quiet chamber was charged with languor. The whilom drowsiness, as if born again of relief, once more seized upon the curtains, furniture, and littered garments. Everything was steeped restfully in the early morning light as it entered through the two windows.

Hélène again stood up close to the bed; on the other side was the doctor, and between them lay Jeanne, lightly sleeping.

"Her father was frequently ill," remarked Hélène softly, continuing her answer to his previous question. "I myself enjoy the best of health."

The doctor, who had not yet looked at her, raised his eyes, and could scarcely refrain from smiling, so hale and hearty was she in every way. She greeted his gaze with her own sweet and quiet smile. Her happiness lay in her good health.

However, his looks were still bent on her. Never had he seen such classical beauty. Tall and commanding, she was a nut-brown Juno, of a nut-brown sunny with gleams of gold. When she slowly turned her head, its profile showed the severe purity of a statue. Her grey eyes and pearly teeth lit up her whole face. Her chin, rounded and somewhat pronounced, proved her to be possesed of common-sense and firmness. But what astonished the doctor was the superbness of her whole figure. She stood there, a model of queenliness, chastity, and modesty.

On her side also she scanned him for a moment. Doctor Deberle's years were thirty-five; his face was clean-shaven and a little long; he had keen eyes and thin lips. As she gazed on him she noticed for the first time that his neck was bare. Thus they remained face to face with Jeanne asleep between them. The distance which but a short time before had appeared immense, now seemed to be dwindling away. Then Hélène slowly wrapped the shawl about her shoulders again, while the doctor hastened to button his coat at the neck.

"Mamma! mamma!" Jeanne stammered in her sleep. She was waking, and on opening her eyes she saw the doctor and became uneasy.

"Mamma, who's that?" was her instant question; but her mother kissed her, and replied: "Go to sleep, darling, you haven't been well. It's only a friend."

The child seemed surprised; she did not remember anything. Drowsiness was coming over her once more, and she fell asleep again, murmuring tenderly: "I'm going to by-by. Goodnight, mamma, dear. If he is your friend he will be mine."

The doctor had removed his medicine-case, and, with a silent bow, he left the room. Hélène listened for a while to the child's breathing, and then, seated on the edge of the bed, she became oblivious to everything around her; her looks and thoughts wandering far away. The lamp, still burning, was paling in the growing sunlight.

## CHAPTER II

### KISSES

NEXT day Hélène thought it right and proper to pay a visit of thanks to Doctor Deberle. The abrupt fashion in which she had compelled him to follow her, and the remembrance of the whole night which he had spent with Jeanne, made her uneasy, for she realized that he had done more than is usually compassed within a doctor's visit. Still, for two days she hesitated to make her call, feeling a strange repugnance towards such a step. For this she could give herself no reasons. It was the doctor himself who inspired her with this hesitancy; one morning she met him, and shrank from his notice as though she were a child. At this excess of timidity she was much annoyed. Her quiet, upright nature protested against the uneasiness which was taking possession of her. She decided, therefore, to go and thank the doctor that very day.

Jeanne's attack had taken place during the small hours of Wednesday morning; it was now Saturday, and the child was quite well again. Doctor Bodlin, whose fears concerning her had prompted him to make an early call, spoke of Doctor Deberle with the respect that an old doctor with a meagre income pays to another in the same district, who is young, rich, and already possessed of a reputation. He did not forget to add, however, with an artful smile, that the fortune had been bequeathed by the elder Deberle, a man whom all Passy held in veneration. The son had only been put to the trouble of inheriting fifteen hundred thousand francs, together with a splendid practice. "He is, though, a very smart fellow," Doctor Bodin hastened to add, "and I shall be honored by having a consulation with him about the precious health of my little friend Jeanne!"

About three o'clock Hélène made her way downstairs with her daughter, and had to take but a few steps along the Rue Vineuse before ringing at the next-door house. Both mother and daughter still wore deep mourning. A servant, in dress-coat and white tie, opened the door. Hélène easily recognized the large entrance-hall, with its Oriental hangings; on each side of it, however, there were now flower-stands, brilliant with a profusion of blossoms. The servant having admitted them to a small drawing-room, the hangings and furniture of which were of a mignonette hue, stood awaiting their pleasure, and Hélène gave her name— Madame Grandjean.

Thereupon the footman pushed open the door of a drawing-room, furnished in yellow and black, of dazzling effect, and, moving aside, announced:

"Madame Grandjean!"

Hélène, standing on the threshold, started back. She had just noticed at the other end of the room a young woman seated near the fireplace on a narrow couch which was completely covered by her ample skirts. Facing her sat an elderly person, who had retained her bonnet and shawl, and was evidently paying a visit.

"I beg pardon," exclaimed Hélène. "I wished to see Doctor Deberle."

She had made the child enter the room before her, and now took her by the hand again. She was both astonished and embarrassed in meeting this young lady. Why had she not asked for the doctor? She well knew he was married.

Madame Deberle was just finishing some story, in a quick and rather shrill voice.

"Oh! it's marvelous, marvelous! She dies with wonderful realism. She clutches at her bosom like this, throws back her head, and her face turns green. I declare you ought to see her, Mademoiselle Aurélie!"

Then, rising up, she sailed towards the doorway, rustling her skirts terribly.

"Be so kind as to walk in, madame," she said with charming graciousness. "My husband is not at home, but I shall be delighted to receive you, I assure you. This must be the pretty little girl who was so ill a few nights ago. Sit down for a moment, I beg of you."

Hélène was forced to accept the invitation, while Jeanne timidly perched herself on the edge of another chair. Madame Deberle again sank down on her little sofa, exclaiming with a pretty laugh:

"Yes, this is my day. I receive every Saturday, you see, and Pierre then announces all comers. A week or two ago he ushered in a colonel suffering from the gout."

"How silly you are, my dear Juliette!" expostulated Mademoiselle Aurélie, the elderly lady, an old friend in straitened circumstances, who had seen her come into the world.

There was a short silence, and Hélène gazed round at the luxury of the apartment, with its curtains and chairs in black and gold, glittering like constellations. Flowers decorated mantel-shelf, piano, and table alike, and the clear light streamed through the windows from the garden, in which could be seen the leafless trees and bare soil. The room had almost a hot-house temperature; in the fireplace one large log was glowing with intense heat. After another glance Hélène recognized that the gaudy colors had a happy effect. Madame Deberle's hair was inky-black, and her skin of a milky whiteness. She was short, plump, slow in her movements, and withal graceful. Amidst all the golden decorations, her white face assumed a vermeil tint under her heavy, sombre tresses. Hélène really admired her.

"Convulsions are so terrible," broke in Madame Deberle. "My Lucien had them when a mere baby. How uneasy you must have been, madame! However, the dear little thing appears to be quite well now."

As she drawled out these words she kept her eyes on Hélène, whose superb beauty amazed and delighted her. Never had she seen a woman with so queenly an air in the black garments which draped the widow's commanding figure. Her admiration found vent in an involuntary smile, while she exchanged glances with Mademoiselle Aurélie. Their admiration was so ingenuously and charmingly expressed, that a faint smile also rippled over Hélène's face.

Then Madame Deberle stretched herself on the sofa. "You were not at the first night at the Vaudeville yesterday, madame?" she asked, as she played with the fan that hung from her waist.

"I never go to the theatre," was Hélène's reply.

"Oh! little Noëmi was simply marvelous! Her death scene is so realistic! She clutches her bosom like this, throws back her head, and her face turns green. Oh! the effect is prodigious."

Thereupon she entered into a minute criticism of the actress's playing, which she upheld against the world; and then she passed to the other topics of the day—a fine art exhibition, at which she had seen some most remarkable paintings; a stupid novel about which too much fuss was being made; a society intrigue which she spoke of to Mademoiselle Aurélie in veiled language. And so she went on from one subject to another, without wearying, her tongue ever ready, as though this social atmosphere were peculiarly her own. Hélène, a stranger to such society, was content to listen, merely interjecting a remark or brief reply now and then.

At last the door was again thrown open and the footman announced: "Madame de Chermette! Madame Tissot!"

Two ladies entered, magnificently dressed. Madame Deberle rose eagerly to meet them, and the train of her black silk gown, heavily decked with trimmings, trailed so far behind her that she had to kick it out of her way whenever she happened to turn round. A confused babel of greetings in shrill voices arose.

"Oh! how kind of you! I declare I never see you!"

"You know we come about that lottery."

"Yes: I know, I know."

"Oh! we cannot sit down. We have to call at twenty houses yet."

"Come now, you are not going to run away at once!"

And then the visitors finished by sitting down on the edge of a couch; the chatter beginning again, shriller than ever.

"Well! what do you think of yesterday at the Vaudeville?"

"Oh! it was splendid!"

"You know she unfastens her dress and lets down her hair. All the effect springs from that."

"People say that she swallows something to make her green."

"No, no, every action is premeditated; but she had to invent and study them all, in the first place."

"It's wonderful."

The two ladies rose and made their exit, and the room regained its tranquil peacefulness. From some hyacinths on the mantel-shelf was wafted an all-prevading perfume. For a time one could hear the noisy twittering of some sparrows quarrelling on the lawn. Before resuming her seat, Madame Deberle proceeded to draw down the embroidered tulle blind of a window facing her, and then returned to her sofa in the mellowed, golden light of the room.

"I beg pardon," she now said. "We have had quite an invasion."

Then, in an affectionate way, she entered into conversation with Hélène. She seemed to know some details of her history, doubtless from the gossip of her servants. With a boldness that was yet full of tact, and appeared instinct with much friendliness, she spoke to Hélène of her husband, and of his sad death at the Hôtel du Var, in the Rue de Richelieu.

"And you had just arrived, hadn't you? You had never been in Paris before. It must be awful to be plunged into mourning, in a strange room, the day after a long journey, and when one doesn't know a single place to go to."

Hélène assented with a slow nod. Yes, she had spent some very bitter hours. The disease which carried off her husband had abruptly declared itself on the day after their arrival, just as they were going out together. She knew none of the streets, and was wholly unaware what district she was in. For eight days she had remained at the bedside of the dying man, hearing the rumble of Paris beneath her window, feeling she was alone, deserted, lost, as though plunged in the depths of an abyss. When she stepped out on the pavement for the first time, she was a widow. The mere recalling of that bare room, with its rows of medicine bottles, and with the travelling trunks standing about unpacked, still made her shudder.

"Was your husband, as I've been told, nearly twice your age?" asked Madame Deberle with an appearance of profound interest, while Mademoiselle Aurélie cocked her ears so as not to lose a syllable of the conversation.

"Oh, no!" replied Hélène. "He was scarcely six years older."

Then she ventured to enter into the story of her marriage, telling in a few brief sentences how her husband had fallen deeply in love with her while she was living with her father, Monsieur Mouret, a hatter in the Rue des Petites-Maries, at Marseilles; how the

Grandjean family, who were rich sugar-refiners, were bitterly opposed to the match, on account of her poverty. She spoke, too, of the ill-omened and secret wedding after the usual legal formalities, and of their hand-to-mouth existence, till the day an uncle on dying left them some ten thousand francs a year. It was then that Grandjean, within whom an intense hatred of Marseilles was growing, had decided on coming to Paris, to live there for good.

"And how old were you when you were married?" was Madame Deberle's next question.

"Seventeen."

"You must have been very beautiful."

The conversation suddenly ceased, for Hélène had not seemed to hear the remark.

"Madame Manguelin!" announced the footman.

A young, retiring woman, evidently ill at ease, was ushered in. Madame Deberle scarcely rose. It was one of her dependents, who had called to thank her for some service performed. The visitor only remained for a few minutes, and left the room with a courtesy.

Madame Deberle then resumed the conversation, and spoke of Abbé Jouve, with whom both were acquainted. The Abbé was a meek officiating priest at Notre Dame de Grâce, the parish church of Passy; however, his charity was such that he was more beloved and more respectfully hearkened to than any other priest in the district.

"Oh, he has such a pious eloquence!" exclaimed Madame Deberle, with a sanctimonious look.

"He has been very kind to us," said Hélène. "My husband had formerly known him at Marseilles. The moment he heard of my misfortune he took charge of everything. To him we owe our settling in Passy."

"He has a brother, hasn't he?" questioned Juliette.

"Yes, a step-brother, for his mother married again. Monsieur Rambaud was also acquainted with my husband. He has started a large business in the Rue de Rambuteau, where he sells oils and other Southern produce. I believe he makes a large amount of money by it." And she added, with a laugh: "The Abbé and his brother make up my court."

Jeanne, sitting on the edge of her chair, and wearied to death, now cast an impatient look at her mother. Her long, delicate, lamb-like face wore a pained expression, as if she disliked all this conversation; and she appeared at times to sniff the heavy, oppressive odors floating in the room, while casting suspicious side-glances at the furniture, as though her own exquisite sensibility warned her of some undefined dangers. Finally, however, she turned a look of tyrannical worship on her mother.

Madame Deberle noticed the child's uneasiness.

"Here's a little girl," she said, "who feels tired at being serious, like a grown-up person. There are some picture-books on the table, dear; they will amuse you."

Jeanne took up an album, but her eyes strayed from it to glance inploringly at her mother. Hélène, charmed by her hostess's excessive kindness, did

not move; there was nothing of the
fidget in her, and she would of her
own accord remain seated for hours.
However, as the servant announced
three ladies in succession—Madame
Berthier, Madame de Guiraud, and
Madame Levasseur—she thought she
ought to rise.

"Oh! pray stop," exclaimed Madame
Deberle; "I must show you my son."

The semi-circle round the fire-place
was increasing in size. The ladies were
all gossiping at the same time. One
of them declared that she was completely broken down, as for five days
she had not gone to bed till four o'clock
in the morning. Another indulged in
a diatribe against wet nurses; she could
no longer find one who was honest.
Next the conversation fell on dress-
makers. Madame Deberle affirmed no
woman tailor could fit you properly;
a man was requisite. Two of the
ladies, however, were mumbling something under their breath, and, a silence
intervening, two or three words became audible. Every one then broke
into a laugh, while languidly waving
their fans.

"Monsieur Malignon!" announced
the servant.

A tall young man, dressed in good
style, was ushered in. Some exclamations greeted him. Madame Deberle,
not taking the trouble to rise, stretched
out her hand and inquired: "Well!
what of yesterday at the Vaudeville?"

"Vile!" was his reply.

"What! vile! She's marvellous
when she clutches her bosom and
throws back her head—"

"Stop! stop! The whole thing is
loathsome in its realism."

And then quite a dispute commenced.
It was easy to talk of realism, but
the young man would have no realism
at all.

"I would not have it in anything,
you hear!" said he, raising his voice.
"No, not in anything! it degrades art."

People would soon be seeing some
fine things on the stage, indeed! Why
didn't Noëmi follow out her actions to
their logical conclusion? And he il-
lustrated his remark with a gesture
which quite scandalized the ladies. Oh,
how horrible! However, when Madame
Deberle had declared that the actress
produced a great effect, and Madame
Levasseur had related how a lady had
fainted in the balcony, everybody
agreed that the affair was a great success; and with this the discussion
stopped short.

The young man sat in an arm-chair,
with his legs stretched out among the
ladies' flowing skirts. He seemed to
be quite at home in the doctor's house.
He had mechanically plucked a flower
from a vase, and was tearing it to
pieces with his teeth. Madame Deberle
interrupted him:

"Have you read the novel which—"

He did not allow her to finish, but
replied, with a superior air, that he
only read two novels in the year.

As for the exhibition of paintings
at the Art Club, it was not worth
troubling about; and then, every topic
being exhausted, he rose and leaned
over Juliette's little sofa, conversing
with her in a low voice, while the
other ladies continued chatting together
in an animated manner.

At length: "Dear me! he's gone,"
exclaimed Madame Bertier turning

round. "I met him only an hour ago in Madame Robinot's drawing-room."

"Yes, and he is now going to visit Madame Lecomte," said Madame Deberle. "He goes about more than any other man in Paris." She turned to Hélène, who had been following the scene, and added: "A very distinguished young fellow he is, and we like him very much. He has some interest in a stockbroking business; he's very rich besides, and well posted in everything."

The other ladies, however, were now going off.

"Good-bye, dear madame. I rely upon you for Wednesday."

"Yes, to be sure; Wednesday."

"Oh, by the way, will you be at that evening party? One doesn't know whom one may meet. If you go, I'll go."

"Ah, well! I'll go, I promise you. Give my best regards to Monsieur de Guiraud.

When Madame Deberle returned she found Hélène standing in the middle of the drawing-room. Jeanne had drawn close to her mother, whose hands she firmly grasped; and thus clinging to her caressingly and almost convulsively, she was drawing her little by little to the doorway.

"Ah, I was forgetting!" exclaimed the lady of the house; and ringing the bell for the servant, she said to him: "Pierre, tell Miss Smithson to bring Lucien here."

During the short interval of waiting that ensued the door was again opened, but this time in a familiar fashion and without any formal anouncement. A good-looking girl of some sixteen years of age entered in company with an old man, short of stature but with a rubicund, chubby face.

"Good-day, sister," was the girl's greeting, as she kissed Madame Deberle.

"Good-day, Pauline! good-day, father!" replied the doctor's wife.

Mademoiselle Aurélie, who had not stirred from her seat beside the fire, rose to exchange greetings with Monsieur Letellier. He owned an extensive silk warehouse on the Boulevard des Capucines. Since his wife's death he had been taking his younger daughter about everywhere, in search of a rich husband for her.

"Were you at the vaudeville last night?" asked Pauline.

"Oh, it was simply marvellous!" repeated Juliette in parrot-fashion, as, standing before a mirror, she rearranged a rebellious curl.

"It is annoying to be so young; one can't go to anything!" said Pauline, pouting like a spoiled child. "I went with papa to the theatre-door at midnight, to find out how the piece had taken."

"Yes, and we tumbled upon Malignon," said the father. "He was extremely pleased with it."

"Really!" exclaimed Juliette. "He was here a minute ago, and declared it vile. One never knows how to take him."

"Have you had many visitors today?" asked Pauline, rushing off to another subject.

"Oh, several ladies; quite a crowd! The room was never once empty. I'm dead-beat—"

Here she abruptly broke off, remembering she had a formal introduction to make:

"My father, my sister—Madame Grandjean."

The conversation was turning on children and the ailments which give mothers so much worry when Miss Smithson, an English governess, appeared with a little boy clinging to her hand. Madame Deberle scolded her in English for having kept them waiting.

"Ah! here's my little Lucien!" exclaimed Pauline as she dropped on her knees before the child, with a great rustling of skirts.

"Now, now, leave him alone!" said Juliette. "Come here, Lucien; come and say good-day to this little lady."

The boy came over very sheepishly. He was no more than seven years old, fat and dumpy, and dressed as coquettishly as a doll. As he saw that they were all looking at him with smiles, he stopped short, and surveyed Jeanne, his blue eyes wide open with astonishment.

"Go on!" urged his mother.

He turned his eyes questioningly on her and advanced a step, evincing all the sullenness peculiar to lads of his age, his head lowered, his thick lips pouting, and his eyebrows bent into a growing frown. Jeanne must have frightened him with the serious look she wore standing there in her black dress. She had not ceased holding her mother's hand, and was nervously pressing her fingers on the bare part of the arm between the sleeve and glove. With head lowered she awaited Lucien's approach uneasily, like a young and timid savage, ready to fly

from his caress. But a gentle push forward from her mother prompted her to step forward.

"Little lady, you will have to kiss him first," Madame Deberle said laughingly. "Ladies always have to begin with him. Oh! the little stupid."

"Kiss him, Jeanne," said Hélène.

The child looked up at her mother; and then, as if conquered by the bashful looks of the little noodle, seized with sudden pity as she gazed on his good-natured face, so dreadfully confused—she smiled divinely. A sudden wave of hidden tenderness rose within her and brightened her features, and she whispered: "Willingly, mamma!"

Then, taking Lucien under the armpits, almost lifting him from the ground, she gave him a hearty kiss on each cheek. He had no further hesitation in embracing her.

"Bravo! capital!" exclaimed the onlookers.

With a bow Hélène turned to leave, accompanied to the door by Madame Deberle.

"I beg you, madame," said she, "to present my heartiest thanks to the doctor. He relieved me of such dreadful anxiety the other night."

"Is Henri not at home?" broke in Monsieur Letellier.

"No, he will be away some time yet," was Juliette's reply. "But you're not going away; you'll dine with us," she continued, addressing Mademoiselle Aurélie, who had risen as if to leave with Madame Grandjean.

The old maid with each Saturday expected a similar invitation, then decided to relieve herself of shawl and bonnet. The heat in the drawing-room was intense, and Monsieur Letellier hastened to open a window, at which he remained standing, struck by the sight of a lilac bush which was already budding. Pauline, meantime, had begun playfully running after Lucien behind the chairs and couches, left in confusion by the visitors.

On the threshold Madame Deberle held out her hand to Hélène with a frank and friendly movement.

"You will allow me," said she. "My husband spoke to me about you, and I felt drawn to you. Your bereavement, your lonely life—in short, I am very glad to have seen you, and you must not be long in coming back."

"I give you my promise, and I am obliged to you," said Hélène, moved by these tokens of affection from a woman whom she had imagined rather flighty. They clasped hands, and each looked into the other's face with a happy smile. Juliette's avowal of her sudden friendship was given with a caressing air. "You are too lovely not to be loved!" she said.

Hélène broke into a merry laugh, for her beauty never engaged her thoughts, and she called Jeanne whose eyes were busy watching the pranks of Lucien and Pauline. But Madame Deberle detained the girl for a moment longer.

"You are good friends henceforth," she said; "you must just say *au revoir*."

Thereupon the two children blew one another a kiss with their finger-tips.

## CHAPTER III

### CONFIDENCE

EVERY Tuesday Hélène had Monsieur Rambaud and Abbé Jouve to dine with her. It was they who, during the early days of her bereavement, had broken in on her solitude, and drawn up their chairs to her table with friendly freedom; their object being to extricate her, at least once a week, from the solitude in which she lived. The Tuesday dinners became established institutions, and the partakers in these little feasts appeared punctually at seven o'clock, serenely happy in discharging what they deemed a duty.

That Tuesday Hélène was seated at the window, profiting by the last gleams of the twilight to finish some needlework, pending the arrival of her guests. She here spent her days in pleasant peacefulness. The noises of the street died away before reaching such a height. She loved this large, quiet chamber, with its substantial luxury, its rosewood furniture and blue velvet curtains. When her friends had attended to her installation, she not having to trouble about anything, she had at first somewhat suffered from all this sombre luxury, in preparing which Monsieur Rambaud had realized his ideal of comfort, much to the admiration of his brother, who had declined the task. She was not long, however, in feeling happy in a home in which, as in her heart, all was sound and simple. Her only enjoyment during her long hours of work was to gaze before her at the vast horizon, the huge pile of Paris, stretching its roofs, like billows, as far as the eye could reach. Her solitary corner overlooked all that immensity.

"Mamma, I can no longer see," said Jeanne, seated near her on a low chair. And then, dropping her work, the child gazed at Paris, which was darkening over with the shadows of night. She rarely romped about, and her mother even had to exert authority to induce her to go out. In accordance with Doctor Bodin's strict injunction, Hélène made her stroll with her two hours each day in the Bois de Boulogne, and this was their only promenade, in eighteen months they had not gone three times into Paris. Nowhere was Jeanne so evidently happy as in their large blue room. Her mother had been obliged to renounce her intention of having her taught music, for the sound of an organ in the silent streets made her tremble and drew tears from her eyes. Her favorite occupation was to assist her mother in sewing linen for the children of the Abbé's poor.

Night had quite fallen when the lamp was brought in by Rosalie, who, fresh from the glare of her range, looked altogether upset. Tuesday's dinner was the one event of the week, which put things topsy-turvy.

"Aren't the gentlemen coming here to-night, madame?" she inquired.

Hélène looked at the timepiece: "It's a quarter to seven; they will be here soon," she replied.

Rosalie was a gift from Abbé Jouve, who had met her at the station on the day she arrived from Orleans, so that she did not know a single street in Paris. A village priest, an old schoolmate of Abbé Jouve's, had sent her to him. She was dumpy and plump, with a round face under her narrow cap, thick black hair, a flat nose, and deep red lips; and she was expert in preparing savory dishes, having been brought up at the parsonage by her godmother, servant to the village priest.

"Here is Monsieur Rambaud at last!" she exclaimed, rushing to open the door before there was even a ring.

Full and broad-shouldered, Monsieur Rambaud entered, displaying an expansive countenance like that of a country notary. His forty-five years had already silvered his hair, but his large blue eyes retained a wondering, artless, gentle expression, akin to a child's.

"And here's his reverence; everybody has come now!" resumed Rosalie, as she opened the door once more.

Whilst Monsieur Rambaud pressed Hélène's hand and sat down without speaking, smiling like one who felt quite at home, Jeanne threw her arms round the Abbé's neck.

"Good-evening, dear friend," said she, "I've been so ill!"

"So ill, my darling?"

The two men at once showed their anxiety, the Abbé especially. He was a short, spare man, with a large head and awkward manners, and dressed in the most careless way; but his eyes, usually half-closed, now opened to their full extent, all aglow with exquisite tenderness. Jeanne relinquished one of her hands to him, while she gave the other to Monsieur Rambaud. Both held her and gazed at her with troubled looks. Hélène was obliged to relate the story of her illness, and the Abbé was on the point of quarreling with her for not having warned him of it. And then they each questioned her. "The attack was quite over now? She had not had another, had she?" The mother smiled as she listened.

"You are even fonder of her than

I am, and I think you'll frighten me in the end," she replied. "No, she hasn't been troubled again, except that she has felt some pains in her limbs and had some headaches. But we shall get rid of these very soon."

The maid then entered to announce that dinner was ready.

The table, sideboard, and eight chairs furnishing the dining-room were of mahogany. The curtains of red repp had been drawn close by Rosalie, and a hanging lamp of white porcelain within a plain brass ring lighted up the tablecloth, the carefully-arranged plates, and the tureen of steaming soup. Each Tuesday's dinner brought round the same remarks, but on this particular day Dr. Deberle served naturally as a subject of conversation. Abbé Jouve lauded him to the skies, though he knew he was no church-goer. He spoke of him, however, as a man of upright character, charitable to a fault, a good father, and a good husband—in fact, one who gave the best of examples to others. As for Madame Deberle she was most estimable, in spite of her somewhat flighty ways, which were doubtless due to her Parisian education. In a word, he dubbed the couple charming. Hélène seemed happy to hear this; it confirmed her own opinions; and the Abbé's remarks determined her to continue the acquaintance, which had at first frightened her.

"You shut yourself up too much!" declared the priest.

"No doubt," echoed his brother.

Héléne beamed on them with her quiet smile, as though to say that they themselves sufficed for all her wants, and that she dreaded new acquaintances. However, ten o'clock struck at last, and the Abbé and his brother took up their hats. Jeanne had just fallen asleep in an easy-chair in the bedroom, and they bent over her, raising their heads with satisfied looks as they observed how tranquilly she slumbered. They stole from the room on tiptoe, and in the lobby whispered their good-byes:

"Till next Tuesday."

"O, by the way," said the Abbé, returning a step or two, "I was forgetting: Mother Fétu is ill. You should go to see her."

"I will go to-morrow," answered Hélène.

The Abbé had a habit of commissioning her to visit his poor. They engaged in all sorts of whispered talks together on this subject, private business which a word or two enabled them to settle together, and which they never referred to in the presence of other persons.

On the morrow Hélène went out alone. She decided to leave Jeanne in the house, as the child had been troubled with fits of shivering since paying a visit of charity to an old man who had become paralyzed. Once out of doors, she followed the Rue Vineuse, turned down the Rue Raynouard, and soon found herself in the Passage des Eaux, a strange, steep lane, like a staircase, pent between garden walls, and conducting from the heights of Passy to the quay. At the bottom of this descent was a dilapidated house, where Mother Fétu lived in an attic lighted by a round window, and furnished with a wretched bed, a rickety table, and a seatless chair.

"Oh! my good lady, my good lady!" she moaned out, directly she saw Hélène enter.

The old woman was in bed. In spite of her wretchedness, her body was plump, swollen out, as it were, while her face was puffy, and her hands seemed numbed as she drew the tattered sheet over her. She had small, keen eyes and a whimpering voice, and displayed a noisy humility in a rush of words.

"Ah! my good lady, how I thank you! Ah, ah! oh, how I suffer. It's just as if dogs were tearing at my side. I'm sure I have a beast inside of me—see, just there! The skin isn't broken; the complaint is internal. But, oh! oh! the pain hasn't ceased for two days past. Good Lord, how is it possible to suffer so much? Ah, my good lady, thank you! You don't forget the poor. It will be taken into account up above; yes, yes, it will be taken into account!"

Hélène had sat down. Noticing on the table a jug of warm *tisane*, she filled a cup which was near at hand, and gave it to the sufferer. Near the jug were placed a packet of sugar, two oranges, and some other comfits.

"Has any one been to see you?" Hélène asked.

"Yes, yes,—a little lady. But she doesn't know. That isn't the sort of stuff I need. Oh, if I could get a little meat! My next-door neighbor would cook it for me. Oh! oh! this pain is something dreadful! A dog is tearing at me—oh, if only I had some broth!"

In spite of the pains which were racking her limbs, she kept her sharp eyes fixed on Hèléne, who was now busy fumbling in her pocket, and on seeing her visitor place a ten-franc piece on the table, she whimpered all the more, and tried to rise to a sitting posture. Whilst struggling, she extended her arm, and the money vanished, as she repeated:

"Gracious Heaven! this is another frightful attack. Oh! oh! I cannot stand such agony any longer! God will requite you, my good lady; I will pray to Him to requite you. Bless my soul, how these pains shoot through my whole body! His reverence Abbé Jouve promised me you would come. It's only you who know what I want. I am going to buy some meat. But now the pain's going down into my legs. Help me; I have no strength left— none left at all!"

The old woman wished to turn over, and Hélène, drawing off her gloves, gently took hold of her and placed her as she desired. As she was still bending over her the door opened, and a flush of surprise mounted to her cheeks as she saw Dr. Deberle entering. Did he also make visits to which he never referred?

"It's the doctor!" blurted out the old woman. "Oh! Heaven must bless you both for being so good!"

The doctor bowed respectfully to Hélène. Mother Fétu had ceased whining on his entrance, but kept up a sibilant wheeze, like that of a child in pain. She had understood at once that the doctor and her benefactress were known to one another; and her eyes never left them, but travelled from one to the other, while her wrinkled face showed that her mind was covertly working. The doctor put some questions to her, and sounded her right side; then, turning to Hélène, who had just sat down, he said:

"She is suffering from hepatic colic. She will be on her feet again in a few days."

And, tearing from his memorandum book a leaf on which he had written some lines, he added, addressing Mother Fétu:

"Listen to me. You must send this to the chemist in the Rue de Passy, and every two hours you must drink a spoonful of the draught he will give you."

The old woman burst out anew into blessings. Hélène remained seated. The doctor lingered gazing at her; but when their eyes had met, he bowed and discreetly took his leave. He had not gone down a flight ere Mother Fétu's lamentations were renewed.

"Ah! he's such a clever doctor! Ah! if his medicine could do me some good! Dandelions and tallow make a good simple for removing water from the body. Yes, yes, you can say you know a clever doctor. Have you known him long? Gracious goodness, how thirsty I am; I feel burning hot. He has a wife, hasn't he? He deserves to have a good wife and beautiful children. Indeed, it's a pleasure to see kind-hearted people good acquaintances."

Héléne had risen to give her a drink.

"I must go now, Mother Fétu," she said. "Good-bye till to-morrow."

"Ah! how good you are! If I only had some linen! Look at my chemise —it's torn in half; and this bed is so dirty. But that doesn't matter. God will requite you, my good lady!"

Next day, on Hélène's entering Mother Fétu's room, she found Dr.

Deberle already there. Seated on the chair, he was writing out a prescription, while the old woman rattled on with whimpering volubility.

"Oh, sir, it now feels like lead in my side—yes, just like lead! It's as heavy as a hundred-pound weight, and prevents me from turning round."

Then, having caught sight of Hélène, she went on without a pause: "Ah, here's the good lady! I told the kind doctor you would come. Though the heavens might fall, said I, you would come all the same. You're a very saint, an angel from paradise, and, oh! so beautiful that people might fall on their knees in the streets to gaze on you as you pass! Dear lady, I am no better; just now I have a heavy feeling here.. Oh, I have told the doctor what you did for me! The emperor could have done no more. Yes, indeed, it would be a sin not to love you —a great sin."

These broken sentences fell from her lips as, with eyes half closed, she rolled her head on the bolster, the doctor meantime smiling at Hélène, who felt very ill at ease.

"Mother Fétu," she said softly, "I have brought you a little linen."

"Oh, thank you, thank you; God will requite you! You're just like this kind, good gentleman, who does more good to poor folks than a host of those who declare it their special work. You don't know what great care he has taken of me for four months past, supplying me with medicine and broth and wine. One rarely finds a rich person so kind to a poor soul! Oh, he's another of God's angels! Dear, dear,

I seem to have quite a house in my stomach!"

In his turn the doctor now seemed to be embarrassed. He rose and offered his chair to Hélène; but although she had come with the intention of remaining a quarter of an hour, she declined to sit down, on the plea that she was in a great hurry.

Meanwhile, Mother Fétu, still rolling her head to and fro, had stretched out her hand, and the parcel of linen had vanished in the bed. Then she resumed:

"Oh, what a couple of good souls you are! I don't wish to offend you; I only say it because it's true. When you have seen one, you have seen the other. Oh, dear Lord! give me a hand and help me to turn round. Kindhearted people understand one another. Yes, yes, they understand one another."

"Good-bye, Mother Fétu," said Hélène, leaving the doctor in sole possession. "I don't think I shall call to-morrow."

The next day, however, found her in the attic again. The old woman was sound asleep, but scarcely had she opened her eyes and recognized Hélène in her black dress sitting on the chair than she exclaimed:

"He has been here—oh, I really don't know what he gave me to take, but I am as stiff as a stick. We were talking about you. He asked me all kinds of questions; whether you were generally sad, and whether your look was always the same. Oh, he's such a good man!"

Her words came more slowly, and she seemed to be waiting to see by the expression of Hélène's face what effect her remarks might have on her, with that wheedling, anxious air of the poor who are desirous of pleasing people. No doubt she fancied she could detect a flush of displeasure mounting to her benefactress's brow, for her huge, puffed-up face, all eagerness and excitement, suddenly clouded over; and she resumed, in stammering accents:

"I am always asleep. Perhaps I have been poisoned. A woman in the Rue de l'Annonciation was killed by a drug which the chemist gave her in mistake for another."

That day Hélène lingered for nearly half an hour in Mother Fétu's room, hearing her talk of Normandy, where she had been born, and where the milk was so good. During the silence she asked the old woman carelessly: "Have you known the doctor a long time?"

Mother Fétu, lying on her back, half-opened her eyes and again closed them.

"Oh, yes!" she answered, almost in a whisper. "For instance, his father attended to me before '48, and he accompanied him then."

"I have been told the father was a very good man."

"Yes, but a little cracked. The son is much his superior. When he touches you you would think his hands were of velvet."

Silence again fell.

"I advise you to do everything he tells you," at last said Hélène. "He is very clever; he saved my daughter."

"To be sure!" exclaimed Mother Fétu, again all excitement. "People ought to have confidence in him. Why, he brought a boy to life again when he was going to be buried! Oh, there aren't two persons like him; you won't stop me from saying that! I am very lucky; I fall in with the pick of good-hearted people. I thank the gracious Lord for it every night. I don't forget either of you. You are mingled together in my prayers. May God in His goodness shield you and grant your every wish! May He load you with His gifts! May He keep you a place in Paradise!"

She was now sitting up in bed with hands clasped, seemingly entreating Heaven with devout fervor. Hélène allowed her to go on thus for a considerable time, and even smiled. The old woman's chatter, in fact, ended by lulling her into a pleasant drowsiness, and when she went off she promised to give her a bonnet and gown, as soon as she should be able to get about again.

Throughout that week Hèléne busied herself with Mother Fétu. Her afternoon visit became an item in her daily life. She felt a strange fondness for the Passage des Eaux. She liked that steep lane for its coolness and quietness and its ever-clean pavement, washed on rainy days by the water rushing down from the heights. A strange sensation thrilled her as she stood at the top and looked at the narrow alley with its steep declivity, usually deserted, and only known to the few inhabitants of the neighboring streets. Then she would venture through an archway dividing a house fronting the Rue Raynouard, and trip down the seven flights of broad steps, in which lay the bed of a pebbly stream occupying half of the narrow way. The walls of the gardens on each side bulged out, coated with a grey, leprous growth; umbrageous trees, dropped over, foliage rained down, here and there an ivy plant thickly mantled the stonework, and the chequered verdure, which only left glimpses of the blue sky above, made the light very soft and greeny. Halfway down Hélène would stop to take breath, gazing at the street-lamp which hung there, and listening to the merry laughter in the gardens, whose doors she had never seen open. At times an old woman panted up with the aid of the black, shiny, iron handrail fixed in the wall to the right; a lady would come, leaning on her parasol as on a walking-stick; or a band of urchins would run down, with a great stamping of feet. But almost always Hélène found herself alone, and this steep, secluded, shady descent was to her a veritable delight—like a path in the depths of a forest. At the bottom she would raise her eyes, and the sight of the narrow, precipitous alley she had just descended made her feel somewhat frightened.

She glided into the old woman's room with the quiet and coolness of the Passage des Eaux clinging to her garments. This woefully wretched den no longer affected her painfully. She moved about there as if in her own rooms, opening the round attic window to admit the fresh air, and pushing the table into a corner if it came in her way. The garret's bareness, its whitewashed walls and rickety furniture, realized to her mind an existence whose simplicity she had sometimes dreamt of in her girlhood. But what especially charmed her was the kindly emotion she experienced there. Playing the part of sick nurse, hearing the constant bewailing of the old woman, all she saw and felt within the four walls left her quivering with deep pity. In the end she awaited with evident impatience Doctor Deberle's customary visit. She questioned him as to Mother Fétu's condition; but from this they glided to other subjects, as they stood near each other, face to face. A closer acquaintance was springing up between them, and they were surprised to find they possessed similar tastes. They understood one another without speaking a word, each heart engulfed in the same overflowing charity. Nothing to Hélène seemed sweeter than this mutual feeling, which arose in such an unusual way, and to which she yielded without resistance, filled as she was with divine pity. At first she had felt somewhat afraid of the doctor; in her own drawing-room she would have been cold and distrustful, in harmony with her nature. Here, however, in this garret they were far from the world, sharing the one chair, and almost happy in the midst of the wretchedness and poverty which filled their souls with emotion. A week passed, and they knew one another as though they had been intimate for years. Mother Fétu's miserable abode was filled with sunshine, streaming from this fellowship of kindness.

The old woman grew better very slowly. The doctor was surprised, and charged her with coddling herself when she related that she now felt a dreadful weight in her legs. She always kept up her monotonous moaning, lying on her back and rolling her head to and fro; but she closed her eyes, as though to give her visitors an opportunity for unrestrained talk. One day she was to all appearance sound asleep, but beneath their lids her little black eyes continued watching. At last, however, she had to rise from her bed; and next day Hélène presented her with the promised bonnet and gown. When the doctor made his appearance that afternoon the old woman's laggard memory seemed suddenly stirred. "Gracious goodness!" said she, 'I've forgotten my neighbor's soup-pot; I promised to attend to it!"

Then she disappeared, closing the door behind her and leaving the couple alone. They did not notice that they were shut in, but continued their conversation. The doctor urged Hélène to spend the afternoon occasionally in his garden in the Rue Vineuse.

"My wife," said he, "must return your visit, and she will in person repeat my invitation. It would do your daughter good."

"But I don't refuse," she replied, laughing. "I do not require to be fetched with ceremony. Only—only— I am afraid of being indiscreet. At any rate, we will see."

Their talk continued, but at last the doctor exclaimed in a tone of surprise: "Where on earth can Mother Fétu have gone? It must be a quarter of an hour since she went to see after her neighbor's soup-pot."

Hélène then saw that the door was shut, but it did not shock her at the moment. She continued to talk of Madame Deberle, of whom she spoke highly to her husband; but noticing that the doctor constantly glanced towards the door, she at last began to feel uncomfortable.

"It's very strange that she does not come back!" she remarked in her turn.

Their conversation then dropped. Hélène, not knowing what to do, opened the window; and when she turned round they avoided looking at one another. The laughter of children came in through the circular window, which, with its bit of blue sky, seemed like a full moon. They could not have been more alone—concealed from all inquisitive looks, with merely this bit of heaven gazing in on them. The voices of the children died away in the distance; and a quivering silence fell. No one would dream of finding them in that attic, out of the world. Their confusion grew apace, and in the end Hélène, displeased with herself, gave the doctor a steady glance.

"I have a great many visits to pay yet," he at once exclaimed. "As she doesn't return, I must leave."

He quitted the room, and Hélène then sat down. Immediately afterwards Mother Fétu returned with many protestations:

"Oh oh! I can scarcely crawl; such a faintness came over me! Has the dear good doctor gone? Well, to be sure, there's not much comfort here! Oh, you are both angels from heaven, coming to spend your time with one so unfortunate as myself! But God in His goodness will requite you. The pain has gone down into my feet to-day, and I had to sit down on a step. Oh, I should like to have some chairs! If I only had an easy-chair! My mattress is so vile too that I am quite ashamed when you come. The whole place is at your disposal, and I would throw myself into the fire if you required it. Yes. Heaven knows it; I always repeat it in my prayers! Oh,

kind Lord, grant their utmost desires to these good friends of mine—in the name of the Father, the Son, and the Holy Ghost!"

As Héléne listened she experienced a singular feeling of discomfort. Mother Fétu's bloated face filled her with disgust. Never before in this stifling attic had she been affected in a like way; its sordid misery seemed to stare her in the face; the lack of fresh air, the surrounding wretchedness, quite sickened her. So she made all haste to leave, feeling hurt by the blessings which Mother Fétu poured after her.

In the Passage des Eaux an additional sorrow came upon her. Halfway up, on the righthand side of the path, the wall was hollowed out, and here there was an excavation, some disused well, enclosed by a railing. During the last two days when passing she had heard the wailings of a cat rising from this well, and now, as she slowly climbed the path, these wailings were renewed, but so pitifully that they seemed instinct with the agony of death. The thought that the poor brute, thrown into the disused well, was slowly dying there of hunger, quite rent Hélène's heart. She hastened her steps, resolving that she would not venture down this lane again for a long time, lest the cat's death-call should reach her ears.

The day was a Tuesday. In the evening, on the stroke of seven, as Hélène was finishing a tiny bodice, the two wonted rings at the bell were heard, and Rosalie opened the door.

"His reverence is first to-night!" she exclaimed. "Oh, here comes Monsieur Rambaud too!"

They were very merry at dinner.

Jeanne was nearly well again now, and the two brothers, who spoiled her, were successful in procuring her permission to eat some salad, of which she was excessively fond, notwithstanding Doctor Bodins formal prohibition. When she was going to bed, the child in high spirits hung round her mother's neck and pleaded:

"Oh! mamma, darling! let me go with you to-morrow to see the old woman you nurse!"

But the Abbé and Monsieur Rambaud were the first to scold her for thinking of such a thing. They would not hear of her going amongst the poor, as the sight affected her too greviously. The last time she had been on such an expedition she had twice swooned, and for three days her eyes had been swollen with tears, that had flowed even in her sleep.

"Oh! I will be good!" she pleaded. "I won't cry, I promise."

"It is quite useless, my darling," said her mother, caressing her. "The old woman is well now. I shall not go out any more; I'll stay all day with you!"

## CHAPTER IV

### BON AMI

DURING the following week Madame Deberle paid a return visit to Madame Grandjean, and displayed an affability that bordered on affection.

"You know what you promised me," she said, on the threshold, as she was going off. "The first fine day we have, you must come down to the garden, and bring Jeanne with you. It is the doctor's strict injunction."

"Very well," Hélène answered, with a smile, "it is understood; we will avail ourselves of your kindness."

Three days later, on a bright February afternoon, she accompanied her daughter down to the garden. The porter opened the door connecting the two houses. At the near end of the garden, in a kind of greenhouse built somewhat in the style of a Japanese pavilion, they found Madame Deberle and her sister Pauline, both idling away their time, for some embroidery, thrown on the little table, lay there neglected.

"Oh, how good of you to come!" cried Juliette. "You must sit down here. Pauline, move that table away! It is still rather cool you know to sit out of doors, but from this pavilion we can keep a watch on the children. Now, little ones, run away and play; but take care not to fall!"

The large door of the pavilion stood open, and on each side were portable mirrors, whose covers had been removed so that they allowed one to view the garden's expanse as from the threshold of a tent. The garden, with a green sward in the centre, flanked by beds of flowers, was separated from the Rue Vineuse by a plain iron railing, but against this grew a thick green hedge, which prevented the curious from gazing in. Ivy, clematis, and woodbine clung and wound around the railings, and behind this first curtain of foliage came a second one of lilacs and laburnums. Even in the winter the ivy leaves and the close network of branches sufficed to shut off the view. But the great charm of the garden lay in its having at the far end a few lofty trees, some magnificent elms, which concealed the grimy wall of a five-story house. Amidst all the neighboring houses these trees gave the spot the aspect of a nook in some park, and seemed to increase the dimensions of this little Parisian garden, which was swept like a drawing-room. Between two of the elms hung a swing, the seat of which was green with damp.

Hélène leaned forward the better to view the scene.

"Oh, it is a hole!" exclaimed Madame Deberle carelessly. "Still, trees are so rare in Paris that one is happy in having half a dozen of one's own."

"No, no, you have a very pleasant place," murmured Hélène.

The sun filled the pale atmosphere that day with a golden dust, its rays streaming slowly through the leafless branches of the trees. These assumed a ruddier tint, and you could see the delicate purple gems softening the cold grey of the bark. On the lawn and along the walks the grass and gravel glittered amidst the haze that seemed to ooze from the ground. No flower was in blossom; only the happy flush which the sunshine cast upon the soil revealed the approach of spring.

"At this time of year it is rather dull," resumed Madame Deberle. "In June it is as cozy as a nest; the trees prevent any one from looking in, and we enjoy perfect privacy." At this point she paused to call: "Lucien, you must come away from that watertap!"

The lad, who was doing the honors of the garden, had led Jeanne towards a tap under the steps. Here he had turned on the water, which he allowed to splash on the tips of his boots. It was a game that he delighted in.

Jeanne, with grave face, looked on while he wetted his feet.

"Wait a moment!" said Pauline, rising. "I'll go and stop this nonsense!"

But Juliette held her back.

"You'll do no such thing; you are even more of a madcap than he is. The other day both of you looked as if you had taken a bath. How is it that a big girl like you cannot remain two minutes seated? Lucien!" she continued directing here eyes on her son, "turn off the water at once!"

The child, in his fright, made an effort to obey her. But instead of turning the tap off, he turned it on all the more, and the water gushed forth with a force and a noise that made him lose his head. He recoiled, splashed up to the shoulders.

"Turn off the water at once!" again ordered his mother, whose cheeks were flushing with anger.

Jeanne, hitherto silent, then slowly, and with the greatest caution, ventured near the tap; while Lucien burst into loud sobbing at sight of this cold stream, which terrified him, and which he was powerless to stop. Carefully drawing her skirt between her legs, Jeanne streched out her bare hands so as not to wet her sleeves, and closed the tap without receiving a sprinkle. The flow instantly ceased. Lucien, astonished and inspired with respect, dried his tears and gazed with swollen eyes at the girl.

"Oh, that child puts me beside myself!" exclaimed Madame Deberle, her complexion regaining its usual pallor, while she stretched herself out, as though wearied to death.

Hélène deemed it right to intervene.

"Jeanne," she called, "take his hand, and amuse yourselves by walking up and down."

Jeanne took hold of Lucien's hand, and both gravely paced the paths with little steps. She was much taller than her companion, who had to stretch his arm up towards her; but this solemn amusement, which consisted in a ceremonious circuit of the lawn, appeared to absorb them and invest them with a sense of great importance. Jeanne, like a genuine lady, gazed about, preoccupied with her own thoughts; Lucien every now and then would venture a glance at her; but not a word was said by either.

"How droll they are!" said Madame Deberle, smiling, and again at her ease. "I must say that your Jeanne is a dear, good child. She is so obedient, so well behaved—"

"Yes, when she is in the company of others," broke in Hélène. "She is a great trouble at times. Still, she loves me, and does her best to be good so as not to vex me."

Then they spoke of children; how girls were more precocious than boys; though it would be wrong to deduce too much from Lucien's unintelligent face. In another year he would doubtless lose all his gawkiness and become quite a gallant. Finally, Madame Deberle resumed her embroidery, making perhaps two stitches in a minute. Hélène, who was only happy when busy, begged permission to bring her work the next time she came. She found her companions somewhat dull, and whiled away the time in examining the Japanese pavilion. The walls and ceiling were hidden by tapestry worked in

gold, with designs showing bright cranes in full flight, butterflies, and flowers and views in which blue ships were tossing upon yellow rivers. Chairs, and ironwood flower-stands were scattered about; on the floor some fine mats were spread; while the lacquered furnishings were littered with trinkets, small bronzes and vases, and strange toys painted in all the hues of the rainbow. At the far end stood a grotesque idol in Dresden china, with bent legs and bare, protruding stomach, which at the least movement shook its head with a terrible and amusing look.

"Isn't it horribly ugly?" asked Pauline, who had been watching Hélène as she glanced round. "I say, sister, you know that all these purchases of yours are so much rubbish! Malignon calls your Japanese museum 'the sixpenny bazaar.' Oh, by the way, talking of him, I met him. He was with a lady, and such a lady — Florence, of the Variétès Theatre."

"Where was it?" asked Juliette immediately. "How I shall tease him!"

"On the boulevards. He's coming here to-day, is he not?"

She was not vouchsafed any reply. The ladies had all at once become uneasy owing to the disappearance of the children, and called to them. However, two shrill voices immediately answered:

"We are here!"

Half hidden by a spindle tree, they were sitting on the grass in the middle of the lawn.

"What are you about?"

"We have put up at an inn," answered Lucien. "We are resting in our room."

Greatly diverted, the women watched them for a time. Jeanne seemed quite contented with the game. She was cutting the grass around her, doubtless with the intention of preparing breakfast. A piece of wood, picked up among the shrubs, represented a trunk. And now they were talking. Jeanne, with great conviction in her tone, was declaring that they were in Switzerland, and that they would set out to see the glaciers, which rather astonished Lucien.

"Ha, here he is!" suddenly exclaimed Pauline.

Madame Deberle turned, and caught sight of Malignon descending the steps. He had scarcely time to make his bow and sit down before she attacked him.

"Oh," she said, "it is nice of you to go about everywhere saying that I have nothing but rubbishy ornaments about me!"

"You mean this little salon of yours? Oh, yes," said he, quite at his ease. "You haven't anything worth looking at here!"

"What! not my china figure?" she asked, quite hurt.

"No, no, everything is quite *bourgeois*. It is necessary for a person to have some taste You wouldn't allow me to select the things—"

"Your taste, forsooth! just talk about your taste!" she retorted, flushing crimson and feeling quite angry. "You have been seen with a lady—"

"What lady?" he asked, surprised by the violence of the attack.

"A fine choice, indeed! I compliment you on it. A girl whom the whole of Paris knows—"

She suddenly paused, remembering Pauline's presence.

"Pauline," she said, "go into the garden for a minute."

"Oh no," retorted the girl indignantly. "It's so tiresome; I'm always being sent out of the way."

"Go into the garden," repeated Juliette, with increased severity in her tone.

The girl stalked off with a sullen look, but stopped all at once to exclaim: "Well, then, be quick over your talk!"

As soon as she was gone, Madame Deberle returned to the charge. "How can you, a gentleman, show yourself in public with that actress Florence? She is at least forty. She is ugly enough to frighten one, and all the gentlemen in the stalls thee and thou her on first nights."

"Have you finished?" called out Pauline, who was strolling sulkily under the trees. "I'm not amusing myself here, you know."

Malignon, however, defended himself. He had no knowledge of this girl Florence; he had never in his life spoken a word to her. They had possibly seen him with a lady: he was sometimes in the company of the wife of a friend of his. Besides, who had seen him? He wanted proofs, witnesses.

"Pauline," hastily asked Madame Deberle, raising her voice, "did you not meet him with Florence?"

"Yes, certainly," replied her sister. "I met them on the boulevards opposite Bignon's."

Thereupon, glorying in her victory over Malignon, whose face wore an embarrassed smile, Madame Deberle called out: "You can come back, Pauline; I have finished."

Malignon, who had a box at the Folies-Dramatiques for the following night, now gallantly placed it at Madame Deberle's service, apparently not feeling the slightest ill-will towards her; moreover, they were always quarreling. Pauline wished to know if she might go to see the play that was running, and as Malignon laughed and shook his head, she declared it was very silly; authors ought to write plays fit for girls to see. She was only allowed such entertainments as *La Dame Blanche* and the classic drama could offer.

Meantime, the ladies had ceased watching the children, and all at once Lucien began to raise terrible shrieks.

"What have you done to him, Jeanne?" asked Hélène.

"I have done nothing, mamma," answered the little girl. "He has thrown himself on the ground."

The truth was, the children had just set out for the famous glaciers. As Jeanne pretended that they were reaching the mountains they had lifted their feet very high, as though to step over the rocks. Lucien, however, quite out of breath with his exertions, at last made a false step, and fell sprawling in the middle of an imaginary icefield. Disgusted, and furious with child-like rage, he no sooner found himself on the ground than he burst into tears.

"Lift him up," called Hélène.

"He won't let me, mamma. He is rolling about."

And so saying, Jeanne drew back, as though exasperated and annoyed by such a display of bad breeding. He did not know how to play; he would certainly cover her with dirt. Her mouth curled, as though she were a duchesss compromising herself by such companionship. Thereupon Madame Deberle, irritated by Lucien's continued wailing, requested her sister to pick him up and coax him into silence. Nothing loth, Pauline ran, cast herself down beside the child, and for a moment rolled on the ground with him. He struggled with her, unwilling to be lifted, but she at last took him up by the arms, and to appease him, said, "Stop crying, you noisy fellow; we'll have a swing!"

Lucien at once closed his lips, while Jeanne's solemn looks vanished, and a gleam of ardent delight illumined her face. All three ran towards the swing, but it was Pauline who took possession of the seat.

"Push, push!" she urged the children; and they pushed with all the force of their tiny hands; but she was heavy, and they could scarcely stir the swing.

"Push!" she urged again. "Oh, the big sillies, they can't!"

In the pavilion, Madame Deberle had just felt a slight chill. Despite the bright sunshine she thought it rather cold, and she requested Malignon to hand her a white cashmere burnous that was hanging from the handle of a window fastening. Malignon rose to wrap the burnous round her shoulders, and they began chatting familiarly on matters which had little interest for Hélène. Feeling fidgety, fearing that Pauline might unwittingly knock the children down, she therefore stepped into the garden, leaving Juliette and the young man to wrangle over some new fashion in bonnets which apparently deeply interested them.

Jeanne no sooner saw her mother than she ran towards her with a wheedling smile, and entreaty in every gesture. "Oh, mamma, mamma!" she implored. "Oh, mamma!"

"No, no, you mustn't!" replied Hélène, who understood her meaning very well. "You know you have been forbidden."

Swinging was Jeanne's greatest delight. She would say that she believed herself a bird; the breeze blowing in her face, the lively rush through the air, the continued swaying to and fro in a motion as rythmic as the beating of a bird's wings, thrilled her with an exquisite pleasure; in her ascent towards cloudland she imagined herself on her way to heaven. But it always ended in some mishap. On one occasion she had been found clinging to the ropes of the swing in a swoon, her large eyes wide open, fixed in a vacant stare, at another time she had fallen to the ground, stiff, like a swallow struck by a shot.

"Oh, mamma!" she implored again. "Only a little, a very, very little!"

In the end her mother, in order to win peace, placed her on the seat. The child's face lit up with an angelic smile, and her bare wrists quivered with joyous expectancy. Hélène swayed her very gently.

"Higher, mamma, higher!" she murmured.

But Hélène paid no heed to her prayer, and retained firm hold of the rope. She herself was glowing all over, her cheeks flushed, and she thrilled with

excitement at very push she gave to the swing. Her wonted sedateness vanished as she thus became her daughter's playmate.

"That will do," she declared after a time, taking Jeanne in her arms.

"Oh, mamma, you must swing now!" the child whispered, as she clung to her neck.

She took a keen delight in seeing her mother flying through the air; as she said, her pleasure was still more intense in gazing at her than in having a swing herself. Hélène, however, asked her laughingly who would push her; when she went in for swinging, it was a serious matter; why, she went higher than the treetops! While she was speaking it happened that Monsieur Rambaud made his appearance under the guidance of the doorkeeper. He had met Madame Deberle in Hélène's rooms, and thought he would not be deemed presuming in presenting himself here when unable to find her. Madame Deberle proved very gracious, pleased as she was with the good-natured air of the worthy man; however, she soon returned to a lively discussion with Malignon.

"*Bon ami* will push you, mamma! *Bon ami* will push you!" Jeanne called out, as she danced round her mother.

"Be quiet! We are not at home!" said her mother with mock gravity.

"Bless me! if it will please you, I am at your disposal," exclaimed Monsieur Rambaud. "When people are in the country—"

Hélène let herself be persuaded. When a girl she had been accustomed to swing for hours, and the memory of those vanished pleasures created a secret craving to taste them once more. Moreover, Pauline, who had sat down with Lucien at the edge of the lawn, intervened with the boldness of a girl freed from the trammels of childhood.

"Of course he will push you, and he will swing me after you. Won't you, sir?"

This determined Hélène. The youth which dwelt within her, in spite of the cold demureness of her great beauty, displayed itself in a charming, ingenuous fashion. She became a thorough school-girl unaffected and gay. There was no prudishness about her. She laughingly declared that she must not expose her legs, and asked for some cord to tie her skirts securely round her ankles. That done, she stood upright on the swing, her arms extended and clinging to the ropes.

"Now, push, Monsieur Rambaud," she exclaimed delightedly. "But gently at first!"

Monsieur Rambaud had hung his hat on the branch of a tree. His broad, kindly face beamed with a fatherly smile. First he tested the strength of the ropes, and, giving a look at the trees, determined to give a slight push. That day Hélène had for the first time abandoned her widow's weeds; she was wearing a grey dress set off with mauve bows. Standing upright, she began to swing, almost touching the ground, and as if rocking to sleep.

"Quicker! quicker!" she exclaimed.

Monsieur Rambaud, with his hands ready, caught the seat as it came back to him, and gave it a more vigorous push. Hélène went higher, each ascent taking her farther. However, despite the motion, she did not lose her sedate-ness; she retained almost an austere demeanor; her eyes shone very brightly in her beautiful, impassive face; her nostrils only were inflated, as though to drink in the air. Not a fold of her skirts was out of place, but a plait of her hair slipped down.

"Quicker! quicker!" she called.

An energetic push gave her increased impetus. Up in the sunshine she flew, even higher and higher. A breeze sprung up with her motion, and blew through the garden; her flight was so swift that they could scarcely distinguish her figure aright. Her face was now all smiles, and flushed with a rosy red, while her eyes sparkled here, then there, like shooting stars. The loosened plait of hair rustled against her neck. Despite the cords which bound them, her skirts now waved about, and you could divine that she was at her ease, her bosom heaving in its free enjoyment as though the air were indeed her natural place.

"Quicker! quicker!"

Monsieur Rambaud, his face red and bedewed with perspiration, exerted all his strength. A cry rang out. Hélène went still higher.

"Oh, mamma! Oh, mamma!" repeated Jeanne in her ecstasy.

She was sitting on the lawn gazing at her mother, her little hands clasped on her bosom, looking as though she herself had drunk in all the air that was stirring. Her breath failed her; with a rythmical movement of the shoulders she kept time with the long strokes of the swing. And she cried, "Quicker! quicker!" while her mother still went higher, her feet grazing the lofty branches of the trees.

"Higher, mamma! oh, higher, mamma!"

But Hélène was already in the very heavens. The trees bent and cracked as beneath a gale. Her skirts, which were all they could see, flapped with a tempestuous sound. When she came back with arms stretched out and bosom distended she lowered her head slightly and for a moment hovered; but then she rose again and sank backwards, her head tilted, her eyes closed, as though she had swooned. These ascensions and descents which made her giddy were delightful. In her flight she entered into the sunshine—the pale yellow February sunshine that rained down like golden dust. Her chestnut hair gleamed with amber tints; and a flame seemed to have leaped up around her, as the mauve bows on her whitening dress flashed like burning flowers. Around her the springtide was maturing into birth, and the purple-tinted gems of the trees showed like delicate lacquer against the blue sky.

Jeanne clasped her hands. Her mother seemed to her a saint with a golden glory around her head, winging her way to paradise, and she again stammered. "Oh, mamma! oh! mamma!"

Madame Deberle and Malignon had now grown interested, and had stepped under the trees. Malignon declared the lady to be very bold.

"I should faint, I'm sure," said Madame Deberle, with a frightened air.

Hèléne heard them, for she dropped these words from among the branches: "Oh, my heart is all right! Give a stronger push, Monsieur Rambaud!"

And indeed her voice betrayed no emotion. She seemed to take no heed of the two men who were onlookers. They were doubtless nothing to her. Her tress of hair had become entangled, and the cord that confined her skirts must have given way, for the drapery flapped in the wind like a flag. She was going still higher.

All at once, however, the exclamation rang out:

"Enough, Monsieur Rambaud, enough!"

Doctor Deberle had just appeared on the house steps. He came forward, embraced his wife tenderly, took up Lucien and kissed his brow. Then he gazed at Hélène with a smile.

"Enough, enough!" she still continued exclaiming.

"Why?" asked he. "Do I disturb you?"

She made no answer; a look of gravity had suddenly come over her face. The swing, still continuing its rapid flights, owing to the impetus given to it, would not stop, but swayed to and fro with a regular motion which still bore Hélène to a great height. The doctor, surprised and charmed, beheld her with admiration; she looked so superb, so tall and strong, with the pure figure of an antique statue whilst swinging thus gently amid the spring sunshine. But she seemed annoyed, and all at once leaped down.

"Stop! stop!" they all cried out.

From Hélène's lips came a dull moan; she had fallen upon the gravel of a pathway, and her efforts to rise were fruitless.

"Good heavens!" exclaimed the doctor, his face turning very pale. "How imprudent!"

They all crowded round her. Jeanne began weeping so bitterly that Monsieur Rambaud, with his heart in his mouth, was compelled to take her in his arms. The doctor, meanwhile, eagerly questioned Hélène.

"Is it the right leg you fell on? Cannot you stand upright?" And as she remained dazed, without answering, he asked: "Do you suffer?"

"Yes, here at the knee; a dull pain," she answered, with difficulty.

He at once sent his wife for his medicine case and some bandages, and repeated:

"I must see, I must see. No doubt it is a mere nothing."

He knelt down on the gravel and Hélène let him do so; but all at once she struggeld to her feet and said: "No, no!"

"But I must examine the place," he said.

A slight quiver stole over her, and she answered in a yet lower tone:

"It is not necessary. It is nothing at all."

He looked at her, at first astounded. Her neck was flushing red; for a moment their eyes met, and seemed to reach each other's soul; he was disconcerted, and slowly rose, remaining near her, but without pressing her further.

Hélène had signed to Monsieur Rambaud. "Fetch Doctor Bodin," she whispered in his ear, "and tell him what has happened to me."

Ten minutes later, when Doctor Bodin made his appearance, she, with superhuman courage, regained her feet, and leaning on him and Monsieur Rambaud, contrived to return home. Jeanne followed, quivering with sobs.

"I shall wait," said Doctor Deberle to his brother physician. "Come down and remove our fears."

In the garden a lively colloquy ensued. Malignon was of opinion that women had queer ideas. Why on earth had that lady been so foolish as to jump down? Pauline, excessively provoked at this accident, which deprived her of a pleasure, declared it was silly to swing so high. On his side Doctor Deberle did not say a word, but seemed anxious.

"It is nothing serious," said Doctor Bodin, as he came down again—"only a sprain. Still, she will have to keep to an easy-chair for at least a fortnight."

Thereupon Monsieur Deberle gave a friendly slap on Malignon's shoulder. He wished his wife to go in, as it was really becoming too cold. For his own part, taking Lucien in his arms, he carried him into the house, covering him with kisses the while.

## CHAPTER V

### A PARIS MORNING

BOTH windows of the bedroom were wide open, and in the depths below the house, which was perched on the very summit of the hill, lay Paris, rolling away in a mighty flat expanse. Ten o'clock struck; the lovely February morning had all the sweetness and perfume of spring.

Hélène reclined in an invalid chair, reading in front of one of the windows, her knee still in bandages. She suffered no pain; but she had been confined to her room for a week past, unable even to take up her customary needlework. Not knowing what to do, she had opened a book which she had found on the table—she, who indulged in little or no reading at any time. This book was the one she used every night as a shade for the night-lamp, the only volume which she had taken within eighteen months from the small but irreproachable library selected by Monsieur Rambaud. Novels usually seemed to her false to life and puerile; and this one, Sir Walter Scott's "Ivanhoe," had at first wearied her to death. However, a strange curiosity had grown upon her, and she was finishing it, at times affected to tears, and at times rather bored, when she would let it slip from her hand for long minutes and gaze fixedly at the far-stretching horizon.

That morning Paris awoke from sleep with a smiling indolence. A mass of vapor, following the valley of the Seine, shrouded the two banks from view. This mist was light and milky, and the sun, gathering strength, was slowly tinging it with radiance. Nothing of the city was distinguishable through this floating muslin. In the hollows the haze thickened and assumed a bluish tint; while over certain broad expanses delicate transparencies appeared, a golden dust, beneath which you could divine the depths of the streets; and up above domes and steeples rent the mist, rearing grey outlines to which clung shreds of the haze which they had pierced. At times cloudlets of yellow smoke would, like giant birds, heavy of wing, slowly soar on high, and then mingle with the atmosphere which seemed to absorb them. And above all this immensity, this mass of cloud, hanging in slumber over Paris, a sky of extreme purity, of a faint and whitening blue, spread out its mighty vault. The sun was climbing the heavens, scattering a spray of soft rays; a pale golden light, akin in hue to the flaxen tresses of a child, was streaming down like rain, filling the atmosphere with the warm quiver of its sparkle. It was like a festival of the infinite, instinct with sovereign peacefulness and gentle gaiety, whilst the city, chequered with golden beams, still remained lazy and sleepy, unwilling to reveal itself by casting off its coverlet of lace.

For eight days it had been Hélène's diversion to gaze on that mighty expanse of Paris, and she never wearied of doing so. It was as unfathomable and varying as the ocean—fair in the morning, ruddy with fire at night, borrowing all the joys and sorrows of the heavens reflected in its depths. A flash of sunshine came, and it would roll in waves of gold; a cloud would darken it and raise a tempest. Its aspect was ever changing. A complete calm would fall, and all would assume an orange hue; gusts of wind would sweep by from time to time, and turn everything livid; in keen, bright weather there would be a shimmer of light on every housetop; whilst when showers fell, blurring both heaven and earth, all would be plunged in chaotic confusion. At her window Hélène experienced all the hopes and sorrows that pertain to the open sea. As the keen wind blew in her face she imagined it wafted a saline fragrance; even the ceaseless noise of the city seemed to her like that of a surging tide beating against a rocky cliff.

The book fell from her hands. She was dreaming, with a far-away look in her eyes. When she stopped reading thus it was from a desire to linger and understand what she had already perused. She took a delight in denying her curiosity immediate satisfaction. The tale filled her soul with a tempest of emotion. Paris that morning was displaying the same vague joy and sorrow as that which disturbed her heart. In this lay a great charm— to be ignorant, to guess things dimly, to yield to slow initiation, with the vague thought that her youth was beginning again.

How full of lies were novels! She was assuredly right in not reading them. They were mere fables, good for empty heads with no proper conception of life. Yet she remained entranced, dreaming unceasingly of the knight Ivanhoe, loved so passionately by two women—Rebecca, the beautiful Jewess, and the noble Lady Rowena. She herself thought she could have loved with the intensity and patient serenity of the latter maiden. To love! to love! She did not utter the words, but they thrilled her through and through in the very thought, astonishing her, and irradiating her face with a smile. In the distance some fleecy cloudlets, driven by the breeze, now floated over Paris like a flock of swans. Huge gaps were being cleft in the fog; a momentary glimpse was given of the left bank, indistinct and clouded, like a city of fairydom seen in a dream; but suddenly a thick curtain of mist swept down, and the fairy city was engulfed, as though by an inundation. And then the vapors, spreading equally over every district, formed, as it were, a beautiful lake, with milky, placid water. There was but one denser streak, indicating the grey, curved course of the Seine. And slowly over those milky, placid waters shadows passed, like vessels with pink sails, which the young woman followed with a dreamy gaze. To love! to love! She smiled as her dream sailed on.

However, she again took up her book. She had reached the chapter describing the attack on the castle, wherein Rebecca nurses the wounded Ivanhoe, and recounts to him the incidents of the fight, which she gazes at from a window. Hélène felt that she was in the midst of a beautiful falsehood, but roamed through it as through some mythical garden, whose trees are laden with golden fruit, and where she imbibed all sort of fancies. Then, at the conclusion of the scene, when Rebecca, wrapped in her veil, exhales her love beside the sleeping knight, Hélène again allowed the book to slip from her hand her heart was so brimful of emotion that she could read no further.

Heavens! could all those things be true? she asked, as she lay back in her easy-chair, numbed by her enforced quiescence, and gazing on Paris, shrouded and mysterious, beneath the golden sun. The events of her life now arose before her, conjured up by the perusal of the novel. She saw herself a young girl in the house of her father, Mouret, a hatter at Marseilles. The Rue des Petites-Maries was black and dismal, and the house, with its vat

of streaming water ready to the hand
of the hatter, exhaled a rank odor of
dampness, even in fine weather. She
also saw her mother, who was ever an
invalid, and who kissed her with pale
lips, without speaking. No gleam of
the sun penetrated into her little room.
Hard work went on around her; only
by dint of toil did her father gain a
workingman's competency. That summed up her early life, and till her
marriage nothing intervened to break
the monotony of days ever the same.
One morning, returning from market
with her mother, a basketful of
vegetables on her arm, she jostled
against young Grandjean. Charles
turned round and followed them. The
love-romance of her life was in this
incident. For three months she was always meeting him, while he, bashful
and awkward, could not pluck up courage to speak to her. She was sixteen
years of age, and a little proud of her
lover, who, she knew, belonged to a
wealthy family. But she deemed him
bad-looking, and often laughed at him,
and no thought of him disturbed her
sleep in the large, gloomy, damp house.
In the end they were married, and this
marriage yet filled her with surprise.
Charles worshipped her, and would fling
himself on the floor to kiss her bare
feet. She beamed on him, her smile full
of kindness, as she rebuked him for
such childishness. Then another dull
life began. During twelve years no
event of sufficient interest had occurred
for her to bear in mind. She was very
quiet and very happy, tormented by no
fever either of body or heart; her whole
attention being given to the daily cares
of a poor household. Charles was still

wont to kiss her fair white feet, while
she showed herself indulgent and
motherly towards him. But other feeling she had none. Then there abruptly
came before her the room in the Hôtel
Du Var, her husband in his coffin, and
her widow's robe hanging over a chair.
She had wept that day as on the winter's night when her mother died. Then
once more the days glided on; for two
months with her daughter she had again
enjoyed peace and happiness. Heaven!
did that sum up everything? What,
then, did that book mean when it spoke
of transcendent loves which illumine
one's existence?

While she thus reflected prolonged
quivers were darting over the sleeping
lake of mist on the horizon. Suddenly
it seemed to burst, gaps appeared, a
rending sped from end to end, betoken-
ing a complete break-up. Then sun,
ascending higher and higher, scattering
its rays in glorious triumph, was vic-
toriously attacking the mist. Little by
little the great lake seemed to dry up,
as though some invisible sluice were
draining the plain. The fog, so dense
but a moment before, was losing its
consistency and becoming transparent,
showing all the bright hues of the rainbow. On the left bank of the Seine all
was of a heavenly blue, deepening into
violet over towards the Jardin des
Plantes. Upon the right bank a pale
pink, flesh-like tint suffused the
Tuileries district; while away towards
Montmartre there was a fiery glow, carmine flaming amid gold. Then, farther
off, the working-men's quarters deepened
to a dusty brick-color, changing more
and more till all became a slatey, bluish
grey. The eye could not yet distinguish

the city, which quivered and receded like those subaqueous depths divined through the crystalline waves, depths with awful forests of huge plants, swarming with horrible things and monsters faintly espied. However, the watery mist was quickly falling. It became at last no more than a fine muslin drapery; and bit by bit this muslin vanished, and Paris took shape and emerged from dreamland.

To love! to love! Why did these words ring in Hélène's ears with such sweetness as the darkness of the fog gave way to light? Had she not loved her husband, whom she had tended like a child? But a bitter memory stirred within her—the memory of her dead father, who had hung himself three weeks after his wife's decease in a closet where her gowns still dangled from their hooks. There he had gasped out his last agony, his body rigid, and his face buried in a skirt, wrapped round by the clothes which breathed of her whom he had ever worshipped. Then Hélène's reverie took a sudden leap. She began thinking of her own home-life, of the month's bills which she had checked with Rosalie that very morning; and she felt proud of the orderly way in which she regulated her household. During more than thirty years she had lived with self-respect and strength of mind. Uprightness alone impassioned her. When she questioned her past, not one hour revealed a sin; in her mind's eye she saw herself ever treading a straight and level path. Truly, the days might slip by; she would walk on peacefully as before, with no impediment in her way. The very thought of this made her stern, and her spirit rose in angry contempt against those lying lives whose apparent heroism disturbs the heart. The only true life was her own, following its course amidst such peacefulness. But over Paris there now only hung a thin smoke, a fine, quivering gauze, on the point of floating away; and emotion suddenly took possession of her. To love! to love! everything brought her back to that caressing phrase—even the pride born of her virtue. Her dreaming became so light, she no longer thought, but lay there, steeped in springtide, with moist eyes.

At last, as she was about to resume her reading, Paris slowly came into view. Not a breath of wind had stirred; it was as if a magician had waved his wand. The last gauzy film detached itself, soared and vanished in the air; and the city spread out without a shadow, under the conquering sun. Hélène, with her chin resting on her hand, gazed on this mighty awakening.

A far-stretching valley appeared, with a myriad of buildings huddled together. Over the distant range of hills were scattered close-set roofs, and you could divine that the sea of houses rolled afar off behind the undulating ground, into the fields hidden from sight. It was as the ocean, with all the infinity and mystery of its waves. Paris spread out as vast as the heavens on high. Burnished with the sunshine that lovely morning, the city looked like a field of yellow corn; and the huge picture was all simplicity, compounded of two colors only, the pale blue of the sky, and the golden reflections of the housetops. The stream of light from the spring sun invested everything with the beauty of a new birth. So pure was the light that the minutest objects became visible. Paris, with its chaotic maze of stone-work, shone as though under glass. From time to time, however, a breath of wind passed athwart this bright, quiescent serenity; and then the out-lines of some districts grew faint, and quivered as if they were being viewed through an invisible flame.

Hélène took interest at first in gazing on the large expanse spread under her windows, the slope of the Trocadéro, and the far-stretching quays. She had to lean out to distinguish the deserted square of the Champ-de-Mars, barred at the farther end by the sombre Military School. Down below, on thoroughfare and pavement on each side of the Seine, she could see the passers-by—a busy cluster of black dots, mov-ing like a swarm of ants. A yellow omnibus shone out like a spark of fire; drays and cabs crossed the bridge, mere child's toys in the distance, with miniature horses like pieces of me-chanism; and amongst others traversing the grassy slopes was a servant girl, with a white apron which set a bright spot in all the greenery. Then Hélène raised her eyes; but the crowd scat-tered and passed out of sight, and even the vehicles looked like mere grains of sand; there remained naught but the gigantic carcass of the city, seemingly untenanted and abandoned, its life lim-ited to the dull trepidation by which it was agitated. There, in the foreground to the left, some red roofs were shin-ing, and the tall chimneys of the Army Bakehouse slowly poured out their smoke; while, on the other side of the river, between the Esplanade and the Champ-de-Mars, a grove of lofty elms clustered, like some patch of a park, with bare branches, rounded tops, and young buds already bursting forth, quite clear to the eye. In the centre of the picture, the Seine spread out and reigned between its grey banks, to which rows of casks, steam cranes, and carts drawn up in line, gave a seaport kind of aspect. Hélène's eyes were always turn-ing towards this shining river, on which boats passed to and fro like birds with inky plumage. Her looks involuntarily followed the water's stately course, which, like a silver band, cut Paris at-wain. That morning the stream rolled liquid sunlight; no greater resplendency could be seen on the horizon. And the young woman's glance encountered first the Pont des Invalides, next the Pont de la Concorde, and then the Pont Royal. Bridge followed bridge, they ap-peared to get closer, to rise one above the other like viaducts forming a flight of steps, and pierced with all kinds of arches; while the river, wending its way beneath these airy structures, showed here and there small patches of its blue robe, patches which became narrower and narrower, more and more indistinct. And again did Hélène raise her eyes, and over yonder the stream forked amidst a jumble of houses; the bridges on either side of the island of La Cité were like mere films stretching from one bank to the other; while the golden towers of Notre-Dame sprang up like boundary-marks of the horizon, beyond which river, buildings, and clumps of trees became naught but sparkling sunshine. Then Hélène, dazzled, withdrew her gaze from this the triumphant heart of Paris, where the whole glory of the city appeared to blaze.

On the right bank, amongst the clustering trees of the Champs-Elysées she saw the crystal buildings of the Palace of Industry glittering with a snowy sheen; farther away, behind the roof of the Madeleine, which looked like a tomb-stone, towered the vast mass of the Opera House; then there were other edifices, cupolas and towers, the Vendôme Column, the church of Saint-Vincent de Paul, the tower of Saint-Jacques; and nearer in, the massive cube-like pavilions of the new Louvre and the Tuileries, half-hidden by a wood of chestnut trees. On the left bank the dome of the Invalides shone with gilding; beyond it the two irregular towers of Saint-Sulpice paled in the bright light; and yet farther in the rear, to the right of the new spires of Sainte-Clotilde, the bluish Panthéon, erect on a height, its fine collonade showing against the sky, overlooked the city, poised in the air, as it were, motionless, with the silken hues of a captive balloon.

Hélène's gaze wandered all over Paris. There were hollows, as could be divined by the lines of roofs; the Butte des Moulins surged upward, with waves of old slates, while the line of the principal boulevards dipped downward like a gutter, ending in a jumble of houses whose tiles even could no longer be seen. At this early hour the oblique sun did not light up the house-fronts looking towards the Trocadéro; not a window-pane of these threw back its rays. The skylights on some roofs alone sparkled with the glittering reflex of mica amidst the red of the adjacent chimney-pots. The houses were mostly of a sombre grey, warmed by reflected beams; still rays of light were transpiercing certain districts, and long streets, stretching in front of Hélène, set streaks of sunshine amidst the shade. It was only on the left that the far-spreading horizon, almost perfect in its circular sweep, was broken by the heights of Montmartre and Père-Lachaise. The details so clearly defined in the foreground, the innumerable denticles of the chimneys, the little black specks of the thousands of windows, grew less and less distinct as you gazed farther and farther away, till everything became mingled in confusion —the pell-mell of an endless city, whose faubourgs, afar off, looked like shingly beaches, steeped in a violet haze under the bright, streaming, vibrating light that fell from the heavens.

Hélène was watching the scene with grave interest when Jeanne burst gleefully into the room.

"Oh, mamma! look here!"

The child had a big bunch of wall-flowers in her hand. She told, with some laughter, how she had waylaid Rosalie on her return from market to peep into her basket of provisions. To rummage in this basket was a great delight to her.

"Look at it, mamma! It lay at the very bottom. Just smell it; what a lovely perfume!"

From the tawny flowers, speckled purple, there came a penetrating odor which scented the whole room. Then Hélène, with a passionate movement, drew Jeanne to her breast, while the nosegay fell on her lap. To love! to love! Truly, she loved her child. Was not that intense love which had pervaded her life till now sufficient for her wants? It ought to satisfy her; it was so gentle, so tranquil; no lassitude could put an end to its continuance. Again she pressed her daughter to her, as though to conjure away thoughts which threatened to separate them. In the meantime Jeanne surrendered herself to the shower of kisses. Her eyes moist with tears, she turned her delicate neck upwards with a coaxing gesture, and pressed her face against her mother's shoulder. Then she slipped an arm round her waist and thus remained, very demure, her cheek resting on Hélène's bosom. The perfume of the wall-flowers ascended between them.

For a long time they did not speak; but at length, without moving, Jeanne asked in a whisper:

"Mamma, you see that rosy-colored dome down there, close to the river; what is it?"

It was the dome of the Institute, and Hélène looked towards it for a moment as though trying to recall the name.

"I don't know, my love," she answered gently.

The child appeared content with this reply, and silence again fell. But soon she asked a second question.

"And there, quite near, what beautiful trees are those?" she said, pointing with her finger towards a corner of the Tuileries garden.

"Those beautiful trees!" said her mother. "On the left, do you mean? I don't know, my love."

"Ah!" exclaimed Jeanne; and after musing for a little while she added with a pout: "We know nothing!"

Indeed they knew nothing of Paris.

During eighteen months it had lain beneath their gaze every hour of the day, yet they knew not a stone of it. Three times only had they gone down into the city; but on returning home, suffering from terrible headaches born of all the agitation they had witnessed, they could find in their minds no distinct memory of anything in all that huge maze of streets.

However, Jeanne at times proved obstinate. "Ah! you can tell me this!" said she: "What is that glass building which glitters there? It is so big you must know it."

She was referring to the Palais de l'Industrie. Hélène, however, hesitated.

"It's a railway station," said she. "No, I'm wrong, I think it is a theatre."

Then she smiled and kissed Jeanne's hair, at last confessing as before: "I do not know what it is, my love."

So they continued to gaze on Paris, troubling no further to identify any part of it. It was very delightful to have it there before them, and yet to know nothing of it; it remained the vast and the unknown. It was as though they had halted on the threshold of a world which ever unrolled its panorama before them, but into which they were unwilling to descend. Paris often made them anxious when it wafted them a hot, disturbing atmosphere; but that morning it seemed gay and innocent, like a child, and from its mysterious depths only a breath of tenderness rose gently to their faces.

Hélène took up her book again while Jeanne, clinging to her, still gazed upon the scene. In the dazzling, tranquil sky no breeze was stirring. The smoke

from the Army Bakehouse ascended perpendicularly in light cloudlets which
vanished far aloft. On a level with the
houses passed vibrating waves of life,
waves of all the life pent up there. The
loud voices of the streets softened
amidst the sunshine into a languid murmur. But all at once a flutter attracted
Jeanne's notice. A flock of white
pigeons, freed from some adjacent dove-
cot, sped through the air in front of
the window; with spreading wings like
falling snow, the birds barred the line
of view, hiding the immensity of Paris.

With eyes again dreamily gazing upward Hélène remained plunged in reverie. She was the Lady Rowena; she
loved with the serenity and intensity of
a noble mind. That spring morning,
that great, gentle city, those early wall-
flowers shedding their perfume on her
lap, had little by little filled her heart
with tenderness.

## CHAPTER VI

### A QUESTION

ONE morning Hélène was arranging
her little library, the various books of
which had got out of order during the
past few days, when Jeanne skipped
into the room, clapping her hands.
"A soldier, mamma! a soldier!" she
cried.

"What? a soldier?" exclaimed her
mother. "What do you want, you and
your soldier?"

But the child was in one of her
paroxysms of extravagant delight; she
only jumped about the more, repeating:
"A soldier! a soldier!" without deigning to give any further explanation. She

had left the door wide open behind her,
and so, as Hélène rose, she was astonished to see a soldier—a very little soldier too—in the ante-room. Rosalie
had gone out, and Jeanne must have
been playing on the landing, though
strictly forbidden to do so by her
mother.

"What do you want, my lad?"
asked Hélène.

The little soldier was very much confused on seeing this lady, so lovely and
fair, in her dressing-gown trimmed with
lace; he shuffled one foot to and fro
over the floor, bowed, and at last
precipitately stammered: "I beg pardon
—excuse—"

But he could get no further, and retreated to the wall, still shuffling his
feet. His retreat was thus cut off, and
seeing the lady awaited his reply with
an involuntary smile, he dived into his
right-hand pocket, from which he
dragged a blue handkerchief, a knife,
and a hunk of bread. He gazed on each
in turn, and thrust them all back again.
Then he turned his attention to the left-
hand pocket, from which were produced
a twist of cord, two rusty nails, and
some pictures wrapped in part of a
newspaper. All these he pushed back to
their resting-place, and began tapping
his thighs with an anxious air. And
again he stammered in bewilderment:
"I beg pardon—excuse—"

But all at once he raised his finger to
his nose, and exclaimed with a loud
laugh: "What a fool I am! I remember
now!"

He then undid two buttons of his
greatcoat, and rummaged in his breast,
into which he plunged his arm up to
the elbow. After a time he drew forth

a letter, which he rustled violently before handing to Hélène, as though to shake some dust from it.

"A letter for me! Are you sure?" said she.

On the envelope were certainly inscribed her name and address in a heavy rustic scrawl, with pothooks and hangers tumbling over one another. When at last she made it all out, after being repeatedly baffled by the extraordinary style and spelling, she could not but smile again. It was a letter from Rosalie's aunt, introducing Zéphyrin Lacour, who had fallen a victim to the conscription, "in spite of two masses having been said by his reverence." However, as Zéphyrin was Rosalie's "intended" the aunt begged that madame would be so good as to allow the young folks to see each other on Sundays. In the three pages which the letter comprised this question was continually cropping up in the same words, the confusion of the epistle increasing through the writer's vain efforts to say something she had not said before. Just above the signature, however, she seemed to have hit the nail on the head, for she had written: "His reverence gives his permission"; and had then broken her pen in the paper, making a shower of blots.

Hélène slowly folded the letter. Two or three times, while deciphering its contents, she had raised her head to glance at the soldier. He still remained close to the wall, and his lips stirred, as though to emphasize each sentence in the letter by a slight movement of the chin. No doubt he knew its contents by heart.

"Then you are Zéphyrin Lacour, are you not?" asked Hélène.

He began to laugh and wagged his head.

"Come in, my lad; don't stay out there."

He made up his mind to follow her, but he continued standing close to the door, while Hélène sat down. She had scarcely seen him in the darkness of the ante-room. He must have been just as tall as Rosalie; a third of an inch less, and he would have been exempted from service. With red hair, cut very short, he had a round, freckled, beardless face, with two little eyes like gimlet holes. His new greatcoat, much too large for him, made him appear still more dumpy, and with his red-trousered legs wide apart, and his large peaked cap swinging before him, he presented both a comical and pathetic sight—his plump, stupid little person plainly betraying the rustic, although he wore a uniform.

Hélène desired to obtain some information from him.

"You left Beauce a week ago?" she asked.

"Yes, madame!"

"And here you are in Paris. I suppose you are not sorry?"

"No, madame."

He was losing his bashfulness, and now gazed all over the room, evidently much impressed by its blue velvet hangings.

"Rosalie is out," Hélène began again, "but she will be here very soon. Her aunt tells me you are her sweetheart."

To this the little soldier vouchsafed no reply, but hung his head, laughing awkwardly, and scraping the carpet with the tip of his boot.

"Then you will have to marry her when you leave the army?" Hélène continued questioning.

"Yes, to be sure!" exclaimed he, his face turning very red. "Yes, of course; we are engaged!" And, won over by the kindly manners of the lady, he made up his mind to speak out, his fingers still playing with his cap. "You know it's an old story. When we were quite children, we used to go thieving together. We used to get switched; oh yes, that's true! I must tell you that the Lacours and the Pichons lived in the same lane, and were next-door neighbors. And so Rosalie and myself were almost brought up together. Then her people died, and her aunt Marguerite took her in. But she, the minx, was already as strong as a demon."

He paused, realizing that he was warming up, and asked hesitatingly:

"But perhaps she has told you all this?"

"Yes, yes; but go on all the same," said Hélène, who was greatly amused.

"In short," continued he, "she was awfully strong, though she was no bigger than a tomtit. It was a treat to see her at her work! How she did get through it! One day she gave a slap to a friend of mine—by Jove! such a slap! I had the mark of it on my arm for a week! Yes, that was the way it all came about. All the gossips declared we must marry one another. Besides, we weren't ten years old before we had agreed on that! And, we have stuck to it, madame, we have stuck to it!"

He placed one hand upon his heart, with fingers wide apart. Hélène, how-

ever, had now become very grave. The idea of allowing a soldier in her kitchen somewhat worried her. His reverence, no doubt, had given his sanction, but she thought it rather venturesome. There is too much license in the country, where lovers indulge in all sorts of pleasantries. So she gave expression to her apprehensions. When Zéphyrin at last gathered her meaning, his first inclination was to laugh, but his awe for Hélène restrained him.

"Oh, madame, madame!" said he, "you don't know her, I can see! I have received slaps enough from her! Of course young men like to laugh! isn't that so? Sometimes I pinched her, and she would turn round and hit me right on the nose. Her aunt's advice always was, 'Look here, my girl, don't put up with any nonsense!' His reverence, too, interfered in it, and maybe that had a lot to do with our keeping up sweethearting. We were to have been married after I had drawn for a soldier. But it was all my eye! Things turned out badly. Rosalie declared she would go to service in Paris, to earn a dowry while she was waiting for me. And so, and so—"

He swung himself about, dangling his cap, now from one hand, now from the other. But still Hélène never said a word, and he at last fancied that she distrusted him. This pained him dreadfully.

"You think, perhaps, that I shall deceive her?" he burst out angrily. "Even, too, when I tell you we are betrothed? I shall marry her, as surely as the heaven shines on us. I'm quite ready to pledge my word in writing.

Yes, if you like, I'll write it down for you."

Deep emotion was stirring him. He walked about the room gazing around in the hope of finding pen and ink. Hélène quickly tried to appease him, but he still went on:

"I would rather sign a paper for you. What harm would it do you? Your mind would be all the easier with it."

However, just at that moment Jeanne, who had again run away, returned, jumping and clapping her hands.

"Rosalie! Rosalie! Rosalie!" she chanted in a dancing tune of her own composition.

Through the open doorway one could hear the panting of the maid as she climbed up the stairs laden with her basket. Zéphyrin started back into a corner of the room, his mouth wide agape from ear to ear in silent laughter, and the gimlet holes of his eyes gleaming with rustic roguery. Rosalie came straight into the room, as was her usual practice, to show her mistress her morning's purchase of provisions.

"Madame," said she, "I've brought some cauliflowers. Look at them! Only eighteen sous for two, it isn't dear, is it?"

She held out the basket half open, but on lifting her head noticed Zéphyrin's grinning face. Surprise nailed her to the carpet. Two or three seconds slipped away; she had doubtless at first failed to recognize him in his uniform. But then her round eyes dilated, her fat little face blanched, and her coarse black hair waved in agitation.

"Oh!" she simply said.

But her astonishment was such that she dropped her basket. The provisions, cauliflowers, onions, apples, rolled on to the carpet. Jeanne gave a cry of delight, and falling on her knees, began hunting for the apples, even under the chairs and the wardrobe. Meanwhile Rosalie, as though paralyzed, never moved, though she repeated:

"What! it's you! What are you doing here? what are you doing here? Say!"

Then she turned to Hélène with the question: "Was it you who let him come in?"

Zéphyrin never uttered a word, but contented himself with winking slily. Then Rosalie gave vent to her emotion in tears; and, to show her delight at seeing him again, could hit on nothing better than to quiz him.

"Oh! go away!" she began, marching up to him. "You look neat and pretty I must say in that guise of yours! I might have passed you in the street, and not even have said: 'God bless you.' Oh! you've got a nice rig-out. You just look as if you had your sentry-box on your back; and they've cut your hair so short that folks might take you for the sexton's poodle. Good heavens! what a fright you are; what a fright!"

Zéphyrin, very indignant, now made up his mind to speak. "It's not my fault that's sure! Oh! if you joined a regiment we should see a few things."

They had quite forgotten where they were; everything had vanished—the room, Hélène and Jeanne, who was still gathering the apples together. With hands folded over her apron, the maid stood upright in front of the little soldier.

"Is everything all right down there?" she asked.

"Oh, yes, excepting Guignard's cow is ill. The veterinary surgeon came and said she'd got the dropsy."

"If she's got the dropsy, she's done for. Excepting that, is everything all right?"

"Yes, yes! The village constable has broken his arm. Old Canivet's dead. And, by the way, his reverence lost his purse with thirty sous in it as he was a-coming back from Gandval. But otherwise, things are all right."

Then silence fell on them and they looked at one another with sparkling eyes, their compressed lips slowly making an amorous grimace. This, indeed, must have been the manner in which they expressed their love, for they had not even stretched out their hands in greeting. Rosalie, however, all at once ceased her contemplation, and began to lament at sight of the vegetables on the floor. Such a nice mess! and it was he who had caused it all! Madame ought to have made him wait on the stairs! Scolding away as fast as she could, she dropped on her knees and began putting the apples, onions, and cauliflowers into the basket again, much to the disgust of Jeanne, who would fain have done it all herself. And as she turned, with the object of betaking herself into her kitchen, never deigning another look in Zéphyrin's direction, Hélène, conciliated by the healthy tranquillity of the lovers, stopped her to say:

"Listen a moment, my girl. Your aunt has asked me to allow this young man to come and see you on Sundays. He will come in the afternoon, and you will try not to let your work fall behind too much."

Rosalie paused, merely turning her head. Though she was well pleased, she preserved her doleful air.

"Oh, madame, he will be such a bother," she declared. But at the same time she glanced over her shoulder at Zéphyrin, and again made an affectionate grimace at him. The little soldier remained for a minute stock-still, his mouth agape from ear to ear with its silent laugh. Then he retired backwards, with his cap against his heart as he thanked Hélène profusely. The door had been shut upon him, when on the landing he still continued bowing.

"Is that Rosalie's brother, mamma?" asked Jeanne.

Hélène was quite embarrassed by the question. She regretted the permission which she had just given in a sudden impulse of kindliness which now surprised her. She remained thinking for some seconds, and then replied, "No, he is her cousin."

"Ah!" said the child gravely.

Rosalie's kitchen looked out on the sunny expanse of Doctor Deberle's garden. In the summer the branches of the elms swayed in through the broad window. It was the cheeriest room of the suite, always flooded with light, which was sometimes so blinding that Rosalie had put up a curtain of blue cotton stuff, which she drew of an afternoon. The only complaint she made about the kitchen was its smallness; and indeed it was a narrow strip of a place, with a cooking-range on the right-hand side, while on the left were the table and dresser. The various utensils and furnishings, however, had all been so well arranged that she had contrived to keep a clear corner beside the window, where she worked in the evening. She took a pride in keeping everything, stewpans, kettles, and dishes, wonderfully clean; and so, when the sun veered round to the window, the walls became resplendent, the copper vessels sparkled like gold, the tin pots showed bright discs like silver moons, while the white-and-blue tiles above the stove gleamed pale in the fiery glow.

On the evening of the ensuing Saturday Hélène heard so great a commotion in the kitchen that she determined to go and see what was the matter.

"What is it?" asked she: "are you fighting with the furniture?"

"I am scouring, madame," replied Rosalie, who sweating and dishevelled, was squatting on the tiled floor and scrubbing it with all the strength of her arms.

This over, she sponged it with clear water. Never had the kitchen displayed such perfection of cleanliness. A bride might have slept in it; all was white as for a wedding. So energetically had she exerted her hands that it seemed as if table and dresser had been freshly planed. And the good order of everything was a sight to see; stewpans and pots taking rank by their size, each on its own hook, even the frying-pan and gridiron shining brightly without one grimy stain. Hélène looked on for a moment in silence, and then with a smile disappeared.

Every Saturday afterwards there was a similar furbishing, a tornado of dust and water lasting for four hours. It was Rosalie's wish to display her neatness to Zéphyrin on the Sunday. That was her reception day. A single cobweb would have filled her with shame; but when everything shone resplendent around her she became amiable, and burst into song. At three o'clock she would again wash her hands and don a cap gay with ribbons. Then the curtain being drawn halfway, so that only the subdued light of a boudoir came in, she awaited Zéphyrin's arrival amidst all this primness, through which a pleasant scent of thyme and laurel was borne.

At half-past three exactly Zéphyrin made his appearance; he would walk about the street until the clocks of the neighborhood had struck the half-hour. Rosalie listened to the beat of his heavy shoes on the stairs, and opened the door the moment he halted on the landing. She had forbidden him to ring the bell. At each visit the same greeting passed between them.

"Is it you?"

"Yes, it's me!"

And they stood face to face, their eyes sparkling and their lips compressed. Then Zéphyrin followed Rosalie; but there was no admission vouchsafed to him till she had relieved him of shako and sabre. She would have none of these in her kitchen; and so the sabre and shako were hidden away in a cupboard. Next she would make him sit down in the corner she had contrived near the window, and thenceforth he was not allowed to budge.

"Sit still there! You can look on, if you like, while I get madame's dinner ready."

But he rarely appeared with empty hands. He would usually spend the morning in strolling with some comrades through the woods of Meudon, lounging lazily about, inhaling the fresh, air which inspired him with regretful memories of his country home. To give his fingers something to do he would cut switches, which he tapered and notched with marvelous figurings, and his steps gradually slackening he would come to a stop beside some ditch, his shako on the back of his head, while his eyes remained fixed on the knife with which he was carving the stick. Then, as he could never make up his mind to discard his switches, he carried them in the afternoon to Rosalie, who would throw up her hands, and exclaim that they would litter her kitchen. But the truth was, she carefully preserved them; and under her bed was gathered a bundle of these switches, of all sorts and sizes.

One day he made his appearance with a nest full of eggs, which he had secreted in his shako under the folds of a handkerchief. Omelets made from the eggs of wild birds, so he declared, were very nice—a statement which Rosalie received with horror; the nest, however, was preserved and laid away in company with the switches. But Zéphyrin's pockets were always full to overflowing. He would pull curiosities from them, transparent pebbles found on the banks of the Seine, pieces of old iron, dried berries, and all sorts of strange rubbish, which not even a ragpicker would have cared for. His chief love, however, was for pictures; as he sauntered along he would seize on all the stray papers that had served as wrappers for chocolate or cakes of soap, and on which were black men, palm-trees, dancing-girls, or clusters of roses. The tops of old broken boxes, decorated with figures of languid, blonde ladies, the glazed prints and silver paper which had once contained sugar-sticks and had been thrown away at the neighboring fairs, were great windfalls that filled his bosom with pride. All such booty was speedily transferred to his pockets, the choicer articles being enveloped in a fragment of an old newspaper. And on Sunday, if Rosalie had a moment's leisure between the preparation of a sauce and the tending of the joint, he would exhibit his pictures to her. They were hers if she cared for them; only as the paper around them was not always clean he would cut them out, a pastime which greatly amused him. Rosalie got angry, as the shreds of paper blew about even into her plates; and it was a sight to see with what rustic cunning he would at last gain possession of her scissors. At times, however, in order to get rid of him, she would give them up without any asking.

Meanwhile some brown sauce would be simmering on the fire. Rosalie watched it, wooden spoon in hand; while Zéphyrin, his head bent and his breadth of shoulder increased by his epaulets, continued cutting out the pictures. His head was so closely shaven that the skin of his skull could be seen; and the yellow collar of his tunic yawned widely behind, displaying his sunburnt neck. For a quarter of an hour at a time neither would utter a syllable. When Zéphyrin raised his head, he watched Rosalie while she took some flour, minced some parsley, or salted and peppered some dish, his eyes betraying the while intense interest. Then, at long

intervals, a few words would escape
him:

"By Jove! that does smell nice!"

The cook, busily engaged, would not
vouchsafe an immediate reply; but
after a lengthy silence she perhaps exclaimed. "You see, it must simmer
properly."

Their talk never went beyond that.
They no longer spoke of their native
place even. When a reminiscence came
to them a word sufficed, and they
chuckled inwardly the whole afternoon.
This was pleasure enough, and by the
time Rosalie turned Zéphyrin out of
doors both of them had enjoyed ample
amusement.

"Come, you will have to go! I must
wait on madame," said she; and restoring him his shako and sabre, she drove
him out before her, afterwards waiting
on madame with cheeks flushed with
happiness; while he walked back to barracks, dangling his arms, and almost intoxicated by the goodly odors of thyme
and laurel which still clung to him.

During his earlier visits Hélène judged
it right to look after them. She popped
in sometimes quite suddenly to give an
order, and there was Zéphyrin always in
his corner, between the table and the
window, close to the stone filter, which
forced him to draw in his legs. The
moment madame made her appearance
he rose and stood upright, as though
shouldering arms, and if she spoke to
him his reply never went beyond a
salute and a respectful grunt. Little
by little Hélène grew somewhat easier;
she saw that her entrance did not disturb them, and that their faces only
expressed the quiet content of patient
lovers.

At this time, too Rosalie seemed even
more wide awake than Zéphyrin. She
had already been some months in Paris,
and under its influence was fast losing
her country rust, though as yet she only
knew three streets—the Rue de Passy,
the Rue Franklin, and the Rue Vineuse.
Zéphyrin, soldier though he was, remained quite a lubber. As Rosalie confided to her mistress, he became more
of a blockhead every day. In the country he had been much sharper. But,
added she, it was the uniform's fault;
all the lads who donned the uniform
became sad dolts. The fact is, his
change of life had quite muddled Zéphyrin, who, with his staring round eyes and
and solemn swagger, looked like a goose.
Despite his epaulets he retained his
rustic awkwardness and heaviness; the
barracks had taught him nothing as yet
of the fine words and victorious at-
titudes of the ideal Parisian fire-eater.
"Yes, madame," Rosalie would wind up
by saying, "you don't need to disturb
yourself; it is not in him to play any
tricks!"

Thus the girl began to treat him in
quite a motherly way. While dressing her
meat on the spit she would preach him
a sermon, full of good counsel as to the
pitfalls he should shun; and he in all
obedience vigorously nodded approval of
each injunction. Every Sunday he had
to swear to her that he had attended
mass, and that he had solemnly repeated his prayers morning and evening.
She strongly inculcated the necessity of
tidiness, gave him a brush down whenever he left her, stitched on a loose button of his tunic, and surveyed him from
head to foot to see if aught were amiss
in his appearance. She also worried her-

self about his health, and gave him cures for all sorts of ailments. In return for her kindly care Zéphyrin professed himself anxious to fill her filter for her; but this proposal was long rejected, through the fear that he might spill the water. One day, however, he brought up two buckets without letting one drop of their contents fall on the stairs, and from that time he replenished the filter every Sunday. He would also make himself useful in other ways, doing all the heavy work and was extremely handy in running to the greengrocer's for butter, had she forgotten to purchase any. At last, even, he began to share in the duties of kitchenmaid. First he was permitted to peel the vegetables; later on the mincing was assigned to him. At the end of six weeks, though still forbidden to touch the sauces, he watched over them with wooden spoon in hand. Rosalie had fairly made him her helpmate, and would sometimes burst out laughing as she saw him, with his red trousers and yellow collar, working busily before the fire with a dishcloth over his arm, like some scullery-servant.

One Sunday Hélène betook herself to the kitchen. Her slippers deadened the sound of her footsteps, and she reached the threshold unheard by either maid or soldier. Zéphyrin was seated in his corner over a basin of steaming broth. Rosalie, with her back turned to the door, was occupied in cutting some long sippets of bread for him. "There, eat away, my dear!" she said. "You walk too much; it is that which makes you feel so empty! There!

have you enough? Do you want any more?"

Thus speaking, she watched him with a tender and anxious look. He, with his round dumpy figure, leaned over the basin, devouring a sippet with each mouthful of broth. His face, usually yellow with freckles, was becoming quite red with the warmth of the steam which circled round him.

"Heavens!" he muttered, "what grand juice! What do you put in it?"

"Wait a minute," she said; "if you like leeks—"

However, as she turned round she suddenly caught sight of her mistress. She raised an exclamation, and then, like Zéphyrin, seemed turned to stone. But a moment afterwards she poured forth a torrent of excuses.

"It's my share, madame—oh, it's my share! I would not have taken any more soup, I swear it! I told him, 'If you would like a bowl of soup, you can have it.' Come, speak up, Zéphyrin; you know that was how it came about!"

The mistress remained silent, and the servant grew uneasy, thinking she was annoyed. Then in quavering tones she continued:

"Oh, he was dying of hunger, madame; he stole a raw carrot for me! They feed him so badly! And then, you know, he had walked goodness knows where all along the river-side. I'm sure, madame, you would have told me yourself to give him some broth!"

Gazing at the little soldier, who sat with his mouth full, not daring to swallow, Hélène felt she could no longer remain stern. So she quietly said:

"Well, well, my girl, whenever the

lad is hungry you must keep him to dinner—that's all. I give you permission."

Face to face with them, she had again felt within her that tender feeling which once already had banished all thoughts of rigor from her mind. They were so happy in that kitchen! the cotton curtain, drawn half-way, gave free entry to the sunset beams. The burnished copper pans set the end wall all aglow, lending a rosy tint to the twilight lingering in the room. And there, in the golden shade the lovers' little round faces shone out, peaceful and radiant, like moons. Their love was instinct with such calm certainty that no neglect was even shown in keeping the kitchen utensils in their wonted order. It blossomed amidst the savory odors of the cooking stove, which heightened their appetites and nourished their hearts.

"Mamma," asked Jeanne, one evening after considerable meditation, "why is it Rosalie's cousin never kisses her?"

"And why should they kiss one another?" asked Hélène in her turn. "They will kiss on their birthdays."

## CHAPTER VII

### TILL NEXT TUESDAY!

THE soup had just been served on the following Tuesday evening, when Hélène, after listening attentively, exclaimed:

"What a downpour! Don't you hear? My poor friends, you will get drenched to-night!"

"Oh, it's only a few drops," said the Abbé quietly, though his old cassock was already wet about the shoulders.

"I've got a good distance to go," said Monsieur Rambaud. "But I shall return home on foot all the same; I like it. Besides, I have my umbrella."

Jeanne was reflecting as she gazed gravely on her last spoonful of vermicelli; and at last her thoughts took shape in words: "Rosalie said you wouldn't come because of the wretched weather; but mamma said you would come. You are very kind; you always come."

A smile lit up all their faces. Hélène addressed a nod of affectionate approval to the two brothers. Out of doors the rain was falling with a dull roar, and violent gusts of wind beat angrily against the window-shutters. Winter seemed to have returned. Rosalie had carefully drawn the red repp curtains; and the small, cosy dining-room, illumined by the steady light of the white hanging-lamp, looked, amidst the buffeting of the storm, a picture of pleasant, affectionate intimacy. On the mahogany sideboard some china reflected the quiet light; and amidst all this indoor peacefulness the four diners leisurely conversed, awaiting the good pleasure of the servant-maid, as they sat round the table, where all, if simple, was exquisitely clean.

"Oh! you are waiting; so much the worse!" said Rosalie familiarly, as she entered with a dish. "These are fillets of sole *au gratin for* Monsieur Rambaud; they require to be lifted at the last moment."

Monsieur Rambaud pretended to be

a gourmand, in order to amuse Jeanne, and give pleasure to Rosalie, who was very proud of her accomplishments as a cook. He turned towards her with the question: "By the way, what have you got for us to-day? You are always bringing in some surprise or other when I am no longer hungry."

"Oh," said she in reply, "there are three dishes as usual, and no more. After the sole you will have a leg of mutton and then some Brussels sprouts. Yes, that's the truth; and there will be nothing else."

From the corner of his eye Monsieur Rambaud glanced towards Jeanne. The child was boiling over with glee, her hands over her mouth to restrain her laughter, while she shook her head, as though to insinuate that the maid was deceiving them. Monsieur Rambaud thereupon clacked his tongue as though in doubt, and Rosalie pretended great indignation.

"You don't believe me because Mademoiselle Jeanne laughs so," said she. "Ah, very well! believe what you like. Stint yourself, and see if you won't have a craving for food when you get home."

When the maid had left the room, Jeanne, laughing yet more loudly, was seized with a longing to speak out.

"You are really too greedy!" she began. "I myself went into the kitchen—" However, she left her sentence unfinished: "No, no, I won't tell; it isn't right, is it, mamma? There's nothing more—nothing at all! I only laughed to cheat you."

This interlude was re-enacted every Tuesday with the same unvarying success. Hélène was touched by the kindliness with which Monsieur Rambaud lent himself to the fun; she was well aware that, with Provençal frugality, he had long limited his daily fare to an anchovy and half-a-dozen olives. As for Abbé Jouve, he never knew what he was eating, and his blunders and forgetfulness supplied an inexhaustible fund for amusement. Jeanne, meditating some prank in this respect, was even now stealthily watching him with glittering epes.

"How nice this whiting is!" she said to him, after they had all been served.

"Very nice, my dear," he answered. "Bless me, you are right—it is whiting; I thought it was turbot."

And then, as everyone laughed, he guilelessly asked why. Rosalie, who had just come into the room again, seemed very much hurt, and burst out:

"A fine thing indeed! The priest in my native place knew much better what he was eating. He could tell the age of the fowl he was carving to a week or so, and didn't require to go into the kitchen to find out what there was for dinner. No, the smell was quite sufficient. Goodness gracious! had I been in the service of a priest like your reverence, I should not know yet even how to turn an omelet."

The Abbé hastened to excuse himself with an embarrassed air, as though his inability to appreciate the delights of the table was a failing he despaired of curing. But, as he said, he had too many other things to think about.

"There! that is a leg of mutton!" exclaimed Rosalie, as she placed on the table the joint referred to.

Everybody once mere indulged in a

peal of laughter, the Abbé Jouve being the first to do so. He bent forward to look, his eyes twinkling with glee.

"Yes, certainly," said he; "it is a leg of mutton. I think I should have known it."

Despite this remark, there was something about the Abbé that day which betokened unusual absent-mindedness. He ate quickly, with the haste of a man who is bored by a long stay at table, and lunches standing when at home. And, having finished, himself, he would wait the convenience of the others, plunged in deep thought and simply smiling in reply to the questions put to him. At every moment he cast on his brother a look in which encouragement and uneasiness were mingled. Nor did Monsieur Rambaud seem possessed of his wonted tranquillity that evening; but his agitation manifested itself in a craving to talk and fidget on his chair, which seemed rather inconsistent with his quiet disposition. When the Brussels sprouts had disappeared, there was a delay in the appearance of the dessert, and a spell of silence ensued. Out of doors the rain was beating down with still greater force, rattling noisily against the house. The dining-room was rather close, and it suddenly dawned on Hélène that there was something strange in the air—that the two brothers had some worry of which they did not care to speak. She looked at them anxiously, and at last spoke:

"Dear, dear! What dreadful rain! isn't it? It seems to be influencing both of you, for you look out of sorts."

They protested, however, that such was not the case, doing their utmost to clear her mind of the notion. And, as Rosalie now made her appearance with an immense dish, Monsieur Rambaud exclaimed, as though to veil his emotion: "What did I say! Still another surprise!"

The surprise of the day was some vanilla cream, one of the cook's triumphs. And thus it was a sight to see her broad, silent grin, as she deposited her burden on the table. Jeanne shouted and clapped her hands.

"I knew it, I knew it! I saw eggs in the kitchen!"

"But I have no more appetite," declared Monsieur Rambaud, with a look of despair. "I could not eat any of it!"

Thereupon Rosalie became grave, full of suppressed wrath. With a dignified air, she remarked: "Oh, indeed! A cream which I made especially for you! Well, well! just try not to eat any of it—yes, try!"

He had to give in and accept a large helping of the cream. Meanwhile Abbé remained thoughtful. He rolled up his napkin and rose before the dessert had come to an end, as was frequently his custom. For a little while he walked about, with his head hanging down; and when Hélène in her turn quitted the table, he cast at Monsieur Rambaud a look of intelligence, and led the young woman into the bedroom. The door being left open behind them, they could almost immediately afterwards be heard conversing together, though the words which they slowly exchanged were indistinguishable.

"Oh, do make haste!" said Jeanne

to Monsieur Rambaud, who seemed incapable of finishing a biscuit. "I want to show you my work."

However, he evinced no haste, though when Rosalie began to clear the table it became necessary for him to leave his chair.

"Wait a little! wait a little!" he murmured, as the child strove to drag him towards the bedroom. And, overcome with embarrassment and timidity, he retreated from the doorway. Then, as the Abbé raised his voice, such sudden weakness came over him that he had to sit down again at the table. From his pocket he drew a newspaper.

"Now," said he, "I'm going to make you a little coach."

Jeanne at once abandoned her intention of entering the adjoining room. Monsieur Rambaud always amazed her by his skill in turning a sheet of paper into all sorts of playthings. Chickens, boats, bishops' mitres, carts, and cages, were all evolved under his fingers. That day, however, so tremulous were his hands that he was unable to perfect anything. He lowered his head whenever the faintest sound came from the adjacent room. Nevertheless, Jeanne took interest in watching him, and leaned on the table on his side.

"Now," said she, "you must make a chicken to harness to the carriage."

Meanwhile, within the bedroom, Abbé Jouve remained standing in the shadow thrown by the lamp-shade upon the floor. Hélène had sat down in her usual place in front of the round table; and, as on Tuesdays she refrained from ceremony with her friends, she had taken up her needlework, and, in the circular glare of light, only her white

hands could be seen sewing a child's cap.

"Jeanne gives you no further worry, does she?" asked the Abbé.

Hélène shook her head before making a reply.

"Doctor Deberle seems quite satisfied," said she. "But the poor darling is still very nervous. Yesterday I found her in her chair in a fainting fit."

"She needs exercise," resumed the priest. "You stay indoors far too much; you should follow the example of other folks and go about more than you do."

He ceased speaking, and silence followed. He now, without doubt, had what he had been seeking,—a suitable inlet for his discourse; but the moment for speaking came, and he was still communing with himself. Taking a chair, he sat down at Hélène's side.

"Hearken to me, my dear child," he began. "For some time past I have wished to talk with you seriously. The life you are leading here can entail no good results. A convent existence such as yours is not consistent with your years; and this abandonment of worldly pleasures is as injurious to your child as it is to yourself. You are risking many dangers—dangers to health, ay, and other dangers, too."

Hélène raised her head with an expression of astonishment. "What do you mean, my friend?" she asked.

"Dear me! I know the world but little," continued the priest, with some slight embarrassment, "yet I know very well that a woman incurs great risk when she remains without a protecting arm. To speak frankly, you keep to your own company too much, and this seclusion in which you hide yourself is not healthful believe me. A day must come when you will suffer from it."

"But I make no complaint; I am very happy as I am," she exclaimed with spirit.

The old priest gently shook his large head.

"Yes, yes, that is all very well. You feel completely happy. I know all that. Only, on the downhill path of a lonely, dreary life, you never know where you are going. Oh! I understand you perfectly you are incapable of doing any wrong. But sooner or later you might lose your peace of mind. Some morning, when it is too late, you will find that blank which you now leave in your life filled by some painful feeling not to be confessed."

As she sat there in the shadow, a blush crimsoned Hélène's face. Had the Abbé, then, read her heart? Was he aware of this restlessness which was fast possessing her—this heart-trouble which thrilled her every-day life, and the existence of which she had till now been unwilling to admit? Her needlework fell on her lap. A sensation of weakness pervaded her, and she awaited from the priest something like a pious complicity which would allow her to confess and particularize the vague feelings which she buried in her innermost being. As all was known to him, it was for him to question her, and she would strive to answer.

"I leave myself in your hands, my friend," she murmured. "You are well

aware that I have always listened to you."

The priest remained for a moment silent, and then slowly and solemnly said:

"My child, you must marry again."

She remained speechless, with arms dangling, in a stupor this counsel brought upon her. She awaited other words, failing, as it were, to understand him. And the Abbé continued putting before her the arguments which should incline her towards marriage.

"Remember, you are still young. You must not remain longer in this out-of-the-way corner of Paris, scarcely daring to go out, and wholly ignorant of the world. You must return to the every-day life of humanity, lest in the future you should bitterly regret your loneliness. You yourself have no idea how the effects of your isolation are beginning to tell on you, but your friends remark your pallor, and feel uneasy."

With each sentence he paused, with the hope that she might break in and discuss his proposition. But no; she sat there as if lifeless, seemingly benumbed with astonishment.

"No doubt you have a child," he resumed. "That is always a delicate matter to surmount. Still, you must admit that even in Jeanne's interest a husband's arm would be of great advantage. Of course, we must find some one good and honorable, who would be a true father—"

However, she did not let him finish. With violent revolt and repulsion she suddenly spoke out: "No, no; I will not! Oh, my friend, how can you advise me thus? Never, do you hear, never!"

Her whole heart was rising; she herself was frightened by the violence of her refusal. The priest's proposal had stirred up that dim nook in her being whose secret she avoided reading, and, by the pain she experienced, she at last understood all the gravity of her ailment. With the open, smiling glance of the priest still bent on her, she plunged into contention.

"No, no; I do not wish it! I love nobody!"

And, as he still gazed at her, she imagined he could read her lie on her face. She blushed and stammered: "Remember, too, I only left off my mourning a fortnight ago. No, it could not be!"

"My child!" quietly said the priest, "I thought over this a great deal before speaking. I am sure your happiness is wrapped up in it. Calm yourself; you need never act against your wishes."

The conversation came to a sudden stop. Hélène strove to keep pent within her bosom the angry protests that were rushing to her lips. She resumed her work, and, with head lowered, contrived to put in a few stitches. And amid the silence, Jeanne's shrill voice could be heard in the dining-room.

"People don't put a chicken to a carriage; it ought to be a horse! You don't know how to make horse, do you?"

"No, my dear; horses are too difficult," said Monsieur Rambaud. "But if you like I'll show you how to make carriages."

This was always the fashion in which their game came to an end. Jeanne, all ears and eyes, watched her kindly playfellow folding the paper into a multitude of little squares, and afterwards she followed his example; but she would make mistakes and then stamp her feet in vexation. However, she already knew how to manufacture boats and bishops' mitres.

"You see," resumed Monsieur Rambaud patiently, "you make four corners like that; then you turn them back—"

With his ears on the alert, he must during the last moment have heard some of the words spoken in the next room; for his poor hands were now trembling more and more, while his tongue faltered, so that he could only half articulate his sentences.

Hélène, who was unable to quiet herself, now began the conversation anew. "Marry again! And whom, pray?" she suddenly asked the priest, as she laid her work down on the table. "You have some one in view, have you not?"

Abbé Jouve rose from his chair and stalked slowly up and down. Without halting, he nodded assent.

"Well! tell me who he is," she said.

For a moment he lingered before her erect, then, shrugging his shoulders, said: "What's the good, since you decline?"

"No matter, I want to know," she replied. "How can I make up my mind when I don't know?"

He did not answer her immediately, but remained standing there, gazing into her face. A somewhat sad smile wreathed his lips. At last he exclaimed, almost in a whisper: "What! have you not guessed?"

No, she could not guess. She tried to do so, with increasing wonder, whereupon he made a single sign— nodding his head in the direction of the dining-room.

"He!" she exclaimed, in a muffled tone, and a great seriousness fell upon her. She no longer indulged in violent protestations; only sorrow and surprise remained visible on her face. She sat for a long time plunged in thought, her gaze turned to the floor. Truly, she had never dreamed of such a thing; and yet, she found nothing in it to object to. Monsieur Rambaud was the only man in whose hand she could put her own honesty and without fear. She knew his innate goodness; she did not smile at his *bourgeois* heaviness. But despite all her regard for him, the idea that he loved her chilled her to the soul.

Meanwhile the Abbé had again begun walking from one to the other end of the room, and on passing the dining-room door he gently called Hélène. "Come here and look!"

She rose and did as he wished.

Monsieur Rambaud had ended by seating Jeanne in his own chair; and he, who had at first been leaning against the table, had now slipped down at the child's feet. He was on his knees before her, encircling her with one of his arms. On the table was the carriage drawn by the chicken, with some boats, boxes, and bishops' mitres.

"Now, do you love me well?" he asked her. "Tell me that you love me well!"

"Of course, I love you well; you know it."

He stammered and trembled, as though he were making some declaration of love.

"And what would you say if I asked you to let me stay here with you always?"

"Oh, I should be quite pleased. We would play together, wouldn't we? That would be good fun."

"Ah, but you know I should always be here."

Jeanne had taken up a boat which she was twisting into a gendarme's hat. "You would need to get mamma's leave," she murmured.

By this reply all his fears were again stirred into life. His fate was being decided.

"Of course," said he. "But if mamma gave me leave, would you say yes, too?"

Jeanne, busy finishing her gendarme's hat, sang out in a rapturous strain: "I would say yes! yes! yes! I would say yes! yes! yes! Come, look how pretty my hat is!"

Monsieur Rambaud, with tears in his eyes, rose to his knees and kissed her, while she threw her arms round his neck. He had entrusted the asking of Hélène's consent to his brother, whilst he himself sought to secure that of Jeanne.

"You see," said the priest, with a smile, "the child is quite content."

Hélène still retained her grave air, and made no further inquiry. The Abbé, however, again eloquently took up his plea, and emphasized his brother's good qualities. Was he not a treasure-trove of a father for Jeanne? She was well acquainted with him; in trusting him she gave no hostages to fortune. Then, as she still remained silent, the Abbé with great feeling and dignity declared that in the step he had taken he had not thought of his brother, but of her and her happiness.

"I believe you; I know how you love me," Hélène promptly answered. "Wait; I want to give your brother his answer in your presence."

The clock struck ten. Monsieur Rambaud made his entry into the bedroom. Wtih outstretched hands she went to meet him.

"I thank you for your proposal, my friend, said she. "I am very grateful; and you have done well in speaking—"

She was gazing calmly into his face, holding his big hand in her grasp. Trembling all over, he dared not lift his eyes. "You will perhaps have to give me a long time."

"Oh! as long as you like—six months, a year, longer if you please," exclaimed he with a light heart, well pleased that she had not forthwith sent him about his business.

His excitement brought a faint smile to her face. "But I intend that we shall still continue friends," said she. "You will come here as usual, and simply give me your promise to remain content till I speak to you about the matter. Is that understood?"

He had withdrawn his hand, and was now feverishly hunting for his hat, signifying his acquiescence by a continuous bobbing of the head. Then, at the moment of leaving, he found his voice once more.

"Listen to me," said he. "You now know that I am there—don't you? Well, whatever happens I shall always be there. That's all the Abbé should have told you. In ten years, if you like; you will only have to make a sign. I shall obey you!"

And it was he who a last time took Hélène's hand and gripped it as though he would crush it. On the stairs the two brothers turned round with the usual good-bye:

"Till next Tuesday!"

"Yes, Tuesday," answered Hélène.

On returning to her room a fresh downfall of rain beating against the shutters filled her with grave concern. Good heavens! what an obstinate downpour, and how wet her poor friends would get! She opened the window and looked down into the street. Sudden gusts of wind were making the gaslights flicker, and amid the shiny puddles and shimmering rain she could see the round fig're of Monsieur Rambaud, as he went off with dancing gait, exultant in the darkness, seemingly caring nothing for the drenching torrent.

Jeanne, however, was very grave, for she had overheard some of her playfellow's last words. She had just taken off her little boots, and was sitting on the edge of the bed in her nightgown, in deep cogitation. On entering the room to kiss her, her mother discovered her thus.

"Good-night, Jeanne; kiss me."

Then, as the child did not seem to hear her, Hélène sank down in front of her, and clasped her round the waist, asking her in a whisper: "So you would be glad if he came to live with us?"

The question seemed to bring no surprise to Jeanne. She was doubtless pondering over this very matter. She slowly nodded her head.

"But you know," said her mother, "he would be always beside us—night and day, at table—everywhere!"

A great trouble dawned in the clear depths of the child's eyes. She nestled her cheek against her mother's shoulder, kissed her neck, and finally, with a quiver, whispered in her ear: "Mamma, would he kiss you?"

A crimson flush rose to Hélène's brow. In her first surprise she was at a loss to answer, but at last she murmurd: "He would be the same as your father, my darling!"

Then Jeanne's little arms tightened their hold, and she burst into loud and grievous sobbing. "Oh! no, no, no!" she cried chokingly. "I don't want it then! Oh! mamma, do please tell him I don't. Go and tell him I won't have it!"

She gasped and threw herself on her mother's bosom, covering her with tears and kisses. Hélène did her utmost to appease her, assuring her she would make it all right; but Jeanne was bent on having a definite answer at once.

"Oh! say no! say no, darling mother! You know it would kill me. Never! Oh, never! Eh?"

"Well, I'll promise it will never be. Now, be good and lie down."

For some minutes longer, the child, speechless with emotion, clasped her mother in her arms, as though powerless to tear herself away, and intent on guarding her against all who might seek to take her from her. After some time Hélène was able to put her to bed; but for a part of the night she had to watch beside her. Jeanne would start violently in her sleep, and every half-hour her eyes would open to make sure of her mother's presence, and then she would doze off again, with her lips pressed to Hélène's hand.

## CHAPTER VIII

### DISCLOSURE

IT was a month of exquisite mildness. The April sun had draped the garden in tender green, light and delicate as lace. Twining around the railing were the slender shoots of the lush clematis, while the budding honeysuckle filled the air with its sweet, almost sugary perfume. On both sides of the trim and close-shaven lawn red geraniums and white stocks gave the flower beds a glow of color; and at the end of the garden the clustering elms, hiding the adjacent houses, reared the green drapery of their branches, whose little leaves trembled with the least breath of air.

For more than three weeks the sky had remained blue and cloudless. It was like a miraculous spring celebrating the new youth and blossoming that had burst into life in Hélène's heart. Every afternoon she went down into the garden with Jeanne. A place was assigned her against the first elm on the right. A chair was ready for her; and on the morrow she would still find on the gravel walk the scattered clippings of thread that had fallen from her work on the previous afternoon.

"You are quite at home," Madame Deberle repeated every evening, displaying for Hélène one of those affections of hers, which usually lasted about six months. "You will come to-morrow, of course; and try to come earlier, won't you?"

Hélène, in truth, felt thoroughly at her ease there. By degrees she became accustomed to this nook of greenery, and looked forward to her afternoon visit with the longing of a child. What charmed her most in this garden was the exquisite trimness of the lawn and flower beds. Not a single weed interfered with the symmetry of the plants. Hélène spent her time there, calmly and restfully. The neatly laid out flower beds, and the network of ivy, withered leaves of which were carefully removed by the gardener, could exercise no disturbing influence on her spirit. Seated beneath the deep shadow of the elm-trees, in this quiet spot which Madame Deberle's presence perfumed with a faint odor of musk, she could have imagined herself in a drawing-room; and only the sight of the blue sky, when she raised her head, reminded her that she was out-of-doors, and prompted her to breathe freely.

Often, without seeing a soul, the two women would thus pass the afternoon, Jeanne and Lucien played at their feet. There would be long intervals of silence, and then Madame Deberle, who disliked reverie, would chatter for hours, quite satisfied with the silent acquiescence of Hélène, and rattling off again if the other even so much as nodded. She would tell endless stories concerning the ladies of her acquaintance, get up schemes for parties during the coming winter, vent magpie opinions on the day's news and the society trifling which filled her narrow brain, the whole intermingled with af-

fectionate outbursts over the children, and sentimental remarks on the delights of friendship. Hélène allowed her to squeeze her hands. She did not always lend an attentive ear; but, in this atmosphere of unceasing tenderness, she showed herself greatly touched by Juliette's caresses, and pronounced her to be a perfect angel of kindness.

Sometimes, to Madame Deberle's intense delight, a visitor would drop in. Since Easter she had ceased receiving on Saturdays, as was usual at this time of the year. But she dreaded solitude, and a casual unceremonious visit paid her in her garden gave her the greatest pleasure. She was now busily engaged in settling on the watering-place where she would spend her holiday in August. To every visitor she retailed the same talk discoursed on the fact that her husband would not accompany her to the seaside; and then poured forth a flood of questions, as she could not make up her mind where to go. She did not ask for herself, however; no, it was all on Lucien's account. When the foppish youth Malignon came he seated himself astride a rustic chair. He, indeed, loathed the country; one must be mad, he would declare, to exile oneself from Paris with the idea of catching influenza beside the sea. However, he took part in the discussions on the merits of the various watering-places, all of which were horrid, said he; apart from Trouville there was not a place worthy of any consideration whatever. Day after day Hélène listened to the same talk, yet without feeling wearied; indeed, she even derived pleasure from this monotony, which lulled her into dreaming of one thing only. The last day of the month came, and still Madame Deberle had not decided where to go.

As Hélène was leaving one evening, her friend said to her: "I must go out to-morrow; but that needn't prevent you from coming down here. Wait for me; I shan't be back late."

Hélène consented; and, alone in the garden, there spent a delicious afternoon. Nothing stirred, save the sparrows fluttering in the trees overhead. This little sunny nook entranced her, and, from that day, her happiest afternoons were those on which her friend left her alone.

A closer intimacy was springing up between the Deberles and herself. She dined with them like a friend who is pressed to stay when the family sits down to table; when she lingered under the elm-trees and Pierre came down to announce dinner, Juliette would implore her to remain, and she sometimes yielded. They were family dinners, enlivened by the noisy pranks of the children. Doctor Deberle and Hélène seemed good friends, whose sensible and somewhat reserved natures sympathized well. Thus it was that Juliette frequently declared: "Oh you two would get on capitally! Your composure exasperates me!"

The doctor returned from his round of visits at about six o'clock every evening. He found the ladies in the garden, and sat down beside them. On the earlier occasions, Hélène started up with the idea of leaving her friends to themselves, but her sudden departure displeased Juliette greatly, and she now perforce had to remain. She became almost a member of this family, which appeared to be so closely united. On the doctor's arrival his wife held up her cheek to him, always with the same loving gesture, and he kissed her; then, as Lucien began clambering up his legs, he kept him on his knees while chatting away. The child would clap his tiny hands on his father's mouth, pull his hair, and play so many pranks that in the upshot he had to be put down, and told to go and play with Jeanne. The fun would bring a smile to Hélène's face, and she neglected her work for the moment, to gaze at father, mother, and child. The kiss of the husband and wife gave her no pain, and Lucien's tricks fliled her with soft emotion. It might have been said that she had found a haven of refuge amidst this family's quiet content.

Meanwhile the sun would sink into the west, gilding the tree tops with its rays. Serene peacefulness fell from the grey heavens. Juliette, whose curiosity was insatiable, even in company with strangers, plagued her husband with ceaseless questions, and often lacked the patience to wait his replies. "Where have you been? What have you been about?"

Thereupon he would describe his round of visits to them, repeat any news of what was going on, or speak of some cloth or piece of furniture he had caught a glimpse of in a shop window. While he was speaking, his eyes often met those of Hélène, but neither turned away the head. They gazed into each other's face for a moment with grave looks, as though heart were being revealed to heart; but after a little they smiled and their eyes dropped. Juliette, fidgety and sprightly, though she would often assume a studied languor, allowed them no opportunity for lengthy conversation, but burst with her interruptions into any talk whatever. Still they exchanged a few words, quite commonplace, slowly articulated sentences which seemed to assume a deep meaning, and to linger in the air after having been spoken. They approvingly punctuated each word the other uttered, as though they had thoughts in common. It was an intimate sympathy that was growing up between them, springing from the depths of their beings, and becoming closer even when they were silent. Sometimes, Juliette, rather ashamed of monopolizing all the talk, would cease her magpie chatter.

"Dear me!" she would exclaim, "you are getting bored, aren't you? We are talking of matters which can have no possible interest for you."

"Oh, never mind me," Hélène answered blithely. "I never tire. It is a pleasure to me to listen and say nothing."

She was uttering no untruth. It was during the lengthy periods of silence that she experienced most delight in being there. With her head bent over her work, only lifting her eyes at long intervals to exchange with the doctor those interminable looks that riveted their hearts the closer, she willingly surrendered herself to the egotism of her emotion. Between herself and him, she now confessed it, there existed a secret sentiment, a something very sweet—all the sweeter because no one in the world shared it with them. But she kept her secret with a tranquil mind, her sense of honor quite unruffled, for no thought of evil ever disturbed her. How good he was to his wife and child! She loved him the more when he made Lucien jump or kissed Juliette on the cheek. Since she had seen him in his own home their friendship had greatly increased. She was now as one of the family; she never dreamt that the intimacy could be broken. And within her own breast she called him Henri—naturally, too, from hearing Juliette address him so. When her lips said "Sir," through all her being "Henri" was re-echoed.

One day the doctor found Hélène alone under the elms. Juliette now went out nearly every afternoon.

"Hello! is my wife with you?" he exclaimed.

"No, she has left me to myself," she answered laughingly. "It is true you have come home earlier than usual."

The children were playing at the other end of the garden. He sat down beside her. Their *tête-à-tête* produced no agitation in either of them. For nearly an hour they spoke of all sorts of matters, without for a moment feeling any desire to allude to the tenderness which filled their hearts. What was the good of referring to that? Did they not well know what might have been said? They had no confession to make. Theirs was the joy of being together, of talking of many things, of surrendering themselves to the pleasure of their isolation with a shadow of regret, in the very spot where every evening he embraced his wife in her presence.

That day he indulged in some joke*

respecting her devotion to work. "Do you know," said he, "I do not even know the color of your eyes? They are always bent on your needle."

She raised her head and looked straight into his face, as was her custom. "Do you wish to tease me?" she asked gently.

But he went on. "Ah! they are grey —grey, tinged with blue, are they not?"

This was the utmost limit to which they dared go; but these words, the first that had sprung to his lips, were fraught with infinite tenderness. From that day onwards he frequently found her alone in the twilight. Despite themselves, and without their having any knowledge of it, their intimacy grew apace. They spoke in an altered voice, with caressing inflections, which were not apparent when others were present. And yet, when Juliette came in, full of gossip about her day in town, they could keep up the talk they had already begun without even troubling themselves to draw their chairs apart. It seemed as though this lovely springtide and this garden, with its blossoming lilac, were prolonging within their hearts the first rapture of love.

Towards the end of the month, Madame Deberle grew excited over a grand idea. The thought of giving a children's ball had suddenly struck her. The season was already far advanced, but the scheme took such hold on her foolish brain that she hurried on the preparations with reckless haste. She desired that the affair should be quite perfect; it was to be a fancy-dress ball. And, in her own home, and in other people's houses, everywhere, in short, she now spoke of nothing but

her ball. The conversations on the subject which took place in the garden were endless. The foppish Malignon thought the project rather stupid, still he condescended to take some interest in it, and promised to bring a comic singer with whom he was acquainted.

One afternoon, while they were all sitting under the trees, Juliette introduced the grave question of costumes which Lucien and Jeanne should wear.

"It is so difficult to make up one's mind," sad she. "I have been thinking of a clown's dress in white satin."

"Oh, that's too common!" declared Malignon. "There will be a round dozen of clowns at your ball. Wait, you must have something novel." Thereupon he began gravely pondering, sucking the head of his cane all the while.

Pauline came up at the moment, and proclaimed her desire to be a soubrette.

'You!" screamed Madame Deberle, in astonishment. "You won't appear in costume at all! Do you think yourself a child, you great stupid? You will oblige me by coming in a white dress."

"Oh, but it would have pleased me so!" exclaimed Pauline, who, despite her eighteen years and plump girlish figure, liked nothing better than to romp with a band of little ones.

Meanwhile Hélène sat at the foot of her tree working away, and raising her head at times to smile at the doctor and Monsieur Rambaud, who stood in front of her conversing. Monsieur Rambaud had now become quite intimate with the Deberle family.

"Well," said the doctor, "and how are you going to dress Jeanne?"

He got no further, for Malignon burst out: "I've got it! I've got it! Lucien must be a marquis of the time of Louis VX."

He waved his cane with a triumphant air; but, as no one of the company hailed his idea with enthusiasm, he appeared astonished. "What, don't you see it? Won't it be for Lucien to receive his little guests? So you place him, dressed as a marquis, at the drawing-room door, with a large bouquet of roses on his coat, and he bows to the ladies."

"But there will be dozens of marquises at the ball!" objected Juliette.

"What does that matter?" replied Malignon coolly. "The more marquises the greater the fun. I tell you it is the best thing you can hit upon. The master of the house must be dressed as a marquis, or the ball will be a complete failure."

Such was his conviction of his scheme's success that at last it was adopted by Juliette with enthusiasm. As a matter of fact, a dress in the Pompadour style, white satin embroidered with posies, would be altogether charming.

"And what about Jeanne?" again asked the doctor.

The little girl had just buried her head against her mother's shoulder in the caressing manner so characteristic of her; and as an answer was about to cross Hélène's lips, she murmured:

"Oh! mamma, you know what you promised me, don't you?"

"What was it?" asked those around her.

Then, as her daughter gave her an imploring look, Hélène laughingly replied: "Jeanne does not wish her dress to be known."

"Yes, that's so," said the child; "you don't create any effect when you tell your dress beforehand."

Every one was tickled with this display of coquetry, and Monsieur Rambaud thought he might tease the child about it. For some time past Jeanne had been ill-tempered with him, and the poor man, at his wits' end to hit upon a mode of again gaining her favor, thought teasing her the best method of conciliation. Keeping his eyes on her face, he several times repeated: "I know, I shall tell, I shall tell!"

Jeanne, however, became quite livid. Her gentle, sickly face assumed an expression of ferocious anger; her brow was furrowed by two deep wrinkles, and her chin drooped with nervous agitation.

"You!" she screamed excitedly; "you will say nothing!" And, as he still feigned a resolve to speak, she rushed at him madly, and shouted out: "Hold your tongue! I will have you hold your tongue! I will I will!"

Hélène had been unable to prevent this fit of blind anger, such as sometimes took possession of the child, and with some harshness exclaimed: "Jeanne, take care; I shall whip you!"

But Jeanne paid no heed, never once heard her. Trembling from head to foot, stamping on the ground, and choking with rage, she again and again repeated, "I will! I will!" in a voice that grew more and more hoarse and broken; and her hands convulsively gripped hold of Monsieur Rambaud's arm, which she twisted with extraordinary strength. In vain did Hélène threaten her. At last, perceiving her inability to quell her by severity, and grieved to the heart by such a display before so many people, she contented herself by saying gently: "Jeanne, you are grieving me very much."

The child immediately quitted her hold and turned her head. And when she caught sight of her mother, with disconsolate face and eyes swimming with repressed tears, she on her side burst into loud sobs, and threw herself on Hélène's neck, exclaiming in her grief: "No, mamma! no, mamma!"

She passed her hands over her mother's face, as though to prevent her weeping. Hélène, however, slowly put her from her, and then the little one, broken-hearted and distracted, threw herself on a seat a short distance off, where her sobs broke out louder than ever. Lucien, to whom she was always held up as example to follow, gazed at her surprised and somewhat pleased. And then, as Hélène folded up her work, apologizing for so regrettable an incident, Juliette remarked to her:

"Dear me! we have to pardon children everything. Besides, the little one has the best of hearts, and is grieved so much, poor darling, that she has been already punished too severely."

So saying she called Jeanne to come and kiss her; but the child remained on her seat, rejecting the offer of forgiveness, and still choking with tears.

Monsieur Rambaud and the doctor, however, walked to her side, and the former, bending over her, asked, in tones husky with emotion: "Tell me, my pet, what has vexed you. What have I done to you?"

"Oh!" she replied, drawing away her hands and displaying a face full of anguish, "you wanted to take my mamma from me!"

"What is this you're talking of?"

"Yes, indeed, the other Tuesday! Oh! you know very well; you were on your knees, and asked me what I should say if you were to stay with us!"

The smile vanished from the doctor's face; his lips became ashy pale, and quivered. A flush, on the other hand, mounted to Monsieur Rambaud's cheek, and he whispered to Jeanne: "But you said yourself that we should always play together?"

"No, no; I did not know at the time," the child resumed excitedly. "I tell you I don't want it. Don't ever speak to me of it again, and then we shall be friends."

Hélène was on her feet now, with her needlework in its basket, and the last words fell on her ear. "Come, let us go up, Jeanne," she said; "your tears are not pleasant company."

She bowed, and pushed the child before her. The doctor, with livid face, gazed at her fixedly. Monsieur Rambaud was in dismay. As for Madame Deberle and Pauline, they had taken hold of Lucien, and were making him turn between them, while excitedly discussing the question of his Pompadour dress.

On the morrow Hélène was left alone under the elms. Madame Deberle was running about in the interests of her ball, and had taken Lucien and Jeanne with her. On the doctor's return home, at an earlier hour than usual, he hurried down the garden steps. However, he did not seat himself, but wandered aimlessly round the young woman, at times tearing strips of bark from the trees with his finger-nails. She lifted her eyes for a moment, feeling anxious at sight of his agitation; and then again began plying her needle with a somewhat trembling hand.

"The weather is going to break up," said she, feeling uncomfortable as the silence continued. "The afternoon seems quite cold."

"We are only in April, remember," he replied, with a brave effort to control his voice.

Then he appeared to be on the point of leaving her, but turned round, and suddenly asked: "So you are going to get married?"

This abrupt question took her wholly by surprise, and her work fell from her hands. Her face blanched, but by a supreme effort of will remained unimpassioned, as though she were a marble statue, fixing dilated eyes upon him. She made no reply, and he continued in imploring tones:

"Oh! pray you, answer me. One word, one only. Are you going to get married?"

"Yes, perhaps. What concern is it of yours?" she retorted, in a tone of icy indifference.

He made a passionate gesture, and exclaimed:

"It is impossible!"

"Why should it be?" she asked, still keeping her eyes fixed on his face.

Her glance stayed the words upon his lips, and he was forced to silence. For a moment longer he remained near her, pressing his hands to his brow, and then fled away, with a feeling of suffocation in his throat, dreading lest he might give expression to his despair; while she, with assumed tranquillity, once more turned to her work.

But the spell of those delicious afternoons was gone. Next day shone fair and sunny, and Hélène seemed ill at ease from the moment she found herself alone with him. The pleasant intimacy, the happy trustfulness, which sanctioned their sitting side by side in blissful security, and revelling in the unalloyed joy of being together, no longer existed. Despite his intense carefulness to give her no cause for alarm, he would sometimes gaze at her and trembled with sudden excitement, while his face crimsoned with a rush of blood. From her own heart had fled its wonted happy calm; quivers ran through her frame; she felt languid; her hands grew weary, and forsook their work.

She now no longer allowed Jeanne to wander from her side. Between himself and her the doctor found this constant onlooker, watching him with large, clear eyes. But what pained Hélène most was that she now felt ill at ease in Madame Deberle's company. When the latter returned of an afternoon, with her hair swept about by the wind, and called her "my dear" while relating the incidents of some shopping expedition, she no longer listened with her former quiet smile. A storm arose from the depths of her soul, stirring up feelings to which she dared not give a name. Shame and spite seemed mingled in them. However, her honorable nature gained the mastery, and she gave her hand to Juliette, but without being able to repress the shudder which ran through her as she pressed her friend's warm fingers.

The weather had now broken up. Frequent rain forced the ladies to take refuge in the Japanese pavilion. The garden, with its whilom exquisite order, became transformed into a lake, and no one dared venture on the walks, on account of the mud. However, whenever the sun peeped out from behind the clouds, the dripping greenery soon dried; pearls hung from each little blossom of the lilac trees; and under the elms big drops fell splashing on the ground.

"At last I've arranged it; it will be on Saturday," said Madame Deberle one day. "My dear, I'm quite tired out with the whole affair. Now, you'll be here at two o'clock, won't you? Jeanne will open the ball with Lucien."

And thereupon, surrendering to a flow of tenderness, in ecstasy over the preparations for her ball, she embraced both children, and, laughingly catching hold of Hélène, pressed two resounding kisses on her cheeks. ,

"That's my reward!" she exclaimed merrily. "You know I deserve it; I have run about enough. You'll see what a success it will be!"

But Hélène remained chilled to the heart, while the doctor, with Lucien clinging to his neck, gazed at them over the child's fair head.

## CHAPTER IX

### PUNCH AND DRAMA

IN THE hall of the doctor's house stood Pierre, in dress coat and white cravat, throwing open the door as each rarriage rolled up. Puffs of dank air rushed in; the afternoon was rainy, and a yellow light illumined the narrow hall, with its curtained doorways and array of green plants. It was only two o'clock, but the evening seemed as near at hand as on a dismal winter's day.

However, as soon as the servant opened the door of the first drawing-room a stream of light dazzled the guests. The shutters had been closed, and the curtains carefully drawn, and no gleam from the dull sky could gain admittance. The lamps standing here and there on the furniture, and the lighted candles of the chandelier and the crystal wall-brackets, gave the apartment somewhat the appearance of a brilliantly illuminated chapel. Beyond the smaller drawing-room, whose green hangings rather softened the glare of the light, was the large black-and-gold one, decorated as magnificently as for the ball which Madame Deberle gave every year in the month of January.

The children were beginning to arrive, while Pauline gave her attention to the ranging of a number of chairs in front of the dining-room doorway, where the door had been removed from its hinges and replaced by a red curtain.

"Papa," she cried, "just lend me a hand! We shall never be ready."

Monsieur Letellier, who, with his arms behind his back, was gazing at the chandelier, hastened to give the required assistance. Pauline carried the chairs about herself. She had paid due deference to her sister's request, and was robed in white; only her dress opened squarely at the neck and displayed her bosom.

"At last we are ready," she exclaimed: "they can come when they like. But what is Juliette dreaming about? She has been ever so long dressing Lucien!"

Just at that moment Madame Deberle entered, leading the little marquis, and everybody present began raising admiring remarks. "Oh, what a love! What a darling he is!" His coat was of white satin embroidered with flowers, his long waistcoat was embroidered with gold, and his knee-breeches were of cherry-colored silk. Lace clustered round his chin and delicate wrists. A sword, a mere toy with a great rose-red knot, rattled against his hip.

"Now you must do the honors," his mother said to him, as she led him into the outer room.

For eight days past he had been repeating his lesson and struck a cavalier attitude with his little legs, his powdered head thrown slighly back, and his cocked hat tucked under his left arm. As each of his lady-guests was ushered into the room, he bowed low, offered his arm, exchanged courteous greetings, and returned to the threshold. Those near him laughed over his intense seriousness in which there was a dash of effrontery. This was the style in which he received Marguerite Tissot, a little lady five years old, dressed in a charming milkmaid costume, with a milk-can hanging at her side; so too did he greet the Berthier children, Blanche and Sophie, the one masquerading as Folly, the other dressed in soubrette style; and he had even the hardihood to tackle Valentine

de Chermette, a tall young lady of some fourteen years, whom her mother always dressed in Spanish costume, and at her side his figure appeared so slight that she seemed to be carrying him along. However, he was profoundly embarrassed in the presence of the Levasseur family, which numbered five girls, who made their appearance in a row of increasing height, the youngest being scarcely two years old, while the eldest was ten. All five were arrayed in Red Riding-Hood costumes, their head-dresses and gowns being in poppy-colored satin with black velvet bands, with which their lace aprons strikingly contrasted. At last Lucien, making up his mind, bravely flung away his three-cornered hat, and led the two elder girls, one hanging on each arm, into the drawing-room, closely followed by the three others. There was a good deal of laughter at it, but the little man never lost his self-possession for a moment.

In the meantime Madame Deberle was taking her sister to task in a corner.

"Good gracious! is it possible! what a fearfully low-necked dress you are wearing!"

"Dear, dear! what have I done now? Papa hasn't said a word," said Pauline coolly. "If you're anxious, I'll put some flowers at my breast."

She plucked a handful of blossoms from a flower-stand where they were growing and allowed them to nestle in her bosom; while Madame Deberle was surrounded by several mammas in stylish visiting-dresses, who were already profuse in their compliments about her ball. As Lucien was passing them, his mother arranged a loose curl of his powdered hair while he stood on tip-toe to whisper in her ear:

"Where's Jeanne?"

"She will be here immediately, my darling. Take good care not to fall. Run away, there comes little Mademoiselle Guiraud. Ah! she is wearing an Alsatian costume."

The drawing-room was now filling rapidly; the rows of chairs fronting the red curtain were almost all occupied, and a hubbub of children's voices was rising. The boys were flocking into the room in groups. There were already three Harlequins, four Punches, a Figaro, some Tyrolese peasants, and a few Highlanders. Young Master Berthier was dressed as a page. Little Guiraud, a mere bantling of two-and-a-half summers, wore his clown's costume in so comical a style that every one as he passed lifted him up and kissed him.

"Here comes Jeanne," exclaimed Madame Deberle, all at once. "Oh, she is lovely!"

A murmur ran round the room; heads were bent forward, and every one gave vent to exclamations of admiration. Jeanne was standing on the threshold of the outer room awaiting her mother, who was taking off her cloak in the hall. The child was robed in a Japanese dress of unusual splendor. The gown, embroidered with flowers and strange-looking birds, swept to her feet, which were hidden from view while beneath her broad waist-ribbon the flaps, drawn aside, gave a glimpse of a green petticoat, watered with yellow. Nothing could be more strangely bewitching than her delicate features seen under the shadow of her hair, coiled above her head with long pins thrust through it, while her chin and oblique eyes, small and sparkling, pictured to the life a young lady of Yeddo, strolling amidst the perfume of tea and benzoin. And she lingered there hesitatingly, with all the sickly languor of a tropical flower pining for the land of its birth.

Behind her, however, appeared Hélène. Both, in thus suddenly passing from the dull daylight of the street into the brilliant glare of the wax candles, blinked their eyes as though blinded, while their faces were irradiated with smiles. The rush of warm air and the perfumes, the scent of violets rising above all else, almost stifled them, and brought a flush of red to their cheeks. Each guest, on passing the doorway, wore a similar air of surprise and hesitancy.

"Why, Lucien! where are you?" exclaimed Madame Deberle.

The boy had not caught sight of Jeanne. But now he rushed forward and seized her arm, forgetting to make his bow. And they were so dainty, so loving, the little marquis in his flowered coat, and the Japanese maiden in her purple embroidered gown, that they might have been taken for two statuettes of Dresden china, daintily gilded and painted, into which life had been suddenly infused.

"You know, I was waiting for you," whispered Lucien. "Oh, it is so nasty to give everybody my arm! Of course, we'll keep beside each other, eh?"

And he sat himself down with her in the first row of chairs, wholly oblivious of his duties as host.

"Oh, I was so uneasy!" purred Juliette into Hélène's ear. "I was beginning to fear that Jeanne had been taken ill."

Hélène proffered an apology; dressing children, said she, meant endless labor. She was still standing in a corner of the drawing-room, one of a cluster of ladies, when her heart told her that the doctor was approaching behind her. He was making his way from behind the red curtain, beneath which he had dived to give some final instructions. But suddenly he came to a standstill. He, too, had divined her presence, though she had not yet turned her head. Attired in a dress of black grenadine, she had never appeared more queenly in her beauty; and a thrill passed through him as he breathed the cool air which she had brought with her from outside, and wafted from her shoulders and arms, gleaming white under their transparent covering.

"Henri has no eyes for anybody," exclaimed Pauline, with a laugh. "Ah, good-day, Henri!"

Thereupon he advanced towards the group of ladies, with a courteous greeting. Mademoiselle Aurélie, who was amongst them, engaged his attention for the moment to point out to him a nephew whom she had brought with her. He was all complaisance. Hélène, without speaking, gave him her hand, encased in its black glove, but he dared not clasp it with marked force.

"Oh! here you are!" said Madame Deberle, as she appeared beside them. "I have been looking for you everywhere. It is nearly three o'clock; they had better begin."

"Certainly; at once," was his reply.

The drawing-room was now crowded. All round it, in the brilliant glare thrown from the chandelier, sat the fathers and mothers, their walking costumes serving to fringe the circle with less vivid colors. Some ladies, drawing their chairs together, formed groups; men standing motionless along the walls filled up the gaps; while in the doorway leading to the next room a cluster of frock-coated guests could be seen crowding together and peering over each other's shoulders. The light fell wholly on the little folks, noisy in their glee, as they rustled about in their seats in the centre of the large room. There were almost a hundred children packed together, in an endless variety of gay costumes, bright with blue and red. It was like a sea of fair heads, varying from pale yellow to ruddy gold, with here and there bows and flowers gleaming vividly—or like a field of ripe grain, spangled with poppies and cornflowers, and waving to and fro as though stirred by a breeze. At times, amidst this confusion of ribbons and lace, of silk and velvet, a face was turned round—a pink nose, a pair of blue eyes, a smiling or pouting little mouth. There were some, no higher than one's boots, who were buried out of sight between big lads of ten years of age, and whom their mothers sought from a distance, but in vain. A few of the boys looked bored and foolish by the side of girls who were busy spreading out their skirts. Some, however, were already very venturesome, jogging the elbows of their fair neighbors with whom they were unacquainted, and laughing in their faces.

But the royalty of the gathering remained with the girls, some of whom, clustering in groups, stirred about in such a way as to threaten destruction to their chairs, and chattered so loudly that the grown-up folks could no longer hear one another speaking. And all eyes were intently gazing at the red curtain.

Slowly was it drawn aside, and in the recess of the doorway appeared a puppet-show. There was a hushed silence. Then all at once Punch sprang in, with so ferocious a yell that baby Guiraud could not restrain a responsive cry of terror and delight. It was one of those bloodthirsty dramas in which Punch, having administered a sound beating to the magistrate, murders the policeman, and tramples with ferocious glee on every law, human and divine. At every cudgelling bestowed on the wooden heads the pitiless audience went into shrieks of laughter and the sharp thrusts delivered by the puppets at each other's breasts, the duels in which they beat a tattoo on one another's skulls as though they were empty pumpkins, the awful havoc of legs and arms, reducing the characters to a jelly, served to increase the roars of laughter which rang out from all sides. But the climax of enjoyment was reached when Punch sawed off the policeman's head on the edge of the stage; an operation provocative of such hysterical mirth that the rows of juveniles were plunged into confusion, swaying to and fro with glee till they all fell on one another. One tiny girl, but four years old, all pink and white, considered the spectacle so entrancing that she pressed her little hands devoutly to her heart. Others burst into applause, while the boys laughed, with mouths agape, their deeper voices mingling with the shrill peals from the girls.

"How amused they are!" whispered the doctor. He had returned to his place near Hélène. She was in high spirits like the children. Behind her, he sat inhaling the intoxicating perfume from her hair. And as one puppet on the stage dealt another an exceptionally hard knock she turned to him and exclaimed: "Do you know it is awfully funny!"

The youngsters, crazy with excitement, were now interfering with the action of the drama. They were giving answers to the various characters. One young lady, who must have been well up in the plot, was busy explaining what would next happen.

"He'll beat his wife to death in a minute! Now they are going to hang him!"

The youngest of the Levasseur girls, who was two years old, shrieked out all at once:

"Mamma, mamma, will they put him on bread and water?"

All sorts of exclamations and reflections followed. Meanwhile Hélène, gazing into the crowd of children, remarked: "I cannot see Jeanne. Is she enjoying herself?"

Then the doctor bent forward, with head perilously near her own, and whispered: "There she is, between that harlequin and the Norman peasant maiden! You can see the pins gleaming in her hair. She is laughing very heartily."

He still leaned towards her, her cool breath playing on his cheek. Till now no confession had escaped them; preserving silence, their intimacy had only been marred for a few days past by a vague sensation of discomfort. But amidst these bursts of happy laughter, gazing upon the little folks before her, Hélène became once more, in sooth, a very child, surrendering herself to her feelings, while Henri's breath beat warm upon her neck. The whacks from the cudgel, now louder than ever, filled her with a quiver which inflated her bosom, and she turned towards him with sparkling eyes.

"Good heavens! what nonsense it all is!" she said each time. "See how they hit one another!"

"Oh! their heads are hard enough!" he replied, trembling.

This was all his heart could find to say. Their minds were fast lapsing into childhood once more. Punch's unedifying life was fostering languor within their breasts. When the drama drew to its close with the appearance of the devil, and the final fight and general massacre ensued, Hélène in leaning back pressed against Henri's hand, which was resting on the back of her arm-chair while the juvenile audience shouting and clapping their hands, made the very chairs creak with their enthusiasm.

The red curtain dropped again, and the uproar was at its height when Malignon's presence was announced by Pauline, in her customary style: "Ah! here's the handsome Malignon!"

He made his way into the room, shoving the chairs aside, quite out of breath.

"Dear me! what a funny idea to close the shutters!" he exclaimed, surprised and hesitating. "People might imagine that somebody in the house was dead." Then, turning towards Madame Deberle, who was approaching him, he continued: "Well, you can boast of having made me run about! Ever since the morning I have been hunting for Perdiguet, you know whom I mean, my singer fellow. But I haven't been able to lay my hands on him, and I have brought you the great Morizot instead."

The great Morizot was an amateur who entertained drawing-rooms by conjuring with juggler-balls. A gipsy table was assigned to him, and on this he accomplished his most wonderful tricks; but it all passed off without the spectators evincing the slightest interest. The poor little darlings were pulling serious faces; some of the tinier mites fell fast asleep, sucking their thumbs. The older children turned their heads towards and smiled towards their parents, who were themselves yawning behind their hands. There was thus a general feeling of relief when the great Morizot decided to take his table away.

"Oh! he's awfully clever," whispered Malignon into Madame Deberle's neck.

But the red curtain was drawn aside once again, and an entrancing spectacle brought all the little folks to their feet.

Along the whole extent of the dining-room stretched the table, laid and bedecked as for a grand dinner, and illumined by the bright radiance of the central lamp and a pair of large candelabra. There were fifty covers laid; in the middle and at either end were shallow baskets, full of flowers; between these towered tall *épergnes*, filled to overflowing with crackers in gilded and colored paper. Then there were mountains of decorated cakes, pyramids of iced fruits, piles of sandwiches, and, less prominent, a whole host of symmetrically disposed plates, bearing sweetmeats and pastry: buns, cream puffs, and *brioches* alternating with dry biscuits, cracknals, and fancy almond cakes. Jellies were quivering in their glass dishes. Whipped creams waited in porcelain bowls. And round the table sparkled the silver helmets of champagne bottles, no higher than one's hand, made specially to suit the little guests. It all looked like one of those gigantic feasts which children conjure up in dreamland—a feast served with the solemnity that attends a repast of grown-up folks—a fairy transformation of the table to which their own parents sat down, and on which the horns of plenty of innumerable pastry-cooks and toy dealers had been emptied.

"Come, come, give the ladies your arms!" said Madame Deberle, her face covered with smiles as she watched the delight of the children.

But the filing off in couples proved a failure. Lucien, who had triumphantly taken Jeanne's arm, went first. But the others following behind fell somewhat into confusion, and the mothers were forced to come and assign them places, remaining close at hand, especially behind the babies, whom they watched lest any mischance should befall them. Truth to tell, the guests at first seemed rather uncomfortable; they looked at one another, felt afraid to lay hands on the good things, and were vaguely disquieted by this new social organization in which everything appeared to be topsy-turvy, the children seated at tables while their parents remained standing. At length the older ones gained confidence and commenced the attack. And when the mothers entered into the fray, and cut up the large cakes, helping those in their vicinity, the feast speedily became very animated and noisy. The exquisite symmetry of the table was destroyed as though by a tempest. The two Berthier girls, Blanche and Sophie, laughed at the sight of their plates, which had been filled with something of everything—jam, custard, cake, and fruit. The five young ladies of the Levasseur family took sole possession of a corner laden with dainties, while Valentine, proud of her fourteen years, acted the lady's part, and looked after the comfort of her little neighbors. Lucien, however, impatient to display his politeness, uncorked a bottle of champagne, but in so clumsy a way that the whole contents spurted over his cherry silk breeches. There was quite a to-do about it.

"Kindly leave the bottles alone! I am to uncork the champagne," shouted Pauline.

She bustled about in an extraordinary fashion, purely for her own amusement. On the entry of a servant with the chocolate pot, she seized it and filled the cups with the greatest glee, as active in the performance as any restaurant waiter. Next she took round some ices and glasses of syrup and water, set them down for a moment to stuff a little baby-girl who had been overlooked, and then went off again asking every one questions.

"What is it you wish, my pet? Eh?

A cake? Yes, my darling, wait a moment; I am going to pass you the oranges. Now eat away, you little stupids, you shall play afterwards."

Madame Deberle, calm and dignified, declared that they ought to be left alone, and would acquit themselves very well.

At one end of the room sat Hélène and some other ladies laughing at the scene which the table presented; all the rosy mouths were eating with the full strength of their beautiful white teeth. And nothing could eclipse in drollery the occasional lapses from the polished behavior of well-bred children to the outrageous freaks of young savages. With both hands gripping their glasses, they drank to the very dregs, smeared their faces, and stained their dresses. The clamor grew worse. The last of the dishes were plundered. Jeanne herself began dancing on her chair as she heard the strains of a quadrille coming from the drawing-room; and on her mother approaching to upbraid her with having eaten too much, she replied: "Oh! mamma, I feel so happy to-day!"

But now the other children were rising as they heard the music. Slowly the table thinned, until there only remained a fat, chubby infant right in the middle. He seemingly cared little for the attractions of the piano; with a napkin round his neck, and his chin resting on the tablecloth—for he was a mere chit —he opened his big eyes, and protruded his lips each time that his mamma offered him a spoonful of chocolate. The contents of the cup vanished, and he licked his lips as the last mouthful went down his throat, with eyes more agape than ever.

"By Jove! my lad, you eat heartily!" exclaimed Malignon, who was watching him with a thoughtful air.

Now came the division of the "surprise" packets. Each child, on leaving the table, bore away one of the large gilt paper twists, the coverings of which were hastily torn off and from them poured forth a host of toys, grotesque hats made of tissue paper, birds and butterflies. But the joy of joys was the possession of a cracker. Every "surprise" packet had its cracker; and these the lads pulled at gallantly, delighted with the noise, while the girls shut their eyes, making many tries before the explosion took place. For a time the sharp crackling of all this musketry alone could be heard; and the uproar was still lasting when the children returned to the drawing-room, where lively quadrille music resounded from the piano.

"I could enjoy a cake," murmured Mademoiselle Aurélie, as she sat down.

At the table, which was now deserted, but covered with all the litter of the huge feast, a few ladies—some dozen or so, who had preferred to wait till the children had retired—now sat down. As no servant could be found, Malignon bustled hither and thither in attendance. He poured out all that remained in the chocolate pot, shook up the dregs of the bottles, and was even successful in discovering some ices. But amidst all these gallant doings of his, he could not quit one idea, and that was—why had they decided on closing the shutters?

"You know," he asserted, "the place looks like a cellar."

Héléne had remained, standing, engaged in conversation with Madame Deberle. As the latter directed her steps towards the drawing-room, her companion prepared to follow, when she felt a gentle touch. Behind her was the doctor, smiling; he was ever near her.

"Are you not going to take anything?" he asked. And the trivial question cloaked so earnest an entreaty that her heart was filled with profound emotion. She knew well enough that each of his words was eloquent of another thing. The excitement springing from the gaiety which pulsed around her was slowly gaining on her. Some of the fever of all these little folks, now dancing and shouting, coursed in her own veins. With flushed cheeks and sparkling eyes, she at first declined.

"No, thank you, nothing at all."

But he pressed her, and in the end, ill at ease and anxious to get rid of him, she yielded.

"Well, then, a cup of tea."

He hurried off and returned with the cup, his hands trembling as he handed it to her. While she was sipping the tea he drew nearer to her, his lips quivering nervously with the confesion springing from his heart. She in her turn drew back from him, and, returning him the empty cup, made her escape while he was placing it on a sideboard, thus leaving him alone in the dining-room with Mademoiselle Aurélie, who was slowly masticating, and subjecting each dish in succession to a close scrutiny.

Within the drawing-room the piano was sending forth its loudest strains, and from end to end of the floor swept the ball with its charming drolleries. A circle of onlookers had gathered round the quadrille party with which Lucien and Jeanne were dancing. The little marquis became rather mixed over the figures; he only got on well when he had occasion to take hold of Jeanne; and then he gripped her by the waist and whirled around. Jeanne preserved her equilibrium, somewhat vexed by his rumpling her dress; but the delights of the dance taking full possession of her, she caught hold of him in her turn and lifted him off his his feet. The white satin coat embroidered with nosegays mingled with the folds of the gown woven with flowers and strange birds, and the two little figures of old Dresden ware assumed all the grace and novelty of some whatnot ornaments. The quadrille over, Hélène summoned Jeanne to her side, in order to rearrange her dress.

"It is his fault, mamma," was the little one's excuse. "He rubs against me—he's a dreadful nuisance."

Around the drawing-room the faces of the parents were wreathed with smiles. As soon as the music began again all the little ones were in motion. Seeing, however, that they were observed they felt distrustful, remained grave, and checked their leaps in order to keep up appearances. Some of them knew how to dance; but the majority were ignorant of the steps, and their limbs were evidently a source of embarrassment to them. But Pauline interposed: "I must see to them! Oh, you little stupids!"

She threw herself into the midst of

the quadrille, caught hold of two of them, one grasping her right hand the other her left, and managed to infuse such life into the dance that the wooden flooring creaked beneath them. The only sounds now audible rose from the hurrying hither and thither of tiny feet beating wholly out of time, the piano alone keeping to the dance measure. Some more of the older people joined in the fun. Hélène and Madame Deberle, noticing some little maids who were to bashful to venture forth, dragged them into the thickest of the throng. It was they who led the figures, pushed the lads forward, and arranged the dancing in rings; and the mothers passed them the youngest of the babies, so that they might make them skip about for a moment, holding them the while by both hands. The ball was now at its height. The dancers enjoyed theselves to their hearts' content, laughing and pushing each other about like some boarding school mad with glee over the absence of the teacher. Nothing, truly, could surpass in unalloyed gaiety this carnival of youngsters, this assemblage of miniature men and women—akin to a veritable microcosm, wherein the fashions of every people mingled with the fantastic creations of romance and drama. The ruddy lips and blue eyes, the faces breathing love, invested the dresses with the fresh purity of childhood. The scene realized to the mind the merry-making of a fairy-tale to which trooped Cupids in disguise to honor the betrothal of some Prince Charming.

"I'm stifling!" exclaimed Malignon. "I'm off to inhale some fresh air."

As he left the drawing-room he threw the door wide open. The daylight from the street then entered in a lurid stream, bedimming the glare of lamps and candles. In this fashion every quarter of an hour Malignon opened the door to let in some fresh air.

Still there was no cessation of the piano-playing. Little Guiraud, in her Alsatian costume, with a butterfly of black ribbon in her golden hair, swung round in the dance with a harlequin twice her height. A Highlander whirled Marquerite Tissot round so madly that she lost her milk-pail. The two Berthier girls, Blanche and Sophie, who were inseparables, were dancing together; the soubrette in the arms of Folly, whose bells were jingling merrily. A glance could not be thrown over the assemblage without one of the Levasseur girls coming into view; the Red Riding-Hoods seemed to increase in number; caps and gowns of gleaming red satin slashed with black velvet everywhere leaped into sight. Meanwhile some of the older boys and girls had found refuge in the adjacent saloon, where they could dance more at their ease. Valentine de Chermette, cloaked in the mantilla of a Spanish señorita, was executing some marvelous steps in front of a young gentleman who had donned evening dress. Suddenly there was a burst of laughter which drew every one to the sight; behind a door in a corner, baby Guiraud, the two-year-old clown, and a mite of a girl of his own age, in peasant costume, were holding one another in a tight embrace for fear of tumbling, and gyrating round and round like a pair of slyboots, with cheek pressed to cheek.

"I'm quite done up," remarked Hélène, as she leaned against the dining-room door.

She fanned her face, flushed with her exertions in the dance. Her bosom rose and fell beneath the transparent grenadine of her bodice. And she was still conscious of Henri's breath beating on her shoulders; he was still close to her — ever behind her. Now it flashed on her that he would speak, yet she had no strength to flee from his avowal. He came nearer and whispered, breathing on her hair: "I love you! oh, how I love you!"

She tingled from head to foot, as though a gust of flame had beaten on her. O God! he had spoken; she could no longer feign the pleasurable quietude of ignorance. She hid behind her fan, her face purple with blushes. The children, whirling madly in the last of the quadrilles, were making the floor ring with the beating of their feet. There were silvery peals of laughter, and bird-like voices gave vent to exclamations of pleasure. A freshness arose from all that band of innocents galloping round and round like little demons.

"I love you!! oh, how I love you!" She shuddered again; she would listen no further. With dizzy brain she fled into the dining-room, but it was deserted, save that Monsieur Letellier sat on a chair, peacefully sleeping. Henri had followed her, and had the hardihood to seize her wrists even at the risk of a scandal, his face convulsed with such passion that she trembled before him. And he still repeated the words:

"I love you! I love you!"

"Leave me," she murmured faintly. "You are mad—"

And, close by, the dancing still went on, with the trampling of tiny feet. Blanche Berthier's bells could be heard ringing in unison with the softer notes of the piano; Madame Deberle and Pauline were clapping their hands, by way of beating time. It was a polka, and Hélène caught a glimpse of Jeanne and Lucien, as they passed by smiling, with arms clasped round each other.

But with a sudden jerk she freed herself and fled to an adjacent room— a pantry into which streamed the daylight. That sudden brightness blinded her. She was terror-stricken — she dared not return to the drawing-room with the tale of passion written so legibly on her face. So, hastily crossing the garden, she climbed to her own home, the noises of the ball-room still ringing in her ears.

## CHAPTER X.

### WITHIN HER SOUL

UPSTAIRS, in her own room, in the peaceful, convent-like atmosphere she found there, Hélène experienced a feeling of suffocation. Her room astonished her, so calm, so secluded, so drowsy did it seem with its blue velvet hangings, while she came to it hotly panting with the emotion which thrilled her. Was this indeed her room, this dreary, lifeless nook, devoid of air? Hastily she threw open a window, and leaned out to gaze on Paris.

The rain had ceased, and the clouds were trooping off like some herd of monsters hurrying in disorderly array into the gloom of the horizon. A blue gap, that grew larger by degrees, had opened up above the city. But Hélène, her elbows trembling on the window-rail, still breathless from her hasty ascent, saw nothing, and merely heard her heart beating against her swelling breast. She drew a long breath, but it seemed to her that the spreading valley with its rivers, its two millions of people, its immense city, its distant hills, could not hold air enough to enable her to breathe peacefully and regularly again.

For some minutes she remained there distracted by the fever of passion which possessed her. It seemed as though a torrent of sensations and confused ideas were pouring down on her, their roar preventing her from hearing her own voice or undertanding aught. There was a buzzing in her ears, and large spots of light swam slowly before her eyes. Then she suddenly found herself examining her gloved hands, and remembering that she had omitted to sew on a button that had come off the left-hand glove. And afterwards she spoke aloud, repeating several times, in tones that grew fainter and fainter: "I love you! I love you! oh, how I love you!"

Instinctively she buried her face in her hands, and pressed her fingers to her eyelids as though to intensify the darkness in which she sought to plunge. It was a wish to annihilate herself, to see no more, to be utterly alone, girt in by the gloom of night. Her breathing grew calmer. Paris blew its mighty breath upon her face; she knew it lay before her, and though she had no wish

to look on it, she felt full of terror at the thought of leaving the window, and of no longer having beneath her that city whose vastness lulled her to rest.

Ere long she grew unmindful of all around her. The love-scene and confusion, despite her efforts, again woke to life in her mind. In the inky darkness Henri appeared to her, every feature so distinct and vivid that she could perceive the nervous twitching of his lips. He came nearer and hung over her. And then she wildly darted back. But, nevertheless, she felt a burning breath on her shoulders and a voice exclaimed: "I love you! I love you!" With a mighty effort she put the phantom to flight, but it again took shape in the distance, and slowly swelled to its whilom proportions; it was Henri once more following her into the dining-room, and still murmuring: "I love you! I love you!" These words rang within her breast with the sonorous clang of a bell; she no longer heard anything but them, pealing their loudest throughout her frame. Nevertheless she desired to reflect, and again strove to escape from the apparition. He had spoken; never would she dare to look on his face again. The brutal passion of the man had tainted the tenderness of their love. She conjured up past hours, in which he had loved her without being so cruel as to say it; hours spent in the garden amidst the tranquillity of the budding springtime. God! he had spoken—the thought clung to her so stubbornly, lowered on her in such immensity and with such weight, that the instant destruction of Paris by a thunderbolt before her eyes would have seemed a trivial matter. Her heart was rent by feelings of indignant protest and haughty anger, commingling with a secret and unconquerable pleasure, which ascended from her inner being and bereft her of her senses. He had spoken, and was speaking still, he sprang up unceasingly before her, uttering those passionate words; "I love you! I love you!"—words that swept into oblivion all her past life as wife and mother.

In spite of her brooding over this vision, she retained some consciousness of the vast expanse which stretched beneath her, beyond the darkness that curtained her sight. A loud rumbling arose, and waves of life seemed to surge up and circle around her. Echoes, odors, and even light streamed against her face, though her hands were still nervously pressed to it.. At times sudden gleams appeared to pierce her closed eyelids, and amidst the radiance she imagined she saw monuments, steeples, and domes standing out in the diffuse light of dreamland. Then she lowered her hands and, opening her eyes, was dazed. The vault of heaven expanded before her, and Henri had vanished.

A line of clouds, a seeming mass of crumbling chalk-hills, now barred the horizon far away. Across the pure, deep blue heavens overhead, merely a few light, fleecy cloudlets were slowly drifting, like a flotilla of vessels with full-blown sails. On the north, above Montmartre, hung a network of extreme delicacy, fashioned as it were of pale-hued silk, and spread over a patch of sky as though for fishing in those tran-quil waters. Westward, however, in the direction of the slopes of Meudon, which Hélène could not see, the last drops of the downpour must still have been obscuring the sun, for, though the sky above was clear, Paris remained gloomy, dismal beneath the vapor of drying house-roofs. It was a city of uniform hue—the bluey-grey of slate, studded with black patches of trees—but withal very distinct, with the sharp outlines of innumerable windows of its houses. The Seine gleamed with the subdued brightness of old silver. The edifices on either bank looked as though they had been smeared with soot. The Tower of St. Jacques rose up like some rust-eaten museum curio, whilst the Panthéon assumed the aspect of a gigantic catafalque above the darkened district which it overlooked. Gleams of light peeped only from the gilding of the dome of the Invalides, like lamps burning in the daytime, sad and vague amidst the crepuscular veil of mourning in which the city was draped. All the usual effects of distance had vanished; Paris resembled a huge yet minutely executed charcoal drawing, showing very vigorously through its cloudy veil, under the limpid heavens.

Glazing upon this dismal city, Hélène reflected that she really knew nothing of Henri. She felt strong and brave now that his image no longer pursued her. A rebellious impulse stirred her soul to reject the mastery which this man had gained over her within a few weeks. No, she did not know him. She knew nothing of him, of his actions or his thoughts; she could not even have determined whether he possessed talent. Perhaps he was even more lacking in qualities of the heart than of the mind. And thus she gave way to every imagining, her heart full of bitterness, ever finding herself confronted by her ignorance, that barrier which separated her from Henri, and checked her in her efforts to know him. She knew nothing, she would never know anything. She pictured him, hissing out those burning words, and creating within her the one trouble which had, till now, broken in on the quiet happiness of her life. Whence had he sprung to lay her life desolate in this fashion? She suddenly thought that but six weeks before she had had no existence for him, and this thought was insufferable. Angels in heaven! to live no more for one another, to pass each other without recognition, perhaps never to meet again! In her despair she clasped her hands, and her eyes filled with tears.

Then Hélène gazed fixedly on the towers of Nôtre-Dame in the far distance. A ray of light from between two clouds tinged them with gold. Her brain was heavy, as though surcharged with all the tumultous thoughts, hurtling within it. It made her suffer; she would fain have concerned herself with the sight of Paris, and have sought to regain her life-peace by turning on that sea of roofs the tranquil glances of past days. To think that at other times, at the same hour, the infinitude of the city —in the stillness of a lovely twilight— had lulled her into tender musing!

At present Paris was brightening in the sunshine. After the first ray had fallen on Notre Dame, others had followed, streaming across the city. The luminary, dipping in the west, rent the clouds asunder, and the various districts spread out, motley with ever-changing lights and shadows. For a time the whole of the left bank was of a leaden hue, while the right was speckled with spots of light which made the verge of the river resemble the skin of some huge beast of prey. Then these resemblances varied and vanished at the mercy of the wind, which drove the clouds before it. Above the burnished gold of the housetops dark patches floated, all in the same direction and with the same gentle and silent motion. Some of them were very large, sailing along with all the majestic grace of an admiral's ship, and surrounded by smaller ones, preserving the regular order of a squadron in line of battle. Then one vast shadow, with a gap yawning like a serpent's mouth, trailed along, and for a while hid Paris, which it seemed ready to devour. And when it had reached the far-off horizon, looking no larger than a worm, a gush of light streamed from a rift in a cloud, and fell into the void which it had left. The golden cascade could be seen descending first like a thread of fine sand, then swelling into a huge cone, and raining in a continuous shower on the Champs-Elysées district, which it inundated with a splashing, dancing radiance. For a long time did this shower of sparks descend, spraying continuously like a fusee.

Ah, well! this love was her fate, and Hélène ceased to resist. She could battle no longer against her feelings. And in ceasing to struggle she tasted immeasurable delight. Why should she grudge herself happiness any longer?

The memory of her past life inspired her with disgust and aversion. How had she been able to drag on that cold, dreary existence, of which she was formerly so proud? A vision rose before her of herself as a young girl living in the Rue des Petites-Maries, at Marseilles, where she had ever shivered; she saw herself a wife, her heart's blood frozen in the companionship of a big child of a husband, with little to take any interest in, apart from the cares of her household; she saw herself through every hour of her life following the same path with the same even tread, without a trouble to mar her peace; and now this monotony in which she had lived, her heart fast asleep, enraged her beyond expression. To think that she had fancied herself happy in thus following her path for thirty years, her passions silent, with naught but the pride of virtue to fill the blank in her existence. How she had cheated herself with her integrity and nice honor, which had girt her round with the empty joys of piety! No, no; she had had enough of it; she wished to live! And an awful spirit of ridicule woke within her as she thought of the behests of reason. Her reason, forsooth! she felt a contemptuous pity for it; during all the years she had lived it had brought her no joy to be compared with that she had tasted during the past hour. She had denied the possibility of stumbling, she had been vain and idiotic enough to think that she would go on to the end without her foot once tripping against a stone. Ah, well! to-day she almost longed to fall. Oh! that she might disappear, after tasting for one

moment the happiness which she had never enjoyed!

Within her soul, however, a great sorrow lingered, a heart-burning and a consciousness of a gloomy blank. Then argument rose to her lips. Was she not free? In her love for Henri she deceived nobody; she could deal as she pleased with her love. Then, did not everything exculpate her? What had been her life for nearly two years? Her widowhood, her unrestricted liberty, her loneliness—everything, she realized, had softened and prepared her for love. Love must have been smouldering within her during the long evenings spent between her two old friends, the Abbé and his brother, those simple hearts whose serenity had lulled it to rest; it had been growing whilst she remained shut up within those narrow walls, far away from the world, and gazed on Paris rumbling noisily on the horizon; it had been growing even when she leaned from that window in the dreamy mood which she had scarce been conscious of, but which little by little had rendered her so weak. And a recollection came to her of that radiant spring morning when Paris had shown out fair and clear, as though in a glass mirror, when it had worn the pure, sunny hue of childhood, as she lazily surveyed it, stretched in her easy-chair with a book upon her knees. That morning love had first awoke—a scarcely perceptible feeling that she had been unable to define, and against which she had believed herself strongly armed. To-day she was in the same place, but devoured by overpowering passion, while before her eyes the dying sun illumined the city with flame. It seemed to her that one day had sufficed for all, that this was the ruddy evening following upon that limpid morning; and she imagined she could feel those fiery beams scorching her heart.

But a change had come over the sky. The sun, in its descent towards the slopes of Meudon, had just burst through the last clouds in all its splendor. The azure vault was illuminated with glory; deep on the horizon the crumbling ridge of chalk clouds, blotting out the distant suburbs of Charenton and Choisy-le-Roi, now reared rocks of a tender pink, outlined with brilliant crimson; the flotilla of cloudlets drifting slowly through the blue above Paris, was decked with purple silks; while the delicate network, seemingly fashioned of white silk thread, above Montmartre, was suddenly transformed into golden cord, whose meshes would snare the stars as soon as they would rise.

Beneath the flaming vault of heaven lay Paris, a mass of yellow, striped with huge shadows. On the vest square below Hèléne, in an orange-tinted haze, cabs and omnibuses crossed in all directions, amidst a crowd of pedestrians, whose swarming blackness was softened and irradiated by splashes of light. The students of a seminary were surrying in serried ranks along the Quai de Billy, and the trail of cassocks acquired an ochraceous hue in the diffuse of light. Farther away, vehicles and foot-passengers faded from view; it was only by their gleaming lamps that you were made aware of the vehicles which, one behind the other, were crossing some distant bridge. On the left the straight, lofty, pink chimneys of the Army Bakehouse were belching forth whirling clouds of flesh-tinted smoke; whilst, across the river, the beautiful elms of the Quai d'Orsay rose up in a dark mass transpierced by shafts of light.

The Seine, whose banks the oblique rays were enfilading, was rolling dancing wavelets, streaked with scattered splashes of blue, green, and yellow; but farther up the river, in lieu of this blotchy coloring, suggestive of an Eastern sea, the waters assumed a uniform golden hue, which became more and more dazzling. You might have thought that some ingot was pouring forth an invisible crucible on the horizon, broadening out with a coruscation of bright colors as it gradually grew colder. And at intervals over this brilliant stream, the bridges, with curves growing ever more slender and delicate, threw, as it were, grey bars, till there came at last a fiery jumble of houses, above which rose the towers of Notre Dame, flaring red like torches. Right and left alike the edifices were all aflame. The glass roof of the Palais de l'Industrie appeared like a bed of glowing embers amidst the Champs-Elysées groves. Farther on, behind the roof of the Madeline, the huge pile of the Opera House shone out like a mass of burnished copper; and the summits of other buildings, cupolas, and towers, the Vendôme column, the church of Saint-Vincent de Paul, the tower of Saint-Jacques, and, nearer in, the pavilions of the new Louvre and the Tuileries, were crowned by a blaze, which lent them the aspect of sacrificial pyres. The dome of the

Invalides was flaring with such brilliancy that you instinctively feared lest it should suddenly topple down and scatter burning flakes over the neighborhood. Beyond the irregular towers of Saint-Sulpice, the Panthéon stood out against the sky in dull splendor, like some royal palace of conflagration reduced to embers. Then, as the sun declined, the pyre-like edivices gradually set the whole of Paris on fire. Flashes sped over the housetops, while black smoke lingered in the valleys. Every frontage turned towards the Trocardèro seemed to be red-hot, the glass of the windows glittering and emitting a shower of sparks, which darted upwards as though some invisible bellows were ever urging the huge conflagration into greater activity. Sheaves of flame were also ever rising afresh from the adjacent districts, where the streets opened, now dark and now all ablaze. Even far over the plain, from a ruddy ember-like glow suffusing the destroyed faubourgs, occasional flashes of flame shot up as from some fire struggling again into life. Ere long a furnace seemed raging, all Paris burned, the heavens became yet more empurpled, and the clouds hung like so much blood over the vast city, colored red and gold.

With the ruddy tints falling upon her, yielding to the passion which was devouring her, Hélène was still gazing upon Paris all ablaze, when a little hand was placed on her shoulder, and she gave a start. It was Jeanne, calling her. "Mamma! mamma!"

She turned her head, and the child went on: "At last! Didn't you hear me before? I have called you at least a dozen times."

The little girl, still in her Japanese costume, had sparkling eyes, and cheeks flushed with pleasure. She gave her mother no time for answer.

"You ran away from me nicely! Do you know, they were hunting for you everywhere? Had it not been for Pauline, who came with me to the bottom of the staircase, I shouldn't have dared to cross the road."

With a pretty gesture, she brought her face close to her mother's lips, and, without pausing, whispered the question: "Do you love me?"

Hélène kissed her somewhat absently. She was amazed and impatient at her early return. Had an hour really gone by since she had fled from the ball-room? However, to satisfy the child, who seemed uneasy, she told her that she had felt rather unwell. The fresh air was doing her good; she only needed a little quietness.

"Oh! don't fear; I'm too tired," murmured Jeanne. "I am going to stop here, and be very, very good. But, mamma dear, I may talk, mayn't I?"

She nestled close to Hélène, full of joy at the prospect of not being undressed at once. She was in ecstasies over her embroidered purple gown and green silk petticoat; and she shook her head to rattle the pendants hanging from the long pins thrust through her hair. At last there burst from her lips a rush of hasty words. Despite her seeming demureness, she had seen everything, heard everything, and remembered everything; and she now made ample amends for her former assumed dignity, silence, and indifference.

"Do you know, mamma, it was an fellow with a grey beard who made Punch move his arms and legs? I saw him well enough when the curtain was drawn aside. Yes, and the little boy Guiraud began to cry. How stupid of him, wasn't it? They told him the policeman would come and put some water in his soup; and at last they had to carry him off, for he wouldn't stop crying. And at lunch, too, Marguerite stained her milkmaid's dress all over with jam. Her mamma wiped it off and said to her: 'Oh, you dirty girl!' She even had a lot of it in her hair. I never opened my mouth, but it did amuse me to see them all rush at the cakes! Were they not bad-mannered, mamma dear?"

She paused for a few seconds, absorbed in some reminiscence, and then asked, with a thoughtful air: "I say, mamma, did you eat any of those yellow cakes with white cream inside? Oh! they were nice! they were nice! I kept the dish beside me the whole time."

Hélène was not listening to this childish chatter. But Jeanne talked to relieve her excited brain. She launched out again, giving the minutest details about the ball, and investing each little incident with the greatest importance.

"You did not see that my waistband came undone just as we began dancing. A lady, whose name I don't know, pinned it up for me. So I said to her: 'Madame, I thank you very much.' But while I was dancing with Lucien the pin ran into him, and he asked me:

'What have you got in front of you that pricks me so?' Of course I knew nothing about it, and told him I had nothing there to prick him. However, Pauline came and put the pin in its proper place. Ah! but you've no idea how they pushed each other about; and one great stupid of a boy gave Sophie a blow on the back which made her fall. The Levasseur girls jumped about with their feet close together. I am pretty certain that isn't the way to dance. But the best of it all came at the end. You weren't there; so you can't know. We all took one another by the arms, and then whirled round; it was comical enough to make one die laughing. Besides, some of the big gentlemen were whirling around as well. It's true; I am not telling fibs. Why, don't you believe me, mamma dear?"

Hélène's continued silence was beginning to vex Jeanne. She nestled closer, and gave her mother's hand a shake. But, perceiving that she drew only a few words from her, she herself, by degrees, lapsed into silence, into thought of the incidents of that ball of which her heart was full. Both mother and daughter now sat mutely gazing on Paris all aflame. It seemed to them yet more mysterious than ever, as it lay there illumined by blood-red clouds, like some city of an old-world tale expiating its lusts under a rain of fire.

"Did you have any round dances?" all at once asked Hélène, as if awakening with a start.

"Yes, yes!" murmured Jeanne, engrossed in her turn.

"And the doctor—did he dance!"

"I should think so; he had a turn with me. He lifted me up and asked me. 'Where is your mamma? where is your mamma?' and then he kissed me."

Hélène unconsciously smiled. What need had she of knowing Henri well? It appeared sweeter to her not to know him—ay, never to know him well—and to greet him simply as the one whose coming she had awaited so long. Why should she feel astonished or disquieted? At the fated hour he had met her on her life-journey. Her frank nature accepted whatever might be in store; and quietude, born of the knowledge that she loved and was beloved, fell on her mind. She told her heart that she would prove strong enough to prevent her happiness from being marred.

But night was coming on and a chilly breeze arose. Jeanne, still plunged in reverie, began to shiver. She reclined her head on her mother's bosom, and, as though the question were inseperably connected with her meditation, she murmured a second time: "Do you love me?"

Then Hélène, her face still glad with smiles, took her head within her hands and for a moment examined her face closely. Next she pressed a long kiss near her mouth, over a ruddy spot on her skin. It was there, she could divine it, that Henri had kissed the child!

The gloomy ridge of the Meudon hills was already partially concealing the disc of the sun. Over Paris the slanting beams of light had yet lengthened. The shadow cast by the dome of the Invalides—increased to stupendous proportions—covered the whole of the Saint Germain district; while the Opera-House, the Saint-Jacques tower, the columns and the steeples, threw streaks of darkness over the right bank dwellings. The lines of house-fronts, the yawning streets, the islands of roofs, were burning with a more sullen glow. The flashes of fire died away in the darkening windows, as though the houses were reduced to embers. Distant bells rang out; a rumbling noise fell on the ears, and then subsided. With the approach of night the expanse of sky grew more vast, spreading a vault of violet, streaked with gold and purple, above the ruddy city. But all at once the conflagration flared afresh with formidable intensity, a last great flame shot up from Paris, illumining its entire expanse, and even its hitherto hidden suburbs. Then it seemed as if a grey, ashy dust were falling; and though the clustering district remained erect, they wore the gloomy, unsubstantial aspect of coals which had ceased to burn.

## CHAPTER XI

### CLOSER FRIENDSHIP

ONE morning in May, Rosalie ran in from the kitchen, dish-cloth in hand, screaming out in the familiar fashion of a favorite servant: "Oh, madame, come quick! His reverence the Abbé is digging the ground down in the doctor's garden."

Hélène made no responsive movement, but Jeanne had already rushed to have a look. On her return, she exclaimed:

"How stupid Rosalie is! he is no

digging at all. He is with the gardener, who is putting some plants into a barrow. Madame Deberle is plucking all her roses."

"'They must be for the church," quietly said Hélène, who was busy with some tapestry-work.

A few minutes later the bell rang, and Abbé Jouve made his appearance. He came to say that his presence must not be expected on the following Tuesday. His evenings would be wholly taken up with the ceremonies incident to the month of May. The parish priest had assigned him the task of decorating the church. It would be a great success. All the ladies were giving him flowers. He was expecting two palm-trees about fourteen feet high, and meant to place them to the right and left of the altar.

"Oh! mamma, mamma!" murmured Jeanne, listening wonderstruck.

"Well," said Hélène, with a smile, "since you cannot come to us, my old friend, we will go to see you. Why, you've quite turned Jeanne's head with your talk about flowers."

She had few religious tendencies; she never even went to mass, on the plea that her daughter's health suffered from the shivering fits which seized her when she came out of a church. In her presence the old priest avoided all reference to religion. It was his wont to say, with good-natured indulgence, that good hearts carve out their own salvation by deeds of loving kindness and charity. God would know when and how to touch her.

Till the evening of the following day Jeanne thought of nothing but the month of Mary. She plagued her mother with questions; she dreamt of the church adorned with a profusion of white roses, filled with thousands of wax tapers, with the sound of angels' voices, and sweet perfumes. And she was very anxious to go near the altar, that she might have a good look at the Blessed Virgin's lace gown, a gown worth a fortune, according to the Abbé. But Hélène bridled her excitement with a threat not to take her should she make herself ill beforehand.

However, the evening came at last, and they set out. The nights were still cold, and when they reached the Rue de l'Annonciation, where the church of Nôtre-Dame-de-Grâce stands, the child was shivering all over.

"The church is heated," said her mother. "We must secure a place near a hot-air pipe."

She pushed open the padded door, and as it gently swung back to its place they found themselves in a warm atmosphere, with brilliant lights streaming on them, and chanting resounding in their ears. The ceremony had commenced, and Hélène, perceiving that the nave was crowded, signified her intention of going down one of the aisles. But there seemed insuperable obstacles in her way; she could not get near the altar. Holding Jeanne by the hand, she for a time patiently pressed forward, but at last, despairing of advancing any farther, took the first unoccupied chairs she could find. A pillar hid half of the choir from view.

"I can see nothing," said the child, grievously discontented. "This is a very nasty place."

However, Hélène signed to her to keep silent, and she lapsed into a fit of sulks. In front of her she could only perceive the broad back of a fat old lady. When her mother next turned towards her she was standing upright on her chair.

"Will you come down!" said Hélène in a low voice. "You are a nuisance."

But Jeanne was stubborn.

"Hist! mamma," she said, "there's Madame Deberle. Look! she is down there in the centre, beckoning to us."

The young woman's annoyance on hearing this made her very impatient, and she shook her daughter, who still refused to sit down. During the three days that had intervened since the ball, Hélène had avoided any visit to the doctor's house on the plea of having a great deal to do.

"Mamma," resumed Jeanne with a child's wonted stubbornness, "she is looking at you; she is nodding good-day to you."

At this intimation Hélène was forced to turn round and exchange greetings; each bowed to the other. Madame Deberle, in a striped silk gown trimmed with white lace, sat in the centre of the nave but a short distance from the choir, looking very fresh and conspicuous. She had brought her sister Pauline, who was now busy waving her hand. The chanting still continued, the elder members of the congregation pouring forth a volume of sound of falling scale, while now and then the shrill voice of the children punctuated the slow, monotonous rhythm of the canticle.

"They want us to go over to them, you see," exclaimed Jeanne, with some triumph in her remark.

"It is useless; we shall be all right here."

"Oh, mamma, do let us go over to them! There are two chairs empty."

"No, no; come and sit down."

However, the ladies smilingly persisted in making signs, heedless to the last degree of the slight scandal they were causing; nay, delighted at being the observed of all observers. Hélène thus had to yield. She pushed the gratified Jeanne before her, and strove to make her way through the congregation, her hands all the while trembling with repressed anger. It was no easy business. Devout female worshippers, unwilling to disturb themselves, glared at her with furious looks, whilst all agape they kept on singing. She pressed on in this style for five long minutes, the tempest of voices ringing around her with ever-increasing violence. Whenever she came to a stand-still, Jeanne, squeezing close beside her, gazed at those cavernous, gaping mouths. However, at last they reached the vacant space in front of the choir, and then had but a few steps to make.

"Come, be quick," whispered Madame Deberle. "The Abbé told me you would be coming, and I kept two chairs for you."

Hélène thanked her, and, to cut the conversation short, at once began turning over the leaves of her missal. But Juliette was as worldly here as elsewhere; as much at her ease, as agreeable and talkative, as in her drawing-room. She bent her head towards Hélène and resumed:

"You have become quite invisible. I intended to pay you a visit to-mor-

row. Surely you haven't been ill, have
you?"

"No, thank you. I've been very
busy."

"Well, listen to me. You must come
and dine with us to-morrow. Quite a
family dinner, you know."

"You are very kind. We will see."

She seemed to retire within herself,
intent on following the service, and on
saying nothing more. Pauline had taken
Jeanne beside her that she might be
nearer the hot-air flue over which she
toasted herself luxuriously, as happy as
any chilly mortal could be. Steeped in
the warm air, the two girls raised themselves inquisitively and gazed around
on everything, the low ceiling with its
woodwork panels, the squat pillars, connected by arches from which hung chandeliers, and the pulpit of carved oak;
and over the ocean of heads which
waved with the rise and fall of the
canticle, their eyes wandered towards
the dark corners of the aisles, towards
the chapels whose gilding faintly gleamed, and the baptistery enclosed by a
railing near the chief entrance. However, their gaze always returned to the
resplendent choir, decorated with brilliant colors and dazzling gilding. A
crystal chandelier, flaming with light,
hung from the vaulted ceiling; immense
candelabra, filled with rows of wax tapers, that glittered amidst the gloom of
the church like a profusion of stars in
orderly array, brought out prominently
the high altar, which seemed one huge
bouquet of foliage and flowers. Over
all, standing amidst a profusion of roses,
a Virgin, dressed in satin and lace, and

crowned with pearls, was holding a
Jesus in long clothes on her arm.

"I say, are you warm?" asked Pauline.
"It's nice, eh?"

But Jeanne, in ecstasy, was gazing on
the Virgin amongst the flowers. The
scene thrilled her. A fear crept over
her that she might do something wrong,
and she lowered her eyes in the endeavor to restrain her tears by fixing
her attention on the black-and-white
pavement. The vibrations of the choir-
boys' shrill voices seemed to stir her
tresses like puffs of air.

Meanwhile, Hélène, with face bent
over her prayer-book, drew herself away
whenever Juliette's lace rustled against
her. She was in no wise prepared for
this meeting. Despite the vow she
had sworn within herself, to be ever
pure in her love for Henri, and never
yield to him, she felt great discomfort
at the thought that she was a traitor-
ess to the confiding, happy woman who
sat by her side. She was possessed by
one idea—she would not go to that
dinner. She sought for reasons which
would enable her to break off these
relations so hateful to her honor. But
the swelling voices of the choristers,
so near to her, drove all reflection from
her mind; she could decide on no precise
course, and surrendered herself to the
soothing influences of the chant, tasting
a pious joy such as she had never before found inside a church.

"Have you been told about Madame
de Cherrmette?" asked Juliette, unable
any longer to restrain her craving for
a gossip.

"No, I know nothing."

"Well, well; just imagine. You have

seen her daughter, so womanish and tall, though she is only fifteen, haven't you? There is some talk about her getting married next year to that dark young fellow who is always hanging to her mother's skirts. People are talking about it with a vengeance."

"Ah!" muttered Hélène, who was not paying the least attention.

Madame Deberle went into particulars, but of a sudden the chant ceased, and the organ-music died away in a moan. Astounded at the loudness of her own voice breaking upon the stillness which ensued, she lapsed into silence. A priest made his appearance at this moment in the pulpit. There was a rustling, and then he spoke. No, certainly not, Hélène would not join that dinner-party. With her eyes fixed on the priest she pictured to herself the next meeting with Henri, that meeting which for three days she had contemplated with terror; she saw him white with anger, reproaching her for hiding herself, and she dreaded lest she might not display sufficient indifference. Amidst her dream the priest had disappeared, his thrilling tones merely reaching her in casual sentences: "No hour could be more ineffable than that when the Virgin, with bent head, answered: 'I am the handmaiden of the Lord!'"

Yes, she would be brave; all her reason had returned to her. She would taste the joy of being loved, but would never avow her love, for her heart told her that such an avowal would cost her peace. And how intensely would she love, without confessing it, gratified by a word, a look from Henri, exchanged at lengthy intervals on the occasion of a chance meeting! It was a dream that brought her some sense of the infinite. The church around her became a friend and comforter. The priest was now exclaiming:

"The angel vanished and Mary plunged into contemplation of the divine mystery working within her, her heart bathed in sunshine and love.

"He speaks very well," whispered Madame Deberle, leaning towards her. "And he's quite young, too, scarcely thirty, don't you think?"

Madame Deberle was effected. Religion pleased her because the emotions it prompted were in good taste. To present flowers for the decoration of churches, to have petty dealings with the priests, who were so polite and discreet, to come to church attired in her best and assume an air of worldly patronage towards the God of the poor —all this had for her special delights; the more so as her husband did not interest himself in religion, and her devotions thus had all the sweetness of forbidden fruit. Hélène looked at her and answered with a nod; her face was ashy white with faintness, while the other's was lit up by smiles. There was a stirring of chairs and a rustling of handkerchiefs, as the priest quitted the pulpit with the final adjuration:

"Oh! give wings unto your love, souls imbued with Christian piety. God has made a sacrifice of Himself for your sakes, your hearts are full of His presence, your souls overflow with His grace!"

Of a sudden the organ sounded again, and the litanies of the Virgin began with their appeals of passionate tenderness. Faint and distant the chanting rolled forth from the side-aisles and the dark recesses of the chapels, as though the earth were giving answer to the angel voices of the chorister-boys. A rush of air swept over the throng, making the flames of the tapers leap, while amongst the flowers, fading as they exhaled their last perfume, the Divine Mother seemed to incline her head to smile on her infant Jesus.

All at once, seized with an instinctive dread, Hélène turned. "You're not ill, Jeanne, are you?" she asked.

The child, with face ashy white and eyes glistening, her spirit borne aloft by the fervent strains of the litanies, was gazing at the altar, where in imagination she could see the roses multiplying and falling in cascades.

"No, no, mamma," she whispered; "I am pleased, I am very well pleased." And then she asked: "But where is our dear old friend?"

She spoke of the Abbé. Pauline caught sight of him; he was seated in the choir, but Jeanne had to be lifted up in order that she might perceive him.

"Oh! He is looking at us," said she; "he is blinking."

According to Jeanne, the Abbé blinked when he laughed inwardly. Hélène hastened to exchange a friendly nod with him. And then the tranquility within her seemed to increase, her future serenity appeared to be assured, thus endearing the church to her and lulling her into a blissful condition of patient endurance. Censers swung before the altar and threads of smoke ascended; the benediction followed, and

the holy monstrance was slowly raised and waved above the heads lowered to the earth. Hélène was still on her knees in happy meditation when she heard Madame Deberle exclaiming: "It's over now; let us go."

There ensued a clatter of chairs and a stamping of feet which reverberated along the arched aisles. Pauline had taken Jeanne's hand, and, walking away in front with the child, began to question her:

"Have you ever been to the theatre?"

"No. Is it finer than this?"

As she spoke, the little one, giving vent to great gasps of wonder, tossed her head as though ready to express the belief that nothing could be finer. To her question, however, Pauline deigned no reply, for she had just come to a standstill in front of a priest who was passing in his surplice. And when he was a few steps away she exclaimed aloud, with such conviction in her tones that two devout ladies of the congregation turned about:

"Oh! what a fine head!"

Héléne, meanwhile, had risen from her knees. She stepped along by the side of Juliette among the crowd which was making its way out with difficulty. Her heart was full of tenderness, she felt languid and enervated, and her soul no longer rebelled at the other being so near. At one moment their bare hands came in contact and they smiled. They were almost stifling in the throng, and Hélène would fain have had Juliette go first. All their old friendship seemed to blossom forth once more.

"Is it understood that we can rely

on you for to-morrow evening?" asked Mademe Deberle.

Hélène no longer had the will to decline. She would see whether it were possible when she reached the street. It finished by their being the last to leave. Pauline and Jeanne already stood on the opposite pavement awaiting them. But a tearful voice brought them to a halt.

"Ah, my good lady, what a time it is since I had the happiness to see you!"

It was Mother Fétu, who was soliciting alms at the church door. Barring Hélène's way, as though she had lain in wait for her, she went on:

"Oh, I have been so very ill always here, in the stomach, you know. Just now I feel as if a hammer were pounding away inside me; and I have nothing at all, my good lady. I didn't dare to send you word about it—May the gracious God repay you!"

Hélène had slipped a piece of money into her hand, and promised to think about her.

"Hello!" exclaimed Madame Deberle, who had remained standing within the porch, "there's someone talking with Pauline and Jeanne. Why, it is Henri."

"Yes, yes," Mother Fétu hastened to add as she turned her ferret-like eyes on the ladies, "it is the good doctor I have seen him there all through the service; he has never budged from the pavement; he has been waiting for you, no doubt. Ah! he's a saint of a man! I swear that to be the truth in the face of God who hears us. Yes, I know you, madame; he is a husband who deserves to be happy. May Heaven hearken to your prayers, may every

blessing fall on you! In the name of the Father, the Son, and the Holy Ghost!"

Amidst the myriad furrows of her face, which was wrinkled like a withered apple, her little eyes kept gleaming in malicious unrest, darting a glance now on Juliette, now on Hélène, so that it was impossible to say with any certainty whom she was addressing while speaking of "the good doctor." She followed them, muttering on without a stop, mingling whimpering entreaty with devout outbursts.

Henri's reserve alike astonished and moved Hélène. He scarcely had the courage to raise his eyes towards her. On his wife quizzing him about the opinions which restrained him from entering a church, he merely explained that to smoke a cigar was his object in coming to meet them; but Hélène understood that he had wished to see her again, to prove to her how wrong she was in fearing some fresh outrage. Doubtless, like herself, he had sworn to keep within the limits of reason. She never questioned whether his sincerity could be real. She simply experienced a feeling of unhappiness at seeing him unhappy. Thus it came about, that on leaving them in the Rue Vineuse, she said cheerfully:

"Well, it is settled then; to-morrow at seven."

In this way the old friendship grew closer than ever, and a charming life began afresh. To Hélène it seemed as if Henri had never yielded to that moment of folly; it was but a dream of hers; each loved the other, but they would never breathe a word of their love, they were content with knowing its existence. They spent delicious hours, in which, without their tongues giving evidence of their passion, they displayed it constantly; a gesture, an inflexion of the voice sufficed, ay, even a silence. Everything insensibly tended towards their love, plunged them more and more deeply into a passion which they bore away with them whenever they parted, which was ever with them, which formed, as it were, the only atmosphere they could breathe. And their excuse was their honesty; with eyes wide open they played this comedy of affection; not even a hand-clasp did they allow each other and their restraint infused unalloyed delight into the simple greetings with which they met.

Every evening the ladies went to church. Madame Deberle was enchanted with the novel pleasure she was enjoying. It was so different from evening dances, concerts, and first nights; she adored fresh sensations, and nuns and priests were now constantly in her company. The store of religion which she had acquired in her schooldays now found new life in her giddy brain, taking shape in all sorts trivial observances, as though she were reviving the games of her childhood. Hélène, who on her side had grown up without any religious training, surrendered herself to the bliss of these services of the month of Mary, happy also in the delight with which they appeared to inspire Jeanne. They now dined earlier; they gave Rosalie no peace lest she should cause them to be late, and prevent their securing good seats. Then they called for Juliette on the way. One day Lucien was taken, but he be-

haved so badly that he was afterward left at home. On entering the warm church, with its glare of wax candles, a feeling of tenderness and calm, which by degrees grew necessary to Hélène, came over her. When doubts sprang up within her during the day, and the thought of Henri filled her with indefinable anxiety, with the evening the church once more brought her peace. The chants arose overflowing with divine passion; the flowers, newly culled, made the close atmosphere of the building still heavier. It was here that she breathed all the first rapture of springtide, amidst that adoration of woman raised to the status of a cult; and her senses swam as she contemplated the mystery of love and purity—Mary, virgin and mother, beaming beneath her wreath of white roses. Each day she remained longer on her knees. She found herself at times with hands joined in entreaty. When the ceremony came to an end, there followed the happiness of the return home. Henri awaited their appearance at the door; the evenings grew warmer, and they wended their way through the dark, still streets of Passy, while scarce a word passed between them.

"How devout you are getting, my dear!" said Madame Deberle, one night, with a laugh.

Yes, it was true; Hélène was widely opening the portals of her heart to pious thoughts. Never could she have fancied that such happiness would attend her love. She returned to the church as to a spot where her heart would melt, for under its roof she could give free vent to her tears, remain thoughtless, plunged in speechless worship. For an

hour each evening she put no restraint
on herself. The bursting love within
her, prisoned throughout the day, at
length escaped from her bosom on the
wings of prayer, amidst the pious
quiver of the throng. The muttered
supplications, the bendings of the knee,
the reverences—words, gestures seemingly interminable—all lulled her to
rest; to her they ever expressed the
same thing; it was always the same
passion speaking in the same phrase, or
the same gesture. She felt a need of
faith, and basked enraptured by the
Divine goodness.

Hélène was not the only person whom
Juliette twitted; she feigned a belief
that Henri himself was becoming religious. What, had he not now entered
the church to wait for them?—he,
atheist and scoffer, who had been wont
to assert that he sought for the soul
with his scalpel, and had not yet discovered its existence! As soon as she
perceived him standing behind a pillar in the shadow of the pulpit, she
would instantly jog Hélène's arm.

"Look, look, he is there already!
Do you know, he wouldn't confess when
we got married! See how funny he
looks; he gazes at us with so comical
an expression; quick, look!"

Hélène did not at the moment raise
her head. The service was coming to
an end, clouds of incense were rising,
and the organ-music pealed forth joyfully. But her neighbor was not a
woman to leave her alone, and she was
forced to speak in answer.

"Yes, yes, I see him," she whispered,
albeit she never turned her eyes.

She had on her own side divined his
presence amidst the song of praise that
mounted from the worshipping throng.
It seemed to her that Henri's breath
was wafted on the wings of the music
and beat against her neck, and she imagined she could see behind her his
glances shedding their light along the
nave and haloing her, as she knelt,
with a golden glory. And then she felt
impelled to pray with such fervor that
words failed her. The expression on
his face was sober, as unruffled as any
husband might wear when looking for
ladies in a church, the same, indeed as
if he had been waiting for them in the
lobby of a theatre. But when they
came together, in the midst of the
slowly-moving crowd of worshippers,
they felt that the bonds of their love
had been drawn closer by the flowers
and the chanting; and they shunned all
conversation, for their hearts were on
their lips.

A fortnight slipped away, and Madame Deberle grew wearied. She ever
jumped from one thing to the other,
consumed with the thirst of doing what
every one else was doing. For the
moment charity bazaars had become
her craze; she would toil up sixty
flights of stairs of an afternoon to beg
paintings of well-known artists, while
her evenings were spent in presiding
over meetings of lady patronesses, with
a bell handy to call noisy members to
order. Thus it happened that one
Thursday evening Hélène and her
daughter went to church without their
companions. On the conclusion of the
sermon, while choristers were commencing the *Magnificat*, the young woman,
forewarned by some impulse of her
heart, turned her head. Henri was
there, in his usual place. Thereupon

she remained with looks riveted to the ground till the service came to an end, waiting the while for the return home.

"Oh, how kind of you to come!" said Jeanne, with all a child's frankness, as they left the church. "I should have been afraid to go alone through these dark streets."

Henri, however, feigned astonishment, asserting that he had expected to meet his wife. Héléne allowed the child to answer him, and followed them without uttering a word. As the trio passed under the porch a pitiful voice sang out: "Charity, charity! May God repay you!"

Every night Jeanne dropped a ten-sou piece into Mother Fétu's hand. When the latter saw the doctor alone with Hélène, she nodded her head knowingly, instead of breaking out into a storm of thanks, as was her custom. The church was now empty, and she began to follow them, mumbling inaudible sentences. Sometimes, instead of returning by the Rue de Passy, the ladies, when the night was fine, went homewards by the Rue Raynouard, the way being thus lengthened by five or six minutes' walk. That night also Hélène turned into the Rue Raynouard, craving for gloom and stillness, and entranced by the loneliness of the long thoroughfare, which was lighted by only a few gas-lamps, without the shadow of a single passer-by falling across its pavement.

At this hour Passy seemed out of the world; sleep had already fallen over it; it had all the quietude of a provincial town. On each side of the street loomed mansions, girls' schools, black and silent, and dining places, from the kitchens of which lights still streamed. There was not however, a single shop to throw the glare of its frontage across the dimness. To Henri and Hélène the loneliness was pregnant with intense charm. He had not ventured to offer her his arm. Jeanne walked between them in the middle of the road, which was gravelled like a walk in some park. At last the houses came to an end, and then on each side were walls, over which spread mantling clematis and clusters of lilac blossoms. Immense gardens parted the mansions, and here and there through the railings of an iron gate they could catch the glimpses of a gloomy background of verdure, against which the tree-dotted turf assumed a more delicate hue. The air was filled with the perfume of irises growing in vases which they could scarce distinguish. All three paced on slowly through the warm spring night, which was steeping them in its odors, and Jeanne, with childish artlessness, raised her face to the heavens, and exclaimed:

"Oh, mamma, see what a number of stars!"

But behind them, like an echo of their own, came the footfall of Mother Fétu. Nearer and nearer she approached, till they could hear her muttering the opening words of the Angelic Salutation "Ave Marie, gratia plena" repeating them over and over again with the same confused persistency. She was telling her beads on her homeward way.

"I have still something left—may I give it to her?" Jeanne asked her mother.

And thereupon, without waiting for

a reply, she left them, running towards the old woman, who was on the point of entering the Passage des Eaux. Mother Fétu clutched at the coin, calling upon all the angels of Heaven to bless her. As she spoke, however, she grasped the child's hand and detained her by her side, then asking in changed tones:

"The other lady is ill, is she not?"

"No," answered Jeanne surprised.

"May Heaven shield her! May it shower its favors on her and her husband! Don't run away yet, my dear little lady. Let me say an *Ave Marie* for your mother's sake and you will join in the 'Amen' with me. Oh! your mother will allow you; you can catch her up."

Meanwhile Henri and H é l è n e trembled as they found themselves left alone in the shadow cast by a line of huge chestnut trees that bordered the road. They quietly took a few steps. The chestnut trees had strewn the ground with their bloom, and they were walking upon this rosy-tinted carpet. On a sudden, however, they came to a stop, their hearts filled with such emotion that they could go no farther.

"Forgive me," said Henri simply.

"Yes, yes," ejaculated Hélène. "But oh! be silent, I pray you."

She had felt his hand touch her own, Jeanne ran towards them at the moment.

"Mamma, mamma!" she cried; "she made me say an *Ave;* she says it will bring you good luck."

The three then turned into the Rue Vineuse, while Mother Fétu crept down the steps of the Passage des Eaux, busy completing her rosary.

The month slipped away. Two or three more services were attended by Madame Deberle. One Sunday, the last one, Henri once more ventured to wait for Hélène and Jeanne. The walk home thrilled them with joy. The month had been one long spell of wondrous bliss. The little church seemed to have entered into their lives to soothe their love and render its way pleasant. At first a great peace had settled on Hélène's soul; she had found happiness in this sanctuary where she imagined she could without shame dwell on her love; however, the undermining had continued, and when her holy rapture passed away she was again in the grip of her passion, held by bonds that would have plucked at her heartstrings had she sought to break them asunder. Henri still preserved his respectful demeanor, but she could not do otherwise than see the passion burning in his face. She dreaded some outburst, and even grew afraid of herself.

One afternoon, going homewards after a walk with Jeanne, she passed along the Rue de l'Annonciation and entered the church. The child was complaining of feeling very tired. Until the last day she had been unwilling to admit that the evening services exhausted her, so intense was the pleasure she derived from them; but her cheeks had grown waxy-pale, and the doctor advised that she should take long walks.

"Sit down here," said her mother. "It will rest you; we'll only stay ten minutes."

She herself walked towards some chairs a short way off, and knelt down. She had placed Jeanne close to a pillar. Workmen were busy at the other end of the nave, taking down the hangings and removing the flowers, the ceremonials attending the month of Mary having come to an end the evening before. With her face buried in her hands Hélène saw nothing and heard nothing; she was eagerly catechising her heart, asking whether she ought not to confess to Abbé Jouve what an awful life had come upon her. He would advise her, perhaps restore her lost peace. Still, within her there arose, out of her very anguish, a fierce flood of joy. She hugged her sorrow, dreading lest the priest might succeed in finding a cure for it. Ten minutes slipped away, then an hour. She was overwhelmed by the strife raging within her heart.

At last she raised her head, her eyes glistening with tears, and saw Abbé Jouve gazing at her sorrowfully. It was he who was directing the workmen. Having recognized Jeanne, he had just come forward.

"Why, what is the matter, my child?" he asked of Hélène, who hastened to rise to her feet and wipe away her tears.

She was at a loss what answer to give; she was afraid lest she should once more fall on her knees and burst into sobs. He approached still nearer, and gently resumed:

"I do not wish to cross-question you, but why do you not confide in me? Confide in the priest and forget the friend."

"Some other day," she said brokenly, "some other day, I promise you."

Jeanne meantime had at first been very good and patient, finding amusement in looking at the stained-glass windows, the statues over the great doorway, and the scenes of the journey to the Cross depicted in miniature bas-reliefs along the aisles. By degrees, however, the cold air of the church had enveloped her as with a shroud; and she remained plunged in a weariness that even banished thought, a feeling of discomfort waking within her with the holy quiet and far-reaching echoes, which the least sound stirred in this sanctuary where she imagined she was going to die. But a grievous sorrow rankled in her heart—the flowers were being borne away. The great clusters of roses were vanishing, and the altar seemed to become more and more bare and chill. The marble looked icy-cold now that no wax-candle shone on it and there was no smoking incense. The lace-robed Virgin moreover was being moved, and after suddenly tottering fell backward into the arms of two workmen. At the sight Jeanne uttered a faint cry, stretched out her arms, and fell back rigid; the illness that had been threatening her for some days had at last fallen upon her.

And when Hélène, in distraction, carried her child, with the assistance of the sorrowing Abbé, into a cab, she turned towards the porch with outstretched, trembling hands.

"It's all this church! it's all this church!" she exclaimed, with a vehemence instinct with regret and self-reproach as she thought of the month of devout delight which she herself had tasted there.

## CHAPTER XII

### THE ATTACK

WHEN evening came Jeanne was somewhat better. She was able to get up, and, in order to remove her mother's fears, persisted in dragging herself into the dining-room, where she took her seat before her empty plate. "I shall be all right," she said, trying to smile. "You know very well that the least thing upsets me. Get on with your dinner, mamma; I want you to eat."

And in the end she pretended an appetite she did not feel, for she observed that her mother sat watching her paling and trembling, without being able to swallow a morsel. She promised to take some jam, and Hélène then hurried through her dinner, while the child, with a never fading smile and her head nodding tremblingly, watched her with worshipping looks. On the appearance of the dessert she made an effort to carry out her promise, but tears welled into her eyes.

"You see I can't get it down my throat," she murmured. "You mustn't be angry with me."

The weariness that overwhelmed her was terrible. Her legs seemed lifeless, her shoulders pained her as though gripped by a hand of iron. But she was very brave through it all, and choked at their source the moans which the shooting pains in her neck awakened. At one moment, however, she forgot herself, her head felt too heavy, and she was bent double by pain. Her mother, as she gazed on her, so faint and feeble, was wholly unable to finish

the pear which she was trying to force down her throat. Her sobs choked her, and throwing down her napkin, she clasped Jeanne in her arms.

"My child! my child!" she wailed, her heart bursting with sorrow, as her eyes ranged round the dining-room where her darling, when in good health, had so often enlivened her by her fondness for tid-bits.

At last Jeanne woke to life again, and strove to smile as of old.

"Don't worry, mamma," said she; "I shall be all right soon. Now that you have done you must put me to bed. I only wanted to see you have your dinner. Oh! I know you; you wouldn't have eaten as much as a morsel of bread."

Hélène bore her away in her arms. She had brought the little crib close to her own bed in the blue room. When Jeanne had stretched out her limbs, and the bedclothes were tucked up under her chin, she declared she felt much better. There were no more complaints about dull pains at the back of her head; but she melted into tenderness, and her passionate love seemed to grow more pronounced. Hélène was forced to caress her, to avow intense affection for her, and to promise that she would again kiss her when she came to bed.

"Never mind if I'm sleeping," said Jeanne. "I shall know you're there all the same."

She closed her eyes and fell into a doze. Hélène remained near her, watching over her slumber. When Rosalie entered on tip-toe to ask permission to go to bed, she answered "Yes" with a nod. At last eleven o'clock struck, and Hélène was still watching there, when she imagined she heard a gentle tapping at the outer door. Bewildered with astonishment, she took up the lamp and left the room to make sure.

"Who is there?"

"'Tis I; open the door," replied a voice in stifled tones.

It was Henri's voice. She quickly opened the door, thinking his coming only natural. No doubt he had but now been informed of Jeanne's illness, and had hastened to her, although she had not summoned him to her assistance, feeling a certain shame at the thought of allowing him to share in attending on her daughter.

However, he gave her no opportunity to speak. He followed her into the dining-room, trembling, with inflamed visage.

"I beseech you, pardon me," he faltered, as he caught hold of her hand. "I haven't seen you for three days past, and I cannot resist the craving to see you."

Hélène withdrew her hand. He stepped back, but, with his gaze still fixed on her, continued: "Don't be afraid; I love you. I would have waited at the door had you not opened it. Oh! I know very well it is simple madness, but I love you, I love you all the same!"

Her face was grave as she listened, eloquent with a dumb reproach which tortured him, and impelled him to pour forth his passionate love.

But Hélène still remained standing, wholly unmoved. At last she spoke. "You know nothing, then?" asked she.

He had taken her hand, and was raising it to his lips, when she started back with a gesture of impatience.

"Oh! leave me!" she exclaimed. "You see that I am not even listening to you. I have something far different to think about!"

Then becoming more composed, she put her question to him a second time. "You know nothing? Well, my daughter is ill. I am pleased to see you; you will dispel my fears."

She took up the lamp and walked on before him, but as they were passing through the doorway, she turned, and looking at him, said firmly:

"I forbid you beginning again here. Oh! you must not!"

He entered behind her, scarcely understanding what had been enjoined on him. His temples throbbed convulsively, as he leaned over the child's little crib.

"She is asleep; look at her," said Hélène in a whisper.

He did not hear her; his passion would not be silenced. She was hanging over the bed in front of him, and he could see her rosy neck, with its wavy hair. He shut his eyes that he might escape the temptation of kissing her, as she said to him:

"Doctor, look at her, she is so feverish. Oh, tell me whether it is serious!"

Then, yielding to professional habit, despite the tempest raging in his brain, he mechanically felt Jeanne's pulse. Nevertheless, so fierce was the struggle that he remained for a time motionless, seemingly unaware that he held this wasted little hand in his own.

"Is it a violent fever?" asked Hélène.

"A violent fever! Do you think so?" he repeated.

The little hand was scorching his own. There came another silence; the physician was awakening within him, and passion was dying from his eyes. His face slowly grew paler; he bent down uneasily, and examined Jeanne.

"You are right; this is a very severe attack," he exclaimed. "My God! the poor child!"

His passion was now dead; he was solely consumed by a desire to be of service to her. His coolness at once returned; he sat down, and was questioning the mother respecting the child's condition previous to this attack of illness, when Jeanne awoke, moaning loudly. She again complained of a terrible pain in the head. The pangs which were darting through her neck and shoulders had attained such intensity that her every movement wrung a sob from her. Hélène knelt on the other side of the bed, encouraging her, and smiling on her, though her heart almost broke at the sight of such agony.

"There's some one there, isn't there, mamma?" Jeanne asked, as she turned round and caught sight of the doctor.

"It is a friend, whom you know." The child looked at him for a time with thoughtful eyes, as if in doubt; but soon a wave of affection passed over her face. "Yes, yes, I know him; I love him very much." And with her coaxing air she added: "You will have to cure me, won't you, sir, to make mamma happy? Oh, I'll be good; I'll drink everything you give me."

The doctor again felt her pulse, while Hélène grasped her other hand; and, as she lay there between them, her eyes travelled attentively from one to the other, as though no such advantageous opportunity of seeing and comparing them had ever occurred before. Then

her head shook with a nervous trembling; she grew agitated; and her tiny hands caught hold of her mother and the doctor with a convulsive grip.

"Do not go away; I'm so afraid. Take care of me; don't let all the others come near me. I only want you, only you two, near me. Come closer up to me, together!" she stammered.

Drawing them nearer, with a violent effort she brought them close to her, still uttering the same entreaty: "Come close, together, together!"

Several times did she behave in the same delirious fashion. Then came intervals of quiet, when a heavy sleep fell on her, but it left her breathless and almost dead. When she started out of these short dozes she heard nothing, saw nothing—a white vapor shrouded her eyes. The doctor remained watching over her for a part of the night, which proved a very bad one. He only absented himself for a moment to procure some medicine. Towards morning, when he was about to leave, Hélène, with terrible anxiety in her face accompanied him into the ante-room.

"Well?" asked she.

"Her condition is very serious," he answered; "but you must not fear; rely on me; I will give you every assistance. I shall come back at ten o'clock."

When Hélène returned to the bedroom she found Jeanne sitting up in bed, gazing round her with bewildered looks.

"You left me! you left me!" she wailed. "Oh! I'm afraid; I don't want to be left all alone."

To console her, her mother kissed her, but she still gazed round the room:

"Where is he?" she faltered. "Oh!

tell him not to go away; I want him to
be here, I want him—"

"He will come back, my darling!"
interrupted Hélène, whose tears were
mingling with Jeanne's own. "He will
not leave us, I promise you. He loves
us too well. Now, be good and lie
down. I'll stay here till he comes back."

"Really? really?" mumured the child,
as she slowly fell back into deep slumber.

Terrible days now began, three weeks
full of awful agony. The fever did not
quit its victim for an hour. Jeanne only
seemed tranquil when the doctor was
present; she put one of her little hands
in his, while her mother held the other.
She seemed to find safety in their presence; she gave each of them an equal
share of her tyrannical worship, as
though she well knew beneath what passionate kindness she was sheltering herself. Her nervous temperament, so exquisite in its sensibility, the keener since
her illness, inspired her, no doubt, with
the thought that only a miraculous effort of their love could save her. As
the hours slipped away she would gaze
on them with grave and searching looks
as they sat on each side of her crib.
Her glances remained instinct with
human passion, and though she spoke
not she told them all she desired by
the warm pressure of her hands, with
which she besought them not to leave
her, giving them to understand what
peace was hers when they were present.
Whenever the doctor entered after having been away her joy became supreme,
and her eyes, which never quitted the
door, flashed with light; and then she
would fall quietly asleep, all her fears
fleeing as she heard her mother and him

moving around her and speaking in
whispers.

On the day after the attack Doctor
Bodin called. But Jeanne suddenly
turned away her head and refused to
allow him to examine her.

"I don't want him, mamma," she
murmured, "I don't want him! I beg
of you."

As he made his appearance on the following day, Hélène was forced to inform
him of the child's dislike, and thus it
came about that the venerable doctor
made no further effort to enter the sick-
room. Still he climbed the stairs every
other day to inquire how Jeanne was
getting on, and sometimes chatted with
his brother professional, Doctor Deberle, who paid him all the deference
due to an elder.

Moreover, it was useless to try to
deceive Jeanne. Her sense had become
wondrously acute. The Abbé and Monsieur Rambaud paid a visit every night;
they sat down and spent an hour in sad
silence. One evening, as the doctor was
going away, Hélène signed to Monsieur
Rambaud to take his place and clasp
the little one's hand, so that she might
not notice the departure of her beloved
friend. But two or three minutes had
scarcely passed ere Jeanne opened her
eyes and quickly drew her hand away.
With tears flowing she declared that
they were behaving ill to her.

"Don't you love me any longer?
won't you have me beside you?" asked
poor Monsieur Rambaud, with tears in
his eyes.

She looked at him, deigning no reply;
it seemed as if her heart was set on
knowing him no more. The worthy
man, grievously pained, returned to his

corner. He always ended by thus gliding into a window-recess, where, half hidden behind a curtain, he would remain during the evening, in a stupor of grief, his eyes the while never quitting the sufferer. The Abbé was there as well, with his large head and pallid face showing above his scraggy shoulders. He concealed his tears by blowing his nose loudly from time to time. The danger in which he saw his little friend lying wrought such havoc within him that his poor were for the time wholly forgotten.

But it was useless for the two brothers to retire to the other end of the room; Jeanne was still conscious of their presence. They were a source of vexation to her, and she would turn round with a harassed look, even though drowsy with fever. Her mother bent over her to catch the words trembling on her lips.

"Oh! mamma, I feel so ill. All this is choking me; send everybody away—quick, quick!"

Hélène with the utmost gentleness then explained to the two brothers the child's wish to fall asleep; they understood her meaning, and quitted the room with drooping heads. And no sooner had they gone than Jeanne breathed with greater freedom, cast a glance round the chamber, and once more fixed a look of infinite tenderness on her mother and the doctor.

"Good-night," she whispered; "I feel well again; stay beside me."

For three weeks she thus kept them by her side. Henri had at first paid two visits each day, but soon he spent the whole night with them, giving every hour he could spare to the child. At the outset he had feared it was a case of typhoid fever; but so contradictory were the symptoms that he soon felt himself involved in perplexity. There was no doubt he was confronted by a disease of the chlorosis type, presenting the greatest difficulty in treatment, with the possibility of very dangerous complications, as the child was almost on the threshold of womanhood. He dreaded first a lesion of the heart and then the setting in of consumption. Jeanne's nervous excitement, wholly beyond his control, was a special source of uneasiness; to such heights of delirium did the fever rise, that the strongest medicines were of no avail. He brought all his fortitude and knowledge to bear on the case, inspired with the one thought that his own happiness and life were at stake. On his mind there had now fallen a great stillness; not once during those three anxious weeks did his passion break its bonds. Hélène's breath no longer woke tremors within him, and when their eyes met they were only eloquent of the sympathetic sadness of two souls threatened by a common misfortune.

Nevertheless every moment brought their hearts nearer. They now lived only with the one idea. No sooner had he entered the bed-chamber than by a glance he gathered how Jeanne had spent the night; and there was no need for him to speak for Hélène to learn what he thought of the child's condition. Besides, with all the innate bravery of a mother, she had forced from him a declaration that he would not deceive her, but allow her to know his fears. Always on her feet, not having had three hours' uninterrupted sleep for three weeks past, she displayed superhuman endurance and composure, and quelled her despair without a tear in order that she might concentrate her whole soul upon the struggle with the dread enemy. Within and without her heart there was nothing but emptiness; the world around her, the usual thoughts of each hour, the consciousness of life itself, had all faded into darkness. Existence held nothing for her. Nothing now bound her to life but her suffering darling and this man who promised her a miracle. It was he, and he only, to whom she looked, to whom she listened, whose most trival words were to her of the first importance, and into whose breast she would fain have transfused her own soul in order to increase his energy. Insensibly, and without break, this idea wrought out its own accomplishment. Almost every evening, when the fever was raging at its worst and Jeanne lay in imminent peril, they were there beside her in silence; and as though eager to remind themselves that they stood shoulder to shoulder struggling against death, their hands met on the edge of the bed in a caressing clasp, while they trembled with solicitude and pity till a faint smile breaking over the child's face, and the sound of quiet and regular breathing, told them that the danger was past. Then each encouraged the other by an inclination of the head. Once again had their love triumphed; and every time the mute caress grew more demonstrative their hearts drew closer together.

One night Hélène divined that Henri was concealing something from her. For ten minutes, without a word crossing his lips, he had been examining Jeanne.

The little one complained of intolerable thirst; she seemed choking, and there was an incessant wheezing in her parched throat. Then a purple flush came over her face, and she lapsed into a stupor which prevented her even from raising her eyelids. She lay motionless; it might have been imagined she was dead but for the sound coming from her throat.

"You consider her very ill, do you not?" gasped Hélène.

He answered in the negative; there was no change. But his face was ashy-white, and he remained seated, overwhelmed by his powerlessness. Thereupon she also, despite the tension of her whole being, sank upon a chair on the other side of the bed.

"Tell me everything. You promised to tell me all. Is she beyond hope?"

He still sat silent, and she spoke again more vehemently:

"You know how brave I am. Have I wept? have I despaired? Speak: I want to know the truth."

Henri fixed his eyes on her. The words came slowly from his lips. "Well," said he, "if in an hour hence she hasn't awakened from this stupor, it will be all over."

Not a sob broke from Hélène; but icy horror possessed her and raised her hair on end. Her eyes turned on Jeanne; she fell on her knees and clasped her in her arms with a superb gesture eloquent of ownership, as though she could preserve her from ill, nestling thus against her shoulder. For more than a minute she kept her face close to the child's, gazing at her intently, eager to give her breath from her own nostrils, ay, and her very life too. The labored breathing of the little sufferer grew shorter and shorter.

"Can nothing be done?" she exclaimed, as she lifted her head. "Why do you remain there? Do something!" But he made a disheartened gesture. "Do something!" she repeated. "There must be something to be done. You are not going to let her die—oh, surely not!"

"I will do everything possible," the doctor simply said.

He rose up, and then a supreme struggle began. All the coolness and nerve of the practitioner had returned to him. Till now he had not ventured to try any violent remedies, for he dreaded to enfeeble the little frame already almost destitute of life. But he no longer remained undecided, and straightway dispatched Rosalie for a dozen leeches. And he did not attempt to conceal from the mother that this was a desperate remedy which might save or kill her child. When the leeches were brought in, her heart failed her for a moment.

"Gracious God! gracious God!" she murmured. "Oh, if you should kill her!"

He was forced to wring consent from her.

"Well, put them on," said she; "but may Heaven guide your hand!"

She had not ceased holding Jeanne, and refused to alter her position, as she still desired to keep the child's little head nestling against her shoulder. With calm features he meantime busied himself with the last resource, not allowing a word to fall from his lips. The first application of the leeches proved unsuccessful. The minutes slipped away. The only sound breaking the stillness of the shadowy chamber was the merciless, incessant tick-tack of the timepiece. Hope departed with every second. In the bright disc of light cast by the lamp, Jeanne lay stretched among the disordered bedclothes, with limbs of waxen pallor. Hélène, with tearless eyes, but choking with emotion, gazed on the little body already in the clutches of death, and to see a drop of her daughter's blood appear, would willingly have yielded up all her own. And at last a ruddy drop trickled down —the leeches had made fast their hold; one by one they commenced sucking. The child's life was in the balance. These were terrible moments, pregnant with anguish. Was that sigh the exhalation of Jeanne's last breath, or did it mark her return to life? For a time Hélène's heart was frozen within her; she believed that the little one was dead; and there came to her a violent impulse to pluck away the creatures which were sucking so greedily; but some supernatural power restrained her, and she remained there with open mouth and her blood chilled within her. The pendulum still swung to and fro; the room itself seemed to wait the issue in anxious expectation.

At last the child stirred. Her heavy eyelids rose, but dropped again, as though wonder and weariness had overcome her. A slight quiver passed over her face; it seemed as if she were breathing. Finally there was a trembling of the lips; and Hélène, in an agony of suspense, bent over her, fiercely awaiting the result.

"Mamma! mamma!" murmured Jeanne.

Henri heard, and walking to the head of the bed, whispered in the mother's ear: "She is saved."

"She is saved! she is saved!" echoed Hélène in stammering tones, her bosom filled with such joy that she fell on the floor close to the bed, gazing now at her daughter and now at the doctor with distracted looks. But she rose and giving way to a mighty impulse, threw herself on Henri's neck.

"I love you!" she exclaimed.

This was her avowal—the avowal imprisoned so long, but at last poured forth in the crisis of emotion which had come upon her. Mother and lover were merged in one; she proffered him her love in a fiery rush of gratitude.

Through her sobs she spoke to him in endearing words, Her tears, dried at their source for three weeks, were now rolling down her cheeks. But at last she fell upon her knees, and took Jeanne in her arms to lull her to deeper slumber against her shoulder; and at intervals whilst her child thus rested she raised to Henri's eyes glistening with passionate tears.

Stretched in her cot, the bedclothes tucked under her chin, and her head, with its dark brown tresses, resting in the centre of the pillow, Jeanne lay, relieved, but prostrate. Her eyelids were closed, but she did not sleep. The lamp, placed on the table, which had been rolled close to the fireplace, lit but one end of the room, and the shade encompassed Hélène and Henri, seated in their customary places on each side of the bed. But the child did not part them; on the contrary, she served as a closer bond between them, and her innocence was intermingled with their

love on this first night of its avowal. At times Hélène rose on tiptoe to fetch the medicine, to turn up the lamp, or give some order to Rosalie; while the doctor, whose eyes never quitted her, would sign to her to walk gently. And when she had sat down again they smiled at one another. Not a word was spoken; all their interest was concentrated on Jeanne, who was to them as their love itself. Sometimes when the coverlet was being pulled up, or the child's head was being raised, their hands met and rested together in sweet forgetfulness. This undesigned, stealthy caress was the only one in which they indulged.

"I am not sleeping," murmured Jeanne. "I know very well you are there."

On hearing her speak they were overjoyed. Their hands parted; beyond this they had no desires. The improvement in the child's condition was to them satisfaction and peace.

"Are you feeling better, my darling?" asked Hélène, when she saw her stirring.

Jeanne made no immediate reply, and when she spoke it was dreamingly.

"Oh, yes! I don't feel anything now. But I can hear you, and that pleases me."

After the lapse of a moment, she opened her eyes with an effort and looked at them. Then an angelic smile crossed her face, and her eyelids dropped once more.

On the morrow, when the Abbé and Monsieur Rambaud made their appearance, Hélène gave way to a shrug of impatience. They were now a disturbing element in her happy nest. As they went on questioning her, shaking with fear lest they might receive bad tidings, she had the cruelty to reply that Jeanne was no better. She spoke without consideration, driven to this strait by the selfish desire of treasuring for herself and Henri the bliss of having rescued Jeanne from death, and of alone knowing this to be so. What was their reason for seeking a share in her happiness? It belonged to Henri and herself, and had it been known to another would have seemed to her impaired in value. To her imagination it would have been as though a stranger were participating in her love.

The priest, however, approached the bed.

"Jeanne, 'tis we, your old friends. Don't you know us?"

She nodded gravely to them in recognition, but she was unwilling to speak to them; she was in a thoughtful mood, and she cast a look full of meaning on her mother. The two poor men went away more heartbroken than on any previous evening.

Three days later Henri allowed his patient her first boiled egg. It was a matter of the highest importance. Jeanne's mind was made up to eat it with none present but her mother and the doctor, and the door must be closed. As it happened, Monsieur Rambaud was present at the moment; and when Hélène began to spread a napkin, by way of tablecloth, on the bed, the child whispered in her ear: "Wait a moment— when he has gone."

And as soon as he had left them she burst out: "Now, quick! quick! It's far nicer when there's nobody but ourselves."

Hélène lifted her to a sitting posture, while Henri placed two pillows behind her to prop her up; and then, with the napkin spread before her and a plate on her knees, Jeanne waited, smiling.

"Shall I break the shell for you?" asked her mother.

"Yes, do, mamma."

"And I will cut you three little bits of bread," added the doctor.

"Oh! four; you'll see if I don't eat four."

It was now the doctor's turn to be addressed endearingly. When he gave her the first slice, she gripped his hand, and as she still clasped her mother's, she rained kisses on both with the same passionate tenderness.

"Come, come; you will have to be good," entreated Hélène, who observed that she was ready to burst into tears; "you must please us by eating your egg."

At this Jeanne ventured to begin; but her frame was so enfeebled that with the second sippet of bread she declared herself wearied. As she swallowed each mouthful, she would say, with a smile, that her teeth were tender. Henri encouraged her, while Hélène's eyes were brimful of tears. Heaven! she saw her child eating! She watched the bread disappear, and the gradual consumption of this egg thrilled her to the heart. To picture Jeanne stretched dead beneath the sheets was a vision of mortal terror; but now she was eating, and eating so prettily, with all an invalid's characteristic dawdling and hesitancy!

"You won't be angry, mamma? I'm doing my best. Why, I'm at my third bit of bread! Are you pleased?"

"Yes, my darling, quite pleased. Oh!

you don't know all the joy the sight gives me!"

And then, in the happiness with which she overflowed, Hélène forgetfully leaned against Henri's shoulder. Both laughed gleefully at the child, but over her face there suddenly crept a sullen flush; she gazed at them stealthily, and drooped her head, and refused to eat any more, her features glooming the while with distrust and anger. At last they had to lay her back in bed again.

## CHAPTER XIII

### QUITE HAPPY?

MONTHS slipped away, and Jeanne was still convalescent. August came, and she had not quitted her bed. When evening fell she would rise for an hour or two; but even the crossing of the room to the window—where she reclined on an invalid-chair and gazed out on Paris, flaming with the ruddy light of the dying sun—seemed too great a strain for her wearied frame. Her attenuated limbs could scarce bear their burden, and she would declare with a wan smile that the blood in her veins would not suffice for a little bird, and that she must have plenty of soup. Morsels of raw meat were dipped in her broth. She had grown to like this mixture, as she longed to be able to go down to play in the garden.

The weeks and the months which slipped by were ever instinct with the same delightful monotony, and Hélène forgot to count the days. She never left the house; at Jeanne's side she forgot the whole world. No news from without reached her ears. Her retreat,

though it looked down on Paris, which with its smoke and noise stretched across the horizon, was as secret and secluded as any cave of holy hermit amongst the hills. Her child was saved, and the knowledge of it satisfied all her desires. She spent her days in watching over her return to health, rejoicing in a shade of bright color returning to her cheeks, in a lively look, or in a gesture of gladness. Every hour made her daughter more like what she had been of old, with lovely eyes and wavy hair. The slower Jeanne's recovery, the greater joy was yielded to Hélène, who recalled the olden days when she had suckled her, and, as she gazed on her gathering strength, felt even a keener emotion than when in the past she had measured her two little feet in her hand to see if she would soon be able to walk.

At the same time some anxiety remained to Hélène. On several occasions she had seen a shadow come over Jeanne's face—a shadow of sudden distrust and sourness. Why was her laughter thus abruptly turned to sulkiness? Was she suffering? was she hiding some quickening of the old pain?

"Tell me, darling, what is the matter? You were laughing just a moment ago, and now you are nearly crying! Speak to me: do you feel a pain anywhere?"

But Jeanne abruptly turned away her head and buried her face in the pillow.

"There's nothing wrong with me," she answered curtly. "I want to be left alone."

And she would lie brooding the whole afternoon, with her eyes fixed on the wall, showing no sign of affectionate repentance, but plunged in a sadness which baffled her forlorn mother. The doctor knew not what to say; these fits of gloom would always break out when he was there, and he attributed them to the sufferer's nervousness. He impressed on Héléne the necessity of crossing her in nothing.

One afternoon Jeanne had fallen asleep. Henri, who was pleased with her progress, had lingered in the room, and was carrying on a whispered conversation with Hélène, who was once more busy with her everlasting needlework at her seat beside the window. Since the terrible night when she had confessed she loved him both had lived on peacefully in the consciousness of their mutual passions, careless of the morrow, and without a thought of the world. Around Jeanne's bed, in this room that still reverberated with her agony, there was an atmosphere of purity which shielded them from any outburst. The child's innocent breath fell on them with a quieting influence. But as the little invalid slowly grew well again, their love in very sympathy took new strength, and they would sit side by side with beating hearts, speaking little, and then only in whispers, lest the little one might be awakened. Their words were without significance, but struck re-echoing chords within the breast of each. That afternoon their love revealed itself in a thousand ways.

"I assure you she is much better," said the doctor. "In a fortnight she will be able to go down to the garden."

Hélène went on stitching quickly.

"Yesterday she was again very sad," she murmured, "but this morning she was laughing and happy. She has given me her promise to be good."

A long silence followed. The child was still plunged in sleep, and their souls were enveloped in a profound peace. When she slumbered thus, their relief was intense; they seemed to share each other's hearts the more.

"Have you not seen the garden yet?" asked Henri. "Just now it's full of flowers."

"The asters are out, aren't they?" she questioned.

"Yes; the flower-bed looks magnificent. The clematises have wound their way up into the elms. It is quite a nest of foliage."

There was another silence. Hélène ceased sewing, and gave him a smile. To their fancy it seemed as though they were strolling together along high-banked paths, dim with shadows, amidst which fell a shower of roses. As he hung over her he drank in the faint perfume of vervain that arose from her dressing-gown. However, all at once a rustling of the sheets disturbed them.

"She is wakening!" exclaimed Hélène, as she started up.

Henri drew himself away, and simultaneously threw a glance towards the bed. Jeanne had but a moment before gripped the pillow with her arms, and, with her chin buried in it, had turned her face towards them. But her eyelids were still shut, and judging by her slow and regular breathing, she had again fallen asleep.

"Are you always sewing like this?" asked Henri, as he came nearer to Hélène.

"I cannot remain with idle hands," she answered. "It is mechanical enough, but it regulates my thoughts. For hours I can think of the same thing without wearying."

He said no more, but his eye dwelt on the needle as the stitching went on almost in a melodious cadence; and it seemed to him as if the thread were carrying off and binding something of their lives together. For hours she could have sewn on, and for hours he could have sat there, listening to the music of the needle, in which, like a lulling refrain, re-echoed one word that never wearied them. It was their wish to live their days like this in that quiet nook, to sit side by side while the child was asleep, never stirring from their places lest they might awaken her. How sweet was that quiescent silence, in which they could listen to the pulsing of hearts, and bask in the delight of a dream of everlasting love!

"How good you are!" were the words which came several times from his lips, the joy her presence gave him only finding expression in that one phrase.

Again she raised her head, never for moment deeming it strange that she should be so passionately worshipped. Henri's face was near her own, and for a second they gazed at one another.

"Let me get on with my work," she said in a whisper. "I shall never have it finished."

But just then an instinctive dread prompted her to turn round, and indeed there lay Jeanne, lowering upon them with deadly pale face and great inky-black eyes. The child had not made the least movement; her chin was still buried in the downy pillow, which she clasped with her little arms. She had only opened her eyes a moment before and was contemplating them.

"Jeanne, what's the matter?" asked Hélène. "Are you ill? do you want anything?"

The little one made no reply, never stirred, did not even lower the lids of her great flashing eyes. A sullen gloom was on her brow, and in her pallid cheeks were deep hollows. She seemed about to throw back her hands as though a convulsion was imminent. Hélène started up, begging her to speak; but she remained obstinately stiff, darting such black looks on her mother that the latter's face became purple with blushes, and she murmured:

"Doctor, see; what is the matter with her?"

Henri had drawn his chair away from Hélène's. He ventured near the bed, and was desirous of taking hold of one of the little hands which so fiercely gripped the pillow. But as he touched Jeanne she trembled in every limb, turned with a start towards the wall, and exclaimed:

"Leave me alone; you, I mean! You are hurting me!"

She pulled the coverlet over her face, and for a quarter of an hour they attempted, without success, to soothe her with gentle words. At last, as they still persevered, she sat up with her hands clasped in supplication: "Oh, please leave me alone; you are tormenting me! Leave me alone!"

Hélène, in her bewilderment, once more sat down at the window, but Henri did not resume his place beside her. They now understood: Jeanne was devoured by jealousy. They were unable to speak another word. For a minute or two the doctor paced up and down in silence, and then slowly quitted the room, well understanding the meaning of the anxious glances which the mother was darting towards the bed. As soon as he had gone, she ran to her daughter's side and pressed her passionately to her breast, with a wild outburst of words.

"Hear me, day pet, I am alone now; look at me, speak to me. Are you in pain? Have I vexed you then? Tell me everything! Is it I whom you are angry with? What are •you troubled about?"

But it was useless to pray for an answer, useless to plead with all sorts of questions; Jeanne declared that she was quite well. Then she started up with a frenzied cry: "You don't love me any more, mamma! you don't love me any more!"

She burst into grievous sobbing, and wound her arms convulsively round her mother's neck, raining greedy kisses on her face. Hélène's heart was rent within her, she felt overwhelmed with unspeakable sadness, and strained her child to her bosom, mingling her tears with her own, and vowing to her that she would never love anybody save herself.

From that da · onward a mere word or glance would suffice to awaken Jeanne's jealousy. While she was in the perilous grip of death some instinct had led her to put her trust in the loving tenderness with which they had shielded and saved her. But now strength was returning to her, and she would allow none to participate in her mother's love. She conceived a kind of spite against the doctor, a spite which

stealthily grew into hate as her health improved. It was hidden deep within her self-willed brain, in the innermost recesses of her suspicious and silent nature. She would never consent to explain things; she herself knew not what was the matter with her; but she felt ill whenever the doctor drew too near to her mother; and would press her hands violently to her bosom. Her torment seemed to sear her very heart, and furious passion choked her and made her cheeks turn pale. Nor could she place any restraint on herself; she imagined every one unjust, grew stiff and haughty, and deigned no reply when she was charged with being very ill-tempered. Hélène, trembling with dismay, dared not press her to explain the source of her trouble; indeed, her eyes turned away whenever this eleven-year-old child darted at her a glance in which was concentrated the premature passion of a woman.

"Oh, Jeanne, you are making me very wretched!" she would sometimes say to her, the tears standing in her eyes as she observed her stifling in her efforts to restrain a sudden bubbling up of mad anger.

But these words, once so potent for good, which had so often drawn the child weeping to Hélène's arms, were now wholly without influence. There was a change taking place in her character. Her humors varied ten times a day. Generally she spoke abruptly and imperiously, addressing her mother as though she were Rosalie, and constantly plaguing her with the pettiest demands. ever impatient and loud in complaint.

"Give me a drink. What a time you take! I am left here dying of thirst!"

And when Hélène handed the glass to her she would exclaim: "There's no sugar in it; I won't have it!"

Then she would throw herself back on her pillow, and a second time push away the glass, with the complaint that the drink was too sweet. They no longer cared to attend her, she would say; they were doing it purposely. Hélène, dreading lest she might infuriate her to a yet greater extent, made no reply, but gazed on her with tears trembling on her cheeks.

However, Jeanne's anger was particularly visible when the doctor made his appearance. The moment he entered the sick-room she would lay herself flat in bed, or sullenly hang her head in the manner of savage brutes who will not suffer a stranger to come near. Sometimes she refused to say a word, allowing him to feel her pulse or examine her while she remained motionless with her eyes fixed on the ceiling. On other days she would not even look at him, but clasp her hands over her eyes with such a gust of passion that to remove them would have necessitated the violent twisting of her arms. One night, as her mother was about to give her a spoonful of medicine, she burst out with the cruel remark: "I won't have it; it will poison me."

Hélène's heart, pierced to the quick, sank within her, and she dreaded to elicit what the remark might mean.

"What are you saying, my child?" she asked. "Do you understand what you are talking about? Medicine is never nice to take. You must drink this."

But Jeanne lay there in obstinate silence, and averted her head in order to get rid of the draught. From that day onward she was full of caprices, swallowing or rejecting her medicines according to the humor of the moment. She would sniff at the phials and examine them suspiciously as they stood on the night-table. Should she have refused to drink the contents of one of them she never forgot its identity, and would have died rather than allow a drop from it to pass her lips. Honest Monsieur Rambaud alone could persuade her at times. It was he whom she now overwhelmed with the most lavish caresses, especially if the doctor were looking on; and her gleaming eyes were turned towards her mother to note if she were vexed by this display of affection towards another.

"Oh, it's you, old friend!" she exclaimed the moment he entered. "Come and sit down near me. Have you brought me any oranges?"

She sat up and laughingly fumbled in his pockets, where goodies were always secreted. Then she embraced him, playing quite a love comedy, while her revenge found satisfaction in the anguish which she imagined she could read on her mother's pallid face. Monsieur Rambaud beamed with joy over his restoration to his little sweetheart's good graces. But Hélène, on meeting him in the ante-room, was usually able to acquaint him with the state of affairs, and all at once he would look at the draught standing on the table and exclaim: "What! are you having syrup?"

Jeanne's face clouded over, and, in a low voice, she replied: "No, no, it's nasty, it's nauseous; I can't take it."

"What! you can't drink this?" questioned Monsieur Rambaud gaily. "I can wager it's very good. May I take a little of it?"

Then without awaiting her permission he poured out a large spoonful, and swallowed it with a grimace that seemed to betoken immeasurable satisfaction.

"How delicious!" he murmured. "You are quite wrong; see, just take a little to try."

Jeanne amused, then made no further resistance. She would drink whatever Monsieur Rambaud happened to taste. She watched his every motion greedily, and appeared to study his features with a view to observing the effects of the medicine. The good man for a month gorged himself in this way with drugs, and, on Hélène gratefully thanking him, merely shrugged his shoulders.

"Oh! it's very good stuff!" he declared, with perfect conviction, making it his pleasure to share the little one's medicines.

He passed his evenings at her bedside. The Abbé, on the other hand, came regularly every second day. Jeanne retained them with her as long as possible, and displayed vexation when she saw them take up their hats. Her immediate dread lay in being left alone with her mother and the doctor, and she would fain have always had company in the room to keep these two apart. Frequently, without reason, she called Rosalie to her. When they were alone with her, her eyes never quitted them, but pursued them into every corner of the bedroom. Whenever their hands came together, her face grew ashy white. If a whispered word was exchanged between them, she started up in anger, demanding to know what had been said. It was a grievance to her that her mother's gown should sweep against the doctor's foot. They could not approach or look at one another without the child falling immediately into violent trembling. The extreme sensitiveness of her innocent little being induced in her an exasperation which would suddenly prompt her to turn round, should she guess that they were smiling at one another behind her. She could divine the times when their love was at its height by the atmosphere wafted around her. It was then that her gloom became deeper, and her agonies were those of nervous women at the approach of a terrible storm.

Every one about Hélène now looked on Jeanne as saved, and she herself had slowly come to recognize this as a certainty. Thus it happened that Jeanne's fits were at last regarded by her as the bad humors of a spoilt child, and as of little or no consequence. A craving to live sprang up within her after the six weeks of anguish which she had just spent. Her daughter was now well able to dispense with her care for hours; and for her, who had so long become unconscious of life, these hours opened up a vista of delight, of peace, and pleasure. She rummaged in her drawers, and made joyous discoveries of forgotten things; she plunged into all sorts of petty tasks, in the endeavor to resume the happy course of her daily existence. And in this upwelling of life her love expanded, and the society of Henri was the reward she allowed herself for the intensity of her past sufferings. In the shelter of that room they deemed themselves beyond the world's ken, and every hindrance in their path was forgotten. The child, to whom their love had proved a terror, alone remained a bar between them.

Jeanne became, indeed, a veritable scourge of their affections. An ever-present barrier, with her eyes constantly upon them, she compelled them to maintain a continued restraint, an affection of indifference, with the result that their hearts were stirred with even greater motion than before. For days they could not exchange a word; they knew intuitively that she was listening even when she was seemingly wrapped in slumber. One evening, when Hélène had quitted the room, with Henri, to escort him to the front door, Jeanne burst out with the cry, "Mamma! mamma!" in a voice shrill with rage. Hélène was forced to return, for she heard the child leap from her bed; and she met her running towards her, shivering with cold and passion. Jeanne would no longer let her remain away from her. From that day forward they could merely exchange a clasp of the hand on meeting and parting. Madame Deberle was now spending a month at the seaside, and the doctor, though he had all his time at his own command, dared not pass more than ten minutes in Hélène's company. Their long chats at the window had come to an end. What particularly tortured their hearts was the fickleness of Jeanne's humor. One night, as the doctor hung over her, she gave way to tears. For a whole day her hate changed to feverish tenderness, and Hélène felt happy once more; but on the morrow, when the doctor entered the room, the child received him with such a display of sourness that the mother besought him with a look to leave them. Jeanne had

fretted the whole night in angry regret over her own good-humor. Not a day passed but what a like scene was enacted. And after the blissful hours the child brought them in her moods of impassioned tenderness these hours of misery fell on them with the torture of the lash.

A feeling of revulsion at last awoke within Hélène. To all seeming her daughter would be her death. Why, when her illness had been put to flight, did the ill-natured child work her utmost to torment her? If one of those intoxicating dreams took possession of her imagination—a mystic dream in which she found herself traversing a country alike unknown and entrancing with Henri by her side—Jeanne's face, harsh and sullen, would suddenly start up before her and thus her heart was ever being rent in twain. The struggle between her maternal affection and her passion became fraught with the greatest suffering.

One evening, despite Hélène's formal edict of banishment, the doctor called. For eight days they had been unable to exchange a word together. She would fain that he had not entered; but he did so on learning that Jeanne was in a deep sleep. They sat down as of old, near the window, far from the glare of the lamp, with the peaceful shadows around them. For two hours their conversation went on in such low whispers that scarcely a sound disturbed the silence of the large room. At times they turned their heads and glanced at the delicate profile of Jeanne, whose little hands, clasped together, were reposing on the coverlet. But in the end they grew forgetful of their surroundings, and their talk incautiously became louder. Then, all at once, Jeanne's voice rang out.

"'Mamma! mamma!" she cried, seized with sudden agitation, as though suffering from nightmare.

She writhed about in her bed, her eyelids still heavy with sleep, and then struggled to reach a sitting posture.

"Hide, I beseech you!" whispered Hélène to the doctor in a tone of anguish. "You will be her death if you stay here."

In an instant Henri vanished into the window-recess, concealed by the blue velvet curtain; but it was in vain, the child still kept up her pitiful cry: "Oh, mamma! mamma! I suffer so much."

"I am here beside you, my darling; where do you feel the pain?"

"I don't know. Oh, see, it is here! Oh, it is scorching me!" With eyes wide open and features distorted, she pressed her little hands to her bosom. "It came on me in a moment. I was asleep, wasn't I? But I felt something like a burning coal."

"But it's all gone now. You're not pained any longer, are you?"

"'Yes, yes, I feel it still."

She glanced uneasily round the room. She was now wholly awake; the sullen gloom crept over her face once more, and her cheeks became livid.

"Are you by yourself, mamma?" she asked.

"Of course I am, my darling!"

Nevertheless Jeanne shook her head and gazed about, sniffing the air, while her agitation visibly increased. "No, you're not; I know you're not. There's some one— Oh, mamma! I'm afraid,

I'm afraid! You are telling me a story; you are not by yourself."

She fell back in bed in an hysterical fit, sobbing loudly and huddling herself beneath the coverlet, as though to ward off some danger. Hélène, crazy with alarm, dismissed Henri without delay, despite his wish to remain and look after the child. But she drove him out forcibly, and on her return clasped Jeanne in her arms while the little one gave vent to the one pitiful cry, with every utterance of which her sobbing was renewed louder than ever: "You don't love me any more! You don't love me any more!"

"Hush, hush, my angel! don't say that," exclaimed the mother in agony. "You are all the world to me. You'll see yet whether I love you or not."

She nursed her until the morning broke, intent on yielding up to her all her heart's affections, though she was appalled at realizing how completely the love of herself possessed this darling child. Next day she deemed a consultation necessary. Doctor Bodin, dropping in as though by chance, subjected the patient with many jokes to a careful examination; and a lengthy discussion ensued between him and Doctor Deberle, who had remained in the adjacent room. Both readily agreed that there were no serious symptoms apparent at the moment, but they were afraid of complex developments, and cross-questioned Hélène for some time. They realized that they were dealing with one of those nervous affections which have a family history, and set medical skill at defiance. She told them, what they already partly knew, that her grandmother was confined in the lunatic asylum of Les Tulettes at a short distance from Plassans, and that her mother had died from galloping consumption, after many years of brain affection and hysterical fits. She herself took more after her father; she had his features and the same gravity of temperament. Jeanne, on the other hand, was the facsimile of her grandmother; but she never would have her strength, commanding figure, or sturdy, bony frame. The two doctors enjoined on her once more that the greatest care was requisite. Too many precautions could not be taken in dealing with chloro-anæmical affections, which tend to develop a multitude of dangerous diseases.

Henri had listened to old Doctor Bodin with a deference which he had never before displayed for a colleague. He besought his advice on Jeanne's case with the air of a pupil who is full of doubt. Truth to tell, this child inspired him with dread; he felt that her case was beyond his science, and he feared lest she might die under his hands and her mother be lost to him forever. A week passed away. He was no longer admitted by Hélène into the little one's presence; and in the end, sad and sick at heart, he broke off his visits of his own accord.

As the month of August verged on its close, Jeanne recovered sufficient strength to rise and walk across the room. The lightness of her heart spoke in her laughter. A fortnight had elapsed since the recurrence of any nervous attack. The thought that her mother was again all her own and would ever cling to her had proved remedy enough. At first distrust had ranked in her mind; while letting Hélène kiss her she had remained uneasy at her least movement, and had imperiously besought her hand before she fell asleep, anxious to retain it in her own during her slumber. But at last, with the knowledge that nobody came near, she had regained confidence, enraptured by the prospect of a reopening of the old happy life when they had sat side by side, working at the window. Every day brought new roses to her cheeks; and Rosalie declared that she was blossoming brighter and brighter every hour.

There were times, however, as night fell, when Hélène broke down. Since her daughter's illness her face had remained grave and somewhat pale, and a deep wrinkle, never before visible, furrowed her brow. When Jeanne caught sight of her in these hours of weariness, despair, and voidness, she herself would feel very wretched, her heart heavy with vague remorse. Gently and silently she would then twine her arms around her neck.

"Are you happy, mother darling? came the whisper.

A thrill ran through Hélène's frame, and she hastened to answer: "Yes, of course, my pet."

Still the child pressed her question: "Are you, oh! are you happy! Quite sure?"

"Quite sure. Why should I feel unhappy?"

With this Jeanne would clasp her closer in her little arms, as though to requite her. She would love her so well, she would say—so well, indeed, that nowhere in all Paris could a happier mother be found.

## CHAPTER XIV

### NOT CONVINCED

DURING August Doctor Deberle's garden was like a well of foliage. The railings were hidden both by the twining branches of the lilac and laburnum trees and by the climbing plants, ivy, honeysuckle, and clematis, w h i c h sprouted everywhere in luxuriance, and glided and intermingled in inextricable confusion, drooping down in leafy canopies, and running along the walls till they reached the elms at the far end, where the verdure was so profuse that you might have thought a tent were stretched between the trees, the elms serving as its giant props. The garden was so small that the least shadow seemed to cover it. At noon the sun threw a disc of yellow light on the centre, illumining the lawn and its two flower-beds. Against the garden steps was a huge rose-bush, laden with hundreds of large tea-roses. In the evening when the heat subsided their perfume became more penetrating, and the air under the elms grew heavy with their warm breath. Nothing could exceed the charm of this hidden, balmy nook, into which no neighborly inquisition could peep, and which brought one a dream of the forest primeval, albeit barrel-organs were playing polkas in the Rue Vineuse, near by.

"Why, madame, doesn't mademoiselle go down to the garden?" Rosalie daily asked. "I'm sure it would do her good to romp about under the trees."

One of the elms had invaded Rosalie's kitchen with its branches. She would pull some of the leaves off as she gazed with delight on the clustering foliage, through which she could see nothing.

"She isn't strong enough yet," was Hélène's reply. "The cold, shady garden might be harmful to her."

Rosalie was in no wise convinced. A happy thought with her was not easily abandoned. Madame must surely be mistaken in imagining that it would be cold or harmful. Perhaps madame's objection sprang rather from the fear that she would be in somebody's way; but that was nonsense. Mademoiselle would of a truth be in nobody's way; not a living soul made any appearance there. The doctor shunned the spot, and as for madame, his wife, she would remain at the seaside till the middle of September. This was so certain that the doorkeeper had asked Zéphyrin to give the garden a rake over, and Zèphyrin and she herself had spent two Sunday afternoons there already. Oh! it was lovely, lovelier than one could imagine.

Hélène, however, still declined to act on the suggestion. Jeanne seemed to have a great longing to enjoy a walk in the garden, which had been the ceaseless topic of her discourse during her illness; but a vague feeling of embarrassment made her eyes droop and closed her mouth on the subject in her mother's presence. At last when Sunday came round again the maid hurried into the room exclaiming breathlessly:

"Oh! madame, there's nobody there, I give you my word! Only myself and Zéphyrin, who is raking! Do let her come. You can't imagine how fine it is outside. Come for a little, only a little while, just to see!"

Her conviction was such that Hélène gave way. She cloaked Jeanne in a shawl, and told Rosalie to take a heavy wrap with her. The child was in an ecstasy, which spoke silently from the depths of her large sparkling eyes; she even wished to descend the staircase without help in order that her strength might be made plain. However, her mother's arms were stretched out behind her, ready to lend support. When they had reached the foot of the stairs and entered the garden, they both gave vent to an exclamation. So little did this umbrageous, thicket-girt spot resemble the trim nook they had seen in the springtime that they failed to recognize it.

"Ah! you wouldn't believe me!" declared Rosalie, in triumphant tones.

The clumps of shrubbery had grown to great proportions, making the paths much narrower, and, in walking, their skirts caught in some of the interwoven branches. To the fancy it seemed some far-away recess in a wood, arched over with foliage, from which fell a greeny light of delightful charm and mystery. Hélène directed her steps towards the elm beneath which she had sat in April.

"But I don't wish her to stay here," said she. "It is shady and coldish."

"Well, well, you will see in a minute," answered the maid.

Three steps farther on they emerged from the seeming forest, and, in the midst of the leafy profusion they found the sun's golden rays streaming on the lawn, warm and still as in a woodland clearing. As they looked up they saw the branches standing out against the blue of the sky with the delicacy of guipure. The tea-roses on the huge bush, faint in the heat, dropped slumberously from their stems. The flower-beds were full of red and white asters, looking with their old-world air like blossoms woven in some ancient tapestry.

"Now you'll see," said Rosalie. "I'm going to put her all right myself."

She had folded and placed the wrap on the edge of a walk, where the shadow came to an end. Here she made Jeanne sit down, covering her shoulders with a shawl, and bidding her stretch out her little legs. In this fashion the shade fell on the child's head, while her feet lay in the sunshine.

"Are you all right, my darling?" Hélène asked.

"Oh, yes," was her answer. "I don't feel cold a bit, you know. I almost think I am sweltering before a big fire. Ah! how well one can breathe! How pleasant it is!"

Thereupon Hélène, whose eyes had turned uneasily towards the closed window-shutters of the house, expressed her intention of returning upstairs for a little while, and loaded Rosalie with a variety of injunctions. She would have to watch the sun; she was not to leave Jeanne there for more than half an hour; and she must not lose sight of her for a moment.

"Don't be alarmed, mamma," exclaimed the child, with a laugh. "There are no carriages to pass along here."

Left to amuse herself, she gathered a handful of gravel from the path at her side, and took pleasure in letting it fall from her clasped hands like a shower of rain. Zéphyrin meantime was raking. On catching sight of madame and her daughter he had slipped on his great-coat, which he had previously hung from the branch of a tree; and in token of respect had stood stock-still, with his rake idle in his hand. Throughout Jeanne's illness he had come every Sunday as usual; but so great had been the caution with which he had slipped into the kitchen, that Hélène would scarcely have dreamt of his presence had not Rosalie on each occasion been deputed as his messenger to inquire about the invalid's progress, and convey his condolences. Yes, so ran her comments, he was now laying claim to good manners; Paris was giving him some polish! And at present here he was, leaning on his rake, and mutely addressing Jeanne with a sympathetic nod. At soon as she saw him, her face broke into smiles.

"I have been very ill," she said.

"Yes, I know, mademoiselle," he replied as he placed his hand on his heart. And inspired with the wish to say something pretty or comical, which might serve to enliven the meeting, he added: "You see, your health has been taking a rest. Now it will indulge in a snore."

Jeanne had again gathered up a handful of gravel, while he, perfectly satisfied, and opening his mouth wide from ear to ear in a burst of silent laughter, renewed his raking with all the strength of his arms. As the rake travelled over the gravel a regular, strident sound arose. When a few minutes had elapsed Rosalie, seeing her little charge absorbed in her amusement, seemingly happy and at ease, drew gradually farther away from her, as though lured

by the grating of this rake. Zéphyrin was now working away in the full glare of the sun, on the other side of the lawn.

"You are sweating like an ox," she whispered to him. "Take off your great-coat. Be quick; mademoiselle won't be offended."

He relieved himself of the garment, and once more suspended it from a branch. His red trousers, supported by a belt round the waist, reached almost to his chest, while his shirt of stout, unbleached linen, held at the neck by a narrow horsehair band, was so stiff that it stuck out and made him look even rounder than he was. He tucked up his sleeves with a certain amount of affectation, as though to show Rosalie a couple of flaming hearts, which, with the inscription "For Ever," had been tattooed on them at the barracks.

"Did you go to mass this morning?" asked Rosalie, who usually tackled him with this question every Sunday.

"To mass! to mass!" he repeated, with a chuckle.

His red ears seemed to stand out from his head, shorn to the very skin, and the whole of his diminutive barrel-like body expressed a spirit of banter. At last the confession came. "Of course I went to mass."

"You are lying," Rosalie burst out violently. "I know you are lying; your nose is twitching. Oh, Zéphyrin, you are going to the dogs—you have left off going to church! Beware!"

His answer, lover-like, was an attempt to put his arm round her waist, but to all appearance she was shocked, for she exclaimed:

"I'll make you put on your coat again if you don't behave yourself. Aren't you ashamed? Why, there's mademoiselle looking at you!"

Thereupon Zéphyrin turned to his raking once more. In truth, Jeanne had raised her eyes towards them. Her amusement was palling on her somewhat; the gravel thrown aside, she had been gathering leaves and plucking grass; but a feeling of indolence crept over her, and now she preferred to do nothing but gaze at the sunshine as it fell on her more and more. A few moments previously only her legs, as far as the knees, had been bathed in this warm cascade of sunshine, but now it reached her waist, the heat increasing like an entrancing caress. What particularly amused her were the round patches of light, of a beautiful golden yellow, which danced over her shawl, for all the world like living creatures. She tossed back her head to see if they were perchance creeping towards her face, and meanwhile clasped her little hands together in the glare of the sunshine. How thin and transparent her hands seemed! The sun's rays passed through them, but all the same they appeared to her very pretty, pinky like shells, delicate and attenuated like the tiny hands of an infant Christ. Then too the fresh air, the gigantic trees around her, and the warmth, had lulled her somewhat into a trance. Sleep, she imagined, had come upon her, and yet she could still see and hear. It all seemed to her very nice and pleasant.

"Mademoiselle, please draw back a bit," said Rosalie, who had approached her. "The sun's heat is too warm for you."

But with a wave of her hand Jeanne declined to stir. For the time her attention was riveted on the maid and the little soldier. She pretended to direct her glances towards the ground, with the intention of making them believe that she did not see them; but in reality, despite her apparent drowsiness, she kept watching them from beneath her long eyelashes.

Rosalie stood near her for a minute or two longer, but was powerless against the charms of the grating rake. Once more she slowly dragged herself towards Zéphyrin, as if in spite of her will. She resented the change in manner which he was now displaying, and yet her heart was bursting with mute admiration. The little soldier had used to good purpose his long strolls with his comrades in the Jardin des Plantes and round the Place du Château-d'Eau, where his barracks stood, and the result was the acquisition of the swaying, expansive graces of the Parisian fire-eater. He had learnt the flowery talk, gallant readiness, and involved style of language so dear to the hearts of the ladies. At times she was thrilled with intense pleasure as she listened to the phrases which he repeated to her with a swagger of the shoulders, phrases full of incomprehensible words that inflamed her cheeks with a flush of pride. His uniform no longer sat awkwardly on him; he swung his arms to and fro with a knowing air, and had an especially noticeable style of wearing his shako on the back of his head, with the result that his round face with its tip of a nose became extremely prominent, while his headgear swayed gently with the rolling of his body. Besides, he was growing quite free and easy, quaffed his dram, and ogled the fair sex. With his sneering ways and affectation of reticence, he now doubtless, knew a great deal more than she did. Paris was fast taking all the remaining rust off him; and Rosalie stood before him, delighted yet angry, undecided whether to scratch his face or let him give utterance to foolish prattle.

Zéphyrin, meanwhile, raking away, had turned the corner of the path. He was now hidden by a big spindle-tree, and was darting side-glances at Rosalie, luring her on against her will with the strokes of his rake. When she had got near him, he pinched her roughly.

"Don't cry out; that's only to show you how I love you!" he said in a husky whisper. "And take that over and above."

So saying he kissed her where he could, his lips lighting somewhere on her ear. Then, as Rosalie gave him a fierce nip in reply, he retaliated by another kiss, this time on her nose. Though she was well pleased, her face turned fiery-red; she was furious that Jeanne's presence should prevent her from giving him a box on the ear.

"I have pricked my finger," she declared to Jeanne as she returned to her, by way of explaining the exclamation that escaped her lips.

However, betwixt the spare branches of the spindle-tree the child had seen the incident. Amid the surrounding greenery the soldier's red trousers and greyish shirt were clearly discernible. She slowly raised her eyes to Rosalie, and looked at her for a moment, while the maid blushed the more. Then Jeanne's gaze fell to the ground again, and she gathered another handful of pebbles, but lacked the will or strength to play with them, and remained in a dreamy state, with her hands resting on the warm ground, amidst the vibrations of the sunrays. Within her a wave of health was swelling and stifling her. The trees seemed to take Titanic shape, and the air was redolent of the perfume of roses. In wonder and delight, she dreamt of all sorts of vague things.

"What are you thinking of, mademoiselle?" asked Rosalie uneasily.

"I don't know—of nothing," was Jeanne's reply. "Yes, I do know. You see, I should like to live to be very old."

However, she could not explain these words. It was an idea, she said, that had come into her head. But in the evening, after dinner, as her dreamy fit fell on her again, and her mother inquired the cause, she suddenly put the question:

"Mamma, do cousins ever marry?"

"Yes, of course," said Hélène. "Why do you ask me that?"

"Oh, nothing; only I wanted to know."

Hélène had become accustomed to these extraordinary questions. The hour spent in the garden had so beneficial an effect on the child that every sunny day found her there. Hélène's reluctance was gradually dispelled; the house was still shut up. Henri never ventured to show himself, and ere long she sat down on the edge of the rug beside Jeanne. However, on the following Sunday morning she found the windows thrown open, and felt troubled at heart.

"Oh! but of course the rooms must be aired," exclaimed Rosalie, as an inducement for them to go down. "I declare to you nobody's there!"

That day the weather was still warmer. Through the leafy screen the sun's rays darted like golden arrows. Jeanne, who was growing strong, strolled about for ten minutes, leaning on her mother's arm. Then, somewhat tired, she turned towards her rug, a corner of which she assigned to Hélène. They smiled at one another, amused at thus finding themselves side by side on the ground. Zéphyrin had given up his raking, and was helping Rosalie to gather some parsley, clumps of which were growing along the end wall.

All at once there was an uproar in the house, and Hélène was thinking of flight, when Madame Deberle made her appearance on the garden-steps. She had just arrived, and was still in her travelling dress, speaking very loudly, and seemingly very busy. But immediately she caught sight of Madame Grandjean and her daughter, sitting on the ground in the front of the lawn, she ran down, overwhelmed them with embraces, and poured a deafening flood of words into their ears.

"What, is it you? How glad I am to see you! Kiss me, my little Jeanne! Poor puss, you've been very ill, have you not? But you're getting better; the roses are coming back to your cheeks! And you, my dear, how often I've thought of you! I wrote to you: did my letters reach you? You must have spent a terrible time: but it's all over now! Will you let me kiss you?"

Hélène was now on her feet, and was forced to submit to a kiss on each cheek and return them. This display of affection, however, chilled her to the heart.

"You'll excuse us for having invaded your garden," she said.

"You're joking," retorted Juliette impetuously. "Are you not at home here?"

But she ran off for a moment, hastened up the stairs, and called across the open rooms: "Pierre, don't forget anything; there are seventeen packages!"

Then, at once coming back, she commenced chattering about her holiday adventures. "Oh! such a splendid season! We went to Trouville, you know. The beach was always thronged with people. It was quite a crush, and people of the highest spheres, you know. I had visitors too. Papa came for a fortnight with Pauline. All the same, I'm glad to get home again. But I haven't given you all my news. Oh! I'll tell you later on!"

She stooped down and kissed Jeanne again; then suddenly becoming serious, she asked:

"Am I browned by the sun?"

"No; I don't see any signs of it," replied Hélène as she gazed at her.

Juliette's eyes were clear and expressionless, her hands were plump, her pretty face was full of amiability; age did not tell on her; the sea air itself was powerless to affect her expression of serene indifference. So far as appearances went, she might have just returned from a shopping expedition in Paris. However, she was bubbling over with affection, and the more loving her outbursts, the more weary, constrained, and ill became Hélène. Jeanne meantime never stirred from the rug, but merely raised her delicate, sickly face, while clasping her hands with a chilly air in the sunshine.

"Wait, you haven't seen Lucien yet," exclaimed Juliette. "You must see him; he has got so fat."

When the lad was brought on the scene, after the dust of the journey had been washed from his face by a servant girl, she pushed and turned him about to exhibit him. Fat and chubby-cheeked, his skin tanned by playing on the beach in the salt breeze, Lucien displayed exuberant health, but he had a somewhat sulky look because he had just been washed. He had not been properly dried, and one cheek was still wet and fiery-red with the rubbing of the towel. When he caught sight of Jeanne he stood stock-still with astonishment. She looked at him out of her poor, sickly face, as colorless as linen against the background of her streaming black hair, whose tresses fell in clusters to her shoulders. Her beautiful, sad, dilated eyes seemed to fill up her whole countenance; and, despite the excessive heat, she shivered somewhat, and stretched out her hands as though chilled and seeking warmth from a blazing fire.

"Well! aren't you going to kiss her?" asked Juliette.

But Lucien looked rather afraid. At length he made up his mind, and very cautiously protruded his lips so that he might not come too near the invalid. This done, he started back expeditiously. Hélène's eyes were brimming over with tears. What health that child enjoyed! whereas her Jeanne was breathless after a walk round the lawn! Some mothers were very fortunate! Juliette all at once understood how cruel Lucien's conduct was, and she rated him soundly.

"Good gracious! what a fool you are! Is that the way to kiss young ladies? You've no idea, my dear, what a nuisance he was at Trouville."

She was getting somewhat mixed. But fortunately for her the doctor now made his appearance, and she extricated herself from her difficulty by exclaiming: "Oh, here's Henri."

He had not been expecting their return until the evening, but she had travelled by an earlier train. She plunged into a discursive explanation, without in the least making her reasons clear. The doctor listened with a smiling face. "At all events, here you are," he said. "That's all that's necessary."

A minute previously he had bowed to Hélène without speaking. His glance for a moment fell on Jeanne, but feeling embarrassed he turned away his head. Jeanne bore his look with a serious face, and unclasping her hands instinctively grasped her mother's gown and drew closer to her side.

"Ah! the rascal," said the doctor, as he raised Lucien and kissed him on each cheek. "Why, he's growing like magic."

"Yes; and am I to be forgotten?" asked Juliette, as she held up her head. Then, without putting Lucien down, holding him, indeed, on one arm, the doctor leaned over to kiss his wife. Their three faces lit up with smiles.

Hélène grew pale, and declared she must now go up. Jeanne, however, was unwilling; she wished to see what might happen, and her glances lingered for a while on the Deberles and then travelled back to her mother. When

Juliette had bent her face upwards to receive her husband's kiss, a bright gleam had come into the child's eyes.

"He's too heavy," resumed the doctor as he set Lucien down again. "Well, was the season a good one? I saw Malignon yesterday, and he was telling me about his stay there. So you let him leave before you, eh?"

"Oh! he's quite a nuisance!" exclaimed Juliette, over whose face a serious, embarrassed expression had now crept. "He tormented us to death the whole time."

"Your father was hoping for Pauline's sake— He hasn't declared his intentions then?"

"What! Malignon!" said she, as though astonished and offended. And then with a gesture of annoyance she added, "Oh! leave him alone; he's cracked! How happy I am to be home again!"

Without any apparent transition, she thereupon broke into an amazing outburst of tenderness, characteristic of her bird-like nature. She threw herself on her husband's breast and raised her face towards him. To all seeming they had forgotten they were not alone.

Jeanne's eyes, however, never quitted them. Her lips were livid and trembled with anger; her face was that of a jealous and revengeful woman. The pain she suffered was so great that she was forced to turn away her head, and in doing so she caught sight of Rosalie and Zéphyrin at the bottom of the garden, still gathering parsley. Doubtless with the intent of being in no one's way, they had crept in among the thickest of the bushes, where both were squatting on the ground. Zéphyrin, with a sly movement had caught hold of one of Rosalie's feet, while she, without uttering a syllable, was heartily slapping him. Between two branches Jeanne could see the little soldier's face, chubby and round as a moon and deeply flushed, while his mouth gaped with an amorous grin. Meantime the sun's rays were beating down vertically, and the trees were peacefully sleeping, not a leaf stirring among them all. From beneath the elms came the heavy odor of soil untouched by the spade. And elsewhere floated the perfume of the last tea-roses, which were casting their petals one by one on the garden steps. Then Jeanne, with swelling heart, turned her gaze on her mother, and seeing her motionless and dumb in presence of the Deberles, gave her a look of intense anguish—a child's look of infinite meaning, such as you dare not question.

But Madame Deberle stepped closer to them, and said: "I hope we shall see each other frequently now. As Jeanne is feeling better, she must come down every afternoon."

Hélène was already casting about for an excuse, pleading that she did not wish to weary her too much. But Jeanne abruptly broke in: "No, No; the sun does me a great deal of good. We will come down, madame. You will keep my place for me, won't you?"

And as the doctor still remained in the background, she smiled towards him.

"Doctor, please tell mamma that the fresh air won't do me any harm."

He came forward, and this man, inured to human suffering, felt on his cheeks a slight flush at being thus gently addressed by the child.

"Certainly not," he exclaimed; "the fresh air will only bring you nearer to good health."

"So you see, mother darling, we must come down," said Jeanne, with a look of ineffable tenderness, whilst a sob died away in her throat.

But Pierre had reappeared on the steps and announced the safe arrival of madame's seventeen packages. Then, followed by her husband and Lucien, Juliette retired, declaring that she was frightfully dirty, and intended to take a bath. When they were alone, Hélène knelt down on the rug, as though about to tie the shawl round Jeanne's neck, and whispered in the child's ear:

"You're not angry with the doctor any longer, then?"

With a prolonged shake of the head the child replied: "No, mamma."

There was a silence. Hélène's hands were seized with an awkward trembling, and she was seemingly unable to tie the shawl. Then Jeanne murmured: "But why does he love other people so? I won't have him love them like that."

And as she spoke, her black eyes became harsh and gloomy, while her little hands fondled her mother's shoulders. Hélène would have replied, but the words springing to her lips frightened her. The sun was now low, and mother and daughter took their departure. Zéphyrin meanwhile had reappeared to view, with a bunch of parsley in his hand, the stalks of which he continued pulling off while darting murderous glances at Rosalie. The maid followed at some distance, in-

spired with distrust now that there was no one present. Just as she stooped to roll up the rug he tried to pinch her, but she retaliated with a blow from her fist which made his back re-echo like an empty cask. Still it seemed to delight him, and he was yet laughing silently when he re-entered the kitchen busily arranging his parsley.

Thenceforth Jeanne was stubbornly bent on going down to the garden as soon as ever she heard Madame Deberle's voice there. All Rosalie's tittle-tattle regarding the next-door house she drank in greedily, ever restless and inquisitive concerning its inmates and their doings; and she would even slip out of the bedroom to keep watch from the kitchen window. In the garden, ensconced in a small arm-chair which was brought for her use from the drawing-room by Juliette's direction, her eyes never quitted the family. Lucien she now treated with great reserve, annoyed it seemed by his questions and antics, especially when the doctor was present. On those occasions she would stretch herself out as if wearied, gazing before her with her eyes wide open. For Hélène the afternoons were pregnant with anguish. She always returned, however, returned in spite of the feeling of revolt which wrung her whole being. Every day when, on his arrival home, Henri printed a kiss on Juliette's hair, her heart leaped in its agony. And at those moments, as if to hide the agitation of her face she pretended to busy herself with Jeanne, she would notice that the child was even paler than herself, with her black eyes glaring and her chin twitching with repressed fury. Jeanne shared in her suffering

When the mother turned away her head, heartbroken, the child became so sad and so exhausted that she had to be carried upstairs and put to bed. She could no longer see the doctor approach his wife without changing countenance; she would tremble, and turn on him a glance full of all the jealous fire of a deserted mistress.

"I cough in the morning," she said to him one day. "You must come and see for yourself."

Rainy weather ensued, and Jeanne became quite anxious that the doctor should commence his visits once more. Yet her health had much improved. To humor her, Hélène had been constrained to accept two or three invitations to dine with the Deberles.

At last the child's heart, so long torn by hidden sorrow, seemingly regained quietude with the complete re-establishment of her health. She would again ask Hélène the old question—"Are you happy, mother darling?"

"Yes, very happy, my pet," was the reply.

And this made her radiant. She must be pardoned her bad temper in the past, she said. She referred to it as a fit which no effort of her own will could prevent, the result of a headache that came on her suddenly. Something would spring up within her—she wholly failed to understand what it was. She was tempest-tossed by a multitude of vague imaginings—nightmares that she could not even have recalled to memory. However, it was past now; she was well again, and those worries would nevermore return.

## CHAPTER XV

### NIGHT

THE night was falling. From the grey heaven, where the first of the stars were gleaming, a fine ashy dust seemed to be raining down on the great city, raining down without cessation and slowly burying it. The hollows were already hidden deep in gloom, and a line of cloud, like a stream of ink, rose upon the horizon, engulfing the last streaks of daylight, the wavering gleams which were retreating towards the west. Below Passy but a few stretches of roof remained visible; and as the wave rolled on, darkness soon covered all.

"What a warm evening!" ejaculated Hélène, as she sat at the window, overcome by the heated breeze which was wafted upwards from Paris.

"A grateful night for the poor," exclaimed the Abbé, who stood behind her. "The autumn will be mild."

That Tuesday Jeanne had fallen into a doze at dessert, and her mother, perceiving that she was rather tired, had put her to bed. She was already fast asleep in her cot, while Monsieur Rambaud sat at the table gravely mending a toy—a mechanical doll, a present from himself, which both spoke and walked, and which Jeanne had broken. He excelled in such work as this. Hélène on her side feeling the want of fresh air—for the lingering heats of September were oppressive—had thrown the window wide open, and gazed with relief on the vast gloomy ocean of darkness that rolled before her. She had pushed an easy-chair to the window in order to be alone, but was suddenly surprised to hear the Abbé speaking to her. "Is the little one warmly covered?" he gently asked. "On these heights the air is always keen."

She made no reply, however; her heart was craving for silence. She was tasting the delights of the twilight hour, the vanishing of all surrounding objects, the hushing of every sound. Gleams, like those of night-lights, tipped the steeples and towers; that on Saint-Augustin died out first, the Panthéon for a moment retained a bluish light, and then the glittering dome of the Invalides faded away, similar to a moon setting in a rising sea of clouds. The night was like the ocean, its extent seemingly increased by the gloom, a dark abyss wherein you divined that a world lay hid. From the unseen city blew a mighty yet gentle wind. There was still a hum; sounds ascended faint yet clear to Hélène's ears—the sharp rattle of an omnibus rolling along the quay, the whistle of a train crossing the bridge of the Pont-du-Jour; and the Seine, swollen by the recent storms, and pulsing with the life of a breathing soul, wound with increased breadth threw the shadows far below. A warm odor streamed upwards from the scorched roofs, while the river amidst this exhalation of the daytime heat, seemed to give forth a cooling breeze. Paris had vanished, sunk in the dreamy repose of a colossus whose limbs the night had enveloped, and who lies motionless for a time, but with eyes wide open.

Nothing affected Hélène more than this momentary pause in the great city's life. For the three months during which she had been a close prisoner, riveted to Jeanne's bedside, she had

had no other companion in her vigil than the huge mass of Paris spreading out towards the horizon. During the summer heats of July and August the windows had almost always been left open; she could not cross the room, could not stir or turn her head, without catching a glimpse of the ever-present panorama. It was there, whatever the weather, always sharing in her griefs and hopes, like some friend who would never leave her side. She was still quite ignorant respecting it; never had it seemed farther away, never had she given less thought to its streets and its citizens,—and yet it peopled her solitude. The sick-room, whose door was kept shut to the outside world, looked out through its two windows upon this city. Often, with her eyes fixed on its expanse, Hélène had wept, leaning on the window-rail in order to hide her tears from her ailing child. One day, too—the very day when she had imagined her daughter to be at the point of death—she had remained for a long time, overcome and choked with grief, watching the smoke which curled up from the Army Bakehouse. Frequently, moreover, in hours of hopefulness she had here confided the gladsome feelings of her heart to the dim and distant suburbs. There was not a single monument which did not recall to her some sensation of joy or sorrow. Paris shared in her own existence; and never did she love it better than when the twilight came, and its day's work over, it surrendered itself to an hour's quietude, forgetfulness, and reverie, whilst waiting for the lighting of its gas.

"What a multitude of stars!" murmured Abbé Jouve. "There are thousands of them gleaming."

He had just taken a chair and sat down at her side. On hearing him, she gazed upwards into the summer night. The heaven was studded with golden lights. On the very verge of the horizon a constellation was sparkling like a carbuncle, while a dust of almost invisible stars sprinkled the vault above as though with glittering sand. Charles's-Wain was slowly turning its shaft in the night.

"Look!" said Hélène in her turn, "look at that tiny bluish star! See— far away up there. I recognize it night after night. But it dies and fades as the night rolls on."

The Abbé's presence no longer annoyed her. Wtih him by her side, she imagined the quiet was deepening around. A few words passed between them after long intervals of silence. Twice she questioned him on the names of the stars—the sight of the heavens had always interested her—but he was doubtful and pleaded ignorance.

"Do you see," she asked, "that lovely star yonder whose lustre is so exquisitely clear?"

"On the left, eh?" he replied—"near another smaller, greenish one? Ah! there are so many of them that my memory fails me."

They again lapsed into silence, their eyes still turned upwards, dazzled, quivering slightly at the sight of that stupendous swarming of luminaries. In the vast depths of the heavens, behind thousands of stars, thousands of others twinkled in ever-increasing multitudes, with the clear brilliancy of gems. The Milky Way was already whitening, displaying its solar specks, so innumerable and so distant that in the vault of the firmament they form but a trailing scarf of light.

"It fills me with fear," said Hélène in a whisper; and that she might see it all no more she bent her head and glanced down on the gaping abyss in which Paris seemed to be engulfed. In its depths not a light could yet be seen; night had rolled over it and plunged it into impenetrable darkness. Its mighty, continuous rumble seemed to have sunk into a softer key.

"Are you weeping?" asked the Abbé, who had heard a sound of sobbing.

"Yes," simply answered Hélène.

They could not see each other. For a long time she continued weeping, her whole being exhaling a plaintive murmur. Behind them, meantime, Jeanne lay at rest in innocent sleep, and Monsieur Rambaud, his whole attention engrossed, bent his grizzled head over the doll which he had dismembered. At times he could not prevent the loosened springs from giving out a creaking noise, a childlike squeaking which his big fingers, though plied with the utmost gentleness, drew from the disordered mechanism. If the doll vented too loud a sound, however, he at once stopped working, distressed and vexed with himself and turning towards Jeanne to see if he had roused her. Then once more he would resume his repairing, with great precautions, his only tools being a pair of scissors and a bodkin.

"Why do you weep, my daughter?" again asked the Abbé. "Can I not afford you some relief?"

"Ah! let me be," said Hélène; "these

tears do me good. By-and-by, by-and-by—"

A stiffling sensation checked any further words. Once before, in this very place, she had been convulsed by a storm of tears; but then she had been alone, free to sob in the darkness till the emotion that wrung her was dried up at its source. However, she knew of no cause of sorrow; her daughter was very well once more, and she had resumed the old monotonous delightful life. But it was as though a keen sense of awful grief had abruptly come upon her; it seemed as if she were rolling into a bottomless abyss which she could not fathom, sinking with all who were dear to her in a limitless sea of despair. She knew not what misfortune hung over her head; but she was without hope, and could only weep.

Similar waves of feeling had swept over her during the month of the Virgin in the church laden with the perfume of flowers. And, as twilight fell, the vastness of Paris filled her with a deep religious impression. The stretch of plain seemed to expand, and a sadness rose up from the two millions of living beings who were being engulfed in darkness. And when it was night, and the city with its subdued rumbling had vanished from view, her oppressed heart poured forth its sorrow, and her tears overflowed, in presence of that sovereign peace. She could have clasped her hands and prayed. She was filled with an intense craving for faith, love, and a lapse into heavenly forgetfulness; and the first glinting of the stars overwhelmed her with sacred terror and enjoyment.

A lengthy interval of silence ensued,

and then the Abbé spoke once more, this time more pressingly.

"My daughter, you must confide in me. Why do you hesitate?"

She was still weeping, but more gently, like a wearied and powerless child.

"The Church frightens you," he continued. "For a time I thought you had yielded your heart to God. But it has been willed otherwise. Heaven has its own purposes. Well, since you mistrust the priest, why should you refuse to confide in the friend?"

"You are right," she faltered. "Yes, I am sad at heart, and need your consolation. I must tell you of it all. When I was a child, I seldom, if ever, entered a church; now I cannot be present at a service without feeling touched to the very depths of my being. Yes; and what drew tears from me just now was that voice of Paris, sounding like a mighty organ, that immeasurable night, and those beauteous heavens. Oh! I would fain believe. Help me; teach me."

Abbé Jouve calmed her somewhat by lightly placing his hand on her own. "Tell me everything," he merely said.

She struggled for a time, her heart wrung with anguish.

"There's nothing to tell, I assure you. I'm hiding nothing from you. I weep without cause, because I feel stifled, because my tears gush out of their own accord. You know what my life has been. No sorrow, no sin, no remorse could I find in it to this hour. I do not know—I do not know—"

Her voice died away, and from the priest's lips slowly came the words, "You love, my daughter!"

She started; she dared not protest. Silence fell on them once more. In the sea of shadows that slumbered before them a light had glimmered forth. It seemed at their feet, somewhere in the abyss, but at what precise spot they would have been unable to specify. And then, one by one, other lights broke through the darkness, shooting into instant life, and remaining stationary, scintillating like stars. It seemed as though thousands of fresh planets were rising on the surface of a gloomy lake. Soon they stretched out in double file, starting from the Trocadéro, and nimbly leaping towards Paris. Then these files were intersected by others, curves were described, and a huge, strange, magnificent constellation spread out. Hélène never breathed a word, but gazed on these gleams of light, which made the heavens seemingly descend below the line of the horizon, as though indeed the earth had vanished and the vault of heaven were on every side. And Hélène's heart was again flooded with emotion, as a few minutes before when Charles's-Wain had slowly begun to revolve round the Polar axis, its shaft in the air. Paris, studded with lights, stretched out, deep and sad, prompting fearful thoughts of a firmament swarming with unknown worlds.

Meanwhile the priest, in the monotonous, gentle voice which he had acquired by years of duty in the confessional, continued whispering in her ear. One evening in the past he had warned her; solitude he had said, would be harmful to her welfare. No one could with impunity live outside the pale of life. She had imprisoned herself too closely, and the door had opened to perilous thoughts.

"I am very old now, my daughter," he murmured, "and I have frequently seen women come to us weeping and praying, with a craving to find faith and religion. Thus it is that I cannot be deceiving myself to-day. These women, who seem to seek God in so zealous a manner, are but souls rendered miserable by passion. It is a man whom they worship in our churches."

She was not listening; a strife was raging in her bosom, amidst her efforts to read her innermost thoughts aright. And at last confession came from her in a broken whisper:

"Oh! yes, I love, and that is all! Beyond that I know nothing—nothing!"

He now forbore to interrupt her; she spoke in short feverish sentences, taking a mournful pleasure in thus confessing her love, in sharing with that venerable priest the secret which had so long burdened her.

"I swear I cannot read my thoughts. This has come to me without my knowing its presence. Perhaps it came in a moment. Only in time did I realize its sweetness. Besides, why should I deem myself stronger than I am? I have made no effort to flee from it; I was only too happy, and to-day I have yet less power of resistance. My daughter was ill; I almost lost her. Well! my love has been as intense as my sorrow; it came back with sovereign power after those days of terror—and it possesses me, I feel transported—"

She shivered and drew a breath.

"In short, my strength fails me. You were right, my friend, in thinking it would be a relief to confide in you.

But, I beseech you, tell me what is happening in the depths of my heart. My life was once so peaceful; I was so happy. A thunderbolt has fallen on me. Why on me? Why not on another? I had done nothing to bring it on; I imagined myself well protected. Ah, if you only knew—I know myself no longer! Help me, save me!"

Then as she became silent, the priest, with the wonted freedom of the confessor, mechanically asked the question:

"The name? tell me his name?"

She was hesitating, when a peculiar noise prompted her to turn her head. It came from the doll which, in Monsieur Rambaud's hands, was by degrees renewing its mechanical life, and had just taken three steps on the table, with a creaking of wheels and springs which showed that there was still something faulty in its works. Then it had fallen on its back, and but for the worthy man would have rebounded onto the ground. He followed all its movements with outstretched hands, ready to support it, and full of paternal anxiety. The moment he perceived Héléne turn, he smiled confidently towards her, as if to give her an assurance that the doll would recover its walking powers. And then he once more dived with scissors and bodkin into the toy. Jeanne still slept on.

Thereupon Hélène, her nerves relaxing under the influence of the universal quiet, whispered a name in the priest's ear. He never stirred; in the darkness his face could not be seen. A silence ensued, and he responded:

"I know it, but I wanted to hear it from your own lips. My daughter, yours must be terrible suffering."

He gave utterance to no truisms on the subject of duty. Hélène, overcome, saddened to the heart by this unemotional pity, gazed once more on the lights which spangled the gloomy veil enshrouding Paris. They were flashing everywhere in myriads, like the sparks that dart over the blackened refuse of burnt paper. At first these twinkling dots had started from the Trocadéro towards the heart of the city. Soon another coruscation had appeared on the left in the direction of Montmartre; then another had burst into view on the right behind the Invalides, and still another, more distant near the Panthéon. From all these centres flights of flames were simultaneously descending.

"You remember our conversation," slowly resumed the Abbé. "My opinion has not changed. My daughter, you must marry."

"I!" she exclaimed, overwhelmed with amazement. "But I have just confessed to you—Oh, you know well I cannot—"

"You must marry," he repeated with greater decision. "You will wed an honest man."

Within the folds of his old cassock he seemed to have grown more commanding. His large comical-looking head, which, with eyes half-closed, was usually inclined towards one shoulder, was now raised erect, and his eyes beamed with such intensity that she saw them sparkling in the darkness.

"You will marry an honest man, who will be a father to Jeanne, and will lead you back to the path of goodness."

"But I do not love him. Gracious Heaven! I do not love him!"

"You will love him, my daughter. He loves you, and he is good in heart."

Hélène struggled, and her voice sank to a whisper as she heard the slight noise that Monsieur Rambaud made behind them. He was so patient and so strong in his hope, that for six months he had not once intruded his love on her. Disposed by nature to the most heroic self-sacrifice, he waited in serene confidence. The Abbé stirred, as though about to turn round.

"Would you like me to tell him everything? He would stretch out his hand and save you. And you would fill him with joy beyond compare."

She checked him, utterly distracted. Her heart revolted. Both of these peaceful, affectionate men, whose judgment retained perfect equilibrium in presence of her feverish passion, were sources of terror to her. What world could they abide in to be able to set at naught that which caused her so much agony? The priest, however, waved his hand with an all-comprehensive gesture.

"My daughter," said he, "look on this lovely night, so supremely still in presence of your troubled spirit. Why do you refuse happiness?"

All Paris was now illumined. The tiny dancing flames had speckled the sea of shadows from one end of the horizon to the other, and now, as in a summer night, millions of fixed stars seemed to be serenely gleaming there. Not a puff of air, not a quiver of the atmosphere stirred these lights, to all appearance suspended in space. Paris, now invisible, had fallen into the depths of an abyss as vast as a firmament. At times, at the base of the Trocadéro, a light—the lamp of a passing cab or omnibus—would dart across the gloom, sparkling like a shooting star; and here amidst the radiance of the gas-jets, from which streamed a yellow haze, a confused jumble of house-fronts and clustering trees—green like the trees in stage scenery—could be vaguely discerned. To and fro, across the Pont des Invalides, gleaming lights flashed without ceasing; far below, across a band of denser gloom, appeared a marvellous train of comet-like coruscations, from whose lustrous tails fell a rain of gold. These were the reflections in the Seine's black waters of the lamps on the bridge. From this point, however, the unknown began. The long curve of the river was merely described by a double line of lights, which ever and anon were coupled to other transverse lines, so that the whole looked like some glittering ladder, thrown across Paris, with its ends on the verge of the heavens among the stars.

To the left there was another trench excavated athwart the gloom; an unbroken chain of stars shone forth down the Champs-Elysées from the Arc-de-Triomphe to the Place de la Concorde, where a new cluster of Pleiades was flashing; next came the gloomy stretches of the Tuileries and the Louvre, the blocks of houses on the brink of the water, and the Hôtel-de-Ville away at the extreme end — all these masses of darkness being parted here and there by bursts of light from some large square or other; and farther and farther away, amidst the endless confusion of roofs, appeared scattered gleams, affording faint glimpses of the hollow of a street below, the corner of some boulevard, or the brilliantly illuminated meeting-place of several thoroughfares. On the opposite bank, on the right, the Esplanade alone could be discerned with any distinctness, its rectangle marked out in flame, like an Orion of a winter's night bereft of his baldrick. The long streets of the Saint-Germain district seemed gloomy with their fringe of infrequent lamps; but the thickly populated quarters beyond were speckled with a multitude of tiny flames, clustering like nebulæ. Away towards the outskirts, girdling the whole of the horizon, swarmed street-lamps and lighted windows, filling these distant parts with a dust, as it were, of those myriads of suns, those planetary atoms which the naked eye cannot discover. The public edifices had vanished into the depths of the darkness, not a lamp marked out their spires and towers. At times you might have imagined you were gazing on some gigantic festival, some illuminated cyclopean monument, with staircases, balusters, windows, pediments, and terraces—a veritable cosmos of stone, whose wondrous architecture was outlined by the gleaming lights of a myriad lamps. But there was always a speedy return of the feeling that new constellations were springing into being, and that the heavens were spreading both above and below.

Hélène, in compliance with the all-embracing sweep of the priest's hand, cast a lingering look over illumined Paris. Here too she knew not the names of those seeming stars. She would have liked to ask what the blaze far below on the left betokened, for she saw it night after night. There were others also which roused her curiosity, and some of them she loved, whilst some inspired her with uneasiness or vexation.

"Father," said she, for the first time employing that appellation of affection and respect, "let me live as I am. The loveliness of the night has agitated me. You are wrong; you would not know how to console me, for you cannot understand my feelings."

The priest stretched out his arms, then slowly dropped them to his side resignedly. And after a pause he said in a whisper:

"Doubtless that was bound to be the case. You call for succor and reject salvation. How many despairing confessions I have received! What tears I have been unable to prevent! Listen, my daughter, promise me one thing only; if ever life should become too heavy a burden for you, think that one honest man loves you and is waiting for you. To regain content you will only have to place your hand in his."

"I promise you," answered Hélène gravely.

As she made the avowal a ripple of laughter burst through the room. Jeanne had just awoke, and her eyes were riveted on her doll pacing up and down the table. Monsieur Rambaud, enthusiastic over the success of his tinkering, still kept his hands stretched out for fear lest any accident should happen. But the doll retained its stability, strutted about on its tiny feet, and turned its head, whilst at every step repeating the same words after the fashion of a parrot.

"Oh! it's some trick or other!" murmured Jeanne, who was still half asleep. "What have you done to it— tell me? It was all smashed, and now it's walking. Give it me a moment; let me see. Oh, you *are* a darling!"

Meanwhile over the gleaming expanse of Paris a rosy cloud was ascending higher and higher. It might have been thought the fiery breath of a furnace. At first it was shadowy-pale in the darkness — a reflected glow scarcely seen. Then slowly, as the evening progressed, it assumed a ruddier hue; and, hanging in the air, motionless above the city, deriving its being from all the lights and noisy life which breathed from below, it seemed like one of those clouds, charged with flame and lighting, which crown the craters of volcanoes.

## CHAPTER XVI

### OPPRESSIVE PERFUMES

THE finger-glasses had been handed round the table, and the ladies were daintily wiping their hands. A momentary silence reigned, while Madame Deberle gazed on either side to see if every one had finished; then, without speaking, she rose, and amidst a noisy pushing back of chairs, her guests followed her example. An old gentleman who had been seated at her right hand hastened to offer her his arm.

"No, no," she murmured, as she led him towards a doorway. "We will now have coffee in the little drawing-room."

The guests, in couples, followed her.

Two ladies and two gentlemen, however, lagged behind the others, continuing their conversation, without thought of joining the procession. The drawing-room reached, all constraint vanished, and the joviality which had marked the dessert made its reappearance. The coffee was already served on a large lacquer tray on a table. Madame Deberle walked round like a hostess who is anxious to satisfy the various tastes of her guests. But it was Pauline who ran about the most, and more particularly waited on the gentlemen. There were a dozen persons present, about the regulation number of people invited to the house every Wednesday, from December onwards. Later in the evening, at ten o'clock, a great many others would make their appearance.

"Monsieur de Guiraud, a cup of coffee," exclaimed Pauline, as she halted in front of a diminutive, baldheaded man. "Ah, no, I remember, you don't take any. Well, then, a glass of Chartreuse?"

But she became confused in discharging her duties, and brought him a glass of cognac. Beaming with smiles, she made the round of the guests, perfectly self-possessed, and looking people straight in the face, while her long train dragged with easy grace behind her. She wore a magnificent gown of white Indian cashmere trimmed with swan's down, and cut square at the bosom. When the gentlemen were all standing up, sipping their coffee, each with cup in hand and chin high in the air, she began to tackle a tall young fellow named Tissot, whom she considered rather handsome.

Hélène had not taken any coffee. She had seated herself apart, with a somewhat wearied expression on her face. Her black velvet gown, unrelieved by any trimming, gave her an air of austerity. In this small drawing-room smoking was allowed, and several boxes of cigars were placed beside her on the pier-table. The doctor drew near; as he selected a cigar he asked her: "Is Jeanne well?"

"Yes, indeed," she replied. "We walked to the Bois to-day, and she romped like a madcap. Oh, she must be sound asleep by now."

They were both chatting in friendly tones, with the smiling intimacy of people who see each other day after day, when Madame Deberle's voice rose high and shrill:

"Stop! stop! Madame Grandjean can tell you all about it. Didn't I come back from Trouville on the 10th of September? It was raining, and the beach had become quite unbearable!"

Three or four of the ladies were gathered round her while she rattled on about her holiday at the seaside. Hélène found it necessary to rise and join the group.

"We spent a month at Dinard," said Madame de Chermette. "Such a delightful place, and such charming society!"

"Behind our chalet was a garden, and we had a terrace overlooking the sea," went on Madame Deberle. "As you know, I decided on taking my landau and coachman with me. It was very much handier when I wanted a drive. Then Madame Levasseur came to see us—"

"Yes, one Sunday," interrupted that lady. "We were at Cabourg. Your establishment was perfect, but a little too dear, I think."

"By the way," broke in Madame Berthier, addressing Juliette, "didn't Monsieur Malignon give you lessons in swimming?"

Hélène noticed a shadow of vexation, of sudden annoyance, pass over Madame Deberle's face. Several times already she had fancied that, on Malignon's name being brought unexpectedly into the conversation, Madame Deberle suddenly seemed perturbed. However, the young woman immediately regained her equanimity.

"A fine swimmer, indeed!" she exclaimed. "The idea of him ever giving lessons to any one! For my part, I have a mortal fear of cold water—the very sight of people bathing curdles my blood."

She gave an eloquent shiver, with a shrug of her plump shoulders, as though she were a duck shaking water from her back.

"Then it's a fable?" questioned Madame de Guiraud.

"Of course; and one, I presume, of his own invention. He detests me since he spent a month with us down there."

People were now beginning to pour in. The ladies, with clusters of flowers in their hair, and round, plump arms, entered smiling and nodding; while the men, each in evening dress and hat in hand, bowed and ventured on some commonplace remark. Madame Deberle, never ceasing her chatter for a moment, extended the tips of her fingers to the friends of the house, many of whom said nothing, but passed on with a bow. However, Mademoiselle Aurélie had just appeared on the scene, and at once went into raptures over Juliette's dress, which was of dark-blue velvet, trimmed with faille silk. At this all the ladies standing round seemed to catch their first glimpse of the dress, and declared it was exquisite, truly exquisite. It came, they learned, from Worth's, and they discussed it for five minutes. The guests who had drunk their coffee had placed their empty cups here and there on the tray and on the pier-tables; only one old gentleman had not yet finished, as between every mouthful he paused to converse with a lady. A warm perfume, the aroma of the coffee and the ladies' dresses intermingled, permeated the apartment.

"You know I have had nothing," remonstrated young Monsieur Tissot with Pauline, who had been chatting with him about an artist to whose studio her father had escorted her with a view to examining the pictures.

"What! have you had nothing? Surely I brought you a cup of coffee?"

"No, mademoiselle, I assure you."

"But I insist on your having something. See, here is some Chartreuse."

Madame Deberle had just directed a meaning nod towards her husband. The doctor, understanding her, thereupon opened the door of a large drawing-room, into which they all filed, while a servant removed the coffee-tray. There was almost a chill atmosphere in this spacious apartment, through which streamed the white light of six lamps and a chandelier with ten wax candles. There were already some ladies there, sitting in a semi-circle

round the fireplace, but only two or three men were present, standing amidst the sea of outspread skirts. And through the open doorway of the smaller drawing-room rang the shrill voice of Pauline, who had lingered behind in company with young Tissot.

"Now that I have poured it out, I'm determined you shall drink it. What would you have me do with it? Pierre has carried off the tray."

Then she entered the larger room, a vision in white, with her dress trimmed with swan's-down. Her ruddy lips parted, displaying her teeth, as she smilingly announced: "Here comes Malignon, the exquisite!"

Hand-shaking and bowing were now the order of the day. Monsieur Deberle had placed himself near the door. His wife, seated with some other ladies on an extremely low couch, rose every other second. When Malignon made his appearance, she affected to turn away her head. He was dressed to perfection; his hair had been curled, and was parted behind, down to his very neck. On the threshold he had stuck an eye-glass in his right eye with a slight grimace, which, according to Pauline, was just the thing; and now he cast a glance around the room. Having nonchalantly and silently shaken hands with the doctor, he made his way towards Madame Deberle, in front of whom he respectfully bent his tall figure.

"Oh, it's you!" she exclaimed, in a voice loud enough to be heard by everybody. "It seems you go in for swimming now."

He did not guess her meaning, but nevertheless replied, by way of a joke:

"Certainly; I once saved a Newfoundland dog from drowning."

The ladies thought this extremely funny, and even Madame Deberle seemed disarmed.

"Well, I'll allow you to save Newfoundlands," she answered, "but you know very well I did not bathe once at Trouville."

"Oh, you're speaking of the lesson I gave you!" he exclaimed. "Didn't I tell you one night in your dining-room how to move your feet and hands about?"

All the ladies were convulsed with mirth — he was delightful! Juliette shrugged her shoulders; it was impossible to engage him in a serious talk. Then she rose to meet a lady whose first visit this was to her house, and who was a superb pianist. Hélène, seated near the fire, her lovely face unruffled by any emotion, looked on and listened. Malignon, especially, seemed to interest her. She saw him execute a strategical movement which brought him to Madame Deberle's side, and she could hear the conversation that ensued behind her chair. Of a sudden there was a change in the tones, and she leaned back to gather the drift of what was being said.

"Why didn't you come yesterday?" asked Malignon. "I waited for you till six o'clock."

"Nonsense; you are mad," murmured Juliette.

Thereupon Malignon loudly lisped: "Oh! you don't believe the story about my Newfoundland! Yet I received a medal for it, and I'll show it to you." Then he added, in a whisper: "You gave me your promise—remember."

A family group now entered the drawing-room, and Juliette broke into complimentary greetings, while Malignon reappeared amongst the ladies, glass in eye. Hélène had become quite pale since overhearing those hastily spoken words. It was as though a thunderbolt, or something equally unforeseen and horrible, had fallen on her. How could thoughts of treachery enter into the mind of that woman whose life was so happy, whose face betrayed no signs of sorrow, whose cheeks had the freshness of the rose? She had always known her to be devoid of brains, displaying an amiable egotism which seemed a guarantee that she would never commit a foolish action. And over such a fellow as Malignon, too! The scenes in the garden of an afternoon flashed back on her memory — she recalled Juliette smiling lovingly as the doctor kissed her hair. Their love for one another had seemed real enough. An inexplicable feeling of indignation with Juliette now pervaded Hélène, as though some wrong had been done herself. She felt humiliated for Henri's sake; she was consumed with jealous rage; and her perturbed feelings were so plainly mirrored in her face Mademoiselle Aurélie asked her: "What is the matter with you? Do you feel ill?"

The old lady had sunk into a seat beside her immediately she had observed her to be alone. She had conceived a lively friendship for Hélène, and was charmed with the kindly manner in which so sedate and lovely a woman would listen for hours to her tittle-tattle.

But Hélène made no reply. A wild desire sprang up within her to gaze on

Henri, to know what he was doing, and what was the expression on his face. She sat up, and glancing round the drawing-room, at last perceived him. He stood talking with a stout, pale man, and looked completely at his ease, his face wearing its customary refined smile. She scanned him for a moment, full of a pity which belittled him somewhat, though all the while she loved him the more with an affection into which entered some vague idea of watching him. Her feelings, still in a whirl of confusion, inspired her with the thought that she ought to bring him back the happiness he had lost.

"Well, well!" muttered Mademoiselle Aurélie; "it will be pleasant if Madame de Guiraud's sister favors us with a song. It will be the tenth time I have heard her sing the 'Turtle-Doves.' That is her stock song this winter. You know that she is separated from her husband. Do you see that dark gentleman down there, near the door? They are most intimate together, I believe. Juliette is compelled to have him here, for otherwise she wouldn't come!"

"Indeed!" exclaimed Hélène.

Madame Deberle was bustling about from one group to another, requesting silence for a song from Madame de Guiraud's sister. The drawing-room was now crowded, some thirty ladies being seated in the centre whispering and laughing together; two, however, had remained standing, and were talking loudly and shrugging their shoulders in a pretty way, while five or six men sat quite at home amongst the fair ones, almost buried beneath the folds of their skirts and trains. A low

"Hush!" ran round the room, the voices died away, and a stolid look of annoyance crept into every face. Only the fans could be heard rustling through the heated atmosphere.

Madame de Guiraud's sister sang, but Hélène never listened. Her eyes were now riveted on Malignon, who feigned an intense love of music, and appeared to be enraptured with the "Turtle Doves." Was it possible? Could Juliette have turned a willing ear to the amorous chatter of the young fop? It was at Trouville, no doubt, that some dangerous game had been played. Malignon now sat in front of Juliette, marking the time of the music by swaying to and fro with the air of one who is enraptured. Madame Deberle's face beamed in admiring complacency, while the doctor, good-natured and patient, silently awaited the last notes of the song in order to renew his talk with the stout, pale man.

There was a murmur of applause as the singer's voice died away, and two or three exclaimed in tones of transport: "Delightful! magnificent!"

Malignon, however, stretching his arms over the ladies' head-dresses, noiselessly clasped his gloved hands, and repeated "Brava! brava!" in a voice that rose high above the others.

The enthusiasm promptly came to an end, every face relaxed and smiled, and a few of the ladies rose, while, with the feeling of general relief, the buzz of conversation began again. The atmosphere was growing much warmer, and the waving fans wafted an odor of musk from the ladies' dresses. At times, amidst the universal chatter, a peal of pearly laughter would ring out, or some word spoken in a loud tone would cause many to turn round. Thrice already had Juliette swept into the smaller drawing-room to request some gentleman who had escaped thither not to desert the ladies in so rude a fashion. They returned at her request, but ten minutes afterwards had again vanished.

"It's intolerable," she muttered, with an air of vexation "not one of them will stay here."

In the meantime Mademoiselle Aurélie was running over the ladies' names for Hélène's benefit, as this was only the latter's second evening visit to the doctor's house. The most substantial people of Passy, some of them rolling in riches, were present. And the old maid leaned towards Hélène and whispered in her ear: "Yes, it seems it's all arranged. Madame de Chermette is going to marry her daughter to that tall fair fellow with whom she has flirted for the last eighteen months. Well, never mind, that will be one mother-in-law who'll be fond of her son-in-law."

She stopped short, and then burst out in a tone of intense surprise: "Good gracious! there's Madame Levasseur's husband speaking to that man. I thought Juliette had sworn never to have them here together."

Hélène's glances slowly travelled round the room. Even amongst such seemingly estimable and honest people as these could there be women of irregular conduct? With her provincial austerity she was astounded at the manner in which wrongdoing was winked at in Paris. She rallied at herself for her own painful repugnance when Juliette had shaken hands with her.

Madame Deberle had now seemingly become reconciled with Malignon; she had curled up her little plump figure in an easy-chair, where she sat listening gleefully to his jests. Monsieur Deberle happened to pass them.

"You're surely not quarrelling tonight?" asked he.

"No," replied Juliette, with a burst of merriment.

"He's talking too much silly nonsense. If you had heard all the nonsense he's been saying!"

There now came some more singing, but silence was obtained with greater difficulty. The aria selected was a duet from *La Favorita*, sung by young Monsieur Tissot and a lady of ripened charms, whose hair was dressed in childish style. Pauline, standing at one of the doors, amidst a crowd of black coats, gazed at the male singer with a look of undisguised admiration, as though she were examining a work of art.

"What a handsome fellow!" escaped from her lips, just as the accompaniment subsided into a softer key, and so loud was her voice that the whole drawing-room heard the remark.

As the evening progressed the guests' faces began to show signs of weariness. Ladies who had occupied the same seat for hours looked bored, though they knew it not—they were even delighted at being able to get bored here. In the intervals between the songs, which were only half listened to, the murmur of conversation again resounded, and it seemed as though the deep notes of the piano were still echoing. Monsieur Letellier related how he had gone to Lyons for the purpose of inspecting some silk he had ordered, and how he had been greatly impressed by the fact that the Saône did not mingle its waters with those of the Rhône. Monsieur de Guiraud, who was magistrate, gave vent to some sententious observations on the need of stemming the vice of Paris. There was a circle round a gentleman who was acquainted with a Chinaman, and was giving some particulars of his friend. In a corner two ladies were exchanging confidences about the failings of their servants; whilst literature was being discussed by those among whom Malignon sat enthroned. Madame Tissot declared Balzac to be unreadable, and Malginon did not deny it, but remarked that here and there at intervals far and few, some very fine passages occurred in Balzac.

"A little silence, please!" all at once exclaimed Pauline; "she's just going to play."

The lady whose talent as a musician had been so much spoken of had just sat down to the piano. In accordance with the rules of politeness, every head was turned towards her. But in the general stillness which ensued the deep voices of the men conversing in the small drawing-room could be heard. Madame Deberle was in despair.

"They are a nuisance!" she muttered. "Let them stay there, if they don't want to come in; but at least they ought to hold their tongues!"

She gave the requisite orders to Pauline, who, intensely delighted, ran into the adjacent apartment to carry out her instructions.

"You must know, gentlemen, that a lady is going to play," she said, with the quiet boldness of a maiden in queenly garb. "You are requested to keep silence."

She spoke in a very loud key, her voice being naturally shrill. And, as she lingered with the men, laughing and quizzing, the noise grew more pronounced than ever. There was a discussion going on among the males, and she supplied additional matter for argument. In the larger drawing-room Madame Deberle was in agony. The guests, moreover, had been sated with music, and no enthusiasm was displayed; so the pianist resumed her seat, biting her lips, notwithstanding the laudatory compliments which the lady of the house deemed it her duty to lavish on her.

Hélène was pained. Henri scarcely seemed to see her; he had made no attempt to approach her, and only at intervals smiled at her from afar. At the earlier part of the evening she had felt relieved by his prudent reserve; but since she had learnt the secret of the two others she wished for something—she know not what—some display of affection, or at least interest, on his part. Her breast was stirred with confused yearnings, and every imaginable evil thought. Did he no longer care for her, that he remained so indifferent to her presence? Oh! if she could have told him everything! If she could appraise him of the unworthiness of the woman who bore his name! Then, while some short, merry catches resounded from the piano, she sank into a dreamy state. She imagined that Henri had driven Juliette from his home, and she was living with him as his wife in some far-away foreign land, the language of which they knew not.

All at once a voice startled her.

"Won't you take anything?" asked Pauline.

The drawing-room had emptied, and the guests were passing into the dining-room to drink some tea. Hélène rose with difficulty. She was dazed; she thought she had dreamt it all—the words she had heard, Juliette's secret intrigue, and its consequences. If it had all been true, Henri would surely have been at her side and ere this both would have quitted the house.

"Will you take a cup of tea?"

She smiled and thanked Madame Deberle, who had kept a place for her at the table. Plates loaded with pastry and sweetmeats covered the cloth, while on glass stands arose two lofty cakes, flanking a large *brioche*. The space was limited, and the cups of tea were crowded together, narrow grey napkins with long fringes lying between each two. The ladies only were seated. They held biscuits and preserved fruits with the tips of their ungloved fingers, and passed each other the cream-jugs and poured out the cream with dainty gestures. Three or four, however, had sacrificed themselves to attend on the men, who were standing against the walls, and, while drinking, taking all conceivable precautions to ward off any push which might be unwittingly dealt them. A few others lingered in the two drawing-rooms, waiting for the cakes to come to them. This was the hour of Pauline's supreme delight. There was a shrill clamor of noisy tongues, peals of laughter mingled with the ringing clatter of

silver plate, and the perfume of musk grew more powerful as it blended with the all-prevading fragrance of the tea.

"Kindly pass me some cake," said Mademoiselle Aurélie to Hélène, close to whom she happened to find herself. "These sweatmeats are frauds!"

She had, however, already emptied two plates of them. And she continued, with her mouth full:

"Oh! some of the people are beginning to go now. We shall be a little more comfortable."

In truth, several ladies were now leaving, after shaking hands with Madame Deberle. Many of the gentlemen had already wisely vanished, and the room was becoming less crowded. Now came the opportunity for the remaining gentlemen to sit down at table in their turn. Mademoiselle Aurélie, however, did not quit her place, though she would much have liked to secure a glass of punch.

"I will get you one," said Hélène, starting to her feet.

"No, no, thank you. You must not inconvenience yourself so much."

For a short time Hélène had been watching Malignon. He had just shaken hands with the doctor, and was now bidding farewell to Juliette at the doorway. She had a lustrous face and sparkling eyes, and by her complacent smile it might have been imagined that she was receiving some commonplace compliments on the evening's success. While Pierre was pouring out the punch at a side-board near the door, Hélène stepped forward in such wise as to be hidden from view by the curtain, which had been drawn back. She listened.

"I beseech you," Malignon was say-

ing, "come the day after to-morrow.
I shall wait for you till three o'clock."

"Why cannot you talk seriously,"
replied Madame Deberle, with a laugh.
"What foolish things you say!"

But with greater determination he
repeated: "I shall wait for you—the
day after to-morrow."

Then she hurriedly gave a whispered
reply:

"Very well—the day after to-
morrow."

Malignon bowed and made his exit.
Madame de Chermette followed in company with Madame Tissot. Juliette,
in the best of spirits, walked with them
into the hall, and said to the former of
these ladies with her most amiable look:

"I shall call on you the day after to-
morrow. I have a lot of calls to make
that day."

Hélène stood riveted to the floor,
her face quite white. Pierre, in the
meanwhile had poured out the punch,
and now handed the glass to her. She
grasped it mechanically and carried it
to Mademoiselle Aurélie, who was
making an inroad on the preserved
fruits.

"Oh, you are far too kind!" exclaimed the old maid. "I should have
made a sign to Pierre. I'm sure it's
a shame not offering the punch to ladies.
Why, when people are my age—"

She got no further, however, for
she observed the ghastliness of Hélène's
face. "You surely are in pain! You
must take a drop of punch!"

"Thank you, it's nothing. The heat
is so oppressive—"

She staggered, and turned aside into
the deserted drawing-room, where she
dropped into an easy-chair. The lamps

were shedding a reddish glare; and the
wax candles in the chandelier, burnt
to their sockets, threatened imminent
destruction to the crystal sconces.
From the dining-room were wafted the
farewells of the departing guests.
Hélène herself had lost all thoughts
of going; she longed to linger where
she was, plunged in thought. So it
was no dream after all; Juliette would
visit that man the day after to-morrow
—she knew the day. Then the thought
struck her that she ought to speak to
Juliette and warn her against sin. But
this kindly thought chilled her to the
heart, and she drove it from her mind
as though it were out of place, and deep
in meditation gazed at the grate, where
a smouldering log was crackling. The
air was still heavy and oppressive with
the perfumes from the ladies' hair.

"What! you are here!" exclaimed
Juliette as she entered. "Well, you are
kind not to run away all at once. At
last we can breathe!"

Hélène was surprised, and made a
movement as though about to rise;
but Juliette went on: "Wait, wait
you are in no hurry. Henri get me my
smelling-salts."

Three or four persons, intimate
friends, had lingered behind the others.
They sat before the dying fire and
chatted with delightful freedom, while
the vast room wearily sank into a doze.
The doors were open, and they saw
the smaller drawing-room empty, the
dining-room deserted, the whole suite
of rooms still lit up and plunged in
unbroken silence. Henri displayed a
tender gallantry towards his wife; he
had run up to their bedroom for her
smelling-salts, which she inhaled with

closed eyes, whilst he asked her if she had not fatigued herself too much. Yes, she felt somewhat tired; but she was delighted—everything had gone off so well. Next she told them that on her reception nights she could not sleep, but tossed about till six o'clock in the morning. Henri's face broke into a smile, and some quizzing followed. Hélène looked at them, and quivered amidst the benumbing drowsiness which little by little seemed to fall upon the whole house.

However, only two guests now remained. Pierre had gone in search of a cab. Hélène remained the last. One o'clock struck. Henri, no longer standing on ceremony rose on tiptoe and blew out two candles in the chandelier which were dangerously heating their crystal sconces. As the lights died out one by one, it seemed like a bedroom scene, the gloom of an alcove spreading over all.

"I am keeping you up!" exclaimed Hélène, as she suddenly rose to her feet. "You must turn me out."

A flush of red dyed her face; her blood, racing through her veins, seemed to stifle her. They walked with her into the hall, but the air there was chilly, and the doctor was somewhat alarmed for his wife in her low dress.

"Go back; you will do yourself harm. You are too warm."

"Very well; good-bye," said Juliette, embracing Hélène, as was her wont in her most endearing moments. "Come and see me oftener."

Henri had taken Hélène's fur coat in his hand, and held it outstretched to assist her in putting it on. When she had slipped her arms into the sleeves, he turned up the collar with a smile, while they stood in front of an immense mirror which covered one side of the hall. They were alone and saw one another in the mirror's depths. For three months, on meeting and parting they had simply shaken hands in a friendly greeting; they would fain that their love had died. But now Hélène was overcome, and sank back into his arms. The smile vanished from his face, which became impassioned, and, still clasping her, he kissed her on the neck. And she, raising her head, returned the kiss.

## CHAPTER XVII

### MOTHER FÉTU

THAT night Hélène was unable to sleep. She turned from side to side in feverish unrest, and whenever a drowsy stupor fell on her senses, the old sorrows would start into new life within her breast. As she dozed and the nightmare increased, one fixed thought tortured her—she was eager to know where Juliette and Malignon would meet. This knowledge, she imagined, would be a source of relief to her. Where, where could it be? Despite herself, her brain throbbed with the thought, and she forgot everything save her craving to unravel this mystery, which thrilled he with secret longings.

When day dawned and she began to dress, she caught herself saying loudly: "It will be to-morrow!"

With one stocking on, and hands

falling helpless to her side she lapsed
for a while into a fresh dreamy fit.
Where, where was it that they had
agreed to meet?

"Good-day, mother, darling!" just
then exclaimed Jeanne who had
awakened in her turn.

As her strength was now returning
to her, she had gone back to sleep in
her cot in the closet. With bare feet
and in her nightdress she came to
throw herself on Hélène's neck, as
was her every-day custom; then back
again she rushed, to curl herself up
in her warm bed for a little while
longer. This jumping in and out
amused her, and a ripple of laughter
stole from under her clothes. Once
more she bounded into the bedroom,
saying: "Good-morning, mammy dear!"

And again she ran off, screaming
with laughter. Then she threw the
sheet over her head, and her cry came,
hoarse and muffled, from beneath it:
"I'm not there! I'm not there!"

But Hélène was in no mood for play,
as on other mornings; and Jeanne,
dispirited, fell asleep again. The day
was still young. About eight o'clock
Rosalie made her appearance to re-
count the morning's chapter of accidents. Oh! the streets were awful
outside; in going for the milk her
shoes had almost come off in the
muddy slush. All the ice was thawing; and it was quite mild too, almost
oppressive. Oh! by the way, she had
almost forgotten! an old woman had
come to see madame the night before.

"Why!" she said, as there came a
pull at the bell, "I expect that's she!"

It was Mother Fétu, but Mother
Fétu transformed, magnificent in a
clean white cap, a new gown, and tar-
tan shawl wrapped round her shoulders.
Her voice, however, still retained its
plaintive tone of entreaty.

"Dear lady, it's only I who have
taken the liberty of calling to ask you
about something!"

Hélène gazed at her, somewhat surprised by her display of finery.

"Are you better, Mother Fétu?"

"Oh yes, yes; I feel better, if I
may venture to say so. You see I always have something queer in my inside; it knocks me about dreadfully,
but still I'm better. Another thing,
too; I've had a stroke of luck; it was
a surprise, you see, because luck hasn't
often come in my way. But a gentleman has made me his housekeeper—
and oh! it's such a story!"

Her words came slowly, and her
small keen eyes glittered in her face,
furrowed by a thousand wrinkles. She
seemed to be waiting for Hélène to
question her; but the young woman
sat close to the fire which Rosalie had
just lit, and paid scant attention to
her, engrossed as she was in her own
thoughts, with a look of pain on her
features.

"What do you want to ask me?"
she at last said to Mother Fétu.

The old lady made no immediate
reply. She was scrutinizing the room,
with its rosewood furniture and blue
velvet hangings. Then, with the
humble and fawning air of a pauper,
she muttered: "Pardon me, madame,
but everything is so beautiful here.
My gentleman has a room like this,
but it's all in pink. Oh! it's such a
story! Just picture to yourself a
young man of good position who has

taken rooms in our house. Of course, it isn't much of a place, but still our first and second floors are very nice. Then, it's so quiet, too! There's no traffic; you could imagine yourself in the country. The workmen have been in the house for a whole fortnight; they have made such a jewel of his room!"

She here paused, observing that Hélène's attention was being aroused.

"It's for his work," she continued in a drawling voice; "he says it's for his work. We have no doorkeeper, you know, and that pleases him. Oh! my gentleman doesn't like doorkeepers, and he is quite right, too!"

Once more she came to a halt, as though an idea had suddenly occurred to her.

"Why, wait a minute; you must know him—of course you must. He visits one of your lady friends!"

"Ah!" exclaimed Hélène, with colorless face.

"Yes, to be sure; the lady who lives close by—the one who used to go with you to church. She came the other day."

Mother Fétu's eyes contracted, and from under the lids she took note of her benefactress's emotion. But Hélène strove to question her in a tone that would not betray her agitation.

"Did she go up?"

"No, she altered her mind; perhaps she had forgotten something. But I was at the door. She asked for Monsieur Vincent, and then got back into her cab again, calling to the driver to return home, as it was too late. Oh!

she's such a nice, lively, and respectable lady. The gracious God doesn't send many such into the world. Why, with the exception of yourself, she's the best—well, well, may Heaven bless you all!"

In this way Mother Fétu rambled on with the pious glibness of a devotee who is perpetually telling her beads. But the twitching of the myriad wrinkles of her face showed that her mind was still working, and soon she beamed with intense satisfaction.

"Ah!" she all at once resumed in inconsequent fashion, "how I should like to have a pair of good shoes! My gentleman has been so very kind, I can't ask him for anything more. You see I'm dressed; still I must get a pair of good shoes. Look at those I have; they are all holes; and when the weather's muddy, as it is to-day, one's apt to get very ill. Yes, I was down with colic yesterday; I was writhing all the afternoon, but if I had a pair of good shoes—"

"I'll bring you a pair, Mother Fétu," said Hélène, waving her towards the door.

Then, as the old woman retired backwards, with profuse curtseying and thanks, she asked her: "At what hour are you alone?"

"My gentleman is never there after six o'clock," she answered. "But don't give yourself the trouble; I'll come myself, and get them from your doorkeeper. But you can do as you please. You are an angel from heaven. God on high will requite you for all your kindness!"

When she had reached the landing

she could still be heard giving vent to her feelings. Hélène sat a long time plunged in the stupor which the information, supplied by this woman with such fortuitous seasonableness, had brought upon her. She now knew the place of assignation. It was a room, with pink decorations, in that old tumble-down house! She once more pictured to herself the staircase oozing with damp, the yellow doors on each landing, grimy with the touch of greasy hands, and all the wretchedness which had stirred her heart to pity when she had gone during the previous winter to visit Mother Fétu; and she also strove to conjure up a vision of that pink chamber in the midst of such repulsive, poverty-stricken surroundings. However, whilst she was still absorbed in her reverie, two tiny warm hands were placed over her eyes, which lack of sleep had reddened, and a laughing voice inquired: "Who is it? who is it?"

It was Jeanne, who had slipped into her clothes without assistance. Mother Fétu's voice had awakened her; and perceiving that the closet-door had been shut, she had made her toilet with the utmost speed in order to give her mother a surprise.

"Who is it? who is it?" she again inquired, convulsed more and more with laughter.

She turned to Rosalie, who entered at the moment with the breakfast.

"You know; don't you speak. Nobody is asking you any question."

"Be quiet, you little madcap!" exclaimed Héléne. "I suppose it's you!"

The child slipped on to her mother's lap, and there, leaning back and swinging to and fro, delighted with the amusement she had devised, she resumed:

"Well, it might have been another little girl! Eh? Perhaps some little girl who had brought you a letter of invitation to dine with her mamma. And she might have covered your eyes, too!"

"Don't be silly," exclaimed Hélène, as she set her on the floor. "What are you talking about? Rosalie, let us have breakfast."

The maid's eyes, however, were riveted on the child, and she commented upon her little mistress being so oddly dressed. To tell the truth, so great had been Jeanne's haste that she had not put on her shoes. She had drawn on a short flannel petticoat which allowed a glimpse of her chemise, and had left her morning jacket open, so that you could see her delicate, undeveloped bosom. With her hair streaming behind her, stamping about in her stockings, which were all awry, she looked charming, all in white like some child of fairyland.

She cast down her eyes to see herself, and immediately burst into laughter.

"Look, mamma, I look nice, don't I? Won't you let me be as I am? It is nice!"

Repressing a gesture of impatience, Hélène, as was her wont every morning, inquired: "Are you washed?"

"Oh, mamma!" pleaded the child, her joy suddenly dashed. "Oh, mamma! it's raining; it's too nasty!"

"Then, you'll have no breakfast. Wash her, Rosalie."

She usually took this office upon herself, but that morning she felt altogether out of sorts, and drew nearer to the fire, shivering, although the weather was so balmy. Having spread a napkin and placed two white china bowls on a small round table, Rosalie had brought the latter close to the fireplace. The coffee and milk steamed before the fire in a silver pot, which had been a present from Monsieur Rambaud. At this early hour the disorderly, drowsy room seemed delightfully homelike.

"Mamma, mamma!" screamed Jeanne from the depths of the closet, "she's rubbing me too hard. It's taking my skin off. Oh dear! how awfully cold!"

Hélène, with eyes fixed on the coffee-pot, remained engrossed in thought. She desired to know everything, so she would go. The thought of that mysterious place of assignation in so squalid a nook of Paris was an ever-present pain and vexation. She judged such taste hateful, but in it she identified Malignon's leaning towards romance.

"Mademoiselle," declared Rosalie, "if you don't let me finish with you, I shall call madame."

"Stop, stop; you are poking the soap into my eyes," answered Jeanne, whose voice was hoarse with sobs. "Leave me alone; I've had enough of it. The ears can wait till to-morrow."

But the splashing of water went on, and the squeezing of the sponge into the basin could be heard. There was a clamor and a struggle, the child was sobbing; but almost immediately afterward she made her appearance, shouting gaily: "It's over now; it's over now!"

Her hair was still glistening with wet, and she shook herself, her face glowing with the rubbing it had received and ex-haling a fresh and pleasant odor. In her struggle to get free her jacket had slipped from her shoulders, her petticoat had become loosened, and her stockings had tumbled down, displaying her bare legs. According to Rosalie, she looked like an infant Jesus. Jeanne, however, felt very proud that she was clean; she had no wish to be dressed again.

"Look at me, mamma; look at my hands, and my neck, and my ears. Oh! you must let me warm myself; I am so comfortable. You don't say anything; surely I've deserved my breakfast to-day."

She had curled herself up before the fire in her own little easy-chair. Then Rosalie poured out the coffee and milk. Jeanne took her bowl on her lap, and gravely soaked her toast in its contents with all the airs of a grown-up person Hélène had always forbidden her to eat in this way, but that morning she remained plunged in thought. She did not touch her own bread, and was satisfied with drinking her coffee. Then Jeanne, after swallowing her last morsel, was stung with remorse. Her heart filled, she put aside her bowl, and gazing on her mother's pale face, threw herself on her neck: "Mamma, are you ill now? I haven't vexed you, have I? —say."

"No, no, my darling, quite the contrary; you're very good," murmured Hélène as she embraced her. "I'm only a little wearied; I haven't slept well. Go on playing: don't be uneasy."

The thought occurred to her that the day would prove a terribly long one. What could she do whilst waiting for the night? For some time past she had abandoned her needlework; sewing had become a terrible weariness. For hours she lingered in her seat with idle hands, almost suffocating in her room, and craving to go out into the open air for breath, yet never stirring. It was this room which made her ill; she hated it, in angry exasperation over the two years which she had spent within its walls; its blue velvet and the vast panorama of the mighty city disgusted her, and her thoughts dwelt on a lodging in some busy street, the uproar of which would have deafened her. Good heavens! how long were the hours! She took up a book, but the fixed idea that engrossed her mind continually conjured up the same visions between her eyes and the page of print.

In the meantime Rosalie had been busy setting the room in order; Jeanne's hair also had been brushed, and she was dressed. While her mother sat at the window, striving to read, the child, who was in one of her moods of obstreperous gaiety, began playing a grand game. She was all alone; but this gave her no discomfort; she herself represented three or four persons in turn with comical earnestness and gravity. At first she played the lady going on a visit. She vanished into the dining-room, and returned bowing and smiling, her head nodding this way and that in the most coquettish style.

"Good-day, madame! How are you, madame? How long it is since I've seen you! A marvellously long time, to be sure! Dear me, I've been so ill madame! Yes; I've had the cholera; it's very disagreeable. Oh! it doesn't show; no, no, it makes you look younger, on my word of honor. And your children, madame? Oh; I've had three since last summer!"

So she rattled on, never ceasing her curtseying to the round table, which doubtless represented the lady she was visiting. Next she ventured to bring the chairs closer together, and for an hour carried on a general conversation, her talk abounding in extraordinary phrases.

"Don't be silly," said her mother at intervals, when the chatter put her out of patience.

"But, mamma, I'm paying my friend a visit. She's speaking to me, and I must answer her. At tea nobody ought to put the cakes in their pockets, ought they?"

Then she turned and began again:

"Good-bye, madame; your tea was delicious. Remember me most kindly to your husband."

The next moment came something else. She was going out shopping in her carriage, and got astride of a chair like a boy.

"Jean, not so quick; I'm afraid. Stop! stop! here is the milliner's! Mademoiselle, how much is this bonnet? Three hundred francs; that isn't dear. But it isn't pretty. I should like it with a bird on it—a bird big like that! Come, Jean, drive me to the grocer's. Have you some honey? Yes, madame, here is some. Oh, how nice it is! But I don't want any of it; give me two sous'worth of sugar. Oh! Jean, look, take care! There! we have had a spill! Mr. Policeman, it was the cart which drove against us. You're not hurt, madame, are you? No, sir, not in the least. Jean, Jean! home now. Gee-up! gee-up. Wait a minute;

I must order some chemises. Three dozen chemises for madame. I want some boots too and some stays. Gee-up! gee-up! Good gracious, we shall never get back again."

Then she fanned herself, enacting the part of the lady who has returned home and is finding fault with her servants. She never remained quiet for a moment; she was in a feverish ecstasy, full of all sorts of whimsical ideas; all the life she knew surged up in her little brain and escaped from it in fragments. Morning and afternoon she thus moved about, dancing and chattering; and when she grew tired, a footstool or parasol discovered in a corner, or some shred of stuff lying on the floor, would suffice to launch her into a new game in which her effervescing imagination found fresh outlet. Persons, places, and incidents were all of her own creation, and she amused herself as much as though twelve children of her own age had been beside her.

But evening came at last. Six o'clock was about to strike. And Hélène, rousing herself from the troubled stupor in which she had spent the afternoon, hurriedly threw a shawl over her shoulders.

"Are you going out, mamma?" asked Jeanne in her surprise.

"Yes, my darling, just for a walk close by. I won't be long; be good."

Outside it was still thawing. The footways were covered with mud. In the Rue de Passy, Hélène entered a boot shop, to which she had taken Mother Fétu on a previous occasion. Then she returned along the Rue Raynouard. The sky was grey, and from the pavement a mist was rising. The street stretched dimly before her, deserted and fear-inspiring, though the hour was yet early. In the damp haze the infrequent gas-lamps glimmered like yellow spots. She quickened her steps, keeping close to the houses, and shrinking from sight as though she were on the way to some assignation. However, as she hastily turned into the Passage des Eaux, she halted beneath the archway, her heart giving way to genuine terror. The passage opened beneath her like some black gulf. The bottom of it was invisible; the only thing she could see in this black tunnel was the quivering gleam of the one lamp which lighted it. Eventually she made up her mind, and grasped the iron railing to prevent herself from slipping. Feeling her way with the tip of her boots she landed successively on the broad steps. The walls, right and left, grew closer, seemingly prolonged by the darkness, while the bare branches of the trees above cast vague shadows, like those of gigantic arms with closed or outstretched hands. She trembled as she thought that one of the garden doors might spring open and a man spring out upon her. There were no passers-by, however, and she stepped down as quickly as possible. Suddenly from out of the darkness loomed a shadow which coughed, and she was frozen with fear; but it was only an old woman creeping with difficulty up the path. Then she felt less uneasy, and carefully raised her dress which had been trailing in the mud. So thick was the latter that her boots were constantly sticking to the steps. At the bottom she turned aside instinctively. From the branches the rain-drops dripped fast into the passage, and the lamp glimmered like that of some miner, hanging to the side of a pit which infiltrations have rendered dangerous.

Hélène climbed straight to the attic she had so often visited at the top of the large house abutting on the Passage. But nothing stirred, although she rapped loudly. In considerable perplexity she descended the stairs again. Mother Fétu was doubtless in the rooms on the first floor, where, however, Hélène dared not show herself. She remained five minutes in the entry, which was lighted by a petroleum lamp. Then again she ascended the stairs hesitatingly, gazing at each door, and was on the point of going away, when the old woman leaned over the balusters.

"What! it's you on the stairs, my good lady!" she exclaimed, "Come in, and don't catch cold out there. Oh! it is a vile place—enough to kill one."

"No, thank you," said Hélène; "I've brought you your pair of shoes, Mother Fétu."

She looked at the door which Mother Fétu had left open behind her, and caught a glimpse of a stove within.

"I'm all alone, I assure you," declared the old woman. "Come in. This is the kitchen here. Oh! you're not proud with us poor folks; we can talk to you!"

Despite the repugnance which shame at the purpose of her coming created within her, Hélène followed her.

"God in Heaven! how can I thank you! Oh, what lovely shoes! Wait, and I'll put them on. There's my whole foot in; it fits me like a glove. Bless the day! I can walk with these without being afraid of the rain. Oh! my good lady, you are my preserver;

you've given me ten more years of life. No, no, it's no flattery; it's what I think, as true as there's a lamp shining on us. No, no, I don't flatter!"

She melted into tears as she spoke, and grasping Hélène's hands kissed them. In a stewpan on the stove some wine was being heated, and on the table, near the lamp, stood a half-empty bottle of Bordeaux with its tapering neck. The only other things placed there were four dishes, a glass, two saucepans, and an earthenware pot. It could be seen that Mother Fétu camped in this bachelor's kitchen, and that the fires were lit for herself only. Seeing Hélène's glance turn towards the stewpan, she coughed, and once more put on her dolorous expression.

"It's gripping me again," she groaned. "Oh! it's useless for the doctor to talk; I must have some creature in my inside. And then, a drop of wine relieves me so. I'm greatly afflicted, my good lady. I wouldn't have a soul suffer from my trouble; it's too dreadful. Well, I'm nursing myself a bit now; and when a person has passed through so much, isn't it fair she should do so? I have been so lucky in falling in with a nice gentleman. May Heaven bless him!"

With this outburst she dropped two large lumps of sugar into her wine. She was now getting more corpulent than ever, and her little eyes had almost vanished from her fat face. She moved slowly with a beatifical expression of felicity. Her life's ambition was now evidently satisfied. For this she had been born. When she put her sugar away again Hélène caught a glimpse of some tid-bits secreted at the bottom of a cupboard—a jar of preserves, a bag of biscuits, and even some cigars, all doubtless pilfered from the gentleman lodger.

"Well, good-bye, Mother Fétu, I'm going away," she exclaimed.

The old lady, however, pushed the saucepan to one side of the stove and murmured: "Wait a minute; this is far too hot, I'll drink it by-and-by. No, no; don't go out that way. I must beg pardon for having received you in the kitchen. Let us go round the rooms."

She caught up the lamp, and turned into a narrow passage. Hélène, with beating heart, followed close behind. The passage, dilapidated and smoky, was reeking with damp. Then a door was thrown open, and she found herself treading a thick carpet. Mother Fétu had already advanced into a room which was plunged in darkness and silence.

"Well?" she asked, as she lifted up the lamp; "it's very nice, isn't it?"

There were two rooms, each of them square, communicating with one another by folding-doors, which had been removed, and replaced by curtains. Both were hung with pink cretonne of a Louis Quinze pattern, picturing chubby-cheeked cupids disporting themselves amongst garlands of flowers. In the first apartment there was a round table, two lounges, and some easy-chairs; and in the second, which was somewhat smaller, most of the space was occupied by the bed. Mother Fétu drew attention to a crystal lamp with gilt chains, which hung from the ceiling. To her this lamp was the veritable acme of luxury.

Then she began explaining things: "You can't imagine what a funny fel-low he is! He lights it up in mid-day, and stays here, smoking a cigar and gazing into vacancy. But it amuses him, it seems. Well, it doesn't matter; I've an idea he must have spent a lot of money in his time."

Hélène went through the rooms in silence. They seemed to her in bad taste. There was too much pink everywhere; the furniture also looked far too new.

"He calls himself Monsieur Vincent," continued the old woman, rambling on. "Of course, it's all the same to me. As long as he pays, my gentleman—"

"Well, good-bye, Mother Fétu," said Hélène, in whose throat a feeling of suffocation was gathering.

She was burning to get away, but on opening a door she found herself threading three small rooms, the bareness and dirt of which were repulsive. The paper hung in tatters from the walls, the ceilings were grimy, and old plaster littered the broken floors. The whole place was pervaded by a smell of long prevalent squalor.

"Not that way! not that way!" screamed Mother Fétu. "That door is generally shut. These are the other rooms which they haven't attempted to clean. My word! it's cost him quite enough already! Yes, indeed, these aren't nearly so nice! Come this way, my good lady—come this way!"

On Hélène's return to the pink boudoir, she stopped to kiss her hand once more.

"You see, I'm not ungrateful! I shall never forget the shoes. How well they fit me! and how warm they are! Why, I could walk half-a-dozen miles with them. What can I beg Heaven to grant you? O Lord, hearken to me, and grant that she may be the happiest of women—in the name of the Father, the Son, and the Holy Ghost!" A devout enthusiasm had suddenly come upon Mother Fétu; she repeated the sign of the cross again and again, and bowed the knee in the direction of the crystal lamp. This done, she opened the door conducting to the landing, and whispered in a changed voice into Hélène's ear:

"Whenever you like to call, just knock at the kitchen door; I'm always there!"

Dazed and glancing behind her as though she were leaving a place of dubious repute, Hélène hurried down the staircase, reascended the Passage des Eaux, and regained the Rue Vineuse, without consciousness of the ground she was covering. The old woman's last words still rang in her ears. In truth, no; never again would she set foot in that house, never again would she bear her charity thither. Why should she ever rap at the kitchen door again? At present she was satisfied; she had seen what was to be seen. And she was full of scorn for herself—for everybody. How disgraceful to have gone there! The recollection of the place with its tawdry finery and squalid surroundings filled her with mingled anger and disgust.

"Well, madame," exclaimed Rosalie, who was awaiting her return on the staircase, "the dinner will be nice. Dear, oh dear! it's been burning for half an hour!"

At table Jeanne plagued her mother with questions. Where had she been? what had she been about? However,

as the answers she received proved somewhat curt, she began to amuse herself by giving a little dinner. Her doll was perched near her on a chair, and in a sisterly fashion she placed half of her dessert before it.

"Now, mademoiselle, you must eat like a lady. See, wipe your mouth. Oh, the dirty little thing! She doesn't even know how to wear her napkin! There, you're nice now. See, here is a biscuit. What do you say? You want some preserve on it. Well, I should think it better as it is! Let me pare you a quarter of this apple!"

She placed the doll's share on the chair. But when she had emptied her own plate she took the dainties back again one after the other and devoured them, speaking all the time as though she were the doll.

"Oh! it's delicious! I've never eaten such nice jam! Where did you get this jam, madame? I shall tell my husband to buy a pot of it. Do those beautiful apples come from your garden, madame?"

She fell asleep while thus playing, and stumbled into the bedroom with the doll in her arms. She had given herself no rest since morning. Her little legs could no longer sustain her—she was helpless and wearied to death. However, a ripple of laughter passed over her face even in sleep; in her dreams she must have been still continuing her play.

At last Hélène was alone in her room. With closed doors she spent a miserable evening beside the dead fire. Her will was failing her; thoughts that found no utterance were stirring within the innermost recesses of her heart. At midnight she wearily sought her bed, but there her torture passed endurance. She dozed, she tossed from side to side as though a fire were beneath her. She was haunted by visions which sleeplessness enlarged to a gigantic size. Then an idea took root in her brain. In vain did she strive to banish it; it clung to her, surged and clutched her at the throat till it entirely swayed her. About two o'clock she rose, rigid, pallid, and resolute as a somnambulist, and having again lighted the lamp she wrote a letter in a disguised hand; it was a vague denunciation, a note of three lines, requesting Doctor Deberle to repair that day to such a place at such an hour; there was no explanation, no signature. She sealed the enevelope and dropped the letter into the pocket of her dress which was hanging over an arm-chair. Then returning to bed, she immediately closed her eyes, and in a few minutes was lying there breathless, overpowered by leaden slumber.

## CHAPTER XVIII

### WHOSE PART?

It was nearly nine o'clock the next morning before Rosalie was able to serve the coffee. Hélène had risen late. She was weary and pale with the nightmare that had broken her rest. She rummaged in the pocket of her dress, felt the letter there, pressed it to the very bottom, and sat down at the table without opening her lips. Jeanne too was suffering from headache, and had a pale, troubled face. She quitted her bed regretfully that morning, without any heart to indulge in play. There

was a sooty color in the sky, and a dim light saddened the room, while from time to time sudden downpours of rain beat against the windows.

"Mademoiselle is in the blues," said Rosalie, who monopolized all the talk. "She can't keep cheerful for two days running. That's what comes of dancing about too much yesterday."

"Do you feel ill, Jeanne?" asked Hélène.

"No, mamma," answered the child. "It's only the nasty weather."

Hélène lapsed once more into silence. She finished her coffee, and sat in her chair, plunged in thought, with her eyes riveted on the flames. While rising she had reflected that it was her duty to speak to Juliette and bid her renounce the afternoon assignation. But how? She could not say. Still, the necessity of the step was impressed on her, and now her one urgent, all-absorbing thought was to attempt it. Ten o'clock struck, and she began to dress. Jeanne gazed at her, and, on seeing her take up her bonnet, clasped her little hands as though stricken with cold, while over her face crept a pained look. It was her wont to take umbrage whenever her mother went out; she was unwilling to quit her side, and craved to go with her everywhere.

"Rosalie," said Hélène, "make haste and finish the room. Don't go out. I'll be back in a moment."

She stooped and gave Jeanne a hasty kiss, not noticing her vexation. But the moment she had gone a sob broke from the child, who had hitherto summoned all her dignity to her aid to restrain her emotion.

"Oh, mademoiselle, how naughty!'

exclaimed the maid by way of consolation. "Gracious powers! no one will rob you of your mamma. You must allow her to see after her affairs. You can't always be hanging to her skirts!"

Meanwhile Hélène had turned the corner of the Rue Vineuse, keeping close to the wall for protection against the rain. It was Pierre who opened the door; but at sight of her he seemed somewhat embarrassed.

"Is Madame Deberle at home?"

"Yes, madame; but I don't know whether—"

Hélène, in the character of a family friend, was pushing past him towards the drawing-room; but he took the liberty of stopping her.

"Wait, madame; I'll go and see."

He slipped into the room, opening the door as little as he could; and immediately afterwards Juliette could be heard speaking in a tone of irritation. "What! you've allowed some one to come in? Why, I forbade it peremptorily. It's incredible! I can't be left quiet for an instant!"

Hélène, however, pushed open the door, strong in her resolve to do that which she imagined to be her duty.

"Oh, it's you!" said Juliette, as she perceived her. "I didn't catch who it was!"

The look of annoyance did not fade from her face, however, and it was evident that the visit was ill-timed.

"Do I disturb you?" asked Hélène.

"Not at all, not at all," answered the other. "You'll understand in a moment. We have been getting up a surprise. We are rehearsing *Caprice* to play it on one of my Wednesdays. We had selected this morning for rehearsal,

thinking nobody would know of it. But you'll stay now? You will have to keep silence about it, that's all."

Then, clapping her hands and addressing herself to Madame Berthier, who was standing in the middle of the drawing-room, she began once more, without paying any further attention to Hélène: "Come, come; we must get on. You don't give sufficient point to the sentence. 'To make a purse unknown to one's husband would in the eyes of most people seem rather more than romantic.' Say that again."

Intensely surprised at finding her engaged in this way, Hélène had sat down. The chairs and tables had been pushed against the wall, the carpet thus being left clear. Madame Berthier, a delicate blonde, repeated her soliloquy, with her eyes fixed on the ceiling in her effort to recall the words; while plump Madame de Guiraud, a beautiful brunette, who had assumed the character of Madame de Léry, reclined in an armchair awaiting her cue. The ladies, in their unpretentious morning gowns, had doffed neither bonnets nor gloves. Seated in front of them, her hair in disorder and a volume of Musset in her hand, was Juliette, in a dressing-gown of white cashmere. Her face wore the serious expression of a stage-manager tutoring his actors as to the tones they should speak in and the by-play they should introduce. The day being dull, the small curtains of embroidered tulle had been pulled aside and swung across the knobs of the window-fastenings, so that the garden could be seen, dark and damp.

"You don't display sufficient emotion," declared Juliette. "Put a little more meaning into it. Every word ought to tell. Begin again: 'I'm going to finish your toilette, my dear little purse.'"

"I shall be an awful failure," said Madame Berthier languidly. "Why don't you play the part instead of me? You would make a delicious Mathilde."

"I! Oh, no! In the first place, one needs to be fair. Besides, I'm a very good teacher, but a bad pupil. But let us get on—let us get on!"

Hélène sat still in her corner. Madame Berthier, engrossed in her part, had not even turned round. Madame de Guiraud had merely honored her with a slight nod. She realized that she was in the way, and that she ought to have declined to stay. If she still remained, it was no longer through the sense of a duty to be fulfilled, but rather by reason of a strange feeling stirring vaguely in her heart's depth's— a feeling which had previously thrilled her in this selfsame spot. The unkindly greeting which Juliette had bestowed on her pained her. However, the young woman's friendships were usually capricious; she worshipped people for three months, threw herself on their necks and seemed to live for them alone; then one morning, without affording any explanation, she appeared to lose all consciousness of being acquainted with them. Without doubt, in this, as in everything else, she was simply yielding to a fashionable craze, an inclination to love the people who were loved by her own circle. These sudden veerings of affection, however, deeply wounded Hélène, for her generous and undemonstrative heart had its ideal in eternity. She often left the Deberles plunged in

sadness, full of despair when she thought how fragile and unstable was the basis of human love. And on this occasion, in this crisis in her life, the thought brought her still keener pain.

"We'll skip the scene with Chavigny," said Juliette. "He won't be here this morning. Let us see Madame de Léry's entrance. Now, Madame de Guiraud, here's your cue." Then she read from her book: "'Just imagine my showing him this purse.'"

"'Oh! it's exceedingly pretty. Let me look at it,'" began Madame de Guiraud in a falsetto voice, as she rose with a silly expression on her face.

When the servant had opened the door to her, Hélène had pictured a scene entirely different from this. She had imagined that she would find Juliette displaying excessive nervousness, with pallid cheeks, hesitating and yet allured, shivering at the very thought of assignation. She had pictured herself imploring her to reflect, till the young woman, choked with sobs, threw herself into her arms. Then they would have mingled their tears together, and Hélène would have quitted her with the thought that Henri was henceforward lost to her, but that she had secured his happiness. However, there had been nothing of all this; she had merely fallen on this rehearsal, which was wholly unintelligible to her; and she saw Juliette before her with unruffled features, like one who has had a good night's rest, and with her mind sufficiently at ease to discuss Madame Berthier's by-play, without troubling herself in the least degree about what she would do in the afternoon. This indifference and frivolity chilled Hélène.

who had come to the house with passion consuming her.

A longing to speak fell on her. At a venture she inquired: "Who will play the part of Chavigny?"

"Why, Malignon, of course," answered Juliette, turning round with an air of astonishment. "He played Chavigny all last winter. It's a nuisance he can't come to the rehearsals. Listen, ladies; I'm going to read Chavigny's part. Unless that's done, we shall never get on."

Thereupon she herself began acting the man's part, her voice deepening unconsciously, whilst she assumed a cavalier air in harmony with the situation. Madame Berthier renewed her warbling tones, and Madame de Guiraud took infinite pains to be lively and witty. When Pierre came in to put some more wood on the fire he slyly glanced at the ladies, who amused him immensely.

Hélène, still fixed in her resolve, despite some heart-shrinking, attempted however to take Juliette aside.

"Only a minute. I've something to say to you."

"Oh, impossible, my dear! You see how much I am engaged. To-morrow, if you have the time."

Hélène said no more. The young woman's unconcern displeased her. She felt anger growing within her as she observed how calm and collected Juliette was, when she herself had endured such intense agony since the night before. At one moment she was on the point of rising and letting things take their course. It was exceedingly foolish of her to wish to save this woman; her nightmare began once more; her

hands slipped into her pocket, and finding the letter there, clasped it in a feverish grasp. Why should she have any care for the happiness of others, when they had no care for her and did not suffer as she did?

"Oh! capital, capital," exclaimed Juliette of a sudden.

Madame Berthier's head was now reclining on Madame de Guiraud's shoulder, and she was declaring through her sobs: "'I am sure that he loves her; I am sure of it!'"

"Your success will be immense," said Juliette. "Say that once more: 'I am sure that he loves her; I am sure of it.' Leave your head as it is. You're divine. Now, Madame de Guiraud, your turn."

"'No, no, my child, it cannot be; it is a caprice, a fancy,'" replied the stout lady.

"Perfect! but oh, the scene is a long one, isn't it? Let us rest a little while. We must have that incident in proper working order."

Then they all three plunged into a discussion regarding the arrangement of the drawing-room. The dining-room door, to the left, would serve for entrances and exits; an easy-chair could be placed on the right, a couch at the farther end, and the table could be pushed close to the fire-place. Hélène, who had risen, followed them about, as though she felt an interest in these scenic arrangements. She had now abandoned her idea of eliciting an explanation, and merely wished to make a last effort to prevent Juliette from going to the place of meeting.

"I intended asking you," she said to her, "if it isn't to-day that you mean to pay Madame de Chermette a visit?"

"Yes, this afternoon."

"Then, if you'll allow me, I'll go with you; it's such a long time since I promised to go to see her."

For a moment Juliette betrayed signs of embarrassment, but speedily regained her self-possession.

"Of course, I should be very happy. Only I have so many things to look after; I must do some shopping first, and I have no idea at what time I shall be able to get to Madame de Chermette's."

"That doesn't matter," said Hélène; "it will enable me to have a walk."

"Listen; I will speak to you candidly. Well, you must not press me. You would be in my way. Let it be some other Monday."

This was said without a trace of emotion, so flatly and with so quiet a smile that Hélène was dumbfounded and uttered not another syllable. She was obliged to lend some assistance to Juliette, who suddenly decided to bring the table close to the fireplace. Then she drew back, and the rehearsal began once more. In a soliloquy which followed the scene, Madame de Guiraud with considerable power spoke these two sentences: " 'But what a treacherous gulf is the heart of man! In truth, we are worth more than they!' "

And Hélène, what ought she to do now? Within her breast the question raised a storm that stirred her to vague thoughts of violence. She experienced an irresistible desire to be revenged on Juliette's tranquillity, as if that self-possession were an insult directed against her own fevered heart. She dreamed of facilitating her fall, that she

might see whether she would always retain this unruffled demeanor. And she thought of herself scornfully as she recalled her delicacy and scruples. Twenty times already she ought to have said to Henri: "I love you; let us go away together." Could she have done so, however, without the most intense emotion? Could she have displayed the callous composure of this woman, who, three hours before her first assignation, was rehearsing a comedy in her own home? Even at this moment she trembled more than Juliette; what maddened her was the consciousness of her own passion amidst the quiet cheerfulness of this drawing room; she was terrified lest she should burst out into some angry speech. Was she a coward, then?

But all at once a door opened, and Henri's voice reached her ear: "Do not disturb yourselves. I'm only passing."

The rehearsal was drawing to a close. Juliette, who was still reading Chavigny's part, had just caught hold of Madame de Guiraud's hand. " 'Ernestine, I adore you!' " she exclaimed with an outburst of passionate earnestness.

" 'Then Madame de Blainville is no longer beloved by you?' " inquired Madame de Guiraud.

However, so long as her husband was present Juliette declined to proceed. There was no need of the men knowing anything about it. The doctor showed himself most polite to the ladies; he complimented them and predicted an immense success. With black gloves on his hands and his face clean-shaven he was about to begin his round of visits. On his entry he had merely greeted Hélène with a slight bow. At the Comédie Français he had seen some very great actress in the character of Madame de Léry, and he acquainted Madame de Guiraud with some of the usual by-play of the scene.

"At the moment when Chavigny is going to throw himself at your feet, you fling the purse into the fire. Dispassionately, you know, without any anger, like a woman who plays with love."

"All right; leave us alone," said Juliette. "We know all about it."

At last, when they had heard him close his study door, she began once more: "'Ernestine, I adore you!'"

Prior to his departure Henri had saluted Hélène with the same slight bow. She sat dumb, as though awaiting some catastrophe. The sudden appearance of the husband had seemed to her ominous; but when he had gone, his courtesy and evident blindness made him seem to her ridiculous. So he also gave attention to this idiotic comedy! And there was no loving fire in his eye as he looked at her sitting there! The whole house had become hateful and cold to her. Here was a downfall; there was nothing to restrain her any longer, for she abhorred Henri as much as Juliette. Within her pocket she held the letter in her convulsive grasp. At last, murmuring "Good-bye for the present," she quitted the room, her head swimming and the furniture seeming to dance around her. And in her ears rang these words, uttered by Madame de Guiraud:

"'Adieu. You will perhaps think badly of me to-day, but you will have some kindly feeling for me to-morrow, and, believe me, that is much better than a caprice.'"

When Hélène had shut the house door and reached the pavement, she drew the letter with a violent, almost mechanical gesture from her pocket, and dropped it into the letter-box. Then she stood motionless for a few seconds, still dazed, her eyes glaring at the narrow brass plate which had fallen back again in its place.

"It is done," she exclaimed in a whisper.

Once more she pictured the rooms hung with pink cretonne. Malignon and Juliette were there together; but all of a sudden the wall was riven open, and the husband entered. She was conscious of no more, and a great calm fell on her. Instinctively she looked around to see if any one had observed her dropping the letter in the box. But the street was deserted. Then she turned the corner and went back home.

"Have you been good, my darling?" she asked as she kissed Jeanne.

The child, still seated on the same chair, raised a gloomy face towards her, and without answering threw both arms around her neck, and kissed her with a great gasp. Her grief indeed had been intense.

At lunch-time Rosalie seemed greatly surprised. "Madame surely went for a long walk!" said she.

"Why do you think so?" asked Hélène.

"Because madame is eating with such an appetite. It is long since madame ate so heartily."

It was true; she was very hungry; with her sudden relief she had felt her stomach empty. She experienced a feeling of intense peace and content. After the shocks of these lest two days a stillness fell upon her spirit, her limbs relaxed and became as supple as though she had just left a bath. The only sensation that remained to her was one of heaviness somewhere, an indefinable load that weighed upon her.

When she returned to her bedroom her eyes were at once directed towards the clock, the hands of which pointed to twenty-five minutes past twelve. Juliette's assignation was for three o'clock. Two hours and a half must still elapse. She made the reckoning mechanically. Moreover, she was in no hurry; the hands of the clock were moving on, and no one in the world could stop them. She left things to their own accomplishment. A child's cap, long since begun, was lying unfinished on the table. She took it up and began to sew at the window. The room was plunged in unbroken silence. Jeanne had seated herself in her usual place, but her arms hung idly beside her.

"Mamma," she said, "I cannot work; it's no fun at all."

"Well, my darling, don't do anything. Oh! wait a minute, you can thread my needles!"

In a languid way the child silently attended to the duty assigned her. Having carefully cut some equal lengths of cotton, she spent a long time in finding the eyes of the needles, and was only just ready with one of them threaded when her mother had finished with the last.

"You see," said the latter gently, "this will save time. The last of my six little caps will be finished to-night."

She turned round to glance at the clock—ten minutes past one. Still nearly two hours. Juliette must now be beginning to dress. Henri had received the letter. Oh! he would certainly go. The instructions were precise; he would find the place without delay. But it all seemed so far off still, and she felt no emotional fever, but went on sewing with regular stitches as industriously as a work-girl. The minutes slipped by one by one. At last two o'clock struck.

A ring at the bell came as a surprise.

"Who can it be, mother darling?" asked Jeanne, who had jumped on her chair. "Oh! it's you!" she continued, as Monsieur Rambaud entered the room. "Why did you ring so loudly? You gave me quite a fright."

The worthy man was in consternation —to tell the truth, his tug at the bell had been a little too violent.

"I am not myself to-day, I'm ill," the child resumed. "You must not frighten me."

Monsieur Rambaud displayed the greatest solicitude. What was the matter with his poor darling? He only sat down, relieved, when Hélène had signed to him that the child was in her dismals, as Rosalie was wont to say. A call from him in the daytime was a rare occurrence, and so he at once set about explaining the object of his visit. It concerned some fellow-townsman of his, an old workman who could find no employment owing to his advanced years, and who lived with his paralytic wife in a tiny little room. Their wretchedness could not be pictured. He himself had gone up that morning to make a personal investigation. Their lodging was a mere hole under the tiles, with a swing window, through whose broken panes the wind beat in. Inside, stretched on a mattress, he had found a woman wrapped in an old curtain, while the man squatted on the floor in a state of stupefaction, no longer finding sufficient courage even to sweep the place.

"Oh! poor things, poor things!" exclaimed Hélène, moved to tears.

It was not the old workman who gave Monsieur Rambaud any uneasiness. He would remove him to his own house and find him something to do. But there was the wife with palsied frame, whom the husband dared not leave for a moment alone, and who had to be rolled up like a bundle; where could she be put? what was to be done with her?

"I thought of you," he went on. "You must obtain her instant admission to an asylum. I should have gone straight to Monsieur Deberle, but I imagined you knew him better and would have greater influence with him. If he would be kind enough to interest himself in the matter, it could all be arranged to-morrow."

Trembling with pity, her cheeks white, Jeanne listened to the tale.

"Oh, mamma!" she murmured with clasped hands, "be kind—get the admission for the poor woman!"

"Yes, yes, of course!" said Hélène, whose emotion was increasing. "I will speak to the doctor as soon as I can; he will himself take every requisite step. Give me their names and the address, Monsieur Rambaud."

He scribbled a line on the table, and said as he rose: "It is thirty-five minutes past two. You would perhaps find the doctor at home now."

She had risen at the same time, and as she looked at the clock a fierce thrill swept through her frame. In truth it was already thirty-five minutes past two, and the hands were still creeping on. She stammered out that the doctor must have started on his round of visits. Her eyes were riveted on the dial. Meantime, Monsieur Rambaud remained standing hat in hand, and beginning his story once more. These poor people had sold everything, even their stove, and since the setting in of winter had spent their days and nights alike without a fire. At the close of December they had been four days without food. Hélène gave vent to a cry of compassion. The hands of the clock now marked twenty minutes to three. Monsieur Rambaud devoted another two minutes to his farewell: "Well, I depend on you," he said. And stooping to kiss Jeanne, he added: "Good-bye, my darling."

"Good-bye; don't worry; mamma won't forget. I'll make her remember."

When Hélène came back from the anteroom, whither she had gone in company with Monsieur Rambaud, the hands of the clock pointed to a quarter to three. Another quarter of an hour and all would be over. As she stood motionless before the fireplace, the scene which was about to be enacted flashed before her eyes: Juliette was already there; Henri entered and surprised her. She knew the room; she could see the scene in its minutest details with terrible vividness. And still affected by Monsieur Rambaud's awful story she felt a mighty shudder rise from her limbs to her face. A voice cried out within her that what she had done—the writing of that letter, that cowardly denunciation—was a crime. The truth came to her with dazzling clearness. Yes, it was a crime she had committed! She recalled to memory the gesture with which she had flung the letter into the box; she recalled it with a sense of stupor such as might come over one on seeing another commit an evil action, without thought of intervening. She was as if awaking from a dream. What was it that had happened? Why was she here, with eyes ever fixed on the hands of that dial? Two more minutes had slipped away.

"Mamma," said Jeanne, "if you like, we'll go to see the doctor together to-night. It will be a walk for me. I feel stifling to-day."

Hélène, however, did not hear; thirteen minutes must yet elapse. But she could not allow so horrible a thing to take place! In this stormy awakening of her rectitude she felt naught but a furious craving to prevent it. She *must* prevent it; otherwise she would be unable to live. In a state of frenzy she ran about her bedroom.

"Ah, you're going to take me!" exclaimed Jeanne joyously. "We're going to see the doctor at once, aren't we, mother darling?"

"No, no," Hélène answered, while she hunted for her boots, stooping to look under the bed.

They were not to be found; but she shrugged her shoulders with supreme indifference when it occurred to her that she could very well run out in the flimsy house-slippers she had on her feet. She was now turning the wardrobe topsy-turvy in her search of her shawl. Jeanne crept up to her with a coaxing air: "Then you're not going to the doctor's, mother darling?"

"No."

"Say that you'll take me all the same. Oh! do take me; it will be such a pleasure!"

But Hélène had at last found her shawl, and she threw it over her shoulders. Good heavens! only twelve minutes left—just time to run. She would go—she would do something, no matter what. She would decide on the way.

"Mamma dear, do please take me with you," said Jeanne in tones that grew lower and more imploring.

"I cannot take you," said Hélène; "I'm going to a place where children don't go. Give me my bonnet."

Jeanne's face blanched. Her eyes grew dim, her words came with a gasp. "Where are you going?" she asked.

The mother made no reply—she was tying the strings of her bonnet.

Then the child continued: "You always go out without me now. You went out yesterday, you went out to-day, and you are going out again. Oh, I'm dreadfully grieved, I'm afraid to be here all alone. I shall die if you leave me here. Do you hear, mother darling. I shall die."

Then bursting into loud sobs, overwhelmed by a fit of grief and rage, she clung fast to Hélène's skirts.

"Come, come, leave me; be good, I'm coming back," her mother repeated.

"No, no! I won't have it!" the child exclaimed through her sobs. "Oh! you don't love me any longer, or you would take me with you. Yes, yes, I am sure you love other people better. Take me with you, take me with you, or I'll stay here on the floor; you'll come back and find me on the floor."

She wound her little arms round her mother's legs; she wept with face buried in the folds of her dress; she clung to her and weighted upon her to prevent her making a step forward. And still the hands of the clock moved steadily on; it was ten minutes to three. Then Hélène thought that she would never reach the house in time, and, nearly distracted, she wrenched Jeanne from her grasp, exclaiming: "What an unbearable child! This is veritable tyranny! If you sob any more, I'll have something to say to you!"

She left the room and slammed the door behind her. Jeanne had staggered back to the window, her sobs suddenly arrested by this brutal treatment, her limbs stiffened, her face quite white. She stretched her hands towards the door, and twice wailed out the words: "Mamma! mamma!" And then she remained where she had fallen on a chair, with eyes staring and features distorted by the jealous thought that her mother was deceiving her.

On reaching the street, Hélène hastened her steps. The rain had ceased, but great drops fell from the house-tops on to her shoulders. She had resolved that she would reflect outside and fix on some plan. But now she was only inflamed with a desire to reach the house. When she reached the Passage des Eaux, she hesitated for just one moment. The descent had become a torrent; the water of the gutters of the Rue Raynouard was rushing down it. And as the stream bounded over the steps, between the close-set walls, it broke here and there into foam, whilst the edges of the stones, washed clear by the downpour, shone out like glass. A gleam of pale light, falling from the gray sky, made the Passage look whiter between the dusky branches of the trees. Hélène went down it, scarcely raising her skirts. The water came up to her ankles. She almost lost her flimsy slippers in the puddles; around her, down the whole way, she heard a gurgling sound, like the murmuring of brooklets coursing through the grass in the depths of the woods.

All at once she found herself on the stairs in front of the door. She stood there, panting in a state of torture. Then her memory came back, and she decided to knock at the kitchen.

"What! is it you?" exclaimed Mother Fétu.

There was none of the old whimper in her voice. Her little eyes were sparkling, and a complacent grin had spread over the myriad wrinkles of her face. All the old deference vanished, and she patted Hélène's hands as she listened to her broken words. The young woman gave her twenty francs.

"May God requite you!" prayed Mother Fétu in her wonted style. "Whatever you please, my dear!"

## CHAPTER XIX

### JULIETTE'S AGITATION

LEANING back in an easy-chair, with his legs stretched out before the huge, blazing fire, Malignon sat waiting. He had considered it a good idea to draw the window-curtains and light the wax candles. The outer room, in which he had seated himself, was brilliantly illuminated by a small chandelier and a pair of candelabra; whilst the other apartment was plunged in shadow, the swinging crystal lamp alone casting on the floor a twilight gleam. Malignon drew out his watch.

"The deuce!" he muttered. "Is she going to keep me waiting again?"

He gave ven to a slight yawn. He had been waiting for an hour already, and it was small amusement to him. However, he rose and cast a glance over his preparations.

The arrangement of the chairs did not please him, and he rolled a couch in front of the fireplace. The cretonne hangings had a ruddy glow, as they reflected the light of the candles; the room was warm, silent, and cozy, while out side the wind came and went in sudden gusts. All at once the young man heard hurried knocks at the door. It was a signal.

"At last!" he exclaimed aloud, his face beaming jubilantly.

He ran to open the door, and Juliette entered, her face veiled, her figure wrapped in a fur mantle. While Malignon was gently closing the door, she stood still for a moment, with the emotion that checked the words on her lips undetected.

However, before the young man had had time to take her hand, she raised her veil, and displayed a smiling face, rather pale, but quite unruffled.

"What! you have lighted up the place!" she exclaimed. "Why? I thought you hated candles in broad daylight!"

Malignon, who had been making ready to clasp her with a passionate gesture that he had been rehearsing, was put somewhat out of countenance by this remark. and hastened to explain that the day was too wretched, and that the windows looked on to waste patches of ground. Besides, night was his special delight.

"Well, one never knows how to take you," she retorted jestingly. "Last spring, at my children's ball, you made such a fuss, declaring that the place was like some cavern, some dead-house. However, let us say that your taste has changed."

She seemed to be paying a mere visit, and affected a courage which slightly deepened her voice. This was the only indication of her uneasiness. At times her chin twitched somewhat, as though she felt some uneasiness in her throat. But her eyes were sparkling, and she tasted to the full the keen pleasure born of her imprudence. She thought of Madame de Chermette, of whom such scandalous stories were related. Good heavens! it seemed strange all the same.

"Let us have a look round," she began.

And thereupon she began inspecting the apartment. He followed in her footsteps, while she gazed at the furniture, examined the walls, looked upwards, and started back, chattering all the time.

"I don't like your cretonne; it is so frightfully common!" said she. "Where did you buy that abominable pink stuff? There's a chair that would be nice if the wood weren't covered with gilding. Not a picture, not a nick-nack—only your chandelier and your candelabra, which are by no means in good style! Ah well, my dear fellow; I advise you to continue laughing at my Japanese pavilion!"

She burst into a laugh, thus revenging herself on him for the old affronts
which still rankled in her breast.

"Your taste is a pretty one, and no
mistake! You don't know that my idol
is worth more than the whole lot of
your things! A draper's shopman
wouldn't have selected that pink stuff.
Was it your idea to fascinate your
washer-woman?"

Malignon felt very much hurt, and
did not answer. He made an attempt
to lead her into the inner room; but she
never entered such gloomy places.
Besides, she could see quite enough;
the one room was worthy of the other.
The whole of it had come from the
Saint-Antoine quarter.

But the hanging lamp was her special
aversion. She attacked it with merciless raillery—what a trashy thing it
was, such as some little work-girl with
no furniture of her own might have
dreamt of! Why, lamps in the same
style could be bought at all the bazaars
at seven francs fifty centimes apiece.

"I paid ninety francs for it," at last
ejaculated Malignon in his impatience.

Thereupon she seemed delighted at
having angered him.

On his self-possession returning, he
inquired: "Won't you take off your
cloak?"

"Oh, yes, I will," she answered; "it
is dreadfully warm here."

She took off her bonnet as well, and
this with her fur cloak he hastened to
deposit in the next room. When he
returned, he found her seated in front
of the fire, still gazing round her. She
had regained her gravity, and was disposed to display a more conciliatory
demeanor.

"It's all very ugly," she said; "still,
you are not amiss here. The two rooms
might have been made very pretty."

"Oh! they're good enough for my
purpose!" he thoughtlessly replied,
with a careless shrug of the shoulders.

The next moment, however, he bitterly regretted these silly words. He
could not possibly have been more im-
pertinent or clumsy. Juliette hung her
head, and a sharp pang darted through
her bosom. Then he sought to turn to
advantage the embarrassment into
which he had plunged her.

"Juliette!" he said pleadingly, as he
leaned towards her.

But with a gesture she forced him to
resume his seat. It was at the seaside,
at Trouville, that Malignon, bored to
death by the constant sight of the sea,
had hit upon the happy idea of falling
in love. One evening he had taken
hold of Juliette's hand She had not
seemed offended; in fact, she had at
first bantered him over it. Soon,
though her head was empty and her
heart free, she imagined that she loved
him. She had, so far, done nearly
everything that her friends did around
her; a lover only was lacking, and curiosity and a craving to be like the others
had impelled her to secure one. How
ever, Malignon was vain enough to
imagine that he might win her by
force of wit, and allowed her time to
accustom herself to playing the part of
a coquette. So, on the first outburst,
which took place one night when they
stood side by side gazing at the sea
like a pair of lovers in a comic opera,
she had repelled him, in her astonishment and vexation that he should spoil

the romance which served as an amusement to her.

On his return to Paris Malignon had vowed that he would be more skliful in his attack. He had just reacquired influence over her, during a fit of boredom which had come on with the close of a wearying winter, when the usual dissipations, dinners, balls, and first-night performances were beginning to pall on her with their dreary monotony. And at last, her curiosity aroused, allured by the seeming mystery and piquancy of an intrigue, she had responded to his entreaties by consenting to meet him. However, so wholly unruffled were her feelings, that she was as little disturbed, seated by the side of Malignon, as when she paid visits to artists' studios to solicit pictures for her charity bazaars.

"Juliette! Juliette!" murmured the young man, striving to speak in caressing tones.

"Come, be sensible," she merely replied; and taking a Chinese fan from the chimney-piece, she resumed — as much at her ease as though she had been sitting in her own drawing-room: "You know we had a rehearsal this morning. I'm afraid I have not made a very happy choice in Madame Berthier. Her 'Mathilda' is a snivelling, insufferable affair. You remember that delightful soliloquy when she addresses the purse—'Poor little thing, I kissed you a moment ago'? Well! she declaims it like a school-girl who has learnt a complimentary greeting. It's so vexatious!"

"And what about Madame de Guiraud?" he asked, as he drew his chair closer and took her hand.

"Oh! she is perfection. I've discovered in her a 'Madame de Léry,' with some sarcasm and animation."

While speaking she surrendered her hand to the young man, and he kissed it between her sentences without her seeming to notice it.

"But the worst of it all, you know," she resumed, "is your absence. In the first place, you might say something to Madame Berthier; and besides, we shall not be able to get a good *ensemble* if you never come."

He had now succeeded in passing his arm round her waist.

"But as I know my part," he murmured.

"Yes, that's all very well; but there's the arrangement of the scenes to look after. It is anything but obliging on your part to refuse to give us three or four mornings."

She was unable to continue, for he was raining a shower of kisses on her neck. At this she could feign ignorance no longer, but pushed him away, tapping him the while with the Chinese fan which she still retained in her hand. Doubtless, she had registered a vow that she would not allow any further familiarity. Her face was now flushed by the heat reflected from the fire, and her lips pouted with the very expression of an inquisitive person whom her feelings astonish. Moreover, she was really getting frightened.

"Leave me alone," she stammered, with a constrained smile. "I shall get angry."

But he imagined that he had moved her, and once more took hold of her hands. To her, however, a voice seemed to be crying out, "No!" It was she herself protesting before she had even answered her own heart.

"No, no!" she said again. "Let me go; you are hurting me!" And thereupon, as he refused to release her, she twisted herself violently from his grasp. She was acting in obedience to some strange emotion; she felt angry with herself and with him. In her agitation some disjointed phrases escaped her lips. Yes, indeed, he rewarded her badly for her trust. What a brute he was! She even called him a coward. Never in her life would she see him again. But he allowed her to talk on, and ran after her with a wicked and brutal laugh. And at last she could do no more than gasp in the mometary refuge which she had sought behind a chair. They were there, gazing at one another, her face transformed by shame and his by passion, when a noise broke through the stillness. At first they did not grasp its significance. A door had opened, some steps crossed the room, and a voice called to them:

"Fly! fly! You will be caught!"

It was Hélène. Astounded, they both gazed at her. So great was their stupefaction that they lost consciousness of their embarrassing situation. Juliette indeed displayed no sign of confusion.

"Fly! fly!" said Hélène again. "Your husband will be here in two minutes."

"My husband!" stammered the young woman; "my husband!—why for what reason?"

She was losing her wits. Her brain was in a turmoil. It seemed to her prodigious that Hélène should be standing there speaking to her of her husband.

But Hélène made an angry gesture.

"Oh! if you think I've time to explain," said she,—"he is on the way here. I give you warning. Disappear at once, both of you."

Then Juliette's agitation became extraordinary. She ran about the rooms like a maniac, screaming out disconnected sentences.

"My God! my God!—I thank you.— Where is my cloak?—How horrid it is, this room being so dark!—Give me my cloak.—Bring me a candle, to help me find my cloak.—My dear, you mustn't mind if I don't stop to thank you.—I can't get my arms into the sleeves—no, I can't get them in—no, I can't!"

She was paralyzed with fear, and Hélène was obliged to assist her with her cloak. She put her bonnet on awry, and did not even tie the ribbons. The worst of it, however, was that they lost quite a minute in hunting for her veil, which had fallen on the floor. Her words came with a gasp, her trembling hands moved about in bewilderment, fumbling over her person to ascertain whether she might be leaving anything behind which might compromise her.

"Oh, what a lesson! what a lesson! Thank goodness, it is well over!"

Malignon was very pale, and made a sorry appearance. His feet beat a tattoo on the ground, as he realized that he was both scorned and ridiculous. His lips could only give utterance to the wretched question:

"Then you think I ought to go away as well?"

Then, as no answer was vouchsafed him, he took up his cane, and went on talking by way of affecting perfect composure. They had plenty of time, said he. It happened that there was another staircase, a small servants' staircase, now never used, but which would yet allow of their descent. Madame Deberle's cab had remained at the door; it would convey both of them away along the quays. And again he repeated: "Now calm yourself. It will be all right. See, this way."

He threw open a door, and the three dingy, dilapidated, little rooms, which had not been repaired and were full of dirt, appeared to view. A puff of damp air entered the boudoir. Juliette, ere she stepped through all that squalor, gave final expression to her disgust.

"How could I have come here?" she exclaimed in a loud voice. "What a hole! I shall never forgive myself."

"Be quick, be quick!" urged Hélène, whose anxiety was as great as her own.

She pushed Juliette forward, but the young woman threw herself sobbing on her neck. She was in the throes of a nervous reaction. She was overwhelmed with shame, and would fain have defended herself, fain have given a reason for being found in that man's company. Then instinctively she gathered up her skirts, as though she were about to cross a gutter. With the tip of his boot Malignon, who had gone on first, was clearing away the plaster which littered the back staircase. The doors were shut once more.

Meantime, Hélène had remained standing in the middle of the sitting-room. Silence reigned there, a warm, close silence, only disturbed by the crackling of the burnt logs. There was a singing in her ears, and she heard nothing. But after an interval, which seemed to her interminable, the rattle of a cab suddenly resounded. It was Juliette's cab rolling away.

Then Hélène sighed, and she made a gesture of mute gratitude. The thought that she would not be tortured by everlasting remorse for having acted despicably filled her with pleasant and thankful feelings. She felt relieved, deeply moved, and yet so weak, now that this awful crisis was over, that she lacked the strength to depart in her turn. In her heart she thought that Henri was coming, and that he must meet some one in this place. There was a knock at the door, and she opened it at once.

The first sensation on either side was one of bewilderment. Henri entered, his mind busy with thoughts of the letter which he had received, and his face pale and uneasy. But when he caught sight of her a cry escaped his lips.

"You! My God! It was you!"

The cry betokened more astonishment than pleasure. But soon there came a furious awakening of his love.

"You love me, you love me!" he stammered. "Ah! it was you, and I did not understand."

He stretched out his arm as he spoke; but Hélène, who had greeted his entrance with a smile, now started back with wan cheeks. Truly she had waited for him; she had promised herself that they would be together for a moment, and that she would invent some fiction. Now, however, full consciousness of the situation flashed upon her; Henri believed it to be an assignation. Yet she had never for one moment desired such a thing, and her heart rebelled.

"Henri, I pray you, release me," said she.

He had grasped her by the wrists, and was drawing her slowly towards him, as though to kiss her. The love that had been surging within him for months, but which had grown less violent owing to the break in their intimacy, now burst forth more fiercely than ever.

"Release me," she resumed. "You are frightening me. I assure you, you are mistaken."

His surprise found voice once more. "Was it not you then who wrote to me?" he asked.

She hesitated for a second. What could she say in answer?

"Yes," she whispered at last.

She could not betray Juliette after having saved her. An abyss lay before her into which she herself was slipping. Henri was now glancing round the two rooms in wonderment at finding them illumined and furnished in such gaudy style. He ventured to question her.

"Are these rooms yours?" he asked. But she remained silent.

"Your letter upset me so," he continued. "Hélène, you are hiding something from me. For mercy's sake, relieve my anxiety!"

She was not listening to him; she was reflecting that he was indeed right in considering this to be an assignation. Otherwise, what could she have been doing there? Why should she have waited for him? She could devise no plausible explanation. She was no longer certain whether she had not given him this rendezvous. A network of chance and circumstance was enveloping her yet more tightly; there

was no escape from it. Each second found her less able to resist.

"You were waiting for me, you were waiting for me!" he repeated passionately, as he bent his head to kiss her. And then as his lips met hers she felt it beyond her power to struggle further; but, as though in mute acquiescence, fell, half swooning and oblivious of the world, upon his neck.

## CHAPTER XX

### THE BURST OF THE STORM

JEANNE, with her eyes fixed on the door, remained plunged in grief over her mother's sudden departure. She gazed around her; the room was empty and silent; but she could still hear the waning sounds of hurrying footsteps and rustling skirts, and last the slamming of the outer door. Then nothing stirred, and she was alone.

All alone, all alone. Over the bed hung her mother's dressing-gown, flung there at random, the skirt bulging out and a sleeve lying across the bolster, so that the garment looked like some person who had fallen down overwhelmed with grief, and sobbing in misery. There was some linen scattered about, and a black neckerchief lay on the floor like a blot of mourning. The chairs were in disorder, the table had been pushed in front of the wardrobe, and amidst it all she was quite alone. She felt her tears choking her as she looked at the dressing-gown which no longer garmented her mother, but was stretched there with the ghastly semblance of death. She clasped her hands, and for the last time wailed, "Mamma! mamma!" The blue velvet hangings, however, deadened the sound. It was all over, and she was alone.

Then the time slipped away. The clock struck three. A dismal, dingy light came in through the windows. Dark clouds were sailing over the sky, which made it still gloomier. Through the panes of glass, which were covered with moisture, Paris could only be dimly seen; the watery vapor blurred it; its far-away outskirts seemed hidden by thick smoke. Thus the city even was no longer there to keep the child company, as on bright afternoons, when, on leaning out a little, it seemed to her as though she could touch each district with her hand.

What was she to do? Her little arms tightened in despair against her bosom. This desertion seemed to her mournful, passing all bounds, characterized by an injustice and wickedness that enraged her. She had never known anything so hateful; it struck her that everything was going to vanish; nothing of the old life would ever come back again. Then she caught sight of her doll seated near her on a chair, with its back against a cushion, and its legs stretched out, its eyes staring at her as though it were a human being. It was not her mechanical doll, but a large one with a pasteboard head, curly hair, and eyes of enamel, whose fixed look sometimes frightened her. What with two years' constant dressing and undressing, the paint had got rubbed off the chin and cheeks, and the limbs, of pink leather stuffed with sawdust had become limp and wrinkled like old

linen. The doll was just now in its night attire, arrayed only in a bedgown, with its arms twisted, one in the air and the other hanging downwards. When Jeanne realized that there was still some one with her, she felt for an instant less unhappy. She took the doll in her arms and embraced it ardently, while its head swung back, for its neck was broken. Then she chattered away to it, telling it that it was Jeanne's best-behaved friend, that it had a good heart, for it never went out and left Jeanne alone. It was, said she, her treasure, her kitten, her dear little pet. Trembling with agitation, striving to prevent herself from weeping again, she covered it all over with kisses.

This fit of tenderness gave her some revengeful consolation, and the doll fell over her arm like a bundle of rags. She rose and looked out, with her forehead against a window-pane. The rain had ceased falling, and the clouds of the last downpour, driven before the wind, were nearing the horizon towards the heights of Père-Lachaise, which were wrapped in gloom; and against this stormy background Paris, illumined by a uniform clearness, assumed a lonely, melancholy grandeur. It seemed to be uninhabited, like one of those cities seen in a nightmare— the reflex of a world of death. To Jeanne it certainly appeared anything but pretty. She was now idly dreaming of those she had loved since her birth. Her oldest sweetheart, the one of her early days at Marseilles, had been a huge cat, which was very heavy; she would clasp it with her little arms, and carry it from one chair to another without provoking its anger in the least; but it had disappeared, and that was the first misfortune she remembered. She had next had a sparrow, but it died; she had picked it up one morning from the bottom of its cage. That made two. She never reckoned the toys which got broken just to grieve her, all kinds of wrongs which had caused her much suffering because she was so sensitive. One doll in particular, no higher than one's hand, had driven her to despair by getting its head smashed; she had cherished it to such a degree that she had buried it by stealth in a corner of the yard; and some time afterwards, overcome by a craving to look on it once more, she had disinterred it, and made herself sick with terror whilst gazing on its blackened and repulsive features.

However, it was always the others who were the first to fail in their love. They got broken; they disappeared. The separation, at all events, was invariably their fault. Why was it? She herself never changed. When she loved any one, her love lasted all her life. Her mind could not grasp the idea of neglect and desertion; such things seemed to her monstrously wicked, and never occurred to her little heart without giving it a deadly pang. She shivered as a host of vague ideas slowly awoke within her. So people parted one day; each went his own way, never to meet or love each other again. With her eyes fixed on the limitless and dreary expanse of Paris, she sat chilled by all that her childish passion could divine of life's hard blows.

Meantime her breath was fast dimming the glass. With her hands she rubbed away the vapor that prevented her from looking out. Several monuments in the distance, wet with the rain, glittered like browny ice. There were lines of houses, regular and distinct, which, with their fronts standing out pale amidst the surrounding roofs, looked like outstretched linen—some tremendous washing spread to dry on fields of ruddy grass. The sky was clearing, and athwart the tail of the cloud which still cloaked the city in gloom the milky ways of the sun were beginning to stream. A brightness seemed to be hesitating over some of the districts; in certain places the sky would soon begin to smile. Jeanne gazed below, over the quay and the slopes of the Trocadéro; the street traffic was about to begin afresh after that violent downpour. The cabs again passed by at a jolting crawl, while the omnibuses rattled along the still lonely streets with a louder noise than usual. Umbrellas were being shut up, and wayfarers, who had taken shelter beneath the trees, ventured from one foot pavement to another through muddy streams which were rushing into the gutters.

Jeanne noticed with special interest a lady and a little girl, both of them fashionably dressed, who were standing beneath the awning of a toy-shop near the bridge. Doubtless they had been caught in the shower, and had taken refuge there. The child would fain have carried away the whole shop, and had pestered her mother to buy her a hoop. Both were now leaving, however, and the child was running along full of glee, driving the hoop before her. At this Jeanne's melancholy returned with intensified force; her doll became hideous. She longed to have a hoop and to be down yonder and run along, while her mother slowly walked behind her and cautioned her not to go too far. Then, however, everything became dim again. At each minute she had to rub the glass clear. She had been enjoined never to open the window; but she was full of rebellious thoughts; she surely might gaze out of the window, if she were not to be taken for a walk. So she opened it, and leaned out like a grown-up person—an imitation of her mother when she esconced herself there and lapsed into silence.

The air was mild, and moist in its mildness, which seemed to her delightful. A darkness slowly rising over the horizon induced her to lift her head. To her imagination it seemed as if some gigantic bird with outstretched wings were hovering on high. At first she saw nothing; the sky was clear; but at last, at the angle of the roof, a gloomy cloud made its appearance, sailing on and speedily enveloping the whole heaven. Another squall was rising before a roaring west wind. The daylight was quickly dying away, and the city grew dark, amidst a livid shimmer, which imparted to the housefronts a rusty tinge.

Almost immediately afterwards the rain fell. The streets were swept by it; the umbrellas were again opened; and the passers-by, fleeing in every direction, vanished like chaff. One old lady gripped her skirts with both hands, while the torrent beat down on her bonnet as though it were falling from a spout. And the rain travelled on;

the cloud kept pace with the water ragefully falling upon Paris: the big drops enfiladed the avenues of the quays, with a gallop like that of a runaway horse, raising a white dust which rolled along the ground at a prodigious speed. They also descended the Champs Elysées, plunged into the long narrow streets of the Saint-Germain district, and at a bound filled up all the open spaces and deserted squares. In a few seconds, behind this veil which grew thicker and thicker, the city paled and seemed to melt away. It was as though a curtain were being drawn obliquely from heaven to earth. Masses of vapor arose too; and the vast, splashing pit-a-pat was as deafening as any rattle of old iron.

Jeanne giddy with the noise, started back. A leaden wall seemed to have been built up before her. But she was fond of rain so she returned, leaned out again, and stretched out her arms to feel the big, cold rain-drops splashing on her hands. This gave her some amusement, and she got wet to the sleeves. Her doll must, of course, like herself, have a headache, and she therefore hastened to put it astride the window-rail, with its back against the side wall. She thought, as she saw the drops pelting down upon it, that they were doing it some good. Stiffly erect, its little teeth displayed in a never-fading smile, the doll sat there, with one shoulder streaming with water, while every gust of wind lifted up its night-dress. Its poor body, which had lost some of its sawdust stuffing, seemed to be shivering.

What was the reason that had prevented her mother from taking her with her? wondered Jeanne. The rain that beat down on her hands seemed a fresh inducement to be out. It must be very nice, she argued, in the street. Once more there flashed on her mind's eye the little girl driving her hoop along the pavement. Nobody could deny that she had gone out with her mamma. Both of them had even seemed to be exceedingly well pleased. This was sufficient proof that little girls were taken out when it rained.

But, then, willingness on her mother's part was requisite. Why had she been unwilling? Then Jeanne again thought of her big cat which had gone away over the houses opposite with its tail in the air, and of the poor little sparrow which she had tempted with food when it was dead, and which had pretended that it did not understand. That kind of thing always happened to her; nobody's love for her was enduring enough. Oh! she would have been ready in a couple of minutes; when she chose she dresesd quickly enough; it was only a question of her boots, which Rosalie buttoned, her jacket, her hat, and it was done. Her mother might easily have waited two minutes for her. When she left home to see her friends, she did not turn her things all topsy-turvy as she had done that afternoon; when she went to the Bois de Boulogne, she led her gently by the hand, and stopped with her outside every shop in the Rue de Passy.

Jeanne could not get to the bottom of it: her black eyebrows frowned, and her delicate features put on a stern, jealous expression which made her resemble some wicked old maid. She felt in a vague way that her mother had gone to some place where children never go. She had not been taken out because something was to be hidden from her. This thought filled her with unutterable sadness, and her heart throbbed with pain.

The rain was becoming finer, and through the curtain which veiled Paris glimpses of buildings were occasionally afforded. The dome of the Invalides, airy and quivering, was the first to reappear through the glittering vibration of the downpour. Next, some of the districts emerged into sight as the torrent slackened; the city seemed to rise from a deluge that had overwhelmed it, its roofs all streaming, and every street filled with a river of water from which vapor still ascended. But suddenly there was a burst of light; a ray of sunshine fell athwart the shower. For a moment it was like a smile breaking through tears.

The rain had now ceased to fall over the Champs Elysées district; but it was sabring the left bank, the Cité, and the far-away suburbs; in the sunshine the drops could be seen flashing down like innumerable slender shafts of steel. On the right a rainbow gleamed forth. As the gush of light streamed across the sky, touches of pink and blue appeared on the horizon, a medley of color, suggestive of a childish attempt at water-color painting. Then there was a sudden blaze—a fall of golden snow, as it were, over a city of crystal. But the light died away, a cloud rolled up, and the smile faded amidst tears; Paris dripped and dripped, with a prolonged sobbing noise, beneath the leaden-hued sky.

Jeanne, with her sleeves soaked, was seized with a fit of coughing. But she was unconscious of the chill that was penetrating her; she was now absorbed in the thought that her mother had gone into Paris. She had come at last to know three buildings—the Invalides, the Panthéon, and the Tower of St.-Jacques. She now slowly went over their names, and pointed them out with her finger without attempting to think what they might be like were she nearer to them. Without doubt, however, her mother was down there; and she settled in her mind that she was in the Panthéon, because it astonished her the most, huge as it was, towering up through the air, like the city's headpiece. Then she began to question herself. Paris was still to her the place where children never go; she was never taken there. She would have liked to know it, however, that she might have quietly said to herself: "Mamma is there; she is doing such and such a thing." But it all seemed to her too immense; it was impossible to find any one there. Then her glance travelled towards the other end of the plain. Might her mother not rather be in one of that cluster of houses on the hill to the left? or nearer in, beneath those huge trees, whose bare branches seemed as dead as firewood? Oh! if she could only have lifted up the roofs! What could that gloomy edifice be? What was that street along which something of enormous bulk seemed to be running? And what could that district be at sight of which she always felt frightened, convinced as she was that people fought one another there? She could not see it distinctly, but, to tell

the truth, its aspects stirred one; it was very ugly, and must not be looked at by little girls.

A host of indefinable ideas and suppositions, which brought her to the verge of weeping, awoke trouble in Jeanne's ignorant, childish mind. From the unknown world of Paris, with its smoke, its endless noises, its powerful, surging life, an odor of wretchedness, filth, and crime seemed to be wafted to her through the mild, humid atmosphere, and she was forced to avert her head, as though she had been leaning over one of those pestilential pits which breathe forth suffocation from their unseen horrors. The Invalides, the Panthéon, the Tower of Saint-Jacques—these she named and counted; but she knew nothing of anything else, and she sat there, terrified and ashamed, with the all-absorbing thought that her mother was among those wicked places, at some spot which she was unable to identify in the depths yonder.

Suddenly Jeanne turend round. She could have sworn that somebody had walked into the bedroom, that a light hand had even touched her shoulder. But the room was empty, still in the same disorder as when Hélène had left. The dressing-gown, flung across the pillow, still lay in the same mournful, weeping attitude. Then Jeanne, with pallid cheeks, cast a glance around, and her heart nearly burst within her. She was alone! she was alone! And, O Heaven, her mother, in forsaking her, had pushed her with such force that she might have fallen to the floor. The thought came back to her with anguish; she again seemed to feel the pain of that outrage on her wrists and shoulders. Why had she been struck? She had been good, and had nothing to reproach herself with. She was usually spoken to with such gentleness that the punishment she had received awoke feelings of indignation within her. She was thrilled by a sensation of childish fear, as in the old times when she was threatened with the approach of the wolf, and looked for it and saw it not: it was lingering in some shady corner, with many other things that were going to overwhelm her. However, she was full of suspicion; her face paled and swelled with jealous fury. Of a sudden, the thought that her mother must love those whom she had gone to see far more than she loved her came upon her with such crushing force that her little hands clutched her bosom. She knew it now; yes, her mother was false to her.

Over Paris a great sorrow seemed to be brooding, pending the arrival of a fresh squall. A murmur travelled through the darkened air, and heavy clouds were hovering overhead. Jeanne, still at the window, was convulsed by another fit of coughing; but in the chill she experienced she felt herself revenged; she would willingly have had her illness return. With her hands pressed against her bosom, she grew conscious of some pain growing more intense within her. It was an agony to which her body abandoned itself. She trembled with fear, and did not again venture to turn round; she felt quite cold at the idea of glancing into the room any more. To be little means to be without strength. What could this new complaint be which

filled her with mingled shame and bitter pleasure? With stiffened body, she sat there as if waiting—every one of her pure and innocent limbs in an agony of revulsion. From the innermost recesses of her being all her woman's feelings were aroused, and there darted through her a pang, as though she had received a blow from a distance. Then with failing heart she cried out chokingly: "Mamma! mamma!" No one could have known whether she called to her mother for aid, or whether she accused her of having inflicted on her the pain which seemed to be killing her.

At that moment the tempest burst. Through the deep and ominous stillness the wind howled over the city, which was shrouded in darkness; and afterwards there came a long-continued crashing—window-shutters beating to and fro, slates flying, chimney-tops and gutter-pipes rattling on to the pavements. For a few seconds a calm ensued; then there blew another gust, which swept along with such mighty strength that the ocean of roofs seemed convulsed, tossing about in waves, and then disappearing in a whirlpool. For a moment chaos reigned. Some enormous clouds, like huge blots of ink, swept through a host of smaller ones, which were scattered and floated like shreds of rag which the wind tore to pieces and carried off thread by thread. A second later two clouds rushed upon one another, and rent one another with crashing reports, which seemed to sprinkle the coppery expanse with wreckage and every time the hurricane thus veered, blowing from every point of the compass, the thunder of opposing navies resounded in the atmosphere, and an awful rending and sinking followed, the hanging fragments of the clouds, jagged like huge bits of broken walls, threatening Paris with imminent destruction. The rain was not yet falling. But suddenly a cloud burst above the central quarters, and a waterspout ascended the Seine. The river's green ribbon, riddled and stirred to its depths by the splashing drops, became transformed into a stream of mud; and one by one, behind the downpour, the bridges appeared to view again, slender and delicately outlined in the mist; while, right and left, the trees edging the grey pavements of the deserted quays were shaken furiously by the wind. Away in the background, over Nôtre-Dame, the cloud divided and poured down such a torrent of water that the island of La Cité seemed submerged. Far above the drenched houses the cathedral towers alone rose up against a patch of clear sky, like floating waifs.

On every side the water now rushed down from the heavens. Three times in succession did the right bank appear to be engulfed. The first fall inundated the distant suburbs, gradually extending its area, and beating on the turrets of Saint-Vincent-de-Paul and Saint-Jacques, which glistened in the rain. Then two other downpours, following in hot haste one upon the other, streamed over Montmartre and the Champs Elysées. At times a glimpse could be obtained of the glass roof of the Palace of Industry, steaming, as it were, under the splashing water; of Saint-Augustin, whose cupola swam in a kind of fog like a clouded moon; of the Madeleine, which spread out its flat roof, looking like some ancient court whose flagstones had been freshly scoured; while, in the rear, the huge mass of the Opera House made one think of a dismasted vessel, which with its hull caught between two rocks, was resisting the assaults of the tempest.

On the left bank of the Seine, also hidden by a watery veil, you perceived the dome of the Invalides, the spires of Sainte-Clotilde, and the towers of Saint-Sulpice, apparently melting away in the moist atmosphere. Another cloud spread out, and from the colonnade of the Panthéon sheets of water streamed down, threatening to inundate what lay below. And from that moment the rain fell upon the city in all directions; one might have imagined that the heavens were precipitating themselves on the earth; streets vanished, sank into the depths, and men reappeared, drifting on the surface, amidst shocks whose violence seemed to foretell the end of the city. A prolonged roar ascended— the roar of all the water rushing along the gutters and falling into the drains. And at last, above muddy-looking Paris, which had assumed with the showers a dingy-yellow hue, the livid clouds spread themselves out in uniform fashion, without stain or rift. The rain was becoming finer, and was falling sharply and vertically; but whenever the wind again rose, the grey hatching was curved into mighty waves, and the raindrops, driven almost horizontally, could be heard lashing the walls with a hissing sound, till, with the fall of the wind, they again fell vertically, peppering the soil with a quiet obstinacy, from the heights of Passy away to the level plain of Charen-

ton. Then the vast city, as though overwhelmed and lifeless after some awful
convulsion, seemed but an expanse of
stony ruins under the invisible heavens.

Jeanne, who had sunk down by the
window, had wailed out once more,
"Mamma! mamma!" A terrible weariness deprived her limbs of their
strength as she lingered there, face to
face with the engulfing of Paris. Amidst
her exhaustion, whilst the breeze played
with her tresses, and her face remained
wet with rain, she preserved some taste
of the bitter pleasure which had made
her shiver, while within her heart there
was a consciousness of some ir-
retrievable woe. Everything seemed to
her to have come to an end; she realized
that she was getting very old. The
hours might pass away, but now she did
not even cast a glance into the room.
It was all the same to her to be forgotten and alone. Such despair possessed the child's heart that all around
her seemed black. If she were scolded,
as of old, when she was ill, it would
surely be very wrong. She was burning
with fever; something like a sick headache was weighing on her. Surely too,
but a moment ago, something had
snapped within her. She could not prevent it; she must inevitably submit to
whatever might be her fate. Besides,
weariness was prostrating her. She had
joined her hands over the window-bar,
on which she rested her head, and,
though at times she opened her eyes to
gaze at the rain, drowsiness was stealing over her.

And still and ever the rain kept beating down; the livid sky seemed dissolving in water. A final blast of wind had
passed by; a monotonous roar could be

heard. Amidst a solemn quiescence the
sovereign rain poured unceasingly upon
the silent, deserted city it had conquered; and behind this sheet of
streaked crystal Paris showed like some
phantom place, with quivering outlines,
which seemed to be melting away. To
Jeanne the scene now brought nothing
beyond sleepiness and horrid dreams,
as though all the mystery and unknown
evil were rising up in vapor to pierce
her through and make her cough. Every
time she opened her eyes she was seized
with a fit of coughing, and would remain
for a few seconds looking at the scene;
which as her head fell back once more,
clung to her mind, and seemed to spread
over her and crush her.

The rain was still falling. What hour
might it be now? Jeanne could not have
told. Perhaps the clock had ceased going. It seemed to her too great a
fatigue to turn round. It was surely at
least a week since her mother had
quitted her. She had abandoned all expectation of her return; she was resigned to the prospect of never seeing
her again. Then she became oblivious of
everything—the wrongs which had been
done her, the pain which she had just
experienced, even the loneliness in which
she was suffered to remain. A weight,
chilly like stone, fell upon her. This
only was certain: she was very unhappy—ah! as unhappy as the poor little
waifs to whom she gave alms as they
huddled together in gateways. Ah!
Heaven! how coughing racked one, and
how penetrating was the cold when
there was no nobody to love one! She
closed her heavy eyelids, succumbing to
a feverish stupor; and the last of her
thoughts was a vague memory of child-

hood, of a visit to a mill, full of yellow wheat, and of tiny grains slipping under millstones as huge as houses.

Hours and hours passed away; each minute was a century. The rain beat down without ceasing, with ever the same tranquil flow, as though all time and eternity were allowed it to deluge the plain. Jeanne had fallen asleep. Close by, her doll still sat astride the iron window-bar; and, with its legs in the room and its head outside, its nightdress clinging to its rosy skin, its eyes glaring, and its hair streaming with water, it looked not unlike a drowned child; and so emaciated did it appear in its comical yet distressing posture of death, that it almost brought tears of pity to the eyes. Jeanne coughed in her sleep; but now she never once opened her eyes. Her head swayed to and fro on her crossed arms, and the cough spent itself in a wheeze without awakening her. Nothing more existed for her. She slept in the darkness. She did not even withdraw her hand, from whose cold, red fingers bright raindrops were trickling one by one into the vast expanse which lay beneath the window. This went on for hours and hours. Paris was slowly waning on the horizon, like some phantom city; heaven and earth mingled together in an indistinguishable jumble; and still and ever with unflagging persistency did the grey rain fall.

## CHAPTER XXI

### JEANNE'S EYES

NIGHT had long gathered in when Hélène returned. From her umbrella the water dripped on step after step, whilst clinging to the balusters she ascended the staircase. She stood for a few seconds outside her door to regain her breath; the deafening rush of the rain still sounded in her ears; she still seemed to feel the jostling of hurrying foot-passengers, and to see the reflections from the street-lamps dancing in the puddles. She was walking in a dream, filled with the surprise of the kisses that had been showered upon her; and as she fumbled for her key she believed that her bosom felt neither remorse nor joy. Circumstances had compassed it all; she could have done naught to prevent it. But the key was not to be found; it was doubtless inside, in the pocket of her other gown. At this discovery her vexation was intense; it seemed as though she were denied admission to her own home. It became necessary that she should ring the bell.

"Oh! it's madame!" exclaimed Rosalie as she opened the door. "I was beginning to feel uneasy."

She took the umbrella, intending to place it in the kitchen sink, and then rattled on:

"Good gracious! what torrents! Zéphyrin, who has just come, was drenched to the skin. I took the liberty, madame, of keeping him to dinner. He has leave till ten o'clock."

Hélène followed her mechanically. She felt a desire to look once more on everything in her home before removing her bonnet.

"You have done quite right, my girl," she answered.

For a moment she lingered on the kitchen threshold, gazing at the bright fire. Then she instinctively opened the door of a cupboard, and promptly shut it again. Everything was in its place, chairs and tables alike; she found them all again, and their presence gave her pleasure.

Zéphyrin had, in the meantime, struggled respectfully to his feet. She nodded to him, smiling.

"I didn't know whether to put the roast on," began the maid.

"Why, what time is it?" asked Hélène.

"Oh, it's close on seven o'clock, madame."

"What! seven o'clock!"

Astonishment riveted her to the floor; she had lost all consciousness of time, and seemed to awaken from a dream.

"And where's Jeanne?" she asked.

"Oh! she has been very good, madame. I even think she must have fallen asleep, for I haven't heard her for some time."

"Haven't you given her a light?"

Embarrassment closed Rosalie's lips; she was unwilling to relate that Zéphyrin had brought her some pictures which had engrossed her attention. Mademoiselle had never made the least stir, so she could scarcely have wanted anything. Hélène, however, paid no further heed to her, but ran into the room, where a dreadful chill fell upon her.

"Jeanne! Jeanne!" she called.

No answer broke the stillness. She stumbled against an armchair. From the dining-room, the door of which she had left ajar, some light streamed across a corner of the carpet. She felt a shiver come over her, and she could have declared that the rain was falling in the room, with its moist breath and continuous streaming. Then, on turning her head, she at once saw the pale square formed by the open window and the gloomy grey of the sky.

"Who can have opened this window?" she cried. "Jeanne! Jeanne!"

Still no answering word. A mortal terror fell on Hélène's heart. She must look out of this window; but as she felt her way towards it, her hands lighted on a head of hair—it was Jeanne's. And then, as Rosalie entered with a lamp, the child appeared with blanched face, sleeping with her cheek upon her crossed arms, while the big raindrops from the roof splashed upon her. Her breathing was scarcely perceptible, so overcome she was with despair and fatigue. Among the lashes of her large, bluey eyelids there were still two heavy tears.

"The unhappy child!" stammered Hélène. "Oh, heavens! she's icy cold! To fall asleep there, at such a time, when she had been expressly forbidden to touch the window! Jeanne, Jeanne, speak to me; wake up, Jeanne!"

Rosalie had prudently vanished. The child, on being raised in her mother's embrace, let her head drop as though she were unable to shake off the leaden slumber that had seized upon her. At last, however, she raised her eyelids; but the glare of the lamp dazzled her, and she remained benumbed and stupid.

"Jeanne, it's I! What's wrong with you? See, I've just come back," said Hélène.

But the child seemingly failed to understand her; in her stupefaction she could only murmur: "Oh! Ah!"

She gazed inquiringly at her mother, as though she failed to recognize her. And suddenly she shivered, growing conscious of the cold air of the room. Her memory was awakening, and the tears rolled from her eyelids to her cheeks. Then she commenced to struggle, in the evident desire to be left alone.

"It's you, it's you! Oh, leave me; you hold me too tight! I was so comfortable."

She slipped from her mother's arms with affright in her face. Her uneasy looks wandered from Hélène's hands to her shoulders; one of those hands was ungloved, and she started back from the touch of the moist palm and warm fingers with a fierce resentment, as though fleeing from some stranger's caress. The old perfume of vervain had died away; Hélène's fingers had surely become greatly attenuated, and her hand was unusually soft. This skin was no longer hers, and its touch exasperated Jeanne.

"Come, I'm not angry with you," pleaded Hélène. "But, indeed, have you behaved well? Come and kiss me."

Jeanne, however, still recoiled from her. She had no remembrance of having seen her mother dressed in that gown or cloak. Besides, she looked so wet and muddy. Where had she come from dressed in that dowdy style.

"Kiss me, Jeanne," repeated Hélène.

But her voice also seemed strange; in Jeanne's ears it sounded louder. Her old heartache came upon her once more, as when an injury had been done her; and unnerved by the presence of what was unknown and horrible to her, divining, however, that she was breathing an atmosphere of falsehood, she burst into sobs.

"No, no, I entreat you! You left me all alone; and oh! I've been so miserable!"

"But I'm back again, my darling. Don't weep any more; I've come home!"

"Oh no, no! it's all over now! I don't wish for you any more! Oh! I waited and waited, and have been so wretched!"

Hélène took hold of the child again, and gently sought to draw her to her bosom; but she resisted stubbornly, plaintively exclaiming:

"No, no; it will never be the same! You are not the same!"

"What! What are you talking of, child?"

"I don't know; you are not the same."

"Do you mean to say that I don't love you any more?"

"I don't know; you are no longer the same! Don't say no. You don't feel the same! It's all over, over, over. I wish to die!"

With blanching face Hélène again clasped her in her arms. Did her looks, then, reveal her secret? She kissed her, but a shudder ran through the child's frame, and an expression of such misery crept into her face that Hélène forbore to print a second kiss upon her brow. She still kept hold of her, but neither of them uttered a word. Jeanne's sobbing fell to a whisper, a nervous revolt stiffening her limbs the while. Hélène's first thought was that much notice ought not to be paid to a child's whims; but to her heart there stole a feeling of secret shame, and the weight of her daughter's body on her shoulder brought a blush to her cheeks. She hastened to put Jeanne down, and each felt relieved.

"Now, be good, and wipe your eyes," said Hélène. "We'll make everything all right."

The child acquiesced in all gentleness, but seemed somewhat afraid and glanced covertly at her mother. All at once her frame was shaken by a fit of coughing. "Good heavens! why, you've made yourself ill now! I cannot stay away from you a moment. Did you feel cold?"

"Yes, mamma; in the back."

"See here; put on this shawl. The dining-room stove is lighted, and you'll soon feel warm. Are you hungry?"

Jeanne hesitated. It was on the tip of her tongue to speak the truth and say no; but she darted a side glance at her mother, and, recoiling, answered in a whisper: "Yes, mamma."

"Ah, well, it will be all right," exclaimed Hélène desirous of tranquillizing herself. "Only, I entreat you, you naughty child, don't frighten me like this again."

On Rosalie re-entering the room to announce that dinner was ready, Hélène severely scolded her. The little maid's head dropped; she stammered out that it was all very true, for she ought to have looked better after mademoiselle. Then, hoping to mollify her mistress, she busied herself in helping her to change her clothes. "Good gracious! madame was in a fine state!" she remarked, as she assisted in removing each mud-stained garment, at which Jeanne glared suspiciously, still racked by torturing thoughts.

"Madame ought to feel comfortable now," exclaimed Rosalie when it was all over. "It's awfully nice to get into dry clothes after a drenching."

Hélène, on finding herself once more in her blue dressing gown, gave vent to a slight sigh, as though a new happiness had welled up within her. She again regained her old cheerfulness; she had rid herself of a burden in throwing off those bedraggled garments. She washed her face and hands; and while she stood there, still glistening with moisture, her dressing-gown buttoned up to her chin, she was slowly approached by Jeanne, who took one of her hands and kissed it.

At table, however, not a word passed between mother and daughter. The fire flared with a merry roar, and there was a look of happiness about the little dining-room, with its bright mahogany and gleaming china. But the old stupor which drove away all thought seemed to have again fallen on Hélène; she ate mechanically, though with an appearance of appetite. Jeanne sat facing her, and quietly watched her over her glass, noting each of her movements. But all at once the child again coughed, and her mother, who had become unconscious of her presence, immediately displayed lively concern.

"Why, you're coughing again! Aren't you getting warm?"

"Oh, yes, mamma; I'm very warm."

Hélène leaned towards her to feel her hand and ascertain whether she was speaking the truth. Only then did she perceive that her plate was still full.

"Why, you said you were hungry. Don't you like what you have there?"

"Oh, yes, mamma; I'm eating away."

With an effort Jeanne swallowed a mouthful. Hélène looked at her for a time, but soon again began dreaming of the fatal room which she had come from. It did not escape the child that her mother took little interest in her now. As the dinner came to an end, her poor wearied frame sank down on the chair, and she sat there like some bent, aged woman, with the dim eyes of one of those old maids for whom love is past and gone.

"Won't mademoiselle have any jam?" asked Rosalie. "If not, can I remove the cloth?"

Hélène still sat there with far-away looks.

"Mamma, I'm sleepy," exclaimed Jeanne in a changed voice. "Will you let me go to bed? I shall feel better in bed."

Once more her mother seemed to awake with a start to consciousness of her surroundings.

"You are suffering, my darling! where do you feel the pain? Tell me."

"No, no; I told you I'm alright! I'm sleepy, and it's already time for me to go to bed."

She left her chair and stood up, as though to prove there was no illness threatening her: but her benumbed feet tottered over the floor on her way to the bed-room. She leaned against the furniture, and her hardihood was such that not a tear came from her, despite the feverish fire darting through her frame. Her mother followed to assist her to bed; but the child had displayed such haste in undressing herself that she only arrived in time to tie up her hair for the night. Without need of any helping hand Jeannie slipped between the sheets, and quickly closed her eyes.

"Are you comfortable?" asked Hélène, as she drew up the bedclothes and carefully tucked her in.

"Yes, quite comfortable. Leave me alone, and don't disturb me. Take away the lamp."

Her only yearning was to be alone in the darkness, that she might reopen her eyes and chew the cud of her sorrows, with no one near to watch her. When the light had been carried away, her eyes opened quite wide.

Nearby, in the meantime, Hélène was pacing up and down her room. She was seized with a wondrous longing to be up and moving about; the idea of going to bed seemed to her insufferable. She glanced at the clock — twenty minutes to nine; what was she to do? She rummaged about in a drawer, but forgot what she was seeking for. Then she wandered to her bookshelves, glancing aimlessly over the books; but the very reading of the titles wearied her. A buzzing sprang up in her ears with the room's stillness; the loneliness, the heavy atmosphere, were as an agony to her. She would fain have had some bustle going on around her, have had some one there to speak to—something, in short, to draw her from herself. She twice listened at the door of Jeanne's little room, from which, however, not even a sound of breathing came. Everything was quiet; so she turned back once more, and amused herself by taking up and replacing whatever came to her hand. Then suddenly the thought flashed across her mind that Zéphyrin must still be with Rosalie. It was a relief to her; she was delighted at the idea of not being alone, and stepped in her slippers towards the kitchen.

She was already in the ante-room, and was opening the glass door of the inner passage, when she detected the re-echoing clap of a swinging box on the ears, and the next moment Rosalie could be heard exclaiming:

"Ha, ha! you think you'll nip me again, do you? Take your paws off!"

"Oh, that's nothing, my charmer!" exclaimed Zéphyrin in his husky, guttural voice. "That's to show how I love you—in this style, you know—"

But at that moment the door creaked, and Hélène, entering, discovered the diminutive soldier and the servant maid seated very quietly at table, with their noses bent over their plates. They had assumed an air of complete indifference; their innocence was certain. Yet their faces were red with blushes, and their eyes aflame, and they wriggled restlessly on their straw-bottomed chairs. Rosalie started up and hurried forward.

"Madame wants something?"

Hélène had no pretext ready to her tongue. She had come to see them, to chat with them, and have their company. However, she felt a sudden shame, and dared not say that she required nothing.

"Have you any hot water?" she asked, after a silence.

"No, madame; and my fire is nearly out. Oh, but it doesn't matter; I'll give you some in five minutes. It boils in no time."

She threw on some charcoal, and then set the kettle in place; but seeing that her mistress still lingered in the doorway, she said:

"I'll bring the water to you in five minutes, madame."

Hélène responded with a wave of the hand.

"I'm not in a hurry for it; I'll wait. Don't disturb yourself, my girl; eat away, eat away. There's a lad who'll have to go back to barracks.'

Rosalie thereupon sat down again. Zéphyrin, who had also been standing, made a military salute, and returned to the cutting of his meat, with his elbows projecting as though to show that he knew how to conduct himself at table. Thus eating together, after madame had finished dinner, they did not even draw the table into the middle of the kitchen, but contented themselves with sitting side by side, with their noses turned towards the wall. A glorious prospect of stewpans was before them. A bunch of laurel and thyme hung near, and a spice-box exhaled a piquant perfume. Around them —the kitchen was not yet tidied—was all the litter of the things cleared away from the dining-room; however, the spot seemed a charming one to these hungry sweethearts, and especially to Zéphyrin, who here feasted on such things as were never seen within the walls of his barracks. The predominant odor was one of toast meat, seasoned with a dash of vinegar—the vinegar of the salad. In the copper pans and iron pots the reflected light from the gas was dancing; and as the heat of the fire was beyond endurance, they had set the window ajar, and a cool breeze blew in from the garden, stirring the blue cotton curtain.

"Must you be in by ten o'clock exactly?" asked Hélène.

"I must, madame, with all deference to you," answered Zéphyrin.

"Well, it's a long way off. Do you take the 'bus'?"

"Oh, yes, madame, sometimes. But you see a good swinging walk is much the best."

She had taken a step into the kitchen, and leaning against the dresser, her arms dangling and her hands clasped over her dressing-gown, she began gossiping away about the wretched weather they had had that day, about the food which was rationed out in barracks, and the high price of eggs. As soon, however, as she had asked a question and their answer had been given the conversation abruptly fell. They experienced some discomfort with her standing thus behind their backs. They did not turn round, but spoke into their plates, their shoulders bent beneath her gaze, while, to conform to propriety, each mouthful they swallowed was as small as possible. On the other hand, Hélène had now regained her tranquillity, and felt quite happy there.

"Don't fret, madame," said Rosalie; "the kettle is singing already. I wish the fire would only burn up a little better!"

She wanted to see to it, but Hélène would not allow her to disturb herself. It would be all right by-and-by. An intense weariness now pervaded the young woman's limbs. Almost mechanically she crossed the kitchen and approached the window, where she observed the third chair, which was very high, and when turned over became a step-ladder. However, she did not sit down on it at once, for she had caught sight of a number of pictures heaped up on a corner of the table.

"Dear me!" she exclaimed, as she took them in her hand, inspired with the wish of gratifying Zéphyrin.

The little soldier gaped with a silent chuckle. His face beamed with smiles, and his eyes followed each picture, his head wagging whenever something especially lovely was being examined by madame.

"That one there," he suddenly remarked, "I found in the Rue du Temple. She's a beautiful woman, with flowers in her basket."

Hélène sat down and inspected the beautiful woman who decorated the gilt and varnished lid of a box of lozenges, every stain on which had been carefully wiped off by Zéphyrin. On the chair a dish-cloth was hanging, and she could not well lean back. She flung it aside, however, and once more lapsed into her dreaming. Then the two sweethearts remarked madame's good nature, and their restraint vanished—in the end, indeed, her very presence was forgotten by them. One by one the pictures had dropped from her hands on to her knees, and, with a vague smile playing on her face, she examined the sweethearts and listened to their talk.

"I say, my dear," whispered the girl, "won't you have some more mutton?"

He answered neither yes nor no, but swung backwards and forwards on his chair as though he had been tickled, then contentedly stretched himself, while she placed a thick slice on his plate. His red epaulets moved up and down, and his bullet-shaped head, with

its huge projecting ears, swayed to and
fro over his yellow collar as though it
were the head of some Chinese idol.
His laughter ran all over him, and he
was almost bursting inside his tunic,
which he did not unbutton, however,
out of respect for madame.

"This is far better than old Rouvet's
radishes!" he exclaimed at last, with
his mouth full.

This was a reminiscence of their
country home; and at thought of it
they burst into immoderate laughter.
Rosalie even had to hold on to the
table to prevent herself from falling.
One day, before their first communion,
it seemed, Zéphyrin had filched three
black radishes from old Rouvet. They
were very tough radishes indeed—tough
enough to break one's teeth; but
Rosalie all the same had crunched her
share of the spoil at the back of the
schoolhouse. Hence it was that every
time they chanced to be taking a meal
together Zéphyrin never omitted to
ejaculate: "Yes, this is better than
old Rouvet's radishes!"

And then Rosalie's laughter would
become so violent that nine times out
of ten her petticoat-string would give
way with an audible crack.

"Hello! has it parted?" asked the
little soldier, with triumph in his tone.

But Rosalie responded with a good
slap.

"It's disgusting to make me break
the string like this!" said she. "I put
a fresh one on every week."

However, he came nearer to her,
intent on some joke or other, by way
of revenging the blow; but with a furious glance she reminded him that her
mistress was looking on. This seemed

to trouble him but little, for he replied
with a rakish wink, as much as to say
that no woman, not even a lady, disliked a little fun. To be sure, when
folks are sweet-hearting, other people
always like to be looking on.

"You have still five years to serve,
haven't you?" asked Hélène, leaning
back on the high wooden-seated chair,
and yielding to a feeling of tenderness.

"Yes, madame; perhaps only four if
they don't need me any longer."

It occurred to Rosalie that her mistress was thinking of her marriage,
and with assumed anger, she broke in:

"Oh! madame, he can stick in the
army for another ten years if he likes
I sha'n't trouble myself to ask the
Government for him. He is becoming
too much of a rake; yes, I believe he's
going to the dogs. Oh! it's useless for
you to laugh—that won't take with me.
When we go before the mayor to get
married, we'll see on whose side the
laugh is!"

At this he chuckled all the more, in
order that he might show himself a
lady-killer before madame, and the
maid's annoyance then became real.

"Oh!" said she, "we know all about
that! You know, madame, he's still
a booby at heart. You've no idea how
stupid that uniform makes them all!
That's the way he goes on with his
comrades; but if I turned him out, you
would hear him sobbing on the stairs.
Oh, I don't care a fig for you, my
lad! Why, whenever I please, won't
you always be there to do as I tell
you?"

She bent forward to observe him
closely; but, on seeing that his good-
natured, freckled face was beginning

to cloud over, she was suddenly moved, and prattled on, without any seeming transition:

"Ah! I didn't tell you that I've received a letter from auntie. The Guignard lot want to sell their house—aye, and almost for nothing too. We might perhaps be able to take it later on."

"By Jove!" exclaimed Zéphyrin, brightening, "we should be quite at home there. There's room enough for two cows."

With this idea they lapsed into silence. They were now having some dessert. The little soldier licked the jam on his bread with a child's greedy satisfaction, while the servant-girl carefully pared an apple with a maternal air.

"Madame!" all at once exclaimed Rosalie, "there's the water boiling now."

Hélène, however, never stirred. She felt herself enveloped by an atmosphere of happiness. She gave a continuance to their dreams, and pictured them living in the country in the Guignards' house and possessed of two cows. A smile came to her face as she saw Zéphyrin sitting there to all appearance so serious, though in reality he was patting Rosalie's knee under the table, whilst she remained very stiff, affecting an innocent demeanor. Then everything became blurred. Hélène lost all definite sense of her surroundings, of the place where she was, and of what had brought her there. The copper pans were flashing on the walls; feelings of tenderness riveted her to the spot; her eyes had a far-away look. She was not affected in any way by

the disorderly state of the kitchen; she had no consciousness of having demeaned herself by coming there all she felt was a deep pleasure, as when a longing has been satisfied. Meantime the heat from the fire was bedewing her pale brow with beads of perspiration, and behind her the wind, coming in through the half-open window, quivered delightfully on her neck.

"Madame, your water is boiling," again said Rosalie. "There will be soon none left in the kettle."

She held the kettle before her, and Hélène, for the moment astonished, was forced to rise. "Oh, yes! thank you!"

She no longer had an excuse to remain, and went away slowly and regretfully. When she reached her room she was at a loss what to do with the kettle. Then suddenly within her there came a burst of passionate love. The torpor which had held her in a state of semi-unconsciousness gave way to a wave of glowing feeling, the rush of which thrilled her as with fire. She quivered, and memories returned to her — memories of her passion and of Henri.

While she was taking off her dressing-gown and gazing at her bare arms, a noise broke on her anxious ear. She thought she had heard Jeanne coughing. Taking up the lamp she went into the closet, but found the child with eyelids closed, seemingly fast asleep. However, the moment the mother, satisfied with her examination, had turned her back, Jeanne's eyes again opened widely to watch her as she returned to her room. There was indeed no sleep for Jeanne, nor had she any desire to sleep. A second fit of coughing racked her bosom, but she buried her head beneath the coverlet and stifled every sound. She might go away for ever now; her mother would never miss her. Her eyes were still wide open in the darkness; she knew everything as though knowledge had come with thought, and she was dying of it all, but dying without a murmur.

## CHAPTER XXII

### TO ITALY!

NEXT day all sorts of practical ideas took possession of Hélène's mind. She awoke impressed by the necessity of keeping watch over her happiness, and shuddering with fear lest by some imprudent step she might lose Henri. At this chilly morning hour, when the room still seemed asleep, she felt that she idolized him, loved him with a transport which pervaded her whole being. Never had she experienced such an anxiety to be diplomatic. Her first thought was that she must go to see Juliette that very morning, and thus obviate the need of any tedious explanations of inquiries which might result in ruining everything.

On calling upon Madame Deberle at about nine o'clock she found her already up, with pallid cheeks and red eyes like the heroine of a tragedy. As soon as the poor woman caught sight of her, she threw herself sobbing upon her neck exclaiming that she was her good angel. She didn't love Malignon, not in the least, she swore it! Gracious heavens! what a foolish affair! It would have killed her —there was no doubt of that! She did not now feel herself to be in the least degree qualified for ruses, lies, and agonies, and the tyranny of a sentiment that never varied. Oh, how delightful did it seem to her to find herself free again! She laughed contentedly; but immediately afterwards there was another outburst of tears as she besought her friend not to despise her. Beneath her feverish unrest a fear lingered; she imagined that her husband knew everything. He had come home the night before trembling with agitation. She overwhelmed Hélène with questions; and Hélène, with a hardihood and facility at which she herself was amazed, poured into her ears a story, every detail of which she invented offhand. She vowed to Juliette that her husband doubted her in nothing. It was she, Hélène, who had become acquainted with everything, and, wishing to save her, had devised that plan of breaking in upon their meeting. Juliette listened to her, put instant credit in the fiction, and, beaming through her tears, grew sunny with joy. She threw herself once more on Hélène's neck. Her caresses brought no embarrassment to the latter; she now experienced none of the honorable scruples that had at one time affected her. When she left her lover's wife after extracting a promise from her that she would try to be calm, she laughed in her sleeve at her own cunning; she was in a transport of delight.

Some days slipped away. Hélène's whole existence had undergone a change; and in the thoughts of every hour she no longer lived in her own home, but with Henri. The only thing that existed for her was that next-door house in which her heart beat. Whenever she could find an excuse to do so she ran thither, and forgot everything in the content of breathing the same air as her lover. In her first rapture the sight of Juliette even flooded her with tenderness; for was not Juliette one of Henri's belongings? He had not, however, again been able to meet her alone. She appeared loth to give him a second assignation. One evening, when he was leading her into the hall, she even made him swear that he would never again visit the house in the Passage des Eaux, as such an act might compromise her.

Meantime, Jeanne was shaken by a short, dry cough, that never ceased, but became severer towards evening every day. She would be then slightly feverish, and she grew weak with the perspiration that bathed her in her sleep. When her mother cross-questioned her, she answered that she wasn't ill, that she felt no pain. Doubtless her cold was coming to an end. Hélène, tranquillized by the explanation, and having no adequate idea of what was going on around her, retained, however, in her bosom, amidst the rapture that made up her life, a vague feeling of sorrow, of some weight that made her heart bleed despite herself. At times, when she was plunged in one of those causeless transports which made her melt with tenderness, an anxious thought would come to her —she imagined that some misfortune was hovering behind her. She turned round, however, and then smiled. People are ever in a tremble when they are too happy. There was nothing there. Jeanne had coughed a moment before, but she

had some *tisane* to drink; there would be no ill effects.

However, one afternoon old Doctor Bodin, who visited them in the character of a family friend, prolonged his stay, and stealthily, but carefully, examined Jeanne with his little blue eyes. He questioned her as though he were having some fun with her, and on this occasion uttered no warning word. Two days later, however, he made his appearance again! and this time, not troubling to examine Jeanne, he talked away merrily in the fashion of a man who has seen many years and many things, and turned the conversation on travelling. He had once served as a military surgeon; he knew every corner of Italy. It was a magnificent country, said he, which to be admired ought to be seen in spring. Why didn't Madame Grandjean take her daughter there? From this he proceeded by easy transitions to advising a trip to the land of the sun, as he styled it. Hélène's eyes were bent on him fixedly. "No, no," he exclaimed, "neither of you is ill! Oh, no, certainly not! Still, a change of air would mean new strength!" Her face had blanched, a mortal chill had come over her at the thought of leaving Paris. Gracious heavens! to go away so far, so far! to lose Henri in a moment, their love to droop without a morrow! Such was the agony which the thought gave her that she bent her head towards Jeanne to hide her emotion. Did Jeanne wish to go away? The child, with a chilly gesture, had intertwined her little fingers. Oh! yes, she would like to go! She would so like to go away into the sunny land, quite alone, she and her mother, quite alone! And over her poor attenuated face with its cheeks burning with fever, there swept the bright hope of a new life. But Hélène would listen to no more; indignation and distrust led her to imagine that all of them—the Abbé, Doctor Bodin, Jeanne herself—were plotting to separate her from Henri. When the old doctor noticed the pallor of her cheeks, he imagined that he had not spoken so cautiously as he might have done, and hastened to declare that there was no hurry, albeit he silently resolved to return to the subject at another time.

It happened that Madame Deberle intended to stop at home that day. As soon as the doctor had gone Hélène hastened to put on her bonnet. Jeanne however, refused to quit the house; she felt better beside the fire; she would be very good, and would not open the window. For some time past she had not teased her mother to be allowed to go with her; still she gazed after her as she went out with a longing look. Then, when she found herself alone, she shrunk into her chair and sat for hours motionless.

"Mamma, is Italy far away?" she asked as Hélène glided towards her to kiss her.

"Oh, very far away, my pet!"

Jeanne clung round her neck, and not letting her rise again at the moment, whispered: "Well, Rosalie could take care of everything here. We should have no need of her. A small travelling-trunk would do for us, you know! Oh! it would be delightful, mother dear! Nobody but us two! I should come back quite plump—like this!"

She puffed out her cheeks and pictured how stout her arms would be.

Hélène's answer was that she would see; and then she ran off with a final injunction to Rosalie to take good care of mademoiselle.

The child coiled herself up in the chimney-corner, gaizng at the ruddy fire and deep in reverie. From time to time she moved her hands forward mechanically to warm them. The glinting of the flames dazzled her large eyes. So absorbed was she in her dreaming that she did not hear Monsieur Rambaud enter the room. His visits had now become very frequent; he came, he would say, in the interests of the poor paralytic women for whom Doctor Deberle had not yet been able to secure admission into the Hospital for Incurables. Finding Jeanne alone, he took a seat on the other side of the fireplace, and chatted with her as thought she were a grown-up person. It was most regrettable; the poor woman had been waiting a week; however, he would go down presently to see the doctor who might perhaps give him an answer. Meanwhile he did not stir.

"Why hasn't your mother taken you with her?" he asked.

Jeanne shrugged her shoulders with a gesture of weariness. It disturbed her to go about visiting other people. Nothing gave her any pleasure now.

"I am getting old," she added, "and I can't be always amusing myself. Mamma finds entertainment out of doors, and I within; so we are not together."

Silence ensued. The child shivered, and held her hands out towards the fire which burnt steadily with a pinky glare; and, indeed, muffled as she was in a huge shawl, with a silk handkerchief round her neck and another encircling her head, she did look like some old dame. Shrouded in all these wraps, it struck one that she was no larger than an ailing bird, panting amidst its ruffled plumage. Monsieur Rambaud, with hands clasped over his knees, was gazing at the fire. Then, turning towards Jeanne, he inquired if her mother had gone out the evening before. She answered with a nod, yes. And did she go out the evening before that and the previous day? The answer was always yes, given with a nod of the head; her mother quitted her every day.

At this the child and Monsieur Rambaud gazed at one another for a long time, their faces pale and serious, as though they shared some great sorrow. They made no reference to it—a chit like her and an old man could not talk of such a thing together; but they were well aware why they were so sad, and why it was a pleasure to them to sit like this on either side of the fireplace when they were alone in the house. It was a comfort beyond telling. They loved to be near one another that their forlornness might pain them less. A wave of tenderness poured into their hearts; they would fain have embraced and wept together.

"You are cold, my dear old friend, I'm certain of it," said Jeanne; "come nearer the fire.

"No, no, my darling; I'm not cold."

"Oh! you're telling a fib; your hands are like ice! Come nearer, or I shall get vexed."

It was now his turn to display his anxious care.

"I could lay a wager they haven't left you any drink. I'll run and make some for you; would you like it? Oh!

I'm a good hand at making it. You would see, if I were your nurse, you wouldn't be without anything you wanted."

He did not allow himself any more explicit hint. Jeanne somewhat sharply declared she was disgusted with *tisane;* she was compelled to drink too much of it. However, now and then she would allow Monsieur Rambaud to flutter round her like a mother; he would slip a pillow under her shoulders, give her the medicine that she had almost forgotten, or carry her into the bedroom in his arms. These little acts of devotion thrilled both with tenderness. As Jeanne eloquenly declared with her sombre eyes, whose flashes disturbed the old man so sorely, they were playing the parts of the father and the little girl while her mother was absent. Then, however, sadness would all at once fall upon them; their talk died away, and they glanced at one another steathily with pitying looks.

That afternoon, after a lengthy silence, the child asked the question which she had already put to her mother: "Is Italy far away?"

"Oh, I should think so," replied Monsieur Rambaud. "It's away over yonder, on the other side of Marseilles, a deuce of a distance! Why do you ask me such a question?"

"Oh! because—" she began gravely. But she burst into loud complaints at her ignorance. She was always ill, and she had never been sent to school. Then they both became silent again, lulled into forgetfulness by the intense heat of the fire.

In the meantime Hélène had found Madame Deberle and her sister Pauline in the Japanese pavilion where they so frequently whiled away the afternoon. Inside it was very warm, a heating apparatus filled it with a stifling atmosphere.

The large windows were shut, and a full view could be had of the little garden, which, in its winter guise, looked like some large sepia drawing, finished with exquisite delicacy, the little black branches of the trees showing clear against the brown earth. The two sisters were carrying on a sharp controversy.

"Now, be quiet, do!" exclaimed Juliette; "it is evidently our interest to support Turkey."

"Oh, I've had a talk about it with a Russian," replied Pauline, who was equally excited. "We are much liked at St. Petersburg, and it is only there that we can find our proper allies."

Juliette's face assumed a serious look, and, crossing her arms, she exclaimed: "Well, and what will you do with the balance of power in Europe?"

The Eastern crisis was the absorbing topic in Paris at that moment; it was the stock subject of conversation, and no woman who pretended to any position could speak with propriety of anything else. Thus, for two days past, Madame Deberle had with passionate fervor devoted herself to foreign politics. Her ideas were very pronounced on the various eventualities which might arise; and Pauline greatly annoyed her by her eccentricity in advocating Russia's cause in opposition to the clear interests of France. Juliette's first desire was to convince her of her folly, but she soon lost her temper.

"Pooh! hold your tongue; you are talking foolishly! Now, if you had only studied the matter carefully with me—"

But she broke off to greet Hélène, who entered at this moment.

"Good-day, my dear! It is very kind of you to call. I don't suppose you have any news. This morning's paper talked of an ultimatum. There has been a very exciting debate in the English House of Commons!"

"No, I don't know anything," answered Hélène, who was astounded by the question. "I go out so little!"

However, Juliette had not waited for her reply, but was busy explaining to Pauline why it was necessary to neutralize the Black Sea; and her talk bristled with references to English and Russian generals, whose names she mentioned in a familiar way and with faultless pronunciation. However, Henri now made his appearance with several newspapers in his hand. Hélène at once realized that he had come there for her sake; for their eyes had sought one another and exchanged a long, meaning glance. And when their hands met it was in a prolonged and silent clasp that told how the personality of each was lost in the other.

"Is there anything in the papers?" asked Juliette feverishly.

"In the papers, my dear?" repeated the doctor; "no there's never anything."

For a time the Eastern Question dropped into the background. There were frequent allusions to some one whom they were expecting, but who did not make his appearance. Pauline remarked that it would soon be three o'clock. Oh! he would come, declared Madame Deberle; he had given such a definite promise; but she never hinted at any name. Hélène listened without understanding; things which had no connection with Henri did not in the least interest her. She no longer brought her work when she now came down into the garden; and though her visits would last a couple of hours, she would take no part in the conversation, for her mind was ever filled with the same childish dream wherein all others miraculously vanished, and she was left alone with him. However, she managed to reply to Juliette's questions, while Henri's eyes, riveted on her own, thrilled her with a delicious langour. At last he stepped behind her with the intention of pulling up one of the blinds, and she fully noticed the tremor that seized him when he brushed against her hair.

"There's a ring at the bell; that must be he!" suddenly exclaimed Pauline.

Then the faces of the two sisters assumed an air of indifference. It was Malignon who made his appearance, dressed with greater care than ever, and having a somewhat serious look. He shook hands; but eschewed his customary jocularity, thus returning, in a ceremonious manner, to this house where for some time he had not shown his face.

While the doctor and Pauline were expostulating with him on the rarity of his visits, Juliette bent down and whispered to Hélène, who, despite her supreme indifference, was overcome with astonishment:

"Ah! you are surprised? Dear me! I am not angry with him at all! he's such a good fellow at heart that nobody could long be angry with him! Just fancy! he has unearthed a husband for Pauline. It's splendid, isn't it?"

"Oh! no doubt," answered Hélène complaisantly.

"Yes, one of his friends, immensely rich, who did not think of getting married, but whom he has sworn to bring here! We were waiting for him to-day to have some definite reply. So, as you will understand, I had to pass over a lot of things. Oh! there's no danger now; we know one another thoroughly."

Her face beamed with a pretty smile, and she blushed slightly at the memories she conjured up; but she soon turned round and took possession of Malignon. Hélène likewise smiled. These accommodating circumstances in life seemed to her sufficient excuse for her own delinquencies. It was absurd to think of tragic melodramas; no, everything wound up with universal happiness. However, while she had thus been indulging in the cowardly, but pleasing, thought that nothing was absolutely indefensible, Juliette and Pauline had opened the door of the pavilion, and were now dragging Malignon in their train into the garden. And, all at once, Hélène heard Henri speaking to her in a low and passionate voice:

"I beseech you, Hélène! Oh! I beseech you—"

She started to her feet, and gazed around her with sudden anxiety. They were quite alone; she could see the three others walking slowly along one of the walks. Henri was bold enough to lay his hand on her shoulder, and she trembled as she felt its pressure.

"As you wish," she stammered, knowing full well what question it was that he desired to ask.

Then, hurriedly, they exchanged a few words.

"At the house in the Passage des Eaux," said he.

"No, it is impossible—I have explained to you, and you swore to me—"

"Well, wherever you like, so that I may see you! In your own house—this evening. Shall I call?"

The idea was repellant to her. But she could only refuse with a sign, for fear again came upon her as she observed the two ladies and Malignon returning. Madame Deberle had taken the young man away under pretext of showing him some clumps of violets which were in full blossom notwithstanding the cold weather. Hastening her steps, she entered the pavilion before the others, her face illumined by a smile.

"It's all arranged," she exclaimed.

"What's all arranged?" asked Hélène, who was still trembling with excitement and had forgotten everything.

"Oh, that marriage! What a riddance! Pauline was getting a bit of a nuisance. However, the young man has seen her and thinks her charming! To-morrow we're all going to dine with papa. I could have embraced Malignon for his good news!"

With the utmost self-possession Henri had contrived to put some distance between Hélène and himself. He also expressed his sense of Malignon's favor, and seemed to share his wife's delight at the prospect of seeing their little sister settled at last. Then he turned to Hélène, and informed her that she was dropping one of her gloves. She thanked him. They could hear Pauline laughing and joking in the garden. She was leaning towards Malignon, murmuring broken sentences in his ear, and bursting into loud laughter as he gave her whispered answers. No doubt he was chatting to her confidentially about her future husband. Standing near the open door of the pavilion, Hélène meanwhile inhaled the cold air with delight.

It was at this moment that in the bedroom up above a silence fell on Jeanne and Monsieur Rambaud, whom the intense heat of the fire filled with languor. The child woke up from the long-continued pause with a sudden suggestion which seemed to be the outcome of her dreamy fit:

"Would you like to go into the kitchen? We'll see if we can get a glimpse of mamma!"

"Very well; let us go," replied Monsieur Rambaud.

Jeanne felt stronger that day, and reaching the kitchen without any assistance pressed her face against a window-pane. Monsieur Rambaud also gazed into the garden. The trees were bare of foliage, and through the large transparent windows of the Japanese pavilion they could make out every detail inside. Rosalie, who was busy attending to the soup, reproached mademoiselle with being inquisitive. But the child had caught sight of her mother's dress; and pointed her out, whilst flattening her face against the glass to obtain a better view. Pauline meanwhile looked up, and nodded vigorously. Then Hélène also made her appearance, and signed to the child to come down.

"They have seen you, mademoiselle," said the servant girl. "They want you to go down."

Monsieur Rambaud opened the window, and every one called him to carry Jeanne downstairs. Jeanne, however, vanished into her room, and vehemently refused to go, accusing her worthy friend of having purposely tapped on the window. It was a great pleasure to her to look at her mother, but she stubbornly declared she would not go near that house; and to all Monsieur Rambaud's questions and entreaties she would only return a stern "Because!" which was meant to explain everything.

"It is not you who ought to force me," she said at last, with a gloomy look.

But he told her that she would grieve her mother very much, and that it was not right to insult other people. He would muffle her up well, she would not catch cold; and, so saying, he wound the shawl round her body, and taking the silk handkerchief from her head, set a knitted hood in its place. Even when she was ready, however, she still protested her unwillingness; and when in the end she allowed him to carry her down, it was with the express provisio that he would take her up again the moment she might feel poorly. The porter opened the door by which the two houses communicated, and when they entered the garden they were hailed with exclamations of joy. Madame Deberle, in particular, displayed a vast amount of affection for Jeanne; she ensconced her in a chair near the stove, and desired that the windows might be closed, for the air she declared was rather sharp for the dear child. Malignon had now left. As Hélène began smoothing the child's dishevelled hair, somewhat ashamed to see her in company muffled up in a shawl

and a hood, Juliette burst out in protest:

"Leave her alone! Aren't we all at home here? Poor Jeanne! we are glad to have her!"

She rang the bell, and asked if Miss Smithson and Lucien had returned from their daily walk. No, they had not yet returned. It was just as well, she declared; Lucien was getting beyond control, and only the night before had made the five Levasseur girls sob with grief.

"Would you like to play at *pigeon volé?*" asked Pauline, who seemed to have lost her head with the thought of her impending marriage. "That wouldn't tire you."

But Jeanne shook her head in refusal. Beneath their drooping lids her eyes wandered over the persons who surrounded her. The doctor had just informed Monsieur Rambaud that admission to the Hospital for Incurables had been secured for his *protégée,* and in a burst of emotion the worthy man clasped his hands as though some great personal favor had been conferred on him. They were all lounging on their chairs, and the conversation became delightfully friendly. Less effort was shown in following up remarks, and there were at times intervals of silence. While Madame Deberle and her sister were busily engaged in discussion, Hélène said to the two men:

"Doctor Bodin has advised us to go to Italy."

"Ah, that is why Jeanne was questioning me!" exclaimed Monsieur Rambaud. "Would it give you any pleasure to go away there?"

Without vouchsafing any answer.

child clasped her little hands upon her bosom, while her pale face flushed with joy. Then, stealthily, and with some fear, she looked towards the doctor; it was he, she understood it, whom her mother was consulting. He started slightly, but retained all his composure. Suddenly, however, Juliette joined in the conversation, wishing, as usual, to have her finger in every pie.

"What's that? Are you talking about Italy? Didn't you say you had an idea of going to Italy? Well, it's a droll coincidence! Why, this very morning, I was teasing Henri to take me to Naples! Just fancy, for ten years now I have been dreaming of seeing Naples! Every spring he promises to take me there, but he never keeps his word!"

"I didn't tell you that I would not go," murmured the doctor.

"What! you didn't tell me? Why, you refused flatly, with the excuse that you could not leave your patients!"

Jeanne was listening eagerly. A deep wrinkle now furrowed her pale brow, and she began twisting her fingers mechanically one after the other.

"Oh! I could entrust my patients for a few weeks to the care of a brother-physician," explained the doctor. "That's to say, if I thought it would give you so much pleasure—"

"Doctor," interrupted Hélène, "are you also of opinion that such a journey would benefit Jeanne?"

"It would be the very thing; it would thoroughly restore her to health. Children are always the better for a change."

"Oh! then," exclaimed Juliette, "we can take Lucien, and we can all go together. That will be pleasant, won't it?"

"Yes, indeed; I'll do whatever you wish," he answered smiling.

Jeanne lowered her face, wiped two big tears of passionate anger and grief from her eyes, and fell back in her chair as though she would fain hear and see no more; while Madame Deberle, filled with ecstasy by the idea of such unexpected pleasure, began chattering noisily. Oh! how kind her husband was! She kissed him for his self-sacrifice. Then, without the loss of a movement, she busied herself with sketching the necessary preparations. They would start the very next week. Goodness gracious; she would never have time to get everything ready. Next she wanted to draw out a plan of their tour; they would need to visit this and that town certainly; they could stay a week at Rome; they must stop at a little country place that Madame de Guiraud had mentioned to her; and she wound up by engaging in a lively discussion with Pauline, who was eager that they should postpone their departure till such time as she could accompany them with her husband.

"Not a bit of it!" exclaimed Juliette; "the wedding can take place when we come back."

Jeanne's presence had been wholly forgotten. Her eyes were riveted on her mother and the doctor. The proposed journey, indeed, now offered inducements to Hélène, as it must necessarily keep Henri near her. In fact, a keen delight filled her heart at the thought of journeying together through the land of the sun, living side by side, and profiting by the hours of freedom. Round her lips wreathed a smile of happy relief; she had so greatly feared that she might lose him; and deemed herself fortunate in the thought that she would carry her love along with her. While Juliette was discoursing of the scenes they would travel through, both Hélène and Henri, indeed, indulged in the dream that they were already strolling through a fairyland of perennial spring, and each told the other with a look that their passion would reign there, aye, wheresoever they might breathe the same air.

In the meantime, Monsieur Rambaud, who with unconscious sadness had slowly lapsed into silence, observed Jeanne's evident discomfort.

"Aren't you well, my darling?" he asked in a whisper.

"No! I'm quite ill! Carry me up again, I implore you."

"But we must tell your mamma."

"Oh, no, no! mamma is busy; she hasn't any time to give to us. Carry me up, oh! carry me up again."

He took her in his arms, and told Hélène that the child felt tired. In answer she requested him to wait for her in her rooms; she would hasten after them. The little one, though light as a feather, seemed to slip from his grasp, and he was forced to come to a standstill on the second landing. She had leaned her head against his shoulder, and each gazed into the other's face with a look of grievous pain. Not a sound broke upon the chill silence of the staircase. Then in a low whisper he asked her:

"You're pleased, aren't you, to go to Italy?"

But she thereupon burst into sobs, declaring in broken words that she no longer had any craving to go, and would

rather die in her own room. Oh! she would not go, she would fall ill, she knew it well. She would go nowhere—nowhere. They could give her little shoes to the poor. Then amidst tears she whispered to him:

"Do you remember what you asked me one night?"

"What was it, my pet?"

"To stay with mamma always—always—always! Well, if you wish so still, I wish so too!"

The tears welled into Monsieur Rambaud's eyes. He kissed her lovingly, while she added in a still lower tone:

"You are perhaps vexed by my getting so angry over it. I didn't understand, you know. But it's you whom I want! Oh! say that it will be soon. Won't you say that it will be soon? I love you more than the other one."

Below in the pavilion, Hélène had begun to dream once more. The proposed journey was still the topic of conversation; and she now experienced an unconquerable yearning to relieve her overflowing heart, and acquaint Henri with all the happiness which was stifling her. So, while Juliette and Pauline were wrangling over the number of dresses that ought to be taken, she leaned towards him and gave him the assignation which she had refused but an hour before.

"Come to-night; I shall expect you."

But as she at last ascended to her own rooms, she met Rosalie flying terror-stricken down the stairs. The moment she saw her mistress, the girl shrieked out:

"Madame! madame! Oh! make haste, do! Mademoiselle is very ill! She's spitting blood!"

## CHAPTER XXIII

### A PAIR OF SHOES

ON rising from the dinner-table the doctor spoke to his wife of a confinement case, in close attendance on which he would doubtless have to pass the night. He quitted the house at nine o'clock, walked down to the riverside, and paced along the deserted quays in the dense nocturnal darkness. A slight moist wind was blowing, and the swollen Seine rolled on in inky waves. As soon as eleven o'clock chimed, he walked up the slopes of the Trocadéro, and began to prowl round the house, the huge square pile of which seemed but a deepning of the gloom. Lights could still be seen streaming through the dining-room windows of Hélène's lodging. Walking round, he noted that the kitchen was also brilliantly lighted up. And at this sight he stopped short in astonishment, which slowly developed into uneasiness. Shadows traversed the blinds; there seemed to be considerable bustle and stir up there. Perhaps Monsieur Rambaud had stayed to dine? But the worthy man never left later than ten o'clock. He, Henri, dared not go up; for what would he say should Rosalie open the door? At last, as it was nearing midnight, mad with impatience and throwing prudence to the winds, he rang the bell, and walked swiftly past the porter's room without giving his name. At the top of the stairs Rosalie received him.

"It's you, sir! Come in. I will go and announce you. Madame must be expecting you."

She gave no sign of surprise on seeing him at this hour. As he entered the dining-room without uttering a word, she resumed distractedly: "Oh! mademoiselle is very ill, sir. What a night! My legs are sinking under me!" Thereupon she left the room, and the doctor mechanically took a seat. He was oblivious of the fact that he was a medical man. Pacing along the quay he had conjured up a vision of a very different reception. And now he was there, as though he were paying a visit, waiting with his hat on his knees. A grievous coughing in the next room alone broke upon the intense silence.

At last Rosalie made her appearance once more, and hurrying across the dining-room with a basin in her hand, merely remarked: "Madame says you are not to go in."

He sat on, powerless to depart. Was their meeting to be postponed till another day, then? He was dazed, as though such a thing had seemed to him impossible. Then the thought came to him that poor Jeanne had very bad health; children only brought on sorrow and vexation. The door, however, opened once more, and Doctor Bodin entered, with a thousand apologies falling from his lips. For some time he chattered away: he had been sent for, but he would always be exceedingly pleased to enter into consultation with his renowned fellow-practitioner.

"Oh! no doubt, no doubt," stammered Doctor Deberle, whose ears were buzzing.

The elder man, his mind set at rest with regard to all questions of professional etiquette, then began to affect a puzzled manner, and expressed his doubts of the meaning of the symptoms.

He spoke in a whisper, and described them in technical phraseology, frequently pausing and winking significantly. There was coughing without expectoration, very pronounced weakness, and intense fever. Perhaps it might prove a case of typhoid fever. But in the meantime he gave no decided opinion, as the anæmic nervous affection, for which the patient had been treated so long, made him fear unforeseen complications.

"What do you think?" he asked, after delivering himself of each remark.

Doctor Deerle answered with evasive questions. While the other was speaking, he felt ashamed at finding himself in that room. Why had he come up?

"I have applied two blisters," continued the old doctor. "I'm waiting the result. But, of course, you'll see her. You will then give me your opinion."

So saying he led him into the bedroom. Henri entered it with a shudder creeping through his frame. It was but faintly lighted by a lamp. There thronged into his mind the memories of other nights, when there had been the same warm perfume, the same close, calm atmosphere, the same deepening shadows shrouding the furniture and hangings. But there was no one now to come to him with outstretched hands as in those olden days. Monsieur Rambaud lay back in an arm-chair exhausted, seemingly asleep. Hélène was standing in front of the bed, robed in a white dressing-gown, but did not turn her head; and her figure, in its death-like pallor, appeared to him extremely tall. Then for a moment's space he gazed on Jeanne. Her weakness was so great that she could not open her eyes without fatigue. Bathed in sweat, she lay in a stupor, her face ghastly, save that a burning flush colored each cheek.

"It's galloping consumption," he exclaimed at last, speaking aloud in spite of himself, and giving no sign of astonishment, as though he had long foreseen what would happen.

Hélène heard him and looked at him. She seemed to be of ice, her eyes were dry, and she was terribly calm.

"You think so, do you?" rejoined Doctor Bodin, giving an approving nod in the style of a man who had not cared to be the first to express this opinion.

He sounded the child once more. Jeanne, her limbs quite lifeless, yielded to the examination without seemingly knowing why she was being disturbed. A few rapid sentences were exchanged between the two physicians. The old doctor murmured some words about amphoric breathing, and a sound such as a cracked jar might give out. Nevertheless, he still affected some hesitation, and spoke, suggestively, of capillary bronchitis. Doctor Deberle hastened to explain that an accidental cause had brought on the illness; doubtless it was due to a cold; however, he had already noticed several times that an anæmical tendency would produce chest diseases. Hélène stood waiting behind him.

"Listen to her breathing yourself," said Doctor Bodin, giving way to Henri.

He leaned over the child, and seemed about to take hold of her. She had not raised her eyelids; but lay there in self-abandonment, consumed by fever. Her open nightdress displayed her childish breast; where as yet there were but slight signs of coming womanhood; and nothing could be more chaste or yet more harrowing than the sight of this dawning maturity on which the Angel of Death had already laid his hand. She had displayed no aversion when the old doctor had touched her. But the moment Henri's fingers glanced against her body she started as if she had received a shock. In a transport of shame she awoke from the coma in which she had been plunged, and, like a maiden in alarm, clasped her poor puny little arms over her bosom, exclaiming the while in quavering tones: "Mamma! mamma!"

Then she opened her eyes, and on recognizing the man who was bending over her, she was seized with terror. Sobbing with shame, she drew the bed-cover over her bosom. It seemed as though she had grown older by ten years during her short agony, and on the brink of death had attained sufficient womanhood to understand that this man, above all others, must not lay hands on her. She wailed out again in piteous entreaty: "Mamma! mamma! I beseech you!"

Hélène, who had hitherto not opened her lips, came close to Henri. Her eyes were bent on him fixedly; her face was a marble. She touched him, and merely said in a husky voice: "Go away!"

Doctor Bodin strove to appease Jeanne, who now shook with a fresh fit of coughing. He assured her that nobody would annoy her again, that every one would go away, to prevent her being disturbed.

"Go away," repeated Hélène, in a deep whisper in her lover's ear. "You see very well that we have killed her!"

Then, unable to find a word in reply, Henri withdrew. He lingered for a moment longer in the dining-room, awaiting he knew not what, something that might possibly take place. But seeing that Doctor Bodin did not come out, he groped his way down the stairs without even Rosalie to light him. He thought of the awful speed with which galloping consumption carried off its victims; the miliary tubercles would rapidly multiply, the stifling sensation would become more and more pronounced; Jeanne would certainly not last another three weeks.

The first of these passed by. In the mighty expanse of heaven before the window, the sun rose and set above Paris, without Hélène being more than vaguely conscious of the pitiless, steady advance of time. She grasped the fact that her daughter was doomed; she lived plunged in a stupor, alive only to the terrible anguish that filled her heart. It was but waiting on in hopelessness, in certainty that death would prove merciless. She could not weep, but paced gently to and fro, tending the sufferer with slow, regulated movements. At times, yielding to fatigue, she would fall upon the chair, whence she gazed at her for hours. Jeanne grew weaker and weaker; painful vomiting was followed by exhaustion; the fever never quitted her. When Doctor Bodin called, he examined her for a little while and left some prescription; but his drooping shoulders, as he left the room, were eloquent of such powerlessness that the mother forbore to accompany him to ask even a question.

On the morning after the illness had

declared itself, Abbé Jouve had made all haste to call. He and his brother now again came every evening, exchanging a mute clasp of the hand with Hélène, and never venturing to ask any news. They had offered to watch by the bedside in succession, but she sent them away when ten o'clock struck; she would have no one in the bedroom during the night. One evening the Abbé, who had seemed absorbed by some idea since the previous day, took her aside.

"There is one thing I've thought of," he whispered. "Her health has put obstacles in the darling child's way; but her first communion might take place here."

His meaning at first did not seem to dawn on Hélène. The thought that, despite all his indulgence, he should now allow his priestly character the ascendant and evince no concern but in spiritual matters, came on her with surprise, and even wounded her somewhat. With a careless gesture she exclaimed: "No, no; I would rather she wasn't worried. If there be a heaven, she will have no difficulty in entering its gates."

That evening, however, Jeanne experienced one of those deceptive improvements in health which fill the dying with illusions as to their condition. Her hearing, rendered more acute by illness, had enabled her to catch the Abbé's words.

"It's you, dear old friend!" said she. "You spoke about the first communion. It will be soon, won't it?"

"No doubt, my darling," he answered. Then she wanted him to come near to speak to her. Her mother had propped her up with the pillow, and she reclined there, looking very little, with a smile on her fever-burnt lips, and the shadow of death already passing over her brilliant eyes.

"Oh! I'm getting on very well," she began. "I could get up if I wanted. But tell me: should I have a white gown and flowers? Will the church be as beautiful as it was in the Month of Mary?"

"More beautiful, my pet."

"Really? Will there be as many flowers, and will there be such sweet chants? It will be soon, soon—you promise me, won't you?"

She was wrapt in joy. She gazed on the curtains of the bed, and murmured in her transport that she was very fond of the good God, and had seen Him while she was listening to the canticles. Even now she could hear organs pealing, see lights that circled round, and flowers in great vases hovering like butterflies before her eyes. Then another fit of coughing threw her back on the pillow. However, her face was still flushed with a smile; she seemed to be unconscious of her cough, but continued:

"I shall get up tomorrow. I shall learn my catechism without a mistake, and we'll all be very happy."

A sob came from Hélène as she stood at the foot of the bed. She had been powerless to weep, but a storm of tears rushed up from her bosom as Jeanne's laughter fell on her ear. Then, almost stifling, she fled into the dining-room, that she might hide her despair. The Abbé followed her. Monsieur Rambaud had at once started up to engage the child's attention.

"Oh dear! mamma cried out! Has she hurt herself?" she asked.

"Your mamma?" he answered. "No, she didn't cry out; she was laughing because you are feeling so well."

In the dining-room, her head bowed dejectedly on the table, Hélène strove to stifle her sobs with her clasped hands. The Abbé hung over her, and prayed her to restrain her emotion. But she raised her face, streaming with tears, and bitterly accused herself. She declared to him that she herself had killed her daughter, and a full confession escaped from her lips in a torrent of broken words. She would never have succumbed to that man had Jeanne remained beside her. It had been fated that she should meet him in that chamber of mystery. God in Heaven! she ought to die with her child; she could live no longer. The priest, terrified, sought to calm her with the promise of absolution.

But there was a ring at the bell, and a sound of voices came from the lobby. Hélène dried her tears as Rosalie made her appearance.

"Madame, it's Doctor Deberle, who—"

"I don't wish him to come in."

"He is asking after mademoiselle."

"Tell him she is dying."

The door had been left open, and Henri had heard everything. Without awaiting the return of the servant-girl, he walked down the stairs. He came up every day, received the same answer, and then went away.

The visits which Hélène received quite unnerved her. The few ladies whose acquaintance she had made at the Deberles' house deemed it their duty to tender her their sympathy. Madame de Chermette, Madame Levasseur, Madame de Guiraud, and others also presented themselves. They made no request to enter, but catechised Rosalie in such loud voices that they could be heard through the thin partitions. Giving way to impatience, Hélène would then receive them in the dining-room, where, without sitting down, she spoke with them very briefly. She went about all day in her dressing-gown, careless of her attire, with her lovely hair merely gathered up and twisted into a knot. Her eyes often closed with weariness; her face was flushed; she had a bitter taste in her mouth; her lips were clammy, and she could scarcely articulate. When Juliette called, she could not exclude her from the bedroom, but allowed her to stay for a little while beside the bed.

"My dear," Madame Deberle said to her one day in friendly tones, "you give way too much. Keep up your spirits."

Hélène was about to reply, when Juliette, wishing to turn her thoughts from her grief, began to chat about the things which were occupying the gossips of Paris: "We are certainly going to have a war. I am in a nice state about it, as I have two cousins who will have to serve."

In this style she would drop in upon them on returning from her rambles through Paris, her brain bursting with all the tittle-tattle collected in the course of the afternoon, and her long skirts whirling and rustling as she sailed through the stillness of the sick-room. It was altogether futile for her to lower her voice and assume a pitiful air; her indifference peeped through all disguise;

it could be seen that she was happy, quite joyous indeed, in the possession of perfect health. Hélène was very downcast in her company, her heart rent by jealous anguish.

"Madame," said Jeanne one evening, "why doesn't Lucien come to play with me?"

Juliette was embarrassed for a moment, and merely answered with a smile.

"Is he ill too?" continued the child.

"No; my darling, he isn't ill; he has gone to school."

Then, as Hélène accompanied her into the ante-room, she wished to apologize for her prevarication.

"Oh! I would gladly bring him; I know that there's no infection. But children get frightened with the least thing, and Lucien is such a stupid. He would just burst out sobbing when he saw your poor angel—"

"Yes, indeed; you are quite right," interrupted Hélène, her heart ready to break with the thought of this woman's gaiety, and her happiness in possessing a child who enjoyed robust health.

A second week had passed away. The disease was following its usual course, robbing Jeanne every hour of some of her vitality. Fearfully rapid though it was, however, it evinced no haste, but, in accomplishing the destruction of that delicate, lovable flesh, passed in turn through each foreseen phase, without skipping a single one of them. Thus the spitting of blood had ceased, and at intervals the cough disappeared. But such was the oppressive feeling which stifled the child that you could detect the ravages of the disease by the difficulty she experienced in breathing. Such

weakness could not withstand so violent an attack; and the eyes of the Abbé and Monsieur Rambaud constantly moistened with tears as they heard her. Day and night under the shelter of the curtains the sound of oppressed breathing arose; the poor darling, whom the slightest shock seemed likely to kill, was yet unable to die, but lived on and on through the agony which bathed her in sweat. Her mother, whose strength was exhausted, and who could no longer bear to hear that rattle, went into the adjoining room and leaned her head against the wall.

Jeanne was slowly becoming oblivious to her surroundings. She no longer saw people, and her face bore an unconscious and forlorn expression, as though she had already lived all alone in some unknown sphere. When they who hovered round her wished to attract her attention, they named themselves that she might recognize them; but she would gaze at them fixedly, without a smile, then turn herself round towards the wall with a weary look. A gloominess was setting over her; she was passing away amidst the same vexation and sulkiness as she had displayed in past days of jealous outbursts. Still, at times the whims characteristic of sickness would awaken her to some consciousness. One morning she asked her mother:

"To-day is Sunday, isn't it?"

"No, my child," answered Hélène; "this is only Friday. Why do you wish to know?"

Jeanne seemed to have already forgotten the question she had asked. But two days later, while Rosalie was in the room, she said to her in a whisper:

"This is Sunday. Zéphyrin is here; ask him to come and see me."

The maid hesitated, but Hélène, who had heard, nodded to her in token of consent. The child spoke again:

"Bring him; come both of you; I shall be so pleased."

When Rosalie entered the sick-room with Zéphyrin, she raised herself on her pillow. The little soldier, with bare head and hands spread out swayed about to hide his intense emotion. He had a great love for mademoiselle, and it grieved him unutterably to see her "shouldering arms on the left," as he expressed it in the kitchen. So, in spite of the previous injunctions of Rosalie, who had instructed him to put on a bright expression, he stood speechless, with downcast face, on seeing her so pale and wasted to a skeleton. He was still as tender-hearted as ever, despite his conquering airs. He could not even think of one of those fine phrases which nowadays he usually concocted so easily. The maid behind him gave him a pinch to make him laugh. But he could only stammer out:

"I beg pardon—mademoiselle and every one here—"

Jeanne was still raising herself with the help of her tiny arms. She widely opened her large, vacant eyes; she seemed to be looking for something; her head shook with a nervous trembling. Doubtless the stream of light was blinding her as the shadows of death gathered around.

"Come closer, my friend," said Hélène to the soldier. "It was mademoiselle who asked to see you."

The sunshine entered through the window in a slanting ray of golden light, in which the dust rising from the carpet could be seen circling. March had come, and the springtime was already budding out of doors. Zéphyrin took one step forward, and appeared in the sunshine; but his round, freckled face had a golden hue, as of ripe corn, while the buttons of his tunic glittered, and his red trousers looked as sanguineous as a field of poppies. At last Jeanne became aware of his presence there; but her eyes again betrayed uneasiness, and she glanced restlessly from one corner to another.

"What do you want, my child?" asked her mother. "We are all here." She understood, however, in a moment. "Rosalie, come nearer. Mademoiselle wishes to see you."

Then Rosalie, in her turn, stepped into the sunlight. She wore a cap, whose strings, carelessly tossed over her shoulders, flapped round her head like the wings of a butterfly. A golden powder seemed to fall on her bristly black hair and her kindly face with its flat nose and thick lips. And for Jeanne there were only these two in the room —the little soldier and the servant-girl, standing elbow to elbow under the ray of sunshine. She gazed at them.

"Well, my darling," began Hélène again, "you do not say anything to them! Here they are together."

Jeanne's eyes were still fixed on them, and her head shook with the tremor of a very aged woman. They stood there like man and wife, ready to take each other's arm and return to their country-side. The spring sun threw its warmth on them, and eager to brighten mademoiselle they ended by smiling into each other's face with a look of mingled embarrassment and tenderness. The very odor of health was exhaled from their plump round figures. Had they been alone, Zéphyrin without doubt would have caught hold of Rosalie, and would have received for his pains a hearty slap. Their eyes showed it.

"Well, my darling, have you nothing to say to them?"

Jeanne gazed at them, her breathing growing yet more oppressed. And still she said not a word, but suddenly burst into tears. Zéphyrin and Rosalie had at once quit the room.

"I beg pardon—mademoiselle and every one—" stammered the little soldier, as he went away in bewilderment.

This was one of Jeanne's last whims. She lapsed into a dull stupor, from which nothing could rouse her. She lay there in utter loneliness, unconscious even of her mother's presence. When Hélène hung over the bed seeking her eyes, the child preserved a stolid expression, as though only the shadow of the curtain had passed before her. Her lips were dumb; she showed the gloomy resignation of the outcast who knows that she is dying. Sometimes she would long remain with her eyelids half closed, and nobody could divine what stubborn thought was thus absorbing her. Nothing now had any existence for her save her big doll, which lay beside her. They had given it to her one night to divert her during her insufferable anguish, and she refused to give it back, defending it with fierce gestures the moment they attempted to take it from her. With its pasteboard head resting on the bolster, the doll was stretched out like an invalid, covered up to the shoulders by the counterpane. There was little doubt the child was nursing it for her burning hands would, from time to time, feel its disjointed limbs of flesh-tinted leather, whence all the sawdust had exuded. For hours her eyes would never stray from those enamel ones which were always fixed, or from those white teeth wreathed in an everlasting smile. She would suddenly grow affectionate, clasp the doll's hands against her bosom and press her cheek against its little head of hair, the caressing contact of which seemed to give her some relief. Thus she sought comfort in her affection for her big doll, always assuring herself of its presence when she awoke from a doze, seeing nothing else, chatting with it, and at times summoning to her face the shadow of a smile, as though she had heard it whispering something in her ear.

The third week was dragged to an end. One morning the old doctor came and remained. Hélène understood him: her child would not live through the day. Since the previous evening she had been in a stupor that deprived her of the consciousness even of her own actions. There was no longer any struggle with death; it was but a question of hours. As the dying child was consumed by an awful thirst, the doctor had merely recommended that she should be given some opiate beverage, which would render her passing less painful; and the relinquishing of all attempts at cure reduced Hélène to a state of imbecility. So long as the medicines had littered the night-table she still had entertained hopes of a miraculous recovery. But now bottles and boxes had vanished, and her last trust was gone. One instinct only inspired her now—to be near Jeanne, never leave her, gaze at her unceasingly. The doctor, wishing to distract her attention from the terrible sight, strove, by assigning some little duties to her, to keep her at a distance. But she ever and ever returned, drawn to the bedside by the physical craving to see. She waited, standing erect, her arms hanging beside her, and her face swollen by despair.

About one o'clock Abbé Jouve and Monsieur Rambaud arrived. The doctor went to meet them, and muttered a few words. Both grew pale, and stood stock-still in consternation, while their hands began to tremble. Hélène had not turned round.

The weather was lovely that day; it was one of those sunny afternoons typical of early April. Jeanne was tossing in her bed. Her lips moved painfully at times with the intolerable thirst which consumed her. She had brought her poor transparent hands from under the coverlet and waved them gently to and fro. The hidden working of the disease was accomplished, she coughed no more, and her dying voice came like a faint breath. For a moment she turned her head, and her eyes sought the light. Doctor Bodin threw the window wide open, and then Jeanne at once became tranquil, with her cheek resting on the pillow and her looks roving over Paris, while her heavy breathing grew fainter and slower.

During the three weeks of her illness she had thus many times turned towards the city that stretched away to the horizon. Her face grew grave, she was musing. At this last hour Paris was smiling under the glittering April sunshine. Warm breezes entered from without, with bursts of urchin's laughter and the chirping of sparrows. On the brink of the grave the child exerted her last strength to gaze again on the scene, and follow the flying smoke which soared from the distant suburbs. She recognized her three friends, the Invalides, the Panthéon, and the Tower of Saint-Jacques; then the unknown began, and her weary eyelids half closed at sight of the vast ocean of roofs. Perhaps she was dreaming that she was growing much lighter and lighter, and was fleeting away like a bird. Now, at last, she would soon know all; she would perch herself on the domes and steeples; seven or eight flaps of her wings would suffice, and she would be able to gaze on the forbidden mysteries that were hidden from children. But a fresh uneasiness fell upon her, and her hands groped about; she only grew calm again when she held her large doll in her little arms against her bosom. It was evidently her wish to take it with her. Her glances wandered far away amongst the chimneys glinting with the run's ruddy light.

Four o'clock struck, and the bluish shadows of evening were already gathering. The end was at hand; there was a stifling, a slow and passive agony. The dear angel no longer had strength to offer resistance. Monsieur Rambaud, overcome, threw himself on his knees, convulsed with silent sobbing, and dragged himself behind a curtain to hide his grief. The Abbé was kneeling at the bedside, with clasped hands, repeating the prayers for the dying.

"Jeanne! Jeanne!" murmured Hélène, chilled to the heart with a horror which sent an icy thrill through her very hair.

She had repulsed the doctor and thrown herself on the ground, leaning against the bed to gaze into her daughter's face. Jeanne opened her eyes, but did not look at her mother. She drew her doll—her last love—still closer. Her bosom heaved with a big sigh, followed by two fainter ones. Then her eyes paled, and her face for a moment gave signs of a fearful anguish. But speedily there came relief; her mouth remained open, she breathed no more.

"It is over," said the doctor, as he took her hand.

Jeanne's big, vacant eyes were fixed on Paris. The long, thin, lamb-like face was still further elongated, there was a sternness on its features, a grey shadow falling from its contracted brows. Thus even in death she retained the livid expression of a jealous woman. The doll, with its head flung back, and its hair dishevelled, seemed to lie dead beside her.

"It is over," again said the doctor, as he allowed the little cold hand to drop.

Hélène, with a strained expression on her face, pressed her hands to her brow as if she felt her head splitting open. No tears came to her eyes; she gazed wildly in front of her. Then a rattling noise mounted in her throat; she had just espied at the foot of the bed a pair of shoes that lay forgotten there. It was all over. Jeanne would never put them on again; the little shoes could be given to the poor. And at the sight Hélène's tears gushed forth; she still knelt on the floor, her face pressed against the dead child's hand, which had slipped down. Monsieur Rambaud was sobbing. The Abbé had raised his voice, and Rosalie, standing at the door of the dining-room, was biting her handkerchief to check the noise of her grief.

At this very moment Doctor Deberle rang the bell. He was unable to refrain from making inquiries.

"How is she now?" he asked.

"Oh, sir!" wailed Rosalie, "she is dead."

He stood motionless, stupefied by the announcement of the end which he had been expecting daily. At last he muttered: "O God! the poor child! what a calamity!"

He could only give utterance to those commonplace but heartrending words. The door shut once more, and he went down the stairs.

## CHAPTER XXIV

### FLOWERS

WHEN Madame Deberle was apprised of Jeanne's death she wept, and gave way to one of the those outbursts of emotion that kept her in a flutter for eight-and-forty hours. Hers was a noisy and immoderate grief. She came and threw herself into Hélène's arms. Then a phrase dropped in her hearing inspired her with the idea of imparting some affecting surroundings to the child's funeral, and soon wholly absorbed her. She offered her services, and declared her willingness to undertake every detail. The mother, worn out with weeping, sat overwhelmed in her chair; Monsieur Rambaud, who was acting in her name, was losing his head. So he accepted the offer with profuse expressions of gratitude. Hélène merely roused herself for a moment to express the wish that there should be some flowers—an abundance of flowers.

Without losing a minute, Madame Deberle sat about her task. She spent the whole of the next day in running from one lady friend to another, bearing the woeful tidings. It was her idea to have a following of little girls all dressed in white. She needed at least thirty, and did not return till she had secured the full number. She had gone in person to the Funeral Administration, discussed the various styles, and chosen the necessary drapery. She would have the garden railings hung with white, and the body might be laid out under the lilac trees, whose twigs were already tipped with green. It would be charming.

"If only it's a fine day to-morrow!" she giddily remarked in the evening when her scurrying to and fro had come to an end.

The morning proved lovely; there was a blue sky and a flood of sunshine, the air was pure and invigorating as only the air of spring can be. The funeral was to take place at ten o'clock. By nine the drapery had been hung up. Juliette ran down to give the workmen her ideas of what should be done. She did not wish the trees to be altogether covered. The white cloth, fringed with silver, formed a kind of porch at the garden gate, which was thrown back against the lilac trees. However, Juliette soon returned to her drawing-room to receive her lady guests. They

were to assemble there to prevent Madame Grandjean's two rooms from being filled to overflowing. Still she was greatly annoyed at her husband having had to go that morning to Versailles—for some consultation or other, he explained, which he could not well neglect. Thus she was left alone, and felt she would never be able to get through with it all. Madame Berthier was the first arrival, bringing her two daughters with her.

"What do you think!" exclaimed Madame Deberle, "Henri has deserted me! Well, Lucien, why don't you say good-day?"

Lucien was already dressed for the funeral, with his hands in black gloves. He seemed astonished to see Sophie and Blanche dressed as though they were about to take part in some church procession. A silk sash encircled the muslin gown of each, and their veils, which swept down to the floor, hid their little caps of transparent tulle. While the two mothers were busy chatting, the three children gazed at one another, bearing themselves somewhat stiffly in their new attire. At last Lucien broke the silence by saying: "Jeanne is dead."

His heart was full, and yet his face wore a smile—a smile born of amazement. He had been very quiet since the evening before, dwelling on the thought that Jeanne was dead. As his mother was up to her ears in business, and took no notice of him, he had plied the servants with questions. Was it a fact, he wanted to know, that it was impossible to move when one was dead?

"She is dead, she is dead!" echoed the two sisters, who looked like rosebuds under their white veils. "Are we going to see her?"

Lucien pondered for a time, and then, with dreamy eyes and open mouth, seemingly striving to divine the nature of this problem which lay beyond his ken, he answered in a low tone:

"We shall never see her again."

However, several other little girls now entered the room. On a sign from his mother Lucien advanced to meet them. Marguerite Tissot, her muslin dress enveloping her like a cloud, seemed a child-Virgin; her fair hair, escaping from underneath her little cap, looked, through the snowy veil, like a tippet figured with gold. A quiet smile crept into every face when the five Levasseurs made their appearance; they were all dressed alike, and trooped along in boarding-school fashion, the eldest first, the youngest last; and their skirts stood out to such an extent that they quite filled one corner of the room. But on little Mademoiselle Guiraud's entry the whispering voices rose to a higher key; the others laughed and crowded round to see her and kiss her. She was like some white turtle-dove with its downy feathers ruffled. Wrapped in rustling gauze, she looked as round as a barrel, but still no heavier than a bird. Her mother even could not find her hands. By degrees the drawing-room seemed to be filling with a cloud of snowballs. Several boys, in their black coats, were like dark spots amidst the universal white. Lucien, now that his little wife was dead, desired to choose another. However, he displayed the greatest hesitation. He would have preferred a wife like Jeanne, taller than himself; but at last he settled on Marguerite, whose hair fascinated him, and to whom he attached himself for the day.

"The corpse hasn't been brought down yet," Pauline muttered at this moment in Juliette's ear.

Pauline was as flurried as though the preliminaries of a ball were in hand. It was with the greatest difficulty that her sister had prevented her from donning a white dress for the ceremony.

"Good gracious!" exclaimed Juliette; "what are they dreaming about? I must run up. Stay with these ladies."

She hastily left the room, where the mothers in their mourning attires sat chatting in whispers, while the children dared not make the least movement lest they should rumple their dresses. When she had reached the top of the staircase and entered the chamber where the body lay, Juliette's blood was chilled by the intense cold. Jeanne still lay on the bed, with clasped hands; and, like Marguerite and the Levasseur girls, she was arrayed in a white dress, white cap, and white shoes. A wreath of white roses crowned the cap, as though she were a little queen about to be honored by the crowd of guests who were waiting below. In front of the window, on two chairs, was the oak coffin lined with satin, looking like some huge jewel casket. The furniture was all in order; a wax taper was burning; the room seemed close and gloomy, with the damp smell and stillness of a vault which has been walled up for many years. Thus Juliette, fresh from the sunshine and smiling life of the outer world, came to a sudden halt, stricken dumb, without the courage to explain that they must needs hurry.

"A great many people have come," she stammered at last. And then, as no answer was forthcoming, she added, just for the sake of saying something: "Henri has been forced to attend a consultation at Versailles; you will excuse him."

Hélène, who sat in front of the bed, gazed at her with vacant eyes. They were wholly unable to drag her from the room. For six-and-thirty hours she had lingered there, despite the prayers of Monsieur Rambaud and the Abbé Jouve, who kept watch with her. During the last two nights she had been weighed to the earth by immeasurable agony. Besides, she had accomplished the grievous task of dressing her daughter for the last time, of putting on those white silk shoes, for she would allow no other to touch the feet of the little angel who lay dead. And now she sat motionless, as though her strength were spent, and the intensity of her grief had lulled her into forgetfulness.

"Have you got some flowers?" she exclaimed after an effort, her eyes still fixed on Madame Deberle.

"Yes, yes, my dear," answered the latter. "Don't trouble yourself about that."

Since her daughter had breathed her last, Hélène had been consumed with one idea—there must be flowers, flowers, an overwhelming profusion of flowers. Each time she saw anybody, she grew uneasy, seemingly afraid that sufficient flowers would never be obtained.

"Are there any roses?" she began again after a pause.

"Yes. I assure you that you will be well pleased."

She shook her head, and once more fell back into her stupor. In the meantime the undertaker's men were waiting on the landing. It must be got over now without delay. Monsieur Rambaud, who was himself affected to such a degree that he staggered like a drunken man, signed to Juliette to assist him in leading the poor woman from the room. Each slipped an arm gently beneath hers, and they raised her up and led her towards the dining-room. But the moment she divined their intentions, she shook them from her in a last despairing outburst. The scene was heartrending. She threw herself on her knees at the bedside and clung passionately to the sheets, while the room re-echoed with her piteous shrieks. But still Jeanne lay there with her face of stone, stiff and icy-cold, wrapped round by the silence of eternity. She seemed to be frowning; there was a sour pursing of the lips, eloquent of a revengeful nature; and it was this gloomy, pitiless look, springing from jealousy and transforming her face, which drove Hélène so frantic. During the preceding thirty-six hours she had not failed to notice how the old spiteful expression had grown more and more intense upon her daughter's face, how more and more sullen she looked the nearer she approached the grave. Oh, what a comfort it would have been if Jeanne could only have smiled on her for the last time!

"No, no!" she shrieked. "I pray you, leave her for a moment. You cannot take her from me. I want to embrace her. Oh, only a moment, only a moment!"

With trembling arms she clasped her

child to her bosom, eager to dispute possession with the men who stood in the ante-room, with their backs turned towards her and impatient frowns on their faces. But her lips were powerless to breathe any warmth on the cold countenance; she became conscious that Jeanne's obstinacy was not to be overcome, that she refused forgiveness. And then she allowed herself to be dragged away, and fell upon a chair in the dining-room, with the one mournful cry, again and again repeated: "My God! My God!"

Monsieur Rambaud and Madame Deberle were overcome by emotion. There was an interval of silence, but when the latter opened the door halfway it was all over. There had been no noise—scarcely a stir. The screws, oiled beforehand, now closed the lid for ever. The chamber was left empty, and a white sheet was thrown over the coffin.

The bedroom door remained open, and no further restraint was put upon Hélène. On re-entering the room she cast a dazed look on the furniture and round the walls. The men had borne away the corpse. Rosalie had drawn the coverlet over the bed to efface the slight hollow made by the form of the little one whom they had lost. Then opening her arms with a distracted gesture and stretching out her hands, Hélène rushed towards the staircase. She wanted to go down, but Monsieur Rambaud held her back, while Madame Deberle explained to her that it was not the thing to do. But she vowed she would behave rationally, that she would not follow the funeral procession. Surely they could allow her to look on;

she would remain quiet in the garden pavilion. Both wept as they heard her pleading. However, she had to be dressed. Juliette threw a black shawl round her to conceal her morning wrap. There was no bonnet to be found; but at last they came across one from which they tore a bunch of red vervain flowers. Monsieur Rambaud, who was chief mourner, took hold of Hélène's arm.

"Do not leave her," whispered Madame Deberle as they reached the garden. "I have so many things to look after!"

And thereupon she hastened away. Hélène meanwhile walked with difficulty, her eyes ever seeking something. As soon as she had found herself out of doors she had drawn a long sigh. Ah! it was a lovely morning! Then she looked towards the iron gate, and caught sight of the little coffin under the white drapery. Monsieur Rambaud allowed her to take but two or three steps forward.

"Now, be brave," he said to her, while a shudder ran through his own frame.

They gazed on the scene. The narrow coffin was bathed in sunshine. At the foot of it, on a lace cushion, was a silver crucifix. To the left the holy-water sprinkler lay in its font. The tall wax tapers were burning with almost invisible flames. Beneath the hangings, the branches of the trees with their purple shoots formed a kind of bower. It was a nook full of the beauty of spring, and over it streamed the golden sunshine irradiating the blossoms with which the coffin was covered. It seemed as if flowers had been raining down; there were clusters of white roses, white camellias, white lilac, white carnations, heaped in a snowy mass of petals; the coffin was hidden from sight, and from the pall some of the white blossoms were falling, the ground being strewn with periwinkles and hyacinths. The few persons passing along the Rue Vineuse paused with a smile of tender emotion before this sunny garden where the little body lay at peace amongst the flowers. There seemed to be a music stealing up from the snowy surroundings; in the glare of light the purity of the blossoms grew dazzling, and the sun flushed hangings, nosegays, and wreaths of flowers, with a very semblance of life. Over the roses a bee flew humming.

"Oh, the flowers! the flowers!" murmured Hélène, powerless to say another word.

She pressed her handkerchief to her lips, and her eyes filled with tears. Jeanne must be warm, she thought, and with this idea a wave of emotion rose in her bosom; she felt very grateful to those who had enveloped her child in flowers. She wished to go forward, and Monsieur Rambaud made no effort to hold her back. How sweet was the scene beneath the cloud of drapery! Perfumes were wafted upwards; the air was warm and still. Hélène stooped down and chose one rose only, that she might place it in her bosom. But suddenly she commenced to tremble, and Monsieur Rambaud became uneasy.

"Don't stay here," he said, as he drew her away. "You promised not to make yourself unwell."

He was attempting to lead her into the pavilion when the door of the drawing-room was thrown open. Pauline was the first to appear. She had undertaken the duty of arranging the funeral procession. One by one the little girls stepped into the garden. Their coming seemed like some sudden outburst of bloom, a miraculous flowering of May. It the open air the white skirts expanded, streaked moire-like by the sunshine with shades of the utmost delicacy. An apple-tree above was raining down its blossoms; gossamer-threads were floating to and fro; the dresses were instinct with all the purity of spring. And their number still increased; they already surrounded the lawn; they yet lightly descended the steps, sailing on like downy balls suddenly expanding beneath the open sky.

The garden was now a snowy mass, and as Hélène gazed on the crowd of little girls, a memory awoke within her. She remembered another joyous season, with its ball and the gay twinkling of tiny feet. She once more saw Marguerite in her milk-girl costume, with her can hanging from her waist; and Sophie, dressed as a waiting-maid, and revolving on the arm of her sister Blanche, whose trappings as Folly gave out a merry tinkle of bells. She thought, too, of the five Levasseur girls, and of the Red Riding-Hoods, whose number had seemed endless, with their ever-recurring cloaks of poppy-colored satin edged with black velvet; while little Mademoiselle Guiraud, with her Alsatian butterfly bow in her hair, danced as if demented opposite a Harlequin twice as tall as herself. To-day they were all arrayed in white. Jeanne, too, was in white, her head laid amongst white flowers on the white satin pillow. The delicate-faced Japanese maiden, with hair transfixed by long pins, and purple tunic embroidered with birds, was leaving them for ever in a gown of snowy white.

"How tall they have all grown!" exclaimed Hélène, as she burst into tears.

They were all there but her daughter; she alone was missing. Monsieur Rambaud led her to the pavilion; but she remained on the threshold, anxious to see the funeral procession start. Several of the ladies bowed to her quietly. The children looked at her, with some astonishment in their blue eyes. Meanwhile Pauline was hovering round, giving orders. She lowered her voice for the occasion, but at times forgot herself.

"Now, be good children! Look, you little stupid, you are dirty already! I'll come for you in a minute; don't stir."

The hearse drove up; it was time to start, but Madame Deberle appeared, exclaiming: "The bouquets have been forgotten! Quick, Pauline, the bouquets!"

Some little confusion ensued. A bouquet of white roses had been prepared for each little girl; and these bouquets now had to be distributed. The children, in an ecstasy of delight, held the great clusters of flowers in front of them as though they had been wax tapers; Lucien, still at Marguerite's side, daintily inhaled the perfume of her blossoms as she held them to his face. All these little maidens, their hands filled with flowers, looked radiant with happiness in the golden light; but suddenly their faces grew grave as they perceived the men placing the coffin on the hearse.

"Is she inside that thing?" asked Sophie in a whisper.

Her sister Blanche nodded assent. Then, in her turn, she said: "For men it's as big as this!"

She was referring to the coffin, and stretched out her arms to their widest extent. However, little Marguerite, whose nose was buried amongst her roses, was seized with a fit of laughter; it was the flowers, said she, which tickled her. Then the others in turn buried their noses in their bouquets to find out if it were so; but they were remonstrated with, and they all became grave once more.

The funeral procession was now filing into the street. At the corner of the Rue Vineuse a woman without a cap, and with tattered shoes on her feet, wept and wiped her cheeks with the corner of her apron. People stood at many windows, and exclamations of pity ascended through the stillness of the street. Hung with white silver-fringed drapery the hearse rolled on without a sound; nothing fell on the ear save the measured tread of the two white horses, deadened by the solid earthen roadway. The bouquets and wreaths, borne on the funeral car, formed a very harvest of flowers; the coffin was hidden by them; every jolt tossed the heaped-up mass, and the hearse slowly sprinkled the street with lilac blossom. From each of the four corners streamed a long ribbon of white watered silk, held by four little girls—Sophie and Marguerite, one of the Levasseur family, and little Mademoiselle Guiraud, who was so small and so uncertain on her legs that her mother walked beside her. The others, in a close body, surrounded the hearse, each bearing her bouquet of roses. They walked slowly, their veils waved, and the wheels rolled on amidst all this muslin, as though borne along on a cloud, from which smiled the tender faces of cherubs. Then behind, following Monsieur Rambaud, who bowed his pale face, came several ladies and little boys, Rosalie, Zéphyrin, and the servants of Madame Deberle. To these succeeded five empty mourning carriages. And as the hearse passed along the sunny street like a car symbolical of springtide, a number of white pigeons wheeled over the mourners' heads.

"Good heavens! how annoying!" exclaimed Madame Deberle when she saw the procession start off. "If only Henri had postponed that consultation! I told him how it would be!"

She did not know what to do with Hélène, who remained prostrate on a seat in the pavilion. Henri might have stayed with her and afforded her some consolation. His absence was a horrible nuisance. Luckily, Mademoiselle Aurélie was glad to offer her services; she had no liking for such solemn scenes, and while watching over Hélène would be able to attend to the luncheon which had to be prepared ere the children's return. So Juliette hastened after the funeral, which was proceeding towards the church by way of the Rue de Passy.

The garden was now deserted; a few workmen only were folding up the hangings. All that remained on the gravelled path over which Jeanne had been carried were the scattered petals of a camellia. And Hélène, suddenly lapsing into loneliness and stillness, was thrilled once more with the anguish of this eternal separation. Once again—only once again!—to be at her darling's side! The never-fading thought that Jeanne was leaving her in anger, with a face that spoke solely of gloomy hatred, seared her heart like a red-hot iron. She well divined that Mademoiselle Aurélie was there to watch her, and cast about for some opportunity to escape and hasten to the cemetery.

"Yes, it's a dreadful loss," began the old maid, comfortably seated in an easy-chair. "I myself should have worshipped children, and little girls in particular. Ah, well! when I think of it I am pleased that I never married. It saves a lot of grief!"

It was thus she thought to divert the mother. She chatted away about one of her friends who had had six children; they were now all dead. Another lady had been left a widow with a big lad who struck her; he might die, and there would be no difficulty in comforting her. Hélène appeared to be listening to all this; she did not stir, but her whole frame quivered with impatience.

"You are calmer now," said Mademoiselle Aurélie, after a time. "Well, in the end we always have to get the better of our feelings."

The dining-room communicated with the Japanese pavilion, and, rising up, the old maid opened the door and peered into the room. The table, she saw, was covered with pastry and cakes. Meantime, in an instant Hélène sped through the garden; the gate was still open, the workmen were just carrying away their ladder.

On the left the Rue Vineuse turns into the Rue des Réservoirs, from which the cemetery of Passy can be entered. On the Boulevard de la Muette a huge retaining wall has been reared, and the cemetery stretches like an immense terrace commanding the heights, the Trocadéro, the avenues, and the whole expanse of Paris. In twenty steps Hélène had reached the yawning gateway, and saw before her the lonely expanse of white gravestones and black crosses. She entered. At the corners of the first walk two large lilac trees were budding. There were but few burials here; weeds grew thickly, and a few cypress trees threw solemn shadows across the green. Hélène hurried straight on; a troop of frightened sparrows flew off, and a grave-digger raised his head towards her after flinging aside a shovelful of earth. The procession had probably not yet arrived from the church; the cemetery seemed empty to her. She turned to the right, and advanced almost to the edge of the terrace parapet; but, on looking round, she saw behind a cluster of acacias the litle girls in white upon their knees before the temporary vault into which Jeanne's remains had a moment before been lowered. Abbé Jouve, with outstretched hand, was giving the farewell benediction. She heard nothing but the dull thud with which the stone slab of the vault fell back into its place. All was over.

Meanwhile, however, Pauline had observed her and pointed her out to Madame Deberle, who almost gave way to anger. "What!" she exclaimed; "she has come. But it isn't at all proper; it's very bad taste!"

So saying she stepped forward, showing Hélène by the expression of her face that she disapproved of her presence. Some other ladies also followed with inquisitive looks. Monsieur Rambaud, however, had already rejoined the bereaved mother, and stood silent by her side. She was leaning against one of the acacias, feeling faint, and weary with the sight of all those mourners. She nodded her head in recognition of their sympathetic words, but all the while she was stifling with the thought that she had come too late; for she had heard the noise of the stone falling back into its place. Her eyes ever turned towards the vault, the step of which a cemetery keeper was sweeping.

"Pauline, see to the children," said Madame Deberle.

The little girls rose from their knees looking like a flock of white sparrows. A few of the tinier ones, lost among their petticoats, had seated themselves on the ground, and had to be picked up. While Jeanne was being lowered down, the older girls had leaned forward to see the bottom of the cavity. It was so dark they had shuddered and turned pale. Sophie assured her companions in a whisper that one remained there for years and years. "At night-time too?" asked one of the little Levasseur girls. "Of course—at night too —always!" Oh, the night! Blanche was nearly dead with the idea. And they all looked at one another with dilated eyes, as if they had just heard some story about robbers. However, when they had regained their feet, and stood grouped around the vault, released from their mourning duties, their cheeks became pink again; it must all be untrue, those stories could only have been told for fun. The spot seemed pleasant, so pretty with its long grass; what capital games they might have had at hide-and-seek behind all the tombstones! Their little feet were already itching to dance away, and their white dresses fluttered like wings. Amidst the graveyard stillness the warm sunshine lazily streamed down, flushing their faces. Lucien had thrust his hand beneath Marguerite's veil, and was feeling her hair and asking if she put anything on it, to make it so yellow. The little one drew herself up, and he told her that they would marry each other some day. To this Marguerite had no objection, but she was afraid that he might pull her hair. His hands were still wandering over it; it seemed to him as soft as highly-glazed letter-paper.

"Don't go so far away," called Pauline.

"Well, we'll leave now," said Madame Deberle. "There's nothing more to be done, and the children must be hungry."

The little girls, who had scattered like some boarding-school at play, had to be marshalled together once more. They were counted, and baby Guiraud was missing; but she was at last seen in the distance, gravely toddling along a path with her mother's parasol. The ladies then turned towards the gateway, driving the stream of white dresses before them. Madame Berthier congratulated Pauline on her marriage, which was to take place during the following month. Madame Deberle informed them that she was setting out in three days' time for Naples, with her husband and Lucien. The crowd now quickly disappeared; Zéphyrin and Rosalie were the last to remain. Then

in their turn they went off, linked together, arm-in-arm, delighted with their outing, although their hearts were heavy with grief. Their pace was slow, and for a moment longer they could be seen at the end of the path, with the sunshine dancing over them.

"Come," murmured Monsieur Rambaud to Hélène.

With a gesture she entreated him to wait. She was alone, and to her it seemed as though a page had been torn from the book of her life. As soon as the last of the mourners had disappeared, she knelt before the tomb with a painful effort. Abbé Jouve, robed in his surplice, had not yet risen to his feet. Both prayed for a long time. Then, without speaking, but with a glowing glance of loving-kindness and pardon, the priest assisted her to rise.

"Give her your arm," he said to Monsieur Rambaud.

Towards the horizon stretched Paris, all golden in the radiance of that spring morning. In the cemetery a chaffinch was singing.

## CHAPTER XXV

### MONSIEUR RAMBAUD

Two years were past and gone. One morning in December the little cemetery lay slumbering in the intense cold. Since the evening before snow had been falling, a fine snow, which a north wind blew before it. From the paling sky the flakes now fell at rarer intervals, light and buoyant, like feathers. The snow was already hardening, and a thick trimming of seeming swan's-down edged the parapet of the terrace.

Beyond this white line lay Paris, against the gloomy grey on the horizon.

Madame Rambaud was still praying on her knees in the snow before the grave of Jeanne. Her husband had but a moment before risen silently to his feet. Hélène and her old lover had been married in November at Marseilles. Monsieur Rambaud had disposed of his business near the Central Markets, and had come to Paris for three days, in order to conclude the transaction. The carriage now awaiting them in the Rue des Réservoirs was to take them back to their hotel, and thence with their travelling-trunks to the railway station. Hélène had made the journey with the one thought of kneeling here. She remained motionless, with drooping head, as if dreaming, and unconscious of the cold ground that chilled her knees.

Meanwhile the wind was falling. Monsieur Rambaud had stepped to the terrace, leaving her to the mute anguish which memory evoked. A haze was stealing over the outlying districts of Paris, whose immensity faded away in this pale, vague mist. Round the Trocadéro the city was of a leaden hue and lifeless, while the last snowflakes slowly fluttered down in pale specks against the gloomy background. Beyond the chimneys of the Army Bakehouse, the brick towers of which had a coppery tint, these white dots descended more thickly; a gauze seemed to be floating in the air, falling to earth thread by thread. Not a breath stirred as the dream-like shower sleepily and rhythmically descended from the atmosphere. As they neared the roofs the flakes seemed to falter in their flight; in myriads they ceaselessly pillowed themselves on one another, in such intense silence that even blossoms shedding their petals make more noise; and from this moving mass, whose descent through space was inaudible, there sprang a sense of such intense peacefulness that earth and life were forgotten. A milky whiteness spread more and more over the whole heavens though they were still darkened here and there by wreaths of smoke. Little by little, bright clusters of houses became plainly visible; a bird's-eye view was obtained of the whole city, intersected by streets and squares, which with their shadowy depths described the framework of the several districts.

Hélène had slowly risen. On the snow remained the imprint of her knees. Wrapped in a large, dark mantle trimmed with fur, she seemed amidst the surrounding white very tall and broad-shouldered. The border of her bonnet, a twisted band of black velvet, looked like a diadem throwing a shadow on her forehead. She had regained her beautiful, placid face with grey eyes and pearly teeth. Her chin was full and rounded, as in the olden days, giving her an air of sturdy sense and determination. As she turned her head, her profile once more assumed statuesque severity and purity. Beneath the untroubled paleness of her cheeks her blood coursed calmly; everything showed that honor was again ruling her life. Two tears had rolled from under her eyelids; her present tranquillity came from her past sorrow. And she stood before the grave on which was reared a simple pillar inscribed with Jeanne's name and two dates, within which the dead child's brief existence was compassed.

Around Hélène stretched the cemetery, enveloped in its snowy pall, through which rose rusty monuments and iron crosses, like arms thrown up in agony. There was only one path visible in this lonely corner, and that had been made by the footmarks of Hélène and Monsieur Rambaud. It was a spotless solitude where the dead lay sleeping. The walks were outlined by the shadowy, phantom-like trees. Ever and anon some snow fell noiselessly from a branch that had been too heavily burdened. But nothing else stirred. At the far end, some little while ago, a black tramping had passed by; some one was being buried beneath this snowy winding-sheet. And now another funeral train appeared on the left. Hearses and mourners went their way in silence, like shadows thrown upon a spotless linen cloth.

Hélène was awaking from her dream when she observed a beggar-woman crawling near her. It was Mother Fétu, the snow deadening the sound of her huge man's boots, which were burst and bound round with bits of string. Never had Hélène seen her weighed down by such intense misery, or covered with filthier rags, though she was fatter than ever, and wore a stupid look. In the foulest weather, despite hard frosts or drenching rain, the old woman now followed funerals in order to speculate on the pity of the charitable. She well knew that amongst the gravestones the fear of death makes people generous; and so she prowled from tomb to tomb, approaching the kneeling mourners at the moment they burst into tears, for she understood that they were then powerless to refuse her. She had entered with the last funeral train, and a moment previously had espied Hélène. But she had not recognized her benefactress, and with gasps and sobs began to relate how she had two children at home who were dying of hunger. Hélène listened to her, struck dumb by this apparition. The children were without fire to warm them; the elder was going off in a decline. But all at once Mother Fétu's words came to an end. Her brain was evidently working beneath the myriad wrinkles of her face, and her little eyes began to blink. Good gracious! it was her benefactress! Heaven, then, had hearkened to her prayers! And without seeking to explain the story about the children, she plunged into a whining tale, with a ceaseless rush of words. Several of her teeth were missing, and she could be understood with difficulty. The gracious God had sent every affliction on her head, she declared. The gentleman lodger had gone away, and she had only just been enabled to rise after lying for three months in bed; yes, the old pain still remained, it now gripped her everywhere; a neighbor had told her that a spider must have got in through her mouth while she was asleep. If she had only had a little fire, she could have warmed her stomach; that was the only thing that could relieve her now. But nothing could be had for nothing—not even a match. Perhaps she was right in thinking that madame had been travelling? That was her own concern, of course. At all events, she looked very well, and fresh, and beautiful. God would requite her for all her kindness. Then, as Hélène began to draw out her purse, Mother Fétu drew breath, leaning against the railing that encircled Jeanne's grave.

The funeral processions had vanished from sight. Somewhere in a grave close at hand a digger, whom they could not see, was wielding his pickaxe with regular strokes. Meanwhile the old woman had regained her breath, and her eyes were riveted on the purse. Then, anxious to extort as large a sum as possible, she displayed considerable cunning, and spoke of the other lady. Nobody could say that she was not a charitable lady; still, she did not know what to do with her money—it never did one much good. Warily did she glance at Hélène as she spoke. And next she ventured to mention the doctor's name. Oh! he was good. Last summer he had again gone on a journey with his wife. Their boy was thriving; he was a fine child. But just then Hélène's fingers, as she opened the purse, began to tremble, and Mother Fétu immediately changed her tone. In her stupidity and bewilderment she had only now realized that the good lady was standing beside her daughter's grave. She stammered, gasped, and tried to bring tears to her eyes. Jeanne, said she, had been so dainty a darling, with such loves of little hands; she could still see her giving her silver in charity. What long hair she had! and how her large eyes filled with tears when she gazed on the poor! Ah! there was no replacing such an angel; there were no more to be found like her, were they even to search the whole of Passy. And when the fine days

came, said Mother Fétu, she would gather some daisies in the moat of the fortifications and place them on her tomb. Then, however, she lapsed into silence frightened by the gesture with which Hélène cut her short. Was it possible, she thought, that she could no longer find the right thing to say? Her good lady did not weep, and only gave her a twenty-sou piece.

Monsieur Rambaud, meanwhile, had walked towards them from the parapet of the terrace. Hélène hastened to rejoin him. At the sight of the gentleman Mother Fétu's eyes began to sparkle. He was unknown to her; he must be a new-comer. Dragging her feet along, she followed Hélène, invoking every blessing of Heaven on her head; and when she had crept close to Monsieur Rambaud, she again spoke of the doctor. Ah! his would be a magnificent funeral when he died, were the poor people whom he had attended for nothing to follow his corpse! He was rather fickle in his loves—nobody could deny that. There were ladies in Passy who knew him well. But all that didn't prevent him from worshipping his wife —such a pretty lady, who, had she wished, might have easily gone wrong, but had given up such ideas long ago. Their home was quite a turtle-doves' nest now. Had madame paid them a visit yet? They were certain to be at home; she had but a few moments previously observed that the shutters were open in the Rue Vineuse. They had formerly had such regard for madame that surely they would be delighted to receive her with open arms!

The old hag leered at Monsieur Rambaud as she thus mumbled away. He listened to her with the composure of a brave man. The memories that were being called up before him brought no shadow to his unruffled face. Only it occurred to him that the pertinacity of the old beggar was annoying Hélène, and so he hastened to fumble in his pocket, in his turn giving her some alms, and at the same time waving her away. The moment her eyes rested on another silver coin Mother Fétu burst into loud thanks. She would buy some wood at once; she would be able to warm her afflicted body—that was the only thing now to give her stomach any relief. Yes, the doctor's home was quite a nest of turtle-doves, and the proof was that the lady had only last winter given birth to a second child—a beautiful little daughter, rosy-cheeked and fat, who must now be nearly fourteen months old. On the day of the baptism the doctor had put a hundred sous into her hand at the door of the church. Ah! good hearts came together. Madame had brought her good luck. Pray God that madame might never have a sorrow, but every good fortune! yes, might that come to pass in the name of the Father, the Son, and the Holy Ghost!

Hélène stood upright gazing on Paris, while Mother Fétu vanished among the tombs, muttering three *Paters* and three *Aves*. The snow had ceased falling; the last of the flakes had fluttered slowly and wearily on to the roofs; and through the dissolving mist the golden sun could be seen tinging the pearly-grey expanse of heaven with a pink glow. Over Montmartre a belt of blue fringed the horizon; but it was so faint and delicate that it seemed but a sha-

dow such as white satin might throw. Paris was gradually detaching itself from amidst the smoke, spreading out more broadly with its snowy expanses the frigid cloak which held it in death-like quiescence. There were now no longer any fleeting specks of white making the city shudder, and quivering in pale waves over the dull-brown house-fronts. Amidst the masses of snow that girt them round the dwellings stood out black and gloomy, as though mouldy with centuries of damp. Entire streets appeared to be in ruins, as if undermined by some gunpowder explosion, with roofs ready to give way and windows already driven in. But gradually, as the belt of blue broadened in the direction of Montmartre, there came a stream of light, pure and cool as the waters of a spring; and Paris once more shone out as under a glass, which lent even to the outlying districts the distinctness of a Japanese picture.

Wrapped in her fur mantle, with her hands clinging idly to the cuffs of the sleeves, Hélène was musing. With the persistency of an echo one thought unceasingly pursued her—a child, a fat, rosy daughter, had been born to them. In her imagination she could picture her at the love-compelling age when Jeanne had commenced to prattle. Baby girls are such darlings when fourteen months old! She counted the months—fourteen: that made two years when she took the remaining period into consideration—exactly the time within a fortnight. Then her brain conjured up a sunny picture of Italy, a realm of dreamland, with golden fruits where lovers wandered through the perfumed nights, with arms round one another's waists. Henri and Juliette were pacing before her eyes beneath the light of the moon. They loved as husband and wife do when passion is once more awakened within them. To think of it—a tiny girl, rosy and fat, its bare body flushed by the warm sunshine, while it strives to stammer words which its mother arrests with kisses! And Hélène thought of all this without any anger; her heart was mute, yet seemingly derived yet greater quietude from the sadness of her spirit. The land of the sun had vanished from her vision; her eyes wandered slowly over Paris, on whose huge frame winter had laid his freezing hand. Above the Panthéon another patch of blue was now spreading in the heavens.

Meanwhile memory was recalling the past to life. At Marseilles she had spent her days in a state of coma. One morning as she went along the Rue des Petites-Maries, she had burst out sobbing in front of the home of her childhood. That was the last occasion on which she had wept. Monsieur Rambaud was her frequent visitor; she felt his presence near her to be a protection. Towards autumn she had one evening seen him enter, with red eyes and in the agony of a great sorrow; his brother, Abbé Jouve, was dead. In her turn she comforted him. What followed she could not recall with any exactitude of detail. The Abbé ever seemed to stand behind them, and influenced by thought of him she succumbed resignedly. When M. Rambaud once more hinted at his wish, she had nothing to say in refusal. It seemed to her that what he asked was

but sensible. Of her own accord, as her period of mourning was drawing to an end, she calmly arranged all the details with him. His hands trembled in a transport of tenderness. It should be as she pleased; he had waited for months; a sign sufficed him. They were married in mourning garb. On the wedding night he, like her first husband, kissed her bare feet—feet fair as though fashioned out of marble. And thus life began once more.

While the belt of blue was broadening on the horizon, this awakening of memory came with an astounding effect on Hélène. Had she lived through a year of madness, then? To-day, as she pictured the woman who had lived for nearly three years in that room in the Rue Vineuse, she imagined that she was passing judgment on some stranger, whose conduct revolted and surprised her. How fearfully foolish had been her act! how abominably wicked! Yet she had not sought it. She had been living peacefully, hidden in her nook, absorbed in the love of her daughter. Untroubled by any curious thoughts, by any desire, she had seen the road of life lying before her. But a breath had swept by, and she had fallen. Even at this moment she was unable to explain it; she had evidently ceased to be herself; another mind and heart had controlled her actions. Was it possible? She had done those things? Then an icy chill ran through her; she saw Jeanne borne away beneath roses. But in the torpor begotten of her grief she grew very calm again, once more without a longing or curiosity, once more proceeding along the path of duty that lay so straight before her. Life had again begun for her, fraught with austere peacefulness and pride of honesty.

Monsieur Rambaud now moved near her to lead her from this place of sadness. But Hélène silently signed to him her wish to linger a little longer. Approaching the parapet she gazed below into the Avenue de la Muette, where a long line of old cabs in the last stage of decay stretched beside the footpath. The hoods and wheels looked blanched, the rusty horses seemed to have been rotting there since the dark ages. Some cabmen sat motionless, freezing within their frozen cloaks. Over the snow other vehicles were crawling along, one after the other, with the utmost difficulty. The animals were losing their foothold, and stretching out their necks, while their drivers with many oaths descended from their seats and held them by the bridle; and through the windows you could see the faces of the patient "fares," reclining against the cushions, and resigning themselves to the stern necessity of taking three-quarters of an hour to cover a distance which in other weather would have been accomplished in ten minutes. The rumblings of the wheels was deadened by the snow; only the voices vibrated upward, sounding shrill and distinct amidst the silence of the streets; there were loud calls, the laughing exclamations of people slipping on the icy paths, the angry whip-cracking of carters, and the snorting of terrified horses. In the distance, to the right, the lofty trees on the quay seemed to be spun of glass, like huge Venetian chandeliers, whose flower-decked arms the designer had whimsically twisted. The icy north wind had transformed the trunks into columns, over which waved downy boughs and feathery tufts, an exquisite tracery of black twigs edged with white trimmings. It was freezing, and not a breath stirred in the pure air.

Then Hélène told her heart that she had known nothing of Henri. For a year she had seen him almost every day; he had lingered for hours and hours near her, to speak to her and gaze into her eyes. Yet she knew nothing of him. Whence had he come? how had he crept into her intimacy? what manner of man was he that she had yielded to him—she who would rather have perished than yield to another? She knew nothing of him; it had all sprung from some sudden tottering of her reason. He had been a stranger to her on the last as on the first day. In vain did she patch together little scattered things and circumstances—his words, his acts, everything that her memory recalled concerning him. He loved his wife and his child; he smiled with delicate grace; he outwardly appeared a well-bred man. Then she saw him again with inflamed visage, and trembling with passion. But weeks passed, and he vanished from her sight. At this moment she could not have said where she had spoken to him for the last time. He had passed away, and his shadow had gone with him. Their story had no other ending. She knew him not.

Over the city the sky had now become blue, and every cloud had vanished. Wearied with her memories, and rejoicing in the purity before her, Hélène raised her head. The blue of the heavens was exquisitely clear, but still very pale in the light of the sun, which hung low on the horizon, and glittered like a silver lamp. In that icy temperature its rays shed no heat on the glittering snow. Below stretched the expanse of roofs—the tiles of the Army Bakehouse, and the slates of the houses on the quay—like sheets of white cloth fringed with black. On the other bank of the river, the square stretch of the Champ-de-Mars seemed a steppe, the black dots of the straggling vehicles making one think of sledges skimming along with tinkling bells; while the elms on the Quai d'Orsay, dwarfed by the distance, looked like crystal flowers bristling with sharp points. Through all the snow-white sea the Seine rolled its muddy waters edged by the ermine of its banks; since the evening before ice had been floating down, and you could clearly see the masses crushing against the piers of the Pont des Invalides, and vanishing swiftly beneath the arches. The bridges, growing more and more delicate with the distance, seemed like the steps of a ladder of white lace reaching as far as the sparkling walls of the Cité, above which the towers of Notre-Dame reared their snow-white crests. On the left the level plain was broken up by other peaks. The Church of Saint-Augustin, the Opera House, the Tower of Saint-Jacques, looked like mountains clad with eternal snow. Nearer at hand the pavilions of the Tuileries and the Louvre, joined together by newly erected buildings, resembled a ridge of hills with spotless summits. On the right, too, were the white tops of the Invalides, of Saint-Sulpice, and the Panthéon, the last in the dim distance, outlining against the sky a palace of fairyland with dressings of bluish marble. Not a sound broke the stillness. Grey-looking hollows revealed the presence of the streets; the public squares were like yawning crevasses. Whole lines of houses had vanished. The fronts of the neighboring dwellings alone showed distinctly with the thousand streaks of light reflected from their windows. Beyond, the expanse of snow intermingled and merged into a seeming lake, whose blue shadows blended with the blue of the sky. Huge and clear in the bright, frosty atmosphere, Paris glittered in the light of the silver sun.

Then Hélène for the last time let her glance sweep over the unpitying city which also remained unknown to her. She saw it once more, tranquil and with immortal beauty amidst the snow, the same as when she had left it, the same as it had been every day for three long years. Paris to her was full of her past life. In its presence she had loved, in its presence Jeanne had died. But this companion of her every-day existence retained on its mighty face a wondrous serenity, unruffled by any emotion, as though it were but a mute witness of the laughter and the tears which the Seine seemed to roll in its flood. She had, according to her mood, endowed it with monstrous cruelty or almighty goodness. To-day she felt that she would be ever ignorant of it, in its indifference and immensity. It spread before her; it was life.

However, Monsieur Rambaud now laid a light hand on her arm to lead her away. His kindly face was troubled, and he whispered:

"Do not give yourself pain."

He divined her every thought, and this was all he could say. Madame Rambaud looked at him, and her sorrow became appeased. Her cheeks were flushed by the cold; her eyes sparkled. Her memories were already far away. Life was beginning again.

"I'm not quite certain whether I shut the big trunk properly," she exclaimed.

Monsieur Rambaud promised that he would make sure. Their train started at noon, and they had plenty of time. Some gravel was being scattered on the streets; their cab would not take an hour. But, all at once, he raised his voice:

"I believe you've forgotten the fishing-rods!" said he.

"Oh, yes; quite!" she answered, surprised and vexed at her forgetfulness. "We ought to have bought them yesterday!"

The rods in question were very handy ones, the like of which could not be purchased at Marseilles. They there owned near the sea a small country house, where they purposed spending the summer. Monsieur Rambaud looked at his watch. On their way to the railway station they would still be able to buy the rods, and could tie them up with the umbrellas. Then he led her from the place, tramping along, and taking short cuts between the graves. The cemetery was empty; only the imprint of their feet now remained on the snow. Jeanne, dead, lay alone, facing Paris, for ever and for ever.

# L'Assommoir

## CHAPTER I

GERVAISE

GERVAISE had waited and watched for Lantier until two in the morning. Then, chilled and shivering she turned from the window and threw herself across the bed, where she fell into a feverish doze with her cheeks wet with tears. For the last week when they came out of the *Veau à deux têtes* where they ate, he had sent her off to bed with the children, and had not appeared until late into the night, and always with a story that he had been looking for work.

This very night, while she was watching for his return, she fancied she saw him enter the ball room of the Grand-Balcon, whose ten windows blazing with lights illuminated as with a sheet of fire, the black lines of the outer Boulevards. She caught a glimpse of Adèle, a pretty brunette who dined at their restaurant, and who was walking a few steps behind him, with her hands swinging as if she had just dropped his arm, rather than pass before the bright light of the globes over the door, in his company.

When Gervaise awoke about five o'clock, stiff and sore, she burst into wild sobs, for Lantier had not come in. For the first time he had slept out. She sat on the edge of the bed, half shrouded in the canopy of faded chintz that hung from the arrow fastened to the ceiling by a string. Slowly, with her eyes suffused with tears, she looked around this miserable *chambre garnie*, whose furniture consisted of a chestnut bureau of which one drawer was absent, three straw chairs and a greasy table, on which was a broken handled pitcher.

Another bedstead—an iron one—had been brought in for the children. This stood in front of the bureau and filled up two-thirds of the room.

A trunk belonging to Gervaise and Lantier stood in the corner wide open, showing its empty sides, while at the bottom a man's old hat lay among soiled shirts and hose. Along the walls, and on the backs of the chairs, hung a ragged shawl, a pair of muddy pantaloons and a dress or two—all too bad for the old clothes man to buy. In the middle of the mantel between two mismated tin candlesticks was a bundle of pawn tickets from the Mont-de-Piété. These tickets were of a delicate shade of rose.

The room was the best in the hotel —the first floor looking out on the Boulevard.

Meanwhile side by side on the same pillow, the two children lay calmly sleeping. Claude, who was eight years old was breathing calmly and regularly with his little hands outside of the coverings, while Etienne, only four, smiled with one arm under his brother's neck.

When their mother's eyes fell on them she had a new paroxysm of sobs, and pressed her handkerchief to her mouth to stifle them. Then with bare feet, not stopping to put on her slippers which had fallen off, she ran to the window, out of which she leaned as she had done half the night, and inspected the sidewalks as far as she could see.

The hotel was on the Boulevard de la Chapelle, at the left of the Barrière Poissonnièrs. It was a two story building, painted a deep red up to the first floor, and had disjointed weather-stained blinds.

Above a lantern with glass sides, was a sign between the two windows:

HOTEL BONCŒUR,

KEPT BY

MARSOULLIER.

in large yellow letters, partially obliterated by the dampness. Gervaise, who was prevented by the lantern from seeing as she desired, leaned out still further, with her handkerchief on her lips. She looked to the right toward the Boulevard de Rochechoumart, where groups of butchers stood with their bloody frocks before their establishments, and the fresh breeze brought in whiffs, a strong animal smell—the smell of slaughtered cattle.

She looked to the left, following the ribbon-like avenue, past the Hospital de Lariboisière, then building. Slowly, from one end to the other of the horizon, did she follow the wall, from behind which in the night time, she had heard strange groans and cries, as if some fell murder were being perpe-

trated. She looked at it with horror, as if in some dark corner—dark with dampness and filth—she should distinguish Lantier,—Lantier lying dead with his throat cut.

When she gazed beyond this gray and interminable wall she saw a great light, a golden mist waving and shimmering with the dawn of a new Parisian day. But it was to the Barrière Poissonnièrs that her eyes persistently returned—watching dully the uninterrupted flow of men and cattle, wagons and sheep which came down from Montmartre and from la Chapelle. There were scattered flocks dashed like waves on the sidewalk by some sudden detention, and an endless succession of laborers going to their work with their tools over their shoulders and their loaves of bread under their arms.

Suddenly Gervaise thought she distinguished Lantier amid this crowd, and she leaned eagerly forward at the risk of falling from the window. With a fresh pang of disappointment she pressed her handkerchief to her lips to restrain her sobs.

A fresh, youthful voice caused her to turn around:

"Lantier has not come in then?"

"No, Monsieur Coupeau," she answered, trying to smile.

The speaker was a tinsmith who occupied a tiny room at the top of the house. His bag of tools was over his shoulder; he had seen the key in the door and entered with the familiarity of a friend.

"You know," he continued, "that I am working now-a-days at the Hospital. What a May this is! The air positively stings one this morning."

As he spoke he looked closely at Gervaise; he saw her eyes were red with tears, and then glancing at the bed, discovered that it had not been disturbed. He shook his head, and going toward the couch where the children lay with their rosy cherub faces, he said in a lower voice:

"You think your husband ought to have been with you, Madame. But don't be troubled, he is busy with politics. He went on like a mad man the other day when they were voting for Eugène Sue. Perhaps he passed the night with his friends abusing that reprobate, Bonaparte."

"No, no," she murmured, with an effort. "You think nothing of that kind. I know where Lantier is only too well. We have our sorrows like the rest of the world!"

Coupeau gave a knowing wink and departed, having offered to bring her some milk if she did not care to go out; she was a good woman, he told her, and might count on him any time when she was in trouble.

As soon as Gervaise was alone, she returned to the window.

From the Barrière, the lowing of the cattle and the bleating of the sheep still came on the keen, fresh morning air. Among the crowd, she recognized the locksmiths by their blue frocks, the masons by their white overalls, the painters by their coats, from under which hung their blouses. This crowd was cheerless. All of neutral tints—grays and blues predominating, with never a dash of color. Occasionally a workman stopped and lighted his pipe, while his companions passed on. There was no laughing, no talking, but they strode on steadily with cadaverous faces, toward that Paris which quickly swallowed them up.

At the two corners of La Rue des Poissonnièrs were two wine shops, where the shutters had just been taken down. Here some of the workmen lingered, crowding into the shop, spitting, coughing, and drinking glasses of brandy and water. Gervaise was watching the place on the left of the street, where she thought she had seen Lantier go in, when a stout woman, bareheaded, and wearing a large apron, called to her from the pavement,

"You are up early! Madame Lantier!"

Gervaise leaned out.

"Ah! Is it you, Madame Boche! Yes, I am up early, for I have much to do to-day."

"Is that so? Well, things don't get done by themselves, that's sure!"

And a conversation ensued between the window and the sidewalk. Madame Boche was the Concierge of the house wherein the restaurant du *Veau à Deux Têtes* occupied the rez de chaussée.

Many times Gervaise had waited for Lantier in the room of this woman, rather than face the men who were eating. The Concierge said she had just been round the corner to arouse a lazy fellow who had promised to do some work, and then went on to speak of one of her lodgers who had come in the night before with some woman, and had made such a noise that every one was disturbed until after three o'clock.

As she gabbled however, she examined Gervaise with considerable curiosity, and seemed, in fact, to have come out under the window for that express purpose.

"Is Monsieur Lantier still asleep?" she asked suddenly.

"Yes, he is asleep," answered Gervaise, with flushing cheeks.

Madame saw the tears come to her eyes, and satisfied with her discovery was turning away, when she suddenly stopped and called out:

"You are going to the lavatory this morning, are you not? All right then, I have some things to wash, and I will keep a place for you next to me, and we can have a little talk!"

Then as if moved by sudden compassion, she added:

"Poor child!—don't stay at that window any longer. You are purple with cold, and will surely make yourself sick!"

But Gervaise did not move. She remained in the same spot for two mortal hours, until the clock struck eight. The shops were now all open. The procession in blouses had long ceased, and only an occasional one hurried along. At the wine shops however, there was the same crowd of men drinking, spitting, and coughing. The workmen in the street had given place to the workwomen. Milliner's apprentices, florists, burnishers, who with thin shawls drawn closely around them, came in bands of three or four, talking eagerly, with gay laughs and quick glances. Occasionally one solitary figure was seen, a pale-faced, serious woman, who walked rapidly, neither looking to the right nor to the left. Then came the clerks, blowing on their fingers to warm them, eating a

roll as they walked; young men, lean and tall, with clothing they had outgrown, and with eyes heavy with sleep; old men, who moved along with measured steps, occasionally pulling out their watches, but able, from many years' practice, to time their movements almost to a second.

The Boulevards at last were comparatively quiet. The inhabitants were sunning themselves. Women with untidy hair and soiled petticoats were nursing their babies in the open air, and an occasional dirty-faced brat fell into the gutter, or rolled over with shrieks of pain or joy.

Gervaise felt faint and ill—all hope was gone. It seemed to her that all was over, and that Lantier would come no more. She looked from the dingy slaughter houses, black with their dirt and loathsome odor, on to the new and staring Hospital, and into the rooms consecrated to Disease and Death. As yet, the windows were not in, and there was nothing to impede her views of the large, empty wards. The sun shone directly in her face and blinded her.

She was sitting on a chair, with her arms dropping drearily at her side, but not weeping, when Lantier quietly opened the door and walked in.

"You have come!" she cried, ready to throw herself on his neck.

"Yes, I have come," he answered, "and what of it? Don't begin any of your nonsense, now!"—and he pushed her aside. Then, with an angry gesture, he tossed his felt hat on the bureau.

He was a small, dark fellow, handsome and well made, with a delicate moustache, which he twisted in his fingers mechanically as he spoke. He wore an old coat, buttoned tightly at the waist, and spoke with a strongly marked Provençal accent.

Gervaise had dropped upon her chair again, and uttered disjointed phrases of lamentation.

"I have not closed my eyes—I thought you were killed! Where have you been all night? I feel as if I were going mad! Tell me, Auguste, where have you been?"

"Oh! I had business," he answered, with an indifferent shrug of his shoulders. "At eight o'clock, I had an engagement with that friend, you know, who is thinking of starting a manufactory of hats. I was detained, and I preferred stopping there. But you know I don't like to be watched and catechised. Just let me alone, will you?"

His wife began to sob. Their voices, and Lantier's noisy movements, as he pushed the chairs about, woke the children. They started up, half naked, with tumbled hair, and hearing their mother cry, they followed her example, rending the air with their shrieks.

"Well, this is lovely music!" cried Lantier, furiously. "I warn you, if you don't all stop, that out of this door I go, and you won't see me again in a hurry! Will you hold your tongue? Good-bye, then; I'll go back where I came from."

He snatched up his hat, but Gervaise rushed toward him, crying:

"No! no!"

And she soothed the children and stifled their cries with kisses, and laid them tenderly back in their bed, and they were soon happy, and merrily playing together. Meanwhile the father, not even taking off his boots, threw himself on the bed with a weary air. His face was white from exhaustion and a sleepless night; he did not close his eyes, but looked around the room.

"A nice looking place, this!" he muttered.

Then examining Gervaise, he said, half aloud and half to himself:

"So! you have given up washing yourself, it seems!"

Gervaise was only twenty-two. She was tall and slender, with delicate features, already worn by hardships and anxieties. With her hair uncombed and shoes down at heel, shivering in her white sack, on which was much dust and many stains from the furniture and wall where it had hung, she looked at least ten years older from the hours of suspense and tears she had passed.

Lantier's word startled her from her resignation and timidity.

"Are you not ashamed?" she said with considerable animation. "You know very well that I do all I can. It is not my fault that we came here. I should like to see you with two children, in a place where you can't get a drop of hot water. We ought as soon as we reached Paris to have settled ourselves at once in a home, that was what you promised.

"Pshaw," he muttered; "you had as much good as I had out of our savings. You ate the fatted calf with me —and it is not worth while to make a row about it now!"

She did not heed his words, but continued:

"There is no need of giving up either. I saw Madame Fauconnier, the laundress in La Rue Neuve. She will take me Monday. If you go in with your friend we shall be afloat again in six months. We must find some kind of a hole where we can live cheaply while we work. That is the thing to do now. Work! work!"

Lantier turned his face to the wall with a shrug of disgust which enraged his wife, who resumed:

"Yes, I know very well that you don't like to work. You would like to wear fine clothes and walk about the streets all day. You don't like my looks since you took all my dresses to the pawnbrokers. Nc, no, Auguste, I did not intend to speak to you about it, but I know very well where you spent the night. I saw you go into the Grand-Balcon with that street walker, Adèle. You have made a charming choice. She wears fine clothes and is clean. Yes, and she has reason to be certainly, there is not a man in that restaurant who does not know her far better than an honest girl should be known!"

Lantier leaped from the bed. His eyes were as black as night and his face deadly pale.

"Yes," repeated his wife, "I mean what I say. Madame Boche will not keep her or her sister in the house any longer, because there are always a crowd of men hanging on the staircase."

Lantier lifted both fists, and then conquering a violent desire to beat her, he seized her in his arms, shook her violently and threw her on the bed where the children were. They at once began to cry again, while he stood for a moment, and then, with the air of a man who finally takes a resolution in regard to which he has hesitated, he said:

"You do not know what you have done, Gervaise. You are wrong—as you will soon discover."

For a moment the voices of the children filled the room. Their mother lying on their narrow couch held them both in her arms, and said over and over again in a monotonous voice:

"If you were not here, my poor darlings! if you were not here! If you were not here!"

Lantier was lying flat on his back with his eyes fixed on the ceiling. He was not listening; his attention was concentrated on some fixed idea. He remained in this way for an hour and more—not sleeping in spite of his evident and intense fatigue. When he turned and leaning on his elbow looked about the room again, he found that Gervaise had arranged the chamber and made the children's bed. They were washed and dressed. He watched her as she swept the room and dusted the furniture.

The room was very dreary still however, with its smoke-stained ceiling, and paper discolored by dampness, and three chairs and dilapidated bureau, whose greasy surface no dusting could clean. Then while she washed herself and arranged her hair before the small mirror, he seemed to examine her arms and shoulders, as if instituting a comparison between herself and some one else. And he smiled a disdainful little smile.

Gervaise was slightly, very slightly lame, but her lameness was perceptible only on such days as she was very tired. This morning, so weary was she from the watches of the night, that she could hardly walk without support.

A profound silence reigned in the room—they did not speak to each other. He seemed to be waiting for something. She, adopting an unconcerned air, seemed to be in haste.

She made up a bundle of soiled linen that had been thrown into a corner behind the trunk, and then he spoke:

"What are you doing? Are you going out?"

At first she did not reply. Then when he angrily repeated the question she answered:

"Certainly I am. I am going to wash all these things. The children cannot live in dirt."

He threw two or three handkerchiefs toward her, and after another long silence he said:

"Have you any money?"

She quickly rose to her feet and turned toward him, in her hand she held some of the soiled clothes.

"Money! Where should I get money unless I had stolen it? You know very well that day before yesterday you got three francs on my black skirt. We have breakfasted twice on that, and money goes fast. No, I have no money. I have four sous for the Lavatory. I cannot make money like other women we know."

He did not reply to this allusion, but rose from the bed, and passed in review the ragged garments hung around the room. He ended by taking down the pantaloons and the shawl and opening the bureau took out a sacque and two chemises. All these he made into a bundle, which he threw at Gervaise.

"Take them," he said, "and make haste back from the pawnbroker's."

"Would you not like me to take the children?" she asked. "Heavens! if pawnbrokers would only make loans on children, what a good thing it would be!"

She went to the Mont-de-Piété, and when she returned, a half hour later, she laid a silver five-franc piece on the mantel-shelf, and placed the ticket with the others between the two candlesticks.

"This is what they gave me," she said, coldly. "I wanted six francs, but they would not give them. They always keep on the safe side there, and yet there is always a crowd."

Lantier did not at once take up the money. He had sent her to the Mont-de-Piété, that he might not leave her without food or money, but when he caught sight of part of a ham wrapped in paper on the table, with half a loaf of bread, he slipped the silver piece into his vest pocket.

"I did not dare go to the milk-woman," explained Gervaise, "because we owe her for eight days. But I shall be back early. You can get some bread and some chops, and have them ready. Don't forget the wine, too."

He made no reply. Peace seemed to be made, but when Gervaise went to the trunk to take out some of Lantier's clothing, he called out:

"No—let that alone."

"What do you mean?" she said,

turning round in surprise. "You can't wear these things again until they are washed! Why shall I not take them?"

And she looked at him with some anxiety. He angrily tore the things from her hands and threw them back into the trunk.

"Confound you!" he muttered. "Will you never learn to obey? When I say a thing I mean it——"

"But why?" she repeated, turning very pale, and seized with a terrible suspicion. "You do not need these shirts—you are not going away. Why should I not take them?"

He hesitated a moment, uneasy under the earnest gaze she fixed upon him.

"Why? Why? Because," he said, "I am sick of hearing you say that you wash and mend for me. Attend to your own affairs, and I will attend to mine."

She entreated him—defended herself from the charge of ever having complained—but he shut the trunk with a loud bang, and then sat down upon it, repeating that he was master at least of his own clothing. Then, to escape from her eyes, he threw himself again on the bed, saying he was sleepy, and that she made his head ache, and finally slept, or pretended to do so.

Gervaise hesitated, she was tempted to give up her plan of going to the Lavatory, and thought she would sit down to her sewing. But at last she was reassured by Lantier's regular breathing, she took her soap and her ball of blueing, and going to the children, who were playing on the floor with some old corks, she said in a low voice:

"Be very good, and keep quiet. Papa is sleeping."

When she left the room there was not a sound except the stifled laughter of the little ones. It was then after ten, and the sun was shining brightly in at the window.

Gervaise, on reaching the Boulevard, turned to the left and followed the Rue de la Goutte-d'Or. As she passed Madame Fauconnier's shop, she nodded to the woman. The Lavatory, whither she went, was in the middle of this street, just where it begins to ascend. Over a large low building towered three enormous reservoirs for water, huge cylinders of zinc strongly made, and in the rear was the drying room, an apartment with very high ceiling, and surrounded by blinds through which the air passed. On the right of the reservoirs a steam engine let off regular puffs of white smoke. Gervaise, habituated apparently to puddles, did not lift her skirts, but threaded her way through the part of *eau de javelle* which encumbered the doorway. She knew the mistress of the establishment, a delicate woman, who sat in a cabinet with glass doors, surrounded by soap and blueing, and packages of bicarbonate of soda.

As Gervaise passed the desk, she asked for her brush and beater, which she had left to be taken care of after her last wash. Then, having taken her number, she went in. It was an immense shed, as it were, with a low ceiling—the beams and rafters unconcealed—and lighted by large windows, through which the daylight streamed. A light gray mist or stream pervaded the room, which was filled with a smell of soap suds and *eau de javelle* combined. Along the central aisle were tubs on either side, and two rows of women with their arms bare to the shoulders, and their skirts tucked up, stood showing their colored stockings and stout laced shoes.

They rubbed and pounded furiously, straightening themselves occasionally to utter a sentence, and then applying themselves again to their task, with the steam and perspiration pouring down their red faces. There was a constant rush of water from the faucets, a great splashing as the clothes were rinsed, and pounding and banging of the beaters, while amid all this noise the steam engine in the corner kept up its regular puffing.

Gervaise went slowly up the aisle, looking to the right and the left. She carried her bundle under her arm and limped more than usual, as she was pushed and jarred by the energy of the women about her.

"Here! this way, my dear," cried Madame Boche, and when the young woman had joined her at the very end where she stood, the Concierge, without stopping her furious rubbing, began to talk in a steady fashion.

"Yes, this is your place. I have kept it for up. I have not much to do. Boche is never hard on his linen, and you, too, do not seem to have much. Your package is quite small. We shall finish by noon, and then we can get something to eat. I used to give my clothes to a woman in La Rue Pelat, but bless my heart! she washed and pounded them all away; and I made up my mind to wash myself. It is

clear gain, you see, and costs only the soap."

Gervaise opened her bundle and sorted the clothes, laying aside all the colored pieces, and when Madame Boche advised her to try a little soda, she shook her head.

"No, no!" she said, "I know all about it!"

"You know?" answered Boche, curiously. "You have washed then, in your own place, before you came here?"

Gervaise, with her sleeves rolled up, showing her pretty, fair arms, was soaping a child's shirt. She rubbed it, and turned it, soaped and rubbed it again. Before she answered she took up her beater and began to use it, accenting each phrase, or rather punctuating them, with her regular blows.

"Yes, yes, washed—I should think I had! ever since I was ten years old. We went to the river side, where I came from. It was much nicer than here. I wish you could see it— a pretty corner under the trees by the running water. Do you know Plassans? near Marseilles?"

"You are a strong one, anyhow!" cried Madame Boche, astonished at the rapidity and strength of the woman. "Your arms are slender, but they are like iron."

The conversation continued until all the linen was well beaten and yet whole! Gervaise then took each piece separately, rinsed it, then rubbed it with soap and brushed it. That is to say, she held the cloth firmly with one hand, and with the other moved the short brush from her, pushing along a dirty foam which fell off into the water below.

As she brushed they talked.

"No, we are not married," said Gervaise. "I do not intend to lie about it. Lantier is not so nice that a woman need be very anxious to be his wife. If it were not for the children! I was fourteen and he was eighteen, when the first one was born. The other child did not come for four years. I was not happy at home. Papa Macquart, for the merest trifle, would beat me. I might have married, I suppose."

She dried her hands, which were red under the white soap suds.

"The water is very hard in Paris," she said.

Madame Boche had finished her work long before, but she continued to dabble in the water merely as an excuse to hear this story, which for two weeks had excited her curiosity. Her mouth was open, and her eyes were shining with satisfaction, at having guessed so well.

"Oh! yes, just as I knew;" she said to herself, "but the little woman talks too much! I was sure, though, there had been a quarrel."

Then aloud:

"He is not good to you, then?"

"He was very good to me once," answered Gervaise, "but since we came to Paris he has changed. His mother died last year, and left him about seventeen hundred francs. He wished to come to Paris, and as Father Macquart was in the habit of hitting me in the face without any warning, I said I would come too, which I did, with the two children. I meant to be a fine laundress, and he was to continue with

his trade as a hatter. We might have been very happy. But you see, Lantier is extravagant; he likes expensive things, and thinks of his amusement before anything else. He is not good for much, anyhow!

"We arrived at the Hôtel Montmartre. We had dinners and carriages, suppers and theatres, a watch for him, a silk dress for me—for he is not selfish when he has money. You can easily imagine therefore, at the end of two months, we were cleaned out. Then it was that we came to Hôtel Boncœur, and that this life began." She checked herself with a strange choking in the throat. Tears gathered in her eyes. She finished brushing her linen.

"I must get my scalding water," she murmured.

But Madame Boche, much annoyed at this sudden interruption to the long desired confidence, called the boy.

"Charles," she said, "it would be very good of you if you would bring a pail of hot water to Madame Lantier, as she is in a great hurry."

The boy brought a bucket full, and Gervaise paid him a sou. It was a sou for each bucket. She turned the hot water into her tub and soaked her linen once more and rubbed it with her hands, while the steam hovered round her blonde head like a cloud.

"Here, take some of this," said the Concierge, as she emptied into the water that Gervaise was using, the remains of a package of bicarbonate of soda. She offered her also some eau de javelle, but the young woman refused, "it was only good," she said, "for grease spots and wine stains."

"I thought him somewhat dissipated," said Madame Boche, referring to Lantier without naming him.

Gervaise, leaning over her tub, and her arms up to the elbows in the soap suds, nodded, in acquiescence.

"Yes," continued the Concierge, "I have seen many little things." But she started back, as Gervaise turned round with a pale face and quivering lips.

"Oh! I know nothing," she continued. "He likes to laugh, that is all, and those two girls who are with us, you know, Adèle and Virginie, like to laugh too, so they have their little jokes together, but that is all there is of it, I am sure."

The young woman with the perspiration standing on her brow, and her arms still dripping, looked her full in the face with earnest, inquiring eyes. Then the Concierge became excited, and struck her breast, exclaiming:

"I tell you I know nothing whatever, nothing more than I tell you!"

Then she added in a gentle voice, "But he has honest eyes, my dear. He will marry you child, I promise that he will marry you!"

Gervaise dried her forehead with her damp hand and shook her head. The two women were silent for a moment; around them too, it was very quiet. The clock struck eleven. Many of the women were seated swinging their feet, drinking their wine and eating their sausages, sandwiched between slices of bread. An occasional economical housewife hurried in with a small bundle under her arm, and a few sounds of the pounder were still heard at intervals; sentences were smothered in the full mouths, or a laugh was uttered, ending in a gurgling sound as the wine was swallowed, while the great machine puffed steadily on. Not one of the women, however, heard it —it was like the very respiration of the Lavatory—the eager breath that drove up among the rafters the floating vapor that filled the room.

The heat gradually became intolerable. The sun shone in on the left through the high windows, imparting to the vapor opaline tints—the palest rose and tender blue fading into soft grays. When the women began to grumble, the boy Charles went from one window to the other, drawing down the heavy linen shades. Then he crossed to the other side, the shady side, and opened the blinds. There was a general exclamation of joy—a formidable explosion of gayety.

All this time Gervaise was going on with her task and had just completed the washing of her colored pieces, which she threw over a trestle to drip; soon small pools of blue water stood on the floor. Then she began to rinse the garments in cold water which ran from a spigot near by.

"You have nearly finished," said Madame Boche. "I am waiting to help you wring them."

"Oh! you are very good! It is not necessary though!" answered the young woman, as she swashed the garments through the clear water. "If I had sheets I would not refuse your offer, however."

Nevertheless she accepted the aid of the Concierge. They took up a brown woolen skirt badly faded, from which poured out a yellow stream as the two women wrung it together. Suddenly Madame Boche cried out:

"Look! There comes Big Virginie! She is actually coming here to wash her rags tied up in a handkerchief."

Gervaise looked up quickly. Virginie was a woman about her own age —larger and taller than herself, a brunette, and pretty in spite of the elongated oval of her face. She wore an old black dress with flounces and a red ribbon at her throat. Her hair was carefully arranged and massed in a blue chenille net.

She hesitated a moment in the centre aisle and half shut her eyes, as if looking for something or somebody, but when she distinguished Gervaise she went toward her with a haughty, insolent air and supercilious smile, and finally established herself only a short distance from her.

"That is a new notion!" muttered Madame Boche, in a low voice. "She was never known before to rub out even a pair of cuffs. She is a lazy creature, I do assure you. She never sews the buttons on her boots. She is just like her sister, that minx of an Adèle, who stays away from the shop two days out of three. What is she rubbing now? A skirt, is it? It is dirty enough, I am sure!"

It was clear that Madame Boche wished to please Gervaise. The truth was she often took coffee with Adèle and Virginie, when the two sisters were in funds. Gervaise did not reply, but worked faster than before. She was now preparing her blueing water in a small tub standing on three legs. She dipped in her pieces, shook them about in the colored water, which was almost a lake in hue, and then wringing them,

she shook them out, and threw them lightly over the high wooden bars.

While she did this she kept her back well turned on Big Virginie. But she felt that the girl was looking at her, and she heard an occasional derisive sniff. Virginie in fact, seemed to have come there to provoke her, and when Gervaise turned around the two women fixed their eyes on each other.

"Let her be," murmured Madame Boche. "She is not the one, now I tell you!"

At this moment, as Gervaise was shaking her last piece of linen, she heard laughing and talking at the door of the Lavatory.

"Two children are here asking for their mother!" cried Charles.

All the women looked around, and Gervaise recognized Claude and Etienne. As soon as they saw her they ran toward her, splashing through the puddles, their untied shoes half off, and Claude, the eldest, dragging his little brother by the hand.

The women as they passed uttered kindly exclamations of pity, for the children were evidently frightened. They clutched their mother's skirts and buried their pretty blonde heads.

"Did papa send you?" asked Gervaise.

But as she stooped to tie Etienne's shoes, she saw on Claude's finger the key of her room, with its copper tag and number.

"Did you bring the key?" she exclaimed, in great surprise. "And why, pray?"

The child looked down on the key hanging on his finger, which he had apparently forgotten. This seemed to remind him of something, and he said, in a clear, shrill voice:

"Papa is gone!"

"He went to buy your breakfast, did he not? And he told you to come and look for me here, I suppose?"

Claude looked at his brother and hesitated. Then he exclaimed:

"Pape has gone, I say. He jumped from the bed, put his things in his trunk, and then he carried his trunk down stairs and put it on a carriage. We saw him—he has gone!"

Gervaise was kneeling, tying the boy's shoe. She rose slowly, with a very white face, and with her hands pressed to either temple, as if she were afraid of her head cracking open. She could say nothing but the same words over and over again:

"Great God! great God! great God!"

Madame Boche, in her turn, interrogated the child eagerly; for she was charmed at finding herself an actor, as it were, in this drama.

"Tell us all about it, my dear. He locked the door, did he? and then he told you to bring the key here?" And then lowering her voice, she whispered in the child's ear.

"Was there a lady in the carriage?" she asked.

The child looked troubled for a moment, but speedily began his story again with a triumphant air.

"He jumped off the bed, put his things in the trunk, and he went away."

Then as Madame Boche made no attempt to detain him, he drew his brother to the faucet, where the two amused themselves in making the water run.

Gervaise could not weep. She felt as if she were stifling. She covered her face with her hands, and turned toward the wall. A sharp, nervous trembling shook her from head to foot. An occasional sobbing sigh, or rather gasp, escaped from her lips, while she pressed her clenched hands more tightly on her eyes, as if to increase the darkness of the abyss in which she felt herself to have fallen.

"Come! come! my child!" muttered Madame Boche.

"If you knew! if you only knew all!" answered Gervaise. "Only this very morning he made me carry my shawl and my chemises to the *Mont-de-Piété*, and that was the money he had for the carriage"—

And the tears rushed to her eyes. The recollection of her visit to the pawnbroker's, of her hasty return with the money in her hand, seemed to let loose the sobs that strangled her, and was the one drop too much. Tears streamed from her eyes and poured down her face. She did not think of wiping them away.

"Be reasonable, child! be quiet," whispered Madame Boche. "They are all looking at you. Is it possible you can care so much for any man? You love him still, although such a little while ago you pretended you did not care for him; and you cry as if your heart would break! O Lord! what fools we women are!"

Then in a maternal tone she added:

"And such a pretty little woman as you are, too. But now I may as well tell you the whole, I suppose? Well! then, you remember when I was talking to you from the sidewalk, and you were at your window? I knew then that it was Lantier who came in with Adéle. I did not see his face, but I knew his coat, and Boche watched and saw him come down stairs this morning. But he was with Adéle, you understand? There is another person who comes to see Virginie twice a week."

She stopped for a moment to take breath, and then went on in a lower tone still.

"Take care! she is laughing at you —the heartless little cat! I bet all her washing is a sham. She has seen her sister and Lantier well off, and then came here to find out how you would take it."

Gervaise took her hands down from her face, and looked around. When she saw Virginie talking and laughing with two or three women, a wild tempest of rage shook her from head to foot. She stooped, with her arms extended, as if feeling for something, and moved along slowly for a step or two, then snatched up a bucket of soap suds and threw it at Virginie.

"You Devil! be off with you!" cried Virginie, starting back. Only her feet were wet.

All the women in the Lavatory hurried to the scene of action. They jumped up on the benches, some with a piece of bread in their hands, others with a bit of soap, and a circle of spectators was soon formed.

"Yes, she is a Devil!" repeated Virginie. "What has got into the fool?"

Gervaise stood motionless, her face convulsed and lips apart. The other continued:

"She got tired of the country, it seems, but she left one leg behind her, at all events."

The women laughed, and Big Virginie, elated at her success, went on in a louder and more triumphant tone:

"Come a little nearer, and I will soon settle you. You had better have remained in the country. It is lucky for you that your dirty soap suds only went on my feet, for I would have taken you over my knees and given you a good spanking, if one drop had gone in my face. What is the matter with her, anyway?" and Big Virginie addressed her audier:e. "Make her tell what I have done to her! Say! Fool— what harm have I ever done to you?"

"You had best not talk so much," answered Gervaise, almost inaudibly; "you know very well where my husband was seen yesterday. Now be quiet, or harm will come to you. I will strangle you—quick as a wink."

"Her husband, she says! Her husband! The lady's husband! As if a looking thing like that had a husband! Is it my fault if he has deserted her? Does she think I have stolen him? Anyway, he was much too good for her. But tell me, some of you, was his name on his collar? Madame has lost her——husband! She will pay a good reward, I am sure, to any one who will carry him back!"

The women all laughed. Gervaise, in a low, concentrated voice, repeated:

"You know very well — you know very well! your sister — yes, I will strangle your sister!"

"Oh! yes, I understand," answered Virginie, "strangle her if you choose. What do I care? and what are you staring at me for? Can't I wash my clothes in peace? Come, I am sick of this stuff! Let me alone!"

Big Virginie turned away, and after five or six angry blows with her beater, she began again:

"Yes, it is my sister, and the two adore each other. You should see them bill and coo together. He has left you, with these dirty-faced imps, and you left three others behind you with three fathers! It was your dear Lantier who told us all that. Ah! he had had quite enough of you—he said so!"

"Miserable fool!" cried Gervaise, white with anger.

She turned, and mechanically looked around on the floor, seeing nothing however, but the small tub of blueing water, she threw that in Virginie's face.

"She has spoiled my dress!" cried Virginie, whose shoulder and one hand was dyed a deep blue. "You just wait a moment!" she added, as she in her turn snatched up a tub and dashed its contents at Gervaise. Then ensued a most formidable battle. The two women ran up and down the room in eager haste, looking for full tubs, which they quickly flung in the faces of each other, and each deluge was heralded and accompanied by a shout.

"Is that enough? Will that cool you off?" cried Gervaise.

And from Virginie:

"Take that! It is good to have a bath once in your life!"

Finally the tubs and pails were all empty, and the two women began to draw water from the faucets. They continued their mutual abuse, while the water was running, and presently it was Virginie who received a bucket-ful in her face. The water ran down her back and over her skirts. She was stunned and bewildered, when suddenly there came another in her left ear, knocking her head nearly off her shoulders—her comb fell and with it her abundant hair.

Gervaise was attacked about her legs. Her shoes were filled with water, and she was drenched above her knees. Presently the two women were deluged from head to foot, their garments stuck to them, and they dripped like umbrellas which have been out in a heavy shower.

"What fun!" said one of the laundresses, as she looked on at a safe distance.

The whole Lavatory were immensely amused, and the women applauded as if at a theatre. The floor was covered an inch deep with water, through which the termagants splashed. Suddenly Virginie discovered a bucket of scalding water standing a little apart, she caught it and threw it upon Gervaise. There was an exclamation of horror from the lookers-on. Gervaise escaped with only one foot slightly burned; but exasperated by the pain, she threw a tub with all her strength at the legs of her opponent. Virginie fell to the ground.

"She has broken her leg!" cried one of the spectators.

"She deserved it," answered another, "for the tall one tried to scald her!"

"She was right, after all, if the blonde had taken away her man!"

Madame Boche rent the air with her exclamations, waving her arms frantically, high above her head. She had taken the precaution to place herself behind a rampart of tubs, with Claude and Etienne clinging to her skirts, weeping and sobbing in a paroxysm of terror and keeping up a cry of "Mamma! Mamma!" When she saw Virginie prostrate on the ground, she rushed to Gervaise and tried to pull her away.

"Come with me!" she urged. "Do be sensible. You are growing so angry that the Lord only knows what the end of all this will be!"

But Gervaise pushed her aside, and the old woman again took refuge behind the tubs with the children. Virginie made a spring at the throat of her adversary, and actually tried to strangle her. Gervaise shook her off, and snatched at the long braid hanging from the girl's head, and pulled it as if she hoped to wrench it off, and the head with it.

The battle began again, this time silent and wordless, and literally tooth and nail. Their extended hands, with fingers stiffly crooked, caught wildly at all in their way, scratching and tearing. The red ribbon and the chenille net worn by the brunette were torn off, the waist of her dress was ripped from throat to belt, and showed the white skin on the shoulder.

Gervaise had lost a sleeve, and her chemise was torn to her waist. Strips of clothing lay in every direction. It was Gervaise who was first wounded. Three long scratches from her mouth to her throat bled profusely, and she fought with her eyes shut lest she should be blinded. As yet Virginie showed no wound. Suddenly Gervaise seized one of her ear-rings — pear-shaped, of yellow glass—she tore it out and brought blood.

"They will kill each other! Separate them," cried several voices.

The women gathered around the combatants; the spectators were divided into two parties—some exciting and encouraging Gervaise and Virginie as if they had been dogs fighting, while others more timid trembled, turned away their heads, and said they were faint and sick. A general battle threatened to take place, such was the excitement.

Madame Boche called to the boy in charge:

"Charles! Charles! Where on earth can he be?"

Finally she discovered him, calmly looking on with his arms folded. He was a tall youth, with a big neck. He was laughing and hugely enjoying the scene. It would be a capital joke, he thought, if the women tore each other's clothes to rags, and if they should be compelled to finish their fight in a state of nudity.

"Are you there, then?" cried Madame Boche, when she saw him. "Come and help us separate them, or you can do it yourself."

"No, thank you," he answered, quietly. "I don't propose to have my own eyes scratched out! I am not here for that. Let them alone! It will do them no harm to let a little of their hot blood out!"

Madame Boche declared she would summon the police, but to this the mistress of the Lavatory, the delicate looking woman with weak eyes, strenuously objected.

"No, no, I will not. It would injure my house!" she said over and over again.

Both women lay on the ground. Suddenly Virginie struggled up to her knees. She had got possession of one of the beaters, which she brandished. Her voice was hoarse and low as she muttered:

"This will be as good for you, as for your dirty linen!"

Gervaise, in her turn, snatched another beater, which she held like a club. Her voice, also, was hoarse and low.

"I will beat your skin," she muttered, "as I would my coarse towels."

They knelt in front of each other in utter silence for at least a minute, with hair streaming, eyes glaring, and distended nostrils. They each drew a long breath.

Gervaise struck the first blow with her beater full on the shoulders of her adversary, and then threw herself over on the side to escape Virginie's weapon, which touched her on the hip.

Thus started they struck each other as laundresses strike their linen, in measured cadence.

The women about them ceased to laugh—many went away, saying they were faint. Those who remained watched the scene with a cruel light in their eyes. Madame Boche had taken Claude and Etienne to the other end of the room, whence came the dreary sound of their sobs which were heard through the dull blows of the beaters.

Suddenly Gervaise uttered a shriek. Virginie had struck her just above the elbow on her bare arm, and the flesh began to swell at once. She rushed at Virginie—her face was so terrible

that the spectators thought she meant to kill her.

"Enough! enough!" they cried.

With almost superhuman strength, she seized Virginie by the waist, bent her forward with her face to the brick floor, and notwithstanding her struggles lifted her skirts and showed the white and naked skin. Then she brought her beater down as she had formerly done at Plassans under the trees on the river side, where her employer had washed the linen of the garrison.

Each blow of the beater fell on the soft flesh with a dull thud, leaving a scarlet mark.

"Oh! oh!" murmured Charles, with his eyes nearly starting from his head.

The women were laughing again by this time, but soon the cry began again of "Enough! enough!"

Gervaise did not even hear. She seemed entirely absorbed, as if she were fulfilling an appointed task, and she talked with strange, wild gayety, recalling one of the rhymes of her childhood:

"Pan! Pan! Margot au lavoir,
Pan! Pan! à coups de battoir;
Pan! Pan! va laver son cœur,
Pan! Pan! tout noir de douleur."

"Take that for yourself, and that for your sister and this for Lantier. And now I shall begin all over again. That is for Lantier—that for your sister—and this for yourself!"

"Pan! Pan! Margot au lavoir!
Pan! Pan! à coups de battoir."

They tore Virginie from her hands. The tall brunette, weeping and sobbing, scarlet with shame, rushed out of the room, leaving Gervaise mistress of the field; who calmly arranged her dress somewhat, and as her arm was stiff, begged Madame Boche to lift her bundle of linen on her shoulder.

While the old woman obeyed, she dilated on her emotions during the scene that had just taken place.

"You ought to go to a doctor and see if something is not broken. I heard a queer sound," she said.

But Gervaise did not seem to hear her, and paid no attention either, to the women who crowded around her with congratulations. She hastened to the door where her children awaited her.

"Two hours!" said the mistress of the establishment, already installed in her glass cabinet. "Two hours and two sous!"

Gervaise mechanically laid down the two sous, and then, limping painfully under the weight of the wet linen which was slung over her shoulder, and dripped as she moved—with her injured arm and bleeding cheek—she went away, dragging after her with her naked arm, the still sobbing and tear-stained Etienne and Claude.

Behind her the Lavatory resumed its wonted busy air, a little gayer than usual from the excitement of the morning. The women had eaten their bread, and drank their wine, and they splashed the water and used their beaters with more energy than usual, as they recalled the blows dealt by Gervaise. They talked from alley to alley—leaning over their tubs. Words and laughs were lost in the sound of running water. The steam and mist were golden in the sun that came in through holes in the curtain. The odor of soap suds grew stronger and stronger.

When Gervaise entered the alley which led to the Hôtel Boncœur her tears choked her. It was a long, dark, narrow alley, with a gutter on one side, close to the wall, and the loathsome smell brought to her mind the recollection of having passed through there with Lantier, a fortnight previous.

And what had that fortnight been? A succession of quarrels and dissensions, the remembrance of which would be forevermore a regret and bitterness.

Her room was empty, filled with the glowing sunlight from the open window. This golden light rendered more apparent the blackened ceiling and the walls with the shabby, dilapidated paper. There was not an article beyond the furniture left in the room, except a woman's fichu that seemed to have caught on a nail near the chimney. The children's bed was pulled out into the centre of the room—the bureau drawers were wide open, displaying their emptiness. Lantier had washed and had used the last of the pomade—two cents worth on the back of a playing card—the dirty water in which he had washed, still stood in the basin. He had forgotten nothing, the corner hitherto occupied by his trunk now seemed to Gervaise a vast desert. Even the small mirror was gone. With a presentiment of evil she turned hastily to the chimney. Yes, she was right, Lantier had carried away the tickets. The pink papers were no longer between the candlesticks!

She threw her bundle of linen into a chair, and stood looking first at one thing and then at another, in a dull agony that no tears came to relieve.

She had but one sou in the world She heard a merry laugh from her boys, who, already consoled, were at the window. She went toward them, and laying a hand on each of their heads, looked out on that scene on which her weary eyes had dwelt so long that same morning.

Yes, it was on that street that she and her children would soon be thrown, and she turned her hopeless despairing eyes toward the outer Boulevards— looking from right to left, lingering at the two extremities, seized by a feeling of terror, as if her life thenceforward was to be spent between a slaughter house and a hospital.

## CHAPTER II

### GERVAISE AND COUPEAU

THREE weeks later, about half past eleven one fine sunny morning, Gervaise and Coupeau, the tinworker, were eating some brandied fruit at the Assommoir.

Coupeau, who was smoking outside, had seen her as she crossed the street with her linen, and compelled her to enter. Her huge basket was on the floor, back of the little table where they sat.

Father Colombe's Tavern, known as the Assommoir, was on the corners of the Rue des Poissonniers and of the Boulevard de Rochechouart. The sign bore the one single word, in long, blue letters,

*DISTILLATION.*

And this word stretched from one end to the other. On either side of the door stood tall oleanders in small casks, their leaves covered thick with dust. The enormous counter with its rows of glasses, its fountain, and its pewter measures, was on the left of the door; and the huge room was ornamented by gigantic casks painted bright yellow, and highly varnished, hooped with shining copper. On high shelves were bottles of liquors, and jars of fruits; all sorts of flasks standing in order concealed the wall, and repeated their pale green or deep crimson tints in the great mirror behind the counter.

The great feature of the house however, was the distilling apparatus, which stood at the back of the room behind an oak railing, on which the tipsy workmen leaned, as they stupidly watched the still, with its long neck and serpentine tubes descending to subterranean regions—a very devil's kitchen.

At this early hour the Assommoir was nearly empty. A stout man in his shirt sleeves—Father Colombe himself—was serving a little girl not more than twelve years old, with four cents worth of liquor in a cup.

The sun streamed in at the door, and lay on the floor, which was black where the men had spat as they smoked. And from the counter—from the casks— from all the room—rose an alcoholic emanation which seemed to intoxicate the very particles of dust floating in the sunshine.

In the meantime, Coupeau rolled a new cigarette. He was very neat and clean, wearing a blouse and a little blue cloth cap, and showing his white teeth as he smiled.

The lower jaw was somewhat prominent, and the nose slightly flat; he had fine brown eyes, and the face of a happy child and good natured animal. His hair was thick and curly. His complexion was delicate still, for he was only twenty-six. Opposite him sat Gervaise in a black gown, leaning slightly forward, finishing her fruit, which she held by the stem.

They were near the street, at the first of the four tables arranged in front of the counter. When Coupeau had lighted his cigar, he placed both elbows on the table and looked at the woman without speaking. Her pretty face had that day, something of the delicate transparency of fine porcelain.

Then continuing something which they apparently had been previously discussing, he said in a low voice:

"Then you say no, do you? Absolutely no?"

"Of course. No, it must be Monsieur Coupeau," answered Gervaise, with a smile. "Surely you do not intend to begin that again here! You promised to be reasonable, too. Had I known, I should certainly have refused your treat."

He did not speak, but gazed at her more intently than before, with tender boldness. He looked at her soft eyes, and dewy lips, pale at the corners, but half parted, allowing one to see the rich crimson within.

She returned his look with a kind and affectionate smile. Finally she said:

"You should not think of such a thing. It is folly! I am an old woman. I have a boy eight years old. What should we do together?"

"Much as other people do, I suppose!" answered Coupeau, with a wink.

She shrugged her shoulders.

"You know nothing about it, Monsieur Coupeau, but I have had some experience. I have two mouths in the house, and they have excellent appetites.

How am I to bring up my children if I trifle away my time? Then, too, my misfortune has taught me one great lesson, which is, that the less I have to do with men, the better!"

She then proceeded to explain all her reasons, calmly and without anger. It was easy to see that her words were the result of grave consideration.

Coupeau listened quietly, saying only at intervals:

"You are hurting my feelings. Yes, hurting my feelings ———"

"Yes, I see that," she answered, "and I am really very sorry for you. If I had any idea of leading a different life from that which I follow to-day, it might as well be with you as with another. You have the look of a good-natured man. But what is the use? I have now been with Madame Fauconnier for a fortnight. The children are going to school, and I am very happy, for I have plenty to do. Don't you see, therefore, that it is best for us to remain as we are?"

And she stooped to pick up her basket.

"You are keeping me here to talk," she said, "and they are waiting for me at my employers'. You will find some other woman, Monsieur Coupeau, far prettier than I, who will not have two children to bring up!"

He looked at the clock, and made her sit down again.

"Wait!" he cried. "It is still thirty-five minutes of eleven. I have twenty-five minutes still, and don't be afraid of my familiarity, for the table is between us! Do you dislike me so very much that you can't stay and talk with me for five minutes?"

She put down her basket, unwilling to seem disobliging, and they talked for some time in a friendly sort of way. She had breakfasted before she left home, and he had swallowed his soup in the greatest haste, and laid in wait for her as she came out. Gervaise, as she listened to him, watched from the windows—between the bottles of brandied fruit—the movement of the crowd in the street, which at this hour—that of the Parisian breakfast—was unusually lively. Workmen hurried into the Bakers, and coming out with a loaf under their arms, they went into the *Veau à Deaux Têtes,* three doors higher up, to breakfast at six sous. Next the Baker's, was a shop where fried potatoes, and mussels with parsley, were sold. A constant succession of shop girls carried off paper parcels of fried potatoes and cups filled with mussels, and others bought bunches of radishes. When Gervaise leaned a little more toward the window, she saw still another shop, also crowded, from which issued a steady stream of children holding in their hands, wrapped in paper, a breaded cutlet, or a sausage, still warm.

A group formed around the door of the Assommoir.

"Say!  Bibi-la-Grillade," asked a voice; "will you stand a drink all around?"

Five workmen went in, and the same voice said:

"Father Colombe, be honest now. Give us honest glasses, and no nut-shells, if you please."

Presently three more workmen entered together, and finally a crowd of blouses passed in between the dusty oleanders.

"You have no business to ask such questions," said Gervaise to Coupeau; "of course I loved him.  But after the manner in which he deserted me"—

They were speaking of Lantier. Gervaise had never seen him again; she supposed him to be living with Virginie's sister—with the friend who was about to start a manufactory for hats.

At first she thought of committing suicide, of drowning herself; but she had grown more reasonable, and had really begun to trust that things were all for the best.  With Lantier she felt sure she never could have done justice to the children, so extravagent were his habits.

He might come, of course, and see Claude and Etienne.  She would not show him the door; only so far as she herself was concerned, he had best not lay his finger on her  And she uttered these words in a tone of determination, like a woman whose plan of life is clearly defined; while Coupeau, who was by no means inclined to give her up lightly, teased and questioned her in regard to Lantier with none too much delicacy, it is true, but his teeth were so white and his face so merry that the woman could not take offence.

"Did you beat him?" he asked, finally.  "Oh! you are none too amiable. You beat people sometimes, I have heard."

She laughed gayly.

Yes, it was true she had whipped that great Virginie.  That day she could have strangled some one with a glad heart.  And she laughed again, because Coupeau told her that Virginie, in her humiliation, had left the Quartier.

Gervaise's face, as she laughed, however, had a certain childish sweetness. She extended her slender, dimpled hands, declaring she would not hurt a fly. All she knew of blows was, that she had received a good many in her life. Then she began to talk of Plassans and of her youth. She had never been indiscreet, nor was she fond of men. When she had fallen in with Lantier she was only fourteen, and she regarded him as her husband. Her only fault, she declared, was that she was too amiable, and allowed people to impose on her, and that she got fond of people too easily; were she to love another man, she should wish and expect to live quietly and comfortably with him always, without any nonsense.

And when Coupeau slyly asked her if she called her dear children nonsense, she gave him a little slap and said that she, of course, was much like other women. But women were not like men, after all; they had their homes to take care of and keep clean; she was like her mother, who had been a slave to her brutal father for more than twenty years!

"My very lameness," she continued—"Your lameness?" interrupted Coupeau, gallantly; "why, it is almost nothing. No one would ever notice it!"

She shook her head. She knew very well that it was very evident, and at forty it would be far worse; but she said softly, with a faint smile, "You have a strange taste, to fall in love with a lame woman!"

He, with his elbows on the table, still coaxed and entreated, but she continued to shake her head in the negative. She listened, with her eyes fixed on the street, seemingly fascinated by the surging crowd.

The shops were being swept—the last frying pan of potatoes was taken from the stove—the pork merchant washed the plates his customers had used, and put his place in order. Groups of mechanics were hurrying out from all the workshops, laughing and pushing each other like so many school-boys, making a great scuffling on the sidewalk with their hob-nailed shoes; while some, with their hands in their pockets, smoked in a meditative fashion, looking up at the sun and winking prodigiously. The sidewalks were crowded, and the crowd constantly added to, by men who poured from the open door—men in blouses and frocks, old jackets and coats, which showed all their defects in the clear morning light.

The bells of the various manufactories were ringing loudly, but the workmen did not hurry. They deliberately lighted their pipes, and then with rounded shoulders slouched along, dragging their feet after them.

Gervaise mechanically watched a group of three, one man much taller than the other two, who seemed to be hesitating as to what they should do next. Finally they came directly to the Assommoir.

"I know them," said Coupeau, "or rather I know the tall one. It is Mes-Bottes, a comrade of mine."

The Assommoir was now crowded with boisterous men. Two glasses rang with the energy with which they brought down their fists on the counter. They stood in rows, with their hands crossed over their stomachs, or folded behind their backs, waiting their turn to be served by Father Colombe.

"Hallo!" cried Mes-Bottes, giving Coupeau a rough slap on the shoulders, "how fine you have got to be with your cigarettes and your linen shirt bosom! Who is your friend that pays for all this? I should like to make her acquaintance."

"Don't be so silly!" returned Coupeau, angrily.

But the other gave a knowing wink.

"Ah! I understand— 'A word to the wise' "—and he turned round with a fearful lurch to look at Gervaise, who shuddered and recoiled. The tobacco smoke—the odor of humanity added to this air heavy with alcohol, was oppressive—and she choked a little and coughed.

"Ah! what an awful thing it is to drink!" she said in a whisper to her friend, to whom she then went on to say, how years before, she had drank anisette with her mother at Plassans, and how it had made her so very sick that ever since that day, she had never been able to endure even the smell of liquors.

"You see," she added, as she held up her glass, "I have eaten the fruit; but I left the brandy, for it would make me ill."

Coupeau also failed to understand how a man could swallow glasses of brandy and water, one after the other. Brandied fruit, now and again, was not bad. As to absinthe and similar abominations, he never touched them —not he, indeed. His comrades might laugh at him as much as they pleased; he always remained on the other side

of the door, when they came in to swallow perdition like that.

His father, who was a tin worker like himself, had fallen one day from the roof of No. 25, in La Rue Coquenaud, and this recollection had made him very prudent ever since. As for himself, when he passed through that street and saw the place, he would sooner drink the water in the gutter, than swallow a drop at the wine shop. He concluded with the sentence:

"You see in my trade, a man needs a clear head and steady legs."

Gervaise had taken up her basket— she had not risen from her chair, however, but held it on her knees, with a dreary look in her eyes as if the words of the young mechanic had awakened in her mind strange thoughts of a possible future.

She answered in a low, hesitating tone, without any apparent connection: "Heavens knows I am not ambitious. I do not ask for much in this world. My idea would be to live a quiet life, and always have enough to eat—a clean place to live in—with a comfortable bed, a table and a chair or two. Yes, I would like to bring my children up in that way, and see them good and industrious. I should not like to run the risk of being beaten—no, that would not please me at all!"

She hesitated, as if to find something else to say, and then resumed:

"Yes, and at the end I should wish to die in my bed in my own home!"

She pushed back her chair and rose. Coupeau argued with her vehemently, and then gave an uneasy glance at the clock. They did not, however, depart at once. She wished to look at the still, and stood for some minutes gazing with curiosity at the great copper machine. The tin worker, who had followed her, explained to her how the thing worked, pointing out with his finger the various parts of the machine, and showed the enormous retort whence fell the clear stream of alcohol. The still, with its intricate and endless coils of wire and pipes had a dreary aspect. Not a breath escaped from it and hardly a sound was heard. It was like some night task performed in daylight, by a melancholy silent workman.

In the meantime Mes-Bottes, accompanied by his two comrades, had lounged to the oak railing, and leaned there until there was a corner of the counter free. He laughed a tipsy laugh as he stood with his eyes fixed on the machine.

"By thunder!" he muttered, "that is a jolly little thing!"

He went on to say that it held enough to keep their throats fresh for a week. As for himself, he should like to hold the end of that pipe between his teeth, and he should like to feel that liquor run down his throat, in a steady stream, until it reached his heels.

The still did its work slowly but surely. There was not a glimmer on its surface—no firelight reflected in its clean colored sides. The liquor dropped steadily, and suggested a persevering stream, which would gradually invade the room, spread over the streets and Boulevard, and finally deluge and inundate Paris itself.

Gervaise shuddered and drew back. She tried to smile, but her lips quivered as she murmured:

"It frightens me—that machine! It makes me feel cold to see that constant drip"——

Then returning to the idea which had struck her as the acme of human happiness, she said:

"Say, do you not think that would be very nice? To work and have plenty to eat—to have a little home all to one's self—to bring up children, and then die in one's bed?"

"And not be beaten," added Coupeau, gayly. "But I will promise never to beat you, Madame Gervaise, if you will agree to what I ask. I will promise also never to drink, because I love you too much! Come now, say yes."

He lowered his voice and spoke with his lips close to her throat, while she, holding her basket in front of her was making a path through the crowd of men.

But she did not say no or shake her head as she had done. She glanced up at him with a half tender smile, and seemed to rejoice in the assurance he gave that he did not drink.

It was clear that she would have said yes, if she had not sworn never to have anything more to do with men.

Finally they reached the door, and went out of the place, leaving it crowded to overflowing. The fumes of alcohol, and the tipsy voices of the men carousing, went out into the street with them.

Mes-Bottes was h e a r d accusing Father Colombe of cheating, by not filling his glasses more than half full, and he proposed to his comrades to go in future to another place, where they could do much better and get more for their money.

"Ah!" said Gervaise, drawing a long

breath when they stood on the sidewalk, "here one can breathe again. Good-bye, Monsieur Coupeau, and many thanks for your politeness. I must hasten now!"

She moved on, but he took her hand and held it fast.

"Go a little way with me. It will not be much further for you. I must stop at my sister's before I go back to the shop."

She yielded to his entreaties, and they walked slowly on together. He told her about his family. His mother, a tailoress, was the housekeeper. Twice she had been obliged to give up her work on account of trouble with her eyes. She was sixty-two on the third of the last month. He was her youngest child. One of his sisters, Madame Lerat, a widow, thirty-six years old, was a flower maker, and lived at Batignolles, in La Rue Des Moines. The other, who was thirty, had married a chain maker—a man by the name of Lorilleux. It was to their rooms that he was now going. They lived in that great house on the left. He ate his dinner every night with them; it was an economy for them all. But he wanted to tell them now, not to expect him that night, as he was invited to dine with a friend.

Gervaise interrupted him suddenly:

"Did I hear your friend call you Cadet-Cassis?"

"Yes. That is a name they have given me, because when they drag me into a wine shop, it is Cassis I always take. I had as lief be called 'Cadet-Cassis' as 'Mes-Bottes,' any time."

"I do not think Cadet-Cassis so very bad," answered Gervaise, and she asked him about his work. How long should he be employed on the new Hospital?

"Oh," he answered, "there was never any lack of work." He had always more than he could do. He should remain in that shop at least a year, for he had yards and yards of gutters to make.

"Do you know," he said, "when I am up there I can see the Hôtel Boncœur. Yesterday you were at the window, and I waved my hand, but you did not see me."

They by this time had turned into La Rue de la Goutte d 'Or. He stopped and looked up.

"There is the house," he said, "and I was born only a few doors further off. It is an enormous place."

Gervaise looked up and down the façade. It was indeed enormous. The house was of five stories, with fifteen windows on each floor. The blinds were black, and with many of the slats broken, which gave an indescribable air of ruin and desolation to the place. Four shops occupied the rez de chaussée. On the right of the door was a large room, occupied as a cookshop. On the left was a charcoal vender, a thread and needle shop, and an establishment for the manufacture of umbrellas.

The house appeared all the higher for the reason, that on either side were two low buildings, squeezed close to it, and stood square, like a block of granite roughly hewn, against the blue sky. Totally without ornament, the house grimly suggested a prison.

Gervaise looked at the entrance, an immense doorway which rose to the height of the second story, and made a deep passage, at the end of which was a large court yard. In the centre of this doorway, which was paved like the street, ran a gutter full of pale, rose colored water.

"Come up," said Coupeau, "they won't eat you."

Gervaise preferred to wait for him in the street, but she consented to go as far as the room of the Concierge, which was within the porch, on the left.

When she had reached this place she again looked up.

Within there were six floors, instead of five, and four regular façades surrounded the vast square of the court yard. The walls were gray—covered with patches of leprous yellow, stained by the dripping from the slate covered roof. The wall had not even a moulding to break its dull uniformity—only the gutters ran across it. The windows had neither shutters nor blinds, but showed the panes of glass which were greenish and full of bubbles. Some were open, and from them hung checked mattresses and sheets to air. Lines were stretched in front of others, on which the family wash was hung to dry —men's shirts, women's chemises and children's breeches! There was a look as if the dwellers under that roof found their quarters too small, and were oozing out at every crack and aperture.

For the convenience of each façade, there was a narrow, high doorway, from which a damp passage led to the rear, where were four stair-cases, with iron railings. These each had one of the first four letters of the alphabet painted at the side.

The Rez de Chaussée was divided into enormous workshops, and lighted by windows black with dust. The forge of a locksmith blazed in one: from another came the sound of a carpenter's plane—while near the doorway a pink stream from a dyeing establishment poured into the gutter. Pools of stagnant water stood in the courtyard, all littered with shavings and fragments of charcoal. A few pale tufts of grass struggled up between the flat stones, and the whole courtyard was lighted but dimly.

In the shade near the water faucet, three small hens were pecking, with the vain hope of finding a worm and Gervaise looked about her, amazed at the enormous place which seemed like a little world, and as interested in the house as if it were a living creature.

"Are you looking for any one?" asked the Concierge, coming to her door considerably puzzled.

But the young woman explained that she was waiting for a friend, and then turned back toward the street. As Coupeau still delayed, she returned to the courtyard, finding in it a strange fascination.

The house did not strike her as especially ugly. At some of the windows were plants—a wall flower, blooming in a pot—a caged canary, who uttered an occasional warble—and several shaving mirrors caught the light and shone like stars.

A cabinet-maker sang, accompanied by the regular whistling sounds of his plane, while from the locksmith's quarters came a clatter of hammers struck in cadence.

At almost all the open windows the laughing, dirty faces of merry children were seen, and women sat, with their calm faces in profile, bending over their work. It was the quiet time—after the morning labors were over, and the men were gone to their work, and the house was comparatively quiet, disturbed only by the sounds of the various trades. The same refrain repeated hour after hour has a soothing effect, Gervaise thought.

To be sure, the courtyard was a little damp. Were she to live there, she should certainly perfer a room on the sunny side.

She went in several steps, and breathed that heavy odor of the homes of the poor—an odor of old dust, of rancid dirt and grease; but as the acridity of the smells from the dye-house predominated, she decided it to be far better than the Hôtel Boncœur.

She selected a window—a window in the corner on the left, where there was a small box planted with scarlet beans, whose slender tendrils were beginning to wind round a little arbor of strings. "I have made you wait too long, I am afraid," said Coupeau, whom she suddenly heard at her side. "They make a great fuss when I do not dine there, and she did not like it to-day, especially as my sister had bought veal. You are looking at this house," he continued. "Think of it—it is always lit from top to bottom. There are a hundred lodgers in it. If I had any furniture I would have had a room in it long ago. It would be very nice here, wouldn't it?"

"Yes," murmured Gervaise, "very nice indeed. At Plassans there were not so many people in one whole street. Look up at that window on the fifth floor—the window, I mean, where those beans are growing. See how pretty that is!"

He, with his usual recklessness, declared he would hire that room for her, and they would live there together.

She turned away with a laugh, and begged him not to talk any more nonsense. The house might stand or fall—they would never have a room in it together.

But Coupeau, all the same, was not reproved when he held her hand longer than was necessary, in bidding her farewell, when they reached Madame Fauconnier's laundry.

For another month the kindly intercourse between Gervaise and Coupeau continued on much the same footing. He thought her wonderfully courageous—declared she was killing herself with hard work all day and sitting up half the night to sew for the children. She was not like the women he had known; she took life too seriously, by far!

She laughed and defended herself modestly. Unfortunately, she said, she had not always been discreet. She alluded to her first confinement when she was not more than fourteen—and to the bottles of anisette she had emptied with her mother—but she had learned much from experience, she said. He was mistaken, however, in thinking she was persevering and strong. She was, on the contrary, very weak, and too easily influenced, as she had discovered to her cost. Her dream had always been, to live in a respectable way, among respectable people; because bad company knocks the life out of a woman. She trembled when she thought of the future, and said she was like a sou thrown up in the air—falling, heads up or down, according to chance—on the muddy pavement. All she had seen, the bad example spread before her childish eyes, had given her valuable lessons. But Coupeau laughed at these gloomy notions and brought back her courage by attempting to put his arm around her waist. She slapped his hands, and he cried out that "for a weak woman, she managed to hurt a fellow considerably!"

As for himself, he was always as merry as a grig, and no fool, either. He parted his hair carefully on one side, wore pretty cravats and patent leather shoes on Sunday, and was as saucy as only a fine Parisian workman can be.

They were of mutual use to each other at the Hôtel Boncœur. Coupeau went for her milk, did many little errands for her, and carried home her linen to her customers, and often took the children out to walk. Gervaise, to return these courtesies, went up to the tiny room where he slept, and in his absence looked over his clothes, sewed on buttons and mended his garments. They grew to be very good and cordial friends. He was to her a constant source of amusement. She listened to the songs he sang, and to their slang and nonsense, which as yet had for her, much of the charm of novelty. But he began to grow uneasy, and his smiles were less frequent. He asked her whenever they met, the same question, "When shall it be?"

She answered invariably with a jest, but passed her days in a fire of indelicate allusions however, which did not bring a flush to her cheek. So long as he was not rough and brutal, she objected to nothing; but one day she was very angry when he, in trying to steal a kiss, tore out a lock of her hair.

About the last of June Coupeau became absolutely morose, and Gervaise was so much disturbed by certain glances he gave her, that she fairly barricaded her door at night. Finally one Tuesday evening, when he had sulked from the previous Sunday, he came to her door at eleven in the evening. At first she refused to open it; but his voice was so gentle, so sad even, that she pulled away the barrier she had pushed against the door for her better protection. When he came in, she was startled, and thought him ill, he was so deadly pale and his eyes were so bright. No, he was not ill, he said, but things could not go on like this; he could not sleep.

"Listen, Madame Gervaise," he exclaimed, with tears in his eyes and a strange choking sensation in his throat. "We must be married at once. That is all there is to be said about it."

Gervaise was astonished and very grave.

"Oh! Monsieur Coupeau, I never dreamed of this, as you know very well, and you must not take such a step lightly."

But he continued to insist—he was certainly fully determined. He had come down to her then, without waiting until morning, merely because he needed a good sleep. As soon as she said yes, he would leave her. But he should not go until he heard that word.

"I cannot say yes in such a hurry," remonstrated Gervaise. "I do not choose to run the risk of your telling me at some future day, that I led you into this. You are making a great mistake, I assure you. Suppose you should not see me for a week—you would forget me entirely. Men sometimes marry for a fancy, and in twenty-four hours would gladly take it all back. Sit down here and let us talk a little."

They sat in that dingy room, lighted only by one candle which they forgot to snuff, and discussed the expediency of their marriage until after midnight—speaking very low, lest they should disturb the children, who were asleep with their heads on the same pillow.

And Gervaise pointed them out to Coupeau. That was an odd sort of dowry to carry a man surely! How could she venture to go to him with such encumbrances? Then too, she was troubled about another thing. People would laugh at him. Her story was known—her lover had been seen, and there would be no end of talk if she should marry now.

To all these good and excellent reasons, Coupeau answered with a shrug of his shoulders. What did he care for talk and gossip? He never meddled with the affairs of others, why should they meddle with his?

Yes, she had children to be sure, and he would look out for them with her. He had never seen a woman in his life, who was so good and so courageous and patient. Besides, that had nothing to do with it! Had she been ugly and lazy, with a dozen dirty children, he would have wanted her, and only her.

"Yes," he continued, tapping her on the knee, "you are the woman I want, and none other. You have nothing to say against that, I suppose?"

Gervaise melted by degrees. Her resolution forsook her, and a weakness of her heart and her senses overwhelmed her in the face of this brutal passion. She ventured only a timid objection or two. Her hands lay loosely folded on her knees, while her face was very gentle and sweet.

Through the open window came the soft air of a fair June night—the candle flickered in the wind—from the street came the sobs of a child, the child of a drunken man, who was lying just in front of the door in the street. From a long distance the breeze brought the notes of a violin, playing at a restaurant for some late marriage festival—a delicate strain it was too, clear and sweet as musical glasses.

Coupeau, seeing that the young woman had exhausted all her arguments, snatched her hands and drew her toward him. She was in one of those moods which she so much distrusted, when she could refuse no one anything. But the young man did not understand this, and he contented himself with simply holding her hands closely in his.

"You say yes, do you not?" he asked.

"How you tease," she replied. "You wish it—well then, yes. Heaven grant that the day will not come when you will be sorry for it."

He started up, lifting her from her feet and kissed her loudly. He glanced at the children.

"Hush!" he said, "we must not wake the boys. Good night."

And he went out of the room. Gervaise, trembling from head to foot, sat for a full hour on the side of her bed without undressing. She was profoundly touched, and thought Coupeau very honest and very kind. The tipsy man in the street uttered a groan like that of a wild beast, and the notes of the violin had ceased.

The next evening, Coupeau urged Gervaise to go with him to call on his sister. But the young woman shrank with ardent fear from this visit to the Lorilleux. She saw perfectly well that her lover stood in dread of these people.

He was in no way dependent on this sister, who was not the eldest either. Mother Coupeau would gladly give her consent, for she had never been known to contradict her son. In the family, however, the Lorilleux were supposed to earn ten francs per day, and this gave them great weight. Coupeau would never venture to marry unless they agreed to accept his wife.

"I have told them about you," he said. "Gervaise—Good Heavens! what a baby you are! Come there, to-night, with me; you will find my sister a little stiff, and Lorilleux is none too amiable. The truth is they are much vexed —because, you see, if I marry, I shall no longer dine with them—and that is their great economy. But that makes no odds; they won't put you out of doors. Do what I ask, for it is absolutely necessary."

These words frightened Gervaise nearly out of her wits. One Saturday evening, however, she consented. Coupeau came for her at half-past eight. She was all ready, wearing a black dress, a shawl with printed palm leaves in yellow, and a white cap with fluted ruffles. She had saved seven francs for the shawl, and two francs fifty centimes for the cap; the dress was an old one, cleaned and made over.

"They expect you," said Coupeau, as they walked along the street, "and

they have become accustomed to the idea of seeing me married. They are really quite amiable to-night. Then, too, if you have never seen a gold chain made, you will be much amused in watching it. They have an order for Monday."

"And have they gold in these rooms?" asked Gervaise.

"I should say so! It is on the walls, on the floors—everywhere!"

By this time they had reached the door, and had entered the courtyard. The Lorilleux lived on the sixth floor— staircase B. Coupeau told her, with a laugh, to keep tight hold of the iron railing and not let it go.

She looked up, half shutting her eyes, and gasped as she saw the height to which the staircase wound. The last gas burner, higher up, looked like a star trembling in a black sky, while two others, on alternate floors, cast long slanting rays down the interminable stairs.

"Ah! Ha!" cried the young man, as they stopped a moment on the second landing, "I smell onion soup; somebody has evidently been eating onion soup about here, and it smells good, too."

It is true. Staircase B, dirty and greasy—both steps and railing with plastering knocked off and showing the laths beneath—was permeated with the smell of cooking. From each landing ran narrow corridors, and on either side were half open doors, painted yellow and black, with finger marks about the lock and handles, and through the open window came the damp, disgusting smell of sinks and sewers mingling with the odor of onions.

Up to the sixth floor came the noises

from the *rez-de-chaussée*—the rattling of dishes being washed—the scraping of saucepans, and all that sort of thing. On one floor Gervaise saw through an open door on which were the words *"Designer and Draughtsman"* in large letters—two men seated at a table, covered with a varnished cloth, they were disputing violently amid thick clouds of smoke from their pipes. The second and third floors were the quietest. Here, through the open doors, came the sound of a cradle rocking—the wail of a baby—a woman's voice—the rattle of a spoon against a cup. On one door she read a placard, *Madame Gaudron, Carder*—on the next —*Monsieur Madinier, Manufacturer of Boxes.*

On the fourth there was a great quarrel going on—blows and oaths; which did not prevent the neighbors opposite from playing cards with their door wide open for the benefit of the air. When Gervaise reached the fifth floor she was out of breath. Such innumerable stairs were a novelty to her. These winding railings made her dizzy. One family had taken possession of the landing— the father was washing plates in a small earthen pan, near the sink, while the mother was scrubbing the baby before putting it to sleep. Coupeau laughingly bade Gervaise keep up her courage; and at last they reached the top, and she looked around to see whence came the clear, shrill voice, which she had heard above all other sounds, ever since her foot touched the first stair. It was a little, old woman, who sang as she worked, and her work was dressing dolls at three cents apiece. Gervaise clung to the railing, all out of breath,

and looked down into the depths below —the gas burner now looked like a star at the bottom of a deep well. The smells, the turbulent life of this great house seemed to rush over her in one tremendous gust. She gasped and turned pale.

"We have not got there yet," said Coupeau, "we have much further to go"; and he turned to the left, and then to the right again. The corridor stretched out before them, faintly lighted by an occasional gas burner— a sucession of doors, like those of a prison or a convent, continued to appear—nearly all wide open, showing the sordid interiors. Finally they reached a corridor that was entirely dark.

"Here we are," said the tin-worker. "Isn't it a journey? Look out for three steps. Hold on to the wall."

And Gervaise moved cautiously for ten paces, or more. She counted the three steps, and then Coupeau pushed open a door, without knocking. A bright light streamed forth. They went in.

It was a long, narrow apartment, almost like a prolongation of the corridor; a woolen curtain, faded and spotted, drawn on one side, divided the room in two.

One compartment, the first—contained a bed, pushed under the corner of the Mansard roof—a stove, still warm from the cooking of the dinner; two chairs, a table and a wardrobe. To place this last piece of furniture where it stood, between the bed and the door, had necessitated sawing away a portion of the ceiling.

The second compartment was the

workshop. At the back, a tiny forge, with bellows—on the right, a vice, screwed against the wall, under an étagère, where were iron tools piled up —on the left, in front of the window, was a small table, covered with pincers, magnifying glasses, tiny scales and shears—all dirty and greasy.

"We have come!" cried Coupeau, going as far as the woolen curtain.

But he was not answered immediately.

Gervaise, much agitated by the idea that she was entering a place filled with gold, stood behind her friend, and did not know whether to speak or retreat.

The bright light which came from a lamp, and also from a brasier of charcoal in the forge, added to her trouble. She saw Madame Lorilleux, a small, dark woman, agile and strong, drawing with all the vigor of her arms—assisted by a pair of pincers—a thread of black metal, which she passed through the holes of a draw-plate held by the vice. Before the desk or table in front of the window, sat Lorilleux, as short as his wife, but with broader shoulders. He was managing a tiny pair of pincers, and doing some work so delicate that it was almost imperceptible. It was he who first looked up, and lifted his head with its scanty, yellow hair. His face was the color of old wax—was long, and had an expression of physical suffering.

"Ah! it is you, is it? Well! well! But we are in a hurry, you understand. We have an order to fill. Don't come into the work-room. Remain in the chamber." And he returned to his work —his face was reflected in a ball filled with water, through which the lamp sent on his work, a circle of the brightest possible light.

"Find chairs for yourselves," cried Madame Lorilleux. "This is the lady, I suppose. Very well! Very well!"

She rolled up her wire, and carried it to the forge, and then she fanned the coals a little to quicken the heat.

Coupeau found two chairs, and made Gervaise seat herself near the curtain. The room was so narrow that he could not sit beside her, so he placed his chair a little behind, and leaned over her to give her the information he deemed desirable.

Gervaise, astonished by the strange reception given her by these people, and uncomfortable under their sidelong glances, had a buzzing in her ears, which prevented her from hearing what was said.

She thought the woman very old-looking for her thirty years, and also extremely untidy, with her hair tumbling over her shoulders and her dirty camisole.

The husband, not more than a year older, seemed to Gervaise really an old man, with thin, compressed lips and bowed figure. He was in his shirt sleeves, and his naked feet were thrust into slippers down at the heel.

She was infinitely astonished at the smallness of the atélier—at the blackened walls and at the terrible heat.

Tiny drops bedewed the waxed forehead of Lorilleux himself, while Madame Lorilleux threw off her sack, and stood in bare arms and chemise half slipped off.

"And the gold?" asked Gervaise softly.

Her eager eyes searched the corners, hoping to discover, amid all the dirt, something of the splendor of which she had dreamed.

But Coupeau laughed.

"Gold?" he said, "Look! here it is—and here—and here again, at your feet."

He pointed in succession to the fine thread with which his sister was busy, and at another package of wire hung against the wall near the vice; then falling down on his hands and knees, he gathered up from the floor, on the tip of his moistened finger, several tiny specks, which looked like needle points.

Gervaise cried out! "That surely was not gold! That black metal, which 'ooked precisely like iron!"

Her lover laughed, and explained to her the details of the manufacture in which his brother-in-law was engaged. The wire was furnished them in coils, just as it hung against the wall, and then they were obliged to heat and re-heat it half a dozen times during their manipulations, lest it should break. Considerable strength and a vast deal of skill was needed, and his sister had both. He had seen her draw out the gold until it was like a hair. She would never let her husband do it, because he always had a cough.

All this time Lorilleux was watching Gervaise stealthily; and after a violent fit of coughing, he said with an air as if he were speaking to himself:

"I make columns"—

"Yes," said Coupeau, in an explanatory voice, "there are four different kind of chains, and his style is called a column."

Lorilleux uttered a little grunt of satisfaction, all the time at work, with the tiny pincers held between very dirty nails.

"Look here, Cadet-Cassis," he said. "This very morning I made a little calculation. I began my work when I was only twelve years old. How many yards do you think I have made, up to this day?"

He lifted his pale face.

"Eight thousand! Do you understand? Eight thousand! Enough to twist around the necks of all the women in this Quartier."

Gervaise returned to her chair entirely disenchanted. She thought it was all very ugly and uninteresting. She smiled in order to gratify the Lorilleux, but she was annoyed and troubled at the profound silence they preserved in regard to her marriage, on account of which she had called there that evening. These people treated her as if she were simply a spectator, whose curiosity had induced Coupeau to bring her to see their work.

They began to talk, it was about the lodgers in the house. Madame Lorilleux asked her brother if he had not heard those Benard people quarrelling as he came up stairs. She said the husband always came home tipsy. Then she spoke of the Designer, who was overwhelmed with debts—always smoking and always quarrelling. The landlord was going to turn out the Coquets, who owed three quarters now, and who would put their furnace out on the landing, which was very dangerous. Mademoiselle Remanjon, as she was going down stairs with a bundle of dolls, was just in season to rescue one of the children from being burned alive.

Gervaise was beginning to find the

place unendurable. The heat was suffocating—the door could not be opened, because the slightest draught gave Lorilleux a cold. As they ignored the marriage question utterly, she pulled her lover's sleeve to signify her wish to depart. He understood, and was himself annoyed at this affectation of silence.

"We are going," he said coldly. "We do not care to interrupt your work any longer."

He lingered a moment, hoping for a word or an allusion. Suddenly he decided to begin the subject himself.

"We rely on you, Lorilleux. You will be my wife's witness," he said.

The man lifted his head in affected surprise, while his wife stood still in the centre of the work-shop.

"Are you in earnest?" he murmured, and then continued as if soliloquizing, "it is hard to know when this confounded Cadet-Cassis is in earnest——"

"We have no advice to give," interrupted his wife. "It is a foolish notion, this marrying, and it never succeeds. Never—no—never."

She drawled out these last words, examining Gervaise from head to foot, as she spoke.

"My brother is free to do as he pleases, of course," she continued. "Of course his family would have liked—— But then people always plan, and things turn out so different. Of course it is none of my business. Had he brought me the lowest of the low, I should have said, 'marry her, and let us live in peace!' He was very comfortable with us, nevertheless. He has considerable flesh on his bones, and does not look as if he had been starved. His soup

was always ready to the minute. Tell 'me, Lorilleux, don't you think that my brother's friend looks like Thérèse—you know whom I mean—that woman opposite, who died of consumption?"

"She certainly does," answered the chain-maker, contemplatively.

"And you have two children, Madame? I said to my brother I could not understand how he could marry a woman wth two children. You must not be angry if I think of his interests, it is only natural. You do not look very strong. Say, Lorilleux, don't you think that Madame looks delicate?"

This courteous pair made no allusion to her lameness, but Gervaise felt it to be in their minds. She sat stiff and still before them, her thin shawl with its yellow palm leaves wrapped closely about her, and answered in monosyllables as if before her judges. Coupeau, realizing her sufferings, cried out:

"This is all nonsense you are talking! What I want to know is, if the day will suit you, July 29th."

"One day is the same as another, to us," answered his sister, severely. "Lorilleux can do as he pleases in regard to being your witness. I only ask for peace."

Gervaise, in her embarrassment, had been pushing about with her feet some of the rubbish on the floor, then fearing she had done some harm, she stooped to ascertain. Lorilleux hastily approached her with a lamp, and looked at her fingers with evident suspicion.

"Take care," he said. "Those small bits of gold stick to the shoes sometimes, and are carried off without your knowing it."

This was a matter of some importance of course, for his employers weighed what they entrusted to him. He showed the hare's foot with which he brushed the particles of gold from the table, and the skin spread on his knees to receive them. Twice each week, the shop was carefully brushed; all the rubbish was kept and burned, and the ashes were examined, where were found each month, twenty-five or thirty francs of gold.

Madame Lorilleux did not take her eyes from the shoes of her guest.

"If Mademoiselle would be so kind," she murmured, with an amiable smile, "and would just look at her soles herself. There is no cause for offense, I am sure!"

Gervaise, indignant and scarlet, reseated herself and held up her shoes for examination. Coupeau opened the door with a gay good night, and she followed him into the corridor after a word or two of polite farewell.

The Lorilleux turned to their work at the end of their room where the tiny forge still glittered. The woman with her chemise slipped off her shoulder, which was red with the reflection from the brasier, was drawing out another wire—the muscles in her throat swelling with her exertions.

The husband, stooping under the green light of the ball of water, was again busy with his pincers, not stopping even to wipe the sweat from his brow.

When Gervaise emerged from the narrow corridors on the sixth landing, she said with tears in her eyes:

"This certainly does not promise very well!"

Coupeau shook his head angrily.

Lorilleux should pay for this evening! Was there ever such a miser. To care if one carried off three grains of gold in the dust on one's shoes. All the stories his sister told were pure fictions and malice. His sister never meant him to marry—his eating with them saved her at least four sous daily. But he did not care whether they appeared on the 29th of July or not, he could get along without them perfectly well.

But Gervaise, as she descended the stair case, felt her heart swell with pain and fear. She did not like the strange shadows on the dimly-lighted stairs. From behind the doors, now closed, came the heavy breathing of sleepers who had gone to their beds, on rising from the table. A faint laugh was heard from one room, while a slender thread of light filtered through the key-hole of the old lady who was still busy with her dolls, cutting out the gauze dresses with squeaking scissors. A child was crying on the next floor, and the smell from the sinks was worse than ever, and seemed something tangible amid this silent darkness. Then in the courtyard, while Coupeau pulled the cord, Gervaise turned and examined the house once more. It seemed enormous as it stood black against the moonless sky. The grey façades rose tall and spectral—the windows were all shut. No clothes fluttered in the breeze; there was literally not the smallest look of life, except in the few windows that were still lighted. From the damp corner of the courtyard came the drip, drip of the fountain. Suddenly, it seemed to Gervaise as if the house were striding toward her and would crush her to the earth.

A moment later she smiled at her foolish fancy.

"Take care!" cried Coupeau.

And as she passed out of the courtyard, she was compelled to jump over a little sea which had run from the dyer's. This time the water was blue, as blue as the summer sky, and the reflection of the lamps carried by the Concierge, was like the stars themselves.

## CHAPTER III

### A MARRIAGE OF THE PEOPLE

GERVAISE did not care for any great wedding. Why should they spend their money so foolishly. Then, too, she felt a little ashamed and did not care to parade their marriage before the whole Quartier. But Coupeau objected. It would never do not to have some festivities—a little drive and a supper perhaps, at a restaurant, he would ask for nothing more. He vowed that no one should drink too much, and finally obtained the young woman's consent and organized a picnic at five francs per head, at the *Moulin d'Argent,* Boulevard de la Chapelle. He was a small wine merchant, who had a garden back of his Restaurant. He made out a list. Among others appeared the names of two of his comrades, Bibi-la-Grillade and Mes-Bottes. It was true that Mes-Bottes crooked his elbow, but he was so deliciously funny that he was always invited to picnics. Gervaise said she, in her turn would bring her employer, Madame Fauconnier—all told there would be fifteen at the table. That was quite enough.

Now as Coupeau was literally penni-

less he borrowed fifty francs from his employer. He first bought his wedding ring, it cost twelve francs out of the shop, but his brother-in-law purchased it for him for nine, at the factory. He then ordered an overcoat, pantaloons and vest from a tailor to whom he paid twenty-five francs on account. His patent leather shoes and his bolivar could last a while longer. Then he put aside his ten francs for the picnic, which was what he and Gervaise must pay; and they had precisely six francs remaining, the price of a Mass at the altar of the poor. He had no liking for those black frocks, and it broke his heart to give these beloved francs to them. But a marriage without a Mass, he had heard, was really no marriage at all.

He went to the church to see if he could not drive a better bargain, and for an hour he fought with a stout little priest in a dirty soutane who, finally declaring that God could never bless such a union, agreed that the Mass should cost only five francs. Thus Coupeau had twenty sous in hand with which to begin the world!

Gervaise in her turn had made her preparations, had worked late into the night and laid aside thirty francs. She had set her heart on a silk mantelette marked thirteen francs, which she had seen in a shop window. She paid for it, and bought for ten francs from the husband of a laundress, who had died in Madame Fauconnier's house, a delaine dress of a deep blue, which she made over entirely. With the seven francs that remained, she bought a rose for her cap, a pair of white cotton gloves, and shoes for Claude. Fortunately both the boys had nice blouses.

She worked for four days mending and making; there was not a hole or a rip in anything. At last the evening before the important day arrived; Gervaise and Coupeau sat together and talked, happy that matters were so nearly concluded. Their arrangements were all made. They were to go to the Mayor's office—the two sisters of Coupeau declared they should remain at home—their presence not being necessary there. Then Mother Coupeau began to weep —saying she wished to go early and hide in a corner—and they promised to take her.

The hour fixed for the party to assemble at the *Moulin d'Argent,* was one o'clock sharp. From then they were to seek an appetite on the Plaine St. Denis and return by rail. Saturday morning, as he dressed, Coupeau thought with some anxiety of his scanty funds, he supposed he ought to offer a glass of wine and a slice of ham to his witnesses, while waiting for dinner; unexpected expenses might arise—no—it was clear that twenty sous was not enough. He consequently, after taking Claude and Etienne to Madame Boche, who promised to appear with them at dinner, ran to his brother-in-law and borrowed ten francs; he did it with reluctance, and the words stuck in his throat, for he half expected a refusal. Lorilleux grumbled and growled, but finally lent the money. But Coupeau heard his sister mutter under her breath, "that is a good beginning."

The civil marriage was fixed for half-past ten. The day was clear, and the sun intensely hot. In order not to excite observation the bridal pair, the mother and the four witnesses separated —Gervaise walked in front, having the arm of Lorilleux, while Monsieur Madinier gave his to Mamma Coupeau; on the opposite sidewalk were Coupeau, Boche and Bibi-la-Grillade. These three wore black frock-coats, and walked with their arms dangling from their rounded shoulders. Boche wore yellow pantaloons. Bibi-la-Grillade's coat was buttoned to the chin, as he had no vest, and a wisp of a cravat was tied around his neck.

Monsieur Madinier was the only one who wore a dress coat, a superb coat with square tails, and people stared as he passed, with the stout Mamma Coupeau in a green shawl and black bonnet with black ribbons. Gervaise was very sweet and gentle, wearing her blue dress and her trim little silk mantle. She listened graciously, to Lorilleux, who, in spite of the warmth of the day, was nearly lost in the ample folds of a loose overcoat. Occasionally she would turn her head and glance across the street with a little smile at Coupeau, who was none too comfortable in his new clothes. They reached the Mayor's office a half hour too early, and their turn was not reached until nearly eleven. They sat in the corner of the office, stiff and uneasy; pushing back their chairs a little, out of politeness, each time one of the clerks passed them, and when the magistrate appeared, they all rose respectfully. They were bidden to sit down again, which they did, and were the spectators of three marriages—the brides in white and the bridesmaids in pink and blue, quite fine and stylish.

When their own turn came Bibi-la-Grillade had disappeared, and Boche hunted him up in the Square, where he had gone to smoke a pipe. All the forms were so quickly completed that the party looked at each other in dismay, feeling as if they had been defrauded of half the ceremony. Gervaise listened with tears in her eyes, and the old lady wept audibly.

Then they turned to the Register and wrote their names in big, crooked letters—all but the newly-made husband, who, not being able to write, contented himself with making a cross.

Then the clerk handed the certificate to Coupeau. He, admonished by a touch of his wife's elbow, presented him with five sous.

It was quite a long walk from the Mayor's office to the church. The men stopped midway to take a glass of beer, and Gervaise and Mamma Coupeau drank some cassis with water. There was not a particle of shade, for the sun was directly above their heads. The Beadle awaited them in the empty church, he hurried them towards a small chapel, asking them indignantly, if they were not ashamed to mock at religion by coming so late. A Priest came towards them, with an ashen face, faint with hunger, preceded by a boy in a dirty surplice. He hurried through the service, gabbling the Latin phrases, with side-long glances at the bridal party. The bride and bridegroom knelt before the altar in considerable embarrassment, not knowing when it was necessary to kneel and when to stand, and not always understanding the gestures made by the clerk.

The witnesses thought it more convenient to stand all the time; while Mamma Coupeau, overcome by her

tears again, shed them on a prayer-book, which she had borrowed from a neighbor.

It was high noon. The last mass was said, and the church was noisy with the movements of the sacristans who were putting the chairs in their places. The centre altar was being prepared for some fête, for the hammers were heard as the decorations were being nailed up. And, in the choking dust raised by the broom of the man who was sweeping the corner of the small altar, the Priest laid his cold and withered hand on the heads of Gervaise and Coupeau with a sulky air, as if he were uniting them as a mere matter of business, or to occupy the time between the two masses.

When the signatures were again affixed to the Register in the vestry, and the party stood outside in the sunshine, they had a sensation as if they had been driven at full speed, and were glad to rest.

"I feel as if I had been at the dentist's. We had no time to cry out before it was all over!"

"Yes," muttered Lorilleux; "they take less than five minutes to do what can't be undone in all one's life! Poor Cadet-Cassis!"

Gervaise kissed her new mother with tears in her eyes, but with smiling lips. She answered the old woman gently:

"Do not be afraid. I will do my best to make him happy. If things turn out ill, it shall not be my fault."

The party went at once to the *Moulin d'Argent*. Coupeau now walked with his wife, some little distnace in advance of the others. They whispered and laughed together, and seemed to see neither the people, nor the houses, nor anything that was going on about them.

At the Restaurant, Coupeau ordered at once some bread and ham; then seeing that Boche and Bibi-la-Grillade were really hungry, he ordered more wine and more meat. His mother could eat nothing, and Gervaise, who was dying of thirst, drank glass after glass of water barely reddened with wine.

"This is my affair," said Coupeau, going to the counter, where he paid four francs, five sous.

The guests began to arrive. Madame Fauconnier, stout and handsome, was the first. She wore a percale gown, écrue ground, with bright figures, a rose-colored cravat, and a bonnet laden with flowers. Then came Mademoiselle Remanjon, in her scanty black dress, which seemed so entirely a part of herself, that it was doubtful if she laid it aside at night. The Gaudron household followed. The husband, enormously stout, looked as if his vest would burst at the least movement; and his wife, who was nearly as huge as himself, was dressed in a delicate shade of violet, which added to her apparent size.

"Ah!" cried Madame Lerat, as she entered; "we are going to have a tremendous shower!" and she bade them all look out the window to see how black the clouds were.

Madame Lerat, Coupeau's eldest sister, was a tall, thin, woman, very masculine in appearance, and talking through her nose; wearing a puce-colored dress, that was much too loose for her. It was profusely trimmed with fringe, which made her look like a lean dog just coming out of the water. She brandished an umbrella as she talked, as if it had been a walking-stick. As she kissed Gervaise, she said:

"You have no idea how the wind blows, and it is as hot as a blast from a furnace!"

Everybody at once declared they had felt the storm coming all the morning. Three days of extreme heat, some one said, always ended in a gust.

"It will blow over," said Coupeau, with an air of confidence; "but I wish my sister would come, all the same."

Madame Lorilleux, in fact, was very late. Madame Lerat had called for her, but she had not then begun to dress; "and," said the widow, in her brother's ear: "you never saw anything like the temper she was in!"

They waited another half-hour. The sky was growing blacker and blacker. Clouds of dust were rising along the street, and down came the rain. And it was in the first shower, that Madame Lorilleux arrived—out of temper and out of breath—struggling with her umbrella, which she could not close.

"I had ten minds," she exclaimed, "to turn back. I wanted you to wait until next Saturday. I knew it would rain to-day—I was certain of it!"

Coupeau tried to calm her, but she quickly snubbed him. Was it he, she would like to know, who was to pay for her dress if it were spoiled?

She wore black silk, so tight that the button-holes were burst out, and it showed white on the shoulders, while the skirt was so scant that she could not take a long step.

The other women, however, looked at her silk with envy.

She took no notice of Gervaise, who

sat by the side of her mother-in-law. She called to Lorilleux, and with his aid carefully wiped every drop of rain from her dress with her handkerchief.

Meanwhile, the shower ceased abruptly, but the storm was evidently not over, for sharp flashes of lightning darted through the black clouds.

Suddenly the rain poured down again. The men stood in front of the door with their hands in their pockets, dismally contemplating the scene. The women crouched together with their hands over their eyes. They were in such terror they could not talk; when the thunder was heard further off, they all plucked up their spirits and became impatient, but a fine rain was falling that looked interminable.

"What are we to do?" cried Madame Lorilleux crossly.

Then Mademoiselle Remanjon timidly observed that the sun perhaps would soon be out, and they might yet go into the country; upon this there was one general shout of derision.

"Nice walking it would be! and how pleasant the grass would be to sit upon!"

Something must be done, however, to get rid of the time until dinner. Bibi-la-Grillade proposed cards, Madame Lerat suggested story telling. To each proposition a thousand objections were offered. Finally when Lorilleux proposed that the party should visit the tomb of Abélard and Héloise his wife's indignation burst forth.

She had dressed in her best, only to be drenched in the rain and to spend the day in a wine shop it seemed! She had had enough of the whole thing and she should go home. Coupeau and Lorilleux held the door, she exclaiming violently:

"Let me go, I tell you I will go!"

Her husband having induced her to listen to reason, Coupeau went to Gervaise, who was calmly conversing with her mother-in-law and Madame Fauconnier.

"Have you nothing to propose?" he asked, not venturing to add any term of endearment.

"No," she said with a smile, "but I am ready to do anything you wish. I am very well suited as I am."

Her face was indeed as sunny as a morning in May. She spoke to every one kindly and sympathetically. During the storm she had sat with her eyes riveted on the clouds, as if by the light of those lurid flashes she was reading the solemn book of the Future.

Monsieur Madinier had proposed nothing, he stood leaning against the counter with a pompous air; he spat upon the ground, wiped his mouth with the back of his hand and rolled his eyes about.

"We could go to the Musée du Louvre, I suppose," and he smoothed his chin while awaiting the effect of this proposition.

"There are antiquities there, statues, pictures,—lots of things—it is very instructive. Have any of you been there?" he asked.

They all looked at each other. Gervaise had never even heard of the place, nor had Madame Fauconnier, nor Boche. Coupeau thought he had been there one Sunday but he was not sure, but Madame Lorilleux, on whom Madinier's air of importance had produced a profound impression, approved of the idea. The day was wasted any way, therefore if a little instruction could be got it would be well to try it. As the rain was still falling they borrowed old umbrellas of every imaginable hue, from the establishment, and started forth for the Musée du Louvre.

There were twelve of them and they walked in couples. Madame Lorilleux with Madinier, to whom she grumbled all the way.

"We know nothing about her" she said, "not even where he picked her up. My husband has already lent them ten francs; and who ever heard of a bride without a single relation. She said she had a sister in Paris. Where is she to-day, I should like to know!"

She checked herself and pointed to Gervaise whose lameness was very perceptible as she descended the hill "Just look at her!" she muttered. "Wooden legs!"

This epithet was heard by Madame Fauconnier who took up the cudgels for Gervaise who, she said, was as neat as a pin and worked like a tiger.

The wedding party coming out of la Rue St. Denis, crossed the Boulevard under their umbrellas amid the pouring rain, driving here and there among the carriages. The drivers as they pulled up their horses, shouted to them to look out, with an oath. On the gray and muddy sidewalk the procession was very conspicuous—the blue dress of the bride—the canary colored breeches of one of the men, Madinier's square tailed coat,—all gave a carnival-like air to the group. But it was the hats of the party that were the most amusing, for they were of all heights, sizes and styles. The shop-keepers on the Boulevard crowded to their windows to enjoy the drollery of the sight. The wedding procession—quite undisturbed by the observation it excited—went gayly on. They stopped for a moment on the Place des Victoire—the bride's shoestring was untied—she fastened it at the foot of the statue of Louis XIV., her friends waiting as she did so.

Finally they reached the Louvre. Here Madinier politely asked permission to take the head of the party; the place was so large, he said, that it was a very easy thing to lose oneself; he knew the prettiest rooms and the things best worth seeing, because he had often been there with an artist, a very intelligent fellow, from whom a great manufacturer of pasteboard boxes bought pictures.

The party entered the museum of Assyrian antiquities. They shivered and walked about, examining the colossal statues—the gods in black marble —strange beasts and monstrosities, half cats and half women This was not amusing, and an inscription in Phenician characters appalled them.—"Who on earth had ever read such stuff as that? it was meaningless nonsense!"

But Madinier shouted to them from the stairs, "Come on! That is nothing! Much more interesting things up here, I assure you!"

The severe nudity of the great staircase cast a gloom over their spirits, an usher in livery added to their awe, and it was with great respect and on the tips of their toes they entered the French gallery.

How many statues! How many pictures! They wished they had all the money they had cost.

In the *Gallerie d'Apollon* the floor excited their admiration; it was smooth as glass, even the feet of the sofas were reflected in it. Madinier bade them look at the ceiling, and at its many beauties of decoration, but they said they dared not look up. Then before entering the *Salon Carré* he pointed to the window and said:

"That is the balcony where Charles IX. fired on the people!"

With a magnificent gesture he ordered his party to stand still in the centre of the *Salon Carré.*

"There are only *chefs-d'œuvres* here," he whispered as solemnly as if he had been in a church.

They walked around the Salon. Gervaise asked the meaning of one of the pictures—the *Noces de Cana*—Coupeau stopped before *La Joconde* declaring that it was like one of his aunts.

Boche and Bibi-la-Grillade snickered and pushed each other at the sight of the nude female figures, and the Gaudrons, husband and wife, stood openmouthed and deeply touched—before Murillo's "Virgin."

When they had been once around the room, Madinier, who was quite attentivet to Madame Lorilleux on account of her silk gown, proposed they should do it over again, it was well worth it, he said.

He never hesitated in replying to any question which she addressed to him in her thirst for information, and when she stopped before "Titian's Mistress," whose yellow hair struck her as like her own, he told her it was a mistress of Henri IV., who was the heroine of a play then running at the Ambigu.

The wedding party finally entered the long gallery devoted to the Italian and Flemish schools of art. The pictures were all meaningless to them and their heads were beginning to ache. They felt a thrill of interest, however, in the copyists with their easels, who painted without being disturbed by spectators. The artists scattered through the rooms had heard that a primitive wedding party were making a tour of the Louvre, and hurried, with laughing faces to enjoy the scene, while the weary bride and bridegroom, accompanied by their friends, clumsily moved about over the shining, resounding floors much like cattle let loose, and with quite as keen an appreciation of the marvellous beauties about them.

The women vowed their backs were broken standing so long, and Madinier, declaring he knew the way said they would leave, after he had shown them a certain room to which he could go with his eyes shut. But he was very much mistaken. Salon succeeded to salon, and finally the party went up a flight of stairs and found themselves among canons and other instruments of war. Madinier, unwilling to confess that he had lost himself, wandered distractedly about, declaring that the doors had been changed. The party began to feel that they were there for life, when suddenly to their great joy, they heard the cry of the janitors resounding from room to room.

"Time to close the doors!"

They meekly followed one of them, and when they were outside, they uttered a sigh of relief as they put up their umbrellas once more, but one and all affected great pleasure at having been to the Louvre.

The clock struck four. There were two hours to dispose of before dinner. The women would have liked to rest, but the men were more energetic, and proposed another walk, during which so tremendous a shower fell, that umbrellas were useless and dresses were irretrievably ruined. Then Monsieur Madinier suggested that they should ascend the column on the Place Vendôme.

"It is not a bad idea," cried the men. And the procession began the ascent of the spiral staircase, which Boche said was so old that he could feel it shake. This terrified the ladies, who uttered little shrieks, but Coupeau said nothing, his arm was around his wife's waist, and just as they emerged upon the platform he kissed her.

"Upon my word!" cried Madame Lorilleux much scandalized.

Madinier again constituted himself master of ceremonies, and pointed out all the monuments, but Madame Fauconnier would not put her foot outside the little door—she would not look down on that pavement for all the world, she said—and the party soon tired of this amusement and descended the stairs. At the foot Madinier wished to pay, but Coupeau interfered and put into the hand of the guard twenty-four sous—two for each person. It was now half past five; they had just time to get to the restaurant, but Coupeau proposed a glass of Vermonth first, and they entered a cabaret for that purpose.

When they returned to the *Moulin d'Argent,* they found Madame Boche, with the two children, talking to Mamma Coupeau, near the table—already spread and waiting. When Gervaise saw Claude and Etienne, she took them both on her knees and kissed them lovingly.

"Have they been good?" she asked.

"I should think Coupeau would feel rather queer!" said Madame Lorilleux, as she looked on grimly.

Gervaise had been calm and smiling all day, but she had quietly watched her husband with the Lorilleux. She thought Coupeau was afraid of his sister—cowardly, in fact. The evening previous, he had said he did not care a sou for their opinion on any subject, and that they had the tongues of vipers; but now he was with them, he was like a whipped hound, hung on their words and anticipated their wishes. This troubled his wife, for it augured ill, she thought, for their future happiness.

"We won't wait any longer for Mes-Bottes," cried Coupeau. "We are all here, but him, and his scent is good! Surely he can't be waiting for us still, at Saint Denis!"

The guests, in good spirits once more, took their seats with a great clatter of chairs.

Gervaise was between Lorilleux and Madinier, and Coupeau between Madame Fauconnier, and his sister, Madame Lorilleux. The others seated themselves.

"No one has asked a blessing," said Boche, as the ladies pulled the table cloth well over their skirts, to protect them from spots.

But Madame Lorilleux frowned at this poor jest. The vermicelli soup, which was cold and greasy, was eaten with noisy haste. Two garçons served them, wearing aprons of a very doubtful white, and greasy vests.

Through the four windows, open on the court-yard and its acacias, streamed the light, soft and warm, after the storm. The trees, bathed in the setting sun, imparted a cool, green tinge to the dingy room, and the shadows of the waving branches and quivering leaves, danced over the cloth.

There were two fly-specked mirrors at either end of the room, which indefinitely lengthened the table spread with thick china. Every time the garçons opened the door into the kitchen, there came a strong smell of burning fat.

"Don't let us all talk at once!" said Boche, as a dead silence fell on the room, broken by the abrupt entrance of Mes-Bottes.

"You are nice people!" he exclaimed. "I have been waiting for you until I am wet through, and have a fish pond in each pocket."

This struck the circle as the height of wit, and they all laughed, while he ordered the garçon to and fro. He devoured three plates of soup and enormous slices of bread. The head of the establishment came and looked in, in considerable anxiety; a laugh ran around the room. Mes-Bottes recalled to their memories a day when he had eaten twelve hard-boiled eggs and drank twelve glasses of wine, while the clock was striking twelve.

There was a brief silence. A waiter placed on the table a rabbit stew in a deep dish. Coupeau turned round.

"Say, boy, is that a gutter rabbit? It mews still."

And the low mewing of a cat seemed indeed to come from the dish. This delicate joke was perpetrated by Coupeau in the throat, without the smallest movement of his lips. This feat always met with such success that he never ordered a meal anywhere without a rabbit stew. The ladies wiped their eyes with their napkins because they laughed so much.

Madame Fauconnier begged for the head—she adored the head; and Boche asked especially for onions.

Madame Lerat compressed her lips and said morosely:

"Of course. I might have known that!"

Madame Lerat was a hard working woman. No man had ever put his nose within her door since her widowhood, and yet her instincts were thoroughly bad—every word uttered by others, bore to her ears a double meaning—a coarse allusion sometimes so deeply vailed that no one but herself could grasp its meaning.

Boche leaned over her with a sensual smile and entreated an explanation. She shook her head.

"Of course," she repeated. "Onions! I knew it!"

Everybody was talking now, each of his own trade. Madinier declared that box-making was an art, and he cited the New Year bonbon boxes, as wonders of luxury. Lorilleux talked of his chains—of their delicacy and beauty. He said that in former times, jewellers wore swords at their sides. Coupeau described a weather-cock, made by one of his comrades, out of tin. Madame Lerat showed Bibi-la-Grillade how a rose stem was made, by rolling the handle of her knife be-tween her bony fingers; and Madame Fauconnier complained loudly of one of her apprentices, who, the night before, had badly scorched a pair of linen sheets.

"It is no use to talk!" cried Lorilleux, striking his fist on the table; "gold is gold!"

A profound silence followed the ut-terance of this truism, amid which arose from the other end of the table, the piping tones of Mademoiselle Reman-jon's voice, as she said:

"And then I sew on the skirt. I stick a pin in the head to hold on the cap, and it is done. They sell for three cents."

She was describing her dolls to Mes-Bottes, whose jaws worked steadily, like machinery.

He did not listen, but he nodded at intervals, with his eyes fixed on the gar-çons, to see that they carried away no dishes that were not emptied.

There had been veal cutlets and string beans served. As a rôti—two lean chickens on a bed of water cresses, were brought in. The room was growing very warm—the sun was lingering on the tops of the acacias, but the room was growing dark. The men threw off their coats, and ate in their shirt sleeves.

"Madame Boche," cried Gervaise, "please don't let those children eat so much."

But Madame Coupeau interposed, and declared that for once in a while, a little fit of indigestion would do them no harm.

Madame Boche accused her husband of holding Madame Lerat's hand under the table.

Madinier talked politics. He was a Republican, and Bibi-la-Grillade and himself were soon in a hot discussion.

"Who cares," cried Coupeau, "whe-ther we have a King, an Emperor, or a President, so long as we earn our five francs per day——!"

Lorilleux shook his head. He was born on the same day as the Comte de Chambord, September 29th, 1820, and this coincidence dwelt in his mind. He seemed to feel that there was a cer-tain connection between the return of the King to France, and his own per-sonal fortunes. He did not say, dis-tinctly, what he expected, but it was clear that it was something very agree able.

The dessert was now on the table—a floating island flanked by two plates of cheese and two of fruit. The float-ing island was a great success. Mes-Bottes ate all the cheese and called for more bread. And then, as some of the custard was left in the dish, he pulled it toward him and ate it as if it had been soup.

"How extraordinary!" said Madinier, filled with admiration.

The men rose to light their pipes, and as they passed Mes-Bottes, asked him how he felt.

Bibi-la-Grillade lifted him from the floor, chair and all.

"Zounds!" he cried, "the fellow's weight has doubled!"

Coupeau declared his friend had only just begun his night's work, that he would eat bread until dawn. The wait-ers, pale with fright, disappeared. Boche went down stairs on a tour of inspection, and stated that the establishment was in a state of confusion, that the proprietor, in consternation, had sent out to all the bakers in the neighborhood; that the house, in fact, had an utterly ruined aspect.

"I should not like to take you to board," said Madame Gaudron.

"Let us have a punch," cried Mes-Bottes.

But Coupeau seeing his wife's troubled face, interfered, and said no one should drink anything more. They had all had enough.

This declaration met with the approval of some of the party, but the others sided with Mes-Bottes.

"Those who are thirsty are thirsty," he said. "No one need drink that does not wish to do so, I am sure," and he added, with a wink, "there will be all the more for those who do!"

Then Coupeau said they would settle the account, and his friend could do as he pleased afterward.

Alas! Mes-Bottes could produce only three francs; he had changed his five-franc piece, and the remainder had melted away somehow on the road from St. Denis. He handed over the three francs, and Coupeau, greatly indignant, borrowed the other two from his brother-in-law, who gave the money secretly, being afraid of his wife.

Monsieur Madinier had taken a plate. The ladies each laid down their five francs quietly and timidly, and then the men retreated to the other end of the room and counted up the amount, and each man added to his subscription five sous for the garçon.

But when Monsieur Madinier sent for the proprietor the little assembly were thrilled, at hearing him say that this was not all, there were "extras."

As this was received with exclamations of rage, he went into explanations. He had furnished twenty-five litres of wine instead of twenty as he agreed. The floating island was an addition, on seeing that the dessert was somewhat scanty, whereupon ensued a formidable quarrel. Coupeau declared he would not pay a sou of the extras.

"There is your money," he said, "take it, and never again will one of us step a foot under your roof!"

"I want six francs more," muttered the man.

The women gathered about in great indignation, not a centime would they give they declared.

Madame Fauconnier had had a wretched dinner—she said she could have had a better one at home for forty sous. Such arrangements always turned out badly, and Madame Gaudron declared aloud, that if people wanted their friends at their weddings they usually invited them out and out.

Gervaise took refuge with her mother-in-law in a distant window, feeling heartily ashamed of the whole scene.

Monsieur Madinier went down stairs with the man and low mutterings of the storm reached the party At the end of a half hour he reappeared, having yielded to the extent of paying three francs, but no one was satisfied, and they all began a discussion in regard to the extras.

The evening was spoiled, as was Madame Lerat's dress; there was no end to the chapter of accidents.

"I know," cried Madame Lorilleux,

"that the garçon spilled gravy from the chickens down my back." She twisted and turned herself before the mirror until she succeeded in finding the spot.

"Yes, I knew it," she cried, "and he shall pay for it as true as I live. I wish I had remained at home!"

She left in a rage, and Lorilleux at her heels.

When Coupeau saw her go, he was in actual consternation, and Gervaise saw that it was best to make a move at once. Madame Boche had agreed to keep the children with her for a day or two.

Coupeau and his wife hurried out, in the hope of overtaking Madame Lorilleux, which they soon did. Lorilleux, with the kindly desire of making all smooth said,

"We will go to your door with you."

"Your door indeed!" cried his wife, and then pleasantly went on to express her surprise that they did not postpone their marriage until they had saved enough to buy a little furniture and move away from that hole, up under the roof.

"But I have given up that room," said her brother. "We shall have the one Gervaise occupies, it is larger."

Madame Lorilleux forgot herself; she wheeled around suddenly.

"What!" she exclaimed. "You are going to live in Wooden Legs' room?"

Gervaise turned pale. This name she now heard for the first time, and it was like a slap in the face. She heard much more in her sister-in-law's exclamation than met the ear. That room to which allusion was made, was the one where she had lived with Lantier for a whole month, where she had wept

such bitter tears, but Coupeau did not understand that, he was only wounded by the name applied to his wife.

"It is hardly wise of you," he said sullenly, "to nickname people after that fashion, as perhaps you are not aware of what you are called in your Quartier. Cow's-Tail is not a very nice name, but they have given it to you on account of your hair. Why should we not keep that room? it is a very good one."

Madame Lorilleux would not answer. Her dignity was sadly disturbed at being called Cow's-Tail.

They walked on in silence until they reached the Hôtel Boncœur; and just as Coupeau gave the two women a push toward each other, and bade them kiss and be friends, a man who wished to pass them on the right, gave a violent lurch to the left, and came between them.

"Look out!" cried Lorilleux, "it is Father Bazouge. He is pretty full to-night."

Gervaise, in great terror, flew toward the door. Father Bazouge was a man of fifty, his clothes were covered with mud, where he had fallen in the street.

"You need not be afraid," continued Lorilleux, "he will do you no harm. He is a neighbor of ours—the third room on the left in our corridor."

But Father Bazouge was talking to Gervaise. "I am not going to eat you, little one," he said. "I have drank too much, I know very well; but when the work is done, the machinery should be greased a little now and then."

Gervaise retreated further into the doorway, and with difficulty kept back a sob. She nervously entreated Coupeau to take the man away.

Bazouge staggered off, muttering as he did so:

"You won't mind it so much one of these days, my dear. I know something about women. They make a great fuss, but they get used to it all the same."

## CHAPTER IV

### A HAPPY HOME

FOUR years of hard and incessant toil followed this day. Gervaise and Coupeau were wise and prudent. They worked hard, and took a little relaxation on Sundays. The wife worked twelve hours of the twenty-four with Madame Fauconnier, and yet found time to keep her own home like waxwork. The husband was never known to be tipsy, but brought home his wages and smoked his pipe at his own window at night before going to bed. They were the bright and shining lights—the good example of the whole Quartier; and as they made jointly about nine francs per day, it was easy to see they were putting by money.

But in the first few months of their married life they were obliged to trim their sails closely, and had some trouble to make both ends meet. They took a great dislike to the Hôtel Boncœur. They longed for a home of their own, with their own furniture. They estimated the cost over and over again, and decided that for three hundred and fifty francs they could venture; but they had little hope of saving such a

sum in less than two years, when a stroke of good luck befell them.

An old gentleman in Plassans sent for Claude, to place him at school. He was a very eccentric old gentleman, fond of pictures and art. Claude was a great expense to his mother, and when Etienne alone was at home, they saved the three hundred and fifty francs in seven months. The day they purchased their furniture they took a long and happy walk together; for it was in important step they had taken—important not only in their own eyes, but in those of the people around them.

For two months they had been looking for an apartment. They wished, of all things, to take one in the old house where Madame Lorilleux lived, but there was not one single room to be rented, and they were compelled to relinquish the idea. Gervaise was reconciled to this more easily, since she did not care to be thrown in any closer contact with the Lorilleux. They looked further. It was essential that Gervaise should be near her friend and employer, Madame Fauconnier, and they finally succeeded in their search, and were indeed in wonderful luck; for they obtained a large room, with a kitchen and tiny bed-room, just opposite the establishment of the laundress. It was a small house, two stories, with one steep staircase, and was divided into two lodgings—the one on the right, the other on the left, while the lower floor was occupied by a carriage maker.

Gervaise was delighted. It seemed to her that she was once more in the country—no neighbors, no gossip, no interference; and from the place where she stood and ironed all day at Madame Fauconnier's, she could see the windows of her own room.

They moved in the month of April. Gervaise was then near her confinement, but it was she who cleaned and put in order her new home. "Every penny was of consequence," she said with pride, now that they should soon have another mouth to feed. She rubbed her furniture, which was of old mahogany, good, but second-hand, until it shone like glass, and was quite broken-hearted when she discovered a scratch. She held her breath if she knocked it when sweeping. The commode was her especial pride—it was so dignified and stately. Her pet dream—which however she kept to herself—was some day to have a clock to put in the centre of the marble slab. If there had not been a baby in prospect, she would have purchased this much coveted article at once; but she sighed and dismissed the thought.

Etienne's bed was placed in the tiny room, almost a closet, and there was room for the cradle by its side. The kitchen was about as big as one's hand; and very dark, but by leaving the door open, one could see pretty well; and as Gervaise had no big dinners to get, she managed comfortably. The large room was her pride. In the morning the white curtains of the alcove were drawn, and the bed-room was transformed into a lovely dining-room, with its table in the middle, the commode and a wardrobe opposite each other. A tiny stove kept them warm in cold weather, for seven sous per day.

Coupeau ornamented the walls with several engravings—one of a Marshal of France on a spirited steed, with his bâton in his hand. Above the commode were the photographs of the family, arranged in two lines, with an antique china bénitier between. On the corners of the commode, a bust of Pascal faced another of Béranger—one grave, the other smiling. It was, indeed, a fair and pleasant home.

"How much do you think we pay here?" Gervaise would ask of each new visitor.

And when too high an estimate was given, she was charmed.

"One hundred and fifty francs—not a penny more," she would exclaim. "Is it not wonderful?"

No small portion of the woman's satisfacton arose from an acacia, which grew in her court-yard, one of whose branches crossed her window, and the scanty foliage was a whole wilderness to her.

Her baby was born one afternoon. She would not allow her husband to be sent for, and when he came gayly into the room, he was welcomed by his pale wife, who whispered to him as he stooped over her:

"My dear, it is a girl."

"All right!" said the tin-worker, jesting to hide his real emotion. "I ordered a girl. You always do just what I want!"

He took up the child.

"Let us have a good look at you, young lady! The down on the top of your head is pretty black, I think. Now you must never squall, but be as good and reasonable always as your papa and mamma."

Gervaise, with a faint smile and sad eyes looked at her daughter. She shook her head. She would have preferred a boy, because boys run less risks in a place like Paris. The nurse took the baby from the father's hands, and told Gervaise she must not talk. Coupeau said he must go and tell his mother and sister the news, but he was famished and must eat something first. His wife was greatly disturbed at seeing him wait upon himself, and she tossed about a little and complained that she could not make him comfortable.

"You must be quiet," said the nurse again.

"It is lucky you are here, or she would be up and cutting my bread for me," said Coupeau.

He finally set forth to announce the news to his family, and returned in an hour with them all.

The Lorilleux, under the influence of the prosperity of their brother and his wife, had become extremely amiable toward them, and only lifted their eyebrows in a significant sort of way, as much as to say that they could tell something if they pleased.

"You must not talk, you understand," said Coupeau, "but they would come and take a peep at you, and I am going to make them some coffee."

He disappeared into the kitchen, and the women discussed the size of the baby and whom it resembled. Meanwhile Coupeau was heard banging round in the kitchen, and his wife nervously called out to him and told him where the things were that he wanted, but her husband rose superior to all difficulties, and soon appeared with the smoking coffee-pot, and they all seated themselves around the table, except the nurse, who drank a cup standing and then departed; all was going well and she was not needed. If she was wanted in the morning, they could send for her.

Gervaise lay with a faint smile on her lips. She only half heard what was said by those about her. She had no strength to speak, it seemed to her that she was dead. She heard the word baptism. Coupeau saw no necessity for the ceremony, and was quite sure too, that the child would take cold. In his opinion, the less one had to do with Priests, the better. His mother was horrified and called him a heathen, while the Lorilleux claimed to be religious people also.

"It had better be on Sunday," said his sister, in a decided tone, and Gervaise consented with a little nod. Everybody kissed her and then the baby, addressing it with tender epithets as if it could understand, and departed.

When Coupeau was alone with his wife, he took her hand and held it while he finished his pipe.

"I could not help their coming," he said, "but I am sure they have given you the headache." And the rough, clumsy man kissed his wife tenderly, moved by a great pity for all she had borne for his sake.

And Gervaise was very happy. She told him so, and said her only anxiety now, was to be on her feet again as soon as possible, for they had another mouth to feed. He soothed her, and asked if she could not trust him to look out for their little one.

In the morning, when he went to his work, he sent Madame Boche to spend the day with his wife, who at night told him she never could consent to lie still any longer and see a stranger going about her room, and the next day she was up, and would not be taken care of again. She had no time for such nonsense! She said it would do for rich women, but not for her, and in another week she was at Madame Fauconniers again, at work.

Madame Lorilleux, who was the baby's godmother, appeared on Saturday evening with a cap and baptism robe, which she had bought cheap, because they had lost their first freshness. The next day Lorilleux, as god-father, gave Gervaise six pounds of sugar. They flattered themselves they knew how to do things properly, and that evening, at the supper given by Coupeau, did not appear empty-handed. Lorilleux came with a couple of bottles of wine under each arm, and his wife brought a large custard which was a specialty of a certain restaurant.

Yes, they knew how to do things—these people—but they also liked to tell of what they did, and they told every one they saw in the next month, that they had spent twenty francs, which came to the ears of Gervaise, who was none too well pleased.

It was at this supper that Gervaise became acquainted with her neighbors on the other side of the house. These were Madame Goujet, a widow, and her son. Up to this time they had exchanged a good morning, when they met on the stairs, or in the street, but as Madame Goujet had rendered some small services on the first day of her illness, Gervaise invited them on the occasion of the baptism.

These people were from the *Departement du Nond*. The mother repaired laces, while the son, a blacksmith by trade, worked in a factory.

They had lived in their present apartment for five years. Beneath the peaceful calm of their lives lay a great sorrow. Goujet, the husband and father, had killed a man in a fit of furious intoxication, and then while in prison, had choked himself with his pockethandkerchief. His widow and child left Lille after this and came to Paris, with the weight of this tragedy on their hearts and heads, and faced the future with indomitable courage and sweet patience. Perhaps they were over proud and reserved, for they held themselves aloof from those about them. Madame Goujet always wore mourning, and her pale serene face was encircled with nun-like bands of white. Goujet was a colossus of twenty-three with a clear fresh complexion, and honest eyes. At the manufactory he went by the name of the Gucule-d'Or, on account of his beautiful blonde beard.

Gervaise took a great fancy to these people, and when she first entered their apartment was charmed with the exquisite cleanliness of all she saw. Madame Goujet opened the door into her son's room to show it to her. It was as pretty and white as the chamber of a young girl. A narrow iron bed, white curtains and quilt, a dressing-table and book-shelves, made up the furniture. A few colored engravings were pinned against the wall and Madame Goujet said that her son was a good deal of a boy still—he liked to look at pictures rather than read. Gervaise sat for an hour with her neighbor, watching her at work with her cushion, its numberless pins and the pretty lace.

The more she saw of her new friends the better Gervaise liked them. They were frugal but not parsimonious. They were the admiration of the neighborhood. Goujet was never seen with a hole or a spot on his garments. He was very polite to all, but a little diffident, in spite of his height and broad shoulders. The girls in the street were much amused to see him look away when they met him—he did not fancy their ways—their forward boldness and loud laughs. One day he came home tipsy. His mother uttered no word of reproach, but brought out a picture of his father which was piously preserved in her wardrobe. And after that lesson Goujet drank no more liquor, though he conceived no hatred for wine.

On Sunday he went out with his mother who was his idol. He went to her with all his troubles and with all his joys as he had done when little.

At first he took no interest in Gervaise, but after a while he began to like her, and treated her like a sister with abrupt familiarity.

Cadet-Cassis—who was a thorough Parisian—thought Gucule d'Or very stupid. What was the sense of turning away from all the pretty girls he met in the street? But this did not prevent the two young fellows from liking each other very heartily.

For three years the lives of these people flowed tranquilly on, without an event. Gervaise had been elevated in the laundry where she worked, had higher wages, and decided to place Etienne at school. Notwithstanding all her expenses of the household, they were able to save twenty and thirty francs each month. When these savings amounted to six hundred francs, Gervaise could not rest, so tormented was she by ambitious dreams. She wished to open a small establishment herself, and hire apprentices in her turn. She hesitated naturally to take the definite steps, and said they would look around for a shop that would answer their purpose; their money in the savings bank was quietly rolling up. She had bought her clock, the object of her ambition; it was to be paid for in a year—so much each month. It was a wonderful clock, rosewood with fluted columns, and gilt mouldings and pendulum. She kept her bank book under the glass shade, and often when she was thinking of her shop, she stood with her eyes fixed on the clock, as if she were waiting for some especial and solemn moment.

The Coupeaus and the Goujets now went out on Sundays together. It was an orderly party with a dinner at some quiet restaurant. The men drank a glass or two of wine, and came home with the ladies and counted up and settled the expenditures of the day before they separated. The Lorilleux were bitterly jealous of these new friends of their brother's. They declared it had a very queer look to see him and his wife always with strangers rather than with his own family, and Madame Lorilleux began to say hateful things again of Gervaise. Madame Lerat on the contrary, took her part, while mamma Coupeau tried to please every one.

The day that Nana—which was the pet name given to the little girl—was three years old, Coupeau on coming in, found his wife in a state of great excitement. She refused to give any explanation, saying in fact there really was nothing the matter, but she finally became so abstracted that she stood still with the plates in her hand, as she laid the table for dinner, and her husband insisted on an explanation.

"If you must know," she said, "that little shop in *la Rue de la Goutte d'Or* is vacant. I heard so only an hour ago and it struck me all of a heap!"

It was a very nice shop in the very house of which they had so often thought. There was the shop itself— a back room—and two others. They were small, to be sure, but convenient and well arranged—only she thought it dear—five hundred francs.

"You asked the price then?"

"Yes, I asked it just out of curiosity," she answered, with an air of indifference, "but it is too dear, decidedly too dear. It would be unwise I think, to take it."

But she could talk of nothing else the whole evening. She drew the plan of the rooms on the margin of a newspaper, and as she talked, she measured the furniture, as if they were to move the next day. Then Coupeau, seeing her great desire to have the place, declared he would see the owner the next morning, for it was possible he would take less than five hundred francs; but how would she like to live so near his sister, whom she detested?

Gervaise was displeased at this, and said she detested no one, and even defended the Lorilleux, declaring they were not so bad, after all. And when Coupeau was asleep, her busy brain was at work arranging the rooms, which as yet they had not decided to hire.

The next day, when she was alone, she lifted the shade from the clock and opened her bank book. Just to think, that her shop and future prosperity lay between those dirty leaves!

Before going to her work she consulted Madame Goujet, who approved of the plan. With a husband like hers, who never drank, she could not fail of success. At noon she called on her sister-in-law to ask her advice, for she did not wish to have the air of concealing anything from the family.

Madame Lorilleux was confounded. What! did Wooden-Legs think of having an establishment of her own! and with an envious heart she stammered out that it would be very well certainly; but when she had recovered herself a little she began to talk of the dampness of the courtyard, and of the darkness of the rez-de-chaussée. Oh! yes, it was a capital place for rheumatism; but of course, if her mind was made up, anything she could say would make no difference.

That night Gervaise told her husband that if he had thrown any obstacles in the way of her taking the shop, she believed she should have fallen sick and died, so great was her longing. But before they came to any decision, they must see if no diminution of the rent could be obtained.

"We can go to-morrow if you say so," was her husband's reply; "you can call for me at six o'clock."

Coupeau was then completing the roof of a three-storied house, and was laying the very last sheets of zinc. It was May, and a cloudless evening. The sun was low in the horizon, and against the blue sky the figure of Coupeau was clearly defined, as he cut his zinc, as quietly as a tailor might have cut out a pair of breeches in his workshop. His assistant, a lad of seventeen, was blowing up the furnace with a pair of bellows, and at each puff a great cloud of sparks arose.

"Put in the irons, Zidore!" shouted Coupeau.

The boy thrust the irons among the coals which showed only a dull pink in the sunlight, and then went to work again with his bellows. Coupeau took up his last sheet of zinc. It was to be placed on the edge of the roof, near the gutter. Just at that spot the roof was very steep. The man walked along in his list slippers much as if he had been at home, whistling a popular melody. He allowed himself to slip a little, and caught at the chimney, calling to Zidore as he did so:

"Why in thunder don't you bring the irons? What are you staring at?"

But Zidore, quite undisturbed, continued to stare at a cloud of heavy black smoke that was rising in the direction of Grenelle. He wondered if it were a fire; but he crawled with the irons toward Coupeau, who began to solder the zinc, supporting himself on the point of one foot, or by one finger, not rashly, but with calm deliberation and perfect coolness. He knew what he could do, and never lost his head. His pipe was in his mouth, and he would occasionally 'urn to spit down into the street below.

"Hallo! Madame Boche!" he cried, as he suddenly caught sight of his old friend crossing the street, "how are you to-day?"

She looked up, laughed, and a brisk conversation ensued between the roof and the street. She stood with her hands under her apron and her face turned up, while he, with one arm round a flue, leaned over the side of the house.

"Have you seen my wife?" he asked.

"No indeed; is she anywhere round?"

"She is coming for me. Is every one well with you?"

"Yes, all well, thanks. I am going to a butcher near here who sells cheaper than up our way."

They raised their voices, because a carriage was passing, and this brought to a neighboring window a little old woman, who stood in breathless horror, expecting to see the man fall from the roof in another minute.

"Well, good-night!" cried Madame Boche, "I must not detain you from your work."

Coupeau turned and took the iron Zidore held out to him. At the same moment Madame Boche saw Gervaise coming toward her, with little Nana trotting at her side. She looked up to the roof to tell Coupeau, but Gervaise closed her lips with an energetic signal, and then as she reached the old Concierge, she said in a low voice, that she was always in deadly terror that her husband would fall. She never dared look at him when he was in such places.

"It is not very agreeable, I admit," answered Madame Boche. "My man is a tailor, and I am spared all this."

"At first," continued Gervaise, "I had not a moment's peace. I saw him in my dreams on a litter; but now I have got accustomed to it somewhat."

She looked up, keeping Nana behind her skirts, lest the child should call out and startle her father, who was at that moment on the extreme edge. She saw the soldering iron. and the tiny flame that rose as he carefully passed it along the edges of the zinc. Gervaise, pale with suspense and fear, raised her hands mechanically with a gesture of supplication. Coupeau ascended the steep roof with a slow step; then glancing down, he beheld his wife.

"You are watching me, are you?" he cried, gayly. "Ah, Madame Boche, is she not a silly one? She was afraid to speak to me. Wait ten minutes, will you?"

The two women stood on the sidewalk, having as much as they could do to restrain Nana, who insisted on fishing in the gutter.

The old woman still stood at the window, looking up at the roof, and waiting.

"Just see her," said Madame Boche. "What is she looking at?"

Coupeau was heard lustily singing; with the aid of a pair of compasses, he had drawn some lines, and now proceeded to cut a large fan, this he adroitly, with his tools, folded into the shape of a pointed mushroom. Zidore was again heating the irons. The sun was setting just behind the house, and the whole western sky was flushed with rose fading to a soft violet, and against this sky, the figures of the two men, immeasurably exaggerated, stood clearly out, as well as the strange form of the zinc which Coupeau was then manipulating.

"Zidore! the irons!"

But Zidore was not to be seen. His master, with an oath, shouted down the scuttle window which was open near by, and finally discovered him two houses off. The boy was taking a walk, apparently, with his scanty blonde hair blowing all about his head.

"Do you think you are in the country?" cried Coupeau, in a fury. "You are another Béranger perhaps—composing verses! Will you have the kindness to give me my irons? Who ever heard the like. Give me my irons, I say!"

The irons hissed as he applied them, and he called to Gervaise:

"I am coming!"

The chimney to which he had fitted this cap was in the centre of the roof. Gervaise stood watching him, soothed by his calm self-possession. Nana clapped her little hands.

"Papa! Papa!" she cried. "Look!"

The father turned—his foot slipped—he rolled down the roof slowly, unable to catch at anything.

"Good God!" he said, in a choked voice, and he fell—his body turned over twice and crashed into the middle of the street with the dull thud of a bundle of wet linen.

Gervaise stood still. A shriek was frozen on her lips. Madame Boche snatched Nana in her arms, and hid her head that she might not see—and the little old woman opposite, who seemed to have waited for this scene in the drama, quietly closed her windows.

Four men bore Coupeau to a druggist's at the corner, where he lay for an hour while a litter was sent for from the Hospital Lariboisière. He was breathing still, but that was all. Gervaise knelt at his side, hysterically sobbing. Every minute or two, in spite of the prohibition of the druggist, she touched him to see if he were still warm. When the litter arrived, and they spoke of the Hospital, she started up, saying, violently:

"No—no!—Not to the Hospital—to our own home."

In vain did they tell her that the expenses would be very great if she nursed him at home.

"No—no!" she said, "I will show them the way. He is my husband, is he not? and I will take care of him myself."

And Coupeau was carried home—and as the litter was borne through the Quartier the women crowded together and extolled Gervaise. "She was a little lame to be sure, but she was very energetic, and she would save her man."

Madame Boche took Nana home, and then went about among her friends to tell the story with interminable details. "I saw him fall," she said. "It was all because of the child; he was going to speak to her, when down he went. Good Lord! I trust I may never see such another sight."

For a week Coupeau's life hung on a thread. His family and his friends expected to see him die from one hour to another. The physician, an experienced physician, whose every visit cost five francs, talked of a lesion, and that word was in itself very terrifying to all but Gervaise, who pale from her vigils, but calm and resolute, shrugged her shoulders, and would not allow herself to be discouraged. Her man's leg was broken, that she knew very well—"but he need not die for that!"—and she watched at his side night and day—forgetting her children, and her home, and everything but him.

On the ninth day, when the physician told her he would recover, she dropped, half fainting, on a chair—and at night she slept for a couple of hours with her head on the foot of his bed.

This accident to Coupeau brought all his family about him. His mother spent the nights there, but she slept in her chair quite comfortably. Madame Lerat came in every evening, after work was over, to make inquiries.

The Lorilleux at first came three or four times each day, and brought an arm-chair for Gervaise; but soon quarrels and discussions arose as to the proper way of nursing the invalid, and Madame Lorilleux lost her temper, and declared that had Gervaise stayed at home, and not gone to pester her husband when he was at work, that the accident would not have happened.

When she saw Coupeau out of danger, Gervaise allowed his family to approach him as they saw fit. His convalesence would be a matter of months. This again was a ground of indignation for Madame Lorilleux.

"What nonsense it was," she said, "for Gervaise to take him home! had he gone to the Hospital he would have recovered as quickly again."

And then she made a calculation of what these four months would cost:—First, there was the time lost, then the physician, the medicines, the wines, and finally the meat for beef-tea. "Yes, it would be a pretty sum to be sure! If they got through it on their savings they would do well; but she believed that the end would be, that they would find themselves head over heels in debt, and they need expect no assistance from his family, for none of them were rich enough to pay for sickness at home!"

One evening Madame Lorilleux was malicious enough to say:

"And your shop, when do you take it? The Concierge is waiting to know what you mean to do."

Gervaise gasped. She had utterly forgotten the shop. She saw the delight of these people when they believed that this plan was given up, and from that day they never lost an occasion of twitting her, on her dream that had toppled over like a house of cards, and she grew morbid, and fancied they were pleased at the accident to their brother which had prevented the realization of their plans.

She tried to laugh, and to show them she did not grudge the money that had been expended in the restoration of her husband's health. She did not withdraw all her savings from the bank at once, for she had a vague hope that some miracle would intervene which would render the sacrifice unnecessary.

Was it not a great comfort, she said to herself and to her enemies, for as such she had begun to regard the Lorilleux, that she had this money now to turn to in this emergency.

Her neighbors next door had been very kind and thoughtful to Gervaise all through her trouble and the illness of her husband.

Madame Goujet never went out without coming to inquire if there was anything she could do, any commission she could execute. She brought innumerable bowls of soup, and even when Gervaise was particularly busy, washed her dishes for her. Goujet filled her buckets every morning with fresh water, and this was an economy of at least two sous, and in the evening came to sit with Coupeau. He did not say much but his companionship cheered

and comforted the invalid. He was tender and compassionate, and was thrilled by the sweetness of Gervaise's voice when she spoke to her husband. Never had he seen such a brave good woman; he did not believe she sat in her chair fifteen minutes in the whole day—she was never tired—never out of temper, and the young man grew very fond of the poor woman as he watched her.

His mother had found a wife for him. A girl whose trade was the same as her own, a lace mender, and as he did not wish to go contrary to her desires he consented that the marriage should take place in September.

But when Gervaise spoke of his future he shook his head.

"All women are not like you, Madame Coupeau," he said, "if they were I should like ten wives."

At the end of two months Coupeau was on his feet again, and could move —with difficulty of course—as far as the window, where he sat with his leg on a chair. The poor fellow was sadly shaken by his accident. He was no philosopher, and he swore from morning until night. He said he knew every crack in the ceiling. When he was installed in his arm chair it was little better. "How long," he asked impatiently, "was he expected to sit there swathed like a mummy?" And he cursed his ill luck. His accident was a cursed shame. If his head had been disturbed by drink it would have been different, but he was always sober and this was the result. He saw no sense in the whole thing!

"My father," he said, "broke his neck. I don't say he deserved it, but I do say there was a reason for it. But I had not drank a drop, and yet over I went, just because I spoke to my child! If there be a Father in Heaven as they say, who watches over us all, I must say He manages things strangely enough sometimes!"

And as his strength returned, his trade grew strangely distasteful to him. It was a miserable business he said, roaming along gutters like a cat. In his opinion there should be a law which should compel every house-owner to tin his own roof. He wished he knew some other trade he could follow, something that was less dangerous.

For two months more Coupeau walked with a crutch, and after a while was able to get into the street and then to the outer Boulevard, where he sat on a bench in the sun. His gayety returned, he laughed again and enjoyed doing nothing. For the first time in his life he felt thoroughly lazy, and indolence seemed to have taken possession of his whole being. When he got rid of his crutches he sauntered about and watched the buildings which were in the process of construction in the vicinity, and he jested with the men and indulged himself in a general abuse of work. Of course he intended to begin again as soon as he was quite well, but at present the mere thought made him feel ill, he said.

In the afternoons Coupeau often went to his sister's apartment; she expressed a great deal of compassion for him and showed every attention. When he was first married, he had escaped from her influence, thanks to his affection for his wife, and her's for him. Now he fell under her thumb again; they brought him back by declaring that he lived in mortal terror of his wife. But the Lorilleux were too wise to disparage her openly, on the contrary they praised her extravagantly, and he told his wife that they adored her, and begged her in her turn to be just to them.

The first quarrel in their home arose on the subject of Etienne. Coupeau had been with his sister. He came in late and found the children fretting for their dinner. He cuffed Etienne's ears, bade him hold his tongue, and scolded for an hour. He was sure he did not know why he let that boy stay in the house, he was none of his; until that day, he had accepted the child as a matter of course.

Three days after this, he gave the boy a kick, and it was not long before the child, when he heard him coming, ran into the Goujets', where there was always a corner at the table for him.

Gervaise had long since resumed her work. She no longer lifted the globe of her clock to take out her bank book, her savings were all gone, and it was necessary to count the sous pretty closely, for there were four mouths to feed, and they were all dependent on the work of her two hands. When any one found fault with Coupeau and blamed him, she always took his part.

"Think how much he has suffered," she said, with tears in her eyes. "Think of the shock to his nerves! Who can wonder that he is a little sour? Wait awhile though until he is perfectly well, and you will see that his temper will be as sweet as it ever was."

And if any one ventured to observe that he seemed quite well, and that he ought to go to work, she would exclaim:

"No indeed, not yet. It would never do." She did not want him down in his bed again. She knew what the doctor had said, and she every day, begged him to take his own time. She even slipped a little silver into his vest pocket. All this Coupeau accepted as a matter of course. He complained of all sorts of pains and aches to gain a little longer period of indolence, and at the end of six months had began to look upon himself as a confirmed invalid.

He almost daily dropped into a wine shop with a friend—it was a place where he could chat a little, and where was the harm? Besides, who ever heard of a glass of wine killing a man. But he swore to himself that he would never touch any thing but wine—not a drop of brandy should pass his lips. Wine was good for one—prolonged one's life, aided digestion—but brandy was a very different matter. Notwithstanding all these wise resolutions, it came to pass more than once that he came in, after visiting a dozen different cabarets, decidedly tipsy. On these occasions, Gervaise locked her doors and declared she was ill, to prevent the Goujets from seeing her husband.

The poor woman was growing very sad. Every night and morning she passed the shop for which she had so ardently longed. She made her calculations over and over again, until her brain was dizzy. Two hundred and fifty francs rent—one hundred and fifty for moving and the apparatus she needed—one hundred francs to keep things going until business began to come in. No, it could not be done under five hundred francs.

She said nothing of this to any one, deterred only by the fear of seeming to regret the money she had spent for her husband during his illness. She was pale and dispirited at the thought that she must work five years at least before she could save that much money.

One evening, Gervaise was alone. Goujet entered—took a chair in silence, and looked at her as he smoked his pipe. He seemed to be revolving something in his mind. Suddenly he took his pipe from his mouth.

"Madame Gervaise," he said, "will you allow me to lend you the money you require?"

She was kneeling at a drawer, laying some towels in a neat pile. She started up, red with surprise. He had seen her standing that very morning for a good ten minutes, looking at the shop; so absorbed that she had not seen him pass.

She refused his offer, however. No, she could never borrow money when she did not know how she could return it, and when he insisted, she replied:

"But your marriage? This is the money you have saved for that."

"Don't worry on that account," he said with a heightened color. "I shall not marry. It was an idea of my mother's, and I prefer to lend you the money."

They looked away from each other. Their friendship had a certain element of tenderness which each silently recognized.

Gervaise accepted finally, and went with Goujet to see his mother, whom he had informed of his intentions. They found her somewhat sad, with her serene, pale face bent over her work.

She did not wish to thwart her son, but she no longer approved of the plan, and she told Gervaise why. With kind frankness, she pointed out to her that Coupeau had fallen into evil habits and was living on her labors, and would in all probability continue to do so. The truth was that Madame Goujet had not forgiven Coupeau for refusing to read during all his long convalescence; this and many other things had alienated her and her son from him, but they had in no degree lost their interest in Gervaise.

Finally it was agreed she should have five hundred francs, and should return the money by paying each month, twenty francs on account.

"Well, well!" cried Coupeau, as he heard of this financial transaction; "we are in luck. There is no danger with us to be sure, but if he were dealing with knaves, he might never see hide or hair of his cash again!"

The next day the shop was taken, and Gervaise ran about with such a light heart, that there was a rumor that she had been cured of her lameness by an operation.

## CHAPTER V

### AMBITIOUS DREAMS

THE Boche couple, on the first of April, moved also, and took the lôge of the great house in la Rue de la Goutte d'-Or. Things had turned out very nicely for Gervaise who, having always got on very comfortable with the Concierge in the house in Rue Neuve, dreaded lest she should fall into the power of some tyrant who would quar-rel over every drop of water that was spilled, and a thousand other trifles like that. But with Madame Boche, all would go smoothly.

The day the lease was to be signed, and Gervaise stood in her new home, her heart swelled with joy. She was finally to live in that house, like a small town, with its intersecting corridors, instead of streets.

She felt a strange timidity—a dread of failure—when she found herself face to face with her enterprise. The struggle for bread was a terrible and an increasing one, and it seemed to her for a moment that she had been guilty of a wild, foolhardy act—like throwing herself into the jaws of a machine; for the planes in the cabinet-maker's shop and the hammers in the lock-smith's were dimly grasped by her as a part of a great whole.

The water that ran past the door that day from the dyer's was pale green. She smiled as she stepped over it, accepting this color as a happy augury. She, with her husband, entered the lôge, where Madame Boche and the owner of the building, Monsieur Mares-cot, were talking on business.

Gervaise, with a thrill of pain, heard Boche advise the landlord to turn out the dress-maker on the third floor, who was behind-hand with her rent. She wondered if she should ever be turned out, and then wondered again at the attitude assumed by these Boche peo-ple, who did not seem to have ever seen her before. They had eyes and ears only for the landlord, who shook hands with his new tenants; but when they spoke of repairs, professed to be in such haste that morning, that it would be necessary to postpone the discussion. They reminded him of certain verbal promises he had made, and finally he consented to examine the premises.

The shop stood with its four bare walls and blackened ceiling. The tenant who had been there had taken away his own counters and cases. A furious discussion took place. Monsieur Marescot said it was for them to embellish the shop.

"That may be," said Gervaise gently; "but surely you cannot call putting on a fresh paper, instead of this that hangs in strips, an embellishment. Whitening the curbing, too, comes under the head of necessary repairs." She only required these two things.

Finally Marescot, with a desperate air, plunged his hands deep in his pockets, shrugged his shoulders, and gave his consent to the repairs on the ceiling, and to the paper, on condition that she would pay for half the paper—and then he hurried away.

When he had departed, Boche clapped Coupeau on the shoulder. "You may thank me for that!" he cried, and then went on to say that he was the real master of the house—that he settled the whole business of the establishment, and it was a nod and look from him that had influenced Monsieur Marescot. That evening, Gervaise, considering themselves in debt to Boche, sent him some wine.

In four days the shop should have been ready for them; but the repairs hung on for three weeks. At first they intended simply to have the paint scrubbed but it was so shabby and worn, that Gervaise repainted at her own expense. Coupeau went every morning, not to work, but to inspect operations; and Boche dropped the vest or pantaloons on which he was working, and gave the benefit of his advice, and the two men spent the whole day smoking and spitting, and arguing over each stroke of the brush. Some days the painters did not appear at all; on others they came and walked off in an hour's time, not to return again.

Poor Gervaise wrung her hands in despair. But finally after two days of energetic labor, the whole thing was done, and the men walked off with their ladders, singing lustily.

Then came the moving, and finally Gervaise called herself settled in her new home and was pleased as a child. As she came up the street she could see her sign afar off.

## CLEAR STARCHER.

### LACES AND EMBROIDERIES

DONE UP WITH ESPECIAL CARE.

The two first words were painted in large yellow letters on a pale blue ground.

In the recessed window shut in at the back by muslin curtains, lay men's shirts, delicate handkerchiefs and cuffs —all these were on blue paper and Gervaise was charmed. When she entered the door all was blue there; the paper represented a golden trellis and blue morning glories. In the centre was a huge table draped with blue bordered cretonne, to hide the trestles.

Gervaise seated herself and looked round, happy in the cleanliness of all about her. Her first glance however was directed to her stove, a sort of furnace whereon ten irons could be heated at once. It was a source of constant anxiety lest her little apprentice should fill it too full of coal and so injure it.

Behind the shop was her bedroom and her kitchen from which a door opened into the court. Nana's bed stood in a little room at the right, and Etienne was compelled to share his with the baskets of soiled clothes. It was all very well except that the place was very damp, and that it was dark by three o'clock in the afternoon in winter.

The new shop created a great excitement in the neighborhood. Some people declared that the Coupeaus were on the road to ruin, they had in fact spent the whole five hundred francs, and were penniless contrary to their intentions. The morning that Gervaise first took down her shutters, she had only six francs in the world, but she was not troubled, and at the end of a week she told her husband after two hours of abstruse calculations, that they had taken in enough to cover their expenses.

The Lorilleux were in a state of rage, and one morning when the apprentice was emptying on the sly, a bowl of starch which she had burned in making, just as Madame Lorilleux was passing, she rushed in and accused her sister-in-law of insulting her. After this all friendly relations were at an end.

"It all looks very strange to me," sniffed Madame Lorilleux; "I can't tell where the money comes from, but I have my suspicions," and she went on to intimate that Gervaise and Goujet were altogether too intimate. This was the groundwork of many fables, she said Wooden Legs was so mild and sweet that she had deceived her to the extent that she had consented to become Nana's god-mother, which had been no small expense; but now things were very different. If Gervaise were dying and asked her for a glass of water she would not give it. She could not stand such people. As to Nana it was different; they would always receive her; the child, of course, was not responsible for her mother's crimes. Coupeau should take a more decided stand, and not put up with his wife's vile conduct.

Boche and his wife sat in judgment on the quarrel, and gave as their opinion that the Lorilleux were much to blame. They were good tenants, of course. They paid regularly. "But," added Madame Boche, "I never could abide jealousy. They are mean people and were never known to offer a glass of wine to a friend."

Mother Coupeau visited her son and daughter successive days, listened to the tales of each, and said never a word in reply.

Gervaise lived a busy life, and took no notice of all this foolish gossip and strife. She greeted her friends with a smile from the door of her shop, where she went for a breath of fresh air. All the people in the neighborhood liked her, and would have called her a great beauty but for her lameness. She was twenty-eight, and had grown plump. She moved more slowly, and when she took a chair to wait for her irons to heat, she rose with reluctance. She was growing fond of good living, that she herself admitted, but she did not regard it as a fault. She worked hard and had a right to good food. Why should she live on potato-parings? Sometimes she worked all night when she had a great deal of work on hand.

She did the washing for the whole house; and for some Parisian ladies, and had several apprentices, beside two laundresses. She was, making money hand over fist, and her good luck would have turned a wiser head than her own. But hers was not turned; she was gentle and sweet, and hated no one except her sister-in-law. She judged everybody kindly, particularly after she had eaten a good breakfast. When people called her good she laughed. Why should she not be good? She had seen all her dreams realized. She remembered what she once said— that she wanted to work hard, have plenty to eat—a home to herself, where she could bring up her chidren —not be beaten, and die in her bed! As to dying in her bed, she added— she wanted that still, but she would put it off as long as possible, "if you please!" It was to Coupeau himself that Gervaise was especially sweet. Never a cross or an impatient word had he heard from her lips, and no one had ever known her complain of him behind his back. He had finally resumed his trade, and as the shop where he worked was at the other end of Paris, she gave him every morning forty sous for his breakfast, his wine and tobacco. Two days out of six, however, Coupeau would meet a friend,

drink up his forty sous, and return to breakfast. Once, indeed, he sent a note, saying that his account at the cabaret exceeded his forty sous—he was in pledge, as it were—would his wife send the money? She laughed and shrugged her shoulders. Where was the harm in her husband's amusing himself a little? A woman must give a man a long rope if she wished to live in peace and comfort. It was not far from words to blows—she knew that very well.

The hot weather had come. One afternoon in June the ten irons were heating on the stove, the door was open into the street, but not a breath of air came in.

"What a melting day!" said Gervaise, who was stooping over a great bowl of starch. She had rolled up her sleeves and taken off her sacque, and stood in her chemise and white skirt; the soft hair in her neck was curling on her white throat. She dipped each cuff in the starch, the fronts of the shirts and the whole of the skirts. Then she rolled up the pieces tightly and placed them neatly in a square basket, after having sprinkled with clear water all those portions which were not starched.

"This basket is for you, Madame Putois," she said; "and you will have to hurry, for they dry so fast in this weather."

Madame Putois was a thin little woman, who looked cool and comfortable in her tightly-buttoned dress. She had not taken her cap off, but stood at the table, moving her irons to and fro with the regularity of an automaton Suddenly she exclaimed:

"Put on your sacque, Clémence; there are three men looking in, and I don't like such things."

Clémence grumbled and growled. What did she care what she liked? She could not and would not roast to suit anybody.

"Clémence, put on your sacque," said Gervaise; "Madame Putois is right— it is not proper."

Clémence muttered, but obeyed, and consoled herself by giving the apprentice, who was ironing hose and towels by her side, a little push. Gervaise had a cap belonging to Madame Boche in her hand, and was ironing the crown with a round ball, when a tall bony woman came in. She was a laundress.

"You have come too soon, Madame Bijard!" cried Gervaise; "I said tonight. It is very inconvenient for me to attend to you at this hour." At the same time, however, Gervaise amiably laid down her work and went for the dirty clothes, which she piled up in the back shop. It took the two women nearly an hour to sort them and mark them with a stitch of colored cotton.

At this moment Coupeau entered. "By Jove!" he said; "the sun beats down on one's head like a hammer." He caught at the table to sustain himself; he had been drinking—a spider's web had caught in his dark hair, where many a white thread was apparent. His under jaw dropped a little, and his smile was good-natured but silly.

Gervaise asked her husband if he had seen the Lorilleux, in rather a severe tone; when he said no, she smiled at him without a word of reproach.

"You had best go and lie down," she said pleasantly, "we are very busy and you are in our way. Did I say thirty-two handkerchiefs, Madame Bijard? Here are two more, that makes thirty-four."

But Coupeau was not sleepy and he preferred to remain where he was. Gervaise called Clémence and bade her to count the linen while she made out the list. She glanced at each piece as she wrote. She knew many of them by the color. That pillow-slip belonged to Madame Boche because it was stained with the pomade she always used, and so on through the whole. Gervaise was seated with these piles of soiled linen about her. Augustine, whose great delight was to fill up the stove had done so now, and it was red hot. Coupeau leaned towards Gervaise.

"Kiss me," he said. "You are a good woman."

As he spoke he gave a sudden lurch and fell among the skirts.

"Do take care," said Gervaise impatiently, "you will get them all mixed again," and she gave him a little push with her foot whereat all the other women cried out.

"He is not like most men," said Madame Putois, "they generally wish to beat you when they come in like this."

Gervaise already regretted her momentary vexation and assisted her husband to his feet and then turned her cheek to him with a smile, but he put his arm round her and kissed her neck. She pushed him aside with a laugh.

"You ought to be ashamed!" she said, but yielded to his embrace, and the long kiss they exchanged before these people, amid the sickening odor of the soiled linen, and the alcoholic fumes of his breath, was the first downward step in the slow descent of their degradation.

Madame Bijard tied up the linen and staggered off under their weight while Gervaise turned back to finish her cap. Alas! The stove and the irons were alike red hot; she must wait a quarter of an hour before she could touch the irons and Gervaise covered the fire with a couple of shovelfuls of cinders. She then hung a sheet before the window to keep out the sun. Coupeau took a place in the corner, refusing to budge an inch, and his wife and all her assistants went to work on each side of the square table. Each woman had at her right a flat brick on which to set her iron. In the centre of the table was a dish of water with a rag and a brush in it, and also a bunch of tall white lilies in a broken jar.

Madame Putois had attacked the basket of linen prepared by Gervaise, and Augustine was ironing her towels, with her nose in the air, deeply interested in a fly that was buzzing about. As to Clémence she was polishing off her thirty-fifth shirt; as she boasted of this great feat, Coupeau staggered toward her.

"Madame," she called, "please keep him away, he will bother me and I shall scorch my shirt."

"Let her be," said Gervaise, without any especial energy, "we are in a great hurry to-day!"

Well! that was not his fault, he did not mean to touch the girl, he only wanted to see what she was about.

"Really," said his wife, looking up from her fluting iron. "I think you had best go to bed."

He began to talk again.

"You need not make such a fuss, Clémence, it is only because these women are here, and——"

But he could say no more, Gervaise quietly laid one hand on his mouth and the other on his shoulder and pushed him toward his room. He struggled a little, and with a silly laugh asked if Clémence was not coming too.

Gervaise undressed her husband and tucked him up in bed as if he had been a child, and then returned to her fluting irons in time to still a grand dispute that was going on about an iron that had not been properly cleaned.

In the profound silence that followed her appearance, she could hear her husband's thick voice.

"What a silly wife I've got! The idea of putting me to bed in broad daylight!"

Suddenly he began to snore, and Gervaise uttered a sigh of relief. She used her fluting-iron for a minute, and then said quietly:

"There is no need of being offended by anything a man does when he is in this state. He is not an accountable being. He did not intend to insult you. Clémence, you know what a tipsy man is—he respects neither father nor mother."

She uttered these words in an indifferent, matter-of-fact way, not in the least disturbed that he had forgotten the respect due to her and to her roof, and really seeing no harm in his conduct.

The work now went steadily on, and Gervaise calculated they would have finished by eleven o'clock. The heat was intense—the smell of charcoal deadened the air; while the branch of white lilies slowly faded, and filled the room with their sweetness.

The day after all this, Coupeau had a frightful head ache, and did not rise until late—too late to go to his work. About noon he began to feel better, and toward evening was quite himself. His wife gave him some silver, and told him to go out and take the air, which meant with him, taking some wine.

One glass washed down another, but he came home as gay as a lark, and quite disgusted with the men he had seen who were drinking themselves to death.

"Where is your lover?" he said to his wife, as he entered the shop. This was his favorite joke. "I never see him nowadays, and must hunt him up."

He meant Goujet, who came but rarely, lest the gossips in the neighborhood should take it upon themselves to gabble. Once in about ten days he made his appearance in the evening, and installed himself in a corner in the back shop, with his pipe. He rarely spoke, but laughed at all Gervaise said. On Saturday evenings the establishment was kept open half the night. A lamp hung from the ceiling, with the light thrown down by a shade. The shutters were put up at the usual time, but as the nights were very warm, the door was left open; and as the hours wore on, the women pulled their jackets open a little more at the throat, and he sat in his corner and looked on as if he were at a theatre.

The silence of the street was broken by a passing carriage. Two o'clock struck—no longer a sound from outside. At half-past two a man hurried past the door, carrying with him a vision of flying arms, piles of white linen, and a glow of yellow light.

Goujet, wishing to save Etienne from Coupeau's rough treatment, had taken him to the place where he was employed, to blow the bellows, with the prospect of becoming an apprentice as soon as he was old enough; and Etienne thus became another tie between the clear starcher and the blacksmith.

All their little world laughed, and told Gervaise that her friend worshipped the very ground she trod upon. She colored and looked like a girl of sixteen.

"Dear boy," she said to herself, "I know he loves me; but never has he said, or will he say, a word of the kind to me!" And she was proud of being loved in this way. When she was disturbed about anything, her first thought was to go to him. When by chance they were left alone together, they were never disturbed by wondering if their friendship verged on love. There was no harm in such affection.

Nana was now six years old and a most troublesome little sprite. Her mother took her every morning to a school in la Rue Polonçeau, to a certain Mademoiselle Josse. Here she did all manner of mischief. She put ashes into the teacher's snuff box, pinned the skirts of her companions together. Twice the young lady was sent home in disgrace, and then taken back again for the sake of the six francs each month. As soon as school hours were over, Nana revenged herself for the hours of enforced quiet she had passed, by making the most frightful din in the courtyard and the shop.

She found able allies in Pauline and Victor Boche. The whole great house resounded with the most extraordinary noises. The thumps of children falling down stairs, little feet tearing up one stair-case and down another, and bursting out on the sidewalk like a band of pilfering, impudent sparrows.

Madame Gaudron alone had nine—dirty, unwashed and unkempt — their stockings hanging over their shoes and the slits in their garments showing the white skin beneath. Another woman on the fifth floor had seven, and they came out in twos and threes from all the rooms. Nana reigned over this band, among which there were some half-grown and others mere infants. Her prime ministers were Pauline and Victor; to them she delegated a little of her authority, while she played mamma—undressed the youngest only to dress them again—cuffed them and punished them at her own sweet will, and with the most fantastic disposition. The band pranced and waded through the gutter that ran from the dye-house and emerged with blue or green legs. Nana decorated herself and the others with shavings from the cabinet makers, which they stole from under the very noses of the workmen.

The courtyard belonged to all of these children apparently, and re-sounded with the clatter of their heels. Sometimes this court-yard, however, was not enough for them, and they spread in every direction to the infinite disgust of Madame Boche, who grumbled all in vain. Boche declared that the children of the poor were as plentiful as mushrooms on a dung-heap, and his wife threatened them with her broom.

One day there was a terrible scene. Nana had invented a beautiful game. She had stolen a wooden shoe belonging to Madame Boche; she bored a hole in it and put in a string, by which she could draw it like a cart. Victor filled it with apple-parings, and they started forth in a procession, Nana drawing the shoe in front, followed by the whole flock, little and big, an imp about the height of a cigar box at the end. They all sang a melancholy ditty full of "ah's" and "oh's." Nana declared this to be always the custom at funerals.

"What on earth are they doing now?" murmured Madame Boche suspiciously, and then she came to the door and peered out.

"Good heavens!" she cried; "it is my shoe they have got."

She slapped Nana, cuffed Pauline and shook Victor. Gervaise was filling a bucket at the fountain, and when she saw Nana with her nose bleeding, she rushed toward the Concierge, and asked how she dared strike her child.

The Concierge replied that any one who had a child like that, had best keep her under lock and key. The end of this was, of course, a complete break between the old friends.

But, in fact, the quarrel had been growing for a month. Gervaise, generous by nature, and knowing the tastes of the Boche people, was in the habit of making them constant presents—oranges, a little hot soup, a cake, or something of the kind. One evening, knowing that the Concierge would sell her soul for a good salad, she took her the remains of a dish of beets and chiccory. The next day she was dumbfounded at hearing from Mademoiselle Remanjon, how Madame Boche had thrown the salad away, saying that she was not yet reduced to eating the leavings of other people! From that day forth, Gervaise sent her nothing more. The Boches had learned to look on her little offerings as their right, and they now felt themselves to be robbed by the Coupeaus.

It was not long before Gervaise realized she had made a mistake—for when she was one day late with her October rent, Madame Boche complained to the proprietor, who came blustering to her shop with his hat on. Of course, too, the Lorilleux extended the right hand of fellowship at once to the Boche people.

There came a day, however, when Gervaise found it necessary to call on the Lorilleux. It was on Mamma Coupeau's account, who was sixty-seven years old, nearly blind and helpless. They must all unite in doing something for her now. Gervaise thought it a burning shame that a woman of her age, with three well-to-do children, should be allowed for a moment to regard herself as friendless and forsaken. And as her husband refused to speak to his sister, Gervaise said she would.

She entered the room like a whirlwind, without knocking. Everything was just as it was on that night when she had been received by them in a fashion which she had never forgotten nor forgiven. "I have come," cried Gervaise, "and I dare say you wish to know why, particularly as we are at daggers-drawn. Well! then, I have come on Mamma Coupeau's account. I have come to ask if we are to allow her to beg her bread from door to door—"

"Indeed!" said Madame Lorilleux, with a sneer, and she turned away.

But Lorilleux lifted his pale face. "What do you mean?" he asked, and as he had understood perfectly, he went on.

"What is this cry of poverty about? The old lady ate her dinner with us yesterday. We do all we can for her, I am sure. We have not the mines of Peru within our reach, but if she thinks she is to run to and fro between our houses, she is much mistaken. I, for one, have no liking for spies." He then added, as he took up his microscope, "When the rest of you agree to give five francs per month toward her support, we will do the same." Gervaise was calmer now—these people always chilled the very marrow in her bones—and she went on to explain her views. Five francs were not enough for each of the old lady's children to pay. She could not live on fifteen francs per month.

"And why not?" cried Lorilleux, "she ought to do so. She can see well enough to find the best bits in a dish before her, and she can do something toward her own maintenance." If he had the means to indulge such laziness he should not consider it his duty to do so, he added.

Then Gervaise grew angry again. She looked at her sister-in-law, and saw her face set in vindictive firmness.

"Keep your money," she cried. "I

will take care of your mother. I found a starving cat in the street the other night and took it in. I can take in your mother too. She shall want for nothing. Good heavens, what people!"

Madame Lorilleux snatched up a saucepan.

"Clear out," she said, hoarsely. "I will never give one sou—no, not one sou toward her keep. I understand you! You will make my mother work for you like a slave, and put my five francs in your pocket! Not if I know it, Madame! And if she goes to live under your roof I will never see her again. Be off with you, I say!"

"What a monster!" cried Gervaise, as she shut the door with a bang.

On the very next day, Madame Coupeau came to her. A large bed was put in the room where Nana slept. The moving did not take long, for the old lady had only this bed, a wardrobe, table, and two chairs. The table was sold, and the chairs new-seated; and the old lady the evening of her arrival washed the dishes and swept up the room, glad to make herself useful. Madame Lerat had amused herself by quarrelling with her sister, to whom she had expressed her admiration of the generosity evinced by Gervaise; and when she saw that Madame Lorilleux was intensely exasperated, she declared she had never seen such eyes in anybody's head as those of the clear-starcher. She really believed one might light paper at them. This declaration naturally led to bitter words, and the sisters parted, swearing they would never see each other again; and since then Madame Lerat had spent most of her evenings at her brother's.

Three years passed away. There were reconciliations and new quarrels. Gervaise continued to be liked by her neighbors: she paid her bills regularly, and was a good customer. When she went out she received cordial greeting on all sides, and she was more fond of going out in these days than of yore. She liked to stand at the corners and chat. She liked to loiter with her arms full of bundles at a neighbor's window and hear a little gossip.

## CHAPTER VI.

### GOUJET AT HIS FORGE

ONE autumnal afternoon Gervaise, who had been to carry a basket of clothes home to a customer who lived a good way off, found herself in La Rue des Poissonnièrs just as it was growing dark. It had rained in the morning, and the air was close and warm. She was tired with her walk, and felt a great desire for something good to eat. Just then she lifted her eyes and seeing the name of the street, she took it into her head that she would call on Goujet at his forge. But she would ask for Etienne, she said to herself. But she did not know the number, but she could find it, she thought. She wandered along and stood bewildered, looking toward Montmartre; all at once she heard the measured click of hammers—and concluded that she had stumbled on the place at last. She did not know where the entrance to the building was, but she caught a gleam of a red light in the distance; she walked toward it and was met by a workman.

"Is it here, sir," she said, timidly, "that my child—a little boy, that is to say—works? A little boy by the name of Etienne?"

"Etienne! Etienne!" repeated the man, swaying from side to side. The wind brought from him to her an intolerable smell of brandy, which caused Gervaise to draw back, and say timidly:

"Is it here that Monsieur Goujet works?"

"Ah! Goujet, yes. If it is Goujet you wish to see, go to the left."

Gervaise obeyed his instructions and found herself in a large room with the forge at the further end. She spoke to the first man she saw, when suddenly the whole room was one blaze of light. The bellows had sent up leaping flames which lighted every crevice and corner of the dusty old building, and Gervaise recognized Goujet before the forge, with two other men. She went toward him.

"Madame Gervaise!" he exclaimed in surprise, his face radiant with joy, and then seeing his companions laugh and wink, he pushed Etienne toward his mother. "You came to see your boy," he said; "he does his duty like a hero."

"I am glad of it," she answered; "but what an awful place this is to get at!"

And she described her journey as she called it, and then asked why no one seemed to know Etienne there.

"Because," said the blacksmith, "he is called Zou Zou here, as his hair is cut as short as a Zouave's."

This visit paid by Gervaise to the Forge was only the first of many others. She often went on Saturdays when she carried the clean linen to Madame Goujet, who still resided in the same house as before. The first year Gervaise had paid them twenty francs each month, or rather the difference between the amount of their washing, seven or eight francs, and the twenty which she agreed upon. In this way she had paid half the money she had borrowed, when one quarter-day, not knowing to whom to turn, as she had not been able to collect her bills punctually, she ran to the Goujets and borrowed the amount of her rent from them. Twice since she had asked a similar favor, so that the amount of her indebtedness now stood at four hundred and twenty-five francs.

Now she no longer paid any cash, but did their washing. It was not that she worked less hard nor that her business was falling off. Quite the contrary; but money had a way of melting away in her hands, and she was content nowadays if she could only make both ends meet. What was the use of fussing, she thought? If she could manage to live that was all that was necessary. She was growing quite stout withal.

Madame Goujet was always kind to Gervaise: not because of any fear of losing her money, but because she really loved her, and was afraid of her going wrong in some way.

The Saturday after the first visit paid by Gervaise to the Forge was also the first of the month. When she reached Madame Goujet's, her basket was so heavy that she panted for two good minutes before she could speak. Every one knows how heavy shirts and such things are.

"Have you brought everything?"

asked Madame Goujet, who was very exacting on this point. She insisted on every piece being returned each week. Another thing she exacted was that the clothes should be brought back always on the same day and hour.

"Everything is here," answered Gervaise, with a smile. "You know I never leave anything behind."

"That is true," replied the elder woman. "You have many faults, my dear; but not that one yet."

And while the laundress emptied her basket, laying the linen on the bed, Madame Goujet paid her many compliments. She never burned her clothes, nor ironed off the buttons, nor tore them; but she did use a trifle too much blueing, and made her shirts too stiff.

"Feel," she said, "it is like pasteboard. My son never complains, but I know he does not like them so."

"And they shall not be so again," said Gervaise. "No one ever touches any of your things but myself, and I would do them over ten times rather than see you dissatisfied."

She colored as she spoke.

"I have no intention of disparaging your work," answered Madame Goujet. "I never saw any one who did up laces and embroideries as you do, and the fluting is simply perfect: the only trouble is a little too much starch, my dear. Guojet does not care to look like a fine gentleman."

She took up her book and drew a pen through the pieces as she spoke. Everything was there. She brought out the bundle of soiled clothes. Gervaise put them in her basket, and hesitated.

"Madame Goujet," she said, at last, "if you do not mind, I should like to have the money for this week's wash."

The account this month was larger than usual, ten francs and over. Madame Goujet looked at her gravely.

"My child," she said, slowly, "it shall be as you wish. I do not refuse to give you the money if you desire it; only this is not the way to get out of debt. I say this with no unkindness, you understand. Only you must take care."

Gervaise, with downcast eyes, received the lesson meekly. "She needed the ten francs to complete the amount due the coal merchant," she said.

But her friend heard this with a stern countenance, and told her she should reduce her expenses; but she did not add, that she too, intended to do the same, and that in future she should do her washing herself, as she had formerly done, if she were to be out of pocket thus.

When Gervaise was on the staircase her heart was light, for she cared little for the reproof now that she had the ten francs in her hand; she was becoming accustomed to paying one debt by contracting another.

Midway on the stairs she met a tall woman coming up with a fresh mackerel in her hand, and behold! it was Virginie, the girl whom she had whipped in the Lavatory. The two looked each other full in the face. Gervaise instinctively closed her eyes, for she thought the girl would slap her in the face with the mackerel. But no; Virginie gave a constrained smile. Then the laundress, whose huge basket filled up the stairway, and who did not choose to be outdone in politeness, said:

"I beg your pardon—"

"Pray don't apologize," answered Virginie, in a stately fashion.

And they stood and talked for a few minutes with not the smallest allusion, however, to the past.

Virginie, then about twenty-nine, was really a magnificent-looking woman; head well-set on her shoulders, and a long, oval face crowned by bands of glossy black hair. She told her history in a few brief words. She was married. Had married the previous spring a cabinet-maker who had given up his trade, and was hoping to obtain a position on the police force. She had just been out to buy this mackerel for him. "He adores them," she said, "and we women spoil our husbands, I think. But come up. We are standing in a draught here."

When Gervaise had in her turn told her story, and added that Virginie was living in the very rooms where she had lived, and where her child was born, Virginie became still more urgent that she should go up. "It is always pleasant to see a place where one has been happy," she said. "She herself had been living on the other side of the water, but had got tired of it, and had moved into these rooms only two weeks ago. She was not settled yet. Her name was Madame Poisson."

"And mine," said Gervaise, "is Coupeau."

Gervaise was a little suspicious of all this courtesy. Might not some terrible revenge be hidden under it all? and she determined to be well on her guard. But as Virginie was so polite just now, she must be polite in her turn.

Poisson, the husband, was a man of thirty-five, with a moustache and imperial; he was seated at a table near the window, making little boxes. His only tools were a pen-knife, a tiny saw, and a glue pot; he was executing the most wonderful and delicate carving, however. He never sold his work, but made presents of it to his friends. It amused him while he was awaiting his appointment.

Poisson rose, and bowed politely to Gervaise, whom his wife called an old friend. But he did not speak—his conversational powers not being his strong point. He cast a plaintive glance at the mackerel, however, from time to time. Gervaise looked around the room, and described her furniture, and where it had stood. How strange it was, after losing sight of each other so long, that they should occupy the same apartment! Virginie entered into new details. He had a small inheritance from his aunt, and she herself sewed a little—made a dress now and then. At the end of a half hour Gervaise rose to depart; Virginie went to the head of the stairs with her, and there both hesitated. Gervaise fancied that Virginie wished to say something about Lantier and Adèle, but they separated without touching on these disagreeable topics.

This was the beginning of a great friendship. In another week Virginie could not pass the shop without going in, and sometimes she remained for two or three hours. At first, Gervaise was very uncomfortable; she thought every time Virginie opened her lips that she should hear Lantier's name. Lantier was in her mind all the time she was with Madame Poisson. It was a stupid thing to do after all, for what on earth did she care what had become of Lantier or of Adèle? but she was none the less curious to know something about them.

Winter had come—the fourth winter that the Coupeaus had spent in La Rue de la Goutte d'Or. This year December and January were especially severe, and after New Year's the snow lay three weeks in the street without melting. There was plenty of work for Gervaise, and her shop was delightfully warm and singularly quiet, for the carriages made no noise in the snow-covered streets. The laughs and shouts of the children were almost the only sounds; they had made a long slide; and enjoyed themselves hugely.

Gervaise took especial pleasure in her coffee at noon. Her apprentices had no reason to complain, for it was hot and strong and unadulterated by chiccory. On the morning of Twelfth Day the clock had struck twelve and then half-past, and the coffee was not ready. Gervaise was ironing some muslin curtains. Clémence, with a frightful cold, was as usual at work on a man's shirt. Madame Putois was ironing a skirt on a board, with a cloth laid on the floor to prevent the skirt from being soiled. Mamma Coupeau brought in the coffee, and as each one of the women took a cup with a sigh of enjoyment, the street door opened, and Virginie came in with a rush of cold air.

"Heavens!" she cried, "it is awful! my ears are cut off!"

"You have come just in time for a cup of hot coffee," said Gervaise, cordially.

"And I shall be only too glad to have it!" answered Virginie, with a shiver. She had been waiting at the grocer's, she said, until she was chilled through and through. The heat of that room was delicious, and then she stirred her coffee, and said she liked the damp, sweet smell of the freshly ironed linen. She and Mamma Coupeau were the only ones who had chairs; the others sat on wooden footstools, so low that they seemed to be on the floor. Virginie suddenly stooped down to her hostess, and said, with a smile:

"Do you remember that day at the Lavatory?"

Gervaise colored; she could not answer. This was just what she had been dreading. In a moment she felt sure she should hear Lantier's name. She knew it was coming. Virginie drew nearer to her. The apprentices lingered over their coffee, and told each other, as they looked stupidly into the street, what they would do if they had an income of ten thousand francs. Virginie changed her seat and took a footstool by the side of Gervaise, who felt weak and cowardly, and helpless to change the conversation, or to stave off what was coming. She breathlessly awaited the next words, her heart big with an emotion which she would not acknowledge to herself.

"I do not wish to give you any pain," said Virginie, blandly. "Twenty times the words have been on my lips, but I hesitated. Pray don't think I bear you any malice."

She tipped up her cup and drank the last drop of her coffee. Gervaise, with her heart in her mouth, waited in a dull agony of suspense, asking herself if Virginie could have forgiven the insult in the Lavatory. There was a glitter in the woman's eyes she did not like.

"You had an excuse," Virginie added, as she placed her cup on the table. "You had been abominably treated. I should have killed some one," and then dropping her little affected tone, she continued more rapidly—

"They were not happy, I assure you, not at all happy. They lived in a dirty street, where the mud was up to their knees. I went to breakfast with them two days after he left you, and found them in the height of a quarrel. You know that Adèle is a wretch. She is my sister, to be sure, but she is a wretch all the same. As to Lantier— well, you know him, so I need not describe him. But for a 'yes' or a 'no,' he would not hesitate to thrash any woman that lives. Oh, they had a beautiful time! their quarrels were heard all over the neighborhood. One day the police were sent for, they made such a hubbub."

She talked on and on, telling things that were enough to make the hair stand up on one's head. Gervaise listened, as pale as death, with a nervous trembling of her lips which might have been taken for a smile. For seven years she had never heard Lantier's name, and she would not have believed that she could have felt any such overwhelming agitation. She could no longer be jealous of Adèle, but she smiled grimly as she thought of the blows she had received in her turn from Lantier, and she would have listened

for hours to all that Virginia had to tell; but she did not ask a question for some time. Finally she said:

"And do they still live in that same place?"

"No, indeed! but I have not told you all yet. They separated a week ago."

"Separated!" exclaimed the clear-starcher.

"Who is separated?" asked Clémence, interrupting her conversation with Mamma Coupeau.

"No one," said Virginie, "or at least no one whom you know."

As she spoke she looked at Gervaise, and seemed to take a positive delight in disturbing her still more. She suddenly asked her, what she would do or say if Lantier should suddenly make his appearance, for men were so strange, no one could ever tell what they would do—Lantier was quite capable of returning to his old love. Then Gervaise interrupted her and rose to the occasion. She answered with grave, dignity that she was married now, and that if Lantier should appear she should ask him to leave. There could never be anything more between them, not even the most distant acquaintance.

"I know very well," she said, "that Etienne belongs to him, and if Lantier desires to see his son, I shall place no obstacle in his way. But as to myself, Madame Poisson, he shall never touch my little finger again! It is finished."

As she uttered these last words she traced a cross in the air to seal her oath; and as if desirous to put an end to the conversation, she called out to her women—

"Do you think the ironing will be

done to-day, if you sit still? To work! to work!"

The women did not move; they were lulled to apathy by the heat and Gervaise herself found it very difficult to resume her labors. Her curtains had dried in all this time, and some coffee had been spilled on them, and she must wash out the spots.

"Au revoir!" said Virginie. "I came out to buy a half-pound of cheese. Poisson will think I am frozen to death!"

The better part of the day was now gone, and it was this way every day—for the shop was the refuge and haunt of all the chilly people in the neighborhood. Gervaise liked the reputation of having the most comfortable room in the Quartier, and she held her receptions—as the Lorilleux and Boche clique said, with a sniff of disdain. She would, in fact, have liked to bring in the very poor whom she saw shivering outside. She became very friendly toward a journeyman painter, an old man of seventy, who lived in a loft of the house, where he shivered with cold and hunger. He had lost his three sons in the Crimea, and for two years his hand had been so cramped by rheumatism that he could not hold a brush.

Whenever Gervaise saw Father Bru she called him in, made a place for him near the stove, and give him some bread and cheese. Father Bru, with his white beard, and his face wrinkled like an old apple, sat in silent content, for hours at a time, enjoying the warmth and the crackling of the coke.

"What are you thinking about?" Gervaise would say, gayly.

"Of nothing—of all sorts of things," he would reply, with a dazed air.

The workwomen laughed, and thought it a good joke to ask if he were in love. He paid little heed to them, but relapsed into silent thought.

From this time Virginie often spoke to Gervaise of Lantier, and one day she said she had just met him. But as the clear-starcher made no reply, Virginie then said no more. But on the next day she returned to the subject, and told her that he had talked long and tenderly of her. Gervaise was much troubled by these whispered conversations in the corner of her shop. The name of Lantier made her faint and sick at heart. She believed herself to be an honest woman. She meant, in every way, to do right and to shun the wrong, because she felt that only in doing so could she be happy. She did not thing much of Coupeau, because she was conscious of no short-comings towards him. But she thought of her friend at the Forge, and it seemed to her that this return of her interest in Lantier, faint and undecided as it was, was an infidelity to Goujet, and to that tender friendship which had become so very precious to her. Her heart was much troubled in these days. She dwelt on that time when her first lover left her. She imagined another day, when, quitting Adèle, he might return to her with that old familiar trunk.

When she went into the street, it was with a spasm of terror. She fancied that every step behind her was Lantier's. She dared not look around, lest his hand should glide about her waist. He might be watching for her at any time. He might come to her door in the afternoon, and this idea brought a cold sweat to her forehead, because he would certainly kiss her on her ear, as he had often teased her by doing in the years gone by. It was this kiss she dreaded. Its dull reverberation deafened her to all outside sounds, and she could hear only the beatings of her own heart. When these terrors assailed her, the Forge was her only asylum, from whence she returned smiling and serene, feeling that Goujet— whose sonorous hammer had put all her bad dreams to flight — would protect her always.

What a happy season this was after all! The clear-starcher always carried a certain basket of clothes to her customer each week, because it gave her a pretext for going into the Forge, as it was on her way. As soon as she turned the corner of the street in which it was situated, she felt as light-hearted as if she were going to the country. The black charcoal dust in the road, the black smoke rising slowly from the chimneys, interested and pleased her as much, as a mossy path through the woods. Afar off the forge was red even at mid-day, and her heart danced in time with the hammers. Goujet was expecting her and making more noise than usual, that she might hear him at a great distance. She gave Etienne a light tap on his cheek, and sat quietly watching these two — this man and boy, who were so dear to her —for an hour without speaking. When the sparks touched her tender skin, she rather enjoyed the sensation. He in his turn, was fully aware of the happiness she felt in being there, and he reserved the work which required skill,

for the time when she could look on in wonder and admiration. It was an idyl that they were unconsciously enacting all that spring, and when Gervaise returned to her home, it was in a spirit of sweet content.

By degrees her unreasonable fears of Lantier were conquered. Coupeau was behaving very badly at this time, and one evening, as she passed the Assommoir, she was certain she saw him drinking with Mes-Bottes. She hurried on lest she should seem to be watching him. But as she hastened she looked over her shoulder. Yes, it was Coupeau who was tossing down a glass of liquor with an air as if it were no new thing. He had lied to her, then; he did drink brandy. She was in utter despair, and all her old horror of brandy returned. Wine she could have forgiven—wine was good for a working man; liquor, on the contrary, was his ruin, and took from him all desire for the food that nourished, and gave him strength for his daily toil. Why did not the government interfere and prevent the manufacture of such pernicious things?

When she reached her home she found the whole house in confusion. Her employés had left their work and were in the court-yard. She asked what the matter was.

"It is Father Bijard beating his wife; he is as drunk as a fool, and he drove her up the stairs to her room, where he is murdering her. Just listen!"

Gervaise flew up the stairs. She was very fond of Madame Bijard, who was her laundress and whose courage and industry she greatly admired. On the sixth floor a little crowd was assembled.

Madame Boche stood at an open door. "Have done!" she cried; "have done! or the police will be summoned."

No one dared enter the room, because Bijard was well known to be like a madman when he was tipsy. He was rarely thoroughly sober; and on the occasional days when he condescended to work, he always had a bottle of brandy at his side. He rarely ate anything, and if a match had been touched to his mouth, he would have taken fire like a torch.

"Would you let her be killed!" exclaimed Gervaise, trembling from head to foot, and she entered the attic room, which was very clean and very bare, for the man had sold the very sheets off the bed to satisfy his mad passion for drink. In this terrible struggle for life, the table had been thrown over, and the two chairs also. On the floor lay the poor woman, with her skirts drenched as she had come from the wash-tub, her hair streaming over her bloody face, uttering low groans at each kick the brute gave her.

The neighbors whispered to each other that she had refused to give him the money she had earned that day. Boche called up the staircase to his wife:

"Come down, I say; let him kill her if he will: it will only make one fool the less in the world!"

Father Bru followed Gervaise into the room, and the two expostulated with the madman. But he turned toward them pale and threatening; a white foam glistened on his lips, and in his faded eyes there was a murderous expression. He grasped Father Bru by the shoulder and threw him over the table, and shook Gervaise until her teeth chattered, and then returned to his wife, who lay motionless, with her mouth wide open and her eyes closed; and during this frightful scene little Lalie, four years old, was in the corner looking on at the murder of her mother. The child's arms were round her sister Henriette, a baby who had just been weaned. She stood with a sad, solemn face, and serious, melancholy eyes, but shed no tears.

When Bijard slipped and fell, Gervaise and Father Bru helped the poor creature to her feet, who then burst into sobs. Lalie went to her side, but she did not cry, for the child was already habituated to such scenes. And as Gervaise went down the stairs, she was haunted by the strange look of resignation and courage in Lalie's eyes —it was an expression belonging to maturity and experience, rather than to childhood.

"Your husband is on the other side of the street," said Clémence, as soon as she saw Gervaise; "he is as tipsy as possible!"

Coupeau reeled in, breaking a square of glass with his shoulder as he missed the doorway. He was not tipsy, but drunk, with his teeth set firmly together, and a pinched expression about the nose. And Gervaise instantly knew that it was the liquor of the Assommoir which had vitiated his blood. She tried to smile, and coaxed him to go to bed. But he shook her off and as he passed her gave her a blow.

He was just like the other—the beast up-stairs who was now snoring, tired out by beating his wife. She was chilled to the heart and desperate. Were all men alike? She thought of Lantier and of her husband, and wondered if there was no happiness in the world.

## CHAPTER VII

### A BIRTHDAY FÊTE

THE 19th of June was the clear-starcher's birthday. There was always an excuse for a fête in the Coupeau mansion—Saints were invented, to serve as a pretext for idleness and festivities. Virginie highly commended Gervaise for living luxuriously. What was the use of her husband drinking up everything? why should she save, for her husband to spend at all the wine-shops in the neighborhood? And Gervaise accepted this excuse. She was growing very indolent and much stouter, while her lameness had perceptibly increased.

For a whole month they discussed the preparation for this fête; they talked over dishes, and licked their lips. They must have something out of the common way. Gervaise was much troubled as to whom she should invite. She wanted exactly twelve at table, not one more nor one less. She, her husband, her mother-in-law, and Madame Lerat were four. The Goujets and Poissons were four more. At first she thought she would not ask her two women, Madame Putois and Clémence, lest it should make them too familiar; but as the entertainment was constantly under discussion before them, she ended by inviting them too. Thus there were ten: she much have two more; she decided on a reconciliation with the

Lorilleux, who had extended the olive-branch several times lately. "Family quarrels were bad things," she said. When the Boche people heard of this, they showed several little courtesies to Gervaise, who felt obliged to urge them to come also. This made fourteen without counting the children. She had never had a dinner like this, and she was both triumphant and terrified.

The 19th fell on a Monday, and Gervaise thought it very fortunate, as she could begin her cooking on Sunday afternoon. On Saturday, while the women hurried through their work, there was an endless discussion as to what the dishes should be. In the last three weeks only one thing had been definitely decided upon—a roast goose stuffed with onions. The goose had been purchased, and Madame Coupeau brought it in that Madame Putois might guess its weight. The thing looked enormous, and the fat seemed to burst from its yellow skin.

"Soup before that, of course," said Gervaise, "and we must have another dish."

Clémence proposed rabbits, but Gervaise wanted something more distinguished. Madame Putois suggested a blanquette du Veau—

That was a new idea. Veal was always good too. Then Madame Coupeau made an allusion to fish, which no one seconded. Evidently fish was not in favor. Gervaise proposed a spare-rib of pork and potatoes, which brightened all their faces, just as Virginie came in like a whirlwind.

"You are just in season. Mamma Coupeau, show her the goose," cried Gervaise.

Virginie admired it, guessed the weight, and laid it down on the ironing-table between an embroidered skirt and a pile of shirts. She was evidently thinking of something else. She soon led Gervaise into the back shop.

"I have come to warn you," she said quickly. "I just met Lantier at the very end of this street, and I am sure he followed me, and I naturally felt alarmed on your account, my dear."

Gervaise turned very pale. What did he want of her? and why on earth should he worry her now amid all the busy preparations for the fête? It seemed as if she never in her life had set her heart on anything that she was not disappointed. Why was it that she could never have a minute's peace?

But Virginie declared that she would look out for her. If Lantier followed her she would certainly give him over to the police. Her husband had been in office now for a month, and Virginie was very dictatorial and aggressive, and talked of arresting every one who displeased her. She raised her voice as she spoke, but Gervaise implored her to be cautious, because her women could hear every word. They went back to the front shop, and she was the first to speak.

"We have said nothing of vegetables," she said, quietly.

"Peas, with a bit of pork," said Virginie, authoritatively.

This was agreed upon with enthusiasm.

The next day at three, Mamma Coupeau lighted the two furnaces belonging to the house, and a third one borrowed from Madame Boche; and at half-past three the soup was gently simmering in a large pot lent by the restaurant at the corner. They had decided to cook the veal and the pork the day previous, as those two dishes could be warmed up so well, and would leave for Monday only the goose to roast and the vegetables. The back shop was ruddy with the glow from the three furnaces—sauces were bubbling with a strong smell of browned flour. Mamma Coupeau and Gervaise, each with large, white aprons, were washing celery, and running hither and thither with pepper and salt, or hurriedly turning the veal with flat wooden sticks made for the purpose. They had told Coupeau pleasantly that his room was better than his company; but they had plenty of people there that afternoon. The smell of the cooking found its way out into the street and up through the house and the neighbors, impelled by curiosity, came down on all sorts of pretexts, merely to discover what was going on.

About five Virginie made her appearance. She had seen Lantier twice. Indeed, it was impossible nowadays to enter the street and not see him. Madame Boche, too, had spoken to him on the corner below. Then Gervaise, who was on the point of going for a sou's worth of fried onions to season her soup, shuddered from head to foot, and said she would not go out ever again. The Concierge and Virginie added to her terror by a succession of stories of men who lay in wait for women, with knives and pistols hidden in their coats.

Such things were read every day in the papers! When such a scamp as Lantier found a woman happy and comfortable, he was always wretched until he had made her so, too. Virginie said she would go for the onions. "Women," she observed sententiously, "should protect each other, as well as serve each other, in such matters." When she returned, she reported that Lantier was no longer there. The conversation around the stove that evening never once drifted from that subject. Madame Boche said that she, under similar circumstances, should tell her husband; but Gervaise was horror-struck at this, and begged her never to breathe one single word about it. Besides, she fancied her husband had caught a glimpse of Lantier from something he had muttered, amid a volley of oaths, two or three nights before. She was filled with dread lest these two men should meet. She knew Coupeau so well, that she had long since discovered that he was still jealous of Lantier; and while the four women discussed the imminent danger of a terrible tragedy, the sauces and the meats hissed and simmered on the furnaces, and they ended by each taking a cup of soup to discover what improvement was desirable.

Monday arrived. Now that Gervaise had invited fourteen to dine, she began to be afraid there would not be room, and finally decided to lay the table, in the shop. She was uncertain how to place the table, which was the ironing table on trestles. In the midst of the hubbub and confusion a customer arrived, and made a scene because her linen had not come home on the Friday previous. She insisted on having every piece that moment— clean or dirty, ironed or rough-dry.

Then Gervaise, to excuse herself, told a lie with wonderful *sang-froid*. It was not her fault. She was cleaning her rooms. Her women would be at work again the next day, and she got rid of her customer, who went away soothed by the promise that her wash should be sent to her early the following morning.

But Gervaise lost her temper, which was not a common thing with her, and as soon as the woman's back was turned, called her by an opprobrious name, and declared that if she did as people wished she could not take time to eat, and vowed she would not have an iron heated that day nor the next, in her establishment. No! not if the Grand Turk himself should come and entreat her on his knees to do up a collar for him. She meant to enjoy herself a little occasionally!

The entire morning was consumed in making purchases. Three times did Gervaise go out and come in, laden with bundles. But when she went the fourth time for the wine she discovered that she had not money enough. She could have got the wine on credit, but she could not be without money in the house, for a thousand little unexpected expenses arise at such times, and she and her mother-in-law racked their brains to know what they should do to get the twenty francs they considered necessary. Madame Coupeau, who had once been house-keeper for an actress, was the first to speak of the Mont-de-Piété. Gervaise laughed gayly.

"To be sure! Why had she not thought of it before?"

She folded her black silk dress and

pined it in a napkin, then she hid the bundle under her mother-in-law's apron and bade her keep it very flat, lest the neighbor's who were so terribly inquisitive should find it out, and then she watched the old woman from the door, to see that no one followed her.

But when Mamma Coupeau had gone a few steps Gervaise called her back into the shop, and, taking her wedding-ring from her finger, said:

"Take this, too, for we shall need all the money we can get to-day."

And when the old woman came back with twenty-five francs she clapped her hands with joy. She ordered six bottles of wine with seals to drink with the roast. The Lorilleux would be green with envy. For a fortnight this had been her idea, to crush the Lorilleux, who were never known to ask a friend to their table; who, on the contrary, locked their doors when they had anything especially to eat. Gervaise wanted to give her a lesson, and would have liked to offer the strangers who passed her door, a seat at her table. Money was a very good thing, and mighty pretty to look at, but it was good for nothing but to spend.

Mamma Coupeau and Gervaise began to lay their table at three o'clock. They had hung curtains before the window, but as the day was warm, the door into the street was open. The two women did not put on a plate or salt-spoon without the avowed intention of worrying the Lorilleux. They had given them seats where the table could be seen to the best advantage, and they placed before them the real china plates.

"No, no, mamma," cried Gervaise, "not those napkins. I have two which are real damask."

"Well! well! I declare!" murmured the old woman. "What will they say to all this?"

And they smiled as they stood at opposite sides of this long table with its glossy white cloth, and its places for fourteen carefully laid. They worshipped there as if it had been a chapel erected in the middle of the shop.

"How false they are!" said Gervaise. "Do you remember how she declared she had lost a piece of one of the chains when she was carrying them home? That was only to get out of giving you your five francs."

"Which I have never had from them but just twice," muttered the old woman.

"I will wager that next month they will invent another tale. That is one reason why they lock their doors when they have a rabbit. They think people might say, 'If you can eat rabbits you can give five francs to your mother!' How mean they are! What do they think would have become of you if I had not asked you to come and live here?"

Her mother-in-law shook her head. She was rather severe in her judgment of the Lorilleux that day, inasmuch as she was influenced by the gorgeous entertainment given by the Coupeaus. She liked the excitement, she liked to cook—she generally lived pretty well with Gervaise; but on those days which occur in all households, when the dinner was scanty and unsatisfactory, she called herself a most unhappy woman, left to the mercy of a daughter-in-law. In the depths of her heart she still loved Madame Lorilleux; she was her eldest child.

"You certainly would have weighed some pounds less with her," continued Gervaise. "No coffee, no tobacco, no sweets. And do you imagine that they would have put two mattresses on your bed?"

"No, indeed," answered the old woman; "but I wish to see them when they first come in—just to see how they look!"

At four o'clock the goose was roasting, and Augustine, seated on a little footstool, was given a long-handled spoon, and bidden to watch and baste it every few minutes. Gervaise was busy with the peas, and Mamma Coupeau, with her head a little confused, was waiting until it was time to heat the veal and the pork. At five the guests began to arrive. Clémence and Madame Putois, gorgeous to behold in their Sunday rig, were the first.

Clémence wore a blue dress and had some geraniums in her hand; Madame was in black, with a bunch of heliotrope. Gervaise, whose hands were covered with flour, put them behind her back, come forward, and kissed them cordially.

After them came Virginie in scarf and hat, though she had only to cross the street; she wore a printed muslin, and was as imposing as any lady in the land. She brought a pot of red carnations, and put both her arms around her friend and kissed her.

The offering brought by Boche was a pot of pansies, and his wife's was mignonette; Madame Lerat's a lemon verbena. The three furnaces filled the room with an overpowering heat, and the frying potatoes drowned their voices. Gervaise was very sweet and smiling, thanking every one for the flowers, at the same time making the dressing for the salad. The perfume of the flowers was perceived above all the smell of cooking.

"Can't I help you?" said Virginie. "It is a shame to have you work so hard for three days on all these things, that we shall gobble up in no time."

"No, indeed," answered Gervaise, "I am nearly through."

The ladies covered the bed with their shawls and bonnets, and then went into the shop that they might be out of the way, and talked through the open door with much noise and loud laughing.

At this moment Goujet appeared, and stood timidly on the threshold with a tall white rose-bush in his arms whose flowers brushed against his yellow beard. Gervaise ran toward him with her cheeks reddened by her furnaces. She took the plant, crying:

"How beautiful!"

He dared not kiss her, and she was compelled to offer her cheek to him; and both were embarrassed. He told her, in a confused way, that his mother was ill with sciatica and could not come. Gervaise was greatly disappointed, but she had no time to say much just then: she was beginning to be anxious about Coupeau—he ought to be in—then, too, where were the Lorilleux? She called Madame Lerat, who had arranged the reconciliation, and bade her go and see.

Madame Lerat put on her hat and shawl with excessive care and departed. A solemn hush of expectation pervaded the room.

Madame Lerat presently reappeared. She had come round by the street to give a more ceremonious aspect to the affair. She held the door open, while Madame Lorilleux, in a silk dress, stood on the threshold. All the guests rose, and Gervaise went forward to meet her sister and kissed her, as had been agreed upon.

"Come in! come in!" she said. "We are friends again."

"And I hope for always," answered her sister-in-law, severely.

After she was ushered in, the same programme had to be followed out with her husband. Neither of the two brought any flowers. They had refused to do so, saying that it would look as if they were bowing down to Wooden Leg. Gervaise summoned Augustine, and bade her bring some wine, and then filled glasses for all the party, and each drank the health of the family.

"It is a good thing before soup," muttered Boche.

Mamma Coupeau drew Gervaise into the next room.

"Did you see her?" she said, eagerly. "I was watching her, and when she saw the table, her face was as long as my arm, and now she is gnawing her lips, she is so mad!"

It was true the Lorilleux could not stand that table, with its white linen, its shining glass, and square piece of bread at each place. It was like a restaurant on the Boulevard, and Madame Lorilleux felt of the cloth stealthily to ascertain if it were new.

"We are all ready," cried Gervaise, reappearing, and pulling down her sleeves over her white arms.

"Where can Coupeau be?" she continued.

"He is always late! he always forgets!" muttered his sister. Gervaise was in despair. Everything would be spoiled. She proposed that someone should go out and look for him. Goujet offered to go, and she said she would accompany him. Virgine followed, all three bare headed. Every one looked at them, so gay and fresh on a week day. Verginie, in her pink muslin, and Gervaise in a white cambric with blue spots, and a gray silk handkerchief knotted round her throat. They went to one wine-shop after another, but no Coupeau. Suddenly, as they went toward the Boulevard, his wife uttered an exclamation.

"What is the matter?" asked Goujet.

The clear-starcher was very pale, and so much agitated that she could hardly stand. Virginie knew at once, and leaning over her, looked in at the restaurant and saw Lantier quietly dining.

"I turned my foot," said Gervaise, when she could speak. Finally, at the Assommoir they found Coupeau and Poisson. They were standing in the centre of an excited crowd. Coupeau, in a gray blouse, was quarrelling with some one, and Poisson, who was not on duty that day, was listening quietly —his red moustache and imperial giving him, however, quite a formidable aspect.

Goujet left the women outside, and going in placed his hand on Coupeau's shoulder, who, when he saw his wife and Virginie, fell into a great rage.

"No, he would not move! He would not stand being followed about by women in this way! They might go home and eat their rubbishy dinner themselves! He did not want any of it!"

To appease him, Goujet was compelled to drink with him, and finally he persuaded him to go with him. But when he was outside, he said to Gervaise:

"I am not going home; you need not think it!"

She did not reply. She was trembling from head to foot. She had been speaking of Lantier to Virginie, and begged the other to go on in front, while the two women walked on either side of Coupeau to prevent him from seeing Lantier as they passed the open window where he sat eating his dinner.

But Coupeau knew that Lantier was there, for he said:

"There's a fellow I know, and you know him, too!"

He then went on to accuse her, with many a coarse word, of coming out to look—not for him—but for her old lover, and then all at once he poured out a torrent of abuse upon Lantier, who, however, never looked up or appeared to hear it.

Virginie at last coaxed Coupeau on, whose rage disappeared when they turned the corner of the street. They returned to the shop, however, in a very different mood from the one in which they had left it, and found the guests, with very long faces, awaiting them.

Coupeau shook hands with the ladies in succession, with difficulty keeping his feet as he did so, and Gervaise, in a choked voice, begged them to take their seats. But suddenly she perceived that Madame Goujet not having come, there was an empty seat next to Madame Lorilleux.

"We are thirteen," she said, much disturbed, as she fancied this to be an additional proof of the misfortune which, for some time, she had felt to be hanging over them.

The ladies, who were seated, started up. Madame Putois offered to leave, because, she said, no one should fly in the face of Destiny; besides, she was not hungry. As to Boche, he laughed, and said it was all nonsense.

"Wait!" cried Gervaise, "I will arrange it."

And rushing out on the sidewalk, she called to Father Bru, who was crossing the street, and the old man followed her into the room.

"Sit there," said the clear-starcher. "You are willing to dine with us, are you not?"

He nodded acquiescence.

"He will do as well as another," she continued, in a low voice. "He rarely, if ever, had as much as he wanted to eat, and it will be a pleasure to us to see him enjoy his dinner."

Goujet's eyes were damp, so much was he touched by the kind way in which Gervaise spoke, and the others felt that it would bring them good luck. Madame Lorilleux was the only one who seemed displeased. She drew her skirts away and looked down with disgusted mien upon the patched blouse at her side.

Gervaise served the soup, and the guests were just lifting their spoons to their mouths, when Virginie noticed that Coupeau had disappeared. He had probably returned to the more congenial society at the Assommoir, and some one said he might stay in the street—certainly no one would go after him; but just as they had swallowed the soup Coupeau appeared bearing two pots, one under each arm—a balsam and a wallflower. All the guests clapped their hands. He placed them on either side of Gervaise, and, kissing her, he said:

"I forgot you, my dear; but all the same I loved you very much."

"Monsieur Coupeau is very amiable to-night; he has taken just enough to make him good-natured," whispered one of the guests.

This little act on the part of the host brought back the smiles to the faces around the table. The wine began to circulate, and the voices of the children were heard in the next room. Etienne, Nana, Pauline, and little Victor Fauconnier were installed at a small table, and were told to be very good.

When the blanquette du Veau was served, the guests were moved to enthusiasm. It was now half-past seven. The door of the shop was shut to keep out inquisitive eyes, and curtains hung before the windows. The veal was a great success; the sauce was delicious, and the mushrooms extraordinarily good. Then came the spare-rib of pork. Of course all these good things demanded a large amount of wine.

In the next room, at the children's table, Nana was playing the mistress of the household. She was seated at the head of the table, and for a while was quite dignified, but her natural gluttony made her forget her good manners when she saw Augustine stealing the peas from the plate, and she slapped the girl vehemently.

"Take care, Mademoiselle," said Augustine, sulkily, "or I will tell your mother that I heard you ask Victor to kiss you."

Now was the time for the goose. Two lamps were placed on the table, one at each end, and the disorder was very apparent: the cloth was stained and spotted. Gervaise left the table, to reappear presently bearing the goose in triumph. Lorilleux and his wife exchanged a look of dismay.

"Who will cut it?" said the clear-starcher. "No, not I: it is too big for me to manage!"

Coupeau said he could do it. After all it was a simple thing enough—he should just tear it to pieces.

There was a cry of dismay.

Madame Lerat had an inspiration.

"Monsieur Poisson is the man," she said; "of course he understands the use of arms," and she handed the sergeant the carving-knife. Poisson made a stiff inclination of his whole body and drew the dish toward him, and went to work in a slow, methodical fashion. As he thrust his knife into the breast, Lorilleux was seized with momentary patriotism, and he exclaimed:

"If it were only a Cossack!"

At last the goose was carved and distributed, and the whole party ate as if they were just beginning their dinner. Presently there was a grand outcry about the heat, and Coupeau opened the door into the street. Gervaise devoured large slices of the breast, hardly speaking, but a little ashamed of her own gluttony in the presence of Goujet. She never forgot old Bru, however, and gave him the choicest morsels, which he swallowed unconsciously, his palate having long since lost the power of distinguishing flavors. Mamma Coupeau picked a bone with her two remaining teeth.

And the wine! Good heavens! how much they drank! A pile of empty bottles stood in the corner. When Madame Putois asked for water, Coupeau himself removed the carafes from the table. No one should drink water, he declared, in his house—did she want to swallow frogs and live things? and he filled up all the glasses. Hypocrites might talk as much as they pleased— the juice of the grape was a mighty good thing and a famous invention!

The guests all laughed and approved; working people must have their wine, they said, and Father Noah had planted the vine for them especially. Wine gave courage and strength for work; and, if it chanced that a man sometimes took a drop too much, in the end it did him no harm, and life looked brighter to him for a time. Goujet himself, who was usually so prudent and absteminous, was becoming a little excited. Boche was growing red and the Lorilleux pair very pale; while Poisson assumed a solemn and severe aspect. The men were all more or less tipsy; and the ladies—well, the less we say of the ladies the better.

Suddenly Gervaise remembered the six bottles of sealed wine she had omitted to serve with the goose as she had intended. She produced them amid much applause. The glasses were filled anew, and Poisson rose and proposed the health of their hostess.

"And fifty more birthdays!" cried Virginie.

"No, no," answered Gervaise, with a smile that had a touch of sadness in it. "I do not care to live to be very old. There comes a time when one is glad to go!"

A little crowd had collected outside, and smiled at the scene, and the smell of the goose pervaded the whole street. The clerks in the grocery opposite licked their lips, and said it was good, and curiously estimated the amount of wine that had been consumed.

None of the guests were annoyed by being the subjects of observation, although they were fully aware of it, and in fact rather enjoyed it. Coupeau catching sight of a familiar face, held up a bottle, which, being accepted with a nod, he sent it out with a glass. This established a sort of fraternity with the street.

In the next room the children were unmanageable. They had taken possession of a saucepan and were drumming on it with spoons. Mamma Coupeau and Father Bru were talking earnestly. The old man was speaking of his two sons who had died in the Crimea. "Ah! had they but lived he would have had bread to eat in his old age!"

Madame Coupeau, whose tongue was a little thick, said:

"Yes; but one has a good deal of unhappiness with children. Many an hour have I wept on account of mine."

Father Bru hardly heard what she said, but talked on half to himself.

"I can't get any work to do. I am too old. When I ask for any, people laugh, and ask if it was I who blacked Henri Quatre's boots. Last year I earned thirty sous by painting a bridge. I had to lie on my back all the time close to the water, and since then I have coughed incessantly." He looked down at his poor stiff hands, and added, "I know I am good for nothing. I wish I was by the side of my boys. It is a great pity that one can't kill one's self when one begins to grow old."

"Really," said Lorilleux, "I cannot see why the government does not do something for people in your condition. Men who are disabled—"

"But workmen are not soldiers," interrupted Poisson, who considered it his duty to espouse the cause of the government. "It is foolish to expect them to do impossibilities."

The dessert was served. In the centre was a pyramid of sponge cake in the form of a temple with melon-like sides, and on the top was an artificial rose, with a butterfly of silver paper hovering over it, held by a gilt wire. Two drops of gum in the heart of the rose stood for dew. On the left was a deep plate with a bit of cheese, and on the other side of the pyramid was a dish of strawberries, which had been sugared and carefully crushed.

In the salad dish there were a few leaves of lettuce left.

"Madame Boche," said Gervaise, courteously, "pray eat these. I know how fond you are of salad."

The Concierge shook her head. There were limits even to her capacities, and she looked at the lettuce with regret. Clémence told how she had once eaten three quarts of watercresses at her breakfast. Madame Putois declared that she enjoyed lettuce with a pinch of salt and no dressing, and as they talked the ladies emptied the salad-bowl.

None of the guests were dismayed at the dessert, although they had eaten so enormously. They had the night before them, too; there was no need of haste. The men lighted their pipes and drank more wine while they watched Gervaise cut the cake. Poisson, who prided himself on his knowledge of the habits of good society, rose and took the rose from the top, and presented it to the hostess amid the loud applause of the whole party. She fastened it just over her heart, and the butterfly fluttered at every movement. A song was proposed—comic songs were a specialty with Boche—and the whole party joined in the chorus. The men kept time with their heels, and the women with their knives on their glasses. The windows of the shop jarred with the noise. Virginie had disappeared twice, and the third time, when she came back, she said to Gervaise:

"My dear, he is still at the restaurant, and pretends to be reading his paper. I fear he is meditating some mischief."

She spoke of Lantier. She had been out to see if he were anywhere in the vicinity. Gervaise became very grave.

"Is he tipsy?" she asked.

"No, indeed; and that is what troubled me. Why on earth should he stay there so long if he is not drinking? My heart is in my mouth, I am so afraid something will happen."

The clear-starcher begged her to say no more. Madame Putois started up and began a fierce piratical song—standing stiff and erect in her black dress, her pale face surrounded by her black lace cap, and gesticulating violently. Poisson nodded approval. He had been to sea, and he knew all about it.

Gervaise, assisted by her mother-in-law, now poured out the coffee. Her guests insisted on a song from her, declaring that it was her turn. She refused. Her face was disturbed and pale, so much so that she was asked if the goose disagreed with her.

Finally she began to sing a plaintive melody, all about dreams and rest. Her eyelids half closed as she ended, and she peered out into the darkness. Then followed a barcarolle from Madame Boche, and a romance from Lorilleux, in which figured, perfumes of Araby—ivory throats—ebony hair—kisses —moonlight and guitars! Clémence followed with a song, which recalled the country with its descriptions of birds and flowers. Virginie brought down the house with her imitation of a vivandière, standing with her hand on her hip, and a wine glass in her hand, which she emptied down her throat as she finished.

But the grand success of the evening was Goujet, who sang in his rich bass the Adieux d'Abd-el-Kader. The words issued from his yellow beard like the call of a trumpet, and thrilled every one around the table.

Virginie whispered to Gervaise:

"I have just seen Lantier pass the door. Good heavens! There he is again, standing still and looking in."

Gervaise caught her breath and timidly turned around. The crowd had increased, attracted by the songs. There were soldiers and shop-keepers, and three little girls, five or six years old, holding each other by the hand, grave and silent, struck with wonder and admiration.

Lantier was directly in front of the door. Gervaise met his eyes, and felt the very marrow of her bones chilled, she could not move hand or foot.

Coupeau called for more wine, and Clémence helped herself to more strawberries. The singing ceased, and the conversation turned upon a woman, who had hung herself the day before in the next street.

It was now Madame Lerat's turn to amuse the company, but she needed to make certain preparations.

She dipped the corner of her napkin into a glass of water and applied it to her temples because she was too warm. Then she asked for a teaspoonful of brandy and wiped her lips.

"I will sing 'L'Enfant du bon Dieu,' " she said, pompously.

She stood up, with her square shoulders like those of a man, and began:

"L'Enfant perdu que sa mère abandonne,
    Troue toujours un asile au Saint lieu,
    Dieu qui le voit, le défend de son trône,
    L'Enfant perdu, c'est L'Enfant du bon Dieu."

She raised her eyes to heaven, and placed one hand on her heart; her voice was not without a certain sympathetic quality, and Gervaise, already quivering with emotion caused by the knowledge of Lantier's presence, could no longer restrain her tears. It seemed to her that she was the deserted child whom le bon Dieu had taken under His care. Clémence, who was quite tipsy, burst into loud sobs. The ladies took out their handkerchiefs and pressed them to their eyes, rather proud of their tenderness of heart.

The men felt it their duty to respect the feeling shown by the women, and were, in fact, somewhat touched themselves. The wine had softened their hearts apparently.

Gervaise and Virginie watched the shadows outside. Madame Boche in her turn now caught a glimpse of Lantier, and uttered an exclamation as she wiped away her fast falling tears. The three women exchanged terrified, anxious glances.

"Good heavens!" muttered Virginie. "Suppose Coupeau should turn around. There would be a murder, I am convinced." And the earnestness of their fixed eyes became so apparent that finally he said:

"What are you staring at?"

And leaning forward he too saw Lantier.

"This is too much," he muttered, "the dirty ruffian! It is too much, and I won't have it!"

As he started to his feet with an oath, Gervaise put her hand on his arm imploringly.

"Put down that knife," she said, "and do not go out, I entreat of you."

Virginie took away the knife, that Coupeau had snatched from the table, but she could not prevent him from going into the street. The other guests saw nothing, so entirely absorbed were they in the touching words which Madame Lerat was still singing.

Gervaise sat with her hands clasped convulsively, breathless with fear, expecting to hear a cry of rage from the street and see one of the two men fall to the ground. Virginie and Madame

Boche had something of the same feeling. Coupeau had been so overcome by the fresh air that when he rushed forward to take Lantier by the collar he missed his footing and found himself seated quietly in the gutter.

Lantier moved aside a little, without taking his hands from his pocket.

Coupeau staggered to his feet again, and a violent quarrel commenced. Gervaise pressed her hands over her eyes; suddenly all was quiet, and she opened her eyes again and looked out.

To her intense astonishment she saw Lantier and her husband talking in a quiet, friendly manner.

Gervaise exchanged a look with Madame Boche and Virginie. What did this mean?

As the women watched them, the two men began to walk up and down in front of the shop. They were talking earnestly. Coupeau seemed to be urging something, and Lantier refusing. Finally Coupeau took Lantier's arm and almost dragged him toward the shop.

"I tell you, you must!" he cried. "You shall drink a glass of wine with us. Men will be men all the world over. My wife and I know that perfectly well."

Madame Lerat had finished her song and seated herself with the air of being utterly exhausted. She asked for a glass of wine. When she sang that song, she said, she was always torn to pieces, and it left her nerves in a terrible state.

Lantier had been placed at the table by Coupeau, and was eating a piece of cake, leisurely dipping it into his glass of wine. With the exception of Madame Boche and Virginie, no one knew him.

The Lorilleux looked at him with some suspicion, which, however, was very far from the mark. An awkward silence followed, broken by Coupeau, who said simply:

"He is a friend of ours!"

And turning to his wife, he added: "Can't you move round a little? Perhaps there is a cup of hot coffee!"

Gervaise looked from one to the other. She was literally dazed. When her husband first appeared with her former lover, she had clasped her hands over her forehead, with that instinctive gesture with which in a great storm one waits for the approach of the thunder-clap.

It did not seem possible that the walls would not fall and crush them all. Then, seeing the two men calmly seated together, it all at once seemed perfectly natural to her. She was tired of thinking about it, and preferred to accept it. Why after all should she worry? No one else did. Every one seemed to be satisfied; why should not she be also?

The children had fallen asleep in the back room, Pauline with her head on Etienne's shoulder. Gervaise started as her eyes fell on her boy. She was shocked at the thought of his father sitting there eating cake without showing the least desire to see his child. She longed to awaken him and show him to Lantier. And then again she had a feeling of passing wonder at the manner in which things settled themselves in this world.

She would not disturb the serenity of matters now, so she brought in the coffee-pot and poured out a cup for Lantier, who received it without even looking up at her, as he murmured his thanks.

"Now it is my turn to sing!" shouted Coupeau.

His song was one familiar to them all, and even to the street, for the little crowd at the door joined in the chorus. The guests within were all more or less tipsy, and there was so much noise that the policemen ran to quell a riot; but when they saw Poisson they bowed respectfully and passed on.

No one of the party ever knew how or at what hour the festivities terminated. It must have been very late, for there was not a human being in the street when they departed. They vaguely remembered having joined hands and danced around the table. Gervaise remembered that Lantier was the last to leave—that he passed her as she stood in the doorway. She felt a breath on her cheek, but whether it was his or the night air she could not tell.

Madame Lerat had refused to return to Batignolles so late, and a mattress was laid on the floor in the shop near the table. She slept there amid the debris of the feast, and a neighbor's cat profited by an open window to establish herself by her side, where she crunched the bones of the goose all night between her fine, sharp teeth.

## CHAPTER VIII

### AN OLD ACQUAINTANCE

THE following Saturday Coupeau, who had not been home to dinner, came in with Lantier about ten o'clock. They had been eating pigs' feet at a restaurant at Montmarte.

"Don't scold, wife," said Coupeau, "we have not been drinking, you see; we can walk perfectly straight;" and he went on to say, how they had met each other quite by accident in the street, and how Lantier had refused to drink with him, saying, that when a man had married a nice little woman, he had no business to throw away his money in that way. Gervaise listened with a faint smile; she had no idea of scolding. Oh, no! it was not worth the trouble, but she was much agitated at seeing the two men together so soon again, and with trembling hands she knotted up her loosened hair.

Her work-women had been gone some time. Nana and Mamma Coupeau were in bed, and Gervaise, who was just closing her shutters when her husband appeared, brought out some glasses and the remains of a bottle of brandy. Lantier did not sit down, and avoided addressing her directly.

When she served him, however, he exclaimed:

"A drop, Madame; a mere drop!"

Coupeau looked at them for a moment, and then expressed his mind fully. They were no fools, he said, nor were they children. The Past was the Past. If people kept up their enmities for nine or ten years, no one would have a soul to speak to soon. As for himself, he was made differently. He knew they were honest people, and he was sure he could trust them.

"Of course," murmured Gervaise, hardly knowing what she said, "of course."

"I regard her as a sister," said Lantier, "only as a sister."

"Give us your hand on that," cried Coupeau, "and let us be good friends in the Future. After all a good heart is better than gold, and I estimate Friendship as above all price."

And he gave himself a little tap on his breast, and looked about for applause, as if he had uttered rather a noble sentiment.

Then the three silently drank their brandy. Gervaise looked at Lantier, and saw him for the first time, for on the night of the fête she had seen him, as it were, through a glass, darkly.

He had grown very stout, and his arms and legs very heavy. But his face was still handsome, although somewhat bloated by liquor and good living. He was dressed with care, and did not look any older than his years. He was thirty-five. He wore gray pantaloons and a dark blue frock-coat like any gentleman, and had a watch and a chain on which hung a ring—a souvenir, apparently.

"I must go," he said, presently.

He was at the door, when Coupeau recalled him to say that he must never pass without coming in to say, "How do you do?"

Meanwhile, Gervaise, who had disappeared, returned, pushing Etienne before her. The boy was half asleep, but smiled as he rubbed his eyes. When he saw Lantier he stared, and looked uneasy from him to Coupeau.

"Do you know this gentleman?" said his mother.

The child looked away, and did not answer, but when his mother repeated the question he made a little sign that he remembered him. Lantier, grave and silent, stood still. When Etienne went toward him, he stooped and kissed the child, who did not look at him but burst into tears, and when he was violently reproached by Coupeau, he rushed away.

"It is excitement," said his mother, who was herself very pale.

"He is usually very good and very obedient," said Coupeau. "I have brought him up well, as you will find out. He will soon get used to you. He must learn something of life, you see, and will understand, one of these days, that people must forget and forgive; and I would cut off my head sooner than prevent a father from seeing his child!"

He then proposed to finish the bottle of brandy. They all three drank together again. Lantier was quite undisturbed, and before he left, he insisted on aiding Coupeau to shut up the shop. Then, as he dusted his hands with his handkerchief, he wished them a careless good-night.

"Sleep well. I am going to try and catch the omnibus. I will see you soon again."

Lantier kept his word, and was seen from that time very often in the shop. He came only when Coupeau was home, and asked for him before he crossed the threshold. Then seated near the window, always wearing a frock coat, fresh linen, and carefully shaved, he kept up a conversation like a man who had seen something of the world. By degrees Coupeau learned something of his life. For the last eight years he had been at the head of a hat manufactory, and when he was asked why he had given it up, he said, vaguely, that he was not satisfied with his partner; he was a rascal, and so on.

But his former position still imparted to him a certain air of importance. He said, also, that he was on the point of concluding an important matter — that certain business houses were in process of establishing themselves, the management of which would be virtually in his hands. In the meantime he had absolutely not one thing to do, but to walk about with his hands in his pocket.

Any day he pleased, however, he could start again. He had only to decide on some house. Coupeau did not altogether believe this tale, and insisted that he must be doing something which he did not choose to tell; otherwise, how did he live?

The truth was that Lantier, excessively talkative in regard to other people's affairs, was very reticent about his own. He lied quite as often as he spoke the truth, and would never tell where he resided. He said he was never at home, so it was of no use for any one to come and see him.

"I am very careful," he said, "in making an engagement. I do not choose to bind myself to a man and find, when it is too late, that he intends to make a slave of me. I went one Monday to Champion at Monrouge. That evening Champion began a political discussion. He and I differed entirely, and on Tuesday I threw up the situation. You can't blame me, I am sure, for not being willing to sell my soul and my convictions for seven francs per day!"

It was now November. Lantier occasionally brought a bunch of violets to Gervaise. By degrees his visits became more frequent. He seemed determined to fascinate the whole house, even the Quartier, and he began by ingratiating himself with Clémence and Madame Putois, showing them both the greatest possible attention.

These two women adored him at the end of a month. Madame Boche, whom he flattered by calling on her in her lôge, had all sorts of pleasant things to say about him.

As to the Lorilleux they were furious when they found out who he was, and declared that it was a sin and a disgrace for Gervaise to bring him into her house. But one fine day Lantier bearded them in their den, and ordered a chain made for a lady of his acquaintance, and made himself so agreeable that they begged him to sit down, and kept him an hour. After this visit they expressed their astonishment that a man so distinguished could ever have seen anything in Wooden Legs to admire. By degrees therefore people had become accustomed to seeing him, and no longer expressed their horror or amazement. Goujet was the only one who was disturbed. If Lantier came in while he was there he at once departed, and avoided all intercourse with him.

Gervaise was very unhappy. She was conscious of a returning inclination for Lantier, and she was afraid of herself and of him. She thought of him constantly; he had taken entire possession of her imagination. But she grew calmer as days passed on, finding that he never tried to see her alone, and that he rarely looked at her, and never laid the tip of his finger on her.

Virginie, who seemed to read her through and through, asked her what

she feared. Was there ever a man more respectful?

But out of mischief or worse, the woman contrived to get the two into a corner one day, and then led the conversation into a most dangerous direction. Lantier, in reply to some question, said in measured tones that his heart was dead, that he lived now only for his son. He never thought of Claude who was away. He embraced Etienne every night, but soon forgot he was in the room, and amused himself with Clémence.

Then Gervaise began to realize that the Past was dead. Lantier had brought back to her the memory of Plassans and the Hotel Boncœur. But this faded away again, and seeing him constantly, the Past was absorbed in the Present. She shook off these memories almost with disgust. Yes, it was all over, and should he ever dare to allude to former years she would complain to her husband.

She began again to think of Goujet, almost unconsciously.

One morning Clémence said that the night before she had seen Lantier walking with a woman who had his arm. Yes, he was coming up La Rue Notre-Dame de Lorette; the woman was a blonde, and no better than she should be. Clémence added that she had followed them until the woman reached a house where she went in. Lantier waited in the street, until there was a window opened, which was evidently a signal, for he went into the house at once.

Gervaise was ironing a white dress; she smiled slightly, and said that she believed a Provençal was always crazy after women, and at night when Lantier appeared, she was quite amused at Clémence who at once attacked him. He seemed to be on the whole rather pleased that he had been seen. The person was an old friend, he said, one whom he had not seen for some time— a very stylish woman, in fact; and he told Clémence to smell of his handkerchief on which his friend had put some of the perfume she used. Just then Etienne came in, and his father became very grave and said that he was in jest—that his heart was dead.

Gervaise nodded approval of this sentiment, but she did not speak.

When spring came Lantier began to talk of moving into that neighborhood. He wanted a furnished, cleanly room. Madame Boche and Gervaise tried to find one for him. But they did not meet with any success. He was altogether too fastidious in his requirements. Every evening at the Coupeaus' he wished he could find people like themselves who would take a lodger.

"You are very comfortable here, I am sure," he would say regularly.

Finally, one night when he had uttered this phrase as usual, Coupeau cried out:

"If you like this place so much, why don't you stay here? We can make room for you."

As he explained that the linen-room could be so arranged that it would be very comfortable, and Etienne could sleep on a mattress in the corner.

"No, no," said Lantier, "it would trouble you too much. I know that you have the most generous heart in the world, but I cannot impose upon you. Your room would be a passage-way to mine, and that would not be agreeable to any of us."

"Nonsense," said Coupeau. "Have we no invention? There are two windows: can't one be cut down to the floor and used as a door? In that case you would enter from the court and not through the shop. You would be by yourself, and we by ourselves."

There was a long silence, broken finally by Lantier.

"If this could be done," he said, "I should like it, but I am afraid you would find yourselves too crowded."

He did not look at Gervaise as he spoke, but it was clear that he was only waiting for a word from her. She did not like the plan at all; not that the thought of Lantier living under their roof disturbed her, but she had no idea where she could put the linen as it came in to be washed and again when it was rough-dry.

But Coupeau was enchanted with the plan. "The rent," he said, "had always been heavy to carry, and now they should gain twenty francs per month." It was not dear for him, and it would help them decidedly. He told his wife that she could have two great boxes made in which all the linen of the Quartier could be piled.

Gervaise still hesitated, questioning Mamma Coupeau with her eyes. Lantier had long since propitiated the old lady by bringing her gum-drops for her cough.

"If we could arrange it, I am sure—" said Gervaise, hesitatingly.

"You are too kind," remonstrated Lantier. "I really feel that it would be an intrusion."

Coupeau flamed out, "Why did she not speak up, he should like to know, instead of stammering and behaving like a fool?"

"Etienne! Etienne!" he shouted.

The boy was asleep with his head on the table. He started up.

"Listen to me. Say to this gentleman, 'I wish it.' Say just those words and nothing more."

"I wish it!" stammered Etienne, half asleep.

Everybody laughed. But Lantier almost instantly resumed his solemn air. He pressed Coupeau's hand cordially.

"I accept your proposition," he said. "It is a most friendly one, and I thank you in my name and in that of my child."

The next morning Marescot, the owner of the house, happening to call, Gervaise spoke to him of the matter. At first he absolutely refused, and was as disturbed and angry as if she had asked him to build on a wing for her especial accommodation. Then, after a minute examination of the premises, he ended by giving his consent, only on condition, however, that he should not be required to pay any portion of the expense, and the Coupeaus signed a paper, agreeing to put everything into its original condition at the expiration of their lease.

That same evening Coupeau brought in a mason, a painter, and a carpenter, all friends and boon companions of his, who would do this little job at night after their day's work was over.

The cutting of the door, the painting, and the cleaning, would come to about cne hundred francs, and Coupeau agreed to pay them as fast as his tenant paid him.

The next question was, how to furnish the room? Gervaise left Mamma Coupeau's wardrobe in it. She added a table and two chairs from her own room. She was compelled to buy a bed and dressing-table, and divers other things, which amounted to one hundred and thirty francs. This she must pay for, ten francs each month. So that for nearly a year they could derive no benefit from their new lodger.

It was early in June that Lantier took possession of his new quarters. Coupeau had offered the night before to help him with his trunk in order to avoid the thirty sous for a fiacre. But the other seemed embarrassed, and said his trunk was heavy, and it seemed as if he preferred to keep it a secret even now where he resided.

He came about three o'clock. Coupeau was not there, and Gervaise, standing at her shop-door, turned white, as she recognized the trunk on the fiacre. It was their old one with which they had travelled from Plassans. Now it was banged and battered, and strapped with cords.

She saw it brought in as she had often seen it in her dreams, and she vaguely wondered if it were the same fiacre which had taken him and Adèle away. Boche welcomed Lantier cordially. Gervaise stood by in silent bewilderment, watching them place the trunk in her lodger's room. Then, hardly knowing what she said, she murmured:

"We must take a glass of wine together—"

Lantier, who was busy untying the

cords on his trunk, did not look up, and she added:

"You will join us, Monsieur Boche!" And she went for some wine and glasses. At that moment she caught sight of Poisson passing the door. She gave him a nod and a wink which he perfectly understood: it meant, when he was on duty, that he was offered a glass of wine; he went round by the court-yard in order not to be seen. Lantier never saw him without some joke in regard to his political convictions, which, however, had not prevented the men from becoming excellent friends.

To one of these jests Boche now replied:

"Did you know," he said, "that when the Emperor was in London he was a policeman, and his special duty was to carry all the intoxicated women to the station-house?"

Gervaise had filled three glasses on the table. She did not care for any wine; she was sick at heart, as she stood looking at Lantier kneeling on the floor by the side of the trunk. She was wild to know what it contained. She remembered that in one corner was a pile of stockings, a shirt or two, and an old hat. Were those things still there? Was she to be confronted with those tattered relics of the Past?

Lantier did not lift the lid however; he rose, and going to the table held his glass high in his hands.

"To your health, Madame!" he said. And Poisson and Boche drank with him.

Gervaise filled their glasses again. The three men wiped their lips with the backs of their hands.

Then Lantier opened his trunk. It was filled with a hodge-podge of papers, books, old clothes, and bundles of linen. He pulled out a saucepan, then a pair of boots followed by a bust of Ledru Rollin with a broken nose—then an embroidered shirt and a pair of ragged pantaloons, and Gervaise perceived a mingled and odious smell of tobacco, leather and dust.

No, the old hat was not in the left corner; in its place was a pin-cushion, the gift of some woman. All at once the strange anxiety with which she had watched the opening of this trunk disappeared, and in its place came an intense sadness as she followed each article with her eyes as Lantier took them out, and wondered which belonged to her time, and which to the days when another woman filled his life.

"Look here, Poisson," cried Lantier, pulling out a small book. It was a scurrilous attack on the Emperor, printed at Brussels, entitled *The Amours of Napoleon III*.

Poisson was aghast. He found no words with which to defend the Emperor. It was in a book—of course therefore, it was true. Lantier, with a laugh of triumph, turned away and began to pile up his books and papers, grumbling a little that there were no shelves on which to put them. Gervaise promised to buy some for him. He owned Louis Blanc's *Histoire de Dix Ans,* all but the first volume, which he had never had; Lamartine's *Les Girondins; The Mysteries of Paris,* and *The Wandering Jew,* by Eugène Sue; without counting a pile of incendiary volumes which he had picked up at book-stalls. His old newspapers he regarded with especial respect. He had collected them with care for years: whenever he had read an article at a café of which he approved, he bought the journal and preserved it. He consequently had an enormous quantity, of all dates and names, tied together without order or sequence.

He laid them all in a corner of the room, saying as he did so:

"If people would study those sheets and adopt the ideas therein, society would be far bettter organized than it now is. Your Emperor and all his minions would come down a bit on the ladder—"

Here he was interrupted by Poisson, whose red imperial and moustache irradiated his pale face.

"And the army," he said, "what would you do with that?"

Lantier became very much excited.

"The army!" he cried. "I would scatter it to the four winds of heaven! I want the military system of the country abolished! I want the abolition of titles and monopolies! I want salaries equalized! I want liberty for every one! Divorces too—"

"Yes; divorces, of course," interposed Boche. "That is needed in the cause of morality."

Poisson threw back his head, ready for an argument, but Gervaise, who did not like discussions, interfered. She had recovered from the torpor into which she had been plunged by the sight of this trunk, and she asked the men to take another glass. Lantier was suddenly subdued and drank his wine, but Boche looked at Poisson uneasily.

"All this talk is between ourselves, is it not?" he said to the policeman.

Poisson did not allow him to finish: he laid his hand on his heart and declared that he was no spy. Their words went in at one ear and out at another. He had forgotten them already.

Coupeau by this time appeared, and more wine was sent for. But Poisson dared linger no longer, and, stiff and haughty, he departed through the courtyard

From the very first Lantier was made thoroughly at home. Lantier had his separate room, private entrance and key. But he went through the shop almost always. The accumulation of linen disturbed Gervaise, for her husband never arranged the boxes he had promised, and she was obliged to stow it away in all sorts of places, under the bed and in the corner. She did not like making up Etienne's mattress late at night either.

Goujet had spoken of sending the child to Lille to his own old master, who wanted apprentices. The plan pleased her, particularly as the boy, who was not very happy at home, was impatient to become his own master. But she dared not ask Lantier, who had come there to live, ostensibly to be near his son. She felt, therefore, that it was hardly a good plan to send the boy away within a couple of weeks after his father's arrival.

When, however, she did make up her mind to approach the subject, he expressed warm approval of the idea, saying that youths were far better in the country than in Paris.

Finally it was decided that Etienne should go, and, when the morning of his departure arrived, Lantier read his son a long lecture and then sent him off, and the house settled down into new habits.

Gervaise became accustomed to seeing the dirty linen lying about, and to seeing Lantier coming in and going out. He still talked with an important air, of his business operations. He went out daily, dressed with the utmost care, and came home declaring that he was worn out with the discussions in which he had been engaged, and which involved the gravest and most important interests.

He rose about ten o'clock, took a walk if the day pleased him, and if it rained he sat in the shop and read his paper. He liked to be there. It was his delight to live surrounded by a circle of worshipping women, and he basked indolently in the warmth and atmosphere of ease and comfort, which characterized the place.

At first Lantier took his meals at the restaurant at the corner, But after a while he dined three or four times a week with the Coupeaus, and finally requested permission to board with them, and agreed to pay them fifteen francs each Saturday. Thus he was regularly installed and was one of the family. He was seen in his shirt sleeves in the shop every morning attending to any little matters, or receiving orders from the customers. He induced Gervaise to leave her own wine merchant and go to a friend of his own. Then he found fault with the bread, and sent Augustine to the Vienna bakery in a distant faubourg. He changed the grocer, but kept the butcher on account of his political opinions. At the end of a month he had instituted a change in the cuisine. Everything was cooked in oil: being a Provençal, that was what he adored. He made the omelettes himself, which were as tough as leather. He superintended Mamma Coupeau, and insisted that the beefsteaks should be thoroughly cooked, until they were like the soles of an old shoe. He watched the salad to see that nothing went in which he did not like. His favorite dish was vermicelli, into which he poured half a bottle of oil. This he and Gervaise eat together, for the others being Parisians, could not be induced to taste it.

By degrees Lantier attended to all those affairs which fall to the share of the master of the house, and to various details of their business in addition. He insisted that if the five francs which the Lorilleux people had agreed to pay toward the support of Mamma Coupeau was not forthcoming, that they should go to law about it. In fact, ten francs was what they ought to pay. He himself would go and see if he could not make them agree to that. He went up at once and asked them in such a way that he returned in triumph with the ten francs. And Madame Lerat, too, did the same, at his representation. Mamma Coupeau could have kissed Lantier's hands, who played the part beside, of an arbiter in the quarrels between the old woman and Gervaise.

The latter, as was natural, sometimes lost patience with the old woman, who retreated to her bed to weep. He would bluster about and ask if they were simpletons to amuse people with their disagreements, and finally induced them to kiss and be friends once more.

He expressed his mind freely in regard to Nana also. In his opinion she was brought up very badly, and here he was quite right; for when her father cuffed her, her mother upheld her, and when in her turn the mother reproved, the father made a scene.

Nana was delighted at this, and felt herself free to do much as she pleased.

She had started a new game at the Farriery opposite. She spent entire days swinging on the shafts of the wagons. She concealed herself, with her troop of followers, at the back of the dark court, redly lighted by the forge, and then would make sudden rushes, with screams and whoops, followed by every child in the neighborhood, reminding one of a flock of martins or sparrows.

Lantier was the only one whose scoldings had any effect. She listened to him graciously. This child of ten years of age, precocious and vicious, coquetted with him as if she had been a grown woman. He finally assumed the care of her education. He taught her to dance and to talk slang!

Thus a year passed away. The whole neighborhood supposed Lantier to be a man of means—otherwise, how did the Coupeaus live as they did? Gervaise, to be sure, still made money; but she supported two men who did nothing, and the shop, of course, did not make enough for that. The truth was that Lantier had never paid one sou, either for board or lodging. He said he would let it run on, and when it amounted to a good sum, he would pay it all at once. After that Gervaise never dared to

ask him for a centime. She got bread, wine and meat on credit; bills were running up everywhere, for their expenditures amounted to three and four francs every day. She had never paid anything, even a trifle on account, to the man of whom she had bought her furniture, nor to Coupeau's three friends who had done the work in Lantier's room. The trades-people were beginning to grumble, and treated her with less politeness.

But she seemed to be insensible to this: she chose the most expensive things, having thrown economy to the winds, since she had given up paying for things at once. She always intended, however, to pay eventually, and had a vague notion of earning hundreds of francs daily in some extraordinary way, by which she could pay all these people.

About the middle of summer Clémence departed, for there was not enough work for two women; she had waited for her money for some weeks. Lantier and Coupeau were quite undisturbed, however. They were in the best of spirits, and seemed to be growing fat over the ruined business.

In the Quartier there was a vast deal of gossip. Everybody wondered as to the terms on which Lantier and Gervaise now stood. The Lorilleux viciously declared that Gervaise would be glad enough to resume her old relations with Lantier, but that he would have nothing to do with her, for she had grown old and ugly. The Boche people took a different view; but while every one declared that the whole arrangement was a most improper one, they finally accepted it as quite a matter of course, and altogether natural.

It is quite possible there were other homes which were quite as open to invidious remarks, within a stone's throw, but these Coupeaus as their neighbors said, were good, kind people. Lantier was especially ingratiating. It was decided, therefore, to let things go their own way undisturbed.

Gervaise lived quietly indifferent to, and possibly entirely unsuspicious of, all these scandals. By-and-by it came to pass that her husband's own people looked on her as utterly heartless. Madame Lerat made her appearance every evening, and she treated Lantier as if he were utterly irresistible, into whose arms any and every woman would be only too glad to fall. An actual league seemed to be forming against Gervaise: all the women insisted on giving her a lover.

But she saw none of these fascinations in him. He had changed, unquestionably, and the external changes were all in his favor. He wore a frock coat, and had acquired a certain polish. But she who knew him so well looked down into his soul through his eyes, and shuddered at much she saw there. She could not understand what others saw in him to admire. And she said so one day to Virginie. Then Madame Lerat and Virginie vied with each other in the stories they told of Clémence and himself—what they did and said whenever her back was turned—and now they were sure, since she had left the establishment, that he went regularly to see her.

"Well, what of it?" asked Gervaise, her voice trembling. "What have I to do with that?"

And she looked into Virginie's dark brown eyes, which were specked with gold, and emitted sparks as do those of cats. But the woman put on a stupid look as she answered:

"Why, nothing, of course; only I should think you would advise him not to have anything to do with such a person."

Lantier was gradually changing his manner to Gervaise. Now, when he shook hands with her, he held her fingers longer than was necessary. He watched her incessantly, and fixed his bold eyes upon her. He leaned over her so closely that she felt his breath on her cheek. But one evening, being alone with her, he caught her in both arms. At that moment Goujet entered. Gervaise wrenched herself free, and the three exchanged a few words as if nothing had happened. Goujet was very pale and seemed embarrassed, supposing that he had intruded upon them, and that she had pushed Lantier aside only because she did not choose to be embraced in public.

The next day Gervaise was miserable, unhappy and restless. She could not iron a handkerchief. She wanted to see Goujet, and tell him just what had happened, but ever since Etienne had gone to Lille, she had given up going to the Forge, as she was quite unable to face the knowing winks with which his comrades received her. But this day she determined to go; and taking an empty basket on her arms she started off, pretending that she was going with skirts to some customers in La Rue des Portes-Blanches.

Goujet seemed to be expecting her,

for she met him loitering on the corner.

"Ah," he said, with a wan smile, "you are going home, I presume?"

He hardly knew what he was saying, and they both turned toward Montmartre without another word. They merely wished to go away from the Forge. They passed several manufactories and soon found themselves with an open field before them. A goat was tethered near by and bleating as it browsed, and a dead tree was crumbling away in the hot sun.

"One might almost think one's self in the country," murmured Gervaise.

They took a seat under the dead tree. The clear-starcher set the basket down at her feet. Before them stretched the heights of Montmartre, with its rows of yellow and gray houses amid clumps of trees, and when they threw back their heads a little they saw the whole sky above, clear and cloudless; but the sunlight dazzled them, and they looked over to the misty outlines of the faubourg, and watched the smoke rising from tall chimneys in regular puffs, indicating the machinery which impelled it. These great sighs seemed to relieve their own oppressed breasts.

"Yes," said Gervaise, after a long silence. "I have been on a long walk, and I came out—"

She stopped: after having been so eager for an explanation she found herself unable to speak, and overwhelmed with shame. She knew that he as well as herself had come to that place with the wish and intention of speaking on one especial subject, and yet neither of them dared to allude to it. The occurrence of the previous evening weighed on both their souls.

Then with a heart torn with anguish, and with tears in her eyes, she told him of the death of Madame Bijard, who had breathed her last that morning after suffering unheard-of agonies.

"It was caused by a kick of Bijard's," she said, in her low, soft voice; "some internal injury. For three days she has suffered frightfully. Why are not such men punished? I suppose, though, if the law undertook to punish all the wretches who kill their wives that it would have too much to do. After all, one kick more or less: what does it matter in the end? And this poor creature, in her desire to save her husband from the scaffold, declared she had fallen over a tub."

Goujet did not speak. He sat pulling up the tufts of grass.

"It is not a fortnight," continued Gervaise, "since she weaned her last baby; and here is that child Lalie, left to take care of two mites. She is not eight years old, but as quiet and sensible as if she were a grown woman; and her father kicks and strikes her too. Poor little soul! There are some persons in this world who seem born to suffer."

Goujet looked at her, and then said suddenly, with trembling lips:

"You made me suffer yesterday."

Gervaise clasped her hands imploringly, and he continued:

"I knew of course how it must end: only you should not have allowed me to think—"

He could not finish. She started up, seeing what his convictions were. She cried out:

"You are wrong! I swear to you that you are wrong! He was going to kiss me, but his lips did not touch me, and it is the very first time that he made the attempt. Believe me, for I swear—on all that I hold most sacred—that I am telling you the truth."

But the blacksmith shook his head. He knew that women did not always tell the truth on such points. Gervaise then became very grave.

"You know me well," she said; "you know that I am no liar. I again repeat that Lantier and I are friends. We shall never be anything more, for if that should ever come to pass, I should regard myself as the vilest of the vile, and should be unworthy of the friendship of a man like yourself." Her face was so honest, her eyes were so clear and frank, that he could do no less than believe her. Once more he breathed freely. He held her hand for the first time. Both were silent. White clouds sailed slowly above their heads with the majesty of swans. The goat looked at them and bleated piteously, eager to be released, and they stood hand in hand on that bleak slope with tears in their eyes.

"Your mother likes me no longer," said Gervaise, in a low voice. "Do not say no;—how can it be otherwise? We owe you so much money."

He roughly shook her arm in his eagerness to check the words on her lips—he would not hear her. He tried to speak, but his throat was too dry; he choked a little, and then he burst out:

"Listen to me," he cried, "I have long wished to say something to you. You are not happy. My mother says things are all going wrong with you, and"—he hesitated; "we must go away together and at once."

She looked at him, not understanding him, but impressed by this abrupt declaration of a love from him, who had never before opened his lips in regard to it.

"What do you mean?" she said.

"I mean," he answered, without looking in her face, "that we two can go away and live in Belgium. It is almost the same to me as home, and both of us could get work and live comfortably."

The color came to her face, which she would have hidden on his shoulder to hide her shame and confusion. He was a strange fellow to propose an elopement. It was like a book, and like the things she heard of in high society. She had often seen and known of the workmen about her, making love to married women, but they did not think of running away with them.

"Ah, Monsieur Goujet!" she murmured; but she could say no more.

"Yes," he said; "we two would live all by ourselves."

But as her self-possession returned, she refused with firmness.

"It is impossible," she said; "and it would be very wrong. I am married, and I have children. I know that you are fond of me, and I love you too much to allow you to commit any such folly as you are talking of, and this would be an enormous folly. No; we must live on as we are. We respect each other now. Let us continue to do so. That is a great deal, and will help us over many a roughness in our paths. And when we try to do right, we are sure of a reward."

He shook his head as he listened to her, but he felt she was right. Suddenly, he snatched her in his arms and kissed her furiously once, and then dropped her and turned abruptly away. She was not angry, but the locksmith trembled from head to foot. He began to gather some of the wild daisies, not knowing what to do with his hands, and tossed them into her empty basket. This occupation amused him and tranquillized him. He broke off the head of the flowers, and when he missed his mark and they fell short of the basket, laughed aloud.

Gervaise sat with her back against the tree, happy and calm. And when she set forth on her walk home, her basket was full of daisies, and she was talking of Etienne.

In reality, Gervaise was more afraid of Lantier than she was willing to admit even to herself. She was fully determined never to allow the smallest familiarity; but she was afraid that she might yield to his persuasions, for she well knew the weakness and amiability of her nature, and how hard it was for her to persist in any opposition to any one.

Lantier, however, did not put this determination on her part to the test. He was often alone with her now, and was always quiet and respectful. Coupeau declared to every one that Lantier was a true friend. There was no nonsense about him; he could be relied upon always and in all emergencies. And he trusted him thoroughly, he declared. When they went out together —the three, on Sundays—he bade his wife and Lantier walk arm-in-arm, while he mounted guard behind, ready to cuff the ears of any one who ventured on a disrespectful glance, a sneer or a wink.

He laughed good-naturedly before Lantier's face, told him he put on a great many airs with his coats and his books, but he liked him in spite of them. They understood each other, he said, and a man's liking for another man is more solid and enduring than his love for a woman.

Coupeau and Lantier made the money fly. Lantier was continually borrowing money from Gervaise; ten francs, twenty francs, whenever he knew there was money in the house. It was always because he was in pressing need for some business matter. But still on those same days he took Coupeau off with him, and at some distant restaurant ordered and devoured such dishes as they could not obtain at home, and these dishes were washed down by bottle after bottle of wine.

Coupeau would have preferred to get tipsy without the food, but he was impressed by the elegance and experience of his friend who found on the *carte* so many extraordinary sauces. He had never seen a man like him, he declared, so dainty and so difficult. He wondered if all Southerners were the same, as he watched him discussing the dishes with the waiter, and sending away a dish that was too salt, or had too much pepper.

Neither could he endure a draught: his skin was all blue if a door was left open, and he made no end of a row until it was closed again.

Lantier was not wasteful in certain

ways, for he never gave a garçon more than two sous after he had served a meal that cost some seven or eight francs.

They never alluded to these dinners the next morning at their simple breakfast with Gervaise. Naturally, people cannot frolic and work too, and since Lantier had become a member of his household, Coupeau had never lifted a tool. He knew every drinking-shop for miles around, and would sit and guzzle, deep into the night, not always pleased to find himself deserted by Lantier, who never was known to be overcome by liquor.

About the first of November, Coupeau turned over a new leaf; he declared he was going to work the next day, and Lantier thereupon preached a little sermon, declaring that labor ennobled man, and in the morning arose before it was light, to accompany his friend to the shop, as a mark of the respect he felt. But when they reached a wineshop on the corner, they entered to take a glass merely to cement good resolutions.

Near the counter they beheld Bibi-la-Grillade smoking his pipe with a sulky air.

"What is the matter, Bibi?" cried Coupeau.

"Nothing!" answered his comrade, "except that I got my walking-ticket, yesterday. Perdition seize all masters!" he added, fiercely.

And Bibi accepted a glass of liquor. Lantier defended the masters. They were not so bad after all: then, too, how were the men to get along without them? "To be sure," continued Lantier, "I manage pretty well, for I don't

have much to do with them myself!"

"Come, my boy," he added, turning to Coupeau, "we shall be late if we don't look out."

Bibi went out with them. Day was just breaking, gray and cloudy. It had rained the night before, and was damp and warm. The street-lamps had just been extinguished. There was one continued tramp of men going to their work.

Coupeau, with his bag of tools on his shoulder, shuffled along: his footsteps had long since lost their ring.

"Bibi," he said, "come with me; the master told me to bring a comrade if I pleased."

"It won't be me, then," answered Bibi. "I wash my hands of them all. No more masters for me, I tell you! But I dare say Mes-Bottes would be glad of the offer."

And as they reached the Assommoir, they saw Mes-Bottes within. Notwithstanding the fact that it was daylight, the gas was blazing in the Assommoir. Lantier remained outside, and told Coupeau to make haste, as they had only ten minutes.

"Do you think I will work for your master?" cried Mes-Bottes. "He is the greatest tyrant in the kingdom. No, I should rather suck my thumbs for a year. You won't stay there, old man! No, you won't stay there three days, now I tell you!"

"Are you in earnest?" asked Coupeau, uneasily.

"Yes, I am in earnest. You can't speak—you can't move. Your nose is held close to the grindstone all the time. He watches you every moment. If you drink a drop, he says you are tipsy, and makes no end of a row!"

"Thanks for the warning. I will try this one day, and if the master bothers me, I will just tell him what I think of him, and turn on my heel and walk out."

Coupeau shook his comrade's hand and turned to depart, much to the disgust of Mes-Bottes, who angrily asked if the master could not wait five minutes. He could not go until he had taken a drink. Lantier entered to join in, and Mes-Bottes stood there with his hat on the back of his head— shabby, dirty and staggering, ordering Father Colombe to pour out the glasses, and not to cheat.

At that moment Goujet and Lorilleux were seen going by. Mes-Bottes shouted to them to come in, but they both refused—Goujet saying he wanted nothing, and the other—as he hugged a little box of gold chains close to his heart—that he was in a hurry.

"Milksops!" muttered Mes-Bottes; "they had best pass their lives in the corner by the fire!"

Returning to the counter, he renewed his attack on Father Colombe, whom he accused of adulterating his liquors.

It was now bright daylight, and the proprietor of the Assommoir began to extinguish the lights. Coupeau made excuses for his brother-in-law, who he said could never drink; it was not his fault, poor fellow! He approved, too, of Goujet, declaring that it was a good thing never to be thirsty. Again he made a move to depart and go to his work, when Lantier, with his dictatorial air, reminded him that he had not paid his score, and that he could not go off in that way, even if it were to his duty.

"I am sick of the words 'work' and 'duty,'" muttered Mes-Bottes.

They all paid for their drinks with the exception of Bibi-la-Grillade, who stooped toward the ear of Father Colombe and whispered a few words. The latter shook his head, whereupon Mes-Bottes burst into a torrent of invectives; but Colombe stood in impassive silence, and when there was a lull in the storm, he said:

"Let your friends pay for you, then —that is a very simple thing to do."

By this time Mes-Bottes was what is properly called howling drunk, and as he staggered away from the counter, he struck the bag of tools which Coupeau had over his shoulder.

"You look like a pedlar with his pack, or a humpback. Put it down!"

Coupeau hesitated a moment; and then slowly and deliberately, as if he had arrived at a decision after mature deliberation, he laid his bag on the ground.

"It is too late to go this morning. I will wait until after breakfast now. I will tell him my wife was sick. Listen, Father Colombe: I will leave my bag of tools under this bench and come for them this afternoon."

Lantier assented to this arrangement. Of course work was a good thing, but friends and good company were better; and the four men stood, first on one foot and then on the other, for more than an hour, and then they had another drink all round. After that a game of billiards was proposed, and they went noisily down the street to the nearest billiard-room, which did not happen to please the fastidious Lantier; who, however, soon recovered his good humor under the effect of the admiration excited in the minds of his friends by his play, which was really very extraordinary.

When the hour arrived for breakfast Coupeau had an idea.

"Let us go and find Bec Sali. I know where he works. We will make him breakfast with us."

The idea was received with applause. The party started forth. A fine drizzling rain was now falling, but they were too warm within to mind this light sprinkling on their shoulders.

Coupeau took them to a factory where his friend worked, and at the door gave two sous to a small boy to go up and find Bec Sali, and to tell him that his wife was very sick and had sent for him.

Bec Sali quickly appeared, not in the least disturbed, as he suspected a joke.

"Ah! ha!" he said, as he saw his friend. "I knew it!" They went to a restaurant and ordered a famous repast of pigs' feet and they sat and sucked the bones and talked about their various employers.

"Will you believe," said Bec Sali, "that mine has had the brass to hang up a bell! Does he think we are slaves to run when he rings it? Never was he so mistaken—"

"I am obliged to leave you!" said Coupeau, rising at last with an important air. "I promised my wife to go to work to-day, and I leave you with the greatest reluctance."

The others protested and entreated, but he seemd so decided that they all accompanied him to the Assommoir to get his tools. He pulled out the bag from under the bench and laid it at his feet, while they all took another drink. The clock struck one and Coupeau kicked his bag under the bench again. He would go to-morrow to the factory; one day really did not make much difference.

The rain had ceased, and one of the men proposed a little walk on the Boulevards to stretch their legs. The air seemed to stupefy them, and they loitered along with their arms swinging at their sides, without exchanging a word. When they reached the wine-shop on the corner of La Rue des Poissonnièrs, they turned in mechanically. Lantier led the way into a small room divided from the public one by windows only. This room was much affected by Lantier, who thought it more stylish by far, than the public one. He called for a newspaper, spread it out, and examined it with a heavy frown. Coupeau and Mes-Bottes played a game of cards, while wine and glasses occupied the centre of the table.

"What is the news?" asked Bibi.

Lantier did not reply instantly; but presently, as the others emptied their glasses, he began to read aloud an account of a frightful murder, to which they listened with eager interest. Then ensued a hot discussion, and argument as to the probable motives for the murder.

By this time the wine was exhausted, and they called for more. About five, all except Lantier were in a state of beastly intoxication, and he found them so disgusting, that as usual, he made his escape without his comrades noticing his defection.

Lantier walked about a little, and

then, when he felt all right, went home, and told Gervaise that her husband was with his friends. Coupeau did not make his appearance for two days. Rumors were brought in that he had been seen in one place and then in another, and always alone. His comrades had apparently deserted him. Gervaise shrugged her shoulders with a resigned air.

"Good heavens!" she said, "what a way to live!" She never thought of hunting him up. Indeed, on the afternoon of the third day, when she saw him through the window of a wineshop, she turned back and would not pass the door. She sat up for him, however, and listened for his step or the sound of his hand fumbling at the lock.

The next morning he came in, only to begin the same thing at night again. This went on for a week; and at last Gervaise went to the Assommoir to make inquiries. Yes, he had been there a number of times, but no one knew where he was just then. Gervaise picked up the bag of tools and carried them home.

Lantier, seeing that Gervaise was out of spirits, proposed that she should go with him to a Café concert. She refused at first, being in no mood for laughing, otherwise she would have consented, for Lantier's proposal seemed to be prompted by the purest friendliness. He seemed really sorry for her trouble, and indeed assumed an absolutely paternal air.

Coupeau had never stayed away like this before, and she continually found herself going to the door, and looking up and down the street. She could not keep to her work, but wandered restlessly from place to place. Had Coupeau broken a limb? Had he fallen into the water? She did not think she could care so very much if he were killed, if this uncertainty were over— if she only knew what she had to expect. But it was very trying to live in this suspense.

Finally, when the gas was lighted, and Lantier renewed his proposition of the café, she consented. After all, why should she not go? Why should she refuse all pleasures because her husband chose to behave in this disgraceful way? If he would not come in, she should go out.

They hurried through their dinner, and as she went out with Lantier at eight o'clock, Gervaise begged Nana and Mamma Coupeau to go to bed early. The shop was closed and she gave the key to Madame Boche, telling her that if Coupeau came in, it would be as well to look out for the lights.

Lantier stood whistling while she gave these directions. Gervaise wore her silk dress, and she smiled as they walked down the street, in alternate shadow and light from the shop windows.

The Café concert was on the Boulevard de Rochechoumart. It had once been a café, and had had a concert-room built on of rough planks.

Over the door was a row of glass globes brilliantly illuminated. Long placards, nailed on wood, were standing quite out in the street by the side of the gutter.

"Here we are!" said Laniter. "Mademoiselle Amanda makes her début tonight."

Bibi-la-Grillade was reading the placard. Bibi had a black eye, as if he had been fighting.

"Hallo!" cried Lantier. "How are you? Where is Coupeau? Have you lost him?"

"Yes, since yesterday. We had a little fight with a waiter at Baquets. He wanted us to pay twice for what we had, and somehow Coupeau and I got separated, and I have not seen him since."

And Bibi gave a great yawn. He was in a disgraceful state of intoxication. He looked as if he had been rolling in the gutter.

"And you know nothing of my husband?" asked Gervaise.

"No, nothing. I think, though, he went off with a coachman."

Lantier and Gervaise passed a very agreeable evening at the Café concert, and when the doors were closed at eleven, they went home in a sauntering sort of fashion. They were in no hurry, and the night was fair, though a little cool. Lantier hummed the air which Amanda had sung, and Gervaise added the chorus. The room had been excessively warm, and she had drank several glasses of wine.

She expressed a great deal of indignation at Mademoiselle Amanda's costume. How did she dare face all those men dressed like that? But her skin was beautiful, certainly, and she listened with considerable curiosity to all that Lantier could tell her about the woman.

"Everybody is asleep," said Gervaise, after she had rung the bell three times.

The door was finally opened; but there was no light. She knocked at the door of the Boche quarters, and asked for her key.

The sleepy Concierge muttered some unintelligible words, from which Gervaise finally gathered that Coupeau had been brought in by Poisson, and that the key was in the door.

Gervaise stood aghast at the disgusting sight that met her eyes as she entered the room where Coupeau lay wallowing on the floor.

She shuddered and turned away. This sight annihilated every ray of sentiment remaining in her heart.

"What am I to do?" she said, piteously. "I can't stay here!"

Lantier snatched her hand.

"Gervaise," he said, "listen to me."

But she understood him, and drew hastily back.

"No, no! Leave me, Auguste. I can manage."

But Lantier would not obey her. He put his arm around her waist, and pointed to her husband as he lay snoring, with his mouth wide open.

"Leave me!" said Gervaise, imploringly; and she pointed to the room where her mother-in-law and Nana slept.

"You will wake them!" she said. "You would not shame me before my child? Pray go!"

He said no more, but slowly and softly kissed her on her ear, as he had so often teased her by doing in those old days. Gervaise shivered, and her blood was stirred to madness in her veins.

"What does that beast care?" she thought. "It is his fault," she murmured; "all his fault. He sends me from his room!"

And as Lantier drew her toward his

door, Nana's face appeared for a moment at the window which lighted her little cabinet.

The mother did not see the child, who stood in her night-dress, pale with sleep. She looked at her father as he lay, and then watched her mother disappear in Lantier's room. She was perfectly grave, but in her eyes burned the sensual curiosity of premature vice.

## CHAPTER IX

### CLOUDS IN THE HORIZON

THAT winter Mamma Coupeau was very ill with an asthmatic attack, which she always expected in the month of December.

The poor woman suffered much, and the depression of her spirits was naturally very great. It must be confessed that there was nothing very gay in the aspect of the room where she slept. Between her bed and that of the little girl there was just room for a chair. The paper hung in strips from the wall. Through a round window near the ceiling came a dreary gray light. There was little ventilation in the room, which made it especially unfit for the old woman, who at night, when Nana was there, and she could hear her breathe, did not complain; but when left alone during the day, moaned incessantly, rolling her head about on her pillow.

"Ah!" she said, "how unhappy I am! It is the same as a prison. I wish I were dead!"

And as soon as a visitor came in—Virginie or Madame Boche—she poured out her grievances. "I should not suffer so much among strangers. I should

like, some times, a cup of tisane, but I can't get it; and Nana—that child whom I have raised from the cradle, disappears in the morning and never shows her face until night, when she sleeps right through and never once asks me how I am, or if she can do anything for me. It will soon be over, and I really believe this clear-starcher would smother me herself—if she were not afraid of the law!"

Gervaise, it is true, was not as gentle and sweet as she had been. Everything seemed to be going wrong with her, and she had lost heart and patience together. Mamma Coupeau had overheard her saying that she was really a great burden. This naturally cut her to the heart, and when she saw her eldest daughter, Madame Lerat, she wept piteously, and declared that she was being starved to death, and when these complaints drew from her daughter's pocket a little silver, she expended it in dainties.

She told the most preposterous tales to Madame Lerat about Gervaise—of her new finery, and of cakes and delicacies eaten in the corner, and many other things of infinitely more consequence. Then in a little while she turned against the Lorilleux, and talked of them in the most bitter manner. At the height of her illness it so happened that her two daughters met one afternoon at her bedside. Their mother made a motion to them to come closer. Then she went on to tell them, between paroxysms of coughing, that her son came home dead-drunk the night before, and that she was absolutely certain that Gervaise spent the night in Lantier's room. "It is all the more disgusting," she added, "because I am certain that Nana heard what was going on quite as well as I did."

The two women did not appear either shocked or surprised.

"It is none of our business," said Madame Lorilleux. "If Coupeau does not choose to take any notice of her conduct, it is not for us to do so."

All the neighborhood were soon informed of the condition of things by her two sisters-in-law, who declared they entered her doors only on their mother's account, who poor thing, was compelled to live amid these abominations.

Every one accused Gervaise now of having perverted poor Lantier. "Men will be men," they said; "surely you can't expect them to turn a cold shoulder to women who throw themselves at their heads. She has no possible excuse; she is a disgrace to the whole street!"

The Lorilleux invited Nana to dinner, that they might question her, but as soon as they began, the child looked absolutely stupid, and they could extort nothing from her.

Amid this sudden and fierce indignation, Gervaise lived — indifferent, dull and stupid. At first she loathed herself, and if Coupeau laid his hand on her she shivered, and ran away from him. But, by degrees, she became accustomed to it. Her indolence had become excessive, and she only wished to be quiet and comfortable.

After all, she asked herself, why should she care? If her lover and her husband were satisfied, why should she not be, too? So the household went on much as usual to all appearance. In reality, whenever Coupeau came in

tipsy, she left and went to Lantier's room to sleep. She was not led there by passion or affection; it was simply that it was more comfortable. She was very like a cat in her choice of soft, clean places.

Mamma Coupeau never dared to speak out openly to the clear-starcher, but after a dispute she was unsparing in her hints and allusions. The first time, Gervaise fixed her eyes on her, and heard all she had to say in profound silence. Then without seeming to speak of herself, she took occasion to say not long afterward that when a woman was married to a man who was drinking himself to death, that a woman was very much to be pitied, and by no means to blame if she looked for consolation elsewhere.

Another time, when taunted by the old woman, she went still further, and declared that Lantier was as much her husband as was Coupeau—that he was the father of two of her children. She talked a little twaddle about the laws of nature, and a shrewd observer would have seen that she—parrot-like—was repeating the words that some other person had put into her mouth. Besides, what were her neighbors doing all about her? They were not so extremely respectable that they had the right to attack her. And then she took house after house, and showed her mother-in-law that while apparently so deaf to gossip, she yet knew all that was going on about her. Yes, she knew —and now seemed to gloat over that, which once had shocked and revolted her.

"It is none of my business, I admit," she cried; "let each person live as he pleases, according to his own light, and let everybody else alone."

One day when Mamma Coupeau spoke out more clearly, she said with compressed lips:

"Now look here: you are flat on your back, and you take advantage of that fact. I have never said a word to you about your own life, but I know it all the same—and it was atrocious! That is all! I am not going into particulars. but remember, you had best not sit in judgment on me!"

The old woman was nearly suffocated with rage and her cough.

The next day Goujet came for his mother's wash while Gervaise was out. Mamma Coupeau called him into her room and kept him for an hour. She read the young man's heart; she knew that his suspicions made him miserable. And in revenge for something that had displeased her, she told him the truth with many sighs and tears, as if her daughter-in-law's infamous conduct was a bitter blow to her.

When Goujet left her room, he was deadly pale, and looked ten years older than when he went in. The old woman had, too, the additional pleasure of telling Gervaise on her return that Madame Goujet had sent word that her linen must be returned to her at once, ironed or unironed. And she was so animated and comparatively amiable that Gervaise scented the truth, and knew instinctively what she had done, and what she was to expect with Goujet. Pale and trembling, she piled the linen neatly in a basket, and set forth to see Madame Goujet. Years had passed since she had paid her friends one penny. The debt still stood at four hundred,

and twenty-five francs. Each time she took the money for her washing she spoke of being pressed just at that time. It was a great mortification for her.

Coupeau was, however, less scrupulous, and said with a laugh, that if she kissed her friend occasionally in the corner, it would keep things straight and pay him well. Then Gervaise, with eyes blazing with indignation, would ask if he really meant that. Had he fallen so low? Neither should he speak of Goujet in that way in her presence.

Every time she took home the linen of these former friends she ascended the stairs with a sick heart.

"Ah! it is you, is it!" said Madame Goujet, coldly, as she opened the door.

Gervaise entered with some hesitation; she did not dare attempt to excuse herself. She was no longer punctual to the hour nor the day—everything about her was becoming perfectly disorderly.

"For one whole week," resumed the lace-mender, "you have kept me waiting. You have told me falsehood after falsehood. You have sent your apprentice to tell me that there was an accident — something had been spilled on the —they would come the next day—and so on. I have been unnecessarily annoyed and worried, besides losing much time. There is no sense in it! Now, what have you brought home? Are the shirts here which you have had for a month, and the skirt which was missing last week?"

"Yes," said Gervaise, almost inaudibly; "yes, the skirt is here. Look at it!"

But Madame Goujet cried out in indignation:

"That skirt did not belong to her, and

she would not have it. This was the crowning touch, if her things were to be changed in this way. She did not like other people's things."

"And the shirts? Where are they? Lost, I suppose. Very well, settle it as you please, but these shirts I must have to-morrow morning!"

There was a long silence. Gervaise was much disturbed by seeing that the door of Goujet's room was wide open. He was there, she was sure, and listening to all these reproaches which she knew to be deserved, and to which she could not reply. She was very quiet and submissive, and laid the linen on the bed as quickly as possible.

Madame Goujet began to examine the pieces.

"Well! well!" she said, "no one can praise your washing nowadays. There is not a piece here that is not dirtied by the iron. Look at this shirt: it is scorched, and the buttons are fairly torn off by the root. Everything comes back—that comes at all, I would say— with the buttons off. Look at that sacque: the dirt is all in it. No, no, I can't pay for such washing as this!"

She stopped talking while she counted the pieces. Then she exclaimed:

"Two pair of stockings, six towels, and one napkin are missing from this week. You are laughing at me, it seems. Now, just understand, I tell you to bring back all you have, ironed or not ironed. If in an hour your woman is not here with the rest, I have done with you, Madame Coupeau!"

At this moment Goujet coughed. Gervaise started. How could she bear being treated in this way before him?

And she stood confused and silent, waiting for the soiled clothes.

Madame Goujet had taken her place and her work by the window.

"And the linen?" said Gervaise, timidly.

"Many thanks," said the old woman. "There is nothing this week."

Gervaise turned pale; it was clear that Madame Goujet meant to take away her custom from her. She sank into a chair. She made no attempt at excuses; she only asked a question.

"Is Monsieur Goujet ill?"

"He is not well; at least he has just come in and is lying down to rest a little."

Madame Goujet spoke very slowly almost solemnly, her pale face encircled by her white cap, and wearing, as usual, her plain, black dress.

And she explained that they were obliged to economize very closely. In future she herself would do their washing. Of course Gervaise must know that this would not be necessary, had she and her husband paid their debt to her son. But, of course, they should submit; they should never think of going to law about it. While she spoke of the debt, her needle moved rapidly to and fro in the delicate meshes of her work.

"But," continued Madame Goujet, "if you were to deny yourself a little, and be careful and prudent, you could soon discharge your debt to us; you live too well, you spend too freely. Were you to give us only ten francs each month—"

She was interrupted by her son who called impatiently, "Mother! come here, will you?"

When she returned she changed the conversation. Her son had undoubtedly begged her to say no more about this money to Gervaise. In spite of her evident determination to avoid this subject, she returned to it again in about ten minutes. She knew from the beginning just what would happen. She had said so at the time and all had turned out precisely as she had prophesied. The tin-worker had drank up the shop, and had left his wife to bear the load by herself. If her son had taken her advice he would never have lent the money. His marriage had f a l l e n through, and he had lost his spirits. She grew very angry as she spoke, and finally accused Gervaise openly of having, with her husband, deliberately conspired to cheat her simple-hearted son.

"M a n y women," she exclaimed, "played the parts of hypocrites and prudes for years, and were found out at the last!"

"Mother! mother!" called Goujet, peremptorily.

She rose, and when she returned, said: "Go in: he wants to see you."

Gervaise obeyed, leaving the door open behind her. She found the room sweet and fresh-looking like that of a young girl, with its simple pictures and white curtains.

Goujet, crushed by what he had heard from Mamma Coupeau, lay at full length on the bed, with pale face and haggard eyes.

"Listen!" he said. "You must not mind my mother's words, she does not understand. You do not owe me anything."

He staggered to his feet, and stood leaning against the bed and looking at her.

"Are you ill?" she said, nervously.

"No, not ill," he answered, "but sick at heart. Sick when I remember what you said and see the truth. Leave me. I cannot bear to look at you."

And he waved her away, not angrily, but with great decision. She went out without a word, for she had nothing to say. In the next room she took up her basket and stood still a moment; Madame Goujet did not look up, but she said:

"Remember, I want my linen at once, and when that is all sent back to me, we will settle the account."

"Yes," answered Gervaise. And she closed the door, leaving behind her all that sweet odor and cleanliness on which she had once placed so high a value. She returned to the shop with her head bowed down, and looking neither to the right nor the left.

Mother Coupeau was sitting by the fire, having left her bed for the first time. Gervaise said nothing to her — not a word of reproach or congratulation. She felt deadly tired — all her bones ached as if she had been beaten. She thought life very hard, and wished that it were over for her.

Gervaise soon grew to care for nothing but her three meals per day. The shop ran itself; one by one her customers left her. Gervaise shrugged her shoulders half indifferently, half insolently; everybody could leave her, she said: she could always get work. But she was mistaken; and soon it became necessary for her to dismiss Madame Putois, keeping no assistant except Augustine, who seemed to grow more and more stupid as time went on. Ruin was fast approaching. Naturally, as indolence and poverty increased, so did lack of cleanliness. No one would ever have known that pretty blue shop in which Gervaise had formerly taken such pride. The windows were unwashed and covered with the mud scattered by the passing carriages. Within it was still more forlorn: the dampness of the steaming linen had ruined the paper; everything was covered with dust; the stove, which once had been kept so bright, was broken and battered. The long ironing-table was covered with wine-stains and grease, looking as if it had served a whole garrison. The atmosphere was loaded with a smell of cooking and of sour starch. But Gervaise was unconscious of it. She did not notice the torn and untidy paper, and having ceased to pay any attention to personal cleanliness, was hardly likely to spend her time in scrubbing the greasy floors. She allowed the dust to accumulate over everything, and never lifted a finger to remove it. Her own comfort and tranquillity was now her first consideration.

Her debts were increasing, but they had ceased to give her any uneasiness. She was no longer honest or straight-forward. She did not care whether she ever paid or not, so long as she got what she wanted. When one shop refused her more credit, she opened an account next door. She owed something in every shop in the whole Quartier. She dared not pass the grocer nor the baker in her own street, and was compelled to make a lengthy circuit each time she went out. The trades-people muttered and grumbled, and

some went so far as to call her a thief and a swindler.

One evening the man who had sold her the furniture for Lantier's room came in with ugly threats.

Such scenes were unquestionably disagreeable. She trembled for an hour after them, but they never took away her appetite.

It was very stupid of these people, after all, she said to Lantier. How could she pay them if she had no money? and where could she get money? She closed her eyes to the inevitable, and would not think of the Future. Mamma Coupeau was well again, but the household had been disorganized for more than a year. In summer there was more work brought to the shop— white skirts and cambric dresses. There were ups and downs, therefore: days when there was nothing in the house for supper, and others when the table was loaded.

Mamma Coupeau was seen almost daily, going out with a bundle under her apron, and returning without it and with a radiant face, for the old woman liked the excitement of going to the Mont-de-Piété.

Gervaise was gradually emptying the house — linen and clothes — tools and furniture. In the beginning she took advantage of a good week, to take out what she had pawned the week before, but after a while she ceased to do that, and sold her tickets. There was only one thing which cost her a pang, and that was selling her clock. She had sworn she would not touch it; not unless she was dying of hunger, and when at last she saw her mother-in-law carry it away, she dropped into a chair and wept like a baby. But when the old woman came back with twenty-five francs, and she found she had five francs more than was demanded by the pressing debt, which had caused her to make the sacrifice, she was consoled, and sent out at once for four sous worth of brandy. When these two women were on good terms, they often drank a glass together sitting at the corner of the ironing-table.

Mamma Coupeau had a wonderful talent for bringing a glass in the pocket of her apron without spilling a drop. She did not care to have the neighbors know, but, in good truth, the neighbors knew very well, and laughed and sneered as the old woman went in and out.

This, as was natural and right, increased the prejudice against Gervaise. Every one said that things could not go on much longer, the end was near.

Amid all this ruin Coupeau thrived surprisingly. Bad liquor seemed to affect him agreeably. His appetite was good in spite of the amount he drank, and he was growing stout. Lantier, however, shook his head, declaring that it was not honest flesh, and that he was bloated. But Coupeau drank all the more after this statement, and was rarely or ever sober. There began to be a strange blueish tone in his complexion. His spirits never flagged. He laughed at his wife when she told him of her embarrassments. What did he care so long as she provided him with food to eat? and the longer he was idle the more exacting he became in regard to this food.

He was ignorant of his wife's infidelity; at least, so all his friends declared. They believed, moreover, that were he

to discover it there would be great trouble. But Madame Lerat, his own sister, shook her head doubtfully, averring that she was not so sure of his ignorance.

Lantier was also in good health and spirits, neither too stout nor too thin. He wished to remain just where he was, for he was thoroughly well satisfied with himself, and this made him critical in regard to his food, as he had made a study of the things he should eat and those he should avoid, for the preservation of his figure. Even when there was not a cent he asked for eggs and cutlets: nourishing and light things were what he required, he said. He ruled Gervaise with a rod of iron, grumbled and found fault far more than Coupeau ever did. It was a house with two masters, one of whom, cleverer by far than the other, took the best of everything. He skimmed the Coupeaus, as it were, and kept all the cream for himself. He was fond of Nana because he liked girls better than boys. He troubled himself little about Etienne.

When people came and asked for Coupeau, it was Lantier who appeared in his shirt-sleeves with the air of the man of the house who is needlessly disturbed. He answered for Coupeau; said it was one and the same thing.

Gervaise did not find this life always smooth and agreeable. She had no reason to complain of her health. She had become very stout. But it was hard work to provide for and please these two men. When they came in, furious and out of temper, it was on her that they wrecked their rage. Coupeau abused her frightfully, and called her by the coarsest epithets. Lantier, on the contrary, was more select in his phraseology, but his words cut her quite as deeply. Fortunately, people become accustomed to almost everything in this world; and Gervaise soon ceased to care for the reproaches and injustice of these two men. She even preferred to have them out of temper with her, for then they let her alone in some degree; but when they were in a good humor, they were all the time at her heels, and she could not find a leisure moment even to iron a cap, so constant were the demands they made upon her. They wanted her to do this, and do that; to cook little dishes for them and wait upon them by inches.

One night she dreamed she was at the bottom of a well. Coupeau was pushing her down with his fists, and Lantier was tickling her to make her jump out quicker. And this she thought was a very fair picture of her life! She said that the people of the Quartier were very unjust after all, when they reproached her for the way of life into which she had fallen. It was not her fault. It was not she who had done it, and a little shiver ran over her as she reflected that perhaps the worst was not yet.

The utter deterioration of her nature was shown by the fact that she detested neither her husband nor Lantier. In a play at the Gaîté, she had seen a woman hate her husband, and poison him for the sake of her lover. This she thought very strange and unnatural. Why could the three not have lived together peaceably? It would have been much more reasonable!

In spite of her debts, in spite of the shifts to which her increasing poverty condemned her, Gervaise would have considered herself quite well off, but for the exacting selfishness of Lantier and Coupeau.

Toward autumn Lantier became more and more disgusted; declared he had nothing to live on but potato-parings, and that his health was suffering. He was enraged at seeing the house so thoroughly cleared out, and he felt that the day was not far off when he must take his hat and depart. He had become accustomed to his den, and he hated to leave it. He was thoroughly provoked that the extravagant habits of Gervaise necessitated this sacrifice on his part. Why could she not have shown more sense? He was sure he didn't know what would become of them. Could they have struggled on six months longer, he could have concluded an affair which would have enabled him to support the whole family in comfort.

One day it came to pass that there was not a mouthful in the house, not even a radish. Lantier sat by the stove in sombre discontent. Finally he started up and went to call on the Poissons, to whom he suddenly became friendly to a degree. He no longer taunted the police officer, but condescended to admit that the Emperor was a good fellow after all. He showed himself especially civil to Virginie, whom he considered a clever woman, and well able to steer her bark through stormy seas.

Virginie one day happened to say in his presence that she should like to establish herself in some business. He approved the plan, and paid her a succession of adroit compliments on her capabilities, and cited the example of several women he knew, who had made or were making their fortunes in this way.

Virginie had the money, an inheritance from an aunt; but she hesitated, for she did not wish to leave the Quartier, and she did not know of any shop she could have. Then Lantier led her into a corner and whispered to her for ten minutes: he seemed to be persuading her to something. They continued to talk together in this way at intervals for several days, seeming to have some secret understanding.

Lantier all this time was fretting and scolding at the Coupeaus, asking Gervaise what on earth she intended to do, begging her to look things fairly in the face. She owed five or six hundred francs to the trades-people about her. She was behind-hand with her rent, and Marescot, the landlord, threatened to turn her out if they did not pay before the first of January.

The Mont-de-Piété had taken everything; there was literally nothing but the nails in the walls left. What did she mean to do?

Gervaise listened to all this at first listlessly, but she grew angry at last and cried out:

"Look here! I will go away to-morrow and leave the key in the door. I had rather sleep in the gutter than live in this way!"

"And I can't say that it would not be a wise thing for you to do!" answered Lantier, insidiously. "I might possibly assist you to find some one to take the lease off your hands whenever you really conclude to leave the shop."

"I am ready to leave it at once!"

cried Gervaise, violently. "I am sick and tired of it."

Then Lantier became serious and business-like. He spoke openly of Virginie, who, he said, was looking for a shop; in fact he now remembered having heard her say that she would like just such a one as this.

But Gervaise shrank back, and grew strangely calm at this name of Virginie.

"She would see," she said; "on the whole she m st have time to think. People said a great many things when they were angry, which on reflection were found not to be advisable."

Lantier rang the changes on this subject for a week; but Gervaise said she had decided to employ some woman and go to work again, and if she were not able to get back her old customers she could try for new ones. She said this merely to show Lantier that she was not so utterly downcast and crushed as he had seemed to take for granted was the case.

He was reckless enough to drop the name of Virginie once more, and she turned upon him in a rage.

"No, no, never!" She had always distrusted Virginie, and if she wanted the shop it was only to humiliate her. Any other woman might have it, but not this hypocrite, who had been waiting for years to gloat over her downfall. No, she understood now only too well the meaning of the yellow sparks in her cat's-eyes. It was clear to her that Virginie had never forgotten the scene in the Lavatory, and if she did not look out there would be a repetition of it.

Lantier stood aghast at this anger, and this torrent of words, but presently he plucked up courage and bade her hold her tongue, and told her she should not talk of his friends in that way. As for himself he was sick and tired of other people's affairs; in future he should let them all take care of themselves, without a word of counsel from him.

January arrived, cold and damp. Mamma Coupeau took to her bed with a violent cold which she expected each year at this time. But those about her said she would never leave the house again, except feet first.

Her children had learned to look forward to her death as a happy deliverance for all. The physician who came once was not sent for again. A little tisane was given her from time to time, that she might not feel herself utterly neglected. She was just alive, that was all. It now became a mere question of time with her; but her brain was clear still, and in the expression of her eyes there were many things to be read— sorrow at seeing no sorrow in those she left behind her, and anger against Nana, who was utterly indifferent to her.

One Monday evening Coupeau came in, as tipsy as usual, and threw himself on the bed, all dressed. Gervaise intended to remain with her mother-in-law part of the night, but Nana was very brave, and said she should hear if her grandmother moved and wanted anything.

About half-past three Gervaise woke with a start; it seemed to her that a cold blast had swept through the room. Her candle had burned down, and she hastily wrapped a shawl around her with trembling hands, and hurried into the next room. Nana was sleeping quietly,

and her grandmother was dead in the bed at her side.

Gervaise went to Lantier and waked him.

"She is dead," she said.

"Well! what of it?" he muttered, half asleep. "Why don't you go to sleep?"

She turned away in silence, while he grumbled at her coming to disturb him, by the intelligence of a death in the house.

Gervaise dressed herself, not without tears, for she really loved the cross old woman whose son lay in the heavy slumbers of intoxication.

When she went back to the room, she found Nana sitting up and rubbing her eyes. The child realized what had come to pass, and trembled nervously in the face of this death of which she had thought much in the last two days, as of something which was hidden from children.

"Get up!" said her mother, in a low voice. "I do not wish you to stay here."

The child slipped from her bed slowly and regretfully, with her eyes fixed on the dead body of her grandmother.

Gervaise did not know what to do with her, nor where to send her. At this moment Lantier appeared at the door. He had dressed himself, impelled by a little shame at his own conduct.

"Let the child go into my room," he said, "and I will help you."

Nana looked first at her mother and then at Lantier, and then trotted with her little bare feet into the next room and slipped into the bed that was still warm.

She lay there wide awake, with blazing cheeks and eyes, and seemed to be absorbed in thought.

While Lantier and Gervaise were silently occupied with the dead, Coupeau lay and snored.

Gervaise hunted in a bureau to find a little crucifix which she had brought from Plassans, when she suddenly remembered that Mamma Coupeau had sold it. They each took a glass of wine, and sat by the stove until daybreak.

About seven o'clock Coupeau woke. When he heard what had happened, he declared they were jesting. But when he saw the body he fell on his knees and wept like a baby. Gervaise was touched by these tears, and found her heart softer toward her husband than it had been for many a long year.

"Courage, old friend!" said Lantier, pouring out a glass of wine as he spoke.

Coupeau took some wine, but he continued to weep, and Lantier went off under pretext of informing the family, but he did not hurry. He walked along slowly, smoking a cigar, and after he had been to Madame Lerat's, he stopped in at a crêmerie to take a cup of coffee, and there he sat for an hour or more in deep thought.

By nine o'clock the family were assembled in the shop, whose shutters had not been taken down. Lorilleux only remained for a few moments, and then went back to his shop. Madame Lorilleux shed a few tears, and then sent Nana to buy a pound of candles.

"How like Gervaise!" she murmured. "She can do nothing in a proper way!"

Madame Lerat went about among the neighbors to borrow a crucifix. She brought one so large that when it was laid on the breast of Mamma Coupeau the weight seemed to crush her.

Then some one said something about holy water, so Nana was sent to the church with a bottle. The room assumed a new aspect. On a small table burned a candle, near it a glass of holy water in which was a branch of box.

"Everything is in order," murmured the sisters; "people can come now as soon as they please."

Lantier made his appearance about eleven. He had been to make inquiries in regard to funeral expenses.

"The coffin," he said "is twelve francs, and if you want a mass, ten francs more. A hearse is paid for, according to its ornaments."

"You must remember," said Madame Lorilleux, with compressed lips, "that Mamma must be buried according to her purse."

"Precisely!" answered Lantier. "I only tell you this as your guide. Decide what you want, and after breakfast I will go and attend to it all."

He spoke in a low voice, oppressed by the presence of the dead. The children were laughing in the court-yard, and Nana singing loudly.

Gervaise said, gently:

"We are not rich, to be sure, but we wish to do what she would have liked. If Mamma Coupeau has left us nothing, it was not her fault, and no reason why we should bury her as if she were a dog. No, there must be a Mass and a hearse."

"And who will pay for it?" asked Madame Lorilleux. "We can't, for we lost much money last week, and I am quite sure you would find it hard work!"

Coupeau, when he was consulted,

shrugged his shoulders with a gesture of profound indifference. Madame Lerat said she would pay her share.

"There are three of us," said Gervaise, after a long calculation; "if we each pay thirty francs we can do it with decency."

But Madame Lorilleux burst our furiously:

"I will never consent to such folly. It is not that I care for the money, but I disapprove of the ostentation. You can do as you please."

"Very well," replied Gervaise, "I will. I have taken care of your mother while she was living, I can bury her now that she is dead."

Then Madame Lorilleux fell to crying, and Lantier had great trouble in preventing her from going away at once, and the quarrel grew so violent, that Madame Lerat hastily closed the door of the room where the dead woman lay, as if she feared the noise would waken her. The children's voices rose shrill in the air with Nana's perpetual "Tra-la-la" above all the rest.

"Heavens! how wearisome those children are with their songs," said Lantier. "Tell them to be quiet, and make Nana come in and sit down."

Gervaise obeyed these dictorial orders, while her sisters-in-law went home to breakfast, while the Coupeaus tried to eat, but they were made uncomfortable by the presence of Death in their crowded quarters. The details of their daily life were disarranged.

Gervaise went to Goujet and borrowed sixty francs, which, added to thirty from Madame Lerat, would pay the expenses of the funeral. In the afternoon several persons came in and looked at the dead woman, crossing themselves as they did so, and shaking Holy Water over the body with the branch of box. They then took their seats in the shop and talked of the poor thing and of her many virtues. One said she had talked with her only three days before, and another asked if it were not possible it was a trance.

By evening the Coupeaus felt it was more than they could bear. It was a mistake to keep a body so long. One has, after all, only so many tears to shed, and that done, grief turns to worry. Mamma Coupeau—stiff and cold—was a terrible weight on them all. They gradually lost the sense of oppression however, and spoke louder.

After a while Monsieur Marescot appeared. He went to the inner room and knelt at the side of the corpse. He was very religious, they saw. He made a sign of the cross in the air and dipped the branch into the holy water and sprinkled the body. Monsieur Marescot having finished his devotions, passed out into the shop and said to Coupeau:

"I came for the two quarters that are due. Have you got the money for me?"

"No, sir; not entirely," said Gervaise, coming forward, excessively annoyed at this scene taking place in the presence of her sisters-in-law. "You see, this trouble came upon us—"

"Undoubtedly," answered her landlord; "but we all of us have our troubles. I cannot wait any longer. I really must have the money. If I am not paid by tomorrow I shall most assuredly take immediate measures to turn you out."

Gervaise clasped her hands imploringly, but he shook his head, saying that discussion was useless; besides, just then it would be a disrespect to the dead.

"A thousand pardons!" he said, as he went out. "But remember that I must have the money to-morrow."

And as he passed the open door of the lighted room, he saluted the corpse with another genuflection.

After he had gone, the ladies gathered around the stove, where a great pot of coffee stood, enough to keep them all awake, for the whole night. The Poissons arrived about eight o'clock; then Lantier, carefully watching Gervaise, began to speak of the disgraceful act committed by the landlord in coming to a house to collect money at such a time.

"He is a thorough hypocrite," continued Lantier; "and were I in Madame Coupeau's place, I would walk off and leave his house on his hands."

Gervaise heard, but did not seem to heed.

The Lorilleux, delighted at the idea that she would lose her shop, declared that Lantier's idea was an excellent one. They gave Coupeau a push and repeated it to him.

Gervaise seemed to be disposed to yield; and then Virginie spoke in the blandest of tones.

"I will take the lease off your hands," she said, "and will arrange the back rent with your landlord."

"No! no! thank you," cried Gervaise, shaking off the lethargy in which she had been wrapped. "I can manage this matter, and I can work. No, no, I say."

Lantier interposed and said, soothingly:

"Never mind! we will talk of it another time—to-morrow, possibly."

The family were to sit up all night. Nana cried vociferously when she was sent into the Boche quarters to sleep; the Poissons remained until midnight. Virginie began to talk of the country: she would like to be buried under a tree, with flowers and grass on her grave. Madame Lerat said, that in her wardrobe—folded up in lavender—was the linen sheet in which her body was to be wrapped.

When the Poissons went away Lantier accompanied them, in order, he said, to leave his bed for the ladies, who could take turns in sleeping there. But the ladies preferred to remain together about the stove.

Madame Lorilleux said she had no black dress, and it was too bad that she must buy one, for they were sadly pinched just at this time. And she asked Gervaise if she was sure that her mother had not a black skirt which would do, one that had been given her on her birthday. Gervaise went for the skirt. Yes, it would do if it were taken in at the waist.

Then Madame Lorrileux looked at the bed and the wardrobe, and asked if there was nothing else belonging to her mother.

Here Madame Lerat interfered. The Coupeaus, she said, had taken care of her mother, and they were entitled to all the trifles she had left. The night seemed endless. They drank coffee, and went by turns to look at the body, lying silent and calm under the flickering light of the candle.

The interment was to take place at half-past ten, but Gervaise would gladly have given a hundred francs, if she had had them, to any one who would have taken Mamma Coupeau away three hours before the time fixed.

"Ah!" she said to herself, "it is no use to disguise the fact: people are very much in the way after they are dead, no matter how much you have loved them!"

Father Bazonge, who was never known to be sober, appeared with the coffin and the pall. When he saw Gervaise he stood with his eyes starting from his head.

"I beg your pardon," he said, "but I thought it was for you;" and he was turning to go away.

"Leave the coffin!" cried Gervaise, growing very pale. Bazonge began to apologize:

"I heard them talking yesterday, but I did not pay much attention. I congratulate you that you are still alive. Though why I do, I do not know, for life is not such a very agreeable thing."

Gervaise listened with a shiver of horror, and a morbid dread that he would take her away and shut her up in his box and bury her. She had once heard him say that he knew a woman who would be only too thankful if he would do exactly that.

"He is horribly drunk," she murmured, in a tone of mingled disgust and terror.

"It will come for you another time," he said, with a laugh; "you have only to make me a little sign. I am a great consolation to women sometimes; and you need not sneer at poor Father Bazonge, for he has held many a fine lady in his arms, and they made no complaint when he laid them down to sleep in the shade of the evergreens."

"Do hold your tongue," said Lorilleux; "this is no time for such talk. Be off with you!"

The clock struck ten. The friends and neighbors had assembled in the shop, while the family were in the back room nervous and feverish with suspense.

Four men appeared—the undertaker, Bazonge, and his three assistants placed the body in the coffin. Bazonge held the screws in his mouth and waited for the family to take their last farewell.

Then Coupeau, his two sisters and Gervaise kissed their mother, and their tears fell fast on her cold face. The lid was put on and fastened down.

The hearse was at the door, to the great edification of the trades-people of the neighborhood, who said under their breath that the Coupeaus had best pay their debts.

"It is shameful," Gervaise was saying at the same moment, speaking of the Lorrileux. "These people have not even brought a bouquet of violets for their mother."

It was true they had come empty-handed—while Madame Lerat had brought a wreath of artificial flowers which was laid on the bier.

Coupeau and Lorilleux, with their hats in their hands, walked at the head of the procession of men. After them followed the ladies, headed by Madame Lorilleux, in her black skirt—wrenched from the dead—her sister trying to cover a purple dress with a large black shawl.

Gervaise had lingered behind to close the shop and give Nana into the charge of Madame Boche, and then ran to overtake the procession, while the little girl stood with the Concierge, profoundly interested in seeing her grandmother carried in that beautiful carriage.

Just as Gervaise joined the procession, Goujet came up a side street and saluted her with a slight bow and with a faint sweet smile. The tears rushed to her eyes. She did not weep for Mamma Coupeau, but rather for herself; but her sisters-in-law looked at her as if she were the greatest hypocrite in the world.

At the church the ceremony was of short duration. The Mass dragged a little because the priest was very old.

The cemetery was not far off, and the cortége soon reached it. A priest came out of a house near by, and shivered as he saw his breath rise with each De Profundis he uttered.

The coffin was lowered, and as the frozen earth fell upon it, more tears were shed, accompanied, however, by sigh of relief.

The procession dispersed outside the gates of the cemetery, and at the very first cabaret Coupeau turned in, leaving Gervaise alone on the sidewalk. She beckoned to Goujet, who was turning the corner.

"I want to speak to you," she said, timidly. "I want to tell you how ashamed I am for coming to you again to borrow money, but I was at my wit's end."

"I am always glad to be of use to you," answered the blacksmith. "But pray never allude to the matter before my mother, for I do not wish to trouble her. She and I think differently on many subjects."

She looked at him sadly and earnestly. Through her mind flitted a vague regret that she had not done as he desired, that she had not gone away with him somewhere. Then a vile temptation assailed her. She trembled.

"You are not angry now?" she said, entreatingly.

"No, not angry, but still heart-sick. All is over between us now and forever." And he walked off with long strides, leaving Gervaise stunned by his words.

"All is over between us!" she kept saying to herself, "and what more is there for me then in life!"

She sat down in her empty, desolate room, and drank a large tumbler of wine. When the others came in, she looked up suddenly, and said to Virginie, gently:

"If you want the shop, take it!"

Virginie and her husband jumped at this, and sent for the Concierge, who consented to the arrangement on condition that the new tenants would become security for the two quarters then due.

This was agreed upon. The Coupeaus would take a room on the sixth floor, near the Lorilleux. Lantier said politely, that if it would not be disagreeable to the Poissins, he should like much to retain his present quarters.

The policeman bowed stiffly, but with every intention of being cordial —and said he decidedly approved of the idea.

Then Lantier withdrew from the discussion entirely, watching Gervaise and Virginie out of the corners of his eye.

That evening when Gervaise was alone again, she felt utterly exhausted. The place looked twice its usual size. It seemed to her that in leaving Mamma Coupeau in the quiet cemetery, she had also left much that was precious to her, a portion of her own life, her pride in her shop, her hopes and her energy. These were not all either that she had buried that day. Her heart was as bare and empty as her walls and her home. She was too weary to try and analyze her sensations, but moved about as if in a dream.

At ten o'clock, when Nana was undressed, she wept, begging that she might be allowed to sleep in her grandmother's bed. Her mother vaguely wondered that the child was not afraid, and allowed her to do as she pleased.

Nana was not timid by nature, and only her curiosity, not her fears, had been excited by the events of the last three days, and she curled herself up with delight in the soft, warm, feather bed.

## CHAPTER X

### DISASTERS AND CHANGES

THE new lodging of the Coupeaus was next that of the Bijards. Almost opposite their door was a closet under the stairs which went up to the roof —a mere hole without light or ventilation, where Father Bru slept.

A chamber and a small room, about as large as one's hand, were all the Coupeaus had now. Nana's little bed stood in the small room, the door of which had to be left open at night, lest the child should stifle.

When it came to the final move Gervaise felt that she could not separate from the commode which she had spent so much time in polishing when first married, and insisted on its going to their new quarters, where it was much in the way and stopped up half the window; and when Gervaise wished to look out into the court, she had not room for her elbows.

The first few days she spent in tears. She felt smothered and cramped; after having had so much room to move about in it seemed to her that she was smothering. It was only at the window she could breathe. The courtyard was not a place calculated to inspire cheerful thoughts. Opposite her was the window which years before had elicited her admiration, where every successive summer, scarlet beans had grown to a fabulous height on slender strings. Her room was on the shady side, and a pot of mignonette would die in a week on her sill.

No, life had not been what she hoped, and it was all very hard to bear.

Instead of flowers to solace her declining years, she would have but thorns. One day, as she was looking down into the court, she had the strangest feeling imaginable. She seemed to see herself standing just near the lôge of the Concierge, looking up at the house and examining it for the first time.

This glimpse of the Past made her feel faint. It was at least thirteen years since she had first seen this huge building—this world within a world. The court had not changed. The façade was simply more dingy. The same clothes seemed to be hanging at the windows to dry. Below, there were the shavings from the cabinet-maker's shop, and the gutter glittered with blue water, as blue and soft in tone as the water she remembered.

But she! Alas! how changed was she! She no longer looked up to the sky. She was no longer hopeful, courageous and ambitious. She was living under the very roof in crowded discomfort, where never a ray of sunshine could reach her, and her tears fell fast in utter discouragement.

Nevertheless, when Gervaise became accustomed to her new surroundings, she grew more content. The pieces of furniture she had sold to Virginie had facilitated her installation. When the fine weather came, Coupeau had an opportunity of going into the country to work. He went and lived three months without drinking — cured for the time being, by the fresh, pure air. It does a man sometimes an infinite deal of good to be taken away from all his old haunts, and from Parisian streets, which always seem to exhale a smell of brandy and of wine.

He came back as fresh as a rose, and he brought four hundred francs, with which he paid the Poissons the amount for which they had become security, as well as several other small but pressing debts. Gervaise had now two or three streets open to her again, which for some time she had not dared to enter.

She now went out to iron by the day, and had gone back to her old mistress, Madame Fauconnier, who was a kind-hearted creature, and ready to do anything for anyone who flattered her adroitly.

With diligence and economy Gervaise could have managed to live comfortably and pay all her debts; but this prospect did not charm her particularly. She suffered acutely in seeing the Poissons in her old shop. She was by no means of a jealous or envious disposition, but it was not agreeable to her to hear the admiration expressed for her successors by her husband's sisters. To hear them, one would suppose that never had so beautiful a shop been seen before. They spoke of the filthy condition of the place when Virginie moved in—who had paid, they declared, thirty francs for cleaning it.

Virginie, after some hesitation, had decided on a small stock of groceries —sugar, tea, and coffee; also bonbons and chocolate. Lantier had advised these because he said the profit on them was immense. The shop was repainted, and shelves and cases were put in, and a counter with scales such as are seen at confectioners'. The little inheritance that Poisson held in reserve was seriously encroached upon. But Virginie was triumphant, for she had her way, and the Lorilleux did not spare Gervaise the description of a case or a jar.

It was said in the street that Lantier had deserted Gervaise—that she gave him no peace running after him; but this was not true, for he went and came to her apartment as he pleased. Scandal was connecting his name and Virginie's. They said Virginie had taken the clear-starcher's lover as well as her shop! The Lorilleux talked of nothing when Gervaise was present but Lantier, Virginie and the shop. Fortunately, Gervaise was not inclined to jealousy, and Lantier's infidelities had hitherto left her undisturbed; but she did not accept this new affair with equal tranquillity. She colored or turned pale as she heard these allusions, but she would not allow a word to pass her lips, as she was fully determined never to gratify her enemies by allowing them to see her discomfiture; but a dispute was heard by the neighbors about this time between herself and Lantier, who went angrily away, and was not seen by any one in the Coupeau quarters for more than a fortnight.

Coupeau behaved very oddly. This blind and complacent husband, who had closed his eyes to all that was going on at home, was filled with virtuous indignation at Lantier's indifference. Then Coupeau went so far as to tease Gervaise in regard to this desertion of her lovers. She had had bad luck, he said, with hatters and blacksmiths—why did she not try a mason?

He said this as if it were a joke, but Gervaise had a firm conviction that he was in deadly earnest. A man who is tipsy from one year's end to the next is not apt to be fastidious; and there are husbands who at twenty are very jealous, and at thirty have grown very complacent, under the influence of constant tippling.

Lantier preserved an attitude of calm indifference. He kept the peace between the Poissons and the Coupeaus. Thanks to him, Virginie and Gervaise affected for each other the most tender regard. He ruled the brunette as he had ruled the blonde, and he would swallow her shop as he had that of Gervaise.

It was in June of this year that Nana partook of her first communion. She was about thirteen, slender and tall as an asparagus plant; and her air and manner was the height of impertinence and audacity.

She had been sent away from the catechism class the year before on account of her bad conduct. And if the Curé did not make a similiar objection this year, it was because he feared she would never come again, and that his refusal would launch on the Parisian pavé another castaway.

Nana danced with joy at the mere thought of what the Lorilleux—as her god-parents—had promised, while Madame Lerat gave the veil and cup, Virginie the purse, and Lantier a prayer-book; so that the Coupeaus looked forward to the day without anxiety.

The Poissons — probably through Lantier's advice—selected this occasion for their house-warming. They invited the Coupeau and the Boche family, as Pauline made her first communion on that day, as well as Nana.

The evening before, while Nana stood in an ecstasy of delight before her presents, her father came in, in an abominable condition. His virtuous resolutions had yielded to the air of Paris, he had fallen into evil ways again, and he now assailed his wife and child with the vilest epithets, which did not seem to shock Nana, for they could fall from her tongue on occasion, with facile glibness.

"I want my soup," cried Coupeau,

"and you two fools are chattering over those fal-lals! I tell you I will sit on them if I am not waited upon, and quickly too."

Gervaise answered impatiently, but Nana, who thought it better taste just then—all things considered—to receive with meekness all her father's abuse, dropped her eyes and did not reply.

"Take that rubbish away!" he cried, with growing impatience, "put it out of my sight, or I will tear it to bits." Nana did not seem to hear him. She took up the tulle-cap and asked her mother what it cost, and when Coupeau tried to snatch the cap, Gervaise pushed him away.

"Let the child alone!" she said, "she is doing no harm!"

Then her husband went into a perfect rage:

"Mother and daughter!" he cried, "a nice pair they make. I understand very well what all this row is for: it is merely to show yourself in a new gown. I will put you in a bag and tie it close round your throat, and you will see if the Curé likes that!"

Nana turned like lightning to protect her treasures. She looked her father full in the face, and, forgetting the lessons taught her by her priest, she said, in a low, concentrated voice: "Beast!" That was all.

After Coupeau had eaten his soup he fell asleep, and in the morning woke quite amiable. He admired his daughter, and said she looked quite like a young lady in her white robe. Then he added, with a sentimental air, that a father on such days was naturally proud of his child. When they were ready to go to the church, and Nana met Pauline in the corridor, she examined the latter from head to foot, and smiled condescendingly on seeing that Pauline had not a particle of *chic*.

The two families started off together, Nana and Pauline in front, each with her prayer-book in one hand and with the other holding down her veil which swelled in the wind like a sail. They did not speak to each other, but keenly enjoyed seeing the shopkeepers run to their doors to see them—keeping their eyes cast down devoutly, but their ears wide open to any compliment they might hear.

Nana's two aunts walked side by side, exchanging their opinions in regard to Gervaise, whom they stigmatized as an irreligious ne'er-do-well, whose child would never have gone to the Holy Communion if it had depended on her.

At the church Coupeau wept all the time. It was very silly, he knew, but he could not help it. The voice of the Curé was pathetic; the little girls looked like white-robed angels; the organ thrilled him, and the incense gratified his senses. There was one especial anthem which touched him deeply. He was not the only person who wept, he was glad to see, and when the ceremony was over, he left the church feeling that it was the happiest day of his life. But an hour later he quarrelled with Lorilleux in a wine-shop because the latter was so hard-hearted.

The house-warming at the Poissons that night was very gay. Lantier sat between Gervaise and Virginie, and was equally civil and attentive to both. Opposite was Poisson with his calm, impassive face, a look he had cultivated since he began his career as a police officer.

But the Queens of the Fête were the two little girls, Nana and Pauline, who sat very erect lest they should crush and deface their pretty white dresses. At dessert there was a serious discussion in regard to the Future of the children. Madame Boche said that Pauline would at once enter a certain manufactory, where she would receive five or six francs per week. Gervaise had not decided yet, for Nana had shown no especial leaning in any direction. She had a good deal of taste, but she was butter-fingered and careless.

"I should make a florist of her," said Madame Lerat. "It is clean work, and pretty work, too."

Whereupon ensued a warm discussion. The men were especially careful of their language out of deference to the little girls, but Madame Lerat would not accept the lesson: she flattered herself she could say what she pleased in such a way, that it could not offend the most fastidious ears.

"Women," she declared, "who followed her trade were more virtuous than others. They rarely made a slip."

"I have no objection to your trade," interrupted Gervaise. "If Nana likes to make flowers let her do so. Say, Nana, would you like it?"

The little girl did not look up from her plate, into which she was dipping a crust of bread. She smiled faintly as she replied:

"Yes, mamma; if you desire it, I have no objection."

The decision was instantly made, and Coupeau wished his sister to take her the very next day to the place where she herself worked—Rue du Caire; and the circle talked gravely of the duties of life. Boche said that Pauline and Nana were now women, since they had been to Communion, and they ought to be serious, and learn to cook and to mend. They alluded to their future marriages, their homes and their children, and the girls touched each other under the table, giggled and grew very red. Lantier asked them if they did not have little husbands already, and Nana blushingly confessed that she loved Victor Fauconnier, and never meant to marry any one else.

Madame Lorilleux said to Madame Boche on their way home:

"Nana is our goddaughter now, but if she goes into that flower business, in six months she will be on the pavé, and we will have nothing to do with her."

Gervaise told Boche that she thought the shop admirably arranged. She had looked forward to an evening of torture, and was surprised that she had not experienced a pang.

Nana, as she undressed, asked her mother if the girl on the next floor, who had been married the week before, wore a dress of muslin like hers.

But this was the last bright day in that household. Two years passed away, and their prospects grew darker and their demoralization and degradation more evident. They went without food and without fire, but never without brandy.

They found it almost impossible to meet their rent, and a certain January came when they had not a penny, and Father Boche ordered them to leave.

It was frightfully cold, with a sharp wind blowing from the north.

Monsieur Marescot appeared in a warm overcoat, and his hands encased in warm woollen gloves, and told them they must go even if they slept in the gutter. The whole house was oppressed with woe, and a dreary sound of lamentation arose from most of the rooms, for half the tenants were behind-hand. Gervaise sold her bed and paid the rent. Nana made nothing as yet, and Gervaise had so fallen off in her work that Madame Fauconnier had reduced her wages. She was irregular in her hours, and often absented herself from the shop for several days together, but was none the less vexed to discover that her old employée, Madame Putois, had been placed above her. Naturally, at the end of the week, Gervaise had little money coming to her.

As to Coupeau, if he worked, he brought no money home, and his wife had ceased to count upon it. Sometimes he declared he had lost it, through a hole in his pocket, or it had been stolen; but after a while he ceased to make any excuses.

But if he had no cash in his pockets it was because he had spent it all in drink. Madame Boche advised Gervaise to watch for him at the door of the place where he was employed and get his wages from him before he had spent them all; but this did no good, as Coupeau was warned by his friends and escaped by a rear door.

The Coupeaus were entirely to blame for their misfortunes, but this is just what people will never admit. It is always ill-luck, or the cruelty of God, or anything in short save the legitimate result of their own vices.

Gervaise now quarrelled with her husband incessantly. The warmth of affection of husband and wife, of parents for their children, and children for their parents had fled, and left them all shivering, each apart from the other.

All three, Coupeau, Gervaise and Nana watched each other with eyes of baleful hate. It seemed as if some spring had broken—the great mainspring that binds families together.

Gervaise did not shudder when she saw her husband lying drunk in the gutter. She would not have pushed him in, to be sure; but if he were out of the way it would be a good thing for everybody. She even went so far as to say one day, in a fit of rage, that she should be glad to see him brought home on a shutter. Of what good was he to any human being? He ate, and he drank, and he slept. His child learned to hate him, and she read the accidents in the papers with the feelings of an unnatural daughter. What a pity it was that her father had not been the man who was killed when that omnibus tipped over!

In addition to her own sorrows and privations, Gervaise, whose heart was not yet altogether hard, was condemned to hear now of the sufferings of others. The corner of the house in which she lived seemed to be consecrated to those who were as poor as herself. No smell of cooking filled the air, which, on the contrary, was laden with the shrill cries of hungry children—heavy with the sighs of weary, heart-broken mothers, and with the oaths of drunken husbands and father.

Gervaise pitied Father Bru from the bottom of her heart; he lay the greater part of the time rolled up in the straw in his den under the staircase leading to the roof. When two or three days elapsed without his showing himself, some one opened the door and looked in, to see if he were still alive.

Yes, he was living; that is, he was not dead. When Gervaise had bread she always remembered him. If she had learned to hate men because of her husband, her heart was still tender toward animals, and Father Bru seemed like one to her. She regarded him as a faithful old dog. Her heart was heavy within her, whenever she thought of him, alone—abandoned by God and man—dying by inches—or drying rather, as an orange dries on the chimney piece.

Gervaise was also troubled by the vicinity of the undertaker Bazonge— a wooden partition alone separated their rooms. When he came in at night she could hear him throw down his glazed hat, which fell, with a dull thud like a shovelful of clay, on the table. The black cloak hung against the wall rustled like the wings of some huge bird of prey. She could hear his every movement, and she spent most of her time listening to him with morbid horror, while he—all unconscious— hummed his vulgar songs and tipsily staggered to his bed, under which the poor woman's sick fancy pictured a dead body concealed.

She had read in some paper a dismal tale of some undertaker who took home with him coffin after coffin— children's coffins—in order to make one trip to the cemetery suffice. When she heard his step, the whole corridor was pervaded to her senses with the odor of dead humanity.

She would as lief have resided at Père La Chaise and watched the moles at their work. The man terrified her; his incessant laughter dismayed her. She talked of moving, but at the same time was reluctant to do so, for there was a strange fascination about Bazonge after all. Had he not told her once that he would come for her and lay her down to sleep in the shadow of waving branches, where she would know neither hunger nor toil?

She wished she could try it for a month. And she thought how delicious it would be in midwinter, just at the time her quarter's rent was due. But alas! this was not possible. The rest and the sleep must be Eternal; this thought chilled her, and her longing for Death faded away before the unrelenting severity of the bonds exacted by Mother Earth.

One night she was sick and feverish, and instead of throwing herself out of the window as she was tempted to do, she rapped on the partition and called loudly—

"Father Bazonge! Father Bazonge!"

The undertaker was kicking off his slippers, singing a vulgar song as he did so.

"What is the matter?" he answered.

But at his voice Gervaise awoke as from a nightmare. What had she done? Had she really tapped? she asked herself, and she recoiled from his side of the wall in chill horror. It seemed to her that she felt the undertaker's hands on her head. No! No! She was not ready. She told herself that she had not intended to call him. It was her elbow that had knocked the wall accidentally, and she shivered from head to foot at the idea of being carried away in this man's arms.

"What is the matter?" repeated Bazonge. "Can I serve you in any way, Madame?"

"No! No! It is nothing!" answered the laundress, in a choked voice. "I am very much obliged."

While the undertaker slept she lay wide awake, holding her breath and not daring to move, lest he should think she called him again.

She said to herself that under no circumstances would she ever appeal to him for assistance, and she said this over and over again with the vain hope of reassuring herself, for she was by no means at ease in her mind.

Gervaise had before her a noble example of courage and fortitude in the Bijard family. Little Lalie, that tiny child—about as big as a pinch of salt —swept and kept her room like wax; she watched over the two younger children with all the care and patience of a mother. This she had done since her father had kicked her mother to death. She had entirely assumed that mother's place, even to receiving the blows which had fallen formerly on that poor woman. It seemed to be a necessity of his nature that when he came home drunk he must have some woman to abuse. Lalie was too small, he grumbled; one blow of his fist covered her whole face, and her skin was so delicate that the marks of his five

fingers would remain on her cheek for days!

He would fly at her like a wolf at a poor little kitten, for the merest trifle. Lalie never answered, never rebelled, and never complained. She merely tried to shield her face, and suppressed all shrieks, lest the neighbors should come; her pride could not endure that. When her father was tired kicking her about the room, she lay where he left her until she had strength to rise, and then she went steadily about her work, washing the children and making her soup, sweeping and dusting, until everything was clean. It was a part of her plan of life to be beaten every day.

Gervaise had conceived a strong affection for this little neighbor. She treated her like a woman who knew something of life. It must be admitted that Lalie was large for her years. She was fair and pale, with solemn eyes for her years. She was fair and pale, with solemn eyes and a delicate mouth. To have heard her talk, one would have thought her thirty. She could make and mend, and she talked of the children as if she had herself brought them into the world. She made people laugh sometimes when she talked, but more often she brought tears to their eyes.

Gervaise did everything she could for her; gave her what she could, and helped the energetic little soul with her work. One day she was altering a dress of Nana's for her, and when the child tried it on, Gervaise was chilled with horror at seeing her whole back purple and bruised—the tiny arm bleeding—all the innocent flesh of childhood martyrized by the brute—her father.

Bazonge might get the coffin ready, she thought, for the little girl could not bear this long. But Lalie entreated her friend to say nothing, telling her that her father did not know what he was doing; that he had been drinking. She forgave him with her whole heart —for madmen must not be held accountable for their deeds. After that, Gervaise was on the watch whenever she heard Bijard coming up the stairs. But she never caught him in any act of absolute brutality. Several times she had found Lalie tied to the foot of the bedstead—an idea that had entered her father's brain, no one knew why—a whim of his disordered brain—disordered by liquor—which probably arose from his wish to tyrannize over the child, even when he was no longer there.

Lalie sometimes was left there all day, and once all night. When Gervaise insisted on untying her, the child entreated her not to touch the knots, saying that her father would be furious if he found the knots had been tampered with.

"And really," she said, with an angelic smile, "she needed rest; and the only thing that troubled her was not to be able to put the room in order. She could watch the children just as well—and she could think—so that her time was not entirely lost." When her father let her free, her sufferings were not over, for it was sometimes more than an hour before she could stand—before the blood circulated freely in her stiffened limbs.

Her father had invented another cheerful game. He heated some sous red-hot on the stove, and laid them on the chimney-piece. He then summoned Lalie and bade her go buy some bread. The child unsuspiciously took up the sous, uttered a little shriek, and dropped them, shaking her poor burned fingers!

Then he would go off in a rage. What did she mean by such nonsense? She had thrown away the money and lost it, and he threatened her with a hiding if she did not find the money instantly. The poor child hesitated, he gave her a cuff on the side of the head. With silent tears streaming down her cheeks, she would pick up the sous and toss them from hand to hand to cool them, as she went down the long flights of stairs.

There was no limit to the strange ingenuity of the man. One afternoon, for example, Lalie having completed playing with the children. The window was open, and the air shook the door so that it sounded like gentle raps.

"It is Mr. Wind," said Lalie; "come in, Mr. Wind—how are you today?"

And she made a low courtesy to Mr. Wind. The children did the same in high glee, and she was quite radiant with happiness, which was not often the case.

"Come in, Mr. Wind!" she repeated; but the door was pushed open by a rough hand, and Bijard entered. Then a sudden change came over the scene. The two children crouched in a corner, while Lalie stood in the centre of the floor frozen stiff with terror, for Bijard held in his hand a new whip, with a long and wicked-looking lash. He laid this whip on the bed, and did not kick either one of the children, but smiled in the most vicious way, showing his two lines of blackened, irregular teeth. He was very drunk and very noisy.

"What is the matter with you fools? Have you been struck dumb? I heard you all talking and laughing merrily enough before I came in. Where are your tongues now? Here! Take off my shoes!"

Lalie, considerably disheartened at not having received her customary kick, turned very pale as she obeyed. He was sitting on the side of the bed. He lay down without undressing, and watched the child as she moved about the room. Troubled by this strange conduct, the child ended by breaking a cup. Then, without disturbing himself, he took up the whip and showed it to her.

"Look here, fool," he said, grimly: "I bought this for you, and it cost me fifty sous; but I expect to get a good deal more than fifty sous' worth of good out of it. With this long lash I need not run about after you, for I can reach you in every corner of the room. You will break the cups, will you? Come, now, jump about a little, and say good-morning to Mr. Wind again!"

He did not even sit up in the bed, but with his head buried in the pillow, snapped the whip with a noise like that made by a postilion. The lash curled round Lalie's slender body—she fell to the floor; but he lashed her again, and compelled her to rise.

"This is a very good thing," he said, coolly, "and saves my getting chilled on cold mornings. Yes, I can reach you in that corner—and in that! Skip, now! Skip!"

A light foam was on his lips, and his suffused eyes were starting from their sockets. Poor little Lalie darted about the room like a terrified bird, but the lash tingled over her shoulders, coiled around her slender legs, and stung like a viper. She was like an India rubber ball bounding from the floor, while her beast of a father laughed aloud and asked her if she had had enough.

The door opened, and Gervaise entered. She had heard the noise. She stood aghast at the scene, and then was seized with noble rage.

"Let her be!" she cried. "I will go myself and summon the police."

Bijard growled like an animal who is disturbed over his prey.

"Why do you meddle?" he exclaimed. "What business is it of yours?"

And with another adroit movement he cut Lalie across the face. The blood gushed from her lip. Gervaise snatched a chair and flew at the brute, but the little girl held her skirts and said it did not hurt much, it would be over soon, and she washed the blood away, speaking gently to the frightened children.

When Gervaise thought of Lalie she was ashamed to complain. She wished she had the courage of this child. She knew that she had lived on dry bread for weeks, and that she was so weak she could hardly stand, and the tears came to the woman's eyes as she saw the precocious mite, who had known nothing of the innocent happiness of her years. And Gervaise took this slender creature for example, whose eyes alone told the story of her misery and hardships, for in the Coupeau family, the vitriol of the Assommoir was doing its work of destruction. Gervaise had seen a whip. Gervaise had learned to dread it, and this dread inspired her with tenderest pity for Lalie. Coupeau had lost the flesh and the bloated look which had been his, and he was thin and emaciated. His complexion was gradually acquiring a leaden hue. His appetite was utterly gone. It was with difficulty that he swallowed a mouthful of bread. His stomach turned against all solid food, but he took his brandy every day. This was his meat as well as his drink, and he touched nothing else.

When he crawled out of his bed in the morning he stood for a good fifteen minutes, coughing and spitting out a bitter liquid that rose in his throat and choked him.

He did not feel any better until he had taken what he called "a good drink," and later in the day his strength returned. He felt strange prickings in the skin of his hands and feet. But lately his limbs had grown heavy. This pricking sensation gave place to the most excruciating cramps, which he did not find very amusing. He rarely laughed now, but often stopped short and stood still on the sidewalk, troubled by a strange buzzing in his ears, and by flashes of light before his eyes. Everything looked yellow to him; the houses seemed to be moving away from him. At other times when the sun was full on his back, he shivered as if a stream of ice-water had been poured down between his shoulders. But the thing he liked the least about himself, was a nervous trembling in his hands, the right hand especially.

"Had he become an old woman, then?" he asked himself, with sudden fury. He tried with all his strength to lift his glass and command his nerves enough to hold it steady. But the glass had a regular tremulous movement from right to left, and left to right again, in spite of all his efforts.

Then he emptied it down his throat, saying that when he had swallowed a dozen more, he should be all right and as steady as a monument. Gervaise told him on the contrary that he must leave off drinking, if he wished to leave off trembling.

He grew very angry, and drank quarts in his eagerness to test the question, finally declaring that it was the passing omnibuses that jarred the house and shook his hand.

In March Coupeau came in one night drenched to the skin. He had been caught out in a shower. That night he could not sleep for coughing. In the morning he had a high fever, and the physician who was sent for, advised Gervaise to send him at once to the hospital.

And Gervaise made no objection; once she had refused to trust her husband to these people; but now she consigned him to their tender mercies without a regret, in fact she should regard it as a mercy.

Nevertheless, when the litter came, she turned very pale, and if she had had even ten francs in her pocket would have kept him at home. She walked to the hospital by the side of the litter, and went into the ward where he was placed. The room looked to her like a miniature Père La Chaise, with its rows of beds on either side, and its path down the middle. She went slowly away, and in the street she turned and looked up. How well she remembered when Coupeau was at work on those gutters, cheerily singing in the morning air! He did not drink in those days, and she, at her window in the Hotel Boncœur, had watched his athletic form against the sky, and both had waved their handkerchiefs. Yes, Coupeau had worked more than a year on this hospital, little thinking that he was preparing a place for himself. Now he was no longer on the roof—he had built a dismal nest within. Good God! was she, and the once happy wife and mother, one and the same? How long ago those days seemed!

The next day when Gervaise went to make inquiries, she found the bed empty. A Sister explained that her husband had been taken to the asylum of Sainte-Anne, because the night before he had suddenly become unmanageable from delirium, and had uttered such terrible howls that it disturbed the inmates of all the beds in that ward. It was the alcohol in his system, she said, which attacked his nerves now, when he was so reduced by the inflammation on his lungs that he could not resist it.

The clear-starcher went home, but how or by what route she never knew. Her husband was mad—she heard these words reverberating through her brain. Life was growing very strange. Nana simply said that he must, of course, be left at the asylum, for he might murder them both.

On Sunday only could Gervaise go to Sainte-Anne. It was a long distance off. Fortunately there was an omnibus which went very near. She got out at La Rue Santé, and bought two oranges that she might not go quite empty-handed.

But when she went in, to her astonishment she found Coupeau sitting up, He welcomed her gayly.

"You are better!" she exclaimed.

"Yes, nearly well," he replied; and they talked together a while, and she gave him the oranges, which pleased and touched him, for he was a different man, now that he drank tisane instead of liquor. She did not dare allude to his delirium, but he spoke of it himself.

"Yes," he said, "I was in a pretty state! I saw rats running all over the floor and the walls, and you were calling me; and I saw all sorts of horrible things! But I am all right now. Once in a while I have a bad dream, but everybody does, I suppose."

Gervaise remained with him until night. When the house surgeon made his rounds at six o'clock, he told him to hold out his hands. They scarcely trembled—an almost impreceptible motion of the tips of his fingers was all. But as the room grew darker, Coupeau became restless. Two or three times he sat up and peered into the remote corners.

Suddenly he stretched out his arms, and seemed to crush some creature on the wall.

"What is it?" asked Gervaise, terribly frightened.

"Rats!" he said, quietly; "only rats!"

After a long silence, he seemed to be dropping off to sleep, with disconnected sentences falling from his lips.

"Dirty beasts! Look out, one is under your skirts!" He pulled the covering hastily over his head, as if to protect himself against the creature he saw.

Then, starting up in mad terror, he screamed aloud. A nurse ran to the bed, and Gervaise was sent away mute with horror at this scene.

But when, on the following Sunday, she went again to the hospital, Coupeau was really well. All his dreams had vanished. He slept like a child, ten hours without lifting a finger. His wife, therefore, was allowed to take him away. The house surgeon gave him a few words of advice before he left, assuring him, if he continued to drink, he would be a dead man in three months. All depended on himself. He could live at home just as he had lived at Sainte-Anne's, and must forget that such things as wine and brandy existed.

"He is right," said Gervaise, as they took their seats in the omnibus.

"Of course he is right," answered her husband. But after a moment's silence he added:

"But then, you know, a drop of brandy now and then never hurts a man: it aids digestion."

That very evening he took a tiny drop, and for a week was very moderate; he had no desire, he said, to end his days at Bicêtre. But he was soon off his guard, and one day his little drop ended in a full glass—to be followed by a second, and so on. At the end of a fortnight he had fallen back in the old rut.

Gervaise did her best, but after all what can a wife do in such circumstances?

She had been so startled by the scene at the asylum, that she had fully determined to begin a regular life again, and hoped that he would assist her and do the same himself. But now she saw that there was no hope—that even the knowledge of the inevitable results could not restrain her husband now.

Then the Hell on earth began again; hopeless and intolerant, Nana asked indignantly, why he had not remained in the asylum. All the money she made, she said, should be spent in brandy, for her father, for the sooner it was ended, the better for them all.

Gervaise blazed out one day, when he lamented his marriage, and told him that it was for her to curse the day when she first saw him. He must remember that she had refused him over and over again. The scene was a frightful one, and one unexampled in the Coupeau annals.

Gervaise, now utterly discouraged, grew more indolent every day. Her room was rarely swept. The Lorilleux said they could not enter it, it was so dirty. They talked all day long over their work of the downfall of Wooden Legs. They gloated over her poverty and her rags.

"Well! well!" they murmured. "A great change has indeed come to that beautiful blonde who was so fine in her blue shop."

Gervaise suspected their comments on her and her acts to be most unkind, but she determined to have no open quarrel. It was for her interest to speak to them when they met, but that was all the intercourse between them.

One Saturday, Coupeau had told his wife he would take her to the circus; he had earned a little money and insisted on indulging himself. Nana was, obliged to stay late at the place where she worked, and would sleep with her aunt, Madame Lerat.

Seven o'clock came, but no Coupeau. Her husband was drinking with his comrades probably. She had washed a cap and mended an old gown with the hope of being presentable. About nine o'clock, in a towering rage, she sallied forth on an empty stomach to find Coupeau.

"Are you looking for your husband?" said Madame Boche. "He is at the Assommoir. Boche has just seen him there."

Gervaise muttered her thanks and went with rapid steps to the Assommoir.

A fine rain was falling. The gas in the tavern was blazing brightly—lighting up the mirrors, the bottles and glasses. She stood at the window and looked in. He was sitting at a table with his comrades. The atmosphere was thick with smoke ,and he looked stupefied and half asleep.

She shivered, and wondered why she should stay there, and so thinking turned away, only to come back twice to look again.

The water lay on the uneven sidewalk in pools, reflecting all the lights from the Assommoir. Finally, she determined on a bold step: she opened the door and deliberately walked up to her husband. After all, why should she not ask him why he had not kept his promise of taking her to the circus? At any rate she would not stay out there in the rain, and melt away like a cake of soap.

"She is crazy!" said Coupeau, when he saw her. "I tell you she is crazy!"

He and all his friends shrieked with laughter, but no one condescended to say what it was that was so very droll. Gervaise stood still, a little bewildered by this unexpected reception. Coupeau was so amiable that she said:

"Come, you know it is not too late to see something."

"Sit down a minute," said her husband, not moving from his seat.

Gervaise saw she could not stand there among all those men, so she accepted the offered chair. She looked at the glasses whose contents glittered like gold. She looked at these dirty, shabby men, and at the others crowding around the counter. It was very warm, and the pipe-smoke thickened the air.

Gervaise felt as if she were choking; her eyes smarted and her head was heavy with the fumes of alcohol. She turned around and saw the still, the machine that created drunkards. That evening the copper was dull and glittered only in one round spot. The shadows of the apparatus on the wall behind were strange and weird—creatures with tails—monsters opening gigantic jaws as if to swallow the whole world.

"What will you take to drink?" said Coupeau.

"Nothing," answered his wife. "You know I have had no dinner!"

"You need it all the more, then! Have a drop of something!"

As she hesitated, Mes-Bottes said, gallantly:

"The lady would like something sweet like herself."

"I like men," she answered, angrily, "who do not get tipsy and talk like fools! I like men who keep their promises!"

Her husband laughed.

"You had better drink your share," he said; "for the devil a bit of a circus will you see to-night."

She looked at him fixedly. A heavy frown contracted her eyebrows. She answered slowly:

"You are right; it is a good idea. We can drink up the money together."

Bibi brought her a glass of anisette. As she sipped it, she remembered all at once the brandied fruit she had eaten in the same place with Coupeau, when he was courting her. That day she had left the brandy and took only the fruit; and now she was sitting there drinking liqueur.

But the anisette was good. When her glass was empty she refused another, and yet she was not satisfied.

She looked around at the infernal machine behind her—a machine that should have been buried ten fathoms deep in the sea. Nevertheless, it had for her a strange fascination, and she longed to quench her thirst with that liquid fire.

"What is that you have in your glasses?" she asked.

"That, my dear," answered her husband, "is Father Colombe's own especial brew. Taste it."

And when a glass of the vitriol was brought to her, Coupeau bade her swallow it down, saying it was good for her.

After she had drank this glass, Gervaise was no longer conscious of the hunger that had tormented her. Coupeau told her they could go to the circus another time, and she felt she had best stay where she was. It did not rain in the Assommoir, and she had come to look upon the scene as rather amusing. She was comfortable and sleepy. She took a third glass, and then put her head on her folded arms, supporting them on the table, and listened to her husband and his friends as they talked.

Behind her the still was at work, with constant drip—drip—and she felt a mad desire to grapple with it as with some dangerous beast, and tear out its heart. She seemed to feel herself caught in those copper fangs, and fancied that those coils of pipe were wound around her own body—slowly but surely crushing out her life.

The whole room danced before her eyes, for Gervaise was now in the condition which had so often excited her pity and indignation with others. She vaguely heard a quarrel arise, and a crash of chairs and tables, and then Father Colombe promptly turned every one into the street.

It was still raining, and a cold sharp wind blowing. Gervaise lost Coupeau—found him—and then lost him again. She wanted to go home, but she could not find her way. At the corner of the street she took her seat by the side of the gutter, thinking herself at her wash-tub. Finally she got home and endeavored to walk straight past the door of the Concierge, within whose room she was vaguely conscious of the Poissons and Lorilleux holding up their hands in disgust at her condition.

She never knew how she got up those six flights of stairs. But when she turned into her own corridor little Lalie ran towards her with loving, extended arms.

"Dear Madame Gervaise," she cried, "papa has not come in; please come and see my children. They are sleeping so sweetly!"

But when she looked up in the face of the clear-starcher she recoiled, trembling from head to foot. She knew only too well that alcoholic smell—those wandering eyes, and convulsed lips.

Then as Gervaise staggered past her without speaking, the child's arms fell at her side, and she looked after her friend with sad and solemn eyes.

## CHAPTER XI

### LITTLE NANA

Nana was growing fast—fair, fresh and dimpled—her skin, velvety like a peach, and eyes so bright that men often asked her if they might not light their pipes at them. Her mass of blonde hair—the color of ripe wheat—looked around her temples as if it were powdered with gold. She had a quaint little trick of sticking out the tip of her tongue between her white teeth, and this habit, for some reason, exasperated her mother.

She was very fond of finery and very coquettish. In this house, where bread was not always to be got, it was difficult for her to indulge her caprices in the matter of costume, but she did wonders. She brought home odds and ends of ribbons, from the shop where she worked, and made them up into bows and knots with which she ornamented her dirty dresses. She was not over particular in washing her feet, but she wore her boots so tight that she suffered martyrdom in honor of Saint Crispin, and if any one asked her what the matter was, when the pain flushed her face suddenly, she always and promptly laid it to the score of the colic.

Summer was the season of her triumphs. In a calico dress that cost five or six francs, she was as fresh and sweet as a spring morning, and made the dull street radiant with her youth and her beauty. She went by the name of "The Little Chicken." One gown in particular suited her to perfection. It was white, with rose-colored dots, without trimming of any kind. The skirt was short and showed her feet. The sleeves were very wide, and displayed her arms to the elbows. She turned the neck away and fastened it with pins—in a corner in the corridor, dreading her father's jests—to exhibit her pretty rounded throat. A rose-colored ribbon, knotted in the rippling masses of her hair, completed her toilet. She was a charming combination of child and woman.

Sundays at this period of her life were her days for coquetting with the public. She looked forward to them all the week through, with a longing for liberty and fresh air.

Early in the morning she began her preparations, and stood for hours in her chemise before the bit of broken mirror nailed by the window, and as every one could see her, her mother would be very much vexed, and ask how long she intended to show herself in that way.

But she, quite undisturbed, went on fastening down the little curls on her forehead with a little sugar and water, and then sewed the buttons on her boots, or took a stitch or two in her frock; bare-footed all this time, and with her chemise slipping off her rounded shoulders.

Her father declared he would exhibit her as the Wild Girl, at two sous a head.

She was very lovely in this scanty costume, the color flushing her cheeks in her indignation at her father's sometimes coarse remarks. She did not dare answer him however, but bit off her thread in silent rage. After breakfast, she went down to the court-yard. The house was wrapped in Sunday quiet—the workshops on the lower floor were closed. Through some of the open windows the tables were seen laid for dinners, the families being on the Fortifications "getting an appetite."

Five or six girls—Nana, Pauline and others—lingered in the court-yard for a time, and then took flight altogether into the streets, and thence to the outer Boulevards. They walked in a line, filling up the whole sidewalk, with ribbons fluttering in their uncovered hair.

They managed to see everybody and everything through their downcast lids. The streets were their native heath as it were, for they had grown up in them. Nana walked in the centre and gave her arm to Pauline; and, as they were the oldest and tallest of the band, they gave the law to the others, and decided where they should go for the day, and what they should do.

Nana and Pauline were deep ones. They did nothing without premeditation. If they ran it was to show their slender ankles, and when they stopped and panted for breath it was sure to be at the side of some youths—young workmen of their acquaintance—who smoked in their faces as they talked. Nana had her favorite, whom she always saw at a great distance—Victor Fauconnier; and Pauline adored a young cabinet-maker, who gave her apples.

Toward sunset the great pleasure of the day began. A band of mountebanks would spread a well-worn carpet, and a circle was formed to look on. Nana and Pauline were always in the thickest of the crowd, their pretty fresh dresses crushed between dirty blouses, but insensible to the mingled odors of dust and alcohol, tobacco and dirt. They heard vile language; it did not disturb them; it was their own tongue —they heard little else. They listened to it with a smile, their delicate cheeks unflushed.

The only thing that disturbed them, was the appearance of their fathers, particularly if these fathers seemed to have been drinking. They kept a good lookout for this disaster.

"Look!" cried Pauline. "Your father is coming, Nana."

Then the girl would crouch on her knees and bid the others stand close around her, and when he had passed on after an inquiring look she would jump up, and they would all utter peals of laughter.

But one day Nana was kicked home by her father, and Boche dragged Pauline away by her ear.

The girls would ordinarily return to the court-yard in the twilight, and establish themselves there with the air of not having been away; and each invented a story with which to greet their questioning parents. Nana now received forty sous per day at the place where she had been apprenticed. The Coupeaus would not allow her to change, because she was there under the supervision of her aunt, Madame Lerat, who had been employed for many years in the same establishment.

The girl went off at an early hour in her little black dress, which was too short and too tight for her, and Madame Lerat was bidden, whenever she was after her time, to inform Gervaise, who allowed her just twenty minutes, which was quite long enough. But she was often seven or eight minutes late, and she spent her whole day coaxing her aunt not to tell her mother. Madame Lerat, who was fond of the girl and understood the follies of youth, did not tell; but, at the same time, she read Nana many a long sermon on her follies, and talked of her own responsibility, and of the dangers a young girl ran in Paris.

"You must tell me everything," she said. "I am too indulgent to you, and if evil should come of it I should throw myself into the Seine. Understand me, my little kitten; if a man should speak to you, you must promise to tell me every word he says. Will you swear to do this?"

Nana laughed an equivocal little laugh. Oh! yes, she would promise. But men never spoke to her: she walked too fast for that. What could they say to her? And she explained her irregularity in coming—her five or ten minutes delay—with an innocent little air. She had stopped at a window to look at pictures, or she had stopped to

talk to Pauline. Her aunt might follow her if she did not believe her.

"Oh! I will watch her. You need not be afraid!" said the widow to her brother. "I will answer for her, as I would for myself!"

The place where the aunt and niece worked side by side, was a large room, with a long table down the centre. Shelves against the wall were piled with boxes and bundles—all covered with a thick coating of dust. The gas had blackened the ceiling. The two windows were so large that the women, seated at the table, could see all that was going on in the street below.

Madame Lerat was the first to make her appearance in the morning, but in another fifteen minutes all the others were there. One morning in July Nana came in last, which, however, was the usual case.

"I shall be glad when I have a carriage!" she said, as she ran to the window without even taking off her hat —a shabby little straw.

"What are you looking at?" asked her aunt, suspiciously. "Did your father come with you?"

"No indeed," answered Nana, carelessly; "nor am I looking at anything. It is awfully warm, and of all things in the world I hate to be in a hurry."

The morning was indeed frightfully hot. The work-women had closed the blinds, leaving a crack, however, through which they could inspect the street, and they took their seats on each side of the table—Madame Lerat at the further end. There were eight girls, four on either side, each with her little pot of glue, her pincers and other tools; heaps of wires of different lengths and sizes lay on the table, spools of cotton, and of different-colored papers, petals and leaves cut out of silk, velvet and satin. In the centre, in a goblet, one of the girls had placed a two sous bouquet, which was slowly withering in the heat.

"Did you know," said Léonie, as she picked up a roseleaf with her pincers, "how wretched poor Caroline is with that fellow who used to call for her regularly every night?"

Before any one could answer, Léonie added:

"Hush! here comes Madame."

And in sailed Madame Titreville, a tall, thin woman, who usually remained below in the shop. Her employées stood in dead terror of her, as she was never known to smile. She went from one to another, finding fault with all: she ordered one woman to pull a marguerite to pieces and make it over, and then went out as stiffly and silently as she had come in.

"Houp! Houp!" said Nana, under her breath, and a giggle ran round the table.

"Really, young ladies," said Madame Lerat, "you will compel me to severe measures."

But no one was listening, and no one feared her. She was very tolerant. They could say what they pleased, provided they put it in decent language.

Nana was certainly in a good school! Her instincts, to be sure, were vicious; but these instincts were fostered and developed in this place, as is too often the case, when a crowd of girls are herded together. It was the story of a basket of apples, the good ones spoiled by those that were already rot-

ten. If two girls were whispering in a corner, ten to one they were telling some story that could not be told aloud.

Nana was not yet thoroughly perverted; but the curiosity which had been her distinguishing characteristic as a child had not deserted her, and she scarcely took her eyes from a girl by the name of Lisa, about whom strange stories were told.

"How warm it is!" she exclaimed, suddenly rising and pushing open the blinds. Léonie saw a man standing on the sidewalk opposite.

"Who is that old fellow," she said. "He has been there a full quarter of an hour."

"Some fool who has nothing better to do, I suppose," said Madame Lerat. "Nana, will you come back to your work? I have told you that you should not go to that window."

Nana took up her violets, and they all began to watch this man. He was well dressed, about fifty, pale and grave. For a full hour he watched the windows.

"Look!" said Léonie, "he has an eyeglass. Oh! he is very *chic*. He is waiting for Augustine." But Augustine sharply answered that she did not like the old man.

"You make a great mistake then," said Madame Lerat, with her equivocal smile.

Nana listened to the conversation which followed—revelling in indecency —as much at home in it, as a fish is in water. All the time her fingers were busy at work. She wound her violet stems, and fastened in the leaves with a slender strip of green paper. A drop of gum—and then behold a bunch of delicate fresh verdure which would fascinate any lady. Her fingers were especially deft by Nature. No instruction could have imparted this quality.

The gentleman had gone away, and the workshop settled down into quiet once more. When the bell rang for twelve, Nana started up, and said she would go out and execute any commissions. Léonie sent for two sous worth of shrimp; Augustine for some fried potatoes; Sophie for a sausage; and Lisa for a bunch of radishes. As she was going out, her aunt said, quietly: "I will go with you. I want something."

Lo! in the lane running up by the shop was the mysterious stranger. Nana turned very red, and her aunt drew her arm within her own, and hurried her along.

So, then, he had come for her! Was not this pretty behavior for a girl of her age? And Madame Lerat asked question after question; but Nana knew nothing of him, she declared, though he had followed her for five days.

Madame Lerat looked at the man out of the corners of her eyes. "You must tell me everything," she said.

While they talked, they went from shop to shop, and their arms grew full of small packages; but they hurried back, still talking of the gentleman.

"It may be a good thing," said Madame Lerat, "if his intentions are only honorable."

The workwomen eat their breakfast on their knees; they were in no hurry, either, to return to their work; when, suddenly, Léonie uttered a low hiss, and, like magic, each girl was busy. Madame Titreville entered the room, and again made her rounds.

Madame Lerat did not allow her niece after this day to set foot on the street without her. Nana at first was inclined to rebel, but on the whole, it rather flattered her vanity to be guarded like a treasure. They had discovered that the man who followed her with such persistency was a manufacturer of buttons, and one night the aunt went directly up to him and told him that he was behaving in a most improper manner. He bowed, and turning on his heel, departed—not angrily by any means, and the next day he did as usual.

One day, however, he deliberately walked between the aunt and the neice, and said something to Nana in a low voice. This frightened Madame Lerat, who went at once to her brother and told him the whole story, whereupon he flew into a violent rage, shook the girl until her teeth chattered, and talked to her as if she were the vilest of the vile.

"Let her be!" said Gervaise, with all a woman's sense. "Let her be! Don't you see that you are putting all sorts of things into her head?"

And it was quite true he had put ideas into her head, and had taught her some things she did not know before, which was very astonishing. One morning, he saw her with something in a paper. It was poudre de riz, which, with a most perverted taste, she was plastering upon her delicate skin. He rubbed the whole of the powder into her hair until she looked like a miller's daughter. Another time she came in with red ribbons to retrim her old hat: he asked her furiously where she got them.

Whenever he saw her with a bit of finery, her father flew at her with insulting suspicious and angry violence. She defended herself and her small possessions with equal violence. One day he snatched from her a little cornelian heart, and ground it to dust under his heel.

She stood looking on, white and stern: for two years she had longed for this heart. She said to herself that she would not bear such treatment long. Coupeau occasionally realized that he had made a mistake; but the mischief was done.

He went every morning with Nana to the shop door, and waited outside for five minutes to be sure that she had gone in. But one morning, having stopped to talk with a friend on the corner for some time, he saw her come out again, and vanish like a flash around the corner. She had gone up two flights higher than the room where she worked, and had sat down on the stairs until she thought him well out of the way.

When he went to Madame Lerat, she told him that she washed her hands of the whole business; she had done all she could, and now he must take care of his daughter himself. She advised him to marry the girl at once, or she would do worse.

All the people in the neighborhood knew Nana's admirer by sight. He had been in the court-yard several times, and once he had been seen on the stairs.

The Lorilleux threatened to move away if this sort of thing went on, and Madame Boche expressed great pity for this poor gentleman whom this scamp of a girl was leading by the nose.

At first, Nana thought the whole thing a great joke, but at the end of a month she began to be afraid of him. Often when she stopped before the jeweller's he would suddenly appear at her side, and ask her what she wanted.

She did not care so much for jewelry or ornaments as she did for many other things. Sometimes as the mud was spattered over her from the wheels of a carriage, she grew faint and sick with envious longings to be better dressed—to go to the theatre—to have a pretty room all to herself. She longed to see another side of life—to know something of its pleasures. The stranger invariably appeared at these moments, but she always turned and fled, so great was her horror of him.

But when winter came, existence became well nigh intolerable. Each evening Nana was beaten, and when her father was tired of this amusement, her mother scolded. They rarely had anything to eat, and were always cold. If the girl bought some trifling article of dress, it was taken from her.

No! This life could not last. She no longer cared for her father. He had thoroughly disgusted her, and now her mother drank too. Gervaise went to the Assommoir nightly—for her husband, she said—and remained there. When Nana saw her mother sometimes, as she passed the window, seated among a crowd of men, she turned livid with rage, because youth has little patience with the vice of intemperance. It was dreary life for her—a comfortless home and a drunken father and mother. A saint on earth could not have remained there, that she knew very well; and she said she would make her escape some fine day, and then perhaps her parents would be sorry, and would admit that they had pushed her out of the nest.

One Saturday, Nana coming in, found her mother and father in a deplorable condition—Coupeau lying across the bed, and Gervaise sitting in a chair, swaying to and fro. She had forgotten the dinner, and one untrimmed candle lighted the dismal scene.

"Is that you, girl?" stammered Gervaise. "Well! your father will settle with you!"

Nana did not reply. She looked around the cheerless room, at the cold stove, at her parents. She did not step across the threshold. She turned and went away.

And she did not come back! The next day, when her father and mother were sober, they each reproached the other for Nana's flight.

This was really a terrible blow to Gervaise, who had no longer the smallest motive for self-control, and she abandoned herself at once to a wild orgie that lasted three days. Coupeau gave his daughter up, and smoked his pipe quietly. Occasionally, however, when eating his dinner, he would snatch up a knife and wave it wildly in the air, crying out that he was dishonored, and then laying it down as suddenly, resumed his seat and his soup.

In this great house, whence each month a girl or two, took flight, this incident astonished no one. The Lorilleux were rather triumphant at the success of their phophecy. Lantier defended Nana.

"Of sourse," he said, "she has done wrong; but bless my hear, what would you have? A girl as pretty as that could not live all her days in such poverty!"

"You know nothing about it!" cried Madame Lorilleux one evening when they were all assembled in the room of the Concierge. "Wooden Legs sold her daughter out and out. I know it! I have positive proof of what I say. The time that the old gentleman was seen on the stairs, he was going to pay the money. Nana and he were seen together at the Ambigu the other night! I tell you I know it!"

They finished their coffee. This tale might or might not be true; it was not improbable, at all events. And after this it was circulated and generally believed in the Quartier, that Gervaise had sold her daughter.

The clear-starcher, meanwhile, was going from bad to worse. She had been dismissed from Madame Fauconnier's, and in the last few weeks had worked for eight laundresses, one after the other—dismissed from all for her untidiness.

As she seemed to have lost all skill in ironing, she went out by the day to wash, and by degrees was intrusted with only the roughest work. This hard labor did not tend to beautify her, either. She continued to grow stouter and stouter in spite of her scanty food and hard labor.

Her womanly pride and vanity had all departed. Lantier never seemed to see her when they met by chance, and she hardly noticed that the liaison which had stretched along for so many years, had ended in a mutual disenchantment.

Lantier had done wisely, so far as he was concerned, in counselling Virginie to open the kind of shop she had. He adored sweets, and could have lived on pralines and gum-drops, sugar-plums and chocolate.

Sugared almonds were his especial delight. For a year his principal food was bon-bons. He opened all the jars, boxes and drawers, when he was left alone in the shop; and often, with five or six persons standing around, he would take off the cover of a jar on the counter, and put in his hand and crunch down an almond. The cover was not put on again, and the jar was soon empty. "It was a habit of his," they all said; besides, "he was subject to a tickling in his throat!"

He talked a great deal to Poisson of an invention of his which was worth a fortune—an umbrella and hat in one; that is to say, a hat which, at the first drops of a shower, would expand into an umbrella.

Lantier suggested to Virginie that she should have Gervaise come in once each week, to wash the floors, shop and the rooms. This she did, and received thirty sous each time. Gervaise appeared on Saturday mornings, with her bucket and brush, without seeming to suffer a single pang at doing this menial work in the house where she had lived as mistress.

One Saturday Gervaise had hard work. It had rained for three days, and all the mud of the streets seemed to have been brought into the shop. Virginie stood behind the counter, with collar and cuffs trimmed with lace. Near her on a low chair lounged Lantier, and he was as usual eating candy.

"Really, Madame Coupeau!" cried Virginie, "can't you do better than that?

You have left all the dirt in the corners. Don't you see? Oblige me by doing that over again."

Gervaise obeyed. She went back to the corner, and scrubbed it again. She was on her hands and knees, with her sleeves rolled up over her her arms. Her old skirt clung close to her stout form, and the sweat poured down her face.

"The more elbow-grease she uses, the more she shines," said Lantier, sententiously, with his mouth full.

Virginie, leaning back in her chair with the air of a princess, followed the progress of the work with half-closed eyes.

"A little more to the right. Remember those spots must all be taken out. Last Saturday, you know, I was not pleased."

And then Lantier and Virginie fell into a conversation, while Gervaise crawled along the floor in the dirt at their feet.

Madame Poisson enjoyed this, for her cat's eyes sparkled with malicious joy, and she glanced at Lantier with a smile. At last she was avenged for that mortification at the Lavatory, which had for years weighed heavy on her soul.

"By the way," said Lantier, addressing himself to Gervaise, "I saw Nana last night."

Gervaise started to her feet with her brush in her hand.

"Yes, I was coming down La Rue des Martyrs. In front of me was a young girl on the arm of an old gentleman. As I passed I glanced at her face, and assure you that it was Nana. She was well dressed, and looked happy."

"Ah!" said Gervaise, in a low, dull voice.

Lantier, who had finished one jar, now began another.

"What a girl that is!" he continued. "Imagine that she made me a sign to follow with the most perfect self-possession. She got rid of her old gentleman in a Café and beckoned me to the door. She asked me to tell her about everybody."

"Ah!" repeated Gervaise.

She stood waiting. Surely this was not all. Her daughter must have sent her some especial message. Lantier ate his sugar-plums.

"I would not have looked at her," said Virginie. "I sincerely trust, if I should meet her, that she would not speak to me, for really it would mortify me beyond expression. I am sorry for you, Madame Gervaise, but the truth is, that Poisson arrests every day a dozen just such girls."

Gervaise said nothing; her eyes were fixed on vacancy. She shook her head slowly, as if in reply to her own thoughts.

"Pray make haste," exclaimed Virginie, fretfully. "I do not care to have this scrubbing going on until midnight."

Gervaise returned to her work. With her two hands clasped around the handle of the brush she pushed the water before her toward the door. After this she had only to rinse the floor after sweeping the dirty water into the gutter.

When all was accomplished she stood before the counter waiting for her money. When Virginie tossed it toward her she did not take it up instantly.

"Then she said nothing else?" Gervaise asked.

"She!" Lantier exclaimed. "who is she? Ah! yes, I remember. Nana! No; she said nothing more."

And Gervaise went away with her thirty sous in her hand—her skirts dripping and her shoes leaving the mark of their broad soles on the sidewalk.

In the Quartier, all the women who drank like herself, took her part, and declared she had been driven to intemperance by her daughter's misconduct. She, too, began to believe this herself, and assumed at times a tragic air, and wished she were dead. Unquestionably she had suffered from Nana's departure. A mother does not like to feel that her daughter will leave her for the first person who asks her to do so.

But she was too thoroughly demoralized to care long, and soon she had but one idea: that Nana belonged to her. Had she not a right to her own property?

She roamed the streets day after day, night after night, hoping to see the girl. That year half the Quartier was being demolished. All one side of the Rue des Poissonnièrs lay flat on the ground. Lantier and Poisson disputed day after day on these demolitions. The one declared that the Emperor wanted to build palaces and drive the lower classes out of Paris, while Poisson, white with rage, said the Emperor would pull down the whole of Paris merely to give work to the people.

Gervaise did not like the improvements either, or the changes in the dingy Quartier, to which she was accustomed. It was, in fact, a little hard for her to see all these embellishments, just when she was going down hill so fast over the piles of brick and mortar, while she was wandering about in search of Nana.

She heard of her daughter several times. There are always plenty of people to tell you things you do not care to hear. She was told that Nana had left her elderly friend for the sake of some young fellow.

She heard too, that Nana had been seen at a ball in the *Grand Salon*—Rue de la Chapelle; and Coupeau and she began to frequent all these places, one after another, whenever they had the money to spend.

But at the end of a month they had forgotten Nana, and went for their own pleasure. They sat for hours, with their elbows on a table—which shook with the movements of the dancers—amused by the sight.

One November night they entered the *Grand Salon,* as much to get warm as anything else. Outside it was hailing, and the rooms were naturally crowded. They could not find a table, and they stood waiting until they could establish themselves. Coupeau was directly in the mouth of the passage, and a young man, in a frock coat, was thrown against him. The youth uttered an exclamation of disgust, as he began to dust off his coat with his handkerchief. The blouse worn by Coupeau was assuredly none of the cleanest.

"Look here, my good fellow!" cried Coupeau, angrily, "those airs are very unnecessary. I would have you to know that the blouse of a working-man can do your coat no harm, if it has touched it!"

The young man turned around and looked at Coupeau from head to foot.

"Learn," continued the angry workman, "that the blouse is the only wear for a man!"

Gervaise endeavored to calm her husband, who, however, tapped his ragged breast, and repeated loudly—

"The only wear for a man, I tell you!"

The youth slipped away and was lost in the crowd.

Coupeau tried to find him, but it was quite impossible; the crowd was too great. The orchestra was playing a quadrille, and the dancers were bringing up the dust from the floor in great clouds, which obscured the gas.

"Look!" said Gervaise, suddenly.

"What is it?"

"Look at that velvet bonnet!"

Quite at the left there was a velvet bonnet, black with plumes, only too suggestive of a hearse. They watched these nodding plumes breathlessly.

"Do you not know that hair?" murmured Gervaise, hoarsely. "I am sure it is she!"

In one second Coupeau was in the centre of the crowd. Yes, it was Nana, and in what a costume! She wore a ragged silk dress, stained and torn. She had no shawl over her shoulders to conceal the fact that half the buttonholes on her dress were burst out. In spite of all her shabbiness the girl was pretty and fresh. Nana, of course, danced on unsuspiciously. Her airs and graces were beyond belief. She courtesied to the very ground, and then in a twinkling threw her foot over her partner's head. A circle was formed and she was applauded vociferously.

At this moment Coupeau fell on his daughter.

"Don't try and keep me back!" he said, "for have her I will!"

Nana turned and saw her father and mother.

Coupeau discovered that his daughter's partner was the young man for whom he had been looking. Gervaise pushed him aside and walked up to Nana and gave her two cuffs on her ears. One sent the plumed hat on the side, the other left five red marks on that pale cheek. The orchestra played on. Nana neither wept nor moved.

The dancers began to grow very angry. They ordered the Coupeau party to leave the room.

"Go!" said Gervaise, "and do not attempt to leave us; for so sure as you do, you will be given in charge of a policeman."

The young man had prudently disappeared.

Nana's old life now began again; for after the girl had slept for twelve hours on a stretch, she was very gentle and sweet for a week. She wore a plain gown and a simple hat, and declared she would like to work at home. She rose early and took a seat at her table by five o'clock the first morning, and tried to roll her violet stems; but her fingers had lost their cunning in the six months in which they had been idle.

Then the glue-pot dried up, the petals and the paper were dusty and spotted; the mistress of the establishment came for her tools and materials, and made more than one scene. Nana relapsed into utter indolence, quarrelling with her mother from morning until night. Of course an end must come to this;

so one fine evening the girl disappeared.

The Lorilleux, who had been greatly amused by the repentance and return of their neice, now nearly died laughing. If she returned again they would advise the Coupeaus to put her in a cage like a canary.

The Coupeaus pretended to be rather pleased, but in their hearts they raged; particularly as they soon learned that Nana was frequently seen in the Quartier. Gervaise declared this was done by the girl to annoy them.

Nana adorned all the balls in the vicinity, and the Coupeaus knew that they could lay their hands on her at any time they chose; but they did not choose, and they avoided meeting her.

But, one night, just as they were going to bed, they heard a rap on the door. It was Nana, who came to ask, as coolly as possible, if she could sleep there. What a state she was in! all rags and dirt. She devoured a crust of dried bread, and fell asleep with a part of it in her hand. This continued for some time, the girl coming and going like a will-of-the-wisp. Weeks and months would elapse without a sign from her, and then she would reappear, without a word to say where she had been, sometimes in rags and sometimes well-dressed. Finally her parents began to take these proceedings as a matter of course. She might come in—they said—or stay out, just as she pleased, provided she kept the door shut. Only one thing exasperated Gervaise now, and that was when her daughter appeared with a bonnet and feathers, and a train. This she would not endure. When Nana came to her it must be as a simple working-woman! None of this dearly-bought finery should be exhibited there, for these trained dresses had created a great excitement in the house.

One day Gervaise reproached her daughter violently for the life she led, and finally, in her rage, took her by the shoulder and shook her.

"Let me be!" cried the girl. "You are the last person to talk to me in that way. You did as you pleased: why can't I do the same?"

"What do you mean?" stammered the mother.

"I have never said anything about it, because it was none of my business; but do you think I did not know where you were when my father lay snoring? Let me alone. It was you who set me the example."

Gervaise turned away pale and trembling, while Nana composed herself to sleep again.

Coupeau's life was a very regular one —that is to say, he did not drink for six months and then yielded to temptation, which brought him up with a round turn and sent him to Sainte-Anne's. When he came out he did the same thing, so that in three years he was seven times at Sainte-Anne's; and each time he came out, the fellow looked more broken and less able to stand another orgie.

The poison had penetrated his entire system. He had grown very thin, his cheeks were hollow, and his eyes inflamed. Those who knew his age shuddered as they saw him pass, bent and decrepit as a man of eighty. The trembling of his hands had so increased that some days he was obliged to use them both, in raising his glass to his lips. This annoyed him intensely, and seemed to be the only symptom of his failing health which disturbed him. He sometimes swore violently at these unruly members, and at others sat for hours looking at these flutttering hands as if trying to discover by what strange mechanism they were moved. And one night Gervaise found him sitting in this way with great tears pouring down his withered cheeks.

The last summer of his life was especially trying to Coupeau. His voice was entirely changed; he was deaf in one ear; and some days he could not see, and was obliged to feel his way up and down-stairs as if he were blind. He suffered from maddening headaches, and sudden pains would dart through his limbs, causing him to snatch at a chair for support. Sometimes after one of these attacks, his arm would be paralyzed for twenty-four hours.

He would lie in bed with even his head wrapped up, silent and moody, like some suffering animal. Then came incipient madness and fever—tearing everything to pieces that came in his way—or he would weep and moan, declaring that no one loved him, that he was a burthen to his wife. One evening when his wife and daughter came in he was not in his bed; in his place lay the bolster carefully tucked in. They found him at last crouched on the floor under the bed, with his teeth chattering with cold and fear. He told them he had been attacked by assassins.

The two women coaxed him back to bed as if he had been a baby.

Coupeau knew but one remedy for all this, and that was a good stout morning dram. His memory had long since fled, his brain had softened. When

Nana appeared after an absence of six weeks, he thought she had been of an errand around the corner. She met him in the street too, very often now, without fear, for he passed without recognizing her. One night in the Autumn Nana went out, saying she wanted some baked pears from the fruiterer's. She felt the cold weather coming on and she did not care to sit before a cold stove. The winter before, she went out for two sous worth of tobacco and came back in a month's time; they thought she would do the same now, but they were mistaken. Winter came and went, as did the spring, and even when June arrived they had seen and heard nothing of her.

She was evidently comfortable somewhere; and the Coupeaus, feeling certain that she would never return, had sold her bed: it was very much in their way and they could drink up the six francs it brought.

One morning Virginie called to Gervaise as the latter passed the shop, and begged her to come in and help a little, as Lantier had had two friends to supper the night before; and Gervaise washed the dishes while Lantier sat in the shop smoking. Presently, he said:

"Oh! Gervaise, I saw Nana the other night."

Virginie, who was behind the counter, opening and shutting drawer after drawer, with a face that lengthened as she found each empty, shook her fist at him indignantly.

She had begun to think he saw Nana very often. She did not speak, but Madame Lerat, who had just come in, said, with a significant look:

"And where did you see her?"

"Oh! in a carriage," answered Lantier with a laugh. "And I was on the sidewalk." He turned toward Gervaise and went on:

"Yes, she was in a carriage, dressed beautifully. I did not recognize her at first, but she kissed her hand to me. Her friend this time must be a vicomte at the least. She looked as happy as a queen."

Gervaise wiped the plate in her hands, rubbing it long and carefully, though it had long since been dry. Virginie, with wrinkled brows, wondered how she could pay two notes which fell due the next day; while Lantier, fat and hearty from the sweets he had devoured, asked himself if these drawers and jars would be filled up again, or if the ruin he anticipated was so near at hand that he should be compelled to pull up stakes at once. There was not another praline for him to crunch, not even a gum-drop.

When Gervaise went back to her room she found Coupeau sitting on the side of the bed weeping and moaning. She took a chair near by and looked at him, without speaking.

"I have news for you," she said at last. "Your daughter has been seen. She is happy and comfortable. Would that I were in her place!"

Coupeau was looking down on the floor intently. He raised his head and said, with an idiotic laugh:

"Do as you please, my dear; don't let me be any hindrance to you. When you are dressed up, you are not so bad-looking after all."

## CHAPTER XII

### POVERTY AND DEGRADATION

THE weather was intensely cold about the middle of January. Gervaise had not been able to pay her rent, due on the first. She had little or no work, and consequently no food to speak of. The sky was dark and gloomy, and the air heavy with the coming of a storm. Gervaise thought it barely possible that her husband might come in with a little money. After all everything is possible, and he had said that he would work. Gervaise after a little, by dint of dwelling on this thought, had come to consider it a certainty. Yes, Coupeau would bring home some money, and they would have a good, hot, comfortable dinner. As to herself, she had given up trying to get work, for no one would have her. This did not much trouble her however, for she had arrived at that point when the mere exertion of moving had become intolerable to her. She now lay stretched on the bed, for she was warmer there.

Gervaise called it a bed. In reality it was only a pile of straw in the corner, for she had sold her bed and all her furniture. She occasionally swept the straw together with a broom, and after all it was neither dustier nor dirtier than everything else in the place. On this straw therefore, Gervaise now lay, with her eyes wide open. How long, she wondered, could people live without eating? She was not hungry, but there was a strange weight at the pit of her stomach. Her haggard eyes wandered about the room in search of anything she could sell. She vaguely wished some one would buy the spider-webs which hung in all the corners. She knew them to be very good for cuts, but she doubted if they had any market value.

Tired of this contemplation, she got up and took her one chair to the window, and looked out into the dingy court-yard.

Her landlord had been there that day, and declared he would only wait one week for his money, and if it were not forthcoming, he would turn them into the street. It drove her wild to see him stand in his heavy overcoat, and tell her so coldly that he should pack her off at once. She hated him with a vindictive hatred, as she did her fool of a husband, and the Lorilleux and Poissons. In fact she hated every one on that especial day.

Unfortunately, people can't live without eating and before the woman's famished eyes floated visions of food. Not of dainty little dishes. She had long since ceased to care for those, and eat all she could get without being in the least fastidious in regard to its quality. When she had a little money, she bought a bullock's heart, or a bit of cheese, or some beans, and sometimes she begged from a restaurant, and made a sort of panada of the crusts they gave her, which she cooked on a neighbor's stove. She was quite willing to dispute with a dog for a bone. Once, the thought of such things would have disgusted her, but at that time she did not—for three days in succession—go without a morsel of food. She remembered how, last week, Coupeau had stolen a half loaf of bread, and sold it, or rather exchanged it for liquor.

She sat at the window looking at the pale sky, and finally fell asleep. She dreamed that she was out in a snowstorm, and could not find her way home. She awoke with a start, and saw that night was coming on. How long the days are when one's stomach is empty! She waited for Coupeau, and the relief he would bring.

The clock struck in the next room. Could it be possible? Was it only three? Then she began to cry. How could she ever wait until seven! After another half hour of suspense, she started up. Yes, they might say what they pleased, but she, at least, would try if she could not borrow ten sous from the Lorilleux.

There was a continual borrowing of small sums in this corridor during the winter; but no matter what was the emergency, no one ever dreamed of applying to the Lorilleux. Gervaise summoned all her courage, and rapped at the door.

"Come in!" cried a sharp voice.

How good it was there! warm and bright with the glow of the forge. And Gervaise smelled the soup, too; and it made her feel faint and sick.

"Ah! it is you, is it?" said Madame Lorilleux. "What do you want?"

Gervaise hesitated. The application for ten sous stuck in her throat, because she saw Boche seated by the stove.

"What do you want?" asked Lorilleux, in his turn.

"Have you seen Coupeau?" stammered Gervaise. "I thought he was here."

His sister answered with a sneer, that they rarely saw Coupeau. They were not rich enough to offer him as many glasses of wine as he wanted in these days.

Gervaise stammered out a disconnected sentence.

"He had promised to come home. She needed food, she needed money."

A profound silence followed. Madame Lorilleux fanned her fire, and her husband bent more closely over his work, while Boche smiled with an expectant air.

"If I could have ten sous," murmured Gervaise.

The silence continued.

"If you would lend them to me," said Gervaise, "I would give them back in the morning."

Madame Lorilleux turned and looked her full in the face, thinking to herself that if she yielded once, that the next day it would be twenty sous, and who could tell where it would stop?

"But, my dear," she cried, "you know we have no money and no prospect of any; otherwise, of course, we would oblige you."

"Certainly," said Lorilleux, "the heart is willing, but the pockets are empty."

Gervaise bowed her head, but she did not leave instantly. She looked at the gold wire on which her sister-in-law was working, and at that in the hands of Lorilleux, and thought that it would take a mere scrap to give her a good dinner. On that day the room was very dirty and filled with charcoal dust, but she saw it resplendent with riches like the shop of a money-changer, and she said once more in a low, soft voice:

"I will bring back the ten sous. I will, indeed!" Tears were in her eyes, but she was determined not to say that she had eaten nothing for twenty-four hours.

"I can't tell you how much I need it," she continued.

The husband and wife exchanged a look. Wooden Legs begging at their door! Well! well! who would have thought it? Why had they not known it was she, when they rashly called out, "Come in?" Really, they could not allow such people to cross their threshold: there was too much that was valuable in the room. They had several times distrusted Gervaise, she looked about so queerly, and now they would not take their eyes off of her.

Gervaise went toward Lorilleux as she spoke.

"Take care!" he said, roughly. "You will carry off some of the particles of gold on the soles of your shoes. It looks really as if you had greased them!"

Gervaise drew back. She leaned against the étagère for a moment, and seeing that her sister-in-law's eyes were fixed on her hands she opened them and said in a gentle, weary voice—the voice of a woman who had ceased to struggle:

"I have taken nothing. You can look for yourself."

And she went away; the warmth of the place and the smell of the soup were unbearable.

The Lorilleux shrugged their shoulders as the door closed. They hoped they had seen the last of her face. She had brought all her misfortunes on her own head, and she had therefore no right to expect any assistance from them. Boche joined in these animadversions, and all three considered themselves avenged for the blue shop and all the rest.

"I know her!" said Madame Lorilleux. "If I had lent her the ten sous she wanted, she would have spent it in liquor."

Gervaise crawled down the corridor with slip-shod shoes and slouching shoulders, but at her door she hesitated: she could not go in: she was afraid. She would walk up and down a little— that would keep her warm. As she passed, she looked in at Father Bru, but to her surprise he was not there; and she asked herself, with a pang of jealousy, if any one could possibly have asked him out to dine. When she reached the Bijards, she heard a groan. She went in.

"What is the matter?" she said.

The room was very clean, and in perfect order. Lalie that very morning had swept and arranged everything. In vain did the cold blast of poverty blow through that chamber, and bring with it dirt and disorder. Ladie was always there; she cleaned, and scrubbed, and gave to everything a look of gentility. There was little money, but much cleanliness within those four walls.

The two children were cutting out pictures in a corner, but Lalie was in bed, lying very straight and pale, with the sheet pulled over her chin.

"What is the matter?" asked Gervaise, anxiously.

Lalie slowly lifted her white lids, and tried to speak.

"Nothing," she said faintly, "nothing, I assure you!" Then, as her eyes closed, she added:

"I am only a little lazy, and am taking my ease."

But her face bore the traces of such frightful agony, that Gervaise fell on her knees by the side of the bed. She knew that the child had had a cough for a month, and she saw the blood trickling from the corners of her mouth.

"It is not my fault," Lalie murmured; "I thought I was strong enough, and I washed the floor; I could not finish the windows, though. Everything but those are clean. But I was so tired that I was obliged to lie down—"

She interrupted herself to say:

"Please see that my children are not cutting themselves with the scissors."

She started at the sound of a heavy step on the stairs; her father noisily pushed open the door. As usual he had drank too much, and in his eyes blazed the lurid flames kindled by alcohol.

When he saw Lalie lying down, he walked to the corner and took up the long whip, from which he slowly unwound the lash.

"This is a good joke!" he said. "The idea of your daring to go to bed at this hour. Come! up with you!"

He snapped the whip over the bed, and the child murmured, softly:

"Do not strike me, papa; I am sure you will be sorry if you do. Do not strike me!"

"Up with you!" he cried; "up with you!"

Then she answered, faintly:

"I cannot, for I am dying."

Gervaise had snatched the whip from Bijard, who stood with his under jaw dropped, glaring at his daughter. What could the little fool mean? Who ever heard of a child dying like that when she had not even been sick? Oh! she was lying!

"You will see that I am telling you the truth," she replied. "I did not tell you as long as I could help it. Be kind to me now, papa, and say good-bye as if you loved me."

Bijard passed his hand over his eyes. She did look very strangely—her face was that of a grown woman. The presence of Death in that cramped room sobered him suddenly. He looked around with the air of a man who had been suddenly awakened from a dream. He saw the two little ones clean and happy, and the room neat and orderly.

He fell into a chair.

"Dear little mother!" he murmured; "dear little mother!"

This was all he said; but it was very sweet to Lalie, who had never been spoiled by over praise. She comforted him. She told him how grieved she was, to go away and leave him, before she had entirely brought up her children. He would watch over them, would he not? And in her dying voice she gave him some little details in regard to their clothes. He—the alcohol having regained its power—listened with round eyes of wonder.

After a long silence, Lalie spoke again:

"We owe four francs and seven sous to the baker. He must be paid. Madame Goudron has an iron that belongs to us; you must not forget it. This evening I was not able to make the soup, but there are bread and cold potatoes."

As long as she breathed, the poor little mite continued to be the mother of the family. She died because her breast was too small to contain so great a heart; and that he lost this precious treasure, was entirely her father's fault. He, wretched creature! had kicked her mother to death, and now just as surely, murdered his daughter.

Gervaise tried to keep back her tears. She held Lalie's hands, and as the bed-clothes slipped away, she re-arranged them. In doing so, she caught a glimpse of the poor little figure. The sight might have drawn tears from a stone. Lalie wore only a tiny chemise over her bruised and bleeding flesh—marks of a lash striped her sides—a livid spot was on her right arm—and from head to foot she was one bruise.

Gervaise was paralyzed at the sight. She wondered if there was a God above, how He could have allowed the child to stagger under so heavy a cross.

"Madame Coupeau," murmured the child, trying to draw the sheet over her. She was ashamed—ashamed for her father.

Gervaise could not stay there. The child was fast sinking. Her eyes were fixed on her little ones, who sat in the corner still cutting out their pictures. The room was growing dark, and Gervaise fled from it. Ah! what an awful thing life was! And how gladly would she throw herself under the wheels of an omnibus, if that might end it!

Almost unconsciously Gervaise took her way to the shop where her husband worked, or rather pretended to work. She would wait for him and get the money before he had a chance to spend it.

It was a very cold corner where she stood. The sounds of the carriages and footsteps were strangely muffled by reason of the fast-falling snow. Gervaise stamped her feet to keep them from freezing. The people who passed offered few distractions, for they hurried by with their coat-collars turned up to their ears. But Gervaise saw several women watching the door of the factory quite as anxiously as herself—they were wives who, like herself, probably wished to get hold of a portion of their husbands' wages. She did not know them, but it required no introduction to understand their business.

The door of the factory remained firmly shut for some time. Then it opened to allow the egress of one workman—then two—three followed, but these were probably those, who well behaved, took their wages home to their wives, for they neither retreated nor started when they saw the little crowd. One woman fell on a pale little fellow, and plunging her hand into his pocket, carried off every sou of her husband's earnings, while he, left without enough to pay for a pint of wine, went off down the street almost weeping.

Some other men appeared, and one turned back to warn a comrade, who came gamely and fearlessly out, having put his silver pieces in his shoes. In vain did his wife look for them in his pockets—in vain did she scold and coax —he had no money, he declared.

Then came another noisy group, elbowing each other in their haste to reach a cabaret, where they could drink away their week's wages. These fellows were followed by some shabby men who were swearing under their breath at the trifle they had received—having been tipsy and absent more than half the week.

But the saddest sight of all was the grief of a meek little woman in black, whose husband, a tall, good-looking fellow, pushed her roughly aside, and walked off down the street with his boon companions, leaving her to go home alone, which she did, weeping her very heart out as she went.

Gervaise still stood watching the entrance. Where was Coupeau? She asked some of the men, who teased her by declaring that he had just gone by the back door. She saw by this time that Coupeau had lied to her; that he had not been at work that day. She also saw that there was no dinner for her. There was not a shadow of hope —nothing but hunger, and darkness, and cold.

She toiled up La Rue des Poissonnièrs, when she suddenly heard Coupeau's voice, and glancing in at the window of a wine-shop, she saw him drinking with Mes-Bottes, who had had the luck to marry the previous summer a woman with some money. He was now therefore, well clothed and fed, and altogether a happy mortal, and Coupeau's admiration. Gervaise laid her hands on her husband's shoulders as he left the cabaret.

"I am hungry," she said softly.

"Hungry, are you? Well, then, eat your fist, and keep the other for to-morrow."

"Shall I steal a loaf of bread?" she asked, in a dull, dreary tone.

Mes-Bottes smoothed his chin, and said in a conciliatory voice:

"No, no! Don't do that: it is against the law. But if a woman manages—"

Coupeau interrupted him with a coarse laugh.

"Yes; a woman, if she had any sense, could always get along, and it was her own fault if she starved."

And the two men walked on toward the outer Boulevard. Gervaise followed them. Again she said:

"I am hungry. You know I have had nothing to eat. You must find me something."

He did not answer, and she repeated her words in a tone of agony.

"Good God!" he exclaimed, turning upon her furiously. "What can I do? I have nothing. Be off with you, unless you want to be beaten."

He lifted his fist—she recoiled and said, with set-teeth:

"Very well, then; I will go and find some man who has a sou."

Coupeau pretended to consider this an excellent joke. Yes, of course, she could make a conquest; by gaslight she was still passably good-looking. If she succeeded he advised her to dine at the Capucin, where there was very good eating.

She turned away with livid lips; he called after her:

"Bring some dessert with you, for I love cake. And, perhaps, you can induce your friend to give me an old coat, for I swear it is cold to-night."

Gervaise, with this infernal mirth ringing in her ears, hurried down the street. She was determined to take this desperate step. She had only a choice between that and theft, and she considered that she had a right to dispose of herself as she pleased. The question of right and wrong did not present itself very clearly to her eyes. "When one is starving is hardly the time," she said to herself, "to philosophize." She walked slowly up and down the Boulevard. This part of Paris was crowded now with new buildings, between whose sculptured façades ran narrow lanes leading to haunts of squalid misery, which were cheek-by-jowl with splendor and wealth.

It seemed strange to Gervaise, that among this crowd who elbowed her, there was not one good Christian to divine her situation, and slip some sous into her hand. Her head was dizzy, and her limbs would hardly bear her weight. At this hour ladies with hats, and well-dressed gentlemen, who lived in these fine new houses, were mingled with the people—with the men and women whose faces were pale and sickly from the vitiated air of the workshops in which they passed their lives. Another day of toil was over, but the days came too often and were too long. One hardly had time to turn over in one's sleep, when the everlasting grind began again.

Gervaise went with the crowd. No one looked at her, for the men were all hurrying home to their dinner. Suddenly she looked up and beheld the Hotel Boncœur. It was empty, the shutters and doors covered with placards, and the whole façade,, weather-stained and decaying. It was there, in that hotel, that the seeds of her present life had been sown. She stood still and looked up at the window of the room she had occupied, and recalled her youth passed with Lantier, and the manner in which he had left her. But she was young then, and soon recovered from the blow. This was twenty years ago, and now what was she?

The sight of the place made her sick, and she turned toward Montmartre.

She passed crowds of workwomen with little parcels in their hands, and children who had been sent to the baker's, carrying four-pound loaves of bread as tall as themselves, which looked like shining brown dolls.

By degrees the crowd dispersed, and Gervaise was almost alone. Every one was at dinner. She thought how delicious it would be, to lie down and never rise again—to feel that all toil was over. And this was the end of her life! Gervaise, amid the pangs of hunger, thought of some of the fête days she had known, and remembered that she had not always been miserable. Once she was pretty, fair and fresh. She had been a kind and admired mistress in her shop. Gentlemen came to it only to see her; and she vaguely wondered where all this youth and this beauty had fled.

Again she looked up: she had reached the abattoirs, which were now being torn down; the fronts were taken away, showing the dark holes within, the very stones of which reeked with blood. Farther on was the hospital with its high, gray walls, with two wings opening out like a huge fan. A door in the wall was the terror of the whole Quartier—the Door of the Dead it was called—through which all the bodies were carried.

She hurried past this solid oak door, and went down to the railroad-bridge, under which a train had just passed, leaving in its rear a floating cloud of smoke. She wished she were on that train, which would take her into the country, and she pictured to herself open spaces, and the fresh air, and expanse of blue sky; perhaps she could live a new life there.

As she thought this, her weary eyes began to puzzle out in the dim twilight the words on a printed hand-bill pasted on one of the pillars of the arch. She read one—an advertisement, offering fifty francs for a lost dog. Some one must have loved the creature very much.

Gervaise turned back again. The street-lamps were being lighted, and defined long lines of streets and avenues. The restaurants were all crowded, and people were eating and drinking. Before the Assommoir stood a crowd waiting their turn, and room within; and as a respectable tradesman passed he said, with a shake of the head, that many a man would be drunk that night in Paris. And over this scene hung the dark sky, low and clouded.

Gervaise wished she had a few sous: she would in that case have gone into this place, and drank until she ceased to feel hungry; and through the window she watched the still, with an angry consciousness that all her misery and all her pain came from that. If she had never touched a drop of liquor all might have been so different.

She started from her reverie; this was the hour of which she must take advantage. Men had dined and were comparatively amiable. She looked around her, and toward the trees where —under the leafless branches—she saw more than one female figure. Gervaise watched them, determined to do what they did. Her heart was in her throat: it seemed to her that she was dreaming a bad dream.

She stood for some fifteen minutes; none of the men who passed looked at her. Finally she moved a little and spoke to one who, with his hands in his pockets, was whistling as he walked.

"Sir," she said, in a low voice, "please listen to me."

The man looked at her from head to foot, and went on whistling louder than before.

Gervaise grew bolder. She forgot everything except the pangs of hunger. The women under the trees walked up and down with the regularity of wild animals in a cage.

"Sir," she said again, "please listen."

But the man went on. She walked toward the Hotel de Boncœur again, past the hospital, which was now brilliantly lighted. There she turned and went back over the same ground—the dismal ground between the slaughterhouses and the place where the sick lay dying. With these two places she seemed to feel bound by some mysterious tie.

"Sir, please listen!"

She saw her shadow on the ground as she stood near a street lamp. It was a grotesque shadow—grotesque because of her ample proportions. Her limp had become, with time and her additional weight, a very decided deformity, and as she moved, the lengthening shadow of herself seemed to be creeping along the sides of the houses with bows and courtesies of mock reverence. Never before had she realized the change in herself. She was fascinated by this shadow. It was very droll, she thought, and she wondered if the men did not think so too.

"Sir, please listen!"

It was growing late. Man after man,

in a beastly state of intoxication, reeled past her; quarrels and disputes filled the air.

Gervaise walked on, half asleep. She was conscious of little except that she was starving. She wondered where her daughter was, and what she was eating, but it was too much trouble to think, and she shivered and crawled on. As she lifted her face she felt the cutting wind, accompanied by the snow, fine and dry like gravel. The storm had come.

People were hurrying past her, but she saw one man walking slowly. She went towards him.

"Sir, please listen!"

The man stopped. He did not seem to notice what she said, but extended his hand and murmured in a low voice—

"Charity, if you please!"

The two looked at each other. Merciful heavens! It was Father Bru begging, and Madame Coupeau doing worse. They stood looking at each other—equals in misery. The aged workman had been trying to make up his mind all the evening to beg, and the first person he stopped was a woman as poor as himself! This was indeed the irony of Fate. Was it not a pity to have toiled for fifty years, and then to beg his bread? To have been one of the most flourishing laundresses in Paris, and then to make her bed in the gutter? They looked at each other once more, and without a word, each went their own way through the fast falling snow, which blinded Gervaise as she struggled on, the wind wrapping her thin skirts around her legs so that she could hardly walk.

Suddenly an absolute whirlwind struck her and bore her breathless and helpless along—she did not even know in what direction. When at last she was able to open her eyes, she could see nothing through the blinding snow, but she heard a step and the outlines of a man's figure. She snatched him by the blouse.

"Sir," she said, "please listen."

The man turned. It was Goujet.

Ah! what had she done to be thus tortured and humiliated? Was God in heaven an angry God always? This was the last dreg of bitterness in her cup. She saw her shadow: her limp, she felt, made her walk like an intoxicated woman, which was indeed hard, when she had not swallowed a drop.

Goujet looked at her, while the snow whitened his yellow beard.

"Come!" he said.

And he walked on, she following him. Neither spoke.

Poor Madame Goujet had died in October of acute rheumatism, and her son continued to reside in the same apartment. He had this night been sitting with a sick friend.

He entered, lighted a lamp, and turned toward Gervaise, who stood humbly on the threshold.

"Come in!" he said, in a low voice, as if his mother could have heard him.

The first room was that of Madame Goujet, which was unchanged since her death. Near the window stood her frame, apparently ready for the old lady. The bed was carefully made, and she could have slept there had she returned from the Cemetery to spend a night with her son. The room was clean, sweet and orderly.

"Come in," repeated Goujet.

Gervaise entered with the air of a woman who is startled at finding herself in a respectable place. He was pale and trembling. They crossed his mother's room softly, and when Gervaise stood within his own, he closed the door.

It was the same room in which he had lived ever since she knew him—small and almost virginal in its simplicity. Gervaise dared not move.

Goujet snatched her in his arms, but she pushed him away faintly.

The stove was still hot and a dish was on the top of it. Gervaise looked toward it. Goujet understood. He placed the dish on the table, poured her out some wine and cut a slice of bread.

"Thank you," she said. "How good you are!"

She trembled to that degree, that she could hardly hold her fork. Hunger gave her eyes the fierceness of a famished beast, and to her head the tremulous motion of senility. After eating a potato she burst into tears, but continued to eat, with the tears streaming down her cheeks and her chin quivering.

"Will you have some more bread?" he asked. "She said "No;" she said "Yes;" she did not know what she said.

And he stood looking at her in the clear light of the lamp. How old and shabby she was! The heat was melting the snow on her hair and clothing, and water was dripping from all her garments. Her hair was very gray and roughened by the wind. Where was the pretty white throat he so well remembered? He recalled the days

when he first knew her, when her skin was so delicate, and she stood at her table, briskly moving the hot irons to and fro. He thought of the time when she had come to the Forge, and of the joy with which he would have welcomed her then to his room. And now she was there!

She finished her bread amid great silent tears, and then rose to her feet.

Goujet took her hand.

"I love you, Madame Gervaise; I love you still," he cried.

"Do not say that," she exclaimed; "for it is impossible."

He leaned toward her.

"Will you allow me to kiss you?" he asked, respectfully.

She did not know what to say, so great was her emotion.

He kissed her, gravely and solemnly, and then pressed his lips upon her gray hair. He had never kissed any one since his mother's death, and Gervaise was all that remained to him of the Past.

He turned away, and throwing himself on his bed, sobbed aloud. Gervaise could not endure this. She exclaimed:

"I love you, Monsieur Goujet, and I understand. Farewell!"

And she rushed through Madame Goujet's room, and then through the street to her home. The house was all dark, and the arched door into the court-yard looked like huge, gaping jaws. Could this be the house where she once desired to reside? Had she been deaf in those days, not to have heard that wail of despair which pervaded the place from top to bottom? From the day when she first set her foot within the house she had steadily gone down hill.

Yes, it was a frightful way to live—so many people herded together, to become the prey of cholera or vice. She looked at the court-yard, and fancied it a Cemetery surrounded by high walls. The snow lay white within it. She stepped over the usual stream from the dyer's, but this time the stream was black, and opened for itself a path through the white snow. The stream was the color of her thoughts. But she remembered when both were rosy.

As she toiled up the six long flights in the darkness, she laughed aloud. She recalled her old dream—to work quietly—have plenty to eat—a little home to herself, where she could bring up her children—never to be beaten—and to die in her bed! It was droll how things had turned out. She worked no more; she had nothing to eat; she lived amid dirt and disorder. Her daughter had gone to the bad, and her husband beat her whenever he pleased. As for dying in her bed, she had none. Should she throw herself out of the window and find one on the pavement below?

She had not been unreasonable in her wishes, surely. She had not asked of Heaven an income of thirty thousand francs, nor a carriage and horses. This was a queer world! And then she laughed again, as she remembered that she had once said, that after she had worked for twenty years, she should retire into the country.

Yes, she would go into the country, for she should soon have her little green corner in Père La Chaise.

Her poor brain was disturbed. She had bidden an eternal farewell to Goujet. They would never see each other again. All was over between them—Love and Friendship too.

As she passed the Bijards, she looked in and saw Lalie lying dead, happy and at peace. It was well with the child. "She is lucky," muttered Gervaise.

At this moment she saw a gleam of light under the undertaker's door. She threw it wide open, with a wild desire that he should take her as well as Lalie. Bazonge had come in that night more tipsy than usual, and had thrown his hat and cloak in the corner, while he lay in the middle of the floor.

He started up, and called out:

"Shut that door! And don't stand there—it is too cold. What do you want?"

Then Gervaise, with arms outstretched, not knowing or caring what she said, began to entreat him with passionate vehemence:

"Oh! take me," she cried; "I can bear it no longer. Take me, I implore you!"

And she knelt before him, a lurid light blazing in her haggard eyes.

Father Bazonge, with garments stained by the dust of the Cemetery, seemed to her as glorious as the sun. But the old man, yet half asleep, rubbed his eyes and could not understand her.

"What are you talking about?" he muttered.

"Take me," repeated Gervaise, more earnestly than before. "Do you remember one night when I rapped on the partition? Afterwards I said I did not, but I was stupid then, and afraid. But I am not afraid now. Here, take my hands—they are not cold with terror. Take me, and put me to sleep, for I have but this one wish now."

Bazonge, feeling that it was not proper to argue with a lady, said:

"You are right. I have buried three women to-day, who would each have given me a jolly little sum out of gratitude, if they could have put their hands in their pockets. But you see, my dear woman, it is not such an easy thing you are asking of me."

"Take me!" cried Gervaise. "Take me! I want to go away!"

"But there is a certain little operation first, you know—" And he pretended to choke and rolled up his eyes.

Gervaise staggered to her feet. He too rejected her and would have nothing to do with her. She crawled into her room and threw herself on her straw. She was sorry she had eaten anything and delayed the work of starvation.

## CHAPTER XIII

### THE HOSPITAL

THE next day Gervaise received ten francs from her son Etienne, who had steady work. He occasionally sent her a little money, knowing that there was none too much of that commodity in his poor mother's pocket.

She cooked her dinner and ate it alone, for Coupeau did not appear, nor did she hear a word of his whereabouts for nearly a week. Finally a printed paper was given her which frightened her at first, but she was soon relieved to find that it simply conveyed to her the information that her husband was at Sainte-Anne's again.

Gervaise was in no way disturbed. Coupeau knew the way back well enough; he would return in due season. She soon heard that he and Mes-Bottes had spent the whole week in dissipation, and she even felt a little angry that they had not seen fit to offer her a glass of wine with all their feasting and carousing.

On Sunday, as Gervaise had a nice little repast ready for the evening, she decided that an excursion would give her an appetite. The letter from the asylum stared her in the face and worried her. The snow had melted, the sky was gray and soft, and the air was fresh. She started at noon, as the days were now short and Sainte-Anne's was a long distance off; but as there were a great many people in the street, she was amused.

When she reached the hospital she heard a strange story. It seems that Coupeau, how no one could say, had escaped from the hospital, and had been found under the bridge. He had thrown himself over the parapet, declaring that armed men were driving him with the point of their bayonets.

One of the nurses took Gervaise up the stairs. At the head she heard terrific howls which froze the marrow in her bones.

"It is he!" said the nurse.

"He? Whom do you mean?"

"I mean your husband. He has gone on like that ever since day before yesterday; and he dances all the time, too. You will see!"

Ah! what a sight it was! The cell was cushioned from the floor to the ceiling, and on the floor were mattresses on which Coupeau danced and howled in his ragged blouse. The sight was terrific. He threw himself wildly against the window and then to the other side of the cell, shaking hands as if he wished to break them off, and fling them in defiance at the whole world. These wild motions are sometimes imitated, but no one who has not seen the real and terrible sight, can imagine its horror.

"What is it? What is it?" gasped Gervaise.

A house-surgeon, a fair and rosy youth, was sitting, calmly taking notes. The case was a peculiar one, and had excited a great deal of attention among the physicians attached to the hospital.

"You can stay a while," he said, "but keep very quiet. He will not recognize you, however."

Coupeau, in fact, did not seem to notice his wife, who had not yet seen his face. She went nearer. Was that really he? She never would have known him, with his blood-shot eyes and distorted features. His skin was so hot that the air was heated around him, and was as if it were varnished— shining and damp with perspiration. He was dancing, it is true, but as if on burning plow-shares: not a motion seemed to be voluntary.

Gervaise went to the young surgeon, who was beating a tune on the back of his chair.

"Will he get well, sir?" she said.

The surgeon shook his head.

"What is he saying? Hark! He is talking now."

"Just be quiet, will you?" said the young man, "I wish to listen."

Coupeau was speaking fast, and looking all about, as if he were examining the underbrush in the Bois de Vincennes.

"Where is it now?" he exclaimed; and then straightening himself, he looked off into the distance.

"It is a fair," he exclaimed, "and lanterns in the trees, and the water is running everywhere; fountains, cascades, and all sorts of things."

He drew a long breath, as if enjoying the delicious freshness of the air.

By degrees, however, his features contracted again with pain, and he ran quickly around the wall of his cell.

"More trickery," he howled. "I knew it!"

He started back with a hoarse cry; his teeth chattered with terror.

"No, I will not throw myself over! All that water would drown me! No, I will not!"

"I am going," said Gervaise to the surgeon. "I canont stay another moment."

She was very pale. Coupeau kept up his infernal dance while she tottered down the stairs, followed by his hoarse voice.

How good it was to breathe the fresh air outside!

That evening every one in the huge house in which Coupeau had lived talked of his strange disease. The Concierge, crazy to hear the details, condescended to invite Gervaise to take a glass of cordial, forgetting that he had turned a cold shoulder upon her for many weeks.

Madame Lorilleux and Madame Poisson were both there also. Boche had heard of a cabinet-maker who had danced the polka until he died. He had drank absinthe.

Gervaise finally, not being able to make them understand her description, asked for the table to be moved, and there, in the centre of the lodge, imitated her husband making frightful leaps and horrible contortions.

"Yes, that was what he did!"

And then everybody said it was not possible that man could keep up such violent exercise for even three hours.

Gervaise told them to go and see, if they did not believe her. But Madame Lorilleux declared that nothing would induce her to set foot within Sainte-Anne's, and Virginie, whose face had grown longer and longer with each successive week that the shop got deeper into debt, contented herself with murmuring, that life was not always gay—in fact, in her opinion, it was a pretty dismal thing. As the wine was finished, Gervaise bade them all good-night. When she was not speaking, she had sat with fixed, distended eyes. Coupeau was before them all the time.

The next day she said to herself when she rose that she would never go to the hospital again: she could do no good. But as mid-day arrived, she could stay away no longer and started forth, without a thought of the length of the walk, so great were her mingled curiosity and anxiety.

She was not obliged to ask a question; she heard the frightful sounds at the very foot of the stairs. The keeper, who was carrying a cup of tisane across the corridor, stopped when he saw her.

"He keeps it up well!" he said.

She went in, but stood at the door, as she saw there were people there. The young surgeon had surrendered his chair to an elderly gentleman wearing several decorations. He was the chief physician of the hospital, and his eyes were like gimlets.

Gervaise tried to see Coupeau over the bald head of that gentleman. Her husband was leaping and dancing with undiminished strength. The perspiration poured more constantly from his brow now, that was all. His feet had worn holes in the mattress with his steady tramp from window to wall.

Gervaise asked herself why she had come back. She had been accused the evening before of exaggerating the picture, but she had not made it strong enough. The next time she imitated him she could do it better. She listened to what the physicians were saying: the house-surgeon was giving the details of the night, with many words which she did not understand; but she gathered that Coupeau had gone on in the same way all night. Finally, he said this was the wife of the patient. Whereupon the surgeon-in-chief turned and interrogated her with the air of a police judge.

"Did this man's father drink?"

"A little, sir. Just as everybody does. He fell from a roof, when he had been drinking, and was killed."

"Did his mother drink?"

"Yes, sir—that is, a little now and then. He had a brother who died in convulsions; but the others are very healthy."

The surgeon looked at her, and said, coldly:

"You drink, too?"

Gervaise attempted to defend herself and deny the accusation.

"You drink," he repeated, "and see

to what it leads. Some day you will be here, and like this."

She leaned against the wall, utterly overcome. The physician turned away. He knelt on the mattress and carefully watched Coupeau; he wished to see if his feet trembled as much as his hands. His extremities vibrated as if on wires. The disease was creeping on, and the peculiar shivering seemed to be under the skin—it would cease for a minute or two and then begin again. The belly and the shoulders trembled like water just on the point of boiling.

Coupeau seemed to suffer more than the evening before. His complaints were curious and contradictory. A million pins were pricking him. There was a weight under the skin; a cold, wet animal was crawling over him. Then there were other creatures on his shoulder.

"I am thirsty," he groaned; "so thirsty."

The house-surgeon took a glass of lemonade from a tray and gave it to him. He seized the glass in both hands, drank one swallow, spilling the whole of it at the same time. He at once spat it out in disgust.

"It is brandy!" he exclaimed.

Then the surgeon, on a sign from his chief, gave him some water, and Coupeau did, the same thing.

"It is brandy!" he cried. "Brandy! Oh, my God!"

For twenty-four hours he had declared that everything he touched to his lips was brandy, and with tears begged for something else—for it burned his throat, he said. Beef-tea was brought to him; he refused it, saying it smelled of alcohol. He seemed to suffer intense and constant agony from the poison which he vowed was in the air. He asked why people were allowed to rub matches all the time under his nose, to choke him with their vile fumes.

The physicians watched Coupeau with care and interest. The phantoms which had hitherto haunted him by night, now appeared before him at midday. He saw spiders' webs hanging from the wall as large as the sails of a man-of war. Then these webs changed to nets, whose meshes were constantly contracting only to enlarge again. These nets held black balls, and they, too, swelled and shrank. Suddenly he cried out—

"The rats! Oh, the rats!"

The balls had been transformed to rats. The vile beasts found their way through the meshes of the nets, and swarmed over the mattress and then disappeared as suddenly as they came.

The rats were followed by a monkey, who went in and came out from the wall, each time so near his face, that Coupeau started back in disgust. All this vanished in the twinkling of an eye. He apparently thought the walls were unsteady and about to fall, for he uttered shriek after shriek of agony.

"Fire! Fire!" he screamed. "They can't stand long. They are shaking! Fire ! Fire! The whole heavens are bright with the light! Help! Help!"

His shrieks ended in a convulsed murmur. He foamed at the mouth. The surgeon-in-chief turned to the assistant.

"You keep the temperature at forty degrees?" he asked.

"Yes, sir."

A dead silence ensued. Then the surgeon shrugged his shoulders.

"Well, continue the same treatment—beef-tea, milk, lemonade, and quinine as directed. Do not leave him, and send for me if there is any change."

And he left the room, Gervaise following close at his heels, seeking an opportunity of asking him if there was no hope. But he stalked down the corridor with so much dignity, that she dared not approach him.

She stood for a moment undecided whether she should go back to Coupeau or not, but hearing him begin again the lamentable cry for water—

"Water, not brandy!"

She hurried on, feeling that she could endure no more that day. In the streets the galloping horses made her start with a s'range fear that all the inmates of Sainte-Anne's were at her heels. She remembered what the physician had said—with what terrors he had threatened her, and she wondered if she already had the disease.

When she reached the house the Concierge and all the others were waiting, and called her into the lodge.

"Was Coupeau still alive?" they asked.

Boche seemed quite disturbed at her answer, as he had made a bet that he would not live twenty-four hours. Every one was astonished. Madame Lorilleux made a mental calculation:

"Sixty hours," she said. "His strength was extraordinary."

Then Boche begged Gervaise to show them once more, what Coupeau did.

The demand became general, and it was pointed out to her that she ought not to refuse, for there were two neighbors there who had not seen her representation the night previous, and who had come in expressly to witness it.

They made a space in the centre of the room, and a shiver of expectation ran through the little crowd.

Gervaise was very reluctant. She was really afraid—afraid of making herself ill. She finally made the attempt, but drew back again hastily.

No, she could not; it was quite impossible. Every one was disappointed, and Virginie went away.

Then every one began to talk of the Poissons. A warrant had been served on them the night before. Poisson was to lose his place. As to Lantier he was hovering around a woman who thought of taking the shop and meant to sell hot tripe. Lantier was in luck as usual.

As they talked, some one caught sight of Gervaise, and pointed her out to the others. She was at the very back of the lodge, her feet and hands trembling, imitating Coupeau in fact. They spoke to her. She stared wildly about as if awaking from a dream, and then left the room.

The next day she left the house at noon, as she had done before. And as she entered Sainte-Anne's she heard the same terrific sounds.

When she reached the cell, she found Coupeau raving mad! He was fighting in the middle of the cell with invisible enemies. He tried to hide himself; he talked and he answered, as if there were twenty persons. Gervaise watched him with distended eyes. He fancied himself on a roof laying down the sheets of zinc. He blew the furnace with his mouth, and he went down on his knees, and made a motion as if he had soldering irons in his hand. He was troubled by his shoes: it seemed as if he thought they were dangerous. On the next roofs stood persons who insulted him by letting quantities of rats loose. He stamped here and there in his desire to kill them, and the spiders, too! he pulled away his clothing to catch the creatures who, he said, intended to burrow under his skin. In another minute he believed himself to be a locomotive, and puffed and panted. He darted toward the window and looked down into the street as if he were on a roof.

"Look!" he said, "there is a travelling circus. I see the lions and the panthers making faces at me. And there is Clémence. Good God! man, don't fire!"

And he gesticulated to the men, who he said were pointing their guns at him.

He talked incessantly, his voice growing louder and louder, higher and higher.

"Ah! it is you, is it? but please keep your hair out of my mouth."

And he passed his hand over his face as if to take away the hair.

"Who is it?" said the keeper.

"My wife, of course."

He looked at the wall, turning his back to Gervaise—who felt very strangely, and looked at the wall to see if she was there! He talked on.

"You look very fine. Where did you get that dress? Come here and let me arrange it for you a little. You devil! there he is again!"

And he leaped at the wall, but the soft cushions threw him back.

"Whom do you see?" asked the young doctor.

"Lantier! Lantier!"

Gervaise could not endure the eyes of the young man, for the scene brought back to her so much of her former life.

Coupeau fancied, as he had been thrown back from the wall in front, that he was now attacked in the rear, and he leaped over the mattress with the agility of a cat. His respiration grew shorter and shorter—his eyes starting from their sockets.

"He is killing her!" he shrieked, "killing her! Just see the blood!"

He fell back against the wall, with his hands wide open before him, as if he were repelling the approach of some frightful object. He uttered two long, low groans, and then fell flat on the mattress.

"He is dead! He is dead!" moaned Gervaise.

The keeper lifted Coupeau. No, he was not dead; his bare feet quivered with a regular motion. The surgeon-in-chief came in, bringing two colleagues. The three men stood in grave silence watching the man for some time. They uncovered him, and Gervaise saw his shoulders and back.

The tremulous motion had now taken complete possession of the body as well as the limbs; and a strange ripple ran just under the skin.

"He is asleep," said the surgeon-in-chief, turning to his colleagues.

Coupeau's eyes were closed, and his his face twitched convulsively. Coupeau might sleep, but his feet did nothing of the kind.

Gervaise, seeing the doctors lay their hands on Coupeau's body, wished to do the same. She approached softly, and placed her hand on his shoulder, and left it there for a minute.

What was going on there? A river seemed hurrying on under that skin. It was the liquor of the Assommoir, working like a mole through muscle, nerves, bone and marrow.

The doctors went away, and Gervaise, at the end of another hour, said to the young surgeon:

"He is dead, sir."

But the surgeon, looking at the feet, said: "No," for those poor feet were still dancing.

Another hour, and yet another passed. Suddenly the feet were stiff and motionless, and the young surgeon turned to Gervaise.

"He is dead," he said.

Death alone had stopped those feet.

When Gervaise went back she was met at the door by a crowd of people, who wished to ask her questions, she thought.

"He is dead," she said, quietly, as she moved on.

But no one heard her. They had their own tale to tell then. How Poisson had nearly murdered Lantier. Poisson was a tiger, and he ought to have seen what was going on long before. And Boche said the woman had taken the shop, and that Lantier was, as usual, in luck again, for he adored tripe.

In the meantime, Gervaise went directly to Madame Lerat and Madame Lorilleux, and said, faintly:

"He is dead—after four days of horror."

Then the two sisters were in duty bound to pull out their handkerchiefs. Their brother had lived a most dissolute life. but then he was their brother.

Boche shrugged his shoulders, and said in an audible voice:

"Pshaw! it is only one drunkard the less!"

After this day Gervaise was not always quite right in her mind, and it was one of the attractions of the house to see her act Coupeau.

But her representations were often involuntary. She trembled at times from head to foot, and uttered little spasmodic cries. She had taken the disease in a modified form at Sainte-Anne's from looking so long at her husband. But she never became altogether like him in the few remaining months of her existence.

She sank lower day by day. As soon as she got a little money from any source whatever, she drank it away at once. Her landlord decided to turn her out of the room she occupied; and as Father Bru was discovered dead one day in his den under the stairs, Monsieur Marescot allowed her to take possession of his quarters. It was there, therefore, on the old straw bed, that she lay waiting for Death to come. Apparently, even Mother Earth would have none of her. She tried several times to throw herself out of the window, but Death took her by bits, as it were. In fact, no one knew exactly when she died, nor exactly what she died of. They spoke of cold and hunger.

But the truth was she died of utter weariness of life, and Father Bazonge came the day she was found dead in her den.

Under his arm he carried a coffin, and he was very tipsy, and as gay as a lark.

"It is foolish to be in a hurry, because one always gets what one wants finally. I am ready to give you all your good pleasure when your time comes. Some want to go, and some want to stay. And here is one who wanted to go, and was kept waiting."

And when he lifted Gervaise in his great, coarse hands, he did it tenderly. And as he laid her gently in her coffin, he murmured, between two hiccoughs:

"It is I—my dear, it is I," said this rough consoler of women. "It is I. Be happy now, and sleep quietly, my dear!"

# The Mysteries of Marseilles

## CHAPTER I

### HOW BLANCHE DE CAZALIS FLED WITH PHILIPPE CAYOL

TOWARDS the close of the month of May, a man about thirty years old was walking rapidly along a path in the Saint-Joseph district, near the Aygalades. He had left his horse in the care of a farmer of the vicinity, and was going in the direction of a large, solidly built square mansion, a sort of country château similar to many found upon the hills of Provence.

He made a turn to avoid the château, and seated himself in the midst of a grove of pines which stretched out behind the dwelling. There, putting aside the branches, he uneasily and excitedly scanned the pathways, seeming to be impatiently awaiting some one. At times, he arose and walked a few steps; then he sat down again, all of a tremble.

This man, tall and strange looking, wore large black side-whiskers. His long face, full of energetic features, possessed a sort of violent and fiery beauty. Suddenly his eyes softened and his strong, thick lips assumed a tender smile. A young girl had just quitted the château, and, bending as if for concealment, was hastening in the direction of the grove of pines.

Panting and rosy, she came beneath the trees. She was scarcely sixteen. Amid the blue ribbons of her straw hat, her youthful visage smiled with a joyous and frightened air. Her flaxen locks fell over her shoulders; her little hands, pressed against her bosom, strove to calm the bounds of her heart.

"How long you have kept me waiting, Blanche," said the young man. "I had given up all hope of seeing you."

And he aided her to seat herself beside him on the moss.

"Pardon me, Philippe," answered the young girl. "My uncle has gone to Aix to purchase a property; but I could not get rid of my governess."

She abandoned herself to the clasp of him she adored, and the two lovers indulged in one of those long chats so silly and so sweet. Blanche was a big baby who played with her admirer as she would have played with a doll. Philippe, ardent and mute, embraced and looked at the young girl with all the transports of ambition and love.

And, as they sat thus, oblivious of the world, they raised their heads and saw that some peasants, who were passing along a neighboring path, were staring and laughing at them. Blanche, startled, drew away from her lover.

"I am lost," said she, growing deadly pale. "Those men will tell my uncle. Ah! in pity save me, Philippe!"

At this cry, the young man arose with a hasty movement.

"If you wish me to save you," replied he, impetuously, "you must marry me. Come, let us fly together. Tomorrow, your uncle will sanction our marriage, and we can enjoy our tenderness forever!"

"Fly—fly," repeated the girl. "Ah! I have not the courage. I am too weak, too timid!"

"I will sustain you, Blanche. We will live a life of love!"

Blanche, without comprehending, without replying, allowed her head to sink upon Philippe's shoulder.

"Oh! I am afraid, I am afraid of the convent," resumed she, in a low tone. "You will love me always?"

"Yes, for I adore you! See, I am on my knees!"

Then, closing her eyes, abandoning herself to her fate, Blanche ran down the hill, leaning on Philippe's arm. As she departed, she gave a last look at the mansion she had quitted, and keen emotion brought great tears into her eyes.

A moment of heedlessness and terror had sufficed to cast her into her lover's arms, crushed and trusting. She loved Philippe with all the new-born ardor of her young blood and with all the madness of her inexperience. She escaped like a school-girl; she went voluntarily, without reflection, regardless of the consequences of her flight. And Philippe led her away, intoxicated with his victory, trembling to feel her walk and pant at his side.

The young man wished to hasten to Marseilles and procure a hackney-coach. But he was afraid to leave Blanche alone upon the highway, and preferred to go on foot with her as far as his mother's country-house. They were a league away from that country-house, which was situated in the district of Saint-Just.

Philippe was forced to abandon his horse, and the two lovers stoutly began their walk. They traversed meadows, cultivated lands and groves of pines, striking across the fields and hurrying onward. It was about four o'clock. The sun, of a glowing yellow, threw before them broad sheets of light. And they hastened forward in the warm air, beneath the heat of the blue sky, urged on by the madness which was gnawing at their hearts. As they passed, the peasants raised their heads and watched their flight with astonishment.

It did not take them an hour to reach the country-house of Philippe's mother. Blanche, worn out, sat down upon a stone bench at the door, while the young man went to procure a priest and send away those who might prove troublesome. Then he returned with the priest and took the young girl into his mother's house where they were married, the man of God exacting a solemn promise from Philippe that, as soon as the civil ceremony could be performed, the nuptial vows should be renewed in church. The priest blessed the newly-wedded pair and departed. Philippe had asked Ayasse, a gardener who was that day working for his mother, to go to Marseilles and find a hackney-coach.

The two lovers were in the fever of their flight. While awaiting the hackney-coach, they remained silent and anxious. Philippe had seated Blanche in a little chair; kneeling before her, he gazed at her a long while and reassured her by gently kissing the hand she abandoned to him.

"You cannot continue to wear that light dress," said he, at last. "How would you like to put on men's clothes?"

Blanche smiled. She felt an infantile joy at the thought of disguising herself.

"My brother is of short stature," continued Philippe. "You shall wear his garments."

It was rare sport. The young girl drew on the pantaloons, laughing heartily. She was charmingly awkward, and Philippe greedily kissed the blushes of her cheeks. When she was dressed, she had the air of a little man, a boy of twelve. She had all the trouble in the world to keep her flood of hair in her hat, and her lover's hands trembled as they tucked in the rebellious curls.

Ayasse at length returned with the hackney-coach. He consented to receive the two fugitives at his domicile at Saint-Barnabé. Philippe took all the money he possessed, and the three quitted the country-house and entered the vehicle.

They stopped the hackney-coach at the bridge of Jarret, and went on foot to Ayasse's dwelling. Philippe had resolved to pass the night in this retreat.

Twilight had come. Transparent shadows fell from the pale sky, and biting odors mounted from the earth, still warm with the sun's last rays. Then a vague fear took possession of Blanche. When, in the growing night, in the voluptuousness of the evening, she found herself alone with her lover, all her terrified young girl's reserve awoke, and she quivered, seized with an unknown dread. She abandoned herself; she was happy and terrified at giving herself up wholly to Philippe. She grew faint; she strove to gain time.

"Listen," said she: "I wish to write to the Abbé Chastanier, my confessor. He will see my uncle, will obtain my pardon from him and will, perhaps, induce him to sanction our marriage. It seems to me that I should tremble less had I his consent."

Philippe smiled at the tender innocence of the last remark.

"Write to the Abbé Chastanier," answered he. "I will acquaint my brother with our retreat. He will come to-morrow and bear your letter."

Then, the night came on, lukewarm and voluptuous. In the sight of Heaven, Blanche was Philippe's wife. She had given herself away, she had not uttered a cry of revolt; she had sinned through ignorance, as Philippe had sinned through ambition and love. Ah! that terrible flight! It was destined to strike the two lovers with misery and give them a world of suffering and regret.

It was thus that Blanche de Cazalis fled with Philippe Cayol one fine evening in May.

## CHAPTER II

### MARIUS CAYOL

MARIUS CAYOL, the brother of Blanche's husband was about twenty-five years of age. He was short, thin and of unobtrusive bearing. His yellowish face, pierced with long and narrow black eyes, lighted up at times with a good-natured smile of devotedness and resignation. He walked, a trifle bent, with infantile hesitation and timidity. When the hatred of evil, the love of right, caused him to straighten up, he became almost handsome.

He had assumed all the hard tasks of the family, allowing his brother to obey his ambitious and impassioned instincts. He crouched beside him, saying, as a matter-of-course, that he was ugly and ought to remain in his ugliness; he added that it was pardonable in Philippe to love to display his lofty stature and the pronounced beauty of his visage. But, on occasion, he showed severity towards that grown-up unruly child, who was his elder and to whom he gave the advice and tenderness of a father.

Their mother, a widow, was without fortune. She lived with difficulty on the wreck of a dowry which her husband had impaired in trade. This money, invested with a banker, gave her a small income which enabled her to educate her two sons. But, when the children had grown up, she showed them her empty hands and brought them face to face with the struggles of life.

The two brothers, thrown thus amid the turmoil of existence, urged on by their different temperaments, took two opposite routes.

Philippe, who had the appetites of wealth and freedom, could not bend himself to work. He wished to gain fortune by a single stroke; he dreamed of making a rich marriage. That was, in his view, an excellent expedient, a speedy way of acquiring an income and a pretty wife. Then he lived in the sunshine; he transformed himself into a lover and even became somewhat of a high liver. He experienced the infinite enjoyment of being finely dressed, of promenading in Marseilles his elegant rudeness, his garments of an original cut, and his glances and words of love. His mother and brother, who indulged him, strove to minister to his caprices. But Philippe acted in good faith: he adored women; it seemed to him perfectly natural to be loved and abducted some fine day by a noble, rich and beautiful young girl.

Marius, while his brother was displaying his good looks, had entered in the capacity of clerk the establishment of M. Martelly, a ship-owner who dwelt in the Rue de la Darse. He was satisfied in the gloom of his office; his whole ambition consisted in gaining a modest competence, in living quietly and unknown. Besides, he felt a secret delight when he aided his mother or his brother. The money he made was dear to him, for he could give it away, make people happy with it and himself taste the profound bliss of devotedness. He had taken the straight road in life, the rugged pathway which leads to peace, joy and dignity.

He had gone to his office when he received the letter in which his brother announced to him his flight and marriage with Mademoiselle de Cazalis. He was seized with dolorous astonishment; he sounded at a glance the abyss into the depths of which the two lovers had cast themselves. He went with the utmost haste to Saint-Barnabé.

The dwelling of the gardener Ayasse had before the door an arbor which formed a little bower; two large mulberry trees, trimmed in the shape of a parasol, stretched out their knotty branches and threw their shadows upon the threshold. Marius found Philippe beneath the arbor, gazing with uneasiness and love at Blanche de Cazelis, seated beside him; the young girl, already weary, was plunged in the oppression of first cares and first delights.

The interview was painful, full of anguish and shame. Philippe had arisen.

"Do you blame me?" asked he, offering his hands to his brother.

"Yes, I blame you," answered Marius, emphatically. "You have committed a rash action. Pride has carried you away and love ruined you. You have not reflected upon the evils you are about to draw down upon your family and yourself."

Philippe showed signs of rebellion.

"You are afraid," said he, bitterly. "I have not calculated; I loved Blanche and Blanche loved me. I said to her: 'Will you be my wife?—will you come with me?' and she came. That's the whole story. Neither of us is culpable."

"Why do you tell an untruth?" resumed Marius, with greater severity. "You are not a child. You well know that your duty was to defend this young girl against herself; you should have stopped her on the brink of the gulf, prevented her from following you. Ah! don't talk to me of love. I know only justice and honor."

Philippe smiled disdainfully. He drew Blanche upon his bosom.

"My poor Marius," said he, "you are a good fellow, but you have never adored a woman; you know nothing of love's fever. Behold my defence."

And he allowed himself to be embraced by Blanche, who clung to him tremblingly. The unfortunate girl felt that her only hope now was in this man. She had married him, she belonged to him; she had followed him as her sovereign master. Now she adored him

like a slave; she crawled towards him, loving and timid.

Marius, in despair, comprehended that he would gain nothing by talking wisdom to the newly wedded couple. He resolved to act by himself; he wished to know all the facts of the case. Philippe answered his questions with docility.

"I have been acquainted with Blanche nearly eight months," said he. "I saw her for the first time at a public fête. She smiled at the crowd, and I thought her smile was addressed to me. From that day I loved her; I sought every occasion to approach her, to talk to her."

"Did you not write to her?" asked Marius.

"Yes, many times."

"Where are your letters?"

"She burned them. Each time I bought a bouquet of Fine, the flower-girl of the Cours Saint-Louis, and slipped my letter among the flowers. The milkmaid Marguerite took the bouquet to Blanche."

"And your letters remained unanswered?"

"At first, Blanche refused the flowers. Then she accepted them; at last, she replied to me. I was mad with love. I dreamed of marrying Blanche, of adoring her forever."

Marius shrugged his shoulders. He drew Philippe a few paces away and there continued the conversation with more firmness in his voice.

"You are an imbecile or a liar," said he, calmly; "you know that M. de Cazalis, a deputy, a millionaire and the all-powerful master in Marseilles, would never have given his niece in marriage to Philippe Cayol, poor, untitled and a republican as the climax of vulgarity. Admit that you have counted upon the scandal attending your flight to force the uncle to give you Blanche's hand."

"And what if I have!" responded Philippe, impetuously. "Blanche loves me; I did not force her to act against her will. She has freely chosen me for her husband."

"Yes, yes, I am aware of that. You repeat it too often for me not to know what I should believe in the premises. But you have not thought of M. de Cazalis' anger; that anger will fall terribly on you and your family—I know the man; this very evening he will have displayed his outraged pride throughout all Marseilles. The best thing you can do will be to take the young girl back to Saint-Joseph."

"No, I will not, I will not. Blanche would never dare to return home. She was in the country scarcely a week; I saw her as often as twice a day in a little grove of pines; we enjoyed in peace the freedom of the fields. Her uncle knew nothing, and the blow must have been severe for him. We cannot present ourselves at this moment."

"Well, listen: give me the letter for the Abbé Chastanier. I will see that priest; if necessary, I will go with him to M. de Cazalis. We must stifle the gossip. I have a task to accomplish, the task of repairing your error. Swear to me that you will not leave this house, that you will await here my orders, my prayers."

"I promise you that I will wait, if no danger threatens me."

Marius took Philippe's hand and looked him squarely in the face.

"Love that child well," said he, in a deep voice, pointing to Blanche; "you can never repair the injury you have done her."

He was about departing when Mademoiselle de Cazalis advanced. She clasped her hands supplicatingly, forcing back her tears.

"Monsieur," stammered she, "if you see my uncle, tell him that I love him. I am married. I wish to remain Philippe's wife and return to our house with him."

Marius bowed calmly.

"Hope," said he.

And he went away, moved and troubled, knowing that he had deceived her and that hope was out of the question.

## CHAPTER III

### THE ABBÉ CHASTANIER

MARIUS, on arriving at Marseilles, hastened to the Saint-Victor Church to which the Abbé Chastanier was attached. Saint-Victor is one of the oldest churches in Marseilles; its black, lofty and embattled walls make it look like a fortress; one might think that it was fashioned entirely with ax strokes by the rude people of the port, who have a special veneration for it.

The young man found the Abbé Chastanier in the sacristy. This priest was a tall old man, with a long, thin face as white as wax; his sad and humble eyes had the vague fixedness of suffering and poverty. He had returned from a burial and was slowly removing his surplice.

His history was brief and sorrowful.

The son of peasants, as mild and innocent as a child, he had taken holy orders, urged on by his mother's pious wishes. In becoming a priest, he had wished to perform an act of humility, of entire devotion. He believed, in the simplicity of his soul, that a minister of God ought to shut himself up in the infinitude of the divine love, renounce the ambition and intrigues of this world and live in the depths of a sanctuary, pardoning sins with one hand and distributing alms with the other.

Ah! the poor abbé! They showed him that simple souls are good only to suffer and remain in the shade! He soon learned that ambition is a sacerdotal virtue, and that young priests frequently love God for the worldly favors distributed by His church. He saw all his seminary comrades use their nails and teeth, and tear off here and there strips of silk and lace. He witnessed these private struggles, these secret intrigues, which make a diocese a little turbulent kingdom. As he remained humbly upon his knees, did not seek to please the ladies, demanded nothing and appeared stupidly pious, they threw him a miserable benefice as one casts a bone to a dog.

He remained thus more than forty years in a small village, situated between Aubagne and Cassis. His church was a sort of barn, whitewashed and glacially bare; in the winter, when the wind broke one of the window panes, the good God was cold for many weeks, as the poor curé did not always possess the few sous required to restore the glass. But he never complained, he lived peacefully in poverty and solitude; he even felt a deep joy in suffering, in feeling himself the brother of the beggars of his parish.

He was sixty when one of his sisters, who was a workwoman at Marseilles, grew infirm. She wrote to him and begged him to come to her. The old priest devoted himself so far as to ask his bishop for a little corner in one of the city churches. He was kept waiting for this little corner several months, and finally was called to Saint-Victor. He was destined to do there, so to speak, all the heavy work, all the labors to which but little fame and profit were attached. He prayed over the coffins of the poor and took them to the cemetery; he even served as sexton upon occasion.

It was then that he began to suffer in earnest. While in his desert, he had been allowed to be simple, poor and old at his ease. Now, he felt that his poverty and innocence were considered a crime, and his heart was torn when he comprehended that there could be servants in the church. He saw plainly that he was looked upon with derision and pity. He bowed his head still lower, made himself more humble and wept to feel his faith shaken by the acts and words of the worldly priests who surrounded him.

Happily, in the evening, he had comfortable hours. He took care of his sister; he consoled himself in his way of devoting himself. He surrounded the poor infirm woman with a thousand little satisfactions. He took refuge beside her and lost himself in his tenderness. Then another joy came to him: M. de Cazalis, who distrusted young abbés, chose him to be the director of his niece. The old priest had hitherto taken charge of no penitent and very rarely confessed any one; he was moved to tears by the proposition of the deputy and questioned him; he loved Blanche as if she had been his own child.

Marius gave him the young girl's letter and watched his face to see what emotions that letter would excite in him. He saw keen grief paint itself there. But the priest did not seem to experience that stupor caused by overwhelming and unexpected news, and Marius thought that Blanche, in confessing herself to him, had avowed the relations existing between her and Philippe.

"You have done well to count upon me, Monsieur," said the Abbé Chastanier to Marius. "But I am very weak and awkward. I should have shown more energy."

The head and hands of the poor man had that gentle and sad trembling peculiar to old people.

"I am at your disposal," continued he. "How can I aid the unhappy child?"

"Monsieur," answered Marius, "I am the brother of the young fool who has fled with and wedded Mademoiselle de Cazalis, and I have sworn to repair the error, to stifle the talk. Will you unite with me? The young girl is lost if her uncle has already handed the case over to justice. Go to him, try to quiet his anger and tell him his niece is about to be restored to him."

"Why did you not bring the child with you? I know the violence of M. de Cazalis; he will desire certainties."

"It is that very violence which has frightened my brother. But we cannot reason now. The facts accomplished

overwhelm us. Rest assured that I am as indignant as you are, and that I fully realize my brother's wretched action. But, in mercy, let us hasten. Afterwards, we will speak of justice and right."

"It is well," said the abbé simply. "I will go with you."

They passed along the Boulevard de la Corderie and reached the Cours Bonaparte, where was situated the deputy's city residence. M. de Cazalis, the day after the flight, had returned to Marseilles, in the morning, a prey to terrible anger and despair.

The Abbé Chastanier stopped Marius at the door of the house.

"Do not enter," said he. "Your visit might, perhaps, be regarded as an insult. Let me act and wait for me."

Marius, for a whole hour, walked the pavement excitedly. He would have preferred to enter, explain the facts himself and ask pardon in Philippe's name. But, while the misfortune of his family was being agitated in that house, he was forced to remain where he was, idle and impatient, in all the anguish of waiting.

At last the Abbé Chastanier appeared. He had been weeping; his eyes were red, his lips quivering.

"M. de Cazalis would listen to nothing," said he, in a troubled voice. "I found him in a blind rage. He has already been to the Procureur du Roi."

What the poor priest did not say was that M. de Cazalis received him with the bitterest reproaches, venting his anger upon him and accusing him, in his fury, of having given evil counsel to his niece. The abbé bent before him; he almost went upon his knees, not defending himself, but asking pity for others.

"Tell me all," cried Marius, in despair."

"It seems," replied the priest, "that the peasant with whom your brother left his horse guided M. de Cazalis in his investigations. This morning a complaint was made, and searches have been instituted at your residence in the Rue Sainte and at your mother's country-house in the district of Saint-Just."

"My God! my God!" groaned Marius.

"M. de Cazalis swears that he will crush your family. I vainly strove to bring him to more merciful feelings. He talks of arresting your mother."

"My mother! Why?"

"He claims that she is an accomplice, that she aided your brother to abduct Mademoiselle Blanche."

"What is to be done—how is the falsity of all this to be proven? Ah! wretched Philippe! This will cause our mother's death."

And Marius began to sob in his clasped hands. The Abbé Chastanier saw his despair with affecting pity; he understood the tenderness and integrity of this poor fellow who wept in the open street.

"Courage, my child," said he.

"You are right, father," cried Marius; "it is courage that I must have. I was a coward this morning. I should have torn the young girl from Philippe's arms and brought her back to her uncle. A voice told me to do this act of justice, and I am punished for not having heeded that voice. They spoke to me of their love and marriage. I allowed myself to be softened."

They were silent for a moment.

"Listen," said Marius, suddenly: "come with me—we two will have sufficient strength to separate them."

"So be it," answered the Abbé Chastanier.

And, without even thinking to take a carriage, they followed the Rue Breteuil, the Quai du Canal, the Quai Napoléon, and ascended the Cannebière. They walked with rapid strides, without speaking.

As they reached the Cours Saint-Louis, a clear voice made them turn their heads. It was Fine, the flower-girl, who was calling Marius.

Joséphine Cougourdan, who was called familiarly by the caressing diminutive of Fine, was one of those dark children of Marseilles, short and plump, whose fine and regular features have preserved all the delicate purity of the Greek type. Her round head rose above slightly sloping shoulders; her pale face between the bands of her black hair expressed a sort of disdainful mockery; there was a passionate energy in her great sombre eyes which a smile now and then softened. She might have been from twenty-two to twenty-four years old.

At fifteen she had been left an orphan, burdened with the support of a brother not more than ten. She had stoutly continued her mother's trade, and, three days after the funeral, still all in tears, was seated in a kiosk of the Cours Saint-Louis, making and selling bouquets as she uttered heavy sighs.

The little flower-girl soon became the spoiled child of Marseilles. She had the popularity of youth and grace. Her flowers, people said, had a sweeter and more penetrating perfume than others.

The gallants thronged about her; she sold them her roses, her violets and her pinks. Thus she was enabled to bring up her brother Cadet and place him, at the age of eighteen, in the employ of a master porter.

The two young folks dwelt upon the Place aux Œufs, in the heart of the popular quarter. Cadet was now a tall fellow who worked on the wharves; Fine, developed, embellished and become a woman, had the lively manners and nonchalant cajolery of the Marseillaises, and reigned, by virtue of her beauty, over all the girls of the people, her companions.

She knew the Cayols from having sold them flowers, and spoke to them with that tender familiarity imparted by the warm air and the soft dialect of Provence. Besides, if all must be told, Philippe of late had so frequently bought roses of her that at last she had grown to feel little thrills in his presence. The young man, a lover by instinct, laughed with her, stared at her so intently as to make her blush and threw her a fragment of a declaration as he passed, all this that he might not lose the habit of loving. And the poor child, who until then had terribly maltreated lovers, allowed herself to be caught by this game. At night she dreamed of Philippe; she asked herself with anguish where all the flowers she sold him could go to.

When Marius stepped up to her, he found her blushing and troubled. She was half hidden behind her bouquets. She looked adorably fresh beneath the large lappets of her little lace cap.

"Monsieur Marius," said she, in a hesitating voice, "is it true that your brother has fled with a young lady, as they have been repeating around me since morning?"

"Who says that?" asked Marius, quickly.

"Everybody. It is the general talk."

As the young man seemed to be as much troubled as she and as he remained silent, Fine continued, with a slight bitterness:

"I have often been told that M. Philippe was inconstant. He spoke too sweetly not to lie."

She was on the point of weeping, but forced back her tears. Then, with dolorous resignation, she added, in a milder tone:

"I see clearly that you are in trouble. If you have need of me, come to me."

Marius looked her in the face and thought he understood the anguish of her heart.

"You are a good girl," cried he. "I thank you and, perhaps, may accept your services."

He gave her hand a strong grasp, as he would have done with a comrade, and hastened to rejoin the Abbé Chastanier, who was waiting for him on the edge of the sidewalk.

"We have no time to lose," said he to the priest. "The rumor of the flight is spreading throughout Marseilles. Let us take a hackney-coach."

It was night when they arrived at St. Barnabé. They found only the wife of the gardener Ayasse, knitting in a low room. This woman tranquilly informed them that the gentleman and the young lady had grown afraid and departed on foot in the direction of Aix. She added that they had taken her son to act as their guide among the hills.

So the last hope was destroyed. Marius, overwhelmed, returned to Marseilles, without hearing the Abbé Chastanier's words of encouragement. He was thinking of the fatal consequences of Philippe's folly; he was protesting against the misfortunes which threatened his family.

"My child," said the priest on quitting him, "I am but a poor man. Dispose of me. I am going to pray."

## CHAPTER IV

### HOW M. DE CAZALIS AVENGED HIS NIECE'S RUNAWAY

THE lovers had fled on Wednesday. The following Friday all Marseilles knew of the affair; the babbling women at the doors ornamented the recital with the most unheard-of commentaries; the nobility were indignant and the citizens made merry over the matter. M. de Cazalis, in his rage, had neglected nothing to augment the noise and make of his niece's flight a frightful scandal.

Clear-sighted people easily guessed the reason of all this anger. M. de Cazalis, deputy of the opposition, had been named at Marseilles by a majority composed of republicans, priests and nobles. Devoted to the legitimist cause, bearing one of the most ancient names of Provence, and bowing humbly before the all-powerful influence of the church, he had felt deep repugnance at flattering the liberals and at accepting their voices. These people, in his view, were clowns and servants who ought to be whipped in public. His indomitable pride suffered at the thought of descending to their level.

He was, however, forced to submit. The republicans placed a high value on their services; once, as a show of disdaining their aid was made, they spoke of embarrassing the election, of causing one of their own number to be named. M. de Cazalis, driven by the circumstances of the case, shut up all his hatred in the depths of his heart, promising himself to be avenged some day. Then ensued shameful intrigues; the clergy took the field, votes were snatched right and left, and, thanks to a thousand reverences and a thousand promises, M. de Cazalis was elected.

And now Philippe Cayol, one of the chiefs of the liberal party, had fallen into his hands. At last he could satisfy his hatred upon one of those clowns who had bargained with him for his election. This man should pay for all; his family should be ruined and crushed; and, as for him, he should be cast into prison, he should be precipitated from the height of his dream of love upon the straw of a dungeon.

What! a common citizen had dared to let himself be loved by the niece of a Cazalis! He had borne her away with him, and now they were running about the highways, playing love's truant. It was a fact that should be made widely known. A man without standing would, perhaps, have preferred to stifle the matter, conceal the deplorable circumstances as much as possible, but a Cazalis, a deputy and a millionaire, had enough influence and pride to cry aloud, without blushing, the shame of his family.

What mattered the fate of a young

girl! Everybody might know that Blanche de Cazalis had been the friend of Philippe Cayol, but nobody, at all events, should say that she was his wife, that she had made a mésalliance by marrying a poor devil without a title. Pride desired that the child should remain disgraced and that her disgrace should be placarded upon the walls of Marseilles.

M. de Cazalis caused to be posted at the corners of the city streets bills in which he promised a reward of ten thousand francs to whoever should bring him his niece and Philippe bound hand and foot. When one loses a blooded dog, one advertises it thus by means of posters.

Among the high classes the matter was noised about with still greater violence. M. de Cazalis exhibited his fury everywhere. He called into requisition all the influence of his friends the priests and nobles. As the guardian of Blanche, who was an orphan and whose fortune he had charge of, he stimulated the investigations of justice and made preparations for the criminal trial. He appeared to be making every effort to give the greatest publicity possible to the free spectacle which was on the eve of commencing.

One of the first steps taken by M. de Cazalis had been to cause the arrest of Philippe Cayol's mother. When the Procureur du Roi presented himself at her house, the poor woman's only answer to all his questions was that she knew not what had become of her son. Her trouble, her anguish and her maternal fears, which made her hesitate, were considered as proofs of complicity. They imprisoned her, seeing in her a hostage and hoping, perhaps, that her son would deliver himself up to free her.

At the news of his mother's arrest, Marius was driven wild. He knew that her health was not good, and his terrified imagination pictured her in the depths of a bare and icy cell; she would die there; she would be tortured there by all the anguish of misery and despair.

Marius was himself disturbed for a moment; but his firm responses and the bail his employer, the shipowner Martelly, offered to enter for him saved him from imprisonment. He wished to remain free to work for the safety of his family.

Little by little, his just mind saw the facts clearly. At first, he had been overwhelmed by Philippe's culpability and had distinguished only his brother's irreparable error; then he had humbled himself, thinking solely of calming Blanche's uncle and giving him every possible satisfaction.

But before the rigor of M. de Cazalis, before the gossip which roused his indignation, Marius had revolted. He had seen the fugitives, he knew that Blanche had followed Philippe of her own free will and he was enraged to hear his brother accused of abduction. Abuse was poured into his ear: Philippe was called a scoundrel and a wretch; his mother experienced no better treatment. At length, the knowledge of the truth forced him to defend the lovers, to take the part of the culprits against justice itself.

Besides, M. de Cazalis' noisy complaints disgusted him. He said that genuine grief was more silent, and that an affair in which a young girl's fate was at stake did not empty itself thus in the public street. And he said this, not because he desired to see his brother escape punishment but because his delicacy was hurt by all this publicity given to a child's misfortune. Further, he fully understood the aim of M. de Cazalis' anger: in striking Philippe, the deputy would strike the clown and the republican, rather than the abductor.

Thus Marius grew angry in his turn. They insulted him through his family, they imprisoned his mother, they tracked his brother like a wild beast, they dragged his dearest affections in the mud and accused them in bad faith and passion. Then, he rose up. The culprit was no longer only the ambitious lover who had fled with a rich young girl, the culprit was also the man who had aroused Marseilles, and who was about to use his overwhelming power to gratify his pride. Since justice charged itself with punishing the first, Marius swore that he would punish the second sooner or later, and that, while awaiting vengeance, he would embarrass his projects and strive to neutralize his influence as a wealthy and titled man.

From that moment, he displayed a feverish energy; he devoted himself wholly to the safety of his brother and his mother. The worst of it was that he could not discover what had become of Philippe. Two days after the flight, he had received a letter from him, in which the fugitive begged him to send him a thousand francs to supply the necessities of travel. This letter was dated at Lambesc.

Philippe had found hospitality there for a few days at the house of M. de Girousse, the son of a former member of the Parliament of Aix, was born in the midst of revolution; from his first breath, he had inhaled the burning of '93, and his blood had always retained a little of the revolutionary fever. He was ill at ease in his hôtel, situated upon the Cours at Aix; the nobility of that town seemed to him to have such outrageous pride and such deplorable inertia that he has passed a harsh judgment on them and preferred to live far from them; his equitable mind and his love of justice and toil had compelled him to accept the fatal march of the times, and he had freely offered his hand to the people, he had accommodated himself to the new tendencies of modern society; he had dreamed for an instant of establishing a manufactory and giving up his title of comte to assume the title of artisan. He felt that there was no longer any nobility but the nobility of toil and talent. Hence he preferred to live alone, removed from his equals; he inhabited, for the greater part of the year, a property he owned near the little town of Lambesc. It was there that he received the fugitives.

Marius was disheartened by Philippe's demand. His savings did not amount to six hundred francs. He went among his friends and strove vainly for two days to borrow the rest of the sum asked for.

As he was despairing one morning, he saw Fine enter his apartment. He had confided, the day before, his troubles to the young girl, whom, since Philippe's flight, he met everywhere upon his path. She incessantly asked him for news of his brother, and always wanted to know if the young lady was still with him.

Fine placed five hundred francs on a table.

"There," said she, blushing. "You can return it to me later. It is some money I put aside to redeem my brother in case he should be drawn as a conscript."

Marius declined to accept.

"You are making me lose time," resumed the young girl, with charming roughness. "I must return immediately to my bouquets. But, if you will permit me, I will come every morning to ask you the news."

And she ran away. Marius sent the thousand francs. Then he learned nothing further; he lived for two whole weeks in complete ignorance of what was taking place. He knew that they were tracking Philippe more eagerly than ever, and that was all. He paid no attention to the grotesque or frightful rumors current on the streets. He had enough terrors of his own, without allowing himself to be frightened by the gossip of a city.

Never had he suffered so much. Anxiety filled his mind almost to bursting; the slightest sound terrified him; he listened constantly, as if he expected to hear bad news. He learned that Philippe had been to Toulon and had narrowly escaped arrest there. The fugitives, the report said, had afterwards returned to Aix. There all trace of them was lost; had they attempted to cross the frontier, or, were they hidden among the hills? No one knew. Marius was the more disturbed because he had been forced to neglect his work at the office of the shipowner

Martelly. If he had not considered himself nailed to his desk by duty, he would have hastened to Philippe's aid and personally looked after his safety. But he dared not quit a house where he was so much needed. M. Martelly showed a sympathy for him altogether paternal. A widower for some years, living with one of his sisters aged twenty-three, he regarded him as a son. The day M. de Cazalis had set afloat the gossip, the ship-owner called Marius into his private office.

"Ah! my friend," said he, "this is a very sad affair. Your brother is lost. We are not powerful enough to save him from the terrible consequences of his folly."

M. Martelly belonged to the liberal party and was even distinguished in its ranks for a violence altogether southern. He had had differences with M. de Cazalis; he knew the man. His lofty probity and immense fortune placed him out of reach of an attack; but his liberalism was of a stately kind; he took a sort of pride in never using his power. He advised Marius to remain quiet and await events; he would second him with all his might when the struggle had commenced.

Marius, who was burning with excitement, was about resolving to ask leave-of-absence of his employer, when Fine, one morning, ran into his chamber, all in tears.

"Monsieur Philippe is arrested!" cried she, sobbing. "They found him, with the young lady, in a country-house in the Trois-bons-Dieux district, a league from Aix."

And as Marius, full of trouble, hastily rushed away to obtain confirmation of the news, which was true, Fine, still bathed in tears, smiled sadly and said, in a low voice:

"At least, the young lady is no longer with him!"

## CHAPTER V

### THE WAY OF THE TRANSGRESSOR

BLANCHE and Philippe quitted the house of the gardener Ayasse at twilight, towards half-past seven o'clock. During the day they had seen gendarmes upon the highway; they were told that they would be arrested in the evening, and fear drove them from their first retreat. Philippe put on a peasant's blouse. Blanche borrowed the costume of a girl of the people from the gardener's wife: a dress of figured red calico and a pink apron; she covered her bosom with a yellow check fichu, and placed over her cap a large coarse straw hat. The gardener's son Victor, a lad of fifteen, accompanied them to guide them across the fields to the Aix highway.

The evening was warmish, with an occasional chill. Warm and biting exhalations arose from the ground and rendered languid the fresh breeze which came at times from the Mediterranean. In the west still lingered the glow as of a conflagration; the rest of the sky, of a sombre blue, was paling little by little, and the stars came out one by one in the darkness, like the trembling lights of a distant town.

The fugitives walked rapidly, with lowered heads, without exchanging a word. They were in haste to reach the desert of the hills. While they were traversing the outskirts of Marseilles,

they met rare passers whom they glanced at with mistrust. Then the broad country spread out before them, and they saw only, here and there, at the sides of the paths, grave and motionless shepherds in the midst of their flocks.

And, in the gloom, in the soft silence of the serene night, they continued to flee. Vague sighs floated about them; stones rolled beneath their feet with sharp sounds. The slumbering country quivered and extended, all black, in the lugubrious monotony of the darkness. Blanche, vaguely terrified, clung to Philippe, quickening her pace that she might not be left behind; she uttered heavy sighs, as she recalled the peaceful nights of her girlhood.

Then came the hills and deep gorges to be crossed. Around Marseilles, the roads are level and pleasant; but, further inland, one encounters those piles of rocks which cut the entire centre of Provence into narrow and sterile valleys. Uncultivated heaths and stony hills, sown with thin clusters of thyme and lavender, now stretched before the fugitives in their sad desolation. The paths ascended and descended along the hills; fragments of rocks encumbered the roads; beneath the bluish serenity of the sky, the scene resembled a sea of flint, an ocean of stone, stricken with eternal immobility in the midst of a hurricane.

Victor, on the lead, softly whistled a Provençal air, as he leaped over the rocks with the agility of a chamois; he had grown from infancy in this desert and knew every corner of it. Blanche and Philippe followed him toilsomely; the young man half carried his companion, whose feet were bruised by the sharp stones of the road. She did not complain, and, when Philippe looked interrogatively into her face in the transparent gloom, she smiled upon him with a sad gentleness.

They had just passed Septèmes, when the worn out young girl fell to the ground. The moon, which was slowly ascending the heavens, displayed her pale visage, bathed in tears. Philippe bent over her with anguish.

"You are weeping," cried he; "you are suffering, my poor, beloved child. Ah! I am a wretch, am I not, to keep you thus with me?"

"Do not say that, Philippe," responded Blanche. "I weep because I am an unhappy girl. See, I can scarcely walk. We would have done better to kneel before my uncle and pray to him with clasped hands."

She made an effort and arose, and they continued their walk through that terrible region. It was not the wild and gay escapade of a couple of lovers: it was a sombre flight, full of anxiety and suffering, the flight of two trembling and silent culprits.

They traversed the territory of Gardanne, and stumbled for nearly five hours over the obstacles of the path. They finally decided to descend to the Aix highway, and there they advanced with less difficulty, but the dust blinded them.

When they were at the top of the rising ground of the Arc, they dismissed Victor. Blanche had travelled six leagues on foot, among the rocks, in less than six hours; she seated herself upon a stone bench at the gate of the town, and declared that she could go no

further. Philippe, who was afraid of being arrested if he remained at Aix, went in quest of a carriage; he found a woman seated in a cart, who consented to take Blanche and himself and conduct them to Lambesc, where she was going.

Blanche, despite the jolts, was soon in a deep slumber and did not awake until they reached the gate of Lambesc. This sleep calmed her blood; she felt rested and stronger. The two lovers quitted the vehicle. The dawn came, a fresh and radiant dawn which filled them with hope. All the phantoms of the night were gone; the fugitives had forgotten the rocks of Septèmes, and walked side by side in the wet grass, intoxicated with their youth and their love.

Not having found M. de Girousse, of whom Philippe had resolved to ask hospitality, they went to the inn, and at last enjoyed a day of peace and quietude. The inn-keeper, thinking that his guests were brother and sister, proposed to prepare two apartments. Blanche smiled; she had now the courage inspired by tenderness.

"One room will do," said she. "Monsieur is my husband."

The following day Philippe went to M. de Girousse, who had returned. He told him everything and asked his advice.

"The deuce!" cried the old noble, "your case is grave. You know that you are a clown; a century ago, M. de Cazalis would have had you hanged for having dared to touch his niece; to-day, he can only have you cast into prison. Rest assured that he will not fail to do it."

"What must I do?"

"What must you do? Send back the young girl to her uncle and gain the frontier as soon as possible."

"You are well aware that I will never do that."

"Then, quietly await your arrest. I have no other counsel to give you."

M. de Girousse had a friendly bluntness which hid the best heart in the world. As Philippe, confused by the roughness of his reception, was about to depart, he recalled him, and, taking his hand:

"My duty," resumed he, with a slight bitterness, "is to have you arrested. I belong to the nobility you have outraged. Listen: I have, on the other side of Lambesc, a small, unoccupied house, the key of which I will give you. Go conceal yourselves there, but say nothing to me about it; otherwise, I shall send the gendarmes after you."

The lovers remained over a week at Lambesc. They lived there in retirement, in the enjoyment of peace which was at times broken by sudden fears. Philippe had received the thousand francs from Marius. Blanche became a little housekeeper, and the twain ate with delight from the same plate.

This new existence seemed like a dream to the young girl. Occasionally she grew dissatisfied, and longed to return to her uncle's home; but she was afraid to speak of this; she felt that she was weak and alone; she had accepted the flight and lacked the courage to retrace her steps.

It was the octave of the Fête-Dieu. One afternoon, as Blanche stood at the window, she saw a procession pass. She knelt and clasped her hands. The young maidens, clad in white, sang in joyous tones, bearing in their midst the banner of the Virgin. At this sight the poor child began to sob; she imagined herself in a snowy robe, among the singers, and her heart bled when she realized that she was a fugitive.

That evening, Philippe received an anonymous note. It warned him that he would be arrested on the following day. He thought he recognized M. de Girousse's handwriting. Then the flight was renewed; it was harder to bear and more wretched than before.

## CHAPTER VI

### HUNTED DOWN

IT WAS a bewildering confusion, a flight without intermission or repose, an incessant terror. Driven right and left by fright, constantly thinking they heard behind them the gallop of horses, passing the nights running about the highways and the days trembling in the filthy chambers of inns, the fugitives traversed Provence many times, hurrying forward and retracing their steps, not knowing where to find an unknown retreat, hidden in the midst of some desert.

They quitted Lambesc on a terribly windy night and went towards Avignon. They had hired a little cart; the blast blinded the horse, and Blanche shivered in her miserable calico dress. As the climax of misfortune, they thought they saw in the distance, at one of the gates of the town, some gendarmes who were scanning the faces of the passers. Terrified, they turned about and went back to Lambesc, through which they merely passed.

They reached Aix, but were afraid to remain there; they resolved to gain the frontier, cost what it might. There they would procure a passport and find safety. Philippe, who was acquainted with a druggist at Toulon, decided that they would go by way of that city; he hoped that his friend would facilitate their flight.

The druggist, a burly, jovial fellow named Jourdan, gave them a hearty welcome. He concealed them in his own chamber, and said he would at once endeavor to get them a passport.

Jourdan had barely left the house when two gendarmes presented themselves.

Blanche nearly fainted; pale, seated in a corner, she restrained her sobs. Philippe, in a choking voice, asked the gendarmes what they wanted.

"Are you the Sieur Jourdan?" demanded one of them, with ill-omened harshness.

"No," answered the young man. "M. Jourdan has gone out, but he will soon return."

"Very good," said the gendarme, coldly.

And he sat down, heavily. The poor fugitives were afraid to look at each other; they were full of terror; they felt unspeakable uneasiness in the presence of these men who had, without doubt, come to seek them. Their torture lasted half an hour. At length Jourdan returned; he grew pale on seeing the gendarmes and answered their questions with inexpressible confusion.

"You must come with us," said one of the men to him.

"Why?" asked Jourdan. "What have I done?"

"You are accused of having cheated at cards, last evening, at a club. You will have to explain matters to the Juge d' Instruction."

A shiver of terror shook Jourdan. His face looked like that of a corpse. He seemed utterly overwhelmed, and, with the docility of a child, followed the gendarmes, who withdrew without even noticing the fright of Blanche and Philippe.

The Jourdan case, at that time, caused a great sensation in Toulon; but no one knew of the private and poignant scene which had taken place at the druggist's house on the day of his arrest.

This scene discouraged Philippe. He realized that he was too weak to escape from that human justice which was tracking him. Besides, he now no longer hoped to procure a passport and could not cross the frontier. Further, it was plain to him that Blanche had begun to be weary. He resolved, therefore, to approach Marseilles and wait, in the vicinity of that city, until M. de Cazalis' anger had somewhat abated. Like all those in utter despair, he entertained at certain moments ridiculous hopes of pardon and happiness.

Philippe had at Aix a relative named Isnard, who kept a mercer's shop. The fugitives, no longer knowing at what door to knock, returned to Aix to ask Isnard for the key of one of his country-houses. Misfortune pursued them: they did not find the mercer at home, and were obliged to hide in an old dwelling on the Cours Sextius, with a cousin of M. de Girousse's farmer

This woman hesitated to receive them, fearing lest, later, her hospitality should be considered a crime; she yielded only when Philippe swore to have her son exempted from military service. The young man was doubtless, in one of his hopeful hours; he already saw himself the nephew of a deputy and made full use of his uncle's power.

In the evening Isnard visited the lovers, and gave them the key of a country-house he possessed on the plain of Puyricard. He owned two besides this: one at Tholonet and the other in the Trois-bons-Dieux district. The keys of these were hidden under certain huge stones which he described to them. He advised them not to sleep two nights in succession beneath the same roof, and promised them that he would make every effort to keep the track of the police.

The lovers departed and took the road which passes beside the Hôpital.

Isnard's country-house was situated to the right of Puyricard, between the village and the Venelles highway. It was one of those hideous little huts built of lime and stones heaped upon each other and adorned with red tiles; there was but a single apartment in it, a sort of filthy stable; remnants of straw were scattered about the floor and huge spider-webs hung from the ceiling.

Philippe and Blanche fortunately had a blanket. They collected the remnants of straw in a corner and spread the blanket over the heap. They passed the night amid the biting exhalations of dampness.

On the morrow they spent the day in the bed of the dried-up torrent of Touloubre. Then, towards evening, they took the Venelles highway, made a circuit to avoid passing through Aix, and reached Tholonet. At eleven o'clock they arrived at the country-house which the mercer possessed below the Oratoire des Jésuites.

This hut was more comfortable than the other. It had two apartments, a kitchen and a dining-room; in the latter was a bed of spun-yarn; the walls were covered with caricatures cut from the Charivari, and strings of onions were suspended from the white-washed beams. The two lovers thought themselves in a palace.

When they awoke in the morning, fear again seized upon them; they climbed the hill and remained until night in the gorges of the Infernets. At that period the precipices of Jaume-garde yet preserved all their sinister horror; the Zola canal had not pierced the mountain, and the fugitives did not venture into that gloomy tunnel of reddish rocks. Blanche and Philippe tasted profound peace in the midst of this desert; they reposed for a long while beside a spring which gushed, limpid and gurgling, from a gigantic block of stone.

With the night returned the cruel necessity of finding a shelter. Blanche could scarcely walk; her wounded feet bled on the pointed and sharp flints. Philippe knew that he could not take her far. He supported her, and slowly they ascended to the plateau which overlooks the Infernets. There stretched out uncultivated plains, vast fields of stones and vague territory hollowed out here and there by abandoned quarries. There is nothing so strangely sinister as that broad landscape with horizons of mournful amplitude, spotted now and again with low and dark verdure; the rocks, like broken limbs, pierce the barren soil; the plain, humped together, seems to have been stricken with death amid the convulsions of frightful agony.

Phillipe hoped to discover a den, a cavern. He had the good fortune to come across a station, one of those little huts in which hunters conceal themselves to wait for the birds of passage. He broke open the door of the cabin without the least scruple, and seated Blanche on a small bench which he felt beneath his hand. Then he went to pull up a large quantity of thyme; the plateau was covered with that humble gray plant, the biting odor of which clings to all the hills of Provence.

Philippe heaped the thyme in the station and made of it thus a sort of straw bed, spreading the blanket upon it.

And the two lovers, upon that miserable couch, gave each other the evening kiss. Ah! what meek suffering and bitter delight that kiss contained!

Philippe's love had become madness. Incessantly obliged to flee, menaced in his dreams of wealth, beneath the blow of an implacable chastisement, the young man rebelled and calmed his rebellion by pressing Blanche in his arms as if he would crush her. The young girl was for him a vengeance; he possessed her as an irate master; he bent her beneath his kisses.

His pride increased. His ambition was largely gratified. A son of the people, he at last controlled the destiny of a daughter of those powerful and haughty men whose equipages had sometimes hurled mud into his face, and he recalled the legends of the country, the vexations of the nobles, the martyrdom of the people, all the cowardice of his fathers before the cruel caprices of the nobility. Then he took vengeance: he stifled Blanche with his caresses.

He had grown to feel a bitter joy in dragging her over the stones of the road. He did not avow these wretched thoughts; he hid from himself the cruelty of his conduct. The truth was that his beloved's anguish and fatigue rendered her dearer and more desirable to him. He would have loved her less in a salon, in the midst of peace. In the evening, when, broken by weariness, she fell beside him, he contemplated her with a cruel joy; the child's sufferings were another spur which augmented his strange love.

The lovers had passed the night amid the filth of the Puyricard country-house. They were there, upon the straw, among the spider-webs, separated, from the world. Around them fell the grand silence of the slumbering heavens. They could love each other in peace; they no longer trembled; they were alone. Philippe would not have exchanged the squalid hut for a royal palace; he said to himself, with transports of pride, that a descendant of the Cazalis family was married to him and was with him in a stable.

And on the morrow and the following days, what keen enjoyment to drag Blanche after him through the deserts of Jaumergarde! He bore away his beloved with all the gentleness of a father and the violence of a wild beast.

He could not sleep in the station: the strong odor of the thyme, upon which he lay drove him mad. He dreamed, wide awake, that M. de Cazalis had received him with tenderness and that he had been named deputy as the successor of his uncle. At times he heard the dolorous sighs of Blanche, who was dozing at his side, feverish and agitated.

The young girl had come to consider her flight with Philippe as a nightmare, full of dolorous terrors. She remained, during the day, stupefied by fatigue; she smiled sadly, but never complained. Her inexperience had made her accept the departure, and her weak character prevented her from demanding that they should return. She belonged body and soul to this man, who was carrying her in his arms; she would have preferred not to walk so much, but she had no idea of quitting Philippe; she continued innocently to believe that her uncle would sanction their marriage, and that it was only necessary to run about among the rocks for a few days longer. She was a big baby, who had had the misfortune to be woman before the proper age.

At sunrise the fugitives quitted their retreat. Their garments began to be terribly torn, and poor Blanche's shoes had holes in them. In the coolness of the morning, amid the sharp perfumes of the plateau which the new-born sunbeams flooded with yellow and pink light, the lovers forgot for an hour their misery and their abandonment. They laughingly declared that they were ferociously hungry.

Then Philippe made Blanche enter the station, and hastened to Tholonet for provisions. He was gone half an hour. When he returned, he found the young girl frightened; she asserted that she had seen wolves pass.

A broad stone slab served as the breakfast table. Blanche and Philippe looked like a couple of Gypsy lovers breakfasting in the open air. After breakfast, the twain walked to the middle of the plateau where they remained all day. They passed there, perhaps, the happiest hours of their love-life.

But, when twilight came on, they were afraid; they did not wish to spend another night in that solitude. The warmish and pure air of the hill had given them hopes and milder thoughts. "Are you weary, my child?" asked Philippe of Blanche.

"Oh! yes," answered the young girl.

"Listen: we will make a last journey. Let us go to the country-house which Isnard owns in the Trois-bons-Dieux district, and remain there until your uncle pardons us or causes my arrest."

"My uncle will pardon us."

"I dare not believe you. At any rate, I desire to flee no longer; you have need of rest. Come; we will walk slowly."

They crossed the plateau, going away from the Infernets, leaving to the right the Château de Saint-Marc, which they saw upon the height. In an hour they reached their destination.

Isnard's country-house was on the hill which stretches to the left of the Vauvenargues highway, when one has passed the Vallon de Repentance. It was a little, two-story cabin; on the first floor there was but one apartment, in which stood a rickety table and three seatless chairs. A wooden ladder led to the chamber above, a sort of garret entirely bare, where the lovers found as the only furniture a wretched mattress placed upon a pile of hay. Isnard had charitably put a white sheet at the foot of the mattress.

Philippe's intention was to go to Aix on the morrow, and obtain information as to M. de Cazalis' designs in regard to himself. He knew that he could not conceal himself much longer; he retired almost in peace, calmed by the soothing words of Blanche, who judged events with a young girl's hopefulness.

For twenty days the fugitives had been running about the fields. For twenty days the gendarmes had been scouring the country, following in their tracks, sometimes taking the wrong road but always brought back to the scent by some trifling circumstance. M. de Cazalis' anger had increased at all these delays; his pride was irritated by each fresh obstacle. At Lambesc the gendarmes had presented themselves a few hours too late; at Toulon the passage of the fugitives had been signaled only the day after their return to Aix; everywhere, Philippe and Blanche escaped as by a miracle. At last, the deputy accused the police of bad faith.

Finally, he was assured that the lovers were in the neighborhood of Aix and were about to be arrested. He hurried to Aix; he wished to assist in the search.

The woman of the Cours Sextius, who had harbored Blanche and Philippe for a few hours, had been stricken with terror; that she might not be accused of complicity, she told all; she said

that the young folks must be concealed in one of Isnard's country-houses.

On being questioned, Isnard calmly denied everything. He declared that he had not seen his relative for several months. This took place at the very time Philippe and Blanche were entering the country-house of the Trois-bons-Dieux district. The mercer could not warn the lovers during the night. At five o'clock the next morning, a commissaire de police knocked at his door and informed him that a search was about to be made at his house and at his three properties.

M. de Cazalis remained at Aix, declaring that he feared he might kill Philippe if he met him face to face. The agents who were directed to visit the Puyricard country-house found the nest empty. Isnard obligingly offered to conduct two gendarmes to his Tholonet property, suspecting that it would be a useless errand. The commissaire de police, accompanied also by two gendarmes, started for the Trois-bons-Dieux district; he took a locksmith with him, Isnard having stated vaguely that the key of the house was hidden under a stone to the right of the door.

It was about six o'clock when the commissaire reached the country-house. All the openings were closed; no sound came from the interior. The commissaire advanced and cried, in a loud voice, pounding upon the door with his fist:

"In the name of the law, open!"

Echo alone answered. Nothing stirred. After several minutes, the commissaire turned to the locksmith and said:

"Pick the lock."

The locksmith went to work. The scraping of the iron broke the silence. Then the shutter of a window opened violently, and amid the golden brightness of the rising sun, his neck and arms bare, appeared Philippe Cayol, disdainful and angry.

"What do you want?" said he, leaning his elbows heavily on the window sill.

At the first blow dealt upon the door by the commissaire, Philippe and Blanche suddenly awoke. Seated on the mattress, amid the tremors of awakening, they heard with anxiety the sound of voices.

The cry, "In the name of the law!" that terrible cry which bursts upon the ears of the guilty like a clap of thunder, nearly deprived the young man of breath. He started up, trembling, dismayed, not knowing what to do. The young girl, her eyes yet heavy with sleep, wrapped herself in the sheet and wept with shame and despair.

Philippe comprehended that all was over, and that he could do nothing but surrender. A sullen revolt stirred in him. So his dreams of wealth were dead: he never would be acknowledged as Blanche's husband; he had carried off an heiress to be cast into prison; at the dénouement, instead of the lordly dwelling of which he had dreamed, he would find a dungeon. Then a cowardly thought came to him: he entertained the idea of leaving his beloved there and fleeing in the direction of Vauvenargues to the gorges of Sainte-Victoire; perhaps he might escape through a window at the back of the country-house. He leaned towards Blanche, and, hesitatingly, told her his

plan in a low voice. The young girl, who was choking with sobs, did not understand him, did not hear him. He saw with anguish that, mentally, she was not in a condition to cover his flight.

At that moment, he heard the sharp sound of the hooks which the locksmith had inserted in the lock. The secret and poignant drama, which was in progress in that bare chamber, had lasted at most two or three minutes.

Philippe felt himself lost, and his irritated pride restored his courage. If he had been armed, he would have defended himself. Then he said to himself that he was not an abductor, that Blanche had chosen to follow and marry him, and that, after all, the shame in the matter was not for him. At this he angrily pushed open the shutter, demanding what was wanted.

"Open the door for us," commanded the commissaire. "We will tell you afterwards what we want."

Philippe came down the wooden ladder and opened the door.

"Are you the Sieur Philippe Cayol?" asked the commissaire.

"Yes," answered the young man, firmly.

"Then I arrest you as guilty of abduction. You have carried off a young girl under sixteen years of age, who should be hidden with you."

Philippe smiled disdainfully.

"The former Mademoiselle Blanche de Cazalis, who is now my wife, is upstairs," said he. "She can declare if there has been violence on my part. I know not what you mean in talking of abduction. I shall, this very day, throw myself at the feet of M. de Cazalis and ask his sanction of his niece's marriage with me."

Blanche, pale and trembling, descended the ladder. She had hastily dressed herself.

"Mademoiselle," said the commissaire to her, "I have orders to take you to your uncle, who is waiting for you at Aix. He is in tears."

"I am very sorry that I displeased my uncle," replied Blanche, with a certain firmness; "but no one must accuse M. Cayol, whom I followed and married of my own free will."

And, turning towards the young man, moved, ready to sob anew:

"Hope, Philippe," continued she; "I love you and will supplicate my uncle to be good to us. Our separation will last only a few days."

Philippe looked at her with a sorrowful air, shaking his head.

"You are a timid and weak child," said he, slowly.

Then he added, in a harsh tone:

"Remember only that you are my wife, that you belong to me through the flesh and through the heart. If you desert me, every hour of your life the remembrance of me will torment you; you will always feel on your lips the fiery stamp of my kisses, and that shall be your punishment."

Blanche wept.

"Love me as I love you," resumed the young man, in a milder voice.

The commissaire put Blanche into a carriage, which he had sent for, and conducted her to Aix, while the two gendarmes took Philippe and led him to the prison of that town.

## CHAPTER VII

### BLANCHE TURNS AGAINST PHILIPPE

THE news of the arrest did not reach Marseilles until the following day. It caused a tremendous sensation. In the afternoon, M. de Cazalis was seen to pass with his niece over the Cannebière. Gossip ran wild; everybody talked of the deputy's triumphant attitude, of Blanche's embarrassment and blushes. M. de Cazalis was the man to exhibit the young girl throughout all Marseilles, in order to let the people know that she was again under his control.

Marius, notified in the morning by Fine, had hurried about the city for hours. The public voice confirmed the news; he was able to seize on the wing all the details of the arrest. The fact, in a brief space, had become legendary, and the shop-keepers and corner idlers related it as if it had been a marvellous story of a century before. The young man, weary of hearing these idle tales, went to his office, his head aching, not knowing upon what to decide.

Unfortunately, M. Martelly was absent and would not return until the following evening. Marius felt the necessity of acting sooner; he wished at once to take some step which would reassure him in regard to his brother's fate. His fears consequent upon the reception of the news had, however, somewhat subsided; he had reflected that, after all, his brother could not be accused of abduction, and that Blanche would be on hand to defend him at any moment. He innocently arrived at the belief that he ought to visit M. de Cazalis to demand of him, in his brother's name, his sanction to Philippe's marriage with his niece.

The next morning, he dressed himself in a complete suit of black and was descending the stairs, when Fine presented herself according to her custom. The poor girl grew deadly pale when Marius informed her of the object of his errand.

"Will you let me accompany you?" asked she, in a supplicating tone. "I will await in the street the answer of the young lady's uncle."

She followed Marius. On reaching the Cours Bonaparte, the young man entered the deputy's house with a firm step and caused himself to be announced.

M. de Cazalis' blind rage had abated. He held his vengeance. He was about to demonstrate the greatness of his power by crushing one of those liberals whom he detested. He now desired only to taste the cruel joy of playing with his prey. He ordered M. Marius Cayol to be admitted. He expected tears and ardent supplications.

The young man found him in the centre of a large salon, standing, with a haughty and implacable air. He advanced towards him, and, without giving him time to speak, said, in a calm and polite tone:

"Monsieur, I have the honor to ask you, in the name of my brother, M. Philippe Cayol, for your sanction to the marriage between him and Mademoiselle Blanche de Cazalis, your niece."

The deptuy was literally thunderstruck. He could not get angry, so grotesquely extravagant did Marius' demand seem to him. Drawing back,

staring the young man in the face and laughing disdainfully, he answered:

"You are mad, Monsieur. I am aware that you are a hard-working and honest fellow, and that is the reason I do not order my servants to put you out of the house. Your brother is a scoundrel, a knave who will be punished according to his desert. What do you want of me?"

Marius, on hearing his brother insulted, felt a ferocious desire to fall like a clown upon the noble personage and beat him with his fists. He restrained himself and continued, in a voice which began to tremble with emotion:

"I have told you what I want, Monsieur. I came here to offer Mademoiselle de Cazalis the only reparation possible—a legal marriage sanctioned by you. Thus the wrong that has been done her will be obliterated."

"We are above wrong!" cried the deputy, contemptuously. "There is no shame for Blanche de Cazalis in having been beloved by a fellow like Philippe Cayol, but there would be shame for her in allying herself with such people as you. I will never sanction that marriage, which, without my consent is null and void!"

"Such people as we are have other ideas in regard to honor. But I do not insist; duty alone dictated to me the offer of reparation which you refuse. Permit me only to add that your niece would, without doubt, urge upon you a different course, if I had the honor of addressing myself to her."

"Do you think so?" said M. de Cazalis, in a jeering tone.

He rang and ordered his niece to be

brought thither immediately. Blanche entered, pale, her eyes red. She looked as if broken by too strong emotions. On perceiving Marius, she trembled.

"Mademoiselle," said her uncle, coldly, "here is a gentleman who formally asks for your hand in the name of the infamous wretch whom I forbear to mention otherwise in your presence. Tell the gentleman what you told me yesterday."

Blanche wavered. She dared not look at Marius. With eyes fixed upon her uncle, all in a tremble, she murmured, in a hesitating and feeble voice:

"I told you that I was abducted by violence, and forced into a marriage, and that I would use every effort to obtain punishment for the odious wrong of which I was the victim."

These words were recited like a lesson learned. Following the example of Saint Peter, Blanche denied her Lord.

M. de Cazalis had not lost his time. The moment his niece was in his power, he brought to bear upon her all his prejudice and all his pride. He realized that she alone could make him win the game. It was imperative that the young girl should lie, that she should stifle the revolts and the cries of her heart, that she should be a yielding and passive instrument in his hands.

For four hours he poured cold and sharp words into her ears. He did not commit the imprudence of showing anger. He spoke with crushing haughtiness, reminding her of the antiquity of her race, talking of his power and his fortune. He displayed exquisite cunning, sketching on one side the picture of a ridiculous and vulgar mésalliance, showing on the other side the noble joys of a rich and great marriage. He attacked the young girl through her coquetry, her vanity, her appetite for luxury and her self-love; he fatigued her, broke her, stupefied her, rendered her what he wished her to be—supple and inert.

After this long interview, this long martyrdom, Blanche was conquered. Perhaps, under her uncle's overwhelming words, her patrician blood at last revolted at the remembrance of Philippe's brutal caresses; perhaps, her childish vanity was aroused at the mention of luxurious toilets, honors of all kinds and wordly delights. Besides, her head was too weak, her heart too cowardly, to resist the deputy's terrible will. Each phrase uttered by M. de Cazalis had struck her, crushed her, filled her with dolorous anxiety. She had loved, followed and married Philippe through weakness; now she had turned against him also through weakness; she was still the same timid and inexperienced soul. She had accepted everything. She had promised everything. She had been eager to escape from the suffocating weight which her uncle's discourse had leaped upon her.

When Marius heard her make her strange declaration, he stood stupefied, filled with terror. He recalled the young girl's attitude at the house of the gardener Ayasse; he saw her hanging about Philippe's neck, faint, trusting and loving.

"Ah! Mademoiselle," cried he, bitterly, "the hidious wrong of which you were the victim appeared to exasperate you less the day you begged me with clasped hands to implore your uncle's pardon and consent. Have you re.

fiected that your falsehood will cause the ruin of the man whom, perhaps, you still love and who is your husband in the sight of God?"

Blanche, rigid, her lips pressed together, stared vaguely before her. "I know not what you mean," answered she, hesitatingly. "I have told no falsehood. I yielded to force. That man deceived and wronged me, and my uncle will avenge the honor of our family."

Marius straightened up. Generous anger added to his short stature and his thin face grew beautiful with justice and truth. He glanced around him, and, with a gesture of contempt, said, in a measured tone:

"And I am in the Cazalis mansion, I am in the home of the descendants of that illustrious family which Provence delights to honor. I knew not that falsehood dwelt within these walls, and did not expect to find calumny and cowardice sheltered here. Oh! you shall hear me to the end. I wish to cast my lackey's dignity into the unworthy faces of my masters!"

Then, turning to the deputy and pointing towards Blanche, who was quivering like a leaf, he resumed:

"That child is innocent; I pardon her weakness. But you, Monsieur, you are a crafty man; you protect maidens by making them liars and cowards; you are, indeed, a noble son of your fathers. If now you were to offer me for my brother your sanction to this marriage with Mademoiselle Blanche de Cazalis, I would refuse it, for I have never lied, I have never committed an evil action, and I should blush to ally myself with such people as you!"

M. de Cazalis bent beneath the young man's fury. At the first insult, he had summoned a tall devil of a lackey, who was standing on the threshold of the door. As the deputy signed to him to throw Marius into the street, the latter continued, with a terrible burst of anger:

"I swear to you that I will cry murder if that man take a step. Let me pass. Some day, Monsieur, I may, perhaps, be able to hurl into your face before everybody the truths I have just spoken in this salon!"

And he departed, with a deliberate and firm step. He no longer saw Philippe's guilt; in his eyes his brother had become a victim whom he wished to save and avenge at any cost. In his upright soul, the smallest falsehood, the least injustice, brought on a tempest. Already the gossip, which M. de Cazalis had set afloat at the time of the flight, had made him assume the defence of the fugitives; now that Blanche had lied and that the deputy was making use of the calumny, he longed to be powerful enough to take justice into his own hands and proclaim the truth in the open street.

He found Fine upon the sidewak. Uneasiness was devouring her.

"Well?" asked the young girl, as soon as she saw him.

"Well!" answered Marius, "those people are miserable liars and proud idiots."

Fine took a long breath. A wave of blood mounted to her cheeks.

"Then," said she, "Monsieur Philippe's marriage with the young lady is not to be acknowledged?"

"The young lady," replied Marius,

with a bitter smile, "claims that Philippe is a scoundrel who abducted her by violence and forced her to marry him! My brother is lost!"

Fine did not understand. She bowed her head, asking herself how the young lady could call her lover a scoundrel. And she thought that she would have been delighted to have been married to Philippe, even through violence. Marius' rage enchanted her: the project for legalizing the marriage had failed.

"Your brother is lost, you say," murmured she, with tender cajolery. "Oh! I will save him—we will save him together!"

## CHAPTER VIII

### THE POWERLESS BROTHER

WHEN, in the evening, Marius related to M. Martelly the interview he had had with M. de Cazalis, the ship-owner said to him, shaking his hand:

"I know not what advice to give you, my friend. I do not wish to fill you with despair; but rest assured that you will be vanquished. It is your duty to engage in the struggle, and I will second you as best I may. Let us admit, however, between ourselves, that we are weak and disarmed in face of an adversary who has on his side the clergy and the nobility. Marseilles and Aix love not the monarchy of July, and these two cities are entirely devoted to a deputy of the opposition who makes war on M. Thiers. They will aid M. de Cazalis in his vengeance; I speak of the leaders; the people will help us, if they can help any one. Our best plan would be to win to our cause an

influential member of the clergy. Do you not know some priest in favor with the bishop?"

Marius answered that he knew the Abbé Chastanier, a poor old fellow who was entirely powerless.

"No matter; see him," said the ship-owner. "The citizens cannot help us; the nobility would thrust us ignominiously into the street, if we asked favors of them. The church remains. It is there we must knock. Take the matter in hand; I will work on my side."

Marius, the next day, went to Saint-Victor. The Abbé Chastanier received him with a sort of terrified embarrassment.

"Do not ask anything of me!" cried he, at the young man's first words. "It is known that I have already meddled with that affair, and I have received grave reproaches. As I have told you, I am only a poor man; I can do nothing but pray God."

The humble attitude of the old priest touched Marius. He was about to depart when the abbé retained him and said, in a low tone:

"Listen: there is a man here, the Abbé Donadéi, who could be useful to you. It is said that he stands on the best footing with Monseigneur. He is a foreign priest, an Italian, I believe, who, in a few months, has won everybody's love."

The Abbé Chastanier paused, hesitating, seeming to interrogate himself. The worthy man thought that he was about to compromise himself terribly, but could not resist the sweet joy of rendering a service.

"Do you wish me to accompany you to his house?" asked he, suddenly.

Marius, who had noticed his brief hesitation, strove to refuse; but the old man was resolved; he no longer heeded his personal peace: he wished to content his heart.

"Come," resumed he. "The Abbé Donadéi lives but a short distance from here, on the Boulevard de la Corderie."

Afte a few minutes' walk, the Abbé Chastanier stopped in front of a small, two-story house, one of those close and discreet houses which have a vague air of mystery.

"This is the place," said he to Marius.

An aged serving-woman answered their summons and introduced them into a little study with sombre hangings, which resembled an austere boudoir.

The Abbé Donadéi received them with supple ease. His pale face, full of cunning and indicative of trickery, did not betray the least astonishment. He offered chairs with a cajoling gesture, half bent, half smiling, doing the honors of his study as a woman would do the honors of her toilet-chamber.

He wore a long black robe, loose at the waist. He had a coquettish look in that plain costume; his white and delicate hands emerged as small as a woman's from broad sleeves, and his shaven visage maintained a tender freshness amid the chestnut curls of his hair. He appeared to be about thirty.

He seated himself in an arm-chair and listened, with smiling gravity, to what Marius had to say. He made him repeat the details of the flight of Philippe and Blanche; the narrative seemed to interest him infinitely.

The Abbé Donadéi was born at Rome. He had an uncle a cardinal. One fine day, that uncle sent him hurriedly to France, without people ever discovering exactly why. On his arrival, the handsome abbé was compelled to enter the little seminary of Aix as professor of living languages. A situation so low down in the scale humiliated him to such a point that he fell ill.

The cardinal was moved and recommended his nephew to the Bishop of Marseilles. Then satisfied ambition cured Donadéi. He entered Saint-Victor, and, as the Abbé Chastanier innocently remarked, had won everybody's love in a few months. His caressing Italian nature and his mild, rosy face made him the delight of the demure lady devotees of the parish. He triumphed particularly when in the pulpit: his slight accent gave a strange charm to his sermons, and, when he opened his arms, he imparted to his hands quivers of emotion which melted the congregation to tears.

Like almost all Italians, he was born for intrigue. He used and abused his uncle's recommendation to the Bishop of Marseilles. Soon he was a power, a hidden power which toils beneath the surface and opens pits for the steps of those it wishes to rid itself of. He became a member of a religious society, all-powerful in Marseilles, and, by his suppleness in smiling and bowing, imposed his will upon his colleagues and made himself the head of a party. Then, he mixed himself up with every event, glided into all affairs; he it was who had caused M. de Cazalis to be named deputy, and he was awaiting a suitable opportunity to demand of him payment for his services. His plan was to work for the success of the rich; later, when he had merited their gratitude, he counted upon making them work in their turn to advance his own fortune.

He questioned Marius with complacency; he seemed from his attention, from the kindness of his reception, to be altogether disposed to aid him in his work of deliverance. The young man allowed himself to be trapped by the amiable mildness of his manners; he opened his soul to him, told him his projects and admitted that the clergy alone could save his brother. Finally, he asked him to use his influence with Monseigneur. Then the Abbé Danadéi arose and, in a tone of austere pleasantry, said:

"Monsieur, my sacred character prohibits me from interfering in this deplorable and scandalous affair. The enemies of the church too often accuse the priests of going out of their sacristies. I can only ask God to pardon your brother."

Marius, in consternation, had also arisen. He realized that he had been tricked by Donadéi. He strove to keep an unmoved countenance.

"I thank you," answered he. "Prayers are very sweet alms for the unfortunate. Ask God that men may do us justice."

He went towards the door, followed by the Abbé Chastanier, who walked with bowed head. Donadéi had affected not to see the old priest.

Upon the threshold, the handsome abbé, recovering all his graceful levity, retained Marius an instant.

"You are employed by M. Martelly, I believe," said he.

"Yes, Monsieur," replied the young man, in astonishment.

"He is a man of high honor, but I know he is not one of our friends. Nevertheless, I cherish the most profound esteem for him. His sister, Mademoiselle Claire, whom I have the honor of directing, is one of our best parishioners."

And as Marius stared at him, finding nothing to say in reply, Donadéi added, coloring slightly:

"She is a charming person, and of exemplary piety."

He bowed with exquisite politeness and gently closed the door. The Abbé Chastanier and Marius, standing alone upon the sidewalk, glanced at each other, and the young man could not avoid shrugging his shoulders. The old priest was confused to see a minister of God play comedy thus. He turned towards his companion and said, hesitatingly:

"My friend, we must not blame God if his ministers are not always what they should be. The young man from whom we have just parted is guilty only of ambition."

He went on thus, excusing Donadéi. Marius looked at him, touched by his goodness, and, despite himself, he compared this poor and modest old man with the powerful and graceful abbé, whose smiles were the law of the diocese. Then he thought that the church loved not her sons with an equal love and that, like all mothers, she spoiled the rosy faces and tricky hearts, and neglected the tender and humble souls who devoted themselves in the shade.

The two visitors were departing, when a carriage stopped before the close and discreet little house. Marius saw M.

de Cazalis descend from this carriage; the deputy hastily entered the Abbé Donadéi's dwelling.

"Look, father," cried the young man; "I am certain that the sacred character of that priest will not prohibit him from working to secure the vengeance of M. de Cazalis."

He was tempted to return to that house, in which God was made to play so miserable a rôle. But he calmed himself; he thanked the Abbé Chastanier and went his way, saying mentally with despair that the last door of safety, that of which the high clergy held the key, had been shut in his face. The next day M. Martelly informed him of an attempt he had made with the leading notary of Marseilles, M. Douglas, a pious man, who, in less than eight years, had become a veritable power through his rich clientèle and his liberal alms. The name of this notary was loved and respected. People spoke with admiration of the virtues of this upright toiler, who lived frugally; they had unbounded confidence in his honesty and in the activity of his intelligence.

M. Martelly had availed himself of his assistance to invest certain funds. He hoped that, if Douglas would lend his support to Marius, the latter would have a portion of the clergy on his side. He went to the house of the notary and asked his aid. Douglas, who seemed greatly preoccupied, stammered out an evasive answer, saying that he was overburdened with business and that he could not struggle against M. de Cazalis.

"I did not insist," said M. Martelly to Marius; "I imagined that your adversary had been before you. I am astonished, however, that M. Douglas, a man of probity, should allow his hands to be tied. Now, my poor friend, I am sure that the game is entirely up."

Marius had no longer the smallest hope. For a month he scoured Marseilles, striving to win to his cause a few influential men. Everywhere he was received coldly, with satirical politeness. M. Martelly was equally unsuccessful. The deputy had rallied all the nobility and the high clergy around him. The citizens, the commercial people, laughed in their sleeves, without taking any action, having an atrocious fear of compromising themselves. As to the masses, they lampooned M. de Cazalis and his niece, not being able otherwise to serve Philippe Cayol.

Time sped on; the preparations for the criminal trial were progressing rapidly. As on the first day, Marius stood alone to defend his brother against M. de Cazalis' hatred and Blanche's complaisant lies. He had constantly beside him M. Martelly, who declared himself powerless, and Fine, whose fiery talk had gained for Philippe the ardent sympathy of the girls of the people.

One morning, Marius learned that his brother and the gardener Ayasse had been indicted, the first as guilty of abduction and the second as accomplice in the crime. Madame Cayol had been released, the proofs against her not being sufficient to hold her for trial.

Marius hastened to embrace his mother. The poor woman had suffered greatly during her imprisonment; her wavering health was greatly impaired.

A few days after her discharge from prison, she gently expired in the arms of her son, who swore amid his sobs to avenge her death.

The funeral occasioned a popular manifestation. Philippe's mother was taken to the Cimetière Saint-Charles, followed by an immense cortège of women of the people, who accused M. de Cazalis, in loud tones, of being the cause of her death. But little was wanting to induce these women to rush to the deputy's house and hurl stones at the windows.

On returning from the burial, Marius, in his little apartment on the Rue Sainte, felt himself alone in the world and wept bitterly. His tears solaced him; he saw the road he must take, clearly traced before his eyes. The evils which overwhelmed him augmented in him the love of truth and the hatred of injustice. He felt that all the rest of his life must be devoted to a holy work.

There was nothing now for him to do in Marseilles. The scene of the drama had changed. The action was to occur at Aix, according to the variations of the trial. Marius wished to be on the spot to follow the different phases of the case and profit by the incidents which might present themselves. He asked M. Martelly for a month's leave-of-absence, which the ship-owner at once granted him.

On the day of his departure, he found Fine in the diligence.

"I am going to Aix with you," said the young girl to him, calmly.

"But this is madness!" cried he. "You are not rich enough to devote yourself thus. And your flowers, who will sell them?"

"Oh! I have put in my place one of my friends, a girl who lives upon the same landing with me on the Place aux Œufs. I said to myself: 'I can be of use to them;' so I put on my handsomest dress and here I am!"

"I thank you with all my soul!" said Marius, simply, in a shaking voice.

## CHAPTER IX

### M. DE GIROUSE GOSSIPS

At Aix, Marius went to the house of Isnard, who dwelt on the Rue d'Italie. The mercer had not been disturbed. A prey of such slight value was, doubtless, disdained.

Fine went straight to the dwelling of the jailer of the prison. She was his niece by marriage. She had her plan. She took with her a huge bouquet of roses which was received with delight. Her pretty smiles and her caressing vivacity made her in two hours her uncle's spoiled child; the jailer was a widower and had two infant daughters of whom Fine immediately became the little mother.

The trial was not to begin until the commencement of the following week. Marius, his hands tied, no longer daring to take a single step, awaited with anguish the opening of the proceedings. At times he was still mad enough to hope for, to count on, an acquittal.

One evening, while walking upon the Cours, he met M. de Girousse, who had come from Lambesc to be present at Philippe's trial. The old gentleman took his arm, and, without uttering a word, led him to his hôtel.

"Now," said he, shutting himself up with him in a large salon, "we are alone, my friend. I can be a plebeian at my ease."

Marius smiled at the rough and peculiar behavior of the comte.

"Well," continued the latter, "you do not ask me to serve you, to defend you against Cazalis! You are intelligent. You understand that I can do nothing against the obstinate and vain nobility to whom I belong. Ah! your brother sought for lofty game!"

M. de Girousse strode about the salon. Suddenly he planted himself before Marius.

"Listen to our history," said he, in an excited voice: "There are, in this town, fifty old fellows like myself, who live apart, cloistered in the depths of a past forever dead. We call ourselves the flower of Provence, and here we are inactive, twirling our thumbs. But we are gentlemen, chivalrous hearts, awaiting with devotion the return of our legitimate princes. Ah! mordieu! we will wait a long while, such a long while that solitude and idleness will kill us before the least sign of a legitimate prince appears. If we had good eyes, we would see the march of events. We cry to the facts: 'You shall go on further!' and the facts calmly pass over our bodies and crush us. I am enraged to see us shut up in an infatuation as ridiculous as heroic. To think that we are almost all rich, that we could almost all become intelligent artisans who could toil for the prosperity of the country, and that we prefer

to mould in the recesses of our hôtels like old wrecks of another age!"

He took breath, and then continued, with greater energy:

"And we are all proud of our empty existence. We do not work out of disdain for toil. We have a holy horror of people whose hands are grimy. Ah! your brother has touched one of our daughters! He will be made to see if he is of the same blood as we are. We will unite together and give a lesson to the clowns; we will take from them the desire to be beloved by our children. Some powerful ecclesiastics will second us: they are fatally bound to our cause. This will be a fine campaign for our vanity."

After an instant's silence, M. de Girousse resumed, jeeringly:

"Our vanity! It has sometimes met with huge impediments. A few years before my birth, a terrible drama was enacted in the hôtel which adjoins mine. M. d' Entrecasteaux, the President of Parliament, assissinated his wife there in her bed; he cut her throat with a razor, urged on, they say, by a passion which he wished to gratify even by the aid of crime. The razor was not found until twenty-five days afterwards, at the extremity of the garden; they found also in the well the victim's jewels, which the murderer had thrown there to make justice believe that the motive of the assassination had been robbery. President d'Entrecasteaux fled and retired, I believe, to Portugal, where he died miserably. The Parliament condemned him for non-appearance to be broken alive upon the wheel. You see that we also have our scoundrels and that the people have no reason to envy us. This cowardly cruelty on the part of one of our number struck, at the time, a heavy blow at our authority. A novelist might make a stirring romance of that bloody and lugubrious history.

"And we also know how to cringe," said M. de Girousse, who had resumed walking. "For example, when Fouché, the regicide, then Duc d'Otrante, was, about 1810, temporarity exiled to our city, all the nobles threw themselves at his feet. I recall an anecdote which shows to what base servility we descended: On the first of January, 1811, a line was formed to offer the former member of the Convention the wish of a happy new year; in the reception salon, they were talking of the extreme cold then prevailing, and one of the visitors expressed fears as to the fate of the olive trees. 'Ah! what do we care about olive trees,' cried one of the noble personages, 'provided that M. the Duc enjoys good health!' See how we are to-day, my friend: humble with the powerful and haughty with the weak. There are, without doubt, exceptions, but they are rare. You can readily understand, that your brother will be convicted. Our pride, which bends before a Fouché, cannot bend before a Cayol. That's logical. Good-evening."

And the comte hastily dismissed Marius. He had grown exasperated while speaking, and was afraid that anger might make him talk foolishness.

The next day, the young man met him again. M. de Girousse, as on the previous evening, led him into his hôtel. He held in his hands a journal containing the names of the jurors who were to try Philippe.

He struck the journal forcibly with his finger.

"Here are the men," cried he, "who are to be entrusted with your brother's fate. Shall I give you a few histories in regard to them? Those histories are curious and instructive."

M. de Girousse had seated himself. He ran his eye over the journal, shrugging his shoulders.

"It is," said he, at last, "a select jury, an assemblage of rich people whose interest it is to serve the cause of M. de Cazalis. They are all more or less church-wardens, more or less frequenters of the salons of the nobility. Nearly all of them have for friends men who pass their mornings in the churches and squeeze money wrongfully out of their customers the rest of the day."

Then he named the jurors one by one, and spoke of the society in which they moved with indignant vehemence.

"Humbert," said he,—"the brother of a merchant of Marseilles, of an oil dealer, an honest man held in high consideration, whom all the poor devils salute. Twenty years ago, their father was only an humble clerk. To-day, the sons are millionaires, thanks to his shrewd speculations. One year, he sold in advance, at the current price, an enormous quantity of oil. A few weeks afterwards, the cold killed the olive trees and the crop was lost; he was ruined if he did not deceive his customers. But our man preferred deception to poverty. While his brethren in the trade delivered sound merchandise at a loss, he bought all the spoiled oil, all the rancid oil, he could find, and made his promised deliveries. His customers complained and grew angry. The speculator coolly replied that he had strictly kept his promises, and that they could demand nothing further of him. The trick was played. All Marseilles knows this history and has not enough bows for this adroit man.

"Gautier—another merchant of Marseilles. He has a nephew, Paul Bertrand, who tricked on a vast scale. This Bertrand was in partnership with a Sieur Aubert, of New York, who sent him cargoes of merchandise to be sold at Marseilles. They were to divide the profits. Our man made a great deal of money at this business, the more because he took care to cheat his partner in each division. One day, a crisis was reached and losses came. Bertrand continued to accept the merchandise which the ships still brought, but refused to pay the drafts Aubert drew upon him, saying that business had proved unfortunate with him and that he was embarrassed. The drafts went back, and returned again with enormous costs added. Then Bertrand calmly declared that he would not pay them, that he was not obliged eternally to remain Aubert's partner and that he owed him nothing. Another sending back of the drafts; new costs, heavy reimbursements for the surprised and indignant New York merchant. The latter, who could sue only by power of attorney, lost the action for damages and interest which he brought against Bertrand; I have been assured that two-thirds of his fortune, twelve hundred thousand francs, were swallowed up in this catastrophe.

Bertrand remains the most honest man in the world; he is a member of all the societies and several congregations; he is envied and honored.

"Dutailly—a grain merchant. There happened in the past to one of his sons in-laws, George Fouque, a misadventure, the scandal of which his friends hastened to stifle. Fouque always so managed it as to cause the cargoes, which the ships brought him, to be found damaged. The insurance companies paid, upon the report of an expert. Weary of paying constantly, these companies entrusted the duty of reporting to an honest baker. who speedily received a visit from Fouque. The latter, while chatting about unimportant matters, slipped some gold pieces into his hand. The baker let the pieces fall and, with a kick, sent them into the middle of the apartment. The scene took place in the presence of a number of persons. Fouque has lost nothing of his credit.

"Delorme—a man who lives in a town near Marseilles. He retired from business long ago. Listen to the details of an infamous action committed by his cousin Mille. Thirty years since, Mille's mother kept a mercer's shop. When the old lady retired, she transferred her stock to one of her clerks, an active and intelligent fellow, whom she regarded almost as a son. The young man, whose name was Michel, soon paid his debt and so increased his trade that he was obliged to take a partner. He chose a Marseilles youth, Jean Martin, who had some money and who seemed to be honorable and industrious. It was a certain fortune which Michel offered his partner. At first, everything went for the best. The profits were augmented yearly, and the two associates each put aside a round sum at the close of every twelvemonth. But Jean Martin, greedy of gain and dreaming of a rapid fortune, said to himself at last that he would make twice as much if he were alone. The matter was difficult to accomplish; Michel, in short, was his benefactor, and the owner of the house, Mme. Mille's son, was his friend. Should the latter prove to be an honest man, Jean Martin would fail in his shameful project. He called on him, counting upon finding a man of his own stamp, and, in fact, he found in him the scoundrel he sought. Martin asked for a new lease in his own name, offering a large sum of money, and, as Mille haggled, he doubled, then tripled the amount. Mille, who is a pedant and a miser, sold himself for the highest possible price; the bargain was concluded. Then, Jean Martin played with Michel the rôle of a hypocrite; he told him that he wished to dissolve their partnership agreement that he might establish himself further away; he even pointed out to him the shop he had hired. Michel, astonished, but not suspecting the infamous proceeding of which he was to be the victim, informed him that he was at liberty to withdraw, and the agreement was annulled. A short time afterwards, Michel's lease expired, and Jean Martin, his new lease in his hand, triumphantly showed his former partner the door. Such crimes escape human justice, but the cowardly and greedy wretches who commit them are condemned by the tribunal of men of

honor. I cannot sufficiently express my contempt for this Mille, who, from infancy had been the friend, the brother, so to speak, of Michel, whom he betrayed in a manner so venal and so base. There are plenty of such foul consciences as his, which bear the weight of an infamous deed lightly. Since we cannot drag into the Cour d'Assises these cunning criminals who cast their friends upon the sidewalk for a bag of hundred-sou pieces, we should post their names in huge letters at the street corners and each passer should spit upon them. That is the ignoble pillory they deserve. Michel, driven almost wild by this treason, established himself in another locality; but, having no longer any customers, he lost the money he had laboriously amassed by thirty years of toil. He died of paralysis amid atrocious suffering, crying out that Mille and Martin were wretches and traitors, and calling upon his sons for vengeance. To-day, his sons are working, are sweating blood and water, to win a position. Mille is allied to the first families of the city; his children are rich; they live luxuriously, surrounded by the devotion and esteem of all.

"Faivre—. His mother took for her second husband a Sieur Chabran, a ship-owner and note shaver. Under pretext of unfortunate speculations, Chabran wrote one day to his numerous creditors that he was forced to suspend payment. Some consented to give him time. The majority wished to prosecute him. Then Chabran hired two young lads, into whose ears for a week he poured a certain lesson; then, flanked by these two little beings, per-

fectly drilled, he visited, one after another, all his creditors, bewailing his
trouble and demanding pity for his
two sons, ragged and without bread.
The trick succeeded marvellously. All
his creditors tore up their notes. The
following day, Chabran was at the
Bourse, calmer and more insolent than
ever. A broker, who was ignorant of
what had taken place, proposed to him
to discount two notes, signed by some
of the very merchants who, the day before, had given quittance to this wretch.
'I will have nothing to do with people
of that class,' he answered, boldly.
Now, Chabran has almost given up
business; he lives in a splendid hôtel,
where he gives sumptuous dinners on
Sundays.

"Gerominot—the President of a club
at which he passes his evenings, and a
usurer of the worst kind. He has
made, they say, a million francs at
that business, which has enabled him
to marry his daughter to a shining
light of finance. His name is Pretigny,
but, since the failure which left in his
hands a capital of three hundred thousand francs, he has called himself
Félix. This adroit scoundrel made,
forty years ago, his first failure, which
put him in condition to buy a house.
His creditors received fifteen per cent.
Ten years later, a second failure permitted him to acquire a superb country
mansion. His creditors received ten
per cent. Scarcely fifteen years ago,
he made a third failure for three hundred thousand francs and offered five
per cent. The creditors having refused
to accept it, he proved to them that
all his property belonged to his wife,
and did not give them a centime."

Marius was discouraged; he made a
gesture of disgust, as if to interrupt
these ignominious revelations.

"You do not believe me, perhaps,"
resumed the terrible comte, with a certain haughtiness. "You are a young
innocent, my friend. I have not finished; I wish you to hear me to the
end."

M. de Girousse jeered with a sinister
heat. His words, loud and hissing, fell
like the crack of a whip upon those
whose foul histories he recited. One
recognized the disdainful gentleman
from the freedom of his speech and
the generous impetuosity of his fury.

He named the jurors turn by turn;
he scanned their lives and those of their
families; he exposed all the shame and
wretchedness in them. Very few, indeed, did he spare. Then he violently
placed himself before Marius and continued, with asperity:

"Did you have the innocence to believe that all those millionaires, all
those parvenus, all those powerful
people, who domineer over and crush
you, were little saints and just men
whose lives were without stain? Those
men make a display, at Marseilles, of
their vanity and their insolence; they
have become devotees and hypocrites;
they have deceived even the honest
folks who salute and esteem them. In
a word, they form an aristocracy of
their own; their past is forgotten; one
sees but their wealth and probity of
recent date. Well, I will tear off the
masks. Listen: This one has made a
fortune by betraying a friend; another
by selling human flesh; another by selling his wife or his daughter; another
by speculating on the misfortunes of

his creditors; another by redeeming at a low figure, after having himself adroitly discredited it, all the stock of a company of which he was the superintendent; another by sinking a ship loaded with stones instead of merchandise, and making the insurance company pay him the price of this strange cargo; another, a partner by verbal agreement, by refusing to share the hazard of an operation as soon as that operation became bad; another by hiding his assets, making two or three failures and living afterwards like a man of means; another by selling for wine extract of logwood or beef's blood; another by forestalling grain on the ocean during the years of scarcity; another by defrauding the revenue on a large scale, by striving to corrupt the employés and by stealing his fill from the administration; another by placing on notes forged signatures of relatives or friends, who were afraid to deny them on the day of maturity, and paid rather than compromise the forger; another by himself burning his factory or his ships, insured beyond their value; another by tearing up and throwing into the fire the notes he snatched from his creditor's hands on the day of payment; another by gambling at the Bourse with the intention of not paying if he lost, and, in fact, by refusing to pay, which did not prevent him from enriching himself, a week afterwards, at the expense of some dupe."

M. de Girousse's breath failed him. He maintained a long silence, allowing his anger to cool. Then his lips again opened and his smile was less bitter: "I am somewhat of a misanthrope,"

said he, mildly, to Marius, who had listened to him with pain and surprise; "I see everything in sombre colors. The reason is that the idleness to which my title condemns me has permitted me to study the pollutions of this district. But know that there are some honest people among us; if they would rise in a body, they could easily crush the scoundrels. I pray God every night that this civil war of virtue against vice may break out at an early day. As for you, count only upon the equity of the magistracy; you will find in it a firm support, independent and loyal. Its members do not crawl like slaves at the bidding of the rich and powerful. I have always had for the magistracy a fanatical respect, for it is the representative of truth and justice on earth."

Marius took leave of M. de Girousse, altogether overwhelmed by the fiery words he had heard. He foresaw that his brother would be pitilessly convicted. The commencement of the proceedings was set down for the following day.

## CHAPTER X

### PHILIPPE'S TRIAL

ALL Aix was excited. Gossip bursts out with strange energy in those quiet little towns, where the curiosity of the idlers has not each day a new aliment. Nothing was talked of but Philippe and Blanche; the adventures of the young lovers were related in the open street; it was loudly asserted that the accused was convicted in advance, and that M. de Cazalis had, either personally or through his friends, demanded his conviction of each juror.

The clergy of Aix lent its support to the deputy, feebly enough, it is true; that clergy then contained eminent and honorable men to whom promoting an injustice was repugnant. A few priests, nevertheless, yielded to the influence coming from the religious society of Marseilles, of which the Abbé Donadéi was, so to speak, the master. These priests strove by visits and shrewd proceedings to bind the hands of the magistracy, the upright and firm spirit of which was feared. They succeeded only in persuading the jurors that the cause of M. de Cazalis was holy.

The nobility strongly aided them in this task. They believed themselves in honor bound to crush Philippe Cayol. They regarded him as a personal enemy, who had dared to make a criminal attempt against the dignity of one of their number, and who had thus insulted them in a body. To see the comtes and marquises agitate themselves, get angry and unite together, one would have thought that the foemen were at the gates of the town. The matter in hand was simply to cause the conviction of a poor devil, guilty of love and ambition.

Philippe also had friends and defenders. All the people declared frankly for him. The lower classes blamed his conduct, censured the means he had employed, and said that he would have done better to have loved and wedded the daughter of some plain citizen like himself; but, while condemning his actions, they noisily defended him against the pride and hatred of M. de Cazalis. It was known in the town that Blanche, before the Juge d'Instruction, had denied her love, and the girls of the people, true Provençales, that is to say devoted and courageous, treated her with insulting contempt. They called her "the renegade;" they assigned infamous motives for her conduct, and did not hesitate to cry out their opinion in the public squares, in the energetic language of the streets.

This noise singularly compromised Philippe's cause. The entire town was in the secret of the drama which was about to be played. Those who were interested in having the accused convicted did not even take the trouble to conceal their proceedings, being certain of their triumph; those who wished to save Marius' brother, feeling themselves weak and disarmed, found solace in shouting, happy to irritate the powerful people whom they had no hope of conquering.

M. de Cazalis had, without shame, dragged his niece to Aix. During the first days, he took a proud delight in exhibiting her upon the Cours. He protested thus against the idea of disgrace which the crowd attached to the young girl's flight; he seemed to say to all: "You see that a clown cannot harm a Cazalis. My niece still towers above you from the height of her title and her fortune!"

But he could not long continue such promenades. The crowd grew angry at his attitude; it insulted Blanche, and was on the point of hurling stones at the uncle and niece. The women especially showed exasperation; they did not comprehend that the young girl was not altogether to be blamed and that she was simply obeying an iron will.

Blanche trembled at the popular fury. She bowed her head that she might not see those women who glared at her with fiery eyes. She was conscious of gestures of contempt behind her; she heard horrible words which she did not understand, and her limbs quaked beneath her; she clung to her uncle's arm that she might not fall. Pale and quivering, she returned to her dwelling one day, declaring that she would go out no more.

The poor child was about to become a mother.

Finally, the proceedings began. From early in the morning, the doors of the Palais-de-Justice were besieged; groups formed in the midst of the Place des Prêcheurs, gesticulating and talking in loud tones. People grew noisy over the probable issue of the trial; they discussed the culpability of Philippe and the attitude of M. de Cazalis and Blanche.

The court-room filled up slowly. Several rows of chairs had been added for persons provided with tickets; these persons were so numerous that nearly all of them were compelled to stand. In the crush were to be seen the flower of the nobility, lawyers, officials—in short, all the notable personages of Aix. Never had an accused drawn such an audience. When the doors were opened to allow the general public to enter, only a few curious persons were able to get in. The others were obliged to stand in the door-ways, in the lobbies and even upon the steps of the Palais. And every

instant there arose from that crowd murmurs and shouts, the sound of which penetrated into the court-room and was augmented there, disturbing the tranquil majesty of the peace.

The ladies had invaded the gallery. They formed up there a compact mass of anxious and smiling faces. Those who were on the first row fanned themselves, leaned over, allowing their gloved hands to rest upon the red velvet of the balustrade. Behind them, in the partial obscurity, mounted packed rows of rosy faces, the bodies belonging to which could not be seen. These rosy faces were as if buried in the midst of laces, ribbons, silks and satins; here and there sparkled the sudden flash of a jewel, when one of the heads was turned. And from that noisy and garrulous crowd fell pearly laughter, soft words and sharp little cries. These ladies were at a play.

When Philippe Cayol was brought in, there was a sudden silence. All the ladies devoured him with their eyes; some of them pointed opera-glasses at him, examining him from head to foot. This tall fellow, whose energetic features announced violent appetites, had a quiet success. The women, who had come to judge of Blanche's taste, doubtless thought the young girl less guilty when they saw the lofty stature and bright looks of her lover.

Philippe's attitude was calm and appropriate. He was clad wholly in black. He seemed to ignore the presence of the two gendarmes who were beside him; he straightened himself and sat down with the grace of a man of the world. Occasionally he glanced at the crowd, tranquilly and without effrontery. He several times raised his eyes to the gallery, and, each time, smiled tenderly in spite of himself; his incorrigible habits of loving and wishing to please resumed possession of him, even in the face of justice.

The bill of indictment was read. This document was very severe on the accused. In it the facts, according to the depositions of M. de Cazalis and his niece, were stated in an able and terrible manner. It was asserted that the young girl had been abducted by violence, that she had clung to an almond tree, and that, during the entire flight, the abductor had been compelled to employ intimidation to cause his victim to follow him. Fnally, a most serious matter was brought forward on the affirmation of Mlle, de Cazalis: she claimed that she had never written to Philippe, and that the two letters presented by the accused were antedated letters which he had forced her to write at Lambesc as a precautionary measure.

When the reading of the bill of indictment was finished, the court-room was filled with a noisy murmur of conversation. Each person, before coming to the Palais, had a version of the affair, and the official recital was discussed in partially subdued voices. Outside, the crowd uttered veritable howls. The President threatened to order the court-room cleared, and silence was gradually re-established.

The questioning of Philippe Cayol was then proceeded with.

When the President had asked him the customary questions and had repeated to him the points of the accusation against him, the young man, without argument, said, in a clear voice:

"I am accused of having been abducted by a young girl!"

These words made the spectators smile. The ladies hid behind their fans to enjoy the joke at their ease. But Philippe's phrase, altogether foolish and absurd as it seemed, contained, nevertheless, the exact truth. The President remarked that the abduction of a man of thirty by a young girl of sixteen was something unheard of.

"Neither have you ever heard," replied Philippe, tranquilly, "of a young girl of sixteen passing along the public highways, traversing towns, meeting hundreds of persons and not thinking of summoning the first passer to deliver her from her jailer!"

And he proceeded to show the utter impossibility of the violence and intimidation of which he was accused. At each hour of the day, Blanche had been free to quit him, to demand aid and relief; if she followed him, it was because she loved him, because she had consented to the flight and marriage. Besides, Philippe displayed the greatest tenderness for the young girl and the greatest deference for M. de Cazalis. He admitted his errors; he merely asked that they should not make him out a base abductor.

The court was adjourned until the following day, which was set apart for hearing the statements of the witnesses.

That evening, the town was in confusion; the ladies spoke of Philippe with affected indignation, the grave men treated him with more or less severity and the masses defended him with energy.

The next day, the crowd at the doors of the Palais-de-Justice was larger and noisier than before. The witnesses were nearly all witnesses for the prosecution. M. de Girousse had not been summoned; they feared the rude freedom of his wit, and, besides, he should rather have been arrested as an accomplice. Marius himself had begged him not to compromise himself in the case. He, like his adversaries, feared the violent spirit of the old comte, who by a whim might spoil everything.

There was but one deposition in favor of Philippe, that of the Lambesc inn-keeper, who declared that Blanche gave her companion the title of husband. This deposition was effaced, so to speak, by those of the other witnesses. Marguerite, the milkmaid, stammered and said that she could not recall having carried Mlle. de Cazalis' letters to the accused. Thus all the witnesses but one served the deputy's interests, either through fear or stupidity and lack of memory.

The speeches began and necessitated another session. Philippe's lawyer defended him with appropriate simplicity. He did not seek to excuse that which was culpable in his client's conduct; he represented him as an ardent and ambitious man, who had allowed himself to be led astray by hopes of wealth and love. But, at the same time, he maintained that the accused could not be convicted of abduction, and that the affair in itself excluded all idea of violence and intimidation.

The speech of the Procureur du Roi was terrible. The defence had counted upon a certain mildness, and the of-ficial's energetic accusations produced a disastrous effect. The jury brought in a verdict of guilty. Philippe was sentenced to an imprisonment of five years and to be publicly exposed in one of the squares of Marseilles. The gardener Ayasse was sent to prison for a few months only.

A confused tumult arose in the court-room. Without, the crowd muttered.

## CHAPTER XI

### BLANCHE AND FINE FACE TO FACE

BLANCHE, hidden in the depths of the gallery, heard Philippe sentenced. She was there by order of her uncle, who wished to crush out whatever tenderness might be lingering in her by showing her her lover between two gendarmes like a thief. An aged female relative had been instructed to take her to this edifying spectacle.

As the two ladies were waiting for their carriage on the steps of the Palais, the crowd, precipitating itself from the building, suddenly separated them. Blanche, dragged into the middle of the Place des Prêcheurs, was recognized by the huckster women, who began to shout at and insult her.

"It is she, it is she!" cried these women. "The renegade, the renegade!"

The poor child, dismayed, not knowing where to flee, was dying with shame and fear, when a young girl with a powerful push scattered the howling group which surrounded her and planted herself at her side.

It was Fine.

The flower-girl also had witnessed the conviction of Philippe. For nearly three hours, she had endured all the agonies of hope and fear; the speech of the Procureur du Roi had overwhelmed her, and she had wept frantically on hearing the sentence pronounced.

She was leaving the Palais, irritated and terribly excited, when she heard the shouts of the huckster women. She comprehended that Blanche was there and that she could take vengeance by abusing her; she ran towards the spot, her fists clenched, with insults on her lips. In her eyes, the young girl was the greatest culprit: she had lied; she had perjured herself and committed a cowardly act. At these thoughts, all Fine's plebeian blood mounted to her face and urged her to cry out and strike.

She precipitated herself upon the crowd; she scattered it to seize upon her prey.

But when she stood before Blanche, when she saw her bent with terror, the quivering and feeble child filled her with pity. She found her so young, so pretty and so delicately fragile that a generous thought of pardon took possession of her heart. With a violent gesture she drove back the women who were shaking their fists at the trembling girl, and, straightening herself up, cried, in a loud, sharp voice:

"Are you not ashamed of yourselves? She is alone, and you are a hundred against her! God has no need of your howls to punish her! Let us pass!"

She had taken Blanche's hand and, in her rage, firmly faced the crowd which murmured and came closer together to bar the passage of the two young girls. Fine waited, her lips pale and trembling. And, as she reassured her companion with a glance, she saw that she was about to become a mother. She grew white as a sheet, and, striding towards the women in the first row, said, in a louder tone:

"Let us pass, I say! Do you not see the poor girl's condition, wretches, and that you will kill her child!"

She repulsed a gross huckster who was sneering. All the other women drew back. Fine's words had suddenly rendered them silent and compassionate. The young girls retired between two hedges of women, among whom ran vague murmurs of regret. Blanche, red with shame, clung with fear to her companion and feverishly hastened her steps.

The flower-girl, to avoid the Rue du Pont-Moreau, then full of people and noise, took the little Rue Saint-Jean. On reaching the Cours, she led Mlle. de Cazalis to her hôtel, the door of which was open. During the walk, she had not uttered a word.

Blanche forced her to enter the vestibule, and there, partially closing the door and almost going upon her knees, she said, in a voice full of emotion:

"Oh! Mademoiselle, I thank you with all my soul for having come to my rescue! Those wicked women would have murdered me!"

"Do not thank me," answered Fine, roughly. "I came like the rest to insult you, to beat you!"

"You!"

"Yes. I hate you; I wish you had died in your cradle!"

Blanche stared at the flower-girl

with astonishment. She drew herself up; her aristocratic instincts rebelled and her lips grew slightly pale with disdain. The two young girls stood face to face, the one with all her frail grace, the other in her fresh and energetic beauty. They contemplated each other silently, feeling surge in them the rivalry of their classes and hearts.

"You are beautiful, you are rich," resumed Fine, bitterly; "why did you steal my lover from me, when you knew that in the end you must despise and hate him? You should have sought in your own sphere; you should have found a stripling as pale and as cowardly as yourself, who would have satisfied your little girl's love. See here: if you aristocrats take our men, we will tear your pink and white faces for you!"

"I do not understand you," stammered Blanche, again seized by fear.

"You do not understand me! Listen, then: I loved Monsieur Philippe. He bought roses of me every morning, and my heart beat as if it would burst when I gave him my bouquets. I know now where those flowers went. I was told one day that he had fled with you. I wept; then I thought you loved him and that he would be happy. But you have put him in prison. Let us not speak of that, or I shall get angry and strike you!"

She paused, panting; then she continued, going close up to the girl, burning with her hot breath Blanche's icy cheeks:

"You do not know how we poor girls love. We love with all our flesh, with all our courage. When we elope with a man, we do not say afterwards that

he took advantage of our weakness. We clasp him tightly in our arms to protect him. Ah! if Monsieur Philippe had loved me, he would not have been betrayed! But I am an unhappy creature, a beggar, an ugly wretch!"

And Fine began to sob, as weak as Mlle. de Cazalis. The latter took her hand, and said, her voice broken by tears:

"In pity, do not accuse me! Will you be my friend—shall I open my heart to you? If you only knew how much I suffer, you would have mercy. I can do nothing; I obey my uncle, who breaks me in his hands of iron. I know I am a coward; but I have not the strength to be otherwise than cowardly. And I love Philippe; he is always in my mind. Truly did he say to me: 'If you desert me, every hour of your life the remembrance of me will torment you, you will always feel on your lips the fiery stamp of my kisses, and that shall be your punishment!' He is here now; he burns me, he will kill me! Awhile ago, when he was sentenced, I felt something leap within me which shook me from head to foot and almost tore me to pieces. I am weeping—do you see? I ask mercy of you."

All Fine's anger had vanished; she sustained Blanche, who was staggering.

"You are right," continued the poor child: "I do not deserve pity. I have stricken the man I love and he will love me no more. Ah! in mercy, if some day he should become your husband, tell him of my tears, ask him to forgive me. What drives me wild is that I can never convince him that I adore him; he would laugh; he could not comprehend the extent of my cowardice. No; do not speak to him of me. Let him forget me—that will be best: I shall be the only one to weep."

There was a dolorous silence.

"And your child?" asked Fine.

"My child!" said Blanche, wildly. "I do not know what will become of it. My uncle will take it from me."

"Would you like me to be a mother to it?"

The flower-girl uttered these words in a grave and tender voice. Mlle. of Cazalis clasped her in her arms in a passionate embrace.

"Oh! how good you are! You can love! Try to see me in Marseilles. When the time comes, I will trust in you."

At that moment, the aged female relative made her appearance, after having in vain searched for Blanche in the crowd. Fine withdrew quickly and hastened up the Cours. As she reached the Place des Carmélites, she saw Marius in the distance, talking with Philippe's lawyer.

The young man was in despair. Never had he imagined that his brother could be sentenced to so severe a punishment. The imprisonment of five years terrified him; but he was still more grievously overwhelmed by the thought of the public exposure in one of the squares of Marseilles. He saw the deputy's hand in this chastisement: M. de Cazalis wished, above all else, to disgrace Philippe, to render him forever unworthy of a woman's love.

Around Marius, the crowd cried out that injustice had been done; the masses with one voice protested against the atrocity of the punishment.

And as the young man, angry and hopeless, talked excitedly with the lawyer, a soft hand was placed upon his arm. He turned quickly and saw Fine beside him, calm and smiling.

"Hope and follow me," said she to him, in a low voice. "Your brother is saved!"

## CHAPTER XII

### FINE'S STRATEGY

WHILE Marius, before the trial, was fruitlessly scouring the town, Fine, on her side, was toiling away at the work of deliverance. She had undertaken a systematic campaign against the conscience of her uncle, the jailer Revertégat.

She had installed herself at his house; she spent the days in the prison. She sought from morning till night to make herself useful, to cause herself to be adored by her relative, who lived alone, like a growling bear, with his two little daughters. She attacked him through his paternal love; she charmingly cajoled the children; she expended all her savings for playthings, sugar-plums and toilet gewgaws. The little ones were not in the habit of being indulged; they acquired a noisy tenderness for their big cousin, who danced them on her knees and distributed such handsome and good things. The father was touched; he thanked Fine effusively.

Despite himself, he yielded to the penetrating influence of the young girl. He grumbled when it was necessary for him to leave the room in which she was-

The flower-girl seemed to have brought with her the sweet odor of her flowers, the freshness of her roses and violets. The jailer's lodge had been delightfully perfumed from the moment of her arrival, when she tripped into it, gay and sprightly; her bright skirts appeared to scatter there light, air and gayety. Everything smiled now in the gloomy apartment, and Revertégat said, with a hearty laugh, that spring had come to live with him. The good man forgot himself amid the caressing effluvia of that spring; his heart softened and, little by little, he laid aside the roughness and severity incident to his vocation.

Fine was too shrewd a girl not to play her rôle with sly prudence. She did nothing hastily; step by step, she led him to pity and lenity. Then, she expressed compassion for Philippe in his presence; she forced him to declare with his own lips that the young man was unjustly kept in prison. When she held Revertégat in her hands, supple and submissive, she asked him if she could not visit the cell of the poor fellow. The jailer dare not say no; he took his niece to the spot, allowed her to enter and remained at the door to keep watch.

Fine stood like a simpleton before Philippe. She stared at him, confused and blushing, oblivious of what she wished to say. The young man recognized her and quickly approached her, with a tender and charmed air.

"You here, my dear child!" cried he. "Ah! how kind you are to come to see me. Will you allow me to kiss your hand?"

Surely, Philippe thought himself in his little apartment on the Rue Sainte, and, perhaps, he was not far from dreaming of a new adventure. The flower-girl, surprised, almost wounded, withdrew her hand and gravely looked at Blanche's lover.

"You are out of your senses, Monsieur Philippe," answered she. "You know well enough that, in my eyes, you are now married. Let us speak of serious things."

She lowered her voice and continued, rapidly:

"The jailer is my uncle, and, for over a week, I have been working for your deliverance. I wished to see you to tell you that your friends have not forgotten you. Hope!"

Philippe, on hearing these welcome words, regretted his gallant reception of his visitor.

"Give me your hand," said he, in an agitated voice. "I ask it as a friend, who wishes to grasp it like an old comrade. Do you pardon me?"

The flower-girl smiled, without answering his question.

"I think," resumed she, "that I can soon throw the door wide open for you. When will you make your escape?"

"Make my escape! But I shall be acquitted. What is the use of flight! If I escaped, I should declare by that very action that I am guilty!"

Fine had not thought of that. In her view, Philippe was convicted in advance; but, all things considered, he was right: they should wait until after the trial. As she maintained silence, pensive and irresolute, Revertégat gave two little knocks upon the door to ask her to quit the cell.

"Well," continued she. addressing the

prisoner, "hold yourself in readiness. If you are convicted, your brother and I will arrange your flight. Have confidence."

She withdrew, leaving Philippe almost in love with her. Now she had time before her in which to win over her uncle. She continued to persue her strategy, amazing the dear man by her kindness and her grace, exciting his pity in regard to the prisoner's lot. She brought into the conspiracy her two little cousins, who, at a word from her, would have quitted their father to follow her. One evening, after having softened Revertégat by all the cajoleries she could invent, she at last asked him squarely for Philippe's freedom.

"Pardieu!" cried the jailer, "if the matter rested only with me, I would at once open the door for him!"

"But it does rest only with you, uncle!" answered Fine, frankly.

"Ah! you think so, do you? If I allowed him to escape, I should lose my place to-morrow and die of hunger with my two daughters."

These words rendered the flower-girl serious.

"But," resumed she, an instant afterwards, "what if I gave you money, if I loved this young man and if I begged you with clasped hands to give him up to me?"

"You! you!" cried the jailer, in astonishment.

He had arisen; he stared at his niece to make sure that she was in earnest. When he saw her grave and moved, he bowed his head, conquered, softened, consenting with a gesture.

"Ma foi!" cried he, "in that case, I would do as you wished. You are too good and too pretty a girl to be refused!"

Fine embraced him and spoke of something else. Now, she was certain of victory. At various times, she resumed the conversation; she accustomed Revereégat to the idea of allowing Philippe to escape. She did not wish to bring her relative to want, and, at first, offered him a recompense of fifteen thousand francs. This offer dazzled the jailer; from that instant, he surrendered himself to her, bound hand and foot.

And this was why Fine had been able to say to Marius, with her cunning smile: "Follow me. Your brother is saved!"

She took the young man to the prison. On the way, she related to him all the details of her campaign; she told him how, little by little, she had won over her uncle. Marius' upright soul at first revolted at the recital of this comedy; it was repugnant to him to think that his brother would owe his safety to flight, to the purchase of a conscience. The idea of duty was so deeply rooted in him that he felt a certain shame at the proposal to pay Revertégat to betray the trust that had been reposed in him. Then he thought of the intrigues employed by M. de Cazalis; he said to himself that after all, he would only be using the same weapons as his adversaries, and he grew calm.

He thanked Fine in a touching way; he knew not how to show her his gratitude. The young girl, happy in her excited joy, scarcely heard his protestations of indebtedness.

They could not see Revertégat until evening. The jailer, at the first words of the conversation, showed Marius his two little daughters, who were playing in a corner of the room.

"Monsieur," he simply said, "there is my excuse. I would not ask for a sou, if I had not those children to keep."

This scene was painful to Maurius. He shortened it as much as possible. He knew that the jailer yielded at once to interest and devotedness, and, if he could not despise him, he felt ill at ease in making such a bargain with him.

However, all was settled in a few minutes. Marius stated that he would depart the following morning for Marseilles, and that he would bring back with him the fifteen thousand francs promised by Fine. He counted upon drawing them from his banker; his mother had left fifty thousand francs, which were deposited with M. Bérard, whose house was one of the strongest and best known in the city. It was decided that the flower-girl should remain at Aix, and there await the young man's return.

He departed, full of hope, already seeing his brother free. As he quitted the diligence at Marseilles, he received unexpected and terrible news which crushed him. The banker Bérard had failed.

## CHAPTER XIII

### A SCOUNDRELLY BANKRUPT

MARIUS hastened to the banker's office. He could not believe the sinister news, for he had the faith of honest hearts. On the way, he said to himself that the rumors which were in circulation were, perhaps, only calumnies, and he cherished wild hopes. The loss of his fortune at this moment was the loss of his brother; it seemed to him that chance could not be so cruel to him; the public must be deceived; Bérard would pay him his money. He must see with his own eyes to be convinced.

When he entered the banking-house, cold anguish seized upon his heart. He saw the terrible reality. The rooms were vacant; the vast apartments, deserted and still, with their closed gratings and their bare desks, appeared funereal to him. A fortune which crumbles away leaves a sad desolation behind it. A vague odor of ruin escaped from the pasteboard boxes, from the papers and from the safe. Seals spread everywhere their white bands and their huge bits of red wax.

Marius passed through three rooms without finding any one. He at last discovered a clerk, who had come to take from a desk some articles belonging to him. This clerk told him in a rough tone that M. Bérard was in his office.

The young man entered, trembling, forgetting to close the door. He perceived the banker, who was tranquilly at work writing letters, arranging papers and adjusting accounts. This man, still young, tall, with a handsome and intelligent face, was dressed with exquisite taste; he wore rings on his fingers; he had a polite and rich air. He looked as if freshly arrayed to receive his customers and personally explain to them his disaster.

Besides, his atitude seemed courageous. He was a resigned victim of circumstances, or rather, an arrant scoundrel who would get out of a scrape by dint of audacity.

On seeing Marius enter, he assumed an air of compunction; he looked his customer squarely in the face, and his countenance expressed a sort of honest sorrow.

"I expected you, my dear Monsieur," said he, in an agitated voice. "You see that I am waiting for all those whose ruin I have caused. I will have courage to the end; I wish every one to see that I have nothing to be ashamed of."

He placed a ledger on his desk and opened it with a certain affectation.

"Here are my accounts," continued he. "My obligations foot up a million and my assets a million, five hundred thousand francs. The court will arrange matters, and I hope my creditors will not suffer too heavy a loss. I am the first to feel the blow: I have lost my fortune and my credit; I have allowed myself to be outrageously robbed by insolent debtors."

Marius had not yet uttered a word. In the presence of Bérard's dejected calmness, in the presence of this mise-en-scène of austere grief, he could not find in his heart a single cry of reproach, a single indignant and furious syllable. He almost pitied this man who thus faced the storm.

"Monsieur," said he, at length, "why did you not notify me when you saw your affairs becoming entangled and going wrong? My mother was a friend of your mother, and, in remembrance of our old relations you should have caused me to withdraw from your house the money you were about to involve.

Your ruin to-day strips me of everything and plunges me in despair."

Bérard advanced hurriedly and seized Marius' hands.

"Do not say that!" cried he, in a piteous tone; "do not overwhelm me! Ah! you little know what cruel regrets are rending me! When I saw the gulf, I strove to cling to the tree branches; I struggled; until the last moment, I hoped to save the amounts deposited with me. You cannot imagine what terrible risks those who handle money run!"

Marius was speechless. What could he say to this man who excused himself by heaping accusations upon his own head? He had no proofs; he dare not call Bérard a swindler; his only course was to retire quietly. Besides, the banker spoke in a voice so woeful, in a fashion so touching and so frank, that he almost felt compassion for him. He hastened to withdraw in order to leave him in peace. His misfortune oppressed him.

As he was returning through the empty rooms, the clerk, who had finished his preparations for the removal of his effects, took up his bundle and hat and followed him. This clerk sneered between his teeth, and, at each step, stared at Marius with a strange air, shrugging his shoulders. Outside, on the pavement, he suddenly addressed him:

"Well," said he, "what do you think of the Sieur Bérard? He is a capital actor, is he not? The office door was left open; I laughed heartily to see his disconsolate looks. He nearly wept, the honest man. Allow me to tell you, Monsieur, that you have permitted yourself to be duped in the most polite fashion!"

"I do not understand you," answered Marius.

"So much the better; that proves you to be an upright and just man. As for me, I quit this swindling shop with profound joy. For a long time I suspected what was going to happen; I foresaw the dénouement of this high comedy of robbery. I have a remarkably keen scent for discovering intrigues in a house."

"Explain yourself."

"Oh! the story is a simple one. I can relate it to you in a few words: Ten years ago, Bérard opened a banking-house. Today I doubt not that from the first he was preparing for a failure. This is the way he reasoned: 'I wish to be rich because I have strong appetites, and I desire to get rich as soon as possible because I am eager to satisfy my appetites. Now, the straight road is rough and long; I prefer to follow the by-ways of trickery and gather up my million in ten years. I will become a banker; I will have a safe as a trap for the funds of the public. Each year, I will steal a round sum. This can go on as long as necessary; I will stop when my pockets are full. Then, I will calmly suspend payment. Of two millions, which shall have been confided to me, I will generously restore two or three hundred thousand francs to my creditors. The rest, hidden in a little corner I know of, will help me to live as I desire, in idleness and pleasure!' Now, do you understand, my dear Monsieur?"

Marius heard the clerk with stupefaction.

"But," said he, "what you tell me is impossible. Bérard this instant informed me that his obligations foot up a million and his assets a million, five hundred thousand francs! We shall all be repaid in full; it is merely a matter of patience."

The clerk gave vent to a torrent of laughter.

"Ah! mon Dieu! how innocent you are!" resumed he. "Do you really believe in those assets of a million, five hundred thousand francs? In the first place, they will deduct Madame Bérard's dowry from that sum. Now, Madame Béraud brought fifty thousand francs to her husband, which the latter has transformed, in the marriage contract, into five hundred thousand francs. As you see, it was a little steal of four hundred and fifty thousand francs. A million remains, and that million is almost entirely represented by worthless notes. The process of getting such notes is exceedingly simple. There are, in Marseilles, people who, for a hundred sous, sell their signatures; this easy and lucrative trade brings them in a good living. Bérard has had a pile of notes signed by these men of straw, and has pocketed the money which he claims to-day to have loaned insolvent debtors. If you get a dividend of ten per cent, you may consider yourself fortunate. And that in eighteen months or two years, when the bankruptcy official shall have finished his labors."

Marius was crushed. Thus the fifty thousand francs, left him by his mother, would dwindle to a ridiculous sum, of no use whatever to him. He must have money immediately, and he was told he would have to wait two years. And his ruin and despair were the work of a scoundrel who had just made a fool of him. Anger took possession of him.

"This Bérard is a rascal," said he, indignantly. "He will be vigorously pursued. We should rid society of these crafty men who enrich themselves by the ruin of others. The jail awaits them."

Again the clerk indulged in a burst of laughter.

"Bérard," answered he, "will perhaps, be sent to prison for a couple of weeks. That's all. You are once more failing to comprehend me! Listen."

The two young men had remained standing upon the sidewalk. The passers pushed against them. They returned to the vestibule of the banking-house.

"You say that the jail awaits Bérard," continued the clerk. "The jail awaits only awkward people. During the ten years he has been maturing and caressing his failure, our man has taken his precautions; such infamy as his is a work of art. His accounts are correct, and he has put the law on his side. He knows in advance the slight risks he runs. The court can at most reproach him with too heavy personal expenses; he will be accused, besides, of having put in circulation a large number of promissory notes, a ruinous method of procuring money. But these faults entail only a derisory punishment. As I have already told you, Bérard will be sent to prison for two weeks or a month at most."

"But," exclaimed Marius, "cannot one proclaim this man's crime in the open street, prove his infamy and cause his conviction?"

"No, that cannot be done! There are no proofs, I tell you. Besides, Bérard has not lost his time; he has forseen everything; he has made powerful friends in Marseilles, thinking that he would, doubtless, some day need their influence. Now, in this city of clubs, he is a sort of inviolable personage; if one should touch a single hair of his head, all his friends would cry out with grief and rage. He can, at the utmost, be imprisoned a brief period for form's sake. When he is set at liberty, he will unearth his little million, display his luxury and easily create for himself a new esteem. Then you will meet him in his carriage, reclining upon cushions, and the wheels of his calèche will splash mud over you; you will see him, indifferent and idle, keeping an expensive house and enjoying all the pleasures of existence. And, to worthily crown his success as a robber, people will bow to him, love him and open for him a new credit of honor and consideration."

Marius kept a ferocious silence. The clerk made him a slight bow and said, as he was about to depart:

"It is thus that the farce is played. I had all this on my heart, and am glad I met you and relieved myself. Now, a word of good advice: Keep secret what I have just told you, bid adieu to your money and do not bother yourself about this wretched affair. Reflect, and you will see that I am right. Farewell."

Marius was alone. A furious desire seized upon him to return to Bérard's office and slap him in the face. All his instincts of justice and probity revolted and urged him to drag the banker into the street, proclaiming his crime. Then disgust succeeded his fury; he thought of his poor mother, shamefully cheated by this man, and from that instant felt only a crushing contempt for him. He followed the clerk's advice; he strode away from the banking-house, striving to forget that he had had money and that a thief had stolen it from him.

In due time, all the clerk's predictions were fulfilled point by point. Bérard was sentenced for simple failure to a month's imprisonment. A year later, his countenance rosy, his bearing easy and insolent, he displayed throughout Marseilles his joyous, rich man's whims. He clinked his gold in the clubs, the restaurants and the theatres—everywhere, in fact, where pleasures were to be bought. And, upon his path, he always found toadies or dupes who bowed to the very ground before him.

## CHAPTER XIV

### A DEFAULTER

MARIUS went mechanically to the harbor. He walked straight on, not knowing whither his feet led him. He was as if stupefied. A single idea surged in his empty head, and that idea repeated, like the murmur of a bell, that he must have fifteen thousand francs at once. He cast around him that vague look of hopeless people; he seemed to search the street to see if he could not find between two paving-stones the sum he needed.

At the harbor, a desire for wealth came to him. The merchandise heaped up along the quays, the ships which brought in fortunes, the noise and the stir of the crowd which was making money irritated him. Never before had he felt his poverty. For a moment he was envious, rebellious and full of jealous bitterness. He asked himself why he was poor, why others were rich.

And constantly the sound of the bell murmured in his head. Fifteen thousand francs! fifteen thousand francs! The very thought of them nearly burst his skull. He could not return with empty hands. His brother was waiting for him. He had only a few hours to save him from infamy. And he could find nothing; his benumbed intelligence did not furnish him with a single practicable idea. He twisted in his powerlessness; he racked his mind vainly; he struggled with rage and anxiety.

Never would he have dared to ask his employer, M. Martelly, for fifteen thousand francs. His salary was too small to guarantee such a loan. Besides, he knew the ship-owner's rigid principles, and feared his reproaches should he admit to him that he wished to buy a conscience. M. Martelly would indignantly refuse him the money.

Suddenly, an idea came to Marius. He would not discuss it with himself, and started in hot haste for his apartment on the Rue Sainte.

In the same house, upon the same landing as himself, dwelt a young employé, named Charles Blétry. Blétry was attached as cashier to the soap manufactory of MM. Daste et Degans.

The two young men being neighbors, a sort of intimacy had arisen between them. Marius had been won by Charles' gentleness; Blétry was an assiduous frequenter of the churches, his conduct was exemplary and he seemed to be of the highest probity.

For two years, however, he had indulged in heavy expenses. He had introduced veritable sumptuousness into his little apartment, purchasing carpets, hangings, mirrors and handsome furniture. Since this change, he had come in later at night and lived more luxuriously; but he had always remained gentle and honest, tranquil and pious.

At first, Marius had been astonished at his neighbor's expenses; he could not comprehend how an employé on a salary of eighteen hundred francs could buy such costly things. But Charles had told him that he had recently come into an inheritance, and that he intended soon to give up his situation to live like a prosperous citizen. He had even put himself at his disposal, offering him his purse without restriction. Marius had refused.

Now, he had thought of this offer. He was going to knock at Charles Blétry's door and ask him to save his brother. A loan of fifteen thousand francs would not, perhaps, embarrass that young man, who seemed to throw money out of the windows. Marius counted upon repaying him little by little, persuaded that his neighbor would grant him the necessary time.

He did not find the clerk in his apartment on the Rue Sainte, and, as he was pressed, he determined to go to the soap manufactory of MM. Daste et Degans. This soap manufactory was situated on the Boulevard des Dames.

When he reached it and asked for Charles Blétry, it seemed to him that the people stared at him with a strange air. The workmen told him roughly to inquire of M. Daste, who was in his office. Marius, astonished at this reception, decided to go to the manufacturer. He found him in conference with three gentlemen, who stopped talking as he entered.

"Can you tell me, Monsieur," asked the young man, "if M. Charles Blétry is at the manufactory?"

Daste exchanged a rapid glance with one of the persons present, a stout gentleman, grave and severe.

"M. Charles Blétry will soon be here," answered he. "Be kind enough to wait for him. Are you one of his friends?"

"Yes," replied Marius, frankly. "He lodges in the same house as myself. I have known him nearly three years."

Silence was maintained for a moment. The young man, thinking that his presence embarrassed the gentlemen, added, bowing and going towards the door:

"I thank you; I will wait outside."

Then the stout gentleman leaned over and said something in a low voice to the manufacturer. M. Daste stopped Marius with a gesture.

"Remain, if you please," said he. "Your presence may be useful to us. You ought to know Blétry's habits; you can, doubtless, give us some information in regard to him!"

Marius, surprised and not understanding, made a gesture of hesitation.

"Pardon," resumed M. Daste, with

great politeness; "I see that my words amaze you."

He pointed to the stout gentleman and continued:

"Monsieur is the commissaire de police of the quarter, and I have just summoned him to arrest Charles Blétry, who, in two years, has stolen from us sixty thousand francs!"

Marius, on hearing Charles accused of robbery, understood everything. He explained to himself the young man's reckless expenses. He thanked Heaven that he had not in the past accepted his offers of service. Never would he have believed that his neighbor could be guilty of a base action. He well knew that there were in Marseilles, as in all the great centres of industry, unworthy employés, young men who robbed their employers to satisfy their vices and their love of luxury; he had often heard of clerks who received a hundred or a hundred and fifty francs a month and who yet found the means to lose enormous sums at the clubs, to throw twenty-franc pieces to beggars and to eat at restaurants and cafés. But Charles had seemed so pious, so modest and honest, and had played the rôle of hypocrite with so much art that Marius had been deceived by these appearances of probity and that he had his doubts even yet, despite M. Daste's formal accusation.

He sat down, awaiting the dénouement of this drama. He could not do otherwise. For half an hour, a dull silence reigned in the office. The manufacturer had begun to write. The commissaire de police and the two agents, mute and as if half asleep, gazed vaguely before them, with a terrible patience.

Such a spectacle would have given honesty to Marius, had he lacked it. Nothing could have been more sinister than those three impassible men; they looked like the inexorable law awaiting crime.

A sound of footsteps was heard; the door opened gently.

"Here is our man," said M. Daste, rising.

Charles Blétry entered, suspecting nothing. He did not even notice the persons who were in the office.

"Do you wish to see me, Monsieur?" asked he, in that drawling tone which employés assume when speaking to their chiefs.

As M. Daste looked him in the face with cutting contempt, he turned and saw the commissaire whom he knew by sight. He grew frightfully pale; he realized that he was lost, and his whole body quivered with shame and fear. He had hurled himself headlong into a trap. Seeing that his terror accused him, he strove to appear calm, to recover a little coolness and audacity.

"Yes, I wish to see you!" cried M. Daste, violently. "You know why, do you not? Ah! wretch, you will rob me no more!"

"I do not know what you mean," stammered Blétry. "I have stolen nothing from you. Of what do you accuse me?"

The commissaire had seated himself at the manufacturer's desk to commit the facts of the case to writing. The two agents guarded the door.

"Monsieur," said the commissaire to Daste, "be kind enough to tell me under what circumstances you detected the defalcations which the Sieur Blétry has, as you assert, committed to your detriment."

Daste then related the story of the robbery. He said that his cashier had sometimes been extraordinarily slow in making certain returns. But as he had unlimited confidence in the young man, he had attributed these delays to the bad faith of the debtors. The first defalcations must have been made at least eighteen months before. Finally, on the preceding day, one of his customers having failed, Daste himself went to demand the payment of a sum of five thousand francs, and learned that Blétry had collected the amount several weeks previously. The manufacturer, frightened, hastily returned to the manufactory and convinced himself, by running over the cashier's books, that he was nearly sixty thousand francs short.

The commissaire afterwards proceeded to question Blétry. The young man, taken unawares and being unable to deny the facts, invented a ridiculous story.

"One day," said he, "I lost a pocketbook containing forty thousand francs. I dared not admit this large loss to M. Daste. Then I began to take money to gamble at the Bourse, hoping to win and reimburse the firm."

The commissaire asked him for details, perplexed him and forced him to contradict himself. Blétry tried another lie.

"You are right," resumed he: "I lost no pocketbook. I prefer to tell everything. The truth is that I myself was robbed. I lodged a young man who was without bread. One night, he vanished, carrying away with him my collection bag; in that bag was a considerable sum of money."

"Do not aggravate your crime by lying," said the commissaire, with that terrifying patience of the police authorities. "You know that we cannot believe you. You are telling us idle tales."

He turned towards Marius and continued:

"I requested M. Daste to detain you, Monsieur, that you might aid us in our task. The accused is your neighbor, you said. Do you know nothing of his manner of living? Can you not conjure him with us to tell the truth?"

Marius was terribly embarrassed. Blétry filled him with pity; he staggered like a drunken man; he supplicated him with a look. The young fellow was not a hardened rogue; he had, without doubt, yielded to temptations, to cowardice of mind and heart. Nevertheless, Marius' conscience made itself heard; it ordered him to tell what he knew. The young man did not reply directly to the commissaire; he preferred to address Blétry himself.

"Listen, Charles," said he: "I know not whether you are guilty or innocent. I have always seen you good and modest. I know that you support your mother and that you are beloved by all who are acquainted with you. If you have committed a folly, admit your blindness; you will cause those who have had esteem and friendship for you to suffer less by frankly accusing yourself and showing sincere repentance."

Marius spoke in a gentle and convincing tone. Blétry, whom the sharp words of the commissaire had left mute and confusedly irritated, bent beneath the austere indulgence of his former friend. He thought of his mother; he thought of that esteem and those friendships which he was about to lose, and a keen emotion took him by the throat. He burst into sobs.

He wept scalding tears in his hands which he held over his face, and, for several minutes, only his terrible groans of despair were heard. It was a complete confession. Everybody remained silent.

"Yes!" cried Blétry, at last, in the midst of his tears, "I did steal and I am a wretch! I did not know what I was doing. It took at first a few hundred francs; then I wanted a thousand, two thousand, five thousand, ten thousand francs at a time. It seemed to me that some one was pushing me on from behind. My needs and my appetites increased constantly."

"But what have you done with all this money?" asked the commissaire.

"I do not know. I gave it away, spent it in riotous living, and lost it at cards. You cannot imagine the whirl I was in. I was calm in my poverty; I aspired to nothing; I loved to pray in the churches, to lead a holy life like an honest man. And yet I have tasted luxury and vice; I have entertained reckless companions; I have bought fine furniture. I was out of my senses!"

"Can you give me the names of the parties you entertained with the money you stole?"

"As if I knew their names! I made their acquaintance here, there and everywhere—in the streets and at the public balls. They came because my pockets were full of gold, and they left me when my pockets were empty. Then I lost much at baccarat at the clubs. What made me a thief was seeing certain young men belonging to fine families throw money out of the windows and wallow in wealth and idleness. I wished to have, like them, boon companions, noisy pleasures, nights of gaming and revelry. I needed thirty thousand francs a year and made but eighteen hundred. Then I stole."

The wretch, stifling, choking with grief, let himself fall upon a chair. Marius approached M. Daste, who himself was moved, and begged him to be indulgent. Afterwards, he hastened to withdraw; this scene made his heart bleed. He left Blétry in a sort of stupor, a kind of nervous prostration. A few months later, he learned that the cashier had been sentenced to five years' imprisonment.

When Marius found himself in the street, he felt greatly relieved. He realized that Heaven had given him a lesson in causing him to witness Blétry's arrest. Several hours before, at the harbor, he had had evil thoughts of fortune; he had felt a sort of hatred for the rich. He had just seen whither such thoughts and such feelings might lead.

And suddenly, he remembered why he went to the soap manufactory. He had now but an hour left him to find the fifteen thousand francs with which to save his brother.

## CHAPTER XV

### PHILIPPE REFUSES TO ESCAPE

Marius mentally acknowledged that he was powerless. He no longer knew where to apply. One does not borrow fifteen thousand francs in an hour, when one is merely a clerk.

He passed slowly down the Rue d'Aix, his brain aching, finding nothing in his benumbed thoughts. Money troubles are terrible; one would rather struggle against an assassin than against the eluding and overwhelming phantom of poverty. Nobody has, up to the present time, been able to invent a hundred-sou piece.

When the young man reached the Cours Belzunce, hopeless and brought to a stand by necessity, he resolved to return empty-handed to Aix. The diligence was about to start; only one place on the impériale was left. Marius took that place joyfully; he preferred to remain in the open air, for anxiety was stifling him and he hoped that the broad country horizons would calm his fever.

It was a sorrowful journey. In the morning he had passed the same trees, the same hills, and the hope which made him smile then threw a mild and delicious brightness over the fields and hillocks. Now, he again saw the same scenes and imparted to them all the sadness of his soul; the country seemed funereal to him. The heavy vehicle rolled onward; the cultivated lands, the groves of pines and the little hamlets stretched out along the highway; and Marius found, in each new landscape, a more sinister mourning, a more poignant grief. Night came on; it appeared to him that the entire region was covered with an immense sheet of black crape.

When he arrived at Aix, he went towards the prison with a lingering step.

He said to himself that, no matter how late he might be, he would still bring the bad news too soon. He entered the jail at nine o'clock in the evening. Revertégat and Fine were playing cards at a corner of the table to kill time.

The flower-girl arose, with a joyous bound, and ran to the young man.

"Well?" asked she, with a bright smile, throwing back her head coquettishly.

Marius dare not reply. He sat down, despairingly.

"Why don't you speak?" cried Fine. "Have you the money?"

"No," answered the young man, simply.

He drew a long breath and told them of Bérard's failure, Blétry's arrest and all the misfortunes which had happened to him at Marseilles. He closed by saying:

"Now, I am only a poor devil. My brother will remain a prisoner."

The flower-girl stood in dolorous surprise. With hands clasped, in that attitude of pity which the women of Provence assume, she murmured, in a low one of lamentation:

"Oh! how hard, how hard!"

She looked at her uncle; she seemed to urge him to speak. Revertégat contemplated the two young people with compassion. They saw that a struggle was taking place in him. Finally, coming to a decision, he said to Marius:

"Listen, Monsieur: My vocation has not so hardened me that I am insensible to the grief of deserving people. I have already told you why I sold you your brother's freedom. But I would not have you think that I am influenced only by the love of money. If unfortunate circumstances prevent you from putting me at present beyond reach of want, I will none the less open the door for Monsieur Philippe. You can help me later; you can pay me the fifteen thousand francs sou by sou, when you are able."

Fine, on hearing these words, clapped her hands. She leaped up on her uncle's neck and kissed him full in the mouth. Marius became grave.

"I cannot accept your devotion," answered he. "I already reproach myself for having made you false to your duty. I refuse to aggravate my responsibility by throwing you, in addition, into the street without a morsel of bread!"

The flower-girl turned towards the young man almost with anger.

"Hold your tongue!" cried she. "Monsieur Philippe must be saved. I wish it. Besides, we can open the prison doors without you. Come, uncle. If Monsieur Philippe consents, his brother will have nothing to say."

Marius followed the young girl and the jailer, who went towards the prisoner's cell. They had taken a dark lantern and glided through the corridors so as not to arouse attention.

They all three entered the cell and closed the door behind them. Philippe was asleep. Revertégat, moved by his niece's tears, had ameliorated as much as possible for the young man the severe regimen of the prison; he had carried to him breakfast and dinner prepared by Fine herself; he had loaned him books and had even given him a supplementary coverlet. The cell had become habitable, and Philippe was not too weary of it; he knew, besides, that preparations for his flight were being made.

He awoke, and put out his hands effusively to his brother and the flower-girl.

"Have you come for me?" asked he, with a smile.

"Yes," replied Fine. "Dress yourself quickly."

Marius was silent. His heart beat with great thumps. He feared lest an ardent desire for freedom might make his brother accept this flight, which he had deemed it his duty to refuse.

"So, all is understood and arranged," resumed Philippe. "I can escape without fear and without remorse. Have you paid the money promised? Why don't you answer me, Marius?"

Fine hurriedly interposed.

"I told you to make haste!" cried she. "What are you uneasy about?"

She had gathered up the young man's garments; she threw them to him, adding that she would wait in the corridor.

Marius stopped her with a gesture.

"Pardon," said he; "I cannot allow my bother to remain in ignorance of our misfortunes."

And, despite Fines impatience, he repeated the particulars of his journey to Marseilles. But he offered no advice; he wished to allow his brother full freedom of choice.

"Then," cried Philippe, overwhelmed, "you have not given the money to the jailer! We are without a sou!"

"Don't trouble yourself about that," said Revertégat, approaching. "You can pay me later."

The prisoner was mute. He thought no more of flight; he thought of poverty and of the sorry figure he would cut thenceforward upon the promenades of Marseilles. No more elegant garments, no more idling about, no more love affairs! Besides, he had chivalrous feelings and poetical ideas which prevented him from accepting the jailer's devotion. He returned to his miserable bed, pulled the coverlet up to his chin and said, in a calm voice:

"Well, I will stay where I am!"

Marius' face was radiant. Fine stood as if stupefied.

Recovering herself, the flower-girl strove to prove the necessity of the flight; she spoke of the public exposure, of the infamy of the pillory. She grew animated; she was beautiful in her anger and Philippe gazed at her with admiration.

"My pretty child," replied he, "you, perhaps, might make me yield if I had not become blind and obstinate in this cell. But, truly, I have already committed enough cowardly actions, without burdening my conscience further. Whatever Heaven ordains will take place! But all is not lost. Marius will deliver me; he will find the money, as you will see. You can come for me when you have paid my ransom. Then, we will fly together and I will embrace you!"

He spoke almost gayly. Marius took his hand.

"Thank you, brother," said he. "Have confidence."

Fine and Revertégat quitted the cell. Philippe and Marius remained alone for several minutes. They had a grave and animated conversation: they talked of Blanche and her child.

When the three visitors to the cell had returned to the jailer's lodge, the flower-girl lost all hope and asked Marius what he was going to do.

"I shall make another attempt to raise the money," replied he. "The trouble is that we are pressed for time and that I do not know any one to whom I can apply for a loan."

"I can aid you a little," asid Revertégat. "There is in this town, a short distance from here, a banker, M. Rostand, who might be induced, perhaps, to lend you a goodly sum. But I forewarn you that this Rostand has the reputation of being a usurer."

Marius had no choice of means.

"I thank you," said he. "I will see Rostand to-morrow morning."

## CHAPTER XVI

### THE USURERS

The Sieur Rostand was a shrewd man. He carried on his infamous business with great ability. To put an honorable stamp upon his vocation, he had opened a banking-house; he paid his license; he was legally established. On occasion, he even knew how to show a little honesty; he loaned money at the same rate as his brethren, the bankers of the town. But, in his establishment, there was, so to speak, a back shop in which he lovingly elaborated his rascalities.

Six months after the opening of his banking-house, he became the manager of a body of usurers, of a scoundrelly band which entrusted him with funds. The combination was of a patriarchal simplicity. People who had the bump of usury and were afraid to operate on their own account, at their own risk and peril, brought him their money and begged him to make the most out of it he could. He thus controlled a rapid circulation of funds to a considerable amount, and could largely take advantage of the needs of borrowers. Those who furnished the money remained in the background. He solemnly engaged to loan at fabulous rates, at fifty, sixty and even eighty per cent. Each month, the capitalists met at his house; he presented his accounts and divided the profits. And he so arranged matters as to keep the largest share for himself, to rob the robbers.

He always sought those doing a small trade. When a merchant, the day before obligation fell due, desired to borrow, he imposed exorbitant conditions upon him. The merchant invariably accepted them. Rostand had thus caused more than fifty failures in ten years. Everything was grist to his mill; he as readily lent a hundred sous to a dealer in vegetables as a thousand francs to a cattle merchant; he systematically sheared the town; he did not lose an opportunity of giving ten francs to secure a return of twenty the next day. He watched the eldest sons of high families, the young reprobates who throw money out of the windows; he filled their hands with gold pieces that they might throw more, and stood below to pick up what fell. He also made trips into the country to tempt the peasants, and, when the harvests failed, tore from them, strip by strip, their farms and their lands.

This house was a veritable trap in which fortunes were swallowed up. People, entire families, whom he had ruined were cited. Everybody knew the secret springs of his trade. They pointed out his capitalists: rich men, former ministerial officials, merchants and even workmen. But they had no proofs. Rostand's license protected him, and he was too cunning to allow himself to be caught at crime.

Once only in his infamous career had he been in danger. The affair made a great noise. A lady belonging to a distinguished family wished to borrow of him quite a large sum; she was very pious and had dissipated her fortune by giving right and left, by bestowing enormous alms. Rostand, who knew that all her property was gone, told her she must sign her brother's name to some notes; having those forgeries in his hands, he was certain of being paid by the brother, who would be interested in avoiding a scandal. The poor lady signed. Charity had ruined her, and the feeble goodness of her character made her succumb. The usurer had made no mistake in his calculation: the first notes were paid; but, as new obligations were constantly being presented, the brother lost patience and determined to look into the affair. He went to Rostand and threatened to prosecute him; he said he would rather see his sister disgraced than allow himself to be robbed with impunity by a thief like him. The usurer was almost frightened out of his wits; he surrendered the notes remaining in his possession. However, he did not lose a sou; he had loaned the money to the lady at a hundred per cent.

From that day, Rostand was extremely prudent. He managed the funds of the scoundrelly band with a craftiness that won him the admiration and confidence of the capitalists. While the latter promenaded in the sunlight, like good people who rob nobody, he remained buried in a large, gloomy office; it was there that the gold pieces of the society shot up and bore fruit. Rostand had grown to passionately love his trade, Certain members of the band used their gains to satisfy their passions, their appetites for luxury and dissipation. His sole delight was in being a crafty knave; he took as much interest in each of his operations as in a poignant drama; he applauded when his sinister comedies succeeded, and then experienced self-satisfaction and the enjoyment of a triumphant author; afterwards, he placed the stolen money on a table and sank into a miserly ecstasy.

Such was the man Revertégat had innocently pointed out to Marius as a person likely to loan him the funds he needed.

The following morning, the young man knocked at Rostand's door about eight o'clock. The house was heavy and square. All the blinds were closed, which gave the front a glacial bareness, an air of mystery and suspicion. An old and toothless woman servant, clad in a rag of dirty calico, partially opened the door.

"Is Monsieur Rostand in?" asked Marius.

"Yes; but he is engaged," answered the servant, without further opening the door.

The impatient young man pushed her aside and entered the vestibule.

"Very well," said he; "I will wait."

The surprised and hesitating servant realized that she could not get rid of such a determined intruder. She decided to take him into the second story, where she left him in a sort of antechamber. The room was small and dark; the walls were covered with greenish paper, which the dampness had discolored in large patches. The only piece of furniture was a straw-bottomed chair; Marius seated himself on it.

In front of him, an open door permitted him to see the interior of an office, in which a clerk was writing with a goose-quill pen, which scratched terribly on the paper. To the left of him was another door, which looked as if it led to the banker's private sanctum.

Marius waited a long while. Pungent odors of old paper lingered around him. The apartment was miserably filthy, and the bareness of the walls gave it a lugubrious aspect. Dust was heaped in the corners, and spiders were spinning their webs on the ceiling. The young man was almost stifled; the scratching of the goose-quill pen, which grew more and more noisy, made him nervous.

Suddenly he heard people talking in the adjoining room, and, as the words reached him clearly and distinctly, he was about to discreetly draw back his chair when certain phrases nailed him to his place. There are conversations to which one can listen; delicacy was not made to protect the privacy of certain men.

A sharp voice, which seemed to be that of the master of the house, said, with a friendly bluntness:

"Messieurs, we are all present; let us talk of serious things. The meeting is called to order. I will render a faithful account of my operations for the month, and we will then proceed to divide the profits."

There was a slight tumult, a sound of individual conversations being brought to a close. Marius, who could not yet understand matters, nevertheless felt a lively curiosity take possession of him; he divined that a strange scene was in progress behind the door.

In truth, the usurer Rostand had assembled his worthy associates of the scoundrelly band. The young man had presented himself at the very hour of the meeting, at the moment the manager was about to exhibit his books, explain his operations and divide what had been cleared.

The sharp voice resumed:

"Before going into details, I must tell you that the results of this month have not been as satisfactory as those of last month. We cleared then, on an average, sixty per cent., but now we have made only fifty-five."

Various exclamations broke forth. One might say that a displeased crowd was protesting in murmurs. There appeared to be at least fifteen persons in the apartment.

"Messieurs," continued Rostand, with a certain jeering bitterness, "I have done all I could; you ought to thank me. The business grows more difficult daily. But here are my accounts; I will rapidly make you acquainted with some of the affairs I have transacted."

A profound silence reigned for several seconds. Then arose a rustling of papers, the slight flapping of the leaves of a ledger. Marius, beginning to comprehend, listened with more attention than ever.

Then Rostand enumerated his operations, giving some explanations in regard to each. He had the noisy and nasal tone of a court tipstaff.

"I loaned," said he, "ten thousand francs to the young Comte de Salvy, a youth of twenty, who will be of age in nine months. He had lost at cards, and his lady-love, it seems, had exacted from him a large sum. I made him sign notes at ninety days for eighteen thousand francs. These notes are dated, as they should be, on the day the debtor will have attained his majority. The Salvys own large estates. It is an excellent affair."

A fawning murmur greeted the usurer's words.

"The next day," continued he, "I received a visit from the Comte's lady-love; she was exasperated, the young man having given her only two or three thousand francs. She swore that she would bring de Salvy to me, bound hand and foot, to obtain another loan. This time, I will demand the cession of a piece of property. We have still nine months to shear the young idiot, whom his mother leaves without money."

Rostand turned the leaves of the ledger. He resumed, after a brief silence:

"Joudier—a cloth merchant, who each month, needs a few hundred francs to meet his obligations. To-day, his stock belongs almost entirely to us. I have again loaned him five hundred francs at sixty per cent. Next month, if he asks me for a sou, I will make him fail and we will seize his merchandise.

"Marianne—a huckster. Every morning, she gets ten francs and returns me fifteen in the evening. I believe she drinks. A small affair, but a sure profit—a fixed income of five francs per day.

"Laurent—a peasant of the Roque-favour district. He has ceded to me, strip by strip, a piece of land he owned near the Arc. The property is worth five thousand francs; it cost us two thousand. I have expelled our man from the premises. His wife and children came to me and wept over their poverty. You will give me credit for all such vexations, will you not?

"André—a miller. He owed us eight hundred francs. I threatened him with a seizure. Then, he hastened to beg me not to ruin him by making public his insolvency. I consented to make the seizure myself without the aid of a bailiff, and took more than twelve hundred francs' worth of furniture and linen: that is I gained over four hundred francs by being humane."

There was a little rustle of satisfaction in the assembly. Marius heard the half-suppressed laughter of those men, who were gloating over Rostand's shrewdness. The banker continued:

"Now, we come to ordinary matters: three thousand francs loaned at forty per cent. to Simon, the merchant; fifteen hundred francs at fifty per cent. to the cattle merchant, Charançon; two thousand francs at eighty per cent. to the Marquis de Cantarel; a hundred francs at thirty-five per cent. to the son of the notary, Tingrey."

And Rostand went on thus for a quarter of an hour, reading out names and figures, enumerating loans which ranged from ten to ten thousand francs, and rates which varied from twenty to a hundred per cent. When he had finished, a hoarse, oily voice said:

"You must have been wrong in your statement a little while ago, my dear friend! You have toiled marvellously, this month. All these transactions are excellent. It is impossible for the profits not to average more than fifty-five per cent. You were surely deceived when you announced that figure."

"I am never deceived," answered the usurer, coldly.

Marius, who had almost glued his ear to the door, thought he noticed indecision in the scoundrel's voice.

"I have not yet told you all," continued Rostand, with embarrassment. "A week ago, we lost twelve thousand francs!"

iA these words, there were terrible exclamations. Marius hoped, for a moment, that the wretches would strangle each other.

"The devil! Listen to me!" cried the banker, amid the tumult. "I make enough money for you to induce you to pardon me, when, by chance, I cause you to lose in a transaction. Besides, it was not my fault. I was robbed!"

He uttered these words with all the indignation of an honest man. When quiet was somewhat restored, he proceeded:

"This is the whole story: Monier, a grain merchant, a solvent man, of whom I had the most favorable information, asked me for twelve thousand francs. I replied that I could not lend them to him, but that I knew an old miser, who would, perhaps, advance them at an exorbitant rate. He returned the next day, and informed me that he was ready to accept all the conditions. I called his attention to the fact that the miser demanded five thousand francs interest for six months. He consented. You see that it was an affair of gold. While I went to get the funds, he seated himself at my desk and signed seventeen notes for a thousand francs each. I glanced over the papers and placed them on the corner of this table. Then, I chatted a few minutes with Monier, who had arisen; after having pocketed the money, he made his preparations to depart. When he had gone, I thought I would lock up his notes. I took the papers in my hand. Just think of it!—the knave had exchanged the notes for a similar package of derisory bills, smeared with ink, to the order of I know not whom, without signature. I was robbed. I nearly had a rush of blood to the head. I ran after the thief, who was tranquilly walking in the sun on the Cours. At the first word I addressed to him, he called me a usurer and threatened to drag me before the commissaire de police. This Monier has the reputation of being an upright and honest man, and, ma foi! I preferred to hold my tongue!"

This recital was frequently interrupted by the angry comments of the assembly.

"Admit, Rostand, that you showed a lack of energy," said the hoarse voice. "Well, we have lost our money, and will only get fifty-five per cent. Another time, you must watch our interests closer. Now, let us divide."

Marius, despite his anguish and his indignation, could not repress a smile. The robbery committed by this Monier struck him as in the highest degree amusing, and, at the bottom of his heart, he applauded the knave who had duped another knave.

He knew now what was Rostand's business. He had not lost a word of what had been said in the adjoining room, and he had easily imagined the scene that had been going on there. Leaning slightly forward on his chair, his ear strained, he had seen with his mind's eye the usurers wrangling, with greedy looks and faces contracted by the evil passions which agitated them. Deep indignation had seized upon him at the recital of Rostand's rascalities; he had felt a desire to enter and strike the man.

He experienced a sort of bitter gayety when he remembered his errand in this den of cut-throats. What innocence, good God! It was here that he had thought to find the fifteen thousand francs necessary to save Philippe, and he had waited for an hour that the banker might turn him into the street like a beggar. Or, perhaps, Rostand would ask of him fifty per cent. and impudently rob him. At this thought, at the thought that on the other side of the door was a reunion of wretches who made money on the poverty and shame of a town, Marius suddenly arose and put his hand on the doorknob.

In the apartment was heard the sharp chink of gold pieces. The usurers were dividing their booty. Each was receiving the profit of a month's cheatery. This money they were counting, the music of which voluptuously tickled their flesh, gave forth at times the sound of sobs; one might say that the usurers' victims were lamenting.

Amid the echoing silence, the banker's voice uttered only amounts with a metallic sharpness. He dealt out a share to each of his partners; he named a sum and let fall a pile of gold pieces, which struck the desk with a ringing sound.

Then Marius turned the door-knob. With pale face and firm, honest looks, he stood for several seconds silently upon the threshold.

The young man had before him a strange spectacle. Rostand was standing in front of his desk; behind him was an open safe from which he took handfuls of gold. Around the desk, seated in a circle, were the members of the scoundrelly band, some awaiting their share, others counting the money they had just received. Every minute, the banker consulted his accounts, stooping over a ledger, letting the money go with the utmost prudence. His worthy partners were staring greedily at his hands.

At the sound made by the door in opening, every head turned with a sudden movement of terror and surprise. And when the usurers perceived Marius, grave and indignant, each instinctively placed his hand over his heap of gold. There was a moment of trouble and stupor.

The young man instantly recognized the wretches. He had met them in the streets, with heads held high, with countenances dignified and honest, and he had even bowed to some of them, who might have saved his brother. They all were rich, honored and influential; among them were former offi-

cials, property-holders, men who assiduously frequented the churches and the salons of the town. Marius, on seeing them thus, debased and contemptible, blanching beneath his glances, made a gesture of disgust and disdain.

Rostand rushed towards the intruder. His eyes snapped excitedly; his thick, wan lips trembled; all his reddish and wrinkled miser's mask expressed a sort of terrified astonishment.

"at do you want?" asked he of Marius, hesitatingly. "It is not customary to enter houses in this way."

"I wanted fifteen thousand francs," the young man, in a cold and jeering tone.

"I have no money," the usurer hastened to reply, moving towards his safe.

"Oh! rest easy; I have abandoned the idea of being robbed. For an hour past, I have been behind that door and have heard all the details of your meeting!"

This declaration fell like the blow of a club, and made all the members of the scoundrelly band turn away their heads. These men yet possessed the shame belonging to their honorable station; some of them hid their faces in their hands. Rostand, who had no reputation to lose, recovered himself little by little. He approached Marius and cried, in a loud voice:

"Who are you? By what right do you steal into my house to listen at the doors? Why do you make your way into my private office, if you have nothing to ask of me?"

"Who am I?" said Marius, in a low, calm tone. "I am an honest man and you are a knave! By what right have

I listened at that door? By the right that people of probity have to unmask and crush scoundrels! Why have I made my way to you? To tell you that you are a wretch and to amply satisfy my indignation!"

Rostand trembled with rage. He did not seek to explain to himself the presence of this avenger, who hurled truths in his face. He was about to cry aloud and fling himself upon Marius, when the latter stopped him with an energetic gesture.

"Be quiet!" thundered he. "I am on the point of going; I am suffocating here. But I did not wish to withdraw without relieving myself a little. Ah! Messieurs, you have a furious appetite. You share among you the tears and despair of families with a terrible gluttony; you gorge yourselves with robberies and rascalities! I am glad to be able to disturb your digestion a trifle, and make you shiver with uneasiness to the depths of your cowardly hearts!"

Rostand strove to interrupt him. He continued, in a more resonant voice:

"Highway robbers have, at least, the merit of courage. They fight, they risk their lives! But you, Messieurs, steal disgracefully in the darkness, you slink ignobly in the by-ways of a contemptible vocation! And, worst of all, you can live without being knaves! You are all rich! You commit villainy, God save the mark! for amusement and the gratification of your tastes!"

Some of the usurers arose, menacingly.

"You have never seen the anger of an honest man, have you?" added Marius, jeeringly. "The truth irritates and frightens you. You are accustomed to be treated with the consideration due to upright people, and, as you have so arranged matters as to hide your infamies and preserve everybody's esteem, you have at last grown to believe in the respect accorded to your hypocrisy! Well, I desired that once in your lives you might be insulted as you deserve, and that is why I came in here!"

The young man saw that he would be murdered if he remained. He retired step by step towards the door, holding the usurers in check with his glance. At the door he paused again.

"I am well aware, Messieurs," said he, "that I cannot drag you before human justice. Your wealth, your influence and your shrewdness render you inviolable. If I were stupid enough to struggle against you, I, certainly, would be the party punished. But, at least, I will not have to reproach myself with having been in the presence of men such as you, without casting my contempt in their faces. Would that my words were a red-hot iron to brand your foreheads with infamy! The crowd in that case would follow you and hoot at you, and then, perhaps, you would profit by the lesson. Divide your gold; if you have the least bit of probity left, it will burn your hands!"

Marius closed the door and departed. When he was in the street, he smiled sadly. He saw life stretch out before him, with all its shame and misery, and said to himself that he was filling in existence the noble and ridiculous rôle of a Don Quixote of justice and honor.

He thought that, perhaps, it would have been better had he not entered

_Rostand's office. He had grown indignant to no purpose whatever; he knew that he would correct no one. But, when indignation urged him on, he altogether lost control of himself; he had attacked the usurers through instinct, as any man would crush base and dangerous reptiles.

## CHAPTER XVII

### TWO INFAMOUS SCOUNDRELS

WHEN Marius related his adventure to the jailer and the flower-girl, the latter exclaimed:

"We have not advanced a step! Why did you get angry? That man, perhaps, would have loaned you the money."

Young girls have infatuations which give them a certain pliancy of conscience; thus Fine, altogether upright as she was, would, doubtless, have turned a deaf ear to Rostand's rascalities, and, on occasion, would even have made use of the secrets chance had confided to her.

Revertégat was somewhat disturbed at having advised Marius to pay a visit to the banker.

"I forewarned you, Monsieur," said he. "I was not ignorant of the rumors in circulation respecting that man, but I attributed a large portion of them to slander. If I had known the whole truth, I never would have sent you to him."

Marius and Fine passed the entire afternoon in framing extravagant plans, in vainly racking their brains for the means of improvising the fifteen thousand francs necessary to secure Philippe's safety.

"What!" cried the young girl, "can we not find in this town a stout heart to extricate us from our embarrassment! Are there no rich people here who lend their money at a reasonable rate? Come now, uncle, help us a little. Name me some available person, that I may cast myself at his feet!"

Revertégat shook his head.

"Yes," answered he, "there are stout hearts here, rich people who, perhaps, might aid you. But you have no claim upon their kindness, you cannot demand money of them on the instant. You must address yourself to the lenders, the note-shavers, and, as you have no solid security to offer, you are compelled to have recourse to the usurers. Oh! I know old misers, old knaves, who would be enchanted to hold you in their claws, or who would throw you into the street as a dangerous beggar."

Fine listened to her uncle. All these money questions were confused in her young head. She had a soul so open and so frank that it seemed to her altogether natural and exceedingly easy to ask for and obtain a large sum in a couple of hours. There were millionaires who could so readily dispose of a few thousand francs without the least trouble.

She persisted.

"Think well," said she to the jailer. "Do you really know of no man whatever with whom we can make an attempt?"

Revertégat gazed with emotion at her anxious countenance. He hesitated to spread the brutal truths of life before this child, full of the hopes of youth. "Indeed," responded he, "I know of no man. I have spoken to you of old misers, of old knaves, who have acquired vast fortunes by shameful means. Like Rostand, they loan a hundred francs to get back a hundred and fifty in three months."

He stopped abruptly and then resumed, in a lower tone:

"Would you like me to tell you the history of one of these men? His name is Roumieu; he was formerly a public official. His specialty was making a terrible hunt after inheritances. Introducing himself into families, called upon by his duties to play the rôle of a confidant and friend, he studied the field and prepared his ambushes. When he encountered a testator of weak and wavering spirit, he became his creature, cozened him, won his favor, little by little, by reverences, cajolery and a shrewd comedy of small cares and filial tenderness. Ah! he was a cunning man! It was a sight to see him put his prey to sleep, make himself supple and winning, worm his way into an old man's friendship. Gradually he drove off the real heirs, the nephews and the cousins; then he wrote a new will which robbed them of their relative's fortune and named him as the sole legatee. He did nothing hastily; he devoted ten years to the attainment of his end, to the proper maturing of his rascalities; he proceeded with feline prudence, crawling in the background unweariedly, and leaping upon his prey only when it lay panting before him, rendered inert by his glances and his caresses! He hunted inheritances as

a tiger hunts a hare, with a silent brutality, a velvety-footed ferocity."

Fine thought she was hearing a tale from "The Arabian Nights;" she listened to her uncle, her eyes wide open with astonishment. Marius had begun to be familiar with roguery.

"And you say that this man has acquired a vast fortune?" said he to the jailer.

"Yes," continued the latter. "Strange examples are cited which prove the extraordinary cunning of Roumieu. For instance, ten or fifteen years ago, he managed to get into the good graces of an old lady who had a fortune of nearly five hundred thousand francs. He actually took possession of her like an evil spirit. The old lady became his slave to such an extent that she refused herself a morsel of bread, in order not to touch the money she wished to leave to this demon who ruled her like a master. She was literally possessed; all the holy water in a church would not have sufficed to exorcise the fiend. A visit from Roumieu plunged her into ecstasies without end; when he bowed to her in the street, she was as if stricken by a fit—she grew red with joy. No one could ever conceive by what flattery, by what adroit and insinuating procedure, the notary had been able to penetrate so far into that heart which excessive piety had closed. When the old lady died, she despoiled her direct heirs and left her five hundred thousand francs to Roumieu. Everybody expected this dénouement."

There was silence for an instant. Revertégat resumed:

"I can cite yet another example. The anecdote contains a cruel comedy and proves Roumieu's rare suppleness. A man named Richard, who had amassed in trade several hundred thousand francs, had retired into the bosom of an honest family, the members of which took care of him and made his old age pleasant. In exchange for this kindly friendship, the former merchant had promised his hosts to leave them his fortune. They lived in that hope; they had numerous children and counted upon establishing them in an honorable fashion. But Roumieu happened to pass that way; he soon became the intimate friend of Richard; he took him occasionally to the country; he accomplished in perfect secrecy his work of taking possession. The family which gave the retired trader a home suspected nothing; the hosts continued to care for their guest, awaiting the inheritance: for fifteen years they had lived thus in delightful quietude, making plans for the future, certain of being happy and rich. Richard died, and, the next day, Roumieu was discovered to be his heir, to the great astonishment and despair of the honest family, robbed of its affection and its rights. Such is the hunter of inheritances. When he walks, his footsteps make no sound: his leaps are too rapid to be noticed; he has already sucked all the blood from his prey before he is seen crouched upon it!"

Fine was shocked.

"No, no," said she, "I will never ask such a man for money. Do you not know of some other lender, uncle?"

"Ah! my poor child," replied the jailer, "all usurers are alike; all of them have some indelible stain on

their lives. I know an old miser, who has a fortune of more than a million francs and lives alone in a dirty and abandoned house. Guillaume buries himself in the depths of his foul-smelling den. The dampness cracks the walls of this vault; the floor is not even paved, and one walks upon a sort of vile muck made of mud and rubbish; spider webs hang from the ceiling, dust covers every object and a dim, lugubrious light enters through the window panes black with grease. The miser seems to sleep in the filth, as the spiders of the beams sleep motionlessly amid their webs. When a victim becomes entangled in the nets he spreads, he draws it to him and sucks the blood from its veins. This man eats nothing but vegetables boiled in water, and never satisfies his hunger. He dresses himself in rags; he leads the life of a beggar and a leper. And all this to keep the money he has already amassed, to constantly augment his treasure. He lends only at a hundred per cent."

Fine turned pale at the hideous spectacle at which her uncle gave her a glimpse.

"But," continued the jailer, "Guillaume has friends who extol his piety. He believes neither in God nor the devil; he would sell Christ a second time if he could; but he has been crafty enough to feign great religious zeal, and this comedy has brought him the esteem of certain narrow-minded and blind people. One meets him crawling in the churches, kneeling behind all the pillars, using buckets of holy water. Question the town, ask what good action this godly personage has ever performed! 'He worships God,' will be the reply; but he robs his fellow-creatures! No one can cite a person he has assisted. He lends at usurious rates, but does not give a sou to the unfortunate. A poor devil might die of hunger at his door, before he would bring him a morsel of bread and a glass of water. If he enjoys any consideration whatever, it is because he has stolen that consideration like everything else belonging to him!"

Revertégat paused, looking at his niece, uncertain as to whether he ought to continue.

"And what if you should be foolish enough to go to such a man!" said he, at length. "I cannot tell everything; I cannot speak of Guillaume's worst faults. This old man has evil instincts; at times, he forgets his avarice. People whisper of shameful orgies, of revolting dissipation—"

"Enough!" cried Marius, sternly.

Fine, blushing and dismayed, hung her head, having no longer either courage or hope.

"I see that money is too dear," resumed the young man, "and that one must sell himself to buy it! Ah! if I only had the time to earn with my own hands the sum we need!"

They all three remained silent, totally unable to find any means of saving Philippe.

## CHAPTER XVIII

### A RAY OF HOPE

THE following morning, Marius, urged by necessity, decided to apply to M. de Girousse. Since he had been endeavoring to raise the money he needed, he had often thought of making application to the old comte. But he had always recoiled from this idea; he feared the gentleman's singular bluntness; he dare not admit to him his poverty; he was ashamed to tell him what was to be done, with the fifteen thousand francs he solicited.

Nothing could be more painful to him than to be obliged to put another party in possession of the secret of his brother's contemplated escape, and M. de Girousse frightened him more than any one else.

When the young man presented himself, the hôtel was empty; the comte had just departed for Lambesc. Marius was almost happy at finding no one, so much did the step he was taking weigh upon him. He stood in the Cours, irresolute, not having the courage to go to Lambesc, disheartened at being brought to a stand.

As he walked away, overwhelmed, with wandering eyes, he met Fine. It was seven o'clock. The flower-girl, wearing her best dress, holding in her hand a small travelling bag, seemed to him resolute and radiant.

"Where are you going?" asked he, in surprise.

"I am going to Marseilles," answered she.

He stared at her with an air of curiosity, questioning her with a look.

"I can tell you nothing," continued she. "I have a project, but am afraid of failing. I shall return this evening. Don't give up all hope yet."

Marius accompanied Fine to the diligence. When the lumbering vehicle started, he followed it for a long while with his eyes; that vehicle bore his last hope and would bring back to him anguish or joy.

Until evening, he hung around the arriving diligences. Only one more was to come, and Fine had not yet apepared. The young man, gnawed by impatience, walking back and forth with a nervous step, trembled lest the flower-girl should not return until the following day.

In the ignorance in which he was, not knowing what this final attempt might be, he felt that he lacked the courage to pass an entire night of anxiety and indecision. He paced the Cours, quivering, a prey to a sort of nightmare.

Finally, he saw the diligence in the distance, in the middle of the Place de la Rotonde. When he heard the wheels rattle over the paving stones, violent palpitations seized upon him. He placed his back against a tree, watching the travellers who got out, one by one, with exasperating deliberation.

Suddenly, he stood as if nailed to the spot. Nearly opposite to him, in an open door-way of the diligence, he had just seen appear the tall figure and pale, sad face of the Abbé Chastanier. When the abbé was upon the sidewalk, he put out his hand and helped a young girl to descend. This young girl was Mademoiselle Blanche de Cazalis.

Behind her, Fine leaped to the pavement with a light bound, without making use of the coach steps. She was radiant.

The two travellers, guided by the flower-girl, went towards the Hôtel des Princes. Marius, who had remained in the darkness of the growing night, followed them mechanically, utterly unable to comprehend matters, as if stupefied.

Fine was ten minutes at most in the hôtel. When she came out, she perceived the young man and ran to him, overcome with wild joy.

"I have suceeeded in bringing them," cried she, clapping her hands; "now, I hope they will obtain what I desire. To-morrow we shall know all about it."

Then, she took Marius' arm, and told him what she had done during her absence.

The day before, she had been struck by the young man's remark to the effect that he regretted not having sufficient time to earn with his own hands the sum he needed.

Besides, her uncle's sadness had proved to her that it was almost impossible to find a lender, a reasonable usurer. The question then rduced itself to gaining time, to striving to postpone as far as possible the period when Philippe would be fastened to the pillory.

What terrified Fine and Marius was this disgraceful exposure, which delivered up culprits to the jeers and insults of the crowd.

The young girl's plan was immediately determined upon, a bold plan which, perhaps, would succeed by reason of its very audacity.

Her project was to go straight to the mansion of M. de Cazalis, to make her way to his neice and to spread out before her the picture of Philippe's exposure, with everything such a spectacle would have of a nature insulting to the young lady.

She would prevail upon her to aid her; they would go together to beg the deputy to intervene; if M. de Cazalis did not consent to ask for Philippe's pardon, he would, perhaps, try to obtain a reprieve. Besides, Fine did not reason concerning her method of procedure; it seemed impossible to her that Blanche's uncle could resist her tears. She had faith in her devotedness.

The poor child dreamed wide awake when she hoped that M. de Cazalis would bend at the last hour. That proud and obstinate man desired Philippe's disgrace, and nothing in the world could have induced him to put an obstacle in the way of the accomplishment of his vengeance. If Fine had been compelled to struggle against him she would have been crushed; she would have utterly wasted her most enchanting smiles and her most touching tears.

Happily for her, circumstanecs aided her. When she presented herself at the deputy's hôtel on the Cours Bonaparte, she was informed that M. de Cazalis had been called to Paris by certain exigencies of his political position. She asked to see Mademoiselle Blanche; the servant vaguely replied that Mademoiselle was absent, that she was travelling.

The flower-girl, greatly embarrassed, was obliged to retire and reflect in the street. All her plans were thrown into disorder; this absence of the uncle and the neice took from her the support upon which she had counted, and there was not a single friend to whom she

could turn. She, however, did not wish to lose her last hope and return to Aix as desperate as on the preceding day, after having made a fruitless journey.

Suddenly, she thought of the Abbé Chastanier. Marius had often spoken to her of the old priest; she knew his kindness, his devotedness. Perhaps he could give her valuable information.

She found him at the hosue of his sister, the aged and infirm workwoman. She opened her heart to him; she explained to him in a few words the motive of her journey to Marseilles. The priest listened to her with marked emotion.

"Heaven has sent you here," answered he. "I think I can, under such circumstances, violate the secret which has been entrusted to me. Mademoiselle Blanche is not travelling. Her uncle, wishing to keep her out of sight and not being able to take her to Paris, hired for her a small house in the village of Saint-Henri. She is living there with a governess. M. de Cazalis, with whom I am again in favor, begged me to make frequent visits to her and gave me extensive authority over her. Would you like me to conduct you to the poor child, whom you will find much changed and greatly dejected?"

Fine accepted with joy. Blanche turned pale when she saw the flower-girl and began to weep bitterly. A slight bluish circle surrounded her eyes; her lips were discolored and her cheeks as white as wax. One could see that a terrible cry, the cry of the heart and the conscience, had broken forth in her and shaken her determination.

When Fine, in a gentle tone and with

compassionate caresses, had made her comprehend that she could, perhaps, save Philippe from a supreme humiliation, she stood firmly up and said, in a broken voice:

"I am ready; dispose of me."

"Well," resumed Fine, eagerly, "aid me in our work of deliverance. I am certain that you will obtain a reprieve, at least, if you try."

"But," observed the Abbé Chastanier, "Mademoiselle Blanche cannot go alone to Aix. I must accompany her. I know that M. de Cazalis, should he hear of this journey, will reproach me in the gravest manner for it. I, however, accept the responsibility of the act, for I firmly believe that I am doing my duty as a man!"

When the flower-girl had obtained the consent of both, she scarcely allowed the old man and the young girl time to make a few preparations. She returned with them to Marseilles, pushed them into the diligence and bore them triumphantly to Aix. The next day, Blanche was to go to the President of the court who had pronounced Philippe's sentence.

Marius, when Fine had finished her recital, kissed her warmly on both cheeks, which made a rosy glow mount to the young girl's forehead.

## CHAPTER XIX

### A REPRIEVE

FINE went to Blanche and the Abbé Chastanier the next morning. She wished to accompany them to the door of the President's hôtel, to learn without delay the result of their undertaking. Marius, realizing that his presence would be painful to Mlle. de Cazalis, moved about the Cours like a soul in torment, following the two young girls and the priest in the distance. When the seekers for mercy had entered the hôtel, the flower-girl noticed the young man and made him a sign to join her. They then waited, without exchanging a word, agitated and anxious.

The President received Blanche with great commisseration. He realized that she was the most cruelly stricken of all in this unfortunate affair. The poor child could not speak; she burst into sobs at the first word she attempted to utter, and her whole suppliant being begged for pity more touchingly than her prayers would have done. The Abbé Chastanier was compelled to explain their presence and present the request.

"Monsieur," said he to the President, "we come to you with clasped hands. Mlle. de Cazalis is already broken by the misfortunes which have overwhelmed her. She prays you in mercy to spare her new humiliation."

"What do you desire of me?" asked the President, in an agitated voice.

"We desire that you may, if possible, prevent an additional trouble. M. Philippe Cayol has been sentenced to public exposure, and that punishment will shortly be inflicted. But the infamy will not fall on him alone; there will be more than one culprit fastened to the pillory: there will also be a poor, suffering child, who asks pity of you. You understand, do you not? The cries of the crowd, the insults, will rebound upon Mlle. de Cazalis; she will be dragged in the mud by the populace, and her name will circulate around the ignoble post, coupled with hateful jeers and foul expressions."

The President seemed deeply touched. He was silent for a moment. Then, as if seized by a sudden idea, he inquired:

"Did M. de Cazalis send you to me? Is he aware of the step you have taken?"

"No," answered the priest, with frank dignity; "M. de Cazalis does not know we are here. Men have interests and passions which carry them away and, sometimes, prevent them from forming a clear judgment of their position. Perhaps, we are acting contrary to the desire of Mlle. Blanche's uncle in coming to solicit your intervention. But goodness and justice are above the passions and the interests of men. Therefore, I have no fear of compromising my sacred character in taking it upon myself to ask you to be good and just."

"You are right, Monsieur," said the President. "I understand the motives which have brought you here, and, as you see, your words have strongly affected me. Unfortunately, I cannot prevent the punishment; it is not in my power to modify a decree of the Cour d'Assises."

Blanche clasped her hands.

"Monsieur," stammered she, "I do not know what you can do for me; but, I pray you, be merciful: think that it is I whom you have sentenced, and try to alleviate my sufferings."

The President took her hands and replied, with paternal gentleness:

"My poor child, I understand everything. My rôle in this affair has been painful. To-day, I am grieved that I cannot say to you: 'Fear nothing; I can set aside the pillory, and you shall not be fastened to the post with the condemned.'"

"Then," resumed the priest, in dismay, "the exposure must soon take place. You are not even permitted to retard the deplorable scene."

The President had risen.

"The Ministre de la Justice, upon the demand of the Procureur Général, can postpone the execution of the sentence," said he, quickly; "do you desire that the exposure shall not occur until the latter part of December? In that event, I shall be happy to prove to you the extent of my compassion and good will."

"Yes, yes," cried Blanche, eagerly. "Postpone the terrible moment as long as possible. I shall, perhaps, be stronger then."

The Abbé Chastanier, who was aware of Marius' projects, thought that, at the President's promise, he ought to retire, without further importunity. He joined Blanche in accepting the offer made to them.

"Very well; it is settled," said the President, accompanying them to the door. "I shall ask that the course of justice be suspended for four months, and I am convinced that my request will be granted. Until then, live in peace, Mademoiselle. Hope; Heaven will, perhaps, send some consolation for your sufferings."

The abbé and Blanche left the house. When Fine perceived them, she ran to meet them.

"Well?" asked she, breathlessly.

"As I told you," answered the Abbé

Chastanier, "the President cannot prevent the execution of the sentence."

The flower-girl turned pale.

"But," the old priest hastened to add, "he has promised to intercede to obtain a postponement of the exposure. You have four months before you in which to work for the prisoner's welfare."

Marius, in spite of himself, had approached the group formed by the young girls and the abbé. The street, silent and solitary, lay white beneath the glowing sun of noon; slight tufts of grass surrounded the shining paving stones, and a single lean dog slunk along in the narrow thread of shade which skirted the house.

When the young man heard the Abbé Chastanier's words, he advanced with a sudden movement and grasped his hands effusively.

"Ah! father," said he, in a trembling voice, "you restore me hope and faith, Since yesterday, I have doubted God! How shall I thank you, how prove to you my gratitude! Now, I feel invincible courage and am certain of saving my brother!"

Blanche, at the sight of Marius, bowed her head. A burning flush mounted to her cheeks. She stood, confused and embarrassed, suffering horribly from the presence of Philippe's brother, who knew her to be a perjurer and whom her uncle and she had plunged in despair. The young man, when his joy had grown somewhat calm, regretted that he had approached. The doleful attitude of Mlle. de Cazalis filled him with pity.

"My brother has been shamefully guilty," said he to her, at last. "But pardon him as I pardon you!"

He could find only those words. He would have liked to speak to her of her child, question her as to the lot in reserve for that poor little being, claim it of her in Philippe's name. But he saw her so overwhelmed that he dare not torture her further.

Without doubt, Fine had comprehended his thoughts. While he walked a few steps with the Abbé Chastanier, she said to Blanche, in a hurried voice:

"Bear in mind that I have offered to be a mother to your child. Now, I love you; I see that you have a stout heart. Make a sign, and I will fly to your aid. Besides, I will watch; I do not wish the poor little creature to suffer from the folly of its parents."

Blanche silently grasped the flower-girl's hand. That was her sole response. Huge tears ran down her cheeks.

Mlle. de Cazalis and the Abbé Chastanier set out immediately for Marseilles. Fine and Marius hastened to the prison. They informed Revertégat that they had four months in which to prepare for the escape, and the jailer swore to them that he would keep his word, no matter on what day or at what hour they should summon him to do so.

Before quitting Aix, the two young people wished to see Philippe, in order to tell him of what had taken place and bid him hope. That night, at eleven o'clock, Revertégat again took them to the cell. Philippe, who was becoming accustomed to prison life, did not seem to them very greatly dejected.

"Provided that you save me from the ignominy of the public exposure," said he to them, "I will consent to everything. I would rather break my head against a wall than be fastened to the infamous pillory!"

Finally, the next day, the diligence bore Marius and Fine back to Marseilles. They were about to continue the struggle on a larger scale. They were about to search the depths of human consciences and see exposed the vices of a great city, given up to all the disorders of modern industry.

## CHAPTER XX

### POLITICS AND JUSTICE

MEANWHILE, political complications had arisen in Marseilles. The liberals had of late received numerous accessions and felt their power. They were thoroughly dissatisfied with the course of M. de Cazalis as a deputy, and his pride and arrogant conduct as an individual utterly disgusted them. Besides, his merciless persecution of Philippe Cayol, whom they recognized as one of their chiefs, filled them with rage, especially as they knew that in disgracing him the deputy was striking the party and taking revenge for having been compelled in the past to pay court to the republicans.

Another election was approaching, and the opposition loudly declared that M. de Cazalis, who was again a candidate, should not be re-chosen deputy. The canvass promised to be unusually bitter and exciting; the adherents of Philippe Cayol were everywhere firing the populace and urging that an overwhelming demonstration against M. de Cazalis be made by the masses. In fact,

the injustice done to Philippe gave signs of being an important issue in the campaign.

Such was the commotion, that the Government, becoming alarmed, had summoned M. de Cazalis to Paris to confer with him respecting the threatening state of affairs.

Marius and Fine returned to Marseilles when the excitement was at its height. The young man was everywhere received by the liberals with enthusiasm which showed plainly that he had suddenly become a person of importance. The masses cheered him in the streets, and wherever he went crowds of girls of the people waved their handkerchiefs in his honor.

Fine was proud of Marius' vast popularity; she neglected no opportunity of adding fuel to the flames by telling the women what a noble fellow he was, and how he had unselfishly devoted himself to the cause of his brother, the victim of aristocratic tyranny.

Marius had not yet decided what steps to take for furthering the object nearest his heart—the raising of the fifteen thousand francs to secure Philippe's liberation—when, early one morning, there was a sharp knock at the door of his apartment on the Rue Sainte.

The young man opened the door; he was filled with amazement to find that the visitor was M. de Girousse.

"You are astonished to see me here, are you not?" said the comte, in his usual abrupt fashion. "Well, you will be still more astonished when you learn my errand!"

M. de Girousse entered the room and took the chair Marius offered him. His eyes sparkled strangely, as he resumed:

"It is in your power to do a little towards bringing the proud and slothful nobles to their senses; at the same time, you can save your brother!"

Marius stared at him in stupefaction. The comte continued:

"Do you not know that you are to-day the most popular man in Marseilles, as M. de Cazalis is the most unpopular? Have you not noticed that the liberals are in the ascendant, that they will surely carry the approaching election? There is your opportunity!"

"I do not understand you," stammered the young man.

"Are you blind!" cried the comte, rising and impatiently pacing the apartment. "The liberals are organized and powerful; they have able leaders; all they need is a suitable and popular candidate. You are that man!"

M. de Girousse stopped in front of Marius and looked him straight in the face.

The young man was astounded. The idea of taking advantage of the political commotion and his personal popularity to oust the deputy from power had never entered his brain.

"But I am no politician," said he; "I am unknown to the leaders of the republicans. Besides, I have not the money to cope with M. de Cazalis in the campaign."

"You are unknown to the leaders of the republicans!" cried M. de Girousse. "Not a bit of it! You are known to all of them; the advisability of your nomination is even at this moment being discussed. As to money, I will aid you to raise all you may require. I came to Marseilles to tell you this,

and also to urge you, if only for your brother's sake, to accept the nomination which will certainly be tendered you."

Marius put his hands to his head in bewilderment. He thought he was dreaming. But a short time before he had been powerless, and M. de Cazalis had towered above him like a giant; now, he was informed that he could humble the arrogant deputy, and that he might speedily have sufficient influence to save Philippe. The comte interrupted his revierie by saying:

"Will you accept the nomination I have spoken of?"

"To help my brother—yes!" replied Marius, with determination.

M. de Girousse then departed, first giving the young man his address in Marseilles, and exacting from him a promise to come to him at once should anything having a political significance occur.

The comte had hardly gone when Fine made her apearance, out of breath and flushed with excitment.

"Do you know what has happened, Marius?" asked she, as soon as she could find words. "No; you could never guess! They say in the streets that the liberals have named you as their candidate for deputy against Blanche's uncle!"

Marius' eyes flashed. Vengeance was, indeed, within his grasp, if nothing more.

"M. de Girousse was here just before you came," said he. "He informed me that my nomination was probable; he also urged me to accept, offered me money to carry on the canvass, and said that my election meant Philippe's safety!"

Fine clapped her hands joyously.
"You will accept?" said she.
"I will!"

During the day, Marius was officially notified of his nomination and accepted. He had grave misgivings as to the step he was taking, but the thought of his brother nerved and sustained him.

The young man at once sought out M. de Girousse and told him the news. The comte grasped him cordially by the hand, asuring him that his success was now only a matter of time.

On both sides, the campaign was pushed with extreme vigor. The nobles and some priests rallied about M. de Cazalis; but the powerful faction of the clergy, headed by the wily Abbé Donadéi, joined the liberal forces. The shrewd Italian had scented the coming storm; with his natural quickness, he saw to which side victory inclined and threw all his weight into the winning scale. M. de Cazalis put in circulation all sorts of slanders in regard to Marius: he was a scoundrel and a reprobate, the terror of honest families, and he deserved to be in prison with his infamous brother; if he had his deserts, he would be pilloried with him. The unscrupulous deputy gave the names of people he had ruined, of others whose peace of mind he had forever destroyed. The liberals retorted by asserting that M. de Cazalis had forced his niece to commit perjury, to turn against the man she loved; that he had deliberately and in cold blood concocted the outrageous plot to disgrace Philippe Cayol; that he was a wretch and a knave; that he had made capital out of Blanche's flight with

which to crush the people in the person of an innocent man, and that he ought to be punished for his crimes instead of being re-elected deputy.

Marius through all this maintained a calm dignity, acting on advice given him by M. de Girousse. But Fine could not be controlled; she was constantly in a fever of excitment, and her enthusiasm for the candidate of the liberals knew no bounds; the indignation she felt at the vile slanders current in regard to Marius fell little short of absolute fury; could she have come in contact with M. de Cazalis, she would have done her best to strangle him.

M. de Girousse did not openly take part in the campaign, but he moved a host of secret springs, making it his business to counteract all the shrewd trickery resorted to by M. de Cazalis and his adherents. Whenever it was known that votes had been purchase for the deputy, the comte promptly furnished money to buy an equal number for Marius. He remained quietly in Marseilles, keeping his eyes and ears wide open.

At length, the election took place, and Marius was triumphantly chosen deputy, M. de Cazalis sustaining an overwhelming defeat.

The first use the new deputy made of his power was to cause Philippe's case to be reopened by the Cour d'Assises at Aix.

Blanche again appeared as a witness. She had ascaped from her uncle's control and, for some time past, had remained in concealment at the house of the Abbé Chastanier's infirm sister in Marseilles, Fine being almost constantly with her and ministering to all her needs like a sister. The poor child stood up in the court-room, pale and trembling, supported on one side by the old priest and on the other by the faithful flower-girl. In an almost inaudible voice, she told the true story of her flight with Philippe, declaring that she had voluntarily followed the young man because she loved him; that she had married him and had always considered herself his wife, and that her statement at the former trial had been dictated to her by her iron-willed uncle, whom she had not had the strength of mind to resist.

The vast audience present received her testimony with murmurs of applause, which were promptly suppressed by the court officials.

Philippe sat in his place, his countenance radiant with joy and hope. On hearing Blanche's evidence, he felt that he loved the young girl more that ever.

The Lambesc inn-keeper repeated that while at his house Mlle. de Cazalis had called Philippe her husband, and Marguerite, the milkmaid, deposed that she now perfectly remembered having carried letters from Mlle. Blanche to her lover.

Marius detailed all that had occurred during his interview with his brother and the young girl at the house of the gardener Ayasse at Saint-Barnabé; he spoke in a firm, manly tone which carried conviction with it.

The result was the acquittal of Philippe Cayol, and the arrest of M. de Cazalis on the charge of conspiracy to ruin the young man. The gardener Ayasse was released from prison by order of the President.

In due course, Philippe was set at liberty. Marius was waiting to receive him, in company with Fine and the Abbé Chastanier. As the jailer Revertégat delivered his prisoner to them, Marius slipped a packet into his hand.

"Take it," said he; "it contains the fifteen thousand francs promised you. I am happy to give you the sum with the knowledge that you have earned it solely by your kindness and that it is not the price of a criminal act!"

It should be stated here that, immediately after Marius' election, the banker Bérard, becoming frightened, had restored to him the fifty thousand francs left by his mother.

Revertégat took the money and silently walked away, but a suspicious moisture in his eyes told that his heart was touched.

Philippe grasped his brother's hand effusively.

"How can I thank you!" he said.

"By making reparation to the young girl you have wronged!" answered Marius, sternly.

"But will she accept me as her husband, after all my baseness?" asked Philippe, greatly agitated.

Fine came forward and Philippe, with a sudden return of his old inclinations, moved as if to kiss her on the cheek.

"No!" said she, repulsing him with an air of sorrow and regret. "In the sight of God, you are the husband of another! You ask if Mlle. Blanche will accept you. I reply that she will!"

The Abbé Chastanier interposed.

"My son," said he, "I have just quitted Mlle. de Cazalis. Rest assured that she will do everything required of her by the laws of God and human justice."

Philippe looked joyously around him. "And I, too, will do everything required of me by the laws of God and human justice!" said he, firmly. "But will M. de Gazalis, proud and haughty as he is, sanction our union?"

"As matters now stand," replied the old priest, "the law will permit us to dispense with his consent."

## CHAPTER XXI

### REPARATION AND REWARD

THE interview between Blanche and Philippe was embarrassing. The young girl scarcely lifted her eyes from the floor when her lover came into her presence; he stood for a moment gazing sorrowfully into her pale and altered face.

"Blanche," said he, at last—"my wife!"

He took her hand and softly caressed it.

Courage returned to the young girl; she raised her eyes and gazed tenderly at her lover, but still not a syllable came from her lips, which seemed dry and parched.

"Blanche," continued Philippe, "give me a word of comfort and hope; tell me that you will be mine; tell me that you will consent to have our already pronounced nuptial vows renewed before the Mayor and in church."

The poor girl blushed scarlet and trembled from head to foot, but her lips remained sealed.

"Blanche! Blanche!" cried the young man, in despair, "is all the love you once felt for me cold and dead in your bosom? You are suffering, child; speak!"

Blanche shuddered.

"Do not recall our old love, Philippe!" said she, in a voice quivering with agony; "it was unblest and unholy! I was a rash, inexperienced girl, and did not know what I was doing!"

"So be it," answered Philippe, solemnly: "let our old love perish; but, from its ashes, may not a new and purer love arise—a love the law will authorize and the church sanctify?—the love which unites two hearts and makes them beat with a single throb!"

"Yes," murmured she, "such a love might arise; but I am unworthy of it. I have betrayed you—I have cast you into prison!"

"But you have also delivered me; you were unjust only because your proud and revengeful uncle compelled you to be so; when you were free to act as you chose, you hastened to my relief, to repair the injury you had inflicted on me. I have long since forgiven you, and now I ask you to forgive me."

Philippe spoke with fire and earnestness. Blanche was deeply moved.

"I, too, forgave you long ago," she replied, in an agitated voice.

"Then love me now and be my wife," said Philippe, eagerly; "think of the pure happiness of wedlock; think that our child will be legitimized."

Mlle. de Cazalis burst into tears. Philippe caught her in his arms; he impressed a burning kiss upon her lips.

"Do not refuse me," he pleaded; "I am sincere—I will make amends for all the bitter past."

The young girl did not seek to free herself; she remained passively in her lover's arms; but she sobbed as if her heart would break.

"Do you consent to be my wife?" continued Philippe; "do you consent to give me an opportunity to prove that I really love you for yourself alone?"

"Yes," murmured Blanche, "for now I know that you speak the truth!"

At that moment there was a discreet knock at the door, and an instant afterwards the Abbé Chastanier entered the apartment. He saw at a glance how matters stood, and a calm smile lighted up his face.

"My children," said he, "I have brought with me a person who ardently desires to see you, that he may in some measure atone for the misery he has caused you. Shall he come in?"

Blanche and Philippe, in surprise, nodded consent. Their surprise deepened to amazement when the old priest, going to the door, ushered in M. de Cazalis in the custody of two court officers. The ex-deputy was humbled and penitent. Blanche ran to him. He took her hands in his and said, in a voice entirely stripped of its usual haughtiness:

"My child, I come to do you tardy justice. I feel that you can never pardon me for all the evil I have done, but I shall strive, at least, to deserve a kind thought from you."

Turning to Philippe, he added:

"You will soon have your revenge, for I shall be convicted and sent to prison; but, before that supreme disgrace prostrates me in the dust, let me say that I withdraw all obstacles to your union with my niece; nay, that I freely consent to that union."

He turned and left the room with the officers. Blanche and Philippe tried in vain to stop him.

"Let him go," said the Abbé Chastanier; "he has repented and made amends. God will blot out his crimes!"

A few evenings after this scene, Marius went to Fine's dwelling on the Place aux Œufs in Marseilles. He was evidently a prey to some strong excitement which he did his best to conceal.

At the door, he met the flower-girl's brother Cadet.

"Cadet," said he, in a rather tremulous voice which he strove to render firm, "is your sister within?"

"Yes," replied the young fellow; "but she is terribly dejected. I think that Monsieur Philippe's approaching marriage with Mlle. de Cazalis has something to do with it!" he added, archly.

"Poor girl!" said Marius. "I know she loved him."

He found Fine busily engaged with her bouquets for the following day; but she went about her work mechanically, and, as her brother had said, she was terribly dejected.

The young deputy spoke some comforting words to her, but his excitement betrayed itself to such an extent that his companion at last noticed it and said:

"What is the matter with you, tonight? Has anything gone wrong?"

"No," replied he; "everything is entirely satisfactory, but, the fact is, I have something important to say to you."

"To me!"

"Ye
"W
b